SILØ STORIES

HUGH HOWEY

wm

WILLIAM MORROW

An Imprint of HarperCollins*Publishers*

Boston New York

Mariner Books
An Imprint of HarperCollins Publishers, registered in the United States of America and/or other jurisdictions.

www.marinerbooks.com

Printed in the United States of America

24 25 26 27 28 LBC 13 12 11 10 9

These stories previously appeared elsewhere, in slightly different form: "In the Air" in *The End Is Nigh,* edited by John Joseph Adams and Hugh Howey; "In the Mountain" in *The End Is Now,* edited by John Joseph Adams and Hugh Howey; "In the Woods" in *The End Has Come,* edited by John Joseph Adams and Hugh Howey.

CONTENTS

IN THE AIR

GEARS WHIR; AN escapement lets loose; wound springs explode a fraction of an inch, and a second hand lurches forward and slams to a stop. All these small violences erupt on John's wrist as the world counts down its final moments, one second at a time.

Less than five minutes. Just a few minutes more, and they would've made it to the exit. They would've been on back roads all the way to the cabin. John stares at the dwindling time and silently curses the fender-bender in Nebraska that set them back. He curses himself for not leaving yesterday or in the middle of the night. But so much to do. The world was about to end, and there was so much to do.

His wife, Barbara, whispers a question, but she has become background noise—much like the unseen interstate traffic whooshing by up the embankment. Huddled on the armrest between them, their nine-year-old daughter, Emily, wants to know why they're pulled off the road, says she doesn't need to pee. A tractor trailer zooms past, air brakes rattling like a machine gun, a warning for everyone to keep their heads down.

John turns in the driver's seat to survey the embankment. He has pulled off Interstate 80 and down the shoulder, but it doesn't feel far enough. There aren't any trees to hide behind. He tries to imagine what's coming but can't. He can't allow himself to believe it. And yet here he is, cranking up the Explorer, ignoring the pleas from the fucking auto-drive to take over and manually steering down the grass toward the concrete piling of a large billboard. The sign high above promises cheap gas and cigarettes. Five minutes. Five minutes, and they'd have made it to the exit. So close.

"Honey, what's going on?"

A glance at his wife. Emily clutches his shoulder as he hits a bump. He waited too long to tell them. It's one of those lies that dragged out and became heavier and heavier the farther he carried it. A tractor-pull lie. And now his wheels are spinning and spitting dirt, and the seconds are ticking down.

He pulls the Explorer around the billboard and backs up until the bumper meets the concrete piling. Killing the ignition silences the annoying beeps from the auto-drive, the seat belt sensors, the GPS warning that they're off the road. The world settles into a brief silence. All the violence is invisible, on a molecular level, the slamming of tiny gears and second hands in whirring watches and little machines swimming in bloodstreams.

"Something very bad is about to happen," John finally says. He turns to his wife, but it is the sight of his daughter that blurs his vision. Emily will be immune, he tells himself. The three of them will be immune. He has to believe this if he allows himself to believe the rest, if he allows himself to believe that it's coming. There is no time left for believing otherwise. A year of doubt, and here he is, that skeptic in the trenches who discovers his faith right as the mortars whistle down.

"You're scaring me," Barbara says.

"Is this where we're camping?" Emily asks, peering through the windshield and biting her lip in disappointment. The back of the Explorer is stuffed with enough gear to camp out for a month. As if that would be long enough.

John glances at his watch. Not long. Not long. He turns again and checks the interstate. It's hot and stuffy in the Explorer. Opening the sunroof, he looks for the words stuck deep in his throat. "I need you to get in the back," he tells Emily. "You need to put your seat belt on, okay? And hold Mr. Bunny tight to your chest. Can you do that for me?"

His voice is shaky. John has seen war and murder. He has participated in plenty of both. But nothing can steel a mind for this. He releases the sunroof button and wipes his eyes. Overhead, the contrail of a passenger jet cuts the square of open blue in half. John shudders to think of what will become of that. There must be tens of thousands of people in the air. Millions of other people driving. Not that it matters. An indiscriminate end is rapidly approaching. All those invisible machines in bloodstreams, counting down the seconds.

"There's something I haven't told you," he tells his wife. He turns to her, sees the worry in her furrowed brow, and realizes that she is ready for any betrayal. She is ready to hear him say that he is married to another woman. That he is gay. That he murdered a prostitute and her body is curled up where the spare tire used to be. That he has been betting on sports, and the reason for the camping gear is that the bank has taken away their home. Barbara is ready for anything. John wishes any of these trivialities were true.

"I didn't tell you before now because . . . because I didn't believe it." He is stammering. He can debrief the president of the United States without missing a beat, but not this. In the backseat, Emily whispers something to Mr. Bunny. John swallows and continues: "I've been a part of something—" He shakes his head. "Something worse than usual. And now . . . that something is about to—" He glances at his watch. It's too late. She'll never get to hear it from him, not when it mattered, not before it was too late. She will have to watch.

He reaches over his shoulder and grabs his seat belt. Buckles up. Glancing up at the passing jet, John says a prayer for those people up in the air. He is thankful that they'll be dead before they strike the earth. On the dashboard, there is a book with *The Order* embossed on the cover. In the reflection of the windshield, it looks vaguely like the word *redo*. If only.

"What have you done?" Barbara asks, and there's a deadness in her voice, a hollow. As if she knows the scope of the horrible things he could do.

John focuses on his watch. The second hand twitches, and the anointed hour strikes. He and his family should be outside Atlanta with the others, not on the side of the road in Iowa. They should be crowding underground with everyone else, the selected few, the survivors. But here they are, on the side of the road, cowering behind a billboard blinking with cheap gas prices, bracing for the end of the world.

For a long while, nothing happens.

Traffic whizzes by unseen; the contrail overhead grows longer; his wife waits for an answer.

The world is on autopilot, governed by the momentum of life, by humanity's great machinations, by all those gears in motion, spinning and spinning.

Emily asks if they can go now. She says she needs to pee.

John laughs. Deep in his chest and with a flood of relief. He feels that cool wave of euphoria like a nearby *zing* telling him that a bullet has passed, that it missed. He was wrong. *They* were wrong. The book, Tracy, all the others. The national convention in Atlanta is nothing more than a convention, one party's picking of a president, just what it was purported to be. There won't be generations of survivors living underground. His government didn't seed all of humanity with microscopic time bombs that will shut down their hosts at the appointed hour. John will now have to go camping with his family. And for weeks and weeks, Barbara will hound him over what this great secret was that made him pull off the interstate and act so strange –

A scream erupts from the backseat, shattering this eyeblink of relief, this last laugh. Ahead, a pickup truck has left the interstate at a sharp angle. A front tire bites the dirt and sends the truck flipping into the air. It goes into the frantic spins of a figure skater, doors flying open like graceful arms, bodies tumbling out lifeless, arms and legs spread, little black asterisks in the open air.

The truck hits in a shower of soil before lurching up again, dented and slower this time. There is motion in the rearview. A tractor trailer tumbles off the blacktop at ninety miles an hour. It is happening. It is really fucking happening. The end of the world.

John's heart stops for a moment. His lungs constrict as if he has stepped naked into a cold shower. But this is only the shock of awareness. The invisible machines striking down the rest of humanity are not alive in him. He isn't going to die, not in that precise moment, not at that anointed hour. His heart and lungs and body are inoculated.

Twelve billion others aren't so lucky.

Two Days Before

The ringtone is both melody and alarm. An old song, danced to in Milan, the composer unknown. It brings back the fragrance of her perfume and the guilt of a one-night stand.

John's palms are sweaty as he swipes the phone and accepts the call. He needs to change that fucking ringtone. Tracy is nothing more than a colleague. Nothing more. But it could've been Pavlov or Skinner who composed that tune, the way it drives him crazy in reflex.

"Hello?" He smiles at Barbara, who is washing dishes, hands covered in suds. It's Wednesday evening. Nothing unusual. Just a colleague calling after hours. Barbara turns and works the lipstick off the rim of a wineglass.

"Have you made up your mind?" Tracy asks. She sounds like a waitress who has returned to his table to find him staring dumbly at the menu, as if this should be simple, as if he should just have the daily special like she suggested half an hour ago.

"I'm sorry, you're breaking up," John lies. He steps out onto the porch and lets the screen door slam shut behind him. Strolling toward the garden, he startles the birds from the low feeder. The neighbor's cat glares at him for ruining dinner before slinking away. "That's better," he says, glancing back toward the house.

"Have you made up your mind?" Tracy asks again. She is asking the impossible. Upstairs on John's dresser, there is a book with instructions on what to do when the world comes to an end. John has spent the past year reading that book from cover to cover. Several times, in fact. The book is full of impossible things. Unbelievable things. No one who reads these things would believe them, not unless they'd seen the impossible before.

Ah, but Tracy has. She believes. And like a chance encounter in Milan – skin touching skin and sparking a great mistake – her brush with this leather book has spun John's life out of control. Whether the book proves false or not, it has already gotten him deeper than he would have liked.

"Our plane leaves tomorrow," he says. "For Atlanta." Technically, this is true. That plane will leave. John has learned from the best how to lie without lying.

A deep pull of air on the other end of the line. John can picture Tracy's lips, can see her elegant neck, can imagine her perfectly, can almost taste the salt on her skin. He needs to change that goddamn ringtone.

"We can guarantee your safety," Tracy says.

John laughs.

"Listen to me. I'm serious. We know what they put in you. Come to Colorado –"

"You mean New Moscow?"

"That's not funny."

"How well do you know these people?" John fights to keep his voice under control. He has looked into the group Tracy is working with. Some of them hold distinguished positions on agency watch lists, including a doctor who poses an actionable threat.

John tells himself it won't matter, that they are too late to stop anything. And he believes this.

"I've known Professor Karpov for years," Tracy insists. "He believes me. He believes you. We're going to survive this thanks to you. And so I would damn well appreciate you being here."

"And my family?"

Tracy hesitates. "Of course. Them too. Tell me you'll be here, John. Hell, forget the tickets I sent and go to the airport right now. Buy new tickets. Don't wait until tomorrow."

John thinks of the two sets of tickets in the book upstairs. He lowers his voice to a whisper. "And tell Barbara what?"

There's a deep breath, a heavy sigh on the other end of the line.

"Lie to her. You're good at that."

The tractor trailer fills the rearview mirror. A bright silver grille looms large, tufts of grass spitting up from the great tires, furrows of soil loosened by yesterday's rain. Time seems to slow. The grille turns as if suddenly uninterested in the Explorer, and the long trailer behind the cab slews to the side, jackknifing. John yells for his family to hold on; he braces for impact. Ahead of him, several other cars are tumbling off the road.

The eighteen-wheeler growls as it passes by. Its trailer misses the concrete pillar and catches the bumper of the Explorer. The world jerks violently. John's head bounces off his headrest as the Explorer is slammed aside like a geek shouldered by a jock in a hallway.

Mr. Bunny hits the dash. There's a yelp from Barbara and a screech from Emily. Ahead of them, the trailer flips and begins a catastrophic roll, the thin metal shell of the trailer tearing like tissue, countless brown packages catapulting into the air and spilling across the embankment.

Time speeds back up, and John can hear tires squealing, cars braking hard on the interstate, a noise like a flock of birds.

It sounds like things are alive out there – still responding to the world – but John knows it's just automated safety features in action. It's the newer cars protecting themselves from the older cars. It's the world slamming to a stop like the second hand inside a watch.

Tracy had told him once that he would last five minutes out here on his own. Turning to check on his wife, John sees a van barreling through the grass toward her side of the car. He yells at Barbara and Emily to move, to get out, *get out*. Fighting for his seat belt, he wonders if Tracy was wrong, if she had overestimated him.

Five minutes seems like an impossibly long time to live.

The Day Before

John likes to tell himself he's a hero. No, it isn't that he likes the telling – he just needs to hear it. He stands in front of the mirror as he has every morning of his adult life, and he whispers the words to himself:

"I am a hero."

There is no conviction. Conviction must be doled out at birth in some limited supply, because it has drained away from him over the years. Or perhaps the conviction was in his fatigues, which he no longer wears. Perhaps it was the pats on the back he used to get in the airport from complete strangers, the applause as the gate attendant allowed him and a few others to board first. Maybe that's where the conviction came from, because he hasn't felt it in a long while.

"I'm a hero," he used to whisper to himself, the words fogging the Plexiglas mask of his clean-room suit, a letter laced with ricin tucked into an envelope and carefully sealed with a wet sponge. The address on the envelope is for an imam causing trouble in Istanbul – but maybe it kills an assistant instead of this imam. Maybe it kills his wife. Or a curious child. "I'm a hero," he whispers, fumbling in that bulky suit, his empty mantra evaporating from his visor.

"I'm a hero," he used to think to himself as he spotted for his sniper. Calling out the klicks to target and the wind, making sure his shooter adjusts for humidity and altitude, he then watches what the bullet does. He tells himself this is necessary as a body sags to the earth. He pats a young man on the shoulder, pounding some of his conviction into another.

In the field, the lies come easy. Lying in bed the next week, at home, listening to his wife breathe, it's hard to imagine that he's the same person. That he helped kill a man. A woman. A family in a black car among a line of black cars. Sometimes the wrong person, the wrong car. These are things he keeps from his wife, and so the details do not seem to live with them. They belong to another. They are a man in Milan with a beautiful woman swinging in the mesmerizing light. They are two people kissing against a door, a room key dropped, happy throats laughing.

John peers at himself in the present, standing in the bathroom, full of wrinkles and regrets. He returns to the bedroom and finds Barbara packing her bags. One of her nice dresses lies flat on the bed, a necklace arranged on top – like a glamorous woman has just vanished. He steels himself to tell her, to tell her that she won't need that dress. This will lead to questions. It will lead to a speech that he has rehearsed ten thousand times, but never once out loud. For one more long minute, as he delays and says nothing, he can feel that they will go to Atlanta and he will do as he has been told. For one more minute, the cabin by the lake is no more than an ache, a dirty thought, a crazy dream. Tracy in Colorado has been forgotten. She may as well be in Milan. John thinks suddenly of other empty dresses. He comes close to confessing in that moment, comes close to telling his wife the truth.

There are so many truths to tell.

"Remember that time we had Emily treated for her lungs?" he

wants to say. "Remember how the three of us sat in that medical chamber and held her hand and asked her to be brave? Because it was so tight in there, and Emily hates to be cooped up? Well, they were doing something to all three of us. Tiny machines were being let into our bloodstream to kill all the other machines in there. Good machines to kill the bad machines. That's what they were doing.

"We are all ticking time bombs," he would tell her, was about to tell her. "Every human alive is a ticking time bomb. Because this is the future of war, and the first person to act wins the whole game. And that's us. That's me. Killing like a bastard from a distance. Doing what they tell me. A payload is a payload. Invisible bullets all heading toward their targets, and none will miss. Everyone is going to die.

"But not us," he will say, because by now Barbara is always crying. That's how he pictures her, every time he rehearses this. She is cunning enough to understand at once that what he says is true. She is never shouting or slapping him, just crying out of sympathy for the soon-to-be dead. "Not us," he promises. "We are all taken care of. I took care of us, just like I always take care of us. We will live underground for the rest of our lives. You and Emily will go to sleep for a long time. We'll have to hold her hand, because it'll be an even smaller chamber that they put her in, but it'll all go by in a flash. Daddy will have to work with all the other daddies. But we'll be okay in the end. We'll all be okay in the end."

This is the final lie. This is the reason he never can tell her, won't tell her even now, will lie and say they're going camping instead, that she needs to pack something more comfortable. It is always here in his rehearsal that he chokes up and tells her what can never be true: "We'll be okay in the end."

And this is when he imagines Barbara nodding and wiping her eyes and pretending to believe him, because she always was the brave one.

• • •

John can see two figures in the van, their bodies slumped outward against the doors, looking like they'd fallen asleep. The van veers toward the Explorer. Emily is already scrambling between the seats to get in his lap as John fumbles with his seat belt. Barbara has her door open. The van fills the frame. His wife is out and rolling as John kicks open his door. Mere seconds pass from the time the van leaves the interstate to him and Emily diving into the grass. Scrambling and crawling, a bang like lightning cracking down around them, the van and the Explorer tumbling like two wrestling bears.

John holds Emily and looks for Barbara. There. Hands clasped on the back of her head, looking up at the Explorer, camping gear tumbling out through busted glass and scattering. There's a screech and the sound of another wreck up on the highway before the world falls eerily silent. John listens for more danger heading their way. All he can hear is Emily panting. He can feel his daughter's breath against his neck.

"Those people," Barbara says, getting up. John hurries to his feet and helps her. Barbara has grass stains on both knees, is looking toward the van and the wreckage of the tractor trailer, obviously wants to assist them. A form slumps out of the van's passenger window. Barbara fumbles her phone from her pocket and starts dialing a number, probably 911.

"No one will answer," John says.

His wife looks at him blankly.

"They're gone," he says, avoiding the word *dead* for Emily's sake. Above him, a contrail lengthens merrily.

"There was a wreck—" His wife points her phone up the embankment toward the hidden blacktop and the now-silent traffic. John steadies her, but he can feel her tugging him up the slope, eager to help those in need.

"They're all gone," he says. "Everyone. Everyone we knew. Everyone is gone."

Barbara looks at him. Emily stares up at him. Wide eyes everywhere. "You knew . . ." his wife whispers, piecing together the sudden stop on the shoulder of the road and what happened after. "How did you know—?"

John is thinking about the Explorer. Their car is totaled. He'll have to get another. There's a vast selection nearby. "Wait here," he says. He hopes everything he packed can be salvaged. As he heads up the embankment, Barbara moves to come with him.

"Keep Emily down here," he tells her, and Barbara gradually understands. Emily doesn't need to see what lies up there on the interstate. As John trudges up the slick grass, he wonders how he expects his daughter to avoid seeing it, avoid seeing the world he helped make.

One Year Before

Smoke curls from Tracy's cigarette as she paces the hotel room in Milan. John lies naked on top of the twisted sheets. The rush of hormones and the buzz of alcohol have passed, leaving him flushed with guilt and acutely aware of what he has done.

"You should move to Italy," Tracy says. She touches the holstered gun on the dresser but does not pick it up. Inhaling, she allows the smoke to drift off her tongue.

"You know I can't," John says. "Even if it weren't for my family . . . I have—"

"Work," Tracy interrupts. She waves her hand as if work were an inconsequential thing harped on by some inferior race. Even when the two of them had worked down the hall from each other in the Pentagon, neither had known what the other did. The confusion had only thickened since, but along with it the professional courtesy not to ask. John feels they both want to know, but tearing clothes off bodies is simpler than exposing hidden lives.

"I do sometimes think about running away from it all," John admits. He considers the project taking most of his time of late, a plan he can only glimpse from the edges, piecing together the odd tasks required of him, similar to how he susses out political intrigue by whom he is hired to remove and who is left alone.

"So why don't you?" Tracy asks.

John nearly blurts out the truth: *Because there won't be anywhere left to run.* Instead, he tells a different truth: "I guess I'm scared."

Tracy laughs as if it's a joke. She taps her cigarette and spills ash onto the carpet, opens one of the dresser drawers and runs her fingers across John's clothes. Before he can say something, she has opened the next drawer to discover the book.

"A Bible," she says, sounding surprised.

John doesn't correct her. He slides from the bed and approaches her from behind in order to get the book. Tracy glances at him in the mirror and blocks him, presses back against him, her bare skin cool against his. John can feel his hormones surge and his resistance flag. He forgets the book, even as Tracy begins flipping through it. She was always curious. It was trouble for them both.

"Looks more interesting than a Bible," she mutters, the cigarette bouncing between her lips. John holds her hips and presses himself against her. She complies by pressing back. "What is this?" she asks.

"It's a book about the end of the world," John says, kissing her neck. This is the same thing he told Barbara. John has come to think of the book as one of those paintings that blurs the closer you get to it. It is safe by being unbelievable. The hidden key to understanding it – knowing who wrote it – was all that needed keeping safe.

Pages are flipped, which fans smoke above their heads.

"A different Bible, then," Tracy says.

"A different Bible," John agrees.

After a few more pages, the cigarette is crushed out. Tracy pulls him back to the bed. Afterward, John sleeps and dreams a strange dream. He is laying Barbara into a crypt deep beneath the soil. There is a smaller coffin there. Emily is already buried, and it is a lie that they'll ever be unearthed. It is a lie that they'll be brought back to life. That's just to get him to go along. John will live on for hundreds of years, every day a torment of being without them, knowing that they are just as dead as the others.

John wakes from this dream once and is only dimly aware that the bedside light is on, smoke curling up toward the ceiling, fanned by the gentle turning of prophetic pages.

The cars are, for the most part, orderly. They sit quietly, most of them electric, only one or two idling and leaking exhaust. They are lined up behind one another as if at any moment the trouble ahead might clear and the traffic will surge forward. Brake lights shine red. Hazards blink. The cars seem alive. Their occupants are not.

John considers the sheer weight of the dead – not just around him on the highway, but an *entire world* of the dead. An entire world slaughtered by men in elected posts who think they know best. How many of those in these cars voted for this? More than half, John thinks grimly.

He tries to remind himself that this is what someone else would've done, some mad dictator or mountain hermit. Eventually. The technology would've trickled out – these machines invisible to the naked eye that are just as capable of killing as they are of healing. When fanatics in basements begin to tinker, the end is near enough in the minds of many. No exotic or radioactive materials to process. Instead, machines that are becoming rapidly affordable, machines that can lay down parts one atom at a time, machines that can build other machines, which build more machines. All it will take is one madman to program a batch that sniffs out people by their DNA before *snuffing* them out.

John remembers his sophomore year of high school when he printed his first gun, how the plastic parts came out warm and slotted neatly together, how the printed metal spring locked into place, how the bullets chambered a little stiff with the first round and then better and better over time.

That was something he could understand, printing a weapon. This . . . this was the next generation's music. These were the kids on his lawn. He was one of their parents pulling the stereo plug before anyone made too much trouble.

John picks out a black SUV in the eastbound lane. A gasser, a Lexus 500. He has always wanted to drive one of these.

Lifeless eyes watch him from either side as he approaches, heads slumped against the glass, blood trickling from noses and ears, just these rivulets of pain. John wipes his own nose and looks at his knuckle. Nothing. He is a ghost, a wandering spirit, an angel of vengeance.

There is a wreck farther ahead, a car on manual that had taken out a few others, the cars around it scattered as their auto-drives had deftly avoided collision. He passes a van with a sticker on the back that shows a family holding hands. He does not look inside. A dog barks from a station wagon. John hesitates, veers from his path toward the SUV and goes over to open the door. The dog does not get out—just looks at him with its head cocked—but at least now it is free. It saddens John to think of how many pets just lost their owners. Like the people stranded up in the sky, there is so much he didn't consider. He heads to the SUV, feeling like he might be sick.

He tries the driver's door on the Lexus and finds it unlocked. A man with a loosened tie sits behind the wheel, blood dripping from his chin. The blood has missed his tie to stain the shirt. A glance in the back shows no baby seat to contend with. John feels a surge of relief. He unbuckles the man and slides him out and to the pavement.

He hasn't seen anything like this since Syria. It's like a chemical attack, these unwounded dead.

Memories from the field surge back, memories of politicians

back when they were soldiers. He gets in and cranks the Lexus, and the whine of the starter reminds him that it's already running. The car has taken itself out of gear. John adjusts the rearview and begins to inch forward and back, working the wheel, until he's sideways in traffic. Once again, he pulls off the interstate and down the embankment.

He heads straight for the wreckage of the Explorer and the van and gets out. Before Barbara and Emily can get to him, he has already pushed the passenger of the van back through the window and has covered him with the sport coat folded up on the passenger seat of the Lexus. John opens the back of the SUV, and Barbara whispers something to Emily. The three of them begin rounding up their gear and luggage and placing it into the car. It is a scavenger hunt for Emily. A box of canned goods has spilled down the embankment, and as she picks up each can and places it into the basket made by clutching the hem of her dress, John feels how wrong all of this is. There is too much normal left in the air. Being alive feels unnatural, a violation. He watches a buzzard swing overhead and land with a final flap of its wings on the top of the billboard. The great black bird seems confused by the stillness. Unsure. Disbelieving its luck.

"Is this ours?" Emily asks. She holds up the small single sideband radio, the antenna unspooled into a tangle.

"Yes," John says. He tries to remember what he was thinking to pack the SSB, what sort of foolish hope had seized him. Barbara says nothing, just works to get everything into the new car. She brushes leaves of grass off her carry-on and nestles it into the Lexus. Her silence is louder than shouted questions. She used to do this when John came home with stitched-up wounds, saying nothing until John feels his skin burn and he has to tell her.

"I wasn't positive—" he begins. He stops as Emily runs over to dump the contents of her dress into the car. He waits until she has moved beyond earshot again. "Part of me hoped nothing would happen, that I'd never have to tell you."

"What happened on the highway?" his wife asks. She shows him her phone. "I can't get anyone . . . Dad won't—"

"Everyone is gone," John says. He repeats this mantra, the one he keeps rolling over and over in his head. "Everyone."

Barbara searches his face. John can feel twelve billion souls staring at him, daring him to make her understand. Even he doesn't understand. Beyond the next exit, maybe the world is continuing along. But he knows this isn't true. Barbara looks at her phone. Her hand is shaking.

"There was no stopping it," John says. "Believe me."

"Who is left? Who can we call?"

"It's just us."

Barbara is silent. Emily returns and stacks cans between the luggage.

"This is because of what you do, isn't it?" Barbara asks. Emily has gone back for more.

John nods. Tears stream down Barbara's cheeks, and she begins to shake. John has seen widows like this, widows the moment they find out that's what they are. It is shock fading to acceptance. He wraps his arms around his wife, can't remember the last time he held her like this.

"Did you do this?" she asks. Her voice is shaking and muffled as he holds her tight.

"No. Not . . . not exactly. Not directly." He watches Emily delight in another find, far down the slope of grass.

"It's something you . . ." Barbara swallows and hunts for the words. ". . . that you went along with."

John can feel himself sag. He can't tell who is propping up whom. Yes, it was something he went along with. That's what he does. He goes along with. In Milan, succumbing to another, never leading. Never leading.

Emily arrives with something blue in her hands. "Is this ours?" she asks.

John pulls away from his wife. He looks down. It's the book.

The Order. "No," he says. "That's nobody's. You can leave that here."

The Day Before

There are two envelopes nestled inside the blue book, two sets of plane tickets. John pulls them both out and studies them, angles them back and forth to watch the printed holograms catch the light. It is raining outside, the wind blowing fat drops against the bedroom window, a sound like fingers tapping to be let in.

He sets the tickets aside and flips through the large book at random. Tracy thought it was the Bible when she first saw it – by dint of it being in a hotel room drawer, no doubt. He thinks about the New Testament and how long people have been writing about the end of the world. Every generation thinks it will be the last. There is some sickness in man, some paranoid delusion, some grandiose morbidity that runs right through to distant ancestors. Or maybe it is the fear in lonely hearts that they might die without company.

John finds the section in the book on security. His future job detail. If he doesn't show, will they promote some other? Or will it mean extra shifts for someone else? John tries to imagine a group of people skipping through time to wait out the cleansing of the Earth. He tries to imagine kissing his wife goodbye as he lays her in a silver coffin. Kissing Emily and telling her it'll all be okay. One last lie to them both before he seals them up.

Because there's no mistaking their ultimate fate. John can feel it in his bones whenever he reads the book. He knows when a person has been doomed by politicians. He knows when they say, "Everything will be all right," that they mean the opposite. The book doesn't say, but it doesn't have to. Not everyone who goes into that bunker will come out alive. If he flies to Atlanta and does his job, he'll never spend another day with his wife and daughter.

Tomorrow will be the last, no matter what, and it'll probably be spent in airports and in economy class.

He weighs the other tickets, the ones to Colorado Springs. Here is folly and madness, a group who thinks they can cheat the system, can survive on their own. Here is a woman who last year asked him to leave his life behind, his wife behind, and start anew someplace else. And now he is being asked again.

John holds the envelopes, one in each hand. It is usually another's life he weighs like this. Not his own. Not his family's. He doesn't want to believe a choice is necessary. Can't stand to think that Emily will never grow up and fall in love, never have kids of her own. Whatever life she has left, a day or years, wouldn't really be living.

He suddenly knows what he has to do. John slams the book shut and takes the tickets with him to the garage. Rummaging around, he finds the old Coleman stove. There's the lantern. The tent. He sniffs the old musky plastic and thinks of the last time they went on a vacation together. Years ago. What he wouldn't give for just one more day like that. One more day, even if it is their last.

He finds a canister and screws it onto the stove, adjusts the knob, presses the igniter. There's a loud click and the pop of gas catching. John watches the blue flames for a moment, remembers the horrible flapjacks he made on that stove years ago: burnt on the outside and raw in the middle. Emily loved them and has asked for her flapjacks like that ever since. He tries. But it's not easy to do things the wrong way on purpose.

John sets both envelopes on the grill, right above the flames, before he can reconsider. It isn't a choice – it's a refusal to choose. He has seen too many folders with assignments in them, too many plane tickets with death on the other end. This is an assignment he can't take. Cheat death or run to the woman he cheated with. He can do neither.

The paper crackles, plastic melts, smoke fills the air and burns his lungs. John takes a deep breath and holds it. He can feel the little buggers inside him, waiting on tomorrow. He can feel the world winding down. Orange flames lick higher as John rummages through the camping gear, gathering a few things, practicing the lies he'll tell to Barbara.

He has only been to the cabin once before, eight years ago. Or has it been nine already? A friend of his from the service had bought the place for an escape, a place to get away when he wasn't deployed. The last time John spoke to Carlos, his friend had complained that the lakeshore was getting crowded with new construction. But standing on the back deck, John sees the same slice of paradise he remembers from a decade prior.

There is a path leading down to the boathouse. The small fishing boat hangs serenely in its water-stained sling. There are clumps of flowers along the path with wire fencing to protect them from the deer. John remembers waking up in the morning all those years ago to find several doe grazing. The venison and fish will never run out. They will soon teem, he supposes. John thinks of the market they passed in the last small town. There won't be anyone else to rummage through the canned goods. It will be a strange and quiet life, and he doesn't like to think of what Emily will do once he and Barbara are gone. There will be time enough to think on that.

The screen door slams as Emily goes back to help unload the Lexus. John wonders for a moment how many others chickened out, decided to stay put in their homes, are now making plans for quiet days. He looks out over the lake as a breeze shatters that mirror finish, and he wishes, briefly, that he'd invited a few others from the program to join him here.

He takes a deep breath and turns to go help unload the car, when a faint rumble overhead grows into a growl. He looks up and searches the sky—but he can't find the source. It sounds like thunder, but there isn't a cloud to be seen. The noise grows and grows until the silver underbelly of a passenger liner flashes above the treetops and rumbles out over the lake. Can't be more than a thousand feet up. The jet is eerily quiet. It disappears into the trees beyond the far bank.

There comes the crack of splitting wood and the bass thud of impact. John waits for the ball of fire and plume of smoke, but of course: the plane is bone dry. Probably overshot Kansas on its way north from Dallas. Thousands of planes would be gliding to earth, autopilots trying in vain to keep them level, engines having sputtered to a stop. The deck creaks as Barbara rushes to his side.

"Was that—?"

He takes her hand in his and watches the distant tree line where birds are stirring. It is strange to think that no one will investigate the crash, that the bodies will never be identified, never seen. Unless he wanders up there out of curiosity one day, or forgets as he tracks deer or a rabbit and then comes across pieces of fuselage. A long life flashes before him, one full of strange quietude and unspoken horrors. A better life than being buried with the rest, he tells himself. Better than crawling into a bunker outside of Atlanta with that blue book. Better than running to Tracy in Colorado and having to explain to Barbara, eventually, what took place in Milan.

The porch shudders from tiny stomping feet. The screen door whacks shut. There is the sound of luggage thudding to the floor, and the porch falls still. John is watching the birds stir in the blue and cloudless sky. His nose itches, and he reaches to wipe it. Barbara sags against him, and John holds her up. They have this moment together, alive and unburied, a spot of blood on John's knuckle.

IN THE MOUNTAIN

"CARRY ON," ONE founder would say to another. To Tracy, it had become a mantra of sorts. Igor had started it, would wave his disfigured hand and dismiss the other founders back to their work. What began as mockery of him became a talisman of strength. *Carry on. Do the job. One foot forward.* A reminder to forge ahead even when the task was gruesome, even when it seemed pointless, even when billions were about to die.

But Tracy knew some things can only be carried so far before they must be set down. Set down or dropped. Dropped and broken.

The world was one of these things. The ten founders carried what they could to Colorado. An existing hole in the mountain there was burrowed even deeper. And when they could do no more, the founders stopped. And they counted the moments as the world plummeted toward the shattering.

The rock and debris pulled from the mountain formed a sequence of hills, a ridge now dusted with snow. The heavy lifters and buses and dump trucks had been abandoned by the mounds of rubble. There was a graveyard hush across the woods, a deep quiet of despair, of a work finished. The fresh snow made no sound as it fell from heavy gray clouds.

Tracy stood with the rest of the founders just inside the gaping steel doors of the crypt they'd built. She watched the snow gather in yesterday's muddy ruts. The crisscross patterns from the busloads of the invited would be invisible by nightfall. Humanity was not yet gone, the world not yet ruined, and already the universe was conspiring to remove all traces.

Anatoly fidgeted by her side. The heavyset physicist exhaled, and a cloud of frost billowed before his beard. On her other side, Igor reached into his heavy coat and withdrew a flash of silver. Tracy stole a glance. The gleaming watch was made more perfect in his mangled hand. Igor claimed he was a descendant and product of Chernobyl. Anatoly had told her it was a chemical burn.

Between Igor's red and fused fingers, the hours ticked down.

"Ten minutes," Igor said to the gathered. His voice was a grumble of distant thunder. Tracy watched as he formed an ugly fist and choked the life out of that watch. His pink knuckles turned the color of the snow.

Tracy shifted her attention to the woods and strained one last time to hear the sound of an engine's whine – the growl of a rental car laboring up that mountain road. She waited for the *crunch-crunch* of hurrying boots. She scanned for the man who would appear between those gray aspens with their peeled-skin bark. But the movies had lied to her, had conditioned her to expect last-minute heroics: a man running, a weary and happy smile, snow flying in a welcome embrace, warm lips pressed to cold ones, both trembling.

"He's not coming," Tracy whispered to herself. Here was a small leak of honesty from some deep and forgotten place.

Igor heard her and checked his watch again. "Five minutes," he said quietly.

And only then, with five minutes left before they needed to get inside, before they needed to shut the doors for good, did it become absolutely certain that he wasn't coming. John had gone to Atlanta with the others, had followed orders like a good soldier, and all that she'd worked to create in Colorado – the fantasy of surviving with him by her side – had been a great delusion. Those great crypt doors would close on her and trap her in solitude. And Tracy felt in that moment that she shouldn't have built this place, that she wouldn't have wasted her time if only she'd known.

"We should get inside," Igor said. He closed the lid on that small watch of his – a click like a cocked gun – and then it disappeared into his heavy coat.

There was a sob among them. A sniff. Patrice suddenly broke from the rest of the founders and ran through the great doors, her boots clomping on concrete, and Tracy thought for a moment that Patrice would keep on running, that she'd disappear into the aspens, but she stopped just beyond the concrete deck, stooped and gathered a handful of fresh snow, and ran back inside, eating some of it from her palms.

Tracy thought of grabbing something as well. A twig. A piece of that bark. A single falling snowflake on her tongue. She scanned the woods for some sight of John as Anatoly guided her inside, deep enough that the founders by the doors could shove the behemoths closed. Four feet thick, solid steel, streaked with rust where the weather had wetted them, they made a hideous screech as they were moved. A cry like a mother wolf out in the gray woods calling for her pups.

The white world slimmed as the doors came together. The view became a column, and then a gap, and then a sliver. There was a heavy and mortal thump as the doors met, steel pressing on steel, and then a darkness bloomed that had to be blinked against to get eyes working again.

Though the doors were now closed, Tracy thought she could still hear the sound of the wolf crying – and realized it was one of the founders making that mournful noise. Tears welled up in her eyes, brought there by a partner's lament. And Tracy remembered being young once and sobbing like that. She remembered the first time a man had broken her heart. It had felt like the end of the entire fucking world.

This day was something like that.

• • •

The mountain was full of the confused. Nearly five thousand people asking questions. Their bags were not yet unpacked; their backs were still sore from the rutted, bumpy ride in the buses. And now the myriad excuses for bringing them there – the retreats, reunions, vacations, emergencies – evaporated as conflicting accounts collided.

With the doors closed, the founders set out to explain. First to family. Later, to all of the invited. Tracy had been given an equal allotment of invitations, and she had used most of them on practical people. Soldiers. Tools of retribution. When the world was clean, all she wanted was to see a bullet in the people who had done this.

Of friends, she had none. Most of her adult life had been spent in Washington or overseas. There was a doorman in Geneva who had always been kind to her. There was the guy who did her taxes. Which was to admit that there was no one. Just her meager family: her father, her sister, and her sister's husband. Three people in all the world. Maybe that was why John's decision hurt so much. He was almost all she had. All she'd *thought* she had.

At least it meant a small audience as she dispensed the horrid truth, the nightmare she'd held inside for more than a year. Tracy hesitated outside the door to her sister's small room. She raised her fist and prepared to knock. Truth waited for her on the other side, and she wasn't sure she was ready.

Her father sat on the bed and wrung his hands while Tracy spoke. Her sister, April, sat next to him, a look of slack confusion on her face. Remy, April's husband, had refused to sit. He stood by his wife, a hand on her shoulder, something between anger and horror in his eyes.

They were all dressed for the camping trip they'd been promised – a week of backpacking, of living in the woods. The gear by the foot of the bed would never be used. The bags and the garb were reminders of Tracy's lies. She listened as the words spilled from her mouth. She listened to herself say what she had rehearsed a hundred times: how the tiny machines used in hospitals to attack cancer – those invisible healers, the same ones that would've saved Mom if they'd been available in time – how those same machines were as capable of killing as they were of healing.

She told her family how those machines were in everyone's blood, in every human being's on Earth. And curing everyone might be possible, but it would only be temporary. Once people knew that it could be done, it was only a matter of time. A switch had been invented that could wipe out every man and woman alive. Any hacker in his basement could flip that switch – which meant someone *would.*

Tracy got through that part without the wailing or hysterics she'd expected, without the questions and confusion from her dad, without anyone pushing past her and banging on the door, screaming to be let out. No one asked her if she belonged to a cult or if she was on drugs or suggested she needed to take a break from whatever work she did in Washington, that she needed to see a professional.

"It was only a matter of time before someone did it," Tracy said again. "And so our government acted before someone else could. So they could control the aftermath."

Remy started to say something, but Tracy continued before he could: "We aren't a part of the group who did this," she said. She looked to her father. "We didn't do this. But we found out about it, and we realized we couldn't stop it. We realized . . . that maybe they were right. That it needed to be done. And so we did the next best thing. We created this place. We invited ourselves along. And those that we could. We'll be okay here. You all were inoculated on the way. You probably felt your ears popping on the bus ride up. Now we'll spend six months here, maybe a year –"

"Six months," Remy said.

"This can't be real." Her sister shook her head.

"It's real," Tracy told April. "I'm sorry. I never wanted to keep this from any of—"

"I don't believe it," Remy said. He glanced around the room as if seeing it for the first time. April's husband was an accountant, was used to columns of numbers in black and white. He was also a survivalist, was used to sorting out the truth on his own. He didn't learn simply by being told. Igor had warned that it would take some people weeks before they believed.

"We are positive," Tracy said. This was a lie; she had her own doubts. She wouldn't be completely sure until the countdown clock hit zero. But there was no use infecting others with her slender hopes. "I realize this is hard to hear. It's hard even for me to grasp. But the war we were bracing for isn't going to come with clouds of fire and armies marching. It's going to be swifter and far worse than that."

"Did *you* do this?" her father asked, voice shaking with age. Even with his encroaching, occasional senility, he knew that Tracy worked for bad agencies full of bad people. There were classified things she had confided to him years ago that he had been willing to shoulder for her. They would likely be the very last things his dementia claimed, little islands of disappointment left in a dark and stormy sea.

"No, Dad, I didn't do this. But I *am* the reason we have this place, a nice place to be together and wait it out."

She flashed back to that night in Milan, to the first time she'd laid eyes on the book with the word *Order* embossed on its cover. It was the same night she made John forget about his wife for a brief moment, the night when all those years of flirtations came to fruition: the bottle of wine, the dancing, that dress – the one she'd gotten in trouble for expensing to her company card. And in his room, after they made love, and hungering for more danger, she had gone to the dresser where she knew his gun would be tucked away, and she'd found that book instead.

If John had stayed in bed, she wouldn't have thought anything more of it. The book was full of the dry text that only lawyers who had become politicians could craft. Emergency procedures. An ops manual of some sort. But the way John had lurched out of bed, it was as if Tracy had let his wife into the room. She remembered the way his hands trembled against her as he asked her to put it away, to come back to bed, like she'd grabbed something far more dangerous than a gun, something cocked and loaded with something much worse than bullets.

After he'd gone to sleep, Tracy had sat on the edge of the bathtub, the book open on the toilet lid, and had turned every page with her phone set to record. Even as she scanned, she saw enough to be afraid.

Enough to *know.*

"I'm sorry," she told her father, unable to stomach the disappointment on his face.

"When—?" April asked.

Tracy turned to her sister, the schoolteacher, who knew only that Tracy worked for the government, who had no idea about all the classified blood on her hands. April was four years older, would always be older than Tracy in all the ways that didn't matter and in none of the ways that did.

"In a few hours," Tracy said. "It'll all be over in a few hours."

"And will we feel anything?" April rubbed her forearm. "What about everyone out there? Everyone we know. They'll just—?"

Remy sat beside his wife and wrapped his arms around her. The air around Tracy grew cold. Even more empty.

"*We* were supposed to be out there when it happened, too," Tracy said. "The four of us. Remember that. We'll talk more later. I have to get to a meeting—"

"A meeting?" April asked. "A *meeting*? To do what? Decide the rest of our lives? Decide who lives and who dies? What kind of meeting?"

And now Remy was no longer embracing his wife. He was restraining her.

"How dare you!" April screamed at Tracy. Their father shivered on the bed, tried to say something, to reach out to his daughters and tell them not to fight. Tracy retreated toward the door. She was wrong about the hysteria, about it not coming. There was just some delay. And as she slipped into the hall and shut the small room on her sister's screaming, she heard that she'd been wrong about her beating on the door as well.

Saving a person seemed simple. But saving them against their will was not. Tracy realized this as she navigated the corridors toward the command room, her sister's screams still with her. She could hear muffled sobs and distant shouting from other rooms as she passed – more people learning the truth. Tracy had thought that preserving a life would absolve all other sins, but the sin of not consulting with that life first was perhaps the only exception. She recalled an ancient argument she'd had with her mother when she was a teenager, remembered yelling at her mom and saying she wished she'd never been born. And she'd meant it. What right did someone else have to make that decision for her? Her mom had always expected her to be grateful simply for having been brought into the world.

Now Tracy had made the same mistake.

She left the apartment wing, those two thousand rooms dug laterally and tacked on to a complex built long ago, and she entered the wide corridors at the heart of the original bunker. The facility had been designed to house fifteen hundred people for five years. The founders had invited more than three times that number, but they wouldn't need to stay as long. The biggest job had been cleaning out and refilling the water and diesel tanks.

The entire place was a buried relic from a different time, a time capsule for a different threat, built for a different end-of-the-world scenario. The facility had been abandoned years ago. It had become a tourist attraction. And then it had fallen into disrepair. The founders chose the location after considering several options.

Igor and Anatoly used their research credentials and leased the space under the auspices of searching for neutrinos, some kind of impossible-to-find subatomic particles. But it was a much different and invisible threat they actually set out to find: the machines that polluted the air and swam through every vein.

Tracy used her key to unlock the cluttered command room. A round table dominated the center of the space. A doughnut of monitors ringed the ceiling above, tangles of wires drooping from them and running off to equipment the engineers had set up. In one corner, a gleaming steel pod stood like some part of an alien ship. It had been built according to stolen plans, was thought at first to be necessary for clearing the small machines from their bloodstreams, but it ended up being some sort of cryo-device, a side project the Atlanta team had undertaken. The only machine Tracy knew how to operate in that room was the coffeemaker. She started a pot and watched the countdown clock overhead tick toward Armageddon.

The other founders trickled in one at a time. Many had red eyes and chapped cheeks. There was none of the chatting, debating, and arguing that had marked their prior meetings in that room. Just the same funereal silence they'd held by the crypt doors.

A second pot was brewed. One of the engineers got the screens running, and they watched the TV feeds in silence. There was speculation among the talking heads that the presidential nomination was not quite the lock everyone had presumed. The excitement in the newsrooms was palpable and eerie. Tracy watched dead men discuss a future that did not exist.

Two minutes.

The talking heads fell silent, and the feeds switched from newsrooms to a stage outside Atlanta. The distant downtown towers gleamed in the background. On the stage, a young girl in a black dress held a microphone and took a deep breath, a little nervous as she began to sing.

The national anthem brought tears to Tracy's eyes. She reminded herself to breathe. And not for the first time, she had an awful premonition that she was wrong, that the book was just a book, that John had believed in something that would not come to pass, and that she would soon be embarrassed in that room with all the people she'd convinced to join her. She would be another in a long line of failed messiahs. Her sister would look at her like she was crazy for the rest of her life. National headlines would mock the kooks in a mountain who had thought the world was going to end. And somehow all of this felt worse than twelve billion dead.

It was a guilty thought, the panic that she might be wrong.

Large red numbers on the clock counted down. No part of her wanted to be right. Either way, her world was ending. When the clock struck all zeroes, Tracy would either be an outcast or a shut-in.

On the array of televisions, the same scene was shown from half a dozen angles, all the various news stations and networks tuned to that young girl in her black dress. One of the screens cut to the obligatory jets screaming in formation overhead. Another screen showed a group of senators and representatives, hands on their goddamn patriotic chests. Tracy searched for John, thought she might see him there near the stage with his suit jacket that showed off his handsome shoulders but also that bulge by his ribs. There were five seconds on the clock. One of the founders started counting, whispering the numbers as they fell.

Three.

Two.

One.

A line of zeroes.

And nothing happened.

"They're still breathing," someone said.

Igor cursed and fumbled for that damned watch of his.

An eternity squeezed itself into a span of three seconds. No one moved.

"Holy shit," someone said.

CNN's feed spun sickeningly to the side, the cameraman whirling, and Tracy realized it was one of the reporters who had cursed. Another screen showed a bright flash, a brief glimpse of a mushroom cloud, and then that monitor went black.

The young girl was no longer singing. She had been replaced with station identifiers and shots of stunned newscasters who stared at their feeds in disbelief. More bright flashes erupted on the last monitor running, which showed a wide vista from some great distance. Three classic and terrifying mushroom clouds rose toward the heavens, shouldering the other clouds aside. And then that last screen succumbed as well, promising impotently to "Be right back."

"Shut it off!" a reporter screamed. He waved at someone off-camera. "Shut it off—"

And then someone did. A switch flipped somewhere, in all those veins, and all the talking heads on all the screens bowed forward or tilted to the side. Blood flowed from the nose of the man who had just been waving. His jaw fell slack; his eyes focused on nothing—a quiet death.

The founders in the command room—no longer breathing—watched in silence. Hands clasped over mouths. Those who had harbored any doubts now believed. All was still. The only things that moved on the screens were the thin red rivulets trickling from noses and ears. There was no one left alive to cut away to, to change the view. And only those ten people huddled around the wire-webbed monitors were left to see.

"Kill it," someone finally said, a terrible slip of the tongue.

Tracy watched as Dmitry fumbled with the controls for the panels. He accidentally changed channels on one of the sets, away from news and into the realm of reruns. There was a sitcom playing: a family around a dinner table, a joke just missed. A bark of canned laughter spilled from the speaker, the illusion that life was still transpiring out there as it always had. But it wasn't just the laughter that was canned now. They all were. All of humanity. What little was left.

“Hey. Wake up.”

Dreams. Nothing more than dreams. A black ghost clawing away at her mother, a wicked witch burying her father and her sister. Tracy sat up in bed, sweating. She felt a hand settle on her shoulder.

“We have a problem,” someone said.

A heavy shadow, framed by the wan light spilling from the hallway.

“Anatoly?”

“Come,” he said. He lumbered out of her small room deep in the mountain. Tracy slid across that double bunk, a bed requisitioned for two, and tugged on the same pants and shirt she’d worn the day before.

The fog of horrible dreams mixed with the even worse images from their first day in the complex. Both swirled in her sleepy brain. Slicing through these was the fear in Anatoly’s voice. The normally unflappable Russian seemed petrified. Was it really only to last a single day, all their schemes to survive the end of the world? Was it a riot already? Orientation the day before had not gone well. Fights had broken out. A crowd had gathered at those four-foot-thick doors, which had been designed just as much to keep people *in* as to keep other dangers out.

Perhaps it was a leak. Air from the outside getting in. Tracy hurried down the hall barefoot, searching her lungs for some burn or itch, touching her upper lip and looking for a bleed. Her last thought as she caught up to Anatoly and they reached the command room together was that the cameras outside the crypt doors would be on, would reveal a lone man, inoculated to the sudden death but slowly dying anyway, banging feebly and begging to be let in—

"Everyone here?" Dmitry asked. The thin programmer scanned the room over his spectacles. There was no real leader among the founders. Tracy held some special status as the originator of the group, she who had found *The Order*. Anatoly was the man who had coordinated the lease and planning of the facility. But Dmitry was the brightest among them, the tinkerer, the one who had deactivated the machines in their blood. Of them all, he seemed to most enjoy the thought of being in charge. No one begrudged him that.

"What is this?" Patrice asked. She knotted her robe across her waist and crossed her arms against the chill in the room.

"The program," Dmitry said. "It . . . has changed."

Someone groaned. Tracy rubbed the sand from her eyes. The gathered braced for Dmitry's usual technobabble, which was bad enough when wide awake.

"Five hundred years," he said. He pushed his glasses up his nose and looked from face to face. "Not six months. Five hundred years."

"Until what?" Sandra asked.

"Until we can go out," Dmitry said. He pointed toward the door. "Until we can go out."

"But you said—"

"I know what I said. And it's all in the book. It says six months. But the program unspooled yesterday. It's dynamic code, a self-assembler, and now there's a clock set to run for five hundred years."

The room was quiet. The recycled air flowing through the overhead vent was the only sound.

"How are you reading this new program?" Igor asked. "Do you have those buggers in here?" He nodded toward the silver pod with all its tubes and wires.

"Of course not. The antennas we put up, I can access the mesh network the machines use to communicate. Are any of you listening to me? The program is set to run for five hundred years. This book"—he pointed to the tome sitting on the large round table—"this isn't a guide for the entire program. It's just for one small part of it, just one shift. I think the cryo-pods are maybe so they can—"

"So how do we change it?" Anatoly asked. "You can tap into the network. How do we turn it all off? So we can leave right now? Or set it back to six months?"

Dmitry let out his breath and shook his head. He had that exasperated air about him that he got when any of the founders asked questions that belied fundamental flaws in their understanding of what, to him, were basic concepts. "What you're asking is impossible. Otherwise I would have done it already. I can program the test machines in my lab, but overcoming the entire network?" He shook his head.

"What does that mean for us?" Tracy asked.

"It means we have a year's worth of food," Dmitry said. "Eighteen months, maybe two years if we ration. And then we all slowly die in here. Or . . ."

"Or what?"

"Or we die quickly out there."

Sharon slapped the table and glared at Dmitry. "We've got fourteen men in the infirmary and another eight in restraints from telling everyone we'll be here for six months and that everyone they know is now dead. Now you're saying we have to tell them that we *lied?* That we brought them here to *starve to death?*"

Tracy sank into one of the chairs. She looked up at Dmitry. "Are you sure about this? You were wrong about the clock the last time. You were a few seconds off. Maybe—"

"It was tape delay," Dmitry said, rubbing his eyes beneath his glasses. "All broadcasters use a time delay. I wasn't wrong. I'm not wrong now. I can show you the code."

One of the founders groaned.

"What were you saying about the pod?"

"I think this is a manual for a single shift," Dmitry said. "And the pod is for—"

"You mean the icebox?" Patrice asked.

"Yes. The cryo-unit is to allow them to stagger the shifts. To last the full five hundred years. I looked over one of the requisitions reports we intercepted, and it all makes sense –"

"Does our pod work?" Anatoly asked.

Dmitry shrugged. "Nobody wanted me to test it, remember? Listen, we have a decision to make –"

"What decision? You're telling us we're all dead."

"Not all of us," Tracy said. She rested her head in her palms, could see that witch from her dreams, shoveling soil on thousands of writhing bodies, hands clawing to get out.

"What do you mean?" Patrice asked.

"I mean we're the same as them." She looked up and pointed to the dead monitors, which had once looked out on the world, on the people with their anthems who had doomed them all. "We have the same decision to make. Our little world, our little mountain, isn't big enough for all of us. So we have a decision to make. The same decision they made. We're no better than them."

"Yes," Dmitry said. "I figure we have eighteen months' worth of food for five thousand mouths. That gives us enough for fifteen people for five hundred years."

"Fifteen people? To do what?"

"To survive," Dmitry said. But the tone of his voice said something more somber and sinister. Tracy tried to imagine all that he was implying. Someone else said it for her.

"And kill everyone else? Our families?"

"No way," someone said. Tracy watched her partners, these founders, fidget. It was the orientation all over again. A fight would break out.

"We can't live that long anyway," Tracy said, attempting to defuse the argument by showing how pointless it all was.

"Generations," Anatoly blurted out. He scratched his beard, seemed to be pondering a way to make some insane plan work. "Have to make sure there's only one birth for every death."

Tracy's eyes returned to the book on the center of the conference table. Others were looking at it as well. She remembered a passage like that inside the book. Several passages now suddenly made more sense. The answer had been there, but none of them had been willing to see it. It's how that book seemed to work.

"I won't be a part of this," Natasha said. "I won't. I'd rather have one year here, with my family, than even consider what you're suggesting."

"Will you still think that a year from now, when the last ration is consumed and we're left watching one another waste away? Either it happens now, or it happens then. Which way is cleaner?"

"We sound just like them," Tracy whispered, mostly to herself. She eyed those monitors again, saw her reflection in one of them.

"The Donner Party," Sherman said. When one of the Russians turned to stare at him, Sherman started to explain. "Settlers heading west two centuries ago. They got trapped in the mountains and had to resort to –"

"I'm familiar with the story. It's not an option."

"I didn't mean it was an *option*." Sherman turned to Natasha. "I mean, that's what we're going to start thinking a year from now. Or eighteen months. Whenever."

Natasha spun a lock of her hair. She dipped the end between her lips and remained silent.

"It would be quick," Dmitry said. "We still have canisters of the test nanos, the ones I built. Those, I can program. We would have to inoculate ourselves first –"

"This is going too fast," Tracy said. "We need to think about this."

"After thirty-six days, we'll be down to fourteen people," Dmitry said. "At the rate we'll be feeding these people, each month we delay means one spot lost. How long do you want to think about it?" He took off his glasses and wiped the condensation from them. It had grown hot in the room. "We're in a lifeboat," he said. "We are drifting to shore, but not as fast as we had hoped. There are too many of us in the boat." He returned the glasses to the bridge of his nose, looked coolly at the others.

"Every one of us should have died yesterday," Anatoly said. "Our families. Us. Every one. None of us should be here. Even this day is a bonus. A year would be a blessing."

"Is it so important that any of us make it to the other side?" Patrice asked. The others turned to her. "I mean, it won't even be us. If we were to do this. It would be our descendants. And what kind of hell are they going to endure in here, living for dozens of generations in this hole, keeping their numbers at fifteen, brothers and sisters coupling? Is that even surviving? What's the point? What's the point if we're just trying to get someone to the other side? No matter what, the assholes in Atlanta will be our legacy now."

"That's why we have to do this," Tracy said.

Dmitry nodded. "Tracy's right. That's *precisely* why we have to do this. So they don't get away with it. Isn't that what we planned from the beginning? Isn't that why we only have enough food for a year but enough guns to slaughter an army?"

"Fifteen people is no army."

"But they'll know," Dmitry said. "They'll carry legends with them. We'll write it all down. We'll make up most of the first fifteen. We'll make sure no one ever forgets—"

"You mean make a religion out of this."

"I mean make a *cause*."

"Or a cult."

"Do we want them to have the world to themselves, the fuckers who did this?"

"We can't decide anything now," Tracy said. She rubbed her temples. "I need to sleep. I need to see my family—"

"No one can know," Anatoly told her.

Tracy shot him a look. "I'm not telling anyone. But we need a day or two before we do anything." She caught the look on Dmitry's face. "Surely we have that much time."

He nodded.

"And you won't program anything without consulting with us first."

Again, a nod.

Sherman laughed, but it was without humor. "Yes," he said. "I need sleep as well." He pointed to Dmitry. "And I want assurances that I'll wake up in the morning."

The following day, Tracy grabbed breakfast from the mess hall and found three founders at a table in the corner. She joined them. No one spoke. Between bites of bread and canned ham, she watched the bustle of strangers weaving through the tables and chairs, introducing themselves to one another, glancing around at their surroundings, and trying to cope with their imprisonment. Their salvation.

The buzz of voices and spoons clicking against porcelain was shattered for a brief moment by an awful release of laughter. Tracy searched for the offender, but it was gone as quickly as it had come. She watched Igor chew his bread, his eyes lifeless, focused beyond the mountain's walls, and knew he was thinking the same thing: They were in a room crowded with ghosts. There was no stopping what they would have to do. And for the first time, Tracy understood all that John had endured those past years. She remembered the way he would glance around in a restaurant, his eyes haunted, the color draining suddenly from his face. *Looking for an exit,* she used to think. *Looking for some way out if it all goes to shit.*

But no – he had been doing this, scanning the people, the bodies all around him. How could he search for an exit when there was none?

Tracy saw her sister and Remy emerge from the serving line, trays in hand. She started to wave them over, then caught herself. When she saw her sister among all those walking dead, she realized what she had to do. She put down her bread and left her tray behind. She needed to find Dmitry. To see if it was possible.

A new *Order* was required, a new book of instructions. Nine of the ten founders and the six they chose would have the rest of their lives to sort out the details, to leave precise instructions. Tracy had already decided she wouldn't go with them. If John were there, maybe it could work, but she couldn't pair off with one of the men in their group.

First she had her own orders to write, her own instructions. This included how to open the great crypt gates, in case there was no one else. She spent her days and nights in the workshop command room, helping Dmitry with the pod, pestering him with questions that he didn't know the answers to. The cryo-pod had been designed for one person. And once they'd realized what it was, it had gone untested. Tracy squeezed inside for a dry fit while Dmitry modified the plumbing.

"Maybe one head over here and the other down there? Legs'll have to go like this."

Dmitry muttered under his breath. He wrestled a piece of tubing onto a small splitter, was having trouble making it fit.

"You need help?" Tracy asked.

"I got it," he said.

"What if . . . something happens to you all and there are no descendants? What if there's no one here to open it?"

"Already working on that," Dmitry said. "The antenna that taps into the mesh network. I can rig it up so when their timer shuts off, the pod will open. So if it's twenty years from now or twenty thousand, as long as this place has power . . ." He finally got the tube on to the fitting. "Don't worry," he said. "I'll take care of it. I have time."

Tracy hoped he was right. She wanted to believe him.

"So what do you think it'll feel like?" she asked. "You think it'll be . . . immediate? Like shutting your eyes at night, and then suddenly the alarm goes off in the morning? Or will it be dream after dream after dream?"

"I don't know." Dmitry shook his head. He started to say something, then turned quietly back to his work.

"What?" Tracy asked. "Is there something you aren't telling me?"

"It's . . . nothing." He set the tubing aside and crossed his arms. Then he turned to her. "Why do you think nobody is fighting for their place in there?" He nodded to the machine.

Tracy hadn't considered that. "Because I asked first?" she guessed.

"Because that thing is a coffin. People have been putting their loved ones in there for years. Nobody wakes up."

"So this is a bad idea?"

Dmitry shrugged. "I think maybe the people who do this, it isn't for the ones *inside* the box."

Tracy lay back in that steel cylinder and considered this, the selfishness of it all. Giving life without asking. Taking life to save some other. "For the last two days," she said, "all I've thought about is what a mistake all this was." She closed her eyes. "Completely pointless. All for nothing."

"That is life," Dmitry said. Tracy opened her eyes to see him waving a tool in the air and staring up at the ceiling. "We do not go out in glory. We leave no mark. What you did was right. What they did was wrong. They're the reason we're in this mess, not you."

Tracy didn't feel like arguing. What was the point? It didn't matter. Nothing mattered. And maybe that's what Dmitry was trying to tell her.

She crawled out of that coffin-within-a-crypt to check the supplies one last time, to make sure the vacuum was holding a seal. Inside the large storage trunk were her handwritten instructions, a set of maps, two handguns, clothing, all of Remy and April's camping gear, and what extra rations would fit.

Five hundred years was a long time to plan for, almost an impossible time to consider. And then it occurred to her that she was wrong about something: She was wrong about the great doors that led into that mountain. This was not a crypt. The dead were on the *outside*. Here was but a bubble of life, trapped in the deep rock. A bubble only big enough now for fifteen people. Fifteen plus two.

Before waking her sister, Tracy stole into her father's room and kissed him quietly on the forehead. She brushed his thinning hair back and kissed him once more. One last time. Wiping tears away, she moved to the neighboring room. Igor and Anatoly were waiting outside the door. They had agreed to help her, had been unhappy with her decision, but she had traded her one precious spot for two questionable others.

They stole inside quietly. The Russians had syringes ready. They hovered over Remy first. It went fast, not enough kicking to stir her sister. April was next. Tracy thought of all she was burdening them with, her sister and Remy. An accountant and a schoolteacher. They would sleep tonight, and when they woke, what would they find? Five hundred years, gone in an instant. A key around their necks. A note from her. An apology.

Igor lifted April, and Tracy helped Anatoly with Remy. They shuffled through dark corridors with their burdens. "Carry on," Tracy whispered, that mantra of theirs, the awful dismissal of all they'd done. But this time, it was with promise. With hope. "Carry on," she whispered to her sister. "Carry on for all of us."

IN THE WOODS

A SLIVER OF LIGHT appeared in the pitch-black—a horizontal crack that ran from one end of April's awareness to the other. There was a deep chill in her bones. Her teeth chattered; her limbs trembled. April woke up cold with metal walls pressed in all around her. A mechanical hum emanated from somewhere behind her head. Another body was wedged in beside her.

She tried to move and felt the tug of a cord on her arm. Fumbling with her free hand, April found an IV. She could feel the rigid lump of a needle deep in her vein. There was another hose along her thigh that ran up to her groin. She patted the cold walls around herself, searching for a way out. She tried to speak, to clear her throat, but like in her nightmares, she made no sound.

The last thing April remembered was going to sleep in an unfamiliar bunk deep inside a mountain. She remembered feeling trapped, being told the world had ended, that she would have to stay there for years, that everyone she knew was gone. She remembered being told that the world had been poisoned.

April had argued with her husband about what to do, whether to flee, whether to even believe what they'd been told. Her sister had said it was the air, that it couldn't be stopped, so a group had planned on riding it out here. They'd brought them in buses to an abandoned government facility in the mountains of Colorado. They said it might be a while before any of them could leave.

The body in the dark by April's feet stirred. There was a foot by her armpit. They were tangled, she and this form. April tried to pull away, to tuck her knees against her chest, but her muscles were slow to respond, her joints stiff. She could feel the chill draining from her, and a dull heat sliding in to take its place – like the tubes were emptying her of death and substituting that frigid void with the warmth of life.

The other person coughed, a deep voice ringing metallic in the small space, hurting her ears. April tried to brace herself with the low ceiling to scoot away from the coughing form, when the crack of light widened. She pushed up more, grunting with the strain, and even more light came in. The ceiling hinged back. The flood of harsh light nearly blinded her. Blinking, eyes watering, ears thrumming from the sound of that noisy pump running somewhere nearby, April woke with all the violence and newness of birth. Shielding her eyes – squinting out against the assault of light – she saw in her blurry vision a man lying still by her feet. It was her husband, Remy.

April wept in relief and confusion. The hoses made it hard to move, but she worked her way closer to him, hands on his shins, thighs, clambering up his body until her head was against Remy's chest. His arms feebly encircled her. Husband and wife trembled from the cold, teeth clattering. April had no idea where in the world they were or how they got there; she just knew they were together.

"Hey," Remy whispered. His lips were blue. He mouthed her name, eyes closed, holding her.

"I'm here," she said. "I'm here."

The warmth continued to seep in. Some came from their naked bodies pressed together; some came directly through her veins. April felt the urge to pee, and her body – almost of its own volition, of some long-learned habit – simply relieved itself. Fluid snaked away from her through one of the tubes. If it weren't for the too-real press of Remy's flesh against her own, she would think this was all a dream.

"What's happening?" Remy asked. He rubbed his eyes with one hand.

"I don't know." April's voice was hoarse. A whisper. "Someone did this to us." Even as she said this, she realized it was obvious, that it didn't need saying. Because she had no memory of being put in that metal canister.

"My eyes are adjusting," she told Remy. "I'm going to open this up some more."

Remy nodded slowly.

Peering up, April saw a curved half-cylinder of gleaming steel hanging over them, a third of the way open. She lifted a quivering leg, got a foot against the hinged lid, and shoved. Their small confines flew open the rest of the way, letting in more light. Flickering bulbs shone down from overhead. The lamps dangled amid a tangle of industrial pipes, traces of wire, air ducts, and one object so out of place that it took a moment to piece together what she was seeing. Suspended from the ceiling, hanging down over their heads, was a large yellow bin: a heavy-duty storage trunk.

"What does that say?" Remy asked. They both squinted up at the object, blinking away cold tears.

April studied the marks of black paint on the yellow tub. She could tell it was a word, but it felt like forever since she'd read anything real, anything not fragmented amid her dreams. When the word crystallized, she saw that it was simply her name.

"April," she whispered. That's all it said.

Before they could get the bin down, she and Remy had to extricate themselves from the steel canister. Why had they been put there? As punishment? But what had they done? The IVs and catheters were terrible clues that they'd been out for more than a mere night, and the stiffness in April's joints and the odor of death in the air—perhaps coming from their very flesh—hinted at it having been more than a week. It was impossible to tell.

"Careful," Remy said, as April peeled away the band that encircled her arm, the band that held the tube in place. It tore like Velcro, not like tape. Were they put away for longer than adhesive would last? The thought was fleeting, too impossible to consider.

"What's that around your neck?" Remy asked.

April patted her chest. She looked down at the fine thread around her neck and saw a key dangling from it. She had sensed it before, but in a daze. Looking back up at the bin, she saw a dull silver lock hanging bat-like from the lip of the bin.

"It's a message," April said, understanding in a haze how the key and the bin and her name were supposed to go together. "Help me out."

Her first hope was that there was food in that bin. Her stomach was in knots, cramped from so deep a hunger. Remy helped her pull her IV out and extract her catheter, and then she helped with his. A spot of purple blood welled up on her arm, and a dribble of fluid leaked from the catheter. Using the lid of the metal pod for balance, April hoisted herself to her feet, stood there for a swaying, unsteady moment, then reached up and touched the large plastic trunk.

It'd been suspended directly over their heads, where they would see it upon waking. A chill ran down April's spine. Whoever had placed them there had known they would wake up on their own, that there wouldn't be anyone around to help them, to explain things, to hand them a key or tell them to look inside the chest. That explained the paint, the thread, the pod cracking open on its own. Had she and Remy been abandoned? Had they been punished? Somehow, she knew her sister had been involved. Her sister who had brought them into the mountain had locked them away yet again, in tighter and tighter confines.

Remy struggled to his feet, grunting from the exertion of simply standing. He surveyed the room. "Looks like junk storage," he whispered, his voice like sandpaper.

"Or a workshop," April said. *Or a laboratory,* she thought to herself. "I think this knot frees the bin. We can lower it down."

"So thirsty," Remy said. "Feels like I've been out for days."

Months, April stopped herself from suggesting. "Help me steady this. I think . . . I have a feeling this is from Tracy."

"Your sister?" Remy held on to April, reached a hand up to steady the swaying bin. "Why do you think that? What have they done to us?"

"I don't know," April said, as she got the knot free. She held the end of the line, which looped up over a paint-flecked pipe above. The line had been wrapped twice, so there was enough friction that even her weak grip could bear the weight of the bin. Lowering the large trunk, she wondered what her sister had done this time. Running away from home to join the army, getting involved with the CIA or FBI or NSA – April could never keep them straight – and now this, whatever this was. Locking thousands of people away inside a mountain, putting her and Remy in a box.

The bin hit the metal pod with a heavy *thunk,* pirouetted on one corner for a moment, then settled until the hoisting rope went slack. April touched the lock. She reached for the key around her neck. The loop was too small to get over her head.

"No clasp," Remy said, his fingertips brushing the back of her neck.

April wrapped a weak fist around the key and tugged with the futile strength of overslept mornings.

The thread popped. April used the key to work the lock loose. Unlatching the trunk, there was a hiss of air and a deep sigh from the plastic container, followed by the perfume scent of life – or maybe just a spot of vacuum to stir away the stale odor of death.

There were folded clothes inside. Nestled on top of the clothes were tins labeled "water" with vials of blue powder taped to each. Remy picked up the small note between the tins, and April recognized the writing. It was her sister's. The note said: "Drink me."

A dreamlike association flitted through April's mind, an image of a white rabbit. She was Alice, tumbling through a hole and into a world both surreal and puzzling. Remy had less hesitation. He popped the tins with the pull tab, took a sip of the water, then studied the vial of powder.

"You think your sister is out to help us?" Remy asked. "Or kill us?"

"Probably thinks she's helping," April said. "And'll probably get us killed." She uncorked one of the vials, dumped it into Remy's tin of water, and stirred with her finger. Her sister wasn't there to argue with, so April skipped to the part where she lost the argument and took a sip.

A foul taste of metal and chalk filled her mouth, but a welcome wetness as well. She drank it all, losing some around the corners of her mouth that trickled down her neck and met again between her bare breasts.

Remy followed suit, trusting her. Setting the empty tin aside, April looked under the clothes. There were familiar camping backpacks there, hers and Remy's. She remembered packing them back at her house in Maryland. Her sister had just said they were going camping in Colorado, to bring enough for two weeks. Along with the packs were stacks of freeze-dried camping MREs; more tins of water; a first-aid kit; plastic pill cylinders that rattled with small white, yellow, and pink pills; and her sister's pocketknife. It was Remy who found the gun and the clips loaded with ammo. At the bottom of the case was an atlas, one of those old AAA road maps of the United States. It was open to a page, a red circle drawn on it with what might've been lipstick. And, finally, there was a sealed note with April's name on it.

She opened the note while Remy studied the map. Skipping to the bottom, April saw her sister's signature, the familiar hurried scrawl of a woman who refused to sit still, to take it easy. She went back to the top and read. It was an apology. A confession. A brief history of the end of the world and Tracy's role in watching it all come to fruition.

"We've been asleep for five hundred years," April told her husband, when she got to that part. She read the words without believing them.

Remy looked up from the atlas and studied her. His face said what she was thinking: *That's not possible.*

Even with the suspicion that they'd been out for months or longer, five hundred years of sleep was beyond the realm of comprehension. The end of the world had been nearly impossible to absorb. Being alive out along the fringe of time, maybe the only two people left on the entire Earth, was simply insane.

April kept reading. Her sister's rough scrawl explained the food situation, that they'd miscalculated the time it would take for the world to be safe again, for the air to be okay to breathe. She explained the need to ration, that there were only enough supplies to get fifteen people through to the other side. She could almost hear her sister's voice as she read, could see her writing this note in growing anger, tears in her eyes, knuckles white around a pen. And then she came to this:

The people who destroyed the world are in Atlanta. I marked their location on the map. If you are reading this, you and whoever else are left in the facility are the only ones alive who know what they did. You're the only ones who can make them pay. For all of us.

I'm sorry. I love you. I never meant for any of this, and no one can take it back—can make it right—but there can be something like justice. A message from the present to the assholes who thought they could get away with this. Who thought they were beyond our reach. Reach them for all of us.

—Tracy

April wiped the tears from her cheeks, tears of sadness and rage. Remy studied the gun in his hand. When April looked to the atlas, she saw a nondescript patch of country circled outside Atlanta. She had no idea what it was her sister expected her to do.

"Did you hear that?" Remy asked.

April turned and stared at the door that led into the room. The handle moved. It tilted down, snapped back up, then tilted again. As if a child were trying to work it, not like it was locked.

"Help me down," Remy said. He started to lift a leg over the lip of the pod.

"Wait." April grabbed her husband's arm. The latch moved again. There was a scratching sound at the door, something like a growl. "The gun," April hissed. "Do you know how to use it?"

A branch snapped in the woods – a sharp crack like a log popping in a fire. Elise stopped and dropped to a crouch, scanned the underbrush. She looked for the white spots. Always easiest to see the white spots along the flank, not the bark-tan of the rest of the hide. Slipping an arrow from her quiver, she notched it into the gut string of her bow. *There.* A buck.

Coal-black eyes studied her between the low branches.

Elise drew back the arrow but kept it pointed at the ground. Deer somehow know when they're being threatened. She has watched them scatter while she took careful aim, until she was letting fly an errant shot at the bouncing white tail that mocked hunters of rabbit and venison alike.

The bow in her hand was Juliette's, once. Elise remembered back when it was made that she couldn't even draw the bow, that her arms had been too weak, too short, too young. But that was forever ago. Elise was nearly as strong as Juliette now. Strong and lean and forest swift. No one in the village had ever caught a rabbit with their bare hands before Elise, and none had done it since.

She and the deer studied one another. Wary. The deer were

learning to be scared of people again. It used to be easy, bringing home a feast. Too easy. But both sides were learning. Remembering how to find that balance. To live like the people in Elise's great books had once lived, with prey growing wary and hunters growing wise.

With one motion, Elise steered the bow up and loosed the arrow with more instinct than aim, with more thought than measure, with six years of practice and habit. The buck reared its head, shook its horns, took a staggering leap to one side, and then collapsed. The heart. They only went down like that with an arrow to the heart. To the spine was faster, and anywhere else might mean half a day of tracking. Elise was too competent with a bow to gloat, wouldn't need to tell anyone how the deer went down. When you ate an animal not from a can but from the flesh, everyone who partook could read the hunt right there on the spit, could tell what had happened.

"Careful," she could hear her brother saying whenever she brought home a deer and provided for her people. "Keep this up, and you'll be mayor one day."

Elise drew out her knife—the one Solo had given to her—and marched through the woods toward her kill. Her quietude was no longer a concern. The hunt was over. But this was a mistake that she too often forgot, that a soft pace was always prudent. Juliette had taught her this. "The hunt is never over," Juliette had said once, while tracking a doe with Elise. "Drop your guard, and what changes in an instant is *who* is doing the hunting."

Elise was reminded of the truth of this by another loud noise to her side. Again, she dropped to a crouch. And again, something was watching her. But this time, it was the most dangerous animal of them all.

April was ready for anything to come through that door. It could be her sister, a mountain bear, a stranger intent on doing them harm. Open to all possibilities, she still wasn't prepared for what appeared.

The battle with the latch was finally won—the door flew open—and some creature entered on all fours. Some half-man, half-beast wildling. The creature sniffed the air, then spotted April and Remy perched inside the steel pod, huddled there beside the large plastic tub.

"Shoot it," April begged.

"What *is* that?" Remy asked.

"Shoot it," she told him again, holding on to her husband's arm.

The beast roared. "FEEF-DEEN!" it growled, with a voice almost like a man's. "Feef-deen!"

And then it was in the air, jumping at them, yellow teeth and white eyes flashing, hands outstretched, hair billowing out wildly, coming to take them.

Remy aimed the gun, but the beast crashed into them before he could pull the trigger. Hair and claws and teeth and snarling. Remy punched the animal, and April tried to shove it away when yellow teeth clamped down on Remy's hand. There was a loud crunch—and her husband screamed and pulled his hand away, blood spurting where two of his fingers had been.

From his other hand came a flash and a roar. Remy flew back into April, who knocked her head against the open lid, nearly blacking out. The animal slumped against the edge of the pod, a clawed hand splayed open, before collapsing to the floor.

"What the fuck!" Remy shouted. He scrambled after the pistol, which had flown from his grip. His other hand was tucked under his armpit, rivulets of blood tracking down his bare ribs.

"Your hand," April said. She pulled one of the clean, folded shirts from the bin and made her husband hold out his hand. She wrapped the shirt as tight as she could and knotted the ends. Blood pooled and turned the fabric red. "Is it dead?" she asked. She braved a glance over the lip of the pod. The beast wasn't moving. And now that she could study it, she saw that it wasn't half-beast at all. It was mostly man. But naked, covered in hair, a scraggly beard, sinewy and lean.

Remy straightened his arms and pointed the gun at the door, his bandaged hand steadying his good one. April saw that there was another beast there. Another person on all fours. Less hairy. A woman.

The woman sniffed the air, studied them, and then peered at the dead man-creature. “Feef-deen,” she said. She snarled, showing her teeth, and her shoulders dipped as she tensed her muscles and readied for a leap. Remy, bless him, didn’t allow her to make the jump. The gun went off again, deafening loud. The woman collapsed. April and Remy watched the door, frozen, and after an agonizing dozen throbs of her pulse, April saw the next one.

“How many bullets do you have?” she asked Remy, wondering where he learned to shoot like that, if it was as easy as he made it seem.

He didn’t answer. He was too busy lining up his shot. But this next creature, another woman, studied the room, the two dead creatures and the two living ones, and made the same noise but without the rage. Without the snarling.

“Feef-deen,” she said, before turning and wandering off. Almost as if satisfied. Almost as if all were right with the world.

“Who goes there?” Elise asked. She watched the shapes beyond the foliage – it appeared to be two men. Pressing an arrow into the dirt, she left the shaft where she could grab it in a hurry, and then withdrew another from her quiver and notched it on to the bowstring. She drew the string taut but kept the arrow aimed to the side. “Rickson? Is that you?”

“Hello,” a voice called. A woman’s voice. “We’re coming out. Don’t shoot.”

A couple stepped around a tree. Elise saw that they were holding hands. They kept their free palms up to show that they were empty. Both wore backpacks. Both looked like they’d been living in the bush for ages, like the people who'd made it out of Silo 37 a few years ago. A thrill ran through Elise with the chance that these were new topsiders.

"Where are you from?" she asked. The couple had stopped twenty paces away. They looked rough. And there were only two of them. Elise recalled how back when she lived in Silo 17, every stranger was to be feared. But the people who dared to free themselves from their silos ended up being good people. It was a truth of the world. The bad people stayed right where they were.

"We've been . . . underground for a long time," the man said.

He didn't give a number. Sometimes they didn't know their number. Sometimes they had to be told by finding their silo on a map; there were fifty of them, the silos, buried underground. Elise fought the temptation to flood this couple with too much all at once. When she was younger, that had been her way. But she was learning to be more than quiet just in the hunt, to be as soft of tongue as she was of foot.

"Are you alone?" she asked, scanning the woods.

"We met another group northwest of here," the man said. He must've run into Debra's scouting party, which had been gone for a week. "They told us the people in charge lived by the coast. We've been looking for them for a long time. A very long time. Can you take us to your city?"

Elise put her notched arrow away and then retrieved the one she'd left in the dirt. "It's a village," she said. "Just a village." The memory of where she used to live, in one of those fifty silos, all cut off from each other, seemed forever ago. That life had grown hazy. Time formed some gulfs that not even recollection could span.

"Do you need help with the deer?" the man asked. "That's a lot of food."

Elise saw that he had a knife on his hip and that both of them bore the shrunken frames of the famished. She wondered what he could possibly know about deer. She'd had to consult her books to learn about deer, how to hunt them, how to clean them, how best to cook them. Maybe he too had pages from his silo's *Legacy,* that great set of books about the old world. Or maybe his silo had a herd of them.

"I'd love the help," she said, putting away the other arrow, comfortable that these people meant no harm and also that she could take the both of them with her bow or knife if she had to. "My name's Elise."

"I'm Remy," the man said, "and this is my wife, April."

Elise closed the distance between them. She shook their hands one at a time, the woman's first. As she shook the man's, she noticed something strange about his hand. He was missing two of his fingers.

Elise and Remy carved the choice cuts of meat and wrapped them in the deer's stripped hide. Elise secured the bundle with bark twine from her pack, and hung the bundle from a thick branch. The couple insisted on carrying the meat, resting it on their shoulders. Elise walked ahead, showing the way back to camp.

She resisted the urge to badger the couple with questions about their silo, how many were left there, what jobs they held, what level they lived on. When she was younger, she would have talked their ears off. But Juliette had a way about topsiders. There were unspoken rules. The people of the buried silos joined the rest when they were ready. They spoke when they were ready. "We all have our demons," Juliette liked to say. "We have to choose when to share them. When to let others in on the wrestling."

Elise often suspected that Juliette was holding out the longest. She had been their mayor for years and years. No one hardly voted for anyone else. But there was something in the woman's frown, a hardness in her eyes, a furrow in her brow, that never relaxed. Juliette was the reason any of them escaped from the silos, and the reason there was something to escape to for the rest. But Elise saw a woman still trapped by something. Held down by demons. Secrets she would never share.

The night fires were times for sharing. Elise told the couple this as they approached camp. She told them about the welcome they would receive, and that they could say as much or as little as they like. "We'll take turns telling you our stories," Elise said. "I'm from Silo 17. There are only a few of us. There are a lot more from Silo 18. Like Juliette."

She glanced back at the couple to see if they were listening. "Like I said, you don't have to say anything if you don't want. Don't have to say what you did or how you got here. Not until you're ready. Don't have to say how many of you are left—"

"Fifteen," the woman said. She'd barely said a word while the deer was being cleaned and packed. But she said this. "There were fifteen of us for the longest time. Now there are only two."

This sobered Elise. She herself had come from a silo that only offered five survivors. She couldn't imagine a world with just two people.

"How many are you?" Remy asked.

Elise turned her head to answer. "We don't count. It's not *really* a rule, but it's basically a rule. Counting was a touchy subject for a lot of our people. Not for me, though. Well, not the same. I came from a silo with very few people. You didn't count so much as glance around the room and see that your family is still there. We have enough people now that there's talk of setting up another village north of here. We're scouting for locations. Some want to see a place that used to be called the Carolinas—"

"Carolinas," Remy said, but he said it differently, with the *i* long like "eye" instead of "eee." Like he was testing the word.

"It's Carolinas," Elise said, correcting him.

Remy didn't try again. His wife said something to him, but Elise couldn't make it out.

"Anyway, that's the sort of thing we vote on now. We all vote. As long as you can read and write. I'm all for the second village, but I don't want to live up there. I know these woods here like the back of my hand."

They reached the first clearing, and Elise steered them toward the larder, where they dropped off the meat. Haney, the butcher's boy, grew excited at the sight of the feast and then at the strangers. He started to pester them with questions, but Elise shooed him away. "I'm taking them to see Juliette," she said. "Leave them alone."

"Juliette's the person in charge here?" the woman asked.

"Yeah," Elise said. "She's our mayor. She has a place near the beach."

She led them there, skirting the square and the market to keep from being waylaid by gawkers. She took the back paths the prowling dogs and mischievous children used. Remy and April followed. Glancing back, Elise saw that April had removed the bag from her back and was clutching it against her chest, the way some parents cradled their children. There was a look of fear and determination on her face. Elise knew that look. It was the hardened visage of someone who has come so far and is near to salvation.

"That's her place," Elise said, pointing up into the last two rows of trees by the beach. There was a small shelter affixed to the trunks with spikes and ropes. It stood two dozen paces off the ground. Juliette had lived inside the earth and upon the ground, but now lived up in the air. "I'm trying to get to heaven," she had told Elise once, joking around. "Just not in a hurry."

Elise thought that explained why Juliette spent so much time out on the beach alone at night, gazing up at the stars.

"There she is," Elise said, pointing down by the surf. "You can leave your bags here if you like."

They elected to carry them. Elise saw them fixate on Juliette, who was standing alone by the surf, watching the tall fishing rods arranged in a line down the beach, monofilament stretching out past the breakers. Farther down the beach, Solo could be seen rigging bait on another line. Charlotte was there as well, casting a heavy sinker into the distance.

Elise had to hurry to catch up with Remy and April. The couple seemed drawn toward Juliette. On a mission. But the woman had that pull on plenty of people. Sensing their presence, the mayor turned and shielded her eyes against the sun, watching the small party approach. Elise thought she saw Juliette stiffen with the sudden awareness that these were strangers, new to the topsides.

"I got a buck," Elise told Juliette. She nodded toward the couple. "And then I met them in the woods. This is April and Remy. And this is our mayor, Juliette. You can call her Jules."

Juliette took the couple in. She brushed the sand from her palms and shook each of theirs in turn, then squeezed Elise's shoulder. A strong wave crashed on the beach and slid up nearly to the line of rods. The tide was coming in. The couple seemed not to be awed by the sight of the ocean, which Elise thought was strange. She still couldn't get used to it. As for them – they could only stare at Juliette.

"Are you in charge of all this?" April asked.

Juliette glanced down the beach toward Solo and Charlotte for a moment. "If you came from a place with a lot of rules and great concern over who is in charge, you'll find we're not so strict here." Juliette rested her hands on her hips. "You both look hungry and tired. Elise, why don't you get them fed and freshened up. They can look around camp when they're ready. And you don't have to tell us your story until you want –"

"I think we'll say our piece now," April said. Elise saw that she was the talkative one now. Remy was holding his tongue. And there was anger in their guises, not relief. Elise had seen this before, the need to vent. She shuffled back a step but wasn't sure why. Maybe it was because Juliette had done the same.

"Very well –" Juliette started to say.

"We aren't here to be saved," April said. She continued to clutch her bag to her chest, like it was a raft keeping her afloat. "We aren't here to live with you. We died a long time ago, when everything was taken from us. We've been dead and walking for years to get here and to tell you this. You didn't get away with it."

"I'm not sure I—" Juliette began.

April dropped her bag to the sand. In her hand was a silver gun. Elise knew straightaway what it was. There were three of them in camp that the men used to hunt; Elise hated the way they spooked the wildlife.

This one was different . . . and trained on Juliette. Elise moved to stand in front of the mayor, but Juliette pushed her away.

"Wait a second," Juliette said.

"No," April said. "We've waited long enough."

"You don't understa—"

But a roar cut off whatever Juliette was about to say. A flash and an explosion of sound. She fell to the beach, a wild wave rushing up nearly to touch her, all so sudden and yet in slow motion. Elise felt her own body startle, like a deer that knows it's in mortal danger. She sensed the whole world around her. Saw Solo and Charlotte stir down the beach and start running. Felt the heat of the sun on her neck, the tickle of sweat on her scalp. Could feel the sand beneath her feet and hear the crying birds. There was an arrow in her hand, her bow coming off her shoulder, a gun swinging around, a man yelling for someone to stop, Elise wasn't sure who.

She only got half a draw before the arrow slipped from her fingers. She loosed it before the trigger could be pulled again. And the shaft lodged in the woman's throat.

More screaming. Gurgling. Blood in the sand. Remy moved to catch his wife. Elise notched another arrow, swift as a hare. By her feet, Juliette did not stir. The man reached for the gun, and Elise put an arrow in his side, hoping not to kill him. He roared and clutched the wound while Elise notched another and knelt by her wounded friend. The man regrouped and went for the gun again, murder in his eyes. For the second time that day, Elise put an arrow through an animal's heart.

The only people moving on the beach were Solo and Charlotte, running their way. Elise dropped her bow and reached for Juliette, who lay on her side, facing away from Elise. Elise held her friend's shoulders and rolled her onto her back. Blood was pooled on Juliette's chest, crimson and spreading. Her lips moved. Elise told her to be strong. She told the strongest person she'd ever known to be extra strong.

Juliette's eyes opened and focused on Elise. They were wet with tears. One tear pooled and broke free, sliding down the wrinkled corner of Juliette's eye. Elise held her friend's hand, could feel Juliette squeezing back.

"It'll be okay," Elise said. "Help is coming. It'll be okay."

And Juliette did something Elise hadn't seen her do in the longest time: She smiled. "It already is," Juliette whispered, blood flecking her lips. "It already is."

Her eyes drifted shut. And then Elise watched as the furrow in her mayor's brow smoothed away and the tension in Jules's clenched jaw relaxed. Something like serenity took hold of the woman. And the demons everywhere – they scattered.

DUST

THE SILO TRILOGY
BY HUGH HOWEY

WOOL

SHIFT

DUST

DUST

HUGH HOWEY

wm

WILLIAM MORROW
An Imprint of HarperCollins*Publishers*
Boston New York

First Mariner Books edition 2016

Mariner Books
An Imprint of HarperCollins Publishers, registered in the United States of America and/or other jurisdictions.

www.marinerbooks.com

Library of Congress Cataloging-in-Publication Data is available.
ISBN 978-0-544-83962-5 (hardback)
ISBN 978-0-544-83826-0 (pbk)

Printed in the United States of America

24 25 26 27 28 LBC 27 26 25 24 23

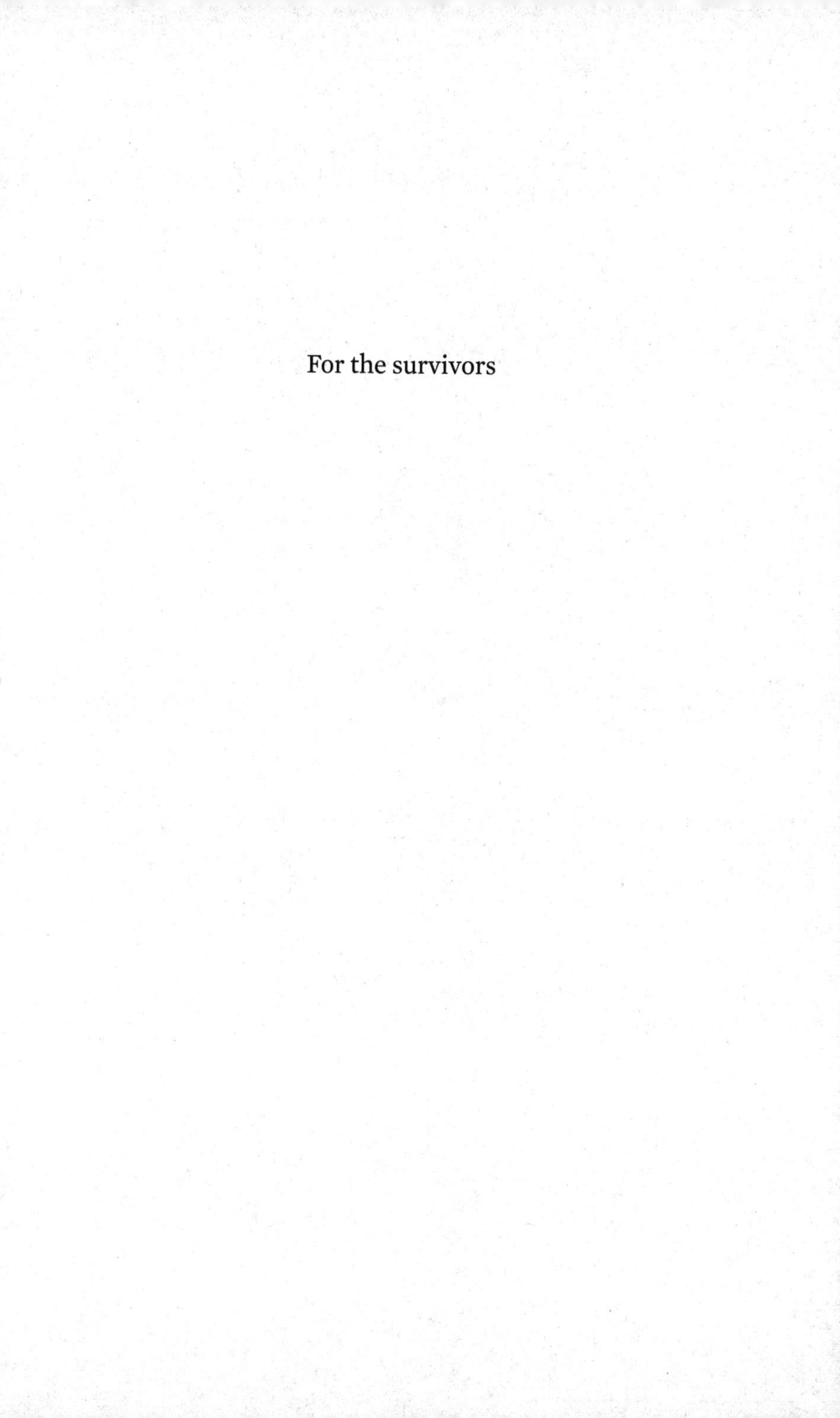

For the survivors

PROLOGUE

"Is anyone there?"

"Hello? Yes. I'm here."

"Ah. Lukas. You weren't saying anything. I thought for a second there . . . that you were someone else."

"No, it's me. Just getting my headset adjusted. Been a busy morning."

"Oh?"

"Yeah. Boring stuff. Committee meetings. We're a bit thin up here at the moment. A lot of reassignments."

"But things have been settling down? No uprisings to report?"

"No, no. Things are getting back to normal. People get up and go to work in the morning. They collapse in their beds at night. We had a big lottery this week, which made a number of people happy."

"That's good. Very good. How's the work on server six coming?"

"Good, thanks. All of your passcodes work. So far it's just more of the same data. Not sure why any of this is important, though."

"Keep looking. Everything's important. If it's in there, there has to be a reason."

"You said that about the entries in these books. But so many of them seem like nonsense to me. Makes me wonder if any of this is real."

"Why? What're you reading?"

"I'm up to volume C. This morning it was about this . . . fungus. Wait a second. Let me find it. Here it is. Cordyceps."

"That's a fungus? Never heard of it."

"Says here it does something to an ant's brain, reprograms it like it's a machine, makes it climb to the top of a plant before it dies—"

"An invisible machine that reprograms brains? I'm fairly certain that's not a random entry."

"Yeah? So what does it mean, then?"

"It means . . . It means we aren't free. None of us are."

"How uplifting. I can see why she makes me take these calls."

"Your mayor? Is that why—? She hasn't answered in a while."

"No. She's away. Working on something."

"Working on what?"

"I'd rather not say. I don't think you'd be pleased."

"What makes you think that?"

"Because I'm not pleased. I've tried to talk her out of this. But she can be a bit . . . obstinate at times."

"If it's going to cause trouble, I should know about it. I'm here to help. I can keep heads turned away—"

"That's just it . . . she doesn't trust you. She doesn't even believe you're the same person every time."

"It is. It's me. The machines do something with my voice."

"I'm just telling you what she thinks."

"I wish she would come around. I really do want to help."

"I believe you. I think the best thing you can do right now is just keep your fingers crossed for us."

"Why is that?"

"Because I've got a feeling that nothing good will come of this."

PART I

THE DIG

Silo 18

1

DUST RAINED IN the halls of Mechanical; it shivered free from the violence of the digging. Wires overhead swung gently in their harnesses. Pipes rattled. And from the generator room, staccato bangs filled the air, bounced off the walls, and brought to mind a time when unbalanced machines spun dangerously.

At the locus of the horrible racket, Juliette Nichols stood with her coveralls zipped down to her waist, the loose arms knotted around her hips, dust and sweat staining her undershirt with mud. She leaned her weight against the excavator, her sinewy arms shaking as the digger's heavy metal piston slammed into the concrete wall of Silo 18 over and over.

The vibrations could be felt in her teeth. Every bone and joint in her body shuddered, and old wounds ached with reminders. Off to the side, the miners who normally manned the excavator watched unhappily. Juliette turned her head from the powdered concrete and saw the way they stood with their arms crossed over their wide chests, their jaws set in rigid frowns, angry perhaps for her appropriating their machine. Or maybe over the taboo of digging where digging was forbidden.

Juliette swallowed the grit and chalk accumulating in her mouth and concentrated on the crumbling wall. There was another possibility, one she couldn't help but consider. Good mechanics and miners had died because of her. Brutal fighting had broken out when she'd refused to clean. How many of these men and women watching her dig had lost a loved one, a best friend, a family member? How many of them blamed her? She couldn't possibly be the only one.

The excavator bucked and there was the clang of metal on metal. Juliette steered the punching jaws to the side as more bones of rebar appeared in the white flesh of concrete. She had already gouged out a veritable crater in the outer silo wall. A first row of rebar hung jagged overhead, the ends smooth like melted candles where she'd taken a blowtorch to them. Two more feet of concrete and another row of the iron rods had followed, the silo walls thicker than she'd imagined. With numb limbs and frayed nerves she guided the machine forward on its tracks, the wedge-shaped piston chewing at the stone between the rods. If she hadn't seen the schematic for herself—if she didn't know there were other silos out there—she would've given up already. It felt as though she were chewing through the very earth itself. Her arms shook, her hands a blur. This was the wall of the silo she was attacking, ramming it with a mind to pierce through the damn thing, to bore clear through to the outside.

The miners shifted uncomfortably. Juliette looked from them to where she was aiming as the hammer bit rang against more steel. She concentrated on the crease of white stone between the bars. With her boot, she kicked the drive lever, leaned into the machine, and the excavator trudged forward on rusted tracks one more inch. She should've taken another break a while ago. The chalk in her mouth was choking her; she was dying for water; her arms needed a rest; rubble crowded the base of the excavator and littered her feet. She kicked a few of the larger chunks out of the way and kept digging.

Her fear was that if she stopped one more time, she wouldn't be able to convince them to let her continue. Mayor or not—a shift head or not—men she had thought fearless had already left the generator room with furrowed brows. They seemed terrified that she might puncture a sacred seal and let in a foul and murderous air. Juliette saw the way they looked at her, knowing she'd been on the outside, as though she were some kind of ghost. Many kept their distance as if she bore some disease.

Setting her teeth, foul-tasting grit crunching between them, she kicked the forward plate once more with her boot. The tracks on the excavator spun forward another inch. One more inch. Juliette cursed the machine and the pain in her wrists. Goddamn the fighting and her friends dead. Goddamn the thought of Solo and the kids all alone, a forever of rock away. And goddamn this mayor nonsense, people looking at her as though she suddenly ran all the shifts on every level, as though she knew what the hell she was doing, as though they had to obey her even as they feared her—

The excavator lurched forward more than an inch, and the pounding hammer bit screamed with a piercing whine. Juliette lost her grip with one hand, and the machine revved up as if fit to explode. The miners startled like fleas, several of them running toward her, shadows converging. Juliette hit the red kill switch, which was nearly invisible beneath a dusting of white powder. The excavator kicked and bucked as it wound down from a dangerous, runaway state.

"You're through! You're through!"

Raph pulled her back, his pale arms, strong from years of mining, wrapping around her numb limbs. Others shouted at her that she was done. Finished. The excavator had made a noise as if a connecting rod had shattered; there had been that dangerous whine of a mighty engine running without friction, without anything to resist. Juliette let go of the controls and sagged into Raph's embrace. A desperation returned, the thought of her friends buried alive in that tomb of an empty silo and her unable to reach them.

"You're through—get back!"

A hand that reeked of grease and toil clamped down over her mouth, protecting her from the air beyond. Juliette couldn't breathe. Ahead of her, a black patch of empty space appeared, the cloud of concrete dissipating.

And there, between two bars of iron, stood a dark void. A void between prison bars that ran two layers deep and all around them, from Mechanical straight to the Up Top.

She was through. *Through.* She now had a glimpse of some other, some different, *outside.*

"The torch," Juliette mumbled, prying Raph's calloused hand from her mouth and hazarding a gulp of air. "Get me the cutting torch. And a flashlight."

2

"DAMN THING'S RUSTED to hell."

"Those look like hydraulic lines."

"Must be a thousand years old."

Fitz muttered the last, the oilman's words whistling through gaps left by missing teeth. The miners and mechanics who had kept their distance during the digging now crowded against Juliette's back as she aimed her flashlight through a lingering veil of powdered rock and into the gloom beyond. Raph, as pale as the drifting dust, stood beside her, the two of them crammed into the conical crater chewed out of the five or six feet of concrete. The albino's eyes were wide, his translucent cheeks bulging, his lips pursed together and bloodless.

"You can breathe, Raph," Juliette told him. "It's just another room."

The pale miner let out his air with a relieved grunt and asked those behind to stop shoving. Juliette passed the flashlight to Fitz and turned from the hole she'd made. She wormed her way through the jostling crowd, her pulse racing from the glimpses of some machine on the other side of the wall. What she had seen was quickly confirmed by the murmuring of others: struts, bolts, hose, plate steel with chips of paint and streaks of rust—a wall of a mechanical beast that went up and to the sides as far as their feeble flashlight beams could penetrate.

A tin cup of water was pressed into her trembling hand. Juliette drank greedily. She was exhausted, but her mind raced. She couldn't wait to get back to a radio and tell Solo. She couldn't wait to tell Lukas. Here was a bit of buried hope.

"What now?" Dawson asked.

The new third-shift foreman, who had given her the water, studied her warily. Dawson was in his late thirties, but working nights had saddled him with extra years. He had the large knotted hands that came from busting knuckles and breaking fingers, some of it from working and some from fighting. Juliette returned the cup to him. Dawson glanced inside and stole the last swig.

"Now we make a bigger hole," she told him. "We get in there and see if that thing's salvageable."

Movement on top of the humming main generator caught Juliette's eye. She glanced up in time to spy Shirly frowning down at her. Shirly turned away.

Juliette squeezed Dawson's arm. "It'll take forever to expand this one hole," she said. "What we need are dozens of smaller holes that we can connect. We need to tear out entire sections at a time. Bring up the other excavator. And turn the men loose with their picks, but keep the dust to a minimum if you can help it."

The third-shift foreman nodded and rapped his fingers against the empty cup. "No blasting?" he asked.

"No blasting," she said. "I don't want to damage whatever's over there."

He nodded, and she left him to manage the dig. She approached the generator. Shirly had her coveralls stripped down to her waist as well, sleeves cinched together, her undershirt wet with the dark inverted triangle of hard work. With a rag in each hand, she worked across the top of the generator, wiping away both old grease and the new film of powder kicked up by the day's digging.

Juliette untied the sleeves of her coveralls and shrugged her arms inside, covering her scars. She climbed up the side of the generator, knowing where she could grab, which parts were hot and which were merely warm. "You need some help?" she asked, reaching the top, enjoying the heat and thrum of the machine in her sore muscles.

Shirly wiped her face with the hem of her undershirt. She shook her head. "I'm good," she said.

"Sorry about the debris." Juliette raised her voice over the hum of the massive pistons firing up and down. There was a day not too long ago when her teeth would've been knocked loose to stand on top of the machine, back when it was unbalanced six ways to hell.

Shirly turned and tossed the muddy white rags down to her shadow, Kali, who dunked them into a bucket of grimy water. It was strange to see the new head of Mechanical toiling away at something so mundane as cleaning the genset. Juliette tried to picture Knox up there doing the same. And then it hit her for the hundredth time that she was *mayor,* and look how she spent her time, hammering through walls and cutting rebar. Kali tossed the rags back up, and Shirly caught them with wet slaps and sprays of suds. Her old friend's silence as she bent back to her work said plenty.

Juliette turned and surveyed the digging party she'd assembled as they cleared debris and worked to expand the hole. Shirly hadn't been happy about the loss of manpower, much less the taboo of breaking the silo's seal. The call for workers had come at a time when their ranks were already thinned by the outbreak of violence. And whether or not Shirly blamed Juliette for her husband's death was irrelevant. Juliette blamed herself, and so the tension stood between them like a cake of grease.

It wasn't long before the hammering on the wall resumed. Juliette spotted Bobby at the excavator's controls, his great muscled arms a blur as he guided the wheeled jackhammer. The sight of some strange machine—some artifact buried beyond the walls—had thrown sparks into reluctant bodies. Fear and doubt had morphed into determination. A porter arrived with food, and Juliette watched the young man with his bare arms and legs study the work intently. The porter left his load of fruit and hot lunches behind and took with him his gossip.

Juliette stood on the humming generator and allayed her doubts. They were doing the right thing, she told herself. She had seen with her own eyes how vast the world was, had stood on a summit and surveyed the land. All she had to do now was show others what was out there. And then they would lean into this work rather than fear it.

3

A HOLE WAS MADE big enough to squeeze through, and Juliette took the honors. A flashlight in hand, she crawled over a pile of rubble and between bent fingers of iron rod. The air beyond the generator room was cool like the deep mines. She coughed into her fist, the dust from the digging tickling her throat and nose. She hopped down to the floor beyond the gaping hole.

"Careful," she told the others behind her. "The ground's not even."

Some of the unevenness was from the chunks of concrete that'd fallen inside—the rest was just how the floor stood. It appeared as though it'd been gouged out by the claws of a giant.

Shining the light from her boots to the dim ceiling high above, she surveyed the hulking wall of machinery before her. It dwarfed the main generator. It dwarfed the oil pumps. A colossus of such proportions was never meant to be built, much less repaired. Her stomach sank. Her hopes of restoring this buried machine diminished.

Raph joined her in the cool and dark, a clatter of rubble trailing him. The albino had a condition that skipped generations. His eyebrows and lashes were gossamer things, nearly invisible. His flesh was as pale as pig's milk. But when he was in the mines, the shadows that darkened the others like soot lent him a healthful complexion. Juliette could see why he had left the farms as a boy to work in the dark.

Raph whistled as he played his flashlight across the machine. A moment later, his whistle echoed back, a bird in the far shadows, mocking him.

"It's a thing of the gods," he wondered aloud.

Juliette didn't answer. She never took Raph as one to listen to the tales of priests. Still, there was no doubting the awe it inspired. She had seen Solo's books and suspected that the same ancient peoples who had built this machine had built the crumbling but soaring towers beyond the hills. The fact that they had built the silo itself made her feel small. She reached out and ran her hand across metal that hadn't been touched nor glimpsed for centuries, and she marveled at what the ancients had been capable of. Maybe the priests weren't that far off after all . . .

"Ye gods," Dawson grumbled, crowding noisily beside them. "What're we to do with this?"

"Yeah, Jules," Raph whispered, respecting the deep shadows and the deeper time. "How're we supposed to dig this thing outta here?"

"We're not," she told them. She scooted sideways between the wall of concrete and the tower of machinery. "This thing is meant to dig its own way out."

"You're assuming we can get it running," Dawson said.

Workers in the generator room crowded the hole and blocked the light spilling in. Juliette steered her flashlight around the narrow gap that stood between the outer silo wall and the tall machine, looking for some way around. She worked to one side, into the darkness, and scrambled up the gently sloping floor.

"We'll get it running," she assured Dawson. "We just gotta figure out how it's supposed to work."

"Careful," Raph warned as a rock kicked loose by her boots tumbled toward him. She was already higher up than their heads. The room, she saw, didn't have a corner or a far wall. It just curled up and all the way around.

"It's a big circle," she called out, her voice echoing between rock and metal. "I don't think this is the business end."

"There's a door over here," Dawson announced.

Juliette slid down the slope to join him and Raph. Another flashlight clicked on from the gawkers in the generator room. Its beam joined hers in illuminating a door with pins for hinges. Dawson wrestled with a handle on the back of the machine. He grunted with effort, and then metal cried out as it reluctantly gave way to muscle.

The machine yawned wide once they were through the door. Nothing prepared Juliette for this. Thinking back to the schematics she'd seen in Solo's underground hovel, she now realized that the diggers had been drawn to scale. The little worms jutting off the low floors of Mechanical were a level high and twice that in length. Massive cylinders of steel, this one sat snug in a circular cave, almost as if it had buried itself. Juliette told her people to be careful as they made their way through the interior. A dozen workers joined her, their voices mingling and echoing in the maze-like guts of the machine, taboo dispelled by curiosity and wonder, the digging forgotten for now.

"This here's for moving the tailings," someone said. Beams of light played on metal chutes of interlocking plates. There were wheels and gears beneath the plates and more plates on the other side that overlapped like the scales on a snake. Juliette saw immediately how the entire chute moved, the plates hinging at the end and wrapping around to the beginning again. The rock and debris could ride on the top as it was pushed along.

Low walls of inch-thick plate were meant to keep the rock from tumbling off. The rock chewed up by the digger would pass through here and out the back, where men would have to wrestle it with barrows.

“It’s rusted all to hell,” someone muttered.

“Not as bad as it should be,” Juliette said. The machine had been there for hundreds of years, at least. She expected it to be a ball of rust and nothing more, but the steel was shiny in places. “I think the room was airtight,” she wondered aloud, remembering a breeze on her neck and the sucking of dust as she pierced through the wall for the first time.

“This is all hydraulic,” Bobby said. There was disappointment in his voice, as though he were learning that the gods cleaned their asses with water too. Juliette was more hopeful. She saw something that could be fixed, so long as the power source was intact. They could get this running. It was made to be simple, as if the gods knew that whoever discovered it would be less sophisticated, less capable. There were treads just like on the excavator but running the length of the mighty machine, axles caked in grease. More treads on the sides and ceiling that must push against the earth as well. What she didn’t understand was how the digging commenced. Past the moving chutes and all the implements for pushing crushed rock and tailings out the back of the machine, they came to a wall of steel that slid up past the girders and walkways into the darkness above.

“That don’t make a lick of sense,” Raph said, reaching the far wall. “Look at these wheels. Which way does this thing run?”

“Those aren’t wheels,” Juliette said. She pointed with her light. “This whole front piece spins. Here’s the pivot.” She pointed to a central axle as big around as two men. “And those round discs there must protrude through to the other side and do the cutting.”

Bobby blew out a disbelieving breath. “Through solid stone?”

Juliette tried to turn one of the discs. It barely moved. A barrel of grease would be needed.

"I think she's right," Raph said. He had the lid raised on a box the size of a double bunk and aimed his flashlight inside. "This here's a gearbox. Looks like a transmission."

Juliette joined him. Helical gears the size of a man's waist lay embedded in dried grease. The gears matched up with teeth that would spin the wall. The transmission box was as large and stout as that of the main generator. Larger.

"Bad news," Bobby said. "Check where that shaft leads."

Three beams of light converged and followed the driveshaft back to where it ended in empty space. The interior cavern of that hulking machine, all that emptiness in which they stood, was a void where the heart of the beast should lie.

"She ain't going nowhere," Raph muttered.

Juliette marched back to the rear of the machine. Beefy struts built for holding a power plant sat bare. She and the other mechanics had been milling about where an engine should sit. And now that she knew what to look for, she spotted the mounts. There were six of them: threaded posts eight inches across and caked in ancient, hardened grease. The matching nut for each post hung from hooks beneath the struts. The gods were communicating with her. Talking to her. The ancients had left a message, written in the language of people who knew machines. They were speaking to her across vast stretches of time, saying: *This goes here. Follow these steps.*

Fitz, the oilman, knelt beside Juliette and rested a hand on her arm. "I am sorry for your friends," he said, meaning Solo and the kids, but Juliette thought he sounded happy for everyone else. Glancing at the rear of the metal cave, she saw more miners and mechanics peering inside, hesitant to join them. Everyone would be happy for this endeavor to end right there, for her to dig no further. But Juliette was feeling more than an urge; she was beginning to feel a purpose. This machine hadn't been hidden from them. It had been safely stowed. Protected. Packed away. Slathered in grease and shielded from the air for a reason beyond her knowing.

"Do we seal it back up?" Dawson asked. Even the grizzled old mechanic seemed eager to dig no further.

"It's waiting for something," Juliette said. She pulled one of the large nuts off its hook and rested it on top of the grease-encased post. The size of the mount was familiar. She thought of the work she'd performed a lifetime ago of aligning the main generator. "She's meant to be opened," she said. "This belly of hers is meant to be opened. Check the back of the machine where we came through. It should come apart so the tailings can get out, but also to let something in. The motor isn't missing at all."

Raph stayed by her side, the beam of his flashlight on her chest so he could study her face.

"I know why they put this here," she told him, while the others left to survey the back of the machine. "I know why they put this next to the generator room."

4

SHIRLY AND KALI were still cleaning the main generator when Juliette emerged from the belly of the digger. Bobby showed the others how the back of the digger opened up, which bolts to remove and how the plates came away. Juliette had them measure the space between the posts and then the mounts of the backup generator to verify what she already knew. The machine they'd uncovered was a living schematic. It really was a message from older times. One discovery was leading to a cascade of others.

Juliette watched Kali wring mud from a cloth before dipping it into a second bucket of slightly less filthy water, and a truth occurred to her: An engine would rot if left for a thousand years. It would only hum if used, if a team of people devoted their lives to the care of it. Steam rose from a hot and soapy manifold as Shirly wiped down the humming main generator, and Juliette saw how they'd been working toward this moment for years. As much as her old friend—and now the Chief of Mechanical—hated this project of hers, Shirly had been assisting all this time. The smaller generator on the other side of the main power plant had another, greater, purpose.

"The mounts look right," Raph told her, a measuring line in

his hand. "You think they used that machine to bring the generator here?"

Shirly tossed down a muddy rag, and a cleaner one was tossed up. Worker and shadow had a rhythm like the humming of pistons.

"I think the spare generator is meant to help that digger *leave*," she told Raph. What she didn't understand was why anyone would send off their backup power source, even for a short time. It would put the entire silo at the whim of a breakdown. They may as well have found a motor crumbling into a solid ball of rust on the other side of the wall. It was difficult to imagine anyone agreeing with the plans coalescing in her mind.

A rag arced through the air and splashed into a bucket of brown water. Kali didn't throw another up. She was staring toward the entrance of the generator room. Juliette followed the shadow's gaze and felt a flush of heat. There, among the black and soiled men and women of Mechanical, an unblemished young man in brilliant silver stood, asking someone for directions. A man pointed, and Lukas Kyle, head of IT, her lover, started off in Juliette's direction.

"Get the backup generator serviced," Juliette told Raph, who visibly stiffened. He seemed to know where this was going. "We need to put her in just long enough to see what that digger does. We've been meaning to unhook and clean out the exhaust manifolds anyway."

Raph nodded, his jaws clenching and unclenching. Juliette slapped his back and didn't dare glance up at Shirly as she strode off to meet Lukas.

"What're you doing down here?" she asked him. She had spoken to Lukas the day before, and he had neglected to mention the visit. His aim was to corner her.

Lukas pulled up short and frowned—and Juliette felt awful

for the tone. There was no embrace, no welcoming handshake. She was too wound up from the day's discoveries, too tense.

"I should ask the same thing," he said. His gaze strayed to the crater carved out of the far wall. "While you're digging holes down here, the head of IT is doing the mayor's work."

"Then nothing's changed," Juliette said, laughing, trying to lighten the mood. But Lukas didn't smile. She rested her hand on his arm and guided him away from the generator and out into the hall. "I'm sorry," she told him. "I was just surprised to see you. You should've told me you were coming. And listen . . . I'm glad to see you. If you need me to come up and sign some things, I'm happy to. If you need me to give a speech or kiss a baby, I'll do that. But I told you last week that I was going to find some way to get my friends out. And since you vetoed my walking back over the hills—"

Lukas's eyes widened at the flippant heresy. He glanced around the hall to see if others were around. "Jules, you're worrying about a handful of people while the rest of the silo grows uneasy. There are murmurs of dissent all through the Up Top. There are echoes of the last uprising you stirred, only now they're aimed at us."

Juliette felt her skin warm. Her hand fell from Lukas's arm. "I wanted no part of that fight. I wasn't even *here* for it."

"But you're here for this one." His eyes were sad, not angry, and Juliette realized the days were as long for him in the Up Top as they were for her down in Mechanical. They'd spent less time talking in the past week than they had while she'd been in Silo 17. They were nearer to one another and in danger of growing apart.

"What would you have me do?" she asked.

"To start with, don't dig. Please. Billings has fielded a dozen complaints from neighbors speculating about what will happen. Some of them are saying that the outside will come to us. A priest from the Mids is holding two Sundays a week now to warn of the dangers, of this vision of his where the dust fills the silo to the brim and thousands die—"

"Priests—" Juliette spat.

"Yes, priests, with people marching from the Top and the Deep both to attend his Sundays. When he finds it necessary to hold three of them a week, we'll have a mob."

Juliette ran her fingers through her hair, rock and rubble tumbling out. She looked at the cloud of fine dust guiltily. "What do people think happened to me outside the silo? My cleaning? What are they saying?"

"Some can scarcely believe it," Lukas said. "It has the makings of legend. Oh, in IT we know what happened, but some wonder if you were sent to clean at all. I heard one rumor that it was an election stunt."

Juliette cursed under her breath. "And news of the other silos?"

"I've been telling others for years that the stars are suns like our own. Some things are too big to comprehend. And I don't think rescuing your friends will change that. You could march your radio friend up to the bazaar and say he came from another silo, and people would just as likely believe you."

"Walker?" Juliette shook her head, but she knew he was right. "I'm not after my friends to prove what happened to me, Luke. This isn't about me. They're living with the dead over there. With ghosts."

"Don't we as well? Don't we dine on our dead? I'm begging you, Jules. Hundreds will die for you to save a few. Maybe they're better off over there."

She took a deep breath and held it a pause, tried her best not to feel angry. "They're not, Lukas. The man I aim to save is half mad from living on his own all these years. The kids over there are having kids of their own. They need our doctors and they need our help. Besides . . . I promised them."

He rewarded her pleas with sad eyes. It was no use. How do you make a man care for those he's never met? Juliette expected the impossible of him, and she was just as much to blame. Did she truly care for the people being poisoned twice on Sundays? Or any of the strangers she had been elected to lead but had never met?

"I didn't want this job," she told Lukas. It was hard to keep the blame out of her voice. Others had wanted her to be mayor, not her. Though not as many as before, it seemed.

"I didn't know what I was shadowing for either," Lukas countered. He started to say something else, but held his tongue as a group of miners exited the generator room, a cloud of dust kicked up from their boots.

"Were you going to say something?" she asked.

"I was going to ask that you dig in secret if you have to dig at all. Or leave these men to it and come—"

He bit off the thought.

"If you were about to say home, this is my home. And are we really no better than the last of them who were in charge? Lying to our people? Conspiring?"

"I fear we are worse," he said. "All they did was keep us alive."

Juliette laughed at that. "Us? They elected to send you and me to die."

Lukas let out his breath. "I meant everyone else. They worked to keep everyone else alive." But he couldn't help it: he cracked a smile while Juliette continued to laugh. She smeared the tears on her cheeks into mud.

"Give me a few days down here," she said. It wasn't a question; it was a concession. "Let me see if we even have the means to dig. Then I'll come kiss your babies and bury your dead—though not in that order, of course."

Lukas frowned at her morbidness. "And you'll tamp down the heresies?"

She nodded. "If we dig, we'll do it quietly." To herself, she wondered if such a machine as she'd uncovered could dig any way but with a growl. "I was thinking of going on a slight power holiday, anyway. I don't want the main generator on a full load for a while. Just in case."

Lukas nodded, and Juliette realized how easy and necessary the lies felt. She considered telling him right then of another idea of hers, one she'd been considering for weeks, all the way back when she was in the doctor's office recovering from her burns. There was something she needed to do up top, but she could see that he was in no mood to be angered further. And so she told him the only part of her plan that she thought he'd enjoy.

"Once things are underway down here, I plan to come up and stay for a while," she said, taking his hand. "Come home for a while."

Lukas smiled.

"But listen here," she told him, feeling the urge to warn. "I've seen the world out there, Luke. I stay up at night listening to Walk's radio. There are a lot of people just like us out there, living in fear, living apart, kept ignorant. I mean to do more than save my friends. I hope you know this. I mean to get to the bottom of what's out there beyond these walls."

The knot in Lukas's throat bobbed up and down. His smile vanished. "You aim too far," he said meekly.

Juliette smiled and squeezed her lover's hand. "Says the man who watches the stars."

Silo 17

5

"SOLO! MR. SOLO!"

The faint voice of a young child worked its way into the deepest of the grow pits. It reached all the way to the cool plots of soil where lights no longer burned and things no longer grew. There, Jimmy Parker sat alone atop the lifeless soil and near to the memory of an old friend.

His hands idly picked clumps of clay and crushed them into powder. If he imagined really hard, he could feel the pinprick of claws through his coveralls. He could hear Shadow's little belly rattling like a water pump. It got harder and harder to imagine as the young voice calling his name grew nearer. The glow of a flashlight cut through the last tangle of plants that the young ones called the Wilds.

"There you are!"

Little Elise made a heap of noise that belied her small size. She stomped over to him in her too-big boots. Jimmy watched her approach and remembered wishing long ago that Shadow could talk. He'd had countless dreams wherein Shadow was a boy with black fur and a rumbly voice. But Jimmy no longer had such dreams. Nowadays, he was thankful for the speechless years with his old friend.

Elise squirmed through the rails of the fence and hugged

Jimmy's arm. The flashlight nearly blinded him as she clutched it against his chest, pointing it up.

"It's time to go," Elise said, tugging at him. "It's time, Mr. Solo."

He blinked against the harsh light and knew that she was right. The youngest among them, little Elise settled more arguments than she started. Jimmy crushed another clump of clay in his hand, sprinkled the soil across the ground, and wiped his palm on his thigh. He didn't want to leave, but he knew they couldn't stay. He reminded himself that it would be temporary. Juliette said so. She said he could come back here and live with all the others who came over. There would be no lottery for a while. There would be lots of people. They would make his old silo whole again.

Jimmy shivered at the thought of so many people. Elise tugged his arm. "Let's go. Let's go," she said.

And Jimmy realized what he was scared of. It wasn't the leaving one day, which was still some time off. It wasn't him setting up home in the Deep, which was nearly pumped dry and no longer frightened him. It was the idea of what he might return to. His home had only grown safer as it had emptied; he had been attacked when it had started filling up again. Part of him just wanted to be left alone, to be Solo.

On his feet, he allowed Elise to lead him back to the landing. She tugged on his calloused hand and pulled him forward with spirit. Outside, she gathered her things by the steps. Rickson and the others could be heard below, their voices echoing up the shaft of quiet concrete. One of the emergency lights was out on that level, leaving a black patch amid the dull green. Elise adjusted the shoulder satchel that held her memory book and cinched the top of her backpack. Food and water, a change of clothes, batteries, a faded doll, her hairbrush—practically everything she owned. Jimmy held the shoulder strap so she could work her arm through, then picked up his own load. The voices of the others faded. The stairwell faintly shook and rang with their footsteps as they headed down, which seemed a fairly odd direction to go in order to get *out*.

"How long before Jewel comes for us?" Elise asked. She took Jimmy's hand, and they spiraled down side by side.

"Not long," Jimmy said, which was his answer for I-don't-know. "She's trying. It's a long way to go. You know how it took a long time for the water to go down and vanish?"

Elise bobbed her head. "I counted the steps," she said.

"Yes, you did. Well, now they have to tunnel their way through solid rock to get to us. That won't be easy."

"Hannah says there'll be dozens and dozens of people after Jewel comes."

Jimmy swallowed. "Hundreds," he said hoarsely. "Thousands, even."

Elise squeezed his hand. Another dozen steps went by, both of them quietly counting. It was difficult for either of them to count so high.

"Rickson says they aren't coming to rescue us, but that they want our silo."

"Yes, well, he sees the bad in people," Jimmy said. "Just like you see the good in them."

Elise looked up at Jimmy. Both of them had lost their count. He wondered if she could imagine what thousands of people would be like. He could barely remember himself.

"I wish he could see the good in people like me," she said.

Jimmy stopped before they got to the next landing. Elise clutched his hand and her swinging satchel and stopped with him. He knelt to be closer to her. When Elise pouted, he could see the gap left by her missing tooth.

"There's a bit of good in all people," Jimmy said. He squeezed Elise's shoulder, could feel a lump forming in his throat. "But there's bad as well. Rickson is probably more right than wrong at times."

He hated to say it. Jimmy hated to fill Elise's head with such things. But he loved her as though she were his own. And he wanted to give her the great steel doors she would need if the silo were to grow full again. It was why he allowed her to cut up the books inside the tin cans and take the pages she liked. It was why he helped her choose which ones were important. The ones he chose were the ones for helping her survive.

"You'll need to start seeing the world with Rickson's eyes," Jimmy said, hating himself for it. He stood and pulled her down the steps this time, no longer counting. He wiped his eyes before Elise noticed him crying, before she asked him one of her easy questions with no easy answers at all.

6

IT WAS DIFFICULT to leave the bright lights and comfort of his old home behind, but Jimmy had agreed to move down to the lower farms. The kids were comfortable there. They quickly resumed their work among the grow plots. And it was closer to the last of the dwindling floods.

Jimmy descended slick steps spotted with fresh rust and listened to the plopping tune of water hitting puddle and steel. Many of the green emergency lights had been drowned by the floods. Even those that worked held murky bubbles of trapped water. Jimmy thought about the fish that used to swim in what now was open air. A few had been found swimming around as the water retreated, even though he'd long ago thought he'd caught them all. Trapped in shallowing pools, they had proved too easy to catch. He had taught Elise how, but she had trouble getting them off the hook. She was forever dropping the slimy creatures back into the water. Jimmy jokingly accused her of doing it on purpose, and Elise admitted she liked catching them more than eating them. He had let her catch the last few fish over and over until he felt too sorry for the poor things to allow it to go on. Rickson and Hannah and the twins had been happy to put these desperate survivors out of their misery and into their bellies.

Jimmy glanced up beyond the rail overhead, picturing his bobber out there in the middle of the air. He imagined Shadow peering down and batting his paw at him, as if Jimmy were now the fish, trapped underwater. He tried to blow bubbles, but nothing came out, just the tickle of his whiskers against his nose.

Further down, a puddle gathered where the stairs bottomed out. The floor was flat here, wasn't sloped to drain. The floods were never meant to get so high. Jimmy flicked on his flashlight, and the beam cut through the dismal darkness deep inside Mechanical. An electrical wire snaked through the open passageway and draped across a security station. A tangle of hose traced along beside it before doubling back on itself. The cable and the hose knew the way to the pumps; they had been left behind by Juliette.

Jimmy followed their trail. His first time to the bottom of the stairs, he had found the plastic dome of her helmet. It was among a raft of trash and debris and sludge, all the foulness left over once the water was gone. He had tried to clean it up as much as he could, had found his small metal washers—the ones that anchored his old paper parachutes—like silver coins among the detritus. Much of the garbage from the floods remained. The only thing he had saved from it all was the plastic dome of her helmet.

The wire and hose turned down a flight of square steps. Jimmy followed them, careful not to trip. Water fell occasionally from the pipes and wires overhead and smacked him on the shoulder and head. The drops twinkled in the beam of his flashlight. Everything else was dark. He tried to imagine being down there when the place was full of water—and couldn't. It was scary enough while dry.

A smack of water right on the crown of his head, and then a tickle as the rivulet raced into his beard. "Mostly dry, I meant,"

Jimmy said, talking to the ceiling. He reached the bottom of the steps. It was only the wire now guiding him along, and tricky to see. He splashed through a thin film of water as he headed down the hall. Juliette said it was important to be there when the pump got done. Someone would have to be around to turn it on and off. Water would continue seeping in, and so the pump needed to do its job, but it was bad for the thing to run dry. Something called an "impeller" would burn, she had told him.

Jimmy found the pump. It was rattling unhappily. A large pipe bent over the lip of a well—Juliette had told him to be careful not to fall in—and there was a sucking, gurgling sound from its depths. Jimmy aimed the flashlight down and saw that the shaft was nearly empty. Just a foot or so of water thrown into turbulence by the fruitless pull of the great pipe.

He pulled his cutters out of his breast pocket and fished the wire out of the thin layer of water. The pump growled angrily, metal clanging on metal, the smell of hot electrics in the air, steam rising from the cylindrical housing that provided the power. Teasing apart the two joined wires, Jimmy severed one of them with his cutters. The pump continued to run for a breath but slowly wound itself down. Juliette had told him what to do. He stripped the cut wire back and twisted the ends. When the basin filled again, Jimmy would have to short out the starter switch by hand, just as she had done all those weeks ago. He and the kids could take turns. They would live above the levels ruined by the floods, tend the Wilds, and keep the silo dry until Juliette came for them.

Silo 18

7

THE ARGUMENT WITH Shirly about the generator went badly. Juliette got her way, but she didn't emerge feeling victorious. She watched her old friend stomp off and tried to imagine being in her place. It had only been a couple of months since her husband, Marck, had died. Juliette had been a wreck for a solid year after losing George. And now some mayor was telling the head of Mechanical that they were taking the backup generator. Stealing it. Leaving the silo at the whim of a mechanical failure. One tooth snaps off one gear, and all the levels descend into darkness, all the pumps fall quiet, until it can be fixed.

Juliette didn't need to hear Shirly argue the points. She could well enough name them herself. Now she stood alone in a dim hallway, her friend's footsteps fading to silence, wondering what in the world she was doing. Even those around her were losing their trust. And why? For a promise? Or was she just being stubborn?

She scratched her arm, one of the scars beneath her coveralls itching, and remembered speaking with her father after almost twenty years of hardheaded avoidance. Neither of them had admitted how dumb they'd been, but it hung in the room like a family quilt. Here was their failing, the source of their drive to accomplish much in life and also the cause of the damage they so often left behind—this injurious pride.

Juliette turned and let herself back into the generator room. A clanging racket along the far wall reminded her of more . . . unbalanced days. The sound of digging was not unlike the warped generator of her past: young and hot and dangerous.

Work was already underway on the backup generator. Dawson and his team had the exhaust coupling separated. Raph worked one of the large nuts on the forward mount with a massive wrench, separating the generator from its ancient mooring. Juliette realized she was really doing this. Shirly had every right to be pissed off.

She crossed the room and stepped through one of the holes in the wall, ducked her head under the rebar, and found Bobby at the rear of the great digger, scratching his beard. Bobby was a boulder of a man. He wore his hair long and in the tight braids miners enjoyed, and his charcoal skin hid the efforts of dark digging. He was in every way his friend Raph's antithesis. Hyla, his daughter and also his shadow, stood quietly at his elbow.

"How goes it?" Juliette asked.

"How goes it? Or how goes this machine?" Bobby turned and studied her a moment. "I'll tell you how this rusted bucket goes. She's not one for turning, not like you need. She's aimed straight as a rod. Not meant to be guided at all."

Juliette greeted Hyla and sized up the progress on the digger. The machine was cleaning up well, was in remarkable shape. She placed a hand on Bobby's arm. "She'll steer," she assured him. "We'll place iron wedges along the wall here on the right-hand side." She pointed to the place. Overhead floodlights from the mines illuminated the dark rock. "When the back end presses on these wedges, it'll force the front to the side." With one hand representing the digger, she pushed on her wrist with the other, cocking her hand to show how it would maneuver.

Bobby reluctantly grumbled his agreement. "It'll be slow going, but that might work." He unfolded a sheet of fine paper, a schematic of all the silos, and studied the path Juliette had drawn. She had stolen the layout from Lukas's hidden office, and her proposed dig traced an arc from Silo 18 to Silo 17, generator room to generator room. "We'll have to wedge it downward as well," Bobby told her. "She's on an incline like she's itchin' to go up."

"That's fine. What's the word on the bracing?"

Hyla studied the two adults and twisted a charcoal in one hand, held her slate in the other. Bobby glanced up at the ceiling and frowned.

"Erik's not so keen on lending what he's got. He says he can spare girders enough for a thousand yards. I told him you'd be wanting five or ten times that."

"We'll have to pull some out of the mines, then." Juliette nodded to Hyla and her slate, suggesting she write that down.

"You mean to start wars down here, do you?" Bobby tugged on his beard, clearly agitated. Hyla stopped scratching on the slate and looked from one of her superiors to the other, not sure what to do.

"I'll talk to Erik," she told Bobby. "When I promise him the pile of steel girders we'll find in the other silo, he'll cave."

Bobby lifted an eyebrow. "Bad choice of words."

He laughed nervously while Juliette gestured to his daughter. "We'll need thirty-six beams and seventy-two risers," she said.

Hyla glanced guiltily at Bobby before jotting this down.

"If this thing moves, it's gonna make a lot of dirt," Bobby said. "Hauling the tailings from here to the crusher down in the mines is gonna make a mess and take as many men as the digging."

The thought of the crushing room where tailings were

ground to powder and vented to the exhaust manifold stirred painful memories. Juliette aimed her flashlight at Bobby's feet, trying not to think of the past. "We won't be expelling the tailings," she told him. "Shaft six is almost directly below us. If we dig straight down, we hit it."

"You mean to fill number six?" Bobby asked, incredulous.

"Six is nearly tapped out anyway. And we double our ore the moment we reach this other silo."

"Erik's gonna blow a gasket. You aren't forgettin' anybody, are you?"

Juliette studied her old friend. "Forgetting anybody?"

"Anyone you're neglecting to piss off."

Juliette ignored the jab and turned to Hyla. "Make a note to Courtnee. I want the backup generator fully serviced before it's brought in. There won't be room to pull the heads and check the seals once it's fitted in here. The ceiling will be too low."

Bobby followed as Juliette continued her inspection of the digger. "You'll be here to look after that, won't you?" he asked. "You'll be here to couple the genset to this monster, right?"

She shook her head. "Afraid not. Dawson will be in charge of that. Lukas is right, I need to go up and make the rounds—"

"Bullshit," Bobby said. "What's this about, Jules? I've never seen you leave a project in half like this, not even if it meant working three shifts."

Juliette turned and gave Hyla that look that all children and shadows know to mean their ears aren't welcome. Hyla stayed back while the two old friends continued on.

"My being down here is causing unrest," Juliette told Bobby, her voice quiet and swallowed by the vastness of the machine around them. "Lukas did the right thing to come get me." She shot the old miner a cold look. "And I'll beat you senseless if that gets back to him."

He laughed and showed his palms. "You don't have to tell me. I'm married."

Juliette nodded. "It's best you all dig while I'm elsewhere. If I'm to be a distraction, then let me be a distraction." They reached the end of a void that the backup generator would soon fill. It was so clever, this arrangement, keeping the delicate engine out where it would be used and serviced. The rest of the digger was just steel and grinding teeth, gears packed tight with grease.

"These friends of yours," Bobby said. "They're worth all this?"

"They are." Juliette studied her old friend. "But this isn't just for them. This is for us too."

Bobby chewed on his beard. "I don't follow," he said after a pause.

"We need to prove this works," she said. "This is only the beginning."

Bobby narrowed his eyes at her. "Well, if it ain't the beginning of one thing," he said, "I would hazard to say it spells the end of another."

8

JULIETTE PAUSED OUTSIDE Walker's workshop and knocked before entering. She had heard tell of him being out and about during the uprising, but this was a cog whose teeth refused to align with anything in her head. As far as she was concerned, it was mere legend, a thing to be disbelieved because it hadn't been seen with her own eyes—similar, she reckoned, to how her jaunt between silos didn't compute for most people. A rumor. A myth. Who was this woman mechanic who claimed to have seen another land? Stories such as these were dismissed—unless legend took seed and sprouted religion.

"Jules!" Walker peered up from his desk, one of his eyes the size of a tomato through his magnifiers. He pulled the lens away, and his eye shrank back to normal. "Good, good. So glad you're here." He waved her over. There was the smell of burning hair in the room, as if the old man had been leaning over his soldering work while careless of his long gray locks.

"I just came to transmit something to Solo," she said. "And to let you know I'll be away for a few days."

"Oh?" Walker frowned. He slotted a few small tools into his leather apron and pressed his soldering iron into a wet sponge. The hiss reminded Juliette of an ill-tempered cat who used to live in the pump room, fussing at her from the darkness. "That Lukas fellow pulling you away?" Walker asked.

Juliette was reminded that Walker was no friend to open spaces, but he was a friend to porters. And they were friendly with his coin.

"That's part of it," she admitted. She pulled out a stool and sank against it, studied her hands, which were scraped and stained with grease. "The other part is that this digging business is going to take a while, and you know how I get when I sit still. I've got another project I've been thinking on. It's going to be even less popular than this one here."

Walker studied her for a moment, glanced up at the ceiling, and then his eyes widened. Somehow, he knew precisely what she was planning. "You're like a bowl of Courtnee's chili," he whispered. "Making trouble at both ends."

Juliette laughed, but also felt a twinge of disappointment that she was so transparent. So predictable.

"I haven't told Lukas yet," she warned him. "Or Peter."

Walker scrunched up his face at the second name.

"Billings," she said. "The new sheriff."

"That's right." He unplugged his soldering iron and dabbed it against the sponge again. "I forget that ain't your job no more."

It hardly ever was, she wanted to say.

"I just want to tell Solo that we're nearly underway with the digging. I need to make sure the floods are under control over there." She gestured to his radio, which could do far more than broadcast up and down a single silo. Like the radio in the room beneath IT's servers, this unit he had built was capable of broadcasting to other silos.

"Sure thing. Shame you aren't leaving in a day or two. I'm almost done with the portable." He showed her a plastic box a little larger than the old radios she and the deputies used to wear on their hips. It still had wires hanging loose and a large external battery attached. "Once I get done with it, you'll be able to switch channels with a dial. It piggybacks the repeaters up and down both silos."

She picked the unit up gingerly, no clue what he was talking about. Walker pointed to a dial with thirty-two numbered positions around it. This she understood.

"Just got to get the old rechargeables to play nice in there. Working on the voltage regulation next."

"You are amazing," Juliette whispered.

Walker beamed. "Amazing are the people who made this the first time. I can't get over what they were able to do hundreds of years ago. People weren't as dumb back then as you'd like to believe."

Juliette wanted to tell him about the books she'd seen, how the people back then seemed as if they were from the future, not the past.

Walker wiped his hands on an old rag. "I warned Bobby and the others, and I think you should know too. The radios won't work so well the deeper they dig, not until they get to the other side."

Juliette nodded. "So I heard. Courtnee said they'll use runners just like in the mines. I put her in charge of the dig. She's thought of just about everything."

Walker frowned. "I heard she wanted to rig this side to blow as well, in case they hit a pocket of bad air."

"That was Shirly's idea. She's just trying to come up with reasons not to dig. But you know Courtnee, once she sets her mind to something, it gets done."

Walker scratched his beard. "As long as she don't forget to feed me, we'll be fine."

Juliette laughed. "I'm sure she won't."

"Well, I wish you luck on your rounds."

"Thanks," she said. She pointed to the large radio set on his workbench. "Can you patch me through to Solo?"

"Sure, sure. Seventeen. Forgot you didn't come down here to chat with me. Let's call your friend." He shook his head. "Have to tell you, from talking to him, he's one odd fellow."

Juliette smiled and studied her old friend. She waited to see if he was joking—decided he was being perfectly serious—and laughed.

"What?" Walker asked. He powered the radio on and handed her the receiver. "What did I say?"

Solo's update was a mixed bag. Mechanical was dry, which was good, but it hadn't taken as long as she'd thought for the flood to pump out. It might be weeks or months to get over there and see what they could salvage, and the rust would set in immediately. Juliette pushed these distant problems out of her mind and concentrated on the things she could lay a wrench on.

Everything she needed for her trip up fit in a small shoulder bag: her good silver coveralls, which she'd barely worn; socks and underwear, both still wet from washing them in the sink; her work canteen, dented and grease-stained; and a ratchet and driver set. In her pockets she carried her multi-tool and twenty chits, even though hardly anyone took payment from her since she turned mayor. The only thing she felt she was missing was a decent radio, but Walker had scrapped two of the functioning units to try and build a new one, and it wasn't ready yet.

With her meager belongings and a feeling like she was abandoning her friends, she left Mechanical behind. The distant clatter from the digging followed her through the hallways and out into the stairwell. Passing through security was like crossing some mental threshold. It reminded her of leaving that airlock all those weeks ago. Like a stopper valve, some things seemed to allow passage in only one direction. She feared how long it might be before she returned. The thought made it difficult to breathe.

She slowly gained height and began passing others on the stairwell, and Juliette could feel them watching her. The glares of people she had once known reminded her of the wind that had buffeted her on the hillside. Their distrustful glances came in gusts—just as quickly, they looked away.

Before long, she saw what Lukas had spoken of. Whatever goodwill her return had wrought—whatever wonder people held for her as someone who had refused to clean and managed to survive the great outside—was crumbling as sure as the concrete being hammered below. Where her return from the outside had brought hope, her plans to tunnel beyond the silo had engendered something else. She could see it in the averted gaze of a shopkeep, in the protective arm a mother wrapped around her child, in the whispers that came and just as suddenly went. Juliette was causing the opposite of hope. She was spreading fear.

A handful of people did acknowledge her with a nod and a "Mayor" as she passed them on the stairwell. A young porter she knew stopped and shook her hand, seemed genuinely thrilled to see her. But when she paused at the lower farms on one-twenty-six for food, and when she sought a bathroom three levels further up, she felt as welcomed as a greaser in the Up Top. And yet she was still among her own. She was their mayor, however unloved.

These interactions gave her second thoughts about seeing Hank, the deputy of the Down Deep. Hank had fought in the uprising and had seen good men and women on both sides give up their lives. As Juliette entered the deputy station on one-twenty, she wondered if stopping was a mistake, if she should just press on. But that was her young self afraid of seeing her father, her young self who buried her head in projects in order to avoid the world. She could no longer be that person. She had a responsibility to the silo and its people. Seeing Hank was the right thing to do. She scratched a scar on the back of her hand and bravely strode into his deputy station. She reminded herself that she was the mayor, not a prisoner being sent to clean.

Hank glanced up from his desk as she entered. The deputy's eyes widened as he recognized her—they had not spoken nor seen each other since she got back. He rose from his chair and took two steps toward her, then stopped, and Juliette saw the same mix of nerves and excitement that she felt and realized she shouldn't have been afraid of coming, that she shouldn't have avoided him until now. Hank reached out his hand timidly, as if worried she might refuse to shake it. He seemed ready to pull it back if it offended. Whatever heartache she had brought him, he still seemed pained at having followed orders and sending her to clean.

Juliette took the deputy's hand and pulled him into an embrace.

"I'm sorry," he whispered, his voice giving out on him.

"Stop that," Juliette said. She let go of the lawman and took a step back, studied his shoulder. "I'm the one who should be apologizing. How's your arm?"

He shrugged his shoulder in a circle. "Still attached," he said. "And if you ever dare apologize to me, I'll have you arrested."

"Truce, then," she offered.

Hank smiled. "Truce," he said. "But I do want to say—"

"You were doing your job. And I was doing the best I could. Now leave it."

He nodded and studied his boots.

"How are things around here? Lukas said there's been grumbling about my work below."

"There's been some acting up. Nothing too serious. I think most people are busy enough patching things up. But yeah, I've heard some talk. You know how many requests we get for transfer out of here and up to the Mids or the Top. Well, I've been getting ten times the normal. Folks don't want to be near what you've got going on, I'm afraid."

Juliette chewed her lip.

"Part of the problem is lack of direction," Hank said. "Don't want to shoulder you with this, but me and the boys down here don't have a clear idea which way is up right now. We aren't getting dispatches from Security like we used to. And your office . . ."

"Has been quiet," Juliette offered.

Hank scratched the back of his head. "That's right. Not that you've been exactly quiet yourself. We can sometimes hear the racket you're making out on the landing."

"That's why I'm visiting," she told him. "I want you to know that your concerns are my concerns. I'm heading up to my office for a week or two. I'll stop by the other deputy stations as well. Things are going to improve around here in a lot of ways."

Hank frowned. "You know I trust you and all, but when you tell people around here that things are going to improve, all they hear is that things are going to change. And for those who are breathing and count that as a blessing, they take that to mean one thing and one thing only."

Juliette thought of all she had planned, in the Up Top as well as the Down Deep. "As long as good men like you trust me, we'll be fine," she said. "Now, I've got a favor to ask."

"You need a place to stay the night," Hank guessed. He waved at the jail cell. "I saved your room for you. I can turn down the cot—"

Juliette laughed. She was happy that they could already joke about what had moments ago been a discomfort. "No," she said. "Thanks, though. I'm supposed to be up at the Mids farms by lights out. I have to plant the first crop in a new patch of soil being turned over." She waved her hand in the air. "It's one of those things."

Hank smiled and nodded.

"What I wanted to ask is that you keep an eye on the stairwell for me. Lukas mentioned there were grumbles up above. I'm going up to soothe them, but I want you to be on the alert if things go sour. We're short-staffed below, and people are on edge."

"You expecting trouble?" Hank asked.

Juliette considered the question. "I am," she said. "If you need to take a shadow or two, I'll budget it."

He frowned. "I normally like having chits thrown my way," he said. "So why does this make me feel uncomfortable?"

"Same reason I'm happy to pay," Juliette said. "We both know you're getting the busted end of the deal."

9

Leaving the deputy's office, Juliette climbed through levels that had seen much of the fighting, and she noticed once more the silo's wounds of war. She rose through ever-worsening reminders of the battles that had been waged in her absence, saw the marks left behind from the fighting, the jagged streaks of bright silver through old paint, the black burns and pockmarks in concrete, the rebar poking through like fractured bone through skin.

She had devoted most of her life to holding that silo together, to keeping it running. This was a kindness repaid by the silo as it filled her lungs with air, gave rise to the crops, and claimed the dead. They were responsible for one another. Without people, this silo would become as Solo's had: rusted and fairly drowned. Without the silo, she would be a skull on a hill, looking blankly to the cloud-filled skies. They needed each other.

Her hand slid up the rail, rough with new welds, her own hand a mess of scars. For much of her life, they had kept each other going, she and the silo. Right up until they'd damn near killed each other. And now the minor hurts in Mechanical she had hoped to repair one day—squealing pumps, spitting pipes, leaks from the exhaust—all paled before the far worse wreckage her leaving had caused. In much the same way that the occasional scars—reminders of youthful missteps—were now lost beneath disfigured flesh, it seemed that one large mistake could bury all the minor ones.

She took the steps one at a time and reached that place where a bomb had ripped a gap in the stairs. A patchwork of metal stretched across the ruin, a web of bar and rail scavenged from landings that now stood narrower than before. Names of those lost in the blast were written here and there in charcoal. Juliette treaded carefully across the mangled metal. Higher up, she saw that the doors to Supply had been replaced. Here, the fighting had been especially bad. The cost these people in yellow had paid for siding with hers in blue.

A Sunday was letting out as Juliette approached the church on ninety-nine. Floods of people spiraled down toward the quiet bazaar she had just passed. Their mouths were pressed tight from hours of serious talk, their joints as stiff as their pressed coveralls. Juliette filed past them and took note of the hostile glances.

The crowds thinned by the time she reached the landing. The small temple was wedged in among the old hydroponic farms and worker flats that used to serve the Deep. It was before her time, but Knox once explained how the temple had sprouted on ninety-nine. It was when his own dad was a boy and protests had arisen over music and plays performed during Sundays. Security had sat back while the protestors swelled into an encampment outside the bazaar. People slept on the treads and choked the stairway until no one could pass. The farm one level up was ravaged in supplying food to these masses. Eventually, they took over much of the hydroponics level. The temple on twenty-eight set up a satellite office, and now that satellite on ninety-nine was bigger than the temple that had sprouted it.

Father Wendel was on the landing as Juliette rounded the last turn. He stood by the door, shaking hands and speaking briefly with each member of his congregation as they left the Sunday service. His white robes fairly emitted a light of their own. They shone much like his bald head, which glistened from the effort of preaching to the crowds. Between head and robes, Wendel seemed to sparkle. Especially to Juliette, who had just left a land of smudge and grease. She felt dirty just seeing such unblemished cloth.

"Thank you, Father," a woman said, bowing slightly, shaking his hand, a child balanced on her hip. The little one's head lolled against her shoulder in perfect slumber. Wendel rested a hand on the child's head and said a few words. The woman thanked him again, moved on, and Wendel shook the next man's hand.

Juliette made herself invisible against the rail while the last handful of churchgoers filed past. She watched a man pause and press a few clinking chits into Father Wendel's open palm. "Thank you, Father," he said, this farewell a chant of sorts. Juliette could smell what she thought was goats on the old man as he filed past and wound his way up, probably back to the pens. He was the last one to leave. Father Wendel turned and smiled at Juliette to let her know he'd been aware of her presence.

"Mayor," he said, spreading his hands. "You honor us. Did you come for the elevens?"

Juliette checked the small watch she wore around her wrist. "This wasn't the elevens?" she asked. She was making good time up the levels.

"It was the tens. We added another Sunday. The toppers come down for late service."

Juliette wondered why those who lived up top would travel so far. She had timed her walk to miss the services entirely, which was probably a mistake. It would be smart for her to hear what was being said that so many found alluring.

"I'm afraid I can only stop for a quick visit," she said. "I'll catch a Sunday on my way back down?"

Wendel frowned. "And when might that be? I heard you were returning to the work God and his people chose you for."

"A few weeks, probably. Long enough to get caught up."

An acolyte emerged on the landing with an ornate wooden bowl. He showed Wendel its contents, and Juliette heard the chits shift against one another. The boy wore a brown cloak, and when he bowed to Wendel, she saw the center of his scalp had been shaved. When he turned to leave, Wendel grabbed the acolyte's arm.

"Pay your respects to your mayor," he said.

"Ma'am." The acolyte bowed. His face showed no expression. Dark eyes under full and dark brows, his lips colorless. Juliette sensed that this young man spent little time outside of the church.

"You don't have to ma'am me," she told him politely. "Juliette." She extended a hand.

"Remmy," the boy said. A hand emerged from his cloak. Juliette accepted it.

"See to the pews," Wendel said. "We have another service yet."

Remmy bowed to both of them and shuffled away. Juliette felt pity for the boy, but she wasn't sure why. Wendel peered across the landing and seemed to listen for approaching traffic. Holding the door, he waved Juliette inside. "Come," he said. "Top up your canteen. I'll bless your journey."

Juliette shook her canteen, which sloshed nearly empty. "Thank you," she said. She followed him inside.

Wendel led her past the reception hall and waved her into the lower chapel, where she'd attended a few Sundays years prior. Remmy busied himself among the rows of benches and chairs, replacing pillows and laying out announcements handwritten on narrow strips of cheap paper. She caught him watching her as he worked.

"The gods miss you," Father Wendel said, letting her know that he was aware how long it'd been since she'd attended a Sunday. The chapel had expanded since she last remembered it. There was the heady and expensive smell of sawdust, of newly shaped wood made from claimed doors and other ancient timbers. She rested her hand on a pew that must've been worth a fortune.

"Well, the gods know where to find me," she answered, taking her hand off the pew. She smiled as she said this, meant it lightly, but saw a flash of disappointment on the father's face.

"I sometimes wonder if you aren't hiding from them as best you can," he said. Father Wendel nodded toward the stained glass behind the altar. The lights behind the glass were full-bright, shards of color thrown against the floor and ceiling. "I read your announcements for every birth and every death up there in my pulpit, and I see in them that you give credit in all things to the gods."

Juliette wanted to say that she didn't even write those announcements. They were written for her.

"But I sometimes wonder if you even believe in the gods, the way you take their rules so lightly."

"I believe in the gods," Juliette said, her temper stoked by this accusation. "I believe in the gods who created this silo. I do. And all the other silos—"

Wendel flinched. "Blasphemy," he whispered, his eyes wide as if her words could kill. He threw a look at Remmy, who bowed and moved toward the hall.

"Yes, blasphemy," Juliette said. "But I believe the gods made the towers beyond the hills and that they left us a way to discover, a way out of here. We have uncovered a tool in the depths of this silo, Father Wendel. A digging machine that could take us to new places. I know you disapprove, but I believe the gods gave us this tool, and I mean to use it."

"This digger of yours is the devil's work, and it lies in the devil's deep," Wendel said. The kindness had left his face. He patted his forehead with a square of fine cloth. "There are no gods like those you speak of, only demons."

This was his sermon, Juliette saw. She was getting his elevens. The people came far to hear this.

She took a step closer. Her skin was warm with anger. "There may be demons among my gods," she agreed, speaking his tongue. "The gods I believe in . . . the gods I worship were the men and women who built this place and more like it. They built this place to protect us from the world they destroyed. They were gods and demons, both. But they left us space for redemption. They meant us to be free, Father, and they gave us the means." She pointed to her temple. "They gave me the means right here. And they left us a digger. They did. There is nothing blasphemous about using it. And I've seen the other silos that you continue to doubt. I've been there."

Wendel took another step back. He rubbed the cross hanging around his neck, and Juliette caught Remmy peeking around the edge of the door, his dark brows casting shadows over his dark eyes.

"We should use all the tools the gods gave us," Juliette said. "Except for the one you wield, this power to make others fear."

"Me?" Father Wendel pressed one palm to his chest. With his other hand, he pointed at her. "*You* are the one spreading fear." He swept his hand at the pews and beyond to the tight rows of mismatched chairs, crates, and buckets at the back of the room. "They crowd in here three Sundays a day to wring their hands over the devil's work you do. Children can't sleep at night for fear that you'll kill us all."

Juliette opened her mouth, but the words would not come. She thought of the looks on the stairwell, thought of that mother pulling her child close, people she knew who no longer said hello. "I could show you books," she said softly, thinking of the shelves that held the Legacy. "I could show you books, and then you'd see."

"There's only one book worth knowing," Wendel said. His eyes darted to the large, ornate tome with its gilded edges that sat on a podium by the pulpit, that sat under a cage of bent steel. Juliette remembered lessons from that book. She'd seen its pages with those occasional and cryptic sentences peeking out amid bars of censored black. She also noticed the way the podium was welded to the steel decking, and not expertly. Fat puckers of paranoid welds. The same gods expected to keep men and women safe couldn't be trusted to look after one book.

"I should leave you to get ready for your elevens," she said, feeling sorry for her outburst.

Wendel uncrossed his arms. She could sense that they had both gone too far and that both knew it. She had hoped to allay doubts and had only worsened them.

"I wish you'd stay," Wendel told her. "At least fill your canteen."

She reached behind her back and unclipped the canteen. Remmy returned with a swish of his heavy brown cloaks, the shaved circle on his head glimmering with perspiration. "I will, Father," Juliette said. "Thank you."

Wendel nodded. He waved to Remmy and said nothing else to her as his acolyte drew water from the chapel fountain. Not a word. His earlier promise to bless her journey had gone forgotten.

10

JULIETTE PARTICIPATED IN a ceremonial planting at the Mids farm, had a late lunch, and continued her laconic pace up the silo. By the time she reached the thirties, the lights were beginning to dim, and she found herself looking forward to a familiar bed.

Lukas was waiting for her on the landing. He smiled a greeting and insisted on taking her shoulder bag, however light.

"You didn't have to wait for me," she said. But in truth, she found it sweet.

"I just got here," he insisted. "A porter told me you were getting close."

Juliette remembered the young girl in light blue coveralls who'd overtaken her in the forties. It was easy to forget that Lukas had eyes and ears everywhere. He held the door open, and Juliette entered a level packed with conflicting memories and feelings. Here was where Knox had died. Here was where Mayor Jahns had been poisoned. Here was where she had been doomed to clean and where doctors had patched her back up.

She glanced toward the conference room and remembered being told that she was mayor. That was where she had suggested to Peter and Lukas that they tell everyone the truth:

that they were not alone in the world. She still thought it a good idea, despite their protestations. But maybe it was better to *show* people rather than tell them. She imagined families taking a grand journey to the Down Deep the way they used to hike up to gaze at the wallscreen. They would travel to her world, thousands of people who had never been, who had no idea what the machines that kept them alive looked like. They would travel down to Mechanical so that they could then pass through a tunnel and see this other silo. On the way, they might marvel at the main generator that now hummed, perfectly balanced. They could marvel at the hole in the ground her friends had made. And then they could contemplate the thrill of filling an empty world so very much like their own, remaking it how they saw fit.

The security gate beeped as Lukas scanned his pass, and Juliette returned from her daydreams. The guard behind the gate waved at her, and Juliette waved back. Beyond him, the halls of IT sat quiet and empty. Most of the workers had gone home for the night. With no one there, Juliette was reminded of Silo 17. She imagined Solo walking around the corner, half a loaf of bread in his hand, crumbs caught in his beard, a happy grin on his face as he spotted her. That hall looked just like this hall, except for the busted light that dangled from its wires in Silo 17.

These two sets of memories jumbled in her head as she followed Lukas back to his private residence. Two worlds with the same layout, two lives lived, one here and one there. The weeks spent with Solo felt like an entire lifetime, such was the bond that formed between two people under strain. Elise might dart out of that office where the kids had set up their home and cling to Juliette's leg. The twins would be arguing over found spoils around the bend. Rickson and Hannah would be stealing a kiss in the dark and whispering of another child.

"—but only if you agree."

Juliette turned to Lukas. "What? Oh, yes. That's fine."

"You didn't hear a word of that, did you?" They reached his door, and he scanned his badge. "It's like you're off in another world sometimes."

Juliette heard concern in his voice, not anger. She took her bag from him and stepped inside. Lukas turned on the lights and threw his ID on the dresser by the bed. "You feeling okay?" he asked.

"Just tired from the climb." Juliette sat on the edge of the bed and untied her laces. She worked her boots off and left them in their usual place. Lukas's apartment was like a second home, familiar and cozy. Her own apartment on level six was a foreign land. She had seen it twice but had never spent a night there. To do so would be to fully accept her role as mayor.

"I was thinking about having a late dinner delivered." Lukas rummaged in his closet and brought out the soft cloth robe that Juliette loved to pull on after a hot shower. He hung it from the hook on the bathroom door. "Do you want me to run you a bath?"

Juliette took a heavy breath. "I reek, don't I?" She sniffed the back of her hand and tried to nose the grease. There was the acidic hint of her cutting torch, the spice of exhaust fumes from the digger—a perfume as tattooed on her flesh as the markings oilmen cut and inked into their arms. All this, despite the fact that she had showered before she left Mechanical.

"No—" Lukas appeared hurt. "I just thought you'd enjoy a bath."

"In the morning, maybe. And I might skip dinner. I've been snacking all day." She smoothed the sheets beside her. Lukas smiled and sat down next to her on the bed. His face bore an expectant grin, that glow in his eyes she saw after they made love—but the look dissipated with her next words: "We need to talk."

His face fell. His shoulders sagged. "We're not going to register, are we?"

Juliette seized his hand. "No, that's not it. Of course we are. Of course." She pressed his hand to her chest, remembering a love that she'd kept hidden from the Pact once before and how that had wrenched her in half. She would never make that mistake again. "It's about the digging," she said.

Lukas took a deep breath, held it for a moment, then laughed. "Only that," he said, smiling. "Amazing that your digging could come as the lesser of two harms."

"I have something else I want to do that you aren't going to like."

He raised an eyebrow. "If this is about trying to spread news of the other silos, about telling people what's out there, you know where Peter and I stand on that. I don't think those words are safe. People won't believe you, and those who do will want to cause trouble."

Juliette thought of Father Wendel and how people could believe amazing things crafted from mere words, how beliefs could form from books. But perhaps they had to *want* to believe those things. And maybe Lukas was right that not everyone would want to believe the truth.

"I'm not going to tell them anything," she told Lukas. "I want to *show* them. There's something I want to do up top, but it requires help from you and your department. I'm going to need some of your men."

Lukas frowned. "I don't like the sound of that." He rubbed her arm. "Why don't we discuss it tomorrow? I just want to enjoy having you here with me tonight. One night where we aren't working. I can pretend I'm just a server tech and you can be . . . not the mayor."

Juliette squeezed his hand. "You're right. Of course. And maybe I should jump in the shower real quick—"

"No, stay." He kissed her neck. "You smell like you. Shower in the morning."

She relented. Lukas kissed her neck again, but when he moved to unzip her coveralls, she asked him to douse the lights. For once, he didn't complain as he often did about not being able to see her. Instead, he left the bathroom light on and shut the door most of the way, leaving the barest of glows. As much as she loved being naked with him, she didn't like to be seen. The patchwork of scars made her look like the slices of mineshaft that cut through granite: a web of white rock standing out from the rest.

But as unattractive as they were to the eyes, they were sensitive to the touch. Each scar was like a nerve ending rising from her own Deep. When Lukas traced them with his fingers—like an electrician following a diagram of wires—wherever he touched was a wrench across two battery terminals. Electricity fluttered through her body as they held each other in the darkness and he explored her with his hands. Juliette could feel her skin grow warm. This would not be a night where they fell fast asleep. Her designs and dangerous plans began to fade under the gentle pressure of his soft touch. This would be a night for traveling back to her youth, of *feeling* rather than thinking, back to simpler times—

"That's strange," Lukas said, stopping what he was doing.

Juliette didn't ask what was strange, hoping he'd forget it. She was too proud to tell him to keep touching her like that.

"My favorite little scar is gone," he said, rubbing a spot on her arm.

Juliette's temperature soared. She was back in the airlock, such was the heat. It was one thing to silently touch her wounds, another to name them. She pulled her arm away and rolled over, thinking this would be a night for sleep after all.

"No, here, let me see," he begged.

"You're being cruel," Juliette told him.

Lukas rubbed her back. "I'm not, I swear. May I please see your arm?"

Juliette sat up in the bed and pulled the sheets over her knees. She wrapped her arms around herself. "I don't like you mentioning them," she said. "And you shouldn't have a favorite." She nodded toward the bathroom, where a faint glow of light leaked out from the cracked door. "Can we please shut that or turn out the light?"

"Jules, I swear to you, I love you just the way you are. I've never seen you any other way."

She took that to mean that he'd never seen her naked before her wounds, not that he'd always found her beautiful. Getting out of bed, she moved to douse the bathroom light herself. She dragged the sheet behind her, leaving Lukas alone and naked on the bed.

"It was on the crook of your right arm," Lukas said. "Three of them crossed and made a little star. I've kissed it a hundred times."

Juliette doused the light and stood alone in the darkness. She could still feel Lukas gazing at her. She could feel people gawking at the scars even when she was fully clothed. She thought of George seeing her like that—and a lump rose in her throat.

Lukas appeared next to her in the pitch black, his arm around her, a kiss lighting on her shoulder. "Come back to bed," he said. "I'm sorry. We can leave the light out."

Juliette hesitated. "I don't like you knowing them so well," she said. "I don't want to be one of your star charts."

"I know," he said. "I can't help it. They're a part of you, the only you I've ever known. Maybe we should have your father take a look—?"

She pulled away from him, only to click the light back on. She studied the crook of her arm in the mirror, first her right arm and then her left, thinking he must be wrong.

"Are you sure it was there?" she asked, studying the web of scars for some bare patch, some piece of open sky.

Lukas took her tenderly by the wrist and elbow, lifted her arm to his mouth, and kissed it.

"Right there," he said. "I've kissed it a hundred times."

Juliette wiped a tear from her eye and laughed in that mix of gasp and sigh that comes from a sad burst of emotion. Locating a particularly offensive knot of flesh, a welt that ran right around her forearm, she showed it to Lukas, forgiving him if not believing him.

"Do this one next," she said.

Silo 1

11

THE SILICON-CARBON BATTERIES the drones ran on were the size of toaster ovens. Charlotte judged each one to weigh between thirty and forty pounds. They had been pulled from two of the drones and wrapped in webbing taken from one of the supply crates. Charlotte gripped one battery in each hand and took lunging squats in a slow lap around the warehouse, her thighs screaming and quivering, her arms numb.

A trail of sweat marked her progress, but she had a long way to go. How had she let herself get so out of shape? All the running and exercise during basic, just to sit at a console and fly a drone, to sit on her butt and play war games, to sit in a cafeteria and eat slop, to sit and read.

She'd gotten overweight, is what. And it hadn't bothered her until she'd woken up in this nightmare. She'd never felt the urge to get up and move around until someone had frozen her stiff for a few hundred years. Now she wanted the body back that she remembered. Legs that worked. Arms that weren't sore just from brushing her teeth. Maybe it was silly of her, thinking she could go back, be who she once was, return to a world she remembered. Or maybe she was being impatient with her recovery. These things took time.

She made it back around to the drones, a full lap. That she

could complete a circuit of the room meant progress. It'd been a few weeks since her brother had woken her, and the routine of eating, exercising, and working on the drones was beginning to seem normal. The insane world she had been woken up to was starting to feel real. And that terrified her.

She lowered the batteries to the ground and took a series of deep breaths. Held them. The routine of military life had been similar. It had prepared her for this, was all that kept her from going crazy. Being cooped up was not new. Living in the middle of a desert wasteland where it wasn't safe to go out was not new. Being surrounded by men she ought to fear was not new. Stationed in Iraq during the Second Iranian War, Charlotte had grown accustomed to these things, to not leaving base, to not wanting to leave her bunk or a bathroom stall. She was used to this struggle to keep sane. It was mental as much as physical exercise that was required.

She showered in one of the stalls down from drone control, toweled off, sniffed each of her three sets of coveralls, and decided it was time to prod Donny into doing laundry again. She pulled on the least offensive of the three, hung the towel to dry from the foot of an upper bunk, and then made up her bed Air Force crisp. Donald had once lived in the conference room at the other end of the warehouse, but Charlotte had almost grown comfortable in the barracks with its ghosts. It felt like home.

Down the hall from the barracks stood a room of pilot stations. Most were covered in plastic sheets. There was a flat desk along the same wall that bore a mosaic of large monitors. It was here that the radio set was being pieced together. Her brother had gathered a jumble of spare parts one at a time from the lower storerooms. It might be decades or even centuries before anyone noticed they were gone.

Charlotte flicked on the light bulb she'd rigged over the table and powered up the set. She could already get quite a few stations. She tuned the knob until she heard static and left it there, waiting on voices. Until then, she pretended it was the sea rolling up onto a beach. Sometimes it was rain on a canopy of fat leaves. Or a crowd of people quietly talking in a dark theater. She pawed through the bin of parts Donald had amassed and looked for a better set of speakers, still needed a microphone or some way to transmit. She wished she was more mechanically inclined. All she knew how to do was plug things together. It was like assembling a rifle or a computer—she just joined anything that would mate and flicked on the power. It had only resulted in smoke the one time. What it mostly took was patience, which she didn't have a lot of. Or time, which she was drowning in.

Footsteps down the hall signaled breakfast. Charlotte turned down the volume and cleared room on the desk as Donny entered, a tray in his hands.

"Morning," she said, getting up to take the tray from him. Her legs felt wobbly from the workout. As her brother stepped into the spill of light from the dangling bulb, she noted his frown. "Everything okay?" she asked.

He shook his head. "We might have a problem."

Charlotte set the tray down. "What is it?"

"I ran into a guy I knew from my first shift. Was stuck on the lift with him. A handyman."

"That's not good." She lifted the dented metal cover from one of the plates. There was an electrical board and a coil of wire beneath. Also, the small driver she'd asked for.

"Your eggs are under the other one."

She set the lid aside and grabbed her fork. "Did he recognize you?"

"I couldn't tell. I kept my head down until he got off. But I knew him as well as I've known anyone in this place. It feels like yesterday that I borrowed tools from him, asked him to change a light for me. Who knows what it feels like for him. That might've been yesterday or a dozen years ago. Memory works weird in this place."

Charlotte took a bite of eggs. Donny had put a touch too much salt on them. She imagined him up there with the shaker, his hand trembling. "Even if he did recognize you," she said around a bite of food, "he might think you're on another shift as yourself. How many people know you as Thurman?"

Donald shook his head. "Not many. But still, this could come crashing down on us at any moment. I'm going to bring some food up from the pantry, more dry goods. Also, I went in and changed the clearance for your badge so you can access the lifts. And I double-checked that no one else could get down here. I'd hate for you to get trapped if something happened to me."

Charlotte moved her eggs around her plate. "I don't like thinking about that," she said.

"Another bit of a problem. The head of this silo is going off shift in a week, which will make things a little complicated. I'm relying on him to orient the next guy to my status. Things have been going a little too smoothly thus far—"

Charlotte laughed and took another bite of eggs. "Too smoothly," she said, shaking her head. "I'd hate to see rough. What's the latest on your favorite silo?"

"The IT head picked up today. Lukas."

Charlotte thought her brother sounded disappointed. "And?" she asked. "Learn anything new?"

"He managed to crack another server. It's more of the same data, everything about its residents, every job they've had, who they're related to, from birth to death. I don't understand how those machines go from that information to this ranked list. It seems like a bunch of noise, like there has to be something else."

He produced a sheet of folded paper, a new printout of the rankings of the silos. Charlotte cleared a space on the work-bench, and he smoothed the report.

"See? The order has changed again. But what determines that?"

She studied the report while she ate, and Donald grabbed one of his folders of notes. He spent a lot of time working in the conference room where he could spread things out and pace back and forth, but Charlotte preferred it when he sat at that drone station. He would sit there for hours sometimes, going through his notes while Charlotte worked on the radio, the two of them listening for chatter among the static.

"Silo Six is back on top again," she muttered. It was like reading the side of a cereal box while she ate, all those numbers that made little sense. One column was labeled *Facility,* which Donald said was what they used to call the silos. Beside each silo was a percentage like a massive dose of daily vitamins: *99.992%, 99.989%, 99.987%, 99.984%*. The last silo with a percentage read *99.974%*. Every silo below this was marked off or had *N/A* listed. Silos 40, 12, 17, and a handful of others were included in that latter category.

"You still think the one on top is the only one that gets to survive?" she asked.

"I do."

"Have you told these people you're talking to? Because they're way down the list."

He just looked at her and frowned.

"You haven't. You're just using them to help you figure all this out."

"I'm not using them. Hell, I saved that silo. I save it every day that I don't report what's going on over there."

"Okay," Charlotte said. She returned to her eggs.

"Besides, they probably figure they're using me. Hell, I think they get more out of our talks than I do. Lukas, the one who heads up their IT, he peppers me with all these questions about the way the world used to be—"

"And the mayor?" Charlotte turned and studied her brother closely. "What does she get out of it?"

"Juliette?" Donald thumbed through a folder. "She enjoys threatening me."

Charlotte laughed. "I would love to hear that."

"If you get that radio sorted, you might."

"And then you'll spend more time working down here? It would be good, you know. Lessen the risk of being recognized." She scraped her plate with her fork, not willing to admit the real reason she wanted him down there more was how empty the place felt when he was gone.

"Absolutely." Her brother rubbed his face, and Charlotte saw how tired he was. Her gaze fell back to the numbers while she ate.

"It makes it seem arbitrary, doesn't it?" she wondered aloud. "If these numbers mean what you think they mean. They're functionally equivalent."

"I doubt the people who planned all this look at it that way. All they need is one of them. It doesn't matter which one. It's like a bunch of spares in a box. You pluck one out, and all you care about is if it'll work. That's it. They just want to see everything is one hundred percent all the way down."

Charlotte couldn't believe that's what they had in mind. But Donny had shown her the Pact and enough of his notes to convince her. All the silos but one would be exterminated. Their own included.

"How long before the next drone is ready?" he asked.

Charlotte took a sip of juice. "Another day or two. Maybe three. I'm really going light with this one. Not even sure if it'll fly." The last two hadn't made it as far as the first. She was getting desperate.

"Okay." He rubbed his face again, his palms muffling his voice. "We're gonna have to decide before too long what we're gonna do. If we do nothing, this nightmare plays out for another two hundred years, and you and I won't last that long." He started to laugh, but it turned into a cough. Donald fished into his coveralls for his handkerchief, and Charlotte looked away. She studied the dark monitors while he had one of his fits.

She didn't want to admit this to him, but her inclination was to let it play out. It seemed as if a bunch of precision machines were in control of humanity's fate, and she tended to trust computers a lot more than her brother did. She had spent years flying drones that could fly themselves, that could make decisions on which targets to hit, could guide missiles to precise locations. She often felt less like a pilot and more like a jockey, a person on a beast that could race along on its own, that only needed someone there to occasionally take the reins or shout encouragement.

She glanced over the numbers on the report again. Hundredths of a percentage point would decide who lived and who died. And most would die. She and her brother would either be asleep or long dead by the time it happened. The numbers made this looming holocaust seem so damn . . . arbitrary.

Donald used the folder in his hand to point at the report. "Did you notice Eighteen moved up two spots?"

She had noticed. "You don't think you've become too . . . attached, do you?"

He looked away. "I have a history with this silo. That's all."

Charlotte hesitated. She didn't want to press further, but she couldn't help herself. "I didn't mean the silo," she said. "You seem . . . different each time you talk to her."

He took a deep breath, let it out slowly. "She was sent to clean," he said. "She's been outside."

For a moment Charlotte thought that was all he was going to say on the matter. As if this were enough, as if it explained everything. He was quiet a pause, his eyes flicking back and forth.

"No one is supposed to come back from that," he finally said. "I don't think the computers take this into account. Not just what she survived, but that Eighteen is hanging in there. By all accounts, they shouldn't be. If they make it through this . . . you wonder if they don't give us the best hope."

"*You* wonder," Charlotte said, correcting him. She waved the piece of paper. "There's no way we're smarter than these computers, brother."

Donald appeared sad. "We can be more compassionate than them," he said.

Charlotte fought the urge to argue. She wanted to point out that he cared about this silo because of the personal contact. If he knew the people behind any of the other silos—if he knew their stories—would he root for them? It would be cruel to suggest this, however true.

Donald coughed into his rag. He caught Charlotte staring at him, glanced at the bloodstained cloth, put it away.

"I'm scared," she told him.

Donald shook his head. "I'm not. I'm not afraid of this. I'm not afraid of dying."

"I know you're not. That's obvious, or you would see someone. But you have to be afraid of something."

"I am. Plenty. I'm afraid of being buried alive. I'm afraid of doing the wrong thing."

"Then do nothing," she insisted. She nearly begged him right then to put a stop to this madness, to their isolation. They could go back to sleep and leave this to the machines and to the God-awful plans of others. "Let's not do anything," she pleaded.

Her brother rose from his seat, squeezed her arm, and turned to leave. "That might be the worst thing," he quietly said.

12

THAT NIGHT, CHARLOTTE awoke from a nightmare of flying. She sat up in her cot, springs crying out like a nest of birds, and could still feel herself swooping down through the clouds, the wind on her face.

Always dreams of flying. Dreams of falling. Wingless dreams where she couldn't steer, couldn't pull up. A plummeting bomb zeroing in on a man with his family, a man turning at the last minute to shield his eyes against the noonday sun, a glimpse of Charlotte's father and mother and brother and herself before impact and loss of signal—

The nest of birds beneath her fell quiet. Charlotte untangled her fists from the sheets, which were damp with all that dreams wrung from terrified flesh. The room hung heavy and somber around her. She could feel the empty bunks all around, that sense that her fellow pilots had been summoned away in the night, leaving her alone. She rose and padded across the hall to the bathroom, feeling her way and sliding the switches up just a fraction to keep the lights dim. She understood sometimes why her brother had lived in the conference room at the other end of the warehouse. Shadows of un-people stalked those halls. She could feel herself pass through the ghosts of the sleeping.

She flushed and washed her hands. There was no going

back to her bunk, no chance of returning to sleep, not after that dream. Charlotte tugged on a pair of the red coveralls Donny had brought her, one of three colors, a little variety for her locked-up life. She couldn't remember what the blue or gold ones were for, but she remembered reactor red. The red coveralls had pouches and slots for tools. She wore them while working, and so they were rarely the cleanest. Loaded up, the coveralls weighed near on twenty pounds, and they rattled as she walked. She zipped up the front and made her way down the hallway.

Curiously, the lights in the warehouse were already on. It had to be in the middle of the night. She was good about turning them off, and nobody else had access to that level. Her mouth suddenly dry, she crept towards the nearby drones under their tarps, the sound of whispers leaking from the shadows.

Beyond the drones—near the tall shelves with boxes of spares and tools and emergency rations—a man knelt over the still form of another. The figure turned at the sound of her jangling tools.

"Donny?"

"Yeah?"

A flush of relief. The sprawling body beneath her brother wasn't a body at all. It was a puffy suit laid out with its arms and legs spread, an empty and lifeless form.

"What time is it?" she asked, rubbing her eyes.

"Late," he said. He dabbed his forehead with the back of his sleeve. "Or early, depending. Did I wake you?"

Charlotte watched as he shifted his body to block her view of the suit. Flopping one leg up, he began to fold the outfit in on itself. A pair of shears and a roll of silvery tape sat by his knees, a helmet, gloves, and a bottle like a dive tank nearby. A pair of boots as well. The fabric whispered as it moved; it was this that she had mistaken for voices.

"Hm? No, you didn't wake me. I got up to go to the bathroom. Thought I heard something."

It was a lie. She had come out to work on a drone in the middle of the night, anything to stay awake, to stay grounded. Donald nodded and pulled a rag from his breast pocket. He coughed into this before stuffing it away.

"What're you doing up?" she asked.

"I was just going through some supplies." Donny made a pile out of the suit parts. "Some things they needed above. Didn't want to risk sending someone else down for them." He glanced at his sister. "You want me to fetch you something hot for breakfast?"

Charlotte hugged herself and shook her head. She hated the reminder of being trapped on that level, needing him to get her things. "I'm getting used to the rations in the crates," she told him. "The coconut bars in the MREs are growing on me." She laughed. "I remember hating them during basic."

"I really don't mind getting you something," Donny said, obviously looking for an excuse to get out of there, some way to change topics. "And I should have the last of what we need for the radio soon. I put in a requisition for a microphone, which I can't find anywhere else. There's one in the comm room that's acting up, which I might steal if nothing else works."

Charlotte nodded. She watched her brother stuff the suit back into one of the large plastic containers. There was something he wasn't telling her. She recognized when he was holding something back. It was what big brothers did.

Crossing to the nearest drone, she pulled the tarp off and laid out a wrench set on the forward wing. She had always been clumsy with tools, but weeks of work on the drones, of persistence if not patience, and she was getting the hang of how they were put together. "So what do they need the suit for?" she asked, forcing herself to sound nonchalant.

"I think it's something to do with the reactor." He rubbed the back of his neck and frowned. Charlotte allowed the lie to echo a bit. She wanted her brother to hear it.

Opening the skin of the drone's wing, Charlotte remembered coming home from basic training with new muscles and weeks of competitive fierceness forged among a squad of men. This was before she'd let herself go while on deployment. Back then, she'd been a wiry and fit teenager, her brother off at graduate school, and his first teasing remark about her new physique had landed him on the sofa, his arm pinned behind his back, laughing and teasing her further.

Laughing, that is, until a sofa cushion had been pressed to the side of his face, and Donny had squealed like a stuck pig. Fun and games had turned into something serious and scary, her brother's fear of being buried alive awakening something primal in him, something she never teased him for and never wanted to see again.

Now she watched as he sealed the bin with the suit inside and slid it back under a shelf. It wasn't needed elsewhere in the silo, she knew. Donald fumbled for his rag, and his coughing resumed. She pretended to be fixated on the drone while he had his fit. Donny didn't want to talk about the suit or the problem with his lungs, and she didn't blame him. Her brother was dying. Charlotte knew her brother was dying, could see him like she saw him in her dreams, turning at the last minute to shield his eyes against the noonday sun. She saw him the way she saw every man in that last instant of their lives. There was Donny's beautiful face on her screen, watching the inevitable fall from the sky.

He was dying, which is why he wanted to stockpile food for her and make sure she could leave. It was why he wanted to make sure she had a radio, so she would have someone to talk to. Her brother was dying, and he didn't want to be buried, didn't want to die down there in that pit in the ground where he couldn't breathe.

Charlotte knew damn well what the suit was for.

Silo 18

13

AN EMPTY CLEANING suit lay spread across the workbench, one of its arms draped over the edge, elbow bent at an unnatural angle. The unblinking visor of the detached helmet gazed silently up at the ceiling. The small screen inside the helmet had been removed to leave a clear plastic window out on the real world. Juliette leaned over the suit, occasional drops of sweat smacking its surface, as she tightened the hex screws that held the lower collar onto the fabric. She remembered the last time she'd built a suit like this.

Nelson, the young IT tech in charge of the cleaning lab, labored at an identical bench on the other side of the workshop. Juliette had selected him as her assistant for this project. He was familiar with the suits, young, and didn't appear to be against her. Not that the first two criteria mattered.

"The next item we need to discuss is the population report," Marsha said. The young assistant—an assistant Juliette had never asked for—juggled a dozen folders until she found the right one. Recycled paper lay strewn across the neighboring workbench, turning an area for building things into a lowly desk. Juliette glanced up and watched as Marsha shuffled through a folder. Her assistant was a slight girl just out of her teens, graced with rosy cheeks and dark hair in tight coils.

Marsha had been the assistant to the last two mayors, a short but tumultuous span of time. Like the gold ID card and the apartment on level six, she had come with the job.

"Here it is," Marsha said. She bit her lip and scanned the report, and Juliette saw that it was printed on one side only. The amount of paper her office went through and repulped could afford to feed an apartment level for a year. Lukas had once joked that it was to keep the recyclers in business. The chance he was right had kept her from laughing.

"Can you hand me those gaskets?" Juliette asked, pointing to Marsha's side of the workbench.

The young girl pointed to a bin of lock washers. And then an assortment of cotter pins. Finally, her hand drifted over the gaskets. Juliette nodded. "Thanks."

"So, we're under five thousand residents for the first time in thirty years," Marsha said, returning to her report. "We've had a lot of . . . passings." Juliette could feel Marsha glance up at her, even as she concentrated on seating the gasket into the collar. "The lottery committee is calling for an official count, just so we can get a sense of—"

"The lottery committee would perform a census every week if they could." Juliette rubbed oil onto the gasket with her finger before seating the other side of the collar.

Marsha laughed politely. "Yes, well, they want to hold another lottery soon. They asked for another two hundred numbers."

"Numbers," Juliette grumbled. Sometimes she thought that was all Lukas's computers were good for, a bunch of tall machines to pull numbers from their whirring butts. "Did you tell them my idea about an amnesty? They do know we're about to double our space, right?"

Marsha shifted uncomfortably. "I told them," she said. "And I told them about the extra space. I don't think they took it so well."

Across the workshop, Nelson looked up from the suit he was working on. It was just the three of them in the old lab where people had once been outfitted to die. Now they were working on something else, a different reason to send people outside.

"Well, what did the committee say?" Juliette asked. "They do know that when we reach this other silo, I'm going to need people to come with me and get it up and running again. The population here is going to dip."

Nelson bent back to his work. Marsha closed the folder on the population report and looked at her feet.

"What did they say to my idea of suspending the lottery?"

"They didn't say anything," Marsha said. She glanced up, and the overhead lights caught the wet film across her eyes. "I don't think many of them believe in your other silo."

Juliette laughed and shook her head. Her hand was trembling as she set the last lock screw into the collar. "It doesn't really matter what the committee believes, does it?" Though she knew this was true of her as well. It was true of anyone. The world out there was the way it was no matter how much doubt or hope or hate a person breathed into it. "The dig is underway. They're clearing three hundred feet a day. I suppose the lottery committee will just have to make the trip down to see for themselves. You should tell them that. Tell them to go see."

Marsha frowned and made a note. "The next thing on the agenda . . ." She grabbed her ledger. "There's been a rash of complaints about—"

There was a knock at the door. Juliette turned, and Lukas entered the Suit Lab, smiling. He waved at Nelson, who saluted back with a 3/8 wrench. Lukas seemed unsurprised to see Marsha there. He clasped her shoulder. "You should just move that big wooden desk of hers down here," he joked. "You've got the porting budget for it."

Marsha smiled and tugged at one of her dark springs. She looked around the lab. "I really should," she said.

Juliette watched her young assistant blush in Lukas's presence and laughed to herself. The helmet locked into the collar with a neat click. Juliette tested the release mechanism.

"Do you mind if I borrow the mayor?" Lukas asked.

"No, I don't mind," Marsha said.

"I do." Juliette studied one of the suit's sleeves. "We're way behind schedule."

Lukas frowned. "There is no schedule. You set the schedule. And besides, have you even gotten permission for this?" He stood beside Marsha and crossed his arms. "Have you even told your assistant what you're planning?"

Juliette glanced up guiltily. "Not yet."

"Why? What're you doing?" Marsha lowered her ledger and studied the suits for what seemed the first time.

Juliette ignored her. She glared at Lukas. "I'm behind schedule because I want to get this done before they complete the dig. They've been on a tear. Hit some soft soil. I'd really like to be down there when they punch through."

"And I'd like for you to be at that meeting today, which you're going to miss if you don't get a move on."

"I'm not going," Juliette said.

Lukas shot a look at Nelson, who set down his wrench, gathered Marsha, and slid out the door. Juliette watched them leave and realized her young Lukas had more authority than she gave him credit for.

"It's the monthly town hall," Lukas said. "The first since your election. I told Judge Picken you'd be there. Jules, you've gotta play mayor or you won't *be* one for much longer—"

"Fine." She raised her hands. "I'm not mayor. I so decree it." She scrawled the air with a driver. "Signed and stamped."

"Not fine. What do you think the next person will make of all this?" He waved his hand at the workbenches. "You think you'll be able to play these games? This room will go right back to what it was built for in the first place."

Juliette bit down the urge to snap at him, to tell him these weren't games she was playing, that it was something far worse.

Lukas looked away from whatever face she was making. His eyes settled on the stack of books piled up by the cot she had brought in. She slept there sometimes when the two of them were disagreeing or when she just needed a place to be alone. Not that she'd slept much recently. She rubbed her eyes and tried to remember the last time she'd gotten four hours in a row. Her nights were spent welding in the airlock. Her days were spent in the Suit Lab or down behind the comm hub. She didn't really sleep anymore—she just passed out here and there.

"We should keep those locked up," Lukas said, indicating the books. "Shouldn't keep them out."

"No one would believe them if they opened them," Juliette said.

"For the paper."

She nodded. He was right. She saw information; others would see money. "I'll take them back down," she promised, and the anger drained away like oil from a cracked casing. She thought of Elise, who had told her over the radio of a book she was making, a single book from all her favorite pages. Juliette needed a book like that. Except where Elise's was probably full of pretty fish and bright birds, Juliette's would catalog darker things. Things in the hearts of men.

Lukas took a step closer. He rested a hand on her arm. "This meeting—"

"I hear they're thinking about a revote," Juliette said, cutting him off. She wiped a loose strand of hair off her face, tucked it behind her ear. "I'm not going to be mayor for long anyway. Which is why I need to get this done. By the time everyone votes again, it shouldn't matter."

"Why? Because you'll be the mayor of a different silo by then? Is that your plan?"

Juliette rested a hand on the domed helmet. "No. Because I'll have my answers by then. Because people will see by then. They'll believe me."

Lukas crossed his arms. He took a deep breath. "I've got to get down to the servers," he said. "If no one's there to answer the call, the lights eventually start flashing in the offices and everyone asks what the hell they're for."

Juliette nodded. She'd seen it for herself. She also knew that Lukas liked the long talks behind the server as much as she did. Except that he was better at it. All her talks led to arguments. He was good at smoothing things over, figuring things out.

"Please tell me you'll go to the meeting, Jules. Promise me you'll go."

She scanned the suit on the other table to see how far along Nelson was. They'd need one more suit for the extra person in the second airlock. If she worked through the night and all day tomorrow—

"For me," he pleaded.

"I'll go."

"Thank you." Lukas glanced at the old clock on the wall, its red arms visible behind hazed plastic. "I'll see you for dinner?"

"Sure."

He leaned forward and kissed her on the cheek. When he turned to go, Juliette began arranging her tools on the leather pad, setting them aside for later. She picked up a clean cloth and wiped her hands. "Oh, and Luke?"

"Yeah?" He paused at the door.

"Tell that fucker I said hello."

14

LUKAS LEFT THE Suit Lab and headed toward the server room on the other side of thirty-four. He passed a tech room that sat empty. The men and women who used to work in there now took up slack in the Down Deep and in Supply where mechanics and workers had lost their lives. People from IT sent to replace those they'd killed.

Juliette's friend Shirly had been left in charge of the aftermath down in Mechanical. She was forever complaining to his office about skeleton shifts, and then complaining again when Lukas reassigned anyone to help. What did she want from him? People, he supposed. Just not his people.

A handful of techs and security personnel standing outside the break room fell silent as Lukas approached. He waved, and hands went up politely. "Sir," someone said, which made him cringe. The chatter resumed only after he rounded the corner, and Lukas remembered being in on conversations like that as his former boss had stormed past.

Bernard. Lukas used to think he understood what it meant to be in charge. You did what you wanted. Decisions were arbitrary. You were cruel for the sake of being cruel. And now he found himself agreeing to worse things than he had ever imagined. Now he knew about a world of such horrors, that maybe men of his ilk weren't suited to lead. It wasn't a thing he could ever say out loud, but perhaps a revote would be for the best. Juliette would make a great lab tech there in IT. Soldering and welding weren't all that different, just matters of scale. And then he tried to imagine her building a suit for someone to clean in, or her sitting idly by while they took orders from another silo on how many births were allowed that week.

It was more likely that a new mayor would mean time apart. Or that he would have to file for a transfer to Mechanical and learn to turn a wrench. From head of IT to a third-shift greaser. Lukas laughed. He coded open the server room door and thought there might be something romantic about that, giving up his job and life to be with her. Maybe something more romantic than going up at night to hunt for stars. He would have to get used to Juliette bossing him around, but that wouldn't be a stretch. Enough degreaser, and her old room down there could be livable. As he wove his way through the servers, he thought of how he had lived in far worse, right there beneath his feet. It was being together that mattered.

The lights overhead weren't yet blinking. He was early or the man named Donald was late. Lukas made his way toward the far wall, passing by several servers with their sides off and wires streaming out. With Donald's help, he was figuring out how to fully access the machines, see what was on them. Nothing exciting yet, but he was making progress.

He stopped at the comm server, which had been his home within a home some lifetime ago. Now it was a different sort of conversation he fell into behind that server. It was a different sort of person on the other end of the line.

One of the rickety wooden chairs from below had been brought up. Lukas remembered climbing the ladder and pushing it ahead of him, Juliette yelling at him that they should lower a rope, the two of them arguing like young porters. Beside the chair, a stack of book tins made a side table of sorts. One of the Legacy books was splayed out on top. Lukas made himself comfortable and picked up the book. He had marked pages by creasing the corners. There were small dots in the margins where he had questions. He flipped through the book and scanned the material while he waited on the call.

What once had been boring about the books was now all he cared about. During his imprisonment—his Rite—he had been forced to read the parts of the Order on human behavior. Now he pored over these sections. And Donald, the voice on the other end of the line, had him fairly convinced that these were more than mere stories, these Robbers Cave boys and Milgrams and Skinners. Some of these things had truly happened.

He had graduated from these stories to find even more lessons in the Legacy books. It was the history of the old world that now commanded his attention. Episodic uprisings had occurred over thousands of years. He and Jules argued over whether or not there could be an end to such cyclic violence. The books suggested such hope was folly. And then Lukas had discovered an entire chapter on the dangers of an uprising's aftermath, the very situation in which they now found themselves. He read about men with strange names—Cromwell, Napoleon, Castro, Lenin—who fought to liberate a people and then enslaved them into something even worse.

They were legends, Juliette insisted. Myths. Like the ghouls parents use to make their children behave. She saw those chapters to mean that tearing a world down was a simple affair; the gravity of human nature tugged willingly. It was the building up afterward that proved complex. It was what to replace injustice with that very few gave thought to. Always with the tearing down, she said, as if the scraps and ashes could be pieced back together.

Lukas disagreed. He thought, and Donald said, that these stories were real. Yes, the revolutions were painful. There would always be a period when things were worse. But eventually, they get better. People learn from their mistakes. This is what he had tried to convince her of one night after a call from Donald had kept them up through the dim time. Jules, of course, had to get in the last word. She had taken him up to the cafeteria and had pointed to the glow over the horizon, to the lifeless hills, to the rare glint of sunlight on decrepit towers. "Here is your world made better," she had told him. "Here is man well learned from his mistakes."

Always with the last word, though Lukas had more to say. "Maybe this is the bad time that comes *before,*" he had whispered into his coffee. And Juliette, for her part, had pretended not to hear.

The pages beneath Lukas's fingers pulsed red. He glanced up at the lights overhead, now flashing with the incoming call. There was a buzzing from the comm server, a blinking indicator over the very first slot. He gathered the headset and untangled the cord, slotted it into the receiver.

"Hello?" he said.

"Lukas." The machine removed all intonation from the voice, all emotion. Except for disappointment. That it was not Juliette who answered elicited a letdown that could be felt if not quite heard. Or perhaps it was all in Lukas's head.

"Just me," he said.

"Very well. Just so you know, I have pressing matters here. Our time is short."

"Okay." Lukas found his place in the book. He skipped down to where they'd previously left off. These talks reminded him of his studies with Bernard, except now he had graduated from the Order to the Legacy. And Donald was swifter than Bernard, more open with his answers. "So . . . I wanted to ask you something about this Rousseau guy—"

"Before we do," Donald said, "I need to implore you again to stop with the digging."

Lukas closed the book on his finger, marking his place. He was glad Juliette had agreed to attend the Town Hall. She got animated whenever this topic came up. Because of an old threat she'd made, Donald seemed to think they were digging toward him, and she made Lukas vow to leave the lie alone. She didn't want them finding out about her friends in 17 or her plans to rescue them. Lukas found the ruse uncomfortable. Where Juliette distrusted this man—who had warned them both that their home could be shut down at any time through mysterious means—Lukas saw someone trying to help them at some cost to himself. Jules thought Donald was scared for his own life. Lukas thought Donald was frightened for *them.*

"I'm afraid that the digging will have to continue," Lukas said. He nearly blurted out: *She won't stop,* but best for there to be some sense of solidarity.

"Well, my people can pick up the vibrations. They know something is happening."

"Can you tell them we're having trouble with our generator? That it's misaligned again?"

There was a disappointed sigh that the computers couldn't touch. "They're smarter than that. What I've done is ordered them not to waste their time looking into it, which is all I can do. I'm telling you, nothing good can come of this."

"Then why are you helping us? Why stick your neck out? Because that's what it seems like you're doing."

"My job is to see that you don't die."

Lukas studied the inside of the server tower, the winking lights, the wires, the boards. "Yeah, but these conversations, going through these books with me, calling every single day like clockwork, why do you do it? I mean . . . what is it that you get out of these conversations?"

There was a pause on the other end of the line, a rare lack of surety from the steady voice of their supposed benefactor.

"It's because . . . I get to help you remember."

"And that's important?"

"Yes. It's important. It is to me. I know what it feels like to forget."

"Is that why these books are here?"

Another pause. Lukas felt that he was stumbling accidentally toward some truth. He would have to remember what was being said and tell Juliette later.

"They are there so that whoever inherits the world—whoever is chosen—will know . . ."

"Know what?" Lukas asked desperately. He feared he was going to lose him. Donald had trod near to this in prior conversations, but had always pulled away.

"To know how to set things right," Donald said. "Look, our time is up. I need to go."

"What did you mean about inheriting the world?"

"Next time. I need to go. Stay safe."

"Yeah," Lukas said. "You too—"

But his headphone had already clicked. The man who somehow knew so much about the old world had signed off.

15

JULIETTE HAD NEVER attended a Town Hall before. Like sows giving birth, she knew such things took place, but had never felt the urge to witness the spectacle. Her first time would be while as mayor, and she hoped it would be her last.

She joined Judge Picken and Sheriff Billings on the raised platform while residents spilled from the hallway and found their seats. The platform they'd put her on reminded her of the stage in the bazaar, and Juliette remembered her father comparing these meetings to plays. She never took him to mean that as a compliment.

"I don't know any of my lines," she whispered cryptically to Peter Billings.

The two of them sat close enough that their shoulders touched. "You'll do fine," Peter said. He smiled at a young woman in the front row, who wiggled her fingers back at him, and Juliette saw that the young sheriff had met someone. Life was continuing apace.

She tried to relax. She studied the crowd. A lot of unfamiliar faces out there. A few she recognized. Three doors led in from the hallway. Two of the doors opened on aisles that sliced through the rows of ancient benches. The third aisle was pressed against the wall. They divided the room into thirds, much as less-well-defined boundaries partitioned the silo. Juliette didn't have to be told these things. The people making their way inside made it obvious.

The Up Top benches in the center of the room were already packed, and more people stood behind the benches at the back of the hall, people she recognized from IT and from the cafeteria. The Mids benches off to one side were half full. Juliette noticed most of these residents sat close to the aisle, as near to the center as possible. Farmers in green. Hydroponic plumbers. People with dreams. The other side of the room was nearly bare. This was for the Down Deep. An elderly couple sat together in the front row of this section, holding hands. Juliette recognized the man, a bootmaker. They had come a long way. Juliette kept waiting for more residents of the Deep to show, but it was too much of a hike. And now she recalled how distant these meetings seemed while working in the depths of the silo. Often, she and her friends only heard what was being discussed and what rules were being passed after it had already happened. Not only was it a far climb, but most of them were too busy surviving the day-to-day to trudge anywhere for a discussion on tomorrows.

When the flow of residents became a trickle, Judge Picken rose to begin the meeting. Juliette prepared to be bored half to death by the proceedings. A quick talk, an introduction, and then they would listen to what ailed the people. Promise to make it better. Get right back to doing the same things.

What she needed to do was get back to work. There was so much that needed accomplishing up at the airlock and down in the Suit Lab. The last thing she wanted to do was listen to minor grievances, a call for a revote, or anyone bitching about her digging. She suspected what was serious to others would feel minor to her. There was something about being sent to one's death and surviving a baptism of fire upon one's return that pushed most squabblings into the deepest recesses of one's mind.

Picken banged his gavel and called the meeting to order. He welcomed everyone and ran down the prepared docket. Juliette squirmed on her bench. She gazed out into the crowd and saw that the vast majority were gazing right back at her rather than watching the judge. She only caught the end of Picken's last sentence because of her name: "—hear from your mayor, Juliette Nichols."

He turned and waved her up to the podium. Peter patted her on the knee for encouragement. As she walked to the podium, the metal decking creaked beneath her boots where it wasn't screwed down tight. That was the only sound. And then someone in the audience coughed. And there was a rustling among the benches as bodies lurched back into motion. Juliette gripped the podium and marveled at the mix of colors facing her, the blues and whites and reds and browns and greens. Scowls above them, she saw. Angry people from all walks of life. She cleared her throat and realized how unprepared she was. She had hoped to say a few words, to thank the people for their concerns, to assure them that she was working tirelessly to forge a new and better life for them. Just give her a chance, she wanted to say.

"Thank you—" she began, and Judge Picken tugged on her arm and pointed to the microphone attached to the podium. Someone in the back shouted that they couldn't hear. Juliette swiveled the microphone closer and saw that the faces in the crowd were the same as those along the stairwell. They were wary of her. Awe, or something like it, had eroded into suspicion.

"I'm here today to listen to your questions. Your concerns," she said, the loudness of her voice startling her. "Before I do, I'd like to say a few things about what we hope to accomplish this year—"

"Did you let poison in here?" someone yelled from the back.

"Excuse me?" Juliette asked. She cleared her throat.

A lady stood up, a baby in her arms. "My child's had a fever ever since you returned!"

"Are the other silos real?" someone shouted.

"What was it like out there?"

A man bolted up from the Mids benches, his face ruddy with rage. "What're you doin' down there that's causing so much noise—?"

A dozen others stood and began shouting as well. Their questions and complaints forged a single noise, an engine of anger. The packed center section spilled outward into the aisles as people needed room to point and wave for attention. Juliette saw her father, standing in the very back, noticeable for his placid demeanor, his worried frown.

"One at a time—" Juliette said. She held her palms out. The crowd lurched forward, and then a shot rang out.

Juliette flinched.

There was another loud bang right beside her, and the gavel was no longer limp in Judge Picken's hand. The wooden disc on the podium leapt and spun as he pounded it back into place, over and over. Deputy Hoyle lurched out of a trance by the door and swam through the crowds in the aisle, urging everyone back into their seats and to hold their tongues. Peter Billings was up from the bench yelling for everyone to be calm as well. Eventually, a tense silence fell over the crowd. But something was whirring in these people. It was like a motor not yet running but one that wanted to, an electrical buzz just beneath the surface, humming and holding back. Juliette chose her words carefully.

"I can't tell you what it's like out there—"

"Can't or won't?" someone asked. This person was silenced by a glare from Deputy Hoyle, who ranged the aisle. Juliette took a deep breath.

"I can't tell you because we don't know." She raised her hands to hold the crowd still a moment. "Everything we've been told about the world beyond our walls has been a lie, a fabrication—"

"How do we know *you're* not the one lying?"

She sought the voice among the crowd. "Because I'm the one admitting that we don't know a damned thing. I'm the one who came here today to tell you that we should go out and see for ourselves. With fresh eyes. With real curiosity. I'm proposing that we do what has never been done, and that's to go and take a sample, to bring back a taste of the air out there and see what's wrong with the world—"

Outbursts from the back drowned out the rest of her sentence. People were up out of their seats again, even as others reached to restrain them. Some were curious now. Some were even more outraged. The gavel barked, and Hoyle loosed his baton and waved it at the front row. But the crowd was beyond calming. Peter stepped forward, a hand on the butt of his gun.

Juliette backed away from the podium. There was a squeal from the speakers as Judge Picken knocked the microphone with his arm. The wooden puck was lost, leaving him to bang on the podium itself, which Juliette saw was marked with half-moon frowns and smiles from past attempts at restoring calm.

Deputy Hoyle had to back up against the stage as the crowd lurched forward, many of them with questions still, most with unbridled fury. Spittle foamed on quivering lips. Juliette heard more accusations, saw the lady with her baby who blamed Juliette for some sickness. Marsha ran to the back of the stage and threw open a metal door painted to look like real wood—and Peter waved Juliette inside, back to the Judge's chambers. She didn't want to go. She wanted to calm these people down, to tell them she meant well, that she could fix this if they would just let her try. But she was being dragged back, past a cloakroom of dark robes that hung like shadows, steered down a hall where pictures of past judges hung askew, to an old metal desk painted to resemble the door.

The shouts were sealed off behind them. The door banging with fists for a moment, Peter cursing. Juliette collapsed into an old leather chair repaired with tape and held her face in her hands. Their anger was her anger. She could feel herself directing it toward Peter and Lukas, who had made her mayor. She could feel herself directing it toward Lukas for begging her to leave the digging and come up top, for making her come to this meeting. As if this rabble could be appeased.

A burst of noise filtered down the hall as the door opened for a moment. Juliette expected Judge Picken to join them. She was surprised to see her father instead.

"Dad."

She rose from the old chair and crossed the room to greet him. Her father wrapped his arms around her, and Juliette found that place in the center of his chest where she could remember finding comfort as a child.

"I heard you might be here," her father whispered.

Juliette didn't say anything. As old as she felt, the years melted away to have him there, to have his arms around her.

"I also heard what you're planning, and I don't want you to go."

Juliette stepped back to study her father. Peter excused himself. The noise from outside wasn't as loud this time when the door cracked, and Juliette realized Judge Picken had allowed her father passage, was out there calming the crowd. Her dad had seen those people react to her, had heard what people had said. She fought back a sudden welling of tears.

"They didn't give me a chance to explain—" she started, swiping at her eyes. "Dad, there are other worlds out there like our own. It's crazy to sit here, fighting amongst ourselves, when there are other worlds—"

"I'm not talking about the digging," her father said. "I heard what you're planning up top."

"You heard . . ." She wiped her eyes again. "Lukas—" she muttered.

"It wasn't Lukas. That technician, Nelson, came by for a check-up, asked me if I was going to be on standby in case anything went wrong. I had to pretend to know what he was talking about. I assume you were going to announce your plans out there just now?" He glanced toward the cloakroom.

"We need to know what's out there," Juliette said. "Dad, they haven't been trying to make it better. We don't know the first thing—"

"Then let the next cleaner see. Let them sample when they're sent out. Not you."

She shook her head. "There won't be anymore cleaning, Dad. Not while I'm mayor. I won't send anyone out there."

He placed a hand on her arm. "And I won't let my daughter go."

She pulled away from him. "I'm sorry," she said. "I have to. I'm taking every precaution. I promise."

Her father's face hardened. He turned his hand over and gazed at his palm.

"We could use your help," she said, hoping to bridge any new rift she feared she was creating. "Nelson's right. It would be nice to have a doctor on the team."

"I don't want any part in this," he said. "Look what happened to you the last time." He glanced at her neck, where the suit's metal collar had left a hook of a scar.

"That was the fire," Juliette told him, adjusting her coveralls.

"And the next time it'll be something else."

They studied one another in that chamber where people were quietly judged, and Juliette felt a familiar temptation to run away from conflict. It was countered by a new desire to bury her face in her father's chest and sob in a way that women her age weren't allowed, that mechanics never could.

"I don't want to lose you again," she told her dad. "You're the only family I've got left. Please support me in this."

It was difficult to say. Vulnerable and honest. A part of Lukas now lived inside of her—this was something he had imparted.

Juliette waited for the reaction and saw her father's face relax. It may have been her imagination, but she thought he moved a step closer, let down his guard.

"I'll give you a check-up before and after," he said.

"Thank you. Oh, speaking of a check-up, there's something else I wanted to ask you about." She worked the long sleeve of her coveralls up her forearm and studied the white marks along her wrist. "Have you ever heard of scars going away with time? Lukas thought—" She looked up at her father. "Do they ever go away?"

Her father took a deep breath and held it awhile. His gaze drifted over her shoulder and far away.

"No," he said. "Not scars. Not even with time."

Silo 1

16

CAPTAIN BREVARD WAS nearly through his seventh shift. Only three more to go. Three more shifts of sitting behind security gates reading the same handful of novels over and over until the yellowed pages gave up and fell out. Three more shifts of whipping his deputies at table tennis—a new deputy on each shift—and telling them that it'd been forever since he'd last played. Three more shifts of the same old food and the same old movies and the same old everything else bland that greeted him when he woke. Three more. He could make it.

Silo 1's Security chief now counted down shifts much as he had once counted down years to retirement. *Let them be uneventful,* was his mantra. The blandness was good. Vanilla was the taste of passing time. Such was his thought as he stood before an open cryopod splattered with dried blood, a foul taste very un-vanilla-like in his mouth.

A pop of blinding light erupted from Deputy Stevens's camera as the young man took another shot of the pod's interior. The body had been removed hours ago. A med tech had been servicing a neighboring pod when he noticed a smear of blood on the lid of this one. He had cleaned half the smear away before he realized what it was. Brevard now studied the tracks that the med tech's cleaning rag had left behind. He took another bitter sip of coffee.

His mug had lost its steam. It was the cold air in that warehouse of bodies. Brevard hated it down there. He hated waking up naked in that place, hated being brought back down and put to sleep, hated what the room did to his coffee. He took another sip. Three shifts left, and then retirement, whatever that meant. Nobody thought along that far. Only to their next shift.

Stevens lowered his camera and nodded toward the exit. "Darcy's back, sir."

The two officers watched as Darcy, the night guard, crossed the hall of cryopods. Darcy had been first on the scene early that morning, had woken Deputy Stevens, who had woken his superior. Darcy had then refused to slag off and get some sleep as ordered. He had instead accompanied the body up to Medical and had volunteered to wait on test results while the other men went over the crime scene. Darcy now waved a piece of paper a bit too enthusiastically as he headed their way.

"I can't stand this guy," Stevens whispered to his chief.

Brevard took a diplomatic sip of his coffee and watched his night guard approach. Darcy was young—late twenties, early thirties—with blond hair and a permanent, goofy grin. Just the sort of inexperienced person police forces loved to place on night shifts when all the bad shit went down. It wasn't logical, but it was tradition. Experience won you deep sleep for when the crazies were out.

"You won't believe what I've got," Darcy said, twenty paces away and more than a touch overeager.

"You've got a match," Brevard said dryly. "The blood on the lid goes with the pod." He nearly added that what Darcy most certainly *didn't* have was a hot cup of coffee for him or Stevens.

"That's part of it," Darcy said, appearing vexed. "How'd you know?" He took a few deep breaths and handed over the report.

"Because matches are exciting," Brevard said, accepting the sheet. "You wave a match in the air like you've got something to say. Lawyers and jury members get excited over a match." *And rookies,* he wanted to add. He wasn't sure what Darcy did before orientation, but it wasn't police work. Glancing down at the report, Brevard saw a standard DNA match, a series of bars lined up with one another, lines drawn between the bars where they were identical. And these two were identical, the DNA on file for the pod and the blood sample taken from the lid.

"Well, there's more," Darcy said. The night guard took another deep breath. He had obviously run down the hall from the lift. "Lots more."

"We think we've got it pieced together," Stevens said with confidence. He nodded toward the open cryopod. "It's pretty clear that a murder took place here. It started—"

"Not a murder," Darcy interjected.

"Give the deputy a chance," Brevard said, lifting his mug. "He's been looking at this for hours."

Darcy started to say something but caught himself. He rubbed under his eyes, seemed exhausted, but nodded.

"Right," Stevens said. He pointed his camera at the cryopod. "Blood on the lid means the struggle began out here. The man we found inside must've been subdued by our killer after a fight, that's how his blood got on the lid. And then he was tossed inside his own cryopod. His hands were bound, I'm assuming at gunpoint, because I didn't note any marks around the wrists, no other sign of struggle. He was shot once in the chest." Stevens pointed to the streaks and spots of blood on the inside of the lid. "We've got splatter here, indicating the victim was sitting up. But the way it ran suggests the lid was shut immediately after. And the coloration tells me that this likely happened on our shift, certainly within the past month."

Brevard watched Darcy's face the entire time, saw how it

scrunched up in disagreement. The kid thought he knew better than the deputy.

"What else?" Brevard asked Stevens, prodding his second-in-command along further.

"Oh, yes. After murdering the victim, our perp inserted an IV and a catheter to keep the body from decomposing, so we're looking at someone with medical training. He might, of course, still be on this shift. Which is why we thought it best to discuss this down here and not around the med team. We'll want to question them one at a time."

Brevard nodded and took a sip of coffee. He waited on the night guard's reaction.

"It wasn't murder," Darcy said, exasperated. "Do you guys want to hear what else I have? For starters, the blood on the lid matches the database entry for the *pod,* just like you said, but it doesn't match the victim. The guy inside is someone else."

Brevard nearly spat out his coffee. He wiped his moustache with his hand. "What?" he asked, not sure that he'd heard correctly.

"The blood on the outside was mixed with saliva. It came from a second person. Doc said it was probably a cough, maybe a chest wound. So our suspect is likely injured."

"Wait. So who's the guy we found in the pod?" Stevens asked.

"They're not sure. They ran his blood, but it seems his records have been tampered with. The guy this pod is registered to, he shouldn't be on the executive wing at all. Should've been in Deep Freeze. And the blood from the *inside* of the lid matches a partial record from the executive files, which would place him in here somewhere—"

"Partial record?" Brevard asked.

Darcy shrugged. "The files are all kinds of fouled up. According to Doctor Whitmore."

"Ah," Deputy Stevens said, snapping his fingers. "I've got it. I know what happened here." He pointed his camera at the pod. "There's a struggle out here, okay? A guy who doesn't want to be put under. He manages to break free, knows how to hack the—"

"Hold up," Brevard said, raising a hand. He could see on Darcy's face that there was more. "Why do you keep insisting this wasn't a murder? We've got a gunshot wound, blood splatter, a closed lid, no weapon, a man with his hands bound, and blood on the lid of this pod, whoever the hell it's registered to. Everything about this screams murder."

"That's what I've been trying to tell you," Darcy said. "It wasn't murder because the guy was plugged in. He was plugged in the entire time, even before he was shot. And the pod was still on and running. This Troy fellow—or whoever it is that we pulled out of there—he's still alive."

17

THE THREE MEN left the pod behind and headed for the medical wing and the operating room. Brevard's mind raced. He didn't need this crap on one of his shifts. This was not vanilla. He imagined the reports he would have to write after this, how much fun it would be to brief the next captain.

"Do you think we should get the Shepherd involved?" Stevens asked, referring to the head executive up on the administration wing, a man who kept mostly to himself.

Brevard scoffed. He coded open the Deep Freeze door and led the men out into the hallway. "I think this is a little below his pay grade, don't you? Shepherd has entire silos to worry about. You can see how it wears on him, how he keeps himself locked up. It's our job to handle cases like this. Even murder."

"You're right," Stevens said.

Darcy, still winded, labored to keep up.

They rode the lift up two levels. Brevard thought about how the body with the gun wound had felt as he had inspected it. The man had been as cold as a stiff in a morgue, but then weren't they all when they first woke up? He thought about all the damage the freezing and thawing produced, how the machines in their blood were supposed to keep them patched together, cell by cell. What if those little machines could do the same for a gunshot wound?

The lift opened on sixty-eight. Brevard could hear voices from the OR. It was difficult to let go of the theories that'd been percolating between him and Stevens for the past hour. It was hard to let go and adapt to everything Darcy had told them. The idea of records being tampered with made this a much more complex problem. Only three shifts to go, and now all this. But if the victim was indeed alive, catching their perp was all but guaranteed. If he was in any condition to talk, he could ID the man who shot him.

The doctor and one of his assistants were in the waiting room outside the little-used OR. Their gloves were off, the doctor's gray hair wild and unkempt as if he'd been running his fingers through it. Both men appeared exhausted. Brevard glanced through the observation window and saw the same man they'd pulled from the pod. He was lying as if asleep, his color completely different, tubes and wires snaking inside a pale blue paper gown.

"I hear we've had an extraordinary turnaround," Brevard said. He crossed to the sink and dumped his coffee down the drain, looked around for a fresh pot and didn't see one. He would've taken on another shift right then for a hot mug, a pack of smokes, and permission to burn them.

The doctor patted his assistant on the arm and gave him instructions. The young man nodded and fished in his pocket for a pair of gloves before backing his way through the door and into the operating room. Brevard watched him check the machines hooked up to the man.

"Can he talk?" Brevard asked.

"Oh, yes," Dr. Whitmore said. He scratched his gray beard. "We had quite the scene up here when he came to. The patient is much stronger than he appears."

"And not quite as dead," Stevens said.

Nobody laughed.

"He was very animated," Dr. Whitmore said. "He insisted his name wasn't Troy. This was before I ran the tests." He nodded at the piece of paper Brevard was now carrying.

Brevard looked to Darcy for confirmation.

"I was using the john," Darcy admitted sheepishly. "I wasn't here when he woke up."

"We gave him a sedative. And I took a blood sample in order to ID him."

"What did you come up with?" Brevard asked.

Dr. Whitmore shook his head. "His records have been expunged. Or so I thought." Taking a plastic cup from one of the cabinets, he ran some water from the sink and took a swig. "They were coming up partials because I don't have access to them. Just rank and cryo level. I remembered seeing this before on my very first shift. It was another guy from the executive wing, and then I remembered where you found this gentleman."

"The executive wing," Brevard said. "But this wasn't his pod, right?" He remembered what Darcy had told him. "The blood on the lid matches the pod, but the man inside is someone else. Wouldn't that suggest someone used their own pod in order to stash a body?"

"If my hunch is correct, it's worse than that." Dr. Whitmore took another sip of water and ran his fingers through his hair. "The name on the executive pod, Troy, matches the swab I took from the lid, but that man should be in Deep Freeze right now. He was put under over a century ago and hasn't been woken up since."

"But that was his blood on the lid," Stevens said.

"Which means he *has* been woken up since," Darcy pointed out.

Brevard glanced at his night-shift officer and realized he'd misjudged the young man. That was the blasted thing about working these shifts with different people every time. You couldn't really get to know anyone, couldn't gauge their worth.

"So the first thing I did was look in the medical records for any strange activity in the Deep Freeze. I wanted to see if anyone had ever been disturbed from there."

Brevard felt uneasy. The doctor was doing all of his work for him. "Did you find anything?" he asked.

Dr. Whitmore nodded. He waved toward the terminal on the waiting room desk. "There has been activity in the Deep Freeze initiated by this office. Not on my shift, mind you. But twice now, people have been woken up from coordinates that place them there. One of them was in the middle of the old Deep Freeze, that storehouse from before orientation."

The doctor paused to allow this to sink in.

It took Brevard a moment. His sleep-deprived night guard proved a hair quicker.

"A woman?" Darcy asked.

Dr. Whitmore frowned. "It's hard to say, but that's my suspicion. I don't have access to this person's records for some reason. I sent Michael down to check, to get a visual on who's in there."

"We could be dealing with a murder of passion," Stevens said.

Brevard grunted in agreement. He was already thinking the same thing. "Say there's a man who can't handle the loneliness. He's been waking up his wife in secret, would probably have to be an administrator to have access. Someone finds out, a non-executive, and so he has to kill the man. But . . . he gets killed instead—" Brevard shook his head. It was getting too complicated. He was too decaffeinated for this.

"Here's the kicker," Dr. Whitmore said.

Brevard groaned in anticipation. He regretted having dumped out his cold coffee. He waved for the news.

"There's been one other case of someone pulled from Deep Freeze, and this guy, I *do* have access to his records." Dr. Whitmore scanned the three security officers. "Anyone wanna guess the guy's name?"

"His name is Troy," Darcy said.

The doctor snapped his fingers, his eyes wide with surprise. "Bingo."

Brevard turned to his night guard. "And how the hell did you come up with that?"

Darcy shrugged. "Everyone loves a match."

"So let me get this straight," Brevard said. "We've got a rogue killer from the Deep Freeze knocking off an administrator, taking his place and likely his codes, and waking up women." The chief turned to Stevens. "Okay, I think you're right. It's time to get Shepherd involved. This just hit his pay grade."

Stevens nodded and turned toward the door. But there was a slap of hurrying boots out in the hall before he could leave. Michael, one of the medical assistants who had helped remove the body from the pod, flew around the corner in a lather and out of air. Resting his hands on his knees, he took several deep breaths, his eyes on his boss.

"I said be quick," Dr. Whitmore said. "I didn't mean for you to race."

"Yessir—" Michael took a series of deep breaths. "Sirs, we've got a problem." The medical assistant looked to the men from Security and grimaced.

"What is it?" Brevard asked.

"It was a woman," Michael said, nodding. "Sure enough. But the readout on her pod was flashing, so I ran a quick check." He scanned their faces, his eyes wild, and Brevard knew. He knew, but someone else beat him to it.

"She's dead," Darcy said.

The assistant nodded vigorously, his hands on his knees. "Anna," he muttered. "The name on the pod was Anna."

The man in the OR with no name tested his restraints, his old and sinewy arms bulging. Dr. Whitmore begged the gentleman to hold still. Captain Brevard stood on the other side of the gurney. He could smell the odor of a man newly awakened, a man left for dead. Wild eyes sought him out among those gathered. The man who had been shot seemed to recognize Brevard as the one in charge.

"Unloose me," the old man said.

"Not until we know what happened," Brevard told him. "Not until you're better."

The leather cuffs around the old man's wrists squeaked as he tested them. "I'll be better when I'm off this damn table."

"You've been shot," Dr. Whitmore said. He rested a hand on his patient's shoulder to calm him.

The old man lowered his head to his pillow, his eyes traveling from doctor to security officer and back again. "I know," he said.

"Do you remember who did it?" Brevard asked.

The man nodded. "His name's Donald." His jaw clenched and unclenched.

"Not Troy?" Brevard asked.

"That's what I meant. Same guy." Brevard watched the old man's hands squeeze into twin fists and then relax. "Look, I'm one of the Heads of this silo. I demand to be released. Check my records—"

"We'll get this sorted out—" Brevard started to say.

The restraints creaked. "Check the damn records," the old man said again.

"They've been tampered with," Brevard told him. "Can you tell us your name?"

The man lay still for a moment, muscles relaxing. He stared up at the ceiling. “Which one?” he asked. “My name is Paul. Most people call me by my last name, Thurman. I used to go by Senator—”

“Shepherd,” Captain Brevard said. “Paul Thurman is the name of the man they call Shepherd.”

The old man narrowed his eyes. “No, I don’t think so,” he said. “I’ve been called a number of things in my time, but never that.”

Silo 17

18

THE EARTH GROWLED. Beyond the walls of the silo, the earth grumbled and the noise steadily grew.

It had begun as a distant thrum a few days ago, had sounded like a hydroponics pump kicking on at the end of a long run of pipe, a vibration that could be felt between the pads of one's feet and the slick metal floor. And then yesterday it had morphed into a steady quake that travelled up Jimmy's knees and bones and into his clenched teeth. Above him, drops of water shivered from pipes, a light drizzle splashing into puddles that had not yet fully dried from the vanishing floods.

Elise squealed and patted the top of her head as she was struck with a drop. She glanced up with a gapped smile and watched for more of the bombardment.

"That's an awful racket," Rickson said. He played his flashlight across the far wall of the old generator room where the noise seemed to originate.

Hannah clapped her hands together and told the twins to get away from the wall. Miles—at least Jimmy thought it was Miles; he could hardly tell the twins apart—had his ear pressed to the concrete, his eyes closed, his mouth agape in concentration. His brother Marcus tugged him back toward the others, face lit up with excitement.

"Get behind me," Jimmy said. His feet tingled from the vibrations. He could feel the noise in his chest as some unseen machine chewed through solid rock.

"How much longer?" Elise asked.

Jimmy tousled her hair and enjoyed the embrace of her worried arms around his waist. "Soon," he told her. The truth was, he didn't know. They'd spent the past two weeks keeping the pump running and Mechanical dry. That morning, they had woken up to find the noise of the digging intolerable. The racket had gotten worse throughout the day, and still the blank wall stood solid before them, still the light rain from wet and shivering pipes continued. The twins splashed in puddles, growing impatient. The baby, inexplicably, slept peacefully in Hannah's arms. They'd been there for hours, listening to the grumbles grow, waiting for something to happen.

The end of the long wait was presaged by mechanical sounds interspersed amid the racket of crushing rock. A squeal of metal joints, the clang of fearsome teeth, the size and breadth of the din becoming confusing as it came from everywhere all at once, from the floor and ceiling and the walls on all sides. Puddles were thrown into chaos. Water flew up from the ground as well as falling from above. Jimmy nearly lost his footing.

"Step back," he yelled over the clamor. He shuffled away from the wall with Elise attached to his hip, the others obeying, wide-eyed and arms out for balance.

A section of concrete fell away, a flat sheet the size of a man. It sloughed off and fell straight down, crumbling into rubble as it hit. Dust filled the air—it seemed to emanate from within the wall itself, concrete releasing powder like a great exhalation.

Jimmy took a few more steps back, and the kids followed, worry replacing excitement. It no longer sounded like an approaching machine—it sounded like hundreds of them. They were everywhere. They were in their chests.

The din reached a furious peak, more concrete falling away, metal screaming as if beaten, great clangs and shots of sparks, and then the great digger broke through, a crack and then a gash appearing in a circular arc like a shadow racing across the wall.

The size of the cut put the noise into perspective. Cutting teeth burst through from the ceiling, spun down beneath the floor, then rose back up on the other side. Iron rods jutted out where they'd been severed. There was the smell of burning metal and chalk. The digger was coming through the wall of level one-forty-two and chewing up a good bit of the concrete above and below. It was boring a hole bigger than a silo level was tall.

The twins whooped and hollered. Elise squeezed Jimmy's ribs so hard he had to work to breathe. The baby stirred in Hannah's arms, but its cries could barely be heard over the tumult. Another great spin from the teeth, another lap from ceiling to floor, and they broke through more fully and revealed themselves to be more like wheels, dozens of discs spinning within a larger disc. A boulder fell from the ceiling and tumbled across the floor toward the larger of the two generators. Jimmy expected the silo itself to come raining down around them.

A light bulb overhead shattered from the vibrations, a glitter of glass amid the drizzle of trapped flood water. "Back!" Jimmy yelled. They were clear across the wide generator room from the digger, but everywhere felt too close. The ground shook, making it difficult to stand. Jimmy felt suddenly afraid. This thing would keep coming, would bore straight through the silo and carry on; it was out of control—

The chewing disc entered the room, sharpened wheels spinning and screaming in the air, rock thrown up on one side and crumbling down from the other. The violence lessened. The squealing of dry metal joints grew less deafening. Hannah cooed to her child, rocking her arms back and forth, eyes wide and fixed on this intrusion into their home.

Somewhere, shouts emerged. They leaked through the falling rock. The rotating disc slowed to a halt, while some of the smaller wheels spun a while longer. Their edges revealed themselves as shiny and new where their battle through the earth had worn them bare. A length of rebar was wrapped around one like a knotted bootlace.

A respite of silence grew. The child fell still once more. A distant clatter and hum—the digger's rumbling belly perhaps—was the only sound.

"Hello?"

A shout from around the digger.

"Yeah, we're through," another voice called. A woman's voice.

Jimmy swept up Elise, who hugged his neck and locked her ankles around his waist. He ran toward the wall of studded steel before him.

"Hey!" Rickson called as he hurried after.

The twins raced along as well.

Jimmy couldn't breathe. It wasn't Elise squeezing him this time—it was the idea of *visitors*. Of people not to be afraid of. Someone he could run *to* rather than from.

Everyone felt it. They raced, grinning, toward the digger's maw.

Between the gap in the wall and the silent disc, an arm emerged, a shoulder, a woman climbing up from the cut tunnel that dipped below the floor.

She pushed herself to her knees, stood up straight, and brushed her hair from her face.

Jimmy pulled up. The group stopped a dozen paces away. A woman. A stranger. She stood in their silo, smiling, covered in dust and grime.

"Solo?" she asked.

Her teeth flashed. She was pretty, even covered in dirt. She walked toward the group and tugged off a pair of thick gloves while someone else crawled out from behind the digger's teeth. An outstretched hand. The baby crying. Jimmy shook the woman's hand, mesmerized by her smile.

"I'm Courtnee," the woman said. She swept her gaze over the children, her smile widening. "You must be Elise." She squeezed the young girl's shoulder, which caused the grip around Jimmy's neck to tighten.

A man emerged from behind the digger, pale as fresh paper with hair just as white, and turned to survey the wall of cutting teeth.

"Where's Juliette?" Jimmy asked, hiking Elise higher on his hip.

Courtnee frowned. "Didn't she tell you? She went outside."

PART II

OUTSIDE

Silo 18

19

JULIETTE STOOD IN the airlock while gas was pumped in around her. The cleaning suit crinkled against her skin. She felt none of the fear from the last time she was sent out, but none of the deluded hope that drove many to exile. Somewhere between pointless dreams and hopeless dread was a desire to know the world. And, if possible, make it better.

The pressure in the airlock grew, and the folds of her suit found every raised scar across her body, wrinkles pressing where wrinkles had once burned. It was a million pricks from a million gentle needles, every sensitive part of her touched all at once, as if this airlock remembered, as if it knew her. A lover's apology.

Clear plastic sheets had been hung over the walls. These began to ripple as they were forced tight around pipes, around the bench where she'd been dressed. Not long now. If anything, she felt excitement. Relief. A long project coming to an end.

She pulled one of the sample containers off her chest and cracked the lid, gathering some of the inert argon for a reference. Screwing the lid back on, she heard a dull and familiar thud within the recesses of the great outer door. The silo opened, and a wisp of fog appeared as pressurized gas pushed its way through, preventing the outside from getting in.

The fog swelled and swirled around her. It pushed at her back, urging her along. Juliette lifted a boot, stepped through the thick outer doors of Silo 18 and was outside once again.

The ramp was just as she remembered it: a concrete plane rising up through the last level of her buried home and toward the surface of the earth. Trapped dirt made slopes of hard corners, and streaks and splatters of mud stained the walls. The heavy doors thumped together behind her, and a dispersing fog rose up toward the clouds. Juliette began her march up the gentle rise.

"You okay?"

Lukas's soft voice filled her helmet. Juliette smiled. It was good to have him with her. She pinched her thumb and finger together, which keyed the microphone in her helmet.

"No one has ever died on the ramp, Lukas. I'm doing just fine."

He whispered an apology, and Juliette's smile widened. It was a different thing altogether to venture out with this support behind her. Much different than being exiled while shamed backs were turned, no one daring to watch.

She reached the top of the ramp, and a feeling of *rightness* overtook her. Without the fear or the digital lies of an electronic visor, she felt what she suspected humans were *meant* to feel: a heady rush of disappearing walls, of raw land spread out in every direction, of miles and miles of open air and tumbling clouds. Her flesh tingled from the thrill of exploration. She had been here twice before, but this was something new. This had purpose.

"Taking my first sample," she said, pinching her glove.

She pulled another of the small containers from her suit. Everything was numbered just like a cleaning, but the steps had changed. Weeks of planning and building had gone into this, a flurry of activity up top while her friends tunneled through the earth. She cracked the lid of the container, held it aloft for a count of ten, and then screwed the cap back on. The top of the vessel was clear. A pair of gaskets rattled inside, and twin strips of heat tape were affixed to the bottom. Juliette pressed waxy sealant around the lip of the lid, making it airtight. The numbered sample went into a flapped pouch on her thigh, joining the one from the airlock.

Lukas's voice crackled through the radio: "We've got a full burn in the airlock. Nelson is letting it cool down before he goes in."

Juliette turned and faced the sensor tower. She fought the urge to lift her hand, to acknowledge the dozens of men and women who were watching on the cafeteria's wallscreen. She looked down at her chest and tried to clear her mind, to remember what she was supposed to do next.

Soil sample. She shuffled away from the ramp and the tower toward a patch of dirt that maybe hadn't seen footsteps in centuries. Kneeling down—the undersuit pinching the back of her knee—she scooped dirt using the shallow container. The soil was packed hard and difficult to dig up, so she brushed more of the surface soil onto the top, filling the dish.

"Surface sample complete," she said, pinching her glove. She screwed the lid on carefully and pressed the ring of wax before sliding it into a pouch on her other thigh.

"Good going," Lukas said. He was probably aiming for encouragement. All she could hear was his intense worry.

"Taking the deep sample next."

She grabbed the tool with both hands. She had built the large T on the top while wearing bulky suit gloves to make sure the grip would be right. With the corkscrew end pressed against the earth, she twisted the handle around and around, leaning her weight into her arms to force the blades through the dense soil.

Sweat formed on her brow. A drop of perspiration smacked her visor and trembled into a little puddle as her arms jerked with effort. A caustic and stiff breeze buffeted her suit, pushing her to the side. When the tool penetrated all the way to the tape mark on the handle, she stood and pulled the T-bar, using her legs.

The plug came free, an avalanche of deep soil spilling off and crumbling into the dry hole. She slid the case over the plug and locked it into place. Everything had the fit and polish of Supply's best. She stowed the tool back in its pouch, slung it around onto her back, and took a deep breath.

"Good?" Lukas asked.

She waved at the tower. "I'm good. Two more samples left. How far along is the airlock?"

"Lemme check."

While Lukas saw how the preparations for her return were going, Juliette trudged toward the nearest hill. Her old footsteps had been worn away by a light rain, but she remembered the path well. The crease in the hill stood like an inviting stairway, a ramp on which two forms still nestled.

She stopped at the base of the hill and pulled out another container with gaskets and heat tape inside. The cap came off easily. She held it up to the wind, allowing whatever blew inside to become trapped. For all they knew, these were the first tests made of the outside air. Reams and reams of bogus reports from previous cleanings had been nothing but numbers used to uphold and justify fears. It was a charade of progress, of efforts being made to right the world, when all they ever cared about was selling the story of how wrong it was.

The only thing more impressive to Juliette than the depths of the conspiracy had been the speed and relief with which its mechanisms had crumbled within IT. The men and women of level thirty-four reminded her of the children of Silo 17, frightened and wide-eyed and desperate for some adult they could cling to and trust. This foray of hers to test the outside air was looked upon with suspicion and fear elsewhere in the silo, but in IT, where they had pretended to do this work for generations, the chance to truly investigate had been seized by many with wild abandon.

Damn!

Juliette slapped the cover on the container. Her mind had wandered; she had forgotten to count to ten, had probably gone twice that.

"Hey, Jules?"

She squeezed her fingers together. "Yeah?" Releasing the mic, she locked the lid tight, made sure it said "2" on the top, and sealed the edges. She put it away with the other container, cursing her inattention.

"The airlock burn is complete. Nelson went in afterward to get things ready for you, but they're saying it's gonna be a while to charge the argon again. Are you sure you're feeling okay?"

She took a moment to survey herself and give an honest answer. A few deep breaths. Wiggled her joints. Looked up at the dark clouds to make sure her vision and balance were normal.

"Yeah. I feel fine."

"Okay. And they are going to go with the flames when you come back. It looks like they really might've been necessary. We were getting some strange readings in the airlock before you left. As a precaution, Nelson is getting a scrub-down in the inner lock right now. We'll have everything prepped for you as fast as we can."

Juliette didn't like the sound of any of that. Her passage through the Silo 17 airlock had been terrifying, but with no lasting consequences. Dumping soup on herself had been enough to survive. The theory they had been working under was that conditions outside weren't as bad as they'd been led to believe, and that the flames were more a deterrent against not leaving the airlock than an actual necessity for cleansing the air. The challenge with this mission of hers was getting back inside without enduring another burn or another stint in the hospital. But she couldn't put the silo at risk, either.

She squeezed her fingers together, thinking suddenly of all that was at stake. "Is there still a crowd up there watching?" she asked Lukas.

"Yeah. There's a lot of excitement in the air. People can't believe this is happening."

"I want you to clear them out," she said.

She let go of her thumb. There was no reply.

"Lukas? Do you read me? I want you to get everyone down to at least level four. Clear out anyone not working on this, okay?"

She waited.

"Yeah," Lukas said. There was a lot of noise in the background. "We're doing that right now. Trying to keep everyone calm."

"Tell them it's just a precaution. Because of the readings in the airlock."

"Doing that."

He sounded winded. Juliette hoped she wasn't causing a panic for no reason.

"I'm going to get the last sample," she said, focusing on the task at hand. They had prepared for the worst. Everything was going to be okay. She was thankful for the crude sensors they'd installed in the airlock. The next time out, she hoped to install a permanent array on the tower. But she couldn't get too far ahead of herself. She approached one of the cleaners at the base of the hill.

The body they'd chosen belonged to Jack Brent. It had been nine years since he'd been sent to clean, having gone mad after his wife's second miscarriage. Juliette knew very little else about him. And that had been her main criterion for the final sample.

She made her way to what was left of the body. The old suit had long turned a dull gray like the soil. What once was a metallic coating flaked away like old paint. The boots were eaten thin, the visor chipped. Jack lay with his arms folded across his chest, legs straight and parallel, almost as if he had taken a nap and had never gotten up. More like he had lain down to gaze at the clear blue sky in his visor.

Juliette pulled the last box out, the one marked "3", and knelt beside the dead cleaner. It spooked her to think that this would've been her fate were it not for Scottie and Walker and the people of Supply who had risked so much. She lifted the sharp blade out of the sample box and cut a square patch from the suit. Setting the blade on the cleaner's chest, she picked up the sample and dropped it into the container. Holding her breath, she grabbed the blade, careful not to nick her own suit, and sliced into the rotted undersuit where it had been exposed across the cleaner's belly.

This last sample had to be prised out with the blade. If there was any flesh inside or gathered with it, she couldn't tell. Everything was thankfully dark beneath the torn and dilapidated suit. But it seemed like nothing but soil in there, blown in amongst the dry bones.

She put the sample in the container and left the blade by the cleaner, no longer needing it and not wanting to risk handling it any further with the bulky gloves. She stood and turned toward the tower.

"You okay?"

Lukas's voice sounded different. Muffled. Juliette exhaled, felt a little dizzy from holding her breath so long.

"I'm fine."

"We're almost ready for you. I'd start heading back."

She nodded, even though he probably couldn't see her at that distance, not even with the tall wallscreens magnifying the world.

"Hey, you know what we forgot?"

She froze and studied the tower.

"What is it?" she asked. "Forgot what?" Sweat trickled down her cheek, tickling her skin. She could feel the lace of scars at the back of her neck where her last suit had melted against her.

"We forgot to send you out with a pad or two," Lukas said. "There's already some build-up visible in here. And you know, while you're out there . . ."

Juliette glared at the tower.

"I'm just saying," Lukas said. "You maybe could have, you know, given it a bit of a cleaning—"

20

JULIETTE WAITED AT the bottom of the ramp. She remembered the last time she'd done this, standing in the same place with a blanket of heat tape Solo had made, wondering if she'd run out of air before the doors opened, wondering if she'd survive what awaited her inside. She remembered thinking Lukas was in there, and then struggling with Bernard instead.

She tried to shake those memories free. Glancing down at her pockets, she made sure the flaps on all the pouches were tightly sealed. Every step of the upcoming decontamination flitted through her mind. She trusted that everything would be in place.

"Here we go," Lukas radioed. Again, his voice was hollow and distant.

On cue, the gears in the airlock door squealed, and a plume of pressurized argon spilled through the gap. Juliette threw herself into the mist, an intense sensation of relief accompanying the move indoors.

"I'm in. I'm in," she said.

The doors thumped shut behind her. Juliette glanced at the inner airlock door, saw a helmet on the other side of the glass porthole, someone peering in, watching. Moving to the ready bench, she opened the airtight box Nelson had installed in her absence. Needed to be quick. The gas chambers and the flames were all automated.

Ripping the sealed pouches off her thighs, she placed them inside. She unslung the borer with its sample and added that as well, then pushed the lid shut and engaged the locks. The practice run-through had helped. Moving in the suit felt comfortable. She had lain in bed at night thinking through each step until they were habit.

Shuffling across the small airlock, she gripped the edge of the immense metal tub she'd welded together. It was still warm from the last bout of flames, but the water Nelson had topped it up with had sapped much of the heat. With a deep and pointless breath, she lowered herself over the edge.

The water flooded against her helmet, and Juliette felt the first real onrush of fear. Her breath quickened. Being outside was nothing like being underwater again. The floods were in her mouth; she could feel herself taking tiny gulps of air, could taste the steel and rust from the steps; she forgot what she was supposed to be doing.

Glimpsing one of the handles at the bottom of the tub, she reached for it and pulled herself down. One boot at a time, she found the bar welded at the other end of the tub and slipped her feet under, held herself to the bottom, trusting that her back was covered. Her arms ached as she strained against the suit's buoyancy. And even through her helmet and beneath that water, she could hear displaced fluid splashing over the lip and onto the airlock floor. She could hear the flames kick on and roar and lick at the tub.

"Three, four, five—" Lukas counted, and a painful memory flashed before her, the dull green emergency lights, the panic in her chest—

"Six, seven, eight—"

She could almost taste the oil and fuel from that final gasp as she emerged, alive, from the flooded depths.

"Nine, ten. Burn complete," he said.

Letting go of the handles and kicking her boots free, she bobbed to the boiling surface, the heat of the water felt through her suit. She fought to get her knees and boots beneath her. Water splashed and steamed everywhere. She feared the longer this next step took, the more the air could attach itself to her, contaminating the second airlock.

She hurried to the door, boots slipping dangerously, the locking wheel already spinning.

Hurry, hurry, she thought to herself.

It opened a crack. She tried to dive through, slipped, landed painfully on the door's jamb. Several gloved hands grabbed at her as she clawed her way forward, the two suited technicians yanking her through before slamming the door shut.

Nelson and Sophia—two of the former suit techs—had brushes ready. They dipped them into a vat of blue neutralizing agent and began scrubbing Juliette down before turning to themselves and each other.

Juliette turned her back and made sure they got that as well. She went to the vat and fished out the third brush, turned and started scrubbing Sophia's suit. And saw that it wasn't Sophia in there.

She squeezed her glove mic. "What the hell, Luke?"

Lukas shrugged, a wince of guilt on his face. She imagined he couldn't stand the thought of someone else risking themselves. Or probably just wanted to be there by the airlock door in case something went wrong. Juliette couldn't blame him; she would've done the same thing.

They scrubbed the second airlock while Peter Billings and a few others looked on from the sheriff's office. Bubbles from the cleaning fluid floated up in the air, then trembled toward the vents where the air inside the new airlock was being pumped into the first. Nelson worked on the ceiling, which they'd kept low on purpose. Less air inside. Less volume. Easier to reach. Juliette searched Nelson's face for any sign of trouble from his time in the inner airlock and blamed the flush and sweat on his energetic scrubbing.

"You've got perfect vacuum," Peter said, using the radio in his office. Juliette motioned to the others, drew her hand across her neck, then closed her fist. They both nodded and went back to scrubbing. While new air was cycled in from the cafeteria, they went over each other one more time, and Juliette finally had a moment to revel in the fact that she was back. Back inside. They had done it. No burns, no hospitals, no contamination. And now they would hopefully learn something.

Peter's voice filled her helmet again: "We didn't want to tell you while you were suiting up, but the dig punched through to the other side about half an hour ago."

Juliette felt a surge of both elation and guilt. She should've been down there. The timing was abysmal, but she had felt her window of opportunity closing there in the Up Top. She resigned herself to being happy for Solo and the kids, relieved by the end of their long ordeal.

The second airlock—with the sealed glass door she'd fashioned from a shower stall—began to open. Behind her, a bright light bloomed inside the old airlock, and the small porthole glowed red. A second round of flames surged and raged in the small room, bathing the spoiled walls, charring the very air, boiling off the water Juliette had spilled on the floor, and throwing the vat into a cauldron of raging steam.

Juliette waved the others out of the new airlock while she eyed the old one warily, remembering. Remembering being in there. Lukas came back and tugged her along, through the door and into the former jail cell where they stripped down to their undersuits for yet another round of showering. As she peeled off the soaking layers, all Juliette could think about was the sealed and fireproof box on the ready bench. She hoped it was worth the risk, that the answers to a host of cruel questions were tucked away, safely inside.

Silo 17

21

THE GREAT DIGGING machine stood quiet and still. Dust fell from where it had chewed through the ceiling, and the large steel teeth and spinning discs gleamed from their journey through solid rock. Between the discs, the digger's face was caked with dirt, debris, torn lengths of rebar, and large rocks. By the edge of the machine, where it jutted out into the heart of Silo 17, there was a black crack that connected two very different worlds.

Jimmy watched as strangers spilled from one of those worlds into his. Burly men with dark beards and yellow smiles, hands black with grease, stepped through and squinted up at the rusted pipes overhead, the puddles on the ground, the calm and quiet organs of a silo that had long ago rumbled and now sat deathly still.

They clasped Jimmy's hand, called him Solo, and squeezed the terrified children. They told him Jules said hello. And then they adjusted the lights on their helmets, which threw golden cones before them, and went splashing off into Jimmy's home.

Elise clutched Jimmy's leg as another group of miners and mechanics squeezed past. Two dogs bounded with them, stopped to sniff at the puddles, then at a trembling Elise, before following their owners. Courtnee—Juliette's friend—finished instructing a group before returning to Jimmy and the kids. Jimmy watched her move. Her hair was lighter than Juliette's, her features sharper, she wasn't quite as tall, but she had that same fierceness. He wondered if all the people from this other world would be the same: the men bearded and covered in soot, the women wild and resourceful.

Rickson rounded up the twins while Hannah cradled her crying baby and tried to soothe it back to sleep. Courtnee handed Jimmy a flashlight.

"I don't have enough lights for all of you," she said, "so you'll want to stick close together." She held her hand over her head. "The tunnel is high enough, just mind the support columns. And the ground is rough, so go slow and stick to the center."

"Why can't we stay here and have the doctor come to us?" Rickson asked.

Hannah shot him a look as she bounced the baby on her hip.

"It's much safer where we're taking you," Courtnee said, glancing around at walls slick and corroded. The way she looked at Jimmy's home made him feel defensive. They'd been getting along just fine for some time now.

Rickson flashed Jimmy a look like he had his own doubts about it being safer on the other side. Jimmy knew what he was scared of. Jimmy had heard the twins talking, and the twins had heard the older kids whispering. Hannah would have to get an implant in her hip like their mothers had. Rickson would be assigned a color and a job other than fending for his family. The young couple were just as wary of these adults as Jimmy was.

Despite their fears, they donned hard hats borrowed from those pouring into their world, clung to one another, and squeezed through the gap. Beyond the digger's teeth, there was a dark tunnel like the Wilds when all the lights were off. But there was a coolness, and an echo to their voices different than the Wilds. The earth seemed to swallow them as Jimmy tried to keep up with Courtnee, and the kids tried to keep up with him.

They entered a metal door and passed through the long digging machine, which was warm inside. Down a narrow corridor, people squeezing past in the other direction, and finally out another door and back into the cool and dark of the tunnel. Men and women shouted to one another, lights dancing from their helmets as they wrestled with piles of rubble that climbed toward the ceiling and out of sight. Rocks shifted and clattered. There were mounds of them on either side, leaving a precarious pathway in the center. Workers filed past, smelling of mud and sweat. There was a boulder taller than Jimmy that the foot traffic had to bend around.

It felt odd to walk straight ahead in one direction like that. They walked and walked without ever bumping into a wall or bending back around. It was unnatural. That lateral void was more frightening than the darkness with its occasional lights. It was scarier than the veil of dust drifting from the ceiling or the occasional rock tumbling down from the piles. It was worse than the strangers bumping past them in the dark, or the steel beams in the middle of the passage that leapt up from the swirling shadows. It was the eeriness of there being nothing to stop them. Walk and walk and walk in one direction, no end to it all.

Jimmy was used to the up-and-down of the spiral staircase. That was normal. This was not. And yet he stumbled along across the rough surface of the chewed rock, past men and women calling to one another in the flash-beam-studded darkness, between piles of earth crowding the narrow center. They overtook men and women carrying parts of machines and lengths of steel taken from his silo, and Jimmy wanted to say something to them. Elise sniffled and said she was scared. Jimmy scooped her up and let her cling to his neck.

The tunnel went on and on. Even when a light could be seen at the end, a rough square of light, it took countless steps to make that bright maw grow larger. Jimmy thought of Juliette walking this far in the outside. It seemed impossible that she had survived such an ordeal. He had to remind himself that he had heard her voice dozens of times since, that she had really done it, had gone off for help and had kept her promise to come back for him. Their two worlds had been made one.

He dodged another steel column in the center of the tunnel. Aiming his flashlight up, he could see the overhead beams these columns supported. The loose rocks crumbling down gave Jimmy new cause for alarm, and he found himself less reluctantly following Courtnee. He pressed forward, toward the promise of light ahead, forgetting what he was leaving behind and where he was going and thinking only about getting out from underneath the tenuously held earth.

Far behind them, a loud crack sounded out, followed by the rumble of shifting rock and then shouts from workers to get out of the way. Hannah brushed past him. He set Elise down, and she and the twins rushed ahead, dancing in and out of the beam of Courtnee's flashlight. Streams of people filed past, lights affixed to their hard hats, heading toward Jimmy's home. He patted his chest reflexively, feeling for the old key that he had put on before leaving the server room. His silo was unprotected. But the fear he could sense in the kids somehow made him stronger. He wasn't as terrified as they were. It was his duty to be strong.

The tunnel came to a blessed end, the twins scampering out first. They startled the gruff men and women in their dark blue coveralls with knee patches of grease and their leather aprons slotted with tools. Eyes grew wide on faces white with chalk and black from soot. Jimmy paused at the mouth of the tunnel and let Rickson and Hannah out first. All work ceased at the sight of the bundle cradled in Hannah's arms. One of the women stepped forward and lifted a hand as if to touch the child, but Courtnee waved her back and told the rest to return to their work. Jimmy scanned the crowd for Juliette, even though he'd been told she was up top. Elise begged to be carried again, her tiny hands stretched up in the air. Jimmy adjusted his pack and obliged, ignoring the pain in his hip. The bag around Elise's neck banged his ribs with its heavy book.

He joined the procession of little ones as they wove through the walls of workers frozen in place, workers who tugged their beards and scratched their heads and watched him as if he were a man from some fictional land. And Jimmy felt at his core that this was a grave mistake. Two worlds had been united, but they were not anything alike. Power surged here. Lights burned steady, and it was crowded with grown men and women. It smelled different. Machines rumbled rather than sat quiet. And the long decades of growing older sloughed off him in a sudden panic as Jimmy hurried to catch up with the others, just one of a number of frightened youth, emerging from shadows and silence into the bright and crowded and noisy.

Silo 18

22

A SMALL BUNKROOM HAD been set up for the kids, with a private room down the hall for Jimmy. Elise was unhappy with the arrangements and clung to one of his hands with both of hers. Courtnee told them she had food being sent down and then they could shower. A stack of clean coveralls sat on one of the bunks, a bar of soap, a few worn children's books. But first, she introduced a tall man in the cleanest pale red coveralls Jimmy could ever remember seeing.

"I'm Dr. Nichols," the man said, shaking Jimmy's hand. "I believe you know my daughter."

Jimmy didn't understand. And then he remembered that Juliette's last name was Nichols. He pretended to be brave while this tall, clean-shaven man peered into his eyes and mouth. Next, a cold piece of metal was pressed to Jimmy's chest, and this man listened intently through his tubes. It all seemed familiar. Something from Jimmy's distant past.

Jimmy took deep breaths as he was told. The children watched warily, and he realized what a model he was for them, a model for normalcy, for courage. He nearly laughed—but he was supposed to be breathing for the doctor.

Elise volunteered to go next. Dr. Nichols lowered himself to his knees and checked the gap of her missing tooth. He asked about fairies, and when Elise shook her head and said she'd never heard of such a thing, a dime was produced. The twins rushed forward and begged to be next.

"Are fairies real?" Miles asked. "We used to hear noises in the farm where we grew up."

Marcus wiggled in front of his brother. "I saw a fairy for real one day," he said. "And I lost twenty teeth when I was young."

"You did?" Dr. Nichols asked. "Can you smile for me? Excellent. Now open your mouth. Twenty teeth, you say."

"Uh-huh," Marcus said. He wiped his mouth. "And every one of them growed back except for the one Miles knocked out."

"It was an accident," Miles complained. He lifted his shirt and asked to have his breaths heard. Jimmy watched Rickson and Hannah huddle together around their infant as they studied the proceedings. He also noted that Dr. Nichols, even as he looked over the two boys, couldn't stop glancing at the baby in Hannah's arms.

The twins were given a dime each after their check-up. "Dimes are good luck for twins," Dr. Nichols said. "Parents put two of these under their pillows in the hopes of having such healthy boys as you."

The twins beamed and scrutinized the coins for any sign of a faded face or portion of a word to suggest they were real. "Rickson used to be a twin too," Miles said.

"Oh?" Dr. Nichols shifted his attention to the older kids sitting side by side on the lower bunk.

"I don't want to take the implant," Hannah said coolly. "My mother had the implant, but it was cut out of her. I don't want to be cut."

Rickson wrapped an arm around her and held her close. He narrowed his eyes at the tall doctor, and Jimmy felt nervous.

"You don't have to take the implant," Dr. Nichols whispered, but Jimmy saw the way he glanced at Courtnee. "Do you mind if I listen to your child's heartbeat? I just want to make sure it's nice and strong—"

"Why wouldn't it be?" Rickson asked, thrusting his shoulders back.

Dr. Nichols studied the boy a moment. "You met my daughter, didn't you? Juliette."

He nodded. "Briefly," he said. "She left soon after."

"Well, she sent me down here because she cares about your health. I'm a doctor. I specialize in children, the youngest of them. I think your child looks very strong and healthy. I just want to be sure." Dr. Nichols held up the metal disc at the end of his hearing tubes and pressed his palm against it. "There. So it'll be nice and warm. Your boy won't even know I'm taking a listen."

Jimmy rubbed his chest where his breathing had been checked and wondered why the doctor hadn't warmed it for *him.*

"For a dime?" Rickson asked.

Dr. Nichols smiled. "How about a few chits, instead?"

"What's a chit?" Rickson asked, but Hannah was already adjusting herself on the bunk so the doctor could have a look.

Courtnee rested a hand on Jimmy's shoulder while the check-ups continued. Jimmy turned to see what she needed.

"Juliette wanted me to call her as soon as you all were over here. I'll be back to check on you in a little while—"

"Wait," Jimmy said. "I'd like to come. I want to speak with her."

"Me too," said Elise, pressing against his leg.

Courtnee frowned. "Okay," she said. "But let's be quick, because you all need to eat and get freshened up."

"Freshened up?" Elise asked.

"If you're going to go up and see your new home, yeah."

"New home?" Jimmy asked.

But Courtnee had already turned to go.

Jimmy hurried out the door and down the hall after Courtnee. Elise grabbed her shoulder bag, the one that held her heavy book, and scampered along beside him.

"What did she mean about a new home?" Elise asked. "When are we going back to our real home?"

Jimmy scratched his beard and wrestled with truth and lies. *We may never go home,* he wanted to say. *No matter where we end up, it may never feel like home again.*

"I think this will be our new home," he told her, keeping his voice from cracking. He reached down and rested his wrinkled hand on her thin shoulder, felt how fragile she was, this flesh that words could crack. "It'll be our home for a time, at least. Until they make our old home better." He glanced ahead at Courtnee, who did not look back.

Elise stopped in the middle of the hallway and peered over her shoulder. When she turned back, the dim lights of Mechanical caught the water in her eyes. Jimmy was about to tell her not to cry when Courtnee knelt down and called Elise over. Elise refused to budge.

"Do you want to come with us to call Juliette and talk with her on the radio?" Courtnee asked.

Elise chewed on her finger and nodded. A tear rolled down her cheek. She clutched the bag with her book in it, and Jimmy remembered kids from another lifetime who used to cling to dolls in the same way.

"After we make this call and you get freshened up, I'll get you some sweetcorn from the pantry. Would you like that?"

Elise shrugged. Jimmy wanted to say that none of the kids

had ever tasted sweetcorn before. He had never heard of the stuff himself. But now he wanted some.

"Let's go call Juliette together," Courtnee said.

Elise sniffed and nodded. She took Jimmy's hand and peered up at him. "What's sweetcorn?" she asked.

"It'll be a surprise," Jimmy said, which was the dead truth.

Courtnee led them down the hall and around a bend. It took a moment for the twists and turns to remind Jimmy of the dark and wet place he'd left behind. Beyond the fresh paint and the humming lights, past the neat wires and the smell of fresh grease, lay a labyrinth identical to the rusted bucket he'd explored the past two weeks. He could almost hear the puddles squish beneath his feet, hear that screaming pump he tended suck at an empty basin—but that was a real noise at his feet. A loud yip.

Elise screamed, and at first Jimmy thought he'd stepped on her. But there at his feet was a large brown rat with a fearsome tail, crying and turning circles.

Jimmy's heart stopped. Elise screamed and screamed, but then he realized it was his voice he was hearing. Elise's arms were latched around his leg, making it difficult to turn and flee. And meanwhile, Courtnee bent over with laughter. Jimmy nearly fainted as Courtnee scooped the giant rat off the ground. When the thing licked at her chin, he realized it wasn't a rat at all but a dog. A juvenile. He'd seen grown dogs in the Mids of his silo when he was a boy, but had never seen a pup. Elise loosened her grip when she saw that the animal meant no harm.

"It's a cat!" Elise cried.

"That's no cat," Jimmy said. He knew cats.

Courtnee was still laughing at him when a young man careened around the corner, panting, summoned no doubt by Jimmy's startled screeches.

"There you are," he said, taking the animal from Courtnee. The pup clawed at the man's shoulder and tried to bite his earlobe. "Damn thing." The mechanic swatted the pup's face away. He gripped it by the scruff of its neck, its legs pawing at the air.

"Is that more of them?" Courtnee asked.

"Same litter," the man said.

"Conner was to put them down weeks ago."

The man shrugged. "Conner's been digging that damn tunnel. But I'll get on him about it." He nodded to Courtnee and marched back the way he'd come, the animal dangling from its scruff.

"Gave you a fright," Courtnee said, smiling at Jimmy.

"Thought he was a rat," Jimmy said, remembering the hordes of them that'd taken over the lower farms.

"We got overrun with dogs when some people from Supply hunkered down here," Courtnee said. She led them down the hall in the direction the man had gone. Elise, for once, was scampering out in front. "They've been busy ever since making more dogs. Found a litter of them myself in the pump room, beneath the heat exchangers. A few weeks ago, another was discovered in the tool lock-up. We'll be finding them in our beds soon enough, damn things. All they do is eat and make mess all over the place."

Jimmy thought of his youth in the server room, eating raw beans out of a can and shitting on the floor grates. You couldn't hate a living thing for . . . living, could you?

The hall ahead came to a dead end. Elise was already exploring to the left as if she were looking for something.

"Walker's workshop is this way," Courtnee said.

Elise glanced back. There was a yip from somewhere, and she turned and carried on.

"Elise," Jimmy called.

She peeked into an open door before disappearing inside. Courtnee and Jimmy hurried after.

When they turned the corner, they found her standing over a parts crate, the man from the hallway placing something back inside. Elise gripped the edge of the crate and bent forward. Yipping and scratching leaked out of the plastic bin.

"Careful, child." Courtnee hurried her way. "They bite."

Elise turned to Jimmy. One of the squirming animals was in her arms, a pink tongue flashing out.

"Put it back," Jimmy said.

Courtnee reached for the animal, but the man corralling the pups already had it by its neck. He dropped the puppy back in with the others and kicked the lid shut with a bang.

"I'm sorry, boss." He slid the crate aside with his foot while Elise made plaintive noises.

"Are you feeding them?" Courtnee asked. She pointed to a pile of scraps on an old plate.

"Conner is. Swear. They're from that dog he took in. You know how he is about the thing. I told him what you said, but he's been putting it off."

"We'll discuss it later," Courtnee said, her eyes darting at young Elise. Jimmy could tell she didn't want to discuss what needed doing in front of the child. "C'mon." She guided Jimmy to the door and back into the hall. He in turn pulled a complaining child after him.

23

A FAMILIAR AND UNPLEASANT odor awaited them at their destination. It was the smell of hot electrics like the humming servers and the stench of unwashed men. For Jimmy, it was a noseful of his old self and his old home. An earful of it too. There was a hiss of static—a familiar, ghostly whisper like his radios made. He followed Courtnee into a room of workbenches and the wreck of countless projects underway or abandoned, it was difficult to tell which.

There was a scattering of computer parts on a counter by the door, and Jimmy thought how his father would have lectured to see them so poorly arranged. A man in a leather smock turned from one of the far benches, a smoking metal wand in his hand, tools studding his chest and poking out of a hundred pockets, a grizzled beard and a wild look in his eyes. Jimmy had never seen such a man in all his life.

"Courtnee," the man said. He pulled a bright length of silver wire from his lips, set the wand down, and waved the smoke from his face. "Is it dinner?"

"It's not yet lunch," Courtnee told him. "I want you to meet two of Juliette's friends. They're from the other silo."

"The other silo." Walker adjusted a lens down over one eye and squinted at his visitors. He got up slowly from his stool.

"I've spoken with you," he said. He wiped his palm on the seat of his coveralls and extended his hand. "Solo, right?"

Jimmy stepped forward and accepted Walker's hand. The two men chewed their beards and studied each other for a moment. "I prefer Jimmy," he said at last.

Walker nodded. "Yes, yes. That's right."

"And I'm Elise." She waved. "Hannah calls me Lily, but I don't like being called Lily. I like Elise."

"It's a good name," Walker agreed. He tugged on his beard and rocked back on his heels, studying her.

"They were hoping to get in touch with Jules," Courtnee said. "And I was supposed to call her and let her know they're here. Is she . . . did everything go okay?"

Walker seemed to snap out of a trance. "What? Oh. Oh, yes." He clapped his hands. "Everything went, it seems. She's back inside."

"What did she go out for?" Jimmy asked. He knew Juliette had been working on something but not what. Just some Project she never wanted to discuss over the radio because she didn't know who might be listening.

"She went to see what was out there, apparently," Walker said. He grumbled something and eyed the open door to his workshop with a scrunched-up nose. He apparently didn't believe this was a valid reason for going anywhere. After an uncomfortable pause, he dropped his gaze to his desk. His old hands deftly lifted an unusual-looking radio, one bristling with knobs and dials. "Let's see if we can raise her," he said.

He called for Juliette, and someone else answered. They said to wait a moment. Walker held the radio out to Jimmy, who took it from him, familiar enough with how they worked.

A voice crackled out of the air: "Yes? Hello—?"

It was Juliette's voice. Jimmy squeezed the button.

"Jules?" He glanced at the ceiling and realized that for the first time in forever, she was above him somewhere, the two of them back under the same top. "Are you there?"

"Solo!" And he didn't correct her. "You're with Walker. Is Courtnee there?"

"Yes."

"Great. That's great. I'm so sorry I wasn't there. I'll be down as soon as I can. They're making up a place for the kids near the farms, more like home. I've just got this . . . one little project to finish first. It should only be a few days."

"It's okay," Jimmy said. He smiled nervously at Courtnee and felt very young all of a sudden. In truth, a few days felt like a very long time. He wanted to see Jules or go home. Or both. "I want to see you soon," he added, changing his mind. "Don't let it be too long."

A burst of static. The sound of radio waves thinking. "It won't be. I promise. Did you see my dad? He's a doctor. I sent him down to check on you and the kids."

"We saw him. He's here." Jimmy glanced down at Elise, who was tugging him toward the door, probably thinking of sweet-corn.

"Good. You said Courtnee was there. Can you put her on?"

Jimmy handed the radio over and saw that his hand was trembling. Courtnee took it. She listened to Juliette say something about the great stairway, and Courtnee updated her on the dig. There was talk of bringing the radio up so Jules could have it, an argument between them on why her father wasn't up top to make sure she and someone named Nelson were okay, a lot that Jimmy didn't understand. He tried to follow along, but his mind wandered. And then he realized Elise was nowhere to be seen.

"Where did that child get off to?" he asked. He ducked down and peered beneath the tool bench, saw nothing but a pile of parts and broken machines. He stood and checked behind one of the tall counters. It was a bad time for playing Hide and Find. He checked the far corner, and a cool taste of panic rose in his throat. Elise was quick to disappear back in his silo, was prone to distraction, just wandered off toward anything shiny or the slightest waft of fruit-smells. But here . . . with strangers and places he didn't know. Jimmy lumbered across the room and peeked between the benches and behind the cluttered shelves, every second cranking up the sound of his heartbeat in his ears.

"She was just—" Walker started to say.

"I'm right here," Elise called. She waved from the hallway, was standing just outside the door. "Can we get back to Rickson? I'm hungry."

"And I promised you sweetcorn," Courtnee said, smiling. Her conversation with Juliette was done. She had missed Jimmy's minute or two of complete and utter panic. On the way to the door, she handed him the strange radio. "Jules wants you to take this with you."

Jimmy accepted it gingerly.

"She said it might be a day or two, but she'll see you at your new place by the lower farms."

"I'm really hungry," Elise called out impatiently. Jimmy laughed and told her to be polite, but his stomach was grumbling too. He joined her in the hallway and saw that she had her large memory book out of her shoulder bag. She clutched it tightly to her chest. Loose and colorful pages she had yet to sew in jutted out at odd angles.

"Follow me," Courtnee said, leading them down the hall. "You are going to love Mama Jean's sweetcorn."

Jimmy felt certain this was true. He hurried along after Courtnee, eager to eat and then see Jules. Behind him, little

Elise trailed along at her own pace. She cradled her large book in both arms—humming quietly to herself because she didn't know how to whistle—her shoulder bag kicking and squirming and making noises of its own.

24

JULIETTE ENTERED THE airlock to retrieve the samples; she could feel the heat from the earlier fire—or else she was imagining it. It could've been her temperature going up inside the suit. Or it may simply have been the sight of that sealed container on the ready bench, its lid now discolored from the lick of flames.

She checked the container with the flat of her glove. The material on her palm didn't grow tacky and stick to the metal; it felt cool to the touch. Over an hour of scrubbing down, changing into new suits, cleaning both airlocks, and now there was a box of clues. A box of outside air, of soil and other samples. Clues, perhaps, to all that was wrong with the world.

She retrieved the box and joined the others beyond the second airlock. A large lead-lined trunk was waiting, its joints sealed, the interior padded. The welded sample box was nestled inside. After the lid was shut, Nelson added a ring of caulk, and Lukas helped Juliette with her helmet. With it off, she realized how labored her breathing had become. Wearing that suit was starting to get to her.

She wiggled out of it while Peter Billings sealed all of the airlocks. His office adjacent to the cafeteria had been a construction site for the past week, and she could tell he would be glad for everyone to be gone. Juliette had promised to remove the inner lock as soon as possible, but that there would most likely be more excursions before that happened. First, she wanted to see about the small pockets of outside air she'd brought into the silo. And it was a long way down to the Suit Lab on thirty-four.

Nelson and Sophia went ahead of them to clear the stairwell. Juliette and Lukas followed after, one hand each on either side of the trunk like porters on a tandem. Another violation of the Pact, Juliette thought. People in silver, porting. How many laws could she break now that she was in a position to uphold them all? How clever could she be in justifying her actions?

Her thoughts drifted from her many hypocrisies to the dig far below, to the news that Courtnee had punched through, that Solo and the kids were safe. She hated that she couldn't be down there with them, but at least her father was. Initially reluctant to play any role in her voyage outside, her father had then resisted leaving her to see to the kids instead. Juliette had convinced him they had taken enough precautions that a checkup of her health was unnecessary.

The trunk swayed and banged against the rail with a jarring clang, and she tried to concentrate on the task at hand.

"You okay back there?" Lukas called.

"How do porters do this?" she asked, switching hands. The weight of the lead-lined trunk pulled down, and its bulk was in the way of her legs. Lukas was lower down and able to walk in the center of the stairway with his arm straight by his side—much more comfortable-looking. She couldn't manage anything similar from higher up. At the next landing, she made Lukas wait while she removed the belt threaded through the waist of her coveralls and tied this to the handle, looping it over her shoulder the way she'd seen a porter do. This allowed her to walk to the side, the weight of the box leaning against her hip, just how they carried those black bags with bodies to be buried.

After a level, it almost grew comfortable, and Juliette could see the appeal of porting. It gave one time to think. The mind grew still while the body moved. But then the thought of black bags and what she and Lukas were porting, and her thoughts found a dark shadow to lie still in.

"How're you doing?" she asked Lukas after two turns of complete silence.

"Fine," he said. "Just wondering what we're carrying here, you know? What's inside the box."

His mind had found similar shadows.

"You think this was a bad idea?" she asked.

He didn't answer. It was hard to tell if that was a shrug, or if he was adjusting his grip.

They passed another landing. Nelson and Sophia had taped the doors off, but faces watched from behind dirty glass. Juliette spotted an elderly woman holding a bright cross against the glass. As she turned, the woman rubbed the cross and kissed it, and Juliette thought of Father Wendel and the idea that she was bringing fear, not hope, to the silo. Hope was what he and the church offered, some place to exist after death. Fear came from the chance that changing the world for the better could possibly make it worse.

She waited until they were beneath the landing. "Hey, Luke?"

"Yeah?"

"Do you ever wonder what happens to us after we're gone?"

"I know what happens to us," he said. "We get slathered in butter and chewed off the cob."

He laughed at his own joke.

"I'm serious. Do you think our souls join the clouds and find some better place?"

His laughter stopped. "No," he said after a long pause. "I think we simply stop being."

They descended a turn and passed another landing, another

door taped off and sealed as a precaution. Juliette realized their voices were drifting up and down a quiet and empty stairwell.

"It doesn't bother me that I won't be around one day," Lukas said after a while. "I don't stress about the fact that I wasn't here a hundred years ago. I think death will be a lot like that. A hundred years from now my life will be just like it was a hundred years ago."

Again, he adjusted his grip or shrugged. It was impossible to say.

"I'll tell you what does last forever." He turned his head to make sure she could hear, and Juliette braced for something corny like "love" or something unfunny like "your casseroles."

"What lasts forever?" she obliged, sure to regret it but sensing that he was waiting for her to ask.

"Our decisions," he said.

"Can we stop a moment?" Juliette asked. There was a burn where the strap rubbed across her neck. She set her end down on a step, and Lukas held his half to keep the trunk level. She checked the knot and stepped around to switch shoulders. "I'm sorry—'our decisions'?" She had lost him.

Lukas turned to face her. "Yeah. Our actions, you know? They last forever. Whatever we do, it'll always be what we did. There's no taking them back."

This wasn't the answer she was expecting. There was sadness in his voice as he said these things, that box resting against his knee, and Juliette was moved by the utter simplicity of his answer. Something resonated, but she wasn't sure what it was. "Tell me more," she said. She looped the strap around her other shoulder and readied to lift it again. Lukas held the rail with one hand and seemed content to rest there a moment longer.

"I mean, the world goes around the sun, right?"

"According to you." She laughed.

"Well, it does. The Legacy and the man from Silo One confirm it."

Juliette scoffed as if neither could be trusted. Lukas ignored her and continued.

"That means we don't exist in one place. Instead, everything we do is left in . . . like a trail out there, a big ring of decisions. Every action we take—"

"And mistake."

He nodded and dabbed at his forehead with his sleeve. "And every mistake. But every good thing we do as well. They are immortal, every single touch we leave behind. Even if nobody sees them or remembers them, that doesn't matter. That trail will always be what happened, what we did, every choice. The past lives on forever. There's no changing it."

"Makes you not want to fuck up," Juliette said, thinking on all the times she had, wondering if this box between them was one more mistake. She saw images of herself in a great loop of space: fighting with her father, losing a lover, going out to clean, a great spiral of hurts like a journey down the stairs with a bleeding foot.

And the stains would never wash out. That's what Lukas was saying. She would always have hurt her father. Was that the way to phrase it? Always have had. It was immortal tense. A new rule of grammar. *Always have had* gotten friends killed. *Always have had* a brother die and a mother take her own life. *Always have had* taken that damn job as sheriff.

There was no going back. Apologies weren't welds; they were just an admission that something had been broken. Often between two people.

"You okay?" Lukas asked. "Ready to go on?"

But she knew he was asking more than if her arm was tired. He had this ability to spot her secret worries. He had a keen vision that allowed him to glimpse the smallest pinprick of hurt through heavy clouds.

"I'm fine," she lied. And she searched her past for some noble deed, for a bloodless tread, for any touch on the world that had left it a brighter place. But when she had been sent to clean, she had refused. Always have had refused. She had turned her back and walked off, and there was no chance of going back and doing it any other way.

Nelson was waiting for them in the Suit Lab. He was already prepped and in his second suit, but with his helmet off. The suit Juliette wore outside and the two used to scrub her down had been left in the airlock. Only the radios installed in the collars had been saved. They were as precious as people, Juliette had joked. Nelson and Sophia had already installed them in this pair of suits; Lukas would have a third radio in the hall.

The trunk went on the floor by a cleared workbench; Juliette and Lukas both shook sensation and blood back into their arms. "You've got the door?" she asked Lukas.

He nodded and threw a last frowning glance at the trunk. Juliette could tell he would rather stay and help. He squeezed her arm and kissed her on the cheek before leaving and closing the door. Juliette sat on her cot and squeezed herself into yet another suit and could hear him and Sophia working seal tape around the door. The vents overhead had already been double-bagged. Juliette reckoned there was far less air in the container than she had allowed inside Silo 17—and she had survived that ordeal—but they were still taking every precaution. They were acting as if even one of those containers had enough poison in it to kill everyone in the silo. It was a condition Juliette had insisted upon.

Nelson zipped up her back and folded the velcro flap over, sealing it tight. She tugged on her gloves. Both of their helmets clicked into place. To give them plenty of air and time, she had pulled an oxygen bottle from the acetylene kit. The flow of air was regulated with a small knob, and the overflow spilled out through a set of double valves. Testing the set-up, Juliette had found they could go for days on the trickle of air from the shared tank.

"You good?" she asked Nelson, testing the volume on her radio.

"Yeah," he said. "Ready."

Juliette appreciated the rapport they had developed, the rhythm of two mechanics on the same shift working the same project night after night. Most of their conversations regarded the project, challenges to overcome, tools to pass back and forth. But she had also learned that Nelson's mother used to work with her father, was a nurse before moving down to the Deep to become a doctor. She also learned that Nelson had built the last two cleaning suits, had fitted Holston before cleaning, had just missed being assigned to her. Juliette had decided that this project was as much for his absolution as hers. He had put in long hours that she didn't think she could expect from anyone else. They were both looking to make things right.

Selecting a flat driver from the tool rack, she began scraping caulk from around the lid of the trunk. Nelson chose another driver and worked his side. When their efforts met, she checked with him, and they pried the lid open to reveal the metal container from the airlock bench. Lifting this out, they rested it on a cleared work surface. Juliette hesitated. From the walls, a dozen cleaning suits looked down on them in silent disapproval.

But they had taken all precautions. Even ludicrous ones. The suits they were wearing had been stripped down of all the excess padding, making it easier to work. The gloves as well. Every concession Lukas had asked for, she had provided. It'd been like Shirly with the backup generator and the dig, going so far as to throttle back the main genny to reduce the power load, even rigging the tunnel with blast charges in case of contamination, whatever it took to allow the project to move forward.

Juliette snapped back to the present as she realized Nelson was waiting on her. She grabbed the lid and hinged it open, pulled out the samples. There were two of air, one control sample of argon from the airlock, one each of surface and deep soil, and one of desiccated human remains. They were each placed on the workbench, and then the metal container was set aside.

"Where do you want to start?" Nelson asked. He grabbed a small length of steel pipe with a piece of chalk slotted into the end, an improvised writing device for gloved hands. A blackboard slate stood ready on the bench to take notes.

"Let's start with the air samples," she said. It had already been several hours in getting the samples down to the lab. Her private fear was that there'd be nothing left of the gaskets by now, nothing to observe. Juliette checked the labels on the containers and found the one marked "2." It'd been taken near the hills.

"There's irony here, you know," Nelson said.

Juliette took the sample container from him and peered through the clear plastic top. "What do you mean?"

"It's just..." He turned and checked the clock on the wall and scratched the time onto the slate, glanced back guiltily at Juliette. "Being allowed to do this, to see what's out there, to even talk about it. I mean, I put your suit together. I was lead tech on the sheriff's suit." He frowned behind his clear dome. Juliette could see a shine on his brow. "I remember helping him get dressed."

It was his third or fourth awkward attempt at an apology, and Juliette appreciated it. "You were just doing your job," she assured him. And then she thought about how powerful that sentiment was, how far down a nasty road that could take a person, shuffling along and simply doing their job.

"But the irony is that this room—" He waved a glove at the suits peering down from the walls. "Even my mom thought this room was here to help people, help cleaners survive for as long as possible, help explore the outside world that nobody's supposed to talk about. And finally, here we are. More than talking about it."

Juliette didn't say anything, but he was right. It was a room of both hope and dread. "What we yearn to find and what's out there are two different things," she eventually said. "Let's stay focused."

Nelson nodded and readied his chalk. Juliette shook the first sample container until the two gaskets inside separated. The durable one from Supply was perfectly whole. The yellow marks on the edge were still there. The other gasket was in far worse shape. Its red marks were already gone, the edges eaten away by the air inside the container. The same was true of the two samples of heat tape adhered to the bottom. The square piece from Supply was intact. She had cut the one from IT into a triangle in order to tell them apart. It had a small hole eaten through it.

"I'd say an eighth gone on the sample two gasket," Juliette said. "One hole in the heat tape three millimeters across. Both Supply samples appear fine."

Nelson wrote her observations down. This was how she had decided to measure the toxicity of the air, by using the seals and heat tape designed to rot out there and compare it to the ones she knew would last. She passed him the container so he could verify and realized that this was their first bit of data. This was confirmation as great as her survival on the outside. The equipment pulled from the cleaning suit storage bays was meant to fail. Juliette felt chills at the momentous nature of this first step.

Already, her mind raced with all the experiments to perform next. And they hadn't yet opened the containers to see what the air inside was like.

"I confirm an eighth of wear on the gasket," Nelson said, peering inside the container. "I would go two and a half mils on the tape."

"Mark two and a half," she said. One way she would change this next time would be to keep their own slates. Her observations might affect his and vice versa. So much to learn. She grabbed the next sample while Nelson scratched his numbers.

"Sample one," she said. "This one was from the ramp." Peering inside, she spotted the whole gasket that had to be from Supply. The other gasket was half worn. It had nearly pinched all the way through in one place. Tipping the container upside down and rattling it, she was able to get the gasket to rest against the clear lid. "That can't be right," she said. "Let's see that lamp."

Nelson swiveled the arm of the worklight toward her. Juliette aimed it upward, bent over the workbench, and twisted her body and head awkwardly to peer past the dilapidated gasket toward the shiny heat tape beyond.

"I . . . I'd say half wear on the gasket. Holes in the heat tape five . . . no, six mils across. I need you to look at this."

Nelson marked down her numbers before taking the sample. He returned the light to his side of the bench. She hadn't expected a huge difference between the two samples, but if one sample was worse, it should be the one from the hills, not the ramp. Not where they were pumping out good air.

"Maybe I pulled them out in the wrong order," she said. She grabbed the next sample, the control. She'd been so careful outside, but she did remember her thoughts being scrambled. She had lost count at one point, had held one of the canisters open too long. That's what it was.

"I confirm," Nelson said. "A lot more wear on these. Are you sure this one was from the ramp?"

"I think I screwed up. I held one of them open too long. Dammit. We might have to throw those numbers out, at least for any comparison."

"That's why we took more than one sample," Nelson said. He coughed into his helmet, which fogged the dome in front of his face. He cleared his throat. "Don't beat yourself up."

He knew her well enough. Juliette grabbed the control sample, cursing herself under her breath, and wondered what Lukas was thinking out there in the hall, listening in on his radio. "Last one," she said, rattling the container.

Nelson waited, chalk poised above the slate. "Go ahead."

"I don't . . ." She aimed the light inside. She rattled the container. Sweat trickled down her jaw and dripped from her chin. "I thought this was the control," she said. She set the sample down and grabbed the next container, but it was full of soil. Her heart was pounding, her head spinning. None of this made sense. Unless she'd pulled the samples out in the wrong order. Had she screwed it all up?

"Yeah, that's the control sample," Nelson said. He tapped the canister she'd just checked with his length of pipe. "It's marked right there."

"Gimme a sec," she said. Juliette took a few deep breaths. She peered inside the control sample once again, which had been collected inside the airlock. It should have captured nothing but argon. She handed the container to Nelson.

"Yeah, that's not right," he said. He shook the container. "Something's not right."

Juliette could barely hear. Her mind raced. Nelson peered inside the control sample.

"I think . . ." He hesitated. "I think maybe a seal fell out when you opened the lid. Which is no big deal. These things happen. Or maybe . . ."

"Impossible," she said. She had been careful. She remembered seeing the seals in there. Nelson cleared his throat and placed the control sample on the workbench. He adjusted the worklight to point directly down into it. Both of them leaned over. Nothing had fallen out, she was sure of it. But then, she had made mistakes. Everyone was capable of them—

"There's only one seal in there," Nelson said. "I really think maybe it fell—"

"The heat tape," Juliette said. She adjusted the light. There was a flash from the bottom of the container where a piece of tape was stuck. The other piece was gone. "Are you telling me that an adhered piece of tape fell out as well?"

"Well then, containers are out of order," he said. "We have them backwards. This makes perfect sense if we got them all backwards. Because the one from the hill isn't quite as worn as the ramp sample. That's what it is."

Juliette had thought of that, but it was an attempt to match what she thought she knew to what she was seeing. The whole point of going out was to confirm suspicions. What did it mean that she was seeing something completely different?

And then it hit her like a wrench to the skull. It hit her like a great betrayal. A betrayal by a machine that was always good to her, like a trusted pump that suddenly ran backwards for no apparent reason. It hit her like a loved one turning his back while she was falling, like some great bond that wasn't simply taken away but never truly existed.

"Luke," she said, hoping he was listening, that he had his radio on. She waited. Nelson coughed.

"I'm here," he answered, his voice thin and distant. "I've been following."

“The argon,” Juliette said, watching Nelson through both of their domes. “What do we know about it?”

Nelson blinked the sweat from his eyes.

“Know what?” Lukas said. “There’s a periodic table in there somewhere. Inside one of the cabinets, I think.”

“No,” Juliette said, raising her voice so she could be sure he heard. “I mean, where does it come from? Are we even sure what it is?”

Silo 1

25

THERE WAS A rattle in Donald's chest, a flapping of some loosely connected thing, an internal alarm that his condition was deteriorating—that he was getting worse. He forced himself to cough, as much as he hated to, as much as his diaphragm was sore from the effort, as much as his throat burned and muscles ached. He leaned forward in his chair and hacked until something deep inside him tore loose and skittered across his tongue, was spat into his square of fetid cloth.

He folded the cloth rather than look and collapsed back into his chair, sweaty and exhausted. He took a deep, less-rattly breath. Another. A handful of cool gasps that didn't quite torture him. Had anything ever felt so great as a painless breath?

Glancing around the room in a daze, he absorbed all that he had once taken for granted: remnants of meals, a deck of cards, a butterflied paperback with browned pages and striated spine—signs of shifts endured but not suffered. He was suffering. He suffered the wait before Silo 18 answered. He studied the schematic of all the other silos that he fretted over. Dead worlds is what he saw. All of them would die except for one. There was a tickle in his throat, and he knew for certain that he would be dead before he decided anything, before he found some way to help or choose or steer the project off its suicidal course. He was the only one who knew or cared—and his knowledge and compassion would be buried with him.

What was he thinking, anyway? That he could fix things? That he could put right a world he had helped destroy? The world was long past fixing. The world was long past setting to right. One glimpse of green fields and blue skies from a drone, and his mind had tumbled out of sorts. Now it'd been so long since that one glimpse that he'd begun to doubt it. He knew how the cleanings worked. He knew better than to trust the vision of some machine.

But foolish hope had him there, in that comm room, reaching out once more. Foolish hope had him dreaming of a stop to it all, some way to let these silos full of people live their own lives, free of all this meddling. It was curiosity as well, wanting to know what was going on in those servers, the last great mystery, one he could explore only with the help of this IT Head he had inducted himself. Donald just wanted answers. He longed for truth and for a painless death for himself and for Charlotte. An end to shifts and dreams. A final resting place, perhaps, up on that hill with a view of Helen's grave. It wasn't too much to hope for, he didn't think.

He checked the clock on the wall. They were late to answer. Fifteen minutes already. Something was happening. He watched the second hand jitter around and realized the entire operation, all of the silos, was like a giant clock. The whole thing ran on automatic. It was winding down.

Invisible machines rode the winds around the planet, destroying anything human, returning the world to wilderness. The people buried underground were dormant seeds that would have to wait another two hundred years before they sprouted. Two hundred years. Donald felt his throat begin to tickle once more and wondered if he had two *days* in him.

At that moment, he only had fifteen minutes. Fifteen minutes before the operators would come back on shift. These sessions of his had grown regular. It was not unusual to clear everyone out for classified discussions, but it was beginning to seem suspicious that he did it every day at the same exact time. He could see the way they looked at one another as they took their mugs and filed out. Probably thought it was some romance. Donald often felt as if it were a romance of sorts. A romance of olden times and truth.

Now he was being stood up. Half of this session had been wasted on listening to the line buzz and go unanswered. Something was happening over there. Something bad. Or maybe he was on edge from the reports of a dead body found in his own silo, some murder the folks in Security were looking into. It was strange that this barely stirred him. He cared more about other silos, had lost all empathy for his own.

There was a click in his ringing headset. "Hello?" he asked, his voice tired and weak. He trusted the machines to make him sound stronger.

There was no reply, just the sound of someone breathing. But that was good enough for an introduction. Lukas never failed to say hello.

"Mayor," he said.

"You know I don't like being called that," she said. She sounded winded, as though she'd been running.

"You prefer Juliette?"

Silence. Donald wondered why he preferred to hear from her. Lukas, he was fond of. He had been there when the young man took his Rite, and Donald admired his curiosity, his study of the Legacy. It filled him with nostalgia to talk about the old world with Lukas. It was a therapy of sorts. And Lukas was the one helping him pry the lid off those servers to study their contents.

With Juliette, the allure was something different. It was the accusations and abuse, which he knew he fully deserved. It was the harsh silences and the threats. There was some part of Donald that wanted her to come end him before his cough could. Humiliation and execution—that was his path to exoneration.

"I know how you're doing it," Juliette finally said, fire in her voice. Venom. "I finally understand. I figured it out."

Donald peeled his headset from one ear and wiped a trickle of sweat. "What do you understand?" he asked. He wondered if Lukas had uncovered something in one of the servers, something to set Juliette off.

"The cleanings," she spat.

Donald checked the clock. Fifteen minutes were going to slip by in a hurry. The person reading that novel would be back soon, as well as the techs in the middle of that game of cards. "I'm happy to talk about the cleanings—"

"I've just been outside," she told him.

Donald covered his microphone and coughed. "Outside where?" he asked. He thought of the tunnel she claimed to be digging, the racket they had been making over there that had recently gone silent. He thought she meant she'd been beyond the boundaries of her silo.

"*Outside* outside. The hills. The world the ancients left behind. I took samples."

Donald leaned forward in his seat. She meant to threaten him, but all he heard was a promise. She meant to torture him, but all he felt was excitement. *Outside*. And to take samples. He dreamed of such a venture. Dreamed of discovering what he had breathed out there, what they had done to the world, if it was getting better or worse. Juliette must think *he* held the answers, but he had nothing but questions.

"What did you find?" he whispered. And he damned the machines that would make him sound disinterested, that would make him sound as if he knew. Why couldn't he just say that he had no idea what was wrong with the world or with himself and please, please help him? Help each other.

"You aren't sending us out there to clean. You're sending something else. I'll tell you what I found—"

To Donald, her voice was the entire universe. The weight of the soil overhead vanished, as did the solidness beneath his feet. It was just him in a bubble, and that voice.

"—we took two samples and another from the airlock that should've been inert gas. We took a sample from the ramp and one from the hills."

Suddenly, he was the silent one. His coveralls clung to him. He waited and waited, but she outlasted him. She wanted him to beg for it. Maybe she knew how lost he was.

"What did you find?" he asked again.

"That you're a lying sack of ratshit. That everything we've been told, any time we've trusted you, we've been fools. We take for granted everything you show us, everything you tell us, and none of it's true. Maybe there were no ancients. You know these goddamn books over here? Burn them all. And you let Lukas believe this crap—"

"The books are real," Donald said.

"Ratshit. Like the argon? Is the argon real? What the hell are you pumping into the airlocks when we go out to clean?"

Donald repeated her question in his head. "What do you mean?" he asked.

"Stop with the games. I know what's going on now. When you send us outside, you pump our airlocks full of something that eats away at us. It takes the seals and gaskets first, and then our bodies. You've got it down to a science, haven't you? Well, I found the camera feeds you hid. I cut them weeks ago. Yeah, that was me. And I saw the power lines coming in. I saw the pipes. The gas is in the pipes, isn't it?"

"Juliette, listen to me—"

"Don't you say my name like you know me. You don't know me. All these talks, telling me how my silo was built like you built it yourself, telling Lukas about a disappeared world like you'd seen it with your own eyes. Were you trying to get us to like you? To think you were our friend? Saying you want to help us?"

Donald watched the clock tick down. The techs would be back soon. He'd have to yell at them to get out. He couldn't leave the conversation like this.

"Stop calling us," Juliette said. "The buzzing and the flashing lights, it's giving us headaches. If you keep doing this every day, I'm going to start tearing shit down, and I've got enough to worry about."

"Listen . . . Please—"

"No, you listen. You are cut off from us. We don't want your cameras, your power, your gas. I'm cutting it all. And no one will ever clean from here again. No more of this bullshit argon. The next time I go out, it'll be with clean air. Now fuck off and leave us to it."

"Juliette—"

But the line was dead.

Donald pulled his headset off and threw it against the desk. Playing cards scattered, and the book fell from its perch, losing someone's place.

Argon? What the hell had come over her? The last time she'd been so angry was when she said she had found some machine, threatened to come after him. But this was something else. Argon. Pumped out with a cleaning. He had no idea what she was talking about. Pumped out with a cleaning—

A bout of dizziness struck him, and Donald sank back into his chair. His coveralls were damp with sweat. He clutched a bloody rag and remembered a fog-filled airlock. He remembered stumbling down a ramp with a jostling crowd, crying for

Helen, the vision of bomb blasts seared in his retinas, Anna and Charlotte tugging him along, while a white cloud billowed out around him.

The gas. He knew how the cleanings went. There was gas to pressurize the airlock. Gas to push against the outside air. Gas to push *out*.

"The dust is in the air," Donald said. He leaned against the counter, his knees weak. The nanos eating away at mankind, they were loosed on the world with every cleaning, little puffs like clockwork, tick-tock with each exile.

The headphones sat there quietly. "I am an ancient," Donald said, using her words. He grabbed the headphones from the desk and repeated into the microphone, loudly, "I am an ancient! I did this!"

He sagged once more against the desk, catching himself before he fell. "I'm sorry," he muttered. "I'm sorry, I'm sorry." Louder, yelling it: "I'm sorry!"

But nobody was listening.

26

CHARLOTTE WORKED THE aileron on the drone's left wing up and down. There was still a bit of play in the cables that guided the flap. She grabbed a work rag hanging from the drone's tail and dabbed the back of her neck. Reaching into her tool bag, she chose a medium driver. Beneath the drone lay a scattering of parts, everything she could find inside that the drone didn't need. The bombing computer, the munitions mounts from the wings, the release servos. She'd taken out every camera but one, had even stripped out some of the bracing struts that helped the drone pull up to a dozen Gs. This would be a straight flight, no stress on the wings. They would go low and fast this time, not caring if the drone was spotted. It was important to see further, to make sure, to verify. Charlotte had spent a week working on the blasted thing, and all she could think about was how quickly the last two had broken down and how lucky that first flight now seemed.

Lying on her back, she worked her shoulders and hips and squirmed beneath the tail of the drone. The access panel was already open, the cables exposed. Every panel would get a fine bead of caulk before it went back together, sealing the machine against the dust. *This'll work,* she told herself as she adjusted the servo arm holding the cable. It would have to. Seeing her brother, the state he was in, had her thinking they didn't have another flight in them. It would be all or nothing. It wasn't just the coughing—he now seemed to be losing his mind.

He had come back from his latest call and had forgotten to bring her dinner. He had also forgotten the last part for the radio he had promised. Now he paced around the drone while she worked, mumbling to himself. He paced down the hall to the conference room and dug through his notes. He stomped back toward the drone, coughing and picking up a conversation she didn't feel a part of.

"—their fear, don't you see? We do it with their fear."

She peeked out from under the drone to see him waving his hands in the air. He looked ashen. There were specks of blood on his coveralls. It was almost time to throw in the towel, get in that lift, turn them both in. Just so he would see someone.

He caught her looking at him.

"Their fear doesn't just color the world they see," he said, his eyes wild. "They poison the world with it. It's a toxin, this fear. They send their own out to clean, and that poisons the world!"

Charlotte didn't know how to respond. She wiggled back out to work the aileron again, thinking of how much faster this would go with two people. She considered asking for his help, but her brother couldn't seem to stand still, much less hold a wrench.

"And this got me thinking, about the gas. I mean, I should have known, right? We pump it into their homes when we're done with them. That's how we end their existence. It's all the same gas. I've done it." Donald walked in a tight circle, jabbing his chest with his finger. He coughed into the crook of his arm. "God knows I've done it. But that's not the only thing!"

Charlotte sighed and pulled her driver back out. Still a touch too loose.

"Maybe they can twist this around, you know?" He began to

wander back to the conference room. "They turned off their cameras. And there was that silo that turned off its demolitions. Maybe they can turn off the gas—"

His voice trailed off with him. Charlotte studied the hallway at the back of the warehouse. The light spilling from the conference room danced with his shadow as he paced back and forth among his notes and charts, walking in circles. They were both stuck in circles. She could hear him cursing. His erratic behavior reminded her of their grandmother, who had gone ungracefully. This would be how she remembered him when he was gone: coughing up blood and babbling nonsense. He would never be Congressman Keene in a pressed suit, never her older and competent brother, never again.

While he agonized over what to do, Charlotte had her own ideas. How about they wake everyone up like Donald had done for her? There were only a hundred or so men on shift at any one time. There were thousands of women asleep. Many thousands. Charlotte thought of the army she could raise. But she wondered if Donny was right—if they would refuse to fight their fathers and husbands and brothers. It took a strange kind of courage to do that.

The light down the hall wavered again with shadows. Pacing back and forth, back and forth. Charlotte took a deep breath and worked the flap on the wing. She thought about his other idea to set the world straight, to clear the air and free the imprisoned. Or at least to give them all a chance. An equal chance. He had likened it to knocking down borders in the old world. There was some saying he repeated about those who had an advantage and wanted to keep it, about the last ones up pulling the ladder after them. "Let's lower the ladders," he had said more than once. Don't let the computers decide. Let the people.

Charlotte still didn't get how that might work. And neither, obviously, did her brother. She wiggled back under the drone and tried to imagine a time when people were born into their jobs, when they had no choice. First sons did what their fathers did. Second sons went to war, to the sea, or to the Church. Any boy who followed was left on his own. Daughters went to the sons of others.

Her wrench slipped off the cable stay—her knuckles banging the fuselage. Charlotte cursed and studied her hand, saw blood welling up. She sucked on her knuckle and remembered another injustice that had once given her pause. She remembered being on deployment and feeling grateful that she was born in the States, not in Iraq. A roll of the dice. Invisible borders drawn on maps that were as real as the walls of silos. Trapped by circumstance. What life you lived was divined by some calculus of your people, your leaders, like computers tallying your fate.

She crawled out once again and tried the wing. The play in the cable was gone. The drone was in the best condition Charlotte could make her. She gathered the wrenches she would no longer need and began slotting them into her tool bag when there was a ding at the end of the shelves, off toward the lifts.

Charlotte froze. Her first thought was of food. The ding meant Donny bringing her food. But her brother's shadow could be seen down the hall.

She heard a lift door slide open. Someone was running. Several someones. Boots rang out like thunder, and Charlotte risked yelling Donald's name. She shouted it down the hall once before rushing around the drone and grabbing the tarp. She spun the tarp like a fisherman's net across the wide wings and the scattering of parts and tools. Had to hide. Hide her work and then herself. Donny had heard her. He would hide as well.

The tarp drifted to the ground on a cushion of trapped air; it billowed out and settled. Charlotte turned toward the hallway to run to Donny just as men spilled from the tall shelves. She fell to the ground at once, certain she'd been spotted. Boots clomped past. Gripping the edge of the tarp, she lifted it slowly and curled her knees against her body. She used her shoulder and hip to wiggle underneath the tarp to join the drone. Donny had heard her call out. He would hear the boots and hide in the bathroom attached to the conference room, hide in the shower. Somewhere. They couldn't know they were down there. How had these people gotten in? Her brother said he had the highest access.

The running receded. They were heading straight to the back of the warehouse, almost as if they knew. Voices nearby. Men talking. Slower footsteps shuffling past the drone. Charlotte thought she heard Donny cry out as he was discovered. Crawling on her belly, she scooted beneath the drone to the other edge of the tarp. The voices were fading, slow footsteps walking past. Her brother was in trouble. She remembered a conversation from a few days prior and wondered if he'd been recognized in the lift. A handyman had seen him. The darkness beneath the tarp closed in around her at the thought of being left alone, of him being taken. She relied on him. She was going crazy enough locked in that warehouse with him to keep her company. Without him—she didn't want to imagine.

Resting her chin on the cool steel plating, she slid her arms forward and lifted the tarp with the backs of her hands. A low sliver of the world was exposed. She could see boots dangerously close. She could smell oil on the decking. Ahead of her, it looked like a man having a hard time walking, another man in silver coveralls helping to support him, their feet shuffling along as if with a single mind.

Beyond them, a hallway was thrown into brightness; all the overhead lights Donny preferred to leave off were now on. Charlotte sucked in her breath as her brother was pulled from the conference room. One of the men in the bright silver coveralls punched him in the ribs. Her brother grunted, and Charlotte felt the blow to her own side. She dropped the tarp with one hand and covered her mouth in horror. The other hand trembled as it lifted the tarp further, not wanting to see but needing to. Her brother was hit again, but the shuffling man waved an arm. She could hear a feeble voice commanding them to stop.

The two men in silver held her brother down on the ground and did as they were told. Charlotte forgot to breathe as she watched the man who shuffled along as if weak—watched him march into the lit hallway. He had white hair as brilliant as the bulbs overhead. He labored to walk, leaned on the young man beside him, arm draped across his back, until he came to a stop by her brother.

Charlotte could see Donny's eyes. He was fifty meters away, but she could see how wide they were. Her brother stared up at this old and feeble man, didn't look away even as he coughed, a bad fit from the blow to his ribs, drowning out something being said by the man who could barely stand.

Her brother tried to speak. He said something over and over, but she couldn't hear. And the thin man with the white hair could barely stand, could barely stand but could still swing his boots. The young man beside him propped him up, and Charlotte watched, cowed and trembling, as a leg was brought back over and over before lashing forward, a heavy boot slamming into her brother with ferocious might, Donny's own legs scrambling to shield himself, hugging his shins as two men pinned him to the ground, giving him nowhere to hide from kick after brutal, stomping, and angry kick.

Silo 18

27

"ARE YOU SURE you should be digging around in there?" Lukas asked.

"Hold the light still," Juliette said. "I've got one more to go."

"But shouldn't we talk about this?"

"I'm just looking, Luke. Except that right now, I can't see a damn thing."

Lukas adjusted the light, and Juliette crawled forward. It was the second time she'd explored beneath the floor grates at the bottom of the server room ladder. It was here that she'd traced the camera feeds over a month ago, soon after Lukas made her mayor. He had shown her how they could see anywhere within the silo, and Juliette had asked who else could see. Lukas had insisted no one until she found the feeds disappearing through a sealed port where the outer edge of the silo wall should be. She remembered seeing other lines in that bundle. Now she wanted to make sure.

She worked the last screw on the cover panel. It came off, exposing the dozens of wires she'd cut, each of them bursting with hundreds of tiny filaments like silver strands of hair. Running parallel to the bundles were thick cables that reminded her of the main feeds from the two generators in Mechanical. There were also two copper pipes buried in there.

"Have you seen enough?" Lukas asked. He crouched down behind her where the floor grating had been removed and aimed the light over her shoulder.

"In the other silo, this level still has power. All of thirty-four has full power with no generator running." She tapped the thick cables with her driver. "The servers over there are still humming as well. And some of the survivors tapped into that power to run pumps and things up and down the silo. I think all that juice comes from here."

"Why?" Lukas asked. He played the light across the bundle and seemed more interested now.

"Because they needed the power for the pumps and grow lights," Juliette said, amazed she had to spell it out.

"No, why are they providing this power in the first place?"

"Maybe they don't trust us to keep things running on our own. Or maybe the servers require more juice than we can generate. I don't know." She leaned to the side and peered back at Lukas. "What I want to know is why they left it running after they tried to kill everyone. Why not shut it off with everything else?"

"Maybe they did. Maybe your friend hacked in here and turned it back on."

Juliette laughed. "No. Not Solo—"

There was a voice down the hall. The crawl space grew dark as Lukas spun the flashlight around. There shouldn't have been anyone else down there.

"It's the radio," he said. "Let me see who it is."

"The flashlight," Juliette called out—but he was already gone. His boots rang and faded down the hallway.

Juliette reached ahead of herself and felt for the copper pipes. They were the right size. Nelson had shown her where the argon tanks were kept. There was a pump and filter mechanism that was supposed to draw a fresh supply of argon from deep within the earth, similar to how the air handlers worked. But now Juliette knew to trust nothing. Pulling out the floor panels and the wall panels behind the tanks, she had discovered two lines feeding into the gas tanks separate from the supply system. A supply system she now suspected did absolutely nothing. Just like with the gaskets and heat tape, the second power feed, the visor of lies, everything had a false front. The truth lay buried beneath.

Lukas stomped back toward her. He knelt down, and the light returned to the crawlspace.

"Jules, I need you to get out of there."

"Please hand me the flashlight," she told him. "I can't see shit." This was going to be another argument like when she'd cut the camera feeds. As if she would cut these pipes without knowing what was in them—

"I need you to get out here. I . . . please."

And she heard it in his voice. Something was wrong. Juliette looked back and caught an eyeful of flashlight.

"One sec," she said. She wiggled back toward him on her palms and the toes of her boots until she reached the open access panel. She left her multi-tool behind.

"What is it?" She sat up and stretched her back, untied her hair, gathered the loose ends, and began tying it back. "Who was that?"

"Your father—" Lukas began.

"Something wrong with my father?"

He shook his head. "No, that was him that called. It . . . one of the kids is gone."

"Missing?" But she knew that wasn't what he meant. "Lukas, what happened?" She stood and dusted off her chest and knees, headed toward the radio.

"They were on their way up to the farms. There was a crowd heading down. One of the kids went over the rails—"

"Fell?"

"Twenty levels," Lukas said.

Juliette couldn't believe this. She grabbed the radio and pressed a palm against the wall, suddenly dizzy. "Who was it?"

"He didn't say."

Before she squeezed the mic, she saw that the set had been left on channel 17 from the last time she'd called Jimmy. Her dad must've been using Walker's new portable. "Dad? Do you read me?"

She waited. Lukas held out his canteen, but Juliette waved him away.

"Jules? Can I get back to you? Something else has just come up."

Her father sounded shaken. There was a lot of static in the line. "I need to know what's going on," she told him.

"Hold on. Elise—"

Juliette covered her mouth.

"—we've lost Elise. Jimmy went looking for her. Baby, we had a problem coming up. There was a crowd heading down. An angry crowd. They knew who I had with me. And Marcus went over the rails. I'm sorry—"

Juliette felt Lukas's hand on her shoulder. She wiped her eyes. "Is he—?"

"I haven't made my way down yet to check. Rickson got hurt in the scuffle. I'm tending to him. Hannah and Miles and the baby are fine. We're at Supply right now. Look, I really need to go. We can't find Elise, and Jimmy took off after her. Someone said they saw her heading up. I don't want you to do anything, but I thought you'd want to know about the boy."

Her hand trembled as she squeezed the mic. "I'm coming down. You're at Supply on one-ten?"

There was a long pause. She knew he was debating whether

or not to argue with her about heading that way. The radio popped as he gave up without a fight.

"I'm at one-ten, yeah. I'm heading down to see about the boy. I'll leave Rickson and the others here. I told Jimmy to bring Elise back here once he finds her."

"Don't leave them there," Juliette said. She didn't know whom they could trust, where they might be safe. "Take them with you. Dad, get them back to Mechanical. Get them home." Juliette wiped her forehead. The entire thing was a mistake. Bringing them over was a mistake.

"Are you sure?" her father asked. "The crowd we ran into. I think they were heading that way."

28

ELISE WAS LOST in the bizarre. She had heard someone call it that, and it was the right name for the place, a place of crowds beyond imagining, a land so wildly strange that its name barely did it justice.

How she found herself there was a bit bewildering. Her puppy had disappeared in a great confrontation of strangers—more people than she thought could exist at one time—and she had chased up the steps after it. One person after another had pointed helpfully upward. A woman in yellow said she saw a man with a dog heading toward the bizarre. Elise had gone up ten levels until she'd reached landing one-hundred.

There had been two men on the landing blowing smoke from their noses. They had said someone just passed through with a dog. They had waved her inside.

Level one-hundred in her home was a scary wasteland of narrow passages and empty rooms scattered with trash and debris and rats. Here it was all of that but full of people and animals and everyone shouting and singing. It was a place of bright colors and awful smells, of people breathing smoke in and out, smoke they held in their fingers and kept going with small sparks of fire. There were men who wore paint on their faces. A woman dressed all in red with a tail and horns who had waved Elise inside a tent, but Elise had turned and ran.

She ran from one fright to another until she was completely lost. There were knees everywhere to bump into. No longer looking for Puppy, now she just wanted out. She crawled beneath a busy counter and cried, but that got her nowhere. It did give her a terribly close view of a fat and hairless animal that made noises like Rickson snoring, though. This animal was led right by her with a rope around its neck. Elise dried her eyes and pulled her book out, looked through pictures until she could name it a pig. Naming things always helped. They weren't nearly so scary after that.

It was Rickson who got her moving again, even though he wasn't there. Elise could hear his loud voice booming through the Wilds telling her there was nothing to be afraid of. He and the twins used to send her on errands through the pitch black when she was just old enough to walk. They would send her for blackberries and plums and delicacies near the stairs when there were people still around to fear. "The littlest ones are the safest," Rickson used to tell her. That was years ago. She wasn't so little anymore.

She put her book away and decided that the dark Wilds with their leafy fingers brushing her neck and the clicking of pumps and chattering teeth were worse than painted people leaking smoke from their noses. With her face chapped from crying, she crawled out from beneath the counter and jostled among the knees. Always turning right—which was the trick to getting through the Wilds in the dark—she found herself in a smoky hallway with loud hisses and a smell in the air like boiling rat.

"Hey, kid, you lost?"

A boy with short-cropped hair and bright green eyes studied her from the edge of a booth. He was older than her, but not by much. As big as the twins. Elise shook her head. She reconsidered and nodded.

The boy laughed. "What's your name?"

"Elise," she said.

"That's a different name."

She shrugged, not sure what to say. The boy caught her eyeing a man beyond him as he lifted strips of sizzling meat with a large fork.

"You hungry?" the boy asked.

Elise nodded. She was always hungry. Especially when she was scared. But maybe that was because she got scared when she went out looking for food, and she went out looking for food when she was hungry. Hard to remember which came first. The boy disappeared behind the counter. He came back with a thick piece of meat.

"Is it rat?" Elise asked.

The boy laughed. "It's pig."

Elise scrunched up her face, remembering the animal that grunted at her earlier. "Does it taste like rat?" she asked, full of hope.

"You say that louder and my dad'll have your hide. You want some or not?" He handed the strip of meat over. "I'm guessing you don't have two chits on you."

Elise accepted the meat and didn't say. She took a small bite, and little bursts of happiness exploded in her mouth. It was better than rat. The boy studied her.

"You're from the Mids, aren't you?"

Elise shook her head and took another bite. "I'm from Silo Seventeen," she said, chewing. Her mouth was full of saliva. She eyed the man cooking the strips of meat. Marcus and Miles should be there to try some.

"You mean level seventeen?" The boy frowned. "You don't look like a topper. No, too dirty to be a topper."

"I'm from the other silo," Elise said. "West of here."

"What's a westophere?" the boy asked.

"West. Where the sun sets."

The boy looked at her funny.

"The sun. It comes up in the east and sets in the west. That's why maps point up. They point up at north." She thought about pulling her book out and showing him the maps of the world, explaining how the sun went around and around, but her hands were covered in grease, and anyway the boy didn't seem interested. "They dug over and rescued us," she explained.

At this, the boy's eyes went wide. "The dig. You're from the other silo. It's real?"

Elise finished the strip of pig and licked her fingers. She nodded.

The boy shoved a hand at her. Elise wiped her palm on her hip and grabbed it with her own.

"My name's Shaw," he said. "You want another piece of pig? Come under the counter. I'll introduce you to my father. Hey, Pa, I want you to meet someone."

"I can't. I'm looking for Puppy."

Shaw scrunched up his face. "Puppy? You'd want the next hall over." He nodded the direction. "But c'mon, pig is much better. Dog is chewy like rat, and puppy is just more expensive than dog but tastes the same."

Elise froze. The pig that went by earlier with a rope around its neck, maybe that one was a pet. Maybe they ate pets, just like Marcus and Miles always wanted to keep a rat for fun, even when everyone else was hungry. "They eat puppy?" she asked this boy.

"If you've got the chits, sure." Shaw grabbed her hand. "Come back to the grill with me. I want you to meet my dad. He says you all aren't real."

Elise pulled away. "I've got to find my puppy." She turned

and scurried through the crowd in the direction the boy had nodded.

"Whaddya mean, *your* puppy—?" he yelled after her.

Around a line of stalls, Elise found another smoky hall. More smells like rat on a stick over an open flame. An old woman wrestled with a bird, two angry wings flapping from her fists. Elise stepped in poop and nearly slipped. The strangeness all around melted with the thought of her puppy gone. She heard someone yell about a dog, and searched for the voice. An older boy, probably Rickson's age, was holding up a piece of red meat, a giant piece with white stripes that looked like bones. There was a pen there and signs with numbers on them. People from the crowd stopped to peer inside. Some of them pointed inside the pen and asked questions.

Elise fought through them toward the sound of yipping. There were live dogs in the pen. She could see through the slats and almost over the top when she was on her tiptoes. A huge animal the size of a pig lunged at the fence and growled at her, and the fence shook. It was a dog, but with a rope around its jaw so it couldn't open. Elise could feel its hot breath blowing out its nose. She scooted out of everyone's way and around the side.

There was a smaller pen in the back. Elise went past the counter to where two young men tended a smoking grill. Their backs were turned. They took something from a woman and handed her a package. Elise grabbed the top of the smaller fence and peered over. There was a dog on its side with five—no, six little animals eating at its belly. She thought they were rats at first, but they were the tiniest of puppies. They made Puppy seem like a grown dog. And they weren't eating the dog—they were sucking like Hannah's baby did at her breast.

Elise was so fixated on the tiny critters that she didn't see the animal at the base of the fence lunge at her until it was too late. A black nose and a pink tongue bounced up and caught her on the jaw. She peered directly down the other side of the fence and saw Puppy, who bounded up at her again.

Elise cried out. Reaching over the fence, she had both hands on the animal, when someone grabbed her from behind.

"Don't think you can afford that one," one of the men behind the counter said.

Elise squirmed in his grip and tried to keep a hold of Puppy.

"Easy now," the man said. "Let it go."

"Let *me* go!" Elise cried.

Puppy slipped from her grasp. Elise wiggled loose, the shoulder strap of her bag yanked over her head. She fell at the man's feet and got back up, reached for Puppy again.

"Well, now," she heard the man say.

Elise reached over the fence and grabbed her pet again. Puppy's feet scratched at the fence to help. His front paws draped over her shoulder, a wet tongue in her ear. Elise turned to find a man towering over her, a bloody white piece of fabric tied over his chest, her Memory Book in his hands.

"What's this?" he asked, thumbing through the pages. A few of the loose papers shuffled free and he grabbed at them frantically.

"That's my book," Elise said. "Give it back."

The man peered down at her. Puppy licked her face.

"Trade you for that one," he said, pointing at Puppy.

"They're both mine," she insisted.

"Naw, I paid for that runt. But this'll do." He weighed her book in his hands, then reached down and steered Elise out of the booth and back toward the crowded hall.

Elise reached for the book. Her bag was being left behind. Puppy nipped her on the hand and nearly squirmed free. She was crying, she realized, as she squealed for the man to give her back her things. He showed his teeth and grabbed her by the hair, was angry now. "Roy! Come grab this runt."

Elise screeched. The boy from outside yelling "dog" to everyone who passed by headed toward her. Puppy was nearly free. She was losing her grip again, and the man was going to rip out her hair.

She lost Puppy, and Elise squealed as the man lifted her off the ground. Then there was a flash, like a dog pouncing, but it was brown coveralls rather than brown fur that flew past, and the large man let out a grunt and fell to the ground. Elise went spilling after.

He no longer had a grip on her hair. Elise saw her bag. Her book. She grabbed both, clutched a handful of loose pages. Shaw was there, the boy who fed her pig. He scooped up Puppy and grinned at Elise.

"Run," he said, flashing his teeth.

Elise ran. She danced away from the boy in the hall and bounced off people in the crowd. Looking over her shoulder, she saw Shaw running after her, Puppy clutched to his chest upside down, paws in the air. The crowd rattled and made room as the men from the stall came after them.

"This way!" Shaw yelled, laughing, as he overtook Elise and turned a corner. Tears streamed from her eyes, but Elise was laughing too. Laughing and terrified and happy to have her book and her pet and getting away and this boy who was nicer to her than the twins. They dashed beneath another of the counters—the smell of fresh fruit—and someone yelled at them. Shaw ran through a dark room with unmade beds, through a kitchen with a woman cooking, then back out into another stall. A tall man with dark skin shook a spatula at them, but they were already out among the crowds, running and laughing and dancing between—

And then someone in the crowd snatched him up. Large and powerful hands jerked the boy into the air. Elise stumbled. Shaw kicked and screamed at this man, and Elise looked up and saw that it was Solo holding him. He smiled down at Elise through his thick beard.

"Solo!" Elise squealed. She grabbed his leg and squeezed.

"This boy got something of yours?" he asked.

"No, he's a friend. Put him down." She scanned the crowd for any sign of the men chasing them. "We should go," she told Solo. She squeezed his leg once more. "I want to go home."

Solo rubbed her head. "And that's just where we're heading."

29

ELISE LET SOLO carry her bag and her book while she clutched Puppy. They made their way through the crowds, out of the bizarre, and back to the stairwell. Shaw trailed after them, even after Solo told the boy to get back to his family. And as Elise and Solo made their way down the stairwell to find the others, she kept glancing back to catch sight of Shaw in his brown coveralls, peeking from around the central post or through the rails of a landing higher up. She thought about telling Solo that he was still there, but she didn't.

A few levels below the bizarre, a porter caught up to them and delivered a message. Jewel was heading down and looking for them. She had half the porters hunting for Elise. And Elise never knew that she'd been missing.

Solo made her drink from his canteen while they waited at the next landing. She then poured a small puddle into his old and wrinkled hands, and Puppy took grateful sips. It took what felt like forever for Jewel to arrive, but when she did, it was in a thunder of hurrying boots. The landing shook. Jewel was all sweaty and out of breath, but Solo didn't seem to care. The two of them hugged, and Elise wondered if they'd ever let go. People came and went from the landing and gave them funny looks as they passed. Jewel was smiling and crying both when they finally released each other. She said something to Solo, and it was his turn to cry. Both of them looked at Elise, and she could see that it was secrets or something bad. Jewel picked her up next and kissed her on the cheek and hugged her until it was hard to breathe.

"It's gonna be okay," she told Elise. But Elise didn't know what was wrong.

"I got Puppy back," she said. And then she remembered that Jewel didn't know about her new pet. She looked down to see Puppy peeing on Jewel's boot, which must be like saying hello.

"A dog," Jewel said. She squeezed Elise's shoulder. "You can't keep her. Dogs are dangerous."

"She's not dangerous!"

Puppy chewed on Elise's hand. Elise pulled away and rubbed Puppy's head.

"Did you get her from the bazaar? Is that where you went?" Jewel looked to Solo, who nodded. Jewel took a deep breath. "You can't take things that don't belong to you. If you got it from a vendor, it'll have to go back."

"Puppy came from the Deep," Elise said. She bent down and wrapped her arms around the dog. "He came from Mechanical. We can take him back there. But not to the bizarre. I'm sorry I took him." She squeezed Puppy and thought about the man holding up the red meat with the white ribs. Jewel turned to Solo again.

"It didn't come from the bazaar," he confirmed. "She plucked it from a box down in Mechanical."

"Fine. We'll straighten this out later. We need to catch up with the others."

Elise could tell that all of them were tired, including her and Puppy, but they set out anyway. The adults seemed eager to get down, and after seeing the bizarre Elise felt the same way. She told Jewel she wanted to go home, and Jewel said that's where they were heading. "We ought to make things how they used to be," Elise told them both.

For some reason that made Jewel laugh. "You're too young to be nostalgic," she said.

Elise asked what nostalgic meant, and Jewel said, "It's where you think the past was better than it really was, only because the present sucks so bad."

"I get nostalgic a lot," Elise declared.

And Jewel and Solo both laughed at that. But then they looked sad after. Elise caught them looking at each other like this a lot, and Jewel kept wiping at her eyes. Finally, Elise asked them what was wrong.

They stopped in the middle of the stairway and told her. Told her about Marcus, who had slipped over the rails when that crazy crowd had knocked her down and Puppy had gotten away. Marcus had fallen and died. Elise looked at the rails beside her and didn't see how Marcus could slip over rails so high. She didn't understand how it had happened, but she knew it was like when their parents had gone off and never came back. It was like that. Marcus would never come laughing through the Wilds again. She wiped her face and felt awful for Miles, who wasn't a twin anymore.

"Is that why we're going home?" she asked.

"It's one of the reasons," Jewel said. "I never should've brought you here."

Elise nodded. There was no arguing with that. Except she had Puppy now, and Puppy had come from here. And no matter what she told Jewel, Elise wasn't giving him back.

Juliette allowed Elise to lead the way. Her legs were sore from the run down; she had nearly lost her footing more than once. Now she was eager to see the kids together and home, couldn't stop blaming herself for what had happened to Marcus. The levels went by full of regrets, and then there was a call on the radio.

"Jules, are you there?"

It was Shirly, and she sounded upset. Juliette pulled the radio from her belt. Shirly must've been with Walker, using one of his sets. "Go ahead," she said. She kept a hand on the rail and followed Elise and Solo. A porter and a young couple squeezed by heading in the other direction.

"What the hell is going on?" Shirly asked. "We just had a mob come through here. Frankie got overrun at the gates. He's in the infirmary. And I've got another two or three dozen people heading through this blasted tunnel of yours. I didn't sign on for this."

Juliette figured it was the same group that led to Marcus's death. Jimmy turned and eyed the radio and its news. Juliette turned down the volume so Elise couldn't hear.

"What do you mean by *another* two or three dozen? Who else is over there?" Juliette asked.

"Your dig team, for one. Some mechanics from third shift who should be sleeping but want to see what's on the other side. And the planning committee you sent."

"The planning committee?" Juliette slowed her pace.

"Yeah. They said you sent them. Said it was okay to inspect the dig. Had a note from your office."

Juliette remembered Marsha saying something about this before the Town Hall. But she had been busy with the suits.

"Did you not send them?" Shirly asked.

"I may have," Juliette admitted. "But this other group, the mob, my dad and them had a run-in on their way down. Someone fell to their death."

There was silence on the other end. And then: "I heard we

had a fall. Didn't know it was related. I tell you, I'm this close to pulling everyone back and shutting this down. Things are out of hand, Jules."

I know, Juliette thought. But she didn't broadcast this. Didn't utter it out loud. "I'll be there soon. On my way now."

Shirly didn't respond. Juliette clipped the radio to her belt and cursed herself. Jimmy hung back to speak with her, allowing Elise to walk further ahead.

"I'm sorry about all of this," Juliette told him.

The two of them walked in silence for a turn of the staircase.

"The people in the tunnel, I saw some of them taking what's not theirs," Jimmy said. "It was dark when they brought us over, but I saw people carrying pipe and equipment from my silo back to this one. Like it was the plan the whole time. But then you said we were going to rebuild my home. Not use it for spares."

"I did. I do. I do mean to rebuild it. As soon as we get down there, I'll talk to them. They aren't taking spares."

"So you didn't tell them it was okay?"

"No. I . . . I may have told them it made sense to come get you and the kids, that the extra silo would mean certain . . . redundancies—"

"That's what a spare is."

"I'll talk to them. I promise. Everything will be all right in the end."

They walked in silence for a while.

"Yeah," Solo finally said. "You keep saying that."

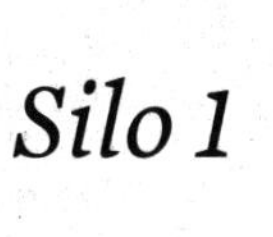

Silo 1

30

CHARLOTTE AWOKE IN darkness, damp with sweat. Cold. The metal decking was cold. Her face was sore from it resting so long on the steel. She worked a half-dead arm from beneath her and rubbed her face, felt the marks there from the diamond plating.

The attack on Donny returned like a dimly remembered dream. She had curled up and waited. Had somehow held back her tears. And whether exhausted from the effort or terrified of moving, she had eventually succumbed to sleep.

She listened for footsteps or voices before cracking the tarp. It was pitch black outside. As black there as under the drone. Like a chick from a nest, she crawled out from beneath the metal bird, her joints stiff, a weight on her chest, a terrible solitude all around her.

Her worklight was somewhere beneath the tarp. She uncovered the drone and patted around, felt some tools, knocked over and noisily scattered a ratchet set. Remembering the drone's headlamp, she felt inside an open access panel, found the test switch, and pressed it. A golden carpet was thrown out in front of the bird's beak. It was enough to find her worklight.

She grabbed this and a large wrench as well. She was no longer safe. A mortar had flown into camp and had leveled a tent, had taken a bunkmate. Another could come whistling down at any time.

She aimed her flashlight toward the lifts, afraid of what they could disgorge without warning. In the silence, she could hear her heartbeat. Charlotte turned and headed for the conference room, for the last place she'd seen him.

There was no sign of struggle on the floor. Inside the conference room, the table was still scattered with notes. Maybe not as many as before. And the several bins scattered among the chairs were gone. Someone had done a poor job of cleaning up. Someone would be back.

Charlotte doused the lights and turned to go. Stepping through the place where he'd been attacked, she saw this time the splattered blood on the wall. She felt the sobs she'd wrestled down before falling asleep rise up to seize her throat, constricting it, wondered if her brother was still alive. She could see the man with the white hair standing there, kicking and kicking, an unholy rage in him. And now she had no one. She hurried through the dark warehouse toward the glowing drone. Pulled from sleep, shown a frightening world, and now she'd been left alone.

The light from the drone's beak spilled across the floor and illuminated a door.

Not quite alone.

Charlotte gathered her wits. She reached into the access panel and turned the drone's headlamp off. She carefully rearranged the tarp. It would no longer do to leave things amiss—she must always assume she might have visitors. With her worklight bobbing, she made for the door, stopped, went back for her tool bag. The drone was now a distant priority. With her tools and light, she hurried past the barracks and to the end of the hall, into the flight room. The workbench on the far wall held a radio pieced together over the weeks. It worked. She and her brother had listened to the chatter from distant worlds. Maybe there was a way to make it transmit. She pawed through the spare parts he had left for her, searching. If nothing else, she could listen. Maybe she could find out what they'd done to him. Maybe she could hear from him—or reach out to another soul.

31

WITH EVERY COUGH, Donald's ribs exploded into a thousand splinters. This shrapnel pierced his lungs and his heart and sent a tidal wave up his spinal column. He was convinced this was taking place inside his body, these bombs of bone and nerve. Already, he missed the simple torture of burning lungs and searing throat. His bruised and cracked ribs now made a mockery of old torments. Yesterday's misery had become nostalgic fondness.

He lay on his cot, bleeding and bruised, having given up on escape. The door was sound, and the space above the ceiling panels led nowhere. He didn't think he was on the admin levels. Maybe Security. Perhaps residential. Or someplace he wasn't familiar with. The hallway outside remained eerily quiet. It could be the middle of the night. Banging on the door was brutal on his aching ribs, and shouting hurt his throat. But the worst pain was imagining what he'd dragged his sister into, what would become of her. When the guards or Thurman came back, he should tell them she was down there, beg for them to be merciful. She had been like a daughter to Thurman, and Donald was the only one to blame for waking her up. Thurman would see that. He would put her back under where she might sleep until the end came for them all. It would be for the best.

Hours passed. Hours of bruised swelling and feeling his pulse throb in a dozen places. Donald tossed and turned, and day and night became even less distinguishable in that buried crypt. A feverish sweat overtook him, one born of regret and fear more than infection. He had nightmares of frozen pods set ablaze, of fire and ice and dust, of flesh melting and bone turning to powder.

Falling in and out of sleep, he had another dream. A dream of a cold night on a wide ocean, of a ship sinking beneath his feet, the deck trembling from the savagery of the sea. Donald's hands were frozen to the wheel of the ship, his breath a fog of lies. Waves lapped over the rails as his command sank deeper and deeper. And all around him on the water were lifeboats ablaze. All the women and children burned out there, screaming, trapped in lifeboats shaped like cryopods that were never meant to reach the shore.

Donald saw that now. He saw it awake—panting, coughing, sweating—as well as in his dreams. He remembered thinking once that the women had been set aside so that there would be nothing to fight over. But the opposite was true. They were there to give the rest of them something to fight *for*. Someone to save. It was for them that men worked these dark shifts, slept through these dark nights, dreaming of what would never be.

He covered his mouth, rolled over in bed, and coughed up blood. Someone to save. The folly of man—the folly of the blasted silos he had helped to build—this assumption that things needed saving. They ought to have been left on their own, both people and the planet. Mankind had the right to go extinct. That's what life did: it went extinct. It made room for the next in line. But individual men had often railed against the natural order. They had their illegally cloned children, their nano treatments, their spare parts, and their cryopods. Individual men like those who did this.

Approaching boots signaled a meal, an end to the interminable nightmare of being asleep with wild thoughts and lying awake with bodily pain. It had to be breakfast, because he was starving. It meant he'd been up for much of the night. He expected the same guard who'd delivered his last meal, but the door cracked open to reveal Thurman. A man in Security silver stood behind him, unsmiling. Thurman entered alone and shut the door, confident that Donald posed no threat to him. He appeared better, fitter, than he had the day before. More time awake, perhaps. Or a flood of new doctors loosed in his bloodstream.

"How long are you keeping me here?" Donald asked, sitting up. His voice was scratchy and distant, the sound of autumn leaves.

"Not long," Thurman said. The old man dragged the trunk away from the foot of the bed and sat on it. He studied Donald intently. "You've only got a few days to live."

"Is that a medical diagnosis? Or a sentencing?"

Thurman raised an eyebrow. "It's both. If we keep you here and leave you untreated, you will die from the air you breathed. We're putting you under, instead."

"God forbid you put me out of my misery."

Thurman seemed to consider this. "I've thought about letting you die in here. I know the pain you're in. I could fix you or let you break all the way down, but I don't have the heart for either."

Donald tried to laugh, but it hurt too much. He reached for the glass of water on the tray and took a sip. A pink spiral of blood danced on the surface as he lowered the glass.

"You've been busy this last shift," Thurman said. "There are drones and bombs missing. We've woken up a few of the people who went into freeze recently to piece together your handiwork. Do you have any idea what you've risked?"

There was something worse than anger in Thurman's voice. Donald couldn't place it at first. Not disappointment. It wasn't any form of rage. The rage had drained from his boots. This was something subdued. It was something like fear.

"What I've risked?" Donald asked. "I've been cleaning up your mess." He sloshed water as he saluted his old mentor. "The silos you damaged. That silo that went black all those years ago. It was still there—"

"Silo Forty. I know."

"And Seventeen." Donald cleared his throat. He grabbed the heel of bread from the tray and took a dry bite, chewed until his jaws ached, chased it with blood-smeared water. He knew so much that Thurman didn't. This occurred to him in that moment. All the talks with the people of 18, the time spent poring over drawings and notes, the weeks of piecing things together, of being in charge. He knew in his present condition that he was no match for Thurman in a fight, but he still felt the stronger of the two. It was his knowledge that made him feel that way. "Seventeen wasn't dead," he said before taking another bite of bread.

"So I've learned."

Donald chewed.

"I'm shutting down Eighteen today," Thurman said quietly. "What that facility has cost us . . ." He shook his head, and Donald wondered if he was thinking of Victor, the head of heads, who had blown his own head off over an uprising that took place there. In the next moment, it occurred to him that the people he'd placed so much hope in were now gone as well. All the time spent smuggling parts to Charlotte, dreaming of an end to the silos, hope of a future under blue skies, all for nothing. The bread felt stale as he swallowed.

"Why?" he asked.

"You know why. You've been talking to them, haven't you?

What did you think was going to become of that place? What were you thinking?" The first hints of anger crept into Thurman's voice. "Did you think they were going to save you? That any of us can be saved? What the hell were you thinking?"

Donald didn't plan on answering, but a response came as reflexively as a cough: "I thought they deserved better than this. I thought they deserved a chance—"

"A chance for what?" Thurman shook his head. "It doesn't matter. It doesn't matter. We planned for enough." He muttered this last to himself. "The shame is that I have to sleep at all, that I can't be here to manage everything. It's like sending drones up when you need to be there yourself, your hand on the yoke." Thurman made a fist in the air. He studied Donald a while. "You're going under first thing in the morning. It's a far cry from what you deserve. But before I'm rid of you, I want you to tell me how you did it, how you ended up here with my name. I can't let that happen again—"

"So now I'm a threat." Donald took another pull of water, flooding the tickle in his throat. He tried to take a deep breath, but the pain in his chest made him double over.

"You aren't, but the next person who does this might be. We tried to think of everything, but we always knew the biggest weakness, the biggest weakness of any system, was a revolt from the top."

"Like Silo Twelve," Donald said. He remembered that silo falling as a dark shadow emerged from its server room. He had witnessed this, had ended that silo, had written a report. "How could you not expect what happened there?" he asked.

"We did. We planned for everything. It's why we have spares. It's why we have the Rite, a chance to try a man's soul, a box to put our ticking time bombs in. You're too young to understand this, but the most difficult task mankind ever tried to master—and that we never quite managed—was how to pass supreme power from one hand to the next." Thurman spread his arms. His old eyes sparkled, the politician in him reawakened. "Until now. We solved it here with the cryopods and the shifts. Power is temporary, and it never leaves the same few hands. There is no transfer of power."

"Congratulations," Donald spat. And he remembered suggesting to Thurman once that he could be President, and Thurman had suggested it would be a demotion. Donald saw that now.

"Yes. It was a good system. Until you managed to subvert it."

"I'll tell you how I did it if you answer something for me." Donald covered his mouth and coughed.

Thurman frowned and waited for him to stop. "You're dying," he said. "We'll put you in a box so you can dream until the end. What could you possibly want to know?"

"The truth. I have so much of it, but still a few holes. They hurt more than the holes in my lungs."

"I doubt that," Thurman said. But he seemed to consider the offer. "What is it you want to know?"

"The servers. I know what's on them. All the details of everyone's lives in the silos, where they work, what they do, how long they live, how many kids they have, what they eat, where they go, everything. I want to know what it's for."

Thurman studied him. He didn't say anything.

"I found the percentages. The list that shuffles. It's the chances that these people survive when they're set free, isn't it? But how does it know?"

"It knows," Thurman said. "And that's what you think the silos do?"

"I think there's a war playing out, yes. A war between all these silos, and only one will win."

"Then what do you need from me?"

"I think there's something else. Tell me, and I'll tell you how

I took your place." Donald sat up and hugged his shins while a coughing fit ravaged his throat and ribs. Thurman waited until he was done.

"The servers do what you say. They keep track of all those lives, and they weigh them. They also decide the lotteries, which means we get to shape these people in a very real way. We increase our odds, allow the best to thrive. It's why the chances keep improving the longer we're at this."

"Of course." Donald felt stupid. He should have known. He had heard Thurman say over and over that they left nothing to chance. And wasn't a lottery just that?

He caught the look Thurman was giving him. "Your turn," he said. "How'd you do it?"

Donald leaned back against the wall. He coughed into his fist while Thurman looked on, wide-eyed and silent. "It was Anna," Donald said. "She found out what you had planned. You were going to put her under after she was done helping you, and she feared she would never wake up again. You gave her access to the systems so she could fix your problem with Forty. She set it up so that I would take your place. And she left a note asking for my help, left it in your inbox. I think she wanted to ruin you. To end this."

"No," Thurman said.

"Oh, yes. And I woke up and didn't understand what she was asking of me. I found out too late. And in the meantime, there were still problems with Silo Forty. When I woke up and started this shift, Forty—"

"Forty was already taken care of," Thurman said.

Donald rested his head back and stared at the ceiling. "They made you think so. Here's what I think. I think Silo Forty hacked the system, that's what Anna found. They hacked their camera feeds so we couldn't know what was going on, a rogue head of IT, a revolt from the top, just like you said. The cutting of the camera feeds was when they went black. But before that, they hacked the gas lines so we couldn't kill them. And before that, they hacked the bombs meant to bring down their silos in case any of this happened. They worked their way backwards. By the time they went black, they were in charge. Like me. Like what Anna did for me."

"How could they—?"

"Maybe she was helping them, I don't know. She helped me. And somehow word spread to others. Or maybe by the time Anna was done saving your ass, she realized they were right and we were wrong. Maybe she left Silo Forty alone in the end to do whatever they pleased. I think she thought they might save us all."

Donald coughed, and thought of all the hero sagas of old, of men and women struggling for righteousness, always with a happy ending, always against impossible odds, always bullshit. Heroes didn't win. The heroes were whoever *happened* to win. History told their story—the dead didn't say a word. All of it was bullshit.

"I bombed Silo Forty before I understood what was going on," Donald said. He gazed at the ceiling, feeling the weight of all those levels, of the dirt and the heavy sky. "I bombed them because I needed a distraction, because I didn't care. I killed Anna because she brought me here, because she saved my life. I did your job for you both times, didn't I? I put down two rebellions you never saw coming—"

"No." Thurman stood. He towered over Donald.

"Yes," Donald said. He blinked away welling tears, could feel a hole in his heart where his anger toward Anna once lay. All that was there now was guilt and regret. He had killed the one who had loved him the most, had fought for the things that were right. He had never stopped to ask, to think, to talk.

"You started this uprising when you broke your own rules,"

he told Thurman. "When you woke her up, you started this. You were weak. You threatened everything, and I fixed it. And goddamn you to hell for listening to her. For bringing me here. For turning me into this!"

Donald closed his eyes. He felt the tickle of escaping tears as they rolled down his temples, and the light through his lids quivered as Thurman's shadow fell over him. He braced for a blow. He tilted his head back, lifted his chin, and waited. He thought of Helen. He thought of Anna. He thought of Charlotte. And remembering, he started to tell Thurman about his sister and where she was hiding before those blows landed, before he was struck as he deserved to be for helping these monsters, for being their unwitting tool at every turn. He started to tell Thurman about Charlotte, but there was a brightening of light through his lids, the slinking away of a shadow, and the slamming of an angry door.

Silo 18

32

LUKAS SENSED SOMETHING was wrong before he slotted the headphones into the jack. The red lights above the servers throbbed red, but it was the wrong time of day. The calls from Silo 1 came like clockwork. This call had come in the middle of dinner. The buzzing and flashing lights had moved to his office and then to the hallway. Sims, the old Security chief, had tracked Lukas down in the break room to let him know someone was getting in touch, and Lukas's first thought was that their mysterious benefactor had a warning for them. Or maybe he was calling to thank them for finally stopping with the digging.

There was a click in his headset as the connection was made. The lights overhead stopped their infernal blinking. "Hello?" he said, catching his breath.

"Who is this?"

Someone different. The voice was the same, but the words were wrong. Why wouldn't this person know who he was?

"This is Lukas. Lukas Kyle. Who is this?"

"Let me speak to the head of your silo."

Lukas stood up straight. "I am the head of this silo. Silo Eighteen of World Order Operation Fifty. Who am I speaking to?"

"You're speaking to the man who dreamed up that World Order. Now get me the head. I have here a . . . Bernard Holland."

Lukas nearly blurted out that Bernard was dead. Everyone knew Bernard was dead. It was a fact of life. He had watched him burn rather than go out to clean, watched him burn rather than allow himself to be saved. But this man didn't know that. And the complexities of life on the other end of that line, that infallible line, caused the room to wobble. The gods weren't omnipotent. Or they didn't sup around the same table. Or the one who called himself Donald was more rogue than even Lukas had believed he might be. Or—as Juliette would claim if she were there—these people were fucking with him.

"Bernard is . . . ah, he is indisposed at the moment."

There was a pause. Lukas could feel the sweat bead up on his forehead and neck, the heat of the servers and the conversation getting to him.

"How long before he's back?"

"I'm not sure. I can, uh, try to get him for you?" His voice lilted at the end of what shouldn't have been a question.

"Fifteen minutes," the voice said. "After that, things are going to go very badly for you and everyone over there. Very badly. Fifteen minutes."

The line clicked dead before Lukas could object or argue for more time. Fifteen minutes. The room continued to wobble. He needed Jules. He would need someone to pretend to be Bernard—maybe Nelson. And what had this man meant when he said he had dreamed up the World Order? That wasn't possible.

Lukas hurried to the ladder and raced down. He grabbed the portable radio from the charging rack and scrambled back up the ladder. He would call Juliette on his way to tracking down Nelson. A different voice would win him some time until he could sort this out. In a way, this was a call he'd always expected, someone wanting to know what in the hell was going on in their silo, but it had never come. He had expected it, and now it took him by surprise.

"Jules?" He reached the top of the ladder and tried the radio. What if she didn't answer? Fifteen minutes. And then what? How bad could they really make it for them in the silo? The other voice—Donald—had tossed around dire and vacuous warnings from time to time. But this felt different. He tried Juliette again. His heart shouldn't be pounding so. He opened the server room door and raced down the hall.

"Can I call you back?" Jules asked, the radio in his palm crackling with her voice. "I've got a nightmare down here. Five minutes?"

Lukas was breathing hard. He dodged around Sims in the hallway, who spun to watch him go. Nelson would be in the Suit Lab. Lukas squeezed the transmit button. "Actually, I could use some help right now. Are you still on your way down?"

"No, I'm here. Just left the kids with my dad. I'm heading to Walker's to get a battery. Are you running? You're not coming down here, are you?"

Deep breaths. "No, I'm looking for Nelson. Someone called, said they need to speak to Bernard, that there would be trouble for us otherwise. Jules—I've got a bad feeling about this."

He rounded the bend and saw that the door to the Suit Lab was open. Strips of seal tape fluttered around the jamb.

"Calm down," Juliette told him. "Take it easy. Who did you say called? And why are you looking for Nelson?"

"I was going to have him talk to this guy, pretend he's Bernard, at least to buy us some time. I don't know who's calling. It sounds like the same guy, but it's not."

"What did he say?"

"He said to get Bernard, said he was the one who dreamed up Operation Fifty. Dammit, Nelson's not here." Lukas glanced around the workbenches and tool cabinets. He remembered passing Sims. The old Security chief had clearance to the server room. Lukas left the Suit Lab and rushed back down the hall.

"Lukas, you aren't making any sense."

"I know, I know. Hey, I'll call you back. I need to catch Sims—"

He jogged down the hallway. Offices flew past, most of them empty, workers who had transferred out of IT or those at dinner. He spotted Sims turning a corner toward the security station.

"Sims!"

The Security chief peered back around the corner, stepped into the hall, and studied Lukas as he ran at him. Lukas wondered how many minutes had passed, how strict this man was going to be.

"I need your help," he said. He pointed to the server room door, which stood at the junction of the two halls. Sims turned and studied the door with him.

"Yeah?"

Lukas entered his code and pushed the door open. Inside, the lights were back to throbbing red. No way it'd been fifteen minutes already. "I need a huge favor," he told Sims. "Look, it's . . . complicated, but I need you to talk to someone for me. I need you to pretend to be Bernard. You knew him well enough, right?"

Sims pulled up. "Pretend to be who?"

Lukas turned and grabbed the larger man's arm, urged him along. "No time to explain. I just need you to answer this guy's questions. It's like a drill. Just be Bernard. Tell yourself that you're Bernard. Act angry or something. And get off the line as quickly as you can. In fact, say as little as possible."

"Who am I talking to?"

"I'll explain afterward. I just need you to get through this.

Fool this guy." He guided Sims to the open server and handed him the headphones. Sims studied them as though he'd never seen a pair. "Just put those over your ears," Lukas said. "I'm going to plug you in. It's like a radio. Remember, you are Bernard. Try to sound like him, okay? Just be him."

Sims nodded. His cheeks were red, a bead of sweat running down his brow. He looked ten years younger and nervous as hell.

"Here you go." Lukas slotted the cord into the jack, thinking that Sims was probably even better for this than Nelson. This would buy them some time until he could figure out what was going on. He watched as Sims flinched, must've heard a greeting in the headphones.

"Hello?" he asked.

"Confident," Lukas hissed. The radio in his hand crackled with Juliette's voice, and he turned down the volume, didn't want it overheard. He would have to call her back.

"Yes, this is Bernard." Sims talked through his nose, high and tight. It sounded more like a man doing a woman's voice than a fair approximation of the former silo head. "This *is* Bernard," Sims said again, more insistently. He turned to Lukas and pleaded with his eyes, looked absolutely helpless. Lukas waved his hand in a small circle. Sims nodded as he listened to something, then pulled the headset off.

"Okay?" Lukas hissed.

Sims held the headset out to Lukas. "He wants to speak to you. I'm sorry. He knows it isn't him."

Lukas groaned. He tucked the radio under his arm, Juliette's voice tiny and distant, and pulled on the headset, slick with sweat.

"Hello?"

"You shouldn't have done that."

"Bernard is . . . I couldn't reach him."

"He's dead. Was it an accident, or was he murdered? What's going on over there? Who's in charge? We've got no feeds over here."

"I'm in charge," Lukas said. He was painfully aware that Sims was studying him. "Everything is just fine over here. I can have Bernard call you—"

"You've been talking with someone over here."

Lukas didn't respond.

"What did he tell you?"

Lukas glanced at the wooden chair and the pile of books. Sims followed his gaze, and his eyes widened at the sight of so much paper.

"We've been talking about population reports," Lukas said. "We put down an uprising. Yes, Bernard was injured during the fighting—"

"I have a machine here that tells me when you're lying."

Lukas felt faint. It seemed impossible, but he believed the man. He turned around and collapsed into the chair. Sims studied him warily. His Security chief could tell that things weren't right.

"We're doing the best we can," Lukas said. "Everything's in order over here. I am Bernard's shadow. I passed the Rite—"

"I know. But I think you've been poisoned. I'm very sorry, son, but this is something I should have done a long time ago. It's for the good of everyone. I truly am sorry." And then, cryptically and softly, almost as if to someone else, the voice uttered the words: "Shut them down."

"Wait—" Lukas said. He turned to Sims, and now they looked helplessly at one another. "Let me—"

Before he could finish, there was a hissing sound above him. Lukas glanced up to find a white cloud billowing down from the vents. An expanding mist. He remembered exhaust fumes like this from long ago, back when he was locked inside the server room and the people in Mechanical tried to divert gas to choke him out. He remembered the feeling that he was going to suffocate inside that room. But this fog was different. It was thick and sinister.

Lukas pulled his undershirt over his mouth and yelled for Sims to come with him. They both dashed through the server room, dodging between the tall black machines, avoiding the cloud where they could. They got to the door that led out to IT, which Lukas figured was airtight. The red light on the panel blinked happily. Lukas didn't remember locking the door. Holding his breath, he punched in his code and waited for the light to turn green. It didn't. He punched it in again, concentrating, feeling lightheaded from not enough air, and the keypad buzzed and blinked at him with its red and solitary eye.

Lukas turned to Sims to complain and saw the large man peering down at his palms. His hands were covered in blood. Blood was pouring from Sims's nose.

33

JULIETTE CURSED THE radio and finally let Walker have a try. Courtnee watched them both with concern. Lukas had come through a couple of times, but all they'd heard was the patter of boots and the hissing of his breathing or some kind of static.

Walker examined the portable. The radio had grown needlessly complex with the knobs and dials he'd added. He fiddled with something and shrugged. "Looks okay to me," he said, tugging on his beard. "Must be on the other end."

One of the other radios on the bench barked. It was the large unit he'd built, the one with the wire dangling from the ceiling. There was a familiar voice followed by a burst of static: "Hello? Anyone? We've got a problem down here."

Juliette raced around the workbench and grabbed the mic before Walker or Courtnee could. She recognized that voice. "Hank, this is Juliette. What's going on?"

"We've got . . . ah, reports from the Mids of some kind of vapor leak. Are you still in that area?"

"No, I'm down in Mechanical. What kind of vapor leak? And from where?"

"In the stairwell, I think. I'm out on the landing right now and don't see anything, but I hear a racket above me. Sounds like a ton of traffic. Can't tell if it's heading up or down. No fire alarm, though."

"Break. Break."

It was another voice cutting in. Juliette recognized it as Peter. He was calling for a pause in the chatter so he could say something.

"Go ahead, Peter."

"Jules, I've got some kind of leak up here as well. It's in the airlock."

Juliette looked to Courtnee, who shrugged. "Confirm that you have smoke in the airlock," she said.

"I don't think it's smoke. And it's in the airlock you added, the new one. Wait. No . . . that's strange."

Juliette found herself pacing between Walker's workbenches. "What's strange? Describe what you're seeing." She imagined an exhaust leak, something from the main generator. They would have to shut it down, and the backup was gone. Fuck. Her worst nightmare. Courtnee frowned at her, was probably thinking the same thing. Fuck, fuck.

"Jules, the yellow door is open. I repeat, the inner airlock door is wide open. And I didn't do it. It was locked just a bit ago."

"What about the smoke?" Juliette asked. "Is it getting worse? Stay low and cover your face. You'll want a wet rag or something—"

"It's not smoke. And it's inside the new door you welded up. That door is still shut. I'm looking through the glass right now. The smoke is all inside there. And I . . . I can see through the yellow door. It's wide open. It's . . . holy shit—"

Juliette felt her heart race. The tone of his voice. She couldn't remember Peter ever uttering a cuss word in all the time she'd known him, and she'd known him through the worst of it. "Peter?"

"Jules, the outer door is open. I say again, the outer airlock door is wide open. I can see straight through the airlock and to . . . what looks like a ramp. I think I'm looking outside. Gods, Juliette, I'm looking straight outside—"

"I need you to get out of there," Juliette said. "Leave everything as it is and get out. Shut the cafeteria door behind you. Seal it up with something. Tape or caulk or something from the kitchen. Do you read?"

"Yes. Yes." His voice was labored. Juliette recalled Lukas telling her something bad was about to happen. She looked to Walker, who still had the new portable in his hand. She needed the old portable. She shouldn't have let him modify the thing. "I need you to raise Luke," she said.

Walker shrugged helplessly. "I'm trying," he said.

"Jules, this is Peter again. I've got traffic heading my way up the stairs. I can hear them. Sounds like half the silo. I don't know why they're heading this way."

Juliette thought of what Hank had said about hearing traffic on the stairwell. If there was a fire, everyone was supposed to man a hose or get to a safe level and wait for assistance. Why would people be running *up*?

"Peter, don't let them near the office. Keep them away from the airlock. Don't let them through."

Her mind whirled. What would she do if she were up there? Have to get in there with a suit on and shut those doors. But that would mean opening the new airlock door. The new airlock door! It shouldn't be there. Forget the sign of smoke, the outside air was now attached to the silo. The outside air—

"Peter?"

"Jules—I . . . I can't stay here. Everyone's acting crazy. They're in the office, Jules. I . . . I don't want to shoot anyone—I can't."

"Listen to me. The vapor. It's the argon, isn't it?"

"It . . . maybe. Yeah. It looked like that. I only saw it fill the airlock the once, when you went out. But yeah—"

Juliette felt her heart sink, her head spin. Her boots no longer touched the floor as she hovered, empty inside, numb and half-deaf. The gas. The poison. The seal missing from the sample canister. That fucker in Silo 1 and his threats. He'd done it. He was killing them all. A thousand useless plans and schemes flitted through Juliette's mind, all of them hopeless and too late. Far too late.

"Jules?"

She squeezed the mic to answer Peter, and then realized the voice was coming from Walker's hands. It was coming from the portable radio.

"Lukas," she gasped. Her vision blurred as she reached for the other radio.

34

"JULES? GODDAMMIT. My volume was down. Can you hear me?"

"I hear you, Lukas. What the hell is going on?"

"Shit. Shit."

Juliette heard clangs and bangs.

"I'm okay. I'm okay. Shit. Is that blood? Okay, gotta get to the pantry. Are you still with me?"

Juliette realized she wasn't breathing. "Are you talking to me? What blood?"

"Yeah, I'm talking to you. Fell down the ladder. Sims is dead. They're doing it. They're shutting us down. My stupid nose. I'm going in the pantry—" The feed turned into static.

"Lukas? Lukas!" She turned to Walker and Courtnee, both watching with wide and wet eyes.

"—no good. Cam't geb recebtion in there." Lukas's voice was garbled as though he were pinching his nose or holding back a sneeze. "Baby, you've gotta seal yourselb off. Can't stob my nose—"

Panic surged through Juliette. Shutting them down. The threats of ending them with the push of a button. Ending them. A silo like Solo's. Maybe a second flitted by, two seconds, and in that brief flash she recalled him telling her stories of the way his silo fell, the rush up top, the spilling out into the open air, the bodies piling up that she had waded through years later. All in an instant, she was transported back and forth through time. This was Silo 17's past; she was witnessing the fall of that silo as it played out in her home. And she had seen their grim future, had seen what was to come of her world. She knew how this ended. She knew that Lukas was already dead.

"Forget the radio," she told him. "Lukas, I want you to forget the radio and seal yourself in that pantry. I'm going to save as many as I can."

She grabbed the other radio, which was tuned to her silo. "Hank, do you read me?"

"Yes—?" She could hear him panting. "Hello?"

"Get everyone down to Mechanical. Everyone you can and as fast as you can. Now."

"I feel like I should be going up," Hank said. "Everyone is storming up."

"No!" Juliette screamed into her radio. Walker startled and dropped the other radio's microphone. "Listen to me, Hank. Everyone you can. Down here. Now!"

She cradled the radio in both hands, glanced around the room to see what else she should grab.

"Are we sealing off Mechanical?" Courtnee asked. "Like before?"

Courtnee must've been thinking about the steel plating welded across security during the holdout. The scars of those joints were still visible, the plating long gone.

"No time for that," Juliette said. She didn't add that it might all be pointless. The air could already be spoiled. No telling how long it took. A part of her mind wanted to focus on all that lay above her, all that she couldn't save, the people and the things as well. Everything good and needed in the world that was now out of reach.

"Grab anything crucial and let's go." She looked to the two of them. "We need to go right now. Courtnee, get to the kids and get them back to their silo—"

"But you said . . . that mob—"

"I don't care about them. Go. And take Walk with you. See that he gets to the dig. I'll meet you there."

"Where are you going?" Courtnee asked.

"To get as many others as I can."

The hallways of Mechanical were strangely devoid of panic. Juliette ran through scenes of normalcy, of people walking to and from their shifts, trolleys of spare parts and heavy pumps, a shower of sparks from someone welding, a flickering flashlight and a passer-by tapping it with their fist. The radio had brought word to her ahead of time. No one else knew.

"Get to the dig," she shouted to everyone she passed. "That's an order. Now. Now. Go."

There was a delayed response. Questions. Excuses. People explained where they were heading, that they were busy, that they didn't have time right then.

Juliette saw Dawson's wife, Raina, who would've been just coming off shift. Juliette grabbed her by the shoulders. Raina's eyes widened, her body stiffened, to be handled like that.

"Get to the classroom," Juliette told her. "Get your kids, get all the kids, and get them through the tunnel. Now."

"What the hell's going on?" someone asked. A few people jostled by in the narrow passageway. One of Juliette's old hands from first shift was there. A crowd was forming.

"Get to the fucking dig," Juliette shouted. "We've got to clear out. Grab everyone you can, your kids, anything you think you need. This is not a drill. Go. Go!"

She clapped her hands. Raina was the first to turn and run, pushing herself through the packed corridor. Those who knew her best leapt into action soon after, rounding up others. Juliette raced toward the stairwell, shouting as she did for everyone to get to the other silo. She vaulted over the security gates, the guard on duty looking up with a startled "Hey!" Behind her, she could hear someone else yelling for everyone to follow, to get moving. Ahead of her, the stairway itself trembled. She could hear welds singing and loose struts rattling. Over this, she could hear the sound of boots stomping her way.

Juliette stood at the bottom of the stairwell and peered up through that wide gap between the stairs and the stairwell's concrete wall. Various landings jutted out overhead, wide bands of steel that became narrow ribbons higher up. The shaft receded into darkness. And then she saw the white clouds like smoke higher up. Maybe from the Mids.

She squeezed the radio.

"Hank?"

No response.

"Hank, come back."

The stairway hummed with the harmonics of heavy but distant traffic. Juliette stepped closer and rested a hand on the rail. It vibrated, numbing her hand. The clanging of boots grew louder. Looking up, she could see hands sliding down the rail above her, could hear voices shouting encouragement and confusion.

A handful of people from the one-thirties spilled down the last turn and seemed confused about where to go next. They had the bewildered look of people who had never known that the stairway ended, that there was this floor of concrete below their homes. Juliette yelled at them to head inside. She turned and shouted into Mechanical for someone to show them the way, to let them through security. They stumbled past, most of them empty-handed, one or two with children clutched to their chests or towed behind, or with bundles cradled in their arms.

They spoke of fire and smoke. A man shuffled down, holding a bloody nose. He insisted that they should be heading up, that they should all be heading up.

"You," Juliette said, grabbing the man by the arm. She studied his face, the crimson dripping from his knuckles. "Where are you coming from? What happened?" She indicated his nose.

"I fell," he said, uncovering his face to talk. "I was at work—"

"Okay. That's fine. Follow the others." She pointed. Her radio barked with a disembodied voice. Shouting. An unholy din. Juliette moved away from the stairs and covered one ear, pressed the radio to the other. It sounded vaguely like Peter. She waited until he was done.

"Can barely hear you!" she yelled. "What's going on?"

She covered her ear again and strained for his words. "—getting through. To the outside. They're getting out—"

Her back found the concrete of the stairwell. She slid down into a crouch. A few dozen people scampered down the stairs. Some stragglers in the yellow of Supply joined them, clutching a few things. Hank arrived, finally, directing traffic, shouting at those who seemed eager to turn back, to head in the other direction. A handful of people from Mechanical came out to help. Juliette concentrated on Peter's voice.

"—can't breathe," he said. "Cloud coming in. I'm in the galley. People pouring up. Everyone. Acting crazy. Falling over. Everyone dead. The outside—"

He gasped and wheezed between every other word. The radio clicked off. Juliette screamed into the handset a few times, but she couldn't raise him. Gazing up the stairwell, she saw the fog overhead. The smoke pouring out into the stairway seemed to thicken. It grew more and more dense as Juliette watched, horrified.

And then something dark punched through—a shadow amid the white. It grew. There was a scream, a terrible peal as it flew down and down, past the landings, on the other side of the stairwell, and then a thudding boom as a person slammed into the deck. The violence of the impact was felt in Juliette's boots.

More screams. This time from those nearby, those dozens spilling down the stairwell, the few who had made it. They crawled over one another in a dash for Mechanical. And the white smoke, it descended down the stairwell like a hammer.

35

JULIETTE FOLLOWED THE others into Mechanical—she was the last one through. The arms on one of the security gates had been busted backward. A crowd surged over the gates while some hopped sideways through the gap. The guard who was meant to prevent this helped people down on the other side and directed them where to go.

Juliette threw herself over and hurried through the crowd toward the bunkroom where the kids had been put up. Someone was clattering around in the break room as she passed, hopefully looting needed things. *Hopefully looting.* The world had gone suddenly mad.

The bunkroom was empty. She assumed Courtnee had already gotten there. No one was getting out of Mechanical, anyway. And it was probably already too late. Juliette doubled back down the hall and headed for the winding stairs that penetrated the levels of Mechanical. She surged with a packed crowd down to the generator room and the site of the dig.

There were piles of tailings and chunks of concrete studded with rebar around the oil rig, which continued to bob its head up and down as if it knew the sad ways of the world, as if depressedly resigned to what was happening, as if saying: "Of course. Of course."

More tailings and rubble from the dig formed piles inside the generator room, everything that hadn't yet been shoveled down the shaft to mine six. There was a scattering of people, but not the crowds Juliette had hoped. The great crowds were likely dead. And then a fleeting thought, an urge to laugh and feel ridiculous, the idea that the smoke was nothing, that the airlock up top had held, that everything was okay and that her friends would soon rib her about this panic she had caused.

But this hope vanished as quickly as it came. Nothing could cut through the metallic fear on her tongue, the sound of Peter's voice telling her that the airlock was wide open, that people were collapsing, Lukas telling her that Sims was dead.

She pushed through the crowd pouring into the tunnel and called out for the children. Then she spotted Courtnee and Walker. Walker was wide-eyed, his jaw sagging. Juliette saw the crowds through his eyes and realized the burden she had left Courtnee with, the challenge of dragging this recluse once again from his lair.

"Have you seen the kids?" she yelled over the crowd.

"They're already through!" Courtnee yelled back. "With your father."

Juliette squeezed her arm and hurried into the darkness. There were lights flashing ahead—the few who had battery-powered flashlights, those with miner's hats on—but between these beams were wide swaths of pitch black. She jostled with the invisible others who materialized solidly out of shadow. Rocks clattered down from the piles of tailings to either side; dust and debris fell from the ceiling, eliciting shrieks and curses. The passage was narrow between the rows of rubble. The tunnel had been made for a handful of people to pass through, no more. Most of the massive hole bored through the earth had been left full of the scraps the digging had generated.

Where logjams formed, some people attempted to scamper

up and along the tops of these piles. This just pushed heaps of dirt and rock down on those between, filling the tunnel with screams and curses. Juliette helped dig someone out and urged everyone to stay in the center, not to shove, even as someone practically climbed over her back.

There were others who tried to turn back, afraid and confused and distrusting of this dark run in a straight line. Juliette and others yelled for them to continue on. A nightmare formed of bumping into the support beams hastily erected in the center of the tunnel, of crawling on hands and knees over tall piles from partial cave-ins, of a baby crying at the top of its lungs somewhere. The adults did a better job of dampening their sobs, but Juliette passed by dozens crying. The journey felt interminable, as if they would crawl and stumble through that tunnel for the rest of time, until the poisonous air caught them from behind.

A jam of foot traffic formed ahead, people shoving at each others' backs, and flashlight beams played over the steel wall of the digger. The end of the tunnel. The access door at the back of the machine was open. Juliette found Raph standing by the door with one of the flashlights, his pale face aglow in the darkness, eyes wide and white.

"Jules!"

She could barely hear him over the voices echoing back and forth in the dark shaft. She made her way to him, asked him who had already passed through.

"It's too dark," he said. "They can only get through one at a time. What the hell is going on? Why all the people? We thought you said—"

"Later," she told him, hoping there would be a later. She doubted it. More likely, there would be piles of bodies at both ends of this silo. That would be the great difference between 17 and 18. Bodies at both ends. "The kids?" she asked, and as soon as she did, she wondered why with all the dead and dying she would concentrate on so few. The mother she never was, she suspected. The primal urge to look after her brood when far more than that was in peril.

"Yeah, quite a few kids came through." He paused and shouted directions to a couple who didn't want to enter the metal door at the back of this digger. Juliette could hardly blame them. They weren't even from Mechanical. What did these people think was going on? Just following the panicked shoutings of others. Probably thought they were lost in the mines. It was a wild experience even for Juliette, who had scaled hills and seen the outside.

"What about Shirly?" Juliette asked.

He aimed his flashlight inside. "Saw her for sure. I think she's in the digger. Directing traffic."

She squeezed Raph's arm, looked back at the writhing darkness of shadowy forms behind her. "Make sure you get through," she told him, and his pale face nodded his consent.

Juliette squeezed into the queue and entered the back of the digger. Cries and shouts rattled within like children screaming into empty soup cans. Shirly was at the back of the power plant, directing the shuffling and shoving mass of people through a crack in the darkness so narrow that everyone had to turn sideways. The lights that'd been rigged up inside the digger to work the tailings were off, the backup generator idle, but Juliette could feel the residual heat from it having been run. She could hear the clicking of metal as it cooled. She wondered if Shirly had been operating the unit in order to move the machine and its power plant back toward Silo 18. She and Courtnee had been arguing over where the digger belonged.

"What the hell?" Shirly asked Juliette when she spotted her.

Juliette felt like bursting into tears. How to explain what she feared, that this was the end of everything they'd ever known? She shook her head and bit her lip. "We're losing the silo," she finally managed. "The outside's getting in."

"So why send them this way?" Shirly had to yell over the clamor of voices. She pulled Juliette to the other side of the generator, away from all the shouting.

"The air is coming down the stairwell," Juliette said. "There's no stopping it. I'm going to seal off the dig."

Shirly chewed on this. "Take down the supports?"

"Not quite. The charges you wanted rigged up—"

Shirly's face hardened. "Those charges are rigged from the other side. I rigged them to seal off *this* side, to seal off *this* silo, to protect us from the air over *here.*"

"Well, now all we *have* is the air over here." Juliette passed Shirly the radio, which was all she'd taken from her home. Shirly cradled it in her arms. She balanced it atop her flashlight, which bloomed against Juliette's chest. In the light that spilled back, Juliette could see a mask of confusion on her poor friend's face. "Watch over everyone," Juliette told her. "Solo and the kids—" She eyed the generator. "The farms here are salvageable. And the air—"

"You're not going to—" Shirly started.

"I'll make sure the last of them get through. There were a few dozen behind me. Maybe another hundred." Juliette grasped her old friend's arms. She wondered if they were still friends. She wondered if there was still that bond between them. She turned to go.

"No."

Shirly grabbed Juliette's arm, the radio falling and clattering to the floor. Juliette tried to yank free.

"I'll be damned," Shirly shouted. She spun Juliette around. "I'll be goddamned if you're leaving me to this, in charge of this. I'll be goddamned—"

There were cries somewhere, from a child or an adult, it was impossible to tell. Just a cacophony of confused and terrified voices echoing in the packed confines of that great steel machine. And in the darkness, Juliette couldn't see the blow coming, couldn't see Shirly's fist. She just felt it on her jaw, marveled at the bright flash of light in the pitch black, and then remembered nothing for a while.

She came to moments or minutes later—it was impossible to tell. Curled up on the steel deck of the digger, the voices around her subdued and far away, she lay still while her face throbbed.

Fewer people. Just the ones who'd made it, and they were moving on through the bowels of the digger. She had been out for a minute or two, it seemed. Maybe longer. Much longer. Someone called her name, was looking for her in the black, but she was invisible curled up on the far side of the generator in the shadow of shadows. Someone called her name.

And then a great boom in the distance. It was like a sheet of three-inch steel falling and banging next to her head. A great rumble in the earth, a tremor felt right through the digger, and Juliette knew. Shirly had gone to the control room and had taken her place. She had set off the charges meant to protect her old home from this new one. She had doomed herself with the others.

Juliette wept. Someone called her name, and Juliette realized it was coming from the radio near her head. She reached for it numbly, her senses scrambled. It was Lukas.

"Luke," she whispered, squeezing the transmit button. His voice meant he was outside the steel locker, the airtight pantry full of food. She thought of Solo surviving for decades on those cans. Lukas could too, if anyone could. "Get back inside," she said, sobbing. "Seal yourself off." She cradled the radio in both hands and remained curled up on the deck.

"I can't," Lukas said. There was coughing, an agonizing wheeze. "I had to . . . had to hear your voice. One last time." The next bout of coughing could be felt in Juliette's own chest, which was full to bursting. "I'm done, Jules. I'm done . . ."

"No." She cried this to herself, and then squeezed the radio. "Lukas, you get inside that pantry right now. Lock it and hold on. Just hold on—"

She listened to him cough and struggle to find his voice. When it came, it was a rattle. "Can't. This is it. This is it. I love you, Jules. I love you . . ."

The last was a whisper, barely more than static. Juliette wept and slapped the floor and screamed at him. She cursed him. She cursed herself. And through the open door of the digger, a cloud of dust billowed in on a cool breeze, and Juliette could taste it on her tongue, on her lips. It was the dry chalk of crushed rock, the remnants of Shirly's blast far down the tunnel, the taste of everything she had ever known . . . dead.

PART III

HOME

Silo 1

36

CHARLOTTE LEANED AWAY from the radio, stunned. She stared at the crackling speaker, listened to the hiss of static, and played the scene over and over in her head. An open door, toxic air leaking in, people dying, a stampede, a silo gone. A silo her brother had labored to save was gone.

Her hand trembled as she reached for the dial. Flipping through channels, she heard other voices from other silos, little snippets of conversation and silence with no context, proof that elsewhere, life continued apace:

"—second time this month this has happened. You let Carol know—"

"—if you'll hold it for me until I get there, I'd sure appre—"

"..."

"—roger that. We have her in custody now—"

Bouts of static between these conversations held the place of silos full of dead air. Silos full of the dead.

Charlotte dialed back to 18. The repeaters were still working up and down that silo; she could tell from the hiss. She listened for that voice to return, the woman calling for everyone to head to the bottom levels. Charlotte had heard someone say her name. It was strange to think she'd heard the voice of this woman her brother was obsessed with, this rogue mayor as he called her, this cleaner-come-home.

It could've been someone else, but Charlotte didn't think so. Those were commands from someone in charge. She imagined a woman huddling down in the depths of a distant silo, someplace dark and lonely, and felt a sudden kinship. What she wouldn't give to be able to transmit rather than just listen, some way to reach out.

Leaning forward, she rubbed the side of the radio where the mic would wire up. It was suspicious that her brother saved this part for last. Almost as if he didn't trust her not to speak with someone. Almost as if he wanted her simply to listen. Or maybe it was himself he was worried about. Perhaps he didn't trust what he would do if he could broadcast his thoughts over the air. This wasn't the heads of the silos listening in, this was anyone with a radio.

Charlotte patted her chest and felt for the ID he had given her, and images flashed before her of a boot rising and falling, of a wall and a floor spotted with blood. In the end, he hadn't been given a chance. But she had to do something. She couldn't sit there listening to static forever, listening to people die. Donny said her ID would work the lifts. The urge to take action was overpowering.

She powered the radio down and covered it with the sheet of plastic. She arranged the chair so it appeared undisturbed and studied the drone control room for signs of habitation. Back at her bunk, she opened her trunk and studied the outfits. She chose reactor red. It fitted her more loosely than the others. Pulling it out, she inspected the name patch. *Stan*. She could be a Stan.

She got dressed and went to the storeroom. There was plenty of grease to be had from the disassembled drone. She collected some on her palm, searched one of the supply bins for a cap, and went to the bathroom. The men's room. Charlotte used to enjoy putting on make-up. That seemed like a different lifetime, a different person. She remembered moving from playing video games to trying to be pretty, shading her cheeks so they didn't look so chubby. This was before basic training made her lean and hard for a brief time. It was before two tours of duty helped her to regain her natural body, get used to that body, accept it, even love it.

She used the grease to deaccentuate her cheekbones. A little on her eyebrows made them appear fuller. A foul-tasting smear on her lips so they weren't so red. It was the opposite of any make-up job she'd ever applied. She stuffed her hair inside the cap and pulled the brim down low, adjusted her coveralls until those looked like folds of fabric rather than breasts.

It was a pathetic disguise. She saw through it immediately. But then, she knew. In a world where women weren't allowed, would any suspect? She wasn't sure. She couldn't know. She longed for Donny to be there so she could ask him. She imagined him laughing at her, which was nearly enough to make her cry.

"Don't you fucking cry," she told the mirror, dabbing at her eyes. She was worried what the crying might do to her make-up. But the tears came anyway. They came and disturbed nothing. They were drops of water gliding over grease.

There was a schematic somewhere. Charlotte searched Donny's folder of notes by the radio and didn't see it. She tried the conference room where her brother had spent much of his time poring through boxes of files. The place was a wreck. Most of his notes had been hauled off. They must be planning on coming back for the rest, probably in the morning. Or they could arrive right then, and Charlotte would have to explain what she was doing there:

"I was sent down here to retrieve . . . uh . . ." Her lowered voice sounded ridiculous. She shuffled through the opened folders and loose pages and tried again, this time with her normal voice just slightly flattened. "I was told to take this to recycling," she explained to nobody. "Oh? And what level is recycling on?" she asked herself. "I have no fucking clue," she admitted. "That's why I'm looking for a map."

She found a map. It wasn't the right one, though. A grid of circles with red lines radiating out to a single point. She only knew it was a map because she recognized the layout with its grid of letters down the side and numbers across the top. The Air Force had once assigned daily targets on grids like these. She would grab a bagel and coffee in the mess hall, and then a man and his family from D-4 would die in a fiery maelstrom. Break for lunch. Ham and cheese on rye.

Charlotte recognized the circles laid out across the grid. It was the silos. She had flown three drones over depressions in hills just like this. The red lines were odd. She traced one with her finger. They reminded her of flight lines. They extended off every silo except for the one near the center, which she thought might be the one she was in. Donald had shown her this layout once on the big table, the one now buried under the loose pages. She folded the map and stuffed it into her breast pocket and kept looking.

The Silo 1 schematic she had seen before seemed lost, but she found the next best thing. A directory. It listed personnel by rank, shift assignment, occupation, living level, and work level. It was the size of a phone book for a small town, a reminder of how many people were taking turns running the silo. Not people—*men*. Scanning the names, Charlotte saw that it was all men. She thought of Sasha, the only other woman who'd gone through boot camp with her. Strange to think that Sasha was dead, that all the men in her regiment, everyone from flight school, all of them were dead.

She found the name of a reactor mechanic and his work level, looked for a pen amid the chaos, found one, and jotted the level number down. Administration, she discovered, was on level thirty-four. A comms officer worked on the same level, which sucked. She hated to think of the comm room right down the hall from the people who ran the joint. A security officer worked on twelve. If Donny was being held, maybe he'd be there. Unless they'd put him back to sleep. Unless he was in whatever passed for a hospital there. Cryo was down below, she thought. She remembered coming up the lift after he'd woken her. She found the level for the main cryo office by locating someone who worked there, but that probably wasn't where the bodies were kept. Was it?

Her notes became a mess of scribbles, a rough outline of what was where above and below her. But where to start in her search? She couldn't find mention of the supply and spares rooms her brother had been raiding, probably because no one actually worked on those levels. Starting over on a fresh piece of paper, she drew a cylinder and made the best schematic she could, filling in the floors she knew from Donny's routine and the ones from the directory. Starting with the cafeteria at the very top, she worked her way down to the cryo office, which was as far down as her notes took her. The empty levels were her best bet. Some of those would be storerooms and warehouses. But the lift could just as easily open to a roomful of men playing cards—or whatever it was they did to kill the time while they killed the world. She couldn't just roll the dice; she needed a plan.

She studied the map and considered her options. One place for sure would have a mic, and that was the comm room. She checked the clock on the wall. Six twenty-five. Dinnertime and end of shift, lots of people moving about. Charlotte touched her face where she had smudged grease to dull her cheekbones. She wasn't thinking straight, probably shouldn't go anywhere until after eleven. Or was it better to be lost in a jostling crowd? What was out there? She paced and debated. "I don't know, I don't know," she said, testing her new voice. It sounded like she had a cold. That was the best way to sound male: like she had a cold.

She returned to the storeroom and studied the lift doors. Someone could burst out right then, and her decision would be made for her. She should wait until later. Returning to the drones, she pulled the tarp off the one she'd been working on and studied the loose panels and scattering of tools. Glancing back at the conference room, she saw Donny curled there on the floor, trying to fend off the kicks with his shins, two men holding him down, a man who could barely stand landing sickening blows.

Picking up a driver, Charlotte slotted it into one of the tool pouches on her coveralls. Not sure what to do, she got to work on the drone, killing time. She would go out later that night when there were fewer people up and less chance of being spotted. First, she would get the next machine ready to fly. Donny wasn't there—his work lay unfinished—but she could soldier on. She could piece things back together, one bolt and one nut at a time. And that night, she would go out and find the part she needed. She would win back her voice and reach out to those people in that stricken silo, if any of them were still alive.

37

THE ARRIVING LIFT struck midnight. Well, five past midnight. That's when Charlotte finally built up enough nerve to venture out, and the lift sent a ding echoing through the armory.

The doors rattled open, and she stepped inside memories of a lost place and time, memories of a normal world where lifts took people to and from work. Clutching the ID card Donny had given her, she felt another pang of doubt. The doors began to close. Charlotte stuck her boot out and allowed the doors to slam against her foot, and the lift opened again. She waited for alarms to sound as the doors tried to close a second time. Maybe she should get off the damn thing and make up her mind, let the lift be on its way, grab another in an hour or two. The doors pinched her boot tentatively, and then retreated, like a monster considering whether to eat her. Charlotte decided she had delayed long enough.

She pressed her ID card to the reader and watched its eye blink green, then pressed the button for level thirty-four. Admin and comms. The lion's den. The doors seemed to sigh gratefully as they finally met. The floors began to flash by.

Charlotte checked the back of her neck and felt a few loose strands of hair. She tucked them into her cap. Admin was a risk—she would stand out in red coveralls meant for the reactor level—but it would be even more awkward to show up where she seemed to belong while not knowing her way around or what she was supposed to do. She patted her pockets to make sure she had her tools, made sure they were visible. They were her cover. Hidden inside a large pouch on her hip, a pistol from one of the storage bins sagged conspicuously. Charlotte's heart raced as the levels flew past. She tried to imagine the world outside that Donald had described, the dry and lifeless wasteland. She imagined the lift going all the way up and opening on those barren hills, the wind howling inside the lift. It might be a relief.

No passengers joined her on the way up. It was a good decision, going this time of night. Thirty-six, thirty-five, and then the lift slowed. The doors opened on a hallway, the lights beyond harsh and bright. She doubted her disguise immediately. A man looked up from a gate a dozen paces distant. There was nothing familiar about this world, nothing like her home of the past few weeks. She tugged the brim of her hat down, aware that it didn't match her coveralls. The important thing was confidence, which she felt none of. Be brash. Direct. She told herself that the days here were full of sameness. Everyone would see what they expected to see. She approached the man and his gate and held out her ID.

"You expected?" the man asked. He pointed to the scanner on her side of the gate. Charlotte swiped the card, not knowing what might happen, fully prepared to run, to pull out the pistol, to surrender, or some confusing mix of all three.

"We're showing a, uh... power drain on this level." Her pretend-sick voice sounded ludicrous to her own ears. But then, she knew her voice better than anyone—she told herself that was why it sounded funny. It might sound normal to someone else. She also hoped a power drain made as little sense to this man as it did to her. "I was sent up to check the comm room. You know where it is?"

A question for him. Tickle his male ego for directions. Charlotte felt a rivulet of sweat run down the nape of her neck and wondered if there were anymore loose strands of hair. She fought the urge to check. Lifting her arm might tighten her coveralls across her chest. Sizing up the large man, she pictured him grabbing her and slamming her to the ground, hands the size of small plates pummeling her.

"Comms? Of course. Yeah. Down the hall to the end, turn left. Second door on your right."

"Thanks." Tipping her hat allowed her to keep her head down. She pushed through the bars with a clack and the tick of some invisible counter.

"Forgetting something?"

She turned. Her hand fell to the pouch by her leg.

"Need you to sign the work log." The guard held out a worn digital tablet, its screen a haze of curling scratches.

"Right." Charlotte took the plastic stylus hanging from a cord of wire repaired with tape. She studied the entry box in the center of the screen. There was a place to write the time and a place to sign her name. She filled in the time and glanced at her chest, already forgetting. Stan. Her name was Stan. She scrawled this messily, tried to make it look casual, handed him the tablet and stylus.

"See you on your way out," the guard said.

Charlotte nodded and hoped her way out would prove just as uneventful.

She followed his directions down the main hall. There was more activity, more sounds than she expected at that time of night. There were lights on in a few of the offices, the squeak of chairs and filing cabinets and keyboards clattering. A door opened down the hall, and a man stepped out, pulled the door shut behind him. Charlotte saw his face, and her legs went numb. She staggered a few steps on stalks of bone and meat, wobbly. Dizzy. Nearly fell.

She lowered her head and scratched the back of her neck, disbelieving. But it was Thurman. Slimmer and older-looking. And then images of Donny curled in a ball and being beaten half to death flooded back. The hallway blurred behind a coat of tears. The white hair, the tall frame. How had she not recognized him then?

"You're a ways from home, aren't you?" Thurman asked.

His voice was sandpaper. It was a familiar scratch. As familiar as her mother's or her father's voice would've been.

"Checking a power drain," Charlotte said, not stopping or turning, hoping he meant her coveralls and not her gender. How could he not hear that it was her voice? How could he not recognize her gait, her frame, the bare patch of skin on the back of her neck, that few square inches of exposed flesh, anything to betray her?

"See to it," he said.

She walked a dozen paces. Two dozen. Sweating. Feeling drunk. She waited until she was at the end of the hall, just starting to make the turn, before glancing back toward the security station. Thurman was there in the distance, speaking with the guard, his white hair like the bare sun. Second door on the right, she reminded herself. She was in danger of forgetting the guard's directions to the comm room, such was the pounding of her heart and the racing of her mind. She took a deep breath and reminded herself why she was there. Seeing Thurman and realizing it was he who had laid into Donny had stunned her. But there was no time for processing that. A door stood before her. She tested the knob, then stepped inside.

• • •

A lone man sat inside the comm room, staring at a bank of monitors and flashing indicators. He turned in his seat as Charlotte entered, a mug in his hand, a great belly wedged between the armrests. Fine wisps of hair had been combed across an otherwise bald head. He peeled back one of the cups from his ear and lifted his eyebrows questioningly.

There had to be half a dozen radio units scattered across the U-shaped arrangement of workbenches and comfortable chairs. An embarrassment of riches. Charlotte just needed one part.

"Yeah?" the radio operator asked.

Charlotte's mouth felt dry. One lie had gotten her past the guard; she had one more fib prepared. She cleared her mind of having seen Thurman in the hallway, of images of him kicking her brother.

"Here to fix one of your units," she said. She pulled a driver from a pocket and briefly imagined having to fight this man, felt a surge of adrenaline. She had to stop thinking like a soldier. She was an electrician. And she needed to get him talking so that she wasn't. "Which is the one with the bum mic?" She waved her driver across the units. Years of piloting drones and working with computers had taught her one thing: there was always a problem machine. Always.

The radio operator narrowed his eyes. He studied her for a moment, then glanced around the room. "You must mean number two," he said. "Yeah. The button's sticky. I'd given up on anyone taking a look." The chair squeaked as he leaned back and locked his fingers behind his head. His armpits were dark stains. "Last guy said it was minor. Not worth replacing. Said to use it until it gave out."

Charlotte nodded and went to the machine he had indicated. It was too easy. She attacked the side panel with her driver, her back to the operator.

"You work down on the reactor levels, right?"

She nodded.

"Yeah. Ate across from you in the cafeteria a while back."

Charlotte waited for him to ask her name again or to resume some conversation he'd had with a different tech. The driver slipped out of her sweaty palm and clattered on the desk. She scooped it back up. She could feel the operator watching her work.

"You think you'll be able to fix it?"

She shrugged. "I need to take it with me. Should have it back tomorrow." She pulled the side panel off and loosened the screw holding the microphone's cord to the casing. The cord itself unplugged from a board inside the machine. On second thought, she undid this board and pulled it out as well. Couldn't remember if she had one installed already, and it made her look as though she really knew what the hell she was doing.

"You'll have it tomorrow? That's great. Really appreciate this."

Charlotte gathered the parts and stood up straight. Pinching the brim of her hat was enough of a goodbye; she turned and headed out the door, leaving too hastily, she suspected. The side panel and screws had been left on the counter. A real tech would've put them back, wouldn't they? She wasn't sure. She knew a few pilots from a different life who would've laughed to have seen her pretending to be technically inclined, modding drones and building radios, putting grease rather than rouge on her face.

The operator said one last thing, but his words were pinched off as she pulled the door shut. She hurried down the hall and toward the main corridor, expecting to round the bend and find Thurman there with a handful of guards, wide shoulders blocking her way. She slotted the driver back into her pocket and coiled the microphone wire up, cradled it and the board to her chest. When she turned the corner, there was no one in the hall except the guard. It took what felt like hours to walk down that corridor to the security gate. It took days. The walls pressed in and throbbed with her heartbeat. Her coveralls clung to her damp skin. Tools rattled, and the gun weighed heavy at her hip. With each step, the lift doors somehow drew two steps further away from her.

She stopped at the gate, remembered the place on the slate to mark her time out, and made a show of checking the guard's clock before scratching the time.

"That was quick," the guard said.

She forced a smile but didn't look up. "Wasn't a big deal." She handed him the tablet and stepped through the clacking gates. Behind her, down the hall, someone closed an office door, boots squeaking on tile. Charlotte marched toward the lifts and jabbed the call button once, twice, wishing the damn thing would hurry. The lift dinged its arrival. There was a clomp of boots behind her.

"Hey!" someone yelled.

Charlotte didn't turn. She hurried inside the lift as someone else clacked through the security gates.

"Hold that for me."

38

A BODY SLAMMED AGAINST the lift doors, a hand jutting inside. Charlotte nearly screamed in fright, nearly slapped at the hand, but then the doors were opening, and a man crowded into the lift beside her, breathing hard.

"Going down, right?"

The name patch on his gray coveralls read *Eren*. He caught his breath while the doors closed. Charlotte's hand was trembling. It took two tries to scan her card. She reached for the button marked "54", but caught herself before pressing it. She had no business being on that level. No one did. The man was watching her, his own card out, waiting for her to decide.

What level for the reactor? She had it written down on a piece of paper inside one of her pockets, but she couldn't very well pull it out and study it. Suddenly, she could smell the grease on her face, could feel herself damp with sweat. Cradling the radio parts in one arm, she pressed one of the lowest levels, trusting that this man would get off before she did and she would have the lift to herself.

"Excuse me," he said, reaching in front of her to swipe his card. Charlotte could smell stale coffee on his breath. He punched the button for level forty-two, and the lift shivered into motion.

"Late shift?" Eren asked.

"Yeah," Charlotte said, keeping her head down and her voice low.

"You just waking up?"

She shook her head. "Night shift."

"No, I mean are you just coming out of freeze? Don't think I've seen you around. I'm the on-shift head right now." He laughed. "For another week, anyway."

Charlotte shrugged. It was boiling hot inside the lift. The numbers were counting down so damn slowly. She should've pressed a nearby floor, gotten off, and waited on the next lift. Too late, now.

"Hey, look at me," the man said.

He knew. He was standing so close. Too close for anything but suspicious scrutiny. Charlotte glanced up; she could feel her breasts press against her coveralls, could feel hair trailing out from her cap, could feel her cheekbones and stubble-free chin, everything that made her a woman, not least of which was her powerful revulsion at this strange man staring at her, this man who had her trapped and powerless in a small lift. She met his gaze, feeling all of this and more. Helpless and afraid.

"What the fuck?" the man said.

Charlotte threw her knee up between his legs, hoping to cripple him, but he turned his hips and jumped back. She caught him on the thigh, instead. She fumbled for the pistol—but the pouch was snapped shut. Never thought she'd need to draw it in a hurry. She got the pouch open and the pistol free as the man slammed into her, knocking the wind out of her lungs and the gun from her hand. The gun and the radio parts clattered to the floor. Boots squeaked as the two of them wrestled, but she was vastly overpowered. His hands gripped her wrists painfully. She screamed, her high-pitched voice a confession. The lift slowed to a stop on his level, and the doors dinged open.

"Hey!" Eren yelled. He tried to drag Charlotte through the doors, but she placed a boot on the panel and kicked off, attempting to wrench free of his grip. "Help!" he shouted over his shoulder and down the dim and empty hall. "Guys! Help!"

Charlotte bit his hand at the base of his thumb. There was a pop as her teeth punctured his flesh, and then the bitter taste of blood. He cursed and lost his grip on her wrist. She kicked him back through the door, lost her cap, felt her hair spill down to her neck as she reached for the gun.

The doors began to close, leaving the man out in the hallway. He lurched from his hands and knees and was back through the doors before they could bang shut. He slammed into Charlotte, and she hit the back wall as the lift continued its merry jaunt down the silo.

A blow caught her in the jaw. Charlotte saw a flash of bright light. She jerked her head back before the next punch landed. The man pressed her against the back of the lift, was grunting like a crazed animal, a sound of fury and terror and startlement. He was trying to kill her, this thing he couldn't understand. She had attacked him, and now he was trying to kill her. A blow to her ribs, and Charlotte cried out and clutched her side. She felt hands around her neck, squeezing, lifting her off the floor. Her palm settled on a driver slotted into her coveralls.

"Hold . . . still," the man grunted through clenched teeth.

Charlotte gagged. Couldn't breathe. Could barely make a sound. Her windpipe was being crushed. Driver in her right fist, she brought it up over his shoulder and slammed it at his face, hoping to scratch him, hoping to scare him, to make him let go. She drove it with all the strength she had left in her, with the last of her consciousness, as the dark tunnel of her vision began to iris shut.

The man saw the strike coming and turned his head to the side, eyes wide as he sought to avoid the blow. She missed his face. The driver buried itself in his neck instead. He lost his grip on her, and Charlotte felt the driver twist and tear inside his throat as she clung to it to keep from falling.

There was a flash of warmth on her face. The lift came to a sudden stop, and both of them fell to the ground. There was a gurgling sound, and the heat on Charlotte's face was the man's blood, which jetted out in crimson spurts. They both gasped for air. Beyond, there was laughter in a hallway, loud voices booming, a gleaming floor that reminded her of the medical wing in which she'd woken up.

She staggered to her feet. The man in gray who had attacked her kicked and squirmed on the ground, his life spilling out of his neck, his eyes wide and beseeching her—anyone—for help. He tried to speak, to cry out to the people down the hall, but it was little more than a gurgle. Charlotte stooped and grabbed him by the collar. The doors were closing. She jammed her boot between them, and they opened again. Tugging on the man—who slipped and slid in his own blood, heels slamming against the floor of the lift—she pulled him into the hallway, made sure his boots were free of the doors. The lift began to close again, threatening to leave her there with him. There was more laughter from a nearby room, a group of men cracking up over some joke. Charlotte dove for the closing doors, stuck her arm between them, and they opened once more. She staggered inside, numb and exhausted.

There was blood everywhere. Her boots slipped in the stuff. Looking at the horror on the ground, she realized something was missing. The pistol. Panic tightened her chest as she glanced up, the doors shuddering together a final time. There was a deafening bang from the gun, hate and fear in a dying man's eyes, and then she was thrown back, a fire erupting in her shoulder.

"Fuck."

Charlotte staggered across the lift, her first thought to get it moving, to flee. She could feel the man on the other side of the door, could picture him clutching his neck with one hand and holding that pistol in the other, could imagine him fumbling for the lift call button, leaving a smear of blood on the wall. She pressed a handful of buttons, marking them with blood, but none of the floors lit up. Cursing, she fumbled for her ID. One arm wouldn't respond. She reached awkwardly across herself with the other, dug the ID out, nearly dropped it, ran it through the scanner.

"Fuck. Fuck," she whispered, her shoulder on fire. She jabbed the button for fifty-four. Home. Her prison had become home, a safe place. By her feet lay the radio parts. The control board was cracked in half from someone's boot. She slid down to her heels, cradling her other arm, fighting the urge to pass out, and scooped up the microphone. She draped this by its cord around the back of her neck, left the other parts. There was blood everywhere. Some of it had to be hers. Reactor red. It blended right in with her coveralls. The lift rose, slowed to a stop, and opened on the dark supply room on fifty-four.

Charlotte staggered out, remembered something, and stepped back inside. She kicked the doors open as they tried to shut, was angry with them now. With her elbow, she tried to wipe the lift buttons clean. There was a smear of blood, a fingerprint, on button fifty-four, a sign pointing to where she had gone. It was no use. The doors again tried to close, and again she kicked them for their effort. Desperate, Charlotte bent and ran her palm through the man's spilled blood, returned to the panel, and covered every button with a great dose of the stuff. Finally, she scanned her ID and pressed the top level, sending the goddamn thing far away, as far away as she could. Staggering out, she collapsed to the ground. The doors began to close, and she was glad to let them.

39

THEY WOULD LOOK for her. She was a fugitive locked in a cage, in a single, giant building. They would hunt her down.

Charlotte's mind raced. If the man she attacked died there in the hallway, she might have until the end of shift before he was discovered and they started looking for her. If he found help, it could be hours. But they had to have heard the gun going off, right? They would save his life. She hoped they would save his life.

She opened a crate where she'd seen a medical kit. Wrong crate. It was the next one. She dug the kit out and undid her coveralls, tearing at the snaps. Wiggling her arms out, she saw the grisly wound. Dark red blood puckered from a hole in her arm and streaked down to her elbow. She reached around and winced as her fingers found the exit. Her arm was numb from the wound down. From the wound up, it was throbbing.

She tore a roll of gauze open with her teeth, then wrapped it under her armpit and around and around, sent the roll behind her neck and across her other shoulder to keep it all in place. Finally, another few laps across the wound. She'd forgotten a pad, a compress, didn't feel like doing it again. Instead, she just made the last wrap as tight as she could tolerate before cinching the end. As far as dressings went, it was a train wreck. Everything from basic training had gone out the window during the fight and after. Just impulse and reflex. Charlotte closed the lid on the bin, saw the blood left on the latch, and realized she'd have to think more clearly to get through this. She opened the case back up, grabbed another roll of gauze, and cleaned up after herself, then checked the floor outside the lifts.

It was a mess. She went back for a small bottle of alcohol, remembered where she'd seen a huge jug of industrial cleaner, grabbed that plus more gauze, wiped everything up. Took her time. Couldn't get in too big a hurry.

The bundle of soiled and stained cloth went back in the bin, the lid kicked shut. Satisfied with the condition of the floor, she hurried to the barracks. Her cot made it obvious that someone lived there. The other mattresses were bare. Before she fixed this, she stripped down, grabbed another pair of coveralls, and went to the bathroom. After washing her hands and face, and the bright spill of blood down her neck and between her breasts, she cleaned the sink and changed. The red coveralls went into her footlocker. If they looked in there, she was screwed.

She pulled the covers off her bed, grabbed her pillow, and made sure everything else was straight. Back in the warehouse, she opened the hangar door on the drone lift and threw her things inside. She went to the shelves and gathered rations and water, added this. Another small medical kit. Inside the bin of first-aid gear, she discovered the microphone, which she must've dropped earlier while grabbing the gauze. This and two flashlights and a spare set of batteries went inside the lift as well. It was the last place anyone would look. The door was practically invisible unless you knew what to search for. It only came up to her knees and was the same color as the wall.

She considered crawling inside right then, would just need to outlast the first thorough search of the level. They would concentrate on the shelving units, the stacks, and think the place was clear, move on to the many other warrens in which she could be hiding. But before she waited that out, there was the microphone coiled up that she had worked so hard to acquire. There was the radio. She had a few hours, she told herself. This wouldn't be the first place they'd check. Surely she had a few hours.

Dizzy from lack of sleep and loss of blood, she made her way to the flight control room and pulled the plastic sheet from the radio. Patting her chest, she remembered she'd changed coveralls. And besides, that driver was gone. She searched the bench for another, found one, and removed the panel from the side of the unit. The board she wasn't sure about was already installed. It was a simple matter of plugging the microphone in. She didn't bother with affixing it to the side panel or closing anything up.

She checked the seating of the control boards. It was a lot like a computer, all the parts slotting together, but she was no electrician. She had no idea if there was anything else, anything missing. And no way in hell was she going on another run for parts. She powered up the unit and selected the channel marked "18".

She waited.

Adjusting the squelch, she brought enough static into the speakers to make sure the unit was on. There was no traffic on the channel. Squeezing the microphone put an end to the static, which was a good sign. Weary and hurting and fearful for herself as well as her brother, Charlotte managed a smile. The click of the microphone back through the speakers was a small victory.

"Can anyone read me?" she asked. She propped one elbow on the desk, her other arm hanging useless by her side. She tried again. "Anyone out there with ears on? Please come back."

Static. Which didn't prove anything. Charlotte could very well imagine the radios sitting miles away in this silo somewhere, all the operators around them slouched over, dead. Her brother had told her about the time he had ended a silo with the press of a button. He had come to her with his eyes shining in the middle of the night and told her all about it. And now this other silo was gone. Or maybe her radio wasn't broadcasting.

She wasn't thinking straight. Needed to troubleshoot before she jumped to conclusions. Reaching for the dial, she immediately thought of the other silo she and her brother had eavesdropped in on, this neighboring silo with a handful of survivors who liked to chat back and forth and play games like Hide and Find with their radios. If she remembered right, the mayor of 18 had somehow transmitted on this other frequency before. Charlotte clicked over to "17" to test her mic, see if anyone would respond, forgetting the late hour. She used her old call sign from the Air Force out of habit.

"Hello. Hello. This is charlie two-four. Anyone read me?"

She listened to static, was about to switch over to another channel when a voice broke through, shaky and distant:

"Yes. Hello? Can you hear us?"

Charlotte squeezed the microphone again, the pain in her shoulder momentarily gone, this connection with a strange voice like a shot of adrenaline.

"I hear you. Yes. You can read me okay?"

"What the hell is going on over there? We can't get through to you. The tunnel . . . there's rubble in the tunnel. No one will respond. We're trapped over here."

Charlotte tried to make sense of this. She double-checked the transmit frequency. "Slow down," she said and took a deep breath, took her own advice. "Where are you? What's going on?"

"Is this Shirly? We're stuck over here in this . . . other place. Everything's rusted. People are panicking. You've gotta get us out of here."

Charlotte didn't know whether to answer or simply power the unit down and try again later. It felt as though she had butted into the middle of a conversation, confusing one of the parties. Another voice chimed in, supporting her theory:

"That's not Shirly," someone said, a woman's voice. "Shirly's dead."

Charlotte adjusted the volume. She listened intently. For a moment, she forgot the man dying in the hallway below, the man she had stabbed, the wound in her arm. She forgot about those who must be coming after her, searching for her. She listened instead with great interest to this conversation on channel 17, this voice that sounded vaguely familiar.

"Who is this?" the first voice—the male voice—asked.

There was a pause. Charlotte didn't know whom he was asking, whom he expected an answer from. She lifted the microphone to her lips, but someone else answered.

"This is Juliette."

The voice was labored and weary.

"Jules? Where are you? What do you mean, Shirly's dead?"

Another burst of static. Another dreadful pause.

"I mean they're all dead," she said. "And so are we."

A burst of static.

"I killed us all."

Silo 17

40

JULIETTE OPENED HER eyes and saw her father. A white light bloomed and passed from one of her eyes to the other. Several faces loomed behind him, peering down at her. Light blue and white and yellow coveralls. What seemed a dream at first gradually coalesced into something real. And what was sensed as nothing more than a nightmare hardened into recollection: Her silo had been shut down. Doors had been opened. Everyone was dead. The last thing she remembered was clutching a radio, hearing voices, and declaring everyone dead. And she had killed them.

She waved the light away and tried to roll onto her side. She was on damp steel plating, someone's undershirt tucked under her head, not on a bed. Her stomach lurched, but nothing came out. It was hollow, cramping, heaving. She made gagging noises and spat on the ground. Her father urged her to breathe. Raph was there, asking her if she'd be all right. Juliette bit down the urge to yell at them all, to yell at the world to leave her the hell alone, to hug her knees and weep for what she'd done. But Raph kept asking if she was okay.

Juliette wiped her mouth with her sleeve and tried to sit up. The room was dark. She was no longer inside the digger. A lambent glow beat from somewhere, like an open flame, the smell of burning biodiesel, a homemade torch. And in the gloom, she saw the dance and swing of flashlights at the ends of disembodied hands and on miners' helmets as her people tended to one another. Small groups huddled here and there. A stunned silence sat like a blanket atop the scattered weeping.

"Where am I?" she asked.

Raph answered. "One of the boys found you in the back of that machine. Said you were curled up. They thought you were dead at first—"

Her father interrupted. "I'm going to listen to your heart. If you can take deep breaths for me."

Juliette didn't argue. She felt young again, young and miserable for breaking something, for disappointing him. Her father's beard twinkled with silver from Raph's flashlight. He plugged his stethoscope into his ears, and she knew the drill. She parted her coveralls. He listened as she swallowed deep gulps of air and let them out slowly. Above her, she recognized enough of the pipes and electrical conduit and exhaust ducts to locate herself. They were in the large pump facility adjacent to the generator room. The ground was wet because all this had been flooded. There must be water trapped above here, a slow leak somewhere, a reservoir gradually emptying. Juliette remembered all the water. She had donned a cleaning suit and had swum past this room in some long-ago life.

"Where are the kids?" she asked.

"They went with your friend Solo," her father said. "He said he was taking them home."

Juliette nodded. "How many others made it?" She took another deep breath and wondered who was still alive. She remembered herding all that she could through the dig. She had seen Courtnee and Walker. Erik and Dawson. Fitz. She remembered seeing families, some of the kids from the classrooms, and that young boy from the bazaar in shopkeep brown coveralls. But Shirly . . . Juliette reached up and gingerly touched her sore jaw. She could hear the blast and feel the rumbles in the ground again. Shirly was gone. Lukas was gone. Nelson and Peter. Her heart couldn't hold it all. She expected it to stop, to quit, while her father was listening to it.

"There's no telling how many made it," Raph said. "Everyone is . . . it's chaos out there." He touched Juliette's shoulder. "There was a group that came through a while back, before everything went nuts. A priest and his congregation. And then a bunch more came after. And then you."

Her father listened intently to her stubborn heartbeat. He moved the metal pad from one corner of her back to another, and Juliette took deep, dutiful breaths. "Some of your friends are trying to figure out how to turn that machine around and dig us out of here," her father said.

"Some are already digging," Raph told her. "With their hands. And shovels."

Juliette tried to sit up. The pain of all she'd lost was hammered by the thought of losing those who remained. "They can't dig," she said. "Dad, it's not safe over there. We have to stop them." She clutched his coveralls.

"You need to take it easy," he said. "I sent someone to fetch you some water—"

"Dad, if they dig, we'll die. Everyone over here will die."

There was silence. It was broken by the slap of boots. A light slashed the darkness up and down, and Bobby arrived with a dented tin canteen sloshing with water.

"We'll die if they dig us out," Juliette said again. She refrained from adding that they were all dead anyway. They were walking corpses in that shell of a silo, that home for madness and rust. But she knew she sounded just as mad as everyone else had, cautioning against digging because the air over here was supposed to be poison. Now they wanted to tunnel to their death as badly as she had wanted to tunnel to hers.

She drank from the canteen, water splashing from her chin to her chest, and considered the lunacy of it all. And then she remembered the congregation that'd come over to exorcise this poisoned silo's demons, or maybe to see the devil's work for themselves. Lowering the canteen, she turned to her father, a looming silhouette in the spill of light from Raph's flashlight.

"Father Wendel and his people," Juliette said. "Was that . . . ? They were the ones who came earlier?"

"They were seen heading up and out of Mechanical," Bobby said. "I heard they were looking for a place to worship. A bunch of the others went up to the farms, heard there was still something growing there. A lot of people are worried about what we'll eat until we get out of here."

"What we'll eat," Juliette muttered. She wanted to tell Bobby that they weren't getting out of there. Ever. It was gone. Everything they had known. The only reason she knew and they didn't is because she had stumbled through the piles of bones and over the mounds of the dead getting into this silo. She had seen what becomes of a fallen world, had heard Solo tell his story of dark days, had listened on the radio as those events played out all over again. She knew the threats, the threats that had now been carried out, all because of her daring.

Raph urged her to sip some more water, and Juliette saw in the flashlit faces around her that these survivors thought they were merely in a spot of trouble, that this was temporary. The truth was that this was likely all that remained of their people, this few hundred who had managed to get through, those lucky enough to live in the Deep, a startled mob from the lower Mids, a congregation of fanatics who had doubted this place. Now they were dispersing, looking to survive what they must hope would be over in a few days, a week, simply concerned with having enough to eat until they were saved.

They didn't yet understand that they *had* been saved. Everyone else was gone.

She handed the canteen back to Raph and started to get up. Her father urged her to stay put, but Juliette waved him off. "We have to stop them from digging," she said, getting to her feet. The seat of her coveralls was damp from the wet floor. There was a leak somewhere, pools of water trapped in the ceilings and the levels above them, slowly draining. It occurred to her that they would need to fix this. And just as quickly, she realized there was no point. Such planning was over. It was now about surviving the next minute, the next hour.

"Which way to the dig?" she asked.

Raph reluctantly pointed with his flashlight. She pulled him along, stopped short when she saw Jomeson, the old pump repairman, huddled against a wall of silent and rusted pumps, his hands cupped in his lap. Jomeson was sobbing to himself, his shoulders pumping up and down like pistons as he gazed into his hands.

Juliette pointed her father to the man and went to his side. "Jomes, are you hurt?"

"I saved this," Jomeson blubbered. "I saved this. I saved this."

Raph aimed his flashlight into the mechanic's lap. A pile of chits glimmered in his palms. Several months' pay. They clinked as his body shook, coins writhing like insects.

"In the mess hall," he said between sniffles and sobs. "In the mess hall while everyone was running. I opened the till. Cans and cans and jars in the larder. And this. I saved this."

"Shhh," Juliette said, resting a hand on his trembling shoulder. She looked to her father, who shook his head. There was nothing to be done for him.

Raph aimed the flashlight elsewhere. Further down, a

mother rocked back and forth and wailed. She clutched a baby to her chest. The child seemed to be okay, its small arm reaching up for its mother, its hand opening and closing, but making no noise. So much had been lost. Everyone had what they could carry and nothing more, just whatever they had grabbed. Jomeson sobbed for what he had grabbed as floodwater trickled from the ceiling, a silo weeping, all but the children crying.

41

JULIETTE FOLLOWED RAPH through the great digger and into the tunnel. They walked a long way over piles of rocks, scampered over avalanches of tailings cascading down from both sides, saw clothes, a single boot, and a half-buried blanket that'd been dropped. Someone's canteen lay forgotten, which Raph collected; he shook it and smiled when it sloshed.

In the distance, open flames bathed rock in orange and red, the raw meat of the earth exposed. A fresh pile of rubble sloped down from a full cave-in of the ceiling, the result of Shirly's sacrifice. Juliette pictured her friend on the other side of those rocks. She saw Shirly slumped over in the generator control room, asphyxiated or poisoned or simply disintegrating in the outside air. This image of a friend lost joined that of Lukas in his small apartment below the servers, his young and lifeless hand relaxed around a silent radio.

Juliette's radio had gone silent as well. There had been that brief transmission in the middle of the night from someone above them, a transmission that woke her up and that she had ended by announcing that everyone was dead. After that call, she had tried to reach Lukas. She had tried him over and over, but it hurt too much to listen to the static. She was killing herself and her battery by trying, had finally switched the unit off, had briefly considered calling on channel 1 to yell at the fucker who had betrayed her, but she didn't want them to know any of her people had survived, that there were more of them out there to kill.

Juliette vacillated between fuming over the evil of what they'd done and mourning the loss of those they'd taken. She leaned against her father and followed Raph and Bobby toward the clinks and thwacks and shouts of digging. Right then, she needed to buy time, to save what was left. Her brain was in survival mode, her body numb and staggering. What she knew for sure was that joining the two silos yet again would mean the death of them all. She had seen the white mist descending the stairwell, knew that this wasn't some harmless gas, had seen what was left of the gasket and heat tape. This was how they poisoned the outside air. It was how they ended worlds.

"Watch yer toes!" someone barked. A miner trundled by with a barrow of rubble. Juliette found herself walking up a sloping floor, the ceiling getting closer and closer. She could make out Courtnee's voice ahead. Dawson's too. Piles of tailings had been hauled away from the collapse to mark the progress already made. Juliette felt torn between the urge to warn Courtnee to stop what she was doing and the desire to jump forward and dig with her own hands, to bend her nails back as she clawed her way toward whatever had happened over there, death be damned.

"Okay, let's clear that top back before we go any further. And what's taking so long with the jack? Can we please get some hydraulics from the genset fed back here? Just because it's dark doesn't mean I can't see you dregs slackin'—"

Courtnee fell silent when she saw Juliette. Her face hardened, her lips pressed tight. And Juliette could sense her friend was wavering between slapping her and hugging her. It stung that she did neither.

"You're up," Courtnee said.

Juliette averted her gaze and studied the piles of stone and rock. Soot swirled and settled from the burning diesel torches. It made the cold air deep inside the earth feel dry and thin, and Juliette worried about the oxygen being burned and whether the sparse farms of Silo 17 could keep up with the demand. And what about all the new lungs—hundreds of pairs of them—sucking that oxygen down as well?

"We need to talk about this," Juliette said, waving at the cave-in.

"We can talk about what the hell happened here after we dig our way back home. If you want to grab a shovel—"

"This rock is the only thing keeping us alive," Juliette said.

Several of those digging had already stopped when they saw who was talking to Courtnee. Courtnee barked at them to get back to work, and they did. Juliette didn't know how to do this delicately. She didn't know how to do it at all.

"I don't know what you're getting at—" Courtnee started.

"Shirly brought the roof down and saved us. If you dig through this, we'll die. I'm sure of it."

"Shirly—?"

"Our home was poisoned, Court. I don't know how to explain it, but it was. People were dying up top. I heard from Peter and—" She caught her breath. "From Luke. Peter saw the outside. The *outside*. The doors had opened and people were dying. And Luke—" Juliette bit her lip until the pain cleared her thoughts. "The first thing I thought of was to get everyone over here, because I knew it was safe here—"

A bark of laughter from Courtnee. "Safe? You think it's . . . ?" She took a step closer to Juliette, and suddenly no one was digging. Juliette's father placed a hand on his daughter's arm and tried to pull her back, but Juliette held her ground.

"You think it's safe over here?" Courtnee hissed. "Where the hell are we? There's a room back there that looks a goddamn lot like our gen room, except that it's a rusted wreck. You think those machines will ever spin again? How much air do we have over here? How much fuel? What about food and water? I give us a few days if we don't get back home. That's a few days of dead-out digging, mostly by hand. Do you have any idea what you've done to us, bringing us over here?"

Juliette withstood the barrage. She welcomed it. She longed to add a few stones of her own.

"I did this," she said. She pulled away from her father and faced the diggers, whom she knew well. She turned and threw her voice down the dark pit from which she'd just come. *"I did this!"* she shouted at the top of her lungs, sending her words barreling toward those she'd damned and doomed. Again, she screamed: *"I did this!"* and her throat burned from the soot and the sting of the admission, her chest cracking open and raw with misery. She felt a hand on her shoulder, her father again. The only sounds, once her echoes died down, were the crackle and whisper of open flames.

"I caused this," she said, nodding. "We shouldn't have come here to begin with. We shouldn't. Maybe my digging is the reason they poisoned us, or my going outside, but the air over here is clean. I promised you all that this place was here and that the air was fine. And now I'm telling you, just as surely, that our home is lost. It is poisoned. Opened to the outside. Everyone we left behind—" She tried to catch her breath, her heart empty, her stomach in knots. Again, her father propped her up. "Yes, it was my fault. My prodding. That's why the man who did this—"

"Man?" Courtnee asked.

Juliette surveyed her former friends, men and women she

had worked alongside for years. "A man, yes. From one of the silos. There are fifty silos just like ours—"

"So you've told us," one of the diggers said gruffly. "So the maps say."

Juliette searched him out. It was Fitz, an oilman and former mechanic. "And do you not believe me, Fitz? Do you now believe that there are only two in all the universe and that they were this near to one another? That the rest of that map is a lie? I am telling you that I stood on a ridge and I saw them with my own eyes. While we stand here in this dark pit choking on fumes, there are tens of thousands of people going about their days, days like we once knew—"

"And you think we should be digging toward them?"

Juliette hadn't considered that. "Maybe," she said. "That might be our only way out of this, if we can reach them. But first we need to know who is over there and if it's safe. It might be as ruined as our silo. Or as empty as this one. Or full of people not at all happy to see us. The air could be toxic when we push through. But I can tell you that there are others."

One of those digging slid down the rubble to join the conversation. "And what if everything is fine on the other side of this pile? Aren't you the one who always has to go look and see?"

Juliette absorbed the blow. "If everything is fine over there, then they will come for us. We will hear from them. I would love for that to be true, for this to happen. I would love to be wrong. But I'm not." She studied their dark faces. "I'm telling you that there's nothing over there but death. You think I don't want to hope? I've lost . . . we've all lost people we love. I listened as men I loved and cared about breathed their last, and you don't think I want to get over there and see for myself? To bury them proper?" She wiped her eyes. "Don't you think for a moment that I don't want to grab a shovel and work three shifts until we're through to them. But I know that I would be burying those of us who are left. We would be tossing this dirt and these rocks right into our own graves."

No one spoke. Somewhere, gravity won a delicate struggle against a rock, and the loose stone tumbled with clacks and clatters toward their feet.

"What would you have us do?" Fitz asked, and Juliette heard an intake of air from Courtnee, who seemed to bristle at the thought of anyone taking advice from her ever again.

"We need a day or two to determine what happened. Like I said, there are a lot of worlds like our own out there. I don't know what they hold, but I know one of them seems to think it's in charge. They have threatened us before, saying they can push a button and end us, and I believe that's what they've done. I believe it's what they did to this other world as well." She pointed down the tunnel to Silo 17. "And yes, it may have been because we dared to dig or because I went outside looking for answers, and you can send me to clean for those sins. I will gladly go. I will clean and die in sight of you. But first, let me tell you what little I know. This silo we're in, it will flood. It is slowly filling even now. We need to power the pumps that keep it dry, and we need to make sure that the farms stay wet, the lights stay on, that we have enough air to breathe." She gestured to one of the torches set into the wall. "We're going through an awful lot of air."

"And where are we supposed to get this power? I was one of the first through to the other side. It's a heap of rust over there!"

"There's power up in the thirties," Juliette said. "Clean power. It runs the pumps and lights in the farms. But we shouldn't rely on that. We brought our own power with us—"

"The backup generator," someone said.

Juliette nodded, thankful to have them listening. For now, at least, they'd stopped digging.

"I'll shoulder the burden for what I've done," Juliette said, and the flames blurred behind a film of tears. "But someone else brought this hell on us. I know who it was. I've spoken with him. We need to survive long enough to make him and his people pay—"

"Revenge," Courtnee said, her voice a harsh whisper. "After all the people who died trying to get some measure of that when you left to clean—"

"Not revenge, no. Prevention." Juliette peered down the dark tunnel and into the gloom. "My friend Solo remembers when this world—his world—was destroyed. It wasn't gods that brought this upon us, but men. Men close enough to talk to by radio. And there are other worlds standing out there beneath their thumbs. Imagine if someone else had acted before now. We would have gone about our lives, never knowing the threat that existed. Our loved ones would be alive right now." She turned back to Courtnee and the others. "We shouldn't go after these people for what they did. No. We should go after them for what they're capable of doing. Before they do it again."

She searched her old friend's eyes for understanding, for acceptance. Instead, Courtnee turned her back on her. She turned away from Juliette and studied the pile of rubble they'd been clearing. A long moment passed, smoke filling the air, orange flames whispering.

"Fitz, grab that torch," Courtnee ordered. There was a moment's hesitation, but the old oilman complied. "Douse that thing," she told him, sounding disgusted with herself. "We're wasting air."

42

ELISE HEARD VOICES down the stairwell. There were strangers in her home. Strangers. Rickson used to frighten her and the twins into behaving by telling them stories of strangers, stories that made them never want to leave their home behind the farms. A long time ago, Rickson used to say, anyone you didn't know was out to kill you and take your things. Even some of those who *did* know you couldn't be trusted. That's what Rickson used to say late at night when the clicking timers made the grow lights go suddenly out.

Rickson told them the story over and over of how he was born because of two people in love—whatever that meant—and that his father had cut a poisoned pill out of his mother's hip, and that's how people had babies. But not all people had babies out of two people in love. Sometimes it was strangers, he said, who came and took whatever they wanted. It was men in those old days, and often what they wanted was for women to make babies, and so they cut poisoned pills right out of their flesh and the women had babies.

Elise didn't have a poisoned pill in her flesh. Not yet. Hannah said they grew in there late like grown-up teeth, which was why it was important to have babies as early as you could. Rickson said this weren't true at all, and that if you were born without a pill in your hip you'd never have one, but Elise didn't know what to believe. She paused on the stairs and rubbed her side, feeling for any bumps there. Tonguing the gap between her teeth in concentration, she felt something hard beneath her gums and growing. It made her want to cry, knowing her body could do foolish things like growing teeth and pills beneath her flesh without her asking. She called up the stairs for Puppy, who had squirmed loose again and had bounded out of sight. Puppy was bad like this. Elise was starting to wonder if puppies were a thing you could own or if they were always running away. But she didn't cry. She clutched the rail and took another step and another. She didn't want babies. She just wanted Puppy to stay with her, and then her body could do whatever it wanted.

A man overtook her on the stairs—it wasn't Solo. Solo had told her to stick close. "Tell *Puppy* to stick close," she would say when Solo caught up to her. It paid to have excuses ready like this. Like pumpkin seeds in pockets. This man overtaking her looked back at her over his shoulder. He was a stranger, but he didn't seem to want her things. He already had things, had a coil of the black and yellow wire that dipped from the ceiling in the farms that Rickson said never to touch. Maybe this man didn't know the rules. It was peculiar to see people she didn't know in her home, but Rickson lied sometimes and was wrong some other times and maybe he lied or was wrong with his scary stories and Solo had been right. Maybe it was a good thing, these strangers. More people to help out and make repairs and dig water trenches in the soil so all the plants got a good drink. More people like Juliette, who had come and made their home better, took them up to where the light was steady and you could heat water for a bath. Good strangers.

Another man spiraled into view with noisy boots. He had a sack bursting with green leaves, the smell of ripe tomatoes and blackberries trailing past. Elise stopped and watched him go.

That's too much to pick all at once, she could hear Hannah saying. Too much. More rules that nobody knew. Elise might have to teach them. She had a book that could teach people how to fish and how to track down animals. And then she remembered that all the fish were gone. And she couldn't even track down one puppy.

Thinking of fish made Elise hungry. She very much wanted to eat right at that moment, and as much as possible. Before there wasn't any left. This hunger was a feeling that came sometimes when she saw the twins eating. Even if she wasn't hungry, she would want some. A lot. Before it was all gone.

She trundled up the steps, her bag with her memory book knocking against her thigh, wishing she'd stayed with the others or that Puppy would just stay put.

"Hey, you."

A man on the next landing peered over the rails and down at her. He had a black beard, only not as messy as Solo's. Elise paused a moment, then continued up the stairs. The man and the landing disappeared from view as she twisted beneath them. He was waiting for her as she reached the landing.

"You get separated from the flock?" the man asked.

Elise cocked her head to the side. "I can't be in a flock," she said.

The man with the dark beard and bright eyes studied her. He wore brown coveralls. Rickson had a pair like them that he wore sometimes. That boy from the bizarre had coveralls like that.

"And why not?" the man asked.

"I'm not a sheep," said Elise. "Sheep make flocks, and there aren't any of them left."

"What's a sheep?" the man asked. And then his bright eyes flashed even brighter. "I seen you. You're one of the kids who lived here, aren't you?"

Elise nodded.

"You can join our flock. A flock is a congregation of people. The members of a church. Do you go to church?"

Elise shook her head. She rested her hand on her memory book, which had a page on sheep, how to raise them and how to care for them. Her memory book and this man disagreed. She felt a hollow in her stomach as she tried to sort out which of them to trust. She leaned toward her book, which was right about so much else.

"Do you want to come inside?" The man waved an arm at the door. Elise peered past him and into the darkness. "Are you hungry?"

Elise nodded.

"We're gathering food. We found a church. The others will be down from the farms soon. Do you want to come in, get something to eat or drink? I picked what I could carry. I'll share it with you." He placed a hand on her shoulder, and Elise found herself studying his forearm, which was thick with dark hair like Solo's but not like Rickson's. Her tummy grumbled, and the farms seemed so far away.

"I need to get Puppy," she said, her voice small in that vast stairwell, a tiny puff of fog in the cool air.

"We'll get your puppy," the man said. "Let's go inside. I want to hear all about your world. It's a miracle, you know. Did you know that you are a miracle? You are."

Elise didn't know this at all. It weren't in any of the books she'd made memories from. But she'd missed a lot of pages. Her stomach grumbled. Her stomach talked to her, and so she followed this man with the dark beard into the dark hall. There were voices ahead, a soothing and quiet mix of hums and whispers, and Elise wondered if this was what a flock sounded like.

Silo 1

43

Charlotte was back to living in a box. A box, but without the cold, without the frosted window, and without the line of bright blue plunged deep into her vein. This box was missing those things and the chance of sweet dreams and the nightmare of waking. It was a plain metal box that dented and sang as she adjusted her weight.

She had made a tidy home of the drone lift, a metal container too low to sit up in, too dark for her to see her hand in front of her face, and too quiet to hear herself think. Twice she had lain there listening to boots on the other side of the door as men hunted for her. She stayed in the lift that night. She waited for them to come back, but they must have many levels to prowl.

She moved every few minutes in a fruitless attempt to make herself comfortable. She went once to use the bathroom when she couldn't hold it anymore, when she feared she would go in her coveralls. To flush or not to flush? Risk the noise or the evidence in the bowl? She flushed, and imagined pipes rattling in some far-off place, someone able to pinpoint where it was coming from.

At the end of the hall, she made sure they hadn't discovered the radio. She expected to find it missing, Donald's notes as well, but all was still there beneath the plastic sheet. Hesitating a moment, Charlotte gathered the folders. They were too valuable to lose. She hurried back to her hole and pushed her things into a corner. Curling up, she pictured boots landing on her brother.

She thought of Iraq. There were dark nights there, lying in her bunk, men coming and going on and off their shifts with whispers and the squeak of springs. Dark nights when she had felt more vulnerable than her drone ever did in the sky. The barracks had felt like an empty parking garage in the dead of night, footsteps in the distance, and her unable to find her car keys. Hiding in that small drone lift felt the same. Like sleeping at night in a darkened garage, in a barracks full of men, wondering what she might wake up to.

She slept little. With a flashlight cradled between her cheek and her shoulder, she went through Donald's folders, hoping the dry reading might help her nod off. In the silence, words and snippets of conversation from the radio returned to her. Another silo had been destroyed. She had listened to their panicked voices, to reports of outer doors being opened, reports of the gas her brother had said he could unleash on these people. She had heard Juliette's voice, heard her say that everyone was dead.

She found a small chart in one of the folders, a map of numbered circles with many of them crossed out. People lived in those circles, Charlotte thought. And now another of them was empty. One more X to scratch. Except Charlotte, like her brother, now felt some connection with these people. She had listened to their voices with him on the radio, had listened to Donald as he recounted his efforts to reach out to them, this one silo that was open to what he had to say, that was helping him hack into their computers to understand what was happening. She had asked him once why he didn't reach out to other silos, and he had said something about those in charge not being safe. They would have turned him in. Somehow, her brother and these people were all rebelling, and now they were gone. This was what happened to those who rebelled. Now it was just Charlotte in darkness and silence.

She flipped through her brother's notes, and her neck began to cramp from holding the flashlight like that. The temperature in the box rose until she was sweating in her coveralls. She couldn't sleep. This was nothing like that other box they put her in. And the more she read, the more she understood her brother's endless pacing, his desire to do something, to put an end to the system in which they were trapped.

Careful with the water and food, taking tiny sips and small bites, she stayed inside for what felt like days but may have been hours. When she needed to go to the bathroom again, she decided to sneak to the end of the hall and try the radio once more. The urge to pee was matched only by the need to know what was going on. There had been survivors. The people of 18 had managed to scamper over the hills and reach another silo. A handful had survived—but how long would they last?

She flushed and listened to the surge of reclaimed water gurgle through overhead pipes. Taking a chance, she went to the drone control room. She left the hall light off and uncovered the radio. There was nothing but static on 18. The same on 17. She turned through a dozen of the other channels until she heard voices and was sure the thing was working. Back to 17, she waited. She could wait forever, she knew. She could wait until they came and found her. The clock on the wall showed that it was just past three, the middle of the night, which she thought was a good thing. They might not be looking for her right then. But then nobody might be listening, either. She squeezed the mic anyway.

"Hello," she said. "Can anyone hear me?"

She nearly identified herself, where she was calling from,

but then wondered if the people in her silo were listening in as well, monitoring all the stations. And what if they were? They wouldn't know where she was transmitting from. Unless they could trace her through the repeaters. Maybe they could. But wasn't this one of the silos crossed off their list? They shouldn't be listening at all. Charlotte moved her tools out of the way and looked for the piece of paper Donny had brought her, the ranking of the silos. It listed at the bottom all of the silos that'd been destroyed—

"Who is this?"

A man's voice spilled from the radio. Charlotte grabbed the mic, wondering if this was someone in her silo transmitting on that frequency.

"I'm . . . Who is this?" she asked, unsure how to answer.

"You down in Mechanical? You know what time it is? It's the middle of the night."

Down in Mechanical. That was the layout of their silos, not hers. Charlotte assumed this was one of the survivors. She also assumed others might be listening in and decided to play it safe.

"Yes, I'm in Mechanical," she said. "What's going on over—I mean, up there?"

"I'm trying to sleep is what, but Court told us to keep this thing on in case she called. We've been wrestling with the water lines. People are staking claims in the farms, marking out plots. Who is this?"

Charlotte cleared her throat. "I'm looking for . . . I was hoping to reach your mayor. Juliette."

"She ain't here. I thought she was down with you. Try in the morning if it ain't an emergency. And tell Court we could use a few more bodies up here. A decent farmer if we've got one. And a porter."

"Uh . . . okay." Charlotte glanced at the clock again, seeing how long she'd have to wait. "Thanks," she said. "I'll try back."

There was no response, and Charlotte wondered why she felt the urge to reach out in the first place. There was nothing she could do for these people. Did she think there was something they could do for her? She studied the radio she'd built, the extra screws and wire scattered around the base, the collection of tools. It was a risk being out and about, but it felt less terrifying than being alone in the drone lift. The risk of discovery was far outweighed by the chance of contact. She would try again in a few hours. Until then, she would try to get some sleep. She covered the radio and considered her old cot in the barracks down the hall, but it was the windowless metal box that claimed her.

44

DONALD'S BREAKFAST ARRIVED with company. They had left him alone the previous day and made him skip a meal. He figured it was some sort of interrogation technique. Same with the boots stomping noisily past in the middle of the night, keeping him up. Anything to throw off his clock, perturb him, make him feel crazy. Or maybe that was day and this was the middle of the night and he hadn't skipped a meal at all. Hard to tell. He had lost track of time. There was a clean circle on the wall and a protruding screw where a clock had once stood.

Two men in security coveralls arrived with Thurman and breakfast. Donald had slept in his coveralls. He pulled his feet up on his cot while the three men packed into his small room. The two security officers regarded him suspiciously. Thurman handed him his tray, which held a plate of eggs, a biscuit, water, and juice. Donald was in incredible pain, but he was also starving. He searched for silverware and saw none, started eating the eggs with his fingers. Hot food made his ribs feel better.

"Check the ceiling panels," one of the security officers said. Donald recognized him. Brevard. He had been chief for almost as long as Donald had been up on shift. Donald could tell Brevard was not his friend.

The other man was younger. Donald didn't recognize him. He was usually up late to avoid being seen, knew the night guard better than these guys. The younger officer scampered on top of the dresser welded to the wall and lifted a ceiling panel. He pulled a flashlight from his hip and shined the light in all directions. Donald had a good idea of what the man was seeing. He had already checked.

"It's blocked," the young officer said.

"You sure?"

"It wasn't him," Thurman said. He had never taken his eyes off of Donald. Thurman waved at the room. "There was blood everywhere. He'd be covered in it."

"Unless he washed up somewhere and changed clothes."

Thurman frowned at the idea. He stood a few paces from Donald, who no longer felt hungry. "Who was it?" Thurman asked.

"Who was what?"

"Don't play dumb. One of my men was attacked, and someone dressed as a reactor tech logged through security right here on this level the same night. They came down this hall, looking for you is my guess. Went to comms, where I know you've been spending your time. There's no way you've been pulling this off on your own. You took someone in, maybe someone from your last shift. Who?"

Donald broke off a piece of biscuit and put it in his mouth to give his lips something to do. Charlotte. What was she doing? Ranging the silo in search of him? Going to comms? She was out of her mind if it was her.

"He knows something," Brevard said.

"I have no idea what you're talking about," Donald said. He took a sip of water and noticed his hand was shaking. "Who was attacked? Are they okay?" He thought of the possibility that it was his sister's blood they had found. What had he done, waking her up? Again, he thought of coming clean and telling them where she was hiding, just so she wouldn't be alone.

"It was Eren," Thurman said. "He got off the late shift, ran for the lift, and was found thirty floors down in a pool of blood."

"Eren's hurt?"

"Eren's dead," Brevard said. "A driver to his neck. One of the lifts is covered in his blood. I want to know where the man who did this—"

Thurman held up a hand, and Brevard fell silent. "Give us a minute," Thurman said.

The young officer standing on the dresser adjusted the ceiling panel until it fell back into place. He jumped down and wiped his hands on his thighs, leaving the dresser covered in lint and snowflakes of styrofoam. The two security men waited outside. Donald recognized one of the office workers passing by before the door shut, nearly called out, wondered what the hell everyone must have thought when they found out he wasn't who he had said he was.

Thurman reached into his breast pocket and procured a folded square of cloth, a fresh rag. He handed this to Donald, who accepted it gratefully. Strange what accounted for a gift. He waited for the need to cough, but it was a rare moment of respite. Thurman held out a plastic bag and kept it open for him. Donald realized what it was for and dug out his other rag, dropped the bloody mess into the bag.

"For analysis, right?"

Thurman shook his head. "There's nothing here we don't already know. Just a . . . gesture. I tried to kill you, you know. It was weak of me to try, and it was because I was weak that I didn't succeed. It turns out you were right about Anna."

"Is Eren really dead?"

Thurman nodded. Donald unfolded the cloth and folded it back up again. "I liked him."

"He was a good man. One of my recruits. Do you know who killed him?"

Donald now saw the cloth for what it was. Bad cop had become good cop. He shook his head. He tried to imagine Charlotte doing these things and couldn't. But then, he couldn't picture her flying drones and dropping bombs or doing fifty push-ups. She was an enigma locked away in his childhood, constantly surprising. "I can't imagine anyone I know killing a man like that. Other than you."

Thurman didn't react to this.

"When do I go under?"

"Today. I have another question."

Donald lifted the water from the tray and took a long pull. The water was cold. It was incredible how good water could taste. He should tell Thurman about Charlotte right then. Or wait until he was going under. What he couldn't do was leave her there alone. He realized Thurman was waiting on him. "Go ahead," he said.

"Do you remember Anna leaving the armory while you were up? I realize you were only with her for a brief time."

"No," Donald said. And it hadn't felt like a brief time. It had felt like a lifetime. "Why? What did she do?"

"Do you remember her talking about gas feeds?"

"Gas feeds? No. I don't even know what that means. Why?"

"We found signs of sabotage. Someone tampered with the feeds between Medical and Population Control." Thurman waved his hand, dismissing what he was about to say. "Like I said, I think you were right about Anna." He turned to leave.

"Wait," Donald said. "I have a question."

Thurman hesitated, his hand on the door.

"What's wrong with me?" Donald asked.

Thurman looked down at the red rag in the plastic bag. "Have you ever seen what the land looks like after a battle?" His voice had grown quiet. Subdued. "Your body is a battlefield now. That's what's going on inside of you. Armies with billions to a side are waging war with one another. Machines that mean to rip you apart and those that hope to keep you together. And their boots are going to turn your body into shrapnel and mud."

Thurman coughed into his fist. He started to pull the door open.

"I wasn't going over the crest that day," Donald said. "I wasn't going out there to be seen. I just wanted to die."

Thurman nodded. "I thought as much later. And I should've let you. But they sounded the alarm. I came up and saw my men struggling with suits and you halfway gone. There was a grenade in my foxhole and years of knowing what I'd do if that ever happened. I threw myself on it."

"You shouldn't have," Donald said.

Thurman opened the door. Brevard was standing on the other side, waiting.

"I know," he said. And then he was gone.

45

DARCY WORKED ON his hands and knees. He dunked his crimson rag into the bucket of red water and wrung it out until it was pink, then went back to scrubbing the mess inside the lift. The walls were already clean, the samples sent out for analysis. While he worked, he grumbled to himself in a mockery of Brevard's voice: "Take samples, Darcy. Clean this up, Darcy. Fetch me a coffee, Darcy." He didn't understand how fetching coffee and mopping up blood had become part of his job description. What he missed were the uneventful night shifts; he couldn't wait for things to get back to normal. Amazing what can begin to feel normal. He almost couldn't smell the copper in the air anymore, and the metallic taste was gone from his tongue. It was like those daily doses in the paper cups, the bland food every day, even the infernal buzzing from the lift with its doors jammed open. All these things to get used to until they disappeared. Things that faded into dull aches like memories from a former life.

Darcy didn't remember much of his old life, but he knew he was good at this job. He had a feeling he used to work security a long time ago, back in a world no one talked about, a world trapped in old films and reruns and dreams. He vaguely remembered being trained to take a bullet for someone else. He had one solid and recurring dream of jogging in the morning, the way the air cooled the sweat from his brow and neck, the chirping of birds, running behind some older man in sweatpants and noticing how this man was going bald. Darcy remembered an earpiece that grew slick and wouldn't stay in place, always falling out of his ear. He remembered watching crowds, the way his heart raced when balloons burst and relic scooters backfired, forever waiting for the chance to take a—

Bullet.

Darcy stopped scrubbing and dabbed his face with his sleeve. He stared at the crack between the floor and the wall of the lift where something bright was lodged, a little stone of metal. He tried to secure it with his fingers, but they wouldn't fit in the crack. A bullet. He shouldn't be touching it anyway.

The rag fell with a splash into the bucket. Darcy grabbed the sample kit from the hallway. The lift continued to buzz and buzz, hating this standing still, wishing it could go places. "Cool your jets," Darcy whispered. He pulled one of the sample bags from the small box inside the kit. The tweezers weren't where they were supposed to be. He dug in the bottom of the kit until he found them, cursed the men on other shifts with no respect for their colleagues. It was like living in a dorm, Darcy thought. No, not the right word, the right memory. Like living in a barracks. It was the semblance of order over an underlying mess. Crisp sheets with folded corners over stained mattresses. That's what this was, people not putting things back where they belonged.

He used the tweezers to grab the bullet and drop it into the plastic bag. It was slightly misshapen but not severely. Hadn't hit anything solid, but it'd hit something. Rubbing the bag around the bullet and holding it up to the light, he saw how a pink stain appeared on the plastic. There was blood on the bullet. He checked the floor to see if he'd slopped any of the bloody water near where the bullet had been wedged, if the blood had perhaps gotten there due to his carelessness.

It hadn't. The man they'd found dead had been stabbed in the neck, but a gun had been discovered nearby. Darcy had sampled the blood inside the lift in a dozen places. A med tech had picked the samples up, and Stevens and the chief had told him that all the samples matched the victim. But now Darcy very likely had a blood sample from the attacker, who was still at large. The man who'd killed Eren. A real clue.

He clutched the sample bag and waited for the express to arrive. He considered for a moment handing this over to Stevens, which would be protocol, but he had found the bullet, knew what it was, had been careful in collecting it. He ought to be the one to see the results.

The express arrived with a cheerful ding. An exhausted-looking man in purple coveralls guided a wheeled bucket out, steered it with the handle of a mop. Instead of calling in his find, Darcy had called down backup. The night custodian. The two men shook hands. Darcy thanked him for staying on shift late, said he owed him a big one. He took the man's place inside the express.

He only had to go down two levels. It felt crazy, taking the express two levels. What the silo needed was stairs. There were so many times he just needed to go up or down a single level and found himself waiting five minutes for a blasted lift. It made no sense. He sighed and pressed the button for the medical wing. Before the doors shut, he heard a wet slap from the mop next door.

Dr. Whitmore's office was crowded. Not with workers—it was just Whitmore and his two med techs busying about—but with bodies. Two extra bodies on slabs. One was the woman discovered dead the day before; Darcy remembered her name being Anna. The other was Eren, the former silo head. Whitmore was at his computer, typing up notes while the lab techs worked on the deceased.

"Sir?"

Whitmore turned. His eyes went from Darcy's face to his hands. "Whatcha got?"

"One more sample. On a bullet. Can you run it for me?"

Whitmore waved at one of the men in the operating room, who exited with his hands held by his shoulders.

"Can you run this for the officer?"

The lab tech didn't seem thrilled. He tugged his bloodstained gloves off with loud thwacks and threw them in the sink to be washed and sterilized. "Let's see it," he said.

The machine didn't take long. It beeped and whirred and made purposeful sounds, and then spit out a piece of paper in jittery fits. The tech reached for the results before Darcy could. "Yup. Got a match. It belongs to . . . Huh. That's weird."

Darcy took the report. There was the bar graph, that unique UPC code of a man's DNA. Amounts and percentages of various blood levels were written in inscrutable code: *IFG, PLT, Hgb.* But where the system should have listed the details of the matching personnel record, it simply said on one of the many lines: *Emer.* The rest of the bio fields were blank.

"Emer," the lab tech said. He crossed to the sink and began washing the gloves and his hands. "That's a weird name. Who would pick a name like that?"

"Where are those other results?" Darcy asked. "From earlier."

The tech nodded to the recycle bin at Dr. Whitmore's feet, who continued to clack away at his keyboard. Darcy sifted through the bin, found one of the results sheets from earlier. He held the two side by side.

"It's not a name," Darcy said. "That would be on the top line.

This is where the location should be." On the other report, the name Eren stood above a line listing the freeze hall and the coordinates of the dead man's storage pod. Darcy remembered what one of the smaller freeze halls was called.

"Emergency Personnel," he said with satisfaction. He had solved a small mystery. He smiled at the room, but the other men had already returned to their work.

Emergency Personnel was the smallest of the freeze halls. Darcy stood outside the metal door, his breath visible in the air and clouding the steel. He entered his code, and the keypad blinked red and buzzed its disapproval. He tried the master security code next, and the doors clunked open and slid into the walls.

His heart raced with a mix of fear and excitement. It wasn't simply being on this trail of clues, it was where that trail was taking him. Emergency Personnel had been set aside for the most extreme of cases, for those times when Security was deemed insufficient. Through a dense haze, he remembered a time when cops stepped aside while heavily armored men emerged from vans and took down a building with military precision. Had that been him? In a former, former life? He couldn't remember. And anyway, these men in the emergency hall were different. Many of them had been up and about recently. Darcy remembered from when he got on shift. They were pilots. He recalled seeing ripples in his mug of coffee one day and finding out that bombs had been dropped from drones. Moving from one pod to the next, he searched for an empty one. Someone had not gone back to sleep when they should have, he suspected. Or someone had been stirred to do bad things.

It was this last possibility that filled him with fear. Who had access to such personnel? Who had the ability to awaken them without anyone knowing? He suspected that no matter whom he reported his findings to, as those findings went up and up the chain of command, they would possibly reach the person or people responsible. It also occurred to him that the man who had been killed was the on-shift head of the entire silo, the head of all the silos. This was big. This was huge. A feud between silo heads? This could get him off coffee-brewing and blood-mopping duty forever.

He was two thirds of the way through the grid of cryopods, making a circuit back and forth, when he started to suspect that he might've been wrong. It was all so tenuous. He was playing at someone else's job. There wouldn't be anyone missing, no grand conspiracy, nobody up killing people—

And then he peered inside a pod with no face there, with no frost on the glass. A palm on the skin of the pod confirmed that it was off. It was the same temperature as the room: cool but not freezing. He checked the display, fearing that it would be off and blank as well, but it showed power. Just no name. Only a number.

Darcy pulled out his report pad and clicked a pen. Only a number. He suspected any name that went with the pod would be classified. But he had his man. Oh, he had his man. And even if he couldn't get a name, he knew where these pilots spent their time when they were on shift. He had a very good idea of where this missing man with his bullet wound might be hiding.

46

CHARLOTTE WAITED UNTIL morning before trying the radio again. This time, she knew what she wanted to say. She also knew her time was short. She had heard people outside the drone lift again that morning, looking for her.

Waiting until she was sure they were gone, she nosed about and saw that they'd cleaned out the rest of Donald's notes in the conference room. She went to the bathroom and took the time to change her bandage, found her arm a scabbed mess. At the end of the hall, she expected to find the radio missing, but the control room was undisturbed. They probably never looked under the plastic sheet, just assumed that everything in the room was part of the drone operations. She uncovered the radio, and the unit buzzed when she powered it on. She arranged Donny's folders across her scattering of tools.

Something Donny had told her came back. He had said they wouldn't live forever, the two of them. They wouldn't live long enough outside the pods to see the results of their actions. And that made it hard to know how best to act. What to do for these people, these three dozen or so silos that were left? Doing nothing doomed so many of them. Charlotte felt her brother's need to pace. She picked up the mic and considered what she was about to do, reaching out to strangers like this. But reaching out was better than just listening. The day before, she had felt like a 911 operator who could only listen while a crime was being committed, unable to respond, powerless to send help.

She made sure the knob was on seventeen, adjusted the volume and squelch until she was rewarded with a soft hiss of static. Somehow, a handful of people had survived the destruction of their silo. Charlotte suspected they had crossed overland. Their mayor—this Juliette her brother had spoken with—had proved it was possible. Charlotte suspected it was this that had drawn her brother's attention. She knew from the suit Donny had been working on that he had dreamed of escaping somehow. These people may have found a way.

She opened his folders and spread out her brother's discoveries. There was a ranking of the silos sorted by their chance of survival. There was a note from the Senator, this suicide pact. And the map of all the silos, not with X's but with the red lines radiating out to a single point. Charlotte arranged the notes and composed herself before making the call. She didn't care if she was discovered. She knew damn well what she wanted to say, what she thought Donny was dying to say but didn't know how.

"Hello, people of Silo Eighteen. People of Silo Seventeen. My name is Charlotte Keene. Can you hear me? Over."

She waited, a rush of adrenaline and a flood of nerves from broadcasting her name, for being so bold. She had very likely just poked the hornets' nest in which she hid. But she had truths to tell. She had been woken up by her brother into a nightmare, and yet she remembered the world from before, a world of blue skies and green grass. She had glimpsed that world with her drone. If she had been born into this, had never known anything else, would she want to be told? To be awoken? Would she want someone to tell her the truth? For a moment, the pain in her shoulder was forgotten. The throbbing was pushed aside by this mix of fear and excitement—

"I'm picking you up nice and clear," someone answered, a man's voice. "You're looking for someone on eighteen? I don't think anyone's up there. Who did you say this was?"

Charlotte squeezed the mic. "My name is Charlotte Keene. Who is this?"

"This is Tom Higgins, head of the Planning Committee. We're up here at the deputy station on seventy-five. We're hearing there's been some kind of collapse, that we shouldn't head back down. What's going on below?"

"I'm not below you," Charlotte said. "I'm in another silo."

"Say again. Who is this? Keene, you say? I don't recognize your name from the census."

"Yes, Charlotte Keene. Is your mayor there? Juliette?"

"You say you're in our silo? Is this someone from the Mids?"

Charlotte started to say something, realized how difficult this was going to be, but another voice cut in. A familiar voice.

"This is Juliette."

Charlotte leaned forward and adjusted the volume. She squeezed the mic. "Juliette, my name is Charlotte Keene. You've been speaking with my brother, Donny. Donald, I mean." She was nervous. She paused to wipe her palms on the leg of her coveralls. When she let go of the mic, the man from earlier could be heard talking on the same frequency:

"—heard our silo is gone. Can you confirm? Where are you?"

"I'm in Mechanical, Tom. I'll come see you when I can. Yes, our silo is gone. Yes, you should stay where you are. Now let me see what this person wants."

"What do you mean, 'gone'? I don't understand."

"Dead, Tom. Everyone is dead. You can tear up your fucking census. Now please stay off the air. In fact, can we change channels?"

Charlotte waited to hear what the man would say. And then she realized the mayor was speaking to her. She hurriedly squeezed the mic before the other voice could step on her transmission.

"I . . . uh, yes. I can transmit on all frequencies."

Again, the head of the planning committee, or whatever he'd called himself, stepped in: "Did you say dead? Was this your doing?"

"Channel eighteen," Juliette said.

"Eighteen," Charlotte repeated. She reached for the knob as a burst of questions spilled from the radio. The man's voice was silenced by a twist of Charlotte's fingers.

"This is Charlotte Keene on channel eighteen, over."

She waited. It felt as though a door had just been pulled tight, a confidant pulled inside.

"This is Juliette. What's this about me knowing your brother? What level are you on?"

Charlotte couldn't believe how difficult this was to get across. She took a deep breath. "Not level. Silo. I'm in Silo One. You've spoken with my brother a few times."

"You're in Silo One. Donald is your brother."

"That's right." And finally, it sounded as if this was established. It was a relief.

"Have you called to gloat?" Juliette asked. There was a sudden spark of life in her voice, a flash of violence. "Do you have any idea what you've done? How many people you've killed? Your brother told me he was capable of this, but I didn't believe him. I never believed him. Is he there?"

"No."

"Well, tell him this. And I hope he believes me when I say it: My every thought right now is how best to kill him, to make sure this never happens again. You tell him that."

A chill spread through Charlotte. This woman thought her brother had brought doom on them. Her palms felt clammy as she cradled the mic. She pressed the button, found it sticking, knocked it against the table until it clicked properly.

"Donny didn't . . . He may already be dead," Charlotte said, fighting back the tears.

"That's a shame. I guess I'll be coming for whoever's next in line."

"No, listen to me. Donny . . . it wasn't him who did this. I swear to you. Some people took him. He wasn't supposed to be talking to you at all. He wanted to tell you something and didn't know how." Charlotte released the mic and prayed that this was getting through, that this stranger would believe her.

"Your brother warned me he could press a button and end us all. Well, that button has been pressed, and my home has been destroyed. People I care about are now dead. If I wasn't coming after you bastards before, I sure as hell am now."

"Wait," Charlotte said. "Listen. My brother is in trouble. He's in trouble because he was talking to you. The two of us . . . we aren't involved in this."

"Yeah, right. You want us talking. Learn what you can. And then you destroy us. It's all games with you. You send us out to clean, but you're just poisoning the air. That's what you're doing. You make us fear each other, fear you, and so we send our own people out, and the world gets poisoned by our hate and our fear, doesn't it?"

"I don't—Listen, I swear to you, I don't know what you're talking about. I . . . this will be hard for you to believe, maybe, but I remember when the world out there was very different. When we could live and breathe out there. And I think part of it can be like that again. Is like that right now. That's what my brother wanted to tell you, that there's hope out there."

A pause. A heavy breath. Charlotte's arm was back to throbbing.

"Hope."

Charlotte waited. The radio hissed at her like an angry breath forced through clenched teeth.

"My home, my people, are dead and you would have me hope. I've seen the hope you dish out, the bright blue skies we pull down over our heads, the lie that makes the exiled do your bidding, clean for you. I've seen it, and thank God I knew to doubt it. It's the intoxication of nirvana. That's how you get us to endure this life. You promise us heaven, don't you? But what do you know of our hell?"

She was right. This Juliette was right. How could such a conversation as this take place? How did her brother manage it? It was alien races who somehow spoke the same tongue. It was gods and mortals. Charlotte was attempting to commune with ants, ants who worried about the twists of their warrens beneath the soil, not the layout of the wider land. She wouldn't be able to get them to see—

But then Charlotte realized this Juliette knew nothing of her own hell. And so she told her.

"My brother was beaten half to death," Charlotte said. "He could very well be dead. It happened before my own eyes. And the man who did it was like a father to us both." She fought to hold it together, to not let the tears creep into her voice. "I'm being hunted right now. They will put me back to sleep or they will kill me, and I don't know that there's a difference. They keep us frozen for years and years while the men work in shifts. There are computers out there that play games and will one day decide which of your silos is allowed to go free. The rest will die. All of the silos but one will die. And there's nothing we can do to stop it."

She fumbled through the folder for the notes, the list of the rankings, and couldn't find it through her blurred vision. She grabbed the map instead. Juliette was saying nothing, was likely just as confused by Charlotte's hell as Charlotte was by hers. But it needed to be said. These awful truths discovered needed to be told. It felt good.

"We . . . Donny and I were only ever trying to figure out how to help you, all of you, I swear. My brother . . . he had an affinity for your people." Charlotte let go of the mic so this person couldn't hear her cry.

"My people," Juliette said, subdued.

Charlotte nodded. She took a deep breath. "Your silo."

There was a long silence. Charlotte wiped her face with her sleeve.

"Why do you think I would trust you? Do you know what you all have done? How many lives you've taken? Thousands are dead—"

Charlotte reached to adjust the volume, to turn it back down.

"—and the rest of us will join them. But you say you want to help. Who the hell are you?"

Juliette waited for her to answer. Charlotte faced the hissing box. She squeezed the mic. "Billions," she said. "Billions are dead."

There was no response.

"We killed so many more than you could ever imagine. The numbers don't even make sense. We killed nearly everyone. I don't think . . . the loss of thousands . . . it doesn't even register. That's why they're able to do it."

"Who? Your brother? Who did this?"

Charlotte wiped fresh tears from her cheeks and shook her head. "No. Donny would never do this. It was . . . you probably don't have the words, the vocabulary. A man who used to be in charge of the world the way it once was. He attacked my brother. He found us." Charlotte glanced at the door, half expecting Thurman to kick it down and barge in, to do the same to her. She had poked the nest, she was sure of it. "He's the one who killed the world and your people. His name is Thurman. He was a . . . something like a mayor."

"Your mayor killed my world. Not your brother, but this other man. Did he kill this world that I'm standing in right now? It's been dead for decades. Did he kill it as well?"

Charlotte realized this woman thought of silos as the entire world. She remembered an Iraqi girl she spoke with once while attempting to get directions to a different town. That was a conversation in a different language about a different world, and it had been simpler than this.

"The man who took my brother killed the wider world, yes." Charlotte saw the memo in the folder, the note labeled *The Pact*. How to explain?

"You mean the world outside the silos? The world where crops grew aboveground and silos held seeds and not people?"

Charlotte let out a held breath. Her brother must've explained more than he let on.

"Yes. That world."

"That world has been dead for thousands of years."

"Hundreds of years," Charlotte said. "And we . . . we've been around a long time. I . . . I used to live in that world. I saw it before it was ruined. The people here in this silo are the ones who did it. I'm telling you."

There was silence. It was the sucking vacuum after a bomb. An admission, clearly stated. Charlotte had done it, what she thought her brother had always wanted to do. Admit to these people what they'd done. Paint a target. Invite retribution. All that they deserved.

"If this were true, I would want all of you dead. Do you understand me? Do you know how we live? Do you know what the world is like outside? Have you seen it?"

"Yes."

"With your own eyes? Because I have."

Charlotte sucked in a deep breath. "No," she admitted. "Not with my own eyes. With a camera. But I've seen further out than any, and I can tell you that it's better out there. I think you're right about us poisoning the world, but I think it's contained. I think there's a great cloud around us. Beyond this cloud is blue skies and a chance at a life. You have to believe me, if I could help you get free, make this right, I would in a heartbeat."

There was a long pause. A very long pause.

"How?"

"I'm not . . . I don't think I'm in a position to help. I'm only saying if I could, I would. I know you're in trouble over there, but I'm not in great shape over here. When they find me, they'll probably kill me. Or something like it. I've done . . ." She touched the driver on the bench, ". . . very bad things."

"My people will want me dead for the part I played in this," Juliette said. "They'll send me to clean, and I won't come back this time. So I guess we have something in common."

Charlotte laughed and wiped her cheeks. "I'm truly sorry," she said. "I'm sorry for the things you're going through. I'm sorry we did this to you all."

There was silence.

"Thank you. I want to believe you, believe that you and your brother weren't the ones who did this. Mostly because someone close to me wanted me to believe your brother was trying to help. So I hope you aren't in the way when I get over there. Now, these bad things you say you've done, have you done them to bad people?"

Charlotte sat up straight. "Yes," she whispered.

"Good. That's a start. And now let me tell you about the world out there. I've loved two men in all my life, and both of them tried to convince me of this, that the world was a good place, that we could make it better. When I found out about the diggers, when I dreamed about tunneling here, I thought this was the way. But it only made things worse. And those two men with all that hope bursting from their breasts? Both of them are dead. That's the world I live in."

"Diggers?" Charlotte asked. She tried to make sense of this. "You got to that other silo through the airlocks. Over the hills."

Juliette didn't answer at first. "I've said too much," she said. "I should go."

"No, wait. Help me understand. You tunneled from one silo to another?" Charlotte leaned forward and spread the notes out again, grabbed the map. Here was one of those puzzles that made no sense until a new rule or piece of information was made available. She traced one of the red lines out beyond the silos to a point labeled *SEED.*

"I think this is important," Charlotte said. She felt a surge of excitement. She saw how the game was supposed to play out, what was to become of this in two hundred years. "You have to believe me when I say this, but I am from the old world. I promise. I've seen it covered with crops that . . . like you say, that grow aboveground. And the world outside that looks ruined, I don't think it stretches like that forever. I've seen a glimpse. And these diggers, you called them. I think I know what they're for. Listen to me. I have a map here that my brother thought was important. It shows a bunch of lines leading to this place marked S-E-E-D."

"Seed," Juliette said.

"Yeah. These lines look like flight lines, which never made sense. But I think they lead to a better place. I think the digger you found wasn't meant to go between silos. I think—"

There was a noise behind her. Charlotte had a difficult time processing it, even though she had expected it for hours, for days. She was so used to being alone, despite the fear that they were coming for her, the perfect knowledge that they were coming for her.

"You think what?" Juliette asked.

Turning, Charlotte watched the door to the drone control room fly open. A man dressed like those who had held her brother down stood in the hallway. He came at her, all alone, shouting for her to hold still, shouting for her to raise her hands. He trained a gun on her.

Juliette's voice spilled from the radio. She asked Charlotte to go on, to tell her what the diggers were for, to answer. But Charlotte was too busy complying with this man, holding one hand over her head and the other as high as the pain would allow. And she knew it was all over.

Silo 17

47

THE GENSET GRUMBLED to life. There was a rattle deep in the belly of the great digger, and then a string of lights flickered on in Silo 17's pump room, in the generator room, and down the main hall. There were whoops and applause from exhausted mechanics, and Juliette realized how important these small victories were. Light shone where once there was dark flood.

For her, every breath was a small victory. Lukas's death was a weight on her chest, as were the losses of Peter and Marsha and Nelson. Everyone in IT she had come to know and forgive was gone. The cafeteria staff. Practically anyone above Supply, all those who hadn't made a run for it. Weights on her chest, every one. She took another deep breath and marveled that breathing was still possible.

Courtnee had taken charge of the mechanics, stepping into the vacuum Shirly had left. She and her team were the ones stringing lights and wires and getting the pumps rigged and automated. Juliette moved about like a ghost. Only a handful seemed to see her. Just her father and a few of her closest friends, loyal to a fault.

She found Walker in the back of the digger, where the tight confines and reliable power made him feel closer to home. He looked over her radio and pronounced it both operational and out of juice. "I could rig up a charger in a few hours," he told her apologetically.

Juliette surveyed the conveyor belt, which had been swept free of dirt and rubble and now served as a workbench for both Walker and the dig team. Walker had several projects underway for Courtnee: pumps to respool and what looked like disassembled mining detonators. Juliette thanked him but told him she was heading up soon; there were chargers in the deputy stations as well as in IT on thirty-four.

Further down the conveyor belt, she noticed members of the dig team poring over a schematic. Juliette gathered the radio and her flashlight from Walker's station, patted him on the back, and joined them.

Erik, the old mine foreman, had a pair of dividers and was marking out distances on the schematic. Juliette squeezed in to get a closer look. It was the silo layout she'd brought down from IT all those weeks ago. It showed a grid of circles, a few of them crossed out. There were markings between two silos to show the route the digger had taken. The schematic had been used by the mining team to chart their way, buttressed by Juliette's best guess on which direction she had walked and how far.

"We could make it to number sixteen in two weeks," Erik calculated.

Bobby grunted. "C'mon. It took longer than that to get here."

"I'm relying on your extra incentive to get out of this place," Erik said.

Someone laughed.

"What if it ain't safe over there?" Fitz asked.

"It probably isn't," Juliette said.

Grime-covered faces turned to acknowledge her.

"You got friends in all of these?" Fitz asked. He practically sneered at her. Juliette could feel the tension among the group. Most of them had gotten their families through, their loved ones and kids and brothers and sisters. But not all.

Juliette squeezed between Bobby and Hyla and tapped one of the circles on the map. "I've got friends right here," she said.

Shadows swayed drunkenly across the map as the bulb overhead swung on its cord. Erik read the label on the circle Juliette had indicated. "Silo One," he said. He traced the three rows of silos between this location and where they currently stood. "That would take a lot longer."

"It's okay," she said. "I'm going alone."

Eyes went from the map to her. The only sound was the rumbling of the genset at the other end of the digger.

"I'll be going overland. And I know you need all the blast charges you can lay hands on, but I saw you had a few cases left over from the dig. I'd love to take enough to pop a hole in the top of this silo."

"What are you talking about?" Bobby asked.

Juliette leaned over the map and traced a path with her finger. "I'm going overland in a modified suit. I'm going to strap as many sticks of blast charge as I can to the door of this silo, and then I'm going to open that motherfucker like a soup can."

Fitz smiled a toothless smile. "What kind of friends you say you got over there?"

"The dead kind," Juliette said. "The people who did this to us live right there. They're the ones who make the world outside unlivable. I think it's time they live in it."

No one spoke for a beat. Until Bobby asked, "How thick are the airlock doors? I mean, you've seen 'em."

"Three, four inches."

Erik scratched his beard. Juliette realized half the men

around that table were doing some kind of figuring. Not a one of them was going to talk her out of this.

"It would take twenty to thirty sticks," someone said.

Juliette searched out the voice and saw a man she didn't recognize. Someone from the Mids who had made it down, maybe. But he was wearing a mechanic's coveralls.

"You all had one-inch plate welded up at the base of the stairwell. We used eight sticks to punch through it. I'd say plan on three to four times that."

"You're a transfer?" Juliette asked.

"Yes, ma'am." He nodded. And looking past the grime to his cropped hair and bright smile, Juliette thought she could see the Up-Topper in there. One of the men sent from IT to bolster the shifts in Mechanical. Someone who had blown open the barrier her friends had erected during the uprising. He knew what he was talking about.

Juliette looked to the others. "Before I go, I'll reach out to a few of these silos, see if any will harbor you. But I've got to warn you, the heads of these joints all work for these people. They'd as likely kill you when you come crashing through their walls as feed you. I don't know what's salvageable here, but you might be better off staying put. Imagine what we would've thought if a few hundred strangers cut their way inside our home and asked to be put up."

"We would've let them," Bobby said.

Fitz sneered. "Easy for you to say, you've got your two kids. What about those of us in the lottery?"

This got several people talking all at once. Erik slapped the conveyor belt with his hand to silence them. "That's enough," he said. He glared at those gathered. "She's right. We need to know where we're headed first. In the meantime, we can start staging. We're gonna want all the supports in the mines of this place, which means a lot of water to pump out and exploring to do."

"How exactly are we going to aim this thing?" Bobby asked. "She was a bitch to steer here. These things aren't fond of turning."

Erik nodded. "Already thought of that. We'll dig around it and give her room enough to spin in place. Court says it's possible to run a set of tracks at a time, a little forward on one side, a little back on the other. She'll creep around as long as there's no earth in the way."

Raph appeared at Juliette's side. He had been hanging back during the discussion. "I'm coming with you," he said.

Juliette realized it wasn't a question. She nodded.

When Erik was done explaining what they needed to do next, workers began to scatter. Juliette caught Erik's attention and showed him her radio. "I'm going to go see Courtnee and my dad before I leave, and I've got some friends that headed off to the farms. I'll have someone bring you down a radio as soon as I find another. And a charger. If I make contact with a silo that'll have you, I'll let you know."

Erik nodded. He started to say something, scanned the faces of those still milling about, then waved her to the side. Juliette handed her radio to Raph and followed.

A few paces away, Erik glanced around and waved her further along. And then further. Until they were at the far end of the tailings facility where the very last bulb swayed and flickered.

"I've heard what some of them are sayin'," Erik said. "I just want you to know it's ratshit, okay?"

Juliette scrunched up her face in confusion. Erik took a deep breath, eyed his workers in the distance. "My wife was working in the one-twenties when this went down. Everyone around her was running up, and as much as she felt the urge to join them, she headed straight down here to our kids. Was the only one on her level to make it. She fought a helluva crowd to get here. People were acting crazy."

Juliette squeezed his arm. "I'm glad she made it." She watched the dangling lights shine in Erik's eyes.

"Goddammit, Jules, listen to what I'm telling you. This morning, I woke up on a rusted sheet of plate steel, a crick in my neck I may live with for the rest of my life, two damn kids sleeping on me like a mattress, and my ass dead numb from the cold—"

Juliette laughed.

"—but Lesley is laying there watching me. Like she's been watching me a long while. And my wife looks around us at this rusted hellhole, and she says thank God we had this place to come to."

Juliette turned away and wiped at her eyes. Erik grabbed her arm and made her face him. He wasn't going to let her retreat like that.

"She hated this dig. Hated it. Hated me taking on a second shift, hated it because of my bitchin' and moanin' over the struts you made me pull, what we did to number six. Hated it because I hated it. You understand?"

Juliette nodded.

"Now, I know the fix we're in as well as most. I don't reckon we'll get anywhere with this next dig, but it'll give us something to do until our time comes. Until then, I'm going to wake up sore next to the woman I love, and if I'm lucky I'll do the same thing the next morning, and every one of those is a gift. This ain't hell. This is what comes before. And you gave us that."

Juliette wiped the tears from her cheeks. Some part of her hated herself for crying in front of him. Another part wanted to throw her arms around his neck and sob. She missed Lukas more powerfully in that moment than she thought herself capable.

"I don't know about this fool's errand you're setting off on, but you take whatever of mine you need. If that means more digging with my bare hands, so be it. You get those fuckers. I want to see them in hell by the time I get there."

48

JULIETTE FOUND HER father in the makeshift clinic he had set up in a cleared-out and rusted storeroom. Raylee, a second-shift electrician nine months pregnant, rested on a bedroll, her husband at her side, both of them with their hands on her belly. Juliette acknowledged the couple and realized their child would be the first—maybe ever—to be born in a different silo from its parents. That child would never know the gleaming Mechanical in which they worked and lived, would never travel up to the bazaar and hear music or see a play, may never gaze at a functioning wallscreen to know the outside world. And if it was a girl, she would face the danger of having children of her own like Hannah had, with no one to tell her otherwise.

"You setting off?" Juliette's father asked.

She nodded. "Just came to tell you goodbye."

"You say that like I'll never see you again. I'll be up to check on the kids once I get things sorted down here. Once we have our new arrival." He smiled at Raylee and her husband.

"Just goodbye for now," Juliette said. She had made the others swear not to tell anyone, especially Court and her father, about what she had planned. As she gave her father a final squeeze, she tried not to let her arms betray her.

"And just so you know," she told him, letting go, "those kids are the nearest thing I'll ever have to children of my own. So whenever I'm not there to look after them, if you can lend Solo a hand . . . Sometimes I think he's the biggest kid of the lot."

"I will. And I know. And I'm sorry about Marcus. I blame myself."

"Don't, Dad. Please don't. Just . . . look after them when I'm too busy to. You know how I can get into some fool project."

He nodded.

"I love you," she said. And then she turned to go before she betrayed herself and her plans any further. In the hallway, Raph shouldered a heavy bag. Juliette grabbed the other. The two of them walked beyond the current string of lights and into the near-darkness, neither of them employing their flashlights, the halls familiar enough, their eyes soon adjusting.

They passed through an unmanned security station. Juliette spotted the breathing hose doubling back on itself, remembered swimming through that very spot. Ahead, the stairwell glowed a dull green from resilient emergency lights, and she and Raph began the long slog up. Juliette had a list in her head of who she needed to see and what she needed to grab on the way. The kids would be in the lower farms, back at their old home. Solo as well. She wanted to see them, and then head up and grab a charger and hopefully another radio at the deputy station. If they were lucky and made good time, she'd be in her old home in the cleaning lab later that night, assembling one last suit.

"You remember to grab the detonators from Walker?" Juliette asked. She felt as though she was forgetting something.

"Yup. And the batteries you wanted. And I topped up our canteens. We're good."

"Just checking."

"How about for modding the suits?" Raph asked. "You sure you have everything up there you need? How many of them are left, anyway?"

"More than enough," Juliette said. She wanted to tell him right then that two suits would be more than enough. She was pretty sure Raph thought he was coming with her the whole way. She was steeling herself for that fight.

"Yeah, but how many? I'm just curious. Nobody was allowed to talk about those things before . . ."

Juliette thought of the stores between thirty-four and thirty-five, the in-floor bunkers that seemed to go on forever. "Two . . . maybe three hundred suits," she told him. "More than I could count. I only modded a couple."

Raph whistled. "That's enough for a few hundred years of cleanings, eh? Assuming you were sending 'em out one a year."

Juliette thought that was about right. And she supposed, now that she knew how the outside air got poisoned, that this was probably the plan: a steady flow of the exiled. Not cleaning, but doing the exact opposite. Making the world dirty.

"Hey, do you remember Gina from Supply?"

Juliette nodded, and the past tense was a busted knuckle. Quite a few from Supply had made it down, but Gina hadn't.

"Did you know we were seeing each other?"

Juliette shook her head. "I didn't. I'm sorry, Raph."

"Yeah."

They made a turn of the staircase.

"Gina did an analysis once of a bunch of spares. You know they had this computer just to tally everything, where it was located, how many were on order, all of that? Well, IT had burned through a few chips for their servers, bang, bang, bang, just one of those weeks where failures crop up all in a row—"

"I remember those weeks," Juliette said.

"Well, Gina wondered how long before they were gonna run out of these chips. This was one of those parts they couldn't make more of, you know? Intricate things. So she looked at the average failure rate, how many they had in the pens, and she came up with two hundred and forty-eight years."

Juliette waited for him to continue. "That number mean something?" she asked.

"Not at first, no. But the number got her curious because she'd run a similar report a few months prior, again out of curiosity, and the number had been close to that. A few weeks later, a bulb goes out in her office. Just a bulb. It winks out while she's working on something, and it got her thinkin'. You've seen the storehouse of bulbs they've got, right?"

"I haven't, actually."

"Well, they're vast. She took me down there once. And . . ."

Raph fell quiet for a few treads.

"Well, the storehouse is about half empty. So Gina runs the figures for a simple bulb for the whole silo and comes up with two hundred and fifty-one years' supply."

"About the same number."

"That's right. And now she's real curious—you'd have loved this about her—she started running reports like this in her spare time, big-ticket items like fuel cells and pregnancy implants and timer chips. And they all converge at right about two-fifty. And that's when she figures we've got that much time left."

"Two hundred and fifty years," Juliette said. "She told you this?"

"Yeah. Me and a few others over drinks. She was pretty drunk, mind you. And I remember . . ." Raph laughed. "I remember Jonny saying that she was remembering the hits and forgetting the misses, and speaking of forgetting the missus, he needed to get back to his. And one of Gina's friends from Supply says that people've been saying stuff like this since her grandmother was around, and they would always be saying that. But

Gina says the only reason this wasn't occurring to everyone at once is because it's early. She said to wait two hundred years or so, and people would be going down into empty caverns to get the last of everything, and then it would be obvious."

"I'm truly sorry she's not here," Juliette said.

"Me too." They climbed a few steps. "But that's not why I'm bringing this up. You said there were a couple hundred suits. Seems like the same count, don't it?"

"It was just a guess," Juliette told him. "I only went down there the couple of times."

"But it seems about right. Don't it seem like a clock ticking down? Either the gods knew how much to stock away, or they don't have plans for us past a certain date. Makes you feel like pig's milk, don't it? Anyhow, that's how it seems to me."

Juliette turned and studied her albino friend, saw the way the green emergency lights gave him a sort of eerie glow. "Maybe," Juliette said. "Gina may've been on to something."

Raph sniffed. "Yeah, but fuckit. We'll be long dead before then."

He laughed at this, his voice echoing up and down the stairs, but the sentiment made Juliette sad. Not just that everyone she knew would be dead before that date ever happened, but that this knowledge made it easier to stomach an awful and morbid truth: Their days were counted. The idea of saving anything was folly, a life especially. No life had ever been truly saved, not in the history of mankind. They were merely prolonged. Everything comes to an end.

49

THE FARMS WERE DARK, the overhead lights sleeping on their distantly clicking timers. Down a long and leafy hall, voices spilled as grow plots were claimed and those claims were just as quickly disputed. Things that were not owned by anyone became owned. It reminded Hannah of troubling times. She clutched her child to her chest and stuck close to Rickson.

Young Miles led the way with his dying flashlight. He beat it in his palm whenever it dimmed, which somehow coaxed more life out of it. Hannah glanced back in the direction of the stairwell. "What's taking Solo so long?" she asked.

Nobody answered. Solo had chased after Elise. It was common enough for her to run off after some distraction, but it was different with all these people everywhere. Hannah was worried.

The child in her arms wailed. It did this when it was hungry. It was allowed to. Hannah clamped down on her own complaints; she was hungry too. She adjusted the child, unhooked one strap of her overalls, and gave the infant access to her breast. The hunger was worse with the pressure of eating for two. And where crops had once brushed against her arms along that hall—where an empty stomach was one of the few things she never need fear—burgeoning plots stood startlingly empty. Ravaged. Owned.

Stalk and leaf rustled like paper as Rickson climbed over the rail and explored the second and third rows, hunting for a tomato or cucumber or any of the berries that had gone wild and had spread through the other crops, their curly arms twining around the stalks of their brethren. He returned noisily and pressed something into Hannah's hand, something small with a soft spot where it had rested on the ground for too long. "Here," he said, and went back to searching.

"Why would they take so much all at once?" Miles asked, digging for food of his own. Hannah sniffed the small offering from Rickson, which smelled vaguely like squash, but underripe. The voices in the distance lifted in argument. She took a small bite and recoiled at the bitter taste.

"They took so much because they aren't family," Rickson said. His voice leaked from behind dark plants that trembled from his passing.

Young Miles aimed his flashlight toward Rickson, who emerged from the rows of cornstalks empty-handed. "But we aren't family," Miles said. "Not really. And we never did this."

Rickson hopped over the rail. "Of course we're family," he said. "We live together and work together like families are supposed to. But not these people, haven't you seen? Seen how they dress differently so they can be told apart? They don't live together. These strangers will fight like our parents fought. Our parents weren't family, either." Rickson untied his hair and collected the loose strands around his face, then tied it all back up. His voice was hushed, his eyes peering into the darkness where voices argued. "They'll do like our parents and fight over food and women until there aren't any of them left. Which means we'll have to fight back if we want to live."

"I don't want to fight," Hannah said. She winced and pulled the baby away from her sore nipple, began working her overalls to switch breasts.

"You won't have to fight," Rickson said. He helped with her overalls.

"They left us alone before," Miles said. "We lived back here for years, and they came and took what they needed and didn't fight us. Maybe these people will do the same."

"That was a long time ago," Rickson said. He watched the baby settle into its mother's breast, then ranged down the railing and into the darkness to forage some more. "They left us alone because we were young and we were theirs. Hannah and I were your age. You and your brother were toddlers. No matter how bad the fighting got, they left us kids alone to live or die by our own devices. It was a gift, the way they abandoned us."

"But they used to come," Miles said. "And bring us things."

"Like Elise and her sister?" Hannah asked. And now she and Rickson had both brought up deceased siblings. That hall was full of the dead and gone, she realized, the plucked-from-above. "There will be fighting," she told Miles, who still didn't seem so sure. "Rickson and I aren't kids any longer." She rocked the baby in her arms, that suckling reminder of just how far from kids they had become.

"I wish they'd just leave," Miles said morosely. He banged the flashlight, which gave forth like a burped baby. "I wish it could all go back to normal. I wish Marcus was here. It don't feel right without him."

"A tomato," Rickson said, emerging victorious from the shadows. He held the red orb in the beam of Miles's light, which threw a blush across all their faces. A knife materialized. Rickson cut the vegetable into thirds, with Hannah getting hers first. Red juice like blood dripped from his hand, from Hannah's lips, and from the knife. They ate in relative quiet, the voices down the hall distant and scary, the knife dripping with life but capable of dripping with worse.

Jimmy cursed himself as he climbed the stairs. He cursed as he used to, with only himself to hear, with words that never had far to travel, moving from his lips to his own ears. He cursed himself and stomped around and around, sending vibrations up and down to mingle with others. Keeping an eye on Elise had turned into a bother. One glance in the other direction, and off she went. Like Shadow used to when all the grow lights popped on at once.

"No, not like Shadow," he mumbled to himself. Shadow had stayed underfoot most days. He had always been tripping over Shadow. Elise was something else.

Another level went past, alone and empty, and Jimmy remembered that this wasn't new. This wasn't sudden. Elise was forever coming and going however she liked. He had just never worried about her when the silo was empty. It made him reconsider what made a place dangerous. Maybe it wasn't the place at all.

"You!"

Jimmy rose to another landing, one-twenty-two. A man waved from the doorway. He had gold coveralls on, which meant something back when things had meaning. It was the first face Jimmy had seen in a dozen levels.

"Have you seen a girl?" Jimmy asked, ignoring the fact that this man seemed to have a question of his own. Jimmy held his hand at his hip. "This high. Seven years old. Missing a tooth." He pointed past his beard at his own teeth.

The man shook his head. "No, but you're the man who used to live here, right? The survivor?" The man had a knife in his hand, which flashed silver like a fish in water. The man in gold then laughed and peered beyond the landing's rail. "I guess we're all survivors, aren't we?" Reaching out, he took hold of one of the rubber hoses Jimmy and Juliette had affixed to the wall to carry off the floods. With a deft swipe of the knife, the hose parted. He began hauling up the lower part, which dangled free far below.

"That was for the floods—" Jimmy began.

"You must know a lot about this place," the man said. "I'm sorry. My name's Terry. Terry Harlson. I'm on the Planning Commi—" He squinted at Jimmy. "Hell, you don't know or care, do you? We're all from the same place to you."

"Jimmy," he said. "My name's Jimmy, but most people call me Solo. And that hose—"

"You have any idea where this power is coming from?" Terry jerked his head at the green lights that dotted the underside of the stairs. "We're up another forty levels from here. Radio there's got power. Some of these wires strung up all over the place got juice too. You do that?"

"Some of it," Jimmy said. "Some was already like that. A little girl named Elise came this way. Did you—?"

"I reckon the power's coming from above, but Tom told me to check down here. He says the power always came from below in our silo, should be the same in this one. Everything else is. But I saw the high-water mark down there where this place was full of water. I don't think power's been coming from there in a while. But you should know, right? This place got any secrets you can tell us about? Love to know about that power."

The hose lay in a coil at the man's feet. The knife was back out, glimmering in his hand. "You ever thought of being on a committee?"

"I need to find my friend," Jimmy said.

Another swipe, but the electrical cord put up more resistance. It was the copper at the center. The man held a loop of the black wire in his hand and sawed back and forth, great muscles bulging beneath an undershirt stained with sweat. After some exertion, the knife burst free, the cord severed in two.

"If your friend ain't with the men in the farms, she's probably up with the chanters. I passed them on my way down. They found a chapel." Terry jabbed the knife skyward before stuffing it away and looping wire around his arm.

"A chapel," Jimmy said. He knew the one. "Thank you, Terry."

"Only fair," the man said, shrugging. "Thanks for telling me where all this power comes from."

"The power—?"

"Yeah, you said it came from above. From level . . ."

"Thirty-four? I said that?"

The man smiled. "I believe you did."

50

ELISE HAD WATCHED the people in the bottom where the floods used to be—the ones who were working to dig their way out and get the power going, get the lights on. She had also seen people at the farms harvesting a bunch of food and figuring out how to get people fed. And now there was this third group of people arranging furniture and sweeping the floors and making things tidy. She had no clue what they were trying to do.

The nice man who had last seen Puppy was off to one side, speaking with another man in a white outfit who had a bald circle in the center of his head even though he looked too young to be bald. The outfit was strange. Like a blanket. Instead of two legs, it had only one, and it was big enough that it swirled around him and made it so you couldn't hardly see his feet. The nice man with the dark whiskers seemed to be arguing a point. The man in the white blanket just frowned and stood there. Now and then, one or both of them would glance at Elise, and she worried they were talking about her. Maybe they were talking about how to find Puppy.

The furniture grew into straight lines, all facing the same way. There weren't any tables like the rooms she used to eat in behind the farms, the places where she would hide under furniture and pretend she was a rat with a whole rat family, all of them talking and twitching their whiskers. Here, it was just chairs and benches facing a wall where a colorful glass picture stood with some of the glass broken out. A man in coveralls worked behind that wall, was visible through the broken glass and hazy behind the part that remained. He spoke to someone else, who passed a black cord through a door. They were working on something, and then a light burst on back there, throwing colorful rays across the room, and a few people moving furniture stopped and stared. Some of them whispered. It sounded like they were all whispering the same thing.

"Elise."

The man with the dark whiskers knelt down beside her. Elise startled and clutched her bag to her chest. "Yes?" she asked, her voice a whisper.

"Have you heard of the Pact?" the man asked. The other man with no hair on the center of his head and the white blanket around his shoulders stood behind, that same frown on his face. Elise imagined that he never smiled.

She nodded. "A pack is a bunch of animals, like deer and dogs and puppies."

The man smiled. "Pact, not pack." But it all sounded the same to Elise. "And dogs and puppies are the same animal."

She didn't feel like correcting him. She'd seen what dogs looked like in her book and in the bizarre, and they were scary. Puppies weren't scary.

"Where did you hear about deer?" the man in the white blanket asked. "Do you have children's books over here?"

Elise shook her head. "We have real books. I've seen deer. They're tall and funny with skinny legs, and they live in the woods."

The man with the whiskers in the orange coveralls didn't seem to care about deer. Not as much as the other man. Elise looked to the door, wondered where everyone she knew was. Where was Solo? He should've been helping her find Puppy.

"The Pact is a very important document," said the man in orange. She suddenly remembered his name was Mr. Rash. He had introduced himself, but she was bad with names. Only ever needed to know a few. Mr. Rash was very nice to her. "The Pact is like a book but only smaller," he was saying. "Similar to how you're like a woman but only smaller."

"I'm seven," Elise said. She wasn't small anymore.

"And you'll be seventeen before you know it." The man with the whiskers reached out and touched Elise's cheek. Elise pulled back, startled, which made the man frown. He turned and looked up at the man in the white blanket, who was studying Elise.

"What books were these?" the man in white asked. "The ones with these animals, they were here in this silo?"

Elise felt her hands drop to her bag and rest protectively there, rest on her Memory Book. She was pretty sure the page with the deer had gone into her book. She liked the things about the green world, the things about fishing and animals and the sun and stars. She bit her lip to keep from saying anything.

The man with the whiskers—Mr. Rash—knelt beside her. He had a sheet of paper and a purple stick of chalk in his hands. He set these on the bench by her leg and rested his hand on Elise's knee. The other man stepped closer.

"If you know of books in this place, it is your duty to God to tell us where they lie," the man in the blanket said. "Do you believe in God?"

Elise nodded. Hannah and Rickson had taught her about God and the night prayers. The world blurred around her, and Elise realized she had tears in her eyes. She swiped them away. Rickson hated it when she cried.

"Where are these books, Elise? How many of them are there?"

"A lot," she said, thinking of all the books she'd stolen pages out of. Solo had been so angry with her when he'd found out she was taking pictures and the how-tos from them. But the how-tos showed her a better way to fish, and then Solo had shown her how to stitch the pages in and out of books proper and they had fished together.

The man in the white blanket knelt down in front of her. "Are these books all over the place?"

"This is Father Remmy," Mr. Rash said, making room for the man with the bald patch and introducing him to Elise. "Father Remmy is going to guide us through these troubling times. We are a flock. We used to follow Father Wendel, but some leave the flock and some join. Like you."

"These books," Mr. Remmy said, who seemed young to be a father, didn't seem all that much older than Rickson. "Are they near us? Where might we find them?" He swept his hand from the wall to the ceiling, had a strange way of talking, a loud voice that could be felt in Elise's chest, a voice that made her want to answer. And his eyes—green like the flooded depths she and Solo used to fish in—made her want to tell the truth.

"All in one place," Elise said, sniffling.

"Where?" the man whispered. He was holding her hands, and the other man was watching this with a funny expression. "Where are the books? It is so important, my daughter. There is only one book, you know. All these others are lies. Now tell me where they are."

Elise thought of the one book in her bag. It was not a lie. But she didn't want this man touching her book. Didn't want him touching her at all. She tried to pull away, but his large hands gripped her more firmly. Something swam behind his eyes.

"Thirty-four," she whispered.

"Level thirty-four?"

Elise nodded, and his hands loosened on hers. As he pulled away, Mr. Rash moved closer and rested a hand on Elise's hand, covering the place the other man had hurt.

"Father, can we . . . ?" Mr. Rash asked.

The man with the bald circle nodded, and Mr. Rash picked up the piece of paper from the bench. One side was printed on. The other side had been written on by hand. There was a purple chalk, and Mr. Rash asked Elise if she could spell, if she knew her letters.

Elise bobbed her head. Her hand once again fell to her bag, guarding her book. She could read better than Miles. Hannah had made sure of that.

"Can you spell your name for me?" the man asked. He showed her the piece of paper. There were lines drawn at the bottom. Two names had already been signed. Another line was blank. "Right here," he said, indicating that line. He pressed the chalk into Elise's hand. She was reading some of the other words, but the writing was messy. It had been written quickly and on a rough surface. Plus, her vision was blurry. "Just your name," he said once more. "Show me."

Elise wanted to get away. She wanted Puppy and Solo and Jewel and even Rickson. She wiped her tears and swallowed a sob that was trying to choke her. If she did what they wanted, she would be free to go. There were more and more people in that room. Some of them were watching her and whispering. She heard a man say that someone else was lucky, that there were more men than women, that people would get left out if they weren't careful. They were watching her and waiting, and the furniture was now straight, the floors swept, some green leaves from plucked plants scattered around the stage.

"Right here," Mr. Rash said. He held her wrist and forced the chalk until it hovered over the line. "Your name." And everyone was watching. Elise knew her letters. She could read better than Rickson. But she could hardly see. She was a fish like she used to catch, under the water, looking up at all these hungry people. But she printed her name. She hoped it would make them go away.

"Good girl."

Mr. Rash bent forward and kissed her on the cheek. People started clapping. And then the man in the white blanket with the fascination for books chanted some words, that voice booming and pretty at the same time. His words felt deep within her chest as he pronounced someone in the name of the Pact, husband and wife.

PART IV
DUST

Silo 1

51

DARCY RODE THE lift up to the armory. He put the small bag with the bullet away and stuffed the blood results into his pocket, stepped out of the lift and fumbled for the wide bank of light switches. Something told him the pilot missing from the cryopod in Emergency Personnel was hiding on this level. It was the level where they'd found the man posing as the Shepherd. It was also where a handful of pilots had been stationed a month or so ago during a flurry of activity. He and Stevens and a few of the others had searched the level several times already, but Darcy had a feeling. It started with the fact that the lift required a security override before it would even bring him to that level.

Only a handful of top personnel and those in Security could manage that sort of override, and on his previous visits Darcy had seen why. Crates of munitions and ammo lined the shelves. There were tarps draped over what appeared to be military drones. Pyramids of bombs sitting on racks. Not anything you wanted the kitchen staff stumbling across when they came down for a can of powdered potatoes and jabbed the wrong button in the lift.

Previous searches hadn't turned up anyone else, but there had to be thousands of places among the tall shelves with their large plastic bins. Darcy peered into these shelves as the lights overhead flickered on. He imagined that he was this pilot, moments after he'd killed a man, arriving there in a lift splattered with blood, on the run and looking for a place to hide.

Crouching, he examined the polished concrete outside the lift. Stepping back and tilting his head, he studied the shine. There was a bit more gleam in front of the door. Perhaps it was from the uneven traffic, the shuffle of boots, the gradual wear. He lowered himself to the floor and took a deep sniff, noted the smell of leaves and pine trees, of lemon and a time forgotten, back when things grew and the world smelled fresh.

Someone had cleaned the floor here. Recently, he thought. He remained crouched and peered through the aisles of weapons and emergency gear, aware that he wasn't alone. What he should do is head straight for Brevard and bring in backup. There was a man in here capable of killing, someonc from Emergency Personnel with military training, someone with access to every weapon in those crates. But this man was also wounded, hiding, and scared. And backup seemed like a bad idea.

It wasn't so much that Darcy was the one who had pieced this together and deserved the credit, it was his increasing certainty that these murders pointed straight to the top. The people involved in this were of the highest rank. Files had been tampered with, Deep Freeze disturbed, neither of which should've been possible. The people he reported to might be involved. And Darcy had stood there propping up the real Shepherd while the old man laid boots into his impostor. Nothing about that was protocol. That shit was personal. He knew the guy that took the beating, used to see him up late shifts all the time, had spoken with him now and then. It was hard to imagine that guy killing people. Everything was upside down.

Darcy pulled his flashlight off his hip and began to search the shelves. He needed something more than a bright light, something more than they assigned to night guards. There were designations on the bins from a different life, one barely remembered. He pried open the lids on several bins—the vacuum seals softly popping—before he found what he was looking for: An H&K .45, a pistol both modern and ancient. Top of the line when it rolled off the factory floor, but those factories were little more than memories. He slotted a clip into the weapon and hoped the ammo was good. He felt more confident with the firearm and crept through the storeroom with renewed purpose, not the cursory laps from the day before when eighty levels needed searching.

He peeked under each of the tarps. Beneath one, he found loose tools and scattered parts, a drone partly disassembled or being repaired. Recent work? It was impossible to tell. There was no dust, but there wouldn't be under the tarp. He walked the perimeter, looked for white foam pellets on the ground from any ceiling panels that may have been disturbed, checked the offices at the very back, looked for any places where the shelves might be scaled, any large bins high up. He headed toward the barracks and noticed the low metal hangar door for the first time.

Darcy made sure the safety was off. He gripped the handle on the door and threw it up, then crouched down and aimed his flashlight and pistol into the gloom.

He very nearly shot up someone's bedroll. There was a rumpled pile of pillows and blankets that looked at first like a person sleeping. He saw more of the folders like the ones he'd helped gather from the conference room. This was probably where the man they'd snagged had been hiding. He'd have to show Brevard and get the place cleaned up. He couldn't imagine living like that, like a rat. He shut the hangar and moved to the door down the wall, the one that led to the barracks. Opening it a crack, Darcy made sure the hall was clear. He moved quietly from room to room, sweeping each. No sign of habitation in the bunkrooms. The bathrooms were still and quiet. Eerie, almost. Leaving the women's, he thought he heard a voice. A whisper. Something beyond the doorway at the very end.

Darcy readied his pistol and stood at the end of the hall. He pressed his ear to the door and listened.

Someone talking. He tried the knob and found it unlocked, took a deep breath. Any sign of a man reaching for a weapon, and he would shoot. He could already hear himself explaining to Brevard what had happened, that he'd had a hunch, had followed a clue, didn't think to ask for backup, had come down and found this man wounded and bleeding. He drew first. Darcy had been protecting himself. One more dead body and another case closed. That was his line if this went badly. All this and more flashed through his mind as he threw the door open and raised his weapon.

A man turned from the end of the room. Darcy yelled for him to freeze as he shuffled closer, his training ingrained and coming as naturally as a heartbeat. "Don't move," he shouted, and the man raised his hands. It was a young man in gray coveralls, one arm over his head and the other held limply at his side.

And then Darcy saw that something was wrong. Everything was wrong. It wasn't a man at all.

"Don't shoot," Charlotte pleaded. She raised one hand and watched this man approach her, a gun aimed at her chest.

"Stand up and step away from the desk," the man said. His voice was unwavering. He gestured with his gun to indicate the wall.

Charlotte glanced at the radio. Juliette asked if she could hear her, asked her to finish what she was saying, but Charlotte didn't test this man by reaching for the transmit button. She eyed the scattering of tools, the drivers, the wire cutters, and remembered the gruesome fight from the day before. Her arm throbbed beneath the gauze wrapping. It hurt to raise her hand even to her shoulder. The man closed the distance between them.

"Both hands up."

His stance—the way he held his gun—reminded her of basic training. She did not doubt that he would shoot her.

"I can't raise it any more than this," she said. Again, Juliette pleaded for her to say something. The man eyed the radio.

"Who're you talking to?"

"One of the silos," she said. She slowly reached for the volume.

"Don't touch it. Against the wall. Now."

She did as he said. Her one consolation was the hope that he would take her to her brother. At least she would know what they'd done with him. Her days of isolation and worry had come to an end. She felt a twinge of relief to have been discovered.

"Turn around and face the wall. Place your hands behind your back. Cross your wrists."

She did this. She also turned to the side and glanced over her shoulder at him, caught a glimpse of a white plastic tie pulled from his belt. "Forehead on the wall," he told her. And then she felt him approach, could smell him, could hear him breathing, and thoughts of spinning around and putting up a fight evaporated as the tie cinched painfully around her wrists.

"Are there any others?" he asked.

She shook her head. "Just me."

"You're a pilot?"

Charlotte nodded. He gripped her elbow and spun her around. "What're you doing here?" Seeing the bandage on her arm, his eyes narrowed. "Eren shot you."

She didn't respond.

"You killed a good man," he said.

Charlotte felt tears well up. She wished he would just take her wherever they were going, put her back to sleep, let her see Donny, whatever came next. "I didn't want to," was her feeble defense.

"How did you get here? You were with the other pilots? It's just . . . women don't . . ."

"My brother woke me," Charlotte said. She nodded at the man's chest, where a Security emblem blazed. "You took him." And she remembered the day they came for Donny, a young man propping up Thurman. She recognized this man in front of her, and more tears came. "Is he . . . still alive?"

The man looked away for a moment. "Yes. Barely."

Charlotte felt tears track down her cheeks.

The man faced her again. "He's your brother?"

She nodded. With her arms strapped behind her, she couldn't wipe her nose, couldn't even reach her shoulder to wipe it on her coveralls. She was surprised this man had come alone, that he wasn't calling for backup. "Can I see him?" she asked.

"I doubt that. They're putting him back under today." He aimed his gun at the radio as Juliette again called for some response. "This isn't good, you know. You've put these people in danger, whoever you're talking to. What were you thinking?"

She studied this man. He looked to be her age, early thirties, looked more like a soldier than a cop. "Where are the others?" she asked. She glanced toward the door. "Why aren't you taking me in?"

"I will. But I want to understand something before I do. How did you and your brother . . . how did you get out?"

"I told you, he woke me." Charlotte glanced at the table where Donny's notes lay. She had left the folders open. The map was on top, the Pact memo visible. The security guard turned to see what she was looking at. He stepped away from her and rested a hand on one of the folders.

"So who woke your brother?"

"Why don't you ask him?" Charlotte was beginning to worry. Him not taking her in felt like a bad thing, like he was operating outside the rules. She had seen men in Iraq operate outside the rules. It was never to do anything good. "Please just take me to see my brother," she said. "I surrender. Just take me in."

He narrowed his eyes at her, then turned his attention back to the folders. "What is all this?" He picked up the map and studied it, set it down and picked up another piece of paper. "We pulled crates of this stuff out of the other room. What the hell are you two working on?"

"Just take me in," Charlotte begged. She was getting scared.

"In a minute." He studied the radio, found the volume, turned it down. He put his back to the desk and leaned against it, the pistol held casually by his hip. He was going to drop his pants, Charlotte realized. He was going to force her to her knees. He hadn't seen a woman in several hundred years, was wanting to understand how to wake them up. That's what he wanted. Charlotte considered running for the door, hoping he might shoot her, hoping he would either miss or hit her square—

"What's your name?" he asked.

Charlotte felt tears roll down her cheeks. Her voice quivered, but she managed to whisper her name.

"Mine's Darcy. Relax. I'm not going to hurt you."

Charlotte began to shake. It was exactly what she imagined a man would say before doing something vile.

"I just want to understand what the hell's going on before I turn you over. Because everything I've seen today suggests this is bigger than you and your brother. Bigger than my job. Hell, for all I know, the moment I take you up to the office, they're going to put me under and put you back to work down here."

Charlotte laughed. She turned her head and wiped the tears hanging from her jaw onto her shoulder. "Not likely," she said. And she began to suspect that this man really wasn't going to hurt her, that he was just as curious as he seemed. Her gaze drifted back to the folders. "Do you know what they have planned for us?" she asked.

"Hard to say. You killed a very important man. You shouldn't be up. They'll put you in Deep Freeze would be my guess. Alive or dead, I don't know."

"No, not what they're gonna do to me and my brother—what they have planned for all of us. What happens after our last shift."

Darcy thought for a moment. "I . . . I don't know. Never thought about it."

She nodded to the folders beside him. "It's all in there. When I go back to sleep, it won't matter if I'm alive or dead. I'll never get up again. Neither will your sister or mom or wife or whoever they have here."

Darcy glanced at the folders, and Charlotte realized his not taking her in right away was an opportunity, not a problem. This is why they couldn't let anyone know the truth. If people knew, they wouldn't stand for it.

"You're making this up," Darcy said. "You don't know what will happen after—"

"Ask your boss. See what he says. Or your boss's boss. And keep asking. Maybe they'll give you a pod down in Deep Freeze next to mine."

Darcy studied her for a heartbeat. He set his pistol down and unbuttoned the top button on his coveralls. And then the next. He kept unbuttoning them down to his waist, and Charlotte knew she'd been right about what he planned to do. She prepared to jump him, to kick him between the legs, to bite him—

Darcy took the folders and slid them around his back, tucked them into his shorts. He began buttoning up his coveralls.

"I'll look into it. Now let's go." He picked up the gun and gestured toward the door, and Charlotte took a grateful breath. She walked around the drone control stations. Inside, she felt torn. She had wanted this man to take her in, but now she wanted to talk more. She had feared him, but now she wanted to trust him. Salvation seemed to come from being arrested, from being put back to sleep, and yet some other salvation seemed to lie within reach.

Her heart pounded as she was marched into the hallway. Darcy shut the door to the control room. She passed the bunk-rooms and the bathrooms, waited at the end of the hall for him to open the door to the armory, her hands useless behind her back.

"I knew your brother, you know," Darcy said as he held the door for her. "He never seemed like the sort. Neither do you."

Charlotte shook her head. "I never wanted to hurt anyone. We were only ever after the truth." She passed through the armory and toward the lift.

"That's the problem with the truth," Darcy said. "Liars and honest men both claim to have it. It puts people in my position in something of a predicament."

Charlotte pulled to a stop. This seemed to startle Darcy, who took a step back and tightened his grip on his pistol. "Let's keep moving," he told her.

"Wait," Charlotte said. "You want the truth?" She turned and nodded at the drones beneath their tarps. "How about you stop trusting what people are telling you? Stop deciding who to believe with your gut. Let me show you. See what's out there for yourself."

52

DONALD'S SIDE WAS a sea of purples, blacks, and blues. He held his undershirt up, his coveralls hanging from his hips, and inspected his ribs in the bathroom mirror. In the center of the bruise there was a patch of orange and yellow. He touched this—barely a brush of his fingertips—and a jolt of electricity shot down his legs and into his knees. He nearly collapsed, and it took a moment to gather his breath. He lowered his shirt gingerly, buttoned his coveralls up, and hobbled back to his cot.

His shins hurt from protecting himself from Thurman's blows. There was a knot on his forearm like a second elbow. And every time a coughing fit seized him, he wanted to die. He tried to sleep. Sleep was a vehicle for passing the time, for avoiding the present. It was a trolley for the depressed, the impatient, and the dying. Donald was all three.

He turned out the light beside his cot and lay in the darkness. The cryopods and shifts were exaggerated forms of sleep, he thought. What seemed unnatural was more a matter of degree than of kind. Cave bears hibernated for a season. Humans hibernated each night. Daytime was a shift, each one endured like a quantum of life, all the short-term planning leading up to another bout of darkness, little thought given to stringing those days into something useful, some chain of valuable pearls. Just another day to survive.

He coughed, which brought bolts of agony to his ribs and flashes of light to his vision. Donald prayed to black out, to pass away, but the gods in charge of his fate were expert torturers. Just enough—but not too much. *Don't kill the man,* he could hear his wounds whispering to one another. *We need him alive so that he can suffer for what he's done.*

The coughing passed with the taste of copper on his lips, blood misting his coveralls—but he didn't care. He laid his head back, soaked in sweat from pain and exertion, and listened to the feeble groans escaping his lips.

Hours or minutes passed. Days. There was a rap at the door, the slide and click of a tumbler, someone flicking on the lights. It would be a guard with dinner or breakfast or some other meaningless designation of time of day. It would be Thurman to lecture him, to grill him, to take him and put him to sleep.

"Donny?"

It was Charlotte. The hall behind her was third-shift dim. As she came to him, a man filled the doorway, one of the security officers. They had discovered her and were locking her up as well. But they were giving him this moment at least. He sat up too quickly, nearly lost his balance, but their arms found one another, both of them wincing in the embrace.

"My ribs," Donald hissed.

"Watch my arm," his sister said.

She untangled herself and stepped back, and Donald was about to ask her what was wrong with her arm, but she pressed a finger to her lips. "Hurry," she said. "This way."

Donald peered past her to the man in the doorway. The guard gazed up and down the hallway, was more concerned about someone coming than about him or his sister escaping.

The ache in Donald's ribs lessened as he realized what was going on.

"We're leaving?" he asked.

His sister nodded and helped him stand. Donald followed her into the hall.

So many questions, but silence was paramount. Now wasn't the time. The security officer closed the door and locked it. Charlotte was already heading toward the lifts. Donald limped after her, barefoot, his left leg singing with every step. They were on the admin level. He passed the accounting offices where spares and supplies were managed; Records, where the major happenings of every silo were tallied and entered into the servers; Population Control, where so many of his reports had once originated. All the offices quiet at what must've been an early-morning hour.

The security station was unmanned. Beyond it, a lift was waiting for them, persistently buzzing in a hold state. Donald noted a strong odor of cleaning agent in the lift. Charlotte slammed the hold button back in, scanned her ID, and pressed the armory level. The guard slid through the closing doors sideways, and Donald noticed the gun in his hand. It wasn't for fear of being discovered by others that he was carrying that gun, Donald realized. They weren't quite free. The young man stood on the other side of the lift and watched him and his sister warily.

"I know you," Donald said. "You work the late shift."

"Darcy," the guard said. He didn't offer his hand. Donald thought of the empty security station and realized this man should've been there.

"Darcy, right. What's going on?" He turned to his sister. A gauze wrapping could be seen peeking out from her short-sleeved undershirt. "Are you okay?"

"I'm fine." She watched the floors light up and slide by with obvious trepidation. "We flew another drone." She turned to Donald, her eyes on fire. "It made it through."

"You saw it?" His wounds were forgotten; the man standing in the lift with the gun was forgotten. It had been so long since that first flight gave him a brief glimpse of blue skies that he had grown to doubt it, had come to think it had never happened at all. The other flights had failed, had never reached as far. The lift slowed as it approached the storehouse.

"The world isn't gone," Charlotte confirmed. "Just our piece of it."

"Let's get off the lift," Darcy said. He waved the gun. "And then I want to understand what the hell is going on. And look, I'm not above having you both locked up before the morning shift comes on. I'll deny we ever talked like this."

Just inside the armory, Donald took a deep, wheezing breath and patted his back pocket. He pulled out the cloth and coughed, bent over to reduce the strain on his ribs. He folded the cloth away quickly so Charlotte couldn't see.

"Let's get you some water," she said, looking to the storehouse of supplies.

Donald waved her off and turned to Darcy. "Why are you helping us?" he asked, his voice hoarse.

"I'm not helping you," Darcy insisted. "I'm hearing you out." He nodded to Charlotte. "Your sister has made some bold claims, and I did a little reading while she put her bird together."

"I gave him some of your notes," Charlotte said. "And the drone flight. He helped me launch it. I put her down in a sea of grass. Real grass, Donny. The sensors held out for another half hour. We just sat there and stared at it."

"But still," Donald said, looking to Darcy. "You don't know us."

"I don't know my bosses, either. Not really. But I saw the beating you took, and it didn't sit right with me. You two are fighting for something, and it might be something bad, something I'm going to stop, but I've noticed a pattern. Any question I ask outside of my duties, and the flow of information stops. They want me to work the night shift and have a fresh pot on in the morning, but I remember being something more in a different life. I was taught to follow orders, but only up to a point."

Donald nodded grimly. He wondered if this young man had been deployed overseas. He wondered if he'd suffered from PTSD, had been on any meds. Something had come back to him, something like a conscience.

"I'll tell you what's going on here," Donald said. He led them away from the lift doors and toward the aisle of supplies that held canned water and MREs. "My old boss—the man you watched give me this limp—explained some things. More than he likely meant to. Most of this is what I've put together, but he filled in some blanks."

Donald lifted the lid on one of the wooden crates his sister had pried open. He winced in pain, and Charlotte rushed to help him. He grabbed a can of water and popped the lid, took a long swig while Charlotte pulled out two more cans. Darcy switched his gun to his other hand to accept a can, and Donald felt the presence of crate after crate of guns around him. He was sick of the things. Somehow, the fear of the one in Darcy's hand was gone. The pain in his chest was a different sort of bullet wound. A quick death would be a blessing.

"We aren't the first people to try and help a silo," Donald said. "That's what Thurman told me. And a lot more makes sense now. C'mon." He led them off that aisle and down another. A light flickered overhead. It would die soon. Donald wondered if anyone would bother to replace it. He found the plastic crate he was looking for hidden among a sea of others, tried to pull it down, and felt a cry from his ribs. He sucked it up and hauled it anyway, his sister helping with one hand, and together they carried it to the conference room. Darcy followed.

"Anna's work," he grunted, hefting the container onto the conference table while Darcy hit the lights. There was a schematic of the silos beneath a thick sheet of glass, and the glass was marked with old wax notes, scratched into illegibility by elbows and folders and glasses of whisky. All of his other notes were gone, but that was okay. He needed to look for something old, something from the past, from his previous shift. He pulled out several folders and flopped them onto the table. Charlotte began looking through them. Darcy remained by the door and glanced occasionally at the floor in the hall, which remained splattered with dried blood.

"There was a silo shut down a while back for broadcasting on a general channel. Not on my shift." He pointed to Silo 10 on the table, which bore the remnants of a red X. "A burst of conscience broadcast on a handful of channels, and then it was shut down. But it was Silo Forty that kept Anna busy for the better part of a year." He found the folder he was looking for, flipped it open. Seeing her handwriting blurred his vision. He hesitated, ran his hands across her words, remembering what he'd done. He had killed the one person trying to help him, the one person who loved him. The one person reaching out to these silos to help. All because of his own guilt and self-loathing for loving her back. "Here's a rundown of the events," he said, forgetting what he was looking for.

"Get to the point," Darcy said. "What's this all about? My shift is up in two hours, and it'll be daylight soon. I'll need both of you under lock and key before then."

"I'm getting there." Donald wiped his eyes and composed himself, waved his hand at a corner of the table. "All of these silos went dark a long time ago. A dozen or so of them. It started with Forty. They must've had some kind of silent revolution. A bloodless one, because we never got any reports. They never acted strange. A lot like what's going on in Eighteen right now—"

"Was," Charlotte said. "I heard from them. They've been shut down."

Donald nodded. "Thurman told me. I meant to say 'was'. Thurman also hinted that they were originally going to build fewer silos but kept adding more for redundancy. There are a few reports I found that suggested this as well. You know what I think? I think they added too many. They couldn't monitor them all closely enough. It's like having a camera on every street corner, but you don't have enough people watching the feeds. And so this one slipped under the rails."

"What do you mean when you say these silos went dark?" Darcy asked. He sidled closer to the table and studied the layout under the glass.

"All the camera feeds went out at the same time. They wouldn't answer our calls. The Order mandated that we shut them down in case they'd gone rogue, so we gassed the place. Popped the doors. And then another silo went dark. And another. The heads on shift here figured that in addition to the camera feeds, they'd sorted out the gas lines as well. So they sent the collapse codes to all of these silos—"

"Collapse codes?"

Donald nodded and drowned a cough with a gulp of water. He wiped his mouth with the back of his sleeve. It was comforting to see all the notes out on the table. The pieces were fitting together.

"The silos were built to fail, and all but one of them will. There's no gravity to take them down, so they had us build them—they had me design them—with great slabs of concrete between the levels." He shook his head. "It never made sense at the time. It made the dig deeper, increased costs, it's an insane amount of concrete. I was told it had something to do with bunker busters or radiation leaks. But it was worse than that. It was so they'd have something to take down. The walls aren't going anywhere—they're tied to the earth." He took another sip of water. "That's why the concrete. And it was because of the gas that they didn't want lifts. Never understood why they had us take them out. Said they wanted the design more 'open.' It's harder to gas a place if you can block off the levels."

He coughed into the crook of his arm, then drew a finger around a portion of the conference table. "These silos were like a cancer. Forty must've communicated with its neighbors, or they just took them offline as well, hacked them remotely. The heads on shift here in our silo started waking people up to deal with it. The collapse codes weren't working, nothing was. Anna figured they'd discovered the blast charges in Forty and had blocked the frequency—something like that."

He paused and remembered the sound of static from her radio, the jargon she'd used that gave him headaches but made her seem so smart and confident. His gaze fell to the corner of the room where a cot once lay, where she used to sneak over in the middle of the night and slip into his arms. Donald finished his water and wished he had something stronger.

"She finally managed to hack the detonators and bring the silos down," he said. "It was this or they were going to risk sending drones up or boots over, which is last-page Order stuff. Back of the book."

"Which is what we've been doing," Charlotte said.

Donald nodded. "I did even more of it before I woke you, back when this level was crawling with pilots."

"So that's what happened to these silos? They were collapsed?"

"That's what Anna said. Everything looked good. The people

in charge over here were relying on her, taking her word. We were all put back to sleep. I figured it was my last snooze, that I'd never wake up again. Deep Freeze. But then I was brought out for another shift, and people were calling me by a different name. I woke up as someone else."

"Thurman," Darcy said. "The Shepherd."

"Yeah, except I was the sheep in that story."

"You were the one who nearly got over the hill?"

Donald saw the way Charlotte stiffened. He returned his attention to the folders and didn't answer.

"This woman you're talking about," Darcy said. "Was she the same one who messed up the database?"

"Yeah. They gave her full access to fix this problem they were having; it was that severe. And her curiosity got her looking in other places. She found this note about what her father and others had planned, realized these collapse codes and gas systems weren't just for emergencies. We were all one big ticking time bomb, every single silo. She realized that she was going to be put in cryo and never wake up again. And even though she could change anything she wanted, she couldn't change her gender. Couldn't make it so that anyone would wake her up, and so she tried to get me to help. She put me in her father's place."

Donald paused and fought back the tears. Charlotte rested her hand on his back. The room was quiet for a long moment.

"But I didn't understand what she wanted me to do. I started digging on my own. And meanwhile, Silo Forty isn't gone at all. The place is still standing. I realize this when another silo goes dark." Donald paused. "I was acting head at the time, wasn't thinking straight, and I signed off on a bombing. Whatever it took to make it all go away. I didn't care about the tremors, being spotted, just ordered it done. We cratered anything over there that was still standing. Drones and bombs started thinning them out."

"I remember," Darcy said. "That was about when I got on shift. There were pilots up in the cafeteria all the time. They worked a lot in the middle of the night."

"And they worked down here. When they were done and went back under, I woke up my sister. I was just waiting for them to leave. I didn't want to drop bombs. I wanted to see what was out there."

Darcy checked the clock on the wall. "And now we've all seen it."

"There's another two hundred years or so before all the silos go down," Donald said. "You ever think about why this silo only has lifts, doesn't have any stairs? You want to know why they call it the express but the damn thing still takes forever to get anywhere?"

"We're rigged to blow," Darcy said. "There's that same mass of concrete between every level."

Donald nodded. This kid was fast. "If they let us walk up a flight of stairs, we'd see. We'd know. And enough people here would know what that was for, what this meant. They might as well put the countdown clock on every desk. People would go insane."

"Two hundred years," Darcy said.

"That might feel like a lot of time to others, but that's a couple naps for us. But see, that's the whole point. They need us dead so no one remembers. This whole thing—" Donald waved at the conference table with the depiction of the silos. "It's as much a time machine as a ticking clock. It's a way of wiping the earth clean and propelling some group of people, some tribe chosen practically at random, into a future where they inherit the world."

"More like sending them back into the past," Charlotte said. "Back into some primitive state."

"Exactly. When I first learned about the nanos, it was something Iran was working on. The idea was to target an ethnic group. We already had machines that could work on a cellular level. This was just the next step. Going after a species is even easier than targeting a race. It was child's play. Erskine, the man who came up with this, said it was inevitable, that someone would eventually do it, create a silent bomb that wipes out all of humanity. I think he was right."

"So what're you looking for in these folders?" Darcy asked.

"Thurman wanted to know if Anna ever left the armory. I'm pretty sure she did. Things would show up down here that I couldn't find on the shelves. And he said something about gas lines—"

"We've got an hour and a half before I need to get you back," Darcy said.

"Yeah, okay. So Thurman found something here in this silo, I think. Something his daughter did, something she snuck out and did. I think she left another surprise. When they gassed Eighteen, Thurman mentioned that they did it right this time. That they undid someone's mess. I thought he was talking about my mess, my fighting to save the place, but it was Anna who had changed things. I think she moved some valves around, or if it's all computerized, just changed some code. There are two types of machines, both of which are in my blood right now. There are those that keep us together, like in the cryopods. And then there are the machines outside around the silos, those we pump inside them to break people down. It's the ultimate haves versus the have-nots. I think Anna tried to flip this around, tried to rig it up so the next silo we shut down would get a dose of what we get. She was playing Robin Hood on a cellular level."

He finally found the report. It was well-worn. It had been looked through hundreds of times.

"Silo Seventeen," he said. "I wasn't around when it was put down, but I looked into this. There was a guy there who answered a call after the place was gassed. But I don't think it was gassed. Not correctly. I think Anna took what we get in our pods to stitch us up and sent that instead."

"Why?" Charlotte asked.

Donald looked up. "To stop the world from ending. To not murder anyone. To show people some compassion."

"So everyone at Seventeen is okay?"

Donald flipped through the pages of the report. "No," he said. "For whatever reason, she couldn't stop the airlock from popping. That's part of the procedure. And with the amount of gas outside, they didn't stand a chance."

"I spoke to someone at Seventeen," Charlotte said. "Your friend . . . that mayor is over there. There are people there. She said they tunneled their way over."

Donald smiled. He nodded. "Of course. Of course. She wanted me to think she was coming after us."

"Well, I think she's coming after us now."

"We need to get in touch with her."

"What we need to do," Darcy said, "is start thinking about the end of this shift. There's going to be a helluva beating in about an hour."

Donald and Charlotte turned to him. He was standing by the door, right near where Donald had been kicked over and over.

"I mean my boss," Darcy said. "He's gonna be pissed when he wakes up and discovers a prisoner escaped during my shift."

Silo 17

53

JULIETTE AND RAPH stopped at the lower deputy station to look for another radio or a spare battery. They found neither. The charging rack was still on the wall, but it hadn't been wired into the makeshift power lines trailing through the stairwell. Juliette weighed whether or not it was worth staying there and getting some juice in the portable or if she should just wait until they got to the Mids station or IT—

"Hey," Raph whispered. "Do you hear something?"

Juliette shined her flashlight deep into the offices. She thought she heard someone crying. "C'mon," she said.

She left the charger alone and headed back toward the holding cells. There was a dark form sitting in the very last cell, sobbing. Juliette thought it was Hank at first, that he had wandered up to the nearest thing like a home to him, only to realize what state this world was in. But the man wore robes. It was Father Wendel who peered up at them from behind the bars. The tears in his eyes caught in the glare of the flashlight. A small candle burned on the bench beside him, wax dripping to the ground.

The door to the holding cell wasn't shut all the way. Juliette pulled it open and stepped inside. "Father?"

The old man looked awful. He had the tattered remains of an ancient book in his hands. Not a book, but a stack of loose pages. There were pages scattered all over the bench and on the floor. As Juliette cast her light down, she could see that she was standing on a carpet of fine print. There was a pattern of black bars across all the pages, sentences and words made unreadable. Juliette had seen pages like this once in a book kept inside a cage, a book where only one sentence in five could be read.

"Leave me," Father Wendel said.

She was tempted to, but she didn't. "Father, it's me, Juliette. What're you doing here?"

Wendel sniffled and sorted through the pages as though he were looking for something. "Isaiah," he said. "Isaiah, where are you? Everything's out of order."

"Where's your congregation?" Juliette asked.

"Not mine anymore." He wiped his nose, and Juliette felt Raph tug on her elbow to leave the man be.

"You can't stay here," she said. "Do you have any food or water?"

"I have nothing. Go."

"C'mon," Raph hissed.

Juliette adjusted the heavy load on her back, those sticks of dynamite. Father Wendel laid out more pages around his boots, checking the front and back of each as he did so.

"There's a group down below planning another dig," she told him. "I'm going to find them a better place, and they're going to get our people out of here. Maybe you could come to one of the farms with us and see about getting some food, see if you can help. The people down below could use you."

"Use me for what?" Wendel asked. He slapped a page down on the bench, and several other pages scattered. "Hellfire or hope," he said. "Take your pick. One or the other. Damnation or salvation. Every page. Take your pick. Take your pick." He looked up at them, beseeching them.

Juliette shook her canteen, cracked the lid, and held it out to Wendel. The candle on the bench sputtered and smoked, shadows growing and shrinking. Wendel accepted the canteen and took a sip. He handed it back.

"Had to see it with my own eyes," he whispered. "I went into the dark to see the devil. I did. Walked and walked, and here it is. Another world. I led my flock to damnation." He twisted up his face, studied one of the pages for a moment. "Or salvation. Take your pick."

Plucking the candle from the bench, he held a page close to it in order to see it better. "Ah, Isaiah, there you are." And with the baritone of a Sunday, he read: "*In the time of my favor I will answer you, and in the day of salvation I will help you; I will keep you and will make you to be a covenant for the people, to restore the land and to reassign its desolate inheritances.*" Wendel touched a corner of the page to the flame and roared again: "Its desolate inheritances!"

The page burned until he had to release it. It moved through the air like an orange, shrinking bird.

"Let's go," Raph hissed, more insistently this time.

Juliette held up a hand. She approached Father Wendel and crouched down in front of him, rested a hand on his knee. The anger she had felt toward him over Marcus was gone. The anger she had felt as he instilled outrage in his people toward her and her digging was gone. Replacing that anger was guilt—guilt from knowing that all of their fears and mistrust had been warranted.

"Father," she said. "Our people will be damned if they stay in this place. I can't help them. I won't be here. They are going to need your guidance if they're to make it to the other side."

"They don't need me," he said.

"Yes, they do. Women in the depths of this silo weep for their babies. Men weep for their homes. They need you." And she knew this was true. It was in the hard times that they needed him the most.

"You will see them through," Father Wendel said. "You will see them through."

"No, I won't. You are their salvation. I am off to damn those who did this. I'm going to send them straight to hell."

Wendel looked up from his lap. Hot wax flowed over his fingers, but he didn't seem to notice. The smell of burnt paper filled the room, and he rested a hand on Juliette's head.

"In that case, my child, I bless your journey."

The trip up the stairwell was heavier with that blessing. Or maybe it was the weight of the explosives on her back, which Juliette knew would've been useful for the tunneling below. They could be used for salvation, but she was using them for damnation. They were like the pages of Wendel's book in that they offered plenty of both. As she approached the farms, she reminded herself that Erik had insisted she take the dynamite. There were others eager to see her pull this off.

She and Raph arrived at the lower farms, and she knew something was wrong the moment they stepped inside. Cracking the door released a surge of heat, a blast of angry air. Her first thought was a fire, and she knew from living in that silo that there were no longer any water hoses that worked. But the bloom of bright lights down the hall and along the outer grow plots hinted at something else.

There was a man lying on the ground by the security gates, his body sideways across the hall. Stripped down to his shorts and undershirt, Juliette didn't recognize Deputy Hank until she was nearly upon him. She was relieved when he moved. He shielded his eyes and tightened his grip on the pistol resting on his chest; sweat soaked his clothes.

"Hank?" Juliette asked. "Are you okay?" She was already feeling sticky herself, and poor Raph seemed liable to wilt.

The deputy sat up and rubbed the back of his neck. He pointed to the security gates. "You get a little shade if you crowd up against them."

Juliette looked down the hall at the lights. They were drawing a ton of power. Every plot appeared to be lit at once. She could *smell* the heat. She could smell the plants roasting in it. She wondered how long the skimpy wiring job in the stairwell could withstand such a draw of current.

"Are the timers stuck? What's going on?"

Hank nodded down the hallway. "People've been staking plots. A fight broke out yesterday. You know Gene Sample?"

"I know Gene," Raph said. "From Sanitation."

Hank frowned. "Gene's dead. Happened when the lights went out. And then they fought over who had rights to bury him, treated poor Gene like fertilizer. Some folks banded together and hired me to restore order. I told them to keep the lights on until things got settled." He wiped the back of his neck. "Before you lay into me, I know it ain't good for the crops, but they were already ravaged. My hope is to sweat these people out, make enough of them move on to give everyone some breathing space. I give it another day."

"In another day, you'll have a fire somewhere. Hank, the wiring outside runs hot enough already with the lights cycling. I'm shocked they can power all of this. When a breaker goes out up on the thirties, you're gonna have nothing but dark for a very long time down here."

Hank peered down the hall. Juliette saw rinds and cores and scraps of food on the other side of the gates. "How're they paying you? In food?"

He nodded. "The food's all gonna go bad. They plucked everything. People were just actin' crazy when they got here. I think a few headed up, but there are all these rumors that the door to this silo is open and if you go up much further, you die. And if you go down, you die. Lots of rumors."

"Well, you need to dispel those rumors," Juliette said. "I'm sure it's better up or down than it is here. Have you seen Solo and the kids, the ones who used to live here? I heard they came up this way."

"Yup. A few of those kids were staking a plot right down the hall before I rigged the lights. But they left a few hours ago." Hank eyed Juliette's wrist. "What time is it, anyway?"

Juliette glanced at her watch. "It's a quarter past two." She saw he was about to ask another question. "In the afternoon," she said.

"Thank you."

"We're going to try and catch up with them," Juliette said. "Can I leave you to handle these lights? You can't draw this much power. And get more people to move up from here. The farms in the Mids are doing much better, or they were when I was here. And if you have people looking for work, they can use hands in Mechanical."

Hank nodded and struggled to his feet. Raph was already heading to the exit, his coveralls spotted with sweat. Juliette clasped Hank on the shoulder before heading off as well.

"Hey," Hank called out. "You said what time it was. But what day is it?"

Juliette hesitated at the door. She turned and saw Hank gazing at her, his hand shielding his eyes. "Does it matter?" she asked. And when Hank didn't respond, she supposed it didn't. All the days were the same now, and every one numbered.

54

JIMMY DECIDED TO search for Elise on two more levels before turning back. He had begun to suspect that he'd missed her, that she'd run inside a level after her animal or to use the bathroom and he'd gone right by. Most likely, she was back at the farms with everyone else while he was stomping up and down the silo alone.

At the next landing, he checked inside the main door, saw nothing but darkness and silence, called out for Elise, and debated going even one level further. Turning back to the stairwell, a flash of brown caught his eye above. He shielded his old eyes and peered up through the green gloom to see a boy peering over the rails at him. The kid waved. Jimmy did not wave back.

He headed for the stairs with a mind of returning to the lower farms, but he soon heard the patter of light footsteps spiraling down toward him. Another kid to look after, he thought. He didn't wait for the boy, but continued along. It took a turn and a half before the child caught up to him.

Jimmy turned to berate the kid for bugging him, but he recognized the boy up close. The brown coveralls and the wiry mop of corn-colored hair. It was the kid who had chased Elise through the bazaar.

"Hey," the boy hissed, breathing hard. "You're that guy."

"I'm that guy," Jimmy agreed. "I suppose you're looking for food. Well, I don't have a thing—"

"No." The kid shook his head. He had to be nine or ten. About the same age as Miles. "I need you to come with me. I need your help."

Everyone needed Jimmy's help. "I'm a bit busy," he said. He turned to go.

"It's Elise," the boy said. "I followed her here. Through the mines. Some people up there won't let her go." He glanced up the stairwell, his voice a whisper.

"You've seen Elise?" Jimmy asked.

The boy nodded.

"What do you mean, people?"

"It's a bunch of them from that church. My dad goes to their Sundays."

"And you say they have Elise?"

"Yeah. And I found her dog. Her dog was trapped behind a busted door a few levels down from here. I penned it up so it couldn't get loose. And then I found where they're keeping Elise. I tried to get to her, but some guy told me to scram."

"Where was this?" Jimmy asked.

The boy pointed up. "Two levels," he said.

"What's your name?"

"Shaw."

"Good work, Shaw." Jimmy hurried to the stairwell and started down.

"I said *up* from here," the boy said.

"I need to grab something," Jimmy told him. "It's not far."

Shaw hurried after him. "Okay. And look, mister, I want you to know how hungry I was. But that I wasn't going to eat the dog."

Jimmy paused and allowed the boy to catch up. "I didn't think you would," he said.

Shaw nodded. "Just so Elise knows," he said. "I want to make sure she knows I would never do that."

"I'll make sure she knows," Jimmy said. "Now c'mon. Let's hurry."

Two levels down, Jimmy peeked inside a dark hallway; he played his flashlight across the walls, then turned guiltily to Shaw, who crowded behind him. "Went too far," Jimmy admitted.

He turned and began climbing back up a level, frustrated with himself. So hard to remember where he put everything. Such a long time ago. He used to have mnemonics for recalling his stashes. He had hidden a rifle way up on level fifty-one. He remembered that because it took a hand to hold the rifle and another finger to pull the trigger. Five and one. That rifle was wrapped in a quilt and buried in the bottom of an old trunk. But he'd left one down here as well. He had carried it down to Supply a lifetime ago; it would've been the trip when he found Shadow. Hadn't carried it all the way back up—not enough hands. One-eighteen. That was it. Not one-nineteen. He hurried up to the landing, his legs getting sore, and went inside the hallway he and Shaw had passed moments prior.

This was it. Apartments. He had left things in lots of them. Poop, mostly. He didn't know you could go in the farms, right in the dirt. The kids taught him that late in life. Elise taught him. Jimmy thought of people doing something bad to Elise, and he remembered what he'd done to people when he was a boy. He'd been young when he'd taught himself to fire a rifle. He remembered the noise it made. He remembered what it did to empty soup cans and people. It made things jump and fall still. Third apartment down on the left.

“Hold this,” he told Shaw, stepping inside the apartment. He handed his flashlight to the boy, who kept it trained in the center of the room. Jimmy grabbed the metal dresser shoved against one wall and pulled it out a ways. Just like yesterday. Except for the thick dust on the top of the dresser. His old bootprints were gone. He climbed up to the top and pushed the ceiling panel up and to the side, asked for the flashlight. A rat squeaked and scattered as he shined the light in there. The black rifle was waiting on him. Jimmy took it down and blew the dust off.

Elise didn’t like her new clothes. They had taken her coveralls from her, saying the color was all wrong, and had wrapped her in a blanket that was sewn up the front and scratchy. She’d asked to leave several times, but Mr. Rash said she had to stay. There were rooms up and down the halls with old beds, and everything smelled awful, but there were people trying to clean it up and make it better. But Elise just wanted Puppy and Hannah and Solo. She was shown a room and was told it would be her new home, but Elise lived beyond the Wilds and never wanted to live anyplace else.

They took her back to the big room where she’d signed her name and had her sit on the bench some more. If she tried to go, Mr. Rash squeezed her wrist. When she cried, he squeezed even harder. They made her sit on a bench they called something else while a man read from a book. The man with the white robes and the bald patch had left, and a new man had taken his place to read from a book. There was a woman off to the side with two other men, and she didn’t look happy. A lot of people on the benches spent time watching this woman instead of the man reading.

Elise was both sleepy and restless. What she wanted to do was get away and nap somewhere else. And then the man was done reading, and he lifted the book up into the air, and everyone around her said the same thing, which was really strange, as if they all knew they were going to say it beforehand, and their voices were funny and hollow like they knew the words but didn't know what they meant.

The man with the book waved the men and the woman up, and it seemed almost like they carried her. There were two tables pushed together back near the colored window with the light shining through it. The woman made a noise as they lifted her to the tables. She had a blanket on like Elise's but bigger, making it easy for the men to expose her bare leg. The people on the benches strained to see better. Elise felt less sleepy than she had before. She whispered to Mr. Rash to find out what they were doing, and he told her to be quiet, not to talk.

The man with the book brought a knife out of his robes. It was long and flashed like a bright fish.

"Be ye fruitful and multiply," he said. He faced the audience, and the woman moved about on the tables, but she couldn't go anywhere. Elise wanted to tell them not to hold her wrists so tight.

"Behold," the man said, reading from the book, "I establish my covenant with you, and with your seed after you." And Elise wondered if they were going to plant something. And he went on and said, "Neither shall all flesh be cut off anymore. And it shall come to pass, when I bring a cloud over the earth, that the blade shall be seen in the cloud."

He held the knife even higher, and the people on the benches mumbled something. Even a boy younger than Elise knew the words. His lips moved like the others'.

The man took the knife to the woman, but he didn't give it to her. There was a man holding her feet and another her wrists, and she tried to be still. And then Elise knew what they were doing. It was the same as her mom and Hannah's mom. And a fearsome scream came from the woman as the knife went in, and Elise couldn't stop watching, and blood came out and down her leg, and Elise could feel it on her own leg, and tried to squirm free, but then it was her wrist being held, and she knew one day this would be her, and the screaming went and went, and the man dug around with the knife and his fingers, a shine of sweat on the top of his head, saying something to the men, who were having trouble with the woman, and there were whispers along the benches, and Elise felt hot, and more blood until the man with the knife erupted with a shout and stood facing the benches with something between his fingers, blood running down his arm to his elbow, his blanket drooping open, a smile on his face as the screams died down.

"Behold!" he shouted.

And the people were clapping. The men bandaged the woman on the table, then brought her down, though she could barely stand. Elise saw that there was another woman by the stage. They were lining up. And the clapping gained a rhythm like when she and the twins would march up the stairs watching each other's feet, *clap, clap* at the same time. The clapping grew louder and louder. Until there was a giant clap that made them all go quiet. A clap that made her heart leap up in her chest.

Heads turned to the back of the room. Elise's ears hurt from the loud bang. Someone shouted and pointed, and Elise turned and saw Solo in the doorway. White powder rained down from the ceiling, and he had something long and black in his hands. Beside him stood Shaw, the boy in the brown coveralls from the bizarre. Elise wondered how he was there.

"Excuse me," Solo said. He scanned the benches until he saw Elise, and his teeth shined through his beard. "I'll be taking that young lady with me."

There were shouts. Men got up from their seats and yelled and pointed, and Mr. Rash shouted something about his wife and property and how dare he interrupt. And the man with the blood and the knife was outraged and stormed down the aisle, which made Solo lift the black thing to his shoulder.

Another clap like it was God doing it with his biggest palms, a bang so loud it made Elise's insides hurt. There was a noise after it, a shattering of glass, and she turned and saw the pretty colored window was even more broke than before.

The people stopped shouting and moving toward Solo, which Elise thought was a very good thing.

"Come along," Solo said to Elise. "Hurry now."

Elise got up from the bench and started toward the aisle, but Mr. Rash grabbed her by the wrist. "She is my wife!" Mr. Rash shouted, and Elise realized this was a bad thing to be. It meant she couldn't leave.

"You do marriages quick," Solo said to the quiet crowd. He waved the black thing at them all, and this seemed to make them nervous. "What about funerals?"

The black thing pointed at Mr. Rash. Elise felt his grip on her loosen. She made it to the aisle and ran past the man with the dripping blood, ran to Solo and Shaw and down the hall.

55

JULIETTE WAS DROWNING again. She could feel the water in her throat, the sting in her eyes, the burn in her chest. As she climbed the stairwell, she could sense the old flood around her, but that wasn't what made her feel as though she couldn't breathe. It was the voices ranging up and down the stairwell shaft, the evidence already of vandalism and theft, the long stretches of wire and pipe gone missing, the scattering of stalk and leaf and soil from those hurrying away with stolen plants.

She hoped to rise above the injustices strewn about her, to escape this last spasm of civility before chaos reigned. It was coming, she knew. But as high as she and Raph climbed, there were people throwing open doors to explore and loot, to claim territory, to yell down from landings some finding or shout up some question. In the depths of Mechanical, she had lamented how few had survived. And now it seemed like so many.

Stopping to fight any of this would be a waste of time. Juliette worried about Solo and the kids. She worried about the razed farms. But the weight of the explosives in her pack gave her purpose, and the calamity surrounding her gave her resolve. She was out to see that this never happened again.

"I feel like a porter," Raph said, wheezing between words.

"If you fall behind, we're heading for thirty-four. Both of the

Mid farms should have food. You can get water from the hydro pumps."

"I can keep up with you," Raph insisted. "Just saying it's unbecoming."

Juliette laughed at the proud miner. She wanted to point out the number of times she'd made this run, always with Solo lagging behind and waving her on, promising he'd catch up. Her mind flashed back to those days, and suddenly her silo was still alive and thriving, churning with civilization, so far away and moving forward without her—but still there and alive.

No more.

But there were other silos, dozens of them, teeming with life and lives. Somewhere, a parent was lecturing a child. A teenager was stealing a kiss. A warm meal was being served. Paper was being recycled into pulp and back into paper; oil was gurgling up and being burned; exhaust was being vented into the great and forbidden outside. All of those worlds were humming forward, each of them ignorant of the others. Somewhere, a person who dared to dream was being sent out to clean. Someone was being buried, another born.

Juliette thought of the children of Silo 17, born into violence, never knowing anything else. That would happen again. It would happen right here. And her annoyance with the Planning Committee and Father Wendel's congregation was misplaced, she thought. Had her mechanics not lashed out? Was she not lashing out right then? What was any group but a bunch of people? And what were people but animals as prone to fear as rats at the sound of boots?

"—catch up with you later, then," Raph called out, his voice distant, and Juliette realized she was pulling away. She slowed and waited for him. Now was not a time for being alone, for climbing without company. And in that silo of solitude, where she had fallen for Lukas because he was there for her in voice and spirit, she missed him more terribly than she ever had. Hope had been stripped away, foolish hope. There was no getting back to him, no seeing him ever again, even as she was deathly sure that she would join him soon enough.

A foray into the second Mids farm won some food, though it was deeper than Juliette remembered. Raph's flashlight revealed signs of recent activity: boot prints in mud that had not yet dried, a watering pipe broken for a drink that continued to drip but had not yet emptied, a stepped-on tomato that was not yet covered in ants. Juliette and Raph took what they could carry—green peppers, cucumbers, blackberries, a precious orange, a dozen underripe tomatoes—enough for a few meals. Juliette ate as many blackberries as she could, for they travelled poorly. She normally shied away from them, hated how they left her fingers stained. But what once was nuisance now seemed a blessing. This was how the last of the supplies went in a hurry, each of a few hundred people taking more than they needed, even the things they didn't truly want.

It wasn't far to thirty-four from the farm. For Juliette, it almost felt like a return home. There would be ample power there, her tools and her cot, a radio, some place to work during this last tremble of a dying people, some place to think, to regret, to build one last suit. The weariness in her legs and back spoke to her, and Juliette realized she was climbing once again in order to escape. It was more than vengeance she was after. This was a flight from the sight of her friends, whom she had failed. It was a hole she was after. But unlike Solo, who had lived in a hole beneath the servers, she was hoping to make a crater on the heads of others.

"Jules?"

She paused halfway across the landing of thirty-four, the doors to IT just ahead. Raph had stopped at the top step. He knelt down and ran his finger across the tread, lifted it to show her something red. Touched his finger to his tongue.

"Tomato," he said.

Someone was already there. The day Juliette had wasted curled up and crying in the belly of the digger haunted her now.

"We'll be fine," she told him. The day she had chased Solo came back to her. She had thundered down these steps, had found the doors barred, had snapped a broom in half getting inside. This time, the doors opened easily. The lights inside were full bright. No sign of anyone.

"Let's go," she said. She hurried quietly and quickly. It wouldn't do to be spotted by people she didn't know, wouldn't want them following her. She wondered if Solo had at least been cautious enough to close up the server room and the grate. But no, at the end of the hall she saw the server room door was open. There were voices somewhere. The stench of smoke. A haze in the air. Or was she losing her mind and imagining Lukas and the gas coming for him? Is that why she was here? Not for the radio, to find a home for her friends, nor to build a suit, but because here was a mirrored place, identical to her own, and maybe Lukas was below, waiting for her, alive in this dead world—

She pushed her way into the server room, and the smoke was real. It gathered at the ceiling. Juliette hurried through the familiar servers. The smoke tasted different than the burnt grease of an overheating pump, the tang of an electrical fire, the scorched rubber of an impeller running dry, the bitterness of motor exhaust. It was a clean burning. She covered her mouth with the crook of her arm, remembered Lukas complaining of fumes, and hurried into the haze.

It was coming from the hatch behind the comm server, a rising column of smoke. There was a fire in Solo's hovel, his bedding, perhaps. Juliette thought of the radio down there, the food. She unzipped her coveralls and pulled her sweat-soaked undershirt up over her face, heard Raph yelling at her not to go as she reached down and lowered herself onto the ladder, practically slid down it until her boots slammed into the grating below.

Staying low, she could just barely see through the haze. She could hear the crackle of flame, a strange and crisp sound. Food and radio and computer and precious schematics on the walls. The one treasure not on her mind as she rushed forward was the books. And it was the books that were burning.

A pile of books, a pile of empty metal tins, a young man in a white robe throwing more books onto the pile, the smell of fuel. He had his back turned, a bald patch on the back of his head glimmering with sweat, but he seemed unconcerned by the blaze. He was feeding it. He returned to the shelves for more to burn.

Juliette ran behind him to Solo's bed and grabbed a blanket, a rat scurrying out of its folds as she lifted it. She hurried toward the fire, eyes stinging, throat burning, and tossed the blanket across the pile of books. The blaze was momentarily swallowed, but it leaked at the seams. The blanket began to smoke. Juliette coughed into her shirt and ran back for the mattress, needed to smother the fire, thought of the empty reservoir of water in the next room, all that was being lost.

The man in the robe spotted her as she lifted the mattress. He howled and threw himself at her. They tumbled into the mattress and the nest of bedding. A boot flashed toward her face, and Juliette jerked her head back. The young man screamed. He was like a white flapping bird loose in the bazaar and swooping at heads. Juliette yelled for him to get away. The blaze leapt higher. She tugged at the mattress, him on top of it, and the man spilled off the other side. Only moments to get the fire under control before all was lost. Only moments. She grabbed Solo's other blanket and beat at the flames. Couldn't fight them and the man both. No time. She coughed and yelled for Raph, and the man in the robes came at her again, his eyes wild, arms flailing. Juliette lowered her shoulder into his stomach, ducked beneath his arms, and the man spilled over her back. He fell to the ground and encircled her legs, dragging her down with him.

Juliette tried to wriggle free, but he was clawing his way from her ankles to her waist. Flames rose behind him. The blanket had caught. The man screamed unholy rage, had lost his mind. Juliette pushed against his shoulders and squirmed on her ass to pull free. She could barely breathe, could barely see. The man on top of her screamed with renewed fervor, and it was his robes on fire. The flames marched up his back and over them both, and Juliette was back in that airlock, a blanket over her head, burning alive.

A boot flew across her face and struck the young priest, and she felt the strength leave the arms clinging to her. Someone pulled her from behind. Juliette kicked free, the smoke too thick now to see. She tried to get her bearings, was coughing uncontrollably, wondered where the radio was, knew it was gone. And someone was tugging her down a narrow hall, Raph's pale face making him little more than a ghost in smoke, urging her up the ladder ahead of him.

The server room was filling with smoke. The fire down below would spread until it ate up all that burned, leaving just charred metal and melted wires behind. Juliette helped Raph out of the ladderway and grabbed the hatch. She threw it on top and saw that it was useless for keeping out the smoke, was a blasted grate.

Raph disappeared behind one of the servers. "Quick!" he yelled. Juliette crawled on her hands and knees and found him pressed against the back of the comm hub, one foot against the server beside it, shoving with all of his might.

Juliette helped him. Aching muscles bulged and burned. They rocked against the unmoving metal, Juliette dimly aware of screws holding the base to the floor, but the weight of the tower helped. Metal groaned. With a heave, screws tore loose and the tall black tower tilted, trembled, and then crashed atop the hole in the ground, covering it.

Juliette and Raph collapsed, coughing, heaving for air. The room was hazy with smoke, but no more was leaking inside. And the screams far below them eventually died out.

Silo 1

56

THERE WERE VOICES outside the drone lift. Boots. Men walking back and forth, searching for them.

Donald and Charlotte clung to one another in the darkness of that low-ceilinged space. Charlotte had looked for some way to secure the door, but it was a featureless wall of metal with just a tiny release for the latch. Donald held back a cough, could feel a tickle in his throat grow until it covered every square inch of his flesh. He kept both hands clasped over his mouth and listened to the muted shouts of "clear" and "all clear".

Charlotte stopped fumbling with the door, and they simply huddled together and tried not to move, for the floor made popping noises any time they shifted their weight. They had spent all day in the small lift, waiting for the search party to come back to their level. Darcy had left to be on shift when everyone woke up. It had been a long day of fitful non-sleep for Donald and his sister, a day when he knew the search party would expand and grow desperate. Now they had a killer on the loose and an escaped prisoner from Deep Freeze, too. He could imagine the consternation this was causing Thurman. He could imagine the beating he would get when they were discovered. He just prayed these boots would go away. But they didn't. They grew nearer.

There was a bang on the metal hangar door, the pounding of an angry fist. Donald could feel Charlotte tense her arm across his back, crushing his cracked ribs. The door moved. Donald tried to push against it to hold it in place, but there was no leverage. The steel squeaked against his sweaty palms. This was it. Charlotte tried to help, but someone was cracking open their hiding spot. A flashlight blinded them both—it shined right in their eyes.

"Clear!" came the yell, close enough that Donald could smell the coffee on Darcy's breath. The door was slammed shut, a palm slapping it twice. Charlotte collapsed. Donald dared to clear his throat.

It was after dinner by the time they finally emerged, tired and starving. It was quiet and dark in the armory. Darcy had said he would try to come back when his shift started, but he had been worried the night shift wouldn't be as quiet as usual, not so suited to slinking away.

Donald and Charlotte hurried down the barracks hall and into separate bathrooms. Donald could hear the pipes rattle as his sister flushed. He ran the sink and coughed up blood, spat and watched the crimson threads spiral down the drain, drank from the tap, spat again, and finally used the bathroom himself.

Charlotte already had the radio uncovered and powered up by the time he got to the end of the hall. She hailed anyone who might hear. Donald stood behind her and watched her switch from channel eighteen to seventeen, repeating the call. No one answered. She left it on seventeen and listened to static.

"How did you raise them the last time?" Donald asked.

"Just like this." She stared at the radio for a moment before turning in her seat to face him, her brow furrowed with worry. Donald expected a thousand questions: How long before they were taken? What were they going to do next? How could they get someplace safe? A thousand questions, but not the one she asked, her voice a sad whisper: "When did you go outside?"

Donald took a step back. He wasn't sure how to answer. "What do you mean?" he asked, but he knew what she meant.

"I heard what Darcy said about you nearly getting over a hill. When was this? Are you still going out? Is that where you go when you leave me? Is that why you're sick?"

Donald slumped against one of the drone control stations. "No," he said. He watched the radio, hoping for some voice to break through the static and save him. But his sister waited. "I only went once. I went . . . thinking I'd never come back."

"You went out there to die."

He nodded. And she didn't get angry with him. She didn't yell or scream like he feared she might, which was why he had never told her before. She simply stood and rushed to him and wrapped her arms around his waist. And Donald cried.

"Why are they doing this to us?" Charlotte asked.

"I don't know. I want to make it stop."

"But not like that." His sister stepped back and wiped her eyes. "Donny, you have to promise me. Not like that."

He didn't reply. His ribs ached from where she'd embraced him. "I wanted to see Helen," he finally said. "I wanted to see where she'd lived and died. It was . . . a bad time. With Anna. Trapped down here." He remembered how he had felt about Anna then, how he felt about her now. So many mistakes. He had made mistakes at every turn. It made it difficult to make anymore decisions, to act.

"There has to be something we can do," Charlotte said. Her eyes lit up. "We could lighten a drone enough to carry us from here. The bunker busters must weigh sixty kilos. If we lighten another drone up, it could carry you."

"And fly it how?"

"I'll stay here and fly it." She saw the look on his face and frowned. "Better that one of us gets out," she said. "You know I'm right. We could launch before daylight, just send you as far as you can go. At least live a day away from this place."

Donald tried to imagine a flight on the back of one of those birds, the wind pelting his helmet, tumbling off in a rough landing, lying in the grass and staring up at the stars. He pulled his rag out and filled it with blood, shook his head as he put it away. "I'm dying," he told her. "Thurman said I have another day or two. He told me that a day or two ago."

Charlotte was silent.

"Maybe we could wake another pilot," he suggested. "I could hold a gun to his head. We could get you and Darcy both out of here."

"I'm not leaving you," his sister said.

"But you would have me go out there alone?"

She shrugged. "I'm a hypocrite."

Donald laughed. "Must be why they recruited you."

They listened to the radio.

"What do you think is going on in all those other silos right now?" Charlotte asked. "You dealt with them. Is it as bad there as it is here?"

Donald considered this. "I don't know. Some of them are happy enough, I suppose. They get married and have kids. They have jobs. They don't know anything beyond their walls, so I guess they don't have some of the stress about what's out there that you and I feel. But I think they have something else that we don't have, this deep feeling that something is wrong with how they're living. Buried, you know. And we understand that, and it chokes us, but they just have this chronic anxiety, I think. I don't know." He shrugged. "I've seen men happy enough here to get through their shifts. I've watched others go mad. I used to . . . I used to play solitaire for hours on my computer upstairs, and that's when my brain was truly off and I wasn't miserable. But then, I wasn't really alive, either."

Charlotte reached out and squeezed his hand.

"I think some of the silos that went dark have it best—"

"Don't say that," Charlotte whispered.

Donald looked up at her. "No, not that. I don't think they're dead, not all of them. I think some of them withdrew and are living how they want quietly enough that no one will come after them. They just want to be left alone, not controlled, free to choose how they live and die. I think it's what Anna wanted them to have. Living down here on this level for a year, trying to find some life without being able to go outside, I think it changed how she viewed all this."

"Or maybe it was being out of that box for a little while," Charlotte said. "Maybe she didn't like what it felt like to be put away."

"Or that," Donald agreed. Again, he thought how things would've been different had he woken her with some trust, had heard her out. If Anna was there to help, everything would be better. It pained him, but he missed her as much as he missed Helen. Anna had saved him, had tried to save others, and Donald had misunderstood and had hated her for both actions.

Charlotte let go of his hand to adjust the radio. She tried hailing someone on both channels, ran her fingers through her hair and listened to static.

"There was a while there when I thought this was a good thing," Donald said. "What they did, trying to save the world. They had me convinced that a mass extinction was inevitable, that a war was about to break out and claim everyone. But you know what I think? I think they knew that if a war broke out between all these invisible machines, that some pockets of people would survive here and there. So they built this. They made sure the destruction was complete so they could control it."

"They wanted to make sure the only pockets of people who survived were in *their* pockets," Charlotte said.

"Exactly. They weren't trying to save the world—they were trying to save themselves. Even if we'd gone extinct, the world would've gone right on along without us. Nature finds a way."

"People find a way," Charlotte said. "Look at the two of us." She laughed. "We're like weeds, aren't we, the two of us? Nature sneaking out along the edge. We're like those silos that wouldn't behave. How did they think they would ever contain all this? That something like this wouldn't happen?"

"I don't know," Donald said. "Maybe the kinds of people who try to shape the world feel like they're smarter than chaos itself."

Charlotte switched the channels back and forth in case someone was answering on one or the other. She seemed exasperated. "They should just let us be," she said. "Just stop and let us grow however we must."

Donald lurched out of his chair and stood up straight.

"What is it?" Charlotte asked. She reached for the radio. "Did you hear something?"

"That's it," Donald told her. "Leave us be." He fumbled for his rag and coughed. Charlotte stopped playing with the radio. "C'mon," he said. He waved at the desk. "Bring your tools."

"For the drone?" she asked.

"No. We need to put together another suit."

"Another suit?"

"For going outside. And you said those bunker busters weigh sixty kilos. Exactly how much is a kilo?"

57

"THIS IS NOT a good plan," Charlotte said. She tightened the breathing apparatus attached to the helmet and grabbed one of the large bottles of air, began fastening the hose to it. "What're we going to do out there?"

"Die," Donald told her. And he saw the look she gave him. "But maybe a week from now. And not here." He had an array of supplies laid out. Satisfied, he began stuffing them into one of the small military backpacks. MREs, water, a first-aid kit, a flashlight, a pistol and two clips, extra ammo, a flint, and a knife.

"How long do you think this air will last?" Charlotte asked.

"Those bottles are for sending troops overground to other silos, so they must have enough to reach the furthest one. We just need to go a little further than that, and we won't be as loaded down." He cinched up the pack and placed it next to the other one.

"It's like we're lightening up a drone."

"Exactly." Picking up a roll of tape, he pulled a folded map out of his pocket and began affixing it to the sleeve of one of the suits.

"Isn't that my suit?"

Donald nodded. "You're a better navigator. I'm going to follow you."

There was a ding on the other side of the shelves from the direction of the lifts. Donald dropped what he was doing and hissed for Charlotte to hurry. They made for the drone lift, but Darcy called out to let them know it was just him. He emerged from the tall shelves with a load in his arms, fresh coveralls and a tray heaped with food.

"Sorry," he said, seeing the panic he'd caused. "It's not like I can warn you." He held out the trays apologetically. "Leftovers from dinner."

He set the trays down, and Charlotte gave him a hug. Donald saw how quickly connections were made in desperate times. Here was a prisoner embracing a guard for not beating her, for showing an ounce of compassion. Donald was glad for the second suit. It was a good plan.

Darcy peered down at the scattering of tools and supplies. "What're you doing?" he asked.

Charlotte checked with her brother. Donald shook his head.

"Look," Darcy said, "I'm sympathetic to your situation. I am. I don't like what's going on around here, either. And the more that comes back—the more I remember about who I was—the more I think I'd be fighting this alongside you. But I'm not all-in with you guys. And this—" He pointed to the suits. "This doesn't look good to me. This doesn't look smart."

Charlotte passed a plate and a fork to Donald. She sat on one of the plastic storage bins and dug into what looked like a canned roast, beets, and potatoes. Donald sat beside her and slid his fork through the slick roast, chopping it up into bites. "Do you remember what you did before all this?" Donald asked. "Is it coming back to you?"

Darcy nodded. "Some. I've stopped taking my meds—"

Donald laughed.

"What? Why's that funny?"

"I'm sorry." Donald apologized and waved his hand. "It's just that . . . it's nothing. It's a good thing. Were you in the army?"

"Yeah, but not for long. I think I was in the Secret Service." Darcy watched them eat for a moment. "What about you two?"

"Air Force," Charlotte said. She jabbed her fork at Donald, whose mouth was full. "Congressman."

"No shit?"

Donald nodded. "More of an architect, really." He gestured at the room around them. "This is what I went to school for."

"Building stuff like this?" Darcy asked.

"Building this," Donald said. He took another bite.

"No shit."

Donald nodded and took a swig of water.

"Who did this to us, then? The Chinese?"

Donald and Charlotte turned to one another.

"What?" Darcy asked.

"We did this," Donald said. "This place wasn't built for a just-in-case. This is what it was designed for."

Darcy looked from one of them to the other, his mouth open.

"I thought you knew. It's all in my notes." *Once you know what to look for,* Donald thought. Otherwise, it was too obvious and audacious to see.

"No. I thought this was like that mountain bunker, where the government goes to survive—"

"It is," Charlotte said. "But this way they get the timing down just right."

Darcy stared down at his boots while Donald and his sister ate. For a last meal, it wasn't all that bad. Donald looked down at the sleeve of the coveralls he'd borrowed from Charlotte and saw the bullet hole in them for the first time. Maybe that was why she had acted as if he was crazy for putting them on. Across from him, Darcy began to slowly nod his head. "Yeah," he said.

"God, yeah. They did this." He looked up at Donald. "I put a guy in Deep Freeze a couple shifts ago. He was yelling all this crazy stuff. A guy from accounting."

Donald set his tray aside. He finished his water.

"He wasn't crazy, was he?" Darcy asked. "That was a good man."

"Probably," Donald said. "He was getting better, at least."

Darcy ran his fingers over his short hair. His attention went back to the scattering of supplies. "The suits," he said. "You're thinking of leaving? Because you know I can't help you do that."

Donald ignored the question. He went to the end of the aisle and retrieved the hand truck. He and Charlotte had already loaded the bunker buster on it. There was a plastic tag dangling from the nose cone that she said he would need to pull before it was armed. She had already removed the altimeter controls and safety overrides. She had called it a "dumb bomb" when she was done. Donald pushed the cart toward the lift.

"Hey," Darcy said. He got up from his bin and blocked the aisle. Charlotte cleared her throat, and Darcy turned to see that she was holding a gun on him.

"I'm sorry," Charlotte said.

Darcy's hand hovered over a bulging pocket. Donald pushed the handcart toward him, and Darcy stepped back.

"We need to discuss this," Darcy said.

"We already have," Donald told him. "Don't move." He stopped the handcart beside Darcy and reached into the young guard's pocket. He withdrew the pistol and stuck it into his own pocket, then asked for Darcy's ID. The young man handed it to him. Donald pocketed this, and then leaned the cart back on its wheels and continued toward the lift.

Darcy followed him at a distance. "Just slow down," he said. "You're thinking of setting that off? C'mon, man. Take it easy. Let's talk. This is a big decision."

"Not arrived at lightly, I promise. The reactor below us powers the servers. The servers control everyone's lives. We're going to set these people free. Let them live and die how they choose."

Darcy laughed nervously. "Servers control their lives? What're you talking about?"

"They pick the lottery numbers," Donald said. "They decide who is worthy to pass themselves along. They cull and shape. They play mock wars to pick a winner. But not for long."

"Okay, but there's just three of us. This is too big for just us to decide. Seriously, man—"

Donald stopped the cart right outside of the lift. He turned to Darcy, saw that his sister had gotten to her feet to stay close to him.

"You want me to name all the times in history that one person led to the death of millions?" Donald asked. "Something like five or a dozen people made this happen. You might be able to trace it back to three. And who knows if one of those men was influencing the other two? Well, if one man can build this, it shouldn't take more than that to bring it all down. Gravity is a bitch until she's on your side." Donald pointed down the aisle. "Now come sit down."

When Darcy didn't move, Donald drew not the guard's gun, but the one from his other pocket that he knew was locked and loaded. The disappointment and hurt on the young man's face before he turned and complied was a physical blow. Donald watched him march back down the aisle, past Charlotte. He caught his sister's arm before she followed, gave her a squeeze and a kiss on the cheek. "Go ahead and get your suit on," he told her.

She nodded, followed Darcy, sat back down on the bin and began to work herself into her suit.

"This isn't happening," Darcy said. He eyed the pistol Charlotte had set aside while she squirmed into her suit.

"Don't even think about it," Donald said. "In fact, you should get busy getting dressed."

The guard and his sister both turned to peer at him quizzically. Charlotte was just getting her legs into her suit. "What're you talking about?" she asked.

Donald picked up the hammer sitting among the tools and showed it to her. "I'm not risking that it doesn't go off," he said.

She tried to stand up, but her feet weren't all the way through the suit legs. "You said you had a way of setting it off remotely!"

"I do. Remotely from you." He aimed the gun at Darcy. "Get dressed. You've got five minutes to get inside that lift—"

Darcy lunged for the gun sitting beside Charlotte. Charlotte was faster and snatched it off the bin. Donald took a step back, and then realized his sister was aiming the gun at him. "*You* get dressed," she told her brother. Her voice was shaky, her eyes shining. "This isn't what we discussed. You promised."

"I'm a liar," Donald said. He coughed into the crook of his arm and smiled. "You're a hypocrite and I'm a liar." He began to back toward the lift, his gun trained on Darcy. "You're not going to shoot me," he told his sister.

"Give me the gun," Darcy told Charlotte. "He'll listen if I'm holding it."

Donald laughed. "You aren't going to shoot me either. That gun's not loaded. Now get dressed. You two get out of here. I'm giving you half an hour. The drone lift takes twenty minutes to get to the top. The best thing to use for jamming the door is an empty bin. I left one over there."

Charlotte was crying and tugging at the legs of her suit, trying to get her feet all the way through. Donald had known she'd never go without him unless he made her, that she'd do something stupid. She would run and embrace him and beg him to come, insist that she would stay there and die with him. The only chance of getting her out had been to leave Darcy with her.

He was a hero. He would save himself and her both. Donald jabbed the call button on the non-express.

"Half an hour," he repeated. He saw that Darcy was already unzipping his suit to get in. His sister was yelling at him and trying to stand up, nearly tripped and fell. She started to kick the suit off rather than put it on the rest of the way. The lift dinged and opened. Donald leaned the cart back and pulled it inside. Tears welled up in his eyes to see the pain he was causing Charlotte. She was halfway down the aisle toward him as the doors began to close.

"I love you," he said. He wasn't sure if she heard him. The doors squeezed shut on the sight of her. He scanned his ID, pressed a button, and the lift began to move.

Silo 17

58

THE COMM HUB COOLED, even as the fire raged below. Wisps of smoke curled out from underneath it. Juliette studied the interior of the great black machine and saw a ruin of broken circuit boards. The long row of headset jacks had shattered, and several of the wires at the base of the machine had stretched and snapped when it tipped over.

"Will it burn out?" Raph asked, eyeing the wisps of smoke.

Juliette coughed. She could still feel the smoke in her throat, could taste those burning pages. "I don't know," she admitted. She watched the lights overhead for any sign of faltering. "What power this silo has runs beneath the grates down there."

"So this silo could go dark as the mines at any time?" Raph scrambled to his feet. "I'm gonna get our bags, have our flashlights handy. And you need to drink some more water."

Juliette watched him trot off. She could feel those books burning beneath her. She could feel the wires inside the radio melting. She didn't think the power would go—hoped it wouldn't go—but so much else was being lost. The large schematics that had helped her find the digger might be ash already. The schematics to help her choose which silo to reach out to, which silo to dig for, gone.

Tall black machines hummed and whirred all around her,

those square-shouldered and unmoved giants. Unmoved save for one. Juliette rose to her feet and studied the fallen server, and the link between those machines and the silos became even more obvious. Here was one collapsed like her home. Like Solo's home. She studied the arrangement of the servers and remembered that their layout was identical to the layout of the silos. Raph returned with both of their bags. He handed Juliette her canteen of water. She took a sip, lost in thought.

"I've got your flashli—"

"Wait," Juliette said. She twisted the cap back onto her canteen and walked between the servers. She went to the back of one and studied the silver plate above the nest of wires. There was a silo symbol there with its three downward-pointing triangles. The number "29" was etched in the center.

"What're you looking for?" Raph asked.

Juliette tapped the plate. "Lukas used to say he needed to work on server six or server thirty or whatever. I remember him showing me how these things were laid out like the silos. We have a schematic right here."

She set off in the direction of servers seventeen and eighteen. Raph followed along. "Should we worry about the power?" he asked.

"There's nothing we can do about that. The decking and walls down there shouldn't get hot enough to catch. When it burns out, we'll go see—" Something caught Juliette's eye as she traced a route between the servers. The wires underneath the floor grates darted in and out of their chutes, running to the bases of the machines. It was a series of red wires amid all the black ones that stopped her.

"What now?" Raph asked. He was watching her as though he were worried. "Hey, are you feeling okay? Because I've seen miners get a rock to their crowns and act loopy for a day—"

"I'm fine," Juliette said. She pointed to the run of wires,

turned and imagined those wires leading from one server to another. "A map," she said.

"Yes," Raph agreed. "A map." He took her by the arm. "Why don't you come sit down? You breathed a lot of smoke—"

"Listen to me. The girl on the radio, the one from Silo One, she said there was a map with these red lines on it. It came up after I told her about the digger. She seemed really excited, said she understood why all the lines went off and converged. This was before the radio stopped working."

"Okay."

"These are the silos," Juliette said. She held out her hands to the tall servers. "C'mere. Look." She hurried around the next row, studied the plates as she searched. Fourteen. Sixteen. Seventeen. "Here we are. And this is where we tunneled. And that's our old silo." She pointed to the next server.

"So you're saying we can choose which of these to call on the radio by seeing who's close? Because we have a map just like this down below. Erik's got one."

"No, I'm saying those red lines on her map are like these wires. See? Tunneling deep underground down there. The diggers weren't meant to go from one silo to the next. Bobby was the one who told me how difficult that thing was to turn. It was aimed somewhere."

"Where?"

"I don't know. I would need that map to tell. Unless—" She turned to Raph, whose pale face she saw was smudged with smoke and soot. "You were on the dig team. How much fuel did that tank in the digger hold?"

He shrugged. "We never measured in gallons. Just topped it up. Court had the tank dipped a few times to see how much we were burning. I remember her saying we would never use up what was in there."

"That's because it was designed to go farther. Much farther.

We need to dip the tank again to get an idea. And Erik's map should show which way that digger was pointing to begin with. If only—" She snapped her fingers. "We've got the other digger."

"I'm not following. Why would we need two diggers? We've only got one generator that works."

Juliette squeezed his arm, could feel herself beaming, her mind racing. "We don't need the other one to dig. We just need to see where it's pointing. If we trace that line on a map and project out where our own digger should've gone, those two lines should cross. And if the fuel supply matches that distance, that's like a confirmation. We can see where and how far this place is that she was telling me about. This seed place. She made it sound like another silo, but one out where the air was—"

There were voices at the other end of the room, someone entering from the hall. Juliette pulled Raph against one of the servers and threw her finger over her mouth. But someone could be heard coming straight for them, a quiet clicking, like fingers tapping on metal. Juliette fought the urge to run, and then a brown shape emerged at her feet, and there was a hiss as a leg was lifted, a stream of urine spattering her boot.

"Puppy!" she heard Elise scream.

Juliette hugged the kids and Solo. She hadn't seen them since her silo fell. They reminded her why she was doing this, what she was fighting for, what was *worth* fighting for. A rage had built up inside of her, a single-minded pursuit of digging through the earth down below and digging for answers outside. And she had lost sight of this, these things worth saving. She had been too concerned with those who deserved to be damned.

This anger melted as Elise clung to her neck and Solo's beard scratched her face. Here was what was left, what they still had, and protecting it was more important than vengeance. That's what Father Wendel had discovered. He had been reading the wrong passages in his book, passages of hate rather than hope. And Juliette had been just as blind. She had been prepared to rush off and leave everyone behind.

Raph joined her and the kids, and they huddled together around one of the servers and discussed what they'd seen of the violence below. Solo had a rifle with him and kept saying they needed to secure the door, needed to hunker down.

"We should hide in here and wait for them to kill each other," he said, a wild look in his eyes.

"Is that how you survived all the years over here?" Raph asked.

Solo nodded. "My father put me away. It was a long time before I left. It was safer that way."

"Your father knew what was going to happen," Juliette said. "He locked you away from it all. It's the same reason we're down here, all of us, living like this. Someone did the same thing a long time ago. They put us away to save us."

"So we should hide again," Rickson said. He looked to the others. "Right?"

"How much food do you have left in the pantry?" Juliette asked Solo. "Assuming the fire didn't get to it."

He pulled on his beard. "Three years' worth. Maybe four. But just for me."

Juliette did the math. "Let's say two hundred people made it over, though I don't think it was that many. What's that? Maybe five days?" She whistled. A new appreciation for all the various farms of her old home dawned on her. To provide for thousands of people for hundreds of years, the balance was meticulous. "We need to stop hiding altogether," she said. "What we need . . ." She studied the faces of these few who trusted her completely. "We need a Town Hall."

Raph laughed, thinking she was joking.

"A what?" Solo asked.

"We need a meeting. With everyone. Everyone left. We need to decide if we're gonna stay hidden or get out of here."

"I thought we were going to dig to another silo," Raph said. "Or dig to this other place."

"I don't think we have time for digging. It would take weeks, and the farms are ravaged. Besides, I've got a better idea. A quicker way."

"What about those sticks of dynamite you've been hauling? I thought we were going after the people who did this."

"That's still an option. Look, we need to do this anyway. We need to get out of here. Otherwise, Jimmy's right. We'll just kill each other. So we need to round everyone up."

"We'll have to do it back down in the generator room," Raph said. "Someplace big enough. Or maybe the farms."

"No." Juliette turned and surveyed the room around her. She saw past the tall servers to the far walls, saw how wide the space was. "We'll do it here. We'll show them this place."

"Here?" Solo asked. "Two hundred people? Here?" He seemed visibly shaken, began tugging on his beard with both hands.

"Where will everyone sit?" Hannah asked.

"How will they see?" Elise wanted to know.

Juliette studied the wide hall with the tall, black machines. Many of them clicked and whirred. Wires trailed from the tops and wove their way through the ceiling. She knew from tracing the camera feeds in her old home that they were all interconnected. She knew how the power fed into the bases, how the side panels came off. She ran her hand across one of the machines Solo had marked with the days of his youth. They had added up to years.

"Go to the Suit Lab and grab my tool bag," she told Solo.

"A Project?" he asked.

She nodded, and Solo disappeared amid the tall machines. Raph and the kids studied her. Juliette smiled. "You kids are going to enjoy this."

With the wires cut from the top and the bolts removed from the base, all it took was a good shove. It went over much easier than the comm hub. Juliette watched with satisfaction as the machine tipped, trembled, and then crashed down with a bang felt through her boots. Miles and Rickson slapped hands and whooped in the manner of boys destroying things. Hannah and Shaw had already moved on to the next server. Elise scampered up on top with a boost from Juliette, wire cutters in her hand, Puppy barking at her to be safe.

"Like cutting hair," Juliette said, watching Elise work.

"We could do Solo's beard next," Elise suggested.

"I doubt he'd like that," Raph said.

Juliette turned to see that the miner had returned from his errand. "I dropped over a hundred notes," he told her. "Couldn't write more than that. My hand was cramping. I sprinkled them around so some will be sure to get to the bottom."

"Good. And you wrote that there was food up here? Enough for everyone?"

He nodded.

"Then we should get that machine off the hatch and make sure we can deliver. Otherwise, we're going to have to raid the farms above us."

Raph followed her to the comm hub. They made sure the smoke wasn't curling up, and Juliette ran her hand along the base, feeling for heat. Solo's hovel was metal on all sides, so her hope was that the fire didn't spread past the pile of books. But there was no telling. The fallen hub made a horrible screech as it was shoved to the side. A cloud of dark smoke billowed out.

Juliette waved her hand over her face and coughed. Raph ran to the other side of the server and made as if to shove it back. "Wait," Juliette said, ducking out of the cloud. "It's clearing."

The server room grew hazy, but there was no great outpouring of smoke. Just a leak from what had been trapped down there. Raph started to lower himself into the hole, but Juliette insisted on going first. She clicked her flashlight on and descended into the dissipating smoke.

She crouched at the bottom and breathed through her undershirt. The beam of her flashlight stood out like a solid thing, as if she could strike someone with it if they came at her. But no one was coming. There was a form in the middle of the hall, still smoldering. The smell was awful. The smoke cleared further, and Juliette yelled up to Raph that it was okay to descend.

He clanged down noisily while Juliette stepped over the body and surveyed the damage in the room. The air was warm and muggy, and it was difficult to breathe. She imagined for a moment what Lukas had gone through, down there and choking. More than smoke brought tears to her eyes.

"Those were books."

Raph joined her and stared at the black patch in the center of the room. He must've seen that they were books when he rescued her, because there was no sign of them left. Those pages were in the air now. They were in their lungs. Juliette choked on memories of the past.

She went to the wall and studied the radio. The metal cage was still bent back from where she'd busted it off the wall so long ago. She flipped the power switch, but nothing happened. The plastic knob was tacky and warm. The insides of the thing were probably a single blob of rubber and copper.

"Where's this food?" Raph asked.

"Through there," Juliette said. "Use a rag on the door."

He went off to explore the apartment and pantry while Juliette studied the remains of an old desk, a misshapen computer monitor sitting in the center, the panel shattered from the heat. There was no sign of Solo's bedding, just a pile of metal boxes that once held books, some of them sagging from the extreme heat. Juliette saw black footprints trailing behind her and realized the rubber on the soles of her boots was melting from the heat. She heard Raph yelling excitedly from the next room. Juliette passed through the door and found him clutching an armload of cans, his chin pressed to the ones on top of the pile, a goofy grin on his face.

"There's shelves of this," he said.

Juliette went to the pantry door and shined her light inside. It was a vast cavern with an odd can here or there. But some of the shelves in the back appeared fuller. "If everyone shows up, it'll last us a few days, no more," she said.

"Maybe we shouldn't have called for everyone."

"No," Juliette said. "We're doing the right thing." She turned to the wall by the small eating table. The fire hadn't made it through the door. The tall schematics the size of blankets hung there, perfectly intact. Juliette flipped through them, looking for the ones she needed. She found them and ripped them free. Folding them up, she heard a muted thud far above them, the sound of another server falling.

59

THEY ARRIVED IN a trickle, and then in clumps, and then in crowds. They marveled at the steady lights in the hallways and explored the offices. None of these people had ever seen the inside of IT. Few of them had spent much time in the Up Top, except on pilgrimages after a cleaning. Families wandered from room to room; kids clutched reams of paper; many came to Juliette or the others with the notes Raph had folded and dropped, asking about the food. In just a few days, they looked different. Coveralls were stained and torn, faces stubbled and gaunt, eyes ringed with dark circles. In just a few days. Juliette saw that they had only a few days more before things grew desperate. Everyone saw that.

Those who arrived early helped prepare the food and push over the last of the servers. The smells of warm vegetables and soup filled the room. Two of the hottest servers, numbers 40 and 38, had been lowered to the ground with their power intact. Open cans were arranged atop their hot sides, the contents of each can simmering. There wasn't enough silverware, so many stood drinking the soups and vegetable juice straight from warm cans.

Hannah helped Juliette set up for the Town Hall while Rickson tended to the baby. One of the schematics was already pinned to the wall, and Hannah was working on the other. Lines were carefully traced with thread, Hannah double-checking Juliette's work. A charcoal was used to mark the route. Juliette watched another group file in. It occurred to her that this was her second Town Hall and that the first hadn't gone so well. It occurred to her that this would most likely be her last.

Most of those gathered were from the farms, but then a few mechanics and miners began to show. Tom Higgins and the Planning Committee arrived from the Mids deputy station. Juliette saw one of them standing on a fallen server with a charcoal and paper, jabbing his finger as he attempted to count heads, cursing the milling crowd for making it difficult. She laughed, and then realized it was important, what he was doing. They would need to know. A cleaning suit lay empty at her feet, one of her props for the Town Hall. They would need to know how many suits and how many people.

Courtnee arrived and squeezed through the crowd, which came as a shock. Juliette beamed and embraced her friend.

"You smell like smoke," Courtnee said.

Juliette laughed. "I didn't think you'd come."

"The note said it was life or death."

"It did?" She looked to Raph.

He shrugged. "Some of them might've said that," he said.

"So what is this?" Courtnee said. "A long climb for some soup? What's going on?"

"I'll tell everyone at once." To Raph: "Can you see about getting everyone in here? And maybe send Miles and Shaw or one of the porters to the stairwell to see if any others are on their way."

While he left, Juliette noticed that everyone was already sitting on the servers, backs to each other, slurping from cans while more were opened and arranged from the great stacks behind Solo. He had taken over popping the cans with some electric contraption that plugged into a floor outlet. Many of those seated were eyeing the pile of food hauled up from the pantry. Many more were eyeing her. The whispers were like an escape of steam.

Juliette fretted and paced as the numbers in the room swelled. Shaw and Miles returned to say the stairway was pretty quiet, maybe a few more heading up. It felt as though an entire day had passed since Juliette and Raph had fought the fire below; she didn't want to glance at her watch and know the truth of the hour. She felt tired. Especially as everyone sat there, tipping their cans to their lips and tapping the bottoms, wiping their faces with their sleeves, watching her. Waiting.

The food had them quiet and momentarily content. The cans had their hands and mouths busy. It had won her some reprieve. Juliette knew it was now or never.

"I know you're wondering what this is all about," she began. "Why we're here." She raised her voice, and the conversations across the fallen servers fell quiet. "And I don't mean here, in this room. I mean this silo. Why did we run? There are a lot of rumors swirling, but I am here to tell you the truth. I have brought you into this most secretive of rooms to tell you the truth. Our silo was destroyed. It was poisoned. Those who did not make it over with us are gone."

There was a hiss of whispers. "Poisoned by who?" someone shouted.

"The same people who put us underground hundreds of years ago. I need you to listen. Please listen."

The crowd quietened.

"Our ancestors were put underground so that we might survive while the world got better. As many of you know, I went outside before our home was taken from us. I sampled the air out there, and I think the farther we get from this place, the better the conditions are. Not only do I suspect this from what we measured, I have heard from another silo that there are blue skies beyond the—"

"Ratshit!" someone yelled. "I heard that was a lie, something they did to your brain before you went to clean."

Juliette found the person who'd said that. It was an older porter, one whose profession was the locus not just of rumors but also of secrets too dangerous to sell. While people whispered again, she saw a new arrival shuffle through the thick metal door at the far end of the room. It was Father Wendel, his arms crossed over his chest, hands stuffed into his sleeves. Bobby bellowed for everyone to shut up, and they gradually did. Juliette waved a greeting to Father Wendel, and heads turned.

"I need you to take some of what I'm about to say on faith," Juliette said. "Some of what I say I know for certain. I know this: We could stay here and make a life, but I don't know for how long. And we would live in fear. Not just fear of each other, but fear that disaster can visit us at any time. They can open our doors without asking, can poison our air without telling, and they can take our lives without warning. And I don't know what kind of life that would be."

The room was as still as death.

"The alternative is to go. But if we do, there's no coming back—"

"Go where?" someone yelled. "Another silo? What if it's worse than this one?"

"Not another silo," Juliette said. She moved to the side so they could see the schematic on the wall. "Here they are. The fifty silos. This one was our home." She pointed, and there was a rustle as everyone strained to see. Juliette felt her throat tighten with emotion at the overwhelming joy and sadness of telling the truth to her people. She slid her finger to the adjacent silo. "This is where we are now."

"So many," she heard someone whisper.

"How far are they?" another asked.

"I drew a line to show how we got here." She pointed. "It may be hard to see from the back. And this line here, this is where our digging machine was pointing." She traced it with her finger so they could see where it led. Her finger went sideways off the map and to the wall. Waving to Elise, Juliette had her come up and press her finger to a spot she'd already marked.

"This schematic is for the silo we're currently in." She moved to the next sheet of paper. "It shows another digging machine at the base—"

"We don't want your digging—"

Juliette turned to the audience. "I don't want to dig either. Honestly, I don't think we have enough fuel left, because we've been burning it since we got here and because we worked the machine hard to get her to turn. And I don't think we have food for more than a week or two, not for everyone. We're not digging. But our schematic matched the size and location of the machine we found back home. It matched it perfectly to scale and even the direction it was pointing. I have a schematic here of this silo and this digger." She ran her hand over the other sheet of paper, then went back to the large map. "When I plot this, look how the line goes between all the other silos, not touching any of them." She walked and slid her finger across the line until she touched Elise's finger. Elise beamed up at her.

"We have a good guess of the fuel we used to get to this silo, and how much remains. We know how much fuel we started with and how fast it burns. And what we determined is that the digger was loaded up with just enough fuel—with maybe ten percent extra—to have taken us directly to this spot." She again touched Elise's finger. "And the diggers are aimed slightly up. We think they were placed here to take us to this point—to get us out of here." She paused. "I don't know when they were going to tell us—if they were ever going to tell us—but I say we don't wait to be asked. I say we go."

"Just go?"

Juliette scanned the audience and saw that it was one of the men from the Planning Committee.

"I think it might be safer out there for us than if we stay. I know what will happen if we stay. I want to see if it's better if we leave."

"You *hope* it's safer," someone said.

Juliette didn't search for the voice. She let her gaze drift across the crowd. Everyone was thinking the same thing, herself included.

"That's right. I hope. I have the word of a stranger. I have whispers from someone I've never met. I have a feeling in my gut, in my heart. I have these lines that cross on a map. And if you think that's not enough, then I agree with you. I've lived my entire life only believing what I can see. I need proof. I need to see results. And even then I need to see them a second and a third time before I get a glimpse of how things truly are. But this is a case where what I know for certain—the life that awaits us here—is not worth living. And there's a chance that a better one can be found elsewhere. I'm willing to go see, but only if enough of you are with me."

"I'm with you," Raph said.

Juliette nodded. The room blurred a little. "I know you are," she said.

Solo raised his hand. With his other, he tugged on his beard. Juliette felt Elise take her hand. Shaw held a squirming puppy, but still managed to raise his.

"How will we get there if we don't aim to dig?" one of the miners hollered.

Juliette bent at the waist to grab something at her feet. While her head was down, she wiped at her eyes. She stood and lifted one of the cleaning suits, held it in one hand, a helmet in the other.

“We’re going outside,” she said.

60

THE FOOD DWINDLED while they worked. It was a grim countdown, these disappearing cans and what had been rounded up from the farms. Not everyone in the silo participated; many never came to the Town Hall; many more simply wandered off, realizing they could grab more grow plots if they hurried. Several mechanics asked for permission to head back down to Mechanical and round up those who had refused to make the climb, to try and convince them to come, to see if Walker could be stirred. Juliette was overjoyed with the prospect of gathering more people to go. She also felt the pressure mount as everyone worked.

The server room became a massive workshop, something like you'd see down the halls of Supply. Nearly a hundred and fifty cleaning suits were laid out, all of them needing to be sized and adjusted. Juliette was sad to see that it was more than they needed, but also a little relieved. It would've been a problem the other way around.

She had shown a dozen mechanics how the valves went together like she and Nelson had used to breathe in the Suit Lab. There weren't enough of the valves in IT, so porters were given samples and sent down to Supply, where Juliette was sure there would be more of these parts otherwise useless for survival. Gaskets, heat tape, and seals were needed. They were also told to secure and haul up the welding kits in both Supply and Mechanical. She showed them the difference between the acetylene bottles and the oxygen and said they wouldn't need the acetylene.

Erik calculated the distance using the chart hanging on the wall and reckoned they could put a dozen people to a bottle. Juliette said to make it ten to be safe. With fifty or so people working on the suits—the fallen servers acting as workbenches as they knelt or sat on the floor—she took a small group up to the cafeteria for what she knew would be a grim job. Just her father, Raph, Dawson, and two of the older porters who she figured had handled bodies before. On the way up, they stopped below the farms and went to the coroner's office past the pump rooms. Juliette found a supply of folded black bags and pulled out five dozen. From there they climbed in silence.

There was no airlock attached to Silo 17, not anymore. The outer door remained cracked open from the fall of the silo decades before. Juliette remembered squeezing through that door twice before, her helmet getting stuck the first time. The only barriers between them and the outside air were the inner airlock door and the door to the sheriff's office. Bare membranes between a dead world and a dying one.

Juliette helped the others remove a tangle of chairs and tables from around the office door. There was a narrow path between them where she had come and gone over a month ago, but they needed more room to work. She warned the others about the bodies inside, but they knew from collecting the bags what they were in for. A handful of flashlights converged on the door as Juliette prepared to open it. They all wore masks and rubber gloves at her father's insistence. Juliette wondered if they should've donned cleaning suits instead.

The bodies inside were just as she remembered them: a tangle of gray and lifeless limbs. The stench of something both foul and metallic filled her mask, and Juliette had a memory of dumping fetid soup on herself to drown the outside air. This was the stench of death and something besides.

They hauled the bodies out one by one and placed them in the funeral bags. It was grisly work. Limp flesh sloughed off bones like a slow roast. "The joints," Juliette cautioned, her voice hot and muffled by her mask. "Armpits and knees."

The bodies held together barely and enough, the tendons and bone doing most of the work. Black zippers were pulled shut with relief. Coughing and gagging filled the air.

Most of the bodies inside the sheriff's office had piled up by the door as if they'd crawled over one another in an attempt to get back inside, back into the cafeteria. Other bodies were in a state of more serene rest. A man slouched over on the tattered remnants of a cot in the open holding cell, just the rusted frame, the mattress long gone. A woman lay in the corner with her arms crossed over her chest as if sleeping. Juliette moved the last of the bodies with her father, and she saw how wide her father's eyes were, how they were fixed on her. She glanced over his shoulder as she shuffled backwards out of the sheriff's office, staring at the airlock door that awaited them all, its yellow skin flaking off in chips of paint.

"This isn't right," her father said, his voice muffled and his mask bobbing up and down with the movement of his jaw. They tucked the body into an open bag and zipped it up.

"We'll give them a proper burial," she assured him, assuming he meant it wasn't right how the bodies were being handled—stacked like bags of dirty laundry.

He removed his gloves and his mask, rested back on his heels, and wiped his brow with the back of his hand. "No. It's these people. I thought you said this place was practically empty when you got here."

"It was. Just Solo and the kids. These people have been dead a long time."

"That's not possible," her father said. "They're too well preserved." His eyes drifted across the bags, wrinkles of concern or confusion in his brow. "I'd say they've been dead for three weeks. Four or five at the most."

"Dad, they were here when I arrived. I crawled over them. I asked Solo about them once, and he said he discovered them years ago."

"That simply can't be—"

"It's probably because they weren't buried. Or the gas outside kept the bugs away. It doesn't matter, does it?"

"It matters plenty when something isn't right like this. There's something not right about this entire silo, I'm telling you." He stood and headed toward the stairwell where Raph was ladling hauled water into scrounged cups and cans. Her father took one for himself and passed one to Juliette. He was lost in thought, she could tell. "Did you know Elise had a twin sister?" her father asked.

Juliette nodded. "Hannah told me. Died in childbirth. The mother passed as well. They don't talk about it much, especially not with her."

"And those two boys. Marcus and Miles. Another set of twins. The eldest boy Rickson says he thought he had a brother, but his father wouldn't talk about it and he never knew his mother to ask her." Her father took a sip of water and peered into the can. Juliette tried to drown the metallic taste on her tongue while Dawson helped with one of the bags. Dawson coughed and looked as though he were about to gag.

"It's a lot of dying," Juliette agreed, worried where her father's thoughts were going. She thought of the brother she never knew. She looked for any sign on her father's face, any indication that this reminded him of his wife and lost son. But he was piecing together some other puzzle.

"No, it's a lot of *living*. Don't you see? Three sets of twins in six births? And those kids are as fit as fiddles with no care. Your friend Jimmy doesn't have a hole in his teeth and can't remember the last time he was sick. None of them can. How do you explain that? How do you explain these bodies piled up like they fell over a few weeks ago?"

Juliette caught herself staring at her arm. She gulped the last of her water, handed the tin to her father, and began rolling up her sleeve. "Dad, do you remember me asking you about scars, about whether or not they go away?"

He nodded.

"A few of my scars have disappeared." She showed him the crook of her arm as if he would know what was no longer there. "I didn't believe Lukas when he told me. But I used to have a mark here. And another here. And you said it was a miracle I survived my burns, didn't you?"

"You received good attention straight away—"

"And Fitz didn't believe me when I told him about the dive I made to fix the pump. He said he's worked flooded mineshafts and has seen men twice my size get sick from breathing air just ten meters deep, much less thirty or forty. He says I would've died if I'd done what I did."

"I don't know the first thing about mining," her father said.

"Fitz does, and he thinks I should be dead. And you think these people should be rotted—"

"They should be bones. I'm telling you."

Juliette turned and gazed at the blank wallscreen. She wondered if it was all a dream. This was what happened to the dying soul; it scrambled for some perch, some stairway to cling to, some way not to fall. She had cleaned and died on that hill outside her silo. She had never loved Lukas at all. Never gotten to know him properly. This was a land of ghosts and fiction, events held together with all the vacant solidarity of dreams, all the nonsense of a drunken mind. She was long dead and only just now realizing it—

"Maybe something in the water," her father said.

Juliette turned away from the blank wall. She reached out to him, held his arms in her hands, then stepped closer. He wrapped his arms around her and she wrapped hers around him. His stubble scratched her cheek, and she fought hard not to cry.

"It's okay," her father said. "It's okay."

She wasn't dead. But things weren't right.

"Not in the water," she said, though she'd swallowed her fair share in that silo. She released her father and watched the first of the bags head to the stairwell. Someone was rigging up spliced electrical cables for rope and running it over the rail to lower a body. Porters be damned, she saw. Even the porters were saying *porters be damned.*

"Maybe it's in the air," she said. "Maybe this is what happens when you don't gas a place. I don't know. But I think you're right that there's something wrong with this silo. And I think it's high time we get out of here."

Her father took a last swig of water. "How long before we leave?" he asked. "And are you sure this is a good idea?"

Juliette nodded. "I'd rather we died out there trying than in here killing each other." And she realized she sounded like all those who had been sent to clean, all the dangerous dreamers and mad fools, those she had mocked and never understood. She sounded like a person who trusted a machine to work without peeking inside, without first tearing it completely apart.

61

CHARLOTTE SLAPPED THE lift door with her palm. She had jabbed the call button right as her brother disappeared, but it was too late. She hopped on one foot to keep her balance, her suit only half on. Down the aisle behind her, Darcy was struggling into his suit. "Will he do it?" Darcy called out.

Charlotte nodded. He would. He had pulled the other suit out for Darcy. This was his plan all along. Charlotte slapped the door again and cursed her brother.

"You need to get dressed," Darcy said.

She turned and sank to the ground, hugged her shins. She didn't want to move. She watched Darcy wriggle into his suit and get the collar over his head. He stood and tried to reach around for the zipper, finally gave up. "Was I supposed to put this backpack on first?" He grabbed one of the bundles her brother had packed and opened it up. He pulled out a can, put it back. Brought out a gun, kept it out. He worked his head and arms back out of the suit. "Charlotte, we've got half an hour. How're we getting out of here?"

Charlotte wiped her cheeks and struggled to her feet. Darcy didn't have the first clue about how to get suited up. She worked her legs into her suit and left the sleeves and collar off, hurried down the aisle toward him. There was a ding behind her.

She stopped and turned, thinking Donald had come back, had changed his mind, forgetting that she had pressed the call button.

Two men in light blue coveralls gaped at her from inside the express lift. One of them peered at the buttons in confusion, looked back to Charlotte—this woman with a silver suit half on and half off—and then the doors slowly closed.

"Shit," Darcy said. "We really need to go."

A panic stirred in Charlotte, an internal countdown. She thought of the way her brother had looked at her from inside the lift, the way he had kissed her goodbye. Her chest felt as though it might implode, but she hurried to Darcy and helped him get his arms out and his pack on. Once he was in fully, she zipped up the back. He helped her do the same, then followed her to the end of the aisle. Charlotte pointed to the low hangar and handed him both helmets. The bin her brother had left was right where he'd said it would be. "Open that door up and jam the bin halfway inside. I'll go start the lift."

She threw open the barracks door and ran down the hall in an awkward waddle, the thick suit crowding her knees. Through the next door. The radio was still on and hissing. She thought of the waste that thing had been, all the time putting it together, collecting the parts, and now she was abandoning it. At the lift control station, she ripped the plastic off and flipped the main controls into the up position. She felt sure she'd given Darcy plenty of time to get it jammed. Another awkward waddle down the hall, past the barracks that'd been her home for these agonizing weeks, out into her armory hell, the last of her birds sulking beneath their tarps, a single chirp ringing out from somewhere. From the lift. The sound of boots storming their way, Darcy yelling at her to get inside the drone lift.

• • •

Donald rode the lift toward the sixty-second floor. When he passed sixty-one, he hit the emergency stop button. The lift jerked to a stop and began buzzing. He steadied the bomb and pulled out the hammer, went ahead and removed the tag. He wasn't sure how much damage it would cause if he detonated it inside the lift, but he would if anyone came for him. He wanted to give his sister enough time, but he was willing to risk everything to put an end to that place. He watched the clock on the lift panel and waited. It gave him plenty of time to think. Fifteen minutes passed without him needing to cough or clear his throat once. He laughed at this and wondered if he was getting better. Then he remembered how his grandfather and his aunt had both gotten better the day before they died. It was probably something like that.

The hammer grew heavy. It was incredible to stand beside something so destructive as that bomb, to lay a hand on a device that could kill so many, change so much. Another five minutes went by. He should go. It was too long. It would take him some time to get to the reactor. He waited another minute, some rational part of his brain aware of what the rest of him was about to do, some buried part that screamed for him to think about this, to be reasonable.

Donald slammed the hold switch before he lost his nerve. The lift lurched. He hoped his sister and Darcy were well on their way.

Charlotte threw herself into the drone lift, her helmet banging on the ceiling, the bottle of air on her back causing her to tip over onto her side. Darcy threw his helmet inside the lift and began crawling in after her. Someone shouted from the armory. Charlotte began to shove at the plastic bin, which was the only thing keeping the lift from closing and heading up. Darcy pushed as well, but it was pinned tight. Another shout from beyond. Darcy fumbled for the pistol he'd taken from the pack. He turned on his side and fired out of the lift, deafening roars from inside that metal can. Charlotte saw men in silver coveralls duck and take cover behind the drones. Another shot rang out, a loud *thwack* inside the lift, the men out there returning fire. Charlotte turned to kick the bin with her feet, but the lid had buckled down where the door had pinched it. It had formed a wedge, wanted to come in with her, not go out. She tried to pull, but there was nothing to cling to.

Darcy yelled for her to stay put. He crawled on his elbows out the door, his gun firing *pop pop pop,* men taking cover, Charlotte cringing. He left the lift and began pushing the bin in from the other side. Charlotte yelled for him to stop, to get back inside. The door would slam shut with him out there. Another shot rang out, the zing of a miss. Darcy kicked the bin with his boot, and it moved several inches.

"Wait!" Charlotte yelled. She scampered to the door, didn't want to go on by herself. "Wait!"

Darcy kicked the bin again. The lift lurched. It was almost free, just a few more inches. Another shot from beyond the drones and no sound of a miss. Just a grunt from Darcy, who fell to his knees, turned and fired wildly behind himself.

Charlotte reached out and tugged on his arm. "Come on!" she yelled.

Darcy reached down and pushed her hands inside the lift. He leaned his shoulder against the bin and smiled at her. And before he shoved the bin inside, he said, "It's okay. I remember who I am, now."

The lift slowed on the reactor level, the doors opened, and Donald pressed a boot to the hand truck and tilted it back. He steered the bomb toward the security gates. The guard there watched him approach, eyebrows up with mild curiosity. Here was everything wrong with everything, Donald thought. Here was a guard not recognizing a murderer because he toted a bomb. Here was a man swiping an ID with Darcy's name on it, a green light, and the ennui of an interminable job as he was waved through the gates. Here was everyone seeing what was coming and ushering hell right along anyway.

"Thank you," Donald said, daring the man to recognize him.

"Good luck with that."

Donald had never seen the reactors before. They were closed off behind large doors and spanned three levels. On any one shift, there were nearly as many men in red as half the others combined. Here was the heart of a soulless machine, which made it the only organ of consequence.

He followed a curving hall lined with thick pipes and heavy cables. He passed two others in reactor red, neither of them noting the holes in the shoulder of his coveralls, or that the bloodstains had begun to brown. Just nods and quick glances at his burden, even quicker glances away lest they be asked to help. One of the hand truck's tires squeaked as if complaining about Donald's plan, unhappy with that terrible load.

Donald stopped outside of the main reactor room. Far enough. He reached into his pocket and pulled out the hammer. He weighed this thing he was about to do. He thought of Helen, who had died the way people were supposed to die. This was how it worked. You lived. You did your best. You got out of the way. You let those who come after you choose. You let them decide for themselves, live their own lives. This was the way.

He raised the hammer with both hands, and a shot rang out. A shot, and a fire in his chest. Donald spun in a lazy circle, the hammer clattering to the ground, and then his legs went out.

He clutched for the bomb, hoping to take it with him, to pull it down. His fingers found the cone, slipped off, caught the hand truck's handle, and they both tumbled. Donald ended up on his back, the bomb slamming flat to the ground with a powerful clang felt through his back, and then rolling lazily and harmlessly toward the wall, out of reach.

The drone lift opened automatically at the end of its long and dark climb. Charlotte hesitated. She looked for some way to lower the lift, to go back down. But the controls were a mile beneath her. The large tank of air on her back knocked against the roof of the lift as she crawled out. Darcy was gone. Her brother was gone. This was not what she wanted.

Overhead, black clouds swirled. She crawled up a sloping ramp, all of it familiar. She had been here before, if not in person. It was the view from her drones, the sight she'd been rewarded with on four flights. With the push of a throttle, she would be up there in those clouds, banking hard and flying free.

But this time, it was with weary muscles that she crawled up the ramp. She reached the top and had to lower herself down to a concrete ledge below. A grounded bird, a flightless traveler, she shinnied down this ledge and dropped to the dirt, a chick plummeting from its nest.

She wasn't sure at first which way to go. And she was thirsty, but her food and water were in a pack and trapped with her inside her suit. She turned and fought for her bearings, checked the map her brother had taped to her arm, and was angry at him for that. Angry and thankful. This was his plan all along.

She studied the map, was used to a digital display, a higher vantage, a flight plan, but the ramp leading down into the earth helped her establish north. Red lines on the map pointed the way. She plodded toward the hills and a better view.

And she remembered this place, remembered being here after a rain when the grass was slick and twin tracks of mud made a brown lacework of that gradual rise. Charlotte remembered being late from the airport. She had topped that very hill, and her brother had raced out to meet her. It was a time when the world was whole. You might look up and see vapor trails from passenger jets inching across the sky. You could drive to fast food. Call a loved one. A settled world existed here.

She passed through the spot where she'd hugged her brother, and any plan of escape wilted. She had little desire to carry on. Her brother was gone. The world was gone. Even if she lived to see green grass and eat one more MRE, cut her lip on one more can of water . . . why?

She trudged up the hill, taking a step only because her other foot had taken a step, tears streaming down her face, wondering why.

Donald's chest was on fire. Warm blood pooled around his neck. He lifted his head and saw Thurman at the end of the hall, marching toward him. Two men from Security were on either side, guns drawn. Donald fumbled in his pocket for his pistol, but it was too late. Too late. Tears welled up, and they were for the people who would live under this system, the hundreds of thousands who would come and go and suffer. He managed to free the pistol but could only raise it a few inches off the ground. These men were coming for him. They would hunt down Charlotte and Darcy out there on the surface. They would swoop down on his sister with their drones. They would take down silo after silo until only one was left, this capricious judgment of souls, of lives run by pitiless servers and soulless code.

Their guns were trained on him, waiting for him to make a move, ready to end his life. Donald put every ounce of his strength into lifting that pistol. He watched Thurman come at him, this man he had shot and killed once before, and he lifted his gun, struggled to raise it, could lift it no more than six inches off the ground.

But it was enough.

Donald steered his arm wide, aimed at the cone of that great bomb designed to bring down monsters such as these, and pulled the trigger. He heard a bang, but he could not tell what from.

The earth lurched and Charlotte fell forward on her hands and knees. There was a *thwump* like a grenade tossed into a deep lake. The hillside shuddered.

Charlotte turned on her side and glanced down the hill. A crack opened along the flat earth. Another. The concrete tower at the center listed to one side, and then the earth yawned open. A crater formed, and then the center of the scooped-out earth between those hills sank and tugged at the land further out, clawed and grabbed at the soil and pulled it down as if it were a giant sinkhole, plumes of white powdered concrete jetting up through the cracks.

The hill rumbled. Sand and tiny rocks slid downward, racing each other toward the bottom as the land became something that *moved.* Charlotte scrambled backwards, up the hill and away from the widening pit, her heart racing and her mind awed.

She turned and rose to her feet and climbed as fast as she could, a hand on the earth in front of her, crouched over, the land slowly becoming solid again. She climbed until she reached the crest, her sobs swallowed by the shock of witnessing this scene of such powerful destruction, the wind strong against her, the suit cold and bulky.

At the top of the hill, she collapsed. “Donny,” she whispered.

Charlotte turned and gazed down at the hole in the world her brother had left. She lay on her back while the dust peppered her suit and the wind screamed against her visor, her view of the world growing more and more blurred, the dust clouding all.

Fulton County, Georgia

62

JULIETTE REMEMBERED A day meant for dying. She had been sent to clean, had been stuffed in a suit similar to this one, and had watched through a narrow visor as a world of green and blue was taken from her, color fading to gray as she crested a hill and saw the true world.

And now, laboring through the wind, the hiss of sand against her visor, the roar of her pulse and heavy breathing trapped in that dome, she watched as brown and gray relented and drained away.

The change was gradual at first. Hints of pale blue. Hard to be sure that's even what it was. She was in the lead group with Raph and her father and the other seven suited figures tethered to the shared bottle of air they lugged between them. A gradual change, and then it became sudden, like stepping through a wall. The haze lifted; a light was thrown; the wind buffeting her from all sides halted as stabs of color erupted, shards of green and blue and pure white, and Juliette was in a world that was almost too vivid, too vibrant, to be believed. Brown grasses like withered rows of corn brushed against her boots, but these were the only dead things in sight. Further away, green grasses stirred and writhed. White clouds roamed the sky. And Juliette saw now that the bright picture books of her youth were in fact faded, the pages muted compared to this.

There was a hand on her back, and Juliette turned to see her father staring wide-eyed at the vista. Raph shielded his eyes against the bright sun, his exhalations fogging his helmet. Hannah smiled down her collar at the bulge cradled to her chest, the empty arms of her suit twisting in the breeze as she held her child. Rickson wrapped his arm around her shoulder and stared at the sky while Elise and Shaw threw their hands up as if they could gather the clouds. Bobby and Fitz set the oxygen bottle down for a moment and simply gaped.

Behind her group, another emerged from the wall of dust. Bodies pierced a veil—and labored and weary faces lit up with wonder and new energy. One figure was being helped along, practically carried, but the sight of color seemed to lend them new legs.

Looking up behind her, Juliette saw a wall of dust reaching into the sky. All along the base, the life that dared approach this choking barrier crumbled, grass turning to powder, occasional flowers becoming brown stalks. A bird turned circles in the open sky, seemed to study these bright intruders in their silvery suits, and then banked away, avoiding danger and gliding through the blue.

Juliette felt a similar tug pulling her toward those grasses and away from the dead land they had crawled out of. She waved to her group, mouthed for them to come on, and helped Bobby with the bottle. Together they lumbered down the slope. After them came others. Each group paused in much the way Juliette had heard cleaners were prone to staggering about. One of the groups carried a body, a limp suit, the looks on their faces sharing grim news. Everywhere else was euphoria, though. Juliette felt it in her fizzing brain, which had planned to die that day; she felt it across her skin, her scars forgotten; she felt it in her tired legs and feet, which now could march to the horizon and beyond.

She waved the other groups down the slope. When she saw a man fiddling with his helmet latches, Juliette motioned for those in his group to stop him, and word spread by hand signal from group to group. Juliette could still hear the hiss from the air bottle in her own helmet, but a new urgency seized her. This was more than hope at their feet, more than blind hope. This was a promise. The woman on the radio had been telling the truth. Donald had truly been trying to help them. Hope and faith and trust had won her people some reprieve, however short. She pulled the map out of a numbered pocket meant for cleaning and consulted the lines. She urged everyone along.

There was another rise ahead, a large and gentle hill. Juliette aimed for this. Elise ranged ahead of her, tugging at the limits of her air hose and kicking up startled insects from the tall grass that came up past her knees. Shaw chased after her, their hoses near to tangling. Juliette heard herself laugh and wondered when she'd last made such a noise.

They struggled up the hill, and the land to either side seemed to grow and widen with the altitude. It wasn't just a hill, she saw as she reached the crest, but rather one more ring of mounded earth. Beyond the summit, the land swooped down into a bowl. Turning to take in the entire view around her, Juliette saw that this single depression was separate from the fifty. Back the way she had come, across a valley of verdant green, rose a wall of dark clouds. Not just a wall, she saw, but a giant dome, the silos at its center. And in the other direction, beyond the ringed hill, a forest like those from the Legacy books, a distant groundcover of giant broccoli heads whose scale was impossible to fathom.

Juliette turned to the others and tapped her helmet with her palm. She pointed to the black birds gliding on the air. Her father lifted a hand and asked her to wait. He understood what she was about to do. He reached for the latches of his own helmet instead.

Juliette felt the same fear he must've felt at the thought of a loved one going first, but agreed to let him. Raph helped with her father's latches, which were nearly impossible to work with the thick gloves. Finally, the dome clicked free. Her father's eyes widened as he took an exploratory breath. He smiled, took another, deeper one, his chest swelling, his hand relaxing, the helmet falling from his fingers and tumbling into the grass.

A frenzy broke, people groping at one another's collars. Juliette set her heavy pack down in the grass and helped Raph, who helped her in turn. When her helmet clicked free, it was the sounds she noticed first. It was the laughter from her father and Bobby, the happy squeals from the children. The smells came next, the odor of the farms and the hydroponic gardens, the scent of healthy soil turned up to claim its seed. And the light, as bright and warm as the grow lights but at a diffused distance, wrapping all around them, an emptiness above her that stretched out into forever, nothing above their heads but far clouds.

Suit collars clanged together with hugs. The groups behind were scurrying faster now, people falling and being helped up, flashes of teeth through domes, wet eyes and trails of tears down cheeks, forgotten bottles of oxygen dragging at the end of taut hoses, one body being carried.

Gloves and suits were torn at, and Juliette realized they'd never hoped for any of this. There were no knives strapped to their chests to cut away at their suits. No plan of ever leaving those silver tombs. They had left the silo in cleaning suits as all cleaners do, because a life cooped up becomes intolerable, and to stagger over a hill, even to death, becomes a great longing.

Bobby managed to tear his glove with his teeth and get a hand free. Fitz did the same. Everyone was laughing and sweating as they managed to work zippers and velcro at each other's backs, shake arms loose, work heads out of ringed collars, tug strenuously at boots. Barefoot and in a colorful array of grimy undersuits, the children squirmed free and tumbled in the grass after one another. Elise set down her dog—which she'd kept pinned to her chest like her own child—and squealed as the animal disappeared in the tall green fronds. She scooped him up again. Shaw laughed and dug her book out of his suit.

Juliette reached down and ran her hands through the grass. It was like weeds from the farms, but bunched together in a solid carpet. She thought of the fruits and vegetables some had packed away inside their suits. It would be important to save the seeds. Already, she was thinking they might last more than the day. More than the week. Her soul soared at the prospect.

Raph grabbed her once he was free of his suit and kissed her on the cheek.

"What the hell?" Bobby roared, spinning in circles with his great arms out and palms up. "What the hell!"

Her father stepped beside her and pointed down the slope, into the basin. "Do you see that?" he asked.

Juliette shielded her eyes and peered into the middle of the depression. There was a mound of green. No, not a mound; a tower. A tower with no antennas but rather some silvery flat roof jutting up and half covered in vines. Tall grass obscured much of the concrete.

The ridge grew crowded with people and laughter, and the grass was soon covered with boots and silver skins. Juliette studied this concrete tower, knowing what they would find inside. Here was the seed of a new beginning. She lifted her bag, heavy with dynamite. She weighed their salvation.

63

"No more than what we need," Juliette cautioned. She saw how the ground outside the concrete tower would soon be littered with more than they could carry. There was clothing and tools, canned food, vacuum-sealed plastic bags of labeled seeds—many of them from plants she'd never heard of. Elise had consulted her book and had pages for only a few of them. Scattered among the supplies were blocks of concrete and rubble from blowing the door open, a door that was designed to be opened from within.

Away from the tower, Solo and Walker wrestled with some kind of fabric enclosure and a set of poles, sorting out how it was supposed to prop itself up. They scratched their beards and debated. Juliette was amazed at how much better Walker was doing. He hadn't wanted out of his suit at first, had stayed in until the oxygen bottle went dry. And then he'd come out in a gasping hurry.

Elise was near them, screaming and chasing through the grass after her animal. Or maybe it was Shaw chasing Elise—it was hard to tell. Hannah sat on a large plastic bin with Rickson, nursing her child and gazing up at the clouds.

The smell of heating food wafted around the tower as Fitz managed to coax a fire from one of the oxygen bottles, a most dangerous method of cooking, Juliette thought. She turned to go back inside and sort through more of the gear, when Courtnee emerged from the bunker with her flashlight in hand and a smile on her face. Before Juliette could ask what she'd found, she saw that the power inside the tower was now on, the lights burning bright.

"What did you do?" Juliette asked. They had explored the bunker down to the bottom—it was only twenty levels deep, and the levels were so crazily packed together that it was more like seven levels tall. At the bottom they had found not a mechanical space but rather a large and empty cavern where twin stairwells bottomed out onto bare rock. It was a landing spot for a digger, someone had guessed. A place to welcome new arrivals. No generator, though. No power. Even though the stairwell and levels were rigged with lights.

"I traced the feed," Courtnee said. "It goes up to those silver sheets of metal on the roof. I'm going to have the boys clear them off, see how they work."

Before long, a moving platform sitting in the middle of the stairwell was made operational. It slid up and down by a series of cables and counterweights and a small motor. Those from Mechanical marveled at the device, and the kids wouldn't get off the thing. They insisted on riding it just one more time. Moving supplies outside and into the grass became far less tiring, though Juliette kept thinking they should leave plenty for the next to arrive, if anyone ever did.

There were those who wanted to live right there, who were reticent to venture any further. They had seeds and more soil than reckoning, and the storerooms could be turned into apartments. It would be a good home. Juliette listened to them debate this.

It was Elise who settled the matter. She opened her book to a map, pointed to the sun and showed them which way was north, and said they should move toward water. She claimed to know how to gather wild fish, said there were worms in the ground and Solo knew how to put them on hooks. Pointing to a page in her memory book, she said they should walk to the sea.

Adults pored over these maps and this decision. There was another round of debates among those who thought they should shelter right there, but Juliette shook her head. "This isn't a home," she said. "It's just a warehouse. Do we want to live in the shadow of that?" She nodded to the dark cloud on the horizon, that dome of dust.

"And what about when others show up?" someone pointed out.

"More reason not to be here," Rickson offered.

More debate. There were just over a hundred of them. They could stay there and farm, get a crop up before the canned goods ran out. Or they could carry what they needed and see if the legends of unlimited fish and of water that stretched to the horizon were true. Juliette nearly pointed out that they could do both, that there were no rules, that there was plenty of land and space, that all the fighting came when things were running low and resources were scarce.

"What's it going to be, Mayor?" Raph asked. "We bedding down here or moving on?"

"Look!"

Someone pointed up the hill, and a dozen heads turned to see. There, over the rise, a figure in a silver suit stumbled down the slope, the grass at their feet already trampled and slick. Someone from their silo who had changed their mind.

Juliette raced through the grass, feeling not fear but curiosity and concern. Someone they'd left behind, someone who had followed them. It could be anyone.

Before she could close the distance, the figure in the suit collapsed. Gloved hands groped to release the helmet, fumbled with the collar. Juliette ran. There was a large bottle strapped to the person's back. She worried they were out of air, wondered what they had rigged up and how.

"Easy," she yelled, dropping behind the struggling figure. She pressed her thumbs into the clasps. They clicked. She pulled the helmet free and heard someone gasping and coughing. They bent forward, wheezing, a spill of sweat-soaked hair, a woman. Juliette rested a hand on this woman's shoulder, did not recognize her at all—thought it was perhaps someone from the congregation or the Mids.

"Breathe easy," she said. She looked up as others arrived. They pulled up short at the sight of this stranger.

The woman wiped her mouth and nodded. Her chest heaved with a deep breath. Another. She brushed the hair off her face. "Thank you," she gasped. She peered up at the sky and the clouds in something other than wonder. In relief. Her eyes focused on and tracked an object, and Juliette turned and gazed up to see another of the birds wheeling lazily in the sky. The crowd around her kept their distance. Someone asked who this was.

"You aren't from our silo, are you?" Juliette asked. Her first thought was that this was a cleaner from a nearby silo who had witnessed their march, had followed them. Her second thought was impossible. It was also correct.

"No," the woman said, "I'm not from your silo. I'm from . . . somewhere quite different. My name is Charlotte."

A glove was offered, a glove and a weary smile. The warmth of that smile disarmed Juliette. To her surprise, she realized that she held no anger or resentment toward this woman, who had told her the truth of this place. Here, perhaps, was a kindred spirit. And more importantly, a fresh start. She regained her composure, smiled back, and shook the woman's hand. "Juliette," she said. "Let me help you out of that."

"You're her," Charlotte said, smiling. She turned her attention to the crowd, to the tower and the piles of supplies. "What is this place?"

"A second chance," Juliette said. "But we aren't staying here. We're heading to the water. You'll come with us, I hope. But I have to warn you, it's a long way."

Charlotte rested her hand on Juliette's shoulder. "That's okay," she said. "I've already come a long way."

EPILOGUE

RAPH SEEMED UNSURE. He held a branch in his hand, weighed it purposefully, his pale face a dance of orange and gold from the flickering fire.

"Just throw the damn thing in," Bobby yelled.

There was laughter, but Raph frowned in consternation. "It's *wood,*" he said, weighing the branch.

"Look around you," Bobby roared. He waved at the dark limbs hanging overhead, the wide trunks. "It's more than we'll ever need."

"Do it, lad." Erik kicked one of the logs, and a burst of sparks buzzed in the air as if startled from their slumber. Finally, Raph threw the branch in with the rest, and the wood began to crackle and spark.

Juliette watched from her bedroll. Somewhere in the woods, an animal made a sound, a sound unlike any she'd ever heard. It was like a crying child, but sonorous and mournful.

"What was that?" someone asked.

In the darkness, they exchanged guesses. They conjured animals from children's books. They listened to Solo recount the many breeds from olden times that he had read about in the Legacy. They gathered around Elise with flashlights and pored through the stitched pages of her book. Everything was a mystery and a wonder.

Juliette lay back and listened to the crackle from the fire, the occasional loud pop from a log, enjoying the heat on her skin, the smell of meat cooking, the peculiar odor of grass and so much soil. And through the canopy overhead, stars twinkled. The bright clouds from before—the ones that had hidden the sun as it set behind the hills—were parted by the breeze. They revealed above her a hundred glittering pricks of light. A thousand. More of them everywhere the longer she looked. They glittered in her tear-filled eyes as she thought of Lukas and the love he had aroused in her. And something hardened in her chest, something that made her jaw clench tight to keep from crying, a renewed purpose in her life, a desire to reach the water on Elise's map, to plant these seeds, to build a home above the ground and live there.

"Jewel? You asleep?"

Elise stood above her, blocking the stars. Puppy's cold nose pressed into Juliette's cheek.

"C'mere," Juliette said. She scooted over and patted her bedroll, and Elise sat down and nestled against her.

"What're you doing?" Elise asked.

Juliette pointed up through the canopy. "I'm looking at the stars," she said. "Each of those is like our sun, but they're a long way away."

"I know the stars," Elise said. "Some of them have names."

"They do?"

"Yeah." Elise rested her head back against Juliette's shoulder and gazed up with her a moment. The unknown thing in the woods howled. "See those?" Elise asked. "Don't those look like a puppy to you?"

Juliette squinted and searched the sky. "Could be," she said. "Yeah, maybe they do."

"We can call those ones Puppy."

"That's a good name," Juliette agreed. She laughed and wiped at her eyes.

"And that one's like a man." Elise pointed at a wide spread of stars, tracing the features. "There's his arms and legs. There's his head."

"I see him," Juliette said.

"You can name him," Elise told her, giving her permission. Deep in the woods, the hidden animal let out another howl, and Elise's puppy made a similar sound. Juliette felt tears roll down her cheeks.

"Not that one," she said quietly. "He already has a name."

The fires settled down as the night wore on. Clouds swallowed stars and tents gobbled children. Juliette watched shadows move in one of the tents, other adults too jittery to sleep. Somewhere, someone was still cooking strips of meat from the animal Solo had shot with his rifle—the long-limbed deer. Juliette had marveled at Solo's transformation these last three days. A man who grew up alone was now a leader of men, more prepared for surviving in this world than any of them. Juliette would ask for another vote soon. Her friend Solo would make an excellent mayor.

In the distance, a silhouette stood over a fire and prodded it with a stick, coaxing more heat from dying embers. Clouds and fire—these two things her people had only ever feared. Fire was death in the silo, and clouds consumed those who dared to leave. And yet, as the clouds closed in overhead and flames were agitated higher, there was comfort in both. The clouds were a roof of sorts, the fire warmth. There was less here to fear. And when a bright star revealed itself through a sudden gap, Juliette's thoughts returned as ever to Lukas.

He had told her once, with his star chart spread across that bed in which they made love, that each of those stars could possibly hold worlds of their own, and Juliette remembered being unable to grasp the thought. It was audacious. Impossible. Even having seen another silo, even having seen dozens of depressions in the earth that stretched to the horizon, she could not imagine entire other worlds existing. And yet, she had returned from her cleaning and had expected others to believe her claims, equally bold—

A stick cracked behind her, a rustle of leaves, and Juliette expected to find Elise returning to complain that she couldn't sleep. Or perhaps it was Charlotte, who had joined her by the fire earlier that night, had remained largely quiet while seeming to have much she wanted to say. But Juliette turned and found Courtnee there, white smoke steaming from something in her hand.

"Mind if I sit?" Courtnee asked.

Juliette made room, and her old friend joined her on the bedroll. She handed Juliette a hot mug of something that smelled vaguely of tea . . . but more pungent.

"Can't sleep?" Courtnee asked.

Juliette shook her head. "Just sitting here thinking about Luke."

Courtnee draped an arm across Juliette's back. "I'm sorry," she said.

"It's okay. Whenever I see the stars up there, it helps put things into perspective."

"Yeah? Help me, then."

Juliette thought how best to do that and realized she hardly had the language. She only had a sense of this vastness—of an infinite possible worlds—that somehow filled her with hope and not despair. Turning that into words wasn't easy.

"All the land we've seen these past days," she said, trying to grasp what she was feeling. "All that space. We don't have a fraction of the time and people to fill it all."

"That's a good thing, right?" Courtnee asked.

"I think so, yeah. And I'm starting to think that those we sent out to clean, they were the good ones. I think there were a lot of good people like them who just kept quiet, who were scared to act. And I doubt there was ever a mayor who didn't want to make more room for her people, didn't want to figure out what was wrong with the outside world, didn't want to suspend the damn lottery. But what could they do, even those mayors? They weren't in charge. Not really. The ones in charge kept a lid on our ambitions. Except for Luke. He didn't stand in the way of me. He supported what I was doing, even when he knew it was dangerous. And so here we are."

Courtnee squeezed her shoulder and took a noisy sip of tea, and Juliette lifted her mug to do the same. As soon as the warm water hit her lips, there was an explosion of flavor, a richness like the smell of the flower stalls in the bazaar and also the upturned loam of a productive grow plot. It was a first kiss. It was lemon and rose. There were sparks in her vision from the heady rush. Juliette's mind shuddered.

"What is this?" she asked, gasping for air. "This is from the supplies we pulled?"

Courtnee laughed and leaned against Juliette. "It's good, right?"

"It's great. It's . . . amazing."

"Maybe we should go back for another load," Courtnee said.

"If we do that, I might not carry anything else."

The two women laughed quietly. They sat together, gazing up at the clouds and the occasional star for a while. The fire nearest them crackled and spat sparks, and a handful of quiet conversations drifted deep into the trees where bugs sang a chorus and some unseen beast howled.

"Do you think we'll make it?" Courtnee asked after a long pause.

Juliette took another sip of the miraculous drink. She imagined the world they might build with time and resources, with no rules but what's best and no one to pin down their dreams.

"I think we'll make it," she finally said. "I think we can make any damn thing we like."

A NOTE TO THE READER

In July of 2011, I wrote and published a short story that brought me into contact with thousands of readers, took me around the world on book tours, and changed my life. I couldn't have dreamed that any of this was about to happen the day I published *Wool*. I thank you for making that journey possible and for accompanying me along the way.

This is not the end, of course. Every story we read, every film we watch, continues on in our imaginations if we allow it. Characters live another day. They grow old and die. New ones are born. Challenges crop up and are dealt with. There is sadness, joy, triumph, and failure. Where a story ends is nothing more than a snapshot in time, a brief flash of emotion, a pause. How and if it continues is up to us.

My only wish is that we leave room for hope. There is good and bad in all things. We find what we expect to find. We see what we expect to see. I have learned that if I tilt my head just right and squint, the world outside is beautiful. The future is bright. There are good things to come.

What do you see?

www.hughhowey.com

SHIFT

THE SILO TRILOGY
BY HUGH HOWEY

WOOL

SHIFT

DUST

SHIFT

HUGH HOWEY

wm

WILLIAM MORROW

An Imprint of HarperCollins*Publishers*

Boston New York

First Mariner Books edition 2016

Mariner Books
An Imprint of HarperCollins Publishers, registered in the United States of America and/or other jurisdictions.

www.marinerbooks.com

Library of Congress Cataloging-in-Publication Data is available.
ISBN 978-0-544-83961-8 (hardback) ISBN 978-0-544-83964-9 (pbk.)

Printed in the United States of America
24 25 26 27 28 LBC 29 28 27 26 25

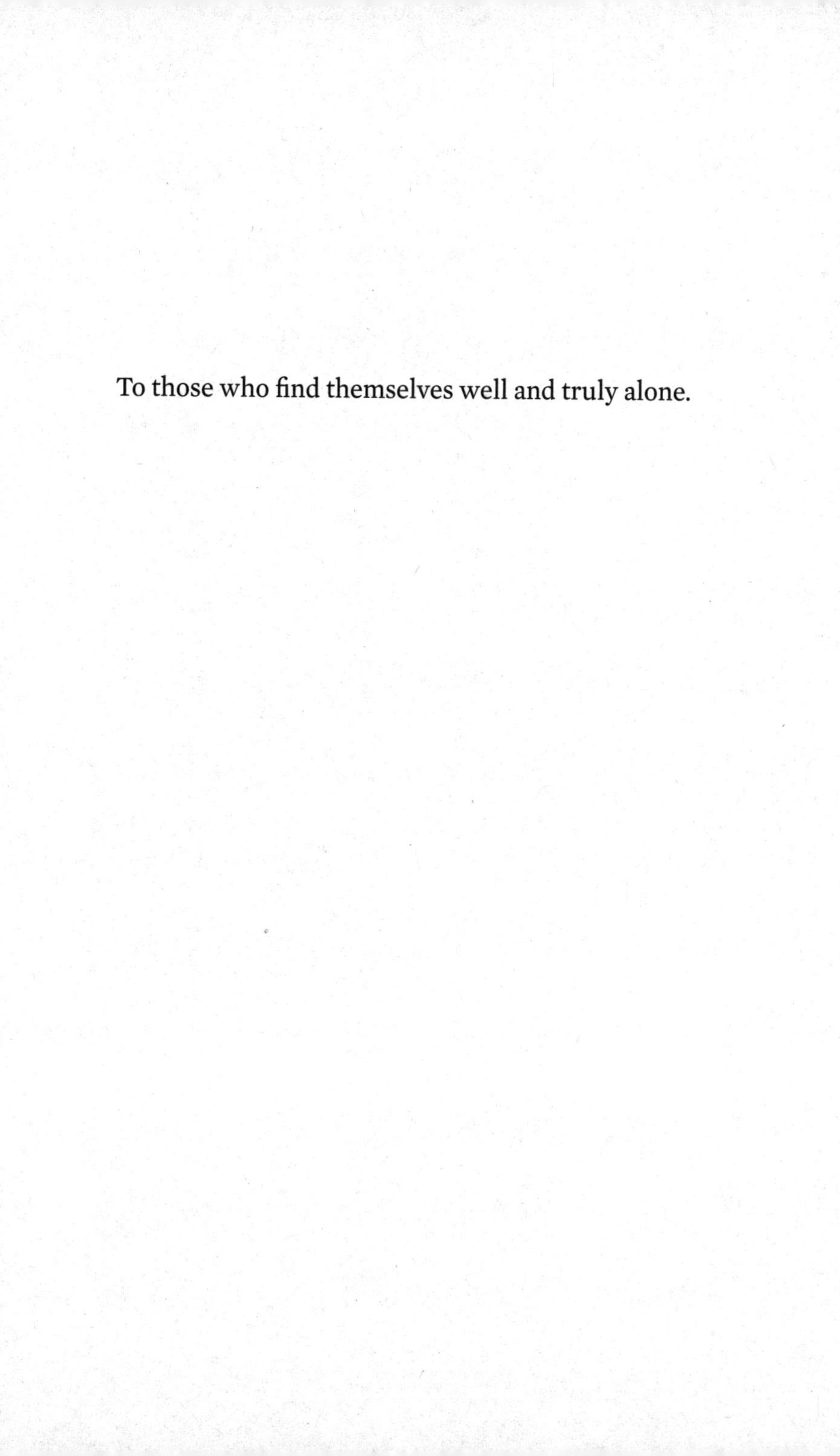

To those who find themselves well and truly alone.

In 2007, the Center for Automation in Nanobiotech (CAN) outlined the hardware and software platforms that would one day allow robots smaller than human cells to make medical diagnoses, conduct repairs, and even self-propagate.

That same year, CBS re-aired a program about the effects of propranolol on sufferers of extreme trauma. A simple pill, it had been discovered, could wipe out the memory of any traumatic event.

At almost the same moment in humanity's broad history, mankind had discovered the means to bring about its utter downfall. And the ability to forget it ever happened.

FIRST SHIFT
LEGACY

PROLOGUE

Year 2110
Beneath the hills of Fulton County, Georgia

TROY RETURNED TO the living and found himself inside of a tomb. He awoke to a world of confinement, a thick sheet of frosted glass pressed near to his face.

Dark shapes stirred on the other side of the icy murk. He tried to lift his arms, to beat on the glass, but his muscles were too weak. He attempted to scream—but could only cough. The taste in his mouth was foul. His ears rang with the clank of heavy locks opening, the hiss of air, the squeak of hinges long dormant.

The lights overhead were bright, the hands on him warm. They helped him sit while he continued to cough, his breath clouding the chill air. Someone had water. Pills to take. The water was cool, the pills bitter. Troy fought down a few gulps. He was unable to hold the glass without help. His hands trembled as memories flooded back, scenes from long nightmares. The feeling of deep time and yesterdays mingled. He shivered.

A paper gown. The sting of tape removed. A tug on his arm, a tube pulled from his groin. Two men dressed in white helped him out of the coffin. Steam rose all around him, air condensing and dispersing.

Sitting up and blinking against the glare, exercising lids long shut, Troy looked down the rows of coffins full of the living that stretched toward the distant and curved walls. The ceiling felt low; the suffocating press of dirt stacked high above. And the years. So many had passed. Anyone he cared about would be gone.

Everything was gone.

The pills stung his throat. He tried to swallow. Memories faded like dreams upon waking, and he felt his grip loosen on everything he'd known.

He collapsed backwards—but the men in the white overalls saw this coming. They caught him and lowered him to the ground, a paper gown rustling on shivering skin.

Images returned; recollections rained down like bombs and then were gone.

The pills would only do so much. It would take time to destroy the past.

Troy began to sob into his palms, a sympathetic hand resting on his head. The two men in white allowed him this moment. They didn't rush the process. Here was a courtesy passed from one waking soul to the next, something all the men sleeping in their coffins would one day rise to discover.

And eventually . . . forget.

1

Year 2049
Washington, DC

THE TALL GLASS trophy cabinets had once served as bookshelves. There were hints. Hardware on the shelves dated back centuries, while the hinges and the tiny locks on the glass doors went back mere decades. The framing around the glass was cherry, but the cases had been built of oak. Someone had attempted to remedy this with a few coats of stain, but the grain didn't match. The color wasn't perfect. To trained eyes, details such as these were glaring.

Congressman Donald Keene gathered these clues without meaning to. He simply saw that long ago there had been a great purge, a making of space. At some point in the past, the Senator's waiting room had been stripped of its obligatory law books until only a handful remained. These tomes sat silently in the dim corners of the glass cabinets. They were shut in, their spines laced with cracks, old leather flaking off like sunburned skin.

A handful of Keene's fellow freshmen filled the waiting room, pacing and stirring, their terms of service newly begun. Like Donald, they were young and still hopelessly optimistic.

They were bringing change to Capitol Hill. They hoped to deliver where their similarly naive predecessors had not.

While they waited their turns to meet with the great Senator Thurman from their home state of Georgia, they chatted nervously amongst themselves. They were a gaggle of priests, Donald imagined, all lined up to meet the Pope, to kiss his ring. He let out a heavy breath and focused on the contents of the case, lost himself in the treasures behind the glass while a fellow representative from Georgia prattled on about his district's Centers for Disease Control and Prevention.

"—and they have this detailed guide on their website, this response and readiness manual in case of, okay, get this—a zombie invasion. Can you believe that? Fucking zombies. Like even the CDC thinks something could go wrong and suddenly we'd all be *eating* each other—"

Donald stifled a smile, fearful its reflection would be caught in the glass. He turned and looked over a collection of photographs on the walls, one each of the Senator with the last four presidents. It was the same pose and handshake in each shot, the same background of windless flags and fancy oversized seals. The Senator hardly seemed to change as the presidents came and went. His hair started white and stayed white; he seemed perfectly unfazed by the passing of decades.

Seeing the photographs side by side devalued each of them somehow. They looked staged. Phony. It was as if this collection of the world's most powerful men had each begged for the opportunity to stand and pose with a cardboard cut-out, a roadside attraction.

Donald laughed, and the congressman from Atlanta joined him.

"I know, right? Zombies. It's hilarious. But think about it, okay? Why would the CDC even *have* this field manual unless—"

Donald wanted to correct his fellow congressman, to tell him what he'd really been laughing about. *Look at the smiles*, he wanted to say. They were on the faces of the *presidents*. The Senator looked as if he'd rather be anyplace else. It looked as if each in this succession of commanders-in-chief knew who the more powerful man was, who would be there long after they had come and gone.

"—it's advice like, everyone should have a baseball bat with their flashlights and candles, right? Just in case. You know, for bashing brains."

Donald pulled out his phone and checked the time. He glanced at the door leading off the waiting room and wondered how much longer he'd have to wait. Putting the phone away, he turned back to the cabinet and studied a shelf where a military uniform had been carefully arranged like a delicate work of origami. The left breast of the jacket featured a wall of medals; the sleeves were folded over and pinned to highlight the gold braids sewn along the cuffs. In front of the uniform, a collection of decorative coins rested in a custom wooden rack, tokens of appreciation from men and women serving overseas.

The two arrangements spoke volumes: the uniform from the past and the coins from those currently deployed, bookends on a pair of wars. One that the Senator had fought in as a youth. The other, a war he had battled to prevent as an older and wiser man.

"—yeah, it sounds crazy, I know, but do you know what rabies does to a dog? I mean, what it *really* does, the biological—"

Donald leaned in closer to study the decorative coins. The number and slogan on each one represented a deployed group. Or was it a battalion? He couldn't remember. His sister Charlotte would know. She was over there somewhere, out in the field.

"Hey, aren't you even a little nervous about this?"

Donald realized the question had been aimed at him. He turned and faced the talkative congressman. He must've been in his mid-thirties, around Donald's age. In him, Donald could see his own thinning hair, his own beginnings of a gut, that uncomfortable slide to middle age.

"Am I nervous about zombies?" Donald laughed. "No. Can't say that I am."

The congressman stepped up beside Donald, his eyes drifting toward the imposing uniform that stood propped up as if a warrior's chest remained inside. "No," the man said. "About meeting *him*."

The door to the reception area opened, bleeps from the phones on the other side leaking out.

"Congressman Keene?"

An elderly receptionist stood in the doorway, her white blouse and black skirt highlighting a thin and athletic frame.

"Senator Thurman will see you now," she said.

Donald patted the congressman from Atlanta on the shoulder as he stepped past.

"Hey, good luck," the gentleman stammered after him.

Donald smiled. He fought the temptation to turn and tell the man that he knew the Senator well enough, that he had been bounced on his knee back when he was a child. Only—Donald was too busy hiding his own nerves to bother.

He stepped through the deeply paneled door of rich hardwoods and entered the Senator's inner sanctum. This wasn't like passing through a foyer to pick up a man's daughter for a date. This was different. This was the pressure of meeting as colleagues when Donald still felt like that same young child.

"Through here," the receptionist said. She guided Donald between pairs of wide and busy desks, a dozen phones chirping in short bursts. Young men and women in suits and crisp blouses double-fisted receivers. Their bored expressions suggested that this was a normal workload for a weekday morning.

Donald reached out a hand as he passed one of the desks, brushing the wood with his fingertips. Mahogany. The aides here had desks nicer than his own. And the decor: the plush carpet, the broad and ancient crown molding, the antique tile ceiling, the dangling light fixtures that may have been actual crystal.

At the end of the buzzing and bleeping room, a paneled door opened and disgorged Congressman Mick Webb, just finished with his meeting. Mick didn't notice Donald, was too absorbed by the open folder he held in front of him.

Donald stopped and waited for his colleague and old college friend to approach. "So," he asked, "how'd it go?"

Mick looked up and snapped the folder shut. He tucked it under his arm and nodded. "Yeah, yeah. It went great." He smiled. "Sorry if we ran long. The old man couldn't get enough of me."

Donald laughed. He believed that. Mick had swept into office with ease. He had the charisma and confidence that went along with being tall and handsome. Donald used to joke that if his friend wasn't so shit with names, he'd be president someday.

"No problem," Donald said. He jabbed a thumb over his shoulder. "I was making new friends."

Mick grinned. "I bet."

"Yeah, well, I'll see you back at the ranch."

"Sure thing." Mick slapped him on the arm with the folder and headed for the exit. Donald caught the glare from the Senator's receptionist and hurried over. She waved him through to the dimly lit office and pulled the door shut behind him.

"Congressman Keene."

Senator Paul Thurman stood from behind his desk and stretched out a hand. He flashed a familiar smile, one Donald had come to recognize as much from photos and TV as from his childhood. Despite Thurman's age—he had to be pushing seventy if he wasn't already there—the Senator was trim and fit. His oxford shirt hugged a military frame; a thick neck bulged out of his knotted tie; his white hair remained as crisp and orderly as an enlisted man's.

Donald crossed the dark room and shook the Senator's hand. "Good to see you, sir."

"Please, sit." Thurman released Donald's hand and gestured to one of the chairs across from his desk. Donald lowered himself into the bright red leather, the gold grommets along the arm like sturdy rivets in a steel beam.

"How's Helen?"

"Helen?" Donald straightened his tie. "She's great. She's back in Savannah. She really enjoyed seeing you at the reception."

"She's a beautiful woman, your wife."

"Thank you, sir." Donald fought to relax, which didn't help. The office had the pall of dusk, even with the overhead lights on. The clouds outside had turned nasty—low and dark. If it rained, he would have to take the tunnel back to his office. He hated being down there. They could carpet it and hang those little chandeliers at intervals, but he could still tell he was below ground. The tunnels in Washington made him feel like a rat scurrying through a sewer. It always seemed as if the roof was about to cave in.

"How's the job treating you so far?"

"The job's good. Busy, but good."

He started to ask the Senator how Anna was doing, but the door behind him opened before he could. The receptionist entered and delivered two bottles of water. Donald thanked her, twisted the cap on his and saw that it had been pre-opened.

"I hope you're not too busy to work on something for me."

Senator Thurman raised an eyebrow. Donald took a sip of water and wondered if that was a skill one could master, that eyebrow lift. It made him want to jump to attention and salute.

"I'm sure I can make the time," he said. "After all the stumping you did for me? I doubt I would've made it past the primaries." He fiddled with the water bottle in his lap.

"You and Mick Webb go back, right? Both Bulldogs."

It took Donald a moment to realize the Senator was referring to their college mascot. He hadn't spent a lot of time at Georgia following sports. "Yessir. Go Dawgs."

He hoped that was right.

The Senator smiled. He leaned forward so that his face caught the soft light raining down on his desk. Donald watched as shadows grew in wrinkles otherwise easy to miss. Thurman's lean face and square chin made him look younger head-on than he did in profile. Here was a man who got places by approaching others directly rather than in ambush.

"You studied architecture at Georgia."

Donald nodded. It was easy to forget that he knew Thurman better than the Senator knew him. One of them grabbed far more newspaper headlines than the other.

"That's right. For my undergrad. I went into planning for my master's. I figured I could do more good governing people than I could drawing boxes to put them in."

He winced to hear himself deliver the line. It was a pat phrase from grad school, something he should have left behind with crushing beer cans on his forehead and ogling asses in skirts. He wondered for the dozenth time why he and the other congressional newcomers had been summoned. When he first got the invite, he thought it was a social visit. Then Mick had bragged about his own appointment, and Donald figured it was some kind of formality or tradition. But now he wondered if this was a power play, a chance to butter up the representatives from Georgia for those times when Thurman would need a particular vote in the lower and *lesser* house.

"Tell me, Donny, how good are you at keeping secrets?"

Donald's blood ran cold. He forced himself to laugh off the sudden flush of nerves.

"I got elected, didn't I?"

Senator Thurman smiled. "And so you probably learned the best lesson there is about secrets." He picked up and raised his water bottle in salute. "*Denial*."

Donald nodded and took a sip of his own water. He wasn't sure where this was going, but he already felt uneasy. He sensed some of the backroom dealings coming on that he'd promised his constituents he'd root out if elected.

The Senator leaned back in his chair.

"Denial is the secret sauce in this town," he said. "It's the flavor that holds all the other ingredients together. Here's what I tell the newly elected: the truth is going to get out—it always does—but it's going to blend in with all the *lies*." The Senator twirled a hand in the air. "You have to deny each lie and every truth with the same vinegar. Let those websites and blowhards who bitch about cover-ups confuse the public *for* you."

"Uh, yessir." Donald didn't know what else to say so he drank another mouthful of water instead.

The Senator lifted an eyebrow again. He remained frozen for a pause, and then asked, out of nowhere: "Do you believe in aliens, Donny?"

Donald nearly lost the water out of his nose. He covered his mouth with his hand, coughed, had to wipe his chin. The Senator didn't budge.

"Aliens?" Donald shook his head and wiped his wet palm on his thigh. "No, sir. I mean, not the abducting kind. Why?"

He wondered if this was some kind of debriefing. Why had

the Senator asked him if he could keep a secret? Was this a security initiation? The Senator remained silent.

"They're not real," Donald finally said. He watched for any twitch or hint. "Are they?"

The old man cracked a smile. "That's the thing," he said. "If they are or they aren't, the chatter out there would be the same. Would you be surprised if I told you they're very much real?"

"Hell, yeah, I'd be surprised."

"Good." The Senator slid a folder across the desk.

Donald eyed it and held up a hand. "Wait. Are they real or aren't they? What're you trying to tell me?"

Senator Thurman laughed. "Of course they're not real." He took his hand off the folder and propped his elbows on the desk. "Have you seen how much NASA wants from us so they can fly to Mars and back? We're not getting to another star. Ever. And nobody's coming here. Hell, why would they?"

Donald didn't know *what* to think, which was a far cry from how he'd felt less than a minute ago. He saw what the Senator meant, how truth and lies seemed black and white, but mixed together, they made everything gray and confusing. He glanced down at the folder. It looked similar to the one Mick had been carrying. It reminded him of the government's fondness for all things outdated.

"This is denial, right?" He studied the Senator. "That's what you're doing right now. You're trying to throw me off."

"No. This is me telling you to stop watching so many science fiction flicks. In fact, why do you think those eggheads are always dreaming of colonizing some other planet? You have any idea what would be involved? It's ludicrous. Not cost-effective."

Donald shrugged. He didn't think it was ludicrous. He twisted the cap back onto his water. "It's in our nature to dream of open space," he said. "To find room to spread out in. Isn't that how we ended up here?"

"Here? In America?" The Senator laughed. "We didn't come here and find open space. We got a bunch of people sick, killed them, and *made* space." Thurman pointed at the folder. "Which brings me to this. I've got something I'd like you to work on."

Donald placed his bottle on the leather inlay of the formidable desk and took the folder.

"Is this something coming through committee?"

He tried to temper his hopes. It was alluring to think of coauthoring a bill in his first year in office. He opened the folder and tilted it toward the window. Outside, storms were gathering.

"No, nothing like that. This is about CAD-FAC."

Donald nodded. *Of course.* The preamble about secrets and conspiracies suddenly made perfect sense, as did the gathering of Georgia congressmen outside. This was about the Containment and Disposal Facility, nicknamed CAD-FAC, at the heart of the Senator's new energy bill, the site that would one day house most of the world's spent nuclear fuel. Or, according to the websites Thurman had alluded to, it was going to be the next Area 51, or the place where a new-and-improved superbomb was being built, or a secure holding facility for libertarians who had purchased one too many guns. Take your pick. There was enough noise out there to hide *any* truth.

"Yeah," Donald said, deflated. "I've been getting some entertaining calls from my district." He didn't dare mention the one about the lizard people. "I want you to know, sir, that privately I'm behind the facility one hundred percent." He looked up at the Senator. "I'm glad I didn't have to vote on it publicly, of course, but it was about time someone offered up their backyard, right?"

"Precisely. For the common good." Senator Thurman took a long pull from his water, leaned back in his chair and cleared his throat. "You're a sharp young man, Donny. Not everyone sees what a boon to our state this'll be. A real lifesaver." He smiled. "I'm sorry, you *are* still going by Donny, right? Or is it Donald now?"

"Either's fine," Donald lied. He no longer enjoyed being called Donny, but changing names in the middle of one's life was practically impossible. He returned to the folder and flipped the cover letter over. There was a drawing underneath that struck him as being out of place. It was . . . too familiar. Familiar, and yet it didn't belong there—it was from another life.

"Have you seen the economic reports?" Thurman asked. "Do you know how many jobs this bill created overnight?" He snapped his fingers. "Forty thousand, just like that. And that's only from Georgia. A lot will be from your district, a lot of shipping, a lot of stevedores. Of course, now that it's passed, our less nimble colleagues are grumbling that *they* should've had a chance to bid—"

"I drew this," Donald interrupted, pulling out the sheet of paper. He showed it to Thurman as if the Senator would be surprised to see that it had snuck into the folder. Donald wondered if this was the Senator's daughter's doing, some kind of a joke or a hello and a wink from Anna.

Thurman nodded. "Yes, well, it needs more detail, wouldn't you say?"

Donald studied the architectural illustration and wondered what sort of test this was. He remembered the drawing. It was a last-minute project for his biotecture class in his senior year. There was nothing unusual or amazing about it, just a large cylindrical building a hundred or so stories tall ringed with glass and concrete, balconies burgeoning with gardens, one side cut away to reveal interspersed levels for housing, working and shopping. The structure was spare where he remembered other classmates being bold, utilitarian where he could've taken risks. Green tufts jutted up from the flat roof—a horrible cliché, a nod to carbon neutrality.

In sum, it was drab and boring. Donald couldn't imagine a design so bare rising from the deserts of Dubai alongside the great new breed of self-sustaining skyscrapers. He certainly couldn't see what the Senator wanted with it.

"More detail," he murmured, repeating the Senator's words. He flipped through the rest of the folder, looking for hints, for context.

"Wait." Donald studied a list of requirements written up as if by a prospective client. "This looks like a design proposal." Words he had forgotten he'd ever learned caught his eye: *interior traffic flow, block plan, HVAC, hydroponics*—

"You'll have to lose the sunlight." Senator Thurman's chair squeaked as he leaned over his desk.

"I'm sorry?" Donald held the folder up. "What exactly are you wanting me to do?"

"I would suggest those lights like my wife uses." He cupped his hand into a tiny circle and pointed at the center. "She gets these tiny seeds to sprout in the winter, uses bulbs that cost me a goddamned fortune."

"You mean grow lights."

Thurman snapped his fingers again. "And don't worry about the cost. Whatever you need. I'm also going to get you some help with the mechanical stuff. An engineer. An entire team."

Donald flipped through more of the folder. "What is this *for*? And why me?"

"This is what we call a *just-in-case* building. Probably'll never get used, but they won't let us store the fuel rods out there unless we put this bugger nearby. It's like this window in my basement I had to lower before our house could pass inspection. It was for . . . what do you call it . . . ?"

"Egress," Donald said, the word flowing back unaided.

"Yes. Egress." He pointed to the folder. "This building is like that window, something we've gotta build so the rest will pass inspection. This will be where—in the unlikely event of an attack or a leak—facility employees can go. A shelter. And it needs to be *perfect* or this project will be shut down faster than a tick's wink. Just because our bill passed and got signed doesn't mean we're home free, Donny. There was that project out west that got okayed decades ago, scored funding. Eventually, it fell through."

Donald knew the one he was talking about. A containment facility buried under a mountain. The buzz on the Hill was that the Georgia project had the same chances of success. The folder suddenly tripled in weight as he considered this. He was being asked to be a part of this future failure. He would be staking his newly won office on it.

"I've got Mick Webb working on something related. Logistics and planning. You two will need to collaborate on a few things. And Anna is taking leave from her post at MIT to lend a hand."

"*Anna?*" Donald fumbled for his water, his hand shaking.

"Of course. She'll be your lead engineer on this project. There are details in there on what she'll need, space-wise."

Donald took a gulp of water and forced himself to swallow.

"There's a lot of other people I could call in, sure, but this project can't fail, you understand? It needs to be like *family*. That's why I want to use people I know, people I can trust." Senator Thurman interlocked his fingers. "If this is the only thing you were elected to do, I want you to do it right. It's why I stumped for you in the first place."

"Of course." Donald bobbed his head to hide his confusion. He had worried during the election that the Senator's endorsement stemmed from old family ties. This was somehow worse.

Donald hadn't been using the Senator at all; it was the *other way around*. Studying the drawing in his lap, the newly elected congressman felt one job he was inadequately trained for melt away—only to be replaced by a *different* job that seemed equally daunting.

"Wait," he said, studying the old drawing. "I still don't get it. Why the grow lights?"

Thurman smiled. "Because," he said. "This building I want you to design for me—it's going to go underground."

2

Year 2110
Silo 1

TROY HELD HIS breath and tried to remain calm while the doctor pumped the rubber bulb. The inflatable band swelled around his bicep until it pinched his skin. He wasn't sure if slowing his breathing and steadying his pulse affected his blood pressure, but he had a strong urge to impress the man in the white overalls. He wanted his numbers to come back *normal.*

His arm throbbed a few beats while the needle bounced and the air hissed out.

"Eighty over fifty." The band made a ripping sound as it was torn loose. Troy rubbed the spot where his skin had been pinched.

"Is that okay?"

The doctor made a note on his clipboard. "It's low, but not outside the norm." Behind him, his assistant labeled a cup of dark gray urine before placing it inside a small fridge. Troy caught sight of a half-eaten sandwich among the samples, not even wrapped.

He looked down at his bare knees sticking out of the blue paper gown. His legs were pale and seemed smaller than he remembered. Bony.

"I still can't make a fist," he told the doctor, working his hand open and shut.

"That's perfectly normal. Your strength will return. Look into the light, please."

Troy followed the bright beam and tried not to blink.

"How long have you been doing this?" he asked the doctor.

"You're my third coming out. I've put two under." He lowered the light and smiled at Troy. "I've only been out myself for a few weeks. I can tell you that the strength will return."

Troy nodded. The doctor's assistant handed him another pill and a cup of water. Troy hesitated. He stared down at the little blue capsule nestled in his palm.

"A double dose this morning," the doctor said, "and then you'll be given one with breakfast and dinner. Please do not skip a treatment."

Troy looked up. "What happens if I don't take it?"

The doctor shook his head and frowned, but didn't say anything.

Troy popped the pill in his mouth and chased it with the water. A bitterness slid down his throat.

"One of my assistants will bring you some clothes and a fluid meal to kick-start your gut. If you have any dizziness or chills, you're to call me at once. Otherwise, we'll see you back here in six months." The doctor made a note, then chuckled. "Well, someone else will see you. My shift will be over."

"Okay." Troy shivered.

The doctor looked up from his clipboard. "You're not cold, are you? I keep it a little extra warm in here."

Troy hesitated before answering. "No, doctor. I'm not cold. Not anymore."

• • •

Troy entered the lift at the end of the hall, his legs still weak, and studied an array of numbered buttons. The orders they'd given him included directions to his office, but he vaguely remembered how to get there. Much of his orientation had survived the decades of sleep. He remembered studying that same book over and over, thousands of men assigned to various shifts, going on tours of the facility before being put under like the women. The orientation felt like yesterday; it was older memories that seemed to be slipping away.

The doors to the lift closed automatically. His apartment was on thirty-seven; he remembered that. His office was on thirty-four. He reached for a button, intending to head straight to his desk, and instead found his hand sliding up to the very top. He still had a few minutes before he needed to be anywhere, and he felt some strange urge, some tug, to get as high as possible, to rise through the soil pressing in from all sides.

The lift hummed into life and accelerated up the shaft. There was a whooshing sound as another car or maybe the counterweight zoomed by. The round buttons flashed as the floors passed. There was an enormous spread of them, seventy in all. The centers of many were dull from years of rubbing. This didn't seem right. It seemed like just yesterday the buttons were shiny and new. Just yesterday, *everything* was.

The lift slowed. Troy palmed the wall for balance, his legs still uncertain.

The door dinged and slid open. Troy blinked at the bright lights in the hallway. He left the lift and followed a short walk toward a room that leaked chatter. His new boots were stiff on his feet, the generic gray overalls itchy. He tried to imagine waking up like this nine more times, feeling this weak and disoriented. Ten shifts of six months each. Ten shifts he hadn't volunteered for. He wondered if it would get progressively easier or if it would only get worse.

The bustle in the cafeteria quieted as he entered. A few heads turned his way. He saw at once that his gray overalls weren't so generic. There was a scattering of colors seated at the tables: a large cluster of reds, quite a few yellows, a man in orange; no other grays.

That first meal of sticky paste he'd been given rumbled once more in his stomach. He wasn't allowed to eat anything else for six hours, which made the aroma from the canned foods overwhelming. He remembered the fare, had lived on it during orientation. Weeks and weeks of the same gruel. Now it would be months. It would be hundreds of years.

"Sir."

A young man nodded to Troy as he walked past, toward the lifts. Troy thought he recognized him but couldn't be sure. The gentleman certainly seemed to have recognized *him*. Or was it the gray overalls that stood out?

"First shift?"

An older gentleman approached, thin, with white and wispy hair that circled his head. He held a tray in his hands, smiled at Troy. Pulling open a recycling bin, he slid the entire tray inside and dropped it with a clatter.

"Come up for the view?" the man asked.

Troy nodded. It was all men throughout the cafeteria. All men. They had explained why this was safer. He tried to remember as the man with the splotches of age on his skin crossed his arms and stood beside him. There were no introductions. Troy wondered if names meant less amid these short six-month shifts. He gazed out over the bustling tables toward the massive screen that covered the far wall.

Whirls of dust and low clouds hung over a field of scattered and mangled debris. A few metal poles bristled from the ground and sagged lifelessly, the tents and flags long vanished. Troy thought of something but couldn't name it. His stomach tightened like a fist around the paste and the bitter pill.

"This'll be my second shift," the man said.

Troy barely heard. His watering eyes drifted across the scorched hills, the gray slopes rising up toward the dark and menacing clouds. The debris scattered everywhere was rotting away. Next shift, or the one after, and it would all be gone.

"You can see farther from the lounge." The man turned and gestured along the wall. Troy knew well enough what room he was referring to. This part of the building was familiar to him in ways this man could hardly guess at.

"No, but thanks," Troy stammered. He waved the man off. "I think I've seen enough."

Curious faces returned to their trays, and the chatter resumed. It was sprinkled with the clinking of spoons and forks on metal bowls and plates. Troy turned and left without saying another word. He put that hideous view behind him—turned his back on the unspoken eeriness of it. He hurried, shivering, toward the lifts, knees weak from more than the long rest. He needed to be alone, didn't want anyone around him this time, didn't want sympathetic hands comforting him while he cried.

3

2049
Washington, DC

DONALD KEPT THE thick folder tucked inside his jacket and hurried through the rain. He had chosen to get soaked crossing the square rather than face his claustrophobia in the tunnels.

Traffic hissed by on the wet asphalt. He waited for a gap, ignored the crossing signals and scooted across.

In front of him, the marble steps of Rayburn, the office building for the House of Representatives, gleamed treacherously. He climbed them warily and thanked the doorman on his way in.

Inside, a security officer stood by impassively while Donald's badge was scanned, red unblinking eyes beeping at bar codes. He checked the folder Thurman had given him, made sure it was still dry, and wondered why such relics were still considered safer than an email or a digital copy.

His office was one floor up. He headed for the stairs, preferring them to Rayburn's ancient and slow lifts. His shoes squeaked on the tile as he left the plush runner by the door.

The hallway upstairs was its usual mess. Two high-schoolers

from the congressional page program hurried past, most likely fetching coffee. A TV crew stood outside of Amanda Kelly's office, camera lights bathing her and a young reporter in a daytime glow. Concerned voters and eager lobbyists were identifiable by the guest passes hanging around their necks. They were easy to distinguish from one another, these two groups. The voters wore frowns and invariably seemed lost. The lobbyists were the ones with the Cheshire Cat grins who navigated the halls more confidently than even the newly elected.

Donald opened the folder and pretended to read as he made his way through the chaos, hoping to avoid conversation. He squeezed behind the cameraman and ducked into his office next door.

Margaret, his secretary, stood up from her desk. "Sir, you have a *visitor*."

Donald glanced around the waiting room. It was empty. He saw that the door to his office was partway open.

"I'm sorry, I let her in." Margaret mimed carrying a box, her hands at her waist and her back arched. "She had a delivery. Said it was from the Senator."

Donald waved her concerns aside. Margaret was older than him, in her mid-forties, and had come highly recommended, but she did have a conspiratorial streak. Perhaps it came with the years of experience.

"It's fine," Donald assured her. He found it interesting that there were a hundred senators, two from his state, but only one was referred to as *the Senator*. "I'll see what it's about. In the meantime, I need you to free up a daily block in my schedule. An hour or two in the morning would be ideal." He flashed her the folder. "I've got something that's going to eat up quite a bit of my time."

Margaret nodded and sat down in front of her computer. Donald turned toward his office.

"Oh, sir . . ."

He looked back. She pointed to her head. "Your *hair,*" she hissed.

He ran his fingers through his hair and drops of water leapt off him like startled fleas. Margaret frowned and lifted her shoulders in a helpless shrug. Donald gave up and pushed his office door open, expecting to find someone sitting across from his desk.

Instead, he saw someone wiggling *underneath* it.

"Hello?"

The door had bumped into something on the floor. Donald peeked around and saw a large box with a picture of a computer monitor on it. He glanced at the desk, saw the display was already set up.

"Oh, hey!"

The greeting was muffled by the hollow beneath his desk. Slender hips in a herringbone skirt wiggled back toward him. Donald knew who it was before her head emerged. He felt a flush of guilt, of anger at her being there unannounced.

"You know, you should have your cleaning lady dust under here once in a while." Anna Thurman stood up and smiled. She slapped her palms together, brushing them off before extending one his way. Donald took her hand nervously. "Hey, stranger."

"Yeah. Hey." Rain dribbled down his cheek and neck, hiding a sudden flush of perspiration. "What's going on?" He walked around his desk to create some space between them. A new monitor stood innocently, a film of protective plastic blurring the screen.

"Dad thought you might need an extra one." Anna tucked a loose clump of auburn hair behind her ear. She still possessed the same alluring and elfin quality when her ears poked out like that. "I volunteered," she explained, shrugging.

"Oh." He placed the folder on his desk and thought about

the drawing of the building he had briefly suspected was from her. And now, here she was. Checking his reflection in the new monitor, he saw the mess he had made of his hair. He reached up and tried to smooth it.

"Another thing," Anna said. "Your computer would be better off *on* your desk. I know it's unsightly, but the dust is gonna choke that thing to death. Dust is *murder* on these guys."

"Yeah. Okay."

He sat down and realized he could no longer see the chair across from his desk. He slid the new monitor to one side while Anna walked around and stood beside him, her arms crossed, completely relaxed. As if they'd seen each other yesterday.

"So," he said. "You're in town."

"Since last week. I was gonna stop by and see you and Helen on Saturday, but I've been so busy getting settled into my apartment. Unboxing things, you know?"

"Yeah." He accidentally bumped the mouse, and the old monitor winked on. His computer was running. The terror of being in the same room with an ex subsided just enough for the timing of the day's events to dawn on him.

"Wait." He turned to Anna. "You were over here *installing* this while your father was asking me if I was interested in his project? What if I'd declined?"

She raised an eyebrow. Donald realized it wasn't something one learned—it was a talent that ran in the family.

"He practically gift-wrapped the election for you," she said flatly.

Donald reached for the folder and riffed the pages like a deck of cards. "The illusion of free will would've been nice, that's all."

Anna laughed. She was about to tousle his hair, he could sense it. Dropping his hand from the folder and patting his jacket pocket, he felt for his phone. It was as though Helen were there with him. He had an urge to call her.

"Was Dad at least gentle with you?"

He looked up to see that she hadn't moved. Her arms were still crossed, his hair untousled—nothing to panic about.

"What? Oh, yeah. He was fine. Like old times. In fact, it's like he hasn't aged a day."

"He doesn't really age, you know." She crossed the room and picked up large molded pieces of foam, then slid them noisily into the empty box. Donald found his eyes drifting toward her skirt and forced himself to look away.

"He takes his nano treatments almost religiously. Started because of his knees. The military covered it for a while. Now he swears by them."

"I didn't know that," Donald lied. He'd heard rumors, of course. It was "Botox for the whole body," people said. Better than testosterone supplements. It cost a fortune, and you wouldn't live forever, but you sure as hell could delay the pain of aging.

Anna narrowed her eyes. "You don't think there's anything *wrong* with that, do you?"

"What? No. It's fine, I guess. I just wouldn't. Wait—why? Don't tell me you've been . . ."

Anna rested her hands on her hips and cocked her head to the side. There was something oddly seductive about the defensive posture, something that whisked away the years since he'd last seen her.

"Do you think I would *need* to?" she asked him.

"No, no. It's not that . . ." He waved his hands. "It's just that *I* don't think I ever would."

A smirk thinned her lips. Maturity had hardened Anna's good looks, had refined her lean frame, but the fierceness from her youth remained. "You say that now," she said, "but wait until your joints start to ache and your back goes out from something as simple as turning your head too fast. Then you'll see."

"Okay. Well." He clapped his hands together. "This has been quite the day for catching up on old times."

"Yes, it has. Now, what day works best for you?" Anna interlocked the flaps on the large box and slid it toward the door with her foot. She walked around the back of the desk and stood beside him, a hand on his chair, the other reaching for his mouse.

"What *day*... ?"

He watched while she changed some settings on his computer and the new monitor flashed to life. Donald could feel the pulse in his crotch, could smell her familiar perfume. The breeze she had caused by walking across the room seemed to stir all around him. This felt near enough to a caress, to a physical touch, that he wondered if he was cheating on Helen right at that very moment while Anna did little more than adjust sliders on his control panel.

"You know how to use this, right?" She slid the mouse from one screen to the other, dragging an old game of solitaire with it.

"Uh, yeah." Donald squirmed in his seat. "Um... what do you mean about a day that works best for me?"

She let go of the mouse. It felt as though she had taken her hand off his thigh.

"Dad wants me to handle the mechanical spaces on the plans." She gestured toward the folder as if she knew precisely what was inside. "I'm taking a sabbatical from the Institute until this Atlanta project is up and running. I thought we'd want to meet once a week to go over things."

"Oh. Well. I'll have to get back with you on that. My schedule here is crazy. It's different every day."

He imagined what Helen would say to him and Anna getting together once a week.

"We could, you know, set up a shared space in AutoCAD," he suggested. "I can link you into my document—"

"We could do that."

"And email back and forth. Or video-chat. You know?"

Anna frowned. Donald realized he was being too obvious. "Yeah, let's set up something like that," she said.

There was a flash of disappointment on her face as she turned for the box, and Donald felt the urge to apologize, but doing so would spell out the problem in neon lights: *I don't trust myself around you. We're not going to be friends. What the fuck are you doing here?*

"You really need to do something about the dust." She glanced back at his desk. "Seriously, your computer is going to choke on it."

"Okay. I will." He stood and hurried around his desk to walk her out. Anna stooped for the box.

"I can get that."

"Don't be silly." She stood with the large box pinned between one arm and her hip. She smiled and tucked her hair behind her ear again. She could've been leaving his dorm room in college. There was that same awkward moment of a morning goodbye in last night's clothes.

"Okay, so you have my email?" he asked.

"You're in the blue pages now," she reminded him.

"Yeah."

"You look great, by the way." And before he could step back or defend himself, she was fixing his hair, a smile on her lips.

Donald froze. When he thawed some time later, Anna was gone, leaving him standing there alone, soaked in guilt.

4

2110
Silo 1

TROY WAS GOING to be late. The first day of his first shift, already a blubbering mess, and he was going to be late. In his rush to get away from the cafeteria, to be alone, he had taken the non-express by accident. Now, as he tried to compose himself, the lift seemed intent on stopping at every floor on the way down to load and unload passengers.

He stood in the corner as the lift stopped again and a man wrestled a cart full of heavy boxes inside. A gentleman with a load of green onions crowded behind him and stood close to Troy for a few stops. Nobody spoke. When the man with the onions got off, the smell remained. Troy shivered, one violent quake that travelled up his back and into his arms, but he thought nothing of it. He got off on thirty-four and tried to remember why he had been upset earlier.

The central lift shaft emptied onto a narrow hallway, which funneled him toward a security station. The floor plan was vaguely familiar and yet somehow alien. It was unnerving to note the signs of wear in the carpet and the patch of dull steel in the middle of the turnstile where thighs had rubbed against it over the years. These were years that hadn't existed for Troy. This wear and tear had shown up as if by magic, like damage sustained from a night of drunkenness.

The lone guard on duty looked up from something he was reading and nodded in greeting. Troy placed his palm on a screen that had grown hazy from use. There was no chit-chat, no small talk, no expectation of forming a lasting relationship. The light above the console flashed green, the pedestal gave a loud click, and a little more sheen was rubbed off the revolving bar as Troy pushed through.

At the end of the hallway, Troy paused and pulled his orders out of his breast pocket. There was a note on the back from the doctor. He flipped it over and turned the little map around to face the right direction; he was pretty sure he knew the way, but everything was dropping in and out of focus.

The red dash marks on the map reminded him of fire safety plans he'd seen on walls somewhere else. Following the route took him past a string of small offices. Clacking keyboards, people talking, phones ringing—the sounds of the workplace made him feel suddenly tired. It also ignited a burn of insecurity, of having taken on a job he surely couldn't perform.

"Troy?"

He stopped and looked back at the man standing in a doorway he'd passed. A glance at his map showed him he'd almost missed his office.

"That's me."

"Merriman." The gentleman didn't offer his hand. "You're late. Step inside."

Merriman turned and disappeared into the office. Troy followed, his legs sore from the walk. He recognized the man, or thought he did. Couldn't remember if it was from the orientation or some other time.

"Sorry I'm late," Troy started to explain. "I got on the wrong lift—"

Merriman raised a hand. "That's fine. Do you need a drink?"

"They fed me."

"Of course." Merriman grabbed a clear thermos off his desk, the contents a bright blue, and took a sip. Troy remembered the foul taste. The older man smacked his lips and let out a breath as he lowered the thermos.

"That stuff's awful," he said.

"Yeah." Troy looked around the office, his post for the next six months. The place, he figured, had aged quite a bit. Merriman, too. If he was a little grayer from the past six months, it was hard to tell, but he had kept the place in order. Troy resolved to extend the same courtesy to the next guy.

"You remember your briefing?" Merriman shuffled some folders on his desk.

"Like it was yesterday."

Merriman glanced up, a smirk on his face. "Right. Well, there hasn't been anything exciting for the last few months. We had some mechanical issues when I started my shift but worked through those. There's a guy named Jones you'll want to use. He's been out a few weeks and is a lot sharper than the last guy. Been a lifesaver for me. He works down on sixty-eight with the power plant, but he's good just about anywhere, can fix pretty much anything."

Troy nodded. "Jones. Got it."

"Okay. Well, I left you some notes in these folders. There have been a few workers we had to deep-freeze, some who aren't fit for another shift." He looked up, a serious expression on his face. "Don't take that lightly, okay? Plenty of guys here would love to nap straight through instead of work. Don't resort to the deep freeze unless you're sure they can't handle it."

"I won't."

"Good." Merriman nodded. "I hope you have an uneventful shift. I've got to run before this stuff kicks in." He took another fierce swig and Troy's cheeks sucked in with empathy. He walked past Troy, slapped him on the shoulder and started to reach for the light switch. He stopped himself at the last minute and looked back, nodded, then was gone.

And just like that, Troy was in charge.

"Hey, wait!" He glanced around the office, hurried out and caught up with Merriman, who was already turning down the main hall toward the security gate. Troy jogged to catch up.

"You leave the light on?" Merriman asked.

Troy glanced over his shoulder. "Yeah, but—"

"Good habits," Merriman said. He shook his thermos. "Form them."

A heavyset man hurried out of one of the offices and labored to catch up with them. "Merriman! You done with your shift?"

The two men shared a warm handshake. Merriman smiled and nodded. "I am. Troy here will be taking my place."

The man shrugged, didn't introduce himself. "I'm off in two weeks," he said, as if that explained his indifference.

"Look, I'm running late," Merriman said, his eyes darting toward Troy with a trace of blame. He pushed the thermos into his friend's palm. "Here. You can have what's left." He turned to go and Troy followed along.

"No thanks!" the man called out, waving the thermos and laughing.

Merriman glanced at Troy. "I'm sorry, did you have a question?" He passed through the turnstile and Troy went through behind him. The guard never looked up from his tablet.

"A few, yeah. You mind if I ride down with you? I was a little . . . behind at orientation. Sudden promotion. Would love to clarify a few things."

"Hey, I can't stop you. You're in charge." Merriman jabbed the call button on the express.

"So, basically, I'm just here in case something goes wrong?"

The lift opened. Merriman turned and squinted at Troy almost as if to gauge if he was being serious.

"Your job is to *make sure* nothing goes wrong." They both stepped into the lift and the car raced downward.

"Right. Of course. That's what I meant."

"You've read the Order, right?"

Troy nodded. *But not for this job,* he wanted to say. He had studied to run just a single silo, not the one that oversaw them all.

"Just follow the script. You'll get questions from the other silos now and then. I found it wise to say as little as possible. Just be quiet and listen. Keep in mind that these are mostly second- and third-generation survivors, so their vocabulary is already a little different. There's a cheat-sheet and a list of forbidden words in your folder."

Troy felt a bout of dizziness and nearly sagged to the ground as weight was added, the lift slowing to a stop. He was still incredibly weak.

The door opened; he followed Merriman down a short hallway, the same one he had emerged from hours earlier. The doctor and his assistant waited in the room beyond, preparing an IV. The doctor looked curiously at Troy, as if he hadn't planned on seeing him again so soon, if ever.

"You finish your last meal?" the doctor asked, waving Merriman toward a stool.

"Every vile drop of it." Merriman unclasped the tops of his overalls and let them flop down around his waist. He sat and held out his arm, palm up. Troy saw how pale Merriman's skin was, the loose tangle of purple lines weaving past his elbow. He tried not to watch the needle go in.

"I'm repeating my notes here," Merriman told him, "but you'll want to meet with Victor in the psych office. He's right across the hall from you. There's some strange things going on in a few of the silos, more fracturing than we thought. Try and get a handle on that for the next guy."

Troy nodded.

"We need to get you to your chamber," the doctor said. His young assistant stood by with a paper gown. The entire procedure looked very familiar. The doctor turned to Troy as if he were a stain that needed scrubbing away.

Troy backed out of the door and glanced down the hall in the direction of the deep freeze. The women and children were kept there, along with the men who couldn't make it through their shifts. "Do you mind if I . . . ?" He felt a very real tug pulling him in that direction. Merriman and the doctor both frowned.

"It's not a good idea—" the doctor began.

"I wouldn't," Merriman said. "I made a few visits the first weeks. It's a mistake. Let it go."

Troy stared down the hallway. He wasn't exactly sure what he would find there, anyway.

"Get through the next six months," Merriman said. "It goes by fast. It all goes by fast."

Troy nodded. The doctor shooed him away with his eyes while Merriman began tugging off his boots. Troy turned, gave the heavy door down the hall one last glance, then headed in the other direction for the lifts.

He hoped Merriman was right. Jabbing the button to call the express, he tried to imagine his entire shift flashing by. And the one after that. And the next one. Until this insanity had run its course, little thought to what came after.

5

2049
Washington, DC

TIME FLEW BY for Donald Keene. Another day came to an end, another week, and still he needed more time. It seemed the sun had just gone down when he looked up and it was past eleven.

Helen. There was a rush of panic as he fumbled for his phone. He had promised his wife he would always call before ten. A guilty heat wedged around his collar. He imagined her sitting around, staring at her phone, waiting and waiting.

It didn't even ring on his end before she picked up.

"There you are," she said, her voice soft and drowsy, her tone hinting more at relief than anger.

"Sweetheart. God, I'm really sorry. I totally lost track of time."

"That's okay, baby." She yawned, and Donald had to fight the infectious urge to do the same. "You write any good laws today?"

He laughed and rubbed his face. "They don't really let me do that. Not yet. I'm mostly staying busy with this little project for the Senator—"

He stopped himself. Donald had dithered all week on the best way to tell her, what parts to keep secret. He glanced at the extra monitor on his desk. Anna's perfume was somehow frozen in the air, still lingering a week later.

Helen's voice perked up: "Oh?"

He could picture her clearly: Helen in her nightgown, his side of the bed still immaculately made, a glass of water within her reach. He missed her terribly. The guilt he felt, despite his innocence, made him miss her all the more.

"What does he have you doing? It's legal, I hope."

"What? Of course it's legal. It's . . . some architectural stuff, actually." Donald leaned forward to grab the finger of gold Scotch left in his tumbler. "To be honest, I'd forgotten how much I love the work. I would've been a decent architect if I'd stuck with it." He took a burning sip and eyed his monitors, which had gone dark to save the screens. He was dying to get back to it. Everything fell away, disappeared, when he lost himself in the drawing.

"Sweetheart, I don't think designing a new bathroom for the Senator's office is why the taxpayers sent you to Washington."

Donald smiled and finished the drink. He could practically hear his wife grinning on the other end of the line. He set the glass back on his desk and propped up his feet. "It's nothing like that," he insisted. "It's plans for that facility they're putting in outside of Atlanta. Just a minor portion of it, really. But if I don't get it just right, the whole thing could fall apart."

He eyed the open folder on his desk. His wife laughed sleepily.

"Why in the world would they have you doing something like that?" she asked. "If it's so important, wouldn't they pay someone who knows what they're doing?"

Donald laughed dismissively, however much he agreed. He couldn't help but feel victim to Washington's habit for assigning jobs to people who weren't qualified for them, like campaign contributors who became ambassadors. "I'm actually quite good at this," he told his wife. "I'm starting to think I'm a better architect than a congressman."

"I'm sure you're wonderful at it." His wife yawned again. "But you could've stayed *home* and been an architect. You could work late *here*."

"Yeah, I know." Donald remembered their discussions on whether or not he should run for office, if it would be worth them being apart. Now he was spending his time away doing the very thing they'd agreed he should give up. "I think this is just something they put us through our first year," he said. "Think of it like your internship. It'll get better. And besides, I think it's a *good* sign he wants me in on this. He sees the Atlanta thing as a family project, something to keep in-house. He actually took notice of some of my work at—"

"*Family* project."

"Well, not *literally* family, more like—" This wasn't how he wanted to tell her. It was a bad start. It was what he got for putting it off, for waiting until he was exhausted and tipsy.

"Is this why you're working late? Why you're calling me after ten?"

"Baby, I lost track of the time. I was on my computer." He looked to his tumbler, saw that it held the barest of sips, just the golden residue that had slid down the glass after his last pull. "This is good news for us. I'll be coming home more often because of this. I'm sure they'll need me to check out the job site, work with the foremen—"

"That *would* be good news. Your dog misses you."

Donald smiled. "I hope you *both* do."

"You know I do."

"Good." He swilled the last drop in the glass and gulped it down. "And listen, I know how you're gonna feel about this, and I swear it's out of my control, but the Senator's daughter is working on this project with me. Mick Webb, too. You remember him?"

Cold silence.

Then, "I remember the Senator's daughter."

Donald cleared his throat. "Yeah, well, Mick is doing some of the organizational work, securing land, dealing with contractors. It's practically his district, after all. And you know neither of us would be where we are today without the Senator stumping for us—"

"What I remember is that you two used to date. And that she used to flirt with you even when I was around."

Donald laughed. "Are you serious? Anna Thurman? C'mon, honey, that was a lifetime ago—"

"I thought you were going to come home more often, anyway. On the weekends." He heard his wife let out a breath. "Look, it's late. Why don't we both get some sleep? We can talk about this tomorrow."

"Okay. Yeah, sure. And sweetheart?"

She waited.

"Nothing's gonna come between us, okay? This is a huge opportunity for me. And it's something I'm really good at. I'd forgotten how good at it I am."

A pause.

"There's a lot you're good at," his wife said. "You're a good husband, and I know you'll be a good congressman. I just don't trust the people you're surrounding yourself with."

"But you know I wouldn't be here if it wasn't for him."

"I know."

"Look, I'll be careful. I promise."

"Okay. I'll talk to you tomorrow. Sleep tight. I love you."

She hung up, and Donald looked down at his phone, saw that he had a dozen emails waiting for him. He decided to ignore them until morning. Rubbing his eyes, he willed himself awake, to think clearly. He shook the mouse to stir his monitors. They could afford to nap, to go dark awhile, but he couldn't.

A wireframe apartment sat in the middle of his new screen. Donald zoomed out and watched the apartment sink away and a hallway appear, then dozens of identical wedge-shaped living quarters squeeze in from the edges. The building specs called for a bunker that could house ten thousand people for at least a year—utter overkill. Donald approached the task as he would any design project. He imagined himself in their place, a toxic spill, a leak or some horrible fallout, a terrorist attack, something that might send all of the facility workers underground where they would have to stay for weeks or months until the area was cleared.

The view pulled back further until other floors appeared above and below, empty floors he would eventually fill with storerooms, hallways, more apartments. Entire other floors and mechanical spaces had been left empty for Anna—

"Donny?"

His door opened—the knock came after. Donald's arm jerked so hard his mouse went skidding off the pad and across his desk. He sat up straight, peered over his monitors and saw Mick Webb grinning at him from the doorway. Mick had his jacket tucked under one arm, tie hanging loose, a peppery stubble on his dark skin. He laughed at Donald's harried expression and sauntered across the room. Donald fumbled for the mouse and quickly minimized the AutoCAD window.

"Shit, man, you haven't taken up day-trading, have you?"

"Day-trading?" Donald leaned back in his chair.

"Yeah. What's with the new set-up?" Mick walked around behind the desk and rested a hand on the back of Donald's chair. An abandoned game of FreeCell sat embarrassingly on the smaller of the two screens.

"Oh, the extra monitor." Donald minimized the card game and turned in his seat. "I like having a handful of programs up at the same time."

"I can see that." Mick gestured at the empty monitors, the wallpaper of cherry blossoms framing the Jefferson Memorial.

Donald laughed and rubbed his face. He could feel his own stubble, had forgotten to eat dinner. The project had only begun a week ago and he was already a wreck.

"I'm heading out for a drink," Mick told him. "You wanna come?"

"Sorry. I've got a little more to do here."

Mick clasped his shoulder and squeezed until it hurt. "I hate to break it to you, man, but you're gonna have to start over. You bury an ace like that, there's no coming back. C'mon, let's get a drink."

"Seriously, I can't." Donald twisted out from his friend's grasp and turned to face him. "I'm working on those plans for Atlanta. I'm not supposed to let anyone see them. It's top secret."

For emphasis, he reached out and closed the folder on his desk. The Senator had told him there would be a division of labor and that the walls of that divide needed to be a mile high.

"Ohhh. *Top secret*." Mick waggled both hands in the air. "I'm working on the same project, asshole." He waved at the monitor. "And you're doing the plans? What gives? My GPA was higher than yours." He leaned over the desk and stared at the taskbar. "AutoCAD? Cool. C'mon, let's see it."

"Yeah, right."

"Come the fuck on. Don't be a child about this."

Donald laughed. "Look, even the people on my team aren't going to see the entire plan. And neither will I."

"That's ridiculous."

"No, it's how government shit like this gets done. You don't see me prying into your part in all this."

Mick waved a hand dismissively. "Whatever. Grab your coat. Let's go."

"Fine, sure." Donald patted his cheeks with his palms, trying to wake up. "I'll work better in the morning."

"Working on a Saturday. Thurman must love you."

"Let's hope so. Just give me a couple of minutes to shut this down."

Mick laughed. "Go ahead. I'm not looking." He walked over to the door while Donald finished up.

When Donald stood to go, his desk phone rang. His secretary wasn't there, so it was someone with his direct line. Donald reached for it and held up a finger to Mick.

"Helen—"

Someone cleared their throat on the other end. A deep and rough voice apologized: "Sorry, no."

"Oh." Donald glanced up at Mick, who was tapping his watch. "Hello, sir."

"You boys going out?" Senator Thurman asked.

Donald turned to the window. "Excuse me?"

"You and Mick. It's a Friday night. Are you hitting the town?"

"Uh, just the one drink, sir."

What Donald wanted to know was how the hell the Senator knew Mick was there.

"Good. Tell Mick I need to see him first thing Monday morning. My office. You too. We need to discuss your first trip down to the job site."

"Oh. Okay."

Donald waited, wondering if that was all.

"You boys will be working closely on this moving forward."

"Good. Of course."

"As we discussed last week, there won't be any need to share details about what you're working on with other project members. The same goes for Mick."

"Yes, sir. Absolutely. I remember our talk."

"Excellent. You boys have a good time. Oh, and if Mick starts blabbing, you have my permission to kill him on the spot."

There was a breath of silence, and then the hearty laugh of a man whose lungs sounded much younger than his years.

"Ah." Donald watched Mick, who had taken out the plug from a decanter to take a sniff. "Okay, sir. I'll be sure to do that."

"Great. See you Monday."

The Senator hung up abruptly. As Donald returned the phone to its cradle and grabbed his coat, his new monitor remained quietly perched on his desk, watching him blankly.

6

2110
Silo 1

TROY'S BEATEN-UP PLASTIC meal tray slid down the line behind the spattered sheet of glass. Once his badge was scanned, a measured portion of canned string beans fell out of a tube and formed a steaming pile on his plate. A perfectly round cut of turkey plopped from the next tube, the ridges still visible from the tin. Mashed potatoes spat out at the end of the line like a spit wad from a child's straw. Gravy followed with an unappetizing squirt.

Behind the serving line stood a heavyset man in white coveralls, hands clasped behind his back. He didn't seem interested in the food. He concentrated on the workers as they lined up for their meals.

When Troy's tray reached the end of the line, a younger man in pale green coveralls and probably not out of his twenties arranged silverware and napkins by the plate. A glass of water was added from a tightly packed tray nearby. The final step was like a ritualized handshake, one Troy remembered from the months of orientation: a small plastic shot glass was handed over, a pill rattling in the bottom, a blurry blue shape barely visible through the translucent cup.

Troy shuffled into place.

"Hello, sir."

A young grin. Perfect teeth. Everyone called him sir, even those much older. It was discomfiting no matter who it came from.

The pill rattled in the plastic. Troy took the cup and tossed the pill down. He swallowed it dry, grabbed his tray and tried not to hold up the line. Searching for a seat, he caught the heavyset man watching him. Everyone in the facility seemed to think Troy was in charge, but he wasn't fooled. He was just another person doing a job, following a script. He found an empty spot facing the screen. Unlike that first day, it no longer bothered him to see the scorched world outside. The view had grown oddly comforting. It created a dull ache in his chest, which was near to feeling *something*.

A mouthful of potatoes and gravy washed away the taste of the pill. Water was never up to the task, could never take away the bitterness. Eating methodically, he watched the sun set on the first week of his first shift. Twenty-five more weeks to go. It was a countable number phrased like that. It seemed shorter than half a year.

An older gentleman in blue overalls with thinning hair sat down diagonally across from him, polite enough not to block the view. Troy recognized the man, had spoken with him once by the recycling bin. When he looked up, Troy nodded in greeting.

The cafeteria hummed pleasantly as they both ate. A few hushed conversations rose and faded. Plastic, glass and metal beat out a rhythmless tune.

Troy glanced at the view and felt there was something

he was supposed to know, something he kept forgetting. He awoke each morning with familiar shapes at the edges of his vision, could feel memories nearby, but by the time breakfast came, they were already fading. By dinner, they were lost. It left Troy with a sadness, a cold sensation, and a feeling like a hollow stomach—different from hunger—like rainy days as a child when he didn't know how to fill his time.

The gentleman across from him slid over a little and cleared his throat. "Things going okay?" he asked.

He reminded Troy of someone. Blotchy skin hung slightly loose around his weathered face. He had a drooping neck, an unsightly pinch of flesh hanging from his Adam's apple.

"Things?" Troy repeated. He returned the smile.

"Anything, I suppose. Just checking in. I go by Hal." The gentleman lifted his glass. Troy did the same. It was as good as a handshake.

"Troy," he said. He supposed to some people it still mattered what they called themselves.

Hal took a long pull from his glass. His neck bobbed, the gulp loud. Self-conscious, Troy took a small sip and worked on the last of his beans and turkey.

"I've noticed some people sit facing it and some sit with their backs to it." Hal jerked his thumb over his shoulder.

Troy looked up at the screen. He chewed his food, didn't say anything.

"I reckon those who sit and watch, they're trying to remember something," Hal said.

Troy swallowed and forced himself to shrug.

"And those of us who don't want to watch," Hal continued. "I figure we're trying our best to forget."

Troy knew they shouldn't be having this conversation, but now it had begun, and he wanted to see where it would lead.

"It's the bad stuff," Hal said, staring off toward the lifts. "Have you noticed that? It's just the bad stuff that slips away. All the unimportant things, we remember well."

Troy didn't say anything. He jabbed his beans, even though he didn't plan on eating them.

"It makes you wonder, don't it? Why we all feel so rotten inside?"

Hal finished up his food, nodded a wordless goodbye, and got up to leave. Troy was left alone. He found himself staring at the screen, a dull ache inside that he couldn't name. It was the time of evening just before the hills disappeared, before they darkened and faded into the cloud-filled sky.

7

2049
Washington, DC

DONALD WAS GLAD he had decided to walk to his meeting with the Senator. The rain from the week before had finally let up, and the traffic in DuPont Circle was at a crawl. Heading up Connecticut and leaning into a stiffening breeze, Donald wondered why the meeting had been moved to Kramerbooks of all places. There were a dozen superior coffee houses much closer to the office.

He crossed a side street and hurried up the short flight of stone steps to the bookshop. The front door to Kramer's was one of those ancient wooden affairs older establishments hung like a boast, a testament to their endurance. Hinges squeaked and actual bells jangled overhead as he pushed open the door, and a young woman straightening books on a center table of bestsellers glanced up and smiled hello.

The cafe, Donald saw, was packed with men and women in business suits sipping from white porcelain cups. There was no sign of the Senator. Donald started to check his phone, see if he was too early, when a Secret Service agent caught his eye.

The agent stood broad-shouldered at the end of an aisle of

books in the small corner of Kramer's that acted as the cafe's bookshop. Donald laughed at how conspicuously hidden the man was: the earpiece, the bulge by his ribs, the sunglasses indoors. Donald headed the agent's way, the wooden boards underfoot groaning with age.

The agent's gaze shifted his way, but it was hard to tell if he was looking at Donald or toward the front door.

"I'm here to see Senator Thurman," Donald said, his voice cracking a little. "I have an appointment."

The agent turned his head to the side. Donald followed the gesture and peered down an aisle of books to see Thurman browsing through the stacks at the far end.

"Ah. Thanks." He stepped between the towering shelves of old books, the light dimming and the smell of coffee replaced with the tang of mildew mixed with leather.

"What do you think of this one?"

Senator Thurman held out a book as Donald approached. No greeting, just the question.

Donald checked the title embossed in gold on the thick leather cover. "Never heard of it," he admitted.

Senator Thurman laughed. "Of course not. It's over a hundred years old—and it's French. I mean, what do you think of the *binding*?" He handed Donald the book.

Donald was surprised by how heavy the volume was. He cracked it open and flipped through a few pages. It felt like a law book, had that same dense heft, but he could see by the white space between lines of dialogue that it was a novel. As he turned a few pages, he admired how thin the individual sheets were. Where the pages met at the spine, they had been stitched together with tiny ropes of blue and gold thread. He had friends who still swore by physical books—not for decoration, but to actually read. Studying the one in his hand, Donald could understand their nostalgic affection.

"The binding looks great," he said, brushing it with the pads of his fingers. "It's a beautiful book." He handed the novel back to the Senator. "Is this how you shop for a good read? You mostly go by the cover?"

Thurman tucked the book under his arm and pulled another from the shelf. "It's just a sample for another project I'm working on." He turned and narrowed his eyes at Donald. It was an uncomfortable gaze. He felt like prey. "How's your sister doing?" he asked.

The question caught Donald off guard. A lump formed in his throat at the mention of her.

"Charlotte? She's . . . she's fine, I guess. She redeployed. I'm sure you heard."

"I did." Thurman slotted the book in his hand back into a gap and weighed the one Donald had appraised. "I was proud of her for re-upping. She does her country proud."

Donald thought about what it cost a family to do a country proud.

"Yeah," he said. "I mean, I know my parents were really looking forward to having her home, but she was having trouble adjusting to the pace back here. It . . . I don't think she'll be able to really *relax* until the war's over. You know?"

"I do. And she may not find peace even then."

That wasn't what Donald wanted to hear. He watched the Senator trace his finger down an ornate spine adorned with ridges, bumps and recessed lettering. The old man's eyes seemed to focus beyond the rows of books.

"I can drop her a line if you want," he said. "Sometimes a soldier just needs to hear that it's okay to see someone."

"If you mean a shrink, she won't do it." Donald recalled the changes in his sister around the time of her sessions. "We already tried."

Thurman's lips pursed into a thin, wrinkled line, his worry

revealing hidden signs of age. "I'll talk to her. I'm familiar enough with the hubris of youth, believe me. I used to have the same attitude when I was younger. I thought I didn't need any help, that I could do everything on my own." He turned to face Donald. "The profession's come a long way. They have pills now that can help her with the battle fatigue."

Donald shook his head. "No. She was on those for a while. They made her too forgetful. And they caused a . . ." He hesitated, didn't want to talk about it. ". . . a *tic*."

He wanted to say tremors, but that sounded too severe. And while he appreciated the Senator's concern—this feeling as if the man was family—he was uncomfortable discussing his sister's problems. He remembered the last time she was home, the disagreement they'd had while going through his and Helen's photographs from Mexico. He had asked Charlotte if she remembered Cozumel from when they were kids, and she had insisted she'd never been. The disagreement had turned into an argument, and he had lied and said his tears were ones of frustration. Parts of his sister's life had been erased, and the only way the doctors could explain it was to say that it must've been something she *wanted* to forget. And what could be wrong with that?

Thurman rested a hand on Donald's arm. "Trust me on this," he said quietly. "I'll talk to her. I know what she's going through."

Donald bobbed his head. "Yeah. Okay. I appreciate it." He almost added that it wouldn't do any good, could possibly cause harm, but the gesture was a nice one. And it would come from someone his sister looked up to, rather than from family.

"And hey, Donny, she's piloting drones." Thurman studied him, seemed to be picking up on his worry. "It's not like she's in any physical danger."

Donald rubbed the spine of a shelved book. "Not physical, no."

They fell silent, and Donald let out a heavy breath. He could hear the chatter from the cafe, the clink of a spoon stirring in some sugar, the clang of bells against the old wooden door, the squeal and hiss of milk being steamed.

He had seen videos of what Charlotte did, camera feeds from the drones and then from the missiles as they were guided in to their targets. The video quality was amazing. You could see people turning to look up to the heavens in surprise, could see the last moments of their lives, could cycle through the video frame by frame and decide—after the fact—if this had been your man or not. He knew what his sister did, what she dealt with.

"I spoke with Mick earlier," Thurman said, seeming to sense that he'd brought up a sore topic. "You two are going to head down to Atlanta and see how the excavation is going."

Donald snapped to. "Of course. Yeah, it'll be good to get the lay of the land. I got a nice head start on my plans last week, gradually filling in the dimensions you set out. You do realize how deep this thing goes, right?"

"That's why they're already digging the foundations. The outer walls should be getting a pour over the next few weeks." Senator Thurman patted Donald's shoulder and nodded toward the end of the aisle, signaling that they were finished looking through books.

"Wait. They're already *digging*?" Donald walked alongside Thurman. "I've only got an outline ready. I hope they're saving mine for last."

"The entire complex is being worked on at the same time. All they're pouring are the outer walls and foundations, the dimensions of which are fixed. We'll fill each structure from the bottom up, the floors craned down completely furnished before we pour the slabs between. But look, this is why I need you boys to go check things out. It sounds like a damned nightmare down there with the staging. I've got a hundred crews from a dozen countries working on top of one another while materials pile up everywhere. I can't be in ten places at once, so I need you to get a read on things and report back."

When they reached the Secret Service agent at the end of the aisle, the Senator handed him the old book with the French embossing. The man in the dark shades nodded and headed toward the counter.

"While you're down there," Thurman said, "I want you to meet up with Charlie Rhodes. He's handling delivery of most of the building materials. See if he needs anything."

"*Charles* Rhodes? As in the governor of Oklahoma?"

"That's right. We served together. And hey, I'm working on transitioning you and Mick into some of the higher levels of this project. Our leadership team is still short a few dozen members. So keep up the good work. You've impressed some important people with what you've put together so far, and Anna seems confident you'll be able to stay ahead of schedule. She says the two of you make a great team."

Donald nodded. He felt a blush of pride—and also the inevitability of extra responsibilities, more bites out of his ever-dwindling time. Helen wouldn't like hearing that his involvement with the project might grow. In fact, Mick and Anna might be the only people he could share the news with, the only ones he could talk to. Every detail about the build seemed to require convoluted layers of clearance. He couldn't tell if it was the fear of nuclear waste, the threat of a terrorist attack, or the likelihood that the project would fall through.

The agent returned and took up a position beside the Senator, shopping bag in hand. He looked over at Donald and seemed to study him through those impenetrable sunglasses. Not for the first time, Donald felt watched.

Senator Thurman shook Donald's hand and said to keep him posted. Another agent materialized from nowhere and formed up on Thurman's flank. They marched the Senator through the jangling door, and Donald only relaxed once they were out of view.

8

2110
Silo 1

THE BOOK OF the Order lay open on his desk, the pages curling up from a spine stitched to last. Troy studied the upcoming procedure once again, his first official act as head of Operation Fifty, and it brought to mind a ribbon-cutting ceremony, a grand display where the man with the shears took credit for the hard work of others.

The Order, he had decided, was more recipe book than operations manual. The shrinks who had written it had accounted for everything, every quirk of human nature. And like the field of psychology, or any field that involved human nature, the parts that made no sense usually served some deeper purpose.

It made Troy wonder what *his* purpose was. How necessary his position. He had studied for a much different job, was meant to be head of a single silo, not all of them. He had been promoted at the last minute, and that made him feel arbitrary, as if anyone could be slotted into his place.

Of course, even if his office was mostly titular, perhaps it served some symbolic purpose. Maybe he wasn't there to lead so much as to provide an illusion to the others that *they were being led.*

Troy skipped back two paragraphs in the Order. His eyes had passed over every word, but none of them had registered. Everything about his new life made him prone to distraction, made him think too much. It had all been perfectly arranged—all the levels and tasks and job descriptions—but for what? For maximum *apathy*?

Glancing up, he could see Victor sitting at his desk in the Office for Psychological Services across the hall. It would be easy enough to walk over there and ask. They, more than any one architect, had designed this place. He could ask them how they had done it, how they had managed to make everyone feel so empty inside.

Sheltering the women and the children played some part; Troy was sure of that. The women and children of Silo 1 had been gifted with a long sleep while the men stayed and took shifts. It removed the passion from the plans, forestalled the chance that the men might fight among themselves.

And then there was the routine, the mind-numbing routine. It was the castration of thought, the daily grind of an office worker who drooled at the clock, punched out, watched TV until sleep overtook him, slapped an alarm three times, did it again. It was made worse by the absence of weekends. There were no free days. It was six months on and *decades* off.

It made him envious of the rest of the facility, all the other silos, where hallways must echo with the laughter of children, the voices of women, the passion and happiness missing from this bunker at the heart of it all. Here, all he saw was stupor, dozens of communal rooms with movies playing in loops on flat-panel TVs, dozens of unblinking eyes in comfortable chairs. No one was truly awake. No one was truly alive. They must have wanted it that way.

Checking the clock on his computer, Troy saw that it was time to go. Another day behind him. Another day closer to the end of his shift. He closed his copy of the Order, locked it away in his desk and headed for the communications room down the hall.

A pair of heads looked up from the radio stations as he walked in, all frowns and lowered brows in their orange coveralls. Troy took a deep breath, pulled himself together. This was an office. It was a job. And he was the man in charge. He just had to keep his shit together. He was there to cut a ribbon.

Saul, one of the lead radio techs, took off his headset and rose to greet him. Troy vaguely knew Saul; they lived on the same executive wing and saw each other in the gym from time to time. While they shook hands, Saul's wide and handsome face tickled some deeper memory, an itch Troy had learned to ignore. Maybe this was someone he had met at his orientation, from before his long sleep.

Saul introduced him to the other tech in comm room orange, who waved and kept his headset on. The name faded immediately. It didn't matter. An extra headset was pulled from a rack. Troy accepted it and lowered it around his neck, keeping the muffs off his ears so he could still hear. Saul found the silvery jack at the end of the headset and ran his fingers across an array of fifty numbered receptacles. The layout and the room reminded Troy of ancient photographs of phone operators back before they were replaced with computers and automated voices.

The mental image of a bygone day mixed and fizzed with his nerves and the shivers brought on by the pills, and Troy felt a sudden bout of giggles bubble beneath the surface. The laughter nearly burst out of him, but he managed to hold it together. It wouldn't be a good sign for the head of overall operations to lurch into hysterics when he was about to gauge the fitness of a future silo head.

"—and you'll just run through the set questions," Saul was telling him. He held out a plastic card to Troy, who was pretty sure he didn't need it but took it anyway. He'd been memorizing the routine for most of the day. Besides, he was sure it didn't matter what he said. The task of gauging a candidate's fitness was better left to the machines and the computers, all the sensors embedded in a distant headset.

"Okay. There's the call." Saul pointed to a single flashing light on a panel studded with flashing lights. "I'm patching you through."

Troy adjusted the muffs around his ears as the tech made the connection. He heard a few beeps before the line clicked over. Someone was breathing heavily on the other end. Troy reminded himself that this young man would be far more nervous than he was. After all, he had to *answer* the questions—Troy simply had to ask them.

He glanced down at the card in his hand, his mind suddenly blank, thankful that he'd been given the thing.

"Name?" he asked the young man.

"Marcus Dent, sir."

There was a quiet confidence in his young voice, the sound of a chest thrust out with pride. Troy remembered feeling that once, a long time ago. And then he thought of the world Marcus Dent had been born into, a legacy *he* would only ever know from books.

"Tell me about your training," Troy said, reading the lines. He tried to keep his voice even, deep, full of command, although the computers were designed to do that for him. Saul made a hoop with his finger and thumb, letting him know he was getting good data from the boy's headset. Troy wondered if his was similarly equipped. Could anyone in that room—or any other room—tell how nervous he was?

"Well, sir, I shadowed under Deputy Willis before transferring to IT Security. That was a year ago. I've been studying the Order for six weeks. I feel ready, sir."

Shadowing. Troy forgot it was called that. He had meant to bring the latest vocabulary card with him.

"What is your primary duty to the . . . silo?" He had nearly said *facility*.

"To maintain the Order, sir."

"And what do you protect above all?"

He kept his voice flat. The best readings would come from not imparting too much emotion into the man being measured.

"Life and Legacy," Marcus recited.

Troy had a difficult time seeing the next question. It was obscured by an unexpected blur of tears. His hand trembled. He lowered the shaking card to his side before anyone noticed.

"And what does it take to protect the things we hold dear?" he asked. His voice sounded like someone else's. He ground his teeth together to keep them from chattering. Something was wrong with him. Powerfully wrong.

"Sacrifice," Marcus said, steady as a rock.

Troy blinked rapidly to clear his vision, and Saul held up his hand to let him know he could continue, that the measures were coming through. Now they needed baselines so the biometrics could tease out the boy's sincerity toward the first questions.

"Tell me, Marcus, do you have a girlfriend?"

He didn't know why that was the first thing that came to mind. Maybe it was the envy that other silos didn't freeze their women, didn't freeze anyone at all. Nobody in the comm room seemed to react or care. The formal portion of the test was over.

"Oh, yessir," Marcus said, and Troy heard the boy's breathing change, could imagine his body relaxing. "We've applied to be married, sir. Just waiting to hear back."

"Well, I don't think you'll have to wait too much longer. What's her name?"

"Melanie, sir. She works here in IT."

"That's great." Troy wiped at his eyes. The shivers passed. Saul waved his finger in a circle over his head, letting him know he could wrap it up. They had enough.

"Marcus Dent," he said, "welcome to Operation Fifty of the World Order."

"Thank you, sir." The young man's voice lifted an octave.

There was a pause, then the sound of a deep breath being taken and held.

"Sir? Is it okay if I ask a question?"

Troy looked to the others. There were shrugs and not much else. He considered the role this young man had just assumed, knew well the sensation of being promoted to new responsibilities, that mix of fear, eagerness, and confusion.

"Sure, son. One question." He figured he was in charge. He could make a few rules of his own.

Marcus cleared his throat, and Troy pictured this shadow and his silo head sitting in a distant room together, the master studying his student.

"I lost my great-grandmother a few years ago," Marcus said. "She used to let slip little things about the world before. Not in a forbidden way, but just as a product of her dementia. The doctors said she was resistant to her medication."

Troy didn't like the sound of this, that third-generation survivors were gleaning anything about the past. Marcus may be newly cleared for such things, but others weren't.

"What's your question?" Troy asked.

"The Legacy, sir. I've done some reading in it as well—not neglecting my studies of the Order and the Pact, of course—and there's something I have to know."

Another deep breath.

"Is everything in the Legacy true?"

Troy thought about this. He considered the great collection of books that contained the world's history—a carefully edited history. In his mind, he could see the leather spines and the gilded pages, the rows and rows of books they had been shown during their orientation.

He nodded and found himself once again needing to wipe his eyes.

"Yes," he told Marcus, his voice dry and flat. "It's true."

Someone in the room sniffled. Troy knew the ceremony had gone on long enough.

"Everything in there is absolutely true."

He didn't add that not every *true thing* was written in the Legacy. Much had been left out. And there were other things he suspected that *none* of them knew, that had been edited out of books and brains alike.

The Legacy was the allowed truth, he wanted to say, the truth that was carried from each generation to the next. But the lies, he thought to himself, were what they carried there in Silo 1, in that drug-hazed asylum charged somehow with humanity's survival.

9

2049
Fulton County, Georgia

THE FRONT-END LOADER let out a throaty blat as it struggled up the hill, a charcoal geyser streaming from its exhaust pipe. When it reached the top, a load of dirt avalanched out of its toothy bucket, and Donald saw that the loader wasn't climbing the hill so much as creating it.

Hills of fresh dirt were taking shape like this all over the site. Between them—through temporary gaps left open like an ordered maze—burdened dump trucks carried away soil and rock from the cavernous pits being hollowed from the earth. These gaps, Donald knew from the topographical plans, would one day be pushed closed, leaving little more than a shallow crease where each hill met its neighbor.

Standing on one of these growing mounds, Donald watched the ballet of heavy machinery while Mick Webb spoke with a contractor about the delays. In their white shirts and flapping ties, the two congressmen seemed out of place. The men in hard hats with the leather faces, calloused hands, and busted knuckles belonged there. He and Mick, blazers tucked under their arms, sweat stains spreading in the humid Georgia heat, were somehow—nominally, at least—supposed to be in charge of that ungodly commotion.

Another loader released a mound of soil as Donald shifted his gaze toward downtown Atlanta. Past the massive clearing of rising hills and over the treetops still stripped bare from fading winter rose the glass-and-steel spires of the old Southern city. An entire corner of sparsely populated Fulton County had been cleared. Remnants of a golf course were still visible at one end where the machines had yet to disturb the land. Down by the main parking lot, a staging zone the size of several football fields held thousands of shipping containers packed with building supplies, more than Donald thought necessary. But he was learning by the hour that this was the way of government projects, where public expectations were as high as the spending limits. Everything was done in excess or not at all. The plans he had been ordered to draw up practically begged for proportions of insanity, and his building wasn't even a necessary component of the facility. It was only there for the worst-case scenario.

Between Donald and the field of shipping containers stood a sprawling city of trailers; a few functioned as offices, but most of them served as housing. This was where the thousands of men and women working on the construction could ditch their hard hats, clock out, and take their well-earned rest.

Flags flew over many of the trailers, the workforce as multinational as an Olympic village. Spent nuclear fuel rods from the world over would one day be buried beneath the pristine soil of Fulton County. It meant that the world had a stake in the project's success. The logistical nightmare this ensured didn't seem to concern the back-room dealers. He and Mick were finding that many of the early construction delays could be traced to language barriers, as neighboring work crews couldn't communicate with one another and had evidently given up trying.

Everyone simply worked on their set of plans, heads down, ignoring the rest.

Beside this temporary city of tin cans sat the vast parking lot he and Mick had trudged up from. He could see their rental car down there, the only quiet and electric thing in sight. Small and silver, it seemed to cower among the belching dump trucks and loaders on all sides. The overmatched car looked precisely how Donald felt, both on that little hill at the construction site and back at the Hill in Washington.

"Two months behind."

Mick smacked him on the arm with his clipboard. "Hey, did you hear me? Two months behind already, and they just broke ground six months ago. How is that even possible?"

Donald shrugged as they left the frowning foremen and trudged down the hill to the parking lot. "Maybe it's because they have elected officials pretending to do jobs that belong to the private sector," he offered.

Mick laughed and squeezed his shoulder. "Jesus, Donny, you sound like a goddamned Republican!"

"Yeah? Well, I feel like we're in over our heads here." He waved his arm at the depression in the hills they were skirting, a deep bowl scooped out of the earth. Several mixer trucks were pouring concrete into the wide hole at its center. More trucks waited in line behind them, their butts spinning impatiently.

"You do realize," Donald said, "that one of these holes is going to hold the building they let *me* draw up? Doesn't that scare you? All this money? All these people. It sure as hell scares me."

Mick's fingers dug painfully into Donald's neck. "Take it easy. Don't go getting all philosophical on me."

"I'm being serious," Donald said. "Billions of taxpayer dollars are gonna nestle in the dirt out there in the shape that *I* drew up. It seemed so . . . *abstract* before."

"Christ, this isn't about you or your plans." He popped Donald with the clipboard and used it to point toward the container field. Through a fog of dust, a large man in a cowboy hat waved them over. "Besides," Mick said, as they angled away from the parking lot, "what're the chances anyone even uses your little bunker? This is about energy independence. It's about the death of coal. You know, it feels like the rest of us are building a nice big house over here, and you're over in a corner stressing about where you're gonna hang the fire extinguisher—"

"*Little bunker?*" Donald held his blazer up over his mouth as a cloud of dust blew across them. "Do you know how many floors *deep* this thing is gonna be? If you set it on the ground, it'd be the tallest building in the world."

Mick laughed. "Not for long it wouldn't. Not if you designed it."

The man in the cowboy hat drew closer. He smiled widely as he kicked through the packed dirt to meet them, and Donald finally recognized him from TV: Charles Rhodes, the governor of Oklahoma.

"You Senator Thawman's boys?"

Governor Rhodes smiled. He had the authentic drawl to go with the authentic hat, the authentic boots and the authentic buckle. He rested his hands on his wide hips, a clipboard in one of them.

Mick nodded. "Yessir. I'm Congressman Webb. This is Congressman Keene."

The two men shook hands. Donald was next. "Governor," he said.

"Got your delivery." He pointed the clipboard at the staging area. "Just shy of a hundred containers. Should have somethin' rollin' in about every week. Need one of you to sign right here."

Mick reached out and took the clipboard. Donald saw an opportunity to ask something about Senator Thurman, something he figured an old war buddy would know.

"Why do some people call him Thawman?" he asked.

Mick flipped through the delivery report, a breeze pinning back the pages for him.

"I've heard others call him that when he wasn't around," Donald explained, "but I've been too scared to ask."

Mick looked up from the report with a grin. "It's because he was an ice-cold killer in the war, right?"

Donald cringed. Governor Rhodes laughed.

"Unrelated," he said. "True, but unrelated."

The governor glanced back and forth between them. Mick passed the clipboard to Donald, tapped a page that dealt with the emergency housing facility. Donald looked over the materials list.

"You boys familiar with his anti-cryo bill?" Governor Rhodes asked. He handed Donald a pen, seemed to expect him to just sign the thing and not look over it too closely.

Mick shook his head and shielded his eyes against the Georgia sun. "Anti-cryo?" he asked.

"Yeah. Aw, hell, this probably dates back before you squirts were even born. Senator Thawman penned the bill that put down that cryo fad. Made it illegal to take advantage of rich folk and turn them into ice cubes. It went to the big court, where they voted five–four, and suddenly tens of thousands of popsicles with more money than sense were thawed out and buried proper. These were people who'd frozen themselves in the hopes that doctors from the future would discover some medical procedure for extracting their rich heads from their own rich asses!"

The governor laughed at his own joke and Mick joined him. A line on the delivery report caught Donald's eye. He turned the clipboard around and showed the governor. "Uh, this shows two thousand spools of fiber optic. I'm pretty sure my plans call for forty spools."

"Lemme see." Governor Rhodes took the clipboard and procured another pen from his pocket. He clicked the top of it three times, then scratched out the quantity. He wrote in a new number to the side.

"Wait, will the price reflect that?"

"Price is the same," he said. "Just sign the bottom."

"But—"

"Son, this is why hammers cost the Pentagon their weight in gold. It's government accounting. Just a signature, please."

"But that's *fifty times* more fiber than we'll need," Donald complained, even as he found himself scribbling his name. He passed the clipboard to Mick, who signed for the rest of the goods.

"Oh, that's all right." Rhodes took the clipboard and pinched the brim of his hat. "I'm sure they'll find a use for it somewhere."

"Hey, you know," Mick said, "I remember that cryo bill. From law school. There were lawsuits, weren't there? Didn't a group of families bring murder charges against the Feds?"

The Governor smiled. "Yeah, but it didn't get far. Hard to prove you killed people who'd already been pronounced dead. And then there were Thawman's bad business investments. Those turned out to be a lifesaver."

Rhodes tucked his thumb in his belt and stuck out his chest.

"Turned out he'd sunk a fortune into one of these cryo companies before digging deeper and reconsidering the . . . *ethical* considerations. Old Thawman may have lost most of his money, but it ended up savin' his ass in Washington. Made him look like some kinda saint, suffering a loss like that. Only defense better woulda been if he'd unplugged his dear momma with all them others."

Mick and the governor laughed. Donald didn't see what was so funny.

"All right, now, you boys take care. The good state of Oklahoma'll have another load for ya in a few weeks."

"Sounds good," Mick said, grasping and pumping that huge Midwestern paw.

Donald shook the governor's hand as well, and he and Mick trudged off toward their rental. Overhead, against the bright blue Southern sky, vapor trails like stretched ropes of white yarn revealed the flight lines of the numerous jets departing the busy hub of Atlanta International. And as the throaty noise of the construction site faded, the chants from the anti-nuke protestors could be heard outside the tall mesh of security fences beyond. They passed through the security gate and into the parking lot, the guard waving them along.

"Hey, you mind if I drop you off at the airport a little early?" Donald asked. "It'd be nice to get a jump on traffic and get down to Savannah with some daylight."

"That's right," Mick said with a grin. "You've got a hot date tonight."

Donald laughed.

"Sure, man. Abandon me and go have a good time with your wife."

"Thanks."

Mick fished out the keys to the rental. "But you know, I was really hoping you'd invite me to come along. I could join you two for dinner, crash at your place, hit some bars like old times."

"Not a chance," Donald said.

Mick slapped the back of Donald's neck and squeezed. "Yeah, well, happy anniversary anyway."

Donald winced as his friend pinched his neck. "Thanks," he said. "I'll be sure to give Helen your regards."

10

2110
Silo 1

TROY PLAYED A hand of solitaire while Silo 12 collapsed. There was something about the game that he found blissfully numbing. The repetition held off the waves of depression even better than the pills. The lack of skill required moved beyond distraction and into the realm of complete mindlessness. The truth was, the player won or lost the very moment the computer shuffled the deck. The rest was simply a process of finding out.

For a computer game, it was absurdly low-tech. Instead of cards, there was just a grid of letters and numbers with an asterisk, ampersand, percent, or plus sign to designate the suit. It bothered Troy not to know which symbol stood for hearts or clubs or diamonds. Even though it was arbitrary, even though it didn't really matter, it frustrated him not to know.

He had stumbled upon the game by accident while digging through some folders. It took a bit of experimenting to learn how to flip the draw deck with the space bar and place the cards with the arrow keys, but he had plenty of time to work things like this out. Besides meeting with department heads, going over Merriman's notes, and refreshing himself on the Order, all he had was time. Time to collapse in his office bathroom and cry until snot ran down his chin, time to sit under a scalding shower and shiver, time to hide pills in his cheek and squirrel them away for when the hurt was the worst, time to wonder why the drugs weren't working like they used to, even when he doubled the dosage on his own.

Perhaps the game's numbing powers were the reason it existed at all, why someone had spent the effort to create it, and why subsequent heads had kept it secreted away. He had seen it on Merriman's face during that lift ride at the end of his shift. The chemicals only cut through the worst of the pain, that indefinable ache. But lesser wounds resurfaced. The bouts of sudden sadness had to be coming from somewhere.

The last few cards fell into place while his mind wandered. The computer had shuffled for a win, and Troy got all the credit for verifying it. The screen flashed *good job!* in large block letters. It was strangely satisfying to be told this by a homemade game—told that he had done a good job. There was a sense of completion, of having *done* something with his day.

He left the message flashing and glanced around his office for something else to do. There were amendments to be made in the Order, announcements to write up for the heads of the other silos, and he needed to make sure the vocabulary in these memos adhered to the ever-changing standards.

He got it wrong himself, often calling them bunkers instead of silos. It was difficult for those who had lived in the time of the Legacy. An old vocabulary, a way of seeing the world, persisted despite the medication. He felt envious of the men and women in the other silos, those who were born and who would die in their own little worlds, who would fall in and out of love, who would keep their hurts in memory, feel them, learn from them, be changed by them. He was jealous of these people even more than he envied the women of his own silo who remained in their long-sleep lifeboats—

There was a knock on his open door. Troy looked up and saw Randall, who worked across the hall in the psych office, standing in the doorway. Troy waved him inside with one hand and minimized the game with the other. He fidgeted with the copy of the Order on his desk, trying to look busy.

"I've got that beliefs report you wanted." Randall waved a folder.

"Oh, good. Good." Troy took the folder. Always with the folders. He was reminded of the two groups that had built that place: the politicians and the doctors. Both were stuck in a prior era, a time of paperwork. Or was it possible that neither group trusted any data they couldn't shred or burn?

"The head of Silo Six has a new replacement picked out and processed. He wants to schedule a talk with you, make the induction formal."

"Oh. Okay." Troy flipped through the folder and saw typed transcripts from the comm room about each of the silos. He looked forward to another induction ceremony. Any task he had already done once before filled him with less dread.

"Also, the population report on Silo Thirty-Two is a little troubling." Randall came around Troy's desk and licked his thumb before sorting through the reports. Troy glanced at his monitor to make sure he'd minimized the game. "They're getting close to the maximum and fast. Doc Haines thinks it might be a bad batch of birth control implants. The head of Thirty-Two, a Biggers . . . Here we go." Randall pulled out the report. "He denies this, says no one with an active implant has gotten pregnant. He thinks the lottery is being gamed or that there's something wrong with our computers."

"Hmm." Troy took the report and looked it over. Silo 32 had crept above nine thousand inhabitants, and the median age had fallen into the low twenties. "Let's set up a call for first thing in the morning. I don't buy the lottery being gamed. They shouldn't even be running the lottery, right? Until they have more space?"

"That's what I said."

"And all the population accounts for every silo are run from the same computer." Troy tried not to make this sound like a question, but it was. He couldn't remember.

"Yup," Randall confirmed.

"Which means we're being lied to. I mean, this doesn't happen overnight, right? Biggers had to see this coming, which means he knew about it earlier, so either he's complicit, or he's lost control over there."

"Exactly."

"Okay. What do we know about Biggers's second?"

"His shadow?" Randall hesitated. "I'd have to pull that file, but I know he's been in place for a while. He was there before we started our shifts."

"Good. I'll speak with him tomorrow. Alone."

"You think we should replace Biggers?"

Troy nodded grimly. The Order was clear on problems that defied explanation: *Start at the top. Assume the explanation is a lie*. Because of the rules, he and Randall were talking about a man being put out of commission as if he were broken machinery.

"Okay, one more thing—"

The thunder of boots down the hallway interrupted the thought. Randall and Troy looked up as Saul bolted into the room, his eyes wide with fear.

"Sirs—"

"Saul. What's going on?"

The communications officer looked like he'd seen a thousand ghosts.

"We need you in the comm room, sir. Right now."

Troy pushed away from his desk. Randall was right behind him.

"What is it?" Troy asked.

Saul hurried down the hallway. "It's Silo Twelve, sir."

The three of them ran past a man on a ladder who was replacing a long light bulb that had gone dim, the large rectangular plastic cover above him hanging open like a doorway to the heavens. Troy found himself breathing hard as he struggled to keep up.

"What *about* Silo Twelve?" he huffed.

Saul flashed a look over his shoulder, his face screwed up with worry. "I think we're losing it, sir."

"What, like contact? You can't reach them?"

"No. Losing *it,* sir. The *silo*. The whole damn thing."

11

2049
Savannah, Georgia

DONALD WASN'T ONE for napkins, but he obeyed decorum by shaking the folded cloth loose and draping it in his lap. Each of the napkins at the other settings around the table had been bent into a decorative pyramid that stood upright amid the silverware. He didn't remember the Corner Diner having cloth napkins when he was in high school. Didn't they used to have those paper napkin dispensers that were all dented up from years of abuse? And those little salt and pepper shakers with the silver caps, even those had gotten fancier. A dish of what he assumed was sea salt sat near the flower arrangement, and if you wanted pepper, you had to wait for someone to come around and crack it on your food for you.

He started to mention this to his wife, and saw that she was gazing past him at the booth behind. Donald turned in his seat, the original vinyl squeaking beneath him. He glanced back at the older couple sitting in the booth where he and Helen had sat on their first date.

"I swear I asked them to reserve it for us," Donald said.

His wife's gaze drifted back to him.

"I think they might've gotten confused when I described which one it was." He stirred the air with his finger. "Or maybe I got turned around when I was on the phone."

She waved her hand. "Sweetie, forget about it. We could be eating grilled cheese at home and I'd be thrilled. I was just staring off into space."

Helen unfolded her own napkin with delicate care, almost as if she were studying the folds, seeing how to piece it back together, how to return a disassembled thing to its original state. The waiter came over in a bustle and filled their glasses with water, careless drips spotting the white tablecloth. He apologized for the wait, and then left them to wait some more.

"This place sure has changed," he said.

"Yeah. It's more grown-up."

They both reached for their waters at the same time. Donald smiled and held his glass up. "Fifteen years to the day that your father made the mistake of extending your curfew."

Helen smiled and tapped her glass against his. "To fifteen more," she said.

They took sips.

"If this place keeps up, we won't be able to afford to eat here in fifteen years," Donald said.

Helen laughed. She had barely changed since that first date. Or maybe it was because the changes were so subtle. It wasn't like coming to a restaurant every five years and seeing the leaps all at once. It was how siblings aged rather than distant cousins.

"You fly back in the morning?" Helen asked.

"Yeah, but to Boston. I have a meeting with the Senator."

"Why Boston?"

He waved his hand. "He's having one of those nano treatments of his. I think he stays locked up in there for a week or so at a time. He still somehow gets his work done—"

"Yeah, by having his minions go out of *their* way—"

"We're not his minions," Donald said, laughing.

"—to come kiss his ring and leave gifts of myrrh."

"C'mon, it's not like that."

"I just worry that you're pushing yourself too hard. How much of your free time are you spending on this project of his?"

A lot, he wanted to say. He wanted to tell his wife how grueling the hours were, but he knew how she would react. "It's not as time-consuming as you'd think."

"Really? Because it seems like it's the only thing I hear you talking about. I don't even know what else it is you do."

Their waiter came past with a tray full of drinks and said it would be just a moment longer. Helen studied the menu.

"I'll be done with my portion of the plans in another few months," he told her. "And then I won't bore you with it anymore."

"Honey, you don't bore me. I just don't want him taking advantage of you. This isn't what you signed up for. You decided *not* to become an architect, remember? Otherwise, you could've stayed home."

"Baby, I want you to know . . ." He dropped his voice. "This project we're working on is—"

"It's really important, I know. You've told me, and I believe you. And then in your moments of self-doubt, you admit that your part in the entire scheme of things is superfluous anyway and will never be used."

Donald forgot they'd had that conversation.

"I'll just be glad when it's done," she said. "They can truck the fuel rods through our *neighborhood* for all I care. Just bury the whole thing and smooth the dirt over and stop talking about it."

This was something else. Donald thought about the phone calls and emails he'd been getting from the district, all the headlines and fear-mongering over the route the spent rods would take from the port as the trucks skirted Atlanta. Every time Helen heard a peep about the project, all she could likely think of was him wasting his time on it rather than doing his real job. Or the fact that he could've stayed in Savannah and done the same work.

Helen cleared her throat. "So . . ." She hesitated. "Was Anna at the job site today?"

She peered over the lip of her glass, and Donald realized, in that moment, what his wife was *really* thinking when the CAD-FAC project and the fuel rods came up. It was the insecurity of him working with *her,* of being so far from home.

"No." He shook his head. "No, we don't really see each other. We send plans back and forth. Mick and I went, just the two of us. He's coordinating a lot of the materials and crews—"

The waiter arrived, pulled his black folio from his apron and clicked his pen. "Can I start you off with drinks?"

Donald ordered two glasses of the house Merlot. Helen declined the offer of an appetizer.

"Every time I bring her up," she said, once their waiter had angled off toward the bar, "you mention Mick. Stop changing the subject."

"Please, Helen, can we not talk about her?" Donald folded his hands together on the table. "I've seen her once since we started working on this. I set it up so that we didn't have to meet, because I knew you wouldn't like it. I have no feelings for her, honey. Absolutely none. Please. This is our night."

"Is working with her giving you second thoughts?"

"Second thoughts about what? About taking on this job? Or about being an architect?"

"About . . . *anything.*" She glanced at the other booth, the booth he should've reserved.

"No. God, no. Honey, why would you even say something like that?"

The waiter came back with their wine. He flipped open his black notebook and eyed the two of them. "Have we decided?"

Helen opened her menu and looked from the waiter to Donald. "I'm going to get my usual," she said. She pointed to what had once been a simple grilled cheese sandwich with fries that now involved fried green heirloom tomatoes, Gruyère cheese, a honey-maple glaze and matchstick frites with tartar.

"And for you, sir?"

Donald looked over the menu. The conversation had him flustered, but he felt the pressure to choose and to choose swiftly.

"I think I'm going to try something different," he said, picking his words poorly.

12

2110
Silo 1

SILO 12 WAS collapsing, and by the time Troy and the others arrived, the communication room was awash in overlapping radio chatter and the stench of sweat. Four men crowded around a comm station normally manned by a single operator. The men looked precisely how Troy felt: panicked, out of their depth, ready to curl up and hide somewhere. It had a calming effect on him. Their panic was his strength. He could fake this. He could hold it together.

Two of the men wore sleepshirts rather than their orange coveralls, suggesting that the late shift had been woken up and called in. Troy wondered how long Silo 12 had been in trouble before they finally came and got *him*.

"What's the latest?" Saul asked an older gentleman, who held a headphone to one ear.

The gentleman turned, his bald head shining in the overhead light, sweat in the wrinkles of his brow, his white eyebrows high with concern. "I can't get anyone to answer the server," he said.

"Give us *just* the feeds from Twelve," Troy said, pointing to one of the other three workers. A man he had met just a week or so ago pulled off his headset and flipped a switch. The speakers in the room buzzed with overlapping shouts and orders. The others stopped what they were doing and listened.

One of the other men, in his thirties, cycled through dozens of video feeds. It was chaos everywhere. There was a shot of a spiral staircase crammed with people pushing and shoving. A head disappeared, someone falling down, presumably being trampled as the rest moved on. Eyes were wide with fear, jaws clenched or shouting.

"Let's see the server room," Troy said.

The man at the controls typed something on his keypad. The crush of people disappeared and was replaced with a calm view of perfectly still cabinets. The server casings and the grating on the floor throbbed from the blinking overhead lights of an unanswered call.

"What happened?" Troy asked. He felt unusually calm.

"Still trying to determine that, sir."

A folder was pressed into his hands. A handful of people gathered in the hallway, peering in. News was spreading, a crowd gathering. Troy felt a trickle of sweat run down the back of his neck, but still that eerie calmness, that resignation to this statistical inevitability.

A desperate voice from one of the radios cut through the rest, the panic palpable:

"—they're coming through. Dammit, they're bashing down the door. They're gonna get through—"

Everyone in the comm room held their breath, all the jitters and activity ceasing as they listened and waited. Troy was pretty sure he knew which door the panicked man was talking about. A lone door stood between the cafeteria and the airlock. It should have been made stronger. A lot of things should have been made stronger.

"—I'm on my own up here, guys. They're gonna get through. Holy shit, they're gonna get through—"

"Is that a deputy?" Troy asked. He flipped through the folder. There were status updates from Silo 12's IT head. No alarms. Two years since the last cleaning. The fear index was pegged at an eight the last time it'd been measured. A little high, but not too low.

"Yeah, I think that's a deputy," Saul said.

The man at the video feed looked back at Troy. "Sir, we're gonna have a mass exodus."

"Their radios are locked down, right?"

Saul nodded. "We shut down the repeaters. They can talk among themselves, but that's it."

Troy fought the urge to turn and meet the curious faces peering in from the hallway. "Good," he said. The priority in this situation was to contain the outbreak: don't let it spread to neighboring cells. This was a cancer. Excise it. Don't mourn the loss.

The radio crackled:

"—they're almost in, they're almost in, they're almost in—"

Troy tried to imagine the stampede, the crush of people, how the panic had spread. The Order was clear on not intervening, but his conscience was muddled. He held out a hand to the radioman.

"Let me speak to him," Troy said.

Heads swiveled his way. A crowd that thrived on protocol sat stunned. After a pause, the receiver was pressed into his palm. Troy didn't hesitate. He squeezed the mic.

"Deputy?"

"Hello? Sheriff?"

The video operator cycled through the feeds, then waved his hand and pointed to one of the monitors. The floor number "72" sat in the corner of the screen, and a man in silver overalls lay slumped over a desk. There was a gun in his hand, a pool of blood around a keyboard.

"That's the sheriff?" Troy asked.

The operator wiped his forehead and nodded.

"Sheriff? What do I do?"

Troy clicked the mic. "The sheriff is dead," he told the deputy, surprised by the steadiness of his own voice. He held the transmit button and pondered this stranger's fate. It dawned on him that most of these silo dwellers thought they were alone. They had no idea about each other, about their true purpose. And now Troy had made contact, a disembodied voice from the clouds.

One of the video feeds clicked over to the deputy, who was gripping a handset, the cord spiraling to a radio mounted on the wall. The floor number in the corner read "1."

"You need to lock yourself in the holding cell," Troy radioed, seeing that the least obvious solution was the best. It was a temporary solution, at least. "Make sure you have every set of keys."

He watched the man on the video screen. The entire room, and those in the hallway, watched the man on the video screen.

The door to the upper security office was just visible in the warped bubble of the camera's view. The edges of the door seemed to bulge outward because of the lens. And then the center of the door bulged *inward* because of the mob. They were beating the door down. The deputy didn't respond. He dropped the microphone and hurried around the desk. His hands shook so violently as he reached for the keys that the grainy camera was able to capture it.

The door cracked along the center. Someone in the comm room drew in an audible breath. Troy wanted to launch into the statistics. He had studied and trained to be on the *other* end of this, to lead a small group of people in the event of a catastrophe, not to lead them *all.*

Maybe that's why he was so calm. He was watching a horror that he should have been in the middle of, that he should have lived and died through.

The deputy finally secured the keys. He ran across the room and out of sight. Troy imagined him fumbling with the lock on the cell as the door burst in, an angry mob forcing their way through the splintered gap in the wood. It was a solid door, strong, but not strong enough. It was impossible to tell if the deputy had made it to safety. Not that it mattered. It was temporary. It was all temporary. If they opened the doors, if they made it out, the deputy would suffer a fate far worse than being trampled.

"The inner airlock door is open, sir. They're trying to get out."

Troy nodded. The trouble had probably started in IT, had spread from there. Maybe the head—but more likely his shadow. Someone with override codes. Here was the curse: a person had to be in charge, had to guard the secrets. Some wouldn't be able to. It was statistically predictable. He reminded himself that it was inevitable, the cards already shuffled, the game just waiting to play out.

"Sir, we've got a breach. The outer door, sir."

"Fire the canisters now," Troy said.

Saul radioed the control room down the hall and relayed the message. The view of the airlock filled with a white fog.

"Secure the server room," Troy added. "Lock it down."

He had this portion of the Order memorized.

"Make sure we have a recent backup just in case. And put them on our power."

"Yessir."

Those in the room who had something to do seemed less anxious than the others, who were left shifting about nervously while they watched and listened.

"Where's my outside view?" Troy asked.

The mist-filled scene of people pushing on one another's backs through a white cloud was replaced by an expansive shot of the outside, of a claustrophobic crowd scampering across a dry land, of people collapsing to their knees, clawing at their faces and their throats, a billowing fog rising up from the teeming ramp.

No one in the comm room moved or said a word. There was a soft cry from the hallway. Troy shouldn't have allowed them to stay and watch.

"Okay," he said. "Shut it down."

The view of the outside went black. There was no point in watching the crowd fight their way back in, no reason to witness the frightened men and women dying on the hills.

"I want to know why it happened." Troy turned and studied those in the room. "I want to know, and I want to know what we do to prevent this next time." He handed the folder and the microphone back to the men at their stations. "Don't tell the other silo heads just yet. Not until we have answers for the questions they'll have."

Saul raised his hand. "What about the people still inside Twelve?"

"The only difference between the people in Silo Twelve and the people in Silo Thirteen is that there won't be future generations growing up in Silo Twelve. That's it. Everyone in all the silos will eventually die. We all die, Saul. Even us. Today was just their day." He nodded to the dark monitor and tried not to picture what was really going on over there. "We knew this would happen, and it won't be the last. Let's concentrate on the others. Learn from it."

There were nods around the room.

"Individual reports by the end of this shift," Troy said, feeling for the first time that he was actually in charge of something. "And if anyone from Twelve's IT staff can be raised, debrief them as much as you can. I want to know who, why, and how."

Several of the exhausted people in the room stiffened before trying to look busy. The gathering in the hallway shrank back as they realized the show was over and the boss was heading their way.

The boss.

Troy felt the fullness of his position for the first time, the heavy weight of responsibility. There were murmurs and sidelong glances as he headed back to his office. There were nods of sympathy and approval, men thankful that they occupied lower posts. Troy strode past them all.

More will try to escape, Troy thought. For all their careful engineering, there was no way to make a thing infallible. The best they could do was plan ahead, stockpile spares, not mourn the dark and lifeless cylinder as it was discarded and others were turned to with hope.

Back in his office, he closed the door and leaned back against it for a moment. His shoulders stuck to his coveralls with the light sweat worked up from the swift walk. He took a few deep breaths before crossing to his desk and resting his hand on his copy of the Order. The fear persisted that they'd gotten it all wrong. How could a room full of doctors plan for everything? Would it really get easier as the generations went along, as people forgot and the whispers from the original survivors faded?

Troy wasn't so sure. He looked over at his wall of schematics, that large blueprint showing all the silos spread out amid the hills, fifty circles spaced out like stars on an old flag he had once served.

A powerful tremor coursed through Troy's body: his shoulders, elbows, and hands twitched. He gripped the edge of his desk until it passed. Opening the top drawer, he picked up a red marker and crossed to the large schematic, the shivers still wracking his chest.

Before he could consider the permanence of what he was about to do, before he could consider that this mark of his would be on display for every future shift, before he could consider that this might become a trend, an action taken by his replacements, he drew a bold "X" through Silo 12.

The marker squealed as it was dragged violently across the paper. It seemed to cry out. Troy blinked away the blurry vision of the red X and sagged to his knees. He bent forward until his forehead rested against the tall spread of papers, old plans rustling and crinkling as his chest shook with heavy sobs.

With his hands in his lap, shoulders bent with the weight of another job he'd been pressured into, Troy cried. He bawled as silently as he could so those across the hall wouldn't hear.

13

2049
RYT Hospital, Dwayne Medical Center

DONALD HAD TOURED the Pentagon once, had been to the White House twice, went in and out of the Capitol building a dozen times a week, but nothing he'd seen in DC prepared him for the security around RYT's Dwayne Medical Center. The lengthy checks hardly made the hour-long meeting with the Senator seem worthwhile.

By the time he passed through the full body scanners leading into the nanobiotech wing, he'd been stripped, given a pair of green medical scrubs to wear, had a blood sample taken, and had allowed every sort of scanner and bright light to probe his eyes and record—so they said—the infrared capillary pattern of his face.

Heavy doors and sturdy men blocked every corridor as they made their way deeper and deeper into the NBT wing. When Donald spotted the Secret Service agents—who had been allowed to keep their dark suits and shades—he knew he was getting close. A nurse scanned him through a final set of stainless steel doors. The nanobiotic chamber awaited him inside.

Donald eyed the massive machine warily. He'd only ever seen

them on TV dramas, and this one loomed even larger in person. It looked like a small submarine that had been marooned on the upper floors of the RYT. Hoses and wires led away from the curved and flawless white exterior in bundles. Studded along the length were several small glass windows that brought to mind the portholes of a ship.

"And you're sure it's safe for me to go in?" He turned to the nurse. "Because I can always wait and visit him later."

The nurse smiled. She couldn't be out of her twenties, had her brown hair wrapped in a knot on the back of her head, was pretty in an uncomplicated way. "It's perfectly safe," she assured him. "His nanos won't interact with your body. We often treat multiple patients in a single chamber."

She led him to the end of the machine and spun open the locking wheel at the end. A hatch opened with a sticky, ripping sound from the rubber seals and let out a slight gasp of air from the difference in pressure.

"If it's so safe, then why are the walls so *thick*?"

A soft laugh. "You'll be fine." She waved him toward the hatch. "There'll be a slight delay and a little buzz after I seal this door, and then the inner hatch will unlock. Just spin the wheel and push to open."

"I'm a little claustrophobic," Donald admitted.

God, listen to himself. He was an adult. Why couldn't he just say he didn't want to go in and have that be enough? Why was he allowing himself to be pressured into this?

"Just step inside please, Mr. Keene."

The nurse placed her hand on the small of Donald's back. Somehow, the pressure of a young and pretty woman watching was stronger than his abject terror of the oversized capsule packed with its invisible machines. He wilted and found himself ducking through the small hatch, his throat constricting with fear.

The door behind him thumped shut, leaving him in a curved space hardly big enough for two. The locks clanked into the jamb. There were tiny silver benches set into the arching walls on either side of him. He tried to stand up, but his head brushed the ceiling.

An angry hum filled the chamber. The hair on the back of his neck stood on end, and the air felt charged with electricity. He looked for an intercom, some way to communicate with the Senator through the inner door so he didn't have to go in any further. It felt as though he couldn't breathe; he needed to get *out*. There was no wheel on the outer door. Everything had been taken out of his control—

The inner locks clanked. Donald lunged for the door and tried the handle. Holding his breath, he opened the hatch and escaped the small airlock for the larger chamber in the center of the capsule.

"Donald!" Senator Thurman looked up from a thick book. He was sprawled out on one of the benches running the length of the long cylinder. A notepad and pen sat on a small table; a plastic tray held the remnants of dinner.

"Hello, sir," he said, barely parting his lips.

"Don't just stand there, get in. You're letting the buggers out."

Against his every impulse, Donald stepped through and pushed the door shut, and Senator Thurman laughed. "You might as well breathe, son. They could crawl right through your skin if they wanted to."

Donald let out his held breath and shivered. It may have been his imagination, but he thought he felt little pinpricks all over his skin, bites like Savannah's no-see-ums on summer days.

"You can't feel 'em," Senator Thurman said. "It's all in your head. They know the difference between you and me."

Donald glanced down and realized he was scratching his arm.

"Have a seat." Thurman gestured to the bench opposite his. He had the same color scrubs on and a few days' growth on his chin. Donald noticed the far end of the capsule opened onto a small bathroom, a showerhead with a flexible hose clipped to the wall. Thurman swung his bare feet off the bench and grabbed a half-empty bottle of water, took a sip. Donald obeyed and sat down, a nervous sweat tickling his scalp. A stack of folded blankets and a few pillows sat at the end of the bench. He saw how the frames folded open into cots but couldn't imagine being able to sleep in this tight coffin.

"You wanted to see me, sir?" He tried to keep his voice from cracking. The air tasted metallic, a hint of the machines on his tongue.

"Drink?" The Senator opened a small fridge below the bench and pulled out a bottle of water.

"Thanks." Donald accepted the water but didn't open it, just enjoyed the cool against his palm. "Mick said he filled you in." He wanted to add that this meeting felt unnecessary.

Thurman nodded. "He did. Met with him yesterday. He's a solid boy." The Senator smiled and shook his head. "The irony is, this class we just swore in? Probably the best bunch the Hill has seen in a very long time."

"The irony?"

Thurman waved his hand, shooing the question away. "You know what I love about this treatment?"

Practically living forever? Donald nearly blurted.

"It gives you time to think. A few days in here, nothing with batteries allowed, just a few books to read and something to write on—it really clears your head."

Donald kept his opinions to himself. He didn't want to admit how uncomfortable the procedure made him, how terrifying it was to be in that room right then. Knowing that tiny machines were coursing through the Senator's body, picking through his individual cells and making repairs, repelled him. Supposedly, your urine turned the color of charcoal once all the machines shut down. He trembled at the thought.

"Isn't that nice?" Thurman asked. He took a deep breath and let it out. "The quiet?"

Donald didn't answer. He realized he was holding his breath again.

Thurman looked down at the book in his lap, then lifted his gaze to study Donald.

"Did you know your grandfather taught me how to play golf?"

Donald laughed. "Yeah. I've seen the pictures of you two together." He flashed back to his grandmother flipping through old albums. She had this outmoded obsession with printing the pictures from her computer and stuffing them in books. Said they became more real once they were displayed like that.

"You and your sister have always felt like family to me," the Senator said.

The sudden openness was uncomfortable. A small vent in the corner of the pod circulated some air, but it still felt warm in there. "I appreciate that, sir."

"I want you in on this project," Thurman said. "All the way in."

Donald swallowed. "Sir. I'm fully committed, I promise."

Thurman raised his hand and shook his head. "No, not like—" He dropped his hand to his lap, glanced at the door. "You know, I used to think you couldn't hide anything anymore. Not in this age. It's all out there, you know?" He waggled his fingers in the air. "Hell, you ran for office and squeezed through that mess. You know what it's like."

Donald nodded. "Yeah, I had a few things I had to own up to."

The Senator cupped his hands into the shape of a bowl. "It's like trying to hold water and not letting a single drop through."

Donald nodded.

"A president can't even get a blow job anymore without the world finding out."

Donald's confused squint had Thurman waving at the air. "Before your time. But here's the thing, here's what I've found, both overseas and in Washington. It's the *unimportant* drips that leak through. The peccadilloes. Embarrassments, not life-and-death stuff. You want to invade a foreign country? Look at D-Day. Hell, look at Pearl Harbor. Or 9/11. Not a problem."

"I'm sorry, sir, I don't see what—"

Thurman's hand flew out, his fingers thudding shut as he pinched the air. Donald thought for a moment that he meant for him to keep quiet, but then the Senator leaned forward and held the pinched pads of his fingers for Donald to see, as if he had snatched a mosquito.

"Look," he said.

Donald leaned closer, but he still couldn't make anything out. He shook his head. "I don't see, sir . . ."

"That's right. And you wouldn't see it coming, either. That's what they've been working on, those snakes."

Senator Thurman released the invisible pinch and studied the pad of his thumb for a moment. He blew a puff of air across it. "Anything these puppies can stitch, they can *unstitch*."

He peered across the pod at Donald. "You know why we went into Iran the first time? It wasn't about nukes, I'll tell you that. I crawled through every hole that's ever been dug in those dunes over there, and those rats had a bigger prize they were chasing than nukes. You see, they've figured out how to attack us without being *seen*, without having to blow themselves up, and with *zero* repercussions."

Donald was sure he didn't have the clearance to hear any of this.

"Well, the Iranians didn't figure it out for themselves so much as steal what Israel was working on." He smiled at Donald. "So, of course, we had to start playing catch-up."

"I don't understa—"

"These critters in here are programmed for my DNA, Donny. Think about that. Have you ever had your ancestry tested?" He looked Donald up and down as if he were surveying a mottled mutt. "What are you, anyway? Scottish?"

"Maybe Irish, sir. I honestly couldn't tell you." He didn't want to admit that it was unimportant to him; it seemed like a topic close to Thurman's heart.

"Well, these buggers can tell. If they ever get them perfected, that is. They could tell you what clan you came from. And that's what the Iranians are working on: a weapon you can't see, that you can't stop, and if it decides you're Jewish, even a *quarter* Jew . . ." Thurman drew his thumb across his own neck.

"I thought we were wrong about that. We never found any NBs in Iran."

"That's because they self-destructed. *Remotely*. Poof." The old man's eyes widened.

Donald laughed. "You sound like one of those conspiracy theorists—"

Senator Thurman leaned back and rested his head against the wall. "Donny, the conspiracy theorists sound like *us*."

Donald waited for the Senator to laugh. Or smile. Neither came.

"What does this have to do with me?" he asked. "Or our project?"

Thurman closed his eyes, his head still tilted back. "You know why Florida has such pretty sunrises?"

Donald wanted to scream. He wanted to beat on the door until they hauled him out of there in a straightjacket. Instead, he took a sip of water.

Thurman cracked an eye. Studied him again.

"It's because the sand from Africa blows clear across the Atlantic."

Donald nodded. He saw what the Senator was getting at. He'd heard the same fear-mongering on the twenty-four-hour news programs, how toxins and tiny machines can circle the globe, just like seeds and pollens have done for millennia.

"It's coming, Donny. I know it is. I've got eyes and ears everywhere, even in here. I asked you to meet me here because I want you to have a seat at the *after* party."

"Sir?"

"You and Helen both."

Donald scratched his arm and glanced at the door.

"It's just a contingency plan for now, you understand? There are plans in place for anything. Mountains for the president to crawl inside of, but we need something else."

Donald remembered the congressman from Atlanta prattling on about zombies and the CDC. This sounded like more of that nonsense.

"I'm happy to serve on any committee you think is important—"

"Good." The Senator took the book from his lap and handed it to Donald. "Read this," Thurman said.

Donald checked the cover. It was familiar, but instead of French script, it read: *The Order*. He opened the heavy tome to a random page and started skimming.

"That's your bible from now on, son. When I was in the war, I met boys no higher than your knee who had the entire Qur'an memorized, every stinkin' verse. You need to do better."

"Memorize?"

"As near as you can. And don't worry, you've got a couple of years."

Donald raised his eyebrows in surprise, then shut the book and studied the spine. "Good. I'll need it." He wanted to know if there would be a raise involved or a ton of committee meetings. This sounded ludicrous, but he wasn't about to refuse the old man, not with his re-election coming up every two years.

"All right. Welcome." Thurman leaned forward and held out his hand. Donald tried to get his palm deep into the Senator's. It made the older man's grip hurt a lot less. "You're free to go."

"Thank you, sir."

He stood and exhaled in relief. Cradling the book, he moved to the airlock door.

"Oh, and Donny?"

He turned back. "Yessir?"

"The National Convention is in a couple of years. I want you to go ahead and pencil it into your schedule. And make sure Helen is there."

Donald felt goosebumps run down his arms. Did that mean a real possibility of promotion? Maybe a speech on the big stage?

"Absolutely, sir." He knew he was smiling.

"Oh, and I'm afraid I haven't been completely honest with you about the critters in here."

"Sir?" Donald swallowed. His smile melted. He had one hand on the hatch's wheel. His mind resumed playing tricks on him, the taste on his tongue metallic, the pricks everywhere on his skin.

"Some of the buggers in here are very much for you."

Senator Thurman stared at Donald for a beat, and then he started laughing.

Donald turned, sweat glassy on his brow as he worked the wheel in the door with a free hand. It wasn't until he secured the airlock, the seals deadening the Senator's laughter, that he could breathe again.

The air around him buzzed, a jolt of static to kill any strays. Donald blew out his breath, harder than usual, and unsteadily walked away.

14

2110
Silo 1

THE SHRINKS KEPT Troy's door locked and delivered his meals while he went through the Silo 12 reports alone. He spread the pages across his keyboard—safely away from the edge of his desk. This way, when stray tears fell, they didn't smudge the paper.

For some reason, Troy couldn't stop crying. The shrinks with the strict meal plans had taken him off his meds for the last two days, long enough to compile his findings with Troy sober, free from the forgetfulness the pills brought about. He had a deadline. After he put his final notes together, they would get him something to cut through the pain.

Images of the dying interfered with his thoughts, the picture of the outside, of people suffocating and falling to their knees. Troy remembered giving the order. What he regretted most was making someone else push the button.

Coming off his meds had brought back other random haunts. He began to remember his father, events from before his orientation. And it worried him that the billions who had been wiped out could be felt as an ache in his gut while the few thousand of Silo 12 who had scrambled to their deaths made him want to curl up and die.

The reports on his keyboard told a story of a shadow who had lost his nerve, an IT head who couldn't see the darkness rising at her feet, and an honest enough Security chief who had chosen poorly. All it took was for a lot of seemingly decent people to put the wrong person in power, and then pay for their innocent choice.

The keycodes for each video feed sat in the margins. It reminded him of an old book he had once known; the references had a similar style.

Jason 2:17 brought up a slice of the feed from the IT head's shadow. Troy followed the action on his monitor. A young man, probably in his late teens or early twenties, sat on a server-room floor. His back was to the camera, the corners of a plastic tray visible in his lap. He was bent over a meal, the bony knots of his spine casting dots of shadow down the back of his overalls.

Troy watched. He glanced at the report to check the timecode. He didn't want to miss it.

In the video, Jason's right elbow worked back and forth. He looked to be eating. The moment was coming. Troy willed himself not to blink, could feel tears coat his eyes from the effort.

A noise startled Jason. The young IT shadow glanced to the side, his profile visible for a moment, an angular and gaunt face from weeks of privation. He grabbed the tray from his lap; it was the first time Troy could spot the rolled-up sleeve. And there, as he fought with the cuff to roll it back down, were the dark parallel lines across his forearm, and nothing on his tray that called for a knife.

The rest of the clip was of Jason speaking to the IT head, her demeanor motherly and tender, a touch on his shoulder, a squeeze of his elbow. Troy could imagine her voice. He had spoken to her once or twice to take down a report. In a few more weeks, they would've scheduled a time to speak with Jason and induct him formally.

The clip ended with Jason descending back into the space beneath the server-room floor, a shadow swallowing a shadow. The head of IT—the *true* head of Silo 12—stood alone for a moment, hand on her chin. She looked so *alive*. Troy had a childlike impulse to reach out and brush his fingers across the monitor, to acknowledge this ghost, to apologize for letting her down.

Instead, he saw something the reports had missed. He watched her body twitch toward the hatch, stop, freeze for a moment, then turn away.

Troy clicked the slider at the bottom of the video to see it again. There she was rubbing her shadow's shoulder, talking to him, Jason nodding. She squeezed his elbow, was concerned about him. He was assuring her everything was fine.

Once he was gone, once she was alone, the doubts and fears overtook her. Troy couldn't know it for sure, but he could *sense* it. She knew a darkness was brewing beneath her feet, and here was her chance to destroy it. It was a mask of concern, a twitch in that direction, reconsidering, turning away.

Troy paused the video and made some notes, jotted down the times. The shrinks would have to verify his findings. Shuffling the papers, he wondered if there was anything he needed to see again. A decent woman had been murdered because she could not bring herself to do the same, to kill in order to protect. And a Security chief had let loose a monster who had mastered the art of concealing his pain, a young man who had learned how to manipulate others, who wanted *out*.

He typed up his conclusions. It was a dangerous age for shadowing, he noted in his report. Here was a boy between his teens and twenties, an age deep in doubts and shallow in control. Troy asked in his report if anyone at that age could ever be ready. He made mention of the first head of IT he had inducted, the question the boy had asked after hearing tales from his demented great-grandmother. Was it right to expose anyone to these truths? Could men at such a fragile age be expected to endure such blows without shattering?

What he didn't add, what he asked himself, was if anyone at *any* age could ever be ready.

There was precedence, he typed, for limiting certain positions of authority by age. And while this would lead to shorter terms—which meant subjecting more unfortunate souls to the abuse of being locked up and shown their Legacy—wasn't it better to go through a damnable process more often rather than take risks such as these?

He knew this report would matter little. There was no planning for insanity. With enough revolutions and elections, enough transfers of power, eventually a madman would take the reins. It was inevitable. These were the odds they had planned for. This was why they had built so many.

He rose from his desk and walked to the door, slapped it soundly with the flat of his palm. In the corner of his office, a printer hummed and shot four pages out of its mouth. Troy took them; they were still warm as he slid them into the folder, these reports on the newly dead and still dying. He could feel the life and warmth draining from those printed pages. Soon, they would be as cool as the air around them. He grabbed a pen from his desk and signed the bottom.

A key rattled in his lock before the door opened.

"Done already?" Victor asked. The gray-haired psychiatrist stood across from his desk, keys jangling as they returned to his pocket. He held a small plastic cup in his hand.

Troy handed him the folder. "The signs were there," he told the doctor, "but they weren't acted upon."

Victor took the folder with one hand and held out the plastic cup with the other.

Troy typed a few commands on his computer and wiped his copy of the videos. The cameras were of no use for predicting and preventing these kinds of problems. There were too many to watch all at once. You couldn't get enough people to sit and monitor an entire populace. They were there to sort through the wreckage, the aftermath.

"Looks good," Victor said, flipping through the folder. The plastic cup sat on Troy's desk, two pills inside. They had increased the dosage to what he had taken at the start of his shift, a little extra to cut through the pain.

"Would you like me to fetch you some water?"

Troy shook his head. He hesitated. Looking up from the cup, he asked Victor a question: "How long do you think it'll take? Silo Twelve, I mean. Before all of those people are gone."

Victor shrugged. "Not long, I imagine. Days."

Troy nodded. Victor watched him carefully. Troy tilted his head back and rattled the pills past his trembling lips. There was the bitter taste on his tongue. He made a show of swallowing.

"I'm sorry that it was your shift," Victor said. "I know this wasn't the job you signed up for."

Troy nodded. "I'm actually glad it was mine," he said after a moment. "I'd hate for it to have been anyone else's."

Victor rubbed the folder with one hand. "You'll be given a commendation in my report."

"Thank you," Troy said. He didn't know what the fuck for.

With a wave of the folder, Victor finally turned to leave and go back to his desk across the hall where he could sit and glance up occasionally at Troy.

And in that brief moment it took for Victor to walk over, with his back turned, Troy spat the pills into the palm of his hand.

Shaking his mouse with one hand, waking up his monitor so

he could boot a game of solitaire, Troy smiled across the hallway at Victor, who smiled back. And in his other hand, still sticky from the outer coating dissolved by his saliva, the two pills nestled in his palm. Troy was tired of forgetting. He had decided to remember.

15

2049
Savannah, Georgia

DONALD SPED DOWN highway 17, a flashing red light on his dash warning him as he exceeded the local speed limit. He didn't care about being pulled over, didn't care about being wired a ticket or his insurance rates creeping up. It all seemed trivial. The fact that there were circuits riding along in his car keeping track of everything he did paled in comparison to the suspicion that machines in his *blood* were doing the same.

The tires squealed as he spiraled down his exit ramp too fast. He merged onto Berwick Boulevard, the overhead lights strobing through the windshield as he flew beneath them. Glancing down at his lap, he watched the gold inlay text on the book throb with the rhythm of the passing lights.

Order. Order. Order.

He had read enough to worry, to wonder what he'd gotten himself mixed up in. Helen had been right to warn him, had been wrong about the scale of the danger.

Turning into his neighborhood, Donald remembered a conversation from long before—he remembered her begging him not to run for office, saying that it would change him, that he couldn't fix anything up there, but that he could sure as hell come home broken.

How right had she been?

He pulled up to the house and had to leave the car by the curb. Her Jeep was in the middle of the driveway. One more habit formed in his absence, a reminder that he didn't live there anymore, didn't have a real home.

Leaving his bags in the trunk, he took just the book and his keys. The book was heavy enough.

The motion light came on as he neared the porch. He saw a form by the window, heard frantic scratching on the other side. Helen opened the door, and Karma rushed out, tail whacking the side of the jamb, tongue lolling, so much bigger in just the few weeks that he'd been away.

Donald crouched down and rubbed her head, let the dog lick his cheek.

"Good girl," he said. He tried to sound happy. The cool emptiness in his chest intensified from being home. The things that should've felt comforting only made him feel worse.

"Hey, honey." He smiled up at his wife.

"You're early."

Helen wrapped her arms around his neck as he stood. Karma sat down and whined at them, tail swishing on the concrete. Helen's kiss tasted like coffee.

"I took an earlier flight."

He glanced over his shoulder at the dark streets of his neighborhood. As if anyone needed to follow him.

"Where're your bags?"

"I'll get 'em in the morning. C'mon, Karma. Let's go inside." He steered his dog through the door.

"Is everything okay?" Helen asked.

Donald went to the kitchen. He set the book down on the island and fished in the cabinet for a glass. Helen watched him with concern as he pulled a bottle of brandy out of the cabinet.

"Baby? What's going on?"

"Maybe nothing," he said. "Lunatics—" He poured three fingers of brandy, looked to Helen and raised the bottle to see if she wanted any. She shook her head. "Then again," he continued, "maybe there's something to it." He took more than a sip. His other hand hadn't left the neck of the bottle.

"Baby, you're acting strange. Come sit down. Take off your coat."

He nodded and let her help him remove his jacket. He slid his tie off, saw the worry on her face, knew it to be a reflection of his own.

"What would you do if you thought it all might end?" he asked his wife. "What would you do?"

"If what? You mean us? Oh, you mean life. Honey, did someone pass away? Tell me what's going on."

"No, not someone. Everyone. Everything."

He tucked the bottle under his arm, grabbed his drink and the book, and went to the living room. Helen and Karma followed. Karma was already on the sofa waiting for him to sit down before he got there, oblivious to anything he was saying, just thrilled for the pack to be reunited.

"It sounds like you've had a very long day," Helen said, trying to find excuses for him.

Donald sat on the sofa and put the bottle and book on the coffee table. He pulled his drink away from Karma's curious nose.

"I have something I have to tell you," he said.

Helen stood in the middle of the room, her arms crossed. "That'd be a nice change." She smiled to let him know she was joking. Donald nodded.

"I know, I know," he said. His eyes fell to the book. "This isn't about that project. And honestly, do you think I enjoy keeping my life from you?"

Helen crossed to the recliner next to the sofa and sat down. "What is this about?" she asked.

"I've been told it's okay to tell you about a . . . promotion. Well, more of an assignment than a promotion. Not an assignment, really, more like being on the National Guard. Just in case—"

Helen reached over and squeezed his knee. "Take it easy," she whispered. Her eyebrows were lowered, confusion and worry lurking in the shadows there.

Donald took a deep breath. He was still revved up from running the conversation over in his head, from driving too fast. In the weeks since his meeting with Thurman he had been reading too much into the book—and too much into that conversation. He couldn't tell if he was piecing something together, or just falling apart.

"How much have you followed what's going on in Iran?" he asked, scratching his arm. "And Korea?"

She shrugged. "I see blurbs online."

"Mmm." He took a burning gulp of the brandy, smacked his lips and tried to relax and enjoy the numbing chill as it travelled through his body. "They're working on ways to take everything out," he said.

"Who? *We* are?" Helen's voice rose. "We're thinking of taking *them* out?"

"No, no—"

"Are you sure I'm allowed to hear this—?"

"No, sweetheart, they're designing weapons to take *us* out. Weapons that can't be stopped, that can't be defended against."

Helen leaned forward, her hands clasped, elbows on her knees. "Is this stuff you're learning in Washington? Classified stuff?"

He waved his hand. “Beyond classified. Look, you know why we went into Iran—”

“I know why they *said* we went in—”

“It wasn’t bullshit,” he said, cutting her off. “Well, maybe it was. Maybe they hadn’t figured it out yet, hadn’t mastered how—”

“Honey, slow down.”

“Yeah.” He took another deep breath. He had an image in mind of a large mountain out west, a concrete road disappearing straight into the rock, thick vault doors standing open as files of politicians crowded inside with their families.

“I met with the Senator a few weeks ago.” He stared down into the ginger-colored liquor in his glass.

“In Boston,” Helen said.

He nodded. “Right. Well, he wants us to be on this alert team—”

“You and Mick.”

He turned to his wife. “No—us.”

“*Us?*” Helen placed a hand on her chest. “What do you mean, us? You and me?”

“Now listen—”

“You’re volunteering *me* for one of his—”

“Sweetheart, I had no idea what this was all about.” He set his glass on the coffee table and grabbed the book. “He gave me this to read.”

Helen frowned. “What is that?”

“It’s like an instruction manual for the—well, for the *after.* I think.”

Helen got up from the recliner and stepped between him and the coffee table. She nudged Karma out of the way, the dog grunting at being disturbed. Sitting down beside him, she put a hand on his back, her eyes shiny with worry.

“Donny, were you drinking on the plane?”

"No." He pulled away. "Just please listen to me. It doesn't matter *who* has them, it only matters *when*. Don't you see? This is the ultimate threat. A world-ender. I've been reading about the possibilities on this website—"

"A website," she said, voice flat with skepticism.

"Yeah. Listen. Remember those treatments the Senator takes? These nanos are like synthetic life. Imagine if someone turned them into a virus that didn't care about its host, that didn't need *us* in order to spread. They could be out there already." He tapped his chest, glanced around the room suspiciously, took a deep breath. "They could be in every one of us right now, little timer circuits waiting for the right moment—"

"Sweetheart—"

"Very bad people are working on this, trying to make this happen." He reached for his glass. "We can't sit back and let them strike first. So we're gonna do it." There were ripples in the liquor. His hand was shaking. "God, baby, I'm pretty sure we're gonna do it before *they* can."

"You're scaring me, honey."

"Good." Another burning sip. He held the glass with both hands to keep it steady. "We should be scared."

"Do you want me to call Dr. Martin?"

"Who?" He tried to make room between them, bumped up against the armrest. "My sister's doctor? The *shrink*?"

She nodded gravely.

"Listen to what I'm telling you," he said, holding up a finger. "These tiny machines are *real*." His mind was racing. He was going to babble and convince her of nothing but his paranoia. "Look," he said. "We use them in medicine, right?"

Helen nodded. She was giving him a chance, a slim one. But he could tell she really wanted to go call someone. Her mother, a doctor, *his* mother.

"It's like when we discovered radiation, okay? The first thing we thought was that this would be a cure, a medical discovery. X-rays, but then people were taking drops of radium like an elixir—"

"They poisoned themselves," Helen said. "Thinking they were doing something good." She seemed to relax a little. "Is this what you're worried about? That the nanos are going to mutate and turn on us? Are you still freaked out from being inside that machine?"

"No, nothing like that. I'm talking about how we looked for medicinal uses first, then ended up building the bomb. This is the *same thing*." He paused, hoping she would get it. "I'm starting to think we're building them too. Tiny machines, just like the ones in the nanobaths that stitch up people's skin and joints. Only *these* would tear people apart."

Helen didn't react. Didn't say a word. Donald realized he sounded crazy, that every bit of this was already online and in podcasts that radiated out from lonely basements on lonely airwaves. The Senator had been right. Mix truth and lies and you couldn't tell them apart. The book on his coffee table and a zombie survival guide would be treated the same way.

"I'm telling you they're real," he said, unable to stop himself. "They'll be able to reproduce. They'll be invisible. There won't be any warning when they're set loose, just dust in the breeze, okay? Reproducing and reproducing, this invisible war will wage itself all around us while we're turned to mush."

Helen remained silent. He realized she was waiting for him to finish, and then she would call her mom and ask what to do. She would call Dr. Martin and get his advice.

Donald started to complain, could feel the anger welling up, and knew that anything he said would confirm her fears rather than convince her of his own.

"Is there anything else?" she whispered. She was looking for permission to leave and make her phone calls, to talk to someone rational.

Donald felt numb. Helpless and alone.

"The National Convention is going to be held in Atlanta." He wiped underneath his eyes, tried to make it look like weariness, like the strain of travel. "The DNC hasn't announced it yet, but I heard from Mick before I got on the flight." He turned to Helen. "The Senator wants us both there, is already planning something big."

"Of course, baby." She rested her hand on his thigh and looked at him as if he were her patient.

"And I'm going to ask that I spend more time down here, maybe do some of my work from home on weekends, keep a closer eye on the project."

"That'd be great." She rested her other hand on his arm.

"I want us to be good to each other," he said. "For whatever time we have left—"

"Shh, baby, it's okay." She wrapped her arm around his back and shushed him again, trying to soothe him. "I love you," she said.

He wiped at his eyes again.

"We'll get through this," she told him.

Donald bobbed his head. "I know," he said. "I know we will."

The dog grunted and nuzzled her head into Helen's lap, could sense something was wrong. Donald scratched the pup's neck. He looked up at his wife, tears in his eyes. "I know we'll get through this," he said, trying to calm himself. "But what about everyone *else*?"

16

2110
Silo 1

TROY NEEDED TO see a doctor. Ulcers had formed in both sides of his mouth, down between his gums and the insides of his cheeks. He could feel them like little wads of tender cotton embedded in his flesh. In the morning, he kept the pill tucked down on the left side. At supper, on the right. On either side, it would burn and dry out his mouth with the bitter bite of the medicine, but he would endure it.

He rarely employed napkins during meals, a bad habit he had formed long ago. They went into his lap to be polite and then onto his plate when he was finished. Now he had a different routine. One quick small bite of something, wipe his mouth, spit out the burning blue capsule, take a huge gulp of water, swish it around.

The hard part was not checking to see if anyone was watching while he spat it out. He sat with his back to the wallscreen, imagining eyes drilling through the side of his head, but he kept his gaze in front of him and chewed his food.

He remembered to use his napkin occasionally, to wipe with both hands, always with both hands, pinching across his mouth, staying consistent. He smiled at the man across from him and made sure the pill didn't fall out. The man's gaze drifted over Troy's shoulder as he stared at the view of the outside world on the screen.

Troy didn't turn to look. There was still the same draw to the top of the silo, the same compulsion to be as high as possible, to escape the suffocating depths, but he no longer felt any desire to see outside. Something had changed.

He spotted Hal at the next table over—recognized his bald and splotchy scalp. The old man was sitting with his back to Troy. Troy waited for him to turn and catch his eye, but Hal never looked around.

He finished his corn and worked on his beets. It had been long enough since spitting out his pill to risk a glance toward the serving line. Tubes spat food; plates rattled on trays; one of the doctors from Victor's office stood beyond the glass serving line, arms crossed, a wan smile on his face. He was scanning the men in line and looking out over the tables. Why? What was there to keep an eye on? Troy wanted to know. He had dozens of burning questions like this. Answers sometimes presented themselves, but they skittered away if he trained his thoughts on them.

The beets were awful.

He ate the last of them while the gentleman across the table stood with his tray. It wasn't long before someone took his place. Troy looked up and down the row of adjoining tables. The vast majority of the workers sat on the *other* side so they could see out. Only a handful sat like Hal and himself. It was strange that he'd never noticed this before.

In the past weeks, it seemed patterns were becoming easier to spot, even as other faculties slipped and stumbled. He cut into a rubbery hunk of canned ham, his knife screeching against his plate, and wondered when he'd get some real sleep.

He couldn't ask the doctors for anything to help, couldn't show them his gums. They might find out he was off his meds. The insomnia was awful. He might doze off for a minute or two, but deep sleep eluded him. And instead of remembering anything concrete, all he had were these dull aches, these bouts of terrible sadness, and the inescapable feeling that something was deeply wrong.

He caught one of the doctors watching him. Troy looked down the table and saw men shoulder to shoulder on the other side, eyeing the view. It wasn't long ago that he'd wanted to sit and stare, mesmerized by the gray hills on the screen. And now he felt sick when he caught even a glimpse; the view brought him close to tears.

He stood with his tray, then worried he was being obvious. The napkin fell from his lap and landed on the floor, and something skittered away from his foot.

Troy's heart skipped a beat. He bent and snatched the napkin, hurried down the line, looking for the pill. He bumped into a chair that had been pulled back from the table, felt all the room's eyes on him.

The pill. He found it and scooped it up with his napkin, the tray teetering dangerously in his palm. He stood and composed himself. A trickle of sweat itched his scalp and ran down the back of his neck. Everyone knew.

Troy turned and walked toward the water fountain, not daring to glance up at the cameras or over at the doctors. He was losing it. Growing paranoid. And there was just over a month left on this shift. A month that would test every inch of will he had left.

Trying to walk naturally with so many eyes on him was impossible. He rested the edge of his tray on the water fountain, stepped on the lever with his foot and topped up his glass. This was why he had gotten up: he was thirsty. He felt like announcing the fact out loud.

Returning to the tables, Troy squeezed between two other workers and sat down facing the screen. He balled up his napkin, felt the pill hidden within its folds, and tucked it between his thighs. He sat there, sipping his water, facing the screen like everyone else, like he was supposed to. But he didn't dare look.

17

2051
Washington, DC

THE FAT RAINDROPS on the canopy outside De'Angelo's restaurant sounded like rhythmless fingers tapping on a drum. The traffic on L Street hissed through puddles gathering against the curb, and the asphalt that flashed between the cars gleamed shiny and black from the streetlights. Donald shook two pills out of a plastic vial and into his palm. Two years on the meds. Two years completely free of anxiety, gloriously numb.

He glanced at the label and thought of Charlotte, of the necessity of fulfilling the prescription under his sister's name, then popped them in his mouth. Donald swallowed. He was sick of the rain, preferred the cleanliness of the snow. Winter had been too warm again.

Keeping out of the foot traffic flowing through the front doors, he cradled his phone against his ear and listened patiently while his wife urged Karma to pee.

"Maybe she doesn't need to go," he suggested. He dropped the vial into his coat pocket and cupped his hand over the phone as the lady beside him wrestled with her umbrella, water flicking everywhere.

Helen continued to cajole Karma with words the poor dog didn't understand. This was typical of Helen and Donald's conversations of late. There was nothing real to say to one another.

"But she hasn't been since *lunch,*" Helen insisted.

"She didn't go somewhere in the house, did she?"

"She's four years old."

Donald forgot. Lately, time felt locked in a bubble. He wondered if his medication was causing that or if it was the workload. Whenever anything seemed . . . off anymore, he always assumed it must be the medication. Before, it could have been the vagaries of life; it could have been anything. Somehow, it felt worse to have something concrete and new to pin it on.

There was shouting across the street, two homeless men yelling at each other in the rain, squabbling over a bag of tin cans. More umbrellas were shaken and more fancy dresses flowed into the restaurant. Here was a city charged with governing all the others, and it couldn't even take care of itself. These things used to worry him more. He patted the capsule in his jacket pocket, a comforting twitch he'd developed.

"She won't go," his wife said exhaustedly.

"Baby, I'm sorry I'm up here and you have all that to take care of. But look, I really need to get inside. We're trying to wrap up final revisions on these plans tonight."

"How is everything going with that? Are you almost done?"

A file of taxis drove by, hunting for fares, fat tires rolling across sheets of water like hissing snakes. Donald watched as one of them slowed to a stop, brakes squealing from the wet. He didn't recognize the man stepping out, coat held over his head. It wasn't Mick.

"Huh? Oh, it's going great. Yeah, we're basically done, maybe a few tweaks here and there. The outer shells are poured, and the lower floors are in—"

"I meant, are you almost done working with *her*?"

He turned away from the traffic to hear better. "Who, Anna? Yeah. Look, I've told you. We've only consulted here and there. Most of it's done electronically."

"And Mick is there?"

"Yup."

Another cab slowed as it passed by. Donald turned, but the car didn't stop.

"Okay. Well, don't work too late. Call me tomorrow."

"I will. I love you."

"Love you—Oh! Good girl! That's a good girl, Karma—"

"I'll talk to you tomorr—"

But the line was already dead. Donald glanced at his phone before putting it away, shivered once from the cool evening and from the moisture in the air. He pressed through the crowd outside the door and made his way to the table.

"Everything okay?" Anna asked. She sat alone at a table with three settings. A wide-necked sweater had been pulled down to expose one shoulder. She pinched her second glass of wine by its delicate stem, a pink half-moon of lipstick on its rim. Her auburn hair was tied up in a bun, the freckles across her nose almost invisible behind a thin veil of make-up. She looked, impossibly, more alluring than she had in college.

"Yeah, everything's fine." Donald twisted his wedding ring with his thumb—a habit. "Have you heard from Mick?" He reached into his pocket and pulled out his phone, checked his texts. He thought of firing off another, but there were already four unanswered messages sitting there.

"Nope. Wasn't he flying in from Texas this morning? Maybe his flight was delayed."

Donald saw that his glass, which he'd left near empty when he made the call outside, had been topped up. He knew Helen would disapprove of him sitting there alone with Anna, even though nothing was going to happen. Nothing ever would.

"We could always do this another time," he suggested. "I'd hate for Mick to be left out."

She set down her glass and studied the menu. "Might as well eat while we're here. Be a little late to find something else. Besides, Mick's logistics are independent of our design. We can send him our materials report later."

Anna leaned to the side and reached for something in her bag, her sweater falling dangerously open. Donald looked away quickly, a flush of heat on the back of his neck. She pulled out her tablet and placed it on top of his manila folder, the screen flashing to life.

"I think the bottom third of the design is solid." She spun the tablet for him to see. "I'd like to sign off on it so they can start layering the next few floors in."

"Well, a lot of these are yours," he said, thinking of all the mechanical spaces at the bottom. "I trust your judgment."

He picked the tablet up, relieved that their conversation hadn't veered away from work. He felt like a fool for thinking Anna had anything else in mind. They had been exchanging emails and updating each other's plans for over two years and there had never been a hint of impropriety. He warned himself not to let the setting, the music, the white tablecloths, fool him.

"There *is* one last-minute change you're not going to like," she said. "The central shaft needs to be modified a little. But I think we can still work with the same general plan. It won't affect the floors at all."

He scrolled through the familiar files until he spotted the difference. The emergency stairwell had been moved from the side of the central shaft to the very middle. The shaft itself seemed smaller, or maybe it was because all the other gear they'd filled it with was gone. Now there was empty space, the discs turned to doughnuts. He looked up from the tablet and saw their waiter approaching.

"What, no lift?" He wanted to make sure he was seeing this right. He asked the waiter for a water and said he'd need more time with the menu.

The waiter bowed and left. Anna placed her napkin on the table and slid over to the adjacent chair. "The board said they had their reasons."

"The medical board?" Donald exhaled. He had grown sick of their meddling and their suggestions, but he had given up fighting with them. He never won. "Shouldn't they be more worried about people falling over these railings and breaking their necks?"

Anna laughed. "You know they're not into that kind of medicine. All they can think about is what these workers might go through, emotionally, if they're ever trapped in there for a few weeks. They wanted the plan to be simpler. More . . . *open*."

"More open." Donald chuckled and reached for his glass of wine. "And what do they mean, trapped for a few weeks?"

Anna shrugged. "You're the elected official. I figure you should know more about this government silliness than I do. I'm just a consultant. I'm just getting paid to lay out the pipes."

She finished her wine, and the waiter returned with Donald's water and to take their orders. Anna raised her eyebrow, a familiar twitch that begged a question: *Are you ready?* It used to mean much more, Donald thought, as he glanced at the menu.

"How about you pick for me?" he finally said, giving up.

Anna ordered, and the waiter jotted down her selections.

"So now they want a single stairwell, huh?" Donald imagined the concrete needed for this, then thought of a spiral design made of metal. Stronger and cheaper. "We can keep the service lift, right? Why couldn't we slide this over and put it in right here?"

He showed her the tablet.

"No. No lifts. Keep everything simple and open. That's what they said."

He didn't like this. Even if the facility would never be used, it should be built as if it might. Why else bother? He'd seen a partial list of supplies they were going to stockpile inside. Lugging them by stair seemed impossible, unless they planned to stock the floors before the prebuilt sections were craned inside. That was more Mick's department. It was one of many reasons he wished his friend were there.

"You know, this is why I didn't go into architecture." He scrolled through their plans and saw all the places where his design had been altered. "I remember the first class we had where we had to go out and meet with mock clients, and they always wanted either the impossible or the downright stupid—or both. And that's when I knew it wasn't for me."

"So you went into politics." Anna laughed.

"Yeah. Good point." Donald smiled, saw the irony. "But hey, it worked for your father."

"My dad went into politics because he didn't know what else to do. He got out of the army, sank too much money into busted venture after busted venture, then figured he'd serve his country some other way."

She studied him a long moment.

"This is *his* legacy, you know." She leaned forward and rested her elbows on the table, bent a graceful finger at the tablet. "This is one of those things they said would never get done, and *he's* doing it."

Donald put the tablet down and leaned back in his chair. "He keeps telling me the same thing," he said. "That this is our legacy, this project. I told him I feel too young to be working on my crowning achievement."

Anna smiled. They both took sips of wine. A basket of bread was dropped off, but neither of them reached for it.

"Speaking of legacies and leaving things behind," Anna asked, "is there a reason you and Helen decided not to have kids?"

Donald placed his glass back on the table. Anna lifted the bottle, but he waved her off. "Well, it's not that we don't want them. We just both went directly from grad school to our careers, you know? We kept thinking—"

"That you'll have forever, right? That you'll always have time. There's no hurry."

"No. It's not that . . ." He rubbed the tablecloth with the pads of his fingers and felt the slick and expensive fabric slide over the other tablecloth hidden below. When they were finished with their meals and out the door, he figured this top layer would be folded back and carried off with their crumbs, a new layer revealed beneath. Like skin. Or the generations. He took a sip of wine, the tannins numbing his lips.

"I think that's it exactly," Anna insisted. "Every generation is waiting longer and longer to pull the trigger. My mom was almost forty when she had me, and that's getting more and more common."

She tucked a loose strand of hair behind her ear.

"Maybe we all think we might be the first generation that simply doesn't die," she continued, "that lives forever." She raised her eyebrows. "Now we all *expect* to hit a hundred and thirty, maybe longer, like it's our right. And so this is my theory—" She leaned closer. Donald was already uncomfortable with where the conversation was going. "Children *used* to be our legacy, right? They were our chance to cheat death, to pass these little bits of ourselves along. But now we hope it can simply be *us*."

"You mean like cloning? That's why it's illegal."

"I don't mean cloning—and besides, just because it's illegal, you and I both know people do it." She took a sip of her wine and nodded at a family in a distant booth. "Look. He has daddy's *everything*."

Donald followed her gaze and watched the kid for a moment, then realized she was just making a point.

"Or how about *my* father?" she asked. "Those nano baths, all the stem-cell vitamins he takes. He truly thinks he's gonna live forever. You know he bought a load of stock in one of those cryo firms years back?"

Donald laughed. "I heard. And I heard it didn't work out so well. Besides, they've been trying stuff like that for years—"

"And they keep getting closer," she said. "All they ever needed was a way to stitch up the cells damaged from the freezing, and now that's not so crazy a dream, right?"

"Well, I hope the people who dream such things get whatever it is they're looking for, but you're wrong about us. Helen and I talk about having kids all the time. I know people having their first kid in their fifties. We've got time."

"Mmm." She finished what was in her glass and reached for the bottle. "You think that," she said. "Everyone thinks they've got all the time left in the world." She leveled her cool gray eyes at him. "But they never stop to ask just how much time that is."

After dinner, they waited under the awning for Anna's car service. Donald declined to share a ride, saying he needed to get back to the office and would just take a cab. The rain hitting the awning had changed, had grown somber.

Her ride pulled up, a shiny black Lincoln, just as Donald's phone began vibrating. He fumbled in his jacket pocket while she leaned in for a hug and kissed his cheek. He felt a flush of heat despite the cool air, saw that it was Mick calling and picked up.

"Hey, you just land or what?" Donald asked.

A pause.

"Land?" Mick sounded confused. There was noise in the background. The driver hurried around the Lincoln to get the door for Anna. "I took a red-eye," Mick said. "My flight got in early this morning. I'm just walking out of a movie and saw your texts. What's up?"

Anna turned and waved. Donald waved back.

"You're getting out of a movie? We just wrapped up our meeting at De'Angelo's. You missed it. Anna said she emailed you like three times."

He glanced up at the car as Anna drew her leg inside. Just a glimpse of her red heels, and then the driver pushed the door shut. The rain on the tinted glass stood out like jewels.

"Huh. I must've missed them. Probably went to junk mail. Not a big deal. We'll catch up. Anyway, I just got out of this trippy movie. If you and I were still in our getting-high days, I would totally force you to blast one with me right now and go to the midnight showing. My mind is totally bent—"

Donald watched the driver hurry around the car to get out of the rain. Anna's window lowered a crack. One last wave, and the car pulled out into light traffic.

"Yeah, well, those days are long gone, my friend," Donald said distractedly. Thunder grumbled in the distance. An umbrella opened with a pop as a gentleman prepared to brave the storm. "Besides," Donald told Mick, "some things are better off back in the past. Where they belong."

18

2110
Silo 1

THE EXERCISE ROOM on level twelve smelled of sweat, of having been used recently. A line of iron weights sat in a jumble in one corner, and a forgotten towel had been left draped over the bar of the bench press, over a hundred pounds of iron discs still in place.

Troy eyed the mess as he worked the last bolt free from the side of the exercise bike. When the cover plate came off, washers and nuts rained down from recessed holes and bounced across the tile. Troy scrambled for them and pushed the hardware into a tidy pile. He peered inside the bike's innards and saw a large cog, its jagged teeth conspicuously empty.

The chain that did all the work hung slack around the cog's axle. Troy was surprised to see it there, would have thought the thing ran on belts. This seemed too fragile. Not a good choice for the length of time it would be expected to serve. It was strange, in fact, to think that this machine was already fifty years old—and that it needed to last centuries more.

He wiped his forehead. Sweat was still beading up from the handful of miles he'd gotten in before the machine broke. Fishing around in the toolbox Jones had loaned him, he found the flathead driver and began levering the chain back onto the cog.

Chains on cogs. *Chains on cogs.* He laughed to himself. Wasn't that the way?

"Excuse me, sir?"

Troy turned to find Jones, his chief mechanic for another week, standing in the gym's doorway.

"Almost done," Troy said. "You need your tools back?"

"Nossir. Dr. Henson is looking for you." He raised his hand, had one of those clunky radios in it.

Troy grabbed an old rag out of the toolbox and wiped the grease from his fingers. It felt good to be working with his hands, getting dirty. It was a welcome distraction, something to do besides checking the blisters in his mouth with a mirror or hanging out in his office or apartment waiting to cry again for no reason.

He left the bike and took the radio from Jones. Troy felt a wave of envy for the older man. He would love to wake up in the morning, put on those denim overalls with the patches on the knees, grab his trusty toolbox and work down a list of repairs. Anything other than sitting around while he waited for something much bigger to break.

Squeezing the button on the side of the radio, he held it up to his mouth.

"This is Troy," he said.

The name sounded strange. In recent weeks, he hadn't liked saying his own name, didn't like hearing it. He wondered what Dr. Henson and the shrinks would say about that.

The radio crackled. "Sir? I hate to disturb you."

"No, that's fine. What is it?" Troy walked back to the exercise bike and grabbed his towel from the handlebars. He wiped his forehead and saw Jones hungrily eyeing the disassembled bike and scattering of tools. When he lifted his brows questioningly, Troy waved his consent.

"We've got a gentleman in our office who's not responding to treatment," Dr. Henson said. "It looks like another deep freeze. I'll need you to sign the waiver."

Jones glanced up from the bike and frowned. Troy rubbed the back of his neck with the towel. He remembered Merriman saying to be careful handing these out. There were plenty of good men who would just as soon sleep through all this mess than serve out their shifts.

"You're sure?" he asked.

"We've tried everything. He's been restrained. Security is taking him down the express right now. Can you meet us down here? You'll have to sign off before he can be put away."

"Sure, sure." Troy rubbed his face with his towel, could smell the detergent in the clean cloth cut through the odor of sweat in the room and the tinge of grease from the open bike. Jones grabbed one of the pedals with his thick hands and gave it a turn. The chain was back on the cog, the machine operational again.

"I'll be right down," Troy said before releasing the button and handing the radio back to the mechanic. Some things were a pleasure to fix. Others weren't.

The express had already passed when Troy reached the lifts; he could see the floor display racing down. He pressed the call button for the other lift and tried to imagine the sad scene playing out below. Whoever it was had his sympathies.

He shook violently, blamed it on the cool air in the hallway and his damp skin. A ping-pong ball clocked back and forth in the rec room around the corner, sneakers squeaking as players chased the next shot. From the same room, a television was playing a movie, the sound of a woman's voice.

Looking down, Troy was self-conscious about his shorts and T-shirt. The only authority he really felt was lent by his coveralls, but there was no time to ride up and change.

The lift beeped and opened, and the conversation inside fell quiet. Troy nodded a greeting, and two men in yellow said hello. The three of them rode in silence for a few levels until the men got off on forty-four, a general living level. Before the doors could close, Troy saw a bright ball skitter across the hallway, two men racing after it. There were shouts and laughter followed by guilty silence when they noticed Troy.

The metal doors squeezed shut on the brief glimpse of lower and more normal lives.

With a shudder, the lift sank deeper into the earth. Troy could feel the dirt and concrete squeezing in from all sides, piling up above. Sweat from nerves mixed with that from his exercise. He was coming out of the other side of the medication, he thought. Every morning, he could feel some semblance of his old self returning, and it lasted longer and longer into the day.

The fifties went by. The lift never stopped on the fifties. Emergency supplies he hoped would never be needed filled the corridors beyond. He remembered parts of the orientation, back when everyone had been awake. He remembered the code names they came up with for everything, the way new labels obscured the past. There was something here nagging him, but he couldn't place it.

Next were the mechanical spaces and the general storerooms, followed by the two levels that housed the reactor. Finally, the most important storage of all: the Legacy, the men and women asleep in their shiny coffins, the survivors from the *before*.

There was a jolt as the lift slowed and the doors chimed open. Troy immediately heard a commotion in the doctor's office, Henson barking commands to his assistant. He hurried down the hallway in his gym attire, sweat cooling on his skin.

When he entered the ready room, he saw an elderly man being restrained on a gurney by two men from Security. It was Hal—Troy recognized him from the cafeteria, remembered speaking with him the first day of his shift and several times since. The doctor and his assistant fumbled through cabinets and drawers, gathering supplies.

"*My name is Carlton!*" Hal roared, his thin arms flailing while unbuckled restraints dangled from the table and swayed from the commotion. Troy assumed they would've had him under control to get him down the lift, wondered if he had broken free when he had come to. Henson and his assistant found what they needed and gathered by the gurney. Hal's eyes widened at the sight of the needle; the fluid inside was a blue the color of open sky.

Dr. Henson looked up and saw Troy standing there in his exercise clothes, paralyzed and watching the scene. Hal screamed once more that his name was Carlton and continued to kick at the air, his heavy boots slamming against the table. The two security men jerked with effort as they held him down.

"A hand?" Henson grunted, teeth clenched as he began to wrestle with one of Hal's arms.

Troy hurried to the gurney and grabbed one of Hal's legs. He stood shoulder to shoulder with the security officers and wrestled with a boot while trying not to get kicked. Hal's legs felt like a bird's inside the baggy overalls, but they kicked like a mule's. One of the officers managed to work a strap across his thighs. Troy leaned his weight on Hal's shin while a second strap was pulled tight.

"What's wrong with him?" he asked. His concerns about himself vanished in the presence of true madness. Or was this where he was heading?

"Meds aren't taking," Henson said.

Or he's not taking them, Troy thought.

The medical assistant used his teeth to pull the cap off the sky-colored syringe. Hal's wrist was pinned. The needle disappeared into his trembling arm, the plunger moving the bright blue liquid into his pale and blotchy flesh.

Troy cringed at the sight of the needle being stabbed into Hal's jerking arm—but the power in the old man's legs faded immediately. Everyone seemed to take deep breaths as he wilted into unconsciousness, his head drifting to the side, one last incomprehensible scream fading into a moan, and then a deep and breathy exhalation.

"What the hell?" Troy wiped his forehead with the back of his arm. He was dripping with sweat, partly from the exertion but mostly from the scene before him, from feeling a man go under like that, sensing the life and will drain from his kicking boots as he was forced asleep. His own body shook with a sudden and violent tremor, gone before he knew it was coming. The doctor glanced up and frowned.

"I apologize for that," Henson said. He glared at the officers, directing his blame.

"We had him no problem," one of them said, shrugging.

Henson turned to Troy. His jowls sagged with disappointment. "I hate to ask you to sign off on this . . ."

Troy wiped his face with the front of his shirt and nodded. The losses had been accounted for—individual losses as well as silos, spares stocked accordingly—but they all stung.

"Of course," he said. This was his job, right? Sign this. Say these words. Follow the script. It was a joke. They were all reading lines from a play none of them could remember. But he was beginning to. He could feel it.

Henson shuffled through a drawer of forms while his assistant unbuckled Hal's overalls. The men from Security asked if they were needed, checked the restraints a final time and were waved away. One of them laughed out loud over something the other said as the sound of their boots faded toward the lift.

Troy, meanwhile, lost himself in Hal's slack face, the slight rise and fall of his old and narrow chest. *Here* was the reward for remembering, he thought. This man had woken up from the routine of the asylum. He hadn't gone crazy; he'd had a sudden bout of *clarity*. He'd cracked open his eyes and seen through the mist.

A clipboard was procured from a peg on the wall, the right form shoved into its metal jaws. Troy was handed a pen. He scratched his name, passed the clipboard back and watched the two doctors work; he wondered if they felt any of what he felt. What if they were all playing the same part? What if each and every one of them was concealing the same doubts, none of them talking because they all felt so completely alone?

"Could you get that one for me?"

The medical assistant was down on his knees, twisting a knob on the base of the table. Troy saw that it was on wheels. The assistant nodded at Troy's feet.

"Of course." Troy crouched down to free the wheel. He was a part in this. It was his signature on the form. It was him twisting the knob that would free the table and allow it to roll down the hall.

With Hal under, the restraints were loosened, his overalls peeled off with care. Troy volunteered with the boots, unknotting the laces and setting them aside. There was no need for a paper gown—his modesty was no longer a concern. An IV needle was inserted and taped down; Troy knew it would plug into the cryopod. He knew what it felt like to have ice crawl through his veins.

They pushed the gurney down the hall and to the reinforced steel doors of the deep freeze. Troy studied the doors. They seemed familiar. He seemed to remember speccing something similar for a project once, but that was for a room full of machines. No—computers.

The keypad on the wall chirped as the doctor entered his code. There was the heavy *thunk* of rods withdrawing into the thick jamb.

"The empties are at the end," Henson said, nodding into the distance.

Rows and rows of gleaming and sealed beds filled the freezing chamber. His eyes fell to the readout screens on the bases of each pod. There were green lights solid with life, no space needed for a pulse or heartbeat, first names only, no way to connect these strangers to their past lives.

Cassie, Catherine, Gabriella, Gretchen.

Made-up names.

Gwynn. Halley. Heather.

Everyone in order. No shifts for them. Nothing for the men to fight over. It would all be done in an instant. Step inside the lifeboat, dream a moment, step out onto dry land.

Another Heather. Duplicates without last names. Troy wondered how that would work. He steered blindly between the rows, the doctor and his assistant chatting about the procedure, when a name caught his peripheral vision and a fierce tremor vibrated through his limbs.

Helen. And another: *Helen.*

Troy lost his grip on the gurney and nearly fell. The wheels squealed to a stop.

"Sir?"

Two Helens. But before him, on a crisp display showing the frozen temps of a deep, deep slumber, another:

Helena.

Troy staggered away from the gurney and Hal's naked body. The echo of the old man's feeble screams came back to him, insisting he was someone named Carlton. Troy ran his hands along the curved top of the cryopod.

She was *here*.

"Sir? We really need to keep moving—"

Troy ignored the doctor. He rubbed the glass shield, the cold inside leaching into his hand.

"Sir—"

A spiderweb of frost covered the glass. He wiped the frozen film of condensation away so he could see inside.

"We need to get this man installed—"

Closed eyes lay inside that cold and dark place. Blades of ice clung to her lashes. It was a familiar face, but this was not his wife.

"Sir!"

Troy stumbled, hands slapping at the cold coffin for balance, bile rising in his throat with remembrance. He heard himself gag, felt his limbs twitch, his knees buckle. He hit the ground between two of the pods and shook violently, spit on his lips, strong memories wrestling with the last residue of the drugs still in his veins.

The two men in white shouted at each other. Footsteps slapped frosted steel and faded toward the distant and heavy door. Inhuman gurgles hit Troy's ears and sounded faintly as though they came from him.

Who was he? What was he doing there? What were any of them doing?

This was not Helen. His name was not Troy.

Footsteps stomped toward him in a hurry. The name was on his tongue as the needle bit his flesh.

Donny.

But that wasn't right, either.

And then the darkness took him, tightening down around anything from his past that his mind deemed too awful to bear.

19

2052
Fulton County, Georgia

Some mash-up of music festival, family reunion, and state fair had descended on the southernmost corner of Fulton County. For the past two weeks, Donald had watched while colorful tents sprang up over a brand-new nuclear containment facility. Fifty state flags flew over fifty depressions in the earth. Stages had been erected, an endless parade of supplies flowing over the rolling hills, golf carts and four-wheelers forming convoys of food, Tupperware containers, baskets of vegetables—some even pulled small enclosed trailers loaded with livestock.

Farmers' markets had been staked out in winding corridors of tents and booths, chickens clucking and pigs snorting, children petting rabbits, dogs on leashes. Owners of the latter guided dozens of breeds through the crowds. Tails wagged happily, and wet noses sniffed the air.

On Georgia's main stage, a local rock band performed a sound check. When they fell quiet to adjust levels, Donald could hear the twangs of bluegrass spilling over from the general direction of North Carolina's delegation. In the opposite direction, someone was giving a speech on Florida's stage while the convoys moved supplies over the rise, and families spread blankets and picnicked on the banks of sweeping bowls. The hills, Donald saw, formed stadium seating, as if they'd been designed for the task.

What he couldn't figure out was where they were putting all those supplies. The tents seemed to keep gobbling them up with no end in sight. The four-wheelers with their little boxed trailers had been rumbling up and down the slopes the entire two weeks he'd been there helping prep for the National Convention.

Mick rumbled to a stop beside him, sitting atop one of the ubiquitous all-terrain vehicles. He grinned at Donald and goosed the throttle while still holding the brakes. The Honda lurched, tires growling against the dirt.

"Wanna go for a ride to South Carolina?" he yelled over the engine. He shifted forward on the seat to make room.

"You got enough gas to make it there?" Donald held his friend's shoulder and stepped on the second set of pegs. He threw his leg over the seat.

"It's just over that hill, you idiot."

Donald resisted the urge to assure Mick he'd been joking. He held on to the metal rack behind him as Mick shifted through the gears. His friend stuck to the dusty highway between the tents until they reached the grass, then angled toward the South Carolina delegation, the tops of the buildings of downtown Atlanta visible off to one side.

Mick turned his head as the Honda climbed the hill. "When is Helen getting here?" he yelled.

Donald leaned forward. He loved the feel of the crisp October morning air. It reminded him of Savannah that time of year, the chill of a sunrise on the beach. He had just been thinking of Helen when Mick asked about her.

"Tomorrow," he shouted. "She's coming on a bus with the delegates from Savannah."

They crested the hill, and Mick throttled back and steered along the ridgeline. They passed a loaded-down ATV heading in the opposite direction. The network of ridges formed an interlocked maze of highways high above each containment facility's sunken bowl.

Peering into the distance, Donald watched the ballet of scooting ATVs weave across the landscape. One day, he imagined, the flat roads on top of the hills would rumble with much larger trucks bearing hazardous waste and radiation warnings.

And yet, seeing the flags waving over the Florida delegation to one side and the Georgia stage to the other, and noting the way the slopes would carry record crowds and afford everyone a perfect view of each stage, Donald couldn't help but think that all the happy accidents had some larger purpose. It was as if the facility had been planned from the beginning to serve the 2052 National Convention, as if it had been built with more than its original goal in mind.

A large blue flag with a white tree and crescent moon swayed lazily over the South Carolina stage. Mick parked the four-wheeler in a sea of other ATVs ringing the large hospitality tent.

Following Mick through the parked vehicles, Donald saw that they were heading toward a smaller tent, which was swallowing a ton of traffic.

"What kind of errand are we on?" he asked.

Not that it mattered. In recent days they'd done a little of everything around the facility: running bags of ice to various state headquarters, meeting with congressmen and senators to see if they needed anything, making sure all the volunteers and delegates were settling into their trailers okay—whatever the Senator needed.

"Oh, we're just taking a little tour," Mick said cryptically. He waved Donald into the small tent where workers were filing through in one direction with their arms loaded and coming out the other side empty-handed.

The inside of the small tent was lit up with floodlights, the ground packed hard from the traffic, the grass matted flat. A concrete ramp led deep into the earth, workers with volunteer badges trudging up one side. Mick jumped into the line heading down.

Donald knew where they were going. He recognized the ramp. He hurried up beside Mick.

"This is one of the rod storage facilities." He couldn't hide the excitement in his voice, didn't even try. He'd been dying to see the other design, either on paper or in person. All he was privy to was his bunker project; the rest of the facility remained shrouded in mystery. "Can we just go *in*?"

As if to answer, Mick started down the ramp, blending with the others.

"I begged for a tour the other day," Donald hissed, "but Thurman spouted all this national security crap—"

Mick laughed. Halfway down the slope, the roof of the tent seemed to recede into the darkness above, and the concrete walls on either side funneled the workers toward gaping steel doors.

"You're not going to see inside one of those other facilities," Mick told him. He put his hand on Donald's back and ushered him through the industrial-looking and familiar entrance chamber. The foot traffic ground to a halt as people took turns entering or leaving through the small hatch ahead. Donald felt turned around.

"Wait." Donald caught glimpses through the hatch. "What the hell? This is my design."

They shuffled forward. Mick made room for the people coming out. He had a hand on Donald's shoulder, guiding him along.

"What're we doing here?" Donald asked. He could've sworn

his own bunker design was in the bowl set aside for Tennessee. Then again, they'd been making so many last-minute changes the past weeks, maybe he'd been mixed up.

"Anna told me you wimped out and skipped the tour of this place."

"That's bullshit." Donald stopped at the oval hatch. He recognized every rivet. "Why would she say that? I was right here. I cut the damn ribbon."

Mick pushed at his back. "Go. You're holding up the line."

"I don't want to go." He waved the people out. The workers behind Mick shifted in place, heavy Tupperware containers in their hands. "I saw the top floor last time," he said. "That was enough."

His friend clasped his neck with one hand and gripped his wrist with the other. As his head was bent forward, Donald had to move along to avoid falling on his face. He tried to reach for the jamb of the interior door, but Mick had his wrist.

"I want you to see what you *built,*" his friend said.

Donald stumbled through to the security office. He and Mick stepped aside to let the congestion they'd caused ease past.

"I've been looking at this damn thing every day for three years," Donald said. He patted his pocket for his pills, wondered if it was too soon to take another. What he didn't tell Mick was that he'd forced himself to envision his design being *above* ground the entire time he'd worked on it, more a skyscraper than a buried straw. No way could he share that with his best friend, tell him how terrified he felt right then with no more than ten meters of dirt and concrete over his head. He seriously doubted Anna had used the phrase "wimped out," but that's exactly what he had done after cutting the ribbon. While the Senator led dignitaries through the complex, Donald had hurried up to find a patch of grass with nothing but bright blue sky above.

"This is really fucking important," Mick said. He snapped his fingers in front of Donald. Two lines of workers filed past. Beyond them, a man sat in a small cubicle, a brush in one hand and a can of paint in the other. He was applying a coat of flat gray to a set of steel bars. A technician behind him worked to wire some kind of massive screen into the wall. Not everything looked as if it was being finished precisely the way Donald had drawn it.

"Donny, listen to me. I'm serious. Today is the last day we can have this talk, okay? I need you to see what you built." Mick's permanent and mischievous grin was gone, his eyebrows tilted. He looked, if anything, sad. "Will you please come inside?"

Taking a full breath and fighting the urge to rush out to the hills and fresh air, away from the stifling crowds, Donald found himself agreeing. It was the look on Mick's face, the feeling that he needed to tell Donald about a loved one who had just passed away, something deathly serious.

Mick patted his shoulder in gratitude as Donald nodded.

"This way."

Mick led him toward the central shaft. They passed through the cafeteria, which was being used. It made sense. Workers sat at tables and ate off plastic trays, taking a break. The smell of food drifted from the kitchens beyond. Donald laughed. He never thought they'd be used at all. Again, it felt as though the convention had given this place a purpose. It made him happy. He thought of the entire complex devoid of life one day, all the workers milling about outside storing away nuclear rods, while this massive building that would have touched the clouds had it been aboveground would sit perfectly empty.

Down a short hallway, the tile gave way to metal grating, and a broad cylinder dove straight through the heart of the facility. Anna had been right. It really was worth seeing.

They reached the railing of the central shaft, and Donald

paused to peer over. The vast height made him forget for a moment that he was underground. On the other side of the landing, a conveyor lift rattled on its gears while a never-ending series of flat loading trays spun empty over the top. It reminded Donald of the buckets on a waterwheel. The trays flopped over before descending back down through the building.

The men and women from outside deposited each of their containers onto one of the empty trays before turning and heading back out. Donald looked for Mick and saw him disappearing down the staircase.

He hurried after, his fear of being buried alive chasing him.

"Hey!"

His shoes slapped the freshly painted stairs, the diamond plating keeping him from skidding off in his haste. He caught up with Mick as they made a full circuit of the thick inner post. Tupperware containers full of emergency supplies—supplies Donald figured would rot, unused—drifted eerily downward beyond the rail.

"I don't want to go any deeper than this," he insisted.

"Two levels down," Mick called back up. "C'mon, man, I want you to see."

Donald numbly obeyed. It would've been worse to make his way out alone.

At the first landing they came to, a worker stood by the conveyor with some type of gun. As the next container passed by, he shot its side with a flash of red, the scanner buzzing. The worker leaned on the railing, waiting for the next one while the container continued its ratcheting plummet.

"Did I miss something?" Donald asked. "Are we still fighting deadlines? What's with all the supplies?"

Mick shook his head. "Deadlines, lifelines," he said.

At least, that's what Donald thought his friend said. Mick seemed lost in thought.

They spiraled down another level to the next landing, ten more meters of reinforced concrete between, thirty-three feet of wasted depth. Donald knew the floor. And not just from the plans he'd drawn. He and Mick had toured a floor like this in the factory where it had been built.

"I've been here before," he told Mick.

Mick nodded. He waved Donald down the hallway until it made a turn. Mick picked one of the doors, seemingly at random, and opened it for Donald. Most of the floors had been prefabbed and furnished before being craned into place. If that wasn't the exact floor the two of them had toured, it had been one of the many just like it.

Once Donald was inside, Mick flicked on the apartment's overhead lights and closed the door. Donald was surprised to see that the bed was made. Stacks of linen were piled up in a chair. Mick grabbed the linens and moved them to the floor. He sat down and nodded to the foot of the bed.

Donald ignored him and poked his head into the small bathroom. "This is actually pretty cool to see," he told his friend. He reached out and turned the knob on the sink, expecting nothing. When clear water gurgled out, he found himself laughing.

"I knew you'd dig it once you saw it," Mick said quietly.

Donald caught sight of himself in the mirror, the joy still on his face. He tended to forget how the corners of his eyes wrinkled up when he smiled. He touched his hair, sprinkles of gray even though he had another five years before he was over that proverbial hill. His job was aging him prematurely. He had feared it might.

"Amazing that we built this, huh?" Mick asked. Donald turned and joined his friend in the tight quarters. He wondered if it was the work they'd been elected to perform that had aged them both or if it had been this one project, this all-consuming build.

"I appreciate you forcing me down here." He almost added that he would love to see the rest, but he figured that would be pushing it. Besides, the crews back in the Georgia tents were probably looking for them already.

"Look," Mick said, "there's something I want to tell you."

Donald looked at his friend, who seemed to be searching for the words. He glanced at the door. Mick was silent. Donald finally relented and sat at the foot of the bed.

"What's up?" he asked.

But he thought he knew. The Senator had included Mick in his other project, the one that had driven Donald to seek help from the doctor. Donald thought of the thick book he had largely memorized. Mick had done the same. And he'd brought him there not just to let him see what they'd accomplished, but to find a spot of perfect privacy, a place where secrets could be divulged. He patted his pocket where he kept his pills, the ones that kept his thoughts from running off to dangerous places.

"Hey," Donald said, "I don't want you saying anything you're not supposed to—"

Mick looked up, eyes wide with surprise.

"You don't need to say *anything,* Mick. Assume I know what *you* know."

Mick shook his head sadly. "You don't," he said.

"Well, assume it anyway. I don't want to know anything."

"I *need* you to know."

"I'd rather not—"

"It's not a secret, man. It's just . . . I want you to know that I love you like a brother. I always have."

The two of them sat in silence. Donald glanced at the door. The moment was uncomfortable, but it somehow filled his heart to hear Mick say it.

"Look—" Donald started.

"I know I'm always hard on you," Mick said. "And hell, I'm

sorry. I really do look up to you. And Helen." Mick turned to the side and scratched at his cheek. "I'm happy for the two of you."

Donald reached across the narrow space and squeezed his friend's arm.

"You're a good friend, Mick. I'm glad we've had this time together, the last few years, running for office, building this—"

Mick nodded. "Yeah. Me too. But listen, I didn't bring you down here to get all sappy like this." He reached for his cheek again, and Donald saw that he was wiping at his eyes. "I had a talk with Thurman last night. He—a few months ago, he offered me a spot on a team, a top team, and I told him last night that I'd rather you take it."

"What? A committee?" Donald couldn't imagine his friend giving up an appointment, *any* kind of appointment. "Which one?"

Mick shook his head. "No, something else."

"What?" Donald asked.

"Look," Mick said, "when you find out about it, and you understand what's going on, I want you to think of me right here." Mick glanced around the room. There were a few breaths of complete silence punctuated by drips of water from the bathroom sink. "If I could choose to be anywhere, *anywhere* in the coming years, it would be right down here with the first group."

"Okay. Yeah, I'm not sure what you mean—"

"You will. Just remember this, all right? That I love you like a brother and that everything happens for a reason. I wouldn't have wanted it any other way. For you or for Helen."

"Okay." Donald smiled. He couldn't tell if Mick was fucking with him or if his friend had consumed a few too many Bloody Marys from the hospitality tent that morning.

"All right." Mick stood abruptly. He certainly moved as though he were sober. "Let's get the hell out of here. This place gives me the creeps."

Mick threw open the door and flicked off the lights.

"Wimping out, eh?" Donald called after his friend.

Mick shook his head and the two of them headed back down the hallway. Behind them, they left the small, random apartment in darkness, its little sink dripping. And Donald tried to sort out how he'd gotten turned around, how the Tennessee tent where he'd cut the ribbon had become the one from South Carolina. He almost had it, his subconscious flashing to a delivery of goods, to fifty times more fiber optic than needed, but the connection was lost.

Meanwhile, containers loaded with supplies rumbled down the mammoth shaft. And empty trays rattled up.

20

2110
Silo 1

TROY WOKE UP in a fog, groggy and disoriented, his head pulsing. He lifted his hands and groped in front of his face, expecting to find the chill of icy glass, the press of domed steel, the doom of a deep freeze. His hands found only empty air. The clock beside his bed showed it was a little after three in the morning.

He sat up and saw that he had on a pair of gym shorts. He couldn't remember changing the night before, couldn't remember going to bed. Planting his feet on the floor, he rested his elbows on his knees, sunk his head into his palms and sat there a moment. His entire body ached.

After a few minutes slipped by, he dressed himself in the dark, buckling up his coveralls. Light would be bad for his headache. It wasn't a theory he needed to test.

The hallway outside was still dimmed for the evening, just bright enough to grope one's way to the shared bathrooms. Troy stole down the hall and headed for the lift.

He hit the "up" button, hesitated, wasn't sure if that was

right. Something tugged at him. He pressed the "down" button as well.

It was too early to go into his office, not unless he wanted to fiddle on the computer. He wasn't hungry, but he could go up and watch the sun rise. The late shift would be up there drinking coffee. Or he could hit the rec room and go for a jog. That would mean going back to his room to change.

The lift arrived with a beep while he was still deciding. Both lights went off, the up and the down. He could take the lift anywhere.

Troy stepped inside. He didn't know where he wanted to go.

The lift closed. It waited on him patiently. Eventually, he figured, it would whisk off to heed some other call, pick up a person with purpose, someone with a destination. He could stand there and do nothing and let that other soul decide.

Running his finger across the buttons, he tried to remember what was on each level. There was a lot he'd memorized, but not everything he knew felt accessible. He had a sudden urge to head for one of the lounges and watch TV, just let the hours slide past until he finally needed to be somewhere. This was how the shift was supposed to go. Waiting and then doing. Sleeping and then waiting. Make it to dinner and then make it to bed. The end was always in sight. There was nothing to rebel against, just a routine.

The lift shook into motion. Troy jerked his hand away from the buttons and took a step back. It didn't show where he was going but it felt as if it had started downwards.

Only a few floors passed before the lift lurched to a halt. The doors opened on a lower apartment level. A familiar face from the cafeteria, a man in reactor red, smiled as he stepped inside.

"Morning," he said.

Troy nodded.

The man turned and jabbed one of the lower buttons, one of

the reactor levels. He studied the otherwise blank array, turned and gave Troy a quizzical look.

"You feeling okay, sir?"

"Hmm? Oh, yeah."

Troy leaned forward and pressed sixty-eight. The man's concern for his well-being must've had him thinking of the doctor, even though Henson wouldn't be on shift for several hours. But there was something else nagging him, something he felt he needed to see, a dream slipping away.

"Must not have taken the first time," he explained, glancing at the button.

"Mmm."

The silence lasted one or two floors.

"How much longer you got?" the reactor mechanic asked.

"Me? Just another couple of weeks. How about you?"

"I just got on a week ago. But this is my second shift."

"Oh?"

The lights counted downward in floors but upward in number. Troy didn't like this; he felt as if the lowest level should be level one. They should count *up*.

"Is the second shift easier?" he asked. The question came out unbidden. It was as though the part of him dying to know was more awake than the part of him praying for silence.

The mechanic considered this.

"I wouldn't say it's easier. How about... less uncomfortable?" He laughed quietly. Troy felt their arrival in his knees, gravity tugging on him. The doors beeped open.

"Have a good one," the mechanic said. They hadn't shared their names. "In case I don't see you again."

Troy raised his palm. "Next time," he said. The man stepped out, and the doors winked shut on the halls to the power plant. With a hum, the lift continued its descent.

The doors dinged on the medical level. Troy stepped out and

heard voices down the corridor. He crept quietly across the tile, and the voices became louder. One was female. It wasn't a conversation; it must have been an old movie. Troy peeked into the main office and saw a man lounging on a gurney, his back turned, a TV set up in the corner. Troy slunk past so as not to disturb him.

The hallway split in two directions. He imagined the layout, could picture the pie-shaped storerooms, the rows of deep-freeze coffins, the tubes and pipes that led from the walls to the bases, from the bases into the people inside.

He stopped at one of the heavy doors and tried his code. The light changed from red to green. He dropped his hand, didn't need to enter this room, didn't feel the urge, just wanted to see if it would work. The urge was elsewhere.

He meandered down the hall past a few more doors. Wasn't he just here? Had he ever left? His arm throbbed. He rolled back his sleeve and saw a spot of blood, a circle of redness around a pinprick scab.

If something bad had happened, he couldn't remember. That part of him had been choked off.

He tried his code on this other pad, this other door, and waited for the light to turn green. This time, he pushed the button that opened the door. He didn't know what it was, but there was something inside that he needed to see.

21

2052
Fulton County, Georgia

LIGHT RAINS ON the morning of the convention left the man-made hills soggy, the new grass slick, but did little to erode the general festivities. Parking lots had been emptied of construction vehicles and mud-caked pickups. Now they held hundreds of idling buses and a handful of sleek black limos, the latter splattered with mud.

The lot where temporary trailers had served as offices and living quarters for construction crews had been handed over to the staffers, volunteers, delegates, and dignitaries who had labored for weeks to bring that day to fruition. The area was dotted with welcoming tents that served as the headquarters for the event coordinators. Throngs of new arrivals filed from the buses and made their way through the CAD-FAC's security station. Massive fences bristled with coils of razor wire that seemed outsized and ridiculous for the convention but made sense for the storing of nuclear material. These barriers and gates held at bay an odd union of protestors: those on the Right who disagreed with the facility's current purpose and those on the Left who feared its future one.

There had never been a National Convention with such energy, such crowds. Downtown Atlanta loomed far beyond the treetops, but the city seemed far removed from the sudden bustle in lower Fulton County.

Donald shivered beneath his umbrella at the top of a knoll and gazed out over the sea of people gathering across the hills, heading toward whichever stage flew their state's flag, umbrellas bobbing and jostling like water bugs.

Somewhere, a marching band blared a practice tune and stomped another hill into mud. There was a sense in the air that the world was about to change—a woman was about to win nomination for president, only the second such nomination in Donald's lifetime. And if the pollsters could be believed, this one had more than a chance. Unless the war in Iran took a sudden turn, a milestone would be reached, a final glass ceiling shattered. And it would happen right there in those grand divots in the earth.

More buses churned through the lot and let off their passengers, and Donald pulled out his phone and checked the time. He still had an error icon, the network choked to death from the overwhelming demand. He was surprised, with so much other careful planning, that the committee hadn't accounted for this and erected a temporary tower or two.

"Congressman Keene?"

Donald startled and turned to find Anna walking along the ridgeline toward him. He glanced down at the Georgia stage but didn't see her ride. He was surprised she would just walk up. And yet, it was like her to do things the difficult way.

"I couldn't tell if that was you," she said, smiling. "Everyone has the same umbrella."

"Yeah, it's me." He took a deep breath, found his chest still felt constricted with nerves whenever he saw her, as though any conversation could get him into trouble.

Anna stepped close as if she expected him to share his umbrella. He moved it to his other hand to give her more space, the drizzle peppering his exposed arm. He scanned the bus lot and searched impossibly for any sign of Helen. She should've been there by now.

"This is gonna be a mess," Anna said.

"It's supposed to clear up."

Someone on the North Carolina stage checked her microphone with a squawk of feedback.

"We'll see," Anna said. She wrapped her coat tighter against the early morning breeze. "Isn't Helen coming?"

"Yeah. Senator Thurman insisted. She's not gonna be happy when she sees how many people are here. She hates crowds. She won't be happy about the mud, either."

Anna laughed. "I wouldn't worry about the conditions of the grounds after this."

Donald thought about all the loads of radioactive waste that would be trucked in. "Yeah." He saw her point.

He peered down the hill again at the Georgia stage. It would be the site of the first national gathering of delegates later that day, all the most important people under one tent. Behind the stage and among the smoking food tents, the only sign of the underground containment facility was a small concrete tower rising up from the ground, a bristle of antennae sprouting from the top. Donald thought of how much work it would take to haul away all the flags and soaked buntings before the first of the spent fuel rods could finally be brought in.

"It's weird to think of a few thousand people from the state of Tennessee stomping around on top of something *we* designed," Anna said. Her arm brushed against Donald's. He stood perfectly still, wondering if it had been an accident. "I wish you'd seen more of the place."

Donald shivered, more from fighting to remain still than

from the cold and moist morning air. He hadn't told anyone about Mick's tour the day before. It felt too sacred. He would probably tell Helen about it and no one else. "It's crazy how much time went into something nobody will ever use," he said.

Anna murmured her agreement. Her arm was still touching his. There was still no sign of Helen. Donald felt irrationally that he would somehow spot her among the crowds. He usually could. He remembered the high balcony of a place they'd stayed in during their honeymoon in Hawaii. Even from up there, he could spot her taking her early morning walks along the foam line, looking for seashells. There might be a few hundred strollers out on the beach, and yet his eyes would be drawn immediately to her.

"I guess the only way they were going to build any of this was if we gave them the right kind of insurance," Donald said, repeating what the Senator had told him. But it still didn't feel right.

"People want to feel safe," Anna said. "They want to know, if the worst happens, they'll have someone—*something*—to fall back on."

Again, Anna rested against his arm. Definitely not an accident. Donald felt himself withdraw and knew she would sense it too.

"I was really hoping to tour one of the *other* bunkers," he said, changing the subject. "It'd be interesting to see what the other teams came up with. Apparently, though, I don't have the clearance."

Anna laughed. "I tried the same thing. I'm dying to see our competition. But I can understand them being sensitive. There's a lot of eyes on this joint." She leaned into him once more, ignoring the space he'd made.

"Don't you feel that?" she asked. "Like there's some huge bull's-eye over this place? I mean, even with the fences and walls down there, you can bet the whole world is gonna be keeping an eye on what happens here."

Donald nodded. He knew she wasn't talking about the convention but about what the place would be used for afterward.

"Hey, it looks like I've got to get back down there."

He turned to follow her gaze, saw Senator Thurman climbing the hill on foot, a massive black golf umbrella shedding the rain around him. The man seemed impervious to the mud and grime in a way no one else was, the same way he seemed oblivious to the passing of time.

Anna reached over and squeezed Donald's arm. "Congrats again. It was fun working together on this."

"Same," he said. "We make a good team."

She smiled. He wondered for a moment if she would lean over and kiss his cheek. It would feel natural in that moment. But it came and went. Anna left his protective cover and headed off toward the Senator.

Thurman lifted his umbrella, kissed his daughter's cheek and watched her descend the hill. He hiked up to join Donald.

They stood beside each other for a pause, the rain dripping off their umbrellas with a muted patter.

"Sir," Donald finally said. He felt newly comfortable in the man's presence. The last two weeks had been like summer camp, where being around the same people almost every hour of the day brought a level of familiarity and intimacy that knowing them casually for years could never match. There was something about forced confinement that brought people together. Beyond the obvious, physical ways.

"Damn rain," was Thurman's reply.

"You can't control everything," Donald said.

The Senator grunted as if he disagreed. "Helen not here yet?"

"No, sir." Donald fished in his pocket and felt for his phone. "I'll message her again in a bit. Not sure if my texts are getting through or not—the networks are absolutely crushed. I'm pretty sure this many people descending on this corner of the county is unprecedented."

"Well, this will be an unprecedented day," Thurman said. "Nothing like it ever before."

"It was mostly your doing, sir. I mean, not just building this place, but choosing not to run. This country could've been yours for the taking this year."

The Senator laughed. "That's true most years, Donny. But I've learned to set my sights higher than that."

Donald shivered again. He couldn't remember the last time the Senator had called him that. Maybe that first meeting in his office, more than two years ago? The old man seemed unusually tense.

"When Helen gets here, I want you to come down to the state tent and see me, okay?"

Donald pulled out his phone and checked the time. "You know I'm supposed to be at the Tennessee tent in an hour, right?"

"There's been a change of plans. I want you to stay close to home. Mick is going to cover for you over there, which means I need you with me."

"Are you sure? I was supposed to meet with—"

"I know. This is a good thing, trust me. I want you and Helen near the Georgia stage with me. And look—"

The Senator turned to face him. Donald peeled his eyes away from the last of the unloading buses. The rain had picked up a little.

"You've contributed more to this day than you know," Thurman said.

"Sir?"

"The world is going to change today, Donny."

Donald wondered if the Senator had been skipping his nano-bath treatments. His eyes seemed dilated and focused on something in the distance. He appeared older somehow.

"I'm not sure I understand—"

"You will. Oh, and a surprise visitor is coming. She should be here any moment." He smiled. "The national anthem starts at noon. There'll be a flyover from the 141st after that. I want you nearby when that happens."

Donald nodded. He had learned when to stop asking questions and just do what the Senator expected of him.

"Yes, sir," he said, shivering against the cold.

Senator Thurman left. Turning his back to the stage, Donald scanned the last of the buses and wondered where in the world Helen was.

22

2110
Silo 1

TROY WALKED DOWN the line of cryopods as if he knew where he was going. It was just like the way his hand had drifted to the button that had brought him to that floor. There were made-up names on each of the panels. He knew this somehow. He remembered coming up with his name. It had something to do with his wife, some way to honor her, or some kind of secret and forbidden link so that he might one day remember.

That all lay in the past, deep in the mist, a dream forgotten. Before his shift there had been an orientation. There were familiar books to read and reread. That's when he had chosen his name.

A bitter explosion on his tongue brought him to a halt. It was the taste of a pill dissolving. Troy stuck out his tongue and scraped it with his fingers, but there was nothing there. He could feel the ulcers on his gums against his teeth but couldn't recall how they'd formed.

He walked on. Something wasn't right. These memories weren't supposed to return. He pictured himself on a gurney, screaming, someone strapping him down, stabbing him with needles. That wasn't him. He was holding that man's boots.

Troy stopped at one of the pods and checked the name. *Helen.* His gut lurched and groped for its medicine. He didn't want to remember. That was a secret ingredient: the *not wanting to remember.* Those were the parts that slipped away, the parts the drugs wrapped their tentacles around and pulled beneath the surface. But now, there was some small part of him that was dying to know. It was a nagging doubt, a feeling of having left some important piece of himself behind. It was willing to drown the rest of him for the answers.

The frost on the glass wiped away with a squeak. He didn't recognize the person inside and moved on to the next pod, a scene from before orientation coming back to him.

Troy recalled halls packed with people crying, grown men sobbing, pills that dried their eyes. Fearsome clouds rose on a video screen. Women were put away for safety. Like a lifeboat, women and children first.

Troy remembered. It wasn't an accident. He remembered a talk in another pod, a bigger pod with another man there, a talk about the coming end of the world, about making *room,* about ending it all before it ended on its own.

A controlled explosion. Bombs were sometimes used to put out fires.

He wiped another frost-covered sheet of glass. The sleeping form in the next chamber had eyelashes that glittered with ice. She was a stranger. He moved on, but it was coming back to him. His arm throbbed. The shakes were gone.

Troy remembered a calamity, but it was all for show. The real threat was in the air, invisible. The bombs were to get people to move, to make them afraid, to get them crying and forgetting. People had spilled like marbles down a bowl. Not a bowl—a *funnel*. Someone explained why they were spared. He remembered a white fog, walking through a white fog. The death was already in them. Troy remembered a taste on his tongue, metallic.

The ice on the next pane was already disturbed, had been wiped away by someone recently. Beads of condensation stood like tiny lenses warping the light. He rubbed the glass and knew what had happened. He saw the woman inside with the auburn hair that she sometimes kept in a bun. This was not his wife. This was someone who wanted that, wanted *him* like that.

"Hello?"

Troy turned toward the voice. The night-shift doctor was heading his way, weaving between the pods, coming for him. Troy clasped his hand over the soreness on his arm. He didn't want to be taken again. They couldn't make him forget.

"Sir, you shouldn't be in here."

Troy didn't answer. The doctor stopped at the foot of the pod. Inside, a woman who wasn't his wife lay in slumber. Wasn't his wife, but had wanted to be.

"Why don't you come with me?" the doctor asked.

"I'd like to stay," Troy said. He felt a bizarre calmness. All the pain had been ripped away. This was more forceful than forgetting. He remembered everything. His soul had been cut free.

"I can't have you in here, sir. Come with me. You'll freeze in here."

Troy glanced down. He had forgotten to put on shoes. He curled his toes away from the floor . . . then allowed them to settle.

"Sir? Please." The young doctor gestured down the aisle. Troy let go of his arm and saw that things were handled as needed. No kicking meant no straps. No shivering meant no needles.

He heard the squeak of hurrying boots out in the hallway. A large man from Security appeared by the open vault door, visibly winded. Troy caught a glimpse of the doctor waving the man down. They were trying not to scare him. They didn't know that he couldn't be scared anymore.

"You'll put me away for good," Troy said. It was something between a statement and a question. It was a realization. He wondered if he was like Hal—like *Carlton*—if the pills would never take again. He glanced toward the far end of the room, knew the empties were kept there. This was where he would be buried.

"Nice and easy," the doctor said.

He led Troy to the exit; he would embalm him with that bright blue sky. The pods slid by as the two of them walked in silence.

The man from Security took deep breaths as he filled the doorway, his great chest heaving against his overalls. There was a squeak from more boots as he was joined by another. Troy saw that his shift was over. Two weeks to go. He'd nearly made it.

The doctor waved the large men out of the way, seemed to hope they wouldn't be needed. They took up positions to either side, seemed to think otherwise. Troy was led down the hallway, hope guiding him and fear flanking him.

"You *know,* don't you?" Troy asked the doctor, turning to study him. "You remember everything."

The doctor didn't turn to face him. He simply nodded.

This felt like a betrayal. It wasn't fair.

"Why are you allowed to remember?" Troy asked. He wanted to know why those dispensing the medicine didn't have to take some of their own.

The doctor waved him into his office. His assistant was there, wearing a sleepshirt and hanging an IV bag bulging with blue liquid.

"Some of us remember," the doctor said, "because we know this isn't a bad thing we've done." He frowned as he helped Troy onto the gurney. He seemed truly sad about Troy's condition. "We're doing good work here," he said. "We're saving the world, not ending it. And the medicine only touches our regrets." He glanced up. "Some of us don't have any."

The doorway was stuffed with security. It overflowed. The assistant unbuckled Troy's overalls. Troy watched numbly.

"It would take a different kind of drug to touch what *we* know," the doctor said. He pulled a clipboard from the wall. A sheet of paper was fed into its jaws. There was a pause, and then a pen was pressed into Troy's palm.

Troy laughed as he signed off on himself.

"Then why me?" he asked. "Why am I here?" He had always wanted to ask this of someone who might know. These were the prayers of youth, but now with a chance of some reply.

The doctor smiled and took the clipboard. He was probably in his late twenties, had come on shift just a few weeks ago. Troy was a few years shy of forty. And yet this man had all the wisdom, all the answers.

"It's good to have people like you in charge," the doctor said, and he seemed to genuinely mean it. The clipboard was returned to its peg. One of the security men yawned and covered his mouth. Troy watched as his coveralls were unsnapped and flopped to his waist. A fingernail makes a distinctive click when it taps against a needle.

"I'd like to think about this," Troy said. He felt a sudden panic wash over him. He knew this needed to happen, but wanted just a few more minutes alone with his thoughts, to savor this brief bout of comprehension. He wanted to sleep, certainly, but not quite yet.

The men in the doorway stirred as they sensed Troy's doubts, could see the fear in his eyes.

"I wish there was some other way," the doctor said sadly. He rested a hand on Troy's shoulder, guided him back against the table. The men from Security stepped closer.

There was a prick on his arm, a deep bite without warning. He looked down and saw the silver barb slide into his vein, the bright blue liquid pumped inside.

"I don't want—" he said.

There were hands on his shins, his knees, weight on his shoulders. The heaviness against his chest was from something else.

A burning rush flowed through his body, chased immediately by numbness. They weren't putting him to sleep. *They were killing him.* Troy knew this as suddenly and swiftly as he knew that his wife was dead, that some other person had tried to take her place. He would go into a coffin *for good* this time. And all the dirt piled over his head would finally serve some purpose.

Darkness squeezed in around his vision. He closed his eyes, tried to yell for it to stop, but nothing came out. He wanted to kick and fight it, but more than mere hands had a hold of him now. He was sinking.

His last thoughts were of his beautiful wife, but the thoughts made little sense—they were the dream world invading.

She's in Tennessee, he thought. He didn't know why or how he knew this. But she was there—and waiting. She was already dead and had a spot hollowed out by her side just for him.

Troy had just one more question, one name he hoped to grope for and seize before he went under, some part of himself to take with him to those depths. It was on the tip of his tongue like a bitter pill, so close that he could taste it—

But then he forgot.

23

2052
Fulton County, Georgia

THE RAIN FINALLY let up just as warring announcements and battling tunes filled the air above the teeming hills. While the main stage was prepped for the evening's gala, it sounded to Donald as though the real action was taking place at all the other states. Opening bands ripped into their sets as the buzz of ATVs subsided to a trickle.

It felt vaguely claustrophobic to be down in the bottom of the bowl by the Georgia stage. Donald sensed an unquenchable urge for height, to be up on the ridge where he could see what was going on. It left him imagining the sight of thousands of guests arrayed across each of the hills, picturing the political fervor in the air everywhere, the gelling of like-minded families celebrating the promise of something new.

As much as Donald wanted to celebrate new beginnings with them, he was mostly looking forward to the *end*. He couldn't wait for the convention to wrap up. The weeks had worn on him. He was looking forward to a real bed, to some privacy, his computer, reliable phone service, dinners out and, most of all: time alone with his wife.

Fishing his phone out of his pocket, he checked his messages for the umpteenth time. They were minutes away from the anthem, and then the flyover from the 141st. He had also heard someone mention fireworks to start the convention off with a bang.

His phone showed that the last half-dozen messages still hadn't gone through. The network was clogged, an error message popping up that he'd never seen before. At least some of the earlier ones looked as if they'd been sent. He scanned the wet banks for her, hoping to see her making her way down, a smile he could spot from any distance.

Someone stepped up beside him. Donald looked away from the hills to see that Anna had joined him by the stage.

"Here we go," she said quietly, scanning the crowd.

She looked and sounded nervous. Maybe it was for her father, who had done so much to arrange the main stage and make sure everyone was in the right place. Glancing back, he saw that people were taking their seats, chairs wiped down from the morning drizzle, not nearly as many people as it seemed before. They must be either working in the tents or off to the other stages. This was the quiet brewing before the—

"*There* she is."

Anna waved her arms. Donald felt his heart swell up into his neck as he turned and followed Anna's gaze. His relief was mixed with the panic of Helen seeing him there with her, the two of them waiting side by side.

Shuffling down the hill was certainly someone familiar. A young woman in a pressed blue uniform, a hat tucked under one arm, a dark head of hair wrapped up in a crisp bun.

"Charlotte?" Donald shielded his eyes from the glare of the

noonday sun filtering through wispy clouds. He gaped in disbelief. All other events and concerns melted away as his sister spotted them and waved back.

"She sure as hell cut this close," Anna muttered.

Donald hurried over to his four-wheeler and turned the key. He hit the ignition, gave the handle some gas, and raced across the wet grass to meet her.

Charlotte beamed as he hit the brakes at the base of the hill. He killed the engine.

"Hey, Donny."

His sister leaned in to him before he could dismount. She threw her arms around his neck and squeezed.

He returned her embrace, worried about denting the creases of her neat uniform. "What the hell are you doing here?" he asked.

She let go and took a step back, smoothed the front of her shirt. The air force dress hat disappeared back under her arm, every motion like an ingrained and precise habit.

"Are you surprised?" she asked. "I thought the Senator would've let it slip by now."

"Hell, no. Well, he said something about a visitor but not who. I thought you were in Iran. Did he swing this?"

She nodded, and Donald felt his cheeks cramping from smiling so hard. Every time he saw her, there came a relief from discovering that she was still the same person. The sharp chin and splash of freckles across her nose, the shine in her eyes that had not yet dulled from the horrible things she'd seen. She had just turned thirty, had been half a world away with no family on her birthday, but she was frozen in his mind as the young teen who had enlisted.

"I think I'm supposed to be on the stage for this thing tonight," she said.

"Of course." Donald smiled. "I'm sure they'll want you on camera. You know, to show support for the troops."

Charlotte frowned. "Oh, God, I'm one of *those* people, aren't I?"

He laughed. "I'm sure they'll have someone from the army, navy, and marines there with you."

"Oh, God. And I'm the *girl.*"

They laughed together, and one of the bands beyond the hills finished their set. Donald scooted forward and told his sister to hop on, his chest suddenly less constricted. There had been a shift in the weather, these breaking clouds, the quieting stages, and now the arrival of family.

He cranked the engine and raced through the least muddy path on the way back to the stage, his sister holding on tight behind him. They pulled up beside Anna, his sister hopping off and into her arms. While they chatted, Donald killed the ignition and checked his phone for messages. Finally, one had gotten through.

Helen: In Tennessee. where r u?

There was a jarring moment as his brain tried to make sense of the message. It was from Helen. What the hell was she doing in *Tennessee*?

Another stage fell silent. It took only a heartbeat or two for Donald to realize that she wasn't hundreds of miles away. She was just over the hill. None of his messages about meeting at the Georgia stage had gone through.

"Hey, I'll be right back."

He cranked the ATV. Anna grabbed his wrist.

"Where are you going?" she asked.

He smiled. "Tennessee. Helen just texted me."

Anna glanced up at the clouds. His sister was inspecting her hat. On the stage, a young girl was being ushered up to the mic. She was flanked by a color guard, and the seats facing the stage were filling up, necks stretched with anticipation.

Before he could react or put the ATV in gear, Anna reached across, twisted the key and pulled it out of the ignition.

"Not now," she said.

Donald felt a flash of rage. He reached for her hands, for the key, but it disappeared behind her back.

"Wait," she hissed.

Charlotte had turned toward the stage. Senator Thurman stood with a microphone in hand, the young girl, maybe sixteen, beside him. The hills had grown deathly quiet. Donald realized what a racket the ATV had been making. The girl was about to sing.

"Ladies and gentlemen, fellow Democrats—"

There was a pause. Donald got off the four-wheeler, took a last glance at his phone, then tucked it away.

"—and our handful of Independents."

Laughter from the crowd. Donald set off at a jog across the flat at the bottom of the bowl. His shoes squished in the wet grass and the thin layer of mud. Senator Thurman's voice continued to roar through the microphone:

"Today is the dawn of a new era, a new time."

He was out of shape, his shoes growing heavy with mud.

"As we gather in this place of future independence—"

By the time the ground sloped upward, he was already winded.

"—I'm reminded of the words from one of our enemies. A Republican."

Distant laughter, but Donald paid no heed. He was concentrating on the climb.

"It was Ronald Reagan who once said that freedom must be fought for, that peace must be earned. As we listen to this anthem, written a long time ago as bombs dropped and a new country was forged, let's consider the price paid for our freedom and ask ourselves if any cost could be too great to ensure that these liberties never slip away."

A third of the way up—and Donald had to stop and catch his breath. His calves were going to give out before his lungs did. He regretted puttering around on the ATV the past weeks while some of the others slogged it on foot. He promised himself he'd get in better shape.

He started back up the hill, and a voice like ringing crystal filled the bowl. It spilled in synchrony over the looming rise. He turned toward the stage below where the national anthem was being sung by the sweetest of young voices—

And he saw Anna hurrying up the hill after him, a scowl of worry on her face.

Donald knew he was in trouble. He wondered if he was dishonoring the anthem by scurrying up the hill. Everyone had assigned places for the anthem and he was ignoring his. He turned his back on Anna and set off with renewed resolve.

"—o'er the ramparts we watched—"

He laughed, out of breath, wondering if these mounds of earth could be considered ramparts. It was easy to see the bowls for what they'd become in the last weeks, individual states full of people, goods and livestock, fifty state fairs bustling at once, all for this shining day, all to be gone once the facility was up and running.

"—and the rockets' red glare, the bombs bursting in air—"

He reached the top of the hill and sucked in deep lungfuls of crisp, clean air. On the stage below, flags swayed idly in a soft breeze. A large screen showed a video of the girl singing about *proof* and *still being there.*

A hand seized his wrist.

"Come back," Anna hissed.

He was panting. Anna was also out of breath, her knees covered in mud and grass stains. She must've slipped on the way up.

"Helen doesn't know where I am," he said.

"—bannerrr yet waaaaave—"

Applause stirred before the end, a compliment. The jets streaking in from the distance caught his eye even before he heard their rumble. A diamond pattern with wing tips nearly touching.

"Get the fuck back down here," Anna yelled. She yanked on his arm.

Donald twisted his wrist away. He was mesmerized by the sight of the jets approaching.

"—o'er the laaand of the freeeeeee—"

That sweet and youthful voice lifted up from fifty holes in the earth and crashed into the thunderous roar of the powerful jets, those soaring and graceful angels of death.

"Let go," Donald demanded, as Anna grabbed him and scrambled to pull him back down the hill.

"—and the hooome of the . . . braaaaave . . ."

The air shook from the grumble of the perfectly timed fly-by. Afterburners screamed as the jets peeled apart and curved upward into the white clouds.

Anna was practically wrestling him, arms wrapped around his shoulders. Donald snapped out of a trance induced by the passing jets, the beautiful rendition of the anthem amplified across half a county, the struggle to spot his wife in the bowl below.

"Goddammit, Donny, we've got to get *down*—"

The first flash came before she could get her hands over his eyes. A bright spot in the corner of his vision in the direction of downtown Atlanta. It was a daytime strike of lightning. Donald turned toward it, expecting thunder. The flash of light had become a blinding glow. Anna's arms were around his waist, jerking him backward. His sister was there, panting, covering her eyes, screaming, "*What the fuck?*"

Another flash of light, starbursts in one's vision. Sirens spilled out of all the speakers. It was the recorded sound of air-raid klaxons.

Donald felt half blinded. Even when the mushroom clouds rose up from the earth—impossibly large to be so distant—it still took a heartbeat to realize what was happening.

They pulled him down the hill. Applause had turned to screams audible over the rise and fall of the blaring siren. Donald could hardly see. He stumbled backward and nearly fell as the three of them slipped and slid down the bowl, the wet grass funneling them toward the stage. The puffy tops of the swelling clouds rose up higher and higher, staying in sight even as the rest of the hills and the trees disappeared from view.

"Wait!" he yelled.

There was something he was forgetting. He couldn't remember what. He had an image of his ATV sitting up on the ridge. He was leaving it behind. How did he get up there? What was happening?

"Go. Go. Go," Anna was saying.

His sister was cussing. She was frightened and confused, just like him. He had never known his sister to be either one.

"The main tent!"

Donald spun around, his heels slipping in the grass, hands

wet with rain and studded with mud and grass. When had he fallen?

The three of them tumbled down the last of the slope as the sound of distant thunder finally reached them. The clouds overhead seemed to race away from the blasts, pushed aside by an unnatural wind. The undersides of the clouds strobed and flashed as if more strikes of lightning were hitting, more bombs detonating. Down by the stage, people weren't running to escape the bowl—they were instead running into the tents, guided by volunteers with waving arms, the markets and food stalls clearing out, the rows of wooden chairs now a heaped and upturned tangle, a dog still tied to a post, barking.

Some people still seemed to be aware, to have their faculties intact. Anna was one of them. Donald saw the Senator by a smaller tent coordinating the flow of traffic. Where was everyone going? Donald felt empty as he was ushered along with the others. It took long moments for his brain to process what he'd seen. Nuclear blasts. The live view of what had forever been resigned to grainy wartime video. Real bombs going off in the real air. Nearby. He had seen them. Why wasn't he completely blind? Was that even what happened?

The raw fear of death overtook him. Donald knew, in some recess of his mind, that they were all dead. The end of all things was coming. There was no outrunning it. No hiding. Paragraphs from a book he'd read came to mind, thousands of memorized paragraphs. He patted his pants for his pills, but they weren't there. Looking over his shoulder, he fought to remember what he'd left behind—

Anna and his sister pulled him past the Senator, who wore a hard scowl of determination, who frowned at his daughter. The tent flap brushed Donald's face, the darkness within interspersed with a few hanging lights. The spots in his vision from the blasts made themselves known in the blackness. There was a crush of people, but not as many as there should've been. Where were the crowds? It didn't make sense until he found himself shuffling downward.

A concrete ramp, bodies on all sides, shoulders jostling, people wheezing, yelling for one another, hands outstretched as the flowing crush drove loved ones away, husband and wife separated, some people crying, some perfectly poised—

Husband and wife.

Helen!

Donald yelled her name over the crowd. He turned and tried to swim against the flowing torrent of the frightened mob. Anna and his sister pulled on him. People fighting to get below pushed from above. Donald was forced downwards, into the depths. He wanted to go under with his wife. He wanted to drown with her.

"Helen!"

Oh, God, he remembered.

He remembered what he had left behind.

Panic subsided and fear took its place. He could see. His vision had cleared. But he could not fight the push of the inevitable.

Donald remembered a conversation with the Senator about how it would all end. There was an electricity in the air, the taste of dead metal on his tongue, a white mist rising around him. He remembered most of a book. He knew what this was, what was happening.

His world was gone.

A new one swallowed him.

SECOND SHIFT
ORDER

24

Silo 1
2212

TROY STARTLED AWAKE from a series of terrible dreams. The world was on fire, and the people who had been sent to extinguish it were all asleep. Asleep and frozen stiff, smoking matches still in their hands, wisps and gray curls of evil deeds.

He had been buried, was enveloped in darkness, could feel the tight walls of his small coffin hemming him in.

Dark shapes moved beyond the frosted glass, the men with their shovels trying to free him.

Troy's eyelids seemed to rip and crack as he fought to open them fully. There was crust in the corners of his eyes, melting frost coursing down his cheek. He tried to lift his arms to wipe it away, but they responded feebly. An IV tugged at his wrist as he managed to raise one hand. He was aware of his catheter. Every inch of his body tingled as he emerged from the numbness and into the cold.

The lid popped with a hiss of air. There was a crack of light to his side that grew as the shadows folded away.

A doctor and his assistant reached in to tend to him. Troy tried to speak but could only cough. They helped him up, brought him the bitter drink. Swallowing took effort. His hands were so weak, arms trembling, that they had to help him with the cup. The taste on his tongue was metallic. It tasted like death.

"Easy," they said when he tried to drink too fast. Tubes and IVs were carefully removed by expert hands, pressure applied, gauze taped to frigid skin. There was a paper gown.

"What year?" he asked, his voice a dry rasp.

"It's early," the doctor said, a different doctor. Troy blinked against the harsh lights, didn't recognize either man tending to him. The sea of coffins around him remained a hazy blur.

"Take your time," the assistant said, tilting the cup.

Troy managed a few sips. He felt worse than last time. It had been longer. The cold was deep within his bones. He remembered that his name wasn't Troy. He was supposed to be dead. Part of him regretted being disturbed. Another part hoped he had slept through the worst of it.

"Sir, we're sorry to wake you, but we need your help."

"Your report—"

Two men were talking at once.

"Another silo is having problems, sir. Silo Eighteen—"

Pills were produced. Troy waved them away. He no longer wished to take them.

The doctor hesitated; the two capsules rested in his palm. He turned to consult with someone else, a third man. Troy tried to blink the world into focus. Something was said. Fingers curled around the pills, filling him with relief.

They helped him up, had a wheelchair waiting. A man stood behind it, his hair as stark white as his coveralls, his square jaw and iron frame familiar. Troy recognized him. This was the man who woke the freezing.

Another sip of water as he leaned against the pod, knees trembling from being weak and cold.

“What *about* Silo Eighteen?” Troy whispered the question as the cup was lowered.

The doctor frowned and said nothing. The man behind the wheelchair studied him intently.

“I know you,” Troy said.

The man in white nodded. The wheelchair was waiting for Troy. Troy felt his stomach twist as dormant parts of him stirred.

“You’re the Thaw Man,” he said, even though this didn’t sound quite right.

The paper gown was warm. It rustled as his arms were guided through the sleeves. The men working on him were nervous. They chattered back and forth, one of them saying a silo was falling, the other that they needed his help. Troy cared only about the man in white. They helped him toward the wheelchair.

“Is it over?” he asked. He watched the colorless man, his vision clearing, his voice growing stronger. He dearly hoped that he had slept through it all.

The Thaw Man shook his head sadly as Troy was lowered into the chair.

“I’m afraid, son,” a familiar voice said, “that it’s only begun.”

25

Silo 18
The Year of the Great Uprising

DEATHDAYS WERE BIRTHDAYS. That's what they said to ease their pain, those who were left behind. An old man dies and a lottery is won. Children weep while hopeful parents cry tears of joy. Deathdays were birthdays, and no one knew this better than Mission Jones.

Tomorrow was his seventeenth. Tomorrow, he would grow a year older. It would also mark seventeen years to the day since his mother died.

The cycle of life was everywhere—it wrapped around all things like the great spiral staircase—but nowhere was it more evident, nowhere could it be seen so clearly that a life given was one taken away, than in him. And so Mission approached his birthday without joy, with a heavy load on his young back, thinking on death and celebrating nothing.

Three steps below him and matching his pace, Mission could hear his friend Cam wheezing from his half of the load. When Dispatch assigned them a tandem, the two boys had flipped a coin—heads for heads—and Cam had lost. That left Mission out in front with a clear view of the stairs. It also gave him rights to set the pace, and his dark thoughts made for an angry one.

Traffic was light on the stairwell that morning. The children were not yet up and heading to school, those of them who still went anymore. A few bleary-eyed shopkeeps staggered to work. There were service workers with grease stains on their bellies and patches sewn into their knees coming off late shifts. One man descended bearing more than a non-porter should, but Mission was in no mood to set down his burden and weigh another's. It was enough to glare at the gentleman, to let him know that he'd been seen.

"Three more to go," he huffed to Cam as they passed the twenty-fourth. His porter's strap was digging into his shoulders, the load a heavy one. Heavier still was its destination. Mission hadn't been back to the farms in near on four months, hadn't seen his father in just as long. His brother, of course, he saw at the Nest now and then, but it'd still been a few weeks. To arrive so near to his birthday would be awkward, but there was no avoiding it. He trusted his father to do as he always had and ignore the occasion altogether, to ignore the fact that he was getting any older.

Past the twenty-fourth they entered another gap between the levels full of graffiti. The noxious odor of home-mixed paint hung in the air. Recent work dribbled in places, parts of it done the night before. Bold letters wrapped across the curving wall of concrete far beyond the stairway railing that read:

THIS IS OUR 'LO.

The slang for Silo felt dated, even though the paint was not yet dry. Nobody said that anymore. Not for years. Further up and much older:

CLEAN THIS, MOTHER—

The rest was obscured in a wash of censoring paint. As if

anyone could read it and not fill in the blank. It was the first half that was the killing offense, anyway.

DOWN WITH THE UP TOP!

Mission laughed at this one. He pointed it out to Cam. Probably painted by some kid born above the Mids and full of self-loathing, some kid who couldn't abide their own good fortune. Mission knew the kind. They were *his* kind. He studied all this graffiti painted over last year's graffiti and that from all the many years before. It was here between the levels, where the steel girders stretched out from the stairwell to the cement beyond, that such slogans went back generations.

THE END IS COMING . . .

Mission marched past this one, unable to argue. The end *was* coming. He could feel it in his bones. He could hear it in the wheezing rattle of the silo with its loose bolts and its rusty joints, could see it in the way people walked of late with their shoulders up around their ears, their belongings clutched to their chests. The end was coming for them all.

His father would laugh and disagree, of course. Mission could hear his father's voice from all the levels away, telling him how people had thought the same thing long before he and his brother were born, that it was the hubris of each generation to think this anew, to think that their time was special, that all things would come to an end with them. His father said it was *hope* that made people feel this, not dread. People talked of the end coming with barely concealed smiles. Their prayer was that when they went, they wouldn't go alone. Their hope was that no one would have the good fortune to come after and live a happy life without them.

Thoughts such as these made Mission's neck itch. He held the hauling strap with one hand and adjusted the 'chief around his neck with the other. It was a nervous habit, hiding his neck when he thought about the end of things.

"You doing okay up there?" Cam asked.

"I'm fine," Mission called back, realizing he'd slowed. He gripped his strap with both hands and concentrated on his pace, on the job. There was a metronome in his head from his shadowing days, a tick-tock, tick-tock for tandem hauls. Two porters with good timing could fall into a rhythm and wind their way up a dozen flights, never feeling a heavy load. Mission and Cam weren't there yet. Now and then one of them would have to shuffle his feet or adjust his pace to match the other. Otherwise, their load might sway dangerously.

Their load. It was easier to think of it that way. Better not to think of it as a body—a dead man.

Mission thought of his grandfather, whom he'd never known. He had died in the uprising of '78, had left behind a son to take over the farm and a daughter to become a chipper. Mission's aunt had quit that job a few years back; she no longer banged out spots of rust and primed and painted raw steel. Nobody did. Nobody bothered. But his father was still farming that same plot of soil, that same plot generations of Jones boys had farmed, forever insisting that things would never change.

"That word means something else, you know," his father had told him once, when Mission had spoken of revolution. "It also means to go around and around. To revolve. One revolution, and you get right back to where you started."

This was the sort of thing Mission's father liked to say when the priests came to bury a man beneath his corn. His dad would pack the dirt with a shovel, say that's how things go, and plant a seed in the neat depression his thumb made.

Mission had told his friends this other meaning of revolution. He had pretended to come up with it himself. It was just the sort of pseudo-intellectual nonsense they regaled each other with late at night on dark landings while they inhaled potato glue out of plastic bags.

His best friend Rodny had been the only one unimpressed. “Nothing changes until we *make* it change,” he had said with a serious look in his eye.

Mission wondered what his best friend was doing now. He hadn’t seen Rodny in months. Whatever he was shadowing for in IT kept him from getting out much.

He thought back to better days, growing up in the Nest with friends tight as a fist. He remembered thinking they would all stay together and grow old in the Up Top. They would live along the same hallways, watch their eventual kids play the way they had.

But they had all gone their separate ways. It was hard to remember who had done it first, who had shaken off the expectations of their parents to follow in their footsteps, but eventually most of them had. Each of them had left home to choose a new fate. Sons of plumbers took up farming. Daughters of the cafeteria learned to sew. Sons of farmers became porters.

Mission remembered being angry when he left home. He remembered a fight with his father, throwing down his shovel, promising he’d never dig a trench again. He’d learned in the Nest that he could be anything he wanted, that he was in charge of his own fate. And so when he grew miserable, he assumed it was the farms that made him feel that way; he assumed it was his family.

He and Cam had flipped a dime back in Dispatch, heads for heads, and Mission had wound up with a dead man’s shoulders pressed against his own. When he lifted his gaze to survey the steps ahead, the back of his skull touched a corpse’s crown through a plastic bag—birthdays and deathdays pressed tight, two halves of a single coin. Mission carried them both, this load meant for two. He took the stairs a pair at a time, a brutal pace, up toward the farm of his youth.

26

THE CORONER'S OFFICE was on thirty-two, just below the dirt farm, tucked away at the end of those dark and damp halls that wound their way beneath the roots. The ceiling was low in that half-level. Pipes hung visible from above and rattled angrily as pumps kicked on and moved nutrients to distant and thirsty roots. Water dripped from dozens of small leaks into buckets and pots. A recently emptied pot banged metallic with each strike. Another overflowed. The floors were slick, the walls damp like sweaty skin.

Inside the coroner's office, the boys lifted the body onto a slab of dented metal, and the coroner signed Mission's work log. She tipped them for the speedy delivery, and when Cam saw the extra chits, his grumpiness over the pace dissolved. Back in the hallway, he bid Mission good day and splashed toward the exit.

Mission watched him go, feeling much more than a year older than his friend. Cam hadn't been told of the evening's plans, the midnight rendezvous of porters. It made him envy the lad for what he didn't know.

Not wanting to arrive at the farms deadheading and have his father lecture him on laziness, Mission stopped by the maintenance room down the hall to see if anything needed carrying up. Winters was on duty, a dark man with a white beard and a knack with pumps. He regarded Mission suspiciously and claimed he hadn't the budget for portering. Mission explained he was going up anyway and that he was glad to take whatever he had.

"In that case . . ." Winters said. He hoisted a huge water pump onto his workbench.

"Just the thing," Mission told him, smiling.

Winters narrowed his eyes as if Mission had worked a bolt loose.

The pump wouldn't fit inside his porter's pack, but the haul straps on the outside of the pack looped nicely across the jutting pipes and sharp fittings. Winters helped him get his arms through the straps and the pump secured to his back. He thanked the old man, which drew another worried frown, and set off and up the half-level. Back at the stairwell, the odor of mildew from the wet halls faded, replaced by the smell of loam and freshly tilled soil, scents of home that pulled Mission back in time.

The landing on thirty-one was crowded as a jam of people attempted to squeeze inside the farms for the day's food. Standing apart from them was a mother in farmer green cradling a wailing child. She had the stains on her knees of a picker and the agitated look of one sent out of the grow plots to soothe her noisy brood. As Mission crowded past, he heard the mother sing the words of a familiar nursery rhyme. She rocked the child frightfully close to the railing, the infant's eyes wide with what looked to Mission like unadulterated fear.

He worked his way through the crowd, and the cries from the infant receded amid the general din. It occurred to Mission how few kids he saw anymore. It wasn't like when he was young. There had been an explosion of newborns after the violence the last generation had wrought, but these days it was just the trickle of natural deaths and the handful of lottery winners. It meant fewer babies crying and fewer parents rejoicing.

He eventually made it through the doors and into the main hall. Using his 'chief, Mission wiped the sweat from his lips. He'd forgotten to top up his canteen a level below, and his mouth was dry. The reasons for pushing so swift a pace felt silly now. It was as if his looming birthday were some deadline to beat, and so the sooner he visited his father and departed, the better. But now, in the wash of sights and sounds from his childhood, his dark and angry thoughts melted away. It was home, and Mission hated how good it felt to be there.

There were a few hellos and waves as he worked his way toward the gates. Some porters he knew were loading sacks of fruits and vegetables to haul up to the cafeteria. He saw his aunt working one of the vending stalls outside the security gate. After giving up chipping, she now performed the questionably legal act of vending, something she'd never shadowed for and had no right to do. Mission did his best not to catch her eye; he didn't want to get sucked into a lecture or have his hair mussed and his 'chief straightened.

Beyond the stalls, a handful of younger kids clustered in the far corner where it was dark, probably dealing seeds, not looking nearly as inconspicuous as they likely thought. The entire scene in the entrance hall was one of a second bazaar, of farmers selling direct, of people crowding in from distant levels to get food they feared would never make it to their shops and stores. It was fear begetting fear, crowds becoming throngs, and it was easy to see how mobs came next.

Working the main security gate was Frankie, a tall, lanky kid Mission had grown up with. Mission wiped his forehead with the front of his undershirt, which was already cool and damp with sweat. "Hey, Frankie," he called out.

"Mission." A nod and a smile. No hard feelings from another kid who'd jumped shadows long ago. Frankie's father worked in security, down in IT. Frankie had wanted to become a farmer, which Mission never understood. Their teacher, Mrs. Crowe, had been delighted and had encouraged Frankie to follow his dreams. And now Mission found it ironic that Frankie had ended up working security for the farms. It was as if he couldn't escape what he'd been born to do.

Mission smiled and nodded at Frankie's shoulder-length hair. "Did someone splash you with grow quick?"

Frankie tucked his hair behind his ear self-consciously. "I know, right? My mother threatens to come up here and knife it in my sleep."

"Tell her I'll hold you down while she does it," Mission said, laughing. "Buzz me through?"

There was a wide gate to the side for wheelbarrows and trolleys. Mission didn't feel like squeezing through the turnstiles with the massive pump strapped to his back. Frankie hit a button, and the gate buzzed. Mission pushed his way through.

"Whatcha haulin'?" Frankie asked.

"Water pump from Winters. How've you been?"

Frankie scanned the crowds beyond the gate. "Hold on a sec," he said, looking for someone. Two farmers swiped their work badges and marched through the turnstiles, jabbering away. Frankie waved over someone in green and asked if they could cover for him.

"C'mon," Frankie told Mission. "Walk me."

The two old friends headed down the main hall toward the bright aura of distant grow lights. The smells were intoxicating and familiar. Mission wondered what those same smells meant to Frankie, who had grown up near the fetid stink of the water plant. Perhaps this reeked to him the way the plant did to Mission. Perhaps the water plant brought back fond memories for Frankie, instead.

"Things are going nuts around here," Frankie whispered once they were away from the gates.

Mission nodded. "Yeah, I saw a few more stalls had sprouted up. More of them every day, huh?"

Frankie held Mission's arm and slowed their pace so they'd have more time to talk. There was the smell of fresh bread from one of the offices. It was too far from the bakery on seven for warm bread, but such was the new way of things. The flour was probably ground somewhere deep in the farms.

"You've seen what they're doing up in the cafeteria, right?" Frankie asked.

"I took a load up that way a few weeks ago," Mission said. He tucked his thumbs under his shoulder straps and wiggled the heavy pump higher onto his hips. "I saw they were building something by the wallscreens. Didn't see what."

"They're starting to grow sprouts up there," Frankie said. "Corn too, supposedly."

"I guess that'll mean fewer runs for us between here and there," Mission said, thinking like a porter. He tapped the wall with the toe of his boot. "Roker'll be pissed when he hears."

Frankie bit his lip and narrowed his eyes. "Yeah, but wasn't Roker the one who started growin' his own beans down in Dispatch?"

Mission wiggled his shoulders. His arms were going numb. He wasn't used to standing still with a load—he was used to moving. "That's different," he argued. "That's food for climbing."

Frankie shook his head. "Yeah, but ain't that hypercritical of him?"

"You mean hypocritical?"

"Whatever, man. All I'm saying is everyone has an excuse.

'We're doing it because they're doing it and someone else started it. So what if we're doing it a little more than they are?' That's the attitude, man. But then we get in a twist when the next group does it a little more. It's like a ratchet, the way these things work."

Mission glanced down the hall toward the glow of distant lights. "I dunno," he said. "The mayor seems to be letting things slide lately."

Frankie laughed. "You really think the mayor's in charge? The mayor's scared, man. Scared and *old*." Frankie glanced back down the hall to make sure nobody was coming. The nervousness and paranoia had been with him since his youth. It'd been amusing when he was younger; now it was sad and a little worrisome. "You remember when we talked about being in charge one day? How things would be different?"

"It doesn't work like that," Mission said. "By the time we're in charge, we'll be old like them and won't care anymore. And then *our* kids can hate *us* for pulling the same crap."

Frankie laughed, and the tension in his wiry frame seemed to subside. "I bet you're right."

"Yeah, well, I need to go before my arms fall off." Mission shrugged the pump higher up his back.

Frankie slapped his shoulder. "Yeah. Good seeing you, man."

"Same." Mission nodded and turned to go.

"Oh, hey, Mish . . ."

He stopped and looked back.

"You gonna see the Crow anytime soon?"

"I'll pass that way tomorrow," he said, assuming he'd live through the night.

Frankie smiled. "Tell her I said hey, wouldya?"

"I will," Mission promised.

One more name to add to the list. If only he could charge his friends for all the messages he ran for them, he'd have way more than the three hundred and eighty-four chits already saved up. Half a chit for every hello he passed to the Crow, and he'd have his own apartment by now. He wouldn't need to stay in the way stations. But messages from friends weighed far less than dark thoughts, so Mission didn't mind them taking up space. They crowded out the other. And Lord knew, Mission hauled his fair share of the heavier kind.

27

IT WOULD'VE MADE more sense and been kinder on Mission's back to drop off the pump before visiting his father, but the whole point of hauling it up was so that his old man would see him with the load. And so he headed into the planting halls and toward the same growing station his grandfather had worked and supposedly his great-grandfather too. Past the beans and the blueberry vines, beyond the squash and the potatoes. In a spot of corn that appeared ready for harvest, he found his old man on his hands and knees looking how Mission would always remember him: with a small spade working the soil, his hands picking at weeds like a habit, the way a girl might curl her fingers in her hair over and over without even knowing she was doing it.

"Father."

His old man turned his head to the side, sweat glistening on his brow under the heat of the grow lights. There was a flash of a smile before it melted. Mission's half-brother Riley appeared behind a back row of corn, a little twelve-year-old mimic of his dad, hands covered in dirt. He was quicker to call out a greeting, shouting "Mission!" as he hurried to his feet.

"The corn looks good," Mission said. He rested a hand on the railing, the weight of the pump settling against his back, and reached out to bend a leaf with his thumb. Moist. The ears were a few weeks from harvest, and the smell took him right back. He saw a midge running up the stalk and killed the parasite with a deft pinch.

"Wadya bring me?" his little brother squealed.

Mission laughed and tussled his brother's dark hair, a gift from the boy's mother. "Sorry, bro. They loaded me down this time." He turned slightly so that Riley—and his father—could see. His brother stepped onto the lowest rail and leaned over for a better look.

"Why dontcha set that down for a while?" his father asked. He slapped his hands together to keep the precious dirt on the proper side of the fence, then reached out and shook Mission's hand. "You're looking good."

"You too, Dad." Mission would've thrust his chest out and stood taller if it didn't mean toppling back on his rear from the weight of the pump. "So what's this I hear about the cafeteria starting in their own sprouts?"

His father grumbled and shook his head. "Corn, too, from what I hear. More goddamn up-sourcing." He jabbed a finger at Mission's chest. "This affects you lads, you know."

His father meant the porters, and there was a tone of having told him so. There was always that tone.

Riley tugged on Mission's overalls and asked to hold his knife. Mission slid the blade from its sheath and handed it over while he studied his father, a silence brewing between them. His dad looked older. His skin was the color of oiled wood, an unhealthy darkness from working too long under the grow lights. It was called a "tan," and you could spot a farmer two landings away because of it.

An intense heat radiated from the bulbs overhead, and the anger Mission carried when he was away from home melted into a hollow sadness. The space his mother had left empty could be felt. It was a reminder to Mission of what his being born had cost. More was the pity he felt for his old man with his damaged skin and dark spots on his nose from years of abuse. These were the signs of all those in green who worked the soil, toiling among the silo's dead.

Mission flashed back to his first solid memory as a boy: wielding a small spade that in those days had seemed to him a giant shovel. He had been playing between the rows of corn, turning over scoops of soil, mimicking his father, when without warning his old man had grabbed his wrist.

"Don't dig there," his father had said with an edge to his voice. This was back before Mission had witnessed his first funeral, before he had seen for himself what was laid beneath the seeds. After that day, he learned to spot the mounds where the soil was darker from having been disturbed.

"They've got you doing the heavy lifting, I see," his father said, breaking the quiet. He assumed the load Mission had carried had been assigned by Dispatch. Mission didn't correct him.

"They let us carry what we can handle," he said. "The older porters get mail delivery. We each haul what we can."

"I remember when I first stepped out of the shadows," his dad said. He squinted and wiped his brow, nodded down the line. "Got stuck with potatoes while my caster went back to plucking blueberries. Two for the basket and one for him."

Not this again. Mission watched as Riley tested the tip of the knife with the pad of his finger. He reached to take back the blade, but his brother twisted away from him.

"The older porters get mail duty because they *can* get mail duty," his father explained.

"You don't know what you're talking about," Mission said, the sadness gone, the anger back. "The old ports have bad knees is why we get the heavy loads. Besides, my bonus pay is judged by the pound and the time I make, so I don't mind."

"Oh, yes." His father waved at Mission's feet. "They pay you in bonuses and you pay them with your knees."

Mission could feel his cheeks tighten, could sense the burn of the welt around his neck.

"All I'm saying, son, is that the older you get and the more seniority you have, you'll earn your own choice of rows to hoe. That's all. I want you to watch out for yourself."

"I'm watching out for myself, Dad."

Riley climbed up, sat on the top rail and flashed his teeth at his reflection in the knife. The kid already had a freckled band of spots across his nose, the start of a farmer's tan. Damaged flesh from damaged flesh, father like son. And Mission could easily picture Riley years hence, on the other side of that rail, all grown up with a kid of his own. It made him thankful that he'd wormed his way out of the farms and into a job he didn't take home every night beneath his fingernails.

"Are you joining us for lunch?" his father asked, sensing perhaps that he was pushing Mission away.

"If you don't mind," Mission said. He felt a twinge of guilt that his father expected to feed him, but he appreciated not having to ask. And it would hurt his stepmom's feelings if he didn't pay her a visit. "I'll have to run afterward, though. I've got a . . . delivery tonight."

His father frowned. "You'll have time to see Allie though, right? She's forever asking about you. The boys here are lined up to marry that girl if you keep her waiting."

Mission wiped his face to hide his expression. Allie was a great friend—his first and briefest romance—but to marry her would be to marry the farms, to return home, to live among the buried dead. "Probably not this time," he said. He felt bad for admitting it.

"Okay. Well, go drop that off. Don't squander your bonus sitting here jawing with us." The disappointment in the old man's voice was hotter than the lights and not so easy to shade. "We'll see you in the feeding hall in half an hour?" He reached out, took his son's hand one more time, and gave it a squeeze. "It's good to see you, son."

"Same." Mission shook his father's hand, then clapped his palms together over the grow pit to knock loose any dirt. Riley reluctantly gave the knife back and Mission slipped it into its sheath. He fastened the clasp around the handle, thinking on how he might need to use it that night. He pondered for a moment if he should warn his father, thought of telling him and Riley both to stay inside until morning, not to dare go out.

But he held his tongue, patted his brother on the shoulder and made his way to the pump room down the hall. As he walked through rows of planters and pickers, he thought about farmers selling their own vegetables in makeshift stalls and grinding their own flour. He thought about the cafeteria growing its own sprouts and corn. And he thought of the recently discovered plans to move something heavy from one landing to another without involving the porters.

Everyone was trying to look after themselves in case the violence returned. Mission could feel it brewing, the suspicion and the distrust, the walls being built. Everyone was trying to get a little less reliant on the others, preparing for the inevitable, hunkering down.

He loosened the straps on his pack as he approached the pump room, and a dangerous thought occurred to him, a revelation: if everyone was trying to get to where they didn't *need* one another, how exactly was that supposed to help them all get along?

28

THE LIGHTS OF the great spiral staircase were dimmed at night so man and silo might sleep. It was in those wee hours when children were long hushed with sing-song lullabies and only those with trouble in mind crept about. Mission held very still in that darkness and waited. Somewhere above him, there came the sound of rope wound tight and sliding across metal, the squeaking of fibers as they gripped steel and strained under some great weight.

A gang of porters huddled with him on the stairway. Mission pressed his cheek against the inner post, the steel cooling his skin. He controlled his breathing and listened for the rope. He well knew the sounds they made, could feel the burn on his neck, that raised weal healed over by the years, a mark glanced at by others but rarely mentioned aloud. And again in that thick gray of the dim-time there came a recognizable squeak as the load from above was steadily lowered.

He waited for the signal. He thought on rope, on his own life—and other forbidden things. There was a book in Dispatch down on seventy-four that kept accounts. In the main way station for all the porters, a massive ledger fashioned out of a fortune in paper was kept under lock and key. It contained a careful tally of certain types of deliveries, handwritten so the information couldn't slip off into wires.

Mission had heard the senior porters kept track of certain kinds of pipe in this ledger, but he didn't know why. Brass too, and various types of fluids and powders coming out of Chemical. Order these—or too much rope—and you were put on the watching list. Porters were the lords of rumor. They knew where everything went. And their whisperings gathered like condensation in Dispatch Main where they were written down.

Mission listened to the rope creak and sing in the darkness. He knew what it felt like to have a length of it cinched tightly around his neck. It seemed strange to him that if you ordered enough to hang yourself, nobody cared. Enough to span a few levels, and eyebrows were raised.

He adjusted his 'chief and thought on this in the dim-time. A man may take his own life, he supposed, as long as he didn't take another's job.

"Ready yourself," came the whisper from above.

Mission tightened the grip on his knife and concentrated on the task at hand. His eyes strained to see in the wan light. He could hear the steady breathing of his fellow porters around him. No doubt they would be squeezing their own knives in anticipation.

The knives came with the job. A porter's knife for slicing open delivered goods, for cutting fruit to eat on the climb, and for keeping peace as its owner strayed across all the silo's heights and depths, taking its dangers two at a time. Now, Mission tensed his in his hand, waiting for the order.

Up the stairwell two full turns, on a dim landing, a group of farmers argued in soft voices as they handled the other end of that rope, performing a porter's job in the dark of night to save a hundred chits or two. Beyond the rail, the rope was invisible in the darkness. He would have to lean out and grope blindly for it.

He felt a ring of heat by his collar, and the hilt of his blade was unsure in his sweaty palm.

"Not yet," Morgan whispered, and Mission felt his old caster's hand on his shoulder, holding him back. Mission cleared his mind. Another soft squeak, the sound of line taking the strain of a heavy generator, and a dense patch of gray drifted through the black. The men above shouted in whispers as they handled the load, as they did in green the work of men in blue.

While the patch of gray inched past, Mission thought of the night's danger and marveled at the fear in his heart. He possessed a sudden care for a life he had once labored to end, a life that never should have been. He thought of his mother and wondered what she was like, beyond the disobedience that had cost her life. That was all he knew of his mom. He knew the implant in her hip had failed, as one in ten thousand might. And instead of reporting the malfunction—and the pregnancy—she had hidden him in loose clothes until it was past the time the Pact allowed a child to be treated as a cyst.

"Ready yourself," Morgan hissed.

The gray mass of the generator crept down and out of sight. Mission clutched his knife and thought of how he should've been cut out of her and discarded. But past a certain date, and one life was traded for another. Such was the Pact. Born behind bars, Mission had been allowed free while his mother had been sent outside to clean.

"Now," Morgan commanded, and Mission startled. Soft and well-worn boots squeaked on the stairs above, the sounds of men lurching into action. Mission concentrated on his part. He pressed himself against the curved rail and reached out into the space beyond. His palm found rope as stiff as steel. He pressed his blade to the taut line.

There was a pop like sinew snapping, the first of the braids parting with just a touch of his sharp blade.

Mission had but a moment to think of those on the landing below, the farmers' accomplices waiting two levels down. Men were storming up the staircase. Mission longed to join them. With the barest of sawing motions, the rope parted the rest of the way, and Mission thought he heard the heavy generator whistle as it picked up speed. There was a ferocious crash a moment later, men screaming in alarm down below. Above, the fighting had broken out.

With one hand on the rail and another gripping his knife, Mission took the stairs three at a time. He rushed to join the melee above, this midnight lesson on breaking the Pact, on doing another's job. Grunts and groans and slapping thuds spilled from the landing, and Mission threw himself into the scuffle, thinking not of consequences, but only of this one fight.

29

Silo 1
2212

THE WHEELCHAIR SQUEAKED as its wheels circled around. With each revolution there was a sharp peal of complaint followed by a circuit of deathly silence. Donald lost himself in this rhythmic sound as he was pushed along. His breath puffed out into the air, the room harboring the same deep chill as his bones.

There were rows and rows of pods stretched out to either side. Names glowed orange on tiny screens, made-up names designed to sever the past from the present. Donald watched them slide by as they pushed him to the exit. His head felt heavy, the weight of remembrance replacing the dreams that coiled away and vanished like wisps of smoke.

The men in the pale blue overalls guided him through the door and into the hallway. He was steered into a familiar room with a familiar table. The wheelchair shimmied as they removed his bare feet from the footrests. He asked how long it'd been, how long he'd been asleep.

"A hundred years," someone said. Which would make a hundred and sixty since orientation. No wonder the wheelchair felt unsteady—it was older than he was. Its screws had worked loose over the long decades that Donald had been asleep.

They helped him stand. His feet were still numb from his hibernation, the cold fading to painful tingles. A curtain was drawn. They asked him to urinate in a cup, which came as glorious relief. The sample was the color of charcoal, dead machines flushed from his system. The paper gown wasn't enough to warm him, even though he knew the cold was in his flesh, not in the room. They gave him more of the bitter drink.

"How long before his head is clear?" someone asked.

"A day," the doctor said. "Tomorrow at the earliest."

They had him sit while they took his blood. An old man in white overalls with hair just as stark stood in the doorway, frowning. "Save your strength," the man in white said. He nodded to the doctor to continue his work and disappeared before Donald could place him in his faltering memory. He felt dizzy as he watched his blood, blue from the cold, as it was taken from him.

They rode a familiar lift. The men around him talked, but their voices seemed distant. Donald felt as though he had been drugged, but he remembered that he had stopped taking their pills. He reached for his bottom lip, finger and mouth both tingling, and felt for an ulcer, that little pocket where he kept his pills unswallowed.

But the ulcer wasn't there. It would've healed in his sleep decades ago. The lift doors parted, and Donald felt more of that dreamtime fade.

They pushed him down another hall, scuff marks on the walls the height of the wheels, black arcs where rubber had once met the paint. His eyes roamed the walls, the ceiling, the tiles, all bearing centuries of wear. It seemed like yesterday that they had been almost new. Now they were heaped with abuse, a sudden crumbling into ruin. Donald remembered designing halls just like these. He remembered thinking they were making something to last for ages. The truth was there all along. The truth was in the design, staring back at him, too insane to be taken seriously.

The wheelchair slowed.

"The next one," a gruff voice behind him said, a familiar voice. Donald was pushed past one closed door to another. One of the orderlies bustled around the wheelchair, a ring of keys jangling from his hip. A key was selected and slotted into the lock with a series of neat clicks. Hinges cried out as the door was pushed inward. The lights inside were turned on.

It was a room like a cell, musky with the scent of disuse. The light overhead flickered before it came on. There was a narrow double bunk in the corner, a side table, a dresser, a bathroom.

"Why am I here?" Donald asked, his voice cracking.

"This will be your room," the orderly said, putting away his keys. His young eyes darted up to the man steering the wheelchair as if seeking assurances for his answer. Another young man in pale blue hurried around and removed Donald's feet from the stirrups and placed them on carpet worn flat by the years.

Donald's last memory was of being chased by snarling dogs with leathery wings, chased up a mountain of bones. But that was a dream. What was his last *real* memory? He remembered a needle. He remembered dying. That felt real.

"I mean—" Donald swallowed painfully. "Why am I . . . *awake*?"

He almost said *alive*. The two orderlies exchanged glances as they helped him from the chair to the lower bunk. The wheelchair squeaked once as it was pushed back into the hallway. The man guiding it paused, his broad shoulders making the doorway appear small.

One of the orderlies held Donald's wrist—two fingers pressing lightly on ice-blue veins, lips moving as he silently counted. The other orderly dropped two pills into a plastic cup and fumbled with the cap on a bottle of water.

"That won't be necessary," the silhouette in the doorway said.

The orderly with the pills glanced over his shoulder as the older man stepped inside the small room and some of the air was displaced. The room shrank. It became more difficult for Donald to breathe.

"You're the Thaw—" Donald whispered.

The old man with the white hair waved a hand at the two orderlies. "Give us a moment," he said.

The one with a grip on Donald's wrist finished his counting and nodded to the other. Unswallowed pills rattled in a paper cup as they were put away. The old man's face had awoken something in Donald, pierced through the muddle of visions and dreams.

"I remember you," Donald said. "You're the Thaw Man."

A smile was flashed, as white as his hair, wrinkles forming around his lips and eyes. The chair in the hallway squeaked as it was pushed away. The door clicked shut. Donald thought he heard the lock engage, but his teeth chattered occasionally and his hearing was still hazy.

"Thurman," the man said, correcting him.

"I remember," Donald said. He remembered his office, the one upstairs and some other office far away, someplace where it still rained, where the grass grew and the cherry blossoms came once a year. This man had been a senator, once.

"That you remember is a mystery we need to solve." The old man tilted his head. "For now, it's good that you do. We *need* you to remember."

Thurman leaned against the metal dresser. He looked as

though he hadn't slept in days. His hair was unkempt, not quite how Donald remembered it. There were dark circles beneath his sad eyes. He seemed much . . . older, somehow.

Donald peered down at his own palms, the springs in the bed making the room feel as though it were swaying. He flashed again to the horrible sight of a man remembering his own name and wanting to be free.

"My name is Donald Keene."

"So you do remember. And you know who I am?" He produced a folded piece of paper and waited for an answer.

Donald nodded.

"Good." The Thaw Man turned and placed the folded piece of paper on the dresser. He arranged it on its bent legs so it tented upward, toward the ceiling. "We need you to remember everything," he said. "Study this report when the fog clears, see if it jars anything loose. Once your stomach is settled, I'll have a proper meal brought down."

Donald rubbed his temples.

"You've been gone for some time," the Thaw Man said. He rapped his knuckles on the door.

Donald wiggled his bare toes against the carpet. The sensation was returning to his feet. The door clicked before swinging open, and the Senator once again blocked the light from the hallway. He became a shadow for a moment.

"Rest, and then we'll get our answers together. There's someone who wants to see you."

The room was sealed tight before Donald could ask what that meant. And somehow, with the door shut and him gone, there was more air to breathe in that small space. Donald took a few deep breaths. Gathering himself, he grabbed the frame of the bed and struggled to his feet. He stood there a moment, swaying.

"Get our answers," he repeated aloud. Someone wanted to see him.

He shook his head, which made the world spin. As if he had any answers. All he had were questions. He remembered the orderlies who woke him saying something about a silo falling. He couldn't remember which one. Why would they wake him for that?

He moved unsteadily to the door, tried the knob, confirmed what he already knew. He went to the dresser where the piece of paper stood on its remembered folds.

"Get some rest," he said, laughing at the suggestion. As if he could sleep. He felt as though he'd been asleep forever. He picked up the piece of paper and unfolded it.

A report. Donald remembered this. It was a copy of a report. A report about a young man doing horrible things. The room twisted around him as if he stood on some great pivot, the memory of men and women trampled and dying, of giving some awful order, faces peering in at him from a hallway somewhere far in the past.

Donald blinked away a curtain of tears and studied the trembling report. Hadn't he written this? He had signed it, he remembered. But that wasn't his name at the bottom. It was his handwriting, but it wasn't his name.

Troy.

Donald's legs went numb. He sought the bed—but collapsed to the floor instead as the memories washed over him. Troy and Helen. Helen and Troy. He remembered his wife. He imagined her disappearing over a hill, her arm raised to the sky where bombs were falling, his sister and some dark and nameless shadow pulling him back as people spilled like marbles down a slope, funneling into some deep hole filled with white mist.

Donald remembered. He remembered all that he had helped do to the world. There was a troubled boy in a silo full of the dead, a shadow among the servers. That boy had brought an end to silo number 12, and Donald had written a report. But Donald—what had he done? He had killed more than a silo full of people; he had drawn the plans that helped end the world. The report in his hand trembled as he remembered. And the tears that fell and struck the paper were tinged a pale blue.

30

A DOCTOR BROUGHT SOUP and bread a few hours later, and a tall glass of water. Donald ate hungrily while the man checked his arm. The warm soup felt good. It slid to his center and seemed to radiate its heat outward. Donald tore at the bread with his teeth and chased it with the water. He ate with the desperation of so many years of fasting.

"Thank you," he said between bites. "For the food."

The doctor glanced up from checking his blood pressure. He was an older man, heavyset, with great bushy eyebrows and a fine wisp of hair that clung to his scalp like a cloud to a hilltop.

"I'm Donald," he said, introducing himself.

There was a wrinkle of confusion on the old man's brow. His gray eyes strayed to his clipboard as if either it or his patient couldn't be trusted. The needle on the gauge jumped with Donald's pulse.

"Who're you?" Donald asked.

"I'm Dr. Sneed," he finally said, though without confidence.

Donald took a long swig on his water, thankful they'd left it at room temperature. He didn't want anything cold inside him ever again. "Where're you from?"

The doctor removed the cuff from Donald's arm with a loud rip. "Level ten. But I work out of the shift office on sixty-eight."

He put his equipment back in his bag and made a note on the clipboard.

"No, I mean where are you *from*? You know . . . before."

Dr. Sneed patted Donald's knee and stood. The clipboard went on a hook on the outside of the door. "You might have some dizziness the next few days. Let us know if you experience any trembling, okay?"

Donald nodded. He remembered being given the same advice earlier. Or was that his last shift? Maybe the repetition was for those who had trouble remembering. He wasn't going to be one of those people. Not this time.

A shadow fell into the room. Donald looked up to see the Thaw Man in the doorway. He gripped the meal tray to keep it from sliding off his knees.

The Thaw Man nodded to Dr. Sneed, but these were not their names. *Thurman,* Donald told himself. Senator Thurman. He knew this.

"Do you have a moment?" Thurman asked the doctor.

"Of course." Sneed grabbed his bag and stepped outside. The door clicked shut, leaving Donald alone with his soup.

He took quiet spoonfuls, trying to make anything of the murmurs on the other side of the door. *Thurman,* he reminded himself again. And not a senator. Senator of what? Those days were gone. Donald had drawn the plans.

The report stood tented on the dresser, returned to its spot. Donald took a bite of bread and remembered the floors he'd laid out. Those floors were now real. They existed. People lived inside them, raising their children, laughing, having fights, singing in the shower, burying their dead.

A few minutes passed before the knob tilted and the door swung inward. The Thaw Man entered the room alone. He pressed the door shut and frowned at Donald. "How're you feeling?"

The spoon clacked against the rim of the bowl. Donald set the utensil down and gripped the tray with both hands to keep them from shaking, to keep them from forming fists.

"You know," Donald hissed, teeth clenched together. "You know what we did."

Thurman showed his palms. "We did what had to be done."

"No. Don't give me that." Donald shook his head. The water in his glass trembled as if something dangerous approached. "The world . . ."

"We saved it."

"That's not true!" Donald's voice cracked. He tried to remember. "There is no world anymore." He recalled the view from the top, from the cafeteria. He remembered the hills a dull brown, the sky full of menacing clouds. "We ended it. We killed everyone."

"They were already dead," Thurman said. "We all were. Everyone dies, son. The only thing that matters is—"

"Stop." Donald waved the words away as if they were buzzing things that could bite him. "There's no justifying this—" He felt spittle form on his lips, wiped it away with his sleeve. The tray on his lap slid dangerously and Thurman moved quickly—quicker than one would expect of a man his age—to catch it. He placed what was left of the meal on the bedside table, and up close, Donald could see that he had gotten older. The wrinkles were deeper, the skin hanging from the bones. He wondered how much time Thurman had spent awake while Donald had slept.

"I killed a lot of men in the war," Thurman said, looking down at the tray of half-eaten food.

Donald found himself focused on the old man's neck. He closed his hands together to keep them still. This sudden admission about killing made it seem as if Thurman could read

Donald's mind, as though this was some kind of a warning for him to stay his murderous plans.

Thurman turned to the dresser and picked up the folded report. He opened it and Donald caught sight of the pale blue smudges, his ice-tinged tears from earlier.

"Some say killing gets easier the longer you're at it," he said. And he sounded sad, not threatening. Donald looked down at his own knees and saw that they were bouncing. He forced his heels against the carpet and tried to pin them there.

"For me, it only got worse. There was a man in Iran—"

"The entire goddamn planet," Donald whispered, stressing each word. This was what he said, but all he could think about was his wife Helen pulled down the wrong hill, everything that had ever existed crumbling to ruin. "We killed everyone."

The Senator took in a deep breath and held it a moment. "I told you," he said. "They were already dead."

Donald's knees began bouncing again. There was no controlling it. Thurman studied the report, seemed unsure of something. The paper faintly shook, but maybe it was the overhead vent blowing, which also stirred his hair.

"We were outside of Kashmar," Thurman said. "This was toward the end of the war, when we were getting our butts kicked and telling the world we were winning. I had a corporal in my squad, our team medic, a James Hannigan. Young. Always cracking jokes but serious when he needed to be. The kind of guy everyone likes. The hardest kind to lose."

Thurman shook his head. He stared off into the distance. The vent in the ceiling quieted, but the report continued to quiver.

"I killed a lot of men during the war, but only once to really save a life. The rest, you never knew what you were doing when you pulled the trigger. Maybe the guy you take out is never gonna find his own target, never hurt a soul. Maybe he's gonna be one of the thousands who drop their rifles and blend in with the civvies, go back to their families, open a kasava stand near the embassy and talk basketball with the troops stationed outside. A good man. You never knew. You're killing these men, and you never knew if you were doing it for a good reason or not."

"How many billions—?" Donald swallowed. He slid to the edge of the bed and reached toward the tray. Thurman knew what he was after and passed the glass of water, half empty. He continued to ignore Donald's complaints.

"Hannigan got hit with shrapnel outside of Kashmar. If we could get him to a medic, it was the kind of wound you survived, the kind you lift your shirt in a bar to show off the scars one day. But he couldn't walk, and it was too hot to send in an airlift. Our squad was hemmed in and would need to fight our way out. I didn't think we could get to a safe LZ in time to save him. But what I knew, because I'd seen it too many damn times before, is that two or three of my men would die trying to get him out. That's what happens when you're lugging a soldier instead of a rifle." Thurman pressed his sleeve to his forehead. "I'd seen it before."

"You left him behind," Donald said, seeing where this was going. He took a sip of water. The surface was agitated.

"No. I killed him." Thurman stared at the foot of the bed. He stared at nothing. "The enemy wouldn't have let him die. Not there, not like that. They would've patched him up so they could catch it on film. They would've stitched up his belly so they could open his throat." He turned to Donald. "I had to make a decision, and I had to make it fast. And the longer I've lived with it, the more I've come to agree with what I did. We lost one man that day. I saved two or three others."

Donald shook his head. "That's not the same as what we—what you—"

"It's precisely the same. Do you remember Safed? What the media called the outbreak?"

Donald remembered Safed. An Israeli town near Nazareth. Near Syria. The deadliest WMD strike of the war. He nodded.

"The rest of the world would've looked just like that. Just like Safed." Thurman snapped his fingers. "Ten billion lights go out all at once. We were already infected, son. It was just a matter of triggering it. Safed was . . . like a beta test."

Donald shook his head. "I don't believe you. Why would anyone do that?"

Thurman frowned. "Don't be naive, son. This life means nothing to some. You put a switch in front of ten billion people, a switch that kills every one of us the moment you hit it, and you'd have thousands of hands racing to be the one. Tens of thousands. It would only be a matter of time. And that switch *existed*."

"No." Donald flashed back to the first conversation he'd ever had with the senator as a member of Congress, after winning office the first time. It had felt like this, the lies and the truth intermingling and shielding one another. "You'll never convince me," he said. "You'll have to drug me or kill me. You'll never convince me."

Thurman nodded as if he agreed. "Drugging you doesn't work. I've read up on your first shift. There's a small percentage of people with some kind of resistance. We'd love to know why."

Donald could only laugh. He settled against the wall behind the cot and nestled into the darkness the top bunk provided. "Maybe I've seen too much to forget," he said.

"No, I don't think so." Thurman lowered his head so he could still make eye contact. Donald took a sip of water, both hands wrapped around the glass. "The more you see—the worse the trauma is—the better the medication works. It makes it easier to forget. Except for some people. Which is why we took a sample."

Donald glanced down at his arm. A small square of gauze had been taped over the spot of blood left by the doctor's needle. He felt a caustic mix of helplessness and fear well up inside him. "You woke me to take my blood?"

"Not exactly." Thurman hesitated. "Your resistance to the meds is something I'm curious about, but the reason you're awake is because I was *asked* to wake you. We are losing silos—"

"I thought that was the plan," Donald spat. "Losing silos. I thought that was what you wanted." He remembered crossing Silo 12 out with red ink, all those many lives lost. They had accounted for this. Silos were expendable. That's what he'd been told.

Thurman shook his head. "Whatever's happening out there, we need to understand it. And there's someone here who . . . who thinks you may have stumbled onto the answer. We have a few questions for you, and then we can put you back under."

Back under. So he wasn't going to be out for long. They had only woken him to take his blood and to peer into his mind, and would then put him back to sleep. Donald rubbed his arms, which felt thin and atrophied. He was dying in that pod. Only more slowly than he would like.

"We need to know what you remember about this report." Thurman held it out. Donald waved the thing away.

"I already looked it over," he said. He didn't want to see it again. He could close his eyes and see the desperate people spilling out onto the dusty land, the people that he had ordered dead.

"We have other medications that might ease the—"

"No. No more drugs." Donald crossed his wrists and spread his arms out, slicing the air with both hands. "Look, I don't have a resistance to your drugs." The truth. He was sick of the lies. "There's no mystery. I just stopped taking the pills."

It felt good to admit it. What were they going to do, anyway? Put him back to sleep? He took another sip of water while he let the confession sink in. He swallowed.

"I kept them in my gums and spat them out later. It's as simple as that. Probably the case with anyone else remembering. Like Hal, or Carlton, or whatever his name was."

Thurman regarded him coolly. He tapped the report against his open palm, seeming to digest this. "We know you stopped taking the pills," he finally said. "And when."

Donald shrugged. "Mystery solved, then." He finished his water and put the empty glass back on the tray.

"The drugs you have a resistance to are not in the pills, Donny. The reason people stop taking the pills is because they begin to remember, not the other way around."

Donald studied Thurman, disbelieving.

"Your urine changes color when you stop taking them. You develop sores on your gums where you hide them. These are the signs we look for."

"What?"

"There are no drugs in the pills, Donny."

"I don't believe you."

"We medicate everyone. There are those of us who are immune. But you shouldn't be."

"Bullshit. I remember. The pills made me woozy. As soon as I stopped taking them, I got better."

Thurman tilted his head to the side. "The reason you stopped taking them was because you were . . . I won't say getting better. It was because the fear had begun leaking through. Donny, the medication is in the water." He waved at the empty glass on the tray. Donald followed the gesture and immediately felt sick.

"Don't worry," Thurman said. "We'll get to the bottom of it."

"I don't want to help you. I don't want to talk about this report. I don't want to see whoever it is you need me to see."

He wanted Helen. All he wanted was his wife.

"There's a chance that thousands will die if you don't help us. There's a chance that you stumbled onto something with this report of yours, even if I don't believe it."

Donald glanced at the door to the bathroom, thought about locking himself inside and forcing himself to throw up, to expunge the food and the water. Maybe Thurman was lying to him. Maybe he was telling the truth. A lie would mean the water was just water. The truth would mean that he did have some sort of resistance.

"I barely remember writing the damn thing," he admitted. And who would want to see him? He assumed it would be another doctor, maybe a silo head, maybe whoever was running this shift.

He rubbed his temples, could feel the pressure building between them. Perhaps he should just do as they wanted and be put back to sleep, back to his dreams. Now and then, he had dreamed of Helen. It was the only place he could be with her.

"Okay," he said. "I'll go. But I still don't understand what I could possibly know." He rubbed his arm where they'd taken the blood. There was an itch there. An itch so deep it felt like a bruise.

Senator Thurman nodded. "I tend to agree with you. But that's not what she thinks."

Donald stiffened. "She?" He searched Thurman's eyes, wondering if he'd heard correctly. "She who?"

The old man frowned. "The one who had me wake you." He waved his hand at the bunk. "Get some rest. I'll take you to her in the morning."

31

HE COULDN'T REST. The hours were cruel, slow and unknowable. There was no clock to mark their passing, no answer to his frustrated slaps on the door. Donald was left to lie in his bunk and stare at the diamond patterns of interlocking wires holding the mattress above him, to listen to the gurgle of water in hidden pipes as it rushed to another room. He couldn't sleep. He had no idea if it was the middle of the night or the middle of the day. The weight of the silo pressed down upon him.

When the boredom grew intolerable, Donald eventually gave in and looked over the report a second time. He studied it more closely. It wasn't the original; the signature was flat, and he remembered using a blue pen.

He skimmed the account of the silo's collapse and his theory that IT heads shadowed too young. His recommendation was to raise the age. He wondered if they had. Maybe so, but the problems were persisting. There was also mention of a young man he had inducted, a young man with a question. This young man's great-grandmother was one of those who remembered, much like Donald. His report suggested allowing one question from each inductee. They were given the Legacy, after all. Why not show them, in that final stage of indoctrination, that there were more truths to be had?

The tiny clicks of a key entering a lock. Thurman opened the door as Donald folded the report away.

"Feeling better?" Thurman asked.

Donald didn't say.

"Can you walk?"

He nodded. A walk. When what he really wanted was to run screaming down the hallway and punch holes in walls. But a walk would do. A walk before his next long sleep.

They rode the lift in silence. Donald noticed Thurman had scanned his badge before pressing the button for level fifty-four. Its number stood bright and new while so many others had been worn away. There was nothing but supplies on that level if Donald remembered correctly, supplies they weren't ever supposed to need. The lift slowed as it approached a level it normally skipped. The doors opened on a cavernous expanse of shelves stocked with instruments of death.

Thurman led him down the middle of it all. There were wooden crates with "ammo" stenciled on the side, longer crates beside them with military designations like "M22" and "M19." There were rows of shelves with armor and helmets, with boxes marked "medical" and "rations," many more boxes unlabeled. And beyond the shelves, tarps covered bulbous and winged forms that he knew to be drones. UAVs. His sister had flown them in a war that now seemed pointless and distant, part of ancient history. But here these relics stood, oiled and covered, reeking of grease and fear.

Beyond the drones, Thurman led the way through a murky dimness that made the storehouse seem to go on forever. At the far end of the wide room, a glow of light leaked from an open-doored office. There were sounds of paper stirring, a chair squeaking as someone turned. Donald reached the doorway and saw, inexplicably, *her* sitting there.

"Anna?"

She sat behind a wide conference table ringed with identical chairs, looked up from a spread of paperwork and a computer monitor. There was no shock on her part, just a smile of acknowledgement and a weariness that her smile could not conceal.

Her father crossed the room while Donald gaped. Thurman squeezed her arm and kissed her on the cheek, but Anna's eyes did not leave Donald's. The old man whispered something to his daughter, then announced that he had work of his own to see to. Donald did not budge until the Senator had left the room.

"Anna—"

She was already around the massive table, wrapping her arms around him. She began whispering things, comforting words as Donald sagged into her embrace, suddenly exhausted. He felt her hand caress the back of his head and come to a rest on his neck. His own arms interlocked around her back.

"What're you doing here?" he whispered.

"I'm here for the same reason you are." She pulled back from the embrace. "I'm looking for answers." She stepped away and surveyed the mess on the table. "To different questions, perhaps."

A familiar schematic—a grid of fifty silos—covered the table. Each silo was like a small plate, all of them trapped under glass. A dozen chairs were gathered around. Donald realized that this was a war room, where generals stood and pushed plastic models and grumbled over lives lost by the thousands. He glanced up at the maps and schematics plastered on the walls. There was an adjoining bathroom, a towel hanging from a hook on the door. A cot had been set up in the far corner and was neatly made. There was a lamp beside it sitting on one of the wooden crates from the storeroom. Extension cords snaked here and there, signs of a room long converted into an apartment of sorts.

He turned to the nearest wall and flipped through some of the drawings. They were three layers deep in places and covered in notes. It didn't look as if a war was being planned. It looked like a scene from the crime shows that used to lull him to sleep in a former life.

"You've been up longer than me," he said.

Anna stood beside him. Her hand alighted on his shoulder, and Donald felt himself startle to be touched at all.

"Almost a year now." Her hand slid down his back before falling away. "Can I get you a drink? Water? I also have a stash of Scotch down here. Dad doesn't know half the stuff they hid away in these crates."

Donald shook his head. He turned and watched as she disappeared into the bathroom and ran the tap. She emerged, sipping from a glass.

"What's going on here?" he asked. "Why am I up?"

She swallowed and waved her glass at the walls. "It's—" She laughed and shook her head. "I was about to say it's nothing, but this is the hell that keeps me out of one box and in another. It doesn't concern you, most of this."

Donald studied the room again. A year, living like this. He turned his attention to Anna, the way her hair was balled up in a bun, a pen sticking out of it. Her skin was pale except for the dark rings beneath her eyes. He wondered how she was able to do this, live like this.

There was a printout on the far wall that matched the table, a grid of circles, the layout of the facilities. A familiar red X had been drawn across what he knew to be Silo 12 in the upper-left corner. There was another X nearby, a new one in what looked to be Silo 10. More lives lost. And in the lower right-hand corner of the grid, a mess that made no sense. The room seemed to wobble as he took a step closer.

"Donny?"

"What happened here?" he asked, his voice a whisper. Anna turned to see what he was looking at. She glanced at the table, and he realized that her paperwork was scattered around the same corner of the facility. The glass surface crawled with notes written in red and blue wax.

"Donny—" She stepped closer. "Things aren't good."

He turned and studied the scrawl of red marks on the wall schematic. There were X's and question marks. There were notes in red ink with lines and arrows. Ten or a dozen of the silos were heavily marked up.

"How many?" he asked, trying to count, to figure the thousands of lives lost. "Are they gone?"

She took a deep breath. "We don't know." She finished her water, walked down the long table and reached into one of the chairs pushed up against it. She procured a bottle and poured a few fingers into her plastic cup.

"It started with Silo Forty," she said. "It went dark about a year ago—"

"Went dark?"

Anna took a sip of the Scotch and nodded. She licked her lips. "The camera feeds went out first. Not at once, but eventually they got them all. We lost contact with the heads over there. Couldn't raise anyone. Erskine was running the shift at the time. He followed the Order and gave the okay to shut the silo down—"

"You mean kill everyone."

Anna shot him a look. "You know what had to be done."

Donald remembered Silo 12. He remembered making that same decision. As if there had been a decision to make. The system ran automatically. Wasn't he just doing what came next, following a set of procedures written down by someone else?

He studied the poster with the red marks. "And the rest of them? The other silos?"

Anna finished the drink with one long pull and gasped for air afterward. Donald caught her eyeing the bottle. "They woke up Dad when Forty-Two went. Two more silos had gone dark by the time he came for me."

Two more silos. "Why you?" he asked.

She tucked a strand of loose hair behind her ear. "Because there was no one else. Because everyone who had a hand in designing this place was either gone or at their wits' end. Because Dad was desperate."

"He wanted to see you."

She laughed. "It wasn't that. Trust me." She waved her empty cup at the arrangement of circles on the table and the spread of papers. "They were using the radios at high frequencies. We think it started with Forty, that maybe their IT head went rogue. They hijacked their antenna and began communicating with the other silos around them, and we couldn't cut them off. They had taken care of that as well. As soon as Dad suspected this, he argued with the others that wireless networks were my specialty. They eventually relented. No one wanted to use the drones."

"Argued with what others? Who knows you're here?" Donald couldn't help but think how dangerous this could get, but maybe that was his own weakness screaming at him.

"My dad, Erskine, Dr. Sneed, his assistants who brought me out. But those assistants won't work another shift—"

"Deep freeze?"

Anna frowned and splashed her cup, and it struck Donald how much had been lost while he had slept. Entire shifts had gone by. Another silo had gone dark, another red X drawn on the map. An entire corner of silos had run into some kind of trouble. Thurman, meanwhile, had been awake for a year, dealing with it. His daughter as well. Donald waved his arm at the room. "You've been stuck in here for a year? Working on this?"

She jerked her head at the door and laughed. "I've been cooped up in worse for a lot longer. But yeah, it sucks. I'm sick of this place." She took another sip, her cup hiding her expression, and Donald wondered if perhaps he was awake because of her weakness just as she might be awake because of her father's. What was next? Him searching the deep freeze for his sister Charlotte?

"We've lost contact with eleven silos so far." Anna peered into her cup. "I think I've got it contained, but we're still trying to figure out how it happened or if anyone's still alive over there. I personally don't think so, but Dad wants to send scouts or drones. Everyone says that's too big a risk. And now it looks like Eighteen is going to burn itself to the ground."

"And I'm supposed to help? What does your father think I know?" He stepped around the planning table and waved for the bottle. Anna splashed her cup and handed the drink to him; she reached for another cup by her monitor while Donald collapsed onto her cot. It was a lot to take in.

"It's not Dad who thinks you know anything. He didn't want you up at all. No one's supposed to come out of deep freeze." She screwed the cap back on the bottle. "It was his boss."

Donald nearly choked on his first sip of the Scotch. He sputtered and wiped his chin with his sleeve while Anna looked on with concern.

"His *boss*?" he asked, gasping for air.

She narrowed her eyes. "Dad told you why you're here, right?"

He fumbled in his pocket for the report. "Something I wrote during my last . . . during my shift. Thurman has a boss? I thought he was in charge."

Anna laughed humorlessly. "Nobody's in charge," she told him. "The system's in charge. It just runs. We built it to just *go*."

She got up from her desk and walked over to join him on the cot. Donald slid over to give her more room.

"Dad was in charge of digging the holes, that was his job. There were three of them who planned most of this. The other two had ideas for how to hide this place. Dad convinced them they should just build it in plain sight. The nuclear containment facility was his idea, and he was in a position to make it happen."

"You said three. Who were the others?"

"Victor and Erskine." Anna adjusted a pillow and leaned back against the wall. "Not their real names, of course. But what does it matter? A name is a name. You can be anyone down here. Erskine was the one who discovered the original threat, who told Victor and Dad about the nanos. You'll meet him. He's been on a double shift with me, working on the loss of these silos, but it's not his area of expertise. Do you need more?" She nodded at his cup.

"No. I'm already feeling dizzy." He didn't add that it wasn't from the alcohol. "I remember a Victor from my shift. He worked across the hall from me."

"The same." She looked away for a moment. "Dad refers to him as the boss, but I've been working with Victor for a while, and he never thought of himself that way. He thought of himself as a steward, joked once about feeling like Noah. He wanted to wake you months ago because of what's happening in Eighteen, but Dad vetoed the idea. I think Victor was fond of you. He talked about you a lot."

"Victor talked about *me*?" Donald remembered the man across the hall from him, the shrink. Anna reached up and wiped underneath her eyes.

"Yes. He was a brilliant man, could tell what you were thinking, what anyone was thinking. He planned most of this. Wrote the Order, the original Pact. It was all his design."

"What do you mean *was*?"

Her lip trembled. She tipped her cup, but there was little left in the bottom.

"Victor's dead," she said. "He shot himself at his desk two days ago."

32

"VICTOR? SHOT HIMSELF?" Donald tried to imagine the composed man who had worked across the hall from him doing such a thing. "Why?"

Anna sniffed and slid closer to Donald. She twisted the empty cup in her hands. "We don't know. He was obsessed with that first silo we lost. Obsessed. It broke my heart to see how he blamed himself. He used to say that he could see certain things coming, that there were . . . probabilistic certainties." She said these two words in a mimic of his voice, which brought the old man's face even more vividly to Donald's mind.

"But it killed him not to know the precise when and where." She dabbed her eyes. "He would've been better off if it'd happened on someone else's shift. Not his. Not where he'd feel guilty."

"He blamed me," Donald said, staring at the floor. "It was on my shift. I was such a mess. I couldn't think straight."

"What? No. Donny, no." She rested a hand on his knee. "There's no one to blame."

"But my report—" He still had it in his hand, folded up and dotted here and there with pale blue.

Anna's eyes fell to the piece of paper. "Is that a copy?" She reached for it, brushed the loose strands of hair off her face.

"Dad had the courage to tell you about this but not about what Vic did." She shook her head. "Victor was strong in some ways, so weak in others." She turned to Donald. "He was found at his desk, surrounded by notes, everything he had on this silo, and your report was on top."

She unfolded the page and studied the words. "Just a copy," she whispered.

"Maybe it was—" Donald began.

"He wrote notes all over the original." She slid her finger across the page. "Right about here, he wrote: 'This is why.'"

"This is why? As in why he did it?" Donald waved his hand at the room. "Shouldn't *this* be why? Maybe he realized he'd made a mistake." He held Anna's arm. "Think about what we've done. What if we followed a crazy man down here? Maybe Victor had a sudden bout of *sanity*. What if he woke up for a second and saw what we'd done?"

"No." Anna shook her head. "We had to do this."

He slapped the wall behind the cot. "That's what everyone keeps saying."

"Listen to me." She placed a hand on his knee, tried to soothe him. "You need to keep it together, okay?" She glanced at the door, a fearful look in her eyes. "I asked him to wake you because I need your help. I can't do this alone. Vic was working on the situation in Silo Eighteen. If Dad has his way, he'll just terminate the place not to have to deal with it. Victor didn't want that. *I* don't want that."

Donald thought of Silo 12, which he'd terminated. But it was already falling, wasn't it? It was already too late. They had opened the airlock. He looked at the schematic on the wall and wondered if it was too late for Silo 18 as well.

"What did he see in my report?" he asked.

"I don't know. But he wanted to wake you weeks ago. He thought you had touched on something."

"Or maybe it was just because I was around at the time."

Donald looked at the room of clues. Anna had been digging, tearing into a different problem. So many questions and answers. His mind was clear, not like last time. He had questions of his own. He wanted to find his sister, find out what happened to Helen, dispel this crazy thought that she was still out there somewhere. He wanted to know more about this damnable place he'd helped build.

"You'll help us?" Anna asked. She rested her hand on his back, and her comforting touch brought back the memory of his wife, of the moments she would soothe and care for him. He startled as if bitten, some part of him thinking for a moment that he was still married, that she was alive out there, maybe frozen and waiting for him to wake her.

"I need . . ." He jumped up and glanced around the room. His eyes fell to the computer on the desk. "I need to look some things up."

Anna rose beside him. "Of course. I can fill you in with what we know so far. Victor left a series of notes. He wrote all over your report. I can show you. And maybe you can convince Dad that he was on to something, that this silo is worth saving—"

"Yes," Donald said. He would do it. But only so he could stay awake. And he wondered for a moment if that was Anna's intention as well. To keep him around, near to her. An hour earlier, all he had wanted was to go back to sleep, to escape the world he had helped create. But now he wanted answers. He would look into Silo 18, but he would find Helen as well. Find out what had happened to her, where she was. He thought of Mick, and Tennessee flashed in his mind. He turned to the wall schematic with all the silos and tried to remember which state went with which number.

"What can we access from here?" he asked. His skin flushed with heat as he thought of the answers at his disposal.

Anna turned toward the door. There were footsteps out there in the darkness.

"Dad. He's the only one with access to this level anymore."

"Anymore?" He turned back to Anna.

"Yeah. Where do you think Victor got the gun?" She lowered her voice. "I was in here when he came down and cracked open one of the crates. I never heard him. Look, my father blames himself for what happened to Victor, and he still doesn't believe this has anything to do with you or your report. But I knew Vic. He wasn't crazy. If there's anything you can do, please. For me."

She squeezed his hand. Donald looked down, didn't realize she'd been holding it. The folded report was in her other hand. The footsteps approached. Donald nodded his assent.

"Thank you," she said. She dropped his hand, grabbed his empty cup from the cot, and nested hers with it. She tucked the cups and the bottle into one of the chairs and slid it under the table. Thurman arrived at the door and rapped the jamb with his knuckles.

"Come in," Anna said, brushing loose hair off her face.

Thurman studied the two of them for a moment. "Erskine is planning a small ceremony," he said. "Just us. Those of us who know."

Anna nodded. "Of course."

Thurman narrowed his eyes and glanced from his daughter to Donald. Anna seemed to take it as a question.

"Donny thinks he can help," she said. "We both think it's best for him to work down here with me. At least until we make some progress."

Donald turned to her in shock. Thurman said nothing.

"We'll need another computer," she added. "If you bring one down, I can set it up."

That, Donald liked the sound of.

"And another cot, of course," Anna added with a smile.

33

Silo 18

MISSION SLUNK AWAY after the scuffle with the farmers, and the rest of the porters scattered. He stole a few hours of sleep at the upper way station on level ten, his nose numb and lips throbbing from a blow he'd taken. Tossing and turning, too restless to stay put, he rose in the dim-time and realized it was too early yet to go to the Nest; the Crow would still be asleep. And so he headed to the cafeteria for a sunrise and a decent breakfast, the coroner's bonus burning in his pockets the way his knuckles burned from their scrapes.

He nursed his aches with a welcomed hot meal, eating with those coming off a midnight shift, and watched the clouds boil and come to life across the hills. The towering husks in the distance—the Crow called them skyscrapers—were the first to catch the rising sun. It was a sign that the world would wake one more day. His birthday, Mission realized. He left his dishes on the table, a chit for whoever cleaned after him, and tried not to think of cleaning at all. Instead, he rushed down the eight flights of stairs before the silo fully woke. He headed toward the Nest, feeling not a day older at all.

Familiar words greeted him at the landing on level nine. There, above the door, rather than a level number it read:

THE CROW'S NEST

The words were painted in bright and blocky letters. They followed the outlines from years and generations prior, color piled on color and letters crooked from more than one young hand's involvement. The children of the silo came and went and left their marks with bristles, but the Old Crow remained.

Her nest comprised the nursery, day school, and classrooms that served the Up Top. She had been perched there for longer than any alive could remember. Some said she was as old as the silo itself, but Mission knew that was just a legend. Nobody knew how old the silo was.

He entered the Nest to find the hallways empty and quiet, the hour early still. There was a soft screech from one classroom as desks were put back into order. Mission caught a glimpse of two teachers conferring in another classroom, their faces scrunched up with worry, probably wondering what to do with a younger version of himself. The scent of strong tea mixed with the odor of paste and chalk. There were rows of metal lockers in dire need of paint and stippled with dents from tiny fists; they transported Mission back to another age. It felt like just yesterday that he had terrorized that hall. He and all his friends whom he didn't see anymore—or at least not as often as he'd like.

The Crow's room was at the far end and adjoined the only apartment on the entire level. The apartment had been built especially for her, converted from a classroom, or so they said. And while she only taught the youngest children anymore, the entire school was hers. This was her nest.

Mission remembered coming to her at various stages of his life. Early on, for comfort, feeling so very far from the farms.

Later, for wisdom, when he was finally old enough to admit he had none. And more than once he had come for both, like the day he had learned the truth of his birth and his mother's death—that she had been sent to clean because of him. Mission remembered that day well. It was the only time he'd ever seen the Old Crow cry.

He knocked on her classroom door before entering and found her at the blackboard that'd been lowered so she could write on it from her chair. Mrs. Crowe stopped erasing yesterday's lessons, turned and beamed at him.

"My boy," she croaked. She waved with the eraser to beckon him closer. A chalky haze filled the air. "My boy, my boy."

"Hello, Mrs. Crowe." Mission passed between the handful of desks to get to her. The power line for her electric chair drooped from the center of the ceiling to a pole that rose up from the chair's back. Mission ducked beneath it as he got closer and bent to give the Crow a hug. His hands wrapped around her, and he breathed in her smell—one of childhood and innocence. The yellow gown she wore, spotted with flowers, was her outfit for Wednesdays, as good as any calendar. It had faded since Mission's time, as all things had.

"I do believe you've grown," she said, smiling up at him. Her voice was barely a whisper, and he recalled how it kept even the young ones quiet so they could hear what was being said. She brought her hand up and touched her own cheek. "What happened to your face?"

Mission laughed and shrugged off his porter's pack. "Just an accident," he said, lying to her like old times. He placed his pack at the foot of one of the tiny desks, could imagine squeezing into the thing and staying for the day's lesson.

"How've you been?" he asked. He studied her face, the deep wrinkles and dark skin like a farmer's but from age rather than grow lights. Her eyes were rheumy, but there was life still behind them. They reminded Mission of the wallscreens on a bright day but in dire need of a cleaning.

"Not so good," Mrs. Crowe said. She twisted the lever on her armrest, and the chair built for her decades ago by some long-gone former student whirred around to face him better. Pulling back her sleeve, she showed Mission a gauze bandage taped to her thin and splotchy arm. "Those doctors came and took my blood away." Her hand shook as she indicated the evidence. "Took half of it, by my reckoning."

Mission laughed. "I'm pretty sure they didn't take half your blood, Mrs. Crowe. The doctors are just looking out for you."

She twisted up her face, an explosion of wrinkles. She didn't seem so sure. "I don't trust them," she said.

Mission smiled. "You don't trust anyone. And hey, maybe they're just trying to figure out why you can't die like everyone else does. Maybe they'll come up with a way for everyone to live as long as you someday."

Mrs. Crowe rubbed the bandage on her withering arm. "Or they're figuring out how to *kill* me," she said.

"Oh, don't be so sinister." Mission reached forward and pulled her sleeve down to keep her from messing with the bandage. "Why would you think such a thing?"

She frowned and declined to answer. Her eyes fell to his near-empty pack. "Day off?" she asked.

Mission turned and followed her gaze. "Hmm? Oh, no. I dropped something off last night. I'll pick up another delivery in a little bit, take it wherever they tell me to."

"Oh, to be so young and free again." Mrs. Crowe spun her chair around and steered it behind her desk. Mission ducked beneath the pivoting wire out of habit; the pole at the back of the chair was made with younger heads in mind. She picked up a container of the vile vegetable pulp she preferred over water and took a sip. "Allie stopped by last week." She set the greenish-black fluid down. "She was asking about you. Wanted to know if you were still single."

"Oh?" Mission could feel his temperature shoot up. Mrs. Crowe had caught them kissing once, back before he knew what kissing was for. She had left them with a warning and a knowing smile. "Everyone's so spread out," Mission said, changing the subject, hoping she might take the hint.

"As it should be." The Crow opened a drawer on her desk and rummaged around, came out with an envelope. Mission could see a half-dozen names scratched out across the thing. It had been used a handful of times. "You're heading down from here? Maybe you could drop off something for Rodny?"

She held out the letter. Mission took it, saw his best friend's name written on the outside, all the other names crossed out.

"I can leave it for him, sure. But the last two times I stopped by there, they said he was unavailable."

Mrs. Crowe nodded as if this was to be expected. "Ask for Jeffery, he's the head of Security down there, one of my boys. You tell him that this is from me and that I said you should hand it to Rodny yourself. In person." She waved her hands in the air, little trembling blurs. "I'll write Jeffery a note."

Mission glanced up at the clock on the wall while she dug into her desk for a pen and ink. Soon the hallways would begin filling with youthful chatter and the opening and slamming of lockers. He waited patiently while she scratched her note and scanned old posters and banners on the walls, the "motivators," as Mrs. Crowe liked to call them.

You can be anything, one of them said. It featured a crude drawing of a boy and a girl standing on a huge mound. The mound was green and the sky blue, just like in the picture books. Another one said: *Dream to your heart's delight*. It had bands of color in a graceful arcing sweep. The Crow had a name for the shape, but he'd forgotten what it was called. Another familiar one: *Go new places.* It featured a drawing of a crow perched in an impossibly large tree, its wings spread as if it were about to take flight.

"Jeffery is the bald one," Mrs. Crowe said. She waved a hand over her own white and thinning hair to demonstrate.

"I know," Mission said. It was a strange reminder that so many of the adults and elders throughout the silo had been her students as well. A locker was slammed in the hallway. Mission remembered when he was a kid how the rows and rows of tiny desks had filled the room. There were cubbies full of rolled mats for nap time, reminding him of the daily routine of clearing a space in the middle of the floor, finding his mat, and drifting off to sleep while the Crow sang forgotten songs. He missed those days. He missed the Old Time stories about a world full of impossible things. Leaning against that little desk, Mission suddenly felt as ancient as the Crow, just as impossibly distant from his youth.

"Give Jeffery this, and then see that Rodny gets my note. From you personally, okay?"

He grabbed his pack and slid both pieces of correspondence into his courier pouch. There was no mention of payment, just the twinge of guilt Mission felt for even thinking of it. Digging into the pack reminded him of the items he had brought her, forgotten due to the previous night's brawl.

"Oh, I brought you these from the farm." He pulled out a few small cucumbers, two peppers and a large tomato, bearing a bruise. He placed them on her desk. "For your veggie drinks," he said.

Mrs. Crowe clasped her hands together and smiled with delight.

"Is there anything else you need next time I'm passing by?"

"These visits," she said, her face a wrinkle of smiles. "All I care about are my little ones. Stop by whenever you can, okay?"

Mission squeezed her arm, which felt like a broomstick tucked into a sleeve. "I will," he said. "And that reminds me: Frankie told me to tell you hello."

"He should come more often," she told him, her voice aquiver.

"Not everyone gets around like I do," he said. "I'm sure he'd like to see you more often as well."

"You tell him," she said. "Tell him I don't have much time left—"

Mission laughed and waved off the morbid thought. "You probably told my grandfather the same thing when he was young, and his father before him."

The Crow smiled as if this were true. "Predict the inevitable," she said, "and you're bound to be right one day."

Mission smiled. He liked that. "Still, I wish you wouldn't talk about dying. Nobody likes to hear it."

"They may not like it, but a reminder is good." She held out her arms, the sleeves of her flowered dress falling away and revealing the bandage once more. "Tell me, what do you see when you look at these hands?" She turned them over, back and forth.

"I see time," Mission blurted out, not sure where the thought came from. He tore his eyes away, suddenly finding her skin to be grotesque. Like shriveled potatoes found deep in the soil long after harvest time. He hated himself for feeling it.

"Time, sure," Mrs. Crowe said. "There's time here aplenty. But there's *remnants* too. I remember things being better, once. You think on the bad to remind yourself of the good."

She studied her hands a moment longer, as if looking for something else. When she lifted her gaze and peered at Mission, her eyes were shining with sadness. Mission could feel his own eyes watering, partly from discomfort, partly due to the somber pall that had been cast over their conversation. It reminded him that today was his birthday, a thought that tightened his neck and emptied his chest. He was sure the Crow knew what day it was. She just loved him enough not to say.

"I was beautiful, once, you know." Mrs. Crowe withdrew her hands and folded them in her lap. "Once that's gone, once it leaves us for good, no one will ever see it again."

Mission felt a powerful urge to soothe her, to tell Mrs. Crowe that she was still beautiful in plenty of ways. She could still make music. Could paint. Few others remembered how. She could make children feel loved and safe, another bit of magic long forgotten.

"When I was your age," the Crow said, smiling, "I could have any boy I wanted."

She laughed, dispelling the tension and casting away the shadows, but Mission believed her, even though he couldn't picture it, couldn't imagine away the wrinkles and the spots and the long strands of hair on her knuckles. Still, he believed her. He always did.

"The world is a lot like me." She lifted her gaze to the ceiling and perhaps beyond. "The world was beautiful once too."

Mission sensed an Old Time story brewing like a storm of clouds. More lockers were slammed in the hallway, little voices gathering.

"Tell me," Mission said, remembering the hours that had passed like eyeblinks at her feet, the songs she sang while children slept. "Tell me about the old world."

The Old Crow's eyes narrowed and settled on a dark corner of the room. Her lips, furrowed with the wrinkles of time, parted and a story began, a story Mission had heard a thousand times before. But it never got old, visiting this land of the Crow's imagination. And as the little ones skipped into the room and slipped into their tiny desks, they too fell silent and gathered around, following along with the widest of eyes and the most open of minds these tales of a world, once beautiful, and now fairly forgotten.

34

THE STORIES MRS. CROWE made up were straight from the children's books. There were blue skies and lands of green, animals like dogs and cats but bigger than people. Juvenile stuff. And yet, these fantastic tales of a better place left Mission angry at the world he lived in. As he left the Up Top behind and wound his way down, past the farms and the levels of his youth, he thought of this better world and was dismayed at the one he knew. The promise of an *elsewhere* highlighted the flaws of the familiar. He had gone off to be a porter, to fly away and be all that he wished, and now what he wished was to be further away than this world would allow.

These were dangerous thoughts. They reminded him of his mother and where she had been sent seventeen years ago to the day.

Past the farms, Mission noted a hint of something burning further down the silo. The air was hazy, and there was the bitter tinge of smoke on the back of his tongue. A trash pile, maybe. Someone who didn't want to pay the fee to have it ported to recycling. Or someone who didn't think the silo would be around long enough to *need* to recycle.

It could be an accident, of course, but Mission doubted it. Nobody thought that way anymore. He could see it on the faces of those on the stairwell. He could see by the way belongings were clutched, children sheltered, that the future of the silo hung in the balance. Last night's fight seemed to prove it.

Mission adjusted his pack and hurried down to the IT levels on thirty-four. When he arrived, there was a crowd gathering on the landing. It was mostly boys his age or a little older, many that he recognized, a lot from the Mids. Several stood with computers tucked under their arms, wires dangling, jostling with the throng. Mission picked his way through. Inside, he found a barrier had been set up just beyond the door. Two men from Security manned the temporary gate and allowed only crumpled IT workers through.

"Delivery," Mission shouted. He worked his way to the front, carefully extracting the note Mrs. Crowe had written. "Delivery for Officer Jeffery."

One of the security men took the note. Mission was pressed against the barrier by the crush behind him. A woman was waved through. She hurried toward the proper security gate leading into the main hall, smoothing her overalls with obvious relief. There were crowds of young men being given instructions in one corner of the wide hall. They stood to attention in neat rank and file, but their wide eyes gave away their obvious fear.

"What the hell is going on?" Mission asked as the barrier was parted for him.

"What the hell isn't?" one of the security guards answered. "Power spike last night took out a load of computers. Every one of our techs is pulling a double. There's a fire down in Mechanical or something, and some kinda violence up in the farms. Did you get the wire?"

Mechanical. That was a long way away to nose a fire. And word was out about last night's raid, making him self-conscious of the cut on his nose. "What wire?" he asked.

The security guard pointed to the groups of boys. "We're hiring. New techs."

All Mission saw were young men, and the guy talking to them was with Security, not IT. The security guard handed the note back to Mission and pointed toward the main gate. The woman from earlier was already beeping her way through, a large and familiar bald head swiveling to watch her ass as she headed down the hall.

"Sir?" he called out as he approached the gate.

Jeffery turned his head, the deep wrinkles and folds of flesh disappearing from his neck.

"Hmm? Oh—" he snapped his fingers, trying to place the name.

"Mission."

He wagged his finger. "That's right. You need to leave something with me, porter?" He held out a palm but seemed disinterested.

Mission handed him the note. "Actually, I have orders from Mrs. Crowe to deliver something in person." He pulled the sealed envelope with the crossed-out names from his courier pouch. "Just a letter, sir."

The old guard glanced at the envelope, then continued reading the note addressed to him. "Rodny isn't available." He shook his head. "I can't give you a timeframe, either. Could be weeks. You wanna leave it with me?"

Again, an outstretched palm, but this time with more interest. Mission pulled the envelope back warily. "I can't. There's no way I can just hand it to him? This is the Crow, man. If it were the mayor asking me, I'd say no problem."

Jeffery smiled. "You were one of her boys too?"

Mission nodded. The head of Security looked past him at a man approaching the gate with his ID out. Mission stepped aside as the gentleman scanned his way through, nodding good morning to Jeffery.

"Tell you what. I'm taking Rodny his lunch in a little bit. When I do, you can come with me, hand him the letter with me standing there, and I won't have to worry about the Crow nipping my hide later. How's that sound?"

Mission smiled. "Sounds good, man. I appreciate it."

The officer pointed across the noisy entrance hall. "Why don't you go grab yourself some water and hang in the conference room. There's some boys in there filling out paperwork." Jeffery looked Mission up and down. "In fact, why don't you fill out an application? We could use you."

"I . . . uh, don't know much about computers," Mission said.

Jeffery shrugged as if that were irrelevant. "Suit yourself. One of the lads will be relieving me in a little bit. I'll come get you."

Mission thanked him again. He crossed the large entrance hall where neat columns and rows of young men listened to barked instructions. Another guard waved him inside the conference room while holding out a sheet of paper and a shard of charcoal. Mission saw that the back of the paper was blank and took it with no plan for filling it out. Half a chit right there in usable paper.

There were a few empty chairs around the wide table. He chose one. A number of boys scribbled with their charcoals on the pages, faces scrunched up in concentration. Mission sat with his back to the only window and placed his sack on the table, kept the letter in his hands. He slid the application inside his pack for future use and studied the Crow's letter for the first time.

The envelope was old but addressed only a handful of times. One edge was worn tissue thin, a small tear revealing a folded piece of paper inside. Peering more closely, Mission saw that it was pulp paper, probably made in the Crow's Nest by one of her kids—water and handfuls of torn paper blended up, pressed down on screens and left overnight to dry.

"Mission," someone at the table hissed.

He looked up to see Bradley sitting across from him. The fellow porter had his blue 'chief tied around his bicep. Mission had thought he was running a regular route in the Down Deep.

"You applying?" Bradley hissed.

One of the other boys coughed into his fist as if he were asking for quiet. It looked as though Bradley was already done with his application.

Mission shook his head. There was a knock on the window behind him and he nearly dropped the letter as he whirled around. Jeffery stuck his head in the door. "Two minutes," the security guard said to Mission. He jabbed his thumb over his shoulder. "I'm just waiting on his tray."

Mission bobbed his head as the door was pulled shut. The other boys looked at him curiously.

"Delivery," Mission explained to Bradley loud enough for the others to hear. He pulled his pack closer and hid the envelope behind it. The boys went back to their scribbling. Bradley frowned and watched the others.

Mission studied the envelope again. Two minutes. How long would he have with Rodny? He tickled the corner of the sealed flap. The milk paste the Crow had used didn't stick very well to the months-old—maybe years-old—dried glue from before. He worked one corner loose without glancing down at the envelope. Instead, he watched Bradley as he disobeyed the third cardinal rule of porting, telling himself this was different, that this was two old friends talking and he was just in the room with them, overhearing.

Even so, his hands trembled as he pulled the letter out. He glanced down, keeping the note hidden. Purple and red string lay strewn in with the dark gray of cheap paper. The writing was in chalk. It meant the words had to be big. White powder gathered in the folds as it shivered loose from the words like dust falling from old pipes:

Soon, soon, the momma bird sings. Take flight, take flight!

Part of an old nursery rhyme. *Beat your wings,* Mission whispered silently, remembering the rest, a story about a young crow learning to be free.

Beat your wings and fly away to brighter things.
Fly, fly with all your might!

He started to check the back for a real note, something beyond this fragment of a rhyme, when someone banged on the window again. Several of the other boys dropped their charcoals, visibly startled. One boy cursed under his breath. Mission whirled around to see Jeffery on the other side of the glass, a covered meal tray balanced on one palm, his bald head jerking impatiently.

Mission folded the letter up and stuffed it back in the envelope. He raised his hand over his head to let Jeffery know he'd be right there, licked one finger and ran it across the sticky paste, resealing the envelope as best he could. "Good luck," he told Bradley, even though he had no clue what the kid thought he was doing. He dragged his pack off the table, was careful to wipe away the chalk dust that had spilled, and hurried out of the conference room.

"Let's go," Jeffery said, clearly annoyed.

Mission hurried after him. He glanced back once at the window, then over at the noisy crowd jostling against the temporary barriers by the door. An IT tech approached the crowd with a computer, wires coiled neatly on top, and a woman reached out desperately from behind the barrier like a mother yearning for her baby.

"Since when did people start bringing their own computers up?" he asked, his profession having made him curious about how things got from there to here and back again. It felt as though this was yet another loop the porters were being cut out of. Roker would have a fit.

"Yesterday. Wyck decided he wouldn't be sending his techs out to fix them anymore. Says it's safer this way. People are being robbed out there and there's not enough security to go around."

They were waved through the gates and wound in silence through the hallways, every office full of clacking sounds or people arguing. Mission saw electrical parts and paper strewn everywhere. He wondered which office Rodny was in and why nobody else was having their food delivered. Maybe his friend was in trouble. That was it. That would make sense of everything. Maybe he had pulled one of his stunts. Did they have a holding cell on thirty-four? He didn't think so. He was about to ask Jeffery if Rodny was in the pen when the old security guard stopped at an imposing steel door.

"Here." He held the tray out to Mission, who stuck the letter between his lips and accepted it. Jeffery glanced back, blocked Mission's view of the door's keypad with his body, and tapped in a code. A series of clunks sounded in the jamb of the heavy door. Fucking right, Rodny was in trouble. What kind of holding cell was this?

The door swung inward. Jeffery grabbed the tray and told Mission to wait there. Mission still had the taste of milk paste on his lips as he watched the Security chief step inside a room that seemed to go back quite a way. The lights inside pulsed as if something was wrong, red warning lights like a fire alarm. Jeffery called out for Rodny while Mission tried to peek around the guard for a better look.

Rodny arrived a moment later, almost as if he were expecting them. His eyes widened when he saw Mission standing there. Mission fought to close his own mouth, which he could feel hanging open at the sight of his friend.

"Hey." Rodny pulled open the heavy door a little further and glanced down the hallway. "What're you doing here?"

"Good to see you too," Mission said. He held out the letter. "The Crow sent this."

"Ah, official business." Rodny smiled. "You're here as a porter, eh? Not a friend?"

Rodny smiled, but Mission could see that his friend was beat. He looked as if he hadn't slept for days. His cheeks were sunk in, dark rings under his eyes, and there was the shadow of a beard on his chin. Hair that Rodny had once taken pains to keep in style had been chopped short. Mission glanced into the room, wondering what they had him doing in there. Tall black metal cabinets were all he could see. They stretched out of sight, neatly spaced.

"You learning to fix refrigerators?" Mission asked.

Rodny glanced over his shoulder. He laughed. "Those are computers."

He still had that condescending tone. Mission nearly reminded his friend that today was his birthday, that they were the same age. Rodny was the only one he ever felt like reminding. Jeffery cleared his throat impatiently, seemed annoyed by the chatter.

Rodny turned to the Security chief. "You mind if we have a few seconds?" he asked.

Jeffery shifted his weight, the stiff leather of his boots squeaking. "You know I can't," he said. "I'll probably get chewed out for allowing even this."

"You're right." Rodny shook his head as if he shouldn't have asked. Mission studied the exchange. Even though it had been months since he'd last seen him, he sensed that Rodny was the same as always. He was in trouble for something, probably being forced to do the most reviled task in all of IT for a brash thing he'd said or done. He smiled at the thought.

Rodny tensed suddenly, as though he'd heard something deep inside the room. He held up a finger to the others and asked them to wait there. "Just a second," he said, rushing off, bare feet slapping on the steel floors.

Jeffery crossed his arms and looked Mission up and down unhappily. "You two grow up down the hall from each other?"

"Went to school together," Mission said. "So what did Rod do? You know, Mrs. Crowe used to make us sweep the entire Nest and clean the blackboards if we cut up in class. We did our fair share of sweeping, the two of us."

Jeffery appraised him for a moment. And then his expressionless face shattered into tooth and grin. "You think your friend is in trouble?" he said. He seemed on the verge of laughing. "Son, you have no idea."

Before Mission could question him, Rodny returned, smiling and breathless.

"Sorry," he said to Jeffery. "I had to get that." He turned to Mission. "Thanks for coming by, man. Good to see you."

That was it?

"Good to see you too," Mission sputtered, surprised that their visit would be so brief. "Hey, don't be a stranger." He went to give his old friend a hug, but Rodny stuck out a hand instead. Mission looked at it for a pause, confused, wondering if they'd grown apart so far, so fast.

"Give my best to everyone," Rodny said, as if he expected never to see any of them again.

Jeffery cleared his throat, clearly annoyed and ready to go.

"I will," Mission said, fighting to keep the sadness out of his voice. He accepted his friend's hand. They shook like strangers, the smile on Rodny's face quivering, the folds of the note hidden in his palm digging sharply into Mission's hand.

35

IT WAS A MIRACLE Mission didn't drop the note as it was passed to him, a miracle that he knew something was amiss, to keep his mouth closed, to not stand there a fool in front of Jeffery and say, "Hey, what's this?" Instead, he kept the wad of paper balled in his fist as he was escorted back to the security station. They were nearly there when someone called "Porter!" from one of the offices.

Jeffery placed a hand on Mission's chest, forcing him to a stop. They turned, and a familiar man strode down the hallway to meet them. It was Mr. Wyck, the head of IT, familiar to most porters. The endless shuffle of broken and repaired computers kept the Upper Dispatch on ten as busy as Supply kept the Lower Dispatch on one-twenty. Mission gathered that may have changed since yesterday.

"You on duty, son?" Mr. Wyck studied the porter's 'chief knotted around Mission's neck. He was a tall man with a tidy beard and bright eyes. Mission had to crane his neck to meet Wyck's gaze.

"Yessir," he said, hiding the note from Rodny behind his back. He pressed it into his pocket with his thumb, like a seed going into soil. "You need something moved, sir?"

"I do." Mr. Wyck studied him for a moment, stroked his beard. "You're the Jones boy, right? The zero."

Mission felt a flash of heat around his neck at the use of the term, a reference to the fact that no lottery number had been pulled for him. "Yessir. It's Mission." He offered his hand. Mr. Wyck accepted it.

"Yes, yes. I went to school with your father. And your mother, of course."

He paused to give Mission time to respond. Mission ground his teeth together and said nothing. He let go of the man's hand before his sweaty palms had a chance to speak for him.

"Say I wanted to move something without going through Dispatch." Mr. Wyck smiled. His teeth were white as chalk. "And say I wanted to avoid the sort of nastiness that took place last night a few levels up . . ."

Mission glanced over at Jeffery, who seemed disinterested in the conversation. It was strange to hear this sort of offer from a man of authority, especially in front of a member of Security, but there was one thing Mission had discovered since emerging from his shadowing days: things only got darker.

"I don't follow," Mission said. He fought the urge to turn and see how far they were from the security gate. A woman emerged from an office down the hall, behind Mr. Wyck. Jeffery made a gesture with his hand and she stopped and kept her distance, out of earshot.

"I think you do, and I admire your discretion. Two hundred chits to move a package a half-dozen levels from Supply."

Mission tried to remain calm. Two hundred chits. A month's pay for half a day's work. He immediately feared this was some sort of test. Maybe Rodny had gotten in trouble for flunking a similar one.

"I don't know—" he said.

"It's an open invitation," Wyck said. "The next porter who

comes through here will get the same offer. I don't care who does it, but only one will get the chits." Wyck raised a hand. "You don't have to answer me. Just show up and ask for Joyce at the Supply counter. Tell her you're doing a job for Wyck. There'll be a delivery report detailing the rest."

"I'll think about it, sir."

"Good." Mr. Wyck smiled.

"Anything else?" Mission asked.

"No, no. You're free to go." He nodded to Jeffery, who snapped back from wherever he'd checked out to.

"Thank you, sir." Mission turned and followed the chief.

"Oh, and happy birthday, son," Mr. Wyck called out.

Mission glanced back, didn't say thanks, just hurried after Jeffery and through the security gate, past the crowds and out onto the landing, down two turns of stairs, where he finally reached into his pocket for the note from Rodny. Paranoid that he might drop it and watch it bounce off the stairs and through the rail, he carefully unfolded the scrap of paper. It looked like the same rag blend Mrs. Crowe's note had been written on, the same threads of purple and red mixed in with the rough gray weave. For a moment, Mission feared the note would be addressed to the Crow rather than to him, maybe more lines of old nursery rhymes. He worked the piece of paper flat. One side was blank; he turned it over to read the other.

It wasn't addressed to anyone. Just two words, which reminded Mission of the way his friend's smile had quivered when they shook hands.

Mission felt suddenly alone. There was the smell of something burning lingering in the stairwell, a tinge of smoke that mixed with the paint from drying graffiti. He took the small note and tore it into ever smaller pieces. He kept tearing until there was nothing left to shred, and then sprinkled the dull confetti over the rail to drift down and disappear into the void.

The evidence was gone, but the message lingered vividly in his mind. The hasty scrawl, the shadowy scratch the edge of a coin or a spoon had made as it was dragged across the paper, two words barely legible from his friend who never needed anybody or asked for anything.

Help me.

And that was all.

36

Silo 1

FINDING THE RIGHT silo was easy enough. Donald could study the old schematic and remember standing on those hills, peering down into the wide bowls that held each facility. The sound of grumbling ATVs came back, the plumes of dust kicked up as they bounced across the ridges where the grass had not yet filled in. He remembered that they had been growing grass over those hills, straw and seed spread everywhere, a task hindsight made both unnecessary and sad.

Standing on that ridge in his memory, he was able to picture the Tennessee delegation. It would be Silo 2. Once he had this, he dug deeper. It took a bit of fumbling to remember how the computer program worked, how to sift through lives that lived in databases. There was an entire history there of each silo if you knew how to read it, but it only went so far. It went back to made-up names, back to the orientation. It didn't stretch to the Legacy beyond. The old world was hidden behind bombs and a fog of mist and forgetting.

He had the right silo, but locating Helen might prove impossible. He worked frantically while Anna sang in the shower.

She had left the bathroom door open, steam billowing out.

Donald ignored what he took to be an invitation. He ignored the throbbing, the yearning, the hormonal rush of being near an ex-lover after centuries of need, and searched instead for his wife.

There were four thousand names in that first generation of Silo 2. Four thousand exactly. Roughly half were female. There were three Helens. Each had a grainy picture taken for her work ID stored on the servers. None of the Helens matched what he remembered his wife looking like, what he *thought* she looked like. Tears came unbidden. He wiped them away, furious at himself. From the shower, Anna sang a sad song from long ago while Donald flipped through random photos. After a dozen, the faces of strangers began to meld together and threaten to erode the vision he held of Helen in his memory. He went back to searching by name. Surely he could guess the name she would've chosen. He had picked Troy for himself those many years ago, a clue leading him back to her. He liked to think she would've done the same.

He tried Sandra, her mother's name, but neither of the two hits were right. He tried Danielle, her sister's name. One hit. Not her.

She wouldn't come up with something random, would she? They had talked once of what they might name their kids. It was gods and goddesses, a joke at first, but Helen had fallen in love with the name Athena. He did a search. Zero hits in that first generation.

The pipes squealed as Anna turned off the shower. Her singing subsided back into a hum, a hymn for the funeral they were about to attend. Donald tried a few more names, anxious to discover something, anything. He would search every night if he had to. He wouldn't sleep until he found her.

"Do you need to shower before the service?" Anna called out from the bathroom.

He didn't want to go to the service, he nearly said. He only knew Victor as someone to fear: the gray-haired man across the hall, always watching, dispensing drugs, manipulating him. At least, that's how the paranoia of his first shift made it all seem.

"I'll go like this," he said. He still wore the beige overalls they'd given him the day before. He flipped through random pictures again, starting at the top of the alphabet. What other name? The fear was that he'd forget what she looked like. Or that she'd look more and more like Anna in his mind. He couldn't let that happen.

"Find anything?"

She snuck up behind him and reached for something on the desk. A towel was wrapped around her breasts and reached the middle of her thighs. Her skin was wet. She grabbed a hairbrush and walked, humming, back to the bathroom. Donald forgot to answer. His body responded to Anna in a way that made him furious and full of guilt.

He was still married, he reminded himself. He would be until he knew what'd happened to Helen. He would be loyal to her forever.

Loyalty.

On a whim, he searched for the name Karma.

One hit. Donald sat up straight. He hadn't imagined a hit. It was their dog's name, the nearest thing he and Helen ever had to a child of their own. He brought up the picture.

"I guess we're all wearing these horrid outfits to the funeral, right?" Anna passed the desk as she snapped up the front of her white overalls. Donald only noticed in the corner of his tear-filled vision. He covered his mouth and felt his body tremble with suppressed sobs. On the monitor, in a tiny square of black and white pixels in the middle of a work badge, was his wife.

"You'll be ready to go in a few minutes, won't you?"

Anna disappeared back into the bathroom, brushing her hair. Donald wiped his cheeks, salt on his lips while he read.

Karma Brewer. There were several occupations listed, with a badge photo for each. *Teacher, School Master, Judge*—more wrinkles in each picture but always the same half-smile. He opened the full file, thinking suddenly what it would've been like to have been on the very first shift in Silo 1, to watch her life unfold next door, maybe even reach out and contact her somehow. A judge. It'd been a dream of hers to be a judge one day. Donald wept while Anna hummed, and through a lens of tears, he read about his wife's life without him.

Married, it said, which didn't throw up any flags at first. Married, of course. To him. Until he read about her death. Eighty-two years old. Survived by Rick Brewer and two children, Athena and Mars.

Rick Brewer.

The walls and ceiling bulged inward. Donald felt a chill. There were more pictures. He followed the links to other files. To her husband's files.

"Mick," Anna whispered behind him.

Donald startled and turned to find her reading over his shoulder. Drying tears streaked his face, but he didn't care. His best friend and his wife. Two kids. He turned back to the screen and pulled up the daughter's file. Athena's. There were several pictures from different careers and phases of her life. She had Helen's mouth.

"Donny. Please don't."

A hand on his shoulder. Donald flinched from it and watched an animation wrought by furious clicks, this child growing into an approximation of his wife, until the girl's own children appeared in her file.

"Donny," Anna whispered. "We're going to be late for the funeral."

Donald wept. Sobs tore through him as if he were made of tissue. "Late," he cried. "A hundred years too late." He sputtered this last, overcome with misery. There was a granddaughter on the screen that was not his, a great-granddaughter one more click away. They stared out at him, all of them, none with eyes like his own.

37

DONALD WENT TO Victor's funeral numb. He rode the lift in silence, watched his boots kick ahead of himself as he teetered forward, but what he found on the medical level wasn't a funeral at all—it was body disposal. They were storing the remains back in a pod because they had no dirt in which to bury their dead. The food in Silo 1 came from cans. Their bodies returned to the same.

Donald was introduced to Erskine, who explained unprompted that the body would not rot. The same invisible machines that allowed them to survive the freezing process and turned their waking piss the color of charcoal would keep the dead as soft and fresh as the living. The thought wasn't a pleasant one. He watched as the man he had known as Victor was prepped for deep freeze.

They wheeled the body down a hall and through a sea of pods. The deep freeze was a cemetery, Donald saw. A grid of bodies laid flat, only a name to feebly encapsulate all that lay within. He wondered how many of the pods contained the dead. Some men must die on their shifts from natural causes. Some must break down and take their own lives as Victor had.

Donald helped the others move the body into the pod. There

were only five of them present, only five who could know how Victor had died. The illusion that someone was in charge must be maintained. Donald thought of his last job, sitting at a desk, hands on a rudderless wheel, pretending. He watched Thurman as the old man kissed his palm and pressed his fingers to Victor's cheek. The lid was closed. The cold of the room fogged their breath.

The others took turns eulogizing, but Donald paid no heed. His mind was elsewhere, thinking of a woman he had loved long ago, of children he had never had. He did not cry. He had sobbed in the lift, with Anna gently holding him. Helen had died almost a century ago. It had been longer than that since he'd lost her over that hill, since missing her messages, since not being able to get through to her. He remembered the national anthem and the bombs filling the air. He remembered his sister Charlotte being there.

His sister. Family.

Donald knew Charlotte had been saved. He was overcome with a fierce urge to find her and wake her, to bring someone he loved back to life.

Erskine paid his final respects. Only five of them present to mourn this man who had killed billions. Donald felt Anna's presence beside him and realized the lack of a crowd was in fact due to her. The five present were the only ones who knew that a woman had been woken. Her father, Dr. Sneed, who had performed the procedure, Anna, Erskine, whom she spoke of as a friend, and himself.

The absurdity of Donald's existence, of the state of the world, swooped down on him in that gathering. He did not belong. He was only there because of a girl he had dated in college, a girl whose father was a senator, whose affections had likely gotten him elected, who had dragged him into a murderous scheme, and had now pulled him from a frozen death. All the great coincidences and marvelous achievements of his life disappeared in a flash. In their place were puppet strings.

"A tragic loss, this."

Donald emerged from his thoughts to discover that the ceremony was over. Anna and her father stood two rows of pods away discussing something. Dr. Sneed was down by the base of the pod, the panel beeping as he made adjustments. That left Donald with Erskine, a thin man with glasses and a British accent. He surveyed Donald from the opposite side of the pod.

"He was on my shift," Donald said inanely, trying to explain why he was present for the service. There was little else he could think to say of the dead man. He stepped closer and peered through the little window at the calm face within.

"I know," Erskine said. This wiry man, probably in his early to mid-sixties, adjusted the glasses on his narrow nose and joined Donald in peering through the small window. "He was quite fond of you, you know."

"I didn't. I mean . . . he never said as much to me."

"He was peculiar that way." Erskine studied the deceased with a smile. "Brilliant perhaps for knowing the minds of others, just not so keen on communicating with them."

"Did you know him from before?" Donald asked. He wasn't sure how else to broach the subject. The *before* seemed taboo with some, freely spoken of by others.

Erskine nodded. "We worked together. Well, in the same hospital. We orbited each other for quite a few years until my discovery." He reached out and touched the glass, a final farewell to an old friend, it seemed.

"What discovery?" He vaguely remembered Anna mentioning something.

Erskine glanced up. Looking closer, Donald thought he may have been in his seventies. It was hard to tell. He had some of the agelessness of Thurman, like an antique that patinas and will grow no older.

"I'm the one who discovered the great threat," he said. It sounded more an admission of guilt than a proud claim. His voice was tinged with sadness. At the base of the pod, Dr. Sneed finished his adjustments, stood and excused himself. He steered the empty gurney toward the exit.

"The nanos." Donald remembered; Anna had said as much. He watched Thurman debate something with his daughter, his fist coming down over and over into his palm, and a question came to mind. He wanted to hear it from someone else. He wanted to see if the lies matched, if that meant they might contain some truth.

"You were a medical doctor?" he asked.

Erskine considered the question. It seemed a simple enough one to answer.

"Not precisely," he said, his accent thick. "I *built* medical doctors. Very small ones." He pinched the air and squinted through his glasses at his own fingers. "We were working on ways to keep soldiers safe, to keep them patched up. And then I found someone else's handiwork in a sample of blood. Little machines trying to do the opposite. Machines made to fight our machines. An invisible battle raging where no one could see. It wasn't long before I was finding the little bastards everywhere."

Anna and Thurman headed their way. Anna donned a cap, her hair in a bun that bulged noticeably through the top. It was little disguise for what she was, useful perhaps at a distance.

"I'd like to ask you about that sometime," Donald said hurriedly. "It might help my . . . help me with this problem in Silo Eighteen."

"Of course," Erskine said.

"I need to get back," Anna told Donald. She set her lips in a thin grimace from the argument with her father, and Donald finally appreciated how trapped she truly was. He imagined a year spent in that warehouse of war, clues scattered across that planning table, sleeping on that small cot, not able even to ride up to the cafeteria to see the hills and the dark clouds or have a meal at the time of her own choosing, relying on others to bring her everything.

"I'll escort the young man up in a bit," Donald heard Erskine say, his hand resting on Donald's shoulder. "I'd like to have a chat with our boy."

Thurman narrowed his eyes but relented. Anna squeezed Donald's hand a final time, glanced at the pod, and headed toward the exit. Her father followed a few paces behind.

"Come with me." Erskine's breath fogged the air. "I want to show you someone."

38

Erskine picked his way through the grid of pods with purpose as though he'd walked the route dozens of times. Donald followed after, rubbing his arms for warmth. He had been too long in that crypt-like place. The cold was leaching back into his bones.

"Thurman keeps saying we were already dead," he told Erskine, attacking the question head-on. "Is that true?"

Erskine looked back over his shoulder. He waited for Donald to catch up, seemed to consider this question.

"Well?" Donald asked. "Were we?"

"I never saw a design with a hundred percent efficiency," Erskine said. "We weren't there yet with our own work, and everything from Iran and Syria was much cruder. Now, North Korea had some elegant designs. I had my money on them. What they had already built could've taken out most of us. That part's true enough." He resumed his walk through the field of sleeping corpses. "Even the most severe epidemics burn themselves out," he said, "so it's difficult to say. I argued for countermeasures. Victor argued for this." He spread his arms over the quiet assembly.

"And Victor won."

"Indeed."

"Do you think he . . . had second thoughts? Is that why . . . ?"

Erskine stopped at one of the pods and placed both hands on its icy surface. "I'm sure we all have second thoughts," he said sadly. "But I don't think Vic ever doubted the rightness of this mission. I don't know why he did what he did in the end. It wasn't like him."

Donald peered inside the pod Erskine had led him to. There was a middle-aged woman inside, her eyelids covered in frost.

"My daughter," Erskine said. "My only child."

There was a moment of silence. It allowed the faint hum of a thousand pods to be heard.

"When Thurman made the decision to wake Anna, all I could dream about was doing the same. But why? There was no reason, no need for her expertise. Caroline was an accountant. And besides, it wouldn't be fair to drag her from her dreams."

Donald wanted to ask if it would ever be fair. What world did Erskine expect his daughter to ever see again? When would she wake to a normal life? A happy life?

"When I found nanos in her blood, I knew this was the right thing to do." He turned to Donald. "I know you're looking for answers, son. We all are. This is a cruel world. It's always been a cruel world. I spent my whole life looking for ways to make it better, to patch things up, dreaming of an ideal. But for every sot like me, there's ten more out there trying to tear things down. And it only takes one of them to get lucky."

Donald flashed back to the day Thurman had given him the Order. That thick book was the start of his plummet into madness. He remembered their talk in that huge chamber, the feeling of being infected, the paranoia that something harmful and invisible was invading him. But if Erskine and Thurman were telling the truth, he'd been infected long before that.

"You weren't poisoning me that day." He looked from the pod to Erskine, piecing something together. "The interview with

Thurman, the weeks and weeks he spent in that chamber having all of those meetings. You weren't infecting us."

Erskine nodded ever so slightly. "We were healing you."

Donald felt a sudden flash of anger. "Then why not heal *everyone*?" he demanded.

"We discussed that. I had the same thought. To me, it was an engineering problem. I wanted to build countermeasures, machines to kill machines before they got to us. Thurman had similar ideas. He saw it as an invisible war, one we desperately needed to take to the enemy. We all saw the battles we were accustomed to fighting, you see. I saw it in the bloodstream, Thurman in the war overseas. It was Victor who set the two of us straight."

Erskine pulled a cloth from his breast pocket and removed his glasses. He rubbed them while he talked, his voice echoing in whispers from the walls. "Victor said there would be no end to it. He pointed to computer viruses to make his case, how one might run rampant through a network and cripple hundreds of millions of machines. Sooner or later, some nano attack would get through, get out of control, and there would be an epidemic built on bits of code rather than strands of DNA."

"So what? We've dealt with plagues before. Why would this be different?" Donald swept his arms at the pods. "Tell me how the solution isn't worse than the problem?"

As worked up as he felt, he also sensed how much angrier he would be if he heard this from Thurman. He wondered if he'd been set up to have a kindlier man, a stranger, take him aside and tell him what Thurman thought he needed to hear. It was hard not to be paranoid about being manipulated, not to feel the strings knotted to his joints.

"Psychology," Erskine replied. He put his glasses back on. "This is where Victor set us straight, why our ideas would never work. I'll never forget the conversation. We were sitting in the cafeteria at Walter Reed. Thurman was there to hand out ribbons, but really to meet with the two of us." He shook his head. "It was crowded in there. If anyone knew the things we were discussing—"

"Psychology," Donald reminded him. "Tell me how this is better. *More* people die this way."

Erskine snapped back to the present. "That's where we were wrong, just like you. Imagine the first discovery that one of these epidemics was man-made—the panic, the violence that would ensue. That's where the end would come. A typhoon kills a few hundred people, does a few billion in damage, and what do we do?" Erskine interlocked his fingers. "We come together. We put the pieces back. But a terrorist's bomb." He frowned. "A terrorist's bomb does the same damage, and it throws the world into turmoil."

He spread his hands open. "When there's only God to blame, we forgive him. When it's our fellow man, we destroy him."

Donald shook his head. He didn't know what to believe. But then he thought about the fear and rage he'd felt when he thought he'd been infected by something in that chamber. Meanwhile, he never worried about the billions of creatures swimming in his gut and doing so since the day he was born.

"We can't tweak the genes of the food we eat without suspicion," Erskine said. "We can pick and choose until a blade of grass is a great ear of corn, but we can't do it with *purpose*. Vic had dozens of examples like these. Vaccines versus natural immunities, cloning versus twins, modified foods. Or course he was perfectly right. It was the man-made part that would've caused the chaos. It would be knowing that people were out to get us, that there was danger in the air we breathed."

Erskine paused for a moment. Donald's mind was racing.

"You know, Vic once said that if these terrorists had an ounce of sense, they would've simply announced what they were working on and then sat back to watch things burn on their own. He said that's all it would take, us knowing that it was happening, that the end of any of us could come silent, invisible, and at any time."

"And so the solution was to burn it all to the ground *ourselves*?" Donald ran his hands through his hair, trying to make sense of it all. He thought of a firefighting technique that always seemed just as confusing to him, the burning of wide swathes of forest to prevent a fire from spreading. And he knew in Iran, when oil wells were set ablaze during the first war, that sometimes the only cure was to set off a bomb, to fight the inferno with something greater.

"Believe me," Erskine said, "I came up with my own complaints. Endless complaints. But I knew the truth from the beginning, it just took me a while to accept it. Thurman was won over more easily. He saw at once that we needed to get off this ball of rock, to start over. But the cost of travel was too great—"

"Why travel through space," Donald interrupted, "when you can travel through time?" He remembered a conversation in Thurman's office. The old man had told him what he was planning that very first day, but Donald hadn't heard.

Erskine's eyes widened. "Yes. That was his argument. He'd seen enough war, I suppose. Me, I didn't have Thurman's experiences or the professional . . . *distance* Vic enjoyed. It was the analogy of the computer virus that wore me down, seeing these nanos like a new cyber war. I knew what they could do, how fast they could restructure themselves, evolve, if you will. Once it started, it would only stop when we were no longer around. And maybe not even then. Every defense would become a blueprint for the next attack. The air would choke with our invisible armies. There would be great clouds of them, mutating and fighting without need of a host. And once the public saw this and *knew* . . ." He left the sentence unfinished.

"Hysteria," Donald muttered.

Erskine nodded.

"You said it might not ever end, even if we were gone. Does that mean they're still out there? The nanos?"

Erskine glanced up at the ceiling. "The world outside isn't just being scrubbed of humans right now, if that's what you're asking. It's being reset. All of our experiments are being removed. By the grace of God, it'll be a very long time indeed before we think to perform them again."

Donald remembered from orientation that the combined shifts would last five hundred years. Half a millennium of living underground. How much scrubbing was necessary? And what was to keep them from heading down that same path a second time? How would any of them unlearn the potential dangers? You don't get the fire back in the box once you've unleashed it.

"You asked me if Victor had regrets—" Erskine coughed into his fist and nodded. "I do think he felt something close to that once. It was something he said to me as he was coming off his eighth or ninth shift, I don't remember which. I think I was heading into my sixth. This was just after the two of you worked together, after that nasty business with Silo Twelve—"

"My first shift," Donald said, since Erskine seemed to be counting. He wanted to add that it was his only shift.

"Yes, of course." Erskine adjusted his glasses. "I'm sure you knew him well enough to know that he didn't show his emotions often."

"He was difficult to read," Donald agreed. He knew almost nothing of the man he had just helped to bury.

"So you'll appreciate this, I think. We were riding the lift together, and Vic turns to me and says how hard it is to sit there at that desk of his and see what we're doing to the men across the hall. He meant you, of course. People in your position."

Donald tried to imagine the man he knew saying such a thing. He wanted to believe it.

"But that's not what really struck me. I've never seen him sadder than when he said the following. He said . . ." Erskine rested a hand on the pod. "He said that sitting there, watching you people work at your desks, getting to know you—he often thought that the world would be a better place with people like you in charge."

"People like me?" Donald shook his head. "What does that even mean?"

Erskine smiled. "I asked him precisely that. His response was that it was a burden doing what he knew to be correct, to be sound and logical." Erskine ran one hand across the pod as if he could touch his daughter within. "And how much simpler things would be, how much better for us all, if we had people brave enough to do what was *right,* instead."

39

THAT NIGHT, ANNA came to him. After a day of numbness and dwelling on death, of eating meals brought down by Thurman and not tasting a bite, of watching her set up a computer for him and spread out folders of notes, she came to him in the darkness.

Donald complained. He tried to push her away. She sat on the edge of the cot and held his wrists while he sobbed and grew feeble. He thought of Erskine's story, on what it meant to do the right thing rather than the correct thing, what the difference was. He thought this as an old lover draped herself across him, her hand on the back of his neck, her cheek on his shoulder, lying there against him while he wept.

A century of sleep had weakened him, he thought. A century of sleep and the knowledge that Mick and Helen had lived a life together. He felt suddenly angry at Helen for not holding out, for not living alone, for not getting his messages and meeting him over the hill.

Anna kissed his cheek and whispered that everything would be okay. Fresh tears flowed down Donald's face as he realized that he was everything Victor had assumed he wasn't. He was a miserable human being for wishing his wife to be lonely so that he could sleep at night a hundred years later. He was a miserable human being for denying her that solace when Anna's touch made him feel so much better.

"I can't," he whispered for the dozenth time.

"Shhh," Anna said. She brushed his hair back in the darkness. And the two of them were alone in that room where wars were waged. They were trapped together with those crates of arms, with guns and ammo, and far more dangerous things.

40

Silo 18

MISSION WOUND HIS way toward Central Dispatch and agonized over what to do for Rodny. He felt afraid for his friend but powerless to help. The door they had him behind was unlike any he'd ever seen: thick and solid, gleaming and daunting. If the trouble his friend had caused could be measured by where they were keeping him—

He shuddered to continue that line of thought. It'd only been a few months since the last cleaning. Mission had been there, had carried up part of the suit from IT, a more haunting experience than porting a body for burial. Dead bodies at least were placed in the black bags the coroners used. The cleaning suit was a different sort of bag, tailored to a living soul that would crawl inside and be forced to die within.

Mission remembered where they had picked up the gear. It'd been a room right down the hall from where Rodny was being kept. Weren't cleanings run by the same department? He shivered. One slip of a tongue could land a body out there, rotting on the hills, and his friend Rodny was known to wag his dangerously.

First his mother, and now his best friend. Mission wondered

what the Pact said about volunteering to clean in one's stead, if it said anything at all. Amazing that he could live under the rules of a document he'd never read. He just assumed others had, all the people in charge, and that they were operating by its codes in good faith.

On fifty-eight, a porter's 'chief tied to the downbound railing caught his attention. It was the same blue pattern as the 'chief worn around his neck, but with a bright red merchant's hem. Duty beckoned, dispelling thoughts that were spiraling nowhere. Mission unknotted the 'chief and searched the fabric for the merchant's stamp. It was Drexel's, the apothecarist down the hall. Light loads and lighter pay, normally. But at least it was downbound, unless Drexel had been careless again with which rail he tied it to.

Mission was dying to get to Central where a shower and a change of clothes awaited, but if anyone spotted him with a flat pack marching past a signal 'chief, he'd hear it from Roker and the others. He hurried inside to Drexel's, praying it wasn't a round of meds going to several dozen individual apartments. His legs ached just at the thought of it.

Drexel was at the counter as Mission pushed open the apothecarist's squeaky door. A large man with a full beard and a balding head, Drexel was something of a fixture in the Mids. Many came to him rather than to the doctors, though Mission wasn't sure how sound a choice that was. Often, it was the man with the most promises who got the chits, not the one who made people better.

A handful of the seemingly sick sat on Drexel's waiting room bench, sniffling and coughing. Mission felt the urge to cover his mouth with his 'chief. Instead, he innocuously held his breath and waited while Drexel filled a small square of paper with ground powder, folding it neatly before handing it to the woman waiting. The woman slid a few chits across the counter.

When she walked away, Mission tossed the signal 'chief on top of the money.

"Ah, Mish. Good to see you, boy. Looking fit as a fiddle." Drexel smoothed his beard and smiled, yellow teeth peering out from cornrows of drooping whiskers.

"Same," Mission said politely, braving a breath. "Got something for me?"

"I do. One sec."

Drexel disappeared behind a wall of shelves crammed full of tiny vials and jars. The apothecarist reappeared with a small sack. "Meds for down below," he said.

"I can take them as far as Central and have Dispatch send them from there," Mission told him. "I'm just finishing up a shift."

Drexel frowned and rubbed his beard. "I suppose that'll do. And Dispatch'll bill me?"

Mission held out a palm. "If you tip," he said.

"Aye, a tip. But only if you solve a riddle." Drexel leaned on the counter, which seemed to sag beneath his bulk. The last thing Mission wanted to hear was another of the old man's riddles and then not get paid. Always an excuse with Drexel to keep a chit on his side of the counter.

"Okay," the apothecarist began, tugging on his whiskers. "Which one weighs more, a bag full of seventy-eight pounds of feathers, or a bag full of seventy-eight pounds of rocks?"

Mission didn't hesitate with his answer. "The bag of feathers," he declared. He'd heard this one before. It was a riddle made for a porter, and he had thought on it long enough between the levels to come up with his own answer, one different from the obvious.

"Incorrect!" Drexel roared, waving a finger. "It isn't the rocks—" His face dimmed. "Wait. Did you say the feathers?" He shook his head. "No, boy, they weigh the *same*."

"The contents weigh the same," Mission told him. "The bag of feathers would have to be bigger. You said they were both full, which means a bigger bag with more material, and so it weighs more." He held out his palm. Drexel stood there, chewing his beard for a moment, thrown off his game.

Begrudgingly, he took two coins from the lady's pay and placed them in Mission's hand. Mission accepted them and stuffed the sack of meds into his pack before cinching it up tight.

"The bigger bag—" Drexel muttered, as Mission hurried off, past the benches, holding his breath again as he went, the pills rattling in his sack.

The apothecarist's annoyance was worth far more than the tip, but Mission appreciated both. The enjoyment faded, however, as he spiraled down through a tense silo. He saw deputies on one landing, hands on their guns, trying to calm down fighting neighbors. The glass on the windows peeking into a shop on forty-two were broken and covered with a sheet of plastic. Mission was pretty sure that was recent. A woman on forty-four sat by the rails and sobbed into her palms, and Mission watched as people passed her by without stopping. On down he went as well, the stairway trembling, the graffiti on the walls warning him of what was yet to come.

He arrived at Central Dispatch to find it eerily quiet, made his way past the sorting rooms with their tall shelves of items needing delivery and went straight to the main counter. He would drop off his current package and pick out his next job before changing and showering. Katelyn was working the counter. There were no other porters queued up. Off licking their wounds, perhaps. Or maybe seeing to their families during this recent spate of violence.

"Hey, Katelyn."

"Mish." She smiled. "You look intact."

He laughed and touched his nose, which was still sore. "Thanks."

"Cam just passed through asking where you were."

"Yeah?" Mission was surprised. He figured his friend would be taking a day off with the bonus from the coroner. "Did he pick something up?"

"Yup. He requested anything heading toward Supply. Was in a better mood than usual, though he seemed miffed to have been left out of last night's adventures."

"He heard about that, huh?" Mission sorted through the delivery list. He was looking for something upbound. Mrs. Crowe would know what to do about Rodny. Maybe she could find out from the mayor what he was being punished for, perhaps put in a good word for him.

"Wait," he said, glancing up at Katelyn. "What do you mean he was in a good mood? And he was heading for *Supply*?" Mission thought of the job he'd been offered by Wyck. The head of IT had said Mission wouldn't be the last to hear of the offer. Maybe he hadn't been the *first*, either. "Where was Cam coming from?"

Katelyn touched her fingers to her tongue and flipped through the old log. "I think his last delivery was a broken computer heading to—"

"That little rat." Mission slapped the counter. "You got anything else heading down? Maybe to Supply or Chemical?"

She checked her computer, fingers clacking furiously, the rest of her perfectly serene. "We're so slow right now," she said apologetically. "I've got something from Mechanical back *up* to Supply. Forty-five pounds. No rush. Standard freight." She peered across the counter at Mission, seeing if he was interested.

"I'll take it," he said. But he didn't plan on heading straight to Mechanical. If he raced, maybe he could beat Cam to Supply and do that other job for Wyck. That was the way in he was looking for. It wasn't the money he wanted, it was having an excuse to go back to thirty-four to collect his pay, another chance to see Rodny, see what kind of help his friend needed, what sort of trouble he was truly in.

41

Mission made record time downbound. It helped that traffic was light, but it wasn't a good sign that he didn't pass Cam on the way. The kid must've had a good head start. Either that, or Mission had gotten lucky and had overtaken him while he was off the stairway for a bathroom break.

Pausing for a moment on the landing outside of Supply, Mission caught his breath and dabbed the sweat from his neck. He still hadn't had his shower. Maybe after he found Cam and took care of this job in Mechanical, he could get cleaned up and get some proper rest. Lower Dispatch would have a change of clothes for him, and then he could figure out what to do about Rodny. So much to think about. A blessing that it took his mind off his birthday.

Inside Supply, he found a handful of people waiting at the counter. No sign of Cam. If the boy had come and gone already, he must've flown, and the delivery must have been heading further down. Mission tapped his foot and waited his turn. Once at the counter, he asked for Joyce, just like Wyck had said. The man pointed to a heavyset woman with long braids at the other end of the counter. Mission recognized her. She handled a lot of the flow of equipment marked special for IT. He waited until she was done with her customer, then asked for any deliveries under the name of Wyck.

She narrowed her eyes at him. "You got a glitch at Dispatch?" she asked. "Done handed that one off." She waved for the next person in line.

"Could you tell me where it was heading?" Mission asked. "I was sent to relieve the other guy. His . . . his mother is sick. They're not sure if she's gonna make it."

Mission winced at the lie. The lady behind the counter twisted her mouth in disbelief.

"Please," he begged. "It really is important."

She hesitated. "It was going six flights down to an apartment. I don't have the exact number. It was on the delivery report."

"Six down." Mission knew the level. One-sixteen was residential except for the handful of less-than-legal businesses being run out of a few apartments. "Thanks," he said. He slapped the counter and hurried toward the exit. It was on his way to Mechanical, anyway. He might be too late for Wyck's delivery, but he could ask Cam if he might pick up the pay for him, offer him a vacation chit in return. Or he could just flat out tell him an old friend was in trouble, and he needed to get through security. If not, he'd have to wait for an IT request to hit Dispatch and be the first to jump on it. And he'd have to hope that Rodny had that much time.

He was four levels down, formulating a dozen such plans, when the blast went off.

The great stairwell lurched as if thrown sideways. Mission slammed against the rail and nearly went over. He wrapped his arms around the trembling steel and held on.

There was a shriek, a chorus of groans. He watched, his head out in the space beyond the railing, as the landing two levels below twisted away from the staircase. The metal sang and cried out as it was ripped free and went tumbling into the depths.

More than one body plummeted after. The receding figures performed cartwheels in space.

Mission tore himself away from the sight. A few steps down from him, a woman remained on her hands and knees, looking up at Mission with wild and frightened eyes. There was a distant crash, impossibly far below.

I don't know, he wanted to say. There was that question in her eyes, the same one pounding in his skull, echoing with the sound of the blast. *What the hell just happened? Is this it? Has it begun?*

He considered running up, away from the explosion, but there were screams coming from below and a porter had a duty to those on the stairwell in need. He helped the woman to her feet and bid her upward. Already the smell of something acrid and the haze of smoke were filling the air. "Go," he urged, and then he spiraled down against the sudden flow of upward traffic. Cam was down there. Where his friend had gone with the package and where the blast had occurred were still coincidence in Mission's rattled mind.

The landing below held a crush of people. Residents and shopkeeps crowded out of the doors and fought for a spot at the rail that they might gaze over at the wreckage one flight further down. Mission fought his way through, yelling Cam's name, keeping an eye out for his friend. A bedraggled couple staggered up to the crowded landing with hollow eyes, clutching the railing and each other. He didn't see Cam anywhere.

He raced down five turns of the central post, his normally deft feet stumbling on the slick treads, around and around. It'd been the level Cam was heading toward, right? Six down. Level one-sixteen. He would be okay. He must be okay. And then the sight of those people tumbling through the air flashed in Mission's mind. It was an image he knew he'd never forget. Surely Cam wasn't among them. The boy was late or early to everything, never right on time.

He made the last turn, and where the next landing should have been was empty space. The rails of the great spiral staircase had been ripped outward before parting. A few of the steps sagged away from the central post, and Mission could feel a pull toward the edge, the void clawing at him. There was nothing there to stop him from going over. The steel felt slick beneath his boots.

Across a gap of torn and twisted steel, the doorway to one-sixteen was missing. In its place stood a pocket of crumbling cement and dark iron bars bent outward like hands reaching for the vanished landing. White powder drifted down from the ceiling beyond the rubble. Unbelievably, there were sounds beyond the veil of dust: coughs and shouts. Screams for help.

"Porter!" someone yelled from above.

Mission carefully slid to the edge of the sloping and bent steps. He held the railing where it had been torn free. It was warm to the touch. Leaning out, he studied the crowd fifty feet above him at the next landing, searching for the person who had called out for him.

Someone pointed when they spotted him leaning out, spotted the 'chief around his neck.

"There he is!" a woman shrieked, one of the mad-eyed women who had staggered past him as he hurried down, one of those who had survived.

"The porter did it!" she yelled.

42

MISSION TURNED AND ran as the stairway thundered and clanged with the descending mob. He stumbled downward, a hand on the inner post, watching for the return of the railing. So much had been pulled away. The stairs were unstable from the damage. He had no idea why he was being chased. It took a full turn of the staircase for the railing to reappear and for him to feel safe at such speeds. It took just as long to realize that Cam was dead. His friend had delivered a package, and now he was dead. He and many others. One glance at his blue 'chief and someone above must've thought it was Mission who'd made the delivery. It very nearly had been.

Another crowd at landing one-seventeen. Tear-streaked faces, a woman trembling, her arms wrapped around herself, a man covering his face, all looking up or down beyond the rails. They had seen the wreckage tumble past. Mission hurried on. Lower Dispatch on one-twenty was the only haven between him and Mechanical. He hurried there as a violent scream approached from above and came much too fast.

Mission startled and nearly fell as the wailing person flew toward him. He waited for someone to tackle him from behind, but the sound whizzed past beyond the rail. Another person. Falling, alive and screaming, plummeting toward the depths.

The loose steps and empty space above had claimed one of those chasing him.

He quickened his pace, leaving the inner post for the outer rail where the curve of the steps was broader and smoother, where the force of his descent tugged him against the steel bar. Here, he could move faster. He tried not to think of what would happen if he came across a gap in the steel. He ran, smoke stinging his eyes, the clang and clamor of his own feet and that of the others above, not realizing at first that the haze in the air wasn't from the ruin he had left behind. The smoke all around him was *rising*.

43

Silo 1

DONALD'S BREAKFAST OF powdered eggs and shredded potatoes had long grown cold. He rarely touched the food brought down by Thurman and Erskine, preferring instead the bland stuff in the unlabeled silver cans he had discovered among the storeroom's vacuum-sealed crates. It wasn't just the matter of trust—it was the rebelliousness of it all, the empowerment that came from taking command of his own survival. He stabbed a yellowish-orange gelatinous blob that he assumed had once been part of a peach and put it in his mouth. He chewed, tasting nothing. He pretended it tasted like a peach.

Across the wide table, Anna fiddled with the dials on her radio and sipped loudly from a mug of cold coffee. A nest of wires ran from a black box to her computer, and a soft hiss of static filled the room.

"It's too bad we can't get a better station," Donald said morosely. He speared another wedge of mystery fruit and popped it into his mouth. Mango, he told himself, just for variety.

"No station is the best station," she said, referring to her hope that the towers of Silo 40 and its neighbors would remain silent. She had tried to explain what she was doing to cut off any unlikely survivors, but little of it made any sense to Donald. A year ago, supposedly, Silo 40 had hacked the system. It was assumed to have been a rogue head of IT. No one else could be expected to possess the expertise and access required of such a feat. By the time the camera feeds were cut, every failsafe had already been severed. Attempts had been made to terminate the silo, but there was no way to verify them. It became obvious these attempts had failed when the darkness started to spread to other silos.

Thurman, Erskine, and Victor had been woken according to protocol, one after the other. Further failsafes proved ineffective, and Erskine worried the hacking had progressed to the level of the nanos, that the machines in the air were being reprogrammed, that everything was in jeopardy. After much cajoling, Thurman had convinced the other two that Anna could help. Her research at MIT had been in wireless harmonics; remote charging technology; the ability to assume control of electronics via radio.

She'd eventually been able to commandeer the collapse mechanism of the afflicted silos. Donald still had nightmares thinking about it. While she described the process, he had studied the wall schematic of a standard silo. He had pictured the blasts that freed the layers of heavy concrete between the levels, sending them like dominoes down to the bottom, crushing everything and everyone in-between. Stacks of concrete thirty feet thick had been cut loose to turn entire societies into rubble. These underground buildings had been designed from the beginning so they could be brought down like any other—and remotely. That such a failsafe was even needed seemed as sick to Donald as the solution was cruel.

All that now remained of those silos was the hiss and crackle of their dead radios, a chorus of ghosts. The silo heads in the rest of the facilities hadn't even been told of the calamity. There would be no red X's on their schematics to haunt their days. The various heads had little contact with each other as it was. The greater worry was of the panic spreading.

But Victor had known. And Donald suspected it was this heavy burden that had led him to take his own life, rather than any of the theories Thurman had offered. Thurman was so in awe of Victor's supposed brilliance that he searched for purpose behind his suicide, some conspiratorial cause. Donald was verging on the sad realization that humanity had been thrown to the brink of extinction by insane men in positions of power following one another, each thinking the others knew where they were going.

He took a sip of tomato juice from a punctured can and reached for two pieces of paper amid the carpet of notes and reports around his keyboard. The fate of Silo 18 supposedly rested on something in these two pages. They were copies of the same report. One was a virgin printout of the report he'd written long ago on the fall of Silo 12. Donald barely remembered writing it. And now he had stared at it so long, the meaning had been squeezed out of it, like a word that, repeated too often, devolves into mere noise.

The other copy showed the notes Victor had scrawled across the face of this report. He had used a red pen, and someone upstairs had managed to pull just this color off in order to make both versions more legible. By copying the red, however, they had also transferred a fine mist and a few splatters of his blood. These marks were gruesome reminders that the report had been atop Victor's desk in the final moments of his life.

After three days of study, Donald was beginning to suspect that the report was nothing more than a scrap of paper. Why else write across the top of it? And yet Victor had told Thurman several times that the key to quelling the violence in Silo 18 lay right there, in Donald's report. Victor had argued for Donald to be pulled from the deep freeze, but hadn't been able to get Erskine or Thurman to side with him. So this was all Donald had: a liar's account of what a dead man had said.

Liars and dead men—two parties unskilled at dispensing the truth.

The scrap of paper with the red ink and rust-colored bloodstains offered little help. There were a few lines that resonated, however. They reminded Donald of how horoscopes were able to land vague and glancing blows, which gave credence to all their other feints.

The One who remembers had been written in bold and confident letters across the center of the report. Donald couldn't help but feel that this referred to him and his resistance to the medication. Hadn't Anna said that Victor spoke of him frequently, that he wanted him awake for testing or questioning? Other musings were vague and dire in equal measure. *This is why,* Victor had written. Also: *An end to them all.*

Had he meant the why of his suicide or the why of Silo 18's violence? And an end to all of what?

In many ways, the cycle of violence in Silo 18 was no different than what took place elsewhere. Beyond being more severe, it was the same waxing and waning of the mobs, of each generation revolting against the last, a fifteen-to-twenty-year cycle of bloody upheaval.

Victor had written much on the subject. He'd left reports behind about everything from primate behavior to the wars of the twentieth and twenty-first centuries. There was one that Donald found especially disturbing. It detailed how primates came of age and attempted to overthrow their fathers, the alpha males. It told of chimps that committed infanticide, males snatching the young from their mothers and taking them into the trees where their arms and legs were ripped, limb for limb, from their small bodies. Victor had written that this put the females back into estrus. It made room for the next generation.

Donald had a hard time believing any of this was true. He had a harder time making sense of a report about frontal lobes and how long they took to develop in humans. Maybe this was important to unraveling some mystery. Or perhaps it was the ravings of a man losing his mind—or a man discovering his conscience and coming to grips with what he'd done to the world.

Donald studied his old report and searched through Victor's notes, looking for the answer. He fell into a routine that Anna had long ago perfected. They slept, ate, and worked. They emptied bottles of Scotch at night, one burning sip at a time, and left them standing like factory smokestacks amid the diagram of silos. In the mornings, they took turns in the shower, Anna brazen with her nakedness, Donald wishing she wouldn't be. Her presence became an intoxicant from the past, and Donald began to assemble a new reality in his mind: he and Anna were working on one more secret project together; Helen was back in Savannah; Mick wasn't making it to the meetings; Donald couldn't raise either of them because his phone wouldn't work.

It was always that his phone didn't work. Just one text getting through on the day of the convention and Helen might be down in the deep freeze, asleep in her pod. He could visit her the way Erskine visited his daughter. They would be together again once all the shifts were over.

In another version of the same dream, Donald imagined that he was able to crest that hill and make it to the Tennessee side. Bombs exploded in the air; frightened people dove into their holes; a young girl sang with a voice so pure. In this fantasy, he and Helen disappeared into the same earth. They had children and grandchildren and were buried together.

Dreams such as these haunted him when he allowed Anna to

touch him, to lie in his cot for an hour before bedtime, just the sound of her breathing, her head on his chest, the smell of alcohol on both their breaths. He would lie there and tolerate it, suffer how good it felt, her hand resting on his neck, and only fall asleep after she grew uncomfortable from the cramped quarters and moved back to her own cot.

In the morning, she would sing in the shower, steam billowing into the war room, while Donald returned to his studies. He would log on to her computer where he was able to dig through the files in Victor's personal directories. He could see when these files had been created, accessed, and how often. One of the oldest and most recently opened was a list with all the silos ranked in order. Number 18 was near the top, but it wasn't clear if this was a measure of trouble or worth. And why rank them to begin with? For what purpose?

He also used Anna's computer to search for his sister Charlotte. She wasn't listed in the pods below, nor under any name or picture that he could find. But she had been there during orientation. He remembered her being led off with the other women and being put to sleep. And now she seemed to have vanished. But to where?

So many questions. He stared at the two reports, the awful, dead sound of static leaking from the radio, the weight of all the earth above pushing down upon him, and he began to wonder, if he fixated on Victor's notes too closely, if perhaps he would reach the same conclusion.

44

WHEN HE COULD no longer look at the notes, Donald went for what had become his customary stroll among the guns and drones in the storeroom. This was his escape from the hiss of the radio static and the cramped confines of their makeshift home, and it was during these laps that he came nearest to clearing his head from his dreams, from the prior night's bottle of Scotch, and from the mix of emotions he was beginning to feel for Anna.

Most of all, he walked those laps and tried to make sense of this new world. He puzzled over what Thurman and Victor had planned for the silos. Five hundred years below ground, and then what? Donald desperately wanted to know. And here was when he felt truly alive: when he was taking action, when he was digging for answers. It was the same fleeting sense of power he had felt from refusing their pills, from staining his fingers blue and tonguing the ulcers that formed in his cheeks.

During these aimless wanderings, he looked through the many plastic crates lining the floors and walls of the huge room. He found the one with the missing firearm, the one he assumed Victor had stolen. The airtight seal was broken and the other guns inside reeked of grease. Some crates, he discovered, contained folded uniforms and suits like astronauts wore, vacuum sealed in thick plastic; others held helmets with large domes and metal collars. There were flashlights with red lenses, food and medical kits, backpacks, rounds and rounds of ammo, and myriad other devices and gadgets he could only guess at. He had found a laminated map in one crate, a chart of the fifty silos. There were red lines that radiated from the silos, one from each, and met at a single point in the distance. Donald had traced the lines with his finger, holding the map up to catch the light spilling from the distant office. He had puzzled over it and then put it back in its place, clues to a mystery he couldn't define.

This time, he stopped during his lap to perform a set of jumping jacks in the wide aisles between the sleeping drones. The exercise had been a struggle just two days ago, but the chill seemed to be melting from his veins. And the more he pushed himself, the more awake and alert he seemed to become. He did seventy-five, ten more than yesterday. After catching his breath, he dropped down to see how many push-ups he could do on his atrophied muscles. And it was here, on the third day of his captivity, his face barely an inch above the steel floor, that he discovered the launch lift, a garage door that barely came to his waist but was wide enough to handle the wingspan of the drones lurking beneath the tarps.

Donald rose from his push-up and approached the low door. The entire storehouse was kept incredibly dim, this wall almost pitch black. He thought about going for one of the flashlights when he saw the red handle. A tug, and the corrugated door slid up into the wall. On his hands and knees, Donald explored the cavity beyond, which went back over a dozen feet. There were no buttons or levers that he could feel along the walls, no method of operating the lift.

Curious, he crawled out to grab a flashlight. As he turned, he spotted another door along the darkened wall. Donald tried the handle and found it unlocked, a dim hallway beyond. He fumbled for a light switch and the overhead bulbs flickered hesitantly. He crept inside and pulled the door shut behind him.

The hallway ran fifty paces to a door at the far end, a pair of doors on either side. More offices, he assumed, similar to the home Anna had carved out in the back of the warehouse. He tried the first door and the odor of mothballs wafted out. Inside, there were rows of bunks, the shuffle of recent footsteps in a layer of dust, and a gap where two small beds formerly lay. The absence of people could be felt. He peeked into the door across the hall and found bathroom stalls and a cluster of showers.

The next two doors were more of the same, except for a row of urinals in the bathroom. Perhaps people had lived down there to keep up with the munitions, but Donald didn't remember anyone coming to that level during his first shift. No, these were quarters kept for another time, much like the machines beneath the tarps. He left the bathroom to the ghosts and checked the door at the end of the hall.

Inside, he found sheets of plastic thrown over tables and chairs, a fine mist of dust settled on top. Donald approached one of the tables and saw the computer display beneath the sheet. The chairs were attached to the desks, and there was something familiar about the knobs and levers. He knelt and fumbled for the edge of the plastic and peeled it up noisily.

The flight controls took him back to another life. Here was the stick his sister had called a yoke, the pedals beneath the seat she had called something else, the throttle and all the other dials and indicators. Donald remembered touring her training facility after she graduated from flight school. They had flown to Colorado for her ceremony. He remembered watching a screen just like this as her drone took to the air and joined a formation of others. He remembered the view of Colorado from the nose of her graceful machine in flight.

He glanced around the room at the dozen or so stations. The

obvious need for the place slammed into him. He imagined voices in the hallway, men and women showering and chatting, towels being snapped at asses, someone looking to borrow a razor, a shift of pilots sitting at these desks where coffee could lie perfectly still in steaming mugs as death was rained down from above.

Donald returned the plastic sheet. He thought of his sister, asleep and hidden some levels below where he couldn't find her, and he wondered if she hadn't been brought there as a surprise for him at all. Maybe she had been brought as a surprise for some future *others*.

And suddenly, thinking of her, thinking of a time lost to dreams and lonely tears, Donald found himself patting his pockets in search of something. Pills. An old prescription with her name on it. Helen had forced him to see a doctor, hadn't she? And Donald suddenly knew why he couldn't forget, why their drugs didn't work on him. The realization came with a powerful longing to find his sister. Charlotte was the why. She was the answer to one of Thurman's riddles.

45

"I WANT TO SEE her first," Donald demanded. "Let me see her, and then I'll tell you."

He waited for Thurman or Dr. Sneed to reply. The three of them stood in Sneed's office on the cryopod wing. Donald had bargained his way down the lift with Thurman, and now he bargained further. He suspected it was his sister's medication that explained why he couldn't forget. He would exchange this discovery for another. He wanted to know where she was, wanted to see her.

Something unspoken passed between the two men. Thurman turned to Donald with a warning. "She will not be woken," he said. "Not even for this."

Donald nodded. He saw how only those who made the laws were allowed to break them.

Dr. Sneed turned to the computer on his desk. "I'll look her up."

"No need," Thurman said. "I know where she is."

He led them out of the office and down the hall, past the main shift rooms where Donald had awoken as Troy all those years ago, past the deep freeze where he had spent a century asleep, all the way to another door just like the others.

The code Thurman entered was different; Donald could tell

by the discordant four-note song the buttons made. Above the keypad in small stenciled letters he made out the words *Emergency Personnel.* Locks whirred and ground like old bones, and the door gradually opened.

Steam followed them inside, the warm air from the hallway hitting the mortuary cool. There were fewer than a dozen rows of pods, perhaps fifty or sixty units in total, little more than a full shift. Donald peered into one of the coffin-like units, the ice a spiderweb of blue and white on the glass, and saw inside a thick and chiseled visage. A frozen soldier, or so his imagination told him.

Thurman led them through the rows and columns before stopping at one of the pods. He rested his hands on its surface with something like affection. His exhalations billowed into the air. It made his white hair and stark beard appear as though they were frosted with ice.

"Charlotte," Donald breathed, peering in at his sister. She hadn't changed, hadn't aged a bit. Even the blue cast of her skin seemed normal and expected. He was growing used to seeing people this way.

He rubbed the small window to clear the web of frost and marveled at his thin hands and seemingly fragile joints. He had atrophied. He had grown older while his sister had remained the same.

"I locked her away like this once," he said, gazing in at her. "I locked her away in my memory like this when she went off to war. Our parents did the same. She was just little Charla."

Glancing away from her, he studied the two men on the other side of the pod. Sneed started to say something, but Thurman placed a hand on the doctor's arm. Donald turned back to his sister.

"Of course, she grew up more than we knew. She was killing people over there. We talked about it years later, after I was in office and she'd figured I'd grown up enough." He laughed and shook his head. "My kid sister, waiting for *me* to grow up."

A tear plummeted to the frozen pane of glass. The salt cut through the ice and left a clear track behind. Donald wiped it away with a squeak, then felt frightened he might disturb her.

"They would get her up in the middle of the night," he said. "Whenever a target was deemed . . . what did she call it? *Actionable.* They would get her up. She said it was strange to go from dreaming to killing. How none of it made sense. How she would go back to sleep and see the video feeds in her mind—that last view from an incoming missile as she guided it into its target—"

He took a breath and gazed up at Thurman.

"I thought it was good that she couldn't be hurt, you know? She was safe in a trailer somewhere, not up there in the sky. But she complained about it. She told her doctor that it didn't feel right, being safe and doing what she did. The people on the front lines, they had fear as an excuse. They had self-preservation. A reason to kill. Charlotte used to kill people and then go to the mess hall and eat a piece of pie. That's what she told her doctor. She would eat something sweet and not be able to taste it."

"What doctor was this?" Sneed asked.

"My doctor," Donald said. He wiped his cheek, but he wasn't ashamed of the tears. Being by his sister's side had him feeling brave and bold, less alone. He could face the past and the future, both. "Helen was worried about my re-election. Charlotte already had a prescription, had been diagnosed with PTSD after her first tour, and so we kept filling it under her name, even under her insurance."

Sneed waved his hand, stirring the air for more information. "What prescription?"

"Propra," Thurman said. "She'd been taking propra, hadn't

she? And you were worried about the press finding out that you were self-medicating."

Donald nodded. "Helen was worried. She thought it might come out that I was taking something for my . . . wilder thoughts. The pills helped me forget them, kept me level. I could study the Order, and all I saw were the words, not the implications. There was no fear." He looked at his sister, understanding finally why she had refused to take the meds. She *wanted* the fear. It was necessary somehow, had made her feel more human.

"I remember you telling me she was on them," Thurman said. "We were in the bookstore—"

"Do you remember your dosage?" Sneed asked. "How long were you on it?"

"I started taking it after I was given the Order to read." He watched Thurman for any hint of expression and got nothing. "I guess that was two or three years before the convention. I took them nearly every day right up until then." He turned to Sneed. "I would've had some on me during orientation if I hadn't lost them on the hill that day. I think I fell. I remember falling—"

Sneed turned to Thurman. "There's no telling what the complications might be. Victor was careful to screen psychotropics from administrative personnel. Everyone was tested—"

"I wasn't," Donald said.

Sneed faced him. "Everyone was tested."

"Not him." Thurman studied the surface of the pod. "There was a last-minute change. A switch. I vouched for him. And if he was getting them in her name, there wouldn't have been anything in his medical records."

"We need to tell Erskine," Sneed said. "I could work with him. We might come up with a new formulation. This could explain some of the immunities in other silos." He turned away from the pod as if he needed to get back to his office.

Thurman looked to Donald. "Do you need more time down here?"

Donald studied his sister for a moment. He wanted to wake her, to talk to her. Maybe he could come back another time just to visit.

"I might like to come back," he said.

"We'll see."

Thurman walked around the pod and placed a hand on Donald's shoulder, gave him a light, sympathetic squeeze. He led Donald toward the door and Donald didn't glance back, didn't check the screen for his sister's new name. He didn't care. He knew where she was, and she would always be Charlotte to him. She would never change.

"You did good," Thurman said. "This is real good." They stepped into the hall, and he shut the thick door behind them. "You may have stumbled on why Victor was so obsessed with that report of yours."

"I did?" Donald didn't see the connection.

"I don't think he was interested in what you wrote at all," Thurman said. "I think he was interested in *you*."

46

THEY RODE THE lift to the cafeteria rather than drop Donald off on fifty-four. It was almost dinnertime, and he could help Thurman with the trays. While the lights behind the level numbers blinked on and off, following their progress up the shaft, Thurman's hunch about Victor haunted him. What if Victor had only been curious about his resistance to the medication? What if there wasn't anything in that report at all?

They rode past level forty, its button winking bright and then going dark, and Donald thought of the silo that had done the same. "What does this mean for Eighteen?" he asked, watching the next number flash by.

Thurman stared at the stainless steel doors, a greasy palm print there from where someone had caught their balance.

"Vic wanted to try another reset on Eighteen. I never saw the point. But maybe he was right. Maybe we give them one more chance."

"What's involved in a reset?"

"You know what's involved." Thurman faced him. "It's what we did to the world, just on a smaller scale. Reduce the population, wipe the computers, their memories, try it all over again. We've done that several times before with this silo. There are risks involved. You can't create trauma without making a mess. At some point, it's simpler and safer to just pull the plug."

"End them," Donald said, and he saw what Victor had been up against, what he had worked to avert. He wished he could speak to the old man. Anna said Victor had spoken of him often. And Erskine had said he wished people like Donald were in charge.

The lift opened on the top level. Donald stepped out and immediately felt strange to be walking among those on their shifts, to be present and at the same time removed from the day-to-day life of Silo 1.

He noticed that no one here looked to Thurman with deference. He was not that shift's head, and no one knew him as such. Just two men, one in white and one in beige, grabbing food and glancing at the ruined wasteland on the wallscreen.

Donald took one of the trays and noticed again that most people sat facing the view. Only one or two ate with their backs to it. He followed Thurman to the lift while longing to speak to these handful, to ask them what they remembered, what they were afraid of, to tell them that it was okay to be afraid.

"Why do the other silos have screens?" he asked Thurman, keeping his voice down. The parts of the facility he'd had no hand in designing made little sense to him. "Why show them what we did?"

"To keep them in," Thurman said. He balanced the tray with one hand and pressed the call button on the express. "It's not that we're showing them what we did. We're showing them what's out there. Those screens and a few taboos are all that contain these people. Humans have this disease, Donny, this compulsion to move until we bump into something. And then we tunnel through that something, or we sail over the edge of the oceans, or we stagger across mountains—"

The lift arrived. A man in reactor red excused himself and

stepped between the two of them. They boarded and Thurman fumbled for his badge. "Fear," he said. "Even the fear of death is barely enough to counter this compulsion of ours. If we didn't show them what was out there, they would go look for themselves. That's what we've always done as a race."

Donald considered this. He thought about his own compulsion to escape the confines of all that pressing concrete, even if it meant death out there. The slow strangulation inside was worse.

"I'd rather see a reset than extinguish the entire silo," Donald said, watching the numbers race by. He didn't mention that he'd been reading up on the people who lived there. A reset would mean a world of loss and heartache, but there would be a chance at life afterward. The alternative was death for them all.

"I'm less and less eager to gas the place, myself," Thurman admitted. "When Vic was around, all I did was argue against wasting our time with any one silo like this. Now that he's gone, I find myself pulling for these people. It's like I have to honor his last wishes. And that's a dangerous trap to fall into."

The lift stopped on twenty and picked up two workers, who ceased a conversation of their own and fell silent for the ride. Donald thought about this process of cleansing a silo only to watch the violence repeat itself. The great wars of old were like this. He remembered two wars in Iran, a new generation unremembering so that sons marched into the battles their fathers had already fought.

The two workers got off at the rec hall, resuming their conversation as the doors closed. Donald remembered how much he enjoyed punishing himself in the weight room. Now he was wasting away with little appetite, nothing to push against, no resistance.

"It makes me wonder sometimes if that was why he did what he did," Thurman said. The lift slid toward fifty-four. "Vic calculated everything. Always with a purpose. Maybe his way of winning this argument of ours was to ensure that he had the last word." Thurman glanced at Donald. "Hell, it's what finally motivated me to wake you."

Donald didn't say out loud how crazy that sounded. He thought Thurman just needed some way to make sense of the unthinkable. Of course, there was another way Victor's death had ended the argument. Not for the first time, Donald imagined that it hadn't been a suicide at all. But he didn't see where such doubts could get him except in trouble.

They got off on fifty-four and carried the trays through the aisles of munitions. As they passed the drones, Donald thought of his sister, similarly sleeping. It was good to know where she was, that she was safe. A small comfort.

They ate at the table in the war room. Donald pushed his dinner around his plate while Thurman and Anna talked. The two reports sat before him—just scraps of paper, he thought. No mystery contained within. He had been looking at the wrong thing, assuming there was a clue in the words, but it was just Donald's *existence* that Victor had remarked upon. He had sat across the hall from Donald and watched him react to whatever was in their water or their pills. And now when Donald looked at his notes, all he saw was a piece of paper with pain scrawled across it amid specks of blood.

Ignore the blood, he told himself. The blood wasn't a clue. It had come after. There were several splatters in a wide space left in the notes. Donald had been studying the senseless. He had been looking for something that wasn't there. He may as well have been staring off into space.

Space. Donald set his fork down and grabbed the other report. Once he ignored the large spots of blood, there was a gap in the notes where nothing had been written. This was what he should've been focused on. Not what was there, but what wasn't.

He checked the other report—the corresponding location of that blank space—to see what was written there. When he found the right spot, his excitement vanished. It was the paragraph that didn't belong, the one about the young inductee whose great-grandmother remembered the old times. It was nothing.

Unless—

Donald sat up straight. He took the two reports and placed them on top of each other. Anna was telling Thurman about her progress with jamming the radio towers, that she would be done soon. Thurman was saying that they could all get off shift in the next few days, get the schedule back in order. Donald held the overlapping reports up to the lights. Thurman looked on curiously.

"He wrote *around* something," Donald muttered. "Not *over* something."

He met Thurman's gaze and smiled. "You were wrong." The two pieces of paper trembled in his hands. "There is something here. He wasn't interested in me at all."

Anna set down her utensils and leaned over to have a look.

"If I had the original, I would've seen it straight away." He pointed to the space in the notes, then slid the top page away and tapped his finger on the one paragraph that didn't belong. The one that had nothing to do with Silo 12 at all.

"Here's why your resets don't work," he said. Anna grabbed the bottom report and read about the shadow Donald had inducted, the one whose great-grandmother remembered the old days, the one who had asked him a question about whether those stories were true.

"Someone in Silo Eighteen remembers," Donald said with

confidence. "Maybe a bunch of people, passing the knowledge in secret from generation to generation. Or they're immune like me. They remember."

Thurman took a sip of his water. He set down the glass and glanced from his daughter to Donald. "More reason to pull the plug," he said.

"No," Donald told him. "No. That's not what Victor thought." He tapped the dead man's notes. "He wanted to find the one who remembers, but he didn't mean me." He turned to Anna. "I don't think he wanted me up at all."

Anna looked up at her father, a puzzled expression on her face. She turned to Donald. "What are you suggesting?"

Donald stood and paced behind the chairs, stepping over the wires that snaked across the tiles. "We need to call Eighteen and ask the head there if anyone fits this profile, someone or some group sowing discord, maybe talking about the world we—" He stopped himself from saying *destroyed*.

"Okay," Anna said, nodding her head. "Okay. Let's say they do know. Let's say we find these people over there like you. What then?"

He stopped his pacing. This was the part he hadn't considered. He found Thurman studying him, the old man's lips pursed.

"We find these people—" Donald said.

And he knew. He knew what it would take to save these people in this distant silo, these welders and shopkeeps and farmers and their young shadows. He remembered being the one on a previous shift to press that button, to kill in order to save.

And he knew he would do it again.

47

Silo 18

MISSION'S THROAT ITCHED and his eyes stung, the smoke growing heavier and the stench stronger as he approached one-twenty and Lower Dispatch. The pursuit from above seemed to have faltered, perhaps from the gap in the rails that had claimed a life.

Cam was dead, of that he felt certain. And how many others had suffered the same fate? A twinge of guilt accompanied the sick thought that the fallen would have to be carried up to the farms in plastic bags. A porter would have to do that job, and it wouldn't be a pretty one.

He shook this thought away as he got within a level of Dispatch. Tears streamed down his face and mixed with the sweat and grime of the long day's descent. He bore bad news. A shower and clean clothes would do little to alleviate the weariness he felt, but there would be protection there, help in clearing up the confusion about the blast. He hurried down the last half-flight and remembered, perhaps due to the rising ash that reminded him of a note torn to confetti, the reason he'd been chasing after Cam in the first place.

Rodny. His friend was locked away in IT, and his plea for help had been lost in the din and confusion of the explosion.

The explosion. Cam. The package. The *delivery*.

Mission wobbled and clutched the railing for balance. He thought of the ridiculous fee for the delivery, a fee that perhaps was never meant to be paid. He gathered himself and hurried on, wondering what was going on in that locked room in IT, what kind of trouble Rodny might be in and how to help him. How, even, to *get* to him.

The air grew thick and it burned to breathe as he arrived at Dispatch. A small crowd huddled on the stairway. They peered across the landing and into the open doors of one-twenty. Mission coughed into his fist as he pushed his way through the onlookers. Had the wreckage from above landed here? Everything seemed intact. Two buckets lay on their sides near the door, and a gray fire hose snaked over the railing and trailed inside. A blanket of smoke clung to the ceiling; it trailed out and up the wall of the stairwell shaft, defying gravity.

Mission pulled his 'chief up over his nose, confused. The smoke was coming from *inside* Dispatch. He breathed in through his mouth, the fabric pressing against his lips and lessening the sting in his throat. Dark shapes moved inside the hallway. He unsnapped the strap that held his knife in place and crossed the threshold, keeping low to stay away from the smoke. The floors were wet and squished with the traffic from deeper inside. It was dark, but beams of light from flashlights danced around further down the hallway.

Mission hurried toward the lights. The smoke was thicker, the water on the floor deeper. Bits of pulp floated on the surface. He passed one of the dormitories, the sorting hall, the front offices.

Lily, an elder porter, ran by in slaps and spray, recognizable only at the last moment as the beam from her flashlight briefly lit her face. There was someone lying in the water, pressed up against the wall. As Mission approached and a passing light played over the form, he saw that they weren't lying there at all. It was Hackett, one of the few dispatchers who treated the young shadows with respect and never seemed to take delight in their burdens. Half of his face remained unscathed, the other half was a seething red blister. Deathdays. Lottery numbers flashed in Mission's vision.

"Porter! Get over here."

It was Morgan's voice, Mission's former caster. The old man's cough joined a chorus of others. The hallway was full of ripples and waves, splashes and hacks, smoke and commands. Mission hurried toward the familiar silhouette, his eyes burning.

"Sir? It's Mission. The explosion—" He pointed at the ceiling.

"I know my own shadows, boy." A light was trained on Mission's eyes. "Get in here and give these lads a hand."

The smell of cooked beans and burned and wet paper was overpowering. There was a hint of fuel behind it all, a smell Mission knew from the Down Deep and its generators. And there was something else: the smell of the bazaar during a pig roast, the foul and unpleasant odor of burned flesh.

The water in the main hall was deep. It lapped up over Mission's halfboots and filled them with muck. Drawers of files were being emptied into buckets. An empty crate was shoved into his hands, beams of light swirling in the mist, his nose burning and running, tears on his cheeks unbidden.

"Here, here," someone said, urging him forward. They warned him not to touch the filing cabinet. Piles of paper went into the crate, heavier than they should be. Mission didn't understand the rush. The fire was out. The walls were black where the flames must have licked at them, and the grow plots along the far wall where rows of beans had run up tall trestles had turned to ash. The trestles stood like black fingers, those that stood at all.

Amanda from Dispatch was there at the filing cabinets, her 'chief wrapped around her hand, managing the drawers as they were emptied. The crate filled up fast. Mission spotted someone emptying the wall safe of its old books as he turned back toward the hallway. There was a body in the corner covered by a sheet. Nobody was in much of a hurry to remove it.

He followed the others to the landing, but they did not go all the way out. The emergency lights in the dorm room were on, mattresses stacked up in the corner. Carter, Lyn, and Jocelyn were spreading the files out on the springs. Mission unloaded his crate and went back for another load.

"What happened?" he asked Amanda as he reached the filing cabinets. "Is this some sort of retribution?"

"The farmers came for the beans," she said. She used her 'chief to wrestle with another drawer. "They came for the beans and they burned it all."

Mission took in the wide swathe of damage. He recalled how the stairwell had trembled during the blast, could still see in his mind the people falling and screaming to their deaths. The months of growing violence had sparked alive as if a switch had been flipped.

"So what do we do now?" Carter asked. He was a powerful porter, in his early thirties, when men find their strength and have yet to lose their joints, but he looked absolutely beat. His hair clung to his forehead in wet clumps. There were black smears on his face, and you could no longer tell what color his 'chief had been.

"Now we burn their crops," someone suggested.

"The crops we eat?"

"Just the upper farms. They're the ones who did this."

"We don't know who did this," Morgan said.

Mission caught his old caster's eye. "In the main hall," he said. "I saw . . . Was that . . . ?"

Morgan nodded. "Roker. Aye."

Carter slapped the wall and barked profanities. "I'll kill 'em!" he yelled.

"So you're . . ." Mission wanted to say *Lower chief,* but it was too soon for that to make sense.

"Aye," Morgan said, and Mission could tell it made little sense to him either.

"People will be carrying whatever they like for a few days," Joel said. "We'll appear weak if we don't strike back." Joel was two years older than Mission and a good porter. He coughed into his fist while Lyn looked on with concern.

Mission had other concerns besides appearing weak. The people above thought a porter had attacked them. And now this assault from the farmers, so far from where they'd been hit the night before. Porters were the nearest thing to a roaming sentry and they were being taken out by someone—purposefully, he thought. Then there were all those boys being recruited into IT. They weren't being recruited to fix computers; they were being hired to break something. The spirit of the silo, perhaps.

"I need to get home," Mission said. It was a slip. He meant to say up top. He worked to unknot his 'chief. The thing reeked of smoke, as did his hands and his coveralls. He would have to find different coveralls, a different color to wear. He needed to get in touch with his old friends from the Nest.

"What do you think you're doing?" Morgan asked. His former caster seemed ready to say something else as Mission tugged the 'chief away. Instead, the old man's eyes fell to the bright red welt around Mission's neck.

"I don't think this is about us at all," Mission said. "I think this is bigger than that. A friend of mine is in trouble. He's at the heart of all that's going wrong. I think something bad is going to happen to him or that he might know something. They won't let him talk to anyone."

"Rodny?" Lyn asked. She and Joel had been two years ahead at the Nest, but they knew Mission and Rodny, both.

Mission nodded. "And Cam is dead," he told the others. He explained what'd happened on his way down, the blast, the people chasing him, the gap in the rails. Someone whispered Cam's name in disbelief. "I don't think anyone cares that we know," Mission added. "I think that's the point. Everyone's supposed to be angry. As angry as possible."

"I need time to think," Morgan said. "To plan."

"I don't think there *is* much time," Mission said. He told them about the new hires at IT. He told Morgan about seeing Bradley there, about the young porter applying for a different job.

"What do we do?" Lyn asked, looking to Joel and the others.

"We take it easy," Morgan said, but he didn't seem so sure. The confidence he displayed as a senior porter and caster seemed shaken now that he was a chief.

"I can't stay down here," Mission said flatly. "You can have every vacation chit I own, but I've got to get up top. I don't know how, but I have to."

48

Before he went anywhere, Mission needed to get in touch with friends he could trust, anyone who might be able to help, the old gang from the Nest. As Morgan urged everyone on the landing back to work, Mission slunk down the dark and smoky hallway toward the sorting room, which had a computer he might be able to use. Lyn and Joel followed, more eager to find out about Rodny than to clean up after the fire.

They checked the monitor at the sorting counter and saw that the computer was down, possibly from the power outage the night before. Mission remembered all those people with their broken computers earlier that morning at IT and wondered if there would be a working machine anywhere on five levels. Since he couldn't send a wire, he picked up the hard line to the other Dispatch offices to see if they could get a message out for him.

He tried Central first. Lyn stood with him at the counter, her flashlight illuminating the dials, piercing the haze of smoke in the room. Joel splashed among the shelves, moving the reusable sorting crates on the bottom higher up to keep them from getting wet. There was no response from Central.

"Maybe the fire got the radio too," she whispered.

Mission didn't think so. The power light was on and the speaker was making that crackling sound when he squeezed the button. He heard Morgan splash past in the hallway, yelling and complaining that his workforce was disappearing. Lyn cupped her hand over her flashlight. "Something is going on at Central," he told Lyn. He had a bad feeling.

The second way station he tried up top finally won a response. "Who's this?" someone asked, their voice shaking with barely concealed panic.

"This is Mission. Who's this?"

"Mission? You're in big trouble, man."

Mission glanced up at Lyn. "Who is this?"

"This is Robbie. They left me alone up here, man. I haven't heard from anybody. But everyone's looking for you. What's going on down there in Lower?"

Joel stopped with the crates and trained his flashlight on the counter.

"Everyone's looking for *me*?" Mission asked.

"You and Cam, a few of the others. There was some kind of fight at Central. Were you there for that? I can't get word from anyone!"

"Robbie, I need you to get in touch with some friends of mine. Can you send out a wire? Something's wrong with our computers down here."

"No, ours are all kind of sideways. We've been having to use the terminal up at the mayor's office. It's the only one working."

"The mayor's office? Okay, I need you to send a couple of wires, then. You got something to write with?"

"Wait," Robbie said. "These are official wires, right? If not, I don't have the authority—"

"Dammit, Robbie, this is important! Grab something to write with. I'll pay you back. They can dock me for it if they want."

Mission glanced up at Lyn, who was shaking her head in disbelief. He coughed into his fist, the smoke tickling his throat.

"All right, all right," Robbie said. "Who'm I sending this to? And you owe me for this piece of paper because that's all I have to write on."

Mission let go of the transmit button to curse the kid. He thought about who would be most likely to get a wire and send it along to the others. He ended up giving Robbie three names, then told him what to write. He would have his friends meet him at the Nest, or meet each other if he couldn't make it there himself. The Nest had to be safe. Nobody would attack the school or the Crow. Once the gang was together, they could figure out what to do. Maybe the Crow would know what to do. The hardest part for Mission would be working out how to join them.

"You got all that?" he asked Robbie when the boy didn't reply.

"Yeah, yeah, man. I think you're gonna be over the character limit, though. This better come out of your pay."

Mission shook his head in disbelief.

"Now what?" Lyn asked as he hung up the receiver.

"I need coveralls," Mission said. He splashed around the counter and joined Joel by the shelves, began looking through the nearest crates. "They're looking for me, so I'm gonna need new colors if I'm getting up there."

"We," Lyn told him. "*We* need new colors. If you're going to the Nest, I'm coming with you."

"Me too," Joel said.

"I appreciate that," Mission said, "but company might make it more dangerous. We'd be more conspicuous."

"Yeah, but they're looking for you," Lyn said.

"Hey, we have a ton of these new whites." Joel pulled the

lid off a sorting bin. "But they'll just make us stand out, won't they?"

"Whites?" Mission headed over to see what Joel was talking about.

"Yeah. For Security. We've been moving a ton of these lately. Came down from Garment a few days ago. No idea why they made up so many."

Mission checked the coveralls. The ones on top were covered in soot, more gray than white. There were dozens of them stacked in the sorting crate. He remembered all the new hires. It was as if they wanted half the silo dressed in white and the other half fighting one another. It made no sense. Unless the idea was to get everyone killed.

"Killed," Mission said. He splashed down the shelves to another crate. "I've got a better idea." He found the right bin—he and Cam had been given one of these just a few days ago. He reached in and pulled out a bag. "How would you two like to make some money?"

Joel and Lyn hurried over to see what he'd found and Mission held up one of the heavy plastic bags with the bright silver zipper and the hauling straps.

"Three hundred and eighty-four chits to divide between you," he promised. "Every chit I own. I just need you for one last tandem."

The two porters played their lights across the object in his hands. It was a black bag. A black bag made for hauls such as these.

49

MISSION SAT ON the counter and worked the laces on his halfboots free. They were soaked, his socks as well. He shucked them off to keep the water out of the bag and to save the weight. Always a porter, thinking about weight. Lyn handed him one of the Security coveralls, an extra precaution. He wiggled out of his porter blues and tugged the whites on while Lyn looked the other way. His knife he strapped back to his waist.

"You guys sure you're up for this?" he asked.

Lyn helped him slide his feet into the bag and worked the inside straps around his ankles. "Are *you* sure?" she asked, cinching the straps.

Mission laughed, his stomach fluttering with nerves. He stretched out and let them work the top straps under his shoulders. "Have you both eaten?"

"We'll be fine," Joel said. "Stop worrying."

"If it gets late—"

"Lie your head back," Lyn told him. She worked the zipper up from his feet. "And don't talk unless we tell you it's okay."

"We'll take a break every twenty or so," Joel said. "We'll bring you into a bathroom with us. You can stretch and get some water."

Lyn worked the zipper up over his chest to his chin, hesitated, then kissed the pads of her fingers and touched his forehead the same way he'd seen countless loved ones and priests bless the dead. "May your steps rise to the heavens," she whispered.

Her wan smile caught in the spill of Joel's flashlight before the bag was sealed up over Mission's face.

"Or at least until Upper Dispatch," Joel added.

They carried him outside and down the hall, and the porters made way for the dead. Several hands reached out and touched Mission through the black plastic, showing respect, and he fought not to flinch or cough. It felt as though the smoke was trapped in the bag with him.

Joel took the lead, which meant Mission's shoulders were pressed against his. He faced upward, his body swaying in time to their steps, the straps beneath his armpits pulling the opposite way from what he was used to. It grew more comfortable as they hit the stairs and began the long spiral up. His feet were lowered until the blood no longer pooled in his head. Lyn carried her half of his weight from several steps below.

The dark and quiet overtook him as they left the chaos of Lower Dispatch. The two porters didn't talk as some tandems might. They saved their breath and kept their thoughts to themselves. Joel set an aggressive pace. Mission could sense it in the gentle swaying of his body, suspended above the steel treads.

As the steps passed, the journey grew more and more uncomfortable. It wasn't the difficulty breathing, for he had been shadowed well to manage his lungs on a long climb. He could also handle the stuffiness from the plastic pressed against his face. Nor was it the dark, for his favorite hour for porting had always been the dim-time, time alone with his thoughts while others slept. It wasn't the stench of plastic and smoke, the tickle in his throat or the pain of the straps.

It was the act of lying still. Of being carried. Of being a burden.

The straps pinched his shoulders until his arms fell numb, and he swayed in the darkness, the sounds of boots on steel, of Joel and Lyn's heavy breathing, as he was lifted up the stairwell. *Too great a burden,* he thought.

He thought of his mother carrying him for all those months with no one to confide in and no one to support her. Not until his father had found out, and by then it was too late to terminate the pregnancy. He wondered how long his father had hated the bulge in her belly, how long he had wanted to cut Mission out like some kind of cancer. Mission had never asked to be carried like that. And he had never wanted to be ported by anyone ever again.

Two years ago to the day. That was the last time he had felt this, this sense of being a burden to all. Two years since he had proved too much for even a rope to bear.

It was a poor knot he had tied. But his hands had been trembling and he had fought to see the knot through a film of tears. When it failed, the knot didn't come free so much as slide, and it left his neck afire and bleeding. His great regret was having jumped from the lower stairwell in Mechanical, the rope looped over the pipes above. If he had gone from a landing, the slipping knot wouldn't have mattered. The fall would've claimed him.

Now he was too scared to try again. He was as scared of trying again as he was of being a burden to another. Was that why he avoided seeing Allie, because she longed to care for him? To help support him? Was that why he ran away from home?

The tears finally came. His arms were pinned, so he couldn't wipe them away. He thought of his mother, about whom he could only piece together a few details. But he knew this of her: she hadn't been afraid of life or death. She had embraced both in an act of sacrifice, giving her own blood for his, a trade he would never feel worthy of.

The silo spun slowly around him; the steps sank one at a time; and Mission endured the suffering. He labored not to sob, seeing himself for the first time in that utter darkness, knowing his soul more fully in that deathly ritual of being ported to his grave, this sad awakening on his birthday.

50

Silo 1

FINDING ONE AMONG ten thousand should've been more difficult. It should have taken months of crawling through reports and databases, of querying the head of 18 and asking for personality profiles, of looking at arrest histories, cleaning schedules, who was related to whom, and all the gossip and chatter compiled from monthly reports.

But Donald found an easier way. He simply searched the database for a facsimile of *himself.*

One who remembered. One full of fear and paranoia. One who tries to blend in but is subversive. He looked for a fear of doctors, teasing out those residents who never went to see them. He looked for someone who shunned medication and found one who did not even trust the water. A part of him expected he might find several people to be causing so much havoc, a pack, and that locating one among them would lead to the rest. He expected to find them young and outraged with some way of handing down what they knew from generation to generation. What he found instead was both eerily similar and not like him at all.

The next morning, he showed his results to Thurman, who stood perfectly still for a long while.

"Of course," he finally said. "Of course."

A hand on Donald's shoulder was all the congratulations he got. Thurman explained that the reset was well underway. He admitted that it had been underway since Donald had been woken, that the head of 18 had taken on new recruits, had sown the seeds of discord. Erskine and Dr. Sneed were working through the night to make changes, to come up with a new formulation, but this component might take weeks. Looking over what Donald had found, he said he was going to make a call to 18.

"I want to come with you," Donald said. "It's my theory after all."

What he wanted to say was that he wouldn't take the coward's way. If someone was to be executed on his account—one life for the sake of many—he didn't want to hide from the decision.

Thurman agreed.

They rode the lift almost as equals. Donald asked why Thurman had started the reset, but he thought he knew the answer.

"Vic won," was Thurman's reply.

Donald thought of all the lives in the database that were now thrown into chaos. He made the mistake of asking how the reset was going, and Thurman told him about the bombs and the violence, how the groups who wore different colors were warring with one another, how these things typically went downhill fast with the barest of nudges, that the formula was as old as time.

"The combustibles are always there," Thurman said. "You'd be surprised at how few sparks it takes."

They exited the lift and walked down a familiar hallway. This was Donald's old commute. Here, he had worked under a different name. He had worked without knowing what he was doing. They passed offices full of people tapping on keyboards and chatting with one another. Half a millennium of people coming on and off shifts, doing what they were told, following orders.

He couldn't help himself as they approached his old office: he paused at the door and peered in. A thin man with a halo of hair that wrapped from ear to ear, just a few wisps on top, looked up at him. He sat there, mouth agape, hand resting on his mouse, waiting for Donald to say or do something.

Donald nodded a sympathetic hello. He turned and looked through the door across the hall where a man in white sat behind a similar desk. The puppeteer. Thurman spoke to him, and he got up from his desk and joined them in the hall. He knew that Thurman was in charge.

Donald followed the two of them to the comm room, leaving the balding man at his old desk to his game of solitaire. He felt a mix of sympathy and envy for the man—for those who didn't remember. As they turned the corner, Donald thought back to those initial bouts of awareness on his first shift. He remembered speaking with a doctor who knew the truth, and having this sense of wonder that anyone could cope with such knowledge. And now he saw that it wasn't that the pain grew tolerable or the confusion went away. Instead, it simply became familiar. It became a part of you.

The comm room was quiet. Heads swiveled as the three of them entered. One of the operators in orange hurriedly removed his feet from his desk. Another took a bite of his protein bar and turned back to his station.

"Get me Eighteen," Thurman said.

Eyes turned to the other man in white, the one supposedly in charge, and he waved his consent. A call was patched through. Thurman held half a headset to one ear while he waited. He caught the expression on Donald's face and asked the operator for another set. Donald stepped forward and took it while the cable was slotted into the receiver. He could hear the familiar beeping of a call being placed, and his stomach fluttered as doubts began to surface. Finally, a voice answered. A shadow.

Thurman asked him to get Mr. Wyck, the silo head.

"He's already coming," the shadow said.

When Wyck joined the conversation, Thurman told the head what Donald had discovered, but it was the shadow who responded. The shadow knew the one they were after. He said he knew the person well. There was something in his voice, some shock or hesitation, and Thurman waved at the operator to get the sensors in his headset going. Suddenly, the monitors were providing feedback like a Rite of Initiation. Thurman conducted the questioning and Donald watched a master at work.

"Tell me what you know," he said. Thurman leaned over the operator and peered at a screen that monitored skin conductivity, pulse, and perspiration. Donald was no expert at reading the charts, but he knew something was up by the way the lines spiked up and down when the shadow spoke. He feared for the young man. He wondered if someone would die then and there.

But Thurman took a softer approach. He got the boy speaking of his childhood, had him admitting to the rage he harbored, a sense of not belonging. The shadow spoke of an upbringing both ideal and frustrating, and Thurman was like a gentle but firm drill sergeant working with a troubled recruit: tearing him down, building him back up.

"You've been fed the truth," he told the young man, referring to the Legacy. "And now you see why the truth must be divvied out carefully or not at all."

"I do."

The shadow sniffed as though he were crying. And yet: the jagged lines on the screen formed less precipitous peaks, less dangerous valleys.

Thurman spoke of sacrifice, of the greater good, of individual lives proving meaningless in the far stretch of time. He took that shadow's rage and redirected it until the torture of being locked up for months with the books of the Legacy was distilled down to its very essence. And through it all, it didn't sound as though the silo head breathed once.

"Tell me what needs to be fixed," Thurman said, after their discussion. He laid the problem at the shadow's feet. Donald saw how this was better than simply handing him the solution.

The shadow spoke of a culture forming that overvalued individuality, of children that wanted to get away from their families, of generations living levels apart and independence stressed until no one relied on anyone and everyone was dispensable.

The sobs came. Donald watched as Thurman's face tightened, and he wondered again if he was about to see the young man put out of his misery. Instead, Thurman released the radio and said to those gathered around, simply, "He's ready."

And what started as an inquiry, a test of Donald's theory, concluded this boy's Rite of Initiation. A shadow became a man. Lines on a screen settled into steel cords of resolve as his anger was given a new focus, a new purpose. His childhood was seen differently. Dangerously.

Thurman gave this young man his first order. Mr. Wyck congratulated the boy and told him he would be allowed to go, would be given his freedom. And later, as Donald and Thurman rode the lift back toward Anna, Thurman declared that in the years to come, this Rodny would make a fine silo head. Even better than the last.

51

THAT AFTERNOON, DONALD and Anna worked to restore order to the war room. They made it ready in case it was called upon in a future shift. All their notes were taken off the walls and filed away into airtight plastic crates, and Donald imagined these would sit on another level somewhere, in another storeroom, to gather dust. The computers were unplugged, all the wiring coiled up, and these were hauled off by Erskine on a cart with squeaky wheels. All that was left were the cots, a change of clothes, and the standard-issue toiletries. Enough to get them through the night and to their meeting with Dr. Sneed the following day.

Several shifts were about to come to a close. For Anna and Thurman, it had been a long time coming. Two full shifts. Almost a year awake. Erskine and Sneed would need a few weeks to finish their work, and by that time the next head would come on, and the schedule would return to normal. For Donald, it had been less than a week awake after a century of sleep. He was a dead man who had blinked his eyes open for but a brief moment.

He took his last shower and his first dose of the bitter drink so that no one would think anything was amiss. But Donald didn't plan on going under again. If he went back to the deep freeze, he knew they would never wake him again. Unless things were so bad that he wouldn't want to be woken anyway. Unless it were Anna once more, lonely, wishing for company and willing to subject him to abuse in order to get it.

That wasn't sleep. That was a body and a mind stored away. There were other choices, more final escapes. Donald had discovered this resolve by following the trail of clues left behind by Victor, and he would soon join him in death.

He walked a final lap amid the guns and drones before finally retiring to his cot. He thought of Helen as he lay there listening to Anna sing in the shower one last time. And he realized the anger he had felt for his wife having lived and loved without him had now dissipated, wiped away by his guilt for coming to find solace in Anna's embrace. And when she came to him that night, straight from the shower with water beading on her flesh, he could not resist any longer. They had the same bitter drink on their breath, that concoction that prepped their veins for the deep sleep, and neither of them cared. Donald succumbed. And then he waited until she had returned to her cot and her breathing had softened before he cried himself to sleep.

When he woke, Anna was already gone, her cot neatly made. Donald did the same, tucking the sheets beneath the mattress and leaving the corners crisp, even though he knew the sheets would be mussed as the cots were returned to their rightful place in the barracks. He checked the time. Anna had been put under during the early morning so as not to be spotted. He had less than an hour before Thurman would come for him. More than enough time.

He went out to the storeroom and approached the drone nearest the hangar door. Yanking the tarp off sent a cloud of dust into the air. He dragged out the empty plastic crate from under one of the wings, opened the low hangar door, and arranged the bin so that it was slightly inside the lift. He lowered the door onto the crate to keep the hangar open.

Hurrying down the hallway, past the empty barracks, he pulled the plastic sheet off the station at the very end. Flipping the plastic cover off the lift switch, he threw it into the up position. The first time he'd done this, the door to the lift would no longer open, but he could hear the platform rumbling upward on the other side of the wall. It hadn't taken long to figure out a solution.

Replacing the plastic sheet, he hurried down the hall, turned the light off and shut the door. He pulled the other bin from under the drone's left wing. Donald stripped and tossed his clothes under the drone. He pulled the thick plastic suit from the bin and sat down to work his feet into the legs. The boots went on next, Donald being careful to seal the cuffs around them. Standing up, he gripped the dangling shoelace stolen from an extra boot. The end had been tied to the zipper on the back of the suit. He pulled it over his shoulder and tugged upward, made sure the zipper went to the top before grabbing the gloves, flashlight, and helmet from the bin.

Suited up, he closed the bin and slid it back under the wing, covered the drone with the tarp. There would only be a single bin out of place when Thurman arrived. Victor had left a mess to discover. Donald would hardly leave a trace.

He crawled inside the lift, pushing the flashlight ahead of him. He could hear the motor straining against the pinned crate like an angry hive of bees. Turning on the flashlight, he took a last look at the storeroom, braced himself, then kicked the plastic tub with both boots.

It budged. He kicked again and there was a thunderous racket as the door slammed shut, and then the shudder of movement. The flashlight jittered and danced. Donald corralled it between his mitts and watched his exhalations fog the inside of his helmet. He had no idea what to expect, but he was causing it. He would control his own fate.

52

THE RIDE UP took much longer than he anticipated. There were moments when he wasn't sure whether or not he was moving. He grew worried that his plan had been discovered, that the misplaced bin had led them to his tracks in the dust, that he was being recalled. He urged the lift to hurry along.

His flashlight gave out. Donald tapped the cylinder in his mitt and worked the switch back and forth. It must've been on a weak charge from its long storage. He was left in the dark, no way of knowing which way was up or down, whether he was rising or falling. All he could do was wait. He knew that this was the right decision. There was nothing worse than being trapped in the darkness, in that pod, unable to do anything more than wait.

Arrival came with a jarring clank. The persistent hum of the motor disappeared, the ensuing quiet haunting. There was a second clank, and then the door opposite the one he'd entered rose slowly. A metal attachment the size of a fist slid forward on a track. Donald scrambled after this, seeing how the drone might be guided forward.

He found himself in a sloping launch bay. He hadn't known what to expect, thought maybe he'd simply arrive above the soil on a barren landscape. But he was in a shaft. Above him, up the slope, a slit was opening, a dim light growing stronger. Beyond this slit, Donald spotted the roiling clouds he knew from the cafeteria. They were the bright gray that came with the sunrise. The doors at the top of the slope continued to slide apart like a maw opening wide.

Donald crawled up the steep slope as quickly as he could. The metal car in the track stopped and locked into place. Donald hurried, imagining he didn't have much time. He stayed off the track in case the launch sequence was automated, but the car never moved, never raced by. He arrived at the open doors exhausted and perspiring and pulled himself out.

The world spread out before him. After a week of living in a windowless chamber, the scale and openness were inspiring. Donald felt like tearing off his helmet and sucking in deep breaths. The oppressive weight of his silo imprisonment had been lifted. Above him were only clouds.

He stood on a round concrete platform. Behind the opening for the launch ramp was a cluster of antennae. He went to these, held on to one of them and lowered himself to the wide ledge below. From here it was a scramble on his belly, trying to hold on to the slick edge with bulky gloves, and then a graceless drop to the dirt.

He scanned the horizon for the city—had to work his way around the tower to find it. From there, he aimed forty-five degrees to the left. He had studied the maps to make sure, but now that he was there, he realized he could've done it by memory. Over there was where the tents had stood, and here the stage, and beyond them the dirt tracks through the struggling beginnings of grass as ATVs buzzed up the hillside. He could almost smell the food that'd been cooking, could hear the dogs barking and children playing, the anthems in the air.

Donald shook off thoughts of the past and made his time count. He knew there was a chance—a very good chance—that someone was sitting at breakfast in the cafeteria. At this very moment, they would be dropping their spoons and pointing at the wallscreen. But he had a head start. They would have to wrestle with suits and wonder if the risk was worth it. By the time they got to him, it would be too late. Hopefully, they would simply leave him be.

He worked his way up the hillside. Movement was a struggle inside the bulky suit. He slipped and fell several times in the slick soil. When a gust of wind hammered the landscape, it peppered his helmet with grit and made a noise like the hiss of Anna's radio. There was no telling how long the suit would last. He knew enough of the cleaning to suspect it wouldn't be forever, but Anna had told him that the machines in the air were designed to attack only certain things. That's why they didn't destroy the sensors, or the concrete, or a properly built suit. And he suspected the suits in Silo 1 would have been built properly.

All he hoped for as he labored up the hill was a view. He was so obsessed and determined to win this that he never thought to look behind him, slipping and scrambling, crawling on his hands and knees the last fifty feet, until he was finally at the summit. He stood and staggered forward, exhausted, breathing heavily. Reaching the edge, he peered down into the adjacent bowl. There, a concrete tower stood like a gravestone, like a monument to Helen. She was buried beneath that tower. And while he could never go to her, never be buried alongside her, he could lie down underneath the clouds and be close enough.

He wanted his helmet off. First, though, his gloves. He tugged one of them free—popping the seal—and dropped it to the soil. The heavy winds sent the glove tumbling down the slope, and the swirling grit stung his hand. The peppering of fine particles burned like a day on a windy beach. Donald began tugging on his other glove, resigned to what would come next, when suddenly he felt a hand grip his shoulder—and he was pulled back from the edge of that gentle rise and the view of his wife's last resting place.

53

DONALD STUMBLED AND FELL. The shock of being touched sent his heart into his throat. He waved his arms to free himself but someone had a grip on his suit. More than one person. They dragged him back until he could no longer see beyond the ridge.

Screams of frustration filled his helmet. Couldn't they see that it was too late? Couldn't they leave him be? He flailed and tried to lunge out of their grip, but he was being pulled inexorably down the hill, back toward Silo 1.

When he fell the next time, he was able to roll over and face them, to get his arms up to defend himself. And there was Thurman standing over him—wearing nothing more than his white coveralls, dust from the dead earth gathering in the old man's gray brow.

"It's time to go!" Thurman yelled into the heavy wind. His voice seemed as distant as the clouds.

Donald kicked his feet and tried to crawl back up the hill but there were three of them there, blocking his way. All in white, squinting against the ferocity of the driving wind and pelting soil.

Donald screamed as they seized him again. He tried to grab rocks and fistfuls of soil as they pulled him along by his boots.

His helmet knocked against the lifeless pack of dirt. He watched the clouds boil overhead as his fingernails were bent back and broken in his struggle for some purchase.

By the time they got him to the flats, Donald was spent. They carried him down a ramp and through the airlock where more men were waiting. His helmet was tossed aside before the outer door fully shut. Thurman stood in a far corner and watched as they undressed him. The old man dabbed at the blood running from his nose. Donald had caught him with his boot.

Erskine was there, Dr. Sneed as well, both of them breathing hard. As soon as they got his suit off, Sneed plunged a needle into Donald's flesh. Erskine held his hand and seemed sad as the liquid spread through Donald's veins.

"A bloody waste," someone said as the fog settled over him.

"Look at this mess."

Erskine placed a hand on Donald's cheek as Donald drifted deeper into the black. His lids grew heavy and his hearing distant.

"Be better if someone like you were in charge," he heard Erskine say.

But it was Victor's voice he heard. It was a dream. No, a memory. A thought from an earlier conversation. Donald couldn't be sure. The waking world of boots and angry voices was too busy being swallowed by the mist of sleep and the fog of dreams. And this time—rather than with a fear of death—Donald went into that darkness gladly. He embraced it hoping it would be eternal. He went with a final thought of his sister, of those drones beneath their tarps, all those things he hoped would never be woken.

54

Silo 18

MISSION FELT BURIED alive. He fell into an uncomfortable trance, the bag growing hot and slick as it trapped his heat and exhalations. Part of him feared he would pass out in there, and Joel and Lyn would discover him dead. Part of him hoped.

The two porters were stopped for questioning on one-seventeen, the landing below the blast that took Cam. Those working to repair the stairwell were on the lookout for a certain porter. Their description was part Cam, part Mission. Mission held deathly still while Joel complained of being stopped with so sensitive and heavy a load. It seemed that they might ask for the bag to be opened, but there were some things nearly as taboo as talk of the outside. And so they were sent on their way with a warning that the rail was out above and that one person had already fallen to their death.

Mission fought off a coughing fit as the voices receded below. He wiggled his shoulders and struggled to cover his mouth to muffle the sound. Lyn hissed at him to be quiet. In the distance, Mission could hear a woman wailing. They passed through the wreckage from hours earlier, and Joel and Lyn gasped at the sight of an entire landing torn free from the stairwell.

Above Supply, on one-zero-seven, they carried Mission into a bathroom, opened the bag and let him work the blood back into his arms. Mission used one of the stalls, took a few sips of water, and assured Joel and Lyn that he was fine in there. All three of them were damp with sweat, and there were still thirty-odd levels to go. Joel especially seemed weary from the climb, or perhaps from seeing the damage wrought by the blast. Lyn was holding up better but was anxious to get going again. She fretted for Rodny and seemed as eager as Mission to get to the Nest.

Mission caught a glance of himself in the mirror with his white coveralls and his porter's knife strapped to his waist. He was the one they were looking for. He drew his knife, held a handful of his hair, and cut through a clump close to his scalp. Lyn saw what he was doing and helped with her own knife. Joel grabbed the trash can from the corner to collect the hair.

It was a rough job, but he looked less like the one they wanted. Before putting his knife away, he cut a few slits in the black bag, right by the zipper. He peeled off his undershirt and wiped the inside of the bag dry before throwing the shirt in the trash can. It reeked of smoke and sweat anyway. Crawling back inside, helping with the straps, they zipped him up and carried him back to the stairway to resume their ascent. Mission was powerless to do anything but worry.

He ran over the events of a very long day. That morning, he had watched the clouds brighten over breakfast, had visited the Crow and delivered her note to Rodny. And then Cam—he had lost a friend. The exhaustion of it all caught up with him, and Mission found himself sliding into unconsciousness.

When he startled awake, it felt but a moment later. His coveralls were damp, the inside of the bag slick with condensation. Joel must have felt him jerk, as he quickly shushed Mission and told him they were coming up on Central.

Mission's heart pounded as he came to and remembered where he was, what they were doing. It felt difficult to breathe. The slits he had cut were lost in the folds of the plastic. He wanted the zipper cracked, just a slice of light, a whisper of fresh air. His arms were pinned and numb from the straps around his shoulders. His ankles were sore from where Lyn was hoisting him from below.

"Can't breathe," he gasped.

Lyn told him to be quiet. But there was a pause, an end to the swaying. Someone fumbled with the bag over his head, a series of tiny clicks from the zipper being lowered a dozen notches.

Mission sucked in cool gasps. The world resumed its swaying, boots striking the stairs in the distance—a commotion somewhere above or below, he couldn't tell. More fighting. More dying. He pictured bodies spinning through the air. He saw Cam leaving the farm sublevels just the day before, a bonus in his pocket, no thought of how little time he had left for spending it.

They rested at Central Dispatch. Mission was let out in the main hallway, which was frighteningly empty. "What the hell happened here?" Lyn asked. She dug her finger into a hole in the wall surrounded by a spiderweb of cracks. There were hundreds of holes like them. Boots rang on the landing and continued past.

"What time is it?" Mission asked, keeping his voice down.

"It's after dinner," Joel said. It meant they were making good time.

Down the hall, Lyn studied a dark patch of what looked to be rust. "Is this blood?" she hissed.

"Robbie said he couldn't reach anyone down here," Mission said. "Maybe they scattered."

Joel took a sip from his canteen. "Or were driven off." He wiped his mouth with his sleeve.

"Should we stay here for the night? You two look beat."

Joel shook his head. He offered Mission his canteen. "I think we need to get past the thirties. Security is everywhere. Hell, you could probably dash up with what you've got on the way they're running about. Might need to clean up your hair a bit."

Mission rubbed his scalp and thought about that. "Maybe I should," he said. "I could be up there before the dim-time." He watched as Lyn disappeared into one of the bunk rooms down the hall. She emerged almost immediately with her hand over her mouth, her eyes wide.

"What is it?" Mission asked, pushing up from a crouch and joining her.

She threw her arms around him and held him away from the door, buried her face into his shoulder. Joel risked a look.

"No," he whispered.

Mission pulled away from Lyn and joined his fellow porter by the door.

The bunks were full. Some lay sprawled on the floor, but it was obvious by the tangle of their limbs—the way arms hung useless from bunks or were twisted beneath them—that these porters weren't sleeping.

They discovered Katelyn among them. Lyn shook with silent sobs as Joel and Mission retrieved Katelyn's body and loaded her into the bag. Mission felt a pang of guilt that she'd been chosen as much for her size as how well loved she'd been. While they were securing the straps and zipping her up, the power in the hallway went out, leaving them in the pitch black.

"What the hell?" Joel hissed.

A moment later, the lights returned but flickered as though an unsteady flame burned in each bulb. Mission wiped the sweat from his forehead and wished he still had his 'chief.

"If you can't make it all the way to the Nest tonight," he said to the others, "stop and stay at the way station and check on Robbie."

"We'll be fine," Joel assured him.

Lyn squeezed his arm before he went. "Watch your steps," she said.

"And you," Mission told them.

He hurried toward the landing and the great stairway beyond. Overhead, the lights flickered like little flames. A sign that something, somewhere, was burning.

55

Mission hurried upbound amid a fog of smoke, his throat on fire. An explosion in Mechanical was whispered to have been the reason for the blackout. Talk swirled of a bent or broken shaft and that the silo was on backup power. He heard such things from half a spiral away as he took the steps two and sometimes three at a time. It felt good to be out and moving, good to have his muscles aching rather than sitting still, to be his own burden.

And he noticed that when anyone saw him, they either fell silent or scattered beyond their landings, even those he knew. At first, he feared it was from recognition. But it was the Security white he wore. Young men just like him thundered up and down the stairwell terrorizing everyone. Only yesterday, they had been farmers, welders, and pumpmen—now they brought order with their dark weapons.

More than once, a group of them stopped Mission and asked where he was going, where his rifle was. He told them that he had been a part of the fighting below and was reporting back. It was something he'd heard another claim. Many of them seemed to know as little as he did and so they let him pass. As ever, the color you wore said everything. People thought they could know you at a glance.

The activity grew thicker near IT. A group of new recruits filed past, and Mission watched over the railing as they kicked in the doors to the level below and stormed inside. He heard screams and then a sharp bang like a heavy steel rod falling to metal decking. A dozen of these bangs, and then less screaming.

His legs were sore, a stitch in his side, as he approached the farms. He caught sight of a few farmers out on the landing with shovels and rakes. Someone yelled something as he passed. Mission quickened his pace, thinking of his father and brother, seeing the wisdom for once in his old man's unwillingness to leave that patch of dirt.

After what seemed like hours of climbing, he reached the quiet of the Nest. The children were gone. Most families were probably holed up in their apartments, cowering together, hoping this madness would pass like others had. Down the hall, several lockers stood open, and a child's backpack lay on the ground. Mission staggered forward on aching legs toward the sound of a familiar, singing voice and the horrid screech of steel on tile.

At the end of the hall, her door stood as welcome and open as always. The singing came from the Crow, whose voice seemed stronger than usual. Mission saw that he wasn't the first to arrive, that his wire had gone out. Frankie and Allie were there, both in the green and white of farm security. They were arranging desks while Mrs. Crowe sang. The sheets had been thrown off the stacks of desks kept in storage along one wall. Those desks now filled the classroom the way Mission remembered from his youth. It was as though the Crow were expecting them to be filled at any time.

Allie was the first to notice Mission's arrival. She turned and spotted him at the door, her bright eyes shining amid her farmer freckles, her dark hair tied back in a bun. She rushed over, and Mission saw how her overalls were bunched up around her boots, the straps knotted at her shoulders to make them shorter. They must've been Frankie's overalls. As she threw herself into his arms, he wondered what the two of them had risked to meet him there.

"Mission, my boy." Mrs. Crowe stopped her singing, smiled and waved him by her side. After a moment, Allie reluctantly loosened her grip.

Mission shook Frankie's hand and thanked him for coming. It took a moment to realize something was different, that his hair had been cut short as well. They both rubbed their scalps and laughed. Humor came easy in humorless times.

"What is this I hear about my Rodny?" the Crow asked. Her chair twitched back and forth, her hand working the controls, her faded blue nightgown tucked under her narrow bones.

Mission drew a deep breath, smoke lingering in his lungs, and told them everything he had seen on the stairwell, about the bombs and the fires and what he had heard of Mechanical, the security forces armed with rifles—until the Crow dispelled his frenzied chatter with a wave of her frail arms.

"Not the fighting," she said. "The fighting I've seen. I could paint a picture of the fighting and hang it from my walls. What of Rodny? What of our boy? Has he got them? Has he made them pay?" She made a small fist and held it aloft.

"No," Mission said. "Got who? He needs our help."

The Crow laughed, which took him aback. He tried to explain. "I gave him your note, and he passed me one in return. It begged for help. They have him locked up behind these great steel doors—"

"Not locked up," the Crow said.

"—like he'd done something wrong—"

"Something *right*," she said, correcting him.

Mission fell silent. He could see knowledge shining behind her old eyes, a sunrise on the day after a cleaning.

"Rodny is in no danger," she said. "He is with the old books. He's with the people who took the world from us."

Allie squeezed Mission's arm. "She's been trying to tell us," she whispered. "Everything's going to be okay. Come, help with the desks."

"But the note . . ." Mission said, wishing he hadn't turned it to confetti.

"The note you gave him was to give him strength. To let him know it was time to begin. Our boy is in a place to hurt them good for what they've done." There was a wildness in the Crow's eyes.

"No," Mission said. "Rodny was afraid. I know my friend, and he was afraid of something."

The Crow's face hardened. She relaxed her fist and smoothed the front of her faded dress. "If that be the case," she said, her voice trembling, "then I judged him most wrongly."

56

THE DIM-TIME APPROACHED while they arranged desks, and the Crow resumed her singing. Allie told him a curfew had been announced, and so Mission lost hope that the others would show up that night. They pulled out mats from the cubbies to rest and plan, and decided to give the others until daybreak. There was much Mission wanted to ask the Crow, but she seemed distracted, her thoughts elsewhere, possessed with a joyousness that made her giddy.

Frankie felt certain he could get them through security and deeper into IT if only he could reach his father. Mission told them how well he'd been able to move about with the whites on. Maybe he could reach Frankie's dad in a pinch. Allie produced fresh fruits harvested from her plot and passed them around. The Crow drank one of her dark green concoctions. Mission grew restless.

He wandered out to the landing, torn between waiting for the others and his anxiety to get going. For all he knew, Rodny was being marched up to his death already. Cleanings tended to settle people down, to follow bouts of unrest, but this was unlike any of the spates of violence he had seen before. This was the burning his father spoke of, the embers of distrust and crumbling trade that jumped up all at once. He had seen this coming, but it had approached with the swiftness of a knife plummeting from the Up Top.

Out on the landing, he heard the sounds of a mob echoing from far below. Holding the landing rail, he could feel the hum of marching boots. He returned to the others and said nothing of it. There was no reason to suspect those boots were coming for them.

Allie looked as though she'd been crying when he got back. Her eyes were moist, her cheeks flushed. The Crow was telling them an Old Time story, her hands painting a scene in the air.

"Is everything all right?" Mission asked.

Allie shook her head as if she'd rather not say.

"What is it?" he said. He held her hand, heard the Crow speaking of Atlantis, another tale of the crumbling and lost city of magic beyond the hills, a bygone day when those ruins shone like a wet dime.

"Tell me," he said. He wondered if the stories were affecting her the way they sometimes did him, making her sad and not knowing why.

"I didn't want to say anything until after," she cried, fresh tears welling up. She wiped them away and the Crow fell silent, her hands dropping into her lap. Frankie sat quietly. Whatever it was, the two of them knew as well.

"Father," Mission said. It had to do with his father. He was gone, he knew it instantly. Allie was close to his father in a way that Mission had never been. And suddenly, he felt a powerful regret for ever having left home. While she wiped her eyes, the words unable to form on her trembling lips, Mission imagined himself on his hands and knees, in the dirt, digging for forgiveness.

Allie bawled, and the Crow hummed a tune of aboveground days. Mission thought of his father, gone, all he longed to say, and wanted nothing more than to hurl himself at the posters on the walls, to tear them down and rip to shreds their urgings to go and be free.

"It's Riley," Allie finally said. "Mish, I'm so sorry."

The Crow ceased her humming. All three of them watched him.

"No," Mission whispered.

"You shouldn't have told him—" Frankie began.

"He ought to know!" Allie demanded. "His father would want him to know."

Mission gazed at a poster of green hills and blue skies. That world blurred with tears as surely as it might with dust. "What happened?" he whispered.

She told him that there'd been an attack on the farms. Riley had begged to go and help fight, had been told no, and had then disappeared. He'd been found with a knife from the kitchen still clutched in his hands.

Mission stood and paced the room, tears splashing from his cheeks. He shouldn't have left. He should have been there. He hadn't been there for Cam, either. Death preceded him in all the places he couldn't be. He had done the same to his mother. And now the end was coming for them all.

A rumble grew from the landing and filled the hallway—the sound of approaching boots. Mission wiped his cheeks. He had given up on any of the others coming and thought it might be Security with their guns. They would ask him where his own gun was before realizing he was an impostor, before shooting them all.

He pushed the door shut, saw that the Crow had no lock on the thing, and wedged a desk under the handle. Frankie hurried to Allie, told her to get behind the Crow's desk. He grabbed the back of the Crow's wheelchair—the overhead wire swinging dangerously—but she insisted she could manage herself, that there was nothing to be afraid of.

Mission knew better. This was Security coming for them—Security or some other mob. He'd travelled the stairwell, knew what was out there.

There was a knock on the door. The handle jiggled. The boots outside quieted as they gathered around. Frankie pressed his finger to his lips, his eyes wide. The wire overhead creaked as it swung back and forth.

The door budged. Mission hoped for a moment that they would go away, that they were just making their rounds. He thought about hiding under the sheets used to cover the desks, but the thought came too late. The door was shoved open, a desk screeching as it skittered across the floor. The first person through was Rodny.

His appearance was as sudden and jarring as a slapped cheek. Rodny wore white overalls with the creases still in them. His hair had been cut short, his face newly shaved, a nick on his chin.

Mission felt as though he were staring into a mirror, the two of them in costume. More men in white crowded behind Rodny in the hallway, rifles in hand. Rodny ordered them back and stepped into the room where all those empty desks lay neatly arranged.

Allie was the first to respond. She gasped with surprise and hurried forward, arms wide as if for an embrace. Rodny held up a palm and told her to stop. His other hand held a small gun, the same the deputies wore. His eyes were not on his friends but on the Old Crow.

"Rodny—" Mission began. His brain attempted to grasp his friend's presence. They had all come together to rescue him, but he looked in little need of it.

"The door," Rodny said over his shoulder.

A man twice Rodny's age hesitated before doing as he was asked and pulling the door shut. This was not the demeanor of a prisoner. Frankie lurched forward before the door shut all the way, calling "Father!" as if he'd seen his old man in the hall with the others.

"We were coming for you," Mission said. He wanted to approach his friend, but there was something dangerous in Rodny's eyes. "Your note—"

Rodny finally looked away from the Crow.

"We were coming to help—" Mission said.

"Yesterday, I needed it," Rodny said. He circled around the desks, the gun at his side, his eyes flicking from face to face. Mission backed up and joined Allie in standing close to the Crow—whether to protect her or feel protected, he couldn't say.

"You shouldn't be here," Mrs. Crowe said with a lecturing tone. "This is not where your fight is. You should be hurting *them*." A thin finger pointed at the door.

The gun in Rodny's hand rose a little.

"What're you doing?" Allie asked, her wide eyes on the gun.

Rodny pointed at the Crow. "Tell them," he said. "Tell them what you've done. What you do."

"What've they done to you?" Mission asked. His friend had changed. It was more than the haircut and uniform. It was in his eyes.

"They showed me—" Rodny swept his gun at the posters on the wall. "That these stories are true." He laughed and turned to the Crow. "And I was angry, just like you said I would be. Angry at what they did to the world. I wanted to tear it all down."

"So do it," the Crow insisted. "Hurt them." Her voice creaked like a door about to slam.

"But now I know. They told me. We got a call. And now I know what you've been doing here—"

"What's this about?" Frankie asked, still in the middle of the room. He moved toward the door. "Why is my father—"

"Stay," Rodny told him. He pushed one of the desks out of

the way and moved down the aisle. "Don't you move." His gun swung from Frankie to the Crow, whose chair shivered in time with her palsied hand. "These sayings on the wall, the stories and songs—you made us what we are. You made us angry."

"You *should* be," she screeched. "You damn well should be!"

Mission moved closer to the Crow. He kept his eye on the gun. Allie knelt and held the old woman's hand. Rodny stood ten paces away, the gun angled at their feet.

"They kill and they kill," the Crow said. "And this will go the way it always has. Wipe it all clean. Bury and burn the dead. And these desks—" Her arm shot up, her quivering finger aimed at the empty desks newly arranged. "These desks will be *full* again."

"No," Rodny said. He shook his head. "No more. It ends here. You won't terrify us anymore—"

"What're you saying?" Mission asked. He stepped close to the Crow, a hand on her chair. "You're the one with the gun, Rodny. You're the one scaring us."

Rodny turned to Mission. "*She* makes us feel this way. Don't you see? The fear and hope go hand in hand. What she sells is no different than the priests, only she gets to us *first*. This talk of a better world. It just makes us hate *this* one."

"No—" Mission hated his friend for uttering such a thing.

"Yes," Rodny said. "Why do you think we hate our fathers? It's because she makes us hate them. Gives us ideas to break free from them. But this won't make it better." He waved his hand. "Not that it matters. What I knew yesterday had me terrified for my life. For all of us. What I know now gives me hope." His gun came up. Mission couldn't believe it. His friend pointed the barrel at the Old Crow.

"Wait—" Mission raised a hand.

"Stand back," Rodny said. "I have to do this."

"No!"

His friend's arm stiffened. The barrel was leveled at a defenseless woman in a mechanical chair, the mother to them all, the one who sang them to sleep in their cribs and on their mats, whose voice followed them through their shadowing days and beyond.

Frankie shoved a desk aside and lurched toward Rodny. Allie screamed. Mission threw himself sideways as the gun roared and flashed. There was a punch to his stomach, a fire in his gut. He crashed to the floor as the gun thundered a second time, the Crow's chair lurching to the side as a spasm gripped her hand.

Mission landed heavily, clutching his stomach. His hands came away sticky and wet.

Lying on his back, he saw the Crow slump over in her chair, a chair that no longer moved. Again, the gun roared. Needlessly. Her body twitched as it was struck. Frankie flew into Rodny and the two men went tumbling. Boots stormed into the room, summoned by the noise.

Allie was there, crying. She kept her hands on Mission's stomach, pressing so hard, and looked back at the Crow. She wailed for them both. Mission tasted blood in his mouth. It reminded him of the time Rodny had punched him as a kid, only playing. They'd only ever been playing. Costumes and pretending to be their fathers.

There were boots everywhere. Shiny and black boots on some, scuffed with wear on others. Those who had fought before and those just learning.

Rodny appeared above Mission, his eyes wide with worry. He told him to hang in there. Mission wanted to say he'd try, but the pain in his stomach was too great. He couldn't speak. They told him to stay awake, but all he'd ever wanted was to sleep. To not be. To not be a burden to anyone.

"Damn you!" Allie screamed, and it was at him, at Mission, not at Rodny. She blubbered that she loved him, and Mission tried to say he knew. He wanted to tell her that she was right all along. He imagined for a moment the kids they would have, the plot of soil if they combined their holdings, the long uninterrupted rows of corn like lives that stretched out for generations. Generations of people staying close to home, there for each other, doing what they knew best, enjoying being a burden to each other.

He wanted to say all these things and more. Much more. But as Allie bent close and he struggled to form the words, all that came out, a whisper amid the din of boots and shouts, was that today was his birthday.

Hush my Darling, don't you cry
I'm going to sing you a lullaby
Though I'm far away it seems
I'll be with you in your dreams.

Hush my Darling, go to sleep
All around you angels keep
In the morn and through the day
They will keep your fears at bay.

Sleep my Darling, don't you cry
I'm going to sing you a lullaby

57

Three Years Later

MISSION CHANGED OUT of his work overalls while Allie readied dinner. He washed his hands, scrubbed the dirt from beneath his fingernails, and watched the mud slide down the drain. The ring on his finger was getting more and more difficult to remove, his knuckles sore and stiff from the hoeing of planting season.

He soaped his hands and finally managed to work the ring off. Remembering the last time he'd lost it down the drain, he set it aside carefully. Allie whistled in the kitchen while she tended the stove. When she cracked the oven, he smelled the pork roast inside. He'd have to say something. They couldn't go buying roasts on no occasion.

His overalls went into the wash. There were lighted candles on the table when he got back to the kitchen. They were for emergencies, for the times when the fools below switched generators and worked on the busted main. Allie knew this. But before he could say anything about the roast or the candles, or tell her that the bean crop wouldn't be what he'd hoped come harvest, he saw the way she was beaming at him. There was only one thing to be that happy about—but it was impossible.

"No," he said. He couldn't allow himself to believe it.

Allie nodded. There were tears in her eyes. By the time he got to her, they were coursing down her cheeks.

"But our ticket is up," he whispered, holding her against him. She smelled like sweet peppers and sage. He could feel her trembling.

Allie sobbed. Her voice broke from being overfull of joy. "Doc says it happened last month. It was in our window, Mish. We're gonna have a baby."

A surge of relief filled Mission to the brim. Relief, not excitement. Relief that everything was legal. He kissed his wife's cheek, salt to go with the pepper and sage. "I love you," he whispered.

"The roast." She pulled away and hurried to the stove. "I was gonna tell you after dinner."

Mission laughed. "You were gonna tell me now or have to explain the candles."

He poured two glasses of water, hands trembling, and set them out while she fixed the plates. The smell of cooked meat made his mouth water. He could anticipate the way the roast would taste. A taste of the future, of what was to come.

"Don't let it get cold," Allie said, setting the plates.

They sat and held hands. Mission cursed himself for not putting his ring back on.

"Bless this food and those who fed its roots," Allie said.

"Amen," said Mission. His wife squeezed his hands before letting go and grabbing her utensils.

"You know," she said, cutting into the roast, "if it's a girl, we'll have to name her Allison. Every woman in my family as far back as we can remember has been an Allison."

Mission wondered how far back her family could remember. It'd be unusual if they could remember very far. He chewed and thought on the name. "Allison it is," he said. And he thought that eventually they would call her Allie too. "But if it's a boy, can we go with Cam?"

"Sure." Allie lifted her glass. "That wasn't your grandfather's name, was it?"

"No. I don't know any Cams. I just like the way it sounds."

He picked up his glass of water, studied it awhile. Or did he know a Cam? Where did he know that name from? There were bits of his past shrouded and hidden from him. There were things like the mark on his neck and the scar on his stomach that he couldn't remember coming to be. Everyone had their share of these things, parts of their bygone days they couldn't recall, but Mission more than most. Like his birthday. It drove him crazy that he couldn't remember when his birthday was. What was so hard about that?

THIRD SHIFT

PACT

58

Silo 1
2345

"SIR?"

There was a clatter of bones beneath his feet. Donald stumbled through the dark, the winged dogs scattering at the sound of voices.

"Can you hear me?"

The haze parted, an eyelid cracking just like the seal of his pod. A bean. Donald was curled inside that pod like a bean.

"Sir? Are you with me?"

Skin so cold. Donald was sitting up, steam rising from his bare legs. He didn't remember going to sleep. He remembered the doctor, remembered being in his office. They were talking. Now he was being woken up.

"Drink this, sir."

Donald remembered this. He remembered waking over and over, but he didn't remember going to sleep. Just the waking. He took a sip, had to concentrate to make his throat work, had to fight to swallow. A pill. There was supposed to be a pill, but it wasn't offered.

"Sir, we had instructions to wake you."

Instructions. Rules. Protocol. Donald was in trouble again. Troy. Maybe it was that Troy fellow. Who was he? Donald drank as much as he could.

"Very good, sir. We're going to lift you out."

He was in trouble. They only woke him when there was trouble. A catheter was removed, a needle from his arm.

"What did I—"

He coughed into his fist. His voice was a sheet of tissue paper, thin and fragile. Invisible.

"What is it?" he asked, shouting to form a whisper.

Two men lifted him up and set him into a wheelchair. A third man held it still. There was a soft blanket instead of a paper gown. There was no rustling this time, no itching on his skin.

"We lost one," someone said.

A silo. A silo was gone. It would be Donald's fault again. "Eighteen," he whispered, remembering his last shift.

Two of the men glanced at each other, mouths open.

"Yes," one of them said, awe in his voice. "From Silo Eighteen, sir. We lost her over the hill. We lost contact."

Donald tried to focus on the man. He remembered losing someone over a hill. *Helen*. His wife. They were still looking for her. There was still hope.

"Tell me," he whispered.

"We're not sure how, but one of them made it out of sight—"

"A cleaner, sir—"

A cleaner. Donald sank into the chair; his bones were as cold and heavy as stone. It wasn't Helen at all.

"—over the hill—" one said.

"—we got a call from Eighteen—"

Donald raised his hand a little, his arm trembling and still half numb from the sleep. "Wait," he croaked. "One at a time. Why did you wake me?" It hurt to talk.

One of the men cleared his throat. The blanket was tucked

up under Donald's chin to stop him from shivering. He hadn't known he was shivering. They were being so reverent with him, so gentle. What was this? He tried to clear his head.

"You told us to wake you—"

"It's protocol—"

Donald's eyes fell to the pod, still steaming as the chill escaped. There was a screen at the base, empty readouts without him in there, just a rising temp. A rising temp and a name. Not his name.

And Donald remembered how names meant nothing unless that was all one had to go by. If nobody remembered each other, if they didn't cross paths, then a name was everything.

"Sir?"

"Who am I?" he asked, reading the little screen, not understanding. This wasn't him. "Why did you wake me?"

"You told us to, Mr. Thurman."

The blanket was wrapped snugly around his shoulders. The chair was turned. They were treating him with respect, as if he had authority. The wheels on this chair did not squeak at all.

"It's okay, sir. Your head will clear soon."

He didn't know these people. They didn't know him.

"The doctor will clear you for duty."

Nobody knew anyone.

"Right this way."

And then anyone could be anybody.

"Through here."

Until it didn't matter who was in charge. One who might do what was correct, another who might do what was right.

"Very good."

One name as good as any other.

59

Silo 17
2312
Hour One

THE LOUD CAME before the quiet. That was a Rule of the World, for the bangs and shouts need somewhere to echo, just as bodies need space in which to fall.

Jimmy Parker was in class when the last of the great Louds began. It was the day before a cleaning. Tomorrow, they would be off from school. For the death of a man, Jimmy and his friends would be gifted a few extra hours of sleep. His father would work overtime down in IT. And tomorrow afternoon, his mother would insist that they go up with his aunt and cousins to watch the bright clouds drift over the clear view of the hills until the sky turned dark as sleep.

Cleaning days were for staying in bed and for seeing family. They were for silencing unrest and quietening the Louds. That's what Mrs. Pearson told them as she wrote the rules from the Pact up on the blackboard. Her chalk clacked and squeaked and left dusty trails of all the whys for which a man could be put to death. Civics lessons on a day before a banishment. Warnings on the eve of graver warnings. Jimmy and his friends fidgeted in their seats and learned rules. Rules of the World that very soon would no longer apply.

Jimmy was sixteen. Many of his friends would move off and shadow soon, but he would need another year of study to follow in his father's footsteps. Mrs. Pearson marked the blackboard and moved on to the seriousness of choosing a life partner, of registering relationships according to the Pact. Sarah Jenkins turned in her seat and smiled back at Jimmy. Civics lessons and biology lessons intermingled, hormones spoken of alongside the laws that governed their excesses. Sarah Jenkins was cute. Jimmy hadn't thought so at the beginning of the year, but now he was seeing it. Sarah Jenkins was cute and would be dead in just a few hours.

Mrs. Pearson asked for a volunteer to read from the Pact, and that's when Jimmy's mother came for him. She burst in unannounced. An embarrassment. The end of Jimmy's world began with hot cheeks and a burning collar and everyone watching. His mom didn't say anything to Mrs. Pearson, didn't excuse herself. She just stormed through the door and hurried among the desks the way she walked when she was angry. She pulled Jimmy from his desk and led him out with his arm in her fist, causing him to wonder what he'd done this time.

Mrs. Pearson didn't speak. Jimmy looked back at his best friend Paul, caught him smiling behind his palm, and wondered why Paul wasn't in trouble too. They rarely got in or out of a fix alone, he and Paul. The only person to utter a word was Sarah Jenkins. "Your backpack!" she cried out just before the classroom door slammed shut, her voice swallowed by the quiet.

There were no other mothers pulling their children down the hallway. If they came, it would be much later. Jimmy's father worked among the computers and knew things. His father knew things before anyone else. This time, it was only moments before. There were others scrambling on the stairwell already.

The noise was frightening. The landing outside the school level thrummed with the vibrations of distant and heavy traffic. A bolt in one of the railing's stanchions rattled as it worked its way loose. It felt as though the silo would simply shake itself apart. Jimmy's mom took him by the sleeve and pulled him toward the spiral staircase as if he was still twelve.

Jimmy pulled against her for a moment, confused. In the past year, he had grown bigger than his mom, as big as his father, and it was strange to be reminded that he had this power, that he was nearly a man. He had left his backpack and his friends behind. Where were they going? The banging from below seemed to be getting louder.

His mother turned as he gave resistance. Her eyes, he saw, were not full of anger. There was no glare, no furrowed brow. They were wide and wet, shiny like the times Grandma and Grandpa had passed. The noise below was frightful, but it was the look in his mother's eyes that placed fear in Jimmy's bones.

"What is it?" he whispered. He hated to see his mother upset. Something dark and empty—like that stray and tailless cat that nobody could catch in the upper apartments—clawed at his insides.

His mother didn't say. She turned and pulled him down the stairs, toward the thundering approach of something awful, and Jimmy realized at once that he wasn't in trouble at all.

They all were.

60

JIMMY HAD NEVER felt the stairs tremble so. The entire spiral staircase seemed to sway. It turned to rubber the way a length of charcoal appears to bend between jiggled fingers, a parlor trick he'd learned in class. Though his feet rarely touched the steps—racing as he was to keep up with his mother—they tingled and felt numb from vibrations transmitted straight from steel to bone. Jimmy tasted fear in his mouth like a dry spoon on his tongue.

There were angry screams from below. Jimmy's mother shouted her encouragement, told him to hurry, and down the staircase they spiraled. They raced toward whatever bad thing was marching upward. "Hurry," she cried again, and Jimmy was more scared of the tremor in her voice than the shuddering of a hundred levels of steel.

He hurried.

They passed twenty-nine. Thirty. People ran by in the opposite direction. A lot of people in coveralls the color of his father's. On the landing of thirty-one, Jimmy saw his first dead body since his grandpa's funeral. It looked as if a tomato had been smashed on the back of the man's head. Jimmy had to skip over the man's arms, which stuck out into the stairwell. He hurried after his mother while some of the red dripped through the landing and splattered and slicked the steps below.

At thirty-two, the shake of the stairs was so great that he could feel it in his teeth. His mother grew frantic as the two of them bumped past more and more people hurrying upward. Nobody seemed to see anyone else. Everyone was looking out for themselves.

The stampede could be heard, a din of a thousand boots. There were loud voices among the ringing footfalls. Jimmy stopped and peered over the railing. Below, as the staircase augered into the depths, he could see the elbows and hands of a jostling crowd jutting out. He turned as someone thundered by. His mother called for him to hurry, for the crowd was already upon them, the traffic growing. Jimmy felt the fear and anger in the people racing past, and it made him want to flee upward with them. But there was his mom yelling for him to come along, and her voice cut through his fear and to the center of his being.

Jimmy shuffled down and took her hand. The embarrassment of earlier was gone. Now he wanted her clutching him. The people who ran past shouted for them to go the other way. Several held pipes and lengths of steel. There were some who were bruised and cut. Blood covered the mouth and chin of one man. A fight somewhere. Jimmy thought that only happened in the Deep. Others seemed simply to be caught up in it all. They were without weapons and were looking over their shoulders. It was a mob scared of a mob. Jimmy wondered what had caused it. What was there to be afraid of?

Loud bangs rang out among the footfalls. A large man knocked into Jimmy's mom and sent her against the railing. Jimmy held her arm, and the two of them stuck to the inner post as they made their way down to thirty-three. "One more to go," she told him, which meant it was his father they were after.

The growing throngs became a crush a few turns above

thirty-four. People pressed four wide where there was only room for two. Jimmy's wrist banged against the inner rail. He wedged himself between the post and those forcing their way up. Moving a few inches at a time—those beside him shoving, jostling and grunting with effort—he felt certain they would all become stuck like that. People crowded in, and he lost his grip on her arm. She surged forward while he remained pinned in place. He could hear her yelling his name below.

A large man, dripping with sweat, jaw slack with fear, was trying to force his way up the downbound side. "Move!" he yelled at Jimmy, as if there were anywhere to go. There was nowhere to go but up. He flattened himself against the center post as the man brushed past. There was a scream by the outer rail, a jolt through the crowd, a series of gasps, someone yelling "Hold on!" and another yelling to let them go, and then a shriek that plummeted away and grew faint.

The wedge of bodies loosened. Jimmy felt sick to his stomach at the thought of someone falling so near to him. He wiggled free and climbed up onto the inner rail, hugged the central post and balanced there, careful not to let his feet slip into the six inches of space between the rail and the post, that gap that kids liked to spit into.

Someone in the crowd immediately took his place on the steps. Shoulders and elbows knocked into his ankles. He remained crouched there, the undersides of the steps above him transmitting the scrapes of shuffling boots from those overhead. He slid his feet along the narrow bar of steel made slick by the rubbing of thousands of palms and worked his way down the railing after his mom. His foot slipped into the gap by the center post. It seemed eager to swallow his leg. Jimmy righted himself, fearful of falling onto the lurching crowd, imagining how he could be tossed across their frenzied arms and slip out into space.

He was half a circuit around the inner post before he found his mom. She had been forced toward the outside by the crowds. "Mom!" he yelled. Jimmy held the edge of the steps above his head and reached over the crowd for her. A woman in the middle of the steps screamed and disappeared, her head sinking below those who took her place. As they trampled her, the woman's screams disappeared. The crowd surged upward. They carried Jimmy's mom a few steps with them.

"Get to your father!" she screamed, cupping her hands around her mouth. "Jimmy!"

"Mom!"

Someone knocked into his shins, and he lost his grip on the stairs overhead. Jimmy waved his arms once, twice, in little circles, trying to keep his balance. He fell inward on the sea of heads and rolled. Someone punched him in the ribs as they protected themselves from his fall.

Another man threw Jimmy aside. He tumbled outward across an undulating platform of sharp elbows and hard skulls, and time slowed to a crawl. There was nothing but empty space and a long fall beyond the crowd, now packed five wide. Jimmy tried to grab one of the hands pushing and shoving at him. His stomach lurched as the space grew nearer. He couldn't see the rail. He heard his mother's voice, a screech recognizable above all the others, as she watched, helpless. Someone screamed to help that boy as he slid down the spiral of heads, rolling and grasping. That boy they were screaming after was him.

Jimmy rolled into open space. He was thrown aside by those trying to protect themselves. He slid between two people—a shoulder catching him on the chin—and he saw the railing at last. He clutched for it, got one hand wrapped around the bar. As his feet tumbled over his head he was twisted around, his shoulder wrenched painfully, but he kept his grip. He hung there, clutching the railing with one hand and one of the vertical stanchions with the other, his feet dangling in the open air.

Someone's hip pinched his fingers against the rail and Jimmy cried out. Hands scrambled at his arms to help, but these people and their concerns were pushed upward by the madness below.

Jimmy tried to pull himself up. He looked down past his kicking feet at the crowds jostling beyond the rail below him. Two turns down was the landing to thirty-four. Again he tried to hoist himself, but there was a fire in his wrenched shoulder. Someone scratched his forearm as they tried to help and then they too were gone, surging upward.

Peering down his chest, between his feet, Jimmy saw that the landing to thirty-four was packed. A crowd spilled out of the jammed stairs and tried to shove their way back in again. Someone barged out of the doors to IT with a cleaning suit on, helmet and everything. They threw themselves into the crowd, silvery arms swimming amid the flesh, everyone trying to get up, more of the bangs and shouts from down below, a sudden pop like the balloons from the bazaar but much, much louder.

Jimmy lost his grip on the railing—his shoulder was too injured to bear the weight any longer. He clutched the stanchion with his other hand as he slid down, sweaty palm on steel adding one more squeal to the uproar of the mob. He was left clutching the edge of the steps at the base of the stanchion. With his feet, he tried to feel for the railing one turn below, but all he felt were angry arms knocking his boots aside. His busted shoulder was alive with pain. He swung down on one hand, dangling for an instant.

Jimmy cried out in alarm. He cried out for his mother, remembering what she'd told him.

Get to your father.

There was no way he was getting back up on the stairwell.

He didn't have the strength. There was no room. Nobody was going to help him. A surging crowd, and yet he hung there all alone.

Jimmy took a deep breath. He dangled a moment longer, glanced down at the packed landing below him, and let go.

61

TWO TURNS OF the spiral staircase flew by. Two turns of wide eyes among the packed and crushing crowd. Jimmy felt the swoosh of wind on his neck grow and grow. His stomach flew up into his throat, and there was a glimpse of a face turning in alarm to watch him plummet past.

Slamming into the crowd on the landing below, he hit with a sickening thud. The man in the silver suit, faceless behind his small visor, was pinned beneath him.

People yelled at him. Others crawled out from underneath him. Jimmy rolled away, an electric shock in his ribs where he'd hit someone, a throbbing pain in one knee, his shoulder burning. Limping, he hurried toward the double doors as another person barged out, a bundle in their arms. They pulled to a halt at the sight of the crowd on the stairs. Someone yelled about the forbidden Outside, and nobody seemed to care. Tomorrow, there was to be a cleaning. Maybe it was too late. Jimmy thought of the extra hours his dad had been putting in. He wondered how many more people would be sent out for all this violence.

He turned back to the stairs and searched for his mom. The screams and shouts for people to move, to get out of the way, made it impossible to hear. But her voice still rang in his ears.

He remembered her last command, the plaintive look on her face, and hurried inside to find his father.

It was chaos beyond the doors, people running back and forth in the halls, loud voices arguing. Yani stood by the security gate, the large officer's hair matted with sweat. Jimmy ran toward him. He clutched his elbow to pin his arm to his chest and keep his shoulder from swinging. The sting in his ribs made it difficult to take in a full breath. His heart was still pounding from the rush of the long fall.

"Yani—" Jimmy leaned against the security gate and gasped for air. It seemed to take a moment for the guard to register his existence. Yani's eyes were wide; they darted back and forth. Jimmy noticed something in his hand, a pistol like the sheriff wore. "I need to get through," Jimmy said. "I need to find Dad."

The officer's wild eyes settled on Jimmy. Yani was a good man, a friend of his father's. His daughter was just two years younger than Jimmy. Their family came over for dinner around the holidays sometimes. But this was not that Yani. Some sort of terror seemed to have him by the throat.

"Yes," he said, bobbing his head. "Your father. Won't let me in. Won't let any of us in. But you—" It seemed impossible, but Yani's eyes grew wilder.

"Can you buzz me—" Jimmy started to ask, nudging the turnstile.

Yani grabbed Jimmy by his collar. Jimmy was no small boy, was growing into his adult frame, but the massive guard practically lifted him over the turnstile as if he were a sack of dirty laundry.

Jimmy struggled in the man's fierce grip. Yani pressed the end of the pistol against Jimmy's chest and dragged him down the hall. "I've got his boy!" he yelled. To whom, it wasn't clear. Jimmy tried to twist free. He was hauled past offices in disarray. The entire level looked cleared out. He thought of all the coveralls in silver and gray on the stairway earlier and feared for a moment that his father had been among those he'd passed. The crowd had been littered with people from this level, as though they'd been leading the charge—or were the ones being chased.

"I can't breathe—" he tried to tell Yani. He got his feet beneath him, clutched the powerful man's forearm, anything to take the pinch off his collar.

"Where'd you assholes go?" Yani screamed, glancing up and down the halls. "I need a hand with this—"

There was a clap like a thousand balloons popping at once, a deafening roar. Jimmy felt Yani lurch sideways as if kicked. The guard's grip relaxed, allowing the blood to rush back to Jimmy's head. Jimmy danced sideways as the large man tumbled over. He crashed to the floor, gurgling and wheezing, the black pistol skittering across the tile.

"Jimmy!"

His father was at the end of the hall, half around a corner, a long black object under his armpit, a crutch that didn't quite reach the floor. The end of this too-short crutch smoked as if it were on fire.

"Hurry, son!"

Jimmy cried out in relief. He stumbled away from Yani, who was writhing on the floor and making awful, inhuman sounds. He ran to his father, limping and clutching his arm.

"Where's your mother?" his dad asked, peering down the hall.

"The stairs—" Jimmy fought for a breath. His pulse had blurred into a steady thrum. "Dad, what's going on?"

"Inside. Inside." He pulled Jimmy down the hall toward a large door of stainless steel. There were shouts from around the corner. Jimmy could see the veins standing out in his father's forehead, trickles of sweat beading beneath his thinning hair. His father keyed a code into the panel by the massive door, and there was a whirring and a series of clunks before it opened a crack. His dad leaned into the door until there was room for the two of them to squeeze through. "C'mon, son. Move."

Down the hall, someone yelled at them to stop. Boots clomped in their direction. Jimmy squeezed through the crack, was worried his dad might close him up in there, all alone, but his old man worked his way through as well then leaned against the inside of the door.

"Push!" he said.

Jimmy pushed. He didn't know why they were pushing, but he'd never seen his dad frightened before. It made his insides feel like jelly. The boots outside stomped closer. Someone yelled his father's name. Someone yelled for Yani.

As the steel door slammed shut, a slap of hands hit the other side. There was a whir and a clunk once more. His dad keyed something into the pad, then hesitated. "A number," he said, gasping for breath. "Four digits. Quick, son, a number you'll remember."

"One two one eight," Jimmy said. Level twelve and level eighteen. Where he went to school and where he lived. His father keyed in the digits. There were muffled yells from the other side, soft ringing sounds from palms slapping futilely against the thick steel.

"Come with me," his father said. "We've got to keep an eye on the cameras, have to find your mother." He slung the black machine over his back, which Jimmy now saw was a bigger version of the pistol. The end was no longer smoking. His father hadn't kicked Yani from a distance; he had shot him.

Jimmy stood motionless while his father set off through the room of large black boxes. It dawned on him that he'd heard of this place, that his father had told him stories of a room full of servers. The machines seemed to watch him as he stood there by the door. They were black sentries, quietly humming, standing guard.

Jimmy left the wall of stainless steel with its muffled slaps and muted shouts and hurried after his father. He had seen his dad's office before, back down the hall and around a bend, but never this place. The room was huge. He favored one leg as he ran the full length of it, trying to pick his way through the servers and keep track of where his dad had gone. At the far wall, he rounded the last black box and found his dad kneeling on the floor as if in prayer. Bringing his hands up around his neck, his dad dug inside his overalls and came out with a thin black cord. Something silver danced on the end of it.

"What about Mom?" Jimmy asked. He wondered how they would let her in with the rest of those guys outside. He wondered why his father was kneeling on the floor like that.

"Listen carefully," his dad said. "This is the key to the silo. There are only two of these. Do not ever lose sight of it, okay?"

Jimmy watched as his father inserted the key into the back of one of the machines. "This is the comm hub," his dad said. Jimmy had no idea what a comm hub was, only that they were going to hide inside of one. That was the plan. Get inside one of the black boxes until the noise went away. His dad turned the key as if unlocking something, did this three more times in three more slots, then pulled the panel away. Jimmy peered inside and watched his dad pull a lever. There was a grinding noise in the floor nearby.

"Keep this safe," his father said. He squeezed Jimmy's shoulder and handed him the lanyard with the key. Jimmy accepted it and studied the jagged piece of silver amid the coil of black cord. One side of the key formed a circle with three wedges inside—the symbol of the silo. He teased the lanyard into a hoop and pulled it down over his head, then watched his dad dig his fingers into the grating by their feet. He lifted out a small rectangle of flooring to reveal darkness underneath.

"Go on. You first," his father said. He waved at the hole in the ground and began unslinging the long pistol from his back. Jimmy shuffled forward and peered down. There were handholds along one wall. It was like a ladder, but much taller than any he'd ever seen.

"C'mon, son. We don't have much time."

Sitting on the edge of the grating, his feet hanging in the void, Jimmy reached for the steel rungs below and began the long descent.

The air beneath the floor was cool, the light dim. The horror and noise of the stairwell seemed to fade, and Jimmy was left with a sense of foreboding, of dread. Why was he being given this key? What was this place? He climbed down mostly using his good arm, made slow but steady progress.

At the bottom of the ladder, he found a narrow passageway. There was a dim pulse of light at the far end. Looking up, he could see the outline of his father making his way down.

"Through there," his father said, indicating the slender hallway. He left the long pistol propped up against the ladder.

Jimmy pointed up. "Shouldn't we cover the—"

"I'll get it on my way out. Let's go, son."

Jimmy turned and worked his way through the passage. There were wires and pipes running in parallel across the ceiling. A light ahead beat crimson. After twenty paces or so, the passage opened on a space that reminded him of the school stockroom. There were shelves along two walls. Two desks as well: one with a computer, the other with an open book. His dad went straight for the computer. "You were with your mother?" he asked.

Jimmy nodded. "She pulled me out of class. We got separated

on the stairs." He rubbed his sore shoulder while his father collapsed heavily into the chair in front of the desk. The computer screen was divided into four squares.

"Where did you lose her? How far up?"

"Two turns above thirty-four," he said, remembering the fall.

Rather than reach for the mouse or keyboard, his father grabbed a black box studded with knobs and switches. There was a wire attached to the box that trailed off to the back of the monitor. In one corner of the screen, Jimmy saw a moving picture of three men standing over someone lying still on the floor. It was real. It was an image, a window, like the cafeteria wallscreen. He was seeing a view of the hallway they'd just left.

"Fucking Yani," his father muttered.

Jimmy's eyes fell from the screen to stare at the back of his dad's head. He'd heard his old man curse before, but never that word. His father's shoulders were rising and falling as he took deep breaths. Jimmy returned his attention to the screen.

The four windows had become twelve. No, sixteen. His father leaned forward, his nose just inches from the monitor, and peered from one square to the next. His old hands worked the black box, which clicked as the knobs and dials were adjusted. Jimmy saw in every square the turmoil he'd witnessed on the stairway. From rail to post, the treads were packed with people. They surged upward. His father traced the squares with a finger, searching.

"Dad—"

"Shhh."

"—what's going on?"

"We've had a breach," he said. "They're trying to shut us down. You said it was two turns above the landing?"

"Yeah. But she was being carried up. It was hard to move. I went over the rail—"

The chair squeaked as his father turned and sized him up. His eyes fell to Jimmy's arm, pinned against his chest. "You fell?"

"I'm okay, Dad. What's going on? Trying to shut what down?"

His father returned his focus to the screen. A few clicks from the black box and the squares flickered and changed. They now seemed to be peering through slightly different windows.

"They're trying to shut down our silo," his father said. "The bastards opened our airlock, said our gas supply was tainted— Wait. There she is."

The many little windows became one. The view shifted slightly. Jimmy could see his mother pinned between a crush of people and the rail. Her mouth and chin were covered in blood. Gripping the rail and fighting for room, she lurched down one laborious step as the crowd coursed in the other direction. It seemed as though everyone in the silo were trying to get top-side, as if that were the only escape.

Jimmy's father slapped the table and stood abruptly. "Wait here," he said. He stepped toward the narrow passage, stopped, looked back at Jimmy, seemed to consider something. There was a strange shine in his eyes.

"Quick, now. Just in case." He hurried in the other direction, past Jimmy and through a door leading out of the room. Jimmy hurried after him, frightened, confused, and limping.

"This is a lot like our stove," his father said, patting an ancient thing in the corner of the next room. "Older model, but it works the same." There was a wild look in his father's eyes. He spun and indicated another door. "Storehouse, bunkroom, showers, all through there. Food enough to last four people for ten years. Be smart, son."

"Dad . . . I don't understand—"

"Tuck that key in," his father said, pointing at Jimmy's chest.

Jimmy had left the lanyard outside of his overalls. "Do not lose that key, okay? What's the number you said you'd never forget?"

"Twelve-eighteen," Jimmy said.

"Okay. Come in here. Let me show you how the radio works."

Jimmy took a last look around this second room. He didn't want to be left alone down there. That's what his father was doing, leaving him down between the levels, hidden in the concrete. The world felt heavy all around him.

"I'll come with you to get her," he said, thinking of those men slapping their hands against the great steel door. His father couldn't go alone, even with the big pistol.

"Don't open the door for anyone but me or your mother," his father said, ignoring his son's pleas. "Now watch closely. We don't have much time." He indicated a box on the wall. The box was locked behind a metal cage, but there were some switches and dials on the outside. "Power's here." His father tapped one of the knobs. "Keep turning this way for volume." His father did this, and the room was filled with an awful hiss. He pulled a device off the wall and handed it to Jimmy. It was attached to the noisy box by a coil of stretchy cord. His dad grabbed another device from a rack on the wall. There were several of them there.

"Hear this? Hear this?" His father spoke into the portable device, and his voice replaced the loud hiss from the box on the wall. "Squeeze that button and talk into the mic." He pointed to the unit in Jimmy's hands. Jimmy did as he was told.

"I hear you," Jimmy said hesitantly, and it was strange to hear his voice emanate from the small unit in his father's hands.

"What's the number?" his dad asked.

"Twelve-eighteen," Jimmy said.

"Okay. Stay here, son." His father appraised him for a moment, then stepped forward and grabbed the back of Jimmy's neck. He kissed his son on the forehead, and Jimmy remembered the last time his father had kissed him like that. It was right before he had disappeared for three months, before his father had become a shadow, back when Jimmy was a little boy.

"When I put the grate back in place, it'll lock itself. There's a handle below to reopen it. Are you okay?"

Jimmy nodded. His father glanced up at the red, pulsing lights and frowned.

"Whatever you do," he said, "do not open that door for anyone but me or your mother. Understand?"

"I understand." Jimmy clutched his arm and tried to be brave. There was another of the long pistols leaning up against the wall. He didn't understand why he couldn't come as well. He reached for the black gun. "Dad—"

"Stay here," his father said.

Jimmy nodded.

"Good man." He rubbed Jimmy's head and smiled, then turned and disappeared down that dark and narrow corridor. The red lights overhead winked on and off, throbbing like a pulse. There was the distant clang of boots on metal rungs, swallowed by the darkness, which soon became silent. And then Jimmy Parker was alone.

62

Silo 1
2345

DONALD COULDN'T FEEL his toes. His feet were bare and had yet to thaw. They were bare, but all around him were boots. Boots everywhere. Boots on the men pushing him through aisles of gleaming pods. Boots standing still while they took his blood and told him to pee. Stiff boots that squeaked in the lift as grown men shifted nervously in place. And up above, a frantic hall greeted them where men stomped by in boots, a hall laden with shouts and nervous, lowered brows. They pushed him to a small apartment and left him alone to clean up and thaw out. Outside his door, more boots clomped up and down, up and down. Hurrying, hurrying. A world of worry, confusion, and noise in which to wake.

Donald remained half asleep, sitting on a bed, his consciousness floating somewhere above the floor. Deep exhaustion gripped him. He was back to aboveground days, back when stirring and waking were two separate things. Mornings when he gained consciousness in the shower or behind the wheel on his way into work, long after he had begun to move. The mind lagged behind the body; it swam through the dust kicked up by numb and shuffling feet. Waking from decades of freezing cold felt like this. Dreams of which he was dimly aware slipped from his grasp, and Donald was eager to let them go.

The apartment they'd brought him to was down the hall from his old office. They had passed it along the way. That meant he was on the operations wing, a place where he used to work. An empty pair of boots sat at the foot of the bed. Donald stared at them numbly. The name "Thurman" wrapped around the back of each ankle in faded black marker. Somehow, these boots were meant for him. They had been calling him Mr. Thurman since he woke up, but that was not who he was. A mistake had been made. A mistake or a cruel trick. Some kind of game.

Fifteen minutes to get ready. That's what they'd said. Ready for what? Donald sat on the double cot, wrapped in a blanket, occasionally shivering. The wheelchair had been left with him. Thoughts and memories reluctantly assembled like exhausted soldiers roused from their bunks in the middle of the night and told to form ranks in the freezing rain.

My name is Donald, he reminded himself. He must not let that go. This was the first and most primal thing. Who he was.

Sensation and awareness gathered. Donald could feel the dent in the mattress the size and shape of another's body. This depression left behind by another tugged at him. On the wall behind the door, a crater stood where the knob had struck, where the door had been flung open. An emergency, perhaps. A fight or an accident. Someone barging inside. A scene of violence. Hundreds of years of stories he wasn't privy to. Fifteen minutes to get his thoughts together.

There was an ID badge on the bedside table with a bar code and a name. No picture, fortunately. Donald touched the badge, remembered seeing it in use. He left it where it was and rose shakily on creaky legs, held the wheelchair for support and moved toward the small bathroom.

There was a bandage on his arm where the doctor had drawn his blood. Dr. Wilson. He'd already given a urine sample but he needed to pee again. Allowing his blanket to fall open, he stood over the toilet. The stream was pink. Donald thought he remembered it being the color of charcoal on his last shift. When he finished, he stepped into the shower to wash off.

The water was hot, his bones cold. Donald shivered in a fog of steam. He opened his mouth and allowed the spray to hit his tongue and fill his cheeks. He scrubbed at the memory of poison on his flesh, a memory that made it impossible to feel clean. For a moment, it wasn't the scalding water burning his skin—it was the air. The outside air. But then he turned off the flow of water and the burning lessened.

He toweled off and found the overalls left out for him. They were too big. Donald shrugged them on anyway, the fabric rough against skin that had lain bare for who knew how long. There was a knock at the door as he worked the zipper up to his neck. Someone called a name that was not his, a name scrawled around the backs of the boots lying perfectly still on the bed, a name that graced the badge sitting on the bedside table.

"Coming," Donald croaked, his voice thin and weak. He slid the badge into his pocket and sat heavily on the bed. He rolled up his cuffs, all that extra material, before pulling the boots on one at a time. He fumbled with the laces, stood, and found that he could wiggle his toes in the space left behind by another.

Many years ago, Donald Keene had been elevated by a simple change in title. Power and importance had come in an instant. For all his life, he had been a man to whom few listened. A man with a degree, a string of jobs, a wife, a modest home. And then one night, a computer tallied stacks of ballots and Donald Keene became Congressman Keene. He became one of hundreds with his hand on some great tiller—a struggle of hands pushing, pulling, and fitfully steering.

It had happened overnight, and it was happening again.

"How're you feeling, sir?"

The man outside his apartment studied Donald with concern. The badge around his neck read *Eren*. He was the Ops head, the one who manned the shrink's desk down the hall.

"Still groggy," Donald said quietly. A gentleman in bright blue overalls raced by and disappeared around the bend. A gentle breeze followed, a stir of air that smelled of coffee and perspiration.

"Are you good to walk? I'm sorry about the rush, but then I'm sure you're used to it." Eren pointed down the hall. "They're waiting in the comm room."

Donald nodded and followed. He remembered these halls being quieter, remembered them without the stomping and the raised voices. There were scuff marks on the walls that he thought were new. Reminders of how much time had passed.

In the comm room, all eyes turned to him. Someone was in trouble—Donald could feel it. Eren led him to a chair, and everyone watched and waited. He sat down and saw that there was a frozen image on the screen in front of him. A button was pressed and the image lurched into motion.

Thick dust tumbled and swirled across the view, making it difficult to see. Clouds flew past in unruly sheets. But there, through the gaps, a figure in a bulky suit could be seen on a forbidding landscape, picking their way up a gentle swell, heading away from the camera. It was someone outside.

He wondered if this was *him* out there, all those years ago. The suit looked familiar. Perhaps they'd caught his foolish act on camera, his attempt to die a free man. And now they'd woken him up to show him this damning bit of evidence. Donald braced for the accusation, for his punishment—

"This was earlier this morning," Eren said.

Donald nodded and tried to calm himself. This wasn't him on the screen. They didn't know who he was. A surge of relief washed over him, a stark contrast to the nerves in the room and the shouts and hurrying boots in the hallway. Donald remembered being told that someone had disappeared over a hill when they'd pulled him from the pod. It was the first thing they'd told him. This was that person on the screen. This was why he'd been woken. He licked his lips and asked who it was.

"We're putting a file together for you now, sir. Should have it soon. What we do know is that there was a cleaning scheduled in Eighteen this morning. Except . . ."

Eren hesitated. Donald turned from the screen and caught the Ops head looking to the others for help. One of the operators—a large man in orange overalls with wiry hair and headphones around his neck—was the first to oblige. "The cleaning didn't go through," the operator said flatly.

Several of the men in boots stiffened. Donald glanced around the room at the crowd that had packed into the small comm center, and he saw how they were watching him. Waiting on him. The Ops head looked down at the floor in defeat. He appeared to be in his late thirties, the same age as Donald, and yet he was waiting to be chastised. These were the men in trouble, not him.

Donald tried to think. The people in charge were looking to *him* for guidance. Something was wrong with the shifts, something very wrong. He had worked with the man they thought he was, the man whose name graced his badge and his boots. Thurman. It felt like yesterday that Donald had stood in that very same comm room and had felt that man's equal but for a moment. He had helped save a silo on his previous shift. And even though his head was groggy and his legs were weak, he knew it was important to uphold this charade. At least until he understood what was going on.

"What direction were they heading?" he asked, his voice a whisper. The others held perfectly still so that the rustle of their overalls wouldn't compete with his words.

A man from the back of the room answered. "In the direction of Seventeen, sir."

Donald composed himself. He remembered the Order, the danger of letting anyone out of sight. These people in their silos with a limited view of the world thought that they were the only ones alive. They lived in bubbles that must not be allowed to burst. "Any word from Seventeen?" he asked.

"Seventeen is gone," the operator beside him said, dispensing more bad news with the same flat voice.

Donald cleared his throat. "Gone?" He searched the faces of the gathered. Foreheads creased with worry. Eren studied Donald, and the operator beside him adjusted his bulk in his seat. On the screen, the cleaner disappeared over the top of the hill and out of view. "What did this cleaner *do*?" he asked.

"It wasn't her," Eren said.

"Seventeen was shut down shifts ago," the operator said.

"Right, right." Donald ran his fingers through his hair. His hand was trembling.

"You feeling all right?" the operator asked. He glanced at the Ops head, then back to Donald. He knew. Donald sensed that this man in orange with the headphones around his neck knew something was wrong.

"Still a bit woozy," Donald explained.

"He's only been up for half an hour," Eren told the operator.

There were murmurs from the back of the room.

"Yeah, okay." The operator settled back into his seat. "It's just . . . he's the Shepherd, you know? I pictured him waking up chewing nails and farting tacks."

Someone just behind Donald's chair chuckled.

"So what're we supposed to do about the cleaner?" a voice asked. "We need permission before we can send anyone out after her."

"She can't have gotten far," someone said.

The comm engineer on the other side of Donald spoke up. He had one side of his headphones still on, the other side pulled off so he could follow the conversation. A sheen of sweat stood out on his forehead. "Eighteen is reporting that her suit was modified," he said. "There's no telling how long it'll last. She could still be out there, sirs."

This caused a chorus of whispers. It sounded like wind striking a visor, peppering it with sand. Donald stared at the screen, at a lifeless hill as seen from Silo Eighteen. The dust came in dark waves. He remembered what it had felt like out there on that landscape, the difficulty of moving in one of those suits, the hard slog up that gentle rise. Who was this cleaner, and where did she think she was going?

"Get me the file on this cleaner as soon as you can," he said. The others fell still and stopped their whispering arguments. Donald's voice was commanding because of its quietude, because of who they thought he was. "And I want whatever we have on Seventeen." He glanced at the operator, whose brow was furrowed by either worry or suspicion. "To refresh my memory," he added.

Eren rested a hand on the back of Donald's chair. "What about the protocols?" he asked. "Shouldn't we scramble a drone or send someone after her? Or shut down Eighteen? There's going to be violence over there. We've never had a cleaning not go through before."

Donald shook his head, which was beginning to clear. He looked down at his hand and remembered tearing off a glove once, there on the outside. He shouldn't be alive. He wondered what Thurman would do, what the old man would order. But he wasn't Thurman. Someone had told him once that people like Donald should be in charge. And now here he was.

"We don't do anything just yet," he said, coughing and clearing his throat. "She won't get far."

The others stared at him with a mixture of shock and acceptance. There finally came a handful of nods. They assumed he knew best. He had been woken up to control the situation. It was all according to protocol. The system could be trusted—it was designed to just *go*. All anyone needed to do was their own job and let others handle the rest.

63

IT WAS A short walk from his apartment to the central offices, which Donald assumed was the point. It reminded him of a CEO's office he'd once seen with an adjoining bedroom. What had seemed impressive at first became sad after realizing why it was there.

He rapped his knuckles on the open door marked *Office of Psychological Services*. He used to think of these people as shrinks, that they were here to keep others sane. Now he knew that they were in charge of the insanity. All he saw on the door anymore was "OPS." Operations. The head of the head of the heads. The office across the hall was where the drudge work landed. Donald was reminded how each silo had a mayor for shaking hands and keeping up appearances, just as the world of before had presidents who came and went. Meanwhile, it was the men in the shadows who wielded the true power, those whose terms had no limits. That this silo operated by the same deceit should not be surprising; it was the only way such men knew how to run anything.

He kept his back to his former office and knocked a little louder. Eren looked up from his computer and a hard mask of concentration melted into a wan smile. "Come in," he said as he rose from his seat. "You need the desk?"

"Yes, but stay." Donald crossed the room gingerly, his legs still half asleep, and noticed that while his own whites were crisp, Eren's were crumpled with the wear of a man well into his six-month shift. Even so, the Ops head appeared vigorous and alert. His beard was neatly trimmed by his neck and only peppered with gray. He helped Donald into the plush chair behind the desk.

"We're still waiting for the full report on this cleaner," Eren said. "The head of Eighteen warned that it's a thick one."

"Priors?" Donald imagined anyone sent to clean would have priors.

"Oh, yeah. The word is that she was a sheriff. Not sure if I'm buying it. Of course, it wouldn't be the first lawman to want out."

"But it would be the first time anyone's gotten out of sight," Donald said.

"From what I understand, yeah." Eren crossed his arms and leaned against the desk. "Nearest anyone got before now was that gentleman you stopped. I reckon that's why protocol says to wake you. I've heard some of the boys refer to you as the Shepherd." Eren laughed.

Donald flinched at the nickname. He was more sheep than shepherd. "Tell me about Seventeen," he said, changing the subject. "Who was on shift when that silo went down?"

"We can look it up." Eren waved a hand at the keyboard.

"My, uh, fingers are still a little tingly," Donald said. He slid the keyboard toward Eren, who hesitated before getting off the desk. The Ops head bent over the keys and pulled up the shift list with a shortcut. Donald tried to follow along with what he was doing on the screen. These were files he didn't have access to, menus he was unfamiliar with.

"Looks like it was Cooper. I think I came off a shift once as he was coming on. Name sounds familiar. I sent someone down to get those files for you as well."

"Good, good."

Eren raised his eyebrows. "You went over the reports on Seventeen on your last shift, right?"

Donald had no clue if Thurman had been up since then. For all he knew, the old man had been awake when it happened. "It's hard to keep everything straight," he said, which was solid truth. "How many years has it been?"

"That's right. You were in the deep freeze, weren't you?"

Donald supposed he was. Eren tapped the desk with his finger, and Donald's gaze drifted to the man across the hall, sitting behind his computer. He remembered what it had been like to be that man nominally in charge, wondering what the doctors in white were discussing across the way. Now he was one of those in white.

"Yes, I was in the deep freeze," Donald said. They wouldn't have moved his body, would they? Erskine or someone could've simply changed entries in a database. Maybe it was that simple. Just a quick hack, two reference numbers transposed, and one man lives the life of another. "I like to be near my daughter," he explained.

"Yeah, I don't blame you." The wrinkles in Eren's brow smoothed. "I've got a wife down there. I still make the mistake of visiting her first thing every shift." He took a deep breath then pointed at the screen. "Seventeen was lost over thirty years ago. I'd have to look it up to be exact. The cause is still unclear. There wasn't any sign of unrest leading up to it, so we didn't have much time to react. There was a cleaning scheduled, but the airlock opened a day early and out of sequence. Could've been a glitch or tampering. We just don't know. Sensors reported a gas purge in the lower levels and then a riot surging up. We pulled the plug as they were scrambling out of the airlock. Barely had time."

Donald recalled Silo 12. That facility had ended in similar

fashion. He remembered people scattering on the hillside, a plume of white mist, some of them turning and fighting to get back inside. "No survivors?" he asked.

"There were a few stragglers. We lost the radio feed and the cameras but continued to put in a routine call over there, just in case anyone was in the safe room."

Donald nodded. By the book. He remembered the calls to 12 after it went down. He remembered nobody answering.

"Someone did pick up the day the silo fell," Eren said. "I think it was some young shadow or tech. I haven't read the transcripts in forever." He paged down on the shift report. "It looks like we sent the collapse codes soon after that call, just as a precaution. So even if the cleaner gets over there, she's gonna find a hole in the ground."

"Maybe she'll keep walking," Donald said. "What silo sits on the other side? Sixteen?"

Eren nodded.

"Why don't you go give them a call?" Donald tried to remember the layout of the silos. These were the kinds of things he'd be expected to know. "And get in touch with the silos on either side of Seventeen, just in case our cleaner takes a turn."

"Will do."

Eren stood, and Donald marveled again at being treated as if he were in charge. It was already beginning to make him feel as if he really were. Just like being elected to Congress, all that awesome responsibility foisted on him overnight—

Eren leaned across the desk and hit two of the function keys on the keyboard, logging himself out of the computer. The Ops head hurried out into the hall while Donald stared at a login and password prompt.

Suddenly he felt very much less in charge.

64

ACROSS THE HALL, a man sat behind a desk that once had belonged to Donald. Donald peered up at this man and found him peering right back. Donald used to gaze across that hallway in the opposite direction. And while this man in his former office—who was heavier than Donald and had less hair—likely sat there playing a game of solitaire, Donald struggled with a puzzle of his own.

His old login of Troy wouldn't work. He tried old ATM codes and they were just as useless. He sat, thinking, worried about performing too many incorrect attempts. It felt like just yesterday that this account had worked. But a lot had happened since then. A lot of shifts. And someone had tampered with them.

It pointed back to Erskine, the old Brit left behind to coordinate the shifts. Erskine had taken a liking to him. But what was the point? What was he expecting Donald to do?

For a brief moment, he thought about standing up and walking out into the hallway and saying, *I am not Thurman or Shepherd or Troy. My name is Donald, and I'm not supposed to be here.*

He should tell the truth. He should rage with the truth, as senseless as it would seem to everyone else. *I am Donald!* he felt like screaming, just as old man Hal once had. They could pin his boots to a gurney and put him back to glorious sleep. They could send him out to the hills. They could bury him like they'd buried his wife. But he would scream and scream until he believed it himself, that he was who he thought he was.

Instead, he tried Erskine's name with his own passkey. Another red warning that the login was incorrect, and the desire to out himself passed as swiftly as it had come.

He studied the monitor. There didn't seem to be a trigger for the number of incorrect tries, but how long before Eren came back? How long before he had to explain that he couldn't log in? Maybe he could go across the hall, interrupt the silo head's game of solitaire and ask him to retrieve his key. He could blame it on being groggy and newly awake. That excuse had been working thus far. He wondered how long he could cling to it.

On a lark, he tried the combination of Thurman and his own passkey of 2156.

The login screen disappeared, replaced by a main menu. The sense that he was the wrong person deepened. Donald wiggled his toes. The extra space in his loose boots gave him comfort. On the screen, a familiar envelope flashed. Thurman had messages.

Donald clicked the icon and scrolled down to the oldest unread message, something that might explain how he had arrived there, something from Thurman's prior shift. The dates went back centuries; it was jarring to watch them scroll by. Population reports. Automated messages. Replies and forwards. He saw a message from Erskine, but it was just a note about the overflow of deep freeze to one of the lower cryopod levels. The useless bodies were stacking up, it seemed. Another message further down was starred as important. Victor's name was in the senders column, which caught Donald's attention. It had to be from before Donald's second shift. Victor was already dead the last time Donald had been woken. He opened the message.

Old friend,

I'm sure you will question what I'm about to do, that you will see this as a violation of our pact, but I see it more as a restructuring of the timeline. New facts have emerged that push things up a bit. For me, at least. Your time will come.

I have in recent days discovered why one of our facilities has seen more than its share of turmoil. There is someone there who remembers, and she both disturbs and confirms what I know of humanity. Room is made that it might be filled. Fear is spread because the clean-up is addicting. Seeing this, much of what we do to one another becomes more obvious. It explains the great quandary of why the most depressed societies are those with the fewest wants. Arriving at the truth, I feel an urge from older times to synthesize a theory and present it to roomfuls of professionals. Instead, I have gone to a dusty room to procure a gun.

You and I have spent much of our adult lives scheming to save the world. Several adult lives, in fact. That deed now done, I ponder a different question, one that I fear I cannot answer and that we were never brave nor bold enough to pose. And so I ask you now, dear friend: was this world worth saving to begin with? Were *we* worth saving?

This endeavor was launched with that great assumption taken for granted. Now I ask myself for the first time. And while I view the cleansing of the world as our defining achievement, this business of saving humanity may have been our gravest mistake. The world may be better off without us. I have not the will to decide. I leave that to you. The final shift, my friend, is yours, for I have worked my last. I do not envy you the choice you will have to make. The pact we formed so long ago haunts me as never before. And I feel that what I'm about to do . . . that this is the easy way.

—Vincent Wayne DiMarco

Donald read the last paragraph again. It was a suicide note. Thurman had known. All along, while Donald wrestled with Victor's fate on his last shift, Thurman had known. He had this note in his possession and hadn't shared it. And Donald had almost grown convinced that Victor had been murdered. Unless the note was a fake—But no, Donald shook that thought away. Paranoia like that could spiral out of control and know no end. He had to cling to something.

He backed out of the message with a heavy heart and scrolled up the list, looking for some other clue. Near the top of the screen was a message with the subject line: *Urgent—The Pact*. Donald clicked the message open. The body was short. It read, simply:

Wake me when you get this.
—Anna
(Locket 20391102)

Donald blinked rapidly at the sight of her name. He glanced across the hall at the silo head and listened for footsteps coming his way. His arms were covered in goosebumps. He rubbed them, wiped underneath his eyes, and read the note a second time.

It was signed *Anna*. It took him a moment to realize that it wasn't to him. It was a note between daughter and father. There was no send date listed, which was curious, but it was sorted near the very top. Perhaps it was from before their last shift together? Maybe the two of them had been awake recently. Donald studied the number at the bottom. *20391102*. It looked like a date. An old date. Inscribed on a locket, perhaps? Something meaningful between the two of them. And what of the mention in the header of this Pact? That was the name the silos used for their constitutions. What could be urgent about that?

Footsteps in the hallway broke his concentration. Eren rounded the corner and covered the office in a few steps. He circled the desk and placed two folders by the keyboard, then glanced at the screen as Donald fumbled with the mouse to minimize the message. "H-How'd it go?" Donald asked. "You got through to everyone?"

"Yeah." Eren sniffed and scratched his beard. "The head of Sixteen took it badly. He's been in that position a long time. Too long, I think. He suggested closing down his cafeteria or shutting off the wallscreen, just in case."

"But he's not going to."

"No, I told him as a last resort. No need to cause a panic. We just wanted them to have a heads-up."

"Good, good." Donald liked someone else thinking. It took the pressure off him. "You need your desk back?" He made a show of logging off.

"No, actually, you're on if you don't mind." Eren checked the clock in the corner of the computer screen. "I can take the afternoon shift. How're you feeling, by the way? Any shakes?"

Donald shook his head. "No. I'm good. It gets easier every time."

Eren laughed. "Yeah. I've seen how many shifts you've taken. And a double a while back. Don't envy you at all, friend. But you seem to be holding up well."

Donald coughed. "Yeah," he said. He picked up the topmost of the two folders and read the tab. "This is what we have on Seventeen?"

"Yep. The thick one is your cleaner." He tapped the other folder. "You might want to check in with the head of Eighteen today. He's pretty shaken up, is shouldering all the blame. Name's Bernard. There are already grumblings from his lower levels about the cleaning not going through, so he's looking at a very probable uprising. I'm sure he'd like to hear from you."

"Yeah, sure."

"Oh, and he doesn't have an official second right now. His last shadow didn't work out, and he's been putting off a replacement. I hope you don't mind, but I told him to hurry that through. Just in case."

"No, no. That's fine." Donald waved his hand. "I'm not here to get in your way." He didn't add that he had absolutely no clue why he was there at all.

Eren smiled and nodded. "Great. Well, if you need anything, call me. And the guy across the hall goes by Gable. He used to hold down a post over here but couldn't cut it. Opted for a wipe instead of a deep freeze when given the choice. Good guy. Team player. He'll be on for a few more months and can get you anything you need."

Donald studied the man across the hall. He remembered the empty sensation of manning that desk, the hollow pit that had filled him. How Donald had ended up there had seemed unusual, a last-minute switch with his friend Mick. It never occurred to him how all the others were selected. To think that any might volunteer for such a post filled him with sadness.

Eren stuck out his hand. Donald studied it a moment, then accepted it.

"I'm really sorry we had to wake you like this," he said, pumping Donald's hand. "But I have to admit, I'm damn sure glad you're here."

65

Silo 17
2312
Day One

THE BOX ON the wall was unrelenting. His father had called it a radio. The noise it made was like a person hissing and spitting. Even the steel cage surrounding it looked like a mouth with its lips peeled back and iron bars for teeth.

Jimmy wanted to silence the radio but was scared to touch it or adjust anything. He waited to hear from his father, who had left him in a strange room, a hidden warren between the silo's levels.

How many more of these secret places were there? He glanced through an open door at the other room his dad had shown him, the one like a small apartment with its stove, table, and chairs. When his parents got back, would they all stay there overnight? How long before the madness cleared from the stairs and he could see his friends again? He hoped it wouldn't be long.

He glared at the hissing black box, patted his chest and felt for the key there. His ribs were sore from the fall, and he could feel a knot forming in his thigh from where he'd landed on someone. His shoulder hurt when he lifted his arm. He turned to the monitor to search for his mother again, but she was no longer on the screen. A jostling crowd moved in jerks and fits. The stairwell shook with more traffic than it was ever meant to hold.

Jimmy reached for the box with the controls his father had used. He twisted one of the knobs and the view changed. It was an empty hall. A faint number "33" stood in the lower left corner of the screen. Jimmy turned the dial once more and got a different hallway. There was a trail of clothes on the ground as if someone had walked by with a leaking laundry bag. Nothing moved.

He tried a different dial and the number on the bottom changed to "32." He was going *up the levels*. Jimmy spun the first dial until he found the stairwell again. Something flashed down and off the bottom of the screen. There were people leaning over the railing with their arms outstretched, mouths open in silent horror. There was no sound, but Jimmy remembered the screams from the woman who fell earlier. This was too far up to be his mother, he consoled himself. His dad would find her and bring her back. His dad had a gun.

Jimmy spun the dials and tried to locate either of his parents, but it seemed that not every angle was covered. And he couldn't figure out how to make the windows multiply. He was decent on a computer—he was going to work for IT like his father someday—but the little box was as unintuitive as the Deeps. He dialed it back down to "34" and found the main hallway. He could see a shiny steel door at the far end of a long corridor. Sprawled in the foreground was Yani. Yani hadn't moved, was surely dead. The men standing over him were gone, and there was a new body at the end of the hall, near the door. The color of his overalls assured Jimmy that it wasn't his father. His father had probably shot that man on his way out. Jimmy wished he hadn't been left alone.

Overhead, the lights continued to blink angry and red, and the image on the screen remained motionless. Jimmy grew restless and paced in circles. He went to the small wooden desk on the opposite wall and flipped through the thick book. It was a fortune in paper, perfectly cut and eerily smooth to the touch. The desk and chair were both made of real wood, not painted to look like that. He could tell by scratching it with his fingernail.

He closed the book and checked the cover. The word *Order* was embossed in shiny letters across the front. He reopened it, and realized he'd lost someone's place. The radio nearby continued to hiss noisily. Jimmy turned and checked the computer screen, but nothing was happening in the hallway. That noise was getting on his nerves. He thought about adjusting the volume, but was scared he might accidentally turn it off. His dad wouldn't be able to get through to him if he messed something up.

He paced some more. There was a shelf of metal containers in one corner that went from floor to ceiling. Pulling one out, Jimmy felt how heavy it was. He played with the latch until he figured out how to open it. There was a soft sigh as the lid came loose, and he found a book inside. Looking at all the containers filling the shelves, Jimmy saw what a pile of chits was there. He returned the book, assuming it was full of nothing but boring words like the one on the desk.

Back at the other desk, he examined the computer underneath and saw that it wasn't turned on. All the lights were dim. He traced the wire from the black box with all the switches and found a different wire led from the monitor to the computer. The machine that made the windows—that could see far distances and around corners—was controlled by something else. The power switch on the computer did nothing. There was a place for a key. Jimmy bent down to inspect the connections on the back, to make sure everything was plugged in, when the radio crackled.

"—need you to report in. Hello—"

Jimmy knocked his head on the underside of the desk. He ran to the radio, which was back to hissing. Grabbing the device at the end of the stretchy cord—the thing his dad had named Mike—he squeezed the button.

"Dad? Dad, is that you?"

He let go and looked to the ceiling. He listened for footsteps and waited for the lights to stop flashing. The monitor showed a quiet hallway. Maybe he should go to the door and wait.

The radio crackled with a voice: "Sheriff? Who is this?"

Jimmy squeezed the button. "This is Jimmy. Jimmy Parker. Who—" The button slipped out of his hand, the static returning. His palms were sweaty. He wiped them on his overalls and got the device under control. "Who is this?" he asked.

"Russ's boy?" There was a pause. "Son, where are you?"

He didn't want to say. The radio continued to hiss.

"Jimmy, this is Deputy Hines," the voice said. "Put your father on."

Jimmy started to squeeze the button to say that his father wasn't there, but another voice chimed in. He recognized it at once.

"Mitch, this is Russ."

Dad! There was a lot of noise in the background, people screaming. Jimmy held the device in both hands. "Dad! Come back, please!"

The radio popped with his father's voice. "James, be quiet. Mitch, I need you to—" Something was lost to the background noise. "—and stop the traffic. People are getting crushed up here."

"Copy."

That was his father talking to the deputy. The deputy was acting as though his old man were in charge.

"We've got a breach up top," his father said, "so I don't know how long you've got, but you're probably the sheriff until the end."

"Copy," Mitch said again. The radio made his voice sound shaky.

"Son—" His father was yelling now, fighting to be heard over some obnoxious din of screams and shouts. "I'm going to get your mother, okay? Just stay there, James. Don't move."

Jimmy turned to the monitor. "Okay," he said. He hung the Mike back on its hook, his hands trembling, and returned to the black box with all the controls. He felt helpless and alone. He should be out there, lending a hand. He wondered how long it would be before his parents returned, before he could see his friends again. He hoped it wouldn't be long.

66

Hours passed, and Jimmy wanted to be anywhere but in that cramped room. He crept down the dark passage to the ladder and peered up at the grating, listening. There was a faint buzzing sound coming and going that he couldn't place. The hiss of the radio could barely be heard from the end of the corridor. He didn't want to be too far away from the radio, but he worried his dad might need him by the door as well. He wanted to be in two places at once.

He went back to the room with the desks. He looked at the long gun propped against the wall, the same as the one his father had used to kill Yani. Jimmy was afraid to touch it. He wished his father hadn't left. It was all Jimmy's fault for being separated from his mom. They should've made it down together. But then he remembered the crush of people on the stairs. If only he'd been faster, they wouldn't have gotten caught up in the crowds. And it occurred to Jimmy that the only reason his mother was there at all was because she had come for him. If it weren't for that, his parents would be down in that room, together and safe.

"James—"

Jimmy spun around. His father's voice was there in the room

with him. It took a moment to realize the static from the radio was gone.

"—son, are you there?"

He lunged for the radio, grabbed the Mike at the end of the cord. It had seemed like hours since he'd heard voices. Too long. As he squeezed the button, a flash of movement caught his eye. Someone was moving on the monitor.

"Dad?" He stretched the cord across the small room and looked closer. His father was outside the steel door, standing at the end of the hall. Yani was still in the foreground, unmoving. The other body was gone. His father had his back to the camera, the portable radio in his hand. "I'm coming!" Jimmy yelled into the radio. He dropped the Mike and dashed for the corridor and the ladder.

"Son! No—"

His father's shouts were cut off by a grunt. Jimmy wheeled around, his boots squeaking. He clutched the desk for balance. On the screen, another man had emerged from around the corner, and his father was doubled over in pain. This man held the long pistol, stooped to retrieve something from the ground, held it to his mouth. It was the portable his father had taken from the room.

"Is this Russ's boy?"

Jimmy stared at the man on the screen. "Yes," he said to the screen. "Don't hurt my dad."

The room was full of static. The lights overhead continued to throb red.

Jimmy cursed himself. They couldn't hear him. He pushed away from the desk and grabbed the dangling Mike. "Please don't hurt him," he said, squeezing the button.

The man turned and looked directly at the camera. It was one of the security guards. There was a bit of movement peeking out from around the corner of the hall, more people out of sight.

"James, is it?"

Jimmy nodded. He watched his dad regain his composure and stand. His father made a gesture to someone out of sight, patted the air with his palm as if to calm someone.

"What's the new code?" the man with the radio asked.

Jimmy didn't want to tell him. But he wanted his father back inside. He wasn't sure what to do.

"The code," the man said. He aimed the gun at Jimmy's dad. Jimmy watched his father say something, then gesture for the portable. The security guard hesitated a moment before handing it over. His father lifted the unit to his mouth.

"They'll kill you," his father said, calm as if he were telling his son to tie his boots. The man with the gun waved an arm, and someone rushed into view to wrestle with his father. "They'll kill us all anyway," his father shouted, struggling to keep hold of the radio. "And they'll kill you the moment you open this door!"

Jimmy screamed as one of the men punched his father. His dad fought back but they punched him again. And then the man with the gun waved the other guy away. The room was full of static, so he couldn't hear the shot, but Jimmy could see the flashes of flame leap out, could see the way his father jerked as he was hit, watched him slump to the ground and become as still as Yani.

Jimmy dropped the Mike and grabbed the edges of the monitor. He yelled at this cruel window on the world while the guards in the silver overalls surveyed the man who had been his father. And then more men appeared from around the corner. They dragged Jimmy's mom behind them, kicking and silently screaming.

67

"No, no, no, no—"

The room was static and pulse. The two men wrestled with Jimmy's mother, who lifted herself off the ground and writhed in their jerking grasps. Her feet kicked and whirled. Jimmy's father lay still as stone beneath her.

"Open this goddamn door!" the man with the portable yelled. The radio on the wall was deafening. Jimmy hated the radio. He ran to it, reached for the dangling cord, then thought better and grabbed the other portable from the rack. One of the knobs said *Power.* He twisted it until it made the hissing sound, turned to the screen and held the small radio to his mouth.

"Don't," Jimmy said, and he realized he was crying. Tears splashed his overalls. "I'm coming."

It was hard to tear himself away from the view of his mother. As he rushed down the dark corridor, he continued to see her kicking and screaming, her boots in the air. He could hear her yelling in the background as the man radioed again: "Tell me the code!"

Jimmy held the portable's wrist strap between his teeth and attacked the ladder, ignoring the pain in his shoulder and knee. He found the release for the grating and threw it aside with a clang. Tossing the portable out, he scrambled after it on his knees. The lights above were on fire. His chest was on fire. His father was as dead as Yani.

"Coming, coming," he said into the radio.

The man yelled something back. All Jimmy could hear was his mother screaming and his heartbeat ringing in his ears. He ran beneath the pulsing lights and between the dark machines. The laces on one of his boots had come undone. They whipped about while he ran, and he thought of his mother's legs, up in the air like that, kicking and fighting.

Jimmy crashed into the door. He could hear muffled shouts on the other side. They came through the radio as well. Jimmy slapped the door with his palm and shouted into his portable: "I'm here, I'm here!"

"The code!" the man screamed.

Jimmy went to the control pad. His hands were shaking, his vision blurred. He imagined his mother on the other side, the gun aimed at her. He could feel his father lying a few feet away, just on the other side of that steel door. Tears streamed down his cheeks. He put in the first two numbers, the level of his home, and hesitated. That wasn't right. It was twelve-eighteen, not eighteen-twelve. Or was it? He put in the other two numbers, and the keypad flashed red. The door didn't open.

"What did you do?" the man yelled through the radio. "Just tell me the code!"

Jimmy fumbled with the portable, brought it to his lips. "Please don't hurt her—" he said.

The radio squawked. "If you don't do as I say, she's dead. Do you understand?"

The man sounded terrified. Maybe he was just as scared as Jimmy. Jimmy nodded and reached for the keypad. He entered the first two numbers correctly, then paused and thought about what his father had said. They would kill him. They would kill him and his mother both if he let these men inside. But it was his mom—

The keypad blinked impatiently. The man on the other side of the door yelled for him to hurry, yelled something about three wrong tries in a row and having to wait another day. Jimmy did nothing, paralyzed with fear. The keypad flashed red and fell silent.

There was a bang on the other side of the door, a blast from a gun. Jimmy squeezed the radio and screamed. When he let go, he could hear his mom shrieking on the other side.

"The next one won't be a warning," the man said. "Now don't touch that pad. Don't touch it again. Just tell me the code. Hurry, boy."

Jimmy blubbered and tried to form the sounds, to tell the man the numbers in the right order, but nothing came out. With his forehead pressed against the wall, he could hear his mother struggling and fighting on the other side.

"The code," the man said, calmer now.

Jimmy heard a grunt. He heard someone yell "Bitch," heard his mother scream for Jimmy not to do it, and then a slap on the other side of the wall, someone pressed up against it, his mother inches away. And then the muffled beeps of numbers being entered, four quick taps of the same number, and an angry buzz from the keypad as a third attempt failed.

More shouts. And then the roar of a gun, louder and angrier with his head pressed to the door. Jimmy screamed and beat his fists against the cold steel. The men were yelling at him through the radio. There were screams coming through the portable, screams leaking through the heavy steel door, but none were made by his mother.

Jimmy slid to the floor, buried the portable against his belly, and curled into a ball as the angry yelling bled through the steel door. His body quivered with sobs, the floor grating rough against his cheek. And while the violence raged, the lights overhead continued to throb at him. They throbbed steady. They weren't like a pulse at all.

68

Silo 1
2345

THERE WAS A plastic bag waiting on Donald's bunk when he got back to his room. He shut the door to block out the cacophony of traffic and office chatter, searched for a lock, and saw that there wasn't one. Here was a lone bedroom among workspaces, a place for men who were always on call, who were up for as long as they were needed.

Donald imagined this was where Thurman stayed when he was called forth in an emergency. He remembered the name on his boots and realized he didn't have to imagine; it was happening.

The wheelchair had been removed, he saw, and a glass of water stood on the nightstand. He tossed the folders Eren had given him on the bed, sat down beside them and picked up the curious plastic bag.

Shift, it read, in large stenciled letters. The clear plastic was heavily wrinkled, a few items appearing inside as inscrutable bulges. Donald slid the plastic seal to the side and peeled open the bag. Turning it over, there was a jingle of metal as a pair of dog tags rattled out, a fine chain slithering after them like a startled snake. Donald inspected the tags and saw that they were Thurman's. Dented and thin, and without the rubber edging he remembered from his sister's tags, they seemed like antiques. Which he supposed they were.

A small pocketknife was next. The handle looked like ivory but was probably a substitute. Donald opened the blade and tested it. Both sides were equally dull. The tip had been snapped off at some point, used to prise something open, perhaps. It had the look of a memento, no longer good for cutting.

The only other item in the bag was a coin, a quarter. The shape and heft of something once so common made it difficult for him to breathe. Donald thought of an entire civilization, gone. It seemed impossible for so much to be wiped out, but then he remembered Roman coins and Mayan coins sitting in museums. He turned this coin over and over and contemplated the only thing unusual about him holding a trinket from a world fallen to ashes—and that was him being around to marvel at the loss. It was supposed to be people who died and cultures that lasted. Now it was the other way around.

Something about the coin caught Donald's attention as he turned it over and over. It was heads on both sides. He laughed and inspected it more closely, wondering if it was a joke item, but the feel of the thing seemed genuine. On one of the sides, there was a faint arc where the stamp had missed its mark. A mistake? Perhaps a gift to Thurman from a friend in the Treasury?

He placed the items on the bedside table and remembered Anna's note to her father. He was surprised not to find a locket in the bag. The note had been marked urgent and had mentioned a locket with a date. Donald folded the bag marked *Shift* and slid it beneath his glass of water. People hurried up and down the hall outside. The silo was in a panic. He supposed if the real Thurman were there, the old man would be storming up and down as well, barking orders, shutting down facilities, ordering lives to be taken.

Donald coughed into the crook of his arm, his throat tickling. Someone had put him in this position. Erskine, or Victor beyond the grave, or maybe a hacker with more nefarious designs. He had nothing to go on.

Lifting the two folders, he thought of the panic roused by a person meandering out of sight. He thought about the violence brewing in the depths of another silo. These were not his mysteries, he thought. What he wanted to know was why he was awake, why he was even *alive*. What exactly was out there beyond those walls? What was the plan for the world once these shifts were over? Would there be a day when the people underground would be set free?

Something didn't sit right with him, imagining how that last shift would play out. There was a nagging suspicion that things wouldn't end so simply. Every layer he'd peeled back so far possessed its share of lies, and he didn't think he was done uncovering them. Perhaps someone had placed him in Thurman's boots to keep digging.

He recalled what Erskine had said about people like himself being in charge. Or was it Victor who said it to Erskine? He couldn't remember. What he did know, patting his pocket for the badge there—a badge that would open doors previously locked to him—was that he was very much in charge now. There were questions he wanted answers to. And now he was in a position to ask them.

Donald coughed into his elbow once more, an itch in his throat that he couldn't quite soothe. He opened one of the folders and reached for his glass. Taking a few gulps of water and beginning to read, he failed to notice the faint stain left behind, the spot of blood in the crook of his elbow.

69

Silo 17
2312
Week One

JIMMY DIDN'T WANT to move. He couldn't move. He remained curled on the steel grating, the lights flashing overhead, on and off, on and off, the color of crimson.

People on the other side of the door yelled at him and at each other. Jimmy slept in fits and starts. There were dull pops from guns and zings that rang against the door. The keypad buzzed. Only a single digit entered, and it buzzed. The whole world was angry with him.

Jimmy dreamt of blood. It seeped under the door and filled the room. It rose up in the shape of his mother and father, and they lectured him, mouths yawning open in anger. But Jimmy couldn't hear.

The yelling on the other side of the door came and went. They were fighting, these men. Fighting to get inside where it was safe. Jimmy didn't feel safe. He felt hungry and alone. He needed to pee.

Standing was the hardest thing he'd ever done. Jimmy's cheek made a tearing sound as he lifted it from the grating. He wiped the drool from the side of his face and felt the ridges there, the deep creases and the places his skin puckered out. His joints were stiff. His eyes were crusted together from crying. He staggered to the far corner of the room and tugged at his coveralls, tried to get them free before he accidentally wet himself.

Urine splashed through the grating and trickled down on bright runs of wires in neat channels. His stomach rumbled and spun inside his belly, but he didn't want to eat. He wanted to waste away completely. He glared up at the lights overhead that drilled into his skull. His stomach was angry with him. Everything was angry with him.

Back at the door, he waited for someone to call his name. He went to the keypad and pressed the number "1." The door buzzed at him immediately. It was angry too.

Jimmy wanted to lie back down on the grating and curl back into a ball, but his stomach said to look for food. Below. There were beds and food below. Jimmy walked in a daze between the black machines. He touched their warm skin for balance, heard them clicking and whirring as if everything were normal. The red lights flashed over and over. Jimmy weaved his way between them until he found the hole in the ground.

He lowered his feet to the rungs of the ladder and noticed the buzzing noise. It came and went in time with the throbbing red lights. He pulled himself out of the shaft and crawled across the floor in pursuit of the sound. It was coming from the server with its back off. His father had called it a comm something. Where had his father gone? Off to find his mother. There was something else—

Jimmy couldn't remember. He patted his chest and felt the key against his breastbone. The buzzing came and went with the flashing lights in perfect synchrony. This machine was making that overhead throb drilling into his skull. He peered inside the machine. A comm hub, that's what his father had called it. There was a headset hanging on a hook. He wished his father were there, but that seemed an impossible wish. Jimmy fumbled with the headset. There was a wire dangling from it. The piece on the end looked like something from computer class. He searched for a place to plug it in and saw a bank of sockets. One of them was blinking. The number "40" was lit up above it.

Jimmy adjusted the headset around his ears. He lined up the jack with the socket and pressed it in until he felt a click. The lights overhead stopped their incessant throbbing and a voice came through, like the radio, only clearer.

"Hello?" the voice said.

Jimmy didn't say anything. He waited.

"Is anyone there?"

Jimmy cleared his throat. "Yes," he said, and it felt strange to talk to an empty room. Stranger even than the radio with its hissing. It felt as though Jimmy were talking to himself.

"Is everyone okay?" the voice asked.

"No," Jimmy said. He remembered the stairs and falling and Yani and something awful on the other side of the door. "No," he said again, wiping tears from his cheeks. "Everyone is *not* okay!"

There was muttering on the other side of the line. Jimmy sniffled. "Hello?" he said.

"What happened?" the voice demanded. Jimmy thought it was an angry voice. Just like the people outside the door.

"Everyone was running—" Jimmy said. He wiped his nose. "They were all heading up. I fell. Mom and Dad—"

"There were casualties?" the man from level forty asked.

Jimmy thought of the body he'd seen on the stairway with the awful wound on his head. He thought of the woman who had gone over the rails, her scream fading to a crisp silence. "Yes," he said.

The voice on the line spat an angry curse, angry but faint. And then: "We were too late." Again, it sounded distant, as if the man were talking to someone else.

"Too late for what?" Jimmy asked.

There was a click, followed by a steady tone. The light above the socket marked "40" went out.

"Hello?"

Jimmy waited.

"Hello?"

He searched inside the box for some button to press, some way to make the voices come back. There were sockets with fifty numbers above them. Why only fifty levels? He glanced at the server behind him and wondered if there were other comm stations to handle the rest of the silo. This one must be for the Up Top. There would be one for the Mids and another for the Deeps. He unplugged the jack, and the tone in the headset fell silent.

Jimmy wondered if he could call another level. Maybe one of the shops near home. He ran his finger down the row looking for "18" and noticed that "17" was missing. There was no jack for "17." He puzzled over this as the overhead lights began to flash once more. Jimmy glanced at level forty's socket, but it remained dark. It was the top level calling. The light over the number "1" blinked on and off. Jimmy glanced at the jack in his hand, lined it up with the socket and pressed it in until he heard a click.

"Hello?" he said.

"What the hell is going on over there?" a voice demanded.

Jimmy shrank within himself. His father had yelled at him like this before, but not for a long time. He didn't answer because he didn't know what to say.

"Is this Jerry? Or Russ?"

Russ was his dad. Jerry was his dad's boss. Jimmy realized he shouldn't be playing with these things.

"This is Jimmy," he said.

"Who?"

"Jimmy. The guy on level forty said they were too late. I told him what happened."

"Too late?" There was some distant talking. Jimmy jiggled the cord in the socket. He was doing something wrong. "How did you get in there?" the man asked.

"My dad let me in," he said, the truth frightened out of him.

"We're shutting you down," the voice said. "Shut them down right now."

Jimmy didn't know what to do. There was a hiss somewhere. He thought it was from the headset until he noticed the white steam coming from the vents overhead. A fog descended toward him. Jimmy waved his hand in front of his face, expecting the sting of smoke like he'd smelled from a fire once as a kid, but the steam didn't smell of anything. It just tasted like a dry spoon in his mouth. Like metal.

"—on my goddamn shift—" the person in his headset said.

Jimmy coughed. He tried to say something back but he had swallowed wrong. The steam stopped leaking from the vents.

"That did it," the man on the other end of the line muttered. "He's gone."

Before Jimmy could say anything else, the winking lights inside the box went dark. There was a click in the headset and then it too fell silent. He pulled the headset off just as a louder *thunk* rang out in the ceiling and the lights in the room turned off. The whirring and clicking of the tall servers around him wound down. The room was pitch black and totally silent. Jimmy couldn't see his own nose, couldn't see his hand as he waved it in front of his face. He thought he'd gone blind, wondered if this was what being dead was like, but then he heard his pulse, a *thump-thump, thump-thump* in his temples.

Jimmy felt a sob catch in his throat. He wanted his mother

and father. He wanted his backpack, which he'd left behind in his classroom like an idiot. For a long while, he sat there, waiting for someone to come to him, for an idea to form on what he should do next. He thought of the ladder nearby and the room below. As he began to crawl toward that hole, cautiously patting the grating ahead of him so he wouldn't fall down the long drop, the clunking in the ceiling came back. There was a blinding flash as the lights overhead wavered, shimmered, blinked on and off several times, then burned steady.

Jimmy froze. The red lights were back to flashing. He went back to the box and looked inside. It was the light over "40" ticking on and off. He thought about answering it, seeing what these people were so angry about, but maybe the power was a warning. Maybe he'd said something wrong.

The lights overhead were like bright heat. They reminded him of the farms, of the time years ago that his class had gone on a trip to the Mids and planted seeds beneath those grow lights.

Jimmy turned to the server with the open back and fumbled for the jack inside. He hated the flashing lights, but he didn't want to get yelled at. So he jabbed the headphone jack into the socket marked "40" until he felt a click.

The lights stopped blinking immediately. There was a muffled voice from the headset, which lay in the bottom of the server. Jimmy ignored that. He took a step away from the machine, watched the overhead lights warily, waited on the bright white ones to shut off again or the angry red ones to return. But everything stayed the same. The jack sat in its socket, the wire dangling, the voice in the headset distant now, unable to be heard.

70

JIMMY WORKED HIS way down the ladder, wondering how long it'd been since he last ate. He couldn't remember. Breakfast before school, but that was a day ago, maybe two. Halfway down the ladder, he thought of himself as a piece of food sliding through some great metal neck. This was what a swallowed bite felt like. At the bottom of the ladder, he stood for a moment in the bowels of the silo, a hollow thing lost in a hollow thing. There would be no end to the silo's hunger, chewing on something empty like him. They would both starve, he thought. His stomach grumbled; he needed to eat. Jimmy staggered down the dark corridor and through the silo's guts.

The radio on the wall continued to hiss. Jimmy turned the volume down until the spitting noise could barely be heard. His father wouldn't be calling him ever again. He wasn't sure how he knew this, but it was a new Rule of the World.

He entered the small apartment. There was a table big enough for four with the pages of a book scattered across it, a needle and thread coiled on top like a snake guarding its nest. Jimmy thumbed the pages and saw that the place where the pages met was being repaired. His stomach hurt, it was so empty. His mind was beginning to ache as well.

Across the room, the ghost of his father stood and pointed

out doors, told him what was behind each. Jimmy patted his chest for the key, took it out, and used it to unlock the pantry across from the stove. Food enough for two people for ten years, that was what his father had told him. Was that right?

The room made a sucking sound as he cracked the pantry door, and there was the tickle of a breeze against his neck. Jimmy found the light switch on the outside of the door—as well as a switch that ran a noisy fan. He turned the fan off, which only reminded him of the radio. Inside the room, he found shelves bulging with cans that receded so far that he had to squint to see the back wall. These were cans like he'd never seen before. He squeezed between the tight shelves and searched up and down, his stomach begging him to choose and be quick about it. *Eat, eat,* his belly growled. Jimmy said to give him a chance.

Tomatoes and beets and squash, stuff he hated. Recipe food. He wanted *food* food. There were entire shelves of corn with labels like colorful sleeves of paper, not the black ink scrawled on a tin that he was used to. Jimmy grabbed one of the cans and studied it. A large man with green flesh smiled at him from the label. Tiny words like those printed in books wrapped all around. The cans of corn were identical. They made Jimmy feel out of place, like he was asleep and dreaming every bit of this.

He kept one of the corn and found an aisle of labeled soups in red and white, grabbed one of those as well. Back in the apartment, he rummaged for an opener. There were drawers around the stove full of spatulas and serving spoons. There was a cabinet with pots and lids. A bottom drawer held charcoal pencils, a spool of thread, batteries bulging with age and covered in gray powder, a child's whistle, a driver, and myriad other things.

He found the can opener. It was rusty and appeared as if it hadn't been used in years. But the dull cutter still sank through the soft tin when he gave it a squeeze, and the handle turned if given enough force. Jimmy worked it all the way around and cursed when the lid sank down into the soup. He fished a knife out of the drawer to lever the lid out with the tip. Food. Finally. He placed a pot onto the stove and turned the burner on, thinking of his apartment, of his mother and father. The soup heated. Jimmy waited, stomach growling, but some part of him was dimly aware that there was nothing he could put inside himself to touch the real ache, this mysterious urge he felt every moment to scream at the top of his lungs or to collapse to the floor and cry.

While he waited for the soup to bubble, he inspected the sheets of paper the size of small blankets hanging on one wall. It looked as if they'd been hung out to dry, and he thought at first that the thick books must be made by folding up or cutting these. But the large sheets were already printed on, the drawings continuous. Jimmy ran his hands down the smooth paper and studied the details of a schematic, an arrangement of circles with fine lines inside each and labels everywhere. There were numbers over the circles. Three of them were crossed out with red ink. Each was labeled a "silo," but that didn't make any sense.

Behind him, a hissing like the radio, like someone calling for him, the whisperings of ghosts. Jimmy turned from the strange drawing to find his soup spitting bubbles, dripping down the edge and sizzling on the glowing-hot burner. He left the large and strange drawing alone.

71

DAYS PASSED UNTIL they threatened to make a week, and Jimmy could glimpse how weeks might eventually become months. Beyond the steel door in the upper room, the men outside were still trying to get in. They yelled and argued over the radio. Jimmy listened sometimes, but all they talked about were the dead and dying and forbidden things, like the great outside.

Jimmy cycled through camera angles of quietude and vast emptiness. Sometimes these still views were interrupted with bursts of activity and violence. Jimmy saw a man held down on the ground and beaten by other men. He saw a woman dragged down a hall, feet kicking. He watched a man attack a child over a loaf of bread. He had to turn the monitor off. His heart raced the rest of the day and into the night, and he resolved not to look at the cameras anymore. That night, alone in the bunk room with all the empty beds, he hardly slept. But when he did, he dreamed of his mother.

The days would be like this, he thought the next morning. Each day would stretch out forever, but their counting would not take long. Their counting would run out for him. His days were numbered and ticking away; he could feel it.

He moved one of the mattresses out into the room with the computer and the radio. There was a semblance of company in that room. Angry voices and scenes of violence were better than the emptiness of the other bunks. He forgot his promise to himself and ate warm soup in front of the cameras, looking for people. He listened to their soft voices bicker on the radio. And when he dreamed that night, his dreams were filled with little square views of a distant past. A younger self stood in those windows, peering back at him.

In forays to the room above, Jimmy crept silently to the steel door and listened to men argue on the other side. They tried codes, three beeping entries at a time, followed by three angry buzzes. Jimmy rubbed the steel door and thanked it for staying shut.

Padding away quietly, he explored the grid of machines. They whirred and clicked and blinked their flashing eyes, but they didn't say anything. They didn't move. Their presence made Jimmy feel even more alone, like a classroom of large boys who all ignored him. Just a handful of days like this and Jimmy felt a new Rule of the World: man wasn't meant to live alone. This was what he discovered, day by day. He discovered it and just as soon forgot, for there was no one around to remind him. He spoke with the machines instead. They clacked back at him and hissed deep in their metal throats that man wasn't supposed to live at all.

The voices on the radio seemed to believe this. They reported deaths and promised more of them for each other. Some of them had guns from the deputy stations. There was a man on the ninety-first who wanted to make sure everyone else knew he had a gun. Jimmy felt like telling this man about the storage facility his key had unlocked beyond the bunk room. There were racks and racks of guns like the one his father had used to kill Yani. And countless boxes of bullets. He felt like telling the entire silo that he had more guns than anyone, that he had the key to the silo, so please stay away, but something told him that these men would just try harder to reach him if he did. So Jimmy kept his secrets to himself.

On the sixth night of being alone, unable to sleep, Jimmy tried to make himself drowsy by flipping through the book on the desk labeled *Order.* It was a strange read, each page referencing other pages, and filled with accounts of all the horrible things that could happen, how to prevent them, how to mitigate inevitable disasters. Jimmy looked for an entry on finding oneself completely and utterly alone. There was nothing in the index. And then Jimmy remembered what was in all the hundreds of metal cases lining the bookshelf beside the desk. Maybe there was something in one of those books that could help him.

He checked the small labels on the lower portion of each tin, went to the *Li–Lo* box for "loneliness." There was a soft sigh as he cracked the tin, like a can of soup sucking at the air. Jimmy slid the book out and flipped toward the back where he thought he'd find the entry.

Instead, he came across the sight of a great machine with large wheels like the wooden toy dog he'd owned as a kid. Fearsome and black with a pointy nose, the machine loomed impossibly large over the man standing in front of it. Jimmy waited for the man to move, but rubbing it, he found it just to be a picture like on his dad's work ID, but one so glossy and vivid in color that it looked to be real.

Locomotive, Jimmy read. He knew these words. The first part meant "crazy." The second part was a person's reason for doing something. He studied this image, wondering what crazy reason someone would have for making this picture. Jimmy carefully turned the page, hoping to find more on this locomotive—

He screamed and dropped the book when the page flopped over. He hopped around and brushed himself with both hands, waiting for the bug to disappear down his shirt or bite him. He stood on his mattress and waited for his heart to stop pounding. Jimmy eyed the flopped-open tome on the ground, expecting a swarm to fly out like the pests in the farms, but nothing moved.

He approached the book and flipped it over with his foot. The damn bug was just another picture, the page folded over and creased where he'd dropped it. Jimmy smoothed the page, read the word "locust" out loud, and wondered just what sort of book this was supposed to be. It was nothing like the children's books he'd grown up with, nothing like the pulp paper they taught with at school.

Flipping the cover over, Jimmy saw that this was different from the book on the desk, which had been embossed with the word *Order*. This one was labeled *Legacy*. He flipped through it a pinch at a time, bright pictures on every page, paragraphs of words and descriptions, a vast fiction of impossible deeds and impossible things, all in a single book.

Not in a single book, he told himself. Jimmy glanced up at the massive shelves bulging with metal tins, each one labeled and arranged in alphabetical order. He searched again for the locomotive, a machine on wheels that dwarfed a grown man. He found the entry and shuffled back to his mattress and his twisted tangle of sheets. A week of solitude was drawing to a close, but there was no chance that Jimmy would be getting any sleep. Not for a very long while.

72

Silo 1
2345

DONALD WAITED IN the comm room for his first briefing with the head of 18. To pass the time, he twisted the knobs and dials that allowed him to cycle through that silo's camera feeds. From a single seat, he had a view of all of the world's residents. He could nudge their fates from a distance if he liked. He could end them all with the press of a button. While he lived on and on, freezing and thawing, these mortals went through routines, lived and died, unaware that he even existed.

"It's like the afterlife," he muttered.

The operator at the next station turned and regarded him silently, and Donald realized he'd spoken aloud. He faced the man, whose bushy black hair looked as though it'd last been combed a century ago. "It's just that . . . it's like a view from the heavens," he explained, indicating the monitor.

"It's a view of something," the operator agreed and took a bite of a sandwich. On his screen, one woman seemed to be yelling at another, a finger jabbed in the other woman's face. It was a sitcom without the laugh track.

Donald worked on keeping his mouth shut. He dialed in

the cafeteria on 18 and watched its people huddle around a wallscreen. It was a small crowd. They gazed out at the lifeless hills, perhaps awaiting their departed cleaner's return, perhaps silently dreaming about what lay beyond those quiet crests. Donald wanted to tell them that she wouldn't be coming back, that there was nothing beyond that rise, even though he secretly shared their dreams. He longed to send up one of the drones to look, but Eren had told him the drones weren't for sightseeing—they were for dropping bombs. They had a limited range, he said. The air out there would tear them to shreds. Donald wanted to show Eren his hand, mottled and pink, and tell him that he'd been out on that hill and back. He wanted to ask if the air outside was really so bad.

Hope. That's what this was. Dangerous hope. He watched the people in the cafeteria staring at the wallscreen and felt a kinship with them. This was how the gods of old got in trouble, how they ended up smitten with mortals and tangled in their affairs. Donald laughed to himself. He thought of this cleaner with her thick folder and how he might've intervened if he'd had the chance. He might've given her a gift of life if he were able. Apollo, doting on Daphne.

The comm officer glanced over at Donald's monitor, that view of the wallscreen, and Donald felt himself being studied. He switched to a different camera. It was the hallway of what looked like a school. Lockers lined either side. A child stood on her tiptoes and opened one of the upper ones, pulled out a small bag, turned and seemed to say something to someone off-camera. Life going on as usual.

"The call's coming through now," the operator behind them said. The man with the sandwich put it away and sat forward. He brushed the crumbs off his chest and switched his view of two women arguing to one of a room full of black cabinets. Donald grabbed a pair of headphones and pulled the two folders off the desk. The one on the top was two inches thick. It was about the missing cleaner. Beneath that was a much thinner folder with a potential shadow's name on it. A man's voice came through his headphones.

"Hello?"

Donald glanced up at his monitor. A figure stood behind one of the black cabinets. He was pudgy and short, unless it was the distortion from the camera lens.

"Report," Donald said. He flipped open the folder marked *Lukas Kyle*. He knew from his last shift that the system would make his voice sound flat, make all their voices sound the same.

"I picked out a shadow as you requested, sir. A good kid. He's done work on the servers before, so his access has already been vetted."

How meek this man. Donald reckoned he would feel the same way, knowing his world could be ended at the press of a button. Fear like that puts a man at odds with his ego.

The operator beside Donald leaned over and peeled back the top page in the folder for him. He tapped his finger on something a few lines down. Donald scanned the report.

"You looked at Mr. Kyle as a possible replacement two years ago." Donald glanced up to watch the man behind the comm server wipe the back of his neck.

"That's right," the head of 18 said. "We didn't think he was ready."

"Your office filed a report on Mr. Kyle as a possible gazer. Says here he's logged a few hundred hours in front of the wallscreen. What's changed your mind?"

"That was a preliminary report, sir. It came from another . . . potential shadow. A bit overeager, a gentleman we found more suited for the security team. I assure you that Mr. Kyle does not dream of the outside. He only goes up at night—" The man cleared his throat, seemed to hesitate. "To look at the stars, sir."

"The stars."

"That's right."

Donald glanced over at the operator beside him, who polished off his sandwich. The operator shrugged. The silo head broke the silence.

"He's the best man for the job, sir. I knew his father. Stern sonofabitch. You know what they say about the treads and the rails, sir."

Donald had no idea what they said about the treads and the rails. It was nothing but stair analogies from these silos. He wondered what this Bernard would say if the man ever saw a lift. The thought nearly elicited a chuckle.

"Your choice of shadow has been approved," Donald said. "Get him on the Legacy as soon as possible."

"He's studying right now, sir."

"Good. Now, what's the latest on this uprising?" Donald felt himself hurrying along, performing rote tasks so he could get back to his more pressing studies.

The silo head glanced back toward the camera. This mortal knew damn well where the eyes of gods lay hidden. "Mechanical is holed up pretty tight. They put up a fight on their retreat down, but we routed them good. There's a . . . bit of a barricade, but we should be through it any time now."

The operator leaned forward and grabbed Donald's attention. He pointed two fingers at his eyes, then at one of the blank screens on the top row, indicating one of the cameras that had gone out during the uprising. Donald knew what he was getting at.

"Any idea how they knew about the cameras?" he asked. "You know we're blind over here from one-forty down, right?"

"Yessir. We . . . I can only assume they've known about them for a while. They do their own wiring down there. I've been in person. It's a nest of pipes and cables. We don't think anyone tipped them off."

"You don't think."

"Nossir. But we're working on getting someone in there. I've got a priest we can send in to bless their dead. A good man. Shadowed with Security. I promise it won't be long."

"Fine. Make sure it isn't. We'll be over here cleaning up your mess, so get the rest of your house in order."

"Yessir. I will."

The three men in the comm room watched this Bernard remove his headset and return it to the cabinet. He wiped his forehead with a rag. While the others were distracted, Donald did the same, wiping the sweat off his brow with a handkerchief he'd requisitioned. He picked up the two folders and studied the operator beside him, who had a fresh trail of breadcrumbs down his overalls.

"Keep a close eye on him," Donald said.

"Oh, I will."

Donald returned his headset to the rack and got up to leave. Pausing at the door, he looked back and saw the screen in front of the operator had divided into four squares. In one, a roomful of black towers stood like silent sentinels. Two women were having a row in another.

73

DONALD TOOK HIS notes and rode the lift to the cafeteria. He arrived to find it was too early for breakfast, but there was still coffee in the dispenser from the night before. He selected a chipped mug from the drying rack and filled it. A gentleman behind the serving line lifted the handle on an industrial washer, and the stainless steel box opened and let loose a cloud of steam. The man waved a dishrag at the cloud, then used it to pull out metal trays that would soon hold reconstituted eggs and slices of freeze-dried toast.

Donald tried the coffee. It was cold and weak but he didn't mind. It suited him. He nodded to the man prepping for breakfast, who dipped his head in reply.

Donald turned and took in the view splayed across the wallscreen. Here was the mystery. The documents in his folders were nothing compared to this. He approached the dusky vista where swirling clouds were just beginning to glow from a sun rising invisibly beyond the hills. He wondered what was out there. People died when they were sent to clean. They died on the hills when silos were shut down. But he had survived. And as far as he knew, so had the men who had dragged him back.

He studied his hand in the dim light leaking from the wallscreen. His palm seemed a little pink to him, a little raw.

But then, he had scrubbed it half a dozen times for the last few nights and each morning. He couldn't shake the feeling that it had been tainted. He pulled his handkerchief out of his pocket and coughed into its folds.

"I'll have potatoes ready in a few minutes," the man behind the counter called out. Another worker in green overalls emerged from the back, cinching an apron around his waist. Donald wanted to know who these people were, what their lives were like, what they were thinking. For six months, they served three meals a day, and then hibernated for decades. Then they did it all over again. They must believe they were heading somewhere. Or did they not care? Was it a case of following the tracks laid down yesterday? A boot in a hole, a boot in a hole, round and round. Did these men see themselves as deck hands on some great ark with a noble purpose? Or were they walking in circles simply because they knew the way?

Donald remembered running for Congress, thinking he was going to do real good for the future. And then he found himself in an office surrounded by a bewildering tempest of rules, memos, and messages, and he quickly learned just to pray for the end of each day. He went from thinking he was going to save the world to passing the time until . . . until time ran out.

He sat down in one of the faded plastic chairs and studied the folder in his pink hand. Two inches thick. *Nichols, Juliette* was written on the tab, followed by an ID number for internal purposes. He could smell the toner from the newly printed pages. It seemed a waste, printing out so much nonsense. Somewhere, down in the vast storeroom, supplies were dwindling. And somewhere else, down the hall from his own office, a person was keeping track of it all, making sure there were just enough potatoes, just enough toner, just enough light bulbs, to get them through to the end.

Donald glanced over the reports. He spread them out across

the empty table and thought of Anna and his last shift as he did so, the way they had smothered that war room with clues. He felt a pang of guilt and regret that Anna so often entered his thoughts before Helen could.

The reports were a welcome distraction while he awaited the sunrise and his food. Here was a story about a cleaner who had been a sheriff, though not for long. One of the top reports in her folder was from the current head of 18, a memo on this cleaner's lack of qualifications. Donald read a list of reasons this woman should not be given a mantle of power, and it was as though he were reading about himself. It seemed the mayor of 18—an old woman called Jahns, a politician like Thurman—had wrangled this woman into the job, had recruited her despite the objections. It wasn't even clear that this Nichols, a mechanic from the lower levels, even *wanted* the job. In another report from the silo head, Donald read about her defiance, culminating in a walk out of sight and a refusal to clean. Again, it felt all too familiar to Donald. Or was he looking for these similarities? Isn't that what people did? Saw in others what they feared to see or hoped to see in themselves?

The hills outside brightened by degrees. Donald glanced up from the reports and studied the mounds of dirt. He remembered the video feed he'd been shown of this cleaner disappearing over a similarly gray dune. Now the panic among his colleagues was that the residents of 18 would be filled with a dangerous sort of hope—the kind of hope that leads to violence. The far graver threat, of course, was that this cleaner had made it to another facility, that those in another silo might discover they were not alone.

Donald did not think it likely. She couldn't have lasted long, and there was little to discover in the direction she had wandered. He pulled out the other folder, the one on Silo 17.

There had been no warning before its collapse, no increase in violence. The population graphs appeared normal. He flipped through pages of typed documents from various division heads downstairs. Everyone had their theory, and of course each saw the collapse through the lens of their own expertise, or attributed it to the incompetence of another division. Population Control blamed a lax IT department. IT blamed a hardware failure. Engineering blamed Programming. And the on-duty comm officer, who liaised with IT and each individual silo head, thought it was sabotage, an attempt to prevent a cleaning.

Donald sensed something familiar about the breakdown of Silo 17, something he couldn't place. The camera feeds had gone out, but not before a brief view of people spilling out of the airlock. There had been an exodus, a panic, mass hysteria. And then a blackout. Comm had placed several calls. The first had been answered by the IT shadow, 17's second-in-charge. There was a short exchange with this Russ fellow, questions fired from both ends, and then Russ had broken the connection.

The follow-up call had gone unanswered for hours. During this time, the silo went dark. And then someone else picked up the line.

Donald coughed into his handkerchief and read this unusual exchange. The officer on duty claimed the respondent sounded young. It was a male, not a shadow or the head, and he had asked a flurry of questions. One stood out to Donald. The person in 17, with only minutes left to live, had asked what was going on down on level forty.

Level forty. Donald didn't need to grab a schematic to check—he had designed the facilities. He knew every level like the back of his hand. Level forty was a mixed-use level with half to housing, a quarter to light agriculture, the rest to commercial. What could be going on down there? And why would this person, who must've been at the limits of survival, care?

He read the exchange again. It almost sounded as though the young man's last contact had been with level forty, as if he'd just spoken with them. Maybe he'd come from down there? It was only six levels away. Donald imagined a frightened boy storming up the stairwell with thousands of others. News of an opened airlock, of death below, people chasing upward. This young man gets to level thirty-four, and the crush of people is too much. IT has already emptied. He finds his way into the server room—

No. Donald shook his head. That wasn't right. None of that felt right. What was it about this that nagged him?

It was the blackout. Donald felt a chill run up his spine. It was the number 40. It was the *silo,* not the level. The report trembled in his hands. He wanted to jump up and pace the cafeteria, but all he had was the germ of a connection, the hint of an outline. He fought to connect the dots before the ideas melted away, disturbed by a rush of adrenalin.

It was *Silo 40* he had spoken with. The boy had found himself at the back of 17's comm station. He didn't know it was a silo calling at all. That would be why he'd called it a level and had wondered what was happening down there. This blackout, this lack of contact, it was just like the silos Anna had been working on.

Anna—

Donald thought about the note she had left, asking Thurman to wake her. She was asleep below. She would know what to do. She should've been woken and put in charge, not him. He gathered the reports and papers and put them back into the proper folders. Workers were beginning to arrive from the lifts. The smell of reconstituted eggs floated out from the kitchen, the swinging doors pumping the aroma with the traffic of the bustling food staff, but Donald had forgotten his hunger.

He glanced up at the wallscreen. Would anyone on shift right now know of Silo 40? Maybe not. They wouldn't have made the same connection. Thurman and the others had kept the outbreak a secret, didn't want to cause a panic. But what if Silo 40 was still out there? What if they'd contacted 17? Anna said the master system had been hacked, that Silo 40 had hacked them. They had cut several facilities off from Silo 1 before Anna and Thurman had been woken to terminate them all. But what if they hadn't? What if this Silo 17 wasn't destroyed? What if it was still there, and this cleaner had stumbled into the bowl to find—

Donald had a sudden urge to go see for himself, to stroll outside and dash up to the top of the hill, suit be damned. He left the wallscreen and headed toward the airlock.

Perhaps he would need to wake Anna, just as Thurman had. He could set her up in the armory. There was a blueprint for doing this from his last shift, only he didn't have anyone he could trust to help. He didn't know the first thing about waking people up. But he was in charge, right? He could demand to know.

He left the cafeteria and approached the silo's airlock, that great yellow door to the open world beyond. The outside wasn't as bad as he had been led to believe. Unless he was simply immune. There were machines in his blood that kept him stitched up when he was frozen. Perhaps they had kept him alive out there. He approached the inner airlock door and peered through the small porthole. The memory of being in there struck him with sudden violence. He tucked the two folders under his elbow and rubbed his arm where the needle had bitten into his flesh long ago, putting him to sleep. What was out there? The light spilling through the holding cell bars flickered as a dust cloud passed, and Donald realized how strange it was that they had a wallscreen in Silo 1. The people here knew what they'd done to the world. Why did they need to see the ruin they'd left behind?

Unless—

Unless the purpose was the same as for the other silos. Unless it was to keep them from going outside, a haunting reminder that the planet was not safe for them. But what did they really know beyond the silos? And how could a man hope to see for himself?

74

IT TOOK A few days of planning and building up the nerve for Donald to make the request, and a few days more for Dr. Wilson to schedule an appointment. During that time he told Eren about his suspicions of Silo 40's involvement. The flurry of activity launched by this simple guess quickly consumed the silo. Donald signed off on a requisition for a bombing run, even though he didn't quite understand what he was signing. Little-used levels of the silo—levels familiar to Donald from before—were reawakened. Days later, he didn't feel the rumble or the ground shake, but others claimed to have. All he found was that a new layer of dust had settled over his things, shaken loose from the ceiling.

The day of his meeting with Dr. Wilson, he stole down to the main cryopod floor to test his code. He still didn't fully trust the disguise offered by his loose overalls and the badge with someone else's name on it. Just the day before, he had seen someone in the gym he thought he recognized from his first shift. It put him in the habit of slinking instead of strutting. And so he shuffled down the hall of frozen bodies and entered his code into the keypad warily. He expected red lights and warning buzzes. Instead, the light above the *Emergency Personnel* label flashed green, and the lock clanked. Donald glanced down the hall to see if anyone was watching as he pulled the door open and slipped inside.

The little-used cryochamber was a fraction of the size of the others and only one level deep. Standing inside the door, Donald could picture how the main deep freeze wrapped around this much smaller room. This was a mere bump along great walls that stretched nearly out of sight. And yet it contained something far more precious. To him, anyway.

He picked his way through the pods and peeked in at the frozen faces. It was difficult to remember being there with Thurman on his previous shift, hard to recall the exact spot, but he eventually found her. He checked the small screen and remembered thinking it didn't matter what her name was, saw that there wasn't one assigned. Just a number.

"Hey, Sis."

His fingertips sang against the glass as he rubbed the frost away. He recalled their parents with sadness. He wondered how much Charlotte knew of this place and Thurman's plans before she came here. He hoped nothing. He liked to think her less culpable than him.

Seeing her brought back memories of her visit to DC. She had wasted a precious furlough on campaigning for Thurman and seeing her brother. Charlotte had given him a hard time when she found out he'd lived in DC for two years and hadn't been to any of the museums. It didn't matter how busy he was, she'd said. It was unforgivable. "They're free," she told him, as if that were reason enough.

So they had gone to the Air and Space Museum together. Donald remembered waiting to get in. He remembered a scale model of the solar system on the sidewalk outside the museum entrance. Although the inner planets were located just a few strides apart, Pluto was blocks away, down past the Hirshhorn Museum, impossibly distant. Now, as he gazed at his sister's frozen form, that day in his memory felt the same way. Impossibly distant. A tiny dot.

Later that afternoon, she had dragged him to the Holocaust Museum. Donald had been avoiding going since moving to Washington. Maybe it was the reason he avoided the National Mall altogether. Everyone told him it was something he had to see. "You must go," they'd say. "It's important." They used words like "powerful" and "haunting." They said it would change his life. They said this—but their eyes warned him.

His sister had pulled him up the steps, his heart heavy with dread. The building had been constructed as a reminder, but Donald didn't want to be reminded. He was on his meds by then to help him forget what he was reading in the Order, to keep him from feeling as though the world might end at any moment. Such barbarisms as that building contained were buried in the past, he'd told himself, never to be unearthed or repeated.

There had been remnants of the museum's sixtieth anniversary still hanging, somber signs and banners. A new wing had been installed, cords and stakes holding up fledgling trees and the air scented with mulch. He remembered seeing a group of tourists file out, dabbing at their eyes and shielding themselves from the sun. He had wanted to turn and run, but his sister had held his hand and the man at the ticket booth had already smiled at him. At least it'd been late in the day, so they couldn't stay long.

Donald rested his hands on the coffin-like pod and remembered the visit, remembered what mulch smelled like. There had been scenes of torture and starvation. A room full of shoes beyond counting. Walls displayed images of naked bodies folded together, lifeless eyes wide open, ribs and genitals exposed, as mounds of people tumbled into a pit, into a hole scooped out of the earth. Donald couldn't bear to look at it. He had tried to focus on the bulldozer instead, to look at the man driving the machine, that serene face, a cigarette between pursed lips, a look of steady concentration. A job. There was no solace to be found anywhere in that scene. The man driving the bulldozer was the most horrific part.

Donald had shrunk away from those grisly exhibits, losing his sister in the darkness. Here was a museum of horrors never to be repeated. Mass burials performed with the opposite of ceremony, with complete apathy. People calmly marched into showers.

He had sought refuge in a new exhibit called *Architects of Death,* drawn to the blueprints, to the promise of the familiar and the ordered. He'd found instead a claustrophobic space wallpapered with schematics of slaughter. That exhibit had been no easier to stomach. There was a wall explaining the movement to deny the Holocaust, even after it had happened.

The array of blueprints had been shown as evidence. That was the purpose of the room. Blueprints that had survived the frantic burnings and purges as the Russians closed in, Himmler's signature on many of them. The layout of Auschwitz, the gas chambers, everything clearly labeled. Donald had hoped the plans would give him relief from what he saw elsewhere in the museum, but then he had learned that Jewish draftsmen had been forced to contribute. Their pens had inked in the very walls around them. They had been coerced into sketching the home of their future abuse.

Donald remembered fumbling for a bottle of pills as the small room spun around him. He remembered wondering how those people could have gone along with it, could have seen what they were drawing and not known. How could they not know, not see what it was for?

Blinking tears away, he noticed where he was standing. The pods in their neat rows were alien to him, but the walls and floor and ceiling were familiar enough. Donald had helped to design this place. It was here because of him. And when he'd tried to get out, to escape, they had brought him back screaming and kicking, a prisoner behind his own walls.

The beeping of the keypad outside chased away these disturbing thoughts. Donald turned as the great slab of steel hinged inward on pins the size of a man's arms. Dr. Wilson, the shift doctor, stepped inside. He spotted Donald and frowned. "Sir?" he called out.

Donald could feel a trickle of sweat work its way down his temple. His heart continued to race from the memory of the exhibition. He felt warm, despite being able to see his breath puff out before him.

"Did you forget about our appointment?" Dr. Wilson asked.

Donald wiped his forehead and rubbed his palm on the seat of his pants. "No, no," he said, fighting to keep the shakiness out of his voice. "I just lost track of time."

Dr. Wilson nodded. "I saw you on my monitor and figured that was it." He glanced at the pod nearest to Donald and frowned. "Someone you know?"

"Hm? No." Donald removed his hand, which had grown cold against the pod. "Someone I worked with."

"Well, are you ready?"

"Yes," Donald said. "I appreciate the refresher. It's been a while since I've gone over the protocols."

Dr. Wilson smiled. "Of course. I've got you lined up with the new reactor tech coming on to his fourth shift. We're just waiting on you." He gestured toward the hall.

Donald patted his sister's pod and smiled. She had waited hundreds of years. Another day or two wouldn't hurt. And then they would see what exactly he had helped to build. The two of them would find out together.

75

Silo 17
2313
Year Two

JIMMY COULDN'T BRING himself to write on the paper. He was drowning in paper, but he didn't dare use even the margins for notes. Those pages were sacrosanct. Those books were too valuable. And so he counted the days using the key around his neck and the black panels of the server labeled "17."

This was his silo, he had learned. It was the number stamped on the inside of his copy of the Order. It was the label on the wall chart of all the silos. He knew what this meant. He might be all alone in his world, *but his was not the only world.*

Every evening before he went to bed, he scratched another bright silver mark in the black paint of the massive server. Jimmy only marked off the days at night. It seemed premature to do it in the mornings.

The Project started sloppily. He had little confidence that the marks would amount to much and so he made them in the middle of the machine and much too large. Two months into his ordeal, he began to run out of room and realized he would need to start adding marks up above, so he had scratched through the ones he'd already made and had gone around to the other side of the server to start anew. Now he made them tiny and neat. Four ticks and then a slash through them, just like his mom used to mark the days in a row that he was good. Six of these in a line to mark what he now thought of as a month. Twelve of these rows with five left over, and he had a year.

He made the final mark in the last set and stepped back. A year took up half the side of a server. It was hard to believe a whole year had gone by, a year of living in the half-level below the servers. He knew this couldn't last. Imagining the other servers covered in scratches was too much to bear. His dad had said there was enough food for ten years for two or four people. He couldn't remember which. That meant at least twenty with him all alone. Twenty years. He stepped around the edge of the server and looked down the aisle between the rows. The massive silver door sat at the very end. At some point, he knew he would have to go out. He would go crazy if he didn't. He was already going crazy. The days were much too full of the same.

He went to the door and listened for some sound on the other side. It was quiet, as it sometimes was, but he could still hear faint bangs echo from his memory. Jimmy thought about entering the four numbers and peeking outside. It was the worst sensation imaginable, not being able to see what was on the other side. When the camera screens had stopped working, Jimmy had felt a primal sense stripped away. He was left with a strong urge to open the door, to crack an eyelid held shut for too long. A year of counting days. Of counting minutes within those days. A boy could only count so long.

He left the keypad alone. Not yet. There were bad people out there, people who wanted in, who wanted to know what was in there, why the power on the level still worked, who he was.

"I'm nobody," Jimmy told them when he had the courage to talk. "Nobody."

He didn't have that courage often. He felt brave enough just listening to the men with the other radios fight. Brave to allow their arguments to fill his world and his head, to hear them argue and report about who had killed whom. One group was working on the farms, another was trying to stop the floods from creeping out of the mines and drowning Mechanical. One had guns and took whatever little bit the others were able to squeeze together. A lone woman called once and screamed for help, but what help could Jimmy be? By his figuring, there were a hundred or more people out there in little pockets, fighting and killing. But they would stop soon. They had to. Another day. A year. They couldn't go on fighting forever, could they?

Maybe they could.

Time had become strange. It was a thing *believed* rather than seen. He had to trust that time was passing at all. There was no dimming of the stairwell and lights-out to signify the coming night. No trips to the top and the glow of sunshine to tell that it was day. There were simply numbers on a computer screen counting so slowly one could scream. Numbers that looked the same day and night. It took careful counting to know a day had passed. The counting let him know that he was alive.

Jimmy thought about playing chase between the servers before he went to bed, but he had done that yesterday. He thought about arranging cans in the order he would eat them, but he already had three months' worth of meals lined up. There was target practice, books to read, a computer to fiddle with, chores to do, but none of that sounded like fun. He knew he would probably just crawl into bed and stare at the ceiling until the numbers told him it was tomorrow. He would think about what to do then.

76

WEEKS PASSED, SCRATCHES accumulated, and the tip of the key around Jimmy's neck wore down. He woke to another morning with crust in his eyes as though he'd been crying in his sleep and took his breakfast—one can of peaches and one of pineapple—up to the great steel door to eat. Unshouldering his gun, Jimmy sat down with his back against server number eight, enjoying the warmth of the busy machine against his spine.

The gun had taken some figuring out. His father had disappeared with the loaded one, and when Jimmy discovered the crates of arms and ammo, the method of inserting the bright casings into the machine had posed a puzzle. He made the task a Project, like his father had used to make their chores and tinkering. Ever since he was little, Jimmy had watched his dad disassemble computers and other electronics, laying out all the pieces—each screw, every bolt, the nuts spun back onto the bolts—in a neat pattern so he knew where they went again. Jimmy had done the same with one of the rifles. And then with a second rifle after he'd accidentally knocked the pieces from the first with his boot.

With the second, he saw where the ammo ended up and how it got there. The spring in the ammo holder was stiff, which made it difficult to load. Later, he learned that this was called a "clip," after reading the entry for "gun" under *G* in the tins full of books. That had come weeks after he'd figured out how the thing worked on his own, with a hole in the ceiling to show for it.

He kept the gun in his lap, across his thighs, and balanced the cans of fruit on the wide part of the stock. The pineapple was his favorite. He had some every day and watched with sadness as the supply on the shelves dwindled. He'd never heard of such a fruit, had to look the thing up in another of the books. The pineapples had led him on a dizzying tour through the book tins. *Be* for "beach" had led to *Oc* for "ocean." This one confused him with its sense of scale. And then the "fish" under *F*. He had forgotten to eat that day as he explored, and the room with the radio and his little mattress had become cluttered with open books and empty tins. It had taken him a week to get things back in order. Countless times since then, he had lost himself in such excursions.

Pulling his rusty can opener and favorite fork from his breast pocket, Jimmy worked the peaches open. There was the whispering pop of air as he made the first cut. Jimmy had learned not to eat the contents if it didn't make that pop. Luckily, the toilets had still been in operation back when he'd learned that lesson. Jimmy missed the toilets something fierce.

He worked his way through the peaches, savoring each bite before drinking down the juice. He wasn't sure if you were supposed to drink that part—the label didn't say—but it was his favorite. He grabbed the pineapples and his opener, was listening for the pop of air, when he heard the keypad on the great steel door beep.

"Little early," he whispered to his visitors. He set the can aside, licked his fork, and put it back in his breast pocket. Cradling the gun against his armpit, he sat and watched for the door to move. One crack and he would open fire.

Instead, he heard four beeps from the keypad as a set of numbers was entered, followed by a buzz to signal that it was the wrong code. Jimmy tightened his grip on the gun while they tried again. The screen on the keypad only had room for four digits. That meant ten thousand combinations if you included all zeros. The door allowed three incorrect attempts before it wouldn't take any more until the following day. Jimmy had learned these things a long time ago. He felt as if his mom had taught him this rule, but that was impossible. Unless she'd done it in a dream.

He listened to the keypad beep with another guess and then buzz once again. One more number down, which meant time was running out. Twelve-eighteen was the code. Jimmy cursed himself for even thinking the number; his finger went to the trigger, waiting. But thoughts couldn't be heard. You had to speak to be heard. He tended to forget this, because he heard himself thinking all the time.

The third and final attempt for the day began, and Jimmy couldn't wait to eat his pineapples. He and these people had this routine, these three tries every morning. Though scary, it was his only daily dose of human contact, and he had come to rely on its regularity. On the server behind him, he had done the math. He assumed they had started at 0000 and were working their way up. Three a day meant they would stumble on the right code on day 406 on the second try. That was less than a month away.

But Jimmy's counting didn't figure for everything. There was the lingering fear that they might skip some numbers, that they had started somewhere else, or that they might get lucky if they were inputting the codes at random. For all Jimmy knew, more than one code could open the door. And since he didn't pay attention to how his father had changed the code, he couldn't move it higher. And what if that only got them closer? Maybe they started at 9999. He could move it lower, of course, hoping to pass one they'd already tried, but what if they hadn't tried it yet? To take action and let them in by accident would be worse than doing nothing and then dying. And Jimmy didn't want to die. He didn't want to die, and he didn't want to kill anyone.

This is how his brain whirled as the next four digits were entered. When the keypad buzzed for the third and final time that day, he relaxed his grip on the gun. Jimmy wiped his sweaty palms off on his thighs and picked up his pineapples.

"Hello, pineapples," he whispered. He bent his head toward his lap and punctured the can, listening closely.

The pineapples whispered back. They told him they were safe to eat.

77

LIFE AT ITS essence, Jimmy learned, was a series of meals and bowel movements. There was some sleep mixed in as well, but little effort was required for that. He didn't learn this great Rule of the World until the water stopped flushing. Nobody thinks about their bowel movements until the water stops flushing. And then it's all one thinks about.

Jimmy started going in the corner of the server room, as far from the door as possible. He peed in the sink until the tap ran out of water and the smell got bad. Once that happened, he tapped into the cistern. The Order told him which page to look on and what to do. It was a dreadfully boring book, but handy at times. Jimmy figured that was the point. The water in the cistern wouldn't last forever, though, so he took to drinking as much of the juice in the bottom of the cans as he could. He hated tomato soup, but he drank a can every day. His pee turned bright orange.

Jimmy was draining the last drops out of a can of apples one morning when the men came to try their codes. It happened so fast. Four numbers, and the keypad beeped. It didn't buzz. It didn't bark or scream or sound angry. It beeped. And a light long red—red for as long as Jimmy could remember—flashed brilliant and scary green.

Jimmy startled. The open can of peaches on his knee leapt

away and tumbled to the ground, juice splashing everywhere. It was two days early for this. It was two days early.

The great steel door made noises. Jimmy dropped his fork and fumbled with the gun. Safety off. A *click* with his thumb, a *thunk* from the door. Voices, voices. Excitement on one side, dread on the other. He pulled the gun against his shoulder and wished he'd practiced yesterday. Tomorrow. Tomorrow was when he was gonna get ready. They were two days too early.

The door made noises, and Jimmy wondered if he'd missed a day or two. There was the time he'd gotten sick and had a fever. There was the day he fell asleep reading and couldn't remember what day it was when he woke. Maybe he'd missed a day. Maybe the people in the hall had skipped a number. The door opened a crack.

Jimmy wasn't ready. His palms were slick on the gun, his heart racing. This was one of those things expected and expected. Expected so hard, with so much fervor and concentration, like blowing up a plastic bag over and over, watching it stretch out big and thin in front of your eyes, knowing it was about to burst, knowing, knowing, and when it comes, it scares you as if it'd never been expected at all.

This was one of those things. The door opened further. There was a person on the other side. A person. And for a moment, for the briefest of pauses, Jimmy reconsidered a year of planning, a calendar of fear. Here was someone to talk to and listen to. Someone to take a turn with the driver and hammer now that the can opener was broke. Someone with a *new* can opener, perhaps. Here was a Project Partner like his dad used to—

A face. A man with an angry sneer. A year of planning, of shooting empty tomato cans, of ringing ears and reloading, of oiling barrels and reading—and now a human face in a crack in the door.

Jimmy pulled the trigger. The barrel leapt upward. And the

angry sneer turned to something else: startlement mixed with sorrow. The man fell down, but another was pushing past him, bursting into the room, something black in his hand.

Again, the barrel leapt and leapt, and Jimmy's eyes blinked with the bangs. Three shots. Three bullets. The running man kept coming, but he had the same sad look on his face, a look fading as he fell, crumbling just a few paces away.

Jimmy waited for the next man. He heard him out there, cursing loudly. And the first man he'd shot was still moving around, like an empty can that danced and danced long after it was hit. The door was open. The outside and the inside were connected. The man who had opened the door lifted his head, something worse than sorrow on his face, and suddenly it was his father out there. His father lying just beyond the door, dying in the hallway. And Jimmy didn't know why that would be.

The cursing grew faint. The man out in the hallway was moving away, and Jimmy took his first full breath since the door had beeped and the light had turned green. He didn't have a pulse; his heart was just one long beat that wouldn't stop. A thrumming like the insides of a whirring server.

He listened to the last man slink away, and Jimmy knew he had his chance to close the door. He got up and ran around the dead man who had fallen inside the server room, a black pistol near his lifeless hand. Lowering his gun, Jimmy prepared to shoulder the door shut, when the thought of tomorrow, or that night, or the next hour occurred to him.

The retreating man now knew the number. He was taking it with him.

"Twelve-eighteen," Jimmy whispered.

He poked his head out the door for a quick look. There was a brief glimpse of a man disappearing into an office. Just a flash of green overalls, and then an empty hall, impossibly long and bright.

The dying man outside the door groaned and writhed. Jimmy ignored him. He pulled the gun against his arm and braced it like he'd practiced. The little notches lined up with each other and pointed toward the edge of the office door. Jimmy imagined a can of soup out there, hovering in the hall. He breathed and waited. The groaning man on the other side of the threshold crawled closer, bloody palms slapping a spot of floor. There was that ache in the center of his skull, an ancient scar across his memories. Jimmy aimed at the nothingness in the hallway and thought of his mother and father. Some part of him knew they were gone, that they had left somewhere and would never return. The notches dropped out of alignment as his barrel trembled.

The man by his feet drew closer. Groans had turned to a hissing. Jimmy glanced down and saw red bubbles frothing on the man's lips. His beard was fuller than Jimmy's and soaked in blood. Jimmy looked away. He watched the spot in the hallway where his rifle was trained and counted.

He was at thirty-two when he felt fingers pawing weakly at his boots.

It was on fifty-one that a head peeked out like a sneaky soup can.

Jimmy's finger squeezed. There was a kick to his shoulder and a blossom of bright red down the hall.

He waited a moment, took a deep breath, then pulled his boot away from the hand reaching up his ankle. He placed his shoulder against a door hanging dangerously open and pushed. Locks whirred and made *thunking* sounds deep within the walls. He only heard them dimly. He dropped his gun and covered his face with his palms while nearby a man lay dying in the server room. Inside the server room. Jimmy wept, and the keypad chirped happily before falling silent, patiently waiting for yet another day.

78

Silo 1
2345

A ROW OF FAMILIAR clipboards hung on the wall in Dr. Wilson's office. Donald remembered scratching his name on them with mock ceremony. He remembered signing off on himself once, authorizing his own deep freeze. There was a twinge of unease at the thought of signing those forms right then. What would he write? His hand would shake as he scribbled someone else's name.

In the middle of the office, an empty gurney brought back bad memories. A fresh sheet had been tucked military crisp on top of it, ready for the next to be put to sleep. Dr. Wilson checked his computer for the next to be woken while his two assistants prepped. One of them stirred two scoops of green powder into a container of warm water. Donald could smell the concoction across the room. It made his cheeks pucker, but he took careful note of which cabinet the powder came from, how much was spooned in, and asked any question that came to mind.

The other assistant folded a clean blanket and draped it over the back of a wheelchair. There was a paper gown. An emergency medical kit was unpacked and repacked: gloves, meds, gauze, bandages, tape. It was all done with a quiet efficiency. Donald was reminded of the men behind the serving counter who laid out breakfast with the same habitual care.

A number was read aloud to confirm who they were waking. This reactor tech, like Donald's sister, had been reduced to a number, a place within a grid, a cell in a spreadsheet. As if made-up names were any better. Suddenly, Donald saw how easily his switch could've taken place. He watched as paperwork was filled out—his signature not needed—and dropped into a box. This was a part of the process he could ignore. There would be no trace of what he had planned.

Dr. Wilson led them out the door. The assistants followed with their wheelchair full of supplies, and Donald trailed behind.

The tech they were waking was two levels down, which meant taking the lift. One of the assistants idly remarked that he had only three days left on his shift.

"Lucky you," the other assistant said.

"Yeah, so be easy with my catheter," he joked, and even Dr. Wilson laughed.

Donald didn't. He was busy wondering what the *final* shift would be like. Nobody seemed to think much past the next shift. They looked forward to one ending and dreaded seeing another. It reminded him of Washington, where everyone he worked alongside hoped to make it to the next term even as they loathed running for another. Donald had fallen into that same trap.

The lift doors opened on another chilled hall. Here were rooms full of shift workers, the majority of the silo's population-in-waiting spread out across two identical levels. Dr. Wilson led them down the hall and coded them through the third door on the right. A hall of sleeping bodies angled off into the distance until it met the concrete skin of the silo. “Twenty down and four over,” he said, pointing.

They made their way to the pod. It was the first time Donald had seen this part of the procedure. He had helped put others under, but had never helped wake anyone up. Storing Victor’s body away was something altogether different. That had been a funeral.

The assistants busied themselves around the pod. Dr. Wilson knelt by the control panel, paused, glanced up at Donald, waiting.

“Right,” Donald said. He knelt and watched over the doctor’s shoulder.

“Most of the process is automated,” the doctor admitted sheepishly. “Frankly, they could replace me with a trained monkey and nobody would know the difference.” He glanced back at Donald as he keyed in his code and pressed a red button. “I’m like you, Shepherd. Only here in case something goes wrong.”

The doctor smiled. Donald didn’t.

“It’ll be a few minutes before the hatch pops.” He tapped the display. “The temperature here will get up to thirty-one Celsius. The bloodstream is getting an injection when this light is flashing.”

The light was flashing.

“An injection of what?” Donald asked.

“Nanos. The freezing procedure would kill a normal human being, which I suppose is why it was outlawed.”

A normal human being. Donald wondered what the hell that made him. He lifted his palm and studied the red splotchiness. He remembered a glove tumbling down a hill.

“Twenty-eight,” Dr. Wilson said. “When it hits thirty, the lid will release. Now’s when I like to go ahead and reset the dial, rather than wait until the end. Just so I don’t forget.” He twisted the dial below the temp readout. "It doesn't stop the process. It only runs one direction once it starts."

"What if something goes wrong?" Donald asked.

Dr. Wilson frowned. "I told you. That's why I'm here."

"But what if something happened to you? Or you got called away?"

The doctor tugged his earlobe, thinking. "I would advise putting them back under until I could get to them." He laughed. "Of course, the nanos might just fix what's wrong before I could. As long as you dial the temp back down, all you have to do is close the lid. But I don't see how that could come up."

Donald did. He watched the temperature tick up to twenty-nine. The two assistants prepped while they waited for the pod to open. One had a towel set aside along with the blanket and the paper gown. The medical kit sat in the wheelchair, the top open. Both men wore blue rubber gloves. One of them peeled off a strip of tape and hung it from the handle of the wheelchair. A packet of gauze was pre-emptively torn open, the bitter drink given a vigorous shake.

"And my code will start the procedure?" Donald asked, thinking of anything he might be missing.

Dr. Wilson chuckled. He placed his hands on his knees and was slow to stand. "I imagine your code would open the airlock. Is there anything you don't have access to?"

A glove was snapped. The hatch hissed as the lock disengaged.

The truth, Donald wanted to say. But he was planning on getting it soon enough.

The lid popped opened a crack, and one of the assistants lifted it the rest of the way. A handsome young man lay inside, his cheeks twitching as he came to. The assistants went to work, and Donald tried to make note of every little part of the procedure. He thought of his sister in a hall above him, lying asleep, waiting.

"Once we get him up to the office," said Dr. Wilson, "we'll check his vitals and take our samples for analysis. If they have any items in their locker, I send one of the boys to retrieve them."

"Locker?" Donald watched as a catheter was removed, a needle extracted from an arm. The tape and gauze were applied while the man in the pod sucked from a straw, wincing from the bitterness as he did so.

"Personal effects. Anything set aside from their previous shift. We retrieve those for them."

The assistants helped the man into the paper gown, then grunted as they lifted him from the steaming pod. Donald moved the medical kit and steadied the wheelchair for them. The blanket was already laid out across the seat. While they settled the man into place, Donald thought of the bag marked *Shift* left on his bed, the one with Thurman's personal effects in them. There had been a small number marked on the bag similar to the one in Anna's note. That number in the note wasn't a date at all.

And then it hit him. *Locket* was a typo. He tried to picture where the R and T were on a keyboard, if this was a likely mistake. Had she meant to say *locker* instead?

The confluence of clues cut through the chill in the room, and for a moment, the idea of waking his sister was forgotten. Other sleeping ghosts were whispering to him, clouding his mind.

79

DONALD HELPED ESCORT the groggy man up to the medical offices while one of the assistants stayed behind to scrub the pod. Not caring to see Dr. Wilson take his samples, Donald volunteered to go and grab the tech's personal items. The assistant gave him directions to one of the storage levels in the heart of the silo.

There were sixteen levels of stores in all, not counting the armory. Donald entered the lift and pressed the worn-out button for the storeroom on fifty-seven. The reactor tech's ID number had been scribbled on a piece of paper. The number from Anna's note to Thurman was vivid in his mind. He had assumed it was a date: November 2nd, 2039. It made the number easy to recall.

The lift slowed to a stop, and Donald stepped through the doors and into darkness. He ran his hand down the bank of light switches along the wall. The bulbs overhead sparked to life with the distant and muted *thunks* of ancient transformers and relays jolting into action. A maze of tall shelves revealed itself in stages as the lights popped on first in the distance, then close, then off to the right, like some mosaic unmasked one random piece at a time. The lockers were in the very back, past the shelves. Donald began the long walk while the last of the bulbs flickered on.

Cliffs of steel shelves laden with sealed plastic tubs swallowed him. The containers seemed to lean in over his head. If he glanced up, he almost expected the shelves to touch high above, to meet like train tracks. Huge swathes of tubs were empty and unlabeled, he saw, waiting for future shifts to fill them. All the notes he and Anna had generated on his last shift would be in tubs like these. They would preserve the tale of Silo 40 and all those unfortunate facilities around them. They would tell of the people of Silo 18 and Donald's efforts to save them. And maybe he shouldn't have. What if this current debacle, this vagabond cleaner, was his fault in some way?

He passed crates sorted by date, by silo, by name. There were cross-cuts between the shelves, narrow aisles wide enough for the carts used to haul blank paper and notebooks out and then bring them back in weighing just a little more from the ink. With relief from his claustrophobia, Donald left the shelves and found the far wall of the facility. He glanced back over his shoulder at how far he'd come, could imagine all the lights going out at once and him not being able to pick his way back to the lift. Maybe he would stagger in circles until he died of thirst. He glanced up at the lights and realized how fragile he was, how reliant on power and light. A familiar wave of fear washed over him, the panic of being buried in the dark. Donald leaned against one of the lockers for a moment and caught his breath. He coughed into his handkerchief and reminded himself that dying wouldn't be the worst of things.

Once the panic faded and he'd fought off the urge to sprint back to the lift, he entered the rows of lockers. There must've been thousands of them. Many were small, like post office boxes, six or so inches to a side and probably as deep as his arm judging by the width of the units. He mumbled the number from Anna's note to himself. Erskine's would be down here as well, and Victor's. He wondered if those men had any secrets squirreled away and reminded himself to come back and check.

The numbers on the lockers ascended as he walked down one of the rows. The first two digits were far from Anna's number. He turned down one of the connecting aisles to search for the correct row and saw a group that started with 43. His ID number started with 44. Perhaps his locker was near here.

Donald imagined it would be empty, even as he found himself honing in on his ID number. He had never carried anything from shift to shift. The numbers marched in a predictable series until he found himself standing before a small metal door with his ID number on it, Troy's ID number. There was no latch, only a button. He pressed it with his knuckle, worried it might have a fingerprint scanner or something equally deserving of his paranoia. What would someone think if they saw Thurman looking in this man's locker? It was easy to forget the ruse. It was similar to the delay between hearing the Senator's name and realizing Donald was the one being spoken to.

There was a soft sigh as the locker cracked open, followed by the squeak of old and unused hinges. The sigh reminded Donald that everything down there—the bins and tubs and lockers—was protected from the air. The good, normal air. Even the air they breathed was caustic and full of invisible things, like corrosive oxygen and other hungry molecules. The only difference between the good air and the bad air was the speed at which they worked. People lived and died too quickly to see the difference.

At least they used to, Donald thought as he reached inside his locker.

Surprisingly, it wasn't empty. There was a plastic bag inside, crinkled and vacuum-packed like Thurman's. Only this bag read

Legacy across the top rather than *Shift*. Inside, he could see a familiar pair of tan slacks and a red shirt. The clothes hammered him with memories. They reminded him of a man he used to be, a world he used to live in. Donald squeezed the bag, which was dense from the absence of air, and glanced up and down the empty aisle.

Why would they keep these things? Was it so he could emerge from deep underground dressed just as he had been when he arrived? Like an inmate staggering out, blinking and shielding his eyes, dressed in outdated fashion? Or was it because storage was the same thing as disposal? There were two entire levels above this one where unrecyclable trash was compacted into cubes as dense as iron and stacked to the ceiling. Where else were they supposed to put their garbage? In a hole in the ground? They lived in a hole in the ground.

Donald puzzled over this as he fumbled with the plastic zipper at the top and slid the bag open. A faint odor of mud and grass escaped, a whiff of bygone days. He opened the bag further, and his clothes blossomed to life as air seeped inside. There was an impulse to change into his old clothes, to pretend that his world wasn't gone. Instead, he decided to shove the bag back into the locker—and then a glimmer caught his eye, a flash of yellow.

Donald dug down past his clothes and reached for the wedding ring. As he was pulling it out, he felt a hard object inside the slacks. He palmed the ring and reached inside again, felt around, squeezed the folds of his clothes. What had he been carrying that day? Not his pills. He'd lost those in a fall. Not the keys to the ATV, Anna had taken those from him. His own keys and wallet had been in his jacket, had never even made it beneath the earth to orientation—

His phone. Donald found it in the pocket of his slacks. The heft of the thing, the curve of the plastic shell, felt right at home in his hand. He returned the bag to the locker, tucked the wedding ring into the pocket of his overalls, and pressed the power button on the old phone. But of course it was dead. Long dead. It hadn't even been working properly the day he'd lost Helen.

Donald placed the phone in his pocket out of habit, the sort of habit that time could not touch. He felt the ring in his pocket and pulled it out, made sure it still fitted, and thought of his wife. Thoughts of Helen led to thoughts of Mick and her having children together. Sadness and sickness intermingled. He stuffed his clothes deep into the locker and shut the door, took the ring off and slipped it into his pocket with the old phone. Donald turned and headed off in search of Anna's locker. He still had to get the tech's personal items as well.

As he tracked down their lockers, something nagged at him, some connection, but he couldn't work out what.

Off to one side, there was a patch of the storeroom still in darkness, a light bulb out, and Donald thought of Silo 40 and the spread of darkness on a previous shift. Eren had brought an end to whatever was going on over there. A bomb had caused dust to shiver from overhead pipes. And now his deep mind whirred and made deeper connections. Something about Anna. Some reason he'd been drawn to his locker. He wrapped his hand around the phone in his pocket and remembered why she'd been woken the last time. He remembered her expertise with wireless systems, with hacking.

In the distance, a light went out with a pop, and Donald felt the darkness closing in on him. There was nothing down here for him, nothing but awful memories and horrible realizations. His heart pounded as it began to come together, a thing he dearly wanted to disbelieve. His phone hadn't worked properly the day the bombs fell; he hadn't been able to contact Helen. And then there were all the times before when he couldn't reach Mick, the nights he and Anna had found themselves alone.

And now they'd been left alone again, in this silo. Mick had changed places with him at the last moment. Donald remembered a conversation in a small apartment. Mick had given him a tour, had taken him down into a room and said to remember him down there, that this was what he wanted.

Donald slapped one of the lockers with his palm, the loud bang drowning out his curse. This should've been Mick over here, freezing and thawing, going steadily mad. Instead, Mick had stolen the domestic life he often teased Donald for living. And he'd had help doing it.

Donald sagged against the lockers. He reached for his handkerchief, coughed into it, imagined his friend consoling Helen. He thought of the kids and grandkids they'd had together. A murderous rage boiled up. All this time, blaming himself for not getting to Helen. All this time, blaming Helen and Mick for the life he'd missed out on. And it was Anna, the engineer. Anna who had hacked his life. She had done this to him. She had brought him here.

80

DONALD RETRIEVED THE items from the other two lockers as if in a dream. Numb, he rode the lift back down to Dr. Wilson's office and dropped off the reactor tech's personal effects. He asked Dr. Wilson for something to help him sleep that night and paid careful attention to where the pills came from. When Wilson left for the lab with his samples, Donald helped himself to more of the pills. Crushing them up, he added two scoops of the powder and made a bitter drink. He had no plan. His actions followed robotically one after the other. There was a cruelness in his life that he wished to end.

Down to the deep freeze. Pushing a loaded-up wheelchair ahead of him, he found her pod effortlessly. Donald traced a finger down the skin of the machine. He touched its smooth surface warily, as if it might cut him. He remembered touching her body like this, always afraid, never quite able to give in or let go. The better it felt, the more it hurt. Each caress had been an affront to Helen.

He pulled his finger back and held it in his other hand to stop some imaginary bleeding. There was danger in being near her. Anna's nakedness was on the other side of that armored shell, and he was about to open it. He glanced around the vast halls of the deep freeze. Crowded, and yet all alone. Dr. Wilson would be in his lab for some while.

Donald knelt by the end of the pod and entered his keycode. Some small part of him hoped it wouldn't work. This was too great a power, the ability to give a life or take it. But the panel beeped. Donald steadied his hand and turned the dial just as he'd been shown.

The rest was waiting. Temperatures rose, and his anger faded. Donald retrieved the drink and gave it a stir. He made sure everything else was in place.

When the lid sighed open, Donald slid his fingers into the crack and lifted it the rest of the way. He reached inside and carefully removed the tubing from the needle in Anna's arm. A thick fluid leaked out of the needle. He saw how the plastic valve on the end worked and turned it until the dripping stopped. Unfolding a blanket from the back of the wheelchair, he tucked it around her. Her body was already warm. Frost dripped down the inner surface of the pod and collected in little channels that served as gutters. The blanket, he realized, was mostly for him.

Anna stirred. Donald brushed the hair off her forehead as her eyes fluttered. Her lips parted, and she let out a soft groan filled with decades of sleep. Donald knew what that stiffness felt like, that deep cold frozen in one's joints. He hated doing this to her. He hated what had been done to him.

"Easy," he said as she began to grope the air with shivering limbs. Her head lolled feebly from side to side, murmuring something. Donald helped her into a sitting position and rearranged the blanket to keep her covered. The wheelchair sat quietly beside him with a medical bag and a thermos. Donald made no move to lift her out and help her into the chair.

Blinking and darting eyes finally settled on Donald. They narrowed in recognition.

"Donny—"

He read his name on her lips as much as heard her.

"You came for me," she whispered.

Donald watched as she trembled; he fought the urge to rub her back or wrap her in his arms.

"What year?" she asked, licking her lips. "Is it time?" Her eyes were now wide and wet with fear. Melting frost slid down her cheeks.

Donald remembered waking like this with his most recent dreams still clouding his thoughts. "It's time for the truth," he said. "You're the reason I'm here, aren't you?"

Anna stared at him blankly, her mind in a fog. He could see it in the twitch of her eyes, the way her dry lips remained parted, the processing delay he knew well from the times they'd done this to him, from the times they had woken him.

"Yes." She nodded ever so slightly. "Father was never going to wake us. The deep freeze—" Her voice was a whisper. "I'm glad you came. I knew you would."

A hand escaped from the blanket and gripped the edge of the pod as if to pull herself out. Donald placed a hand on her shoulder. He turned and grabbed the thermos from the wheelchair. Peeling her hand from the lip of the pod, he pressed the drink into her palm. She wiggled her other arm free and held the thermos against her knees.

"I want to know why," he said. "Why did you bring me *here*? To this place." He looked around at the pods, these unnatural graves that kept death at bay.

Anna gazed at him. She studied the thermos and the straw. Donald let go of her arm and reached into his pocket. He pulled out the phone. Anna shifted her attention to that.

"What did you do that day?" he asked. "You kept me from her, didn't you? And the night we met to finalize the plans—all the times Mick missed a meeting—that was you as well."

A shadow slid across Anna's face. Something deep and dark registered. Donald had expected a harsh defiance, steel resolve, denials. Anna looked sad instead.

"So long ago," she said, shaking her head. "I'm sorry, Donny, but it was so long ago." Her eyes flitted beyond him toward the door as if she were expecting danger. Donald glanced back over his shoulder and saw nothing. "We have to get out of here," she croaked, her voice feeble and distant. "Donny, my father, they made a pact—"

"I want to know what you did," he said. "Tell me."

She shook her head. "What Mick and I did—Donny, it seemed like the right thing at the time. I'm sorry. But I need to tell you something else. Something more important." Her voice was small and quiet. She licked her lips and glanced at the straw, but Donald kept a hand on her arm. "Dad woke me for another shift while you were in the deep freeze." She lifted her head and fixed her eyes on him. Her teeth chattered together while she collected her thoughts. "And I found something—"

"Stop," Donald said. "No more stories. No lies. Just the truth."

Anna looked away. A spasm surged through her body, a great shiver. Steam rose from her hair, and condensation raced down the skin of the pod in sudden bursts of speed.

"It was meant to be this way," she said. The admission was in the way she said it, her refusal to look at him. "It was meant to be. You and me together. We built this."

Donald seethed with renewed rage. His hands trembled more than hers.

Anna leaned forward. "I couldn't stand the thought of you dying over there, alone."

"I wouldn't have been alone," he hissed through clenched teeth. "And you don't get to decide such things." He gripped the edge of the pod with both hands and squeezed until his knuckles turned white.

"You need to hear what I have to say," Anna said.

Donald waited. What explanation or apology was there? She had taken from him what little her father had left behind. Thurman had destroyed the world, and Anna had destroyed Donald's. He waited to hear what she had to say.

"My father made a pact," she said, her voice gaining strength. "We were never to be woken. We need to get out of here. I need your help—"

This again. She didn't care that she had destroyed him. Donald felt his rage subside. It dissipated throughout his body, a part of him, a powerful surge that came and went like an ocean wave, not strong enough to hold itself up, crashing down with a hiss and a sigh.

"Drink," he told her, lifting her arm gently. "Then you can tell me. You can tell me how I can help you."

Anna blinked. Donald reached for the straw and steered it to her lips. Lips that would tell him anything, keep him confused, use him so that she might feel less hollow, less alone. He had heard enough of her lies, her brand of poison. To give her an ear was to give her a vein.

Anna's lips closed around the straw, and her cheeks dented as she sucked. A column of foul green surged up the straw.

"So bitter," she whispered after her first swallow.

"Shhh," Donald told her. "Drink. You need this."

She did, and Donald held the thermos for her. Anna paused between sips to tell him they needed to get out of there, that it wasn't safe. He agreed and guided the straw back to her lips. The danger was her.

There was still some of the drink left when she gazed up at him, confused. "Why am I . . . feeling sleepy?" she asked. Anna blinked slowly, fighting to keep her eyes open.

"You shouldn't have brought me here," Donald said. "We weren't meant to live like this."

Anna lifted an arm, reached out and seized Donald's shoulder. Awareness seemed to grip her. Donald sat on the edge of the pod and put an arm around her. As she slumped against him, he flashed back to the night of their first kiss. Back in college, her with too much to drink, falling asleep on his frat house sofa, her head on his shoulder. And Donald had stayed like that for the rest of the night, his arm trapped and growing numb while a party thrummed and finally faded. They had woken the next morning, Anna stirring before he did. She had smiled and thanked him, called him her guardian angel and had given him a kiss.

That seemed several ages ago. Eons. Lives weren't supposed to drag on so long. But Donald remembered as if it were yesterday the sound of Anna breathing that night. He remembered from their last shift, sharing a cot, her head on his chest as she slept. And then he heard her, right then in that moment as she took in one last, sudden, trembling lungful. A gasp. Her body stiffened for a pause, and then cold and trembling fingernails sank into his shoulder. And Donald held her as that grip slowly relaxed, as Anna Thurman breathed her very last.

81

Silo 17
2318
Year Seven

SOMETHING BAD WAS happening with the cans. Jimmy couldn't be sure at first. He had noticed little brown spots on a can of beets months ago and hadn't thought anything of it. Now, more and more cans were covered with them. And some of the contents tasted a little different too. That part may have been his imagination, but he was for sure getting sick to his stomach more often, which was making the server room smell awful. He didn't like going anywhere near the poop corner—the flies were getting bad over there—which meant defecating further and further out. Eventually he would be going everywhere, and the flies didn't carry away his waste as fast as he made it.

He knew he needed to get out. He hadn't heard any activity in the halls of late, no one trying the door. But the room that had once felt like a prison now felt like the only safe place to be. And the idea of leaving, once desirable, now turned his insides to water. The routines were all he knew. Doing something different seemed insane.

He put it off for two days by making a Project out of preparing.

He took his favorite rifle apart and oiled all the pieces before putting it back together. There was a box of lucky ammo where very few had failed or jammed during games of Kick the Can, so he emptied two clips and filled them with only these magic bullets. A spare set of overalls was turned into a backpack by knotting the arms to the legs for loops and cinching up the neck. The zipper down the front made for a nice enclosure. He filled this with two cans of sausage, two of pineapple and two of tomato juice. He didn't think he'd be gone that long, but he couldn't know.

Patting his chest, he made sure he had his key around his neck. It never came off, but he habitually patted his chest anyway to make sure it was there. A purple bruise on his sternum hinted that he did this too often. He placed a fork and a rusty driver in his breast pocket, the latter for jabbing open the cans. Jimmy really needed to find a can opener. That and batteries for his flashlight were the highest of priorities. The power had only gone out twice over the years, but both times had left him terrified of the dark. And checking to make sure his flashlight worked all the time tended to wear down the batteries.

Scratching his beard, he thought of what else he would need. He didn't have much water left in the cistern, but maybe he'd find some out there, so he threw in two empty bottles from years prior. These took some digging. He had to rummage behind the hill of empty cans in one corner of the storeroom, the flies pestering him and yelling at him to leave them alone.

"I see you, I see you," he told them. "Buzz off."

Jimmy laughed at his own joke.

In the kitchen, he grabbed the large knife, the one he hadn't broken the tip off, and put that in his pack as well. By the time he worked up his nerve to leave on the second day, he decided it was too late to get started. So he took his gun apart and oiled it up one more time and promised himself that he would leave in the morning.

Jimmy didn't sleep well that night. He left the radio on in case there was any chatter, and the hissing made him dream of the air from the outside leaking in through the great steel door. He woke up more than once gasping for a breath and found it difficult to get back to sleep.

In the morning, he checked the cameras, but they were still not working. He wished he had the one of the hallway. All it showed was black. He told himself there was no one there. But soon he would be. He was about to go outside. *Outside.*

"It's okay," he told himself. He grabbed his rifle, which reeked of oil, and lifted his homemade pack, which he thought suddenly he could wear as clothes in a pinch, if he had to. He laughed some more and headed for the ladder.

"C'mon, c'mon," he said, urging himself as he climbed up. He tried to whistle, was normally a very good whistler, but his mouth was too dry. He hummed a tune his parents had used to sing to him instead.

The pack and the gun were heavy. Dangling from the crook of his elbow, they made it difficult to unlock the hatch at the top of the ladder. But he finally managed. He stuck his head out and paused to admire the gentle hum of the machines. Some of them made little clicking sounds as if their innards were busy. He'd taken most of the backs off over the years to peer inside and see if any contained secrets, but they all looked like the guts of the computers his dad used to build.

The stench of his own waste greeted him as he moved between the tall towers. That wasn't how you were supposed to greet someone, he thought. The black boxes radiated an awful heat, which only made the smell worse.

He stood in front of the great steel door and hesitated. Jimmy's world had been shrinking every day. First he had been comfortable on these two levels, the room with the black machines and the labyrinth beneath. And then he'd only been comfortable below. And then even the dark passageway and the tall ladder had frightened him. And soon, he had limited himself to the back room with all the beds and the storerooms with their funny smells, until the only place he felt safe was on his makeshift cot by the computer desk, the sound of the radio crackling in the background.

And now he stood before that door his father had dragged him through, the place where he'd killed three men, and he thought about his world expanding.

His palms were damp as he reached for the keypad. A part of him feared the air outside would be toxic, but he was probably breathing the same air, and people had lived for years out there, talking now and then on the radio. He keyed in the first two digits, level twelve, then thought about the next two. Eighteen. Jimmy imagined going home and getting some different clothes, using the bathroom in a toilet. He pictured his mother sitting on his parents' bed, waiting for him. He saw her lying on her back, arms crossed, nothing but bones.

His hand trembled as he reached for the 1 and hit the 4 instead. He wiped his hands on his thighs and waited for the keypad to time out with a buzz. "There's no one on the other side," he told himself. "No one. I'm alone. I'm alone."

Somehow, this comforted him.

He entered the two digits again for school, and then the digits of his home.

The keypad beeped. The door began to make noises. And Jimmy Parker took a step back. He thought of school and his friends, wondered if any of them were still alive. If *anyone* was still alive. He hooked his finger under the strap of his rifle and pulled it over his head, tucked it against his shoulder. The door clanked free. All he had to do was pull.

82

THERE WERE SIGNS of life and death waiting for him in the hall. A charred ring on the tile and a scatter of ash marked the corpse of an old fire. The outside of the steel door was lined with scratches and marked with dents. The latter reminded him of his misses during Kick the Can, the ineffectual kiss of bullet against solid steel. Right by his feet, Jimmy noticed a stain on the floor—a patch of dappled brown—and remembered a man dying there. Jimmy looked away from these signs of the living and the dying and stepped into the hall.

As he began to pull the door shut, something made him hesitate. Jimmy wondered if perhaps his code wouldn't work from the outside. What if the door locked and he could never get back in? He checked the keypad and saw the gouges around its steel plate where someone had tried to prise it off the wall. He was reminded how desperately so many others had wanted in over the years. Remembering this made him feel crazy for wanting out.

Before he could worry further, he shut the steel door and his heart sank a little as the gears whirred and the locks slid into the wall. There was a hollow *thunk,* the sound of awful finality.

Jimmy rushed to the keypad, his chest pounding in his throat, the feeling of men running down all three hallways to get him, blood-curdling screams and bludgeoning weapons held high over their heads—

He entered the code, and the door whirred open. Pushing on the handle, he took a few deep breaths of home . . . and nearly gagged on the smell of his own waste warmed by the hot servers.

There was no one running down the halls. He needed a new can opener. He needed to find a toilet that worked. He needed overalls that weren't worn to tatters. He needed to breathe and find another stash of canned food and water.

Jimmy reluctantly closed the door again. And even though he had just tested the keypad, the fear that he would never get back inside returned. The gears would be worn out. The code would only work from the outside once per day, once per year. A part of him knew—the obsessive part of him knew—that he could check the code a hundred times and still worry it wouldn't work the very next. He could check forever and never be satisfied. His pulse pounded in his ears as he tore himself from the door.

The hallway was brightly lit. Jimmy kept his rifle against his arm and slid silently past ransacked offices. Everything was quiet except for the buzzing of one light fixture on its last leg and the flutter of a piece of paper on a desk beneath a blowing vent. The security station was unmanned. Jimmy crawled over the gate, remembering Yani, imagining the stairwell outside crowded with people, a man in a cleaning suit barging out and wading into the masses, but when he opened the door and peered outside, the landing was empty.

It was also dim. Only the green emergency lights were on. Jimmy shut the door slowly so that the rusty hinges would groan rather than squeal. There was an object on the grating by his feet. Jimmy nudged it with his boot, a white cylinder the length of his forearm with knobby ends. A bone. He recognized it from the jumble of a man who had wasted away by the servers, dragged close to his piles of shit.

Jimmy felt with keen surety that his own bones would be exposed someday. Perhaps this day. He would never make it back inside his sturdy little home beneath the servers. And this frightened him less than it should have. The heady rush of being out in the open, the cool air and the green glow of the stairwell, even the remnants of another human being, were a sudden and welcome relief from the claustrophobia of being imprisoned. What had once been his pen—the floors and levels of the silo—was now the great outside. Here was a land of infinite death and of hopeful opportunity.

83

HE HAD NO great plan, no real direction, but the tug was upward. His flashlight was running out of juice, so he knew to explore the levels cautiously. Groping in an apartment, he fumbled for a toilet, relieved himself the way God intended, and was disheartened by the lack of a flush. The sink didn't run either. Neither did the wash nozzle beside the toilet, which left him using a bedsheet in perfect darkness.

He started up. There was a general store on nineteen, just below his home. He would check there for batteries, though he feared most useful things would have been consumed by now. The garment district would have overalls, though. He felt sure of that. A plan was forming.

Until a vibration in the steps altered it.

Jimmy stopped and listened to the clang of footsteps. They were coming from above. He could see the next landing jutting off overhead, one turn around the central post. It was nearer than the landing below. So he ran, rifle clattering against the jugs tied to his makeshift backpack, boots clomping awkwardly on the treads, both fearful and relieved not to be alone.

He yanked the doors open on the next landing and pulled them to, leaving a small crack. Pressing his cheek against the door, he peered through the gap, listening. The clanging grew louder and louder. Jimmy held his breath. A figure flew by, hand squeaking along the railing, and then another figure close behind, shouting threats. Both were little more than blurs. He remained in the darkness at the end of a strange and silent hall until the noise faded and he could feel things creeping across the tile toward him, hands with claws reaching through the inky black to tangle up in his wild and long hair, and Jimmy found himself back on the landing in the dull green glow of emergency lights, panting and not knowing what to believe.

He was alone, one way or the other. Even if people survived around him, the only company one found was the kind that chased you or killed you.

Upward again, listening more closely for footfalls, keeping a hand on the rail for a vibration, he spiraled his way past the water plant on thirty-two, the dirt farm on thirty-one, past sanitation on twenty-six, keeping to the green light and aiming for the general store. The muscles in his legs grew warm from the use, but in a good way. He passed familiar landmarks, levels from another life with an accumulation of wear and a tangle of wires and pipes. The world had grown as rusty as his memory of it.

He arrived at the general store to find it mostly bare, except for the remains of someone trapped under a spilled stand of shelves. The boots sticking out were small, a woman's or a child's. White ankle bones spanned the gap between boot and cuff. There were goods trapped underneath the shelf alongside the person, but Jimmy felt no urge to investigate. He searched the scattering of items on the other shelves for batteries or a can opener. There were toys and trinkets and useless things. Jimmy sensed that many a shadow had fallen over those goods. He saved his flashlight by sneaking out in the darkness.

Searching his old apartment wasn't worth the juice either. It no longer felt like home. There was a sadness inside that he couldn't name, a sense that he had failed his parents, an old ache in the center of his mind like he used to get from sucking on ice. Jimmy left the apartment and continued up. Something still called to him from above. And it wasn't until he got within half a spiral from the schoolhouse that he knew what it was. The distant past was reaching out to him. The day it all began. His classroom, where he could last remember seeing his mother, where his friends still sat in his disordered mind, where if he remained, if he could just go back and sit at his desk and unwind events once more, they would have to come out differently.

84

Jimmy kept his flashlight powered up as he made his way to the classroom. There was no going back, he quickly saw. There, in the middle of the room, lay his old backpack. Several of the desks were askew, the neat rows snapped like broken bones, and Jimmy could see in his mind his friends rushing out, could see the paths they took, could watch them spill toward the door. They had taken their bags with them. Jimmy's remained and lay still as a corpse.

A step inside, the room aglow from his flashlight, he felt Mrs. Pearson look up from a book, smile and say nothing. Barbara sat at her desk, right by the door. Jimmy remembered her hand in his during a class trip to the livestock pens. It was on the way back, after the strange smells of so many animals, hands reaching through bars to stroke fur and feather and fat, hairless pigs. Jimmy had been fourteen, and something about the animals had excited or changed him. So that when Barbara hung back at the end of the corkscrew of classmates making their way up the staircase and had reached for his hand, he hadn't pulled back.

That prolonged touch was a taste of what-might-have-been with another. He brushed the surface of Barbara's desk with his fingertips and left tracks through the dust. Paul's desk—his best friend's—was one of those that had been disturbed. He stepped through the gap it left, seeing everyone leaving at once, his mother giving him a head start, until he stood in the center of the room, by his bag, completely alone.

"I am all alone," he said. "I am solitude."

His lips were dry and stuck together. They tore apart when he spoke as if opened for the very first time.

Approaching his bag, he noticed that it had been gutted. He knelt down and tossed open the flap. There was a scrap of plastic that his mom had used and reused to wrap his lunch, but his lunch was long gone. Two cornbars and an oatmeal brownie. Amazing how he remembered some things and not others.

He dug deeper, wondering if they'd taken much else. The calculator his father had built from scratch was still in there, as were the glass figurine soldiers his uncle had given him on his thirteenth birthday. He took the time to transfer everything from his makeshift bag to his old backpack. The zipper was stiff, but it still worked. He studied the knotted coveralls and decided they were in worse shape than the ones he had on, so he left them.

Jimmy stood and surveyed the room, sweeping his flashlight across the chaos. On the blackboard, he saw someone had left their mark. He played the light across the scene and saw the word *fuck* written over and over. It looked like a string of letters like that, *fuckfuckfuckfuck*.

Jimmy found the erasing rag behind Mrs. Pearson's desk. It was stiff and crusty, but the words still came off. Left behind was a smear, and Jimmy remembered the happy days of writing on the board in front of the class. He remembered writing assignments. Mrs. Pearson complimented him on his poetry once, probably just to be nice. Licking his lips, he fished a nub of old chalk from the tray and thought of something to write. There were no nerves from standing before the class. No one was watching. He was well and truly all alone.

I am Jimmy, he wrote on the board, the flashlight casting a strange halo, a ring of dim light, as he wrote. The nub of chalk clicked and clacked as he made each stroke. It squeaked and groaned between the clicks. The noise was like company, and yet he wrote a poem of being alone, a mechanical act from bygone days:

The ghosts are watching. The ghosts are watching. They watch
me stroll alone.
The corpses are laughing. The corpses are laughing. They go
quiet when I step over them.
My parents are missing. My parents are missing. They are
waiting for me to come home.

He wasn't sure about that last line. Jimmy ran the light across what he'd written, which he didn't think was very good. More wouldn't make it better, but he wrote more, anyway.

The silo is empty. The silo is empty. It's full of death from pit
to rim.
My name was Jimmy, my name was Jimmy. But nobody calls
me any longer.
I am alone, the ghosts are watching, and solitude makes me
stronger.

The last part was a lie, he knew, but it was poetry, so it didn't count. Jimmy stepped away from the board and studied the words with his flickering flashlight. The words trailed off to the side and dipped down, each line sagging more than the last, the letters getting smaller toward the end of each sentence. It was a problem he always had with the blackboard. He started big and seemed to shrink as he went. Scratching the beard on his chin, he wondered what this said of him, what it portended.

There was a lot wrong with what he'd written, he thought. The fifth line was untrue, the one about nobody calling him Jimmy. Above the poem, he had written *I am Jimmy.* He still thought of himself as Jimmy.

He grabbed the stiff rag he'd left in the chalk tray, stood before his poem, and went to erase the line that wasn't right. But something stopped him. It was the fear of making the poem worse by attempting to fix it, the fear of taking a line away and having nothing good to put in its place. This was his voice, and it was too rare a thing to quash.

Jimmy felt Mrs. Pearson's eyes upon him. He felt the eyes of his classmates. The ghosts were watching, the corpses laughing, while he studied the problem on the board.

When the solution came, it brought a familiar thrill of arriving at the right place, of connecting the dots. Jimmy reached up and slapped the dusty rag against the board and erased the first thing he'd written. The words *I am Jimmy* disappeared into a white smear and a tumbling haze of powder. He set the rag aside and began to write a truth in its place.

I am Solitude, he started to write. He liked the sound of that. It sounded poetic and full of meaning. But like poetry was wont to do, the words had a mind of their own; his deep thoughts intervened, and so he wrote something different. He shortened it to two little neat circles, a swerve, and a slash. Grabbing his bag, he left the room and his old friends behind. All that remained was a poem and the call to be remembered, a mark to prove he'd been there.

I am Solo.

And a haze of chalk fell through the air like the ghost of unwritten words.

85

Silo 1
2345

DONALD STEERED THE empty wheelchair back to Dr. Wilson's office. A damp blanket was draped over the armrests and dragged across the tile. He felt numb. His dream that morning had been to give life, not take it. The permanence of what he'd done began to set in, and Donald found it difficult to swallow, to breathe. He stopped in the hallway and took stock of what he'd become. Unknowing architect. Prisoner. Puppet. Hangman. He wore a different man's clothes. His transformation horrified him. Tears welled up in his eyes, and he wiped them away angrily. All it took was thinking of Helen and Mick, of the life taken from him. Everything leading up to that point in time, to him awakening in that silo, had been someone else's doing. He could feel parted strings dangling from his elbows and knees. He was a loose puppet steering an empty wheelchair back to where it belonged.

Donald parked the chair and set the brakes. He took the plastic vial out of his pocket and considered stealing another dose or two. Sleep would be hard to come by, he feared.

The vial went back into the cabinet full of empties. Donald turned to go when he saw the note left in the middle of the gurney:

You forgot this.
—Wilson

The note was stuck to a slender folder. Donald remembered handing it to Dr. Wilson along with the reactor tech's belongings. The trip to the other two lockers had been a blur. All he could remember was clutching his phone, facts coming together, realizing that Anna had played Mick and Thurman to engineer a last-minute switch that made no sense, that could only happen with a daughter bending her father's ear. Thus his life had been stolen away.

The folder had been in the locker Anna had mentioned to her father in the message. It seemed inconsequential now. Donald balled up the note from Dr. Wilson and tossed it in the recycling bin. He grabbed the folder with the intention of staggering back to his cot and searching for sleep. But he found himself opening it up instead.

There was a single sheet of paper inside. An old sheet of paper. It had yellowed, and the edges were rough where bits had flaked off over the years. Below the single-spaced typing there were five signatures, a mix of florid and subdued penmanship. At the top of the document, boldly typed, it read: RE: THE PACT.

Donald glanced up at the door. He turned and went to the small desk with the computer, placed the folder by the keyboard, and sat down. Anna's note to her father had the same words in the subject line, along with *Urgent*. He had read the note a dozen times to try and divine its meaning. And the number in the note had led him to this folder.

He was familiar enough with the Pact of the silos, the governing document that kept each facility in line, that managed their populations with lotteries, that dictated their punishments from fines to cleanings. But this was too brief to be that Pact. It looked like a memo from his days on Capitol Hill.

Donald read:

All—

It has been previously discussed that ten facilities would suffice for our purposes, and that a time frame of one century would perform an adequate cleanse. With members of this pact both familiar with budget underruns and how battle plans prove fruitless upon first firing, it should surprise no one that facts have changed our forecast. We are now calling for thirty facilities and a two-century time frame. The tech team assures me their progress makes the latter feasible. These figures may be revisited once again.

There was also discussion in the last meeting of allowing two facilities to reach E-Day for redundancy (or the possibility of holding one facility back in reserve). That has been deemed inadvisable. Having all baskets in one egg is better than the danger of allowing two or more eggs to hatch. As it is a source of growing contention, this amendment to the original Pact shall be hereby undersigned by all founding persons and considered law. I will take it upon myself to work E-shift and pull the lever. Long-term survivability prospects are at 42 percent in the latest models. Marvelous progress, everyone.

—V

Donald scanned the signatures a second time. There was Thurman's simple scrawl, recognizable from countless memos and bills on the Hill. Another signature that might be Erskine's.

One that looked like Charles Rhodes, the swaggering Oklahoma governor. Illegible others. There was no date on the memo.

He read over it again. Understanding dawned slowly, full of doubts at first, but solidifying. There was a list he remembered from his previous shift, a ranking of silos. Number 18 had been near the top. It was why Victor had fought so hard to save the facility. This decision he mentions in the memo, pulling the lever. Had he said something about this in his note to Thurman? In his admission before he killed himself? Victor had grown unsure of whether or not he could make some decision.

Baskets in one egg. That wasn't how the saying went. Donald leaned back in the chair, and one of the light bulbs in Dr. Wilson's desk lamp flickered. Bulbs were not meant to last so long. They went dark, but there were redundancies.

One egg. Because what would they do to each other if more than one were allowed to hatch?

The list.

The reason it all fell together for Donald so easily was because he already knew. Had always known. How could it be otherwise? They had no plan, these bastards, of allowing the men and women of the silos to go free. No. There could be only one. For what would they do to each other if they met hundreds of years hence on the hills outside? Donald had drawn this place. He should've always known. He was an architect of death.

He thought about the list, the rankings of the silos. The one at the top was the only one that mattered. But what was their metric? How arbitrary would that decision be? All those eggs slaughtered except for one. With what hope? What plan? That the differences and struggles among a silo's people can be overcome? And yet the differences between the silos themselves was too much?

Donald coughed into his trembling hand. He understood

what Anna was trying to tell him. And now it was too late. Too late for answers. This was the way of life and death, and in a place that ignored both, he'd forgotten. There was no waking anyone. Just confusion and grief. His only ally, gone.

But there was another he could wake, the one he'd hoped to from the beginning. This was a grave power, this ability to bestir the dead. Donald shivered as he realized what the Pact truly meant, this pact between the madmen who had conspired to destroy the world.

"It's a suicide pact," he whispered, and the concrete walls of the silo closed in around him; they wrapped him like the shell of an egg. An egg never meant to be hatched. For they were the most dangerous of them all, this pit of vipers, and no world would ever be safe with them in it. The women and children were in lifeboats only to urge the men of Silo 1 to keep working their shifts. But they were all meant to drown. Every last one of them.

86

Silo 17
2323
Year Twelve

SOLO DIDN'T SET out one day to plumb the silo's depths—it simply happened. He had explored enough in both directions over the years, had hidden from the sound of others fighting, had found the messes they left behind, but such encounters grew rarer, and so his explorations grew bolder. It was curiosity as much as gravity and despair that drove him down. It was these things that ended his days alone.

He scavenged as he went. On one-twenty he discovered the lower farms and the signs of those who had lived there. This was farther than he'd ever been before. Those who had survived the early days had rigged the farms with wires and makeshift pipes. Solo took some carrots and beets from the overgrowth and left with the feeling of ghosts watching him. Outside, realizing how close he was to fabled Supply—the subject of so much radio chatter—he spiraled deeper. Supply was the land of plenty, or so they used to say. The promise of batteries and a can opener tugged him along.

The door to Supply was locked. Solo felt eyes on him as

he crouched by the entrance and pressed his ear against the cool steel. There was a thrumming he felt as much as heard. It seemed far away, like the lungs of the silo somewhere distant rattling and wheezing. He tried the door again. It wouldn't budge. There were no locks visible on the outside, just the standard vertical handles big enough for one hand to grab and pull.

Solo retreated to the staircase. He lightly gripped the railing with both hands and listened. He listened hard. Eventually, he heard his own pulse in his ears. That's when he knew he was listening best.

No ghosts. No tremble to the rail. He checked his rifle, made sure the safety was off, then pulled it tight against his shoulder. He aimed for the place between the double doors where the handles met. He pictured a can sitting there, imagined kicking it, tried not to see the chest of a man. He squeezed the trigger so lightly and gradually that when the bullet exploded out of the barrel, it startled him. The boom of the shot reverberated up and down the silo. A loud crack, and then a dozen echoes. Solo took aim again and fired a second round. A third. BOOM. BOOM. The ghosts would be everywhere cowering, he figured. He was Solo, but his rifle gave him noisy company.

He slipped the rifle strap over his head and tried the doors. One of them moved a little. Solo stepped back and kicked the door, even though they opened outward, just to put some violence into whatever bits continued to hold. When he pulled it the next time, the door came free with a grinding noise. Debris rained out of the insides and clattered onto the landing. The holes on the inside of the door were much larger than the holes on the outside, and the metal was bright and shiny where it had peeled away. Sharp to the touch, too, Solo discovered, sucking on his finger.

The silence within Supply seemed powerful after the boom of his rifle. Solo approached the counter that stretched from wall to wall. There were places he could crawl under where the counter wasn't solid. Then he saw the metal hinges and how the surface lifted up and folded away so he could step through.

Behind the counter were tall shelves and aisles littered with odds and ends. Solo thought he heard a scratching noise, but it was just one of the doors pulling itself shut on its spring-loaded hinges. He tiptoed through the debris and removed his rifle from his back. Just in case.

The bins on the shelves had been rummaged through. Many were missing altogether. Some were upside down, their contents scattered across the floor. To Solo's eye, Supply looked like little more than a bolt and screw store. Bins full of machined metal—rivets, nuts, bolts, washers, hooks, and hinges. He dipped his hand into a tub of tiny washers and scooped up a fistful, allowed them to spill out between his fingers. They made a clumsy song as they landed.

Farther down the aisle, the parts became larger. There were pumps and lengths of pipe, bins full of attachments to split the pipe, make it turn corners, and cap it. Solo made mental note of where things were. He thought of all the incredible Projects he could start.

Beyond the aisles, a corridor stretched in both directions with doors on either side. It was dark down the halls. He fished his flashlight from his breast pocket and trained the feeble beam on the pitch black. He should be searching the shelves for another battery, but something tugged him down the corridor. There was something wrong. Trash on the ground. It was the smell of tomatoes. The canned kind, the kind that smelled sweet like the sauce it was preserved in, not sweet like the vine.

He bent and picked up a discarded can. Red tomato paste clung to the lid. Dabbing it with his finger, he found it wet, not hardened like he knew it got within days. Solo touched his finger to his tongue, the taste a jolt to his senses, awareness a shock to his nerves. He clutched his rifle and pulled the strap over his head, wedged the stock against his shoulder. Holding the flashlight and the grip of the gun in the same hand, he balanced the barrel on top of the light. The barrel split the beam in two where it hit the ceiling, leaving a dark shadow above him.

Solo trained the sights down the hall and listened. His flashlight wavered. He crept down a corridor that seemed to be holding its breath.

The doorknobs he tried were all unlocked. He pushed the doors inward, his finger resting on the trigger, finding rooms full of shadows. There were machines on stands with no power. Cutting and welding machines, shaping and joining machines, all splashed with orange rust. They revealed themselves only as his flashlight danced across them. For a split second, each machine loomed in the darkness as a man with his arms up and ready to pounce. There were more doors off the backs of these rooms. A labyrinth of storerooms. Debris scattered everywhere. Evidence of the original exodus was lost amid the struggle to survive ever since.

One of the rooms smelled funny, like hot electrics, like the smell of his rifle after a shell was ejected. The walls in that room were charred black. The darkness swallowed his flashlight's beam. He moved to the next door, leaving far behind the wan green emergency light trickling from the stairwell and through the tall shelves of bolts and screws.

An ominous glow emanated from down the hall. An open door. Solo thought he heard something. He stilled his breathing and waited. Not a whisper, just his heartbeat, probably nothing. He thought of the thousands who had lived in the silo before. How many like him had survived? How many tended the remnants of the farms, scraped the insides of cans with the flat of a knife, digging for those calories at the bottom, watching for spots of rust? Maybe it was just him anymore. Just Solo.

The next door leaked a faint spill of light. Solo approached warily, annoyed at his boots for squeaking, and nudged the door open with the end of his barrel. He remembered what it felt like to kick a man from a distance, to watch the blood spurt from his chest. His flashlight blinked on and off, the battery acting up again. Solo let go of his rifle and knocked the light against his thigh until the beam woke up. He peered into the room, searching for the source of the glow.

A wedge of light sliced up from the floor, a wedge of light from a glowing circle. It was the lens of another flashlight.

Solo sucked in a shallow breath at the fortuitous discovery. He hurried forward, scattering cans and wads of trash, and crouched by the lit flashlight. He flicked his own flashlight off and tucked it into his pocket, picked up this other one. It shone brightly. He aimed it around the room, excited. This was what he had come for. Better than just batteries, a new flashlight as well. The batteries inside would last him years if he was careful, if he conserved. But they wouldn't last him more than a few days if he accidentally left it on.

A few days.

A bucket of cold water spilled down Solo's spine. The darkness all around him crowded closer. He heard imagined whispers from the shadows, and the flashlight was warm in his grip. Had it been warm when he picked it up?

He stood. An empty can clattered noisily from his boot. Solo realized how much of a racket he was making, how much light and life he had brought into this dark and deathly place. He backed toward the door, pulled his gun against his shoulder, the feeling of hands coming at him from every direction, long fingernails of the unkempt about to sink into his flesh.

He nearly dropped the flashlight as he turned to run. The rifle knocked against the doorjamb and pressed into his finger. There was a blinding flash in the coal-dark corridor, a bang like the end of the world, a kick from the rifle. And then Solo was running. Running back toward the shelves with their trickle of stairlight. Running away while imaginary things chased him, no room in his startled mind for the truth that he had brought terror to those who lived there, that his swinging new flashlight, bright and harmonious, had left someone else in the echoing bang and the pitch black that he had left behind.

87

HE FLED FROM Supply and headed deeper, a second flashlight his reward for the scare. On one-twenty-eight, he stopped in an apartment to empty his bladder, which seemed to fill whenever he was afraid. There was a thought of getting some rest on the apartment's bare mattress, but he suspected it wasn't yet nighttime. It was just the fading adrenaline that made him feel sleepy.

Back on the landing, he considered his options. He had seen almost all that was left of the silo. It was just him and the ghosts. He had plenty of notes in his head on where things were, had discovered a second farm full of food, had found the water stock on one-twelve, had used his gun to bust open a door. Still no can opener, but he could make do with his driver and hammer. Things were looking up the more he explored down, so that's the way he went.

A dozen levels deeper, the temperature really began to dip. The air grew cool and moist and blossomed in clouds when he blew his breath. An emergency fire hose had been left out on one-thirty-six, unspooled from its little rusted closet. The hose lay tangled on the landing. Water dripped from the nozzle, and Solo could hear the plummeting impacts ring out like tiny bells somewhere farther below. He was almost at the end. The Deep. He had never been to the Deep before.

He filled his water jug from the nozzle. Normally, even a slight crack from those valves would let loose a powerful torrent. Solo was able to open this one all the way, and even then he had to lift the tangle of hose from the landing and coax out half a jugful. He took a few sips, wincing at the bitter taste of the hose's fabric, then screwed the lid back on the jug. It hung from his pack, which jangled with the odds and ends he'd picked up since he'd left home the day before. Along with the rifle, it was a lot to carry.

Solo peered over the railing and spotted the bottom of the silo below: the floor of the Deep, slick and shiny. All he knew of Mechanical—the levels beneath the last twist of the stairway—was that power and air came from there. Since there was still some of both, maybe that meant people. Solo clutched his rifle warily. He wasn't sure if he ever wanted to see people again, ever.

He twisted his way down another few flights, his boots clomp-clomping. Anyone with an ear pressed to the railing would hear his progress. The thought sent chills down his arms. Solo imagined ten thousand people lining the rail, noses touching the crowns of those before them, all listening to him as he descended, an uninterrupted spiral of disembodied noggins attuned to his every move.

"Go away, ghosts," he whispered. He hugged the inner rail, just in case. The steps made less noise near the post. He flashed back to years ago when there'd been no space on the steps, when it'd been hard to breathe as people packed in around him, and his mother had yelled for him to go on without her. Solo felt sixteen again, except his tears disappeared into his beard where before he could wipe them away. He was sixteen again. Would always be sixteen.

His boots splashed into cold water. Solo startled and lost his grip on the rail. He slid, fought for balance, and fell to one knee, water soaking him up to his crotch, his rifle slipping off his shoulder, his bag getting wet.

Cursing, he struggled to his feet. Water dripped from the barrel of his rifle, a stream of liquid bullets. His coveralls were freezing cold and clung to his skin where they'd gotten soaked. Solo wiped at his eyes, which were full of tears, and wondered briefly if all that water at his feet had come from his years of crying.

"Stupid," he said. It was a stupid thought. The water had probably drained from all the toilets that didn't work. Or maybe this is where they flushed to, and now the mechanics weren't around to filter it and pump it back to the Top.

He retreated up a step and watched the agitated surface slowly settle. This was the shiny floor he'd seen from above. Peering through its murky surface—a colorful film across the top with all the colors that existed—he saw that the stairs spiraled out of sight and into the dark depths of the water. The silo was flooded.

Solo watched where the water met the railing and waited to see if the flood was rising. If so, it was far slower than he could tell.

One of the doors on level one-thirty-seven moved back and forth with the waves his splashing had caused. The water was two feet or more above the level of the landing. It was that high inside the door as well. The entire silo was filling up with water, he thought. It had taken years for it to get this high. Would it go on forever? How long before it filled his home up on thirty-four? How long before it reached the top?

Thinking of slowly drowning elicited a strange sound from Solo's mouth, a noise like a sad whimper. His clothes dripped water back to where it had come from, and then Solo heard the whimpering sound again. It wasn't coming from him at all.

He crouched down and peered into the flooded level, listening. There. The sound of someone crying. It was coming from inside the flooded levels, and Solo knew he was not alone.

88

IT SOUNDED LIKE an infant. Solo peered down at the water. He would have to wade through it to get inside the level. The dim green lights overhead lent the world a ghostly pallor. The air was cold, and the water colder.

He retreated up the steps and left his heavy pack on one of the dry treads—toward the outside, where the steps were wider. He lowered himself, his gun clattering on the stairs. The cuffs of his coveralls were soaked. He rolled them up over his calves, then began unknotting the laces of his boots.

He listened for the cry again. It did not come. He wondered if he would be braving the wet and cold for something he'd imagined, for another ghost who would disappear as soon as he paid it any mind. He dumped the water out of his boots before setting them aside. He pulled off his socks—his big toe poking through a hole in one of them. He squeezed and twisted these, then draped them across the railing to dry.

He left his bag four steps above the waterline. Surely it wasn't coming up fast enough to worry. It didn't appear to have moved since he'd arrived. He glanced at the doorway again, noted the height of the waterline, and imagined the flood surging up while he was trapped inside. Solo shivered, and not from the cold. He thought he heard the baby cry again.

He was enough years old to have a baby, he thought. He did the math. He rarely did this math. Was he twenty-six? Twenty-seven? Another birthday had come and gone with no one to remind him. No sweetbread, no candle lit and just as quickly blown out. "Blow it quick," his mother used to say. His father would barely get the thing lit before Jimmy leaned forward to puff it out. Just an instant of fire, barely a warming of the wax, and the family candle would be put away for his father, whose birthday came next.

A silly tradition, he thought. But supposedly each family had as many birthdays among them as there was wax. The Parker candle was many generations old and not yet half gone. Jimmy used to think he'd live forever if he blew swiftly enough. He and his parents would all live forever. But none of that was true. It would only be him until he died, and so the candle had been a lie.

He stepped into the water and waded toward the door, his feet shocked half-numb from the cold. The colorful film on the surface of the water swirled and mixed and flowed around the stanchions that held up the landing rail. Solo paused and peered beyond the landing. It seemed strange to be so high off the bottom of the silo and see this fluid stretching out to the concrete walls. If he were to fall over, would the water slow his plummet to the bottom? Or would he bob on the surface like that bit of trash over there? He thought he would sink. The most water he'd ever been in before was a tubful, and he'd sat right on the bottom. He was sinking up to his shins right then. The fear of slipping through some unseen crack and dropping to his death caused him to shuffle his feet cautiously. He fought to feel the metal grating beneath his soles, even as his feet grew colder and colder. Something silver seemed to flash beneath the grating, but he thought it was just his reflection or the dance of the metallic sheen on the surface.

"You better be worth this," he told the ghost of some baby down the hall.

He listened for the ghost to call back, but it was no longer crying. The light beyond the doors fell away to blackness, so he pulled his flashlight out of his chest pocket and turned it on. The layer of rippling water caught the beam and magnified it. Waves of light danced across the ceiling in a display so mesmerizing and beautiful that Solo forgot the freezing water. Or perhaps it was that his feet no longer had any feeling at all.

"Hello?" he called out.

His voice echoed softly back to him. He played the light down the hall, which branched off in three directions. Two of the paths curved around as if to meet on the other side of the stairwell. It was one of the hub-and-spoke levels. Solo laughed. *Bi* for *Bicycles*. He thought of that entry and realized where the words *hub and spoke* came from. These were magical discoveries, how old words came to be—

A cry.

For certain, this time, or he truly was losing his senses. Solo spun around and aimed his flashlight down the curving corridor. He waited. Silence. The whisper of ripples as they crashed into the hallway wall. He picked his way toward the noise, throwing up new waves with the push of his shins. He floated like a ghost. He couldn't feel his feet.

It was an apartment level. But why would anyone live down here with the waters seeping in? He paused outside a community rec room and dispelled pockets of darkness with his flashlight. There was a tennis table in the middle of the room. Rust reached up the steel legs as if the water had chased it there. The paddles were still on the warped surface of the rotting green table. *Green for grass,* Solo thought. The Legacy books made his own world look different to him.

Something bumped into his shin, and Solo startled. He aimed

his light down and saw a foam cushion floating by his feet. He pushed it away and waded toward the next door.

A community kitchen. He recognized the layout of wide tables and all the chairs. Most of the chairs lay on their sides, partly submerged. A few legs stuck up where chairs had been overturned. There were two stoves in the corner and a wall of cabinets. The room was dark; almost none of the light from the stairwell trickled back this far. Solo imagined that if his batteries died, he would have to grope to find his way out. He should've brought the new flashlight, not his old one.

A cry. Louder this time. Near. Somewhere in the room.

Solo waved his flashlight about but couldn't see every corner at once. Cabinets and countertops. A spot of movement, he thought. He trained his light back a little, and something moved on one of the counters. It leapt straight up, the sound of claws scratching as it caught itself on an open cabinet above the counter, then the whisking of a bushy tail before a black shadow disappeared into the darkness.

89

A CAT! A LIVING thing. A living thing he need not fear, that could do him no harm. Solo trudged into the room, calling, “Kitty, kitty, kitty.” He recalled neighbors trying to corral that tailless animal that lived down the hall from his old apartment.

Something rummaged around in the cabinets. One of the closed doors rattled open and banged shut again. He could only see a spot at a time, wherever he aimed the flashlight. His shins brushed against something. He aimed the beam down to see trash and debris floating in the water. There was a squeak and a splash. Searching with the flashlight, he saw a V of ripples behind what he took for a swimming rat. Solo no longer wanted to be in that room. He shivered and rubbed his arm with his free hand. The cat made a racket inside the cabinet.

“Here, kitty,” he said with less gusto. Reaching into his breast pocket, he pulled out one of his ration bars and tore the packaging off with his teeth. Taking a stale bite for himself, he chewed and held the rest out in front of him. The silo had been dead for twelve years. He wondered how long cats lived, how this one had made it so long. And eating what? Or were old cats having new cats? Was this a new cat?

His bare feet brushed through something beneath the water. The reflection of the light made it difficult to see, and then a white bone broke the surface before sinking again. There was a loose jumble of someone's remains around his ankles.

Solo pretended it was just trash. He reached the cabinet that was making all the noise, grabbed a handle and pulled it open. There was a hiss from the shadows. Cans and rotting boxes shifted about as the cat retreated further. Solo broke off a piece of stale bar and set it on the shelf. He waited. There was another squeak from the corner of the room, the sound of water lapping at furniture, a stillness inside the cabinet. He kept the flashlight down so as not to spook the animal.

Two eyes approached like bobbing lights. They fixed themselves on Solo for a small eternity. He began to seriously wonder if his feet might fall off from the cold. The eyes drew closer and diverted downward. It was a black cat, the color of wet shadow, slick as oil. The piece of ration bar crunched as the cat chewed.

"Good kitty," he whispered, ignoring the scattered bones beneath his feet. He broke off another small piece of the bar and held it out. The cat withdrew a pace. Solo set the food on the edge and watched as the animal came forward more quickly this time. The next piece, the cat took from his palm. He offered the last piece, and as the cat came to accept it, Solo tried to pick it up with both hands. And this thing, this company he hoped would do him no harm, latched on to one of his arms and sank its claws into his flesh.

Solo screamed and threw up his hands. The flashlight tumbled end over end in the air. There was a splash as the cat disappeared. A shriek and a hiss, a violent noise, Solo fumbling beneath the water for the dull glow of the light, which flickered once, twice, then left him in darkness.

He groped blindly, seized a solid cylinder and felt the knobby ends where the leg sockets into the hip. He dropped the bone in disgust. Two more bones before he found the flashlight, which was toast. He retrieved it anyway as the sound of frantic splashing approached. His arms were on fire; he had seen blood on them in the last of the spinning light. And then something was against his leg, up his shin, claws stinging his thighs, the damn cat climbing him as if he were the leg of a table.

Solo reached for the poor animal to get its claws out of his flesh. The cat was soaked and hardly felt bigger around than his flashlight. It trembled in his arms and rubbed itself against a dry patch of his coveralls, mewing in complaint. It began to sniff at his breast pocket.

Solo held the animal with one forearm across his chest, making a perch, and reached inside his pocket for the other ration bar. It was perfectly dark in the room, so dark it made his ears ache. He ripped the package free and held the bar steady. Tiny paws wrapped around his hand, and there was a crunching sound.

Jimmy smiled. He worked his way toward where he thought the door might be, bumping through furniture and old bones as he went, Solo no more.

90

Silo 1
2345

Donald's apartment had transformed into a cave, a cave where notes lay strewn like bleached bones, where the carcasses of folders decorated his walls, and where boxes of more notes were ordered up from archives like fresh kill. Weeks had passed. The stomping in the halls had dwindled. Donald lived alone with ghosts and slowly pieced together the purpose of what he'd helped to build. He was beginning to see it, the entire picture, zooming out of the schematic until the whole was laid bare.

He coughed into a pink rag and resumed examination of his latest find. It was a map he'd come across once before in the armory, a map of all the silos with a line coming out of each and converging at a single point. Here was one of many mysteries left. The document was labeled *Seed,* but he could find nothing else about it.

Donald could hear Anna whispering to him. She had been trying to tell him something. The note in Thurman's account, she was trying to say, had been left for him. So obvious now. She could never be woken, not a woman. She needed him, needed his help. Donald imagined her piecing all of this together on some recent shift, alone and terrified, scared of her own father, no one left to turn to. So she had taken her father out of power, had entrusted Donald, had switched him with another man for the second time, and had left him a note to wake her. And what did Donald do instead?

There was a knock on his door.

"Who is it?" Donald asked, his voice not sounding like his own.

The door opened a crack. "It's Eren, sir. We've got a call from 18. The shadow is ready."

"Just a second."

Donald coughed into his handkerchief. He rose slowly and moved to the bathroom, stepping over two trays of old dishes. He emptied his bladder, flushed and studied himself in the mirror. Gripping the edge of the counter, he grimaced at his reflection, this man with scraggly hair and the start of a beard. He looked half crazed, and yet people still trusted him. That made them crazier than he was. Donald smiled a yellowing smile and thought of the long history of madmen who remained in charge simply because no one would challenge them.

Hinges squealed as Eren poked his head in the door.

"I'm coming," Donald said. He stomped across the reports, leaving a trail of footprints behind, and a bloody palm print on the edge of the counter.

"They're calling the shadow now, sir," Eren said to him in the hall. "You want to freshen up?"

"No," Donald said. "I'm good." He stood in the doorway, struggling to remember what this meeting was about. A Rite of Initiation. He remembered those, thought it was something Gable would handle. "Why am I needed again?" he asked. "Shouldn't our head be conducting this?" Donald remembered being the one to conduct such a Rite on his first shift.

Eren popped something into his mouth and chewed. He shook his head. "You know, with all that reading you're doing in there, you could bone up on the Order a bit. It sounds like it's changed since the last time you read it. The ranking officer on shift completes the Rite. That would normally be me—"

"But since I'm up, it's me." Donald pulled his door shut. The two of them started down the hall.

"That's right. The heads here do less and less every shift. There have been . . . problems. I'll sit in with you though, help you get through the script. Oh, and you wanted to know when the pilots were heading off shift. The last one is going under right now. They're just straightening up down there."

Donald perked up at this. Finally. What he'd been waiting for. "So the armory's empty?" he asked, unable to hide his delight.

"Yessir. No more flight requisitions. I know you didn't like chancing them to begin with."

"Right, right." Donald waved his hand as they turned the corner. "Restrict access to the armory once they're done. Nobody should be able to get in there but me."

Eren slowed his pace. "Just you, sir?"

"For as long as I'm on shift," Donald said.

They passed Gable in the hall, who had three cups of coffee nestled in a web of fingers. Gable smiled and nodded. Donald remembered fetching coffee for people when he was head of the silo. Now, that was near enough all the head did. Donald couldn't help but think his first shift was partly to blame.

Eren lowered his voice. "You know the story behind him, right?" He took another bite of something and chewed.

Donald glanced over his shoulder. "Who, Gable?"

"Yeah. He was in Ops until a few shifts back. Broke down. Tried to get himself into deep freeze. The duty doc at the time talked him into a demotion. We were losing too many people, and the shifts were starting to get some overlap." Eren paused and took another bite. There was a familiar scent. Eren caught him watching and held out something. "Bagel?" he asked. "They're fresh baked."

Donald could smell it. Eren tore off a piece. It was still warm. "I didn't know they could make these," he said, popping the morsel into his mouth.

"New chef just came on shift. He's been experimenting with all kinds of stuff. He—"

Donald didn't hear the rest. He chewed on memories. A cool day in DC, Helen up to visit, had the dog with her, drove all the way from Savannah. They walked around the Lincoln Memorial a week too early for the cherry blossoms, but there were still spots of color dotted here and there. They had stopped for fresh bagels, still warm, the smell of coffee—

"Put an end to this," Donald said, indicating the rest of Eren's bagel.

"Sir?"

They were nearly at the bend in the hall that led to the comm room. "I don't want this chef experimenting anymore. Have him stick to the usual."

Eren seemed confused. After some hesitation, he nodded. "Yes, sir."

"Nothing good can come of this," Donald explained. And while Eren agreed more strenuously this time, Donald realized he had begun to think like the people he loathed. A veil of disappointment fell over Eren's face, and Donald felt a sudden urge to take it back, to grab the man by the shoulders and ask him what the hell they thought they were doing, all this misery and heartache. They should eat memory foods, of course, and talk about the days they'd left behind.

Instead, he said nothing, and they continued down the hall in quiet and discomfort.

"Quite a few of our silo heads came from Ops," Eren said after a while, steering the conversation back to Gable. "I was a comm officer for my first two shifts, you know. The guy I took over for, the Ops head from the last shift, was from Medical."

"So you're not a shrink?" Donald asked.

Eren laughed, and Donald thought of Victor, blowing his brains out. This wasn't going to last, this place. There were cracked tiles in the center of the hall. Tiles that had no replacement. The ones at the edge were in much better shape. He stopped outside the comm room and surveyed the wear on this centuries-old place. There were scuff marks low on the walls, hand-high, shoulder-high, fewer anywhere else. The traffic patterns on the floors throughout the facility showed where people walked. The wear on that place, like on its people, was not evenly distributed.

"Are you okay, sir?" Eren asked.

Donald held up his hand. He could sense those in the comm room were waiting on him. But he was thinking on how an architect designs a structure to last. A certain calculus was used, an averaging of forces and wear across an entire structure, letting every beam and rivet shoulder its share of the load. All together, the resulting building could take the force of a hurricane, an earthquake, with plenty of redundancies to boot. But real stress and strain weren't as kind as the hurricanes computers simulated. Hidden in those calculus winds were hurtling rods of steel and two by fours. And where they slammed it was like bombs going off. Just as the center of a hall bore an unfortunate share of strain, some people would be on shift for the worst of it.

"I believe they're waiting on us, sir."

Donald looked away from the scuff marks to Eren, this young man with bright eyes and bagel on his breath, his hair full of color, an upturn at the corners of his mouth, a wan smile like a scar of hope.

"Right," Donald said. He waved Eren inside the comm room before following behind, stepping dead center like everyone else.

91

DONALD FAMILIARIZED HIMSELF with the script while Eren plopped into the chair beside him and pulled a headset on. The software would mask their voices, make them featureless and the same. The silo heads need not know when one man went off shift and another replaced him. It was always the same voice, the same person, as far as they were concerned.

The shift operator lifted a mug and took a sip. Donald could see something written on the mug with a marker. It said: *We're #1.* Donald wondered if whoever wrote it meant the silo. The operator set the mug down and twirled his finger for Donald to begin.

Donald covered his mic and cleared his throat. He could hear someone talking on the other end of the line as a distant headset was pulled on. There was a script to follow for the first half. Donald remembered most of it. Eren turned to the side and polished off the bagel guiltily. When the operator gave them the thumbs-up, Eren gestured to Donald to do the honors, and all Donald could think about was getting this over with and getting down to that empty armory.

"Name," he said into his mic.

"Lukas Kyle," came the reply.

Donald watched the graphs jump with readings taken from

the headset. He felt sorry for this person, signing on to head a silo rated near the bottom. It all seemed hopeless, and here Donald was going through the motions. "You shadowed in IT," he said.

There was a pause. "Yessir."

The boy's temperature was up. Donald could read it on the display. The operator and Eren were comparing notes and pointing to something. Donald checked the script. It listed easy questions everyone knew the answers to.

"What is your primary duty to the silo?" he asked, reading the line.

"To maintain the Order."

Eren raised a hand as the readouts spiked. When they settled, he gave Donald the sign to continue.

"What do you protect above all?" Even with the software helping, Donald tried to keep his voice flat. There was a jump on one of the graphs. Donald's thoughts drifted to the news of the pilots gone from his space, a space that he felt belonged to him. He would get through this and set his alarm clock. Tonight. Tonight.

"Life and Legacy," the shadow recited.

Donald lost his place. It took a moment to find the next line. "What does it take to protect these things we hold so dear?"

"It takes sacrifice," the shadow said after a brief pause.

The comm head gave Donald and Eren an okay signal. The formal readings were over. Now to the baseline, to get off script. Donald wasn't sure what to say. He nodded to Eren, hoping he'd take over.

Eren covered his mic for a second as if he was about to argue, but shrugged. "How much time have you had in the Suit Labs?" he asked the shadow, studying the monitor in front of him.

"Not much, sir. Bernar—Uh, my boss, he's wanting me to schedule time in the labs after, you know . . ."

"Yes. I do know." Eren nodded. "How's that problem in your lower levels going?"

"Um, well, I'm only kept apprised of the overall progress, and it sounds good." Donald heard the shadow clear his throat. "That is, it sounds like progress is being made, that it won't be much longer."

A long pause. A deep breath. Waveforms relaxed. Eren glanced at Donald. The operator waved his finger for them to keep going.

Donald had a question, one that touched on his own regrets. "Would you have done anything differently, Lukas?" he asked. "From the beginning?"

There were red spikes on the monitors, and Donald felt his own temperature rise. Maybe he was asking something too close to home.

"Nossir," the young shadow said. "It was all by the Order, sir. Everything's under control."

The comm head reached to his controls and muted all of their headsets. "We're getting borderline readings," he told them. "His nerves are spiking. Can you push him a little more?"

Eren nodded. The operator on the other side of him shrugged and took a sip from his #1 mug.

"Settle him down first, though," the comm head said.

Eren turned to Donald. "Congratulate him and then see if you can get him emotional. Level him out and then tweak him."

Donald hesitated. It was all so artificial and manipulative. He forced himself to swallow. The mics were unmuted.

"You are next in line for the control and operation of Silo 18," he said stiffly, sad for what he was dooming this poor soul to.

"Thank you, sir." The shadow sounded relieved. Waveforms collapsed as if they'd struck a pier.

Now Donald fought for some way to push the young man.

The comm head waving at him didn't help. Donald glanced up at the map of the silos on the wall. He stood, the headphone cord stretching, and studied the several silos marked out, the one there with the number "12." Donald considered the seriousness of what this young man had just taken on, what his job entailed, how many had died elsewhere because their leaders had let them down.

"Do you know the worst part of my job?" Donald asked. He could feel those in the comm room watching him. Donald was back on his first shift, initiating that other young man. He was back on his first shift, shutting a silo down.

"What's that, sir?" the voice asked.

"Standing here, looking at a silo on this map, and drawing a red cross through it. Can you imagine what that feels like?"

"I can't, sir."

Donald nodded. He appreciated the honest answer. He remembered what it felt like to watch those people spill out of 12 and perish on the landscape. He blinked his vision clear. "It feels like a parent losing thousands of children all at once," he said.

The world stood still for a heartbeat or two. The operator and the comm head were both fixated on their monitors, looking for a crack. Eren watched Donald.

"You will have to be cruel to your children so as not to lose them," Donald said.

"Yessir."

Waveforms began to pulse like gentle surf. The comm head gave Donald the thumbs-up. He had seen enough. The boy had passed, and now the Rite was truly over.

"Welcome to Operation Fifty of the World Order, Lukas Kyle," Eren said, reading from the script and taking over from Donald. "Now, if you have a question or two, I have the time to answer, but briefly."

Donald remembered this part. He had a hand in this. He settled back into his chair, suddenly exhausted.

"Just one, sir. And I've been told it isn't important, and I understand why that's true, but I believe it will make my job here easier if I know." The young man paused. "Is there . . . ?" A new red spike on his graph. "How did this all begin?"

Donald held his breath. He glanced around the room, but everyone else was watching their monitors as if any question was as good as another.

Donald responded before Eren could. "How badly do you wish to know?" he asked.

The shadow took in a breath. "It isn't crucial," he said, "but I would appreciate a sense of what we're accomplishing, what we survived. It feels like it gives me—gives us a purpose, you know?"

"The reason *is* the purpose," Donald told him. This was what he was beginning to learn from his studies. "Before I tell you, I'd like to hear what you think."

He thought he could hear the shadow gulp. "What I think?" Lukas asked.

"Everyone has ideas," Donald said. "Are you suggesting you don't?"

"I think it was something we saw coming."

Donald was impressed. He had a feeling this young man knew the answer and simply wanted confirmation. "That's one possibility," he agreed. "Consider this . . ." He thought how best to phrase it. "What if I told you that there were only fifty silos in all the world, and that we are in this infinitely small corner of it?"

On the monitor, Donald could practically watch the young man think, his readings oscillating up and down like the brain's version of a heartbeat.

"I would say that we were the only ones . . ." A wild spike on the monitor. "I'd say we were the only ones who *knew*."

“Very good. And why might that be?”

Donald wished he had the jostling lines on the screen recorded. It was serene, watching another human being clutch after his vanishing sanity, his disappearing doubts.

“It’s because . . . It’s not because we knew.” There was a soft gasp on the other end of the line. “It’s because we *did it*.”

“Yes,” Donald said. “And now you know.”

Eren turned to Donald and placed his hand over his mic. “We’ve got more than enough. The kid checks out.”

Donald nodded. “Our time is up, Lukas Kyle. Congratulations on your assignment.”

“Thank you.” There was a final flutter on the monitors.

“Oh, and Lukas?” Donald said, remembering the young man’s predilection for staring at the stars, for dreaming, for filling himself with dangerous hope.

“Yessir?”

“Going forward, I suggest you concentrate on what’s beneath your feet. No more of this business with the stars, okay, son? We know where most of them are.”

92

Silo 17
2327
Year Sixteen

JIMMY WASN'T SURE how the algebra worked, but feeding two mouths was more than just twice the work. And yet—it felt like less than half the chore. He suspected it had to do with how nice it was to provide for something besides himself. The satisfaction of seeing the cat eat and of it growing used to him made him relish meals and travel outside more often.

It had been a rough start, though. The cat had been skittish after its rescue. Jimmy had dried himself off with a towel scavenged two levels up, and the cat had acted insane as he dried it off after. It seemed to both love and hate the process, rolling around one minute and batting at Jimmy's hands the next. Once dry, the animal had blossomed to twice its wet size. And yet he was still pathetic and hungry.

Jimmy found a can of beans beneath a mattress. The can wasn't too rusty. He opened it with his driver and fed the slick pods to the cat one at a time while his own feet thawed, tingling like electricity the entire time.

After the beans, the cat had taken to following him wherever he went to see what he might find next. It made the hunt for food fun, rather than a never-ending war against his own growling stomach. Fun, but also lots of work. Up the staircase they went, him back in his boots, the cat silently pawing behind and sometimes ahead.

Jimmy had learned early on to trust the cat's balance. The first few times it rubbed itself against the outer stanchions, even twisting itself beyond them and back through as it ascended the steps, Jimmy nearly had a heart attack. The cat seemed to have a death wish, or just an ignorance of what it meant to fall. But he soon learned to trust the cat even as the cat began to trust him.

And that first night, as he lay huddled under his tarp in the lower farms, listening to pumps and lights click on and off and noises he mistook for others in hiding, the cat tucked itself under his arm and curled against the crook his belly made when his legs were bent and began to rattle like a pump on loose mounts.

"You were lonely, huh?" Jimmy had whispered. He had grown uncomfortable but was unwilling to move. A cramp had formed in his neck while a different tightness disappeared from deep in his gut, a tightness he didn't know was there until it was gone.

"I was lonely too," he had told the cat softly, fascinated by how much more he talked with the animal around. It was better than talking to his shadow and pretending it was a person.

"That's a good name," Jimmy had whispered. He didn't know what people named cats, but Shadow would work. Like the shadows in which he'd found the thing, another spot of blackness to follow Jimmy around. And that night, years back, the two of them had fallen asleep amid the clicking pumps, the dripping water, the buzzing insects and all the stranger sounds deep within the farms that Jimmy preferred not to name.

• • •

That was years ago. Now, cat hair and beard hair gathered together in the spines of the Legacy books. Jimmy trimmed his beard while he read about snakes. The scissors made crunching noises as he pinched a load of hair, held it away from his chin and hacked it off with the dull shears. He sprinkled most of the hair in an empty can. The rest drifted down among the pages, large swoops of meddling punctuation mingling with hair from the cat, who kept walking back and forth under his arms, arching his back, and stepping across the sentences.

"I'm trying to read," Jimmy complained. But he put down the scissors and dutifully stroked the animal from neck to tail, Shadow pressing his spine up into Jimmy's palm. He meowed and made that grumbling sound as if his heart were going to burst and begged for more.

Tiny claws clenched into little fists and punctured a photo of a corn snake, and Jimmy guided the animal toward the floor. Shadow lay on his back with his feet in the air, watching Jimmy carefully. It was a trap. Jimmy could rub his belly for only a moment before the cat would suddenly decide he hated this and attack his wrist. Jimmy didn't understand cats that well, but he'd read the entry on them a dozen times. One thing he hated to learn was that they didn't live as long as humans. He tried not to think of that day. On that day he would go back to being Solo, and he much preferred being Jimmy. Jimmy talked more. Solo was the one with the wild thoughts, the one who gazed over the rails, who spat toward the Deep and watched as his spit trembled and tore itself apart from the wild speeds of its racing fall.

"Are you bored?" Jimmy asked Shadow.

Shadow looked at him as though he were bored. It was similar to the look that said he was hungry.

"Wanna go explore?"

The cat's ear twitched, which was enough of a sign.

Jimmy decided to check up top again. He had only been once since the days went dark, and just for a peek. If there was a working can opener in the silo, it would be there. An end to crusty drivers and slicing his hands on roughly opened lids.

They set out after lunch with a short break at the farms. When they got to the cafeteria, they found it perfectly silent and glowing in the green cast from the stairwell. Shadow scampered up the last steps alone, intrepid as usual. Jimmy headed straight for the kitchen and found it a looted wreck.

"Who took all the openers?" he called out to Shadow.

But Shadow wasn't there. Shadow was off to the far wall, acting agitated.

Jimmy ranged behind the serving line and sorted through the forks, eager to replace his usual one, when he heard the mewing. He peered across the wide cafeteria hall and saw Shadow rubbing back and forth against a closed door.

"Keep it down," Jimmy yelled to Shadow. Didn't the cat know he'd only bring trouble making such a racket? But Shadow wasn't listening. He mewed and mewed and scratched his claws at the door and stretched until Jimmy relented. Jimmy hurried through the maze of upturned chairs and crooked tables to see what the fuss was about.

"Is it food?" he asked. With Shadow, it was almost always food. His companion was drawn to meals like a magnet, which Jimmy had come to find quite handy. Approaching the door, he saw the remnants of a rope looped around the handle, the years reducing it to tatters. Jimmy tried the handle and found it unlocked. He eased it open.

The room beyond was dark, none of the emergency lights lit like at the top of the stairwell. Jimmy fumbled for his flashlight while Shadow disappeared through the cracked door, his tail swishing into the void.

There was a startled hiss just as the flashlight came on. Jimmy paused, a boot nearly through the door, as the cone of his flashlight fell upon a face staring up at him with open and lifeless eyes. Bodies shifted against the door, and an arm flopped out against his foot.

Jimmy screamed and fell backward. He kicked at the pale and fleshy hand and called for Shadow, who came screeching out the door, fur standing on end. There was the taste of metal on Jimmy's tongue, a rush of adrenalin as he scrambled to get the door shut. He lifted the limp arm and shoved it back inside, the clothes disintegrating at his touch, the flesh beneath whole and spongy.

Open mouths and curled fingers were the last things he saw. Piles of bodies, as fresh as the morning dead, frozen where they'd crawled over one another, hands reaching for the door.

Once it clicked shut, Jimmy began sliding tables and chairs against the door. He created a huge tangle of them, tossing more chairs on top of the pile, shivering and cursing beneath his beard while Shadow spun in circles.

"Gross, gross, gross," he told Shadow, whose hair had not yet settled. He studied his barricade against the piles of dead and hoped it would be adequate, that he hadn't let out too many ghosts. The remnants of old rope swayed on the door's handle, and Jimmy thanked whomever had kept these people at bay.

"Let's go," he said, and Shadow swished against his leg for comfort. There was no view to see on the wallscreen, no food or tools of any use. He'd had quite enough of up top, which suddenly felt crowded to the walls with the dead.

93

Besides food, Shadow had a nose for trouble. A nose for causing it. Jimmy woke one morning to an awful screeching sound, a pathetic and plaintive hiss spilling down the corridor. Jimmy had climbed the ladder half asleep to find Shadow stuck near the top rung. He didn't know how the cat had got there, and the cat didn't know how to get down. Jimmy released the hatch over their heads and threw it aside. He watched as Shadow clawed up the metal mesh behind the ladder, his back pressed against the rungs, and scampered over the top.

Two mornings later, the same thing happened, and that's when Jimmy decided to leave the hatch open all the time. He was sick of opening and closing it as he came and went, and Shadow liked being able to explore the server room whenever he liked. There hadn't been any fighting in a long time and the great steel door still winked red.

Shadow loved the servers. Most times, Jimmy would find him up on server number forty, where the metal was so hot that Jimmy could barely touch it. But Shadow didn't mind. He slept up there or peered over the edge at the ground far below, watching for bugs on which to pounce.

Other times, Jimmy found him standing in the corner where that man he'd shot all that time ago had wasted away. Shadow liked to sniff the rust stains and touch his tongue to the grating. It was for these freedoms that the hatch remained off. And this was how, when the power went out big-time, the bad men got inside. This was how Jimmy woke up one morning with a stranger standing over his bed.

The outage had woken him in the middle of the night. Jimmy slept with the lights on, keeping the ghosts at bay. He even liked a little of the radio static to fill the room, so he couldn't hear any whisperings. When the silence and darkness hit at once with a loud thump, Jimmy had startled awake and scrambled for his flashlight, stepping on Shadow's tail in the process. He waited for the lights to come on, but they remained off. Too tired to think what to do, he went back to sleep, both hands wrapped around his flashlight, Shadow curling up warily against his neck.

The noise of someone coming down the ladder was what stirred him later. Jimmy was dimly aware of a presence in the room. It was a sensation he often felt, but this presence seemed to change the way the silence bounced around, the way even the noise of his breathing echoed. He opened his eyes to find a flashlight shining down on him, a man standing at the foot of his bed.

Jimmy screamed, and the man pounced as if to silence him. A bearded snarl of yellowed teeth caught the beam of light, and then the arc of a steel rod.

There was a flash of pain in Jimmy's shoulder. The man hauled back to hit him again with his length of pipe. Jimmy got his arms up to protect his head. The pipe cracked him on the wrist. There was a screech and a hiss by his head, and then a darting black shape amid the shadows.

The man with the pipe screamed and dropped his flashlight, which doused itself in the bedsheets. Jimmy scrambled away, his mind unable to come to grips with a person in his home. A person in his home. The fear of years and years became real in an instant. He had loosened his precautions. All the venturing out. *Slack, slack,* he told himself, crawling on his hands and knees.

Shadow let out an awful screech, the noise he made when his tail got stepped on. A howl of pain followed. Jimmy felt anger rise up and mix with his fear. He crawled toward the corner, banged into the desk, reached for where it should be propped—

His hands settled around the gun. It'd been years since he'd fired it. Couldn't remember if it was even loaded. But he could still swing it like a club if he had to. He cradled it against his shoulder and waved the barrel through the pitch black. Shadow screeched again. There was a thump of a small body hitting something hard. Jimmy couldn't breathe or swallow. He couldn't see anything but the dim glow of light rising up from the folds of his bed.

He pointed the barrel at a patch of blackness that seemed to move and squeezed the trigger. There was a blinding flash of light from the muzzle, a roar that filled the small space to the seams. In that brief strobe flashed the searing image of a man whirling toward him. Another wild shot. Another glimpse of this stranger in Jimmy's space, a thin man with a long beard and white eyes. And now Jimmy knew where he was, and the third shot did not zing. Its impact was lost in screams. The screams filled the darkness, and then a final shot put an end to even these.

Shadow's eyes glowed beneath the desk. He peered out warily at Jimmy and his new flashlight.

"You okay?" Jimmy asked.

The cat blinked.

"Stay here," Jimmy whispered.

He cradled the flashlight between his cheek and shoulder and checked the clip. Before he left, he nudged the man who was bleeding on his sheets. Jimmy felt a strange numbness at seeing someone down there, even dead. He listened for more intruders as he stole his way toward the ladder.

The power outage and this attack were no coincidence, he told himself. Someone had gotten the door open. They had figured the keypad or pulled a breaker. Jimmy hoped this man had done it alone. He didn't recognize the face, but a lot of years had passed. Beards got long and turned gray. The silver overalls hinted at someone who might know how to break in. The pain in his shoulder and wrist hinted at these being no friends of his.

There was no one on the ladder. Jimmy slipped the rifle over his shoulder and doused the flashlight so no one would see him coming. His palms made the softest of rings on the metal rungs. He was halfway up when he felt Shadow slithering and clacking his way up between the ladder and the wall.

Jimmy hissed at the cat to stay put but it disappeared ahead of him. At the top of the ladder, Jimmy unslung his rifle and held it in one hand. With the other, he pressed the flashlight against his stomach and turned it on. Peeling the lens away from his overalls a little at a time, he cast just enough glow to pick his way through the servers.

There was a noise ahead of him, Shadow or another person, he couldn't tell. Jimmy hesitated before continuing on. It took forever to cross the wide room with the dark machines like this. He could hear them still clacking, still whirring, still putting off heat. But when he got close to the door, the keypad was no longer blinking its sentinel light at him. And there was a void beyond the gleaming door—a door that stood halfway open.

More noise outside. The rustle of fabric, of a person moving. Jimmy killed the flashlight and steadied his rifle. He could taste the fear in his mouth. He wanted to call out for these people to leave him alone. He wanted to say what he had done to all those who came inside. He wanted to drop his gun and cry and beg never to have to do it again.

He poked his head into the hall and strained to see in the darkness, hoped this other person couldn't see him back. The hall contained nothing but the sound of two people breathing. There was a growing awareness that a dark space was shared with another.

"Hank?" someone whispered.

Jimmy turned and squeezed the trigger. There was a flash of light. The rifle kicked him in the shoulder. He retreated into the server room and waited for screams and stomping boots. He waited what felt like forever. Something touched his boot, and Jimmy screamed. It was Shadow purring and rubbing against him.

Chancing his flashlight, he peered around the corner and allowed some light to dribble out. There was a form there, a person on their back. He checked the deep and dark hallways and saw nothing. "Leave me alone!" he yelled out to all the ghosts and more solid things.

Not even his echo called back.

Jimmy looked over this second man only to discover it wasn't a man at all. It was a woman. Her eyes had thankfully fallen shut. A man and a woman coming for his food, coming to steal from him. It made Jimmy angry. And then he saw the woman's swollen and distended belly and got doubly angry. It wasn't as if they were hurting for food, he thought.

94

JIMMY LOCATED THE breaker the bad people had tampered with and had gotten the power back on, but there was no fixing the door. Two days of playing with the wires hanging from the keypad had gotten him nowhere. It made a night of sound sleep impossible, even with the grate back in place. Shadow climbed to the top of the ladder at night and mewed and mewed, and that wouldn't do. And so Jimmy decided that they needed to get away. It gave them an excuse to go do one of their favorite things. He and Shadow went fishing.

The two of them sat on the lowest of the dry landings while Jimmy watched flashes of silver dart below, watched the fish twist beneath and through the flooded stairs. They looked like flashlights aimed from the drowned deep, like beams pointed skyward toward him and Shadow as the two of them peered over the edge of the landing.

Shadow's black tail swished back and forth in the air. His paws hugged the edge of the rusted steel grating, whiskers twitching. For all his consternation, however, Jimmy's bobber remained unmoved.

"Not hungry today," Jimmy said. He whistled a tune for the fish, a catching-fish tune, and Shadow peered up at him, a critic with an unreadable face. Jimmy's stomach growled. "I don't mean us," he told Shadow. "We're plenty hungry. I mean the fish."

Jimmy was hungry from digging for worms all morning. They were hard to find among the overgrowth of the farms. It was hot work when the lights were on, but it kept his mind off the people he'd hurt. He'd been so consumed by that and the promise of a day fishing that he hadn't eaten the veggies that were right there as he dug with his shovel. It was a lot of damn work, catching these fish. First, you had to catch the worms! Jimmy wondered, if the fish liked them so much, why he and Shadow didn't save themselves the trouble and just eat worms. But when he'd held one out, the cat had looked at him like he was crazy.

"I'm not crazy," he had assured Shadow.

He found himself insisting this more and more.

While Jimmy explained that it was the fish that weren't hungry that day, Shadow went back to studying the darting swimmers below. Jimmy did the same. They reminded him of spilled mercury, of a thermometer he broke years back. They changed directions and moved so fast.

He grabbed his pole, lifted his bobber out of the water, and checked the hook. The worm was still on there. Good thing. He only had a few left, and the nearest dirt was a dozen flights up. He lowered the line back into the water, the ping-pong ball resting on the surface. He had learned about fishing from the Legacy. Learned how to tie knots and fix a bobber and sinker, what kind of bait to use, all these instructions that came in perfect handy. It was as if the people who wrote those books somehow knew these things would be important some day.

He watched the fish swim and wondered how they'd gotten in the water. The tanks were a bunch of levels up above the farms, and now they were empty of fish. Jimmy had checked. All he found was algae that looked awful but that made the water in the vats taste pretty good. There were cups and jugs and even the beginnings of a hose to carry the water off to other levels, a Project someone had abandoned years back. Jimmy wondered if they'd dumped the fish over the railing, and now here they were. However it'd happened, he was glad.

There were only a dozen or so of them left. They didn't breed as fast as he could catch them. And the ones that remained were the hardest to catch. They'd watched what happens. They'd seen. They were like Jimmy in those early days, watching the people spiral up to their deaths. They knew like his mother had known that they didn't want to go that way. So they nibbled and nibbled until the worms were gone, but sometimes they couldn't help themselves. They'd get a taste and take a bite instead of a nibble, and then Jimmy would have them up in the air, dripping and dancing, flopping on the rusted grate until he could wrangle their slippery flesh in his fist and work the hook loose.

First, though, the waiting. Jimmy's bobber sat motionless on the rainbow-hued water. Shadow mewed impatiently.

"Listen to you," Jimmy said. "Two years ago, you didn't know what a fish tasted like."

Shadow crouched down on his belly and pawed at the air between the landing and the water as if to say, *I used to catch these all the time.*

"I'm sure you did," Jimmy said, rolling his eyes. He watched the water, which had come up quite a ways since his first time down. The level he had rescued Shadow from was now completely gone. Fish likely lived in the room he'd found Shadow in. He peered down at his feline friend, a new thought coming to him.

"Is that what you were doing in there all that time ago?" he asked.

Shadow looked up at him with a face full of innocence.

"You devil."

The cat licked his paw, turned a circle, and watched for the bobber to move.

It moved.

Jimmy gave the pole a yank and felt resistance, the weight of a fish on his hook. He squealed and lifted the pole and reached out over the rail to grab the line. Shadow mewed and danced and tried to help by swiping at the air and swishing his tail.

"Here, here," Jimmy told the fish. He hauled the line up and rested the pole against the railing, reached over and grabbed more line, the flopping of the fish causing it to dig into his fingers. "Easy, now." He pursed his lips, could never feel like he'd truly caught one of the buggers until he got them over the rail and above the grate of the landing. Sometimes they spit the hook and got the worm for free and laughed at him as they splashed back home.

"Here we go," he told Shadow. He lowered the fish to the metal and got a boot on its tail. He hated this part. The fish looked so upset. This was when he would change his mind and wish he could throw the thing back, but Shadow was already swirling around his legs and swishing his tail. Jimmy held the fish still with his boot and dug the homemade hook out of its lip. The little barb he'd made by bending the needle back before pounding a new point made it hard to get free, but Jimmy had learned that this was the point.

"The point," he said, laughing at his own joke.

Shadow told him to hurry up.

Jimmy tossed the hook and line over the top of the rail to get it out of the way. The fish threw itself against the grating a few times. It peered up at him with its wide eye, its mouth panting frantically. Jimmy reached for his knife.

"I'm sorry," he said. "So, so sorry."

He stuck the knife in the fish's head to stop its pain. He looked away while he did this. So much death. Lifetimes of death. But Shadow was already acting so happy. The life dribbled out of the fish and into the water below. The handful of fish that remained darted up to gobble at the places the blood hit the water, and Jimmy wondered why they did that. There was none of this that he enjoyed, not the digging for worms, nor the long hike, nor the setting of hooks, nor the killing, nor the cleaning—but he did it anyway.

He cleaned the fish the way the Legacy showed, a slice behind the gills, and then a swipe along the bone toward the tail. Two runs of the knife like this, and he had two pieces of meat. He left the scales on, since Shadow never touched that part. Both fillets went onto a chipped plate near the stairwell.

Shadow spun in circles a few times, his belly making that thrumming noise, then began tearing at the flesh with his teeth.

Jimmy retired to the other end of the railing. He had a towel there. He wiped his hands of the foul slickness and sat down, his back against the closed doors of level one-thirty-one, and watched the cat eat. Silvery shapes darted below. The landing and all else seemed calm in the pale green glow of the emergency stairwell lights.

Before long, there wouldn't be any fish left. Another year at this rate, and Jimmy figured he'd catch them all.

"But not the last one," he told himself as he watched Shadow eat. Jimmy hadn't tasted a fish yet and didn't think he ever would. The catching of them was too much work, little of it fun, much of it disgusting. But he thought, when he came down one day with his rod and his jar of dirt and worms and saw only one fish remained, that he would leave it alone. Just the one, he thought. It would be scared enough down there. No need to go yanking it out into the frightful air. Just let the poor thing be.

95

Silo 1
2345

DONALD SET HIS alarm for three in the morning, but there was little chance of him falling asleep. He'd waited weeks for this. A chance to give a life rather than take one. A chance at redemption and a chance for the truth, a chance to satisfy his growing suspicions.

He stared at the ceiling and considered what he was about to do. It wasn't what Erskine or Victor had hoped he would do if someone like him was in charge, but those men had got a lot wrong, least of all who he was. This wasn't the end of the end of the world. This was the beginning of something else. An end to the not knowing what was out there.

He studied his hand in the dim light spilling from the bathroom and thought of the outside. At two-thirty, he decided he'd waited long enough. He got up, showered and shaved, put on a fresh pair of coveralls, tugged on his boots. He grabbed his badge, clipped it to his collar, and left his apartment with his head up and his shoulders back. Long strides took him down a hall with a few lights still on and the distant clatter of a keyboard, someone working late. The door to Eren's office was closed. Donald called for the lift and waited.

Before heading all the way down, he checked to see if it would be all for naught by scanning his badge and pressing the shiny button marked fifty-four. The light flashed and the lift lurched into motion. So far, so good. The lift didn't stop until it reached the armory. The doors opened on a familiar darkness studded with tall shadows—black cliffs of shelves and bins. Donald held his hand on the edge of the door to keep it from shutting and stepped out into the room. The vastness of the space could somehow be felt, as though the echoes of his racing pulse were being swallowed by the distance. He waited for a light to flick on at the far end, for Anna to walk out brushing her hair or with a bottle of Scotch in her hand, but nothing in that room moved. Everything was quiet and still. The pilots and the temporary activity were gone.

He returned to the lift and pressed another button. The lift sank. It drifted past more storage levels, past the reactor. The doors cracked open on the medical wing. Donald could feel the tens of thousands of bodies arranged all around him, all facing the ceiling, eyelids closed. Some of them were well and truly dead, he thought. One was about to be woken.

He went straight to the doctor's office and knocked on the jamb. The assistant on duty lifted his head from behind the monitor. He wiped his eyes behind his glasses, adjusted them on his nose, and blinked at Donald.

"How's it going?" Donald asked.

"Hmm? Good. Good." The young man shook his wrist and checked his watch, an ancient thing. "We got someone going into deep freeze? I didn't get a call. Is Wilson up?"

"No, no. I just couldn't sleep." Donald pointed at the ceiling. "I went to see if anyone was up at the cafeteria, then figured since I was restless, I might as well come down here and see if you wanted me to finish out your shift. I can sit and watch a film as well as anyone."

The assistant glanced at his monitor and laughed guiltily. "Yeah." He checked his watch again, had somehow already forgotten what it just told him. "Two hours left. I wouldn't mind slagging off. You'll wake me if anything pops up?" He stood and stretched, covered his yawn with his hand.

"Of course."

The medical assistant staggered out from behind the desk. Donald stepped around and pulled the seat away, sat down and propped up his feet as though he wouldn't be going anywhere for hours.

"I owe you one," the young man said, collecting his coat from the back of the door.

"Oh, we're even," Donald said under his breath as soon as the man was gone.

He waited for the lift to chime before launching into action. There was a plastic drink container on the drying rack by the sink. He grabbed this and filled it with water, the musical pitch of the vessel filling like a rising anxiety.

The lid came off the powder. Two scoops. He stirred with one of the long plastic tongue depressors and twisted the lid on, put the powder back in the fridge. The wheelchair wouldn't budge at first. He saw that the brakes were on, the little metal arms pressing into the soft rubber. He freed these, grabbed one of the blankets from the tall cabinet and a paper gown, tossed them onto the seat. Just like before. But he'd do it right this time. He collected the medical kit, made sure there was a fresh set of gloves.

The wheelchair rattled out the door and down the hall, and Donald's palms felt sweaty against the handles. To keep the front wheels silent, he rocked the chair back on its large rubber tires. The small wheels spun lazily in the air as he hurried.

He entered his code into the keypad and waited for a red light, for some impediment, some blockade. The light winked green. Donald pulled the door open and swerved between the pods toward the one that held his sister.

There was a mix of anticipation and guilt. This was as bold a step as his run up that hill in a suit. The stakes were higher for involving family, for waking someone into this harsh world, for subjecting her to the same brutality Anna had foisted upon him, that Thurman had foisted upon her, on and on, a never-ending misery of shifts.

He left the wheelchair in place and knelt by the control pad. Hesitant, he lurched to his feet and peered through the glass porthole, just to be sure.

She looked so serene in there, probably wasn't plagued by nightmares like he was. Donald's doubts grew. And then he imagined her waking up on her own; he imagined her conscious and beating on the glass, demanding to be let out. He saw her feisty spirit, heard her demand not to be lied to, and he knew that if she were standing there with him, she would ask him to do it. She would rather know and suffer than be left asleep in ignorance.

He crouched by the keypad and entered his code. The keypad beeped cheerfully as he pressed the red button. There was a click from within the pod, like a valve opening. He turned the dial and watched the temperature gauge, waited for it to start climbing.

Donald rose and stood by the pod, and time slowed to a crawl. He expected someone to come find him before the process was complete. But there was another clack and a hiss from the lid. He laid out the gauze and the tape. He separated the two rubber gloves and began pulling them on, a cloud of chalk misting the air as he snapped the elastic.

He opened the lid the rest of the way.

His sister lay on her back, her arms by her sides. She had not yet moved. A panic seized him as he went over the procedure again. Had he forgotten something? Dear God, had he killed her?

Charlotte coughed. Water trailed down her cheeks as the frost on her eyelids melted. And then her eyes fluttered open weakly before returning to thin slits against the light.

"Hold still," Donald told her. He pressed a square of gauze to her arm and removed the needle. He could feel the steel slide beneath the pad and his fingers as he extracted it from her arm. Holding the gauze in place, he took a length of tape hanging from the wheelchair and applied it across. The last was the catheter. He covered her with the towel, applied pressure and slowly removed the tube. And then she was free of the machine, crossing her arms and shivering. He helped her into the paper gown, left the back open.

"I'm lifting you out," he said.

Her teeth clattered in response.

Donald shifted her feet toward her butt to tent her knees. Reaching down beneath her armpits—her flesh cool to the touch—and another arm under her legs, he lifted her easily. It felt like she weighed so little. He could smell the cast-stink on her flesh.

Charlotte mumbled something as he placed her in the wheelchair. The blanket was draped across so that she sat on the fabric rather than the cold seat. As soon as she was settled, he wrapped the blanket around her. She chose to remain in a ball with her arms wrapped around her shins rather than place her feet on the stirrups.

"Where am I?" she asked, her voice a sheet of crackling ice.

"Take it easy," Donald told her. He closed the lid on the pod, tried to remember if there was anything else, looked for anything he'd left behind. "You're with me," he said as he pushed her toward the exit. That was where both of them were: with each other. There was no home, no place on the earth to welcome one to anymore, just a hellish nightmare in which to drag another soul for sad company.

96

THE HARDEST PART was making her wait to eat. Donald knew what it felt like to be that hungry. He put her through the same routine he'd endured a number of times: made her drink the bitter concoction, made her use the bathroom to flush her system, had her sit on the edge of the tub and take a warm shower, then put her in a fresh set of clothes and a new blanket.

He watched as she finished the last of the drink. Her lips gradually faded to pink from pale blue. Her skin was so white. Donald couldn't remember if she'd been so pale before orientation. Maybe it had happened overseas, sitting in those dark trailers with only the light of a monitor to bathe in.

"I need to go make an appearance," he told her. "Everyone else will be getting up. I'll bring you breakfast on my way back down."

Charlotte sat quietly in one of the leather chairs around the old war planning table, her feet tucked up under her. She tugged at the collar of the overalls as if they itched her skin. "Mom and Dad are gone," she said, repeating what he'd told her earlier. Donald wasn't sure what she would and wouldn't remember. She hadn't been on her stress medications as long or as recently as him. But it didn't matter. He could tell her the truth. Tell her and hate himself for doing it.

"I'll be back in a little bit. Just stay here and try to get some rest. Don't leave this room, okay?"

The words echoed hollow as he hurried through the warehouse and toward the lift. He remembered hearing from others as soon as they woke him that he should get some rest. Charlotte had been asleep for three centuries. As he scanned his badge and waited for the lift, Donald thought on how much time had passed and how little had changed. The world was still the ruin they'd left it. Or if it wasn't, they were about to find out.

He rode up to the operations level and checked in with Eren. The Ops head was already at his desk, surrounded by files, one hand tangled in his hair, his elbow on piles of paperwork. There was no steam from his mug of coffee. He'd been at his desk for a while.

"Thurman," he said, glancing up.

Donald startled and glanced down the hall, looking for someone else.

"Any progress with 18?"

"I, uh . . ." Donald tried to remember. "Last I heard, they'd breached the barrier in the lowest levels. The head over there thinks the fighting will be over in a day or two."

"Good. Glad the shadow is working out. Scary time not to have one. There was this one time on my third shift I think it was when we lost a head while he was between shadows. Helluva time finding a recruit." Eren leaned back in his chair. "The mayor wasn't an option; the head of Security was as bright as a lump of coal; so we had to—"

"I'm sorry to interrupt," Donald said, pointing down the hall. "I need to get back to—"

"Oh, of course." Eren waved his hand, seemed embarrassed. "Right. Me too."

"—just a lot to do this morning. Grabbing breakfast and then I'll be in my room." He jerked his head toward the empty office across the hall. "Tell Gable I took care of myself, okay? I don't want to be disturbed."

"Sure, sure." Eren shooed him with his hand.

Donald spun back to the lift. Up to the cafeteria. His stomach rumbled its agreement. He'd been up all night without eating. He'd been up and empty for far too long.

97

HE WAS PUSHING the time limit by letting her eat an hour early, but it was difficult to say no. Donald encouraged her to take small bites, to slow down. And while Charlotte chewed, he brought her up to date. She knew about the silos from orientation. He told her about the wallscreens, about the cleaners, that he had been woken because someone had disappeared. Charlotte had a hard time grasping these things. It took saying them several times until they became strange even to his ears.

"They let them see outside, these people in the other silos?" she asked, chewing on a small bite of biscuit.

"Yeah. I asked Thurman once why we put them there. You know what he told me?"

Charlotte shrugged and took a sip of water.

"They're there to keep them from wanting to leave. We have to show them death to keep them in. Otherwise, they'll always want to see what's over the rise. Thurman said it's human nature."

"But some of them go anyway." She wiped her mouth with her napkin, picked up her fork, her hand trembling, and pulled Donald's half-eaten breakfast toward her.

"Yeah, some of them go anyway," Donald said. "And you need to take it easy." He watched her dig into his eggs and thought about his own trip up the drone lift. He was one of those people who had gone anyway. It wasn't something she needed to know.

"We have one of those screens," Charlotte said. "I remember watching the clouds boil." She looked up at Donald. "Why do we have one?"

Donald reached quickly for his handkerchief and coughed into its folds. "Because we're human," he answered, tucking the cloth away. "If we think there's no point in going out there—that we'll die if we go—we'll stay here and do what we're told. But I know of a way to see what's out there."

"Yeah?" Charlotte scraped the last of his eggs onto her fork and lifted them to her mouth. She waited.

"And I'm going to need your help."

They pulled the tarp off one of the drones. Charlotte ran a trembling hand down its wing and walked unsteadily around the machine. Grabbing the flap on the back of a wing, she worked it up and down. She did the same for the tail. The drone had a black dome and nose that gave it something like a face. It sat silently, unmoving, while Charlotte inspected it.

Donald noticed that three of the other drones were missing—the floor glossy where their tarps used to drape. And the neat pyramid of bombs in the munitions rack was missing a few from the top. Signs of the armory's use these past weeks. Donald went to the hangar door and worked it open.

"No hardware?" Charlotte asked. She peered under one of the wings where bad things could be attached.

"No," Donald said. "Not for this." He ran back and helped her push. They steered the drone toward the open maw of the lift. The wings just barely fitted.

"There should be a strap or a linkage," she said. She lowered herself gingerly and crawled behind the drone, worked her way beneath the wing.

"There's something in the floor," Donald said, remembering the nub that moved along the track. "I'll get a light."

He retrieved a flashlight from one of the bins, made sure it had a charge and brought it back to her. Charlotte hooked the drone into the launch mechanism and squirmed her way out. She seemed slow to stand and he lent her his hand.

"And you're sure this lift'll work?" She brushed hair, still wet from the shower, off her face.

"Very sure," Donald said. He led her down the hall, past the barracks and bathrooms. Charlotte stiffened when he led her into the piloting room and pulled back the plastic sheets. He flipped the switch on the lift controls. She stared blankly at one of the stations with its joysticks, readouts and screens.

"You can operate this, right?" he asked.

She broke from her trance and stared at him a moment, then nodded her head. "If they'll power up."

"They will." He watched the light above the lift controls flash while Charlotte settled behind one of the stations. The room felt overly quiet and empty with all those other stations sitting under sheets of plastic. The dust was gone from them, Donald saw. The place was recently lived in. He thought of the requisitions he'd signed for flights, each one at considerable cost. He thought of the risk of them being spotted in the wallscreens, the need to fly deep in the swirling clouds. Eren had stressed the one-use nature of the drones. The air outside was bad for them, he'd said. Their range was limited. Donald had thought about why this might be as he'd dug through Thurman's files.

Charlotte flicked several switches, the neat clicks breaking the silence, and the control station whirred to life.

"The lift takes a while," he told her. He didn't say how he knew, but he thought back to that ride up all those years ago. He remembered his breath fogging the dome of his helmet as he rose to what he had hoped might be his death. Now he had a different hope. He thought of what Erskine had told him about wiping the earth clean. He thought about Victor's suicide note to Thurman. This project of theirs was about resetting life. And Donald, whether by madness or reason, had grown convinced that the effort was more precise than anyone had rights to imagine.

Charlotte adjusted her screen. She flicked a switch, and a light bloomed on the monitor. It was the glare of the steel door of the lift, lit up by the drone's headlamp and viewed by its cameras.

"It's been so long," she said. Donald looked down and saw that her hands were trembling. She rubbed them together before returning them to the controls. Wiggling in her seat, she located the pedals with her feet, and then adjusted the brightness of the monitor so it wasn't so blinding.

"Is there anything I can do?" Donald asked.

Charlotte laughed and shook her head. "No. Feels strange not to be filing a flight plan or anything. I usually have a target, you know?" She looked back at Donald and flashed a smile.

He squeezed her shoulder. It felt good to have her around. She was all he had left. "Your flight plan is to fly as far and as fast as you can," he told her. His hope was that without a bomb, the drone would go further. His hope was that the limited range wasn't preprogrammed somehow. There was a flashing light from the lift controls. Donald hurried over to check them.

"The door's coming up," Charlotte said. "I think we've got daylight."

Donald hurried back over. He glanced out the door and down the hall, thinking he'd heard something.

"Engine check," Charlotte said. "We've got ignition."

She wiggled in her seat. The overalls he'd stolen for her were too big, were bunched around her arms. Donald stood behind her and watched the monitor, which showed a view of swirling skies up a sloped ramp. He remembered that view. It became difficult to breathe, seeing that. The drone was pulled from the lift and arranged on the ramp. Charlotte hit another switch.

"Brakes on," she said, her leg straightening. "Applying thrust."

Her hand slid forward. The camera view dipped as the drone strained against its brakes.

"Been a long time since I've done this without a launcher," she said nervously.

Donald was about to ask if that was a problem when she shifted her feet and the view on the screen lifted. The metal shaft vibrated and began to race by. The swirling clouds filled the viewscreen until that was all that existed. Charlotte said, "Lift-off," and worked the yoke with her right hand. Donald found himself leaning to the side as the drone banked and the ground came briefly into view before all was swallowed by thick clouds.

"Which way?" she asked. She flicked a switch and the terrain below stood out by radar, by something that could pierce the clouds.

"I don't think it matters," he said. "Just straight." He leaned closer to watch the strange but familiar landscape slide by. There were the great divots he had helped create. There was another tower down in the middle of a depression. The remnants of the convention—the tents and fairgrounds and stages—were long gone, eaten by the tiny machines in the air. "Just a straight line," he said, pointing. It was a theory, a crazy idea, but he needed to see for himself before he dared say anything.

The pattern of depressions ended in the distance. The clouds thinned occasionally, giving him a true glimpse of the ground. Donald strained to see beyond the bowls when Charlotte let go of the throttle and reached for a bank of dials and indicators. "Uh . . . I think we have a problem." She flipped a switch back and forth. "I'm losing oil pressure."

"No." Donald watched the screen as the clouds swirled and the land seemed to heave upward. It was too early. Unless he'd missed some step, some precaution. "Keep going," he breathed, as much to the machine as to its pilot.

"She's handling screwy," Charlotte said. "Everything feels loose."

Donald thought of all the drones in the hangar. They could launch another. But he suspected the result would be the same. He might be resistant to whatever was out there, but the machines weren't. He thought of the cleaning suits, the way things were meant to break down at a certain time, a certain place. Invisible destroyers so precise that they could let loose their vengeance as soon as a cleaner hit a hill, reached a particular altitude, as soon as they dared to rise up. He reached for his cloth and coughed into it, and had a vague memory of workers scrubbing the airlock after pulling him back inside.

"You're at the edge," he said, pointing to the last of the silos on the radar as the bowl disappeared beneath the drone's camera. "Just a little further."

But in truth, he had no idea how much further it might take. Maybe you could fly straight around the world and right back where you started, and that still wouldn't be far enough.

"I'm losing lift," Charlotte said. Her hands were twin blurs. They went from the controls to switches and back again.

"Engine two is out," she said. "I'm in a glide. Altitude oh-two-hundred."

It looked like far less on the screen. They were beyond the last of the hills now. The clouds had thinned. There was a scar in the earth, a trench that may have been a river, black sticks like charred bones that stuck up in sharp points like pencil lead—all that remained of ancient trees, perhaps. Or the steel girders of a large security fence, eaten away by time.

"Go, go," he whispered. Every second aloft provided a new sight, a new vista. Here was a breath of freedom. Here was an escape from hell.

"Camera's going. Altitude oh-one-fifty."

There was a bright flash on the screen like the shock of dying electrics. A purplish cast followed from the frying sensors, then a wash of blue where once there was nothing but browns and grays.

"Altitude fifty feet. Gonna touch down hard."

Donald blinked away tears as the drone plummeted and the earth rushed up to meet the machine. He blinked away tears at the sight on the monitor, nothing wrong with the camera at all.

"Blue—" he said.

It was an utterance of confirmation just before a vivid green landscape swallowed the dying drone. The monitor faded from color to darkness. Charlotte released the controls and cursed. She slapped the console with her palm. But as she turned and apologized to Donald, he was already wrapping his arms around her, squeezing her, kissing her cheek.

"Did you see it?" he asked, his voice a breathless whisper. "Did you see?"

"See what?" Charlotte pulled away, her face a hardened mask of disappointment. "Every gauge was toast there at the end. Blasted drone. Probably been sitting too long—"

"No, no," Donald said. He pointed to the screen, which was now dark and lifeless. "You did it," he said. "I saw it. There were blue skies and green grass out there, Charla! I saw it!"

98

Silo 17
2331
Year Twenty

WITHOUT WANTING TO, Solo became an expert in how things broke down. Day by day, he watched steel and iron crumble to rust, watched paint peel and orange flecks curl up, saw the black dust gather as metal eroded to powder. He learned what rubber hoses felt like as they hardened, dried up and cracked. He learned how adhesives failed, things appearing on the floor that once were affixed to walls and ceilings, objects moved suddenly and violently by the twin gods of gravity and dilapidation. Most of all, he learned how bodies rot. They didn't always go in a flash—like a mother pushed upward by a jostling crowd or a father sliding into the shadows of a darkened corridor. Instead, they were often chewed up and carried off in invisible pieces. Time and maggots alike grew wings; they flew and flew and took all things with them.

Solo tore a page from one of the boring articles in the *Ri–Ro* book and folded it into a tent. The silo, he thought, belonged to the insects in many ways. Wherever the bodies were gathered, the insects swarmed in dark clouds. He had read up on them in the books. Somehow, maggots turned into flies. White and writhing became black and buzzing. Things broke down and changed.

He threaded lengths of string into the folded piece of paper to give something to hang the weight on. This was when Shadow would normally get in the way, would come and arch his back against Solo's arm, step on whatever he was doing, make him annoyed and make him laugh at the same time. But Shadow didn't interrupt.

Solo made small knots in the string to keep them from pulling through. The paper was doubled over across the holes so it wouldn't tear. He knew well how things broke down. He was an expert in things he wished he could unlearn. Solo could tell at a glance how long it'd been since someone had died.

The people he'd killed years back had been stiff when he moved them, but this only lasted a while. People soon swelled up and stank. Their bodies let off gasses and the flies swarmed. The flies swarmed and the maggots feasted.

The stench would make his eyes water and his throat burn. And the bodies would soon grow soft. Solo had to move some bodies on the stairs once, tangled where they lay and difficult to step over, and the flesh came right apart. It became like cottage cheese he'd had back when there was still milk and goats to get it from. Flesh came apart once the person was no longer inside, holding themselves together. Solo concentrated on holding himself together. He tied the other ends of the strings to one of the small metal washers from Supply. Chewing his tongue, he made the finest of knots.

String and fabric didn't last either, but clothes stayed around longer than people. Within a year, it was clothes and bones that were left. And hair. The hair seemed to go last. It clung to bones and sometimes hung over empty and gazing sockets. The hair made it worse. It lent bones an identity. Beards on most, but not on the young or on the women.

Within five years, even the clothes would break down. After ten, it was mostly bones. These days, so very long after the silo had gone dark and quiet—over twenty years since he'd been shown the secret lair beneath the servers—it was only the bones. Except for up in the cafeteria. The rot everywhere else made those bodies behind that door all the more curious.

Solo held up his parachute, a paper tent with little strings fastened to a tiny washer. He had dozens and dozens of bits of string lying in tangles across the open book. A handful of washers remained. He gave one of the strings on his parachute a tug and thought of the bodies up in the cafeteria. Behind that door, there were dead people who wouldn't break down like the others. When he and Shadow had first discovered them, he'd assumed they'd recently passed. Dozens of them, dying together and piled on one another as though they'd been tossed in there or had been crawling atop the others. The door to the forbidden outside was just beyond them, Solo knew. But he hadn't gone that far. He had closed the door and left in a hurry, spooked by the lifeless eyeballs and the strange feeling of seeing a face other than his own peering back at him like that. He had left the bodies and not come back for a long time. He had waited for them to become bones. They never had.

He went to the rail and peered over, made sure the piece of paper was tented, ready to grab the air. There was a cool updraft from the flooded deep. Solo leaned out beyond the third-level railing, the fine paper pinched in one hand, the washer resting in his other palm. He wondered why some people rotted and others kept going. What made them break down?

"Break down," he said aloud. He liked the way his voice sounded sometimes. He was an expert in how things broke down. Shadow should've been there, rubbing against his ankles, but he wasn't.

"I'm an expert," Solo told himself. "Breaking down, breaking down." He stretched out his arms and released the parachute, watched it plummet for a moment before the strings went taut. And then it bobbed and twisted in the air as it sank into the dwindling depths. "Down down down," he called after the parachute. All the way to the bottom. Sinking until it splashed invisible or got caught up along the way.

Solo knew well how bodies rot. He scratched his beard and squinted after the disappearing chute, then sat back down and crossed his legs, the knee torn completely out of his old overalls. He mumbled to himself, delaying what needed to be done, his Project for the day, and instead tore another page from the shrinking book, trying not to think about yet another carcass that would soon dwindle with time.

99

THERE HAD BEEN items Solo spent days and weeks searching for. There had been some things he'd needed that had consumed his hunts for years. Often, he found useful things much later, when he needed them no longer. Like the time he had come across a stash of razors. A great big bin of them in a doctor's office. All the important stuff—the bandages, medicine, the tape—had long ago been snagged by those fighting over the scraps. But a bin of new razors, many of the blades still shiny, taunted him. He had long before resigned himself to his beard, but there had been times before that when he would've killed for a razor.

Other times, he found a thing before he even knew he needed it. The machete was like that. A great blade found beneath the body of a man not long dead. Solo had taken it simply so nobody else would have the murderous thing. He had locked himself below the server room for three days, terrified of the sight of another still-warm body. That had been many years ago. It took a while longer for the farms to thicken up where the machete became necessary. By then, he had taken to leaving his gun behind—no longer any use for it—and the machete became a constant companion, something found before he knew he needed it.

Solo set the last of the parachutes free and watched as it narrowly missed the landing on level nine. The folded paper vanished out of sight. He thought of the things Shadow had helped him find over the years, mostly food. But there was one time when Shadow had run off with a mind of his own. It was on a trip down to Supply when Shadow had raced ahead and had disappeared across a landing. Solo had followed with his flashlight.

The cat had mewed and mewed by a door—Solo wary of another pile of bodies—but the apartment had been empty. Up on the kitchen counter, twirling, pawing at a cabinet full of little cans. Ancient and spotted with rust, but with pictures of cats on them. A madness in Shadow, and there, with a short cord plugged into the wall, a battered contraption, a mechanized can opener.

Solo smiled and gazed over the rail, thinking on the things found and lost over the years. He remembered pressing the button on the top of that gadget the first time, how Shadow had whipped into a frenzy, how neatly the tops had come off. He remembered not being impressed at all with the food in the cans, but Shadow had a mind of his own.

Solo turned and studied the book with the torn pages, feeling sad. He was out of washers, so he left the book behind and reluctantly headed down to the farms. He was off to do what needed to be done.

Hacking at the greenery with his machete, Solo marveled that the farms hadn't long ago rotted to ruin without people around to tend them. But the lights were rigged to come on and off, and more than half of them still could. Water continued to dribble from pipes. Pumps kicked on and off with angry buzzes and loud grumbles. Electricity stolen from his realm below was brought up on wires that snaked the stairwell walls. Nothing worked perfectly, but Solo saw that man's relationship to the crops mostly consisted of eating them. Now it was only him eating. Him and the rats and the worms.

He carried his burden through the thickest plots, needing to reach the far corners of the farm where the lights no longer burned, where the soil was cool and damp, where nothing grew anymore. A special place. Away from his weekly trips to gather food. A place he would come to as a destination rather than simply pass because it was along the way.

Leaving the heat of the lights, he entered a dark place. He liked it back here. It reminded him of the room beneath the servers, a private and safe place where one could hide and not be disturbed. And there, scattered among other abandoned and forgotten tools, a shovel. A thing he needed right when he needed it. This was the other way of finding things. It was when the silo was in a gifting mood. It wasn't a mood the silo got into often.

Solo knelt and placed his burden by the edge of the three-railing fence. The body in the bag had gone into that stiff phase. Soon it would soften. After that—

Solo didn't want to think after that. He was an expert in some things he'd rather not know.

He collected the shovel and scampered over the top rail—it was too dark to hunt for the gate. The shovel growled and crunched through the dirt. He lifted each scoop into the air. Soft sighs and little piles slid out. Some things you found just when you needed them, and Solo thought of the years that had passed so swiftly with his friend. He already missed the way Shadow rubbed on his shin while he worked, always in the way but clever enough not to be stepped on, coming in a flash whenever Solo broke out in a whistle, there at just the right time. A thing found, before he even knew he needed it.

100

Silo 1
2345

DONALD'S BOOTS ECHOED in the lower-level shift storage, where thousands of pods lay packed together like gleaming stones. He stooped to check another nameplate. He had lost count of his position down the aisle and was worried he'd have to start over again. Bringing a rag to his mouth, he coughed. He wiped his lip and carried on. Something heavy and cold weighed down one pocket and pressed against his thigh. Something heavy and cold lay within his chest.

He finally found the pod marked *Troy*. Donald rubbed the glass and peered inside. There was a man in there, older than he seemed. Older than Donald remembered. A blue cast overwhelmed pale flesh. White hair and white brows possessed an azure tint.

Donald studied the man, hesitated, reconsidered. He had come there with no wheelchair, no medical kit. Just a cold heaviness. A slice of truth and a desire to know more. Sometimes a thing needed opening before closure was found.

He bent by the control pad and repeated the procedure that had freed his sister. He thought of Charlotte up in the barracks as he entered his code. She couldn't know what he was doing down there. She couldn't know. Thurman had been like a second father to them both.

The dial was turned to the right. Numbers blinked, then ticked up a degree. Donald stood and paced. He circled that pod with a name on it, the name of a man they'd turned him into, this sarcophagus that now held his creator. The cold in Donald's heart spread into his limbs while Thurman warmed. Donald coughed into a rag stained pink. He tucked it back into his pocket and drew out the length of cord.

A report from Victor's files came to him as he stood there, roles reversed, thawing the Thaw Man. Victor had written of old experiments where guards and prisoners switched places, and the abused soon became the abuser. Donald found the idea detestable, that people could change so swiftly. He found the results unbelievable. But he had seen good men and women arrive on the Hill with noble intentions, had seen them change. He had been given a dose of power on this shift and could feel its allure. His discovery was that evil men arose from evil systems, and that any man had the potential to be perverted. Which was why some systems needed to come to an end.

The temperature rose and the lid was triggered. It opened with a sigh. Donald reached in and lifted it the rest of the way. He half expected a hand to shoot out and snatch his wrist but there was just a man lying inside, still and steaming. Just a man, pathetic and naked, a tube running into his arm, another between his legs. Muscles sagged. Pale flesh gathered in folds of wrinkles. Hair clung in wisps. Donald took Thurman's hands and placed them together. He looped the cord around Thurman's wrists, threaded it between his hands and around the loops of cord, then cinched a knot to draw the loops tight. Donald stood back and watched his wrinkled eyelids for any sign of life.

Thurman's lips moved. They parted and seemed to take a first, experimental gasp. It was like watching the dead become reanimated, and Donald appreciated for the first time the miracle of these machines. He coughed into his fist as Thurman stirred. The old man's eyes fluttered open, melted frost tracking from their corners, lending him a degree of false humanity. Wrinkled hands came up to wipe away the crust and Donald knew what that felt like, lids that wouldn't fully part, that felt as though they'd grown together. A grunt spilled out as Thurman struggled with the cord. He came to more fully and saw that all was not right.

"Be still," Donald told him. He placed a hand on the old man's forehead, could feel the chill still in his flesh. "Easy."

"Anna—" Thurman whispered. He licked his lips, and Donald realized he hadn't even brought water, hadn't brought the bitter drink. There was no doubting what he was there to do.

"Can you hear me?" he asked.

Thurman's eyelids fluttered open again; his pupils dilated. He seemed to focus on Donald's face, eyes flicking back and forth in stunted recognition.

"Son . . . ?" His voice was hoarse.

"Lie still," Donald told him, even as Thurman turned to the side and coughed into his bound hands. He peered at the cord knotted around his wrists, his expression confused. Donald turned and checked the door in the distance. "I need you to listen to me."

"What's going on here?" Thurman gripped the edge of the pod and tried to pull himself upright. Donald fished into his pocket for the pistol. Thurman gaped at the black steel as the barrel was leveled on him. His awareness thawed in an instant. He remained perfectly still, only his eyes moving as he met Donald's gaze. "What year is it?" he asked.

"Another two hundred years before you kill us all," Donald said. The barrel trembled with hatred. He wrapped his other hand around the grip and took half a step back. Thurman was weak and bound but Donald was taking no chances. The old man was like a coiled snake on a cold morning. Donald couldn't help but think of what he would be capable of as the day warmed.

Thurman licked his lips and studied Donald. Curls of steam rose from the old man's shoulders. "Anna told you," he finally said.

Donald had a sadistic urge to tell him that Anna was dead. He felt a prideful twinge and wanted to insist that he'd figured it out for himself. He simply nodded instead.

"You have to know this is the only way," Thurman whispered.

"There are a thousand ways," Donald said. He moved the gun to his other hand and dried his sweaty palm on his overalls.

Thurman glanced at the gun, then searched the room beyond Donald for help. After a pause, he settled back against the pod. Steam rose from within the unit, but Donald could see him begin to shiver against the cold.

"I used to think you were trying to live forever," Donald said.

Thurman laughed. He inspected the knotted cord once more, looked at the needle and tube hanging from his arm. "Just long enough."

"Long enough for what? To whittle humanity down to nothing? To let one of these silos go free and then sit here and kill the rest?"

Thurman nodded. He pulled his feet closer and hugged his shins. He looked so thin and fragile without his overalls on, without his proud shoulders thrown back.

"You saved all these people just to kill most of them. And us as well."

Thurman whispered a reply.

"Louder," Donald said.

The old man mimed taking a drink. Donald showed him the gun. It was all he had. Thurman tapped his chest and tried to speak again, and Donald took a wary step closer. "Tell me why," Donald said. "I'm the one in charge here. Me. Tell me or I swear I'll let everyone out of their silos right now."

Thurman's eyes became slits. "Fool," he hissed. "They'll kill each other."

His voice was barely audible. Donald could hear all the cryo-pods around them humming. He stepped even closer, more confident with each passing moment that this was the right thing to do.

"I know what you think they'll do to one another," Donald said. "I know about this great cleanse, this reset." He jabbed the gun at Thurman's chest. "I know you see these silos as starships taking people to a better world. I've read every note and memo and file you have access to. But this is what I want to hear from you before you die—"

Donald felt his legs wobble. A coughing fit seized him. He fumbled for his cloth but pink spittle struck the silver pod before he could cover his mouth. Thurman watched. Donald steadied himself, tried to remember what he'd been saying.

"I want to know why all the heartache," Donald said, his voice scratchy, his throat on fire. "All the miserable lives coming and going, the people down here you plan on killing, on never waking. Your own daughter . . ." He searched Thurman's face for some reaction. "Why not freeze us for a thousand years and wake us when it's done? I know now what I helped you build. I want to know why we couldn't sleep through it all. If you wanted a better place for us, why not take us there? Why the suffering?"

Thurman remained perfectly still.

"Tell me why," Donald said. His voice cracked but he pretended to be okay. He lifted the barrel, which had drooped.

"Because no one can know," Thurman finally said. "It has to die with us."

"What has to die?"

Thurman licked his lips. "Knowledge. The things we left out of the Legacy. The ability to end it all with the flip of a switch."

Donald laughed. "You think we won't discover them again? The means to destroy ourselves?"

Thurman shrugged his naked shoulders. The steam rising from them had dissipated. "Eventually. Which is a longer time than right now."

Donald waved his gun at the pods all around him. "And so all this goes as well. We're supposed to choose one tribe, one of your starships to land, and everything else is shut down. That's the pact you made?"

Thurman nodded.

"Well, someone broke your pact," Donald said. "Someone put me here in your place. I'm the shepherd now."

Thurman's eyes widened. His gaze traveled from the gun to the badge clipped on Donald's collar. Clattering teeth were silenced by the clenching and unclenching of his jaw. "No," he said.

"I never asked for this job," Donald said, more to himself than to Thurman. He steadied the barrel. "For any of these jobs."

"Me neither," Thurman replied, and Donald was again reminded of those prisoners and those guards. This could be him in that pod. It could be anyone standing there with that gun. It was the system.

There were a hundred other things he wanted to ask or say. He wanted to tell this man how much like a father he'd been to him, but what did that mean when fathers could be as abusive as they were loving? He wanted to scream at Thurman for the damage he'd done to the world, but some part of Donald knew the damage had been done long before and that it was irreversible. And finally, there was a part of him that wanted to beg for help, to free this man from his pod; a part that wanted to take his place, to curl up inside and go back to sleep—a part that found being the prisoner was so much easier than remaining on guard. But his sister was up above, recovering. They both had more questions that needed answering. And in a silo not far away, a transformation was taking place, the end of an uprising, and Donald wanted to see how that played out.

All this and more raced through Donald's mind. It wouldn't be long before Dr. Wilson returned to his desk and possibly glanced at a screen just as the right camera cycled through. And even as Thurman's mouth parted to say something, Donald realized that waking the old man to hear his excuses had been a mistake. There was little to learn here.

Thurman leaned forward. "Donny," he said. He reached out with bound wrists for the pistol in Donald's hand. His arms moved slowly and feebly, not with the hope—Donald didn't think—of snatching the gun away, but possibly with the desire to pull it close, to press it against his chest or his mouth the way Victor had, such was the sadness in the old man's eyes.

Thurman reached past the lip of the pod and groped for the gun, and Donald very nearly handed it to him, just to see what he would do with it.

He pulled the trigger instead. He pulled the trigger before he could regret it.

The bang was unconscionably loud. There was a bright flash, a horrid noise echoing out across a thousand sleeping souls, and then a man slumping down into a coffin.

Donald's hand trembled. He remembered his first days in office, all this man had done for him, that meeting very early on. He had been hired for a job for which he was barely qualified. He had been hired for a job he could not at first discern. That first morning, waking up a congressman, realizing he and only a handful of others stood at the helm of a powerful nation, had filled him with as much fear as accomplishment. And all along, he had been an inmate asked to erect the walls of his own asylum.

This time would be different. This time, he would accept responsibility and lead without fear. Him and his sister in secret. They would find out what was wrong with the world and fix it. Restore order to all that had been lost. An experiment had begun in another silo, a changing of the guard, and Donald intended to see the results.

He reached up and closed the lid on the pod. There was pink spittle on its shiny surface. Donald coughed once and wiped his mouth. He stuffed the pistol in his pocket and walked away from the pod, his heart racing from what he'd done. And the pod with a dead man inside—it quietly hummed.

101

Silo 17
2345
Year Thirty-Four

SOLO WORKED THE rope through the handles of the empty plastic jugs. They rattled together and made a kind of sonorous music. He collected his canvas bag and stood there a moment, scratching his beard, forgetting something. What had he forgotten? Patting his chest, he made sure he had the key. It was an old habit from years ago that he couldn't shake. The key, of course, was no longer there. He had tucked it in a drawer when things no longer needed locking, when there was no one left to be afraid of.

He took two bags of empty soup and veggie cans with him—hardly a dent in the massive pile of garbage. With his hands full and every step causing a clang and a clatter, he carried his things down the dark passage to the shaft of light at the far end.

It took two trips up the ladder to unload everything. He passed between the black machines, many of which had gone silent over the years, succumbing to the heat, perhaps. The filing cabinet had to be moved before the door would open. The silo had no locks and no people—but no dummies, either. He pulled the heavy door, could feel his father's presence as always, and stepped out into the wide world crowded with nothing but ghosts and things so bad he couldn't remember them.

The hallways were bright and empty. Solo waved to where he knew the cameras were as he passed. He often thought that he'd see himself on the monitors one day, but the cameras had quit working forever ago. And besides, there'd have to be two of him for that to happen. One to stand there and wave, another down by the monitors. He laughed at how silly he was. He was Solo.

Stepping out on the landing brought fresh air and a troubling sense of height. Solo thought of the rising water. How long before it reached him? Too long, he thought. He would be gone by then. But it was sad to think of his little home under the servers full of water one day. All the empty cans in the great pile by the shelves would float to the top. The computer and the radio would gurgle little bubbles of air. That made him laugh, thinking of them gurgling and the cans bobbing around on the surface, and he no longer cared if it happened or not. He tossed both bags of empty cans over the railing and listened for them to crunch down on the landing at forty-two. They dutifully did. He turned to the stairs.

Up or down? Up meant tomatoes, cucumbers and squash. Down meant berries, corn and digging for potatoes. Down required more cooking. Solo marched up.

He counted the steps as he went. "Eight, nine, ten," he whispered. Each of the stairs was different. There were a lot of stairs. They had all kinds of company, all kinds of fellow stairs, like friends, to either side. More things just like them. "Hello, step," he said, forgetting to count. The step said nothing. He didn't speak whatever they spoke, the ringing singing of lonely boots clanging up and down.

A noise. Solo heard a noise. He stopped and listened, but usually the noises knew when he was doing that and they got shy. This was another of those noises. He heard things that weren't there all the time. There were pumps and lights wired all over the place that turned on and off at their whim and choosing. One of these pumps had sprung a leak years ago, and Solo had fixed it himself. He needed a new Project. He was doing a lot of the same ones over and over, like chopping his beard when it got to his chest, and all of these Projects were boring.

Only one break to drink and pee before he reached the farms. His legs were good. Stronger, even, than when he was younger. The hard things got easier the more you did them. It didn't make it any more fun to do the hard things, though. Solo wished they would just be easy the first time.

He rounded the last bend before the landing on twelve, was just about to start whistling a harvest tune, when he saw that he'd left the door open. He wasn't sure how. Solo never left the door open. Any doors.

There was something propped up in the corner against the rail. It looked like scrap material from one of his Projects. A broken piece of plastic pipe. He picked it up. There was water in it. Solo sniffed the tube. It smelled funny, and he started to dump the water over the rail when the pipe slipped from his fingers. He froze and waited for the distant clatter. It never came.

Clumsy. He cursed himself for being forgetful and clumsy. Left a door open. He was headed inside when he saw what was holding it open. A black handle. He reached for it, saw that it was a knife plunged down through the grating.

There was a noise inside, deep within the farms. Solo stood very still for a moment. This was not his knife. He was not this forgetful. He pulled the blade out and allowed the door to close as a thousand thoughts flitted through his waking mind. A rat couldn't do something like this. Only a person could. Or a powerful ghost.

He should do something. He should tie the handles together or wedge something under the doors, but he was too afraid. He turned and ran instead. He ran down the stairs, jugs clattering together, his empty pack flopping on his back, someone else's knife clutched in his hand. When the jugs caught on the railing the rope snagged, and he tugged twice before giving up and letting them go. His hole. He had to get to his hole. Breathing heavily, he hurried on, the clangs and vibrations of some *other* disrupting his solitude. He didn't have to stop to listen for them. This was a loud ghost. Loud and solid. Solo thought of his machete, which had snapped in half years ago. But he had this knife. This knife. Around and around the stairs he went, sorely afraid. Down to the landing. Wrong landing! Thirty-three. One more to go. Stopped counting, stopped counting. He nearly stumbled, he ran so fast. Sweating. Home.

He slammed the doors behind him and took a deep breath, hands on his knees. Scooping the broom off the ground, he slid it through the handles on the door. It kept the quiet ghosts at bay. He hoped it would work on the noisy ones.

Solo pushed through the busted security gate and hurried down the halls. One of the lights overhead was out. A Project. But no time. He reached the metal door and heaved. Ran inside. Stopped and ran back. He leaned on the door and pushed it closed. He got low and put his shoulder into the filing cabinet, slid that against the door, an awful screech. He thought he heard footsteps outside. Someone fast. Sweat dripped off his nose. He clutched the knife and ran, through the servers. There was a squeal behind him, metal on metal. Solo was not alone. They had come for him. They were coming, coming. He could taste the fear in his mouth like metal. He raced to the grate, wished he'd left it open. At least the locks were broken. Rusted. No, that wasn't good. He needed the locks. Solo lowered himself down the ladder and grabbed the grating, began to pull it over his head. He would hide. Hide. Like the early years. And then someone was tugging the grate from his hand. He was swiping at them with the knife. There was a startled scream, a woman, breathing heavy and looking down at him, telling him to take it easy.

Solo trembled. His boot slipped a little on the ladder. But he held. He held very still while this woman talked to him. Her eyes were wide and alive. Her lips moved. She was hurt, didn't want to hurt him back. She just wanted his name. She was happy to see him. The wetness in her eyes was from being happy to see him. And Solo thought—maybe—that he himself was like a shovel or a can opener or any of those rusty things lying about. He was something that could be found. He could be found. And someone had.

EPILOGUE

2345
Silo 1

DONALD SAT IN the otherwise empty comm room. He had every station to himself, had sent the others to lunch and ordered those who weren't hungry to take a break. And they listened to him. They called him Shepherd, knew nothing else about him except that he was in charge. They came on and off shift, and they did as he ordered.

A blinking light on the neighboring comm station signaled Silo 6 attempting to make a call. They would have to wait. Donald sat and listened to the ringing in his headset as he placed a call of his own.

It rang and rang. He checked the cord, traced it to the jack, made sure it was plugged in correctly. Between two of the comm stations lay an unfinished game of cards, hands set aside from Donald ordering everyone out. There was a discard pile with a queen of spades on top. Finally, a click in his headset.

"Hello?" he said.

He waited. He thought he could hear someone breathing on the other line.

"Lukas?"

"No," the voice said. It was a softer voice. And yet harder, somehow.

"Who is this?" he asked. He was used to talking to Lukas.

"It doesn't matter who this is," the woman said. And Donald knew perfectly well. He looked over his shoulders, made sure he was still alone, then leaned forward in his chair.

"We're not used to hearing from mayors," he said.

"And I'm not used to being one."

Donald could practically hear the woman sneer at him. "I didn't ask for my job," he confided.

"And yet here we are."

"Here we are."

There was a pause.

"You know," Donald said, "if I were any good at my job, I'd press a button right now and shut your silo down."

"Why don't you?"

The mayor's voice was flat. Curious. It sounded like a real question rather than a dare.

"I doubt you'd believe me if I told you."

"Try me," she said. And Donald wished he still had the folder on this woman. He had carried it everywhere his first weeks on shift. And now, when he needed it—

"A long time ago," he told her, "I saved your silo. It would be a shame to end it now."

"You're right. I don't believe you."

There was a noise in the hallway. Donald removed one of the cups from his ears and glanced over his shoulder. His comm engineer stood outside the door with a thermos in one hand, a slice of bread in the other. Donald raised his finger and asked him to wait.

"I know where you've been," Donald told this mayor, this woman sent to clean. "I know what you've seen. And I—"

"You don't know the first thing about what I've seen," she spat, her words sharp as razors.

Donald felt his temperature rise. This was not the conversation he wanted to have with this woman. He wasn't prepared. He cupped his hand over the microphone, could sense that he was both running out of time and losing her.

"Be careful," he said. "That's all I'm saying—"

"Listen to me," she told him. "I'm sitting over here in a roomful of truth. I've seen the books. I'm going to dig until I get to the heart of what you people have done."

Donald could hear her breathing.

"I know the truth you're looking for," he said quietly. "You may not like what you find."

"*You* may not like what I find, you mean."

"Just . . . be careful." Donald lowered his voice. "Be careful where you go digging."

There was a pause. Donald glanced over his shoulder at the engineer, who took a sip from his thermos.

"Oh, we'll be careful where we dig," this Juliette finally answered. "I'd hate for you to hear us coming."

WOOL

THE SILO TRILOGY
BY HUGH HOWEY

WOOL

SHIFT

DUST

WOOL

HUGH HOWEY

WILLIAM MORROW
An Imprint of HarperCollins*Publishers*
Boston New York

First Mariner Books edition 2020

Mariner Books
An Imprint of HarperCollins Publishers, registered in the United States of America and/or other jurisdictions.

www.marinerbooks.com

Library of Congress Cataloging-in-Publication Data
Names: Howey, Hugh, author.
Title: Wool / Hugh Howey.
Description: First Mariner Books edition. | Boston :
Houghton Mifflin Harcourt, 2020. | Series: The Silo trilogy |
"A John Joseph Adams Book/Mariner Books."
Identifiers: LCCN 2020023879 (print) | LCCN 2020023880 (ebook) |
ISBN 9780358447849 (trade paperback) |
ISBN 9780358447832 (hardcover) | ISBN 9780358447955 (ebook)
Subjects: GSAFD: Science fiction.
Classification: LCC PS3608.O9566 W66 2020 (print) |
LCC PS3608.O9566 (ebook) | DDC 813/.6—dc23
LC record available at https://lccn.loc.gov/2020023879
LC ebook record available at https://lccn.loc.gov/2020023880

Printed in the United States of America

24 25 26 27 28 LBC 20 19 18 17 16

For those who dare to hope.

CONTENTS

PART 1

HOLSTON

1

THE CHILDREN WERE playing while Holston climbed to his death; he could hear them squealing as only happy children do. While they thundered about frantically above, Holston took his time, each step methodical and ponderous, as he wound his way around and around the spiral staircase, old boots ringing out on metal treads.

The treads, like his father's boots, showed signs of wear. Paint clung to them in feeble chips, mostly in the corners and undersides, where they were safe. Traffic elsewhere on the staircase sent dust shivering off in small clouds. Holston could feel the vibrations in the railing, which was worn down to the gleaming metal. That always amazed him: how centuries of bare palms and shuffling feet could wear down solid steel. One molecule at a time, he supposed. Each life might wear away a single layer, even as the silo wore away that life.

Each step was slightly bowed from generations of traffic, the edge rounded down like a pouting lip. In the center, there was almost no trace of the small diamonds that once gave the treads their grip. Their absence could only be inferred from the pattern to either side, the small pyramidal bumps rising from the flat steel with their crisp edges and flecks of paint.

Holston lifted an old boot to an old step, pressed down, and did it again. He lost himself in what the untold years had done, the ablation of molecules and lives, layers and layers ground to fine dust. And he thought, not for the first time, that neither life nor staircase had been meant for such an existence. The tight confines of that long spiral, threading through the buried silo like a straw in a glass, had not been built for such abuse. Like much of their cylindrical home, it seemed to have been made for other purposes, for functions long since forgotten. What was now used as a thoroughfare for thousands of people, moving up and down in repetitious daily cycles, seemed more apt in Holston's view to be used only in emergencies and perhaps by mere dozens.

Another floor went by—a pie-shaped division of dormitories. As Holston ascended the last few levels, this last climb he would ever take, the sounds of childlike delight rained down even louder from above. This was the laughter of youth, of souls who had not yet come to grips with where they lived, who did not yet feel the press of the earth on all sides, who in their minds were not buried at all, but *alive*. Alive and unworn, dripping happy sounds down the stairwell, trills that were incongruous with Holston's actions, his decision and determination to go *outside*.

As he neared the upper level, one young voice rang out above the others, and Holston remembered being a child in the silo—all the schooling and the games. Back then, the stuffy concrete cylinder had felt, with its floors and floors of apartments and workshops and hydroponic gardens and purification rooms with their tangles of pipes, like a vast universe, a wide expanse one could never fully explore, a labyrinth he and his friends could get lost in forever.

But those days were more than thirty years distant. Holston's childhood now felt like something two or three lifetimes ago, something someone else had enjoyed. Not him. He had an entire lifetime as sheriff weighing heavy, blocking off that past. And more recently, there was this third stage of his life — a secret life beyond childhood and being sheriff. It was the last layers of himself ground to dust; three years spent silently waiting for what would never come, each day longer than any month from his happier lifetimes.

At the top of the spiral stairway, Holston's hand ran out of railing. The curvy bar of worn steel ended as the stairwell emptied into the widest rooms of the entire silo complex: the cafeteria and the adjoining lounge. The playful squeals were level with him now. Darting bright shapes zagged between scattered chairs, playing chase. A handful of adults tried to contain the chaos. Holston saw Emma picking up scattered chalk and crayon from the stained tiles. Her husband, Clarke, sat behind a table arranged with cups of juice and bowls of cornflour cookies. He waved at Holston from across the room.

Holston didn't think to wave back, didn't have the energy or the desire. He looked past the adults and playing children to the blurry view beyond, projected on the cafeteria wall. It was the largest uninterrupted vista of their inhospitable world. A morning scene. Dawn's dim light coated lifeless hills that had hardly changed since Holston was a boy. They sat, just as they always had, while he had gone from playing chase among the cafeteria tables to whatever empty thing he was now. And beyond the stately rolling crests of these hills, the top of a familiar and rotting skyline caught the morning rays in feeble glints. Ancient glass and steel stood distantly where people, it was suspected, had once lived aboveground.

A child, ejected from the group like a comet, bumped into Holston's knees. He looked down and moved to touch the kid

—Susan's boy—but just like a comet the child was gone again, pulled back into the orbit of the others.

Holston thought suddenly of the lottery he and Allison had won the year of her death. He still had the ticket; he carried it everywhere. One of these kids—maybe he or she would be two by now and tottering after the older children—could've been theirs. They had dreamed, like all parents do, of the double fortune of twins. They had tried, of course. After her implant was removed, they had spent night after glorious night trying to redeem that ticket, other parents wishing them luck, other lottery hopefuls silently praying for an empty year to pass.

Knowing they only had a year, he and Allison had invited superstition into their lives, looking to anything for help. Tricks, like hanging garlic over the bed, that supposedly increased fertility; two dimes under the mattress for twins; a pink ribbon in Allison's hair; smudges of blue dye under Holston's eyes—all of it ridiculous and desperate and fun. The only thing crazier would have been to *not* try everything, to leave some silly séance or tale untested.

But it wasn't to be. Before their year was even out, the lottery had passed to another couple. It hadn't been for a lack of trying; it had been a lack of time. A sudden lack of *wife*.

Holston turned away from the games and the blurry view and walked toward his office, situated between the cafeteria and the silo's airlock. As he covered that ground, his thoughts went to the struggle that once took place there, a struggle of ghosts he'd had to walk through every day for the last three years. And he knew, if he turned and hunted that expansive view on the wall, if he squinted past the ever-worsening blur of cloudy camera lenses and airborne grime, if he followed that dark crease up the hill, that wrinkle that worked its way over the muddy dune toward the city beyond, he could pick out her quiet form. There, on that hill, his wife could be seen. She lay like a sleeping boulder, the air and toxins wearing away at her, her arms curled under her head.

Maybe.

It was difficult to see, hard to make out clearly even back before the blurring had begun anew. And besides, there was little to trust in that sight. There was much, in fact, to doubt. So Holston simply chose not to look. He walked through that place of his wife's ghostly struggle, where bad memories lay eternal, that scene of her sudden madness, and entered his office.

"Well, look who's up early," Marnes said, smiling.

Holston's deputy closed a metal drawer on the filing cabinet, a lifeless cry singing from its ancient joints. He picked up a steaming mug, then noted Holston's solemn demeanor. "You feeling okay, boss?"

Holston nodded. He pointed to the rack of keys behind the desk. "Holding cell," he said.

The deputy's smile drooped into a confused frown. He set down the mug and turned to retrieve the key. While his back was turned, Holston rubbed the sharp, cool steel in his palm one last time, then placed the star flat on the desk. Marnes turned and held out the key. Holston took it.

"You need me to grab the mop?" Deputy Marnes jabbed a thumb back toward the cafeteria. Unless someone was in cuffs, they only went into the cell to clean it.

"No," Holston said. He jerked his head toward the holding cell, beckoning his deputy to follow.

He turned, the chair behind the desk squeaking as Marnes rose to join him, and Holston completed his march. The key slid in with ease. There was a sharp clack from the well-built and well-maintained inner organs of the door. The barest squeak from the hinges, a determined step, a shove and a clank, and the ordeal was over.

"Boss?"

Holston held the key between the bars. Marnes looked down at it, unsure, but his palm came up to accept it.

"What's going on, boss?"

"Get the mayor," Holston said. He let out a sigh, that heavy breath he'd been holding for three years.

"Tell her I want to go outside."

2

THE VIEW FROM the holding cell wasn't as blurry as it had been in the cafeteria, and Holston spent his final day in the silo puzzling over this. Could it be that the camera on that side was shielded against the toxic wind? Did each cleaner, condemned to death, put more care into preserving the view they'd enjoyed on their last day? Or was the extra effort a gift to the *next* cleaner, who would spend their final day in that same cell?

Holston preferred this last explanation. It made him think longingly of his wife. It reminded him why he was there, on the wrong side of those bars, and willingly.

As his thoughts drifted to Allison, he sat and stared out at the dead world some ancient peoples had left behind. It wasn't the best view of the landscape around their buried bunker, but it wasn't the worst, either. In the distance, low rolling hills stood, a pretty shade of brown, like coffee mash with just the right amount of pig's milk in it. The sky above the hills was the same dull gray of his childhood and his father's childhood and his grandfather's childhood. The only moving feature on the landscape was the clouds. They hung full and dark over the hills. They roamed free like the herded beasts from the picture books.

The view of the dead world filled up the entire wall of his cell, just like all the walls on the silo's upper level, each one full of a different slice of the blurry and ever-blurrier wasteland beyond. Holston's little piece of that view reached from the corner by his cot, up to the ceiling, to the other wall, and down to the toilet. And despite the soft blur—like oil rubbed on a lens—it looked like a scene one could stroll out into, like a gaping and inviting hole oddly positioned across from forbidding prison bars.

The illusion, however, convinced only from a distance. Leaning closer, Holston could see a handful of dead pixels on the massive display. They stood stark white against all the brown and gray hues. Shining with ferocious intensity, each pixel (Allison had called them "stuck" pixels) was like a square window to some brighter place, a hole the width of a human hair that seemed to beckon toward some better reality. There were dozens of them, now that he looked closer. Holston wondered if anyone in the silo knew how to fix them, or if they had the tools required for such a delicate job. Were they dead forever, like Allison? Would all of the pixels be dead eventually? Holston imagined a day when half of the pixels were stark white, and then generations later when only a few gray and brown ones remained, then a mere dozen, the world having flipped to a new state, the people of the silo thinking the outside world was on fire, the only *true* pixels now mistaken for malfunctioning ones.

Or was that what Holston and his people were doing even now?

Someone cleared their throat behind him. Holston turned and saw Mayor Jahns standing on the other side of the bars, her hands resting in the belly of her overalls. She nodded gravely toward the cot.

"When the cell's empty, at night when you and Deputy Marnes are off duty, I sometimes sit right there and enjoy that very view."

Holston turned back to survey the muddy, lifeless landscape. It only looked depressing compared to scenes from the children's books — the only books to survive the uprising. Most people doubted those colors in the books, just as they doubted purple elephants and pink birds ever existed, but Holston felt that they were truer than the scene before him. He, like some others, felt something primal and deep when he looked at those worn pages splashed green and blue. Even so, when compared to the stifling silo, that muddy gray view outside looked like some kind of salvation, just the sort of open air men were born to breathe.

"Always seems a little clearer in here," Jahns said. "The view, I mean."

Holston remained silent. He watched a curling piece of cloud break off and move in a new direction, blacks and grays swirling together.

"You get your pick for dinner," the mayor said. "It's tradition —"

"You don't need to tell me how this works," Holston said, cutting Jahns off. "It's only been three years since I served Allison her last meal right here." He reached to spin the copper ring on his finger out of habit, forgetting he had left it on his dresser hours ago.

"Can't believe it's been that long," Jahns murmured to herself. Holston turned to see her squinting at the clouds displayed on the wall.

"Do you miss her?" Holston asked venomously. "Or do you just hate that the blur has had so much time to build?"

Jahns's eyes flashed his way a moment, then dropped to the floor. "You know I don't want this, not for any view. But rules are the rules —"

"It's not to be blamed," Holston said, trying to let the anger go. "I know the rules better than most." His hand moved, just a little, toward the missing badge, left behind like his ring. "Hell, I enforced those rules for most my life, even after I realized they were bullshit."

Jahns cleared her throat. "Well, I won't ask why you chose this. I'll just assume it's because you'd be unhappier here."

Holston met her gaze, saw the film on her eyes before she was able to blink it away. Jahns looked thinner than usual, comical in her gaping overalls. The lines in her neck and radiating from her eyes were deeper than he remembered. Darker. And he thought the crack in her voice was genuine regret, not just age or her ration of tobacco.

Suddenly, Holston saw himself through Jahns's eyes, a broken man sitting on a worn bench, his skin gray from the pale glow of the dead world beyond, and the sight made him dizzy. His head spun as it groped for something reasonable to latch on to, something that made sense. It seemed a dream, the predicament his life had become. None of the last three years seemed true. Nothing seemed true anymore.

He turned back to the tan hills. In the corner of his eye, he thought he saw another pixel die, turning stark white. Another tiny window had opened, another clear view through an illusion he had grown to doubt.

Tomorrow will be my salvation, Holston thought savagely, *even if I die out there.*

"I've been mayor too long," Jahns said.

Holston glanced back and saw that her wrinkled hands were wrapped around the cold steel bars.

"Our records don't go back to the beginning, you know. They don't go back before the uprising a century and a half ago, but since then no mayor has sent more people to cleaning than I have."

"I'm sorry to burden you," Holston said dryly.

"I take no pleasure in it. That's all I'm saying. No pleasure at all."

Holston swept his hand at the massive screen. "But you'll be the first to watch a clear sunset tomorrow night, won't you?" He hated the way he sounded. Holston wasn't angry about his death, or life, or whatever came after tomorrow, but resentment over Allison's fate still lingered. He continued to see inevitable events from the past as avoidable, long after they'd taken their course. "You'll all love the view tomorrow," he said, more to himself than the mayor.

"That's not fair at all," Jahns said. "The law is the law. You broke it. You knew you were breaking it."

Holston looked at his feet. The two of them allowed a silence to form. Mayor Jahns was the one who eventually spoke.

"You haven't threatened yet to *not* go through with it. Some of the others are nervous that you might not do the cleaning because you aren't saying you won't."

Holston laughed. "They'd feel better if I said I *wouldn't* clean the sensors?" He shook his head at the mad logic.

"Everyone who sits there says they aren't gonna do it," Jahns told him, "but then they do. It's what we've all come to expect—"

"Allison never threatened that she wouldn't do it," Holston reminded her, but he knew what Jahns meant. He himself had been sure Allison wouldn't wipe the lenses. And now he thought he understood what she'd been going through as she sat on that very bench. There were larger things to consider than the act of cleaning. Most who were sent outside were caught at something, were surprised to find themselves in that cell, their fate mere hours away. Revenge was on their mind when they said they wouldn't do it. But Allison and now Holston had bigger worries. Whether or not they'd clean was inconsequential; they had arrived here because they wanted, on some insane level, to *be* here. All that remained was the curiosity of it all. The wonder of the outside world beyond the projected veil of the wallscreens.

"So, are you planning on going through with it or not?" Jahns asked directly, her desperation evident.

"You said it yourself." Holston shrugged. "Everyone does it. There must be some reason, right?"

He pretended not to care, to be disinterested in the *why* of the cleaning, but he had spent most of his life, the past three years especially, agonizing over the why. The question drove him nuts. And if his refusing to answer Jahns caused pain to those who had murdered his wife, he wouldn't be upset.

Jahns rubbed her hands up and down the bars, anxious. "Can I tell them you'll do it?" she asked.

"Or tell them I won't. I don't care. It sounds like either answer will mean the same to them."

Jahns didn't reply. Holston looked up at her, and the mayor nodded.

"If you change your mind about the meal, let Deputy Marnes know. He'll be at the desk all night, as is tradition . . ."

She didn't need to say. Tears came to Holston's eyes as he remembered that part of his former duties. He had manned that desk twelve years ago when Donna Parkins was put to cleaning, eight years ago when it was Jack Brent's time. And he had spent a night clinging to the bars, lying on the floor, a complete wreck, three years ago when it was his wife's turn.

Mayor Jahns turned to go.

"Sheriff," Holston muttered before she got out of earshot.

"I'm sorry?" Jahns lingered on the other side of the bars, her gray, bushy brows hanging over her eyes.

"It's Sheriff Marnes now," Holston reminded her. "Not Deputy."

Jahns rapped a steel bar with her knuckles. "Eat something," she said. "And I won't insult you by suggesting you get some sleep."

3

Three Years Earlier

"YOU'VE GOTTA BE *kidding* me," Allison said. "Honey, listen to this. You won't believe this. Did you know there was more than *one* uprising?"

Holston looked up from the folder spread across his lap. Around him, scattered piles of paper covered the bed like a quilt—stacks and stacks of old files to sort through and new complaints to manage. Allison sat at her small desk at the foot of the bed. The two of them lived in one of the silo condos that had been subdivided only twice over the decades. It left room for luxuries like desks and wide nonbunk beds.

"And how would I have known about that?" he asked her. His wife turned and tucked a strand of hair behind her ear. Holston jabbed a folder at her computer screen. "All day long you're unlocking secrets hundreds of years old, and I'm supposed to know about them before *you* do?"

She stuck out her tongue. "It's an expression. It's my way of informing you. And why don't you seem more curious? Did you hear what I just said?"

Holston shrugged. "I never would've assumed the one uprising we know about was the first—just that it was the most recent. If I've learned one thing from my job, it's that no crime or crazy mob is ever all that original." He picked up a folder by his knee. "You think this is the first water thief the silo's known? Or that it'll be the last?"

Allison's chair squealed on the tile as she turned to face him. The monitor on the desk behind her blinked with the scraps and fragments of data she had pulled from the silo's old servers, the remnants of information long ago deleted and overwritten countless times. Holston still didn't understand how the retrieval process worked, or why someone smart enough to come up with it was dumb enough to love him, but he accepted both as truth.

"I'm piecing together a series of old reports," she said. "If true, they mean something like our old uprising used to take place regularly. Like once every generation or so."

"There's a lot we don't know about the old times," Holston said. He rubbed his eyes and thought about all the paperwork he wasn't getting done. "Maybe they didn't have a system for cleaning the sensors, you know? I'll bet back then, the view upstairs just got blurrier and blurrier until people went crazy, there'd be a revolt or something, and then they'd finally exile a few people to set things straight. Or maybe it was just natural population control, you know, before the lottery."

Allison shook her head. "I don't think so. I'm starting to think . . ." She paused and glanced down at the spread of paperwork around Holston. The sight of all the logged transgressions seemed to make her consider carefully what she was about to say. "I'm not passing judgment, not saying anyone was right or wrong or anything like that. I'm just suggesting that maybe the servers weren't wiped out by the rebels during the uprising. Not like we've always been told, anyway."

That got Holston's attention. The mystery of the blank servers, the empty past of the silo's ancestors, haunted them all. The erasure was nothing more than fuzzy legend. He closed the folder he was working on and set it aside. "What do you think caused it?" he asked his wife. "Do you think it was an accident? A fire or a power outage?" He listed the common theories.

Allison frowned. "No," she said. She lowered her voice and looked around anxiously. "I think *we* wiped the hard drives. Our ancestors, I mean, *not* the rebels." She turned and leaned toward the monitor, running her finger down a set of figures Holston couldn't discern from the bed. "Twenty years," she said. "Eighteen. Twenty-four." Her finger slid down the screen with a squeak. "Twenty-eight. Sixteen. Fifteen."

Holston plowed a path through the paperwork at his feet, putting the files back in stacks as he worked his way toward the desk. He sat on the foot of the bed, put a hand on his wife's neck, and peered over her shoulder at the monitor.

"Are those dates?" he asked.

She nodded. "Just about every two decades, there's a major revolt. This report cataloged them. It was one of the files deleted during the most recent uprising. *Our* uprising."

She said *our* like either of them or any of their friends had been alive at the time. Holston knew what she meant, though. It was the uprising they had been raised in the shadow of, the one that seemed to have spawned them — the great conflict that hung over their childhoods, over their parents and grandparents. It was the uprising that filled whispers and occupied sideways glances.

"And what makes you think it was us, that it was the good guys who wiped the servers?"

She half turned and smiled grimly. "Who says we are the good guys?"

Holston stiffened. He pulled his hand away from Allison's neck. "Don't start. Don't say anything that might —"

"I'm kidding," she said, but it wasn't a thing to kid about.

It was two steps from traitorous, from *cleaning.* "My theory is this," she said quickly, stressing the word *theory.* "There's generational upheaval, right? I mean for over a hundred years, maybe longer. It's like clockwork." She pointed at the dates. "But then, during the great uprising—the only one we've known about till now—someone wiped the servers. Which, I'll tell you, isn't as easy as pressing a few buttons or starting a fire. There's redundancies on top of redundancies. It would take a concerted effort, not an accident or any sort of rushed job or mere sabotage—"

"That doesn't tell you who's responsible," Holston pointed out. His wife was a wizard with computers, no doubt, but sleuthing was not her bag; it was his.

"What tells me something," she continued, "is that there were uprisings every generation for all this time, but there hasn't been an uprising *since.*" Allison bit her lip.

Holston sat up straight. He glanced around the room and allowed her observation to sink in. He had a sudden vision of his wife yanking his sleuthing bag out of his hands and making off with it.

"So you're saying . . ." He rubbed his chin and thought this through. "You're saying that someone wiped out our history to stop us from repeating it?"

"Or worse." She reached out and held his hand with both of hers. Her face had deepened from seriousness to something more severe. "What if the reason for the revolts was right there on the hard drives? What if some part of our known history, or some data from the outside, or maybe the knowledge of whatever it was that made people move in here long, long ago—what if that information built up some kind of pressure that made people lose their marbles, or go stir-crazy, or just want *out?*"

Holston shook his head. "I don't want you thinking that way," he cautioned her.

"I'm not saying they were right to go nuts," she told him, back to being careful. "But from what I've pieced together so far, this is my theory."

Holston gave the monitor an untrusting glance. "Maybe you shouldn't be doing this," he said. "I'm not even sure *how* you're doing it, and maybe you shouldn't be."

"Honey, the information is there. If I don't piece it together now, somebody else will at some point. You can't put the genie back in the bottle."

"What do you mean?"

"I've already published a white paper on how to retrieve deleted and overwritten files. The rest of the IT department is spreading it around to help people who've unwittingly flushed something they needed."

"I still think you should stop," he said. "This isn't the best idea. I can't see any good coming of it—"

"No good coming from the truth? Knowing the truth is always good. And better that it's us discovering it than someone else, right?"

Holston looked at his files. It'd been five years since the last person was sent to cleaning. The view of the outside was getting worse every day, and he could feel the pressure, as sheriff, to find someone. It was growing, like steam building up in the silo, ready to launch something out. People got nervous when they thought the time was near. It was like one of those self-fulfilling prophecies where the nerves finally made someone twitch, then lash out or say something regretful, and then they'd find themselves in a cell, watching their last blurry sunset.

Holston sorted through the files all around him, wishing there was something in them. He would put a man to his death tomorrow if it meant releasing that steam. His wife was poking some great, overly full balloon with a needle, and Holston wanted to get that air out of it before she poked too far.

4

Present Time

HOLSTON SAT ON THE lone steel bench in the airlock, his brain numb from lack of sleep and the surety of what lay before him. Nelson, the head of the cleaning lab, knelt in front of him and worked a leg of the white hazard suit over Holston's foot.

"We've played around with the joint seals and added a second spray-on lining," Nelson was saying. "It should give you more time out there than anyone has had before."

This registered with Holston, and he remembered watching his wife go about her cleaning. The top floor of the silo with its great screens showing the outside world was usually empty for cleanings. The people inside couldn't bear to watch what they'd done—or maybe they wanted to come up and enjoy a nice view without seeing what it took to get it. But Holston had watched; there was never any doubt that he would. He couldn't see Allison's face through her silver-masked helmet, couldn't see her thin arms through the bulky suit as she scrubbed and scrubbed with her wool pads, but he knew her walk, her mannerisms. He had watched her finish the job, taking her time and doing it well, and then she had stepped back, looked in the camera one last time, waved at him, then turned to walk away. Like others before her, she had lumbered toward a nearby hill and had begun climbing up, trudging toward the dilapidated spires of that ancient and crumbling city just visible over the horizon. Holston hadn't moved the entire time. Even as she fell on the side of the hill, clutching her helmet, writhing while the toxins first ate away the spray-on linings, then the suit, and finally his wife, he hadn't moved.

"Other foot."

Nelson slapped his ankle. Holston lifted his foot and allowed the tech to bunch the rest of the suit around his shins. Looking at his hands, at the black carbon undersuit he wore against his skin, Holston pictured it all dissolving off his body, sloughing away like flakes of dried grease from a generator's pipe while the blood burst from his pores and pooled up in his lifeless suit.

"If you'll grab the bar and stand—"

Nelson was walking him through a routine he'd seen twice before. Once with Jack Brent, who had been belligerent and hostile right up to the end, forcing him as sheriff to stand guard by the bench. And once with his wife, whom he had watched get ready through the airlock's small porthole. Holston knew what to do from watching these others, but he still needed to be told. His thoughts were elsewhere. Reaching up, he grabbed the trapezelike bar hanging above him and pulled himself upright. Nelson grabbed the sides of the suit and yanked them up to Holston's waist. Two empty arms flapped at either side.

"Left hand here."

Holston numbly obeyed. It was surreal to be on the other side of this—this mechanical death-walk of the condemned. Holston had often wondered why people complied, why they just went along. Even Jack Brent had done what he was told, as foulmouthed and verbally abusive as he'd been. Allison had done it quietly, just like this, Holston thought as he inserted one hand and then the other. The suit came up, and Holston thought that maybe people went along with it because they couldn't believe it was happening. None of it was real enough to rebel against. The animal part of his mind wasn't made for this, to be calmly ushered to a death it was perfectly aware of.

"Turn."

He did.

There was a tug at the small of his back, and then a noisy zipping sound up to his neck. Another tug, another zip. Two layers of futility. The crunch of industrial Velcro over the top. Pats and double-checks. Holston heard the hollow helmet slide off its shelf; he flexed his fingers inside the puffy gloves while Nelson checked over the dome's innards.

"Let's go over the procedure one more time."

"It's not necessary," Holston said quietly.

Nelson glanced toward the airlock door leading back to the silo. Holston didn't need to look to know someone was likely watching. "Bear with me," Nelson said. "I have to do it by the book."

Holston nodded, but he knew there wasn't any "book." Of all the mystic oral traditions passed through silo generations, none matched the cultlike intensity of the suit makers and the cleaning techs. Everyone gave them their space. The cleaners might perform the physical act, but the techs were the people who made it possible. These were the men and women who maintained the view to that wider world beyond the silo's stifling confines.

Nelson placed the helmet on the bench. "You got your scrubbers here." He patted the wool pads stuck to the front of the suit.

Holston pulled one off with a ripping sound, studied the whorls and curls of the rough material, then stuck it back on.

"Two squirts from the cleaning bottle before you scrub with the wool, then dry with this towel, then put the ablating films on last." He patted the pockets in order, even though they were clearly labeled and numbered — upside down so Holston could read them — and color-coded.

Holston nodded and met the tech's eyes for the first time. He was surprised to see fear there, fear he had learned well to notice in his profession. He almost asked Nelson what was wrong before it occurred to him: the man was worried all these instructions were for naught, that Holston would walk out — like everyone in the silo feared all cleaners would — and not do his duty. Not clean up for the people whose rules, rules against dreaming of a better place, had doomed him. Or was Nelson worried that the expensive and laborious gear he and his colleagues had built, using those secrets and techniques handed down from well before the uprising, would leave the silo and rot to no purpose?

"You okay?" Nelson asked. "Anything too tight?"

Holston glanced around the airlock. *My life is too tight,* he wanted to say. *My skin is too tight. The walls are too tight.*

He just shook his head.

"I'm ready," he whispered.

It was the truth. Holston was oddly and truly very much ready to go.

And he remembered, suddenly, how ready his wife had been as well.

5

Three Years Earlier

"I WANT TO GO OUT. I want to go out. Iwanttogoout."

Holston arrived at the cafeteria in a sprint. His radio was still squawking, Deputy Marnes yelling something about Allison. Holston hadn't even taken the time to respond, had just bolted up three flights of stairs toward the scene.

"What's going on?" he asked. He swam through the crowd by the door and found his wife writhing on the cafeteria floor, held down by Connor and two food staff employees. "Let her go!" He slapped their hands off his wife's shins and was nearly rewarded by one of her boots to his chin. "Settle down," he said. He reached for her wrists, which were twisting this way and that to get out of the desperate grips of grown men. "Baby, what the *hell* is going on?"

"She was running for the airlock," Connor said through grunts of exertion. Percy corralled her kicking feet, and Holston didn't stop him. He saw now why three men were needed. He leaned close to Allison, making sure she saw him. Her eyes were wild, peeking through a curtain of disheveled hair.

"Allison, baby, you've gotta settle down."

"I want to go out. I want to go out." Her voice had quieted, but the words kept tumbling out.

"Don't say that," Holston told her. Chills ran through his body at the sound of the grave utterances. He held her cheeks. "Baby, don't say that!"

But some part of him knew, in a jolting flash, what it meant. He knew it was too late. The others had heard. Everyone had heard. His wife had signed her own death certificate.

The room spun around Holston as he begged Allison to be quiet. It was like he had arrived at the scene of some horrible accident — some mishap in the machine shop — to find a person he loved wounded. Arrived to find them alive and kicking, but knowing at a glance that the injury was fatal.

Holston felt warm tears streak down his cheeks as he tried to wipe the hair from her face. Her eyes finally met his, stopped their fevered swirling and locked onto his with awareness. And for a moment, just a second, before he could wonder if she'd been drugged or abused in any way, a spark of calm clarity registered there, a flash of sanity, of cool calculation. And then it was blinked away and her eyes went wild again as she begged to be let out, over and over.

"Lift her up," Holston said. His husband eyes swam behind tears while he allowed his dutiful sheriff-self to intervene. There was nothing for it but to lock her up, even as he wanted no more than room enough to scream. "That way," he told Connor, who had both hands under her twisting shoulders. He nodded toward his office and the holding cell beyond. Just past that, down at the end of the hall, the bright yellow paint on the great airlock door stood out, serene and menacing, silent and waiting.

Once in the holding cell, Allison immediately calmed. She sat on the bench, no longer struggling or blabbering, as if she'd only stopped by to rest and enjoy the view. Holston was now the writhing wreck. He paced outside the bars and blubbered unanswered questions while Deputy Marnes and the mayor handled his procedural work. The two of them were treating Holston and his wife *both* like patients. And even as Holston's mind spun with the horror of the past half hour, in the back of his sheriff brain, where he was always alert for the rising tensions in the silo, he was dimly aware of the shock and rumors trembling through walls of concrete and rebar. The enormous pent-up pressure of the place was now hissing through the seams in whispers.

"Sweetheart, you've gotta talk to me," he pleaded again and again. He stopped his pacing and twisted the bars in his hands. Allison kept her back to him. She gazed at the wallscreen, at the brown hills and gray sky and dark clouds. Now and then a hand came up to brush hair out of her face, but otherwise she didn't move or speak. Only when Holston's key had gone into the lock, not long after they had wrestled her in and shut the door, did she utter a single *don't* that had convinced him to remove it.

While he pleaded and she ignored, the machinations of the looming cleaning gyred through the silo. Techs rumbled down the hallway as a suit was sized and readied. Cleaning tools were prepped in the airlock. A canister hissed somewhere as argon was loaded into the flushing chambers. The commotion of it sporadically rumbled past the holding cell where Holston stood gazing at his wife. Chattering techs went dreadfully silent as they squeezed past; they didn't even seem to *breathe* in his presence.

Hours passed and Allison refused to talk—behavior that created its own stir in the silo. Holston spent the entire day blubbering through the bars, his brain on fire with confusion and agony. It had happened in a single moment, the destruction of all that he knew. He tried to wrap his brain around it while Allison sat in the cell, gazing out at the dismal land, seemingly pleased with her far worse status as a cleaner.

It was after dark when she finally spoke, after her last meal had been silently refused for the final time, after the techs had finished in the airlock, closing the yellow door and retiring for a sleepless night. It was after his deputy had gone for the night, patting Holston on the shoulder twice. What felt like many hours after that, when Holston was near to passing out in fatigue from his crying and hoarse remonstrations, long after the hazy sun had settled over the hills visible from the cafeteria and lounge—the hills that hid the rest of that distant, crumbling city—in the near-dark left in the holding cell, Allison whispered something almost inaudible: "It's not real."

That's what Holston *thought* he heard. He stirred.

"Baby?" He gripped the bars and pulled himself up to his knees. "Honey," he whispered, wiping the crust from his cheeks.

She turned. It was like the sun changing its mind and rising back over the hills. That she'd acknowledged him gave him hope. It choked him up, causing him to think this had all been a sickness, a fever, something they could have Doc write up to excuse her for everything she'd uttered. She'd never meant it. She was saved just by snapping out of it, and Holston was saved just by seeing her turn to him.

"Nothing you see is real," she said quietly. She seemed calm of body even as her craziness continued, condemning her with forbidden words.

"Come talk to me," Holston said. He waved her to the bars.

Allison shook her head. She patted the cot's thin mattress beside her.

Holston checked the time. It was long past visiting hours. He could be sent to cleaning just for doing what he was about to do.

The key went into the lock without hesitation.

A metallic click rang out impossibly loud.

Holston stepped inside with his wife and sat beside her. It killed him to not touch her, to not wrap her up or drag her out to some safe place, back to their bed, where they could pretend it had all been a bad dream.

But he didn't dare move. He sat and twisted his hands together while she whispered:

"It doesn't have to be real. Any of this. None of this." She looked to the screen.

Holston leaned so close he could smell the dried sweat from the day's struggle. "Baby, what's going on?"

Her hair stirred with the breath from his words. She reached out and rubbed the darkening display, feeling the pixels.

"It could be morning right now and we'd never know. There could be people outside." She turned and looked at him. "They could be watching us," she said with a sinister grin.

Holston held her gaze. She didn't seem crazy at all, not like earlier. Her *words* were crazy, but she didn't seem to be. "Where did you get that idea?" he asked. He thought he knew, but he asked anyway. "Did you find something on the hard drives?" He'd heard that she had run straight from her lab toward the airlock, already barking her madness. Something had happened while she was at work. "What did you find?"

"There's more deleted than just from the uprising," she whispered. "Of course there would be. Everything is deleted. All the recent stuff, too." She laughed. Her voice got suddenly loud and her eyes lost focus. "E-mails you never sent me, I bet!"

"Honey." Holston dared to reach for her hands, and she didn't pull away. He held them. "What did you find? Was it an e-mail? Who was it from?"

She shook her head. "No. I found the programs they use. The ones that make pictures on the screens that look so *real*." She looked back to the quickening dusk. "IT," she said. "Eye. Tee. They're the ones. They *know*. It's a secret that only they know." She shook her head.

"What secret?" Holston couldn't tell if this was nonsense or important. He only knew that she was talking.

"But now I know. And you will too. I'll come back for you, I swear. This'll be different. We'll break the cycle, you and me. I'll come back and we'll go over that hill together." She laughed. "If it's there," she said loudly. "If that hill is there and it's green, we'll go over it together."

She turned to him.

"There is no uprising, not really, there's just a gradual leak. Just the people who know, who want out." She smiled. "They get to go out," she said. "They get just what they ask for. I know why they clean, why they say they won't but why they do. I know. I know. And they never come back; they wait and wait and wait, but I won't. I'll come right back. This'll be different."

Holston squeezed her hands. Tears were dripping off his cheeks. "Baby, why are you doing this?" He felt like she wanted to explain herself now that the silo was dark and they were all alone.

"I know about the uprisings," she said.

Holston nodded. "I know. You told me. There were others —"

"No." Allison pulled away from him, but it was only to make space so she could look him in the eyes. Hers were no longer wild, as before.

"Holston, I know why the uprisings took place. I know *why.*"

Allison bit her lower lip. Holston waited, his body tense.

"It was always over the doubt, the suspicion, that things weren't as bad out there as they seemed. You've felt that, right? That we could be *anywhere,* living a lie?"

Holston knew better than to answer, to even twitch. Broaching this subject led to cleaning. He sat frozen and waited.

"It was probably the younger generations," Allison said. "Every twenty years or so. They wanted to push further, to explore, I think. Don't you ever feel that urge? Didn't you when you were younger?" Her eyes lost focus. "Or maybe it was the couples, newly married, who were driven to madness when they were told they couldn't have kids in this damned limited world of ours. Maybe they were willing to risk everything for that chance . . ."

Her eyes focused on something far away. Perhaps she was seeing that lottery ticket they had yet to redeem and now never would. She looked back at Holston. He wondered if he could be sent to cleaning even for his silence, for not yelling her down as she uttered every one of the great forbidden words.

"It could even have been the elderly residents," she said, "cooped up too long, no longer afraid in their final years, maybe wanting to move out and make room for the others, for the few precious grandchildren. Whoever it was, whoever, every uprising took place because of this doubt, this feeling, that *we're* in the bad place right *here*." She looked around the cell.

"You can't say that," Holston whispered. "That's the great offense—"

Allison nodded. "Expressing any desire to leave. Yes. The great offense. Don't you see why? Why is that so forbidden? Because all the uprisings started with that desire, that's why."

"You get what you ask for," Holston recited, those words drilled into his head since youth. His parents had warned him—their only precious child—never to want out of the silo. Never even to *think* it. Don't let it cross your mind. It was instant death, that thought, and it would be the destruction of their one and only.

He looked back at his wife. He still didn't understand her madness, this decision. So she had found deleted programs that could make worlds on computer screens look real. What did that mean? Why do this?

"Why?" he asked her. "Why do it this way? Why didn't you

come to me? There has to be a better way to find out what's going on. We could start by telling people what you're finding on those drives—"

"And be the ones who start the next great uprising?" Allison laughed. Some of the madness was still there, or maybe it was just an intense frustration and boiling anger. Perhaps a great, multigenerational betrayal had pushed her to the edge. "No thanks," she said, her laughter subsiding. "Damn them if they stay here. I'm only coming back for *you.*"

"You don't come *back* from this," Holston said angrily. "You think the banished are still out there? You think they choose not to come back because they feel betrayed by us?"

"Why do you think they do the cleaning?" Allison asked. "Why do they pick up their wool and set to work without hesitation?"

Holston sighed. He felt the anger in him draining away. "No one knows why," he said.

"But why do you *think?*"

"We've talked about this," he said. "How many times have we discussed this?" He was sure all couples whispered their theories when they were alone. He looked past Allison as he remembered those times. He looked to the wall and saw the moon's position and read in it the night's hour. Their time was limited. His wife would be gone tomorrow. That simple thought came often, like lightning from stormy clouds.

"Everyone has theories," he said. "We've shared ours countless times. Let's just—"

"But now you know something new," Allison told him. She let go of his hand and brushed the hair from her face. "You and I know something new, and now it all makes sense. It makes perfect sense. And tomorrow I'll know for sure." Allison smiled. She patted Holston's hand as if he were a child. "And one day, my love, you will know it, too."

6

Present Time

THE FIRST YEAR WITHOUT her, Holston had waited, buying into her insanity, distrusting the sight of her on that hill, hoping she'd come back. He'd spent the first anniversary of her death scrubbing the holding cell clean, washing the yellow airlock door, straining for some sound, some knock, that would mean the ghost of his wife was back to set him free.

When it didn't happen, he began to consider the alternative: going out after her. He had spent enough days, weeks, months going through her computer files, reading some of what she had pieced together, making sense of half of it, to become half-mad himself. His world was a lie, he came to believe, and without Allison in it he had nothing to live for even if it were truth.

The second anniversary of her departure was his year of cowardice. He had walked to work, the poisonous words in his mouth—his desire to go out—but he had choked them down at the last second. He and Deputy Marnes had gone on patrol that day with the secret of how near he'd come to death burning inside of him. That was a long year of cowardice, of letting Allison down. The first year had been her failure; last year had been his. But no more.

Now, one more year later, he was alone in the airlock, wearing a cleaning suit, full of doubts and convictions. The silo was sealed off behind him, that thick yellow door bolted tight, and Holston thought that this was *not* how he'd thought he'd die, or what he had hoped would become of him. He had thought he would remain in the silo forever, his nutrients going as the nutrients of his parents had: into the soil of the eighth-floor dirt farm. It seemed a lifetime ago that he had dreamed of a family, of his own child, a fantasy of twins or another lottery win, a wife to grow old with—

A klaxon sounded on the other side of the yellow doors, warning everyone but him away. He was to stay. There was nowhere else for him to go.

The argon chambers hissed, pumping the room full of the inert gas. After a minute of this, Holston could feel the pressure of the air as it crinkled the cleaning suit tight around his joints. He breathed the oxygen circulating inside his helmet and stood before the other door, the forbidden door, the one to the awful outside world, and waited.

There was a metal groan from pistons deep within the walls. The sacrificial plastic curtains covering the interior of the airlock wrinkled from the pressure of the built-up argon. These curtains would be incinerated inside the airlock while Holston cleaned. The area would be scrubbed before nightfall, made ready for the next cleaning.

The great metal doors before him shuddered, and then a shaft of incredible space appeared at their joint, widening as the doors withdrew into the jamb. They wouldn't open all the way, not like they were once designed to—the risk of invading air had to be minimized.

An argon torrent hissed through the gap, dulling to a roar as the space grew. Holston pressed close, as horrified at himself for not resisting as he'd previously been perplexed by the actions of others. Better to go out, to see the world one time with his own eyes, than to be burned alive with the plastic curtains. Better to survive a few moments more.

As soon as the opening was wide enough, Holston squeezed through, his suit catching and rubbing at the doors. There was a veil of fog all around him as the argon condensed in the less pressurized air. He stumbled forward blindly, pawing through the soft cloud.

While he was still in that mist, the outer doors groaned and began closing. The klaxon howls behind were swallowed by the press of thick steel against thick steel, locking him and the toxins out while cleansing fires began to rage inside the airlock, destroying any contamination that had leaked its way inside.

Holston found himself at the bottom of a concrete ramp, a ramp that led *up*. His time felt short—there was a constant reminder thrumming in the back of his skull—*hurry! Hurry!* His life was ticking away. He lumbered up the ramp, confused that he wasn't already aboveground, so used as he was to seeing the world and the horizon from the cafeteria and lounge, which were on the same level as the airlock.

He shuffled up the narrow ramp, walls of chipped concrete to either side, his visor full of a confusing, brilliant light. At the top of the ramp, Holston saw the heaven into which he'd been condemned for his simple sin of hope. He whirled around, scanning the horizon, his head dizzy from the sight of so much green!

Green hills, green grass, green carpet beneath his feet. Holston whooped in his helmet. His mind buzzed with the sight. Hanging over all the green, there was the exact hue of blue from the children's books, the white clouds untainted, the movement of living things flapping in the air.

Holston turned around and around, taking it in. He had a sudden memory of his wife doing the same; he had watched her awkwardly, slowly turning, almost as if she were lost or confused or considering whether to do the cleaning at all.

The cleaning!

Holston reached down and pulled a wool pad from his chest. The cleaning! He knew, in a dizzying rush, a torrent of awareness, why, why. *Why!*

He looked where he always assumed the tall circular wall of the uppermost silo floor would be, but of course that wall was buried. All that stood behind him was a small mound of concrete, a tower no more than eight or nine feet tall. A metal ladder ran up one side; antennae bristled from the top. And on the side facing him — on all the sides he saw as he approached — were the wide, curving, fish-eye lenses of the silo's powerful cameras.

Holston held out his wool and approached the first. He imagined the view of himself from inside the cafeteria, staggering forward, becoming impossibly large. He had watched his wife do the same thing three years ago. He remembered her waving, he had thought at the time for balance, but had she been telling him something? Had she been grinning like a fool, as wide as he was grinning now, while she remained hidden behind that silver visor? Had her heart been pounding with foolish hope while she sprayed, scrubbed, wiped, applied? Holston knew the cafeteria would be empty; there was no one left who loved him enough to watch, but he waved anyway. And for him, it wasn't the raw anger he imagined many might have cleaned with. It wasn't the knowledge that they in the silo were condemned and the condemned set free; it wasn't the feeling of betrayal that guided the wool in his hand in small, circular motions. It was pity. It was raw pity and unconstrained joy.

The world blurred, but in a good way, as tears came to Holston's eyes. His wife had been right: the view from inside was a lie. The hills were the same — he'd recognize them at a glance after so many years of living with them—but the colors were all wrong. The screens inside the silo, the programs his wife had found, they somehow made the vibrant greens look gray, they somehow removed all signs of life. Extraordinary life!

Holston polished the grime off the camera lens and wondered if the gradual blurring was even real. The grime certainly was. He saw it as he rubbed it away. But was it simple dirt, rather than some toxic, airborne grime? Could the program Allison discovered modify only what was already seen? Holston's mind spun with so many new facts and ideas. He was like an adult child, born into a wide world, so much to piece together all at once that his head throbbed.

The blur is real, he decided as he cleaned the last of the smear from the second lens. It was an overlay, like the false grays and browns the program must have used to hide that green field and this blue sky dotted with puffy white. They were hiding from them a world so beautiful, Holston had to concentrate not to just stand still and gape at it.

He worked on the second of the four cameras and thought about those untrue walls beneath him, taking what they saw and modifying it. He wondered how many people in the silo knew. *Any* of them? What kind of fanatical devotion would it take to maintain this depressing illusion? Or was this a secret from *before* the last uprising? Was it an unknown lie perpetuated through the generations—a fibbing set of programs that continued to hum away on the silo computers with nobody aware? Because if someone knew, if they could show anything, why not something nice?

The uprisings! Maybe it was just to prevent them from happening over and over again. Holston applied an ablative film to the second sensor and wondered if the ugly lie of an unpleasant outside world was some misguided attempt to keep people from *wanting* out. Could someone have decided that the truth was worse than a loss of power, of control? Or was it something deeper and more sinister? A fear of unabashed, free, many-as-you-like children? So many horrible possibilities.

And what of Allison? Where was she? Holston shuffled around the corner of the concrete tower toward the third lens, and the familiar but strange skyscrapers in the distant city came into view. Only, there were more buildings than usual there. Some stood to either side, and an unfamiliar one loomed in the foreground. The others, the ones he knew by heart, were whole and shining, not twisted and jagged. Holston gazed over the crest of the verdant hills and imagined Allison walking over them at any minute. But that was ridiculous. How would she know he'd been expelled on this day? Would she remember the anniversary? Even after he'd missed the last two? Holston cursed his former cowardice, the years wasted. He would have to go to *her,* he decided.

He had a sudden impulse to do just that, to tear off his helmet and bulky suit and scamper up the hill in nothing but his carbon undersuit, breathing in deep gulps of crisp air and laughing all the way to his waiting wife in some vast, unfathomable city full of people and squealing children.

But no, there were appearances to keep, illusions to maintain. He wasn't sure why, but it was what his wife had done, what all the other cleaners before him had done. Holston was now a member of that club, a member of the *out* group. There was a press of history, of *precedent,* to obey. They had known best. He would complete his performance for the *in* group he had just joined. He wasn't sure why he was doing it, only that everyone before him had, and look at the secret they all shared. That secret was a powerful drug. He knew only to do what he had been told, to follow the numbers on the pockets, to clean mechanically while he considered the awesome implications of an outside world so big one couldn't live to see it all, couldn't breathe all the air, drink all the water, eat all the food.

Holston dreamed of such things while he dutifully scrubbed the third lens, wiped, applied, sprayed, then moved to the last. His pulse was audible in his ears; his chest pounded in that constricting suit. Soon, soon, he told himself. He used the second wool pad and polished the grime off the final lens. He wiped and applied and sprayed a final time, then put everything back in its place, back in the numbered pouches, not wanting to spoil the gorgeous and healthy ground beneath his feet. Done, Holston stepped back, took one last look at the nobodies not watching from the cafeteria and lounge, then turned his back on those who had turned their backs on Allison and all the others before her. There was a reason nobody came back for the people inside, Holston thought, just as there was a reason everyone cleaned, even when they said they wouldn't. He was free; he was to join the others, and so he strolled toward that dark crease that ran up the hill, following in his wife's footsteps, aware that some familiar boulder, long sleeping, no longer lay there. That, too, Holston decided, had been nothing more than another awful pixelated lie.

7

HOLSTON WAS A dozen paces up the hill, still marveling at the bright grass at his feet and the brilliant sky above, when the first pang lurched in his stomach. It was a writhing cramp, something like intense hunger. At first, he worried he was going too fast, first with the cleaning and now with his impatient shuffling in that cumbersome suit. He didn't want to take it off until he was over the hill, out of sight, maintaining whatever illusion the walls in the cafeteria held. He focused on the tops of the skyscrapers and resigned himself to slowing down, to calming down. One step at a time. Years and years of running up and down thirty flights of stairs should have made this nothing.

Another cramp, stronger this time. Holston winced and stopped walking, waiting for it to pass. When did he eat last? Not at all yesterday. Stupid. When did he last use the bathroom? Again, he couldn't remember. He might need to get the suit off earlier than he'd hoped. Once the wave of nausea passed, he took a few more steps, hoping to reach the top of the hill before the next bout of pain. He only got another dozen steps in before it hit him, more severe this time, worse than anything he'd ever felt. Holston retched from the intensity of it, and now his dry stomach was a blessing. He clutched his abdomen as his knees gave out in a shiver of weakness. He crashed to the ground and groaned. His stomach was burning, his chest on fire. He managed to crawl forward a few feet, sweat dripping from his forehead and splashing on the inside of his helmet. He saw sparks in his vision; the entire world went bright white, several times, like lightning strikes. Confused and senseless, he crawled ever upward, moving laboriously, his startled mind still focused on his last clear goal: cresting that hill.

Again and again, his view shimmered, his visor letting in a solid bright light before it flickered away. It became difficult to see. Holston ran into something before him, and his arm folded, his shoulder crashing to the ground. He blinked and gazed forward, up the hill, waiting for a clear sight of what lay ahead, but saw only infrequent strobes of green grass.

And then his vision completely disappeared. All was black. Holston clawed at his face, even as his stomach tangled in a new torturous knot. There was a glow, a blinking in his vision, so he knew he wasn't blind. But the blinking seemed to be coming from *inside* his helmet. It was his *visor* that had become suddenly blind, not him.

Holston felt for the latches on the back of the helmet. He wondered if he'd used up all his air. Was he asphyxiating? Being poisoned by his own exhalations? Of course! Why would they give him more air than he needed for the cleaning? He fumbled for the latches with his bulky gloves. They weren't meant for this. The gloves were part of his suit, his suit a single piece zipped up twice at the back and Velcroed over. It wasn't meant to come off, not without help. Holston was going to die in it, poison himself, choke on his own gases, and now he knew true fear of containment, a true sense of being closed in. The silo was nothing to this as he scrambled for release, as he writhed in pain inside his tailored coffin. He squirmed and pounded at the latches, but his padded fingers were too big. And the blindness made it worse, made him feel smothered and trapped. Holston retched again in pain. He bent at the waist, hands spread in the dirt, and felt something sharp through his glove.

He fumbled for the object and found it: a jagged rock. A tool. Holston tried to calm himself. His years of enforcing calm, of soothing others, of bringing stability to chaos, came back to him. He gripped the rock carefully, terrified of losing it to his blindness, and brought it up to his helmet. There was a brief thought of cutting away his gloves with the rock, but he wasn't sure his sanity or air would last that long. He jabbed the point of the rock at his armored neck, right where the latch should have been. He heard the crack as it landed. *Crack. Crack.* Pausing to probe with his padded finger, retching again, Holston took more careful aim. There was a click instead of a crack. A sliver of light intruded as one side of the helmet came free. Holston was choking on his exhalations, on the stale and used air around him. He moved the rock to his other hand and aimed for the second latch. Two more cracks before it landed, and the helmet popped free.

Holston could *see*. His eyes burned from the effort, from not being able to breathe, but he could see. He blinked the tears away and tried to suck in a deep, crisp, revitalizing lungful of blue air.

What he got instead was like a punch to the chest. Holston gagged. He threw up spittle and stomach acid, the very lining of him trying to flee. The world around him had gone brown. Brown grass and gray skies. No green. No blue. No life.

He collapsed to one side, landing on his shoulder. His helmet lay open before him, the visor black and lifeless. There was no looking through the visor. Holston reached for it, confused. The outside of the visor was coated silver, the other side was nothing. No glass. A rough surface. Wires leading in and out of it. A display gone dark. Dead pixels.

He threw up again. Wiping his mouth feebly, looking down

the hill, he saw the world with his naked eyes as it *was,* as he'd always known it to be. Desolate and bleak. He let go of the helmet, dropping the lie he had carried out of the silo with him. He was dying. The toxins were eating him from the inside. He blinked up at the black clouds overhead, roaming like beasts. He turned to see how far he had gotten, how far it was to the crest of the hill, and he saw the thing he had stumbled into while crawling. A boulder, sleeping. It hadn't been there in his visor, hadn't been a part of the lie on that little screen, running one of the programs Allison had discovered.

Holston reached out and touched the object before him, the white suit flaking away like brittle rock, and he could no longer support his head. He curled up in pain from the slow death overtaking him, holding what remained of his wife, and thought, with his last agonizing breath, what this death of his must look like to those who could see, this curling and dying in the black crack of a lifeless brown hill, a rotting city standing silent and forlorn over him.

What would they see, anyone who had chosen to watch?

PART 2

PROPER GAUGE

8

HER KNITTING NEEDLES rested in a leather pouch in pairs, two matching sticks of wood, side by side like the delicate bones of the wrist wrapped in dried and ancient flesh. Wood and leather. Artifacts like clues handed down from generation to generation, innocuous winks from her ancestors, harmless things like children's books and wood carvings that managed to survive the uprising and the purge. Each clue stood as a small hint of a world beyond their own, a world where buildings stood aboveground like the crumbling ruins visible over the gray and lifeless hills.

After much deliberation, Mayor Jahns selected a pair of needles. She always chose carefully, for proper gauge was critical. Too small a needle, and the knitting would prove difficult, the resulting sweater too tight and constricting. Too large a needle, on the other hand, would create a garment full of large holes. The knitting would remain loose. One would be able to see straight through it.

Her choice made, the wooden bones removed from their leather wrist, Jahns reached for the large ball of cotton yarn. It was hard to believe, weighing that knot of twisted fibers, that her hands could make of it something ordered, something useful. She fished for the end of the yarn, dwelling on how things came to be. Right now, her sweater was little more than a tangle and a thought. Going back, it had once been bright fibers of cotton blooming in the dirt farms, pulled, cleaned, and twisted into long strands. Even further, and the very substance of the cotton plant itself could be traced to those souls who had been laid to rest in its soil, feeding the roots with their own leather while the air above baked under the full glory of powerful grow lights.

Jahns shook her head at her own morbidity. The older she got, the quicker her mind went to death. Always, in the end, the thoughts of death.

With practiced care, she looped the end of the yarn around the point of one needle and crafted a triangle-shaped web with her fingers. The tip of the needle danced through this triangle, casting the yarn on. This was her favorite part, casting on. She liked beginnings. The first row. Out of nothing comes something. Since her hands knew what to do, she was free to glance up and watch a gust of morning wind chase pockets of dust down the slope of the hill. The clouds were low and ominous today. They loomed like worried parents over these smaller darting eddies of windswept soil, which tumbled like laughing children, twirling and spilling, following the dips and valleys as they flowed toward a great crease where two hills collided to become one. Here, Jahns watched as the puffs of dust splashed against a pair of dead bodies, the frolicking twins of dirt evaporating into ghosts, solid playful children returning once more to dreams and scattered mist.

Mayor Jahns settled back in her faded plastic chair and watched the fickle winds play across the forbidding world outside. Her hands worked the yarn into rows, requiring only occasional glances to keep her place. Often, the dust flew toward the silo's sensors in sheets, each wave causing her to cringe as if a physical blow were about to land. This assault of blurring grime was difficult to watch at any time, but especially brutal the day after a cleaning. Each touch of dust on the clouding lenses was a violation, a dirty man touching something pure. Jahns remembered what that felt like. And sixty years later, she sometimes wondered if the misting of grime on those lenses, if the bodily sacrifice needed to keep them clean, wasn't even more painful for her to abide.

"Ma'am?"

Mayor Jahns turned away from the sight of the dead hills cradling her recently deceased sheriff. She turned to find Deputy Marnes standing by her side.

"Yes, Marnes?"

"You asked for these."

Marnes placed three manila folders on the cafeteria table and slid them toward her through the scattered crumbs and juice stains of last night's cleaning celebration. Jahns set her knitting aside and reluctantly reached for the folders. What she really wanted was to be left alone a little longer to watch rows of knots become something. She wanted to enjoy the peace and quiet of this unspoiled sunrise before the grime and the years dulled it, before the rest of the upper silo awoke, rubbed the sleep from their eyes and the stains from their consciences, and came up to crowd around her in their own plastic chairs and take it all in.

But duty beckoned: she was mayor by choice, and the silo needed a sheriff. So Jahns put aside her own wants and desires and weighed the folders in her lap. Caressing the cover of the first one, she looked down at her hands with something between pain and acceptance. The backs of them appeared as dry and crinkled as the pulp paper hanging out of the folders. She glanced over at Deputy Marnes, whose white mustache was flecked with the occasional black. She remembered when the colors were the other way around, when his tall, thin frame was a mark of vigor and youth rather than gaunt fragility. He was handsome still, but only because she knew him from long ago, only because her old eyes still remembered.

"You know," she told Marnes, "we could do this different this time. You could let me promote you to sheriff, hire yourself a deputy, and do this proper."

Marnes laughed. "I've been deputy almost as long as you've been mayor, ma'am. Don't figure on being nothing else but dead one day."

Jahns nodded. One of the things she loved about having Marnes around was that his thoughts could be so black as to make hers shine gray. "I fear that day is rapidly approaching for us both," she said.

"Truer than true, I reckon. Never figured to outlive so many. Sure as sin don't see me outliving you." Marnes rubbed his mustache and studied the view of the outside. Jahns smiled at him, opened the folder on top, and studied the first bio.

"That's three decent candidates," Marnes said. "Just like you asked for. Be happy to work with any of them. Juliette, I think she's in the middle there, would be my first pick. Works down in Mechanical. Don't come up much, but me and Holston . . ." Marnes paused and cleared his throat.

Jahns glanced over and saw that her deputy's gaze had crept toward that dark crook in the hill. He covered his mouth with a fist of sharp knuckles and faked a cough.

"Excuse me," he said. "As I was sayin', the sheriff and me worked a death down there a few years back. This Juliette — I think she prefers Jules, come to think of it — was a right shiner. Sharp as a tack. Big help on this case, good at spotting details, handling people, being diplomatic but firm, all that. I don't think she comes up past the eighties much. A down-deeper for sure, which we ain't had in a while."

Jahns sorted through Juliette's folder, checking her family tree, her voucher history, her current pay in chits. She was listed as a shift foreman with good marks. No history in the lottery.

"Never married?" Jahns asked.

"Nope. Something of a johnboy. A wrencher, you know? We were down there a week, saw how the guys took to her. Now, she could have her pick of them boys but chooses not to. Kind of person who leaves an impression but prefers to go it alone."

"Sure seems like she left an impression on you," Jahns said, regretting it immediately. She hated the jealous tone in her own voice.

Marnes shifted his weight to his other foot. "Well, you know me, Mayor. I'm always sizing up candidates. Anything to keep from bein' promoted."

Jahns smiled. "What about the other two?" She checked the names, wondering if a down-deeper was a good idea. Or possibly worried about Marnes's having a crush. She recognized the name on the top folder. Peter Billings. He worked a few floors down in Judicial, as a clerk or a judge's shadow.

"Honestly, ma'am? They're filler to make it seem fair. Like I said, I'd work with them, but I think Jules is your girl. Been a long time since we had a lass for a sheriff. Be a popular choice with an election comin' up."

"That won't be why we choose," Jahns said. "Whoever we decide on will probably be here long after we're gone—" She stopped herself as she recalled having said the same thing about Holston, back when he'd been chosen.

Jahns closed the folder and returned her attention to the wallscreen. A small tornado had formed at the base of the hill, the gathering dust whipped into an organized frenzy. It built some steam, this small wisp, as it swelled into a larger cone, spinning and spinning on a wavering tip like a child's top as it raced toward sensors that fairly sparkled in the wan rays of a clear sunrise.

"I think we should go see her," Jahns finally said. She kept the folders in her lap, fingers like rolled parchment toying with the rough edges of handmade paper.

"Ma'am? I'd rather us fetch her up here. Do the interview in your office like we've always done. It's a long way down to her and an even longer way back up."

"I appreciate the concern, Deputy, I do. But it's been a long while since I've been much past the fortieth. My knees are no excuse not to see my people—" The mayor stopped. The tornado of dust wavered, turned, and headed straight for them. It grew and grew—the wide angle of the lens distorting it into a monster much larger and more fierce than she knew it to actually be—and then it blew over the sensor array, the entire cafeteria descending into a brief darkness until the zephyr caromed past, retreating across the screen in the lounge and leaving behind it a view of the world now tainted with a slight, dingy film.

"Damn those things," Deputy Marnes said through gritted teeth. The aged leather of his holster squeaked as he rested his hand on the butt of his gun, and Jahns imagined the old deputy out on that landscape, chasing the wind on thin legs while pumping bullets into a cloud of fading dust.

The two of them sat silent a moment, surveying the damage. Finally, Jahns spoke.

"This trip won't be about the election, Marnes. It won't be for votes, either. For all I know, I'll run again unopposed. So we won't make a deal of it, and we'll travel light and quiet. I want to *see* my people, not be seen by them." She looked over at him, found that he was watching her. "It'll be for me, Marnes. A getaway."

She turned back to the view.

"Sometimes . . . sometimes I just think I've been up here too long. The both of us. I think we've been *anywhere* too long . . ."

The ringing of morning footsteps on the spiral staircase gave her pause, and they both turned toward the sound of life, the sound of a waking day. And she knew it was time to start getting the images of dead things out of her mind. Or at least to bury them for a while.

"We'll go down and get us a proper gauge of this Juliette, you and me. Because sometimes, sitting here, looking out on what the world makes us do—it needles me deep, Marnes. It needles me straight through."

They met after breakfast in Holston's old office. Jahns still thought of it as his, a day later. It was too early for her to think of the room as anything else. She stood beyond the twin desks and old filing cabinets and peered into the empty holding cell while Deputy Marnes gave last-minute instructions to Terry, a burly security worker from IT who often held down the fort while Marnes and Holston were away on a case. Standing dutifully behind Terry was a teenager named Marcha, a young girl with dark hair and bright eyes who was apprenticing for work in IT. She was Terry's shadow; just about half of the workers in the silo had one. They ranged in age from twelve to twenty, these ever-present sponges absorbing the lessons and techniques for keeping the silo operational for at least one generation more.

Deputy Marnes reminded Terry how rowdy people got after a cleaning. Once the tension was released, people tended to live it up a little. They thought, for a few months at least, that anything went.

The warning hardly needed saying—the revelry in the next room could be heard through the shut door. Most residents from the top forty were already packed into the cafeteria and lounge. Hundreds more from the mids and the down deep would trickle up throughout the day, asking for time off work and turning in holiday chits just to see the mostly clear view of the world outside. It was a pilgrimage for many. Some came up only once every few years, stood around for an hour muttering that it looked the same as they remembered, then shooed their children down the stairs ahead of them, fighting the upward-surging crowds.

Terry was left with the keys and a temporary badge. Marnes checked the batteries in his wireless, made sure the volume on the office unit was up, and inspected his gun. He shook Terry's hand and wished him luck. Jahns sensed it was almost time for them to go and turned away from the empty cell. She said goodbye to Terry, gave Marcha a nod, and followed Marnes out the door.

"You feel okay leaving right after a cleaning?" she asked as they stepped out into the cafeteria. She knew how rowdy it would get later that night, and how testy the crowd would become. It seemed an awful time to drag him away on a mostly selfish errand.

"Are you kidding? I need this. I need to get away." He glanced toward the wallscreen, which was obscured by the crowds. "I still can't figure what Holston was thinking, can't reckon why he never talked to me about all that was going on in that head of his. Maybe by the time we get back, I won't feel him in the office anymore, 'cause right now I can't hardly breathe in there."

Jahns thought about this as they fought through the crowded cafeteria. Plastic cups sloshed with a mix of fruit juices, and she smelled the sting of tub-brewed alcohol in the air but ignored it. People were wishing her well, asking her to be careful, promising to vote. News of their trip had leaked out faster than the spiked punch, despite their hardly telling anyone. Most were under the impression that it was a goodwill trip. A reelection campaign. The younger silo residents, who only remembered

Holston as sheriff, were already saluting Marnes and giving him that honorific title. Anyone with wrinkles around their eyes knew better. They nodded to the duo as they passed through the cafeteria and wished them a different sort of unspoken luck. *Keep us going,* their eyes said. *Make it so my kids live as long as me. Don't let it unravel, not just yet.*

Jahns lived under the weight of this pressure, a burden brutal on more than knees. She kept quiet as they made their way to the central stairwell. A handful called for her to make a speech, but the lone voices did not gain traction. No chant formed, much to her relief. What would she say? That she didn't know why it all held together? That she didn't even understand her own knitting, how if you made knots, and if you did it right, things just worked out? Would she tell them it took only one snip for it all to unravel? One cut, and you could pull and pull and turn that garment into a pile. Did they really expect her to understand, when all she did was follow the rules, and somehow it kept working out, year after year after year?

Because she didn't understand what held it together. And she didn't understand their mood, this celebration. Were they drinking and shouting because they were safe? Because they'd been spared by fate, passed over for cleaning? Her people cheered while a good man, her friend, her partner in keeping them alive and well, lay dead on a hill next to his wife. If she gave a speech, if it weren't full of the forbidden, it would be this: that no two better people had ever gone to cleaning of their own free will, and what did that say about the lot of them who remained?

Now was not the time for speeches. Or for drinking. Or for being merry. Now was the hour of quiet contemplation, which was one of the reasons Jahns knew she needed to get away. Things had changed. Not just by the day, but by the long years. She knew better than most. Maybe old lady McLane down in

Supply knew, could see it coming. One had to live a long time to be sure, but now she was. And as time marched on, carrying her world faster than her feet could catch up, Mayor Jahns knew that it would soon leave her completely behind. And her great fear, unspoken but daily felt, was that this world of theirs probably wouldn't stagger very far along without her.

9

JAHNS'S WALKING STICK made a conspicuous ring as it impacted each metal step. It soon became a metronome for their descent, timing the music of the stairwell, which was crowded and vibrating with the energy of a recent cleaning. All the traffic seemed to be heading upward, save for the two of them. They jostled against the flow, elbows brushing, cries of "Hey, Mayor!" followed by nods to Marnes. And Jahns saw it on their faces: the temptation to call him sheriff tempered by their respect for the awful nature of his assumed promotion.

"How many floors you up for?" Marnes asked.

"Why, you tired already?" Jahns glanced over her shoulder to smirk at him, saw his bushy mustache twisted up in a smile of his own.

"Going down ain't a problem for me. It's the going back up I can't stand."

Their hands briefly collided on the twisted railing of the spiral staircase, Jahns's hand trailing behind her, Marnes's reaching ahead. She felt like telling him she wasn't tired at all, but she did feel a sudden weariness, an exhaustion more mental than physical. She had a childish vision of more youthful times and pictured Marnes scooping her up and carrying her down the staircase in his arms. There would be a sweet release of strength and responsibility, a sinking into another's power, no need to feign her own. This was not a remembrance of the past – it was a future that had never happened. And Jahns felt guilty for even thinking it. She felt her husband beside her, his ghost perturbed by her thoughts –

"Mayor? How many you thinking?"

The two of them stopped and hugged the rail as a porter trudged up the stairs. Jahns recognized the boy, Connor, still in his teens but already with a strong back and steady stride. He had an array of bundles strapped together and balanced on his shoulders. The sneer on his face was not from exhaustion or pain, but annoyance. Who were all these people suddenly on his stairwell? These tourists? Jahns thought of something encouraging to say, some small verbal reward for these people who did a job her knees never could, but he was already gone on his strong young feet, carrying food and supplies up from the down deep, slowed only by the crush of traffic attempting to worm up through the silo for a peek of the clear and wide outside.

She and Marnes caught their breath for a moment between flights. Marnes handed her his canteen, and she took a polite sip before passing it back.

"I'd like to do half today," she finally answered. "But I want to make a few stops on the way."

Marnes took a swig of water and began twisting the cap back on. "House calls?"

"Something like that. I want to stop at the nursery on twenty."

Marnes laughed. "Kissin' babies? Mayor, ain't nobody gonna vote you out. Not at your age."

Jahns didn't laugh. "Thanks," she said with a mask of false pain. "But no, not to kiss babies." She turned her back and resumed walking; Marnes followed. "It's not that I don't trust your professional opinion about this Jules lady. You haven't picked anything but a winner since I've been mayor."

"Even . . . ?" Marnes interrupted.

"Especially him," Jahns said, knowing what he was thinking. "He was a good man, but he had a broken heart. That'll take even the best of them down."

Marnes grunted his agreement. "So what're we checkin' at the nursery? This Juliette weren't born on the twentieth, not if I recall—"

"No, but her father works there now. I thought, since we were passing by, that we'd get a feel for the man, get some insight on his daughter."

"A father for a character witness?" Marnes laughed. "Don't reckon you'll get much of an impartial there."

"I think you'll be surprised," Jahns said. "I had Alice do some digging while I was packing. She found something interesting."

"Yeah?"

"This Juliette character still has every vacation chit she's ever earned."

"That ain't rare for Mechanical," Marnes said. "They do a lot of overtime."

"Not only does she not get out, she doesn't have visitors."

"I still don't see where you're going with this."

Jahns waited while a family passed. A young boy, six or seven probably, rode on his father's shoulders with his head ducked to avoid the undersides of the stairs above. The mother brought up the rear, an overnight bag draped over her shoulder, a swaddled infant cradled in her arms. It was the perfect family, Jahns thought. Replacing what they took. Two for two. Just what the lottery aimed for and sometimes provided.

"Well then, let me tell you where I'm going with this," she told Marnes. "I want to find this girl's father, look him in the eyes, and ask him why, in the nearly twenty years since his daughter moved to Mechanical, he hasn't visited her. Not once."

She looked back at Marnes, saw him frowning at her beneath his mustache.

"And why she hasn't once made her way up to see him," she added.

The traffic thinned as they made their way into the teens and past the upper apartments. With each step down, Jahns dreaded having to reclaim those lost inches on the way back up. This was the easy part, she reminded herself. The descent was like the uncoiling of a steel spring, pushing her down. It reminded Jahns of nightmares she'd had of drowning. Silly nightmares, considering she'd never seen enough water to submerge herself in, much less enough that she couldn't stand up to breathe. But they were like the occasional dreams of falling from great heights, some legacy of another time, broken fragments unearthed in each of their sleeping minds that suggested: *We weren't supposed to live like this.*

And so the descent, this spiraling downward, was much like the drowning that swallowed her at night. It felt inexorable and inextricable. Like a weight pulling her down combined with the knowledge that she'd never be able to claw her way back up.

They passed the garment district next, the land of multicolored coveralls and the place her balls of yarn came from. The smell of the dyes and other chemicals drifted over the landing. A window cut into the curving cinder blocks looked through to a small food shop at the edge of the district. It had been ransacked by the crowds, shelves emptied by the crushing demand of exhausted hikers and the extra post-cleaning traffic. Several porters crowded up the stairs with heavy loads, trying their best to satisfy demand, and Jahns recognized an awful truth about yesterday's cleaning: the barbaric practice brought more than psychological relief, more than just a clear view of the outside —it also buttressed the silo's economy. There was suddenly an excuse to travel. An excuse to trade. And as gossip flowed, and family and old friends met again for the first time in months or perhaps years, there was a vitality injected into the entire silo. It was like an old body stretching and loosening its joints, blood flowing to the extremities. A decrepit thing was becoming *alive* again.

"Mayor!"

She turned to find Marnes almost out of sight around the spiral above her. She paused while he caught up, watching his feet as he hurried.

"Easy," he said. "I can't keep up if you take off like that."

Jahns apologized. She hadn't been aware of any change in her pace.

As they entered the second tier of apartments, down below the sixteenth floor, Jahns realized she was already in territory she hadn't seen in almost a year. There was the rattle here of younger legs chasing along the stairwell, getting tangled up in the slow climbers. The grade school for the upper third was just above the nursery. From the sound of all the traffic and voices, school had been canceled. Jahns imagined it was a combination of knowing how few would turn up for class (with parents taking their kids up to the view) plus how many teachers would want to do the same. They passed the landing for the school, where chalk games of Hop and Square-Four were blurred from the day's traffic, where kids sat hugging the rails, skinned knees poking out, feet swinging below the jutting landings, and where catcalls and eager shouts faded to secret whispers in the presence of adults.

"Glad we're almost there, I need a rest," Marnes said as they spiraled down one more flight to the nursery. "I just hope this feller is available to see us."

"He will be," Jahns said. "Alice wired him from my office that we were coming."

They crossed traffic at the nursery landing and caught their breath. When Marnes passed his canteen, Jahns took a long pull and then checked her hair in its curved and dented surface.

"You look fine," he said.

"Mayoral?"

He laughed. "And then some."

Jahns thought she saw a twinkle in his old brown eyes when he said this, but it was probably the light bouncing off the canteen as he brought it to his lips.

"Twenty floors in just over two hours. Don't recommend the pace, but I'm glad we're this far already." He wiped his mustache and reached around to try to slip the canteen back into his pack.

"Here," Jahns said. She took the canteen from him and slid it into the webbed pouch on the rear of his pack. "And let me do the talking in here," she reminded him.

Marnes lifted his hands and showed his palms, as if no other thought had ever crossed his mind. He stepped past her and pulled one of the heavy metal doors open, the customary squeal of rusted hinges not coming as expected. The silence startled Jahns. She was used to hearing the chirp of old doors up and down the staircase as they opened and closed. They were the stairwell's version of the wildlife found in the farms, ever present and always singing. But these hinges were coated in oil, rigorously maintained. The signs on the walls of the waiting room reinforced the observation. They demanded silence in bold letters, accompanied by pictures of fingers over lips and circles with slashes through open mouths. The nursery evidently took its quietude seriously.

"Don't remember so many signs last time I was here," Marnes whispered.

"Maybe you were too busy yapping to notice," Jahns replied.

A nurse glared at them through a glass window, and Jahns elbowed Marnes.

"Mayor Jahns to see Peter Nichols," she told the woman.

The nurse behind the window didn't blink. "I know who you are. I voted for you."

"Oh, of course. Well, thank you."

"If you'll come around." The woman hit a button on her desk and the door beside her buzzed faintly. Marnes pushed on the door, and Jahns followed him through.

"If you'll don these."

The nurse — Margaret, according to the hand-drawn tag on her collar — held out two neatly folded white cloth robes. Jahns accepted them both and handed one to Marnes.

"You can leave your bags with me."

There was no refusing Margaret. Jahns felt at once that she was in this much younger woman's world, that she had become her inferior when she passed through that softly buzzing door. She leaned her walking stick against the wall, took her pack off and lowered it to the ground, then shrugged on the robe. Marnes struggled with his until Margaret helped, holding the sleeve in place. He wrestled the robe over his denim shirt and held the loose ends of the long fabric waist tie as if its working was beyond his abilities. He watched Jahns knot hers, and finally made enough of a mess of it for the robe to hold fairly together.

"What?" he asked, noticing the way Jahns was watching him. "This is what I've got cuffs for. So I never learned to tie a knot, so what?"

"In sixty years," Jahns said.

Margaret pressed another button on her desk and pointed down the hall. "Dr. Nichols is in the nursery. I'll let him know you're coming."

Jahns led the way. Marnes followed, asking her, "Why is that so hard to believe?"

"I think it's cute, actually."

Marnes snorted. "That's an awful word to use on a man my age."

Jahns smiled to herself. At the end of the hall, she paused before a set of double doors before pushing them open a crack. The light in the room beyond was dim. She opened the door further, and they entered a sparse but clean waiting room. She remembered a similar one from the mid levels where she had waited with a friend to be reunited with her child. A glass wall looked into a room that held a handful of cribs and bassinets. Jahns's hand dropped to her hip. She rubbed the hard nub of her now-useless implant, inserted at birth and never removed, not once. Being in that nursery reminded her of all she had lost, all she had given up for her work. For her ghosts.

It was too dark inside the nursery to see if any of the small beds stirred with newborns. She was notified of every birth, of course. As mayor, she signed a letter of congratulations and a birth certificate for each one, but the names ran together with the days. She could rarely remember what level the parents lived on, if it was their first or second. It made her sad to admit it, but those certificates had become just more paperwork, another rote duty.

The shadowy outline of an adult moved among the small cribs, the shiny clamp of a clipboard and the flash of a metal pen winking in the light of the observation room. The dark shape was obviously tall, with the gait and build of an older man. He took his time, noting something as he hovered over a crib, the two shimmers of metal uniting to jot a note. When he was done, he crossed the room and passed through a wide door to join Marnes and Jahns in the waiting room.

Peter Nichols was an imposing figure, Jahns saw. Tall and

lean, but not like Marnes, who seemed to fold and unfold unsure limbs to move about. Peter was lean like a habitual exerciser, like a few porters Jahns knew who could take the stairs two at a time and make it look like they'd been expressly designed for such a pace. It was height that lent confidence. Jahns could feel it as she took Peter's outstretched hand and let him pump it firmly.

"You came," Dr. Nichols said simply. It was a cold observation. There was only a hint of surprise. He shook Marnes's hand, but his eyes returned to Jahns. "I explained to your secretary that I wouldn't be much help. I'm afraid I haven't seen Juliette since she became a shadow twenty years ago."

"Well, that's actually what I wanted to talk to you about." Jahns glanced at the cushioned benches where she imagined anxious grandparents, aunts, and uncles waited while parents were united with their newborns. "Could we sit?"

Dr. Nichols nodded and waved them over.

"I take each of my appointments for office very seriously," Jahns explained, sitting across from the doctor. "At my age, I expect most judges and lawmen I install to outlive me, so I choose carefully."

"But they don't always, do they?" Dr. Nichols tilted his head, no expression on his lean and carefully shaven face. "Outlive you, I mean."

Jahns swallowed. Marnes stirred on the bench beside her.

"You must value family," Jahns said, changing the subject, realizing this was just another observation, no harm meant. "To have shadowed so long and to choose such a demanding line of work."

Nichols nodded.

"Why do you and Juliette never visit? I mean, not once in twenty years. She's your only child."

Nichols turned his head slightly, his eyes drifting to the

wall. Jahns was momentarily distracted by the sight of another form moving behind the glass, a nurse making the rounds. Another set of doors led off to what she assumed were the delivery rooms, where right now a convalescing new mother was probably waiting to be handed her most precious possession.

"I had a son as well," Dr. Nichols said.

Jahns felt herself reaching for her bag to procure the folders within, but it wasn't by her side. This was a detail she had missed, a brother.

"You couldn't have known," Nichols said, correctly reading the shock on Mayor Jahns's face. "He didn't survive. Technically, he wasn't born. The lottery moved on."

"I'm sorry . . ."

She fought the urge to reach over and hold Marnes's hand. It had been decades since the two of them had purposefully touched, even innocently, but the sudden sadness in the room punctured that intervening time.

"His name was going to be Nicholas, my father's father's name. He was born prematurely. One pound eight ounces."

The clinical precision in his voice was somehow sadder than an outpouring of emotion might have been.

"They intubated, moved him into an incubator, but there were . . . complications." Dr. Nichols looked down at the backs of his hands. "Juliette was thirteen at the time. She was as excited as we were, if you can imagine, to have a baby brother on the way. She was one year out from shadowing her mother, who was a delivery nurse." Nichols glanced up. "Not here in this nursery, mind you, but in the old mid-level nursery, where we both worked. I was still an intern then."

"And Juliette?" Mayor Jahns still didn't understand the connection.

"There was a failure with the incubator. When Nicholas—"

The doctor turned his head to the side and brought his hand halfway to his eyes but was able to compose himself. "I'm sorry. I still call him that."

"It's okay."

Mayor Jahns was holding Deputy Marnes's hand. She wasn't sure when or how that had happened. The doctor didn't seem to notice or, more likely, care.

"Poor Juliette." He shook his head. "She was distraught. She blamed Rhoda at first, an experienced delivery nurse who had done nothing but work a miracle to give our boy the slim chance he had. I explained this. I think Juliette knew. She just needed someone to hate." He nodded to Jahns. "Girls that age, you know?"

"Believe it or not, I remember." Jahns forced a smile and Dr. Nichols returned it. She felt Marnes squeeze her hand.

"It wasn't until her mother died that she took to blaming the incubator that had failed. Well, not the incubator, but the poor condition it was in. The general state of rot all things become."

"Your wife died from the complications?" It was another detail Jahns felt she must have missed from the file.

"My wife killed herself a week later."

Again, the clinical detachment. Jahns wondered if this was a survival mechanism that had kicked in after these events, or a personality trait already in place.

"Seems like I would remember that," Deputy Marnes said, the first words he'd uttered since introducing himself to the doctor.

"Well, I wrote the certificate myself. So I could put whatever cause I wanted —"

"And you admit to this?" Marnes seemed ready to leap off the bench. To do what, Jahns could hardly guess. She held his arm to keep him in place.

"Beyond the statute of limitations? Of course. I admit it. It was a worthless lie, anyway. Juliette was smart, even at that age. She knew. And this is what drove her —" He stopped himself.

"Drove her what?" Mayor Jahns asked. "Crazy?"

"No." Dr. Nichols shook his head. "I wasn't going to say that. It's what drove her away. She applied for a change in casters. Demanded to move down to Mechanical, to enter the shop as a shadow. She was a year too young for that sort of placement, but I agreed. I signed off on it. I thought she'd go, get some deep air, come back. I was naïve. I thought the freedom would be good for her."

"And you haven't seen her since?"

"Once. For her mother's funeral, just a few days later. She marched up on her own, attended the burial, gave me a hug, then marched back down. All without rest, from what I've heard. I try to keep up with her. I have a colleague in the deep nursery who will wire now and then with a bit of news. It's all focus, focus, focus with her."

Nichols paused and laughed.

"You know, when she was young, all I saw was her mother in her. But she grew up to be more like me."

"Is there anything you know that would preclude her from or make her ill suited for the job of silo sheriff? You do understand what's involved with the job, right?"

"I understand." Nichols looked over at Marnes, his eye drifting to the copper badge visible through the open, shoddily tied robe, down to the bulge of a pistol at his side. "All the little lawmen throughout the silo have to have someone up top, giving commands, is that it?"

"More or less," Jahns said.

"Why her?"

Marnes cleared his throat. "She helped us with an investigation once —"

"Jules? She was up here?"

"No. We were down there."

"She has no training."

"None of us have," Marnes said. "It's more of a . . . political office. A citizen's post."

"She won't agree to it."

"Why not?" Jahns asked.

Nichols shrugged. "You'll see for yourself, I suppose." He stood. "I wish I could give you more time, but I really should get back." He glanced at the set of double doors. "We'll be bringing a family in soon —"

"I understand." Jahns rose and shook his hand. "I appreciate your seeing us."

He laughed. "Did I have a choice?"

"Of course."

"Well, I wish I'd known that sooner."

He smiled, and Jahns saw that he was joking, or attempting to. As they parted company and walked back down the hallway to collect their things and return the robes, Jahns found herself more and more intrigued by this nomination of Marnes's. It wasn't his style, a woman from the down deep. A person with baggage. She wondered if his judgment was perhaps clouded by *other* factors. And as he held the door for her, leading out to the main waiting room, Mayor Jahns wondered if she was going along with him because *her* judgment was clouded as well.

10

It was lunchtime, but neither of them was powerfully hungry. Jahns nibbled on a cornbar while she walked, priding herself on "eating on the climb" like a porter. They continued to pass these tradesmen, and Jahns's esteem of their profession grew and grew. She had a strange pang of guilt from heading down under such a light load while these men and women trudged up carrying so much. And they moved so *fast*. She and Marnes pressed themselves against the rail as a downward porter apologetically stomped past. His shadow, a girl of fifteen or sixteen, was right behind him, loaded down with what looked to be sacks of garbage for the recycling center. Jahns watched the young girl spiral out of sight, her sinewy and smooth legs hanging miles out of her shorts, and suddenly felt very old and very tired.

The two of them fell into a rhythmic pace, the reach of each foot hovering over the next tread, a sort of collapsing of the bones, a resignation to gravity, falling to that foot, sliding the hand, extending the walking stick forward, repeat. Doubt crept into Jahns around the thirtieth floor. What had seemed a fine adventure at sunrise now seemed a mighty undertaking. Each step was performed reluctantly, with the knowledge of how grueling it would be to win that elevation back.

They passed the upper water treatment plant on thirty-two, and Jahns realized she was seeing portions of the silo that were practically new to her. It had been a lifetime ago that she'd been this deep, a shameful thing to admit. And in that time, changes had been made. Construction and repairs were ongoing. Walls were a different color than she remembered. But then, it was hard to trust one's memory.

The traffic on the stairs lightened as they neared the IT floors. Here were the most sparsely populated levels of the silo, where fewer than two dozen men and women – but mostly men – operated within their own little kingdom. The silo servers took up almost an entire floor, the machines slowly reloading with recent history, having been wiped completely during the uprising. Access to them was now severely restricted, and as Jahns passed the landing on the thirty-third, she swore she could hear the mighty thrumming of all the electricity they consumed. Whatever the silo had been, or had been originally designed for, she knew without asking or being told that these strange machines were some organ of primacy. Their power draw was a constant source of contention during budget meetings. But the necessity of the cleaning, the fear of even talking about the outside and all the dangerous taboos that went with it, gave IT incredible leeway. They housed the labs that made the suits, each one tailored to the person waiting in the holding cell, and this alone set them apart from all else.

No, Jahns told herself, it wasn't simply the taboo of the cleaning, the fear of the outside. It was the hope. There was this unspoken, deadly hope in every member of the silo. A ridiculous, fantastical hope. That maybe not for them, but perhaps for their children, or their children's children, life on the outside would be possible once again, and that it would be the work of IT and the bulky suits that emerged from their labs that would make it all possible.

Jahns felt a shiver even to think it. Living outside. The childhood conditioning was that strong. Maybe God would hear her thoughts and rat her out. She imagined herself in a cleaning suit, a far too common thought, placing herself into the flexible coffin to which she had condemned so many.

On the thirty-fourth, she slipped off onto the landing. Marnes joined her, his canteen in hand. Jahns realized she'd been drinking out of his all day while hers had stayed strapped to her back. There was something childlike and romantic about this, but also something practical. It was more difficult to reach one's own water than it was to grab that of the other from their pack.

"You need a break?" He passed the canteen, which had two swallows left in it. Jahns took one of them.

"This is our next stop," she said.

Marnes looked up at the faded number stenciled over the doorway. He had to know what floor they were on, but it was as if he needed to double-check.

Jahns returned his canteen. "In the past, I've always wired them to get the okay on my nominations. It was something Mayor Humphries did before me, and Mayor Jeffers before him." She shrugged. "Way of the world."

"I didn't know they had to approve." He took the last swallow and patted Jahns on the back, twirled his finger for her to turn around.

"Well, they've never rejected any of my nominations." Jahns felt her canteen tugged out of her pouch, Marnes's canteen shoved in its place. Her pack felt a smidgen lighter. She realized Marnes wanted to carry her water and share it until it too was empty. "I think the unwritten rule is there just so we'll carefully consider every judge and lawman, knowing there's some informal oversight."

"So this time you're doing it in person."

She turned back around to face her deputy. "I figured we

were passing this way . . ." She paused while a young couple hurried up the stairs behind Marnes, holding hands and taking the treads two at a time. "And that it might feel even more conspicuous *not* to stop and check in."

"Check in," Marnes said. Jahns half expected him to spit over the railing; the tone seemed to require such punctuation. She suddenly felt another of her weaknesses exposed.

"Think of it as a goodwill mission," she said, turning toward the door.

"I'm gonna think of it as a fact-finding raid," Marnes muttered, following her.

Jahns could tell that, unlike at the nursery, they would not be buzzed through and sent back into the mysterious depths of IT. While they waited to be seen, she watched as even a member of the staff, identifiable from their silver overalls, was patted down and searched just to *leave* the wing and exit toward the stairs. A man with a wand — a member of IT's own internal security detail — seemed to have the job of checking everyone who passed through the metal gates. The receptionist on the outside of the gates was deferent enough, however, and seemed pleased to have the mayor for a visit. She expressed her condolences for the recent cleaning, an odd thing to say but something Jahns wished she heard more often. They were shown to a small conference room attached to the main foyer, a place, she supposed, for meeting with various departments without putting them through the hassle of passing through security.

"Look at all this space," Marnes whispered once they were alone in the room together. "Did you see the size of that entrance hall?"

Jahns nodded. She looked around the ceiling and walls for some peephole, something to confirm the creepy sensation that she was being watched. She set her bag and walking stick down and collapsed wearily into one of the plush chairs. When it moved, she realized the thing was on wheels. Nicely oiled wheels.

"Always wanted to check this place out," Marnes said. He peered through the glass window that looked back into the wide foyer. "Every time I've passed this place—and it's only been a dozen times or so—I've been curious to see what's inside."

Jahns nearly asked him to stop talking but worried that it would hurt his feelings.

"Boy, he's coming in a hurry. Must be because of you."

Jahns turned and looked out the window to see Bernard Holland heading their way. He disappeared from view as he approached the door, the handle flicked down, and the small man whose job it was to keep IT running smoothly strode into the room.

"Mayor."

Bernard was all teeth, the front ones crooked. He had a wispy mustache that hung down in a weak attempt to hide this flaw. Short, portly, and with a pair of glasses perched on his small nose, he looked every bit the technical expert. Above all, to Jahns at least, he looked *smart*.

He reached for Jahns's hand as she rose from the chair, the blasted thing nearly scooting out from underneath her as she pressed down on the armrests.

"Careful," Bernard said, grabbing her elbow to steady her. "Deputy." He nodded toward Marnes while Jahns regained her balance. "It's an honor to have you down. I know you don't take these trips often."

"Thanks for seeing us on short notice," Jahns said.

"Of course. Please, make yourselves comfortable." He swept his hand over the lacquered conference table. It was nicer than the one in the mayor's office, though Jahns assuaged herself by assuming it was shiny from being less frequently employed. She sat in the chair warily, then reached into her bag and produced the set of files.

"Straight to business, as always," Bernard said, sitting beside her. He pushed his small round spectacles up his nose and glided forward on the chair until his plump belly met the desk. "Always appreciated that about you. We are, as you can imagine with yesterday's unfortunate events, as busy as ever. Lots of data to go through."

"How's that going?" Jahns asked while she arranged the material in front of her.

"Some positives and negatives, as always. Readouts from some of the seal sensors showed improvement. Atmospheric levels of eight of the known toxins have declined, though not by much. Two have risen. Most have remained unchanged." He waved his hand. "It's a lot of boring technical stuff, but it'll all be in my report. I should have it ported up before you get back to your office."

"That'll be fine," Jahns said. She wanted to say something else, to acknowledge his department's hard work, to let him know that another cleaning had been successful, God knew why. But it was Holston out there, the closest thing she'd ever had to a shadow, the only man she'd ever seen running for her office when she was dead and feeding the roots of the fruit trees. It was too soon to mention it, much less applaud it.

"I normally wire this sort of thing to you," she said, "but since we were passing by, and you won't be up for the next committee meeting for, what, another three months . . . ?"

"The years go fast," Bernard said.

"I just figured we could informally agree to this now, so I could offer our best candidate the job." She glanced up at Marnes. "Once she accepts, we can finish the paperwork on our way back up, if you don't mind." She slid the folder toward

Bernard and was surprised when he produced one of his own, rather than accept hers.

"Well, let's go over this," Bernard said. He opened his folder, licked his thumb, and flipped through a few pieces of high-quality paper. "We were wired about your visit, but your list of candidates didn't hit my desk until this morning. Otherwise, I would have tried to save you the trip down and back up." He pulled out a piece of paper devoid of creases. It didn't even look bleached. Jahns wondered where IT got such things while her office was held together with cornflour paste. "I'm thinking, of the three names listed here, that Billings is our man."

"We may consider him next—" Deputy Marnes started to say.

"I think we should consider him now." He slid the paper toward Jahns. It was an acceptance contract. There were signatures at the bottom. One line was left blank, the mayor's name neatly printed underneath.

She had to catch her breath.

"You've already contacted Peter Billings about this?"

"He accepted. The judge's robe was going to be a little stifling for him, being so young and full of energy. I thought he was a fine choice for that role, but I think he's an even better one now for the job of sheriff."

Jahns remembered Peter's judicial nomination process. It had been one of the times she'd gone along with Bernard's suggestion, seeing it as a trade for a future pick of her own. She studied the signature, Peter's hand familiar from his various notes sent up on behalf of Judge Wilson, under whom he currently shadowed. She imagined one of the porters who had flown past them on the steps that day, apologizing as they went, rushing this very piece of paper down.

"I'm afraid Peter is currently third on our list," Mayor Jahns finally said. Her voice suddenly felt tired. It sounded frail and weak in the cavernous and wasteful space of that underused and outsized conference room. She looked up at Marnes, who was glaring at the contract, his jaw clenching and unclenching.

"Well, I think we both know Murphy's name is on this list for flattery. He's too old for the job—"

"Younger than me," Marnes interrupted. "I hold up just fine."

Bernard tilted his head. "Yes, well, your first choice simply won't do, I'm afraid."

"And why is that?" Jahns asked.

"I'm not sure how . . . *thorough* your background check has been, but we've had enough problems with this candidate that I recognized her name. Even though she's from Maintenance."

Bernard said this last word like it was full of nails and might gut him to spit it out.

"What kinda problems?" Marnes demanded.

Jahns shot the deputy a look of warning.

"Nothing we would have wanted to report, mind you." Bernard turned to Marnes. There was venom in the small man's eyes, a raw hatred for the deputy, or perhaps for the star on his chest. "Nothing worth involving the *law*. But there have been some . . . creative requisitions from her office, items rerouted from our use, improper claims of priority and the like." Bernard took a deep breath and folded his hands together on top of the folder in front of him. "I wouldn't go as far as calling it *stealing*, per se, but we have filed complaints with Deagan Knox as head of Mechanical to inform him of these . . . irregularities."

"That's it?" Marnes growled. "Requisitions?"

Bernard frowned. He spread his hands on the folder. "That's it? Have you been listening? The woman has practically stolen goods, has had items rerouted from *my* department. It's not clear if these are even for silo use. They could be for personal gain. God knows, the woman uses more than her allowance of electricity. Maybe she trades for chits—"

"Is this a formal accusation?" Marnes asked. He made a show

of pulling his pad from his pocket and clicking his mechanical pen.

"Ah, no. As I said, we would not want to trouble your office. But, as you can see, this is not the sort of person to enter a career in high law. It's what I expect of a mechanic, to be honest, which is where, I'm afraid, this candidate should stay." He patted the folder as if putting the issue to rest.

"That's your suggestion," Mayor Jahns said.

"Why, yes. And I think since we have such a fine candidate ready and willing to serve and already living in the up top—"

"I'll take your *suggestion* into account." Jahns took the crisp contract from the table and deliberately folded it in half, pinching the crease with her fingernails as she slid them down its length. She stuck the piece of paper in one of her folders while Bernard watched, horrified.

"And since you have no *formal* complaints about our first candidate, I will take this as tacit approval to speak with her about the job." Jahns stood and grabbed her bag. She slid the folders into the outside pouch and secured the flap, then grabbed her walking stick from where it leaned against the conference table. "Thank you for seeing us."

"Yes, but—" Bernard scooted away from the table and hurried after her as Jahns made for the door. Marnes got up and followed, smiling.

"What should I tell Peter? He's of the assumption that he starts anytime!"

"You should never have told him anything," Jahns said. She stopped in the foyer and glared at Bernard. "I gave you my list in confidence. You betrayed that. Now, I appreciate all you do for the silo. You and I have a long and peaceable history working together, overseeing what might be the most prosperous age our people have known—"

"Which is why—" Bernard began.

"Which is why I'm forgiving this trespass," Mayor Jahns said. "This is *my* job. My people. They elected me to make these kinds of decisions. So my deputy and I will be on our way. We will give our top choice a fair interview. And I will be sure to stop by on my way up in case there is anything to sign."

Bernard spread his hands in defeat. "Very well," he said. "I apologize. I only hoped to expedite the process. Now, please, rest a little, you are our guests. Let me get you some food, maybe some fruit?"

"We'll be on our way," Jahns said.

"Fine." He nodded. "But at least some water? Top up your canteens?"

Jahns remembered one of them was already empty, and they had a few more flights to go.

"That would be a kind gesture," she said. She signaled to Marnes, who turned so she could grab his canteen from his pack. Then she turned her back so he could grab hers as well. Bernard waved to one of his workers to come fetch them and fill them up, but the entire time he kept his eyes on this curious and intimate exchange.

11

THEY WERE ALMOST down to the fifties before Jahns could think straight. She imagined she could feel the weight of Peter Billings's contract in her pack. Marnes muttered his own complaints from a few steps behind, bitching about Bernard and trying to keep up, and Jahns realized she was fixated now. The weariness in her thighs and calves had become compounded by the growing sense that this trip was more than a mistake: it was probably futile. A father who warns her that his daughter won't accept. Pressure from IT to choose another. Now each step of their descent was taken with dread. Dread and yet a new certainty that Juliette was the person for the job. They would have to convince this woman from Mechanical to take the post, if only to show Bernard, if only to keep this arduous journey from becoming a total waste.

Jahns was old, had been mayor a long time, partly because she got things done, partly because she prevented worse things from happening, but mostly because she rarely made a ruckus. She felt like it was about time – now, while she was old enough for the consequences not to matter. She glanced back at Marnes and knew the same went for him. Their time was almost up. The best, the most important thing they could do for the silo was to make sure their legacy endured. No uprisings. No abuses of power. It was why she had run unopposed the last few elections. But now she could sense that she was gliding to the finish while stronger and younger runners were preparing to overtake her. How many judges had she signed off on at Bernard's request? And now the sheriff, too? How long before Bernard was mayor? Or worse: a puppet master with strings interwoven throughout the silo.

"Take it easy," Marnes huffed.

Jahns realized she was going too fast. She slowed her pace.

"That bastard's got you riled up," he said.

"And you better be as well," she hissed back at him.

"You're passing the gardens."

Jahns checked the landing number and saw that he was right. If she'd been paying attention, she would've noticed the smell. When the doors on the next landing flew open, a porter bearing sacks of fruit on each shoulder strode out, the scent of lush and wet vegetation accompanying him and overpowering her.

It was past dinnertime, and the smell was intoxicating. The porter, even though overburdened, saw that they were leaving the stairwell for the landing and held the door open with a planted foot as his arms bulged around the weight of the large sacks.

"Mayor," he said, bowing his head and then nodding to Marnes as well.

Jahns thanked him. Most of the porters looked familiar to her: she'd seen them over and over as they delivered throughout the silo. But they never stayed in one place long enough for her to catch and remember a name, a normally keen skill of hers. She wondered, as she and Marnes entered the hydroponic farms, if the porters made it home every night to be with their families. Or did they even have families? Were they like the priests? She was too old and too curious not to know these things. But then, maybe it took a day on the stairwell to appreciate their job, to notice them fully. The porters were like the air she breathed, always there, always serving, so necessary as to be ubiquitous and taken for granted. But now the weariness of the descent had opened her senses completely to them. It was like a sudden drop in the oxygen, triggering her appreciation.

"Smell those oranges," Marnes said, snapping Jahns out of her thoughts. He sniffed the air as they passed through the low garden gates. A staff member in green overalls waved them through. "Bags here, Mayor," he said, gesturing to a wall of cubbies sporadically filled with shoulder bags and bundles.

Jahns complied, leaving her kit in one of the cubbies. Marnes pushed hers to the back and added his to the same one. Whether it was to save space or merely his habitual protectiveness, Jahns found the act as sweet as the air inside the gardens.

"We have reservations for the evening," Jahns told the worker.

He nodded. "One flight down for the rooms. I believe they're still getting yours ready. Are you here just for a visit or to eat?"

"A little of both."

The young man smiled. "Well, by the time you've had a bite, your rooms should be available."

Rooms, Jahns thought. She thanked the young man and followed Marnes into the garden network.

"How long since you were here?" she asked the deputy.

"Wow. A while back. Four years or so?"

"That's right." Jahns laughed. "How could I forget? The heist of the century."

"I'm glad you think it's funny," Marnes said.

At the end of the hallway, the twisting spiral of the hydroponic gardens diverted off both ways. This main tunnel snaked through two levels of the silo, curving mazelike all the way to the edges of the distant concrete walls. The constant sound of water dripping from the pipes was oddly soothing, the splatters echoing off the low ceiling. The tunnel was open on either side, revealing the bushy green of plants, vegetables, and small trees growing amid the lattice of white plastic pipes, twine strung everywhere to give the creeping vines and stems something to hold on to. Men and women with their young shadows, all in green overalls, tended to the plants. Sacks hung around their necks bulged with the day's harvest, and the cutters in their hands clacked like little claws that were a biological part of them. The pruning was mesmerizingly adroit and effortless, the sort of ability that came only from day after week after year of practice and repetition.

"Weren't you the first one to suggest the thievery was an inside job?" Jahns asked, still laughing to herself. She and Marnes followed the signs pointing toward the tasting and dining halls.

"Are we really going to talk about this?"

"I don't know why it's embarrassing. You've got to laugh about it."

"With time." He stopped and gazed through the mesh fencing at a stand of tomatoes. The powerful odor of their ripeness made Jahns's stomach grumble.

"We were really hyped up to make a bust at the time," Marnes said quietly. "Holston was a mess during all of this. He was wiring me every night for an update. I've never seen him want to take someone down so bad. Like he really needed it, you know?" He wrapped his fingers in the protective grate and stared past the vegetables as if into the years gone by. "Looking back, it's almost like he knew something was up with Allison. Like he saw the madness coming." Marnes turned to Jahns. "Do you remember what it was like before she cleaned? It had been so long. Everyone was on edge."

Jahns had long since stopped smiling. She stood close to

Marnes. He turned back to the plants, watched a worker snip off a red ripe tomato and place it in her basket.

"I think Holston wanted to let the air out of the silo, you know? I think he wanted to come down and investigate the thefts himself. Kept wiring me every day for reports like a life depended on it."

"I'm sorry to bring it up," Jahns said, resting a hand on his shoulder.

Marnes turned and looked at the back of her hand. His bottom lip was visible below his mustache. Jahns could picture him kissing her hand. She pulled it away.

"It's fine," he said. "Without all that baggage, I guess it is pretty funny." He turned and continued down the hallway.

"Did they ever figure out how it got in here?"

"Up the stairwell," Marnes said. "Had to be. Though I heard one person suggest that a child could've stolen one to keep as a pet and then released it up here."

Jahns laughed. She couldn't help herself. "One rabbit," she said, "confounding the greatest lawman of our time and making off with a year's salary of greens."

Marnes shook his head and chuckled a little. "Not the greatest," he said. "That was never me." He peered down the hallway and cleared his throat, and Jahns knew perfectly well who he was thinking of.

After a large and satisfying dinner, they retired a level down to the guest rooms. Jahns had a suspicion that extra pains had been taken to accommodate them. Every room was packed, many of them double- and triple-booked. And since the cleaning had been scheduled well before this last-minute interview adventure of theirs, she suspected rooms had been bumped around to make space. The fact that they had been given separate rooms, the mayor's with two beds, made it worse. It wasn't just the waste, it was the arrangement. Jahns was hoping to be more . . . inconvenienced.

And Marnes must've felt the same way. Since it was still hours before bedtime, and they were both buzzing from a fine meal and strong wine, he asked her to his small room so they could chat while the gardens settled down.

His room was tastefully cozy, with only a single twin bed, but nicely appointed. The upper gardens were one of just a dozen large private enterprises. All the expenses for their stay would be covered by her office's travel budget, and that money as well as the fares of the other travelers helped the establishment afford finer things, like nice sheets from the looms and a mattress that didn't squeak.

Jahns sat on the foot of the bed. Marnes took off his holster, placed it on the dresser, and plopped onto a changing bench just a few feet away. While she kicked off her boots and rubbed her sore feet, he went on and on about the food, the waste of separate rooms, brushing his mustache down with his hand as he spoke.

Jahns worked her thumbs into the soreness in her heels. "I feel like I'm going to need a week of rest at the bottom before we start the climb up," she said during a pause.

"It's not all that bad," Marnes told her. "You watch. You'll be sore in the morning, but once you start moving, you'll find that you're stronger than you were today. And it's the same on the way up. You just lean into each step, and before you know it, you're home."

"I hope you're right."

"Besides, we'll do it in four days instead of two. Just think of it as an adventure."

"Trust me," Jahns said. "I already am."

They sat quietly for a while, Jahns resting back on the pillows, Marnes staring off into space. She was surprised to find how calming and natural it was, just being in a room, alone, with him. The talk wasn't necessary. They could just *be*. No badge, no office. Two people.

"You don't take a priest, do you?" Marnes finally asked.

"No." She shook her head. "Do you?"

"I haven't. But I've been thinking about it."

"Holston?"

"Partly." He leaned forward and rubbed his hands down his thighs like he was squeezing the soreness out of them. "I'd like to hear where they think his soul has gone."

"It's still with us," Jahns said. "That's what they'd say, anyway."

"What do you believe?"

"Me?" She pushed herself up from the pillows and rested on one elbow, watching him watch her. "I don't know, really. I keep too busy to think about it."

"Do you think Donald's soul is still here with us?"

Jahns felt a shiver. She couldn't remember the last time someone had uttered his name.

"He's been gone more years than he was ever my husband," she said. "I've been married more to his ghost than to him."

"That don't seem like the right thing to say."

Jahns looked down at the bed, the world a little blurry. "I don't think he'd mind. And yes, he's still with me. He motivates me every day to be a good person. I feel him watching me all the time."

"Me too," Marnes said.

Jahns looked up and saw that he was staring at her.

"Do you think he'd want you to be happy? In all things, I mean?" He stopped rubbing his legs and sat there, hands on his knees, until he had to look away.

"You were his best friend," Jahns said. "What do you think he'd want?"

He rubbed his face, glanced toward the closed door as a laughing child thundered down the hallway. "I reckon he only ever wanted you to be happy. That's why he was the man for you."

Jahns wiped her eyes while he wasn't looking and peered curiously down at her wet fingers.

"It's getting late," she said. She slid to the edge of the small bed and reached down for her boots. Her bag and stick were waiting for her by the door. "And I think you're right. I think I'll be a little sore in the morning, but I think I'll feel stronger, eventually."

12

ON THE SECOND and final day of their descent into the down deep, the novel gradually became the habitual. The clank and thrum of the great spiral staircase found a rhythm. Jahns was able to lose herself in her thoughts, daydreaming so serenely that she would glance up at the floor number, seventy-two, eighty-four, and wonder where a dozen landings went. The kink in her left knee was even soothed away, whether by the numbness of fatigue or an actual return to health, she didn't know. She took to using the walking stick less, finding it only held up her pace as it often slipped between the treads and got caught there. With it tucked under her arm, it felt more useful. Like another bone in her skeleton, holding her together.

When they passed the ninetieth floor, with the stench of fertilizer and the pigs and other animals that produced this useful waste, Jahns pressed on, skipping the tour and lunch she'd planned, thinking only briefly of the small rabbit that somehow had escaped from another farm, made it twenty floors up without being spotted, and ate its fill for three weeks while it confounded half a silo.

Technically, they were already in the down deep when they reached ninety-seven. The bottom third. But even though the silo was mathematically divided into three sections of forty-eight floors each, her brain didn't work that way. Floor one hundred was a better demarcation. It was a milestone. She counted the floors down until they reached the first landing with three digits and stopped for a break.

Marnes was breathing deeply, she noticed. But she felt great. Alive and renewed in the way she had hoped the trip would make her feel. The futility, dread, and exhaustion from the day before were gone. All that remained was a small twinge of fear that these dour feelings could return, that this exuberant elation was a temporary high, that if she stopped, if she thought on it too long, it would spiral away and leave her dark and moody once more.

They split a small loaf of bread between them, sitting on the metal grating of the wide landing with their elbows propped up on the railings, their feet swinging over empty space, like two kids cutting class. Level one hundred teemed with people coming and going. The entire floor was a bazaar, a place for exchanging goods, for cashing in work chits for whatever was needed or merely coveted. Workers with their trailing shadows came and went, families yelled for one another among the dizzying crowds, merchants barked their best deals. The doors remained propped open for the traffic, letting the smells and sounds drift out onto the double-wide landing, the grating shivering with excitement.

Jahns reveled in the anonymity of the passing crowd. She bit into her half of the loaf, savoring the fresh yeastiness of bread baked that morning, and felt like just another person. A younger person. Marnes cut her a piece of cheese and a slice of apple and sandwiched them together. His hand touched hers as he passed it to her. Even the bread crumbs in his mustache were part of the moment's perfection.

"We're way ahead of schedule," Marnes said before taking a bite of fruit. It was just a pleasant observation. A pat on their elderly backs. "I figure we'll hit one-forty by dinner."

"Right now, I'm not even dreading the climb out," Jahns said. She finished the cheese and apple and chewed contentedly. Everything tasted better while climbing, she decided. Or in pleasant company, or amid the music leaking out of the bazaar, some beggar strumming his uke over the noise of the crowd.

"Why don't we come down here more often?" she asked.

Marnes grunted. "Because it's a hundred flights down? Besides, we've got the view, the lounge, the bar at Kipper's. How many of these people come up to any of that more than once every few years?"

Jahns chewed on that and on her last bite of bread.

"Do you think it's natural? Not wandering too far from where we live?"

"Don't follow," Marnes said around a bite of food.

"Pretend, just as a hypothetical, mind you, that people lived in those ancient aboveground silos poking up over the hillside. You don't think they would move around so little, do you? Like stay in the same silo? Never wander over here or up and down a hundred flights of stairs?"

"I don't think on those things," Marnes said. Jahns took it as a hint that she shouldn't, either. It was impossible sometimes to know what could and couldn't be said about the outside. Those were discussions for spouses, and maybe the walk and the day together yesterday had gotten to her. Or maybe she was as susceptible to the post-cleaning high as anyone else: the sense that some rules could be relaxed, a few temptations courted, the release of pressure in the silo giving excuse for a month of jubilant wiggling in one's own skin.

"Should we get going?" Jahns asked as Marnes finished his bread.

He nodded, and they stood and collected their things. A woman walking by turned and stared, a flash of recognition on her face, gone as she hurried to catch up with her children.

It was like another world down here, Jahns thought to herself. She had gone too long without a visit. And even as she promised herself not to let that happen again, some part of her knew, like a rusting machine that could feel its age, that this journey would be her last.

Floors drifted in and out of sight. The lower gardens, the larger farm in the one-thirties, the pungent water treatment plant below that. Jahns found herself lost in thought, remembering her conversation with Marnes the night before, the idea of Donald living with her more in memory than reality, when she came to the gate at one-forty.

She hadn't even noticed the change in the traffic, the preponderance of blue denim overalls, the porters with more satchels of parts and tools than clothes, food, or personal deliveries. But the crowd at the gate showed her that she'd arrived at the upper levels of Mechanical. Gathered at the entrance were workers in loose blue overalls spotted with age-old stains. Jahns could nearly peg their professions by the tools they carried. It was late in the day, and she assumed most were returning home from repairs made throughout the silo. The thought of climbing so many flights of stairs and *then* having to work boggled her mind. And then she remembered she was about to do that very thing.

Rather than abuse her station or Marnes's power, they waited in line while the workers checked through the gate. As these tired men and women signed back in and logged their travel and hours, Jahns thought of the time she had wasted ruminating about her own life during the long descent, time she should've spent polishing her appeal to this Juliette. Rare nerves twisted her gut as the line shuffled forward. The worker ahead of them showed his ID, the card colored blue for Mechanical. He scratched his information on a dusty slate. When it was their turn, they pushed through the outer gate and showed their golden IDs. The station guard raised his eyebrows, then seemed to recognize the mayor.

"Your Honor," he said, and Jahns didn't correct him. "Weren't expecting you this shift." He waved their IDs away and reached for a nub of chalk. "Let me."

Jahns watched as he spun the board around and wrote their names in neat print, the side of his palm collecting dust from the old film of chalk below. For Marnes, he simply wrote "Sheriff," and again, Jahns didn't correct him.

"I know she wasn't expecting us until later," Jahns said, "but I wonder if we could meet with Juliette Nichols now."

The station guard turned and looked behind him at the digital clock that recorded the proper time. "She won't be off the generator for another hour. Maybe two, knowing her. You could hit the mess hall and wait."

Jahns looked at Marnes, who shrugged. "Not entirely hungry yet," he said.

"What about seeing her at work? It would be nice to see what she does. We'd try our best to stay out of the way."

The guard lifted his shoulders. "You're the mayor. I can't say no." He jabbed the nub of chalk down the hall, the people lined up outside the gate shifting impatiently as they waited. "See Knox. He'll get someone to run you down."

The head of Mechanical was a man hard to miss. Knox amply filled the largest set of overalls Jahns had ever seen. She wondered if the extra denim cost him more chits and how a man managed to keep such a belly full. A thick beard added to his scope. If he smiled or frowned at their approach, it was impossible to know. He was as unmoved as a wall of concrete.

Jahns explained what they were after. Marnes said hello,

and she realized they must've met the last time he was down. Knox listened, nodded, and then bellowed in a voice so gruff, the words were indistinguishable from one another. But they meant something to someone, as a young boy materialized from behind him, a waif of a kid with unusually bright orange hair.

"Gitemoffandowntojules," Knox growled, the space between the words as slender as the gap in his beard where a mouth should have been.

The young boy, young even for a shadow, waved his hand and darted away. Marnes thanked Knox, who didn't budge, and they followed after the boy.

The corridors in Mechanical, Jahns saw, were even tighter than elsewhere in the silo. They squeezed through the end-of-shift traffic, the concrete blocks on either side primed but not painted, and rough where they brushed against her shoulder. Overhead, parallel and twisting runs of pipe and wire conduit hung exposed. Jahns felt the urge to duck, despite the half foot of clearance; she noticed many of the taller workers walking with a stoop. The lights overhead were dim and spaced well apart, making the sensation of tunneling deeper and deeper into the earth overwhelming.

The young shadow with the orange hair led them around several turns, his confidence in the route seemingly habitual. They came to a flight of stairs, the square kind that made right turns, and went down two more levels. Jahns heard a rumbling grow louder as they descended. When they left the stairwell on one-forty-two, they passed an odd contraption in a wide-open room just off the hallway. A steel arm the size of several people end to end was moving up and down, driving a piston through the concrete floor. Jahns slowed to watch its rhythmic gyrations. The air smelled of something chemical, something rotten. She couldn't place it.

"Is this the generator?"

Marnes laughed in a patronizing, uniquely manly way.

"That's a pump," he said. "Oil well. It's how you read at night."

He squeezed her shoulder as he walked past, and Jahns forgave him instantly for laughing at her. She hurried after him and Knox's young shadow.

"The generator is that thrumming you hear," Marnes said. "The pump brings up oil, they do something to it in a plant a few floors down, and then it's ready to burn."

Jahns vaguely knew some of this, possibly from a committee meeting. She was amazed, once again, at how much of the silo was alien to even her, she who was supposed to be – nominally at least – running things.

The persistent grumbling in the walls grew louder as they neared the end of the hall. When the boy with the orange hair pulled open the doors, the sound was deafening. Jahns felt wary about approaching further, and even Marnes seemed to stall. The kid waved them forward with frantic gestures, and Jahns found herself willing her feet to carry her toward the noise. She wondered, suddenly, if they were being led *outside*. It was an illogical, senseless idea, born of imagining the most dangerous threat she could possibly summon.

As she broke the plane of the door, cowering behind Marnes, the boy let the door slam shut, trapping them inside with the onslaught. He pulled headphones – no wires dangling from them – from a rack by the wall. Jahns followed his lead and put a pair over her own ears. The noise was deadened, remaining only in her chest and nerve endings. She wondered why, for what cause, this rack of ear protection would be located *inside* the room rather than outside.

The boy waved and said something, but it was just moving lips. They followed him along a narrow passageway of steel grating, a floor much like the landings on each silo floor. When the hallway turned, one wall fell away and was replaced with a railing of three horizontal bars. A machine beyond reckoning loomed on the other side. It was the size of her entire apartment and office put together. Nothing seemed to be moving at first, nothing to justify the pounding she could feel in her chest and across her skin. It wasn't until they fully rounded the machine that she saw the steel rod sticking out of the back of the unit, spinning ferociously and disappearing into another massive metal machine that had cables as thick as a man's waist rising up toward the ceiling.

The power and energy in the room were palpable. As they reached the end of the second machine, Jahns finally saw a solitary figure working beside it. A young-looking woman in overalls, a hard hat on, brown braided hair hanging out the back, was leaning into a wrench nearly as long as she was tall. Her presence gave the machines a terrifying sense of scale, but she didn't seem to fear them. She threw herself into her wrench, her body frightfully close to the roaring unit, reminding Jahns of an old children's tale where a mouse pulled a barb out of an imaginary beast called an elephant. The idea of a woman this size fixing a machine of such ferocity seemed absurd. But she watched the woman work while the young shadow slipped through a gate and ran up to tug on her overalls.

The woman turned, not startled, and squinted at Jahns and Marnes. She wiped her forehead with the back of one hand, her other hand swinging the wrench around to rest on her shoulder. She patted the young shadow on the head and walked out to meet them. Jahns saw that the woman's arms were lean and well defined with muscle. She wore no undershirt, just blue overalls cut high up over her chest, exposing a bit of olive skin that gleamed with sweat. She had the same dark complexion as the farmers who worked under grow lights, but it could have been as much from the grease and grime if her denims were any indication.

She stopped short of Jahns and Marnes, and nodded at them. She smiled at Marnes with a hint of recognition. She didn't offer a hand, for which Jahns was grateful. Instead, she pointed toward a door by a glass partition and then headed that way herself.

Marnes followed on her heels like a puppy, Jahns close behind. She turned to make sure the shadow wasn't underfoot, only to see him scurrying off the way he had come, his hair glowing in the wan overhead lights of the generator room. His duty, as far as he was concerned, was done.

Inside the small control room, the noise lessened. It dropped almost to nothing as the thick door was shut tight. Juliette pulled off her hard hat and earmuffs and dropped them on a shelf. Jahns took hers away from her head tentatively, heard the noise reduced to a distant hum, and removed them all the way. The room was tight and crowded with metal surfaces and winking lights unlike anything she had ever seen. It was strange to her that she was mayor of this room as well, a thing she hardly knew existed and certainly couldn't operate.

While the ringing in Jahns's ears subsided, Juliette adjusted some spinning knobs, watching little arms waver under glass shields. "I thought we were doing this tomorrow morning," she said, concentrating intently on her work.

"We made better time than I'd hoped."

Jahns looked to Marnes, who was holding his ear protection in both hands, shifting uncomfortably.

"Good to see you again, Jules," he said.

She nodded and leaned down to peer through the thick glass window at the gargantuan machines outside, her hands darting over the large control board without needing to look, adjusting large black dials with faded white markings.

"Sorry about your partner," she said, glancing down at a bank of readouts. She turned and studied Marnes, and Jahns saw that this woman, beneath the sweat and grime, was beautiful. Her face was hard and lean, her eyes bright. She had a fierce intelligence you could measure from a distance. And she peered at Marnes with utmost sympathy, visible in the furrow of her brow. "Really," she said. "I'm terribly sorry. He seemed like a good man."

"The best," Marnes sputtered, his voice cracking.

Juliette nodded as if that was all that needed saying. She turned to Jahns.

"That vibration you feel in the floor, Mayor? That's a coupling when it's barely two millimeters off. If you think it feels bad in here, you should go put your hands on the casing. It'll jiggle your fingers numb immediately. Hold it long enough, and your bones will rattle like you're coming apart."

She turned and reached between Jahns and Marnes to throw a massive switch, then turned back to the control board. "Now imagine what that generator is going through, shaking itself to pieces like that. Teeth start grinding together in the transmission, small bits of metal shavings cycle through the oil like sandpaper grit. Next thing you know, there's an explosion of steel and we've got no power but whatever the backup can spit out."

Jahns held her breath.

"You need us to get someone?" Marnes asked.

Juliette laughed. "None of this is news or different from any other shift. If the backup unit wasn't being torn down for new gaskets, and we could go to half power for a week, I could pull that coupler, adjust the mounts, and have her spinning like a top." She shot a look at Jahns. "But since we have a mandate for full power, no interruptions, that's not happening. So I'm going to keep tightening bolts while they keep trying to shake loose, and try to find the right revolutions in here to keep her fairly singing."

"I had no idea, when I signed that mandate—"

"And here I thought I'd dumbed down my report enough to make it clear," Juliette said.

"How long before this failure happens?"

Jahns suddenly realized she wasn't here interviewing this woman. The demands were heading in the opposite direction.

"How long?" Juliette laughed and shook her head. She finished a final adjustment and turned to face them with her arms crossed. "It could happen right now. It could happen a hundred years from now. The point is: it's *going* to happen, and it's entirely preventable. The goal shouldn't be to keep this place humming along for our lifetimes"—she looked pointedly at Jahns—"or our current term. If the goal ain't forever, we should pack our bags right now."

Jahns saw Marnes stiffen at this. She felt her own body react, a chill coursing across her skin. This last line was dangerously close to treason. The metaphor only half saved it.

"I could declare a power holiday," Jahns suggested. "We could stage it in memory of those who clean." She thought more about this. "It could be an excuse to service more than your machine here. We could—"

"Good luck getting IT to power down shit," Juliette said. She wiped her chin with the back of her wrist, then wiped this on her overalls. She looked down at the grease transferred to the denim. "Pardon my language, Mayor."

Jahns wanted to tell her it was quite all right, but the woman's attitude, her power, reminded her too much of a former self that she could just barely recall. A younger woman who dispensed with niceties and got what she wanted. She found herself glancing over at Marnes. "Why do you single out their department? For the power, I mean."

Juliette laughed and uncrossed her arms. She tossed her hands toward the ceiling. "Why? Because IT has, what, three floors out of one-forty-four? And yet they use up over a quarter of all the power we produce. I can do the math for you—"

"That's quite all right."

"And I don't remember a server ever feeding someone or saving someone's life or stitching up a hole in their britches."

Jahns smiled. She suddenly saw what Marnes liked about this woman. She also saw what he had once seen in her younger self, before she married his best friend.

"What if we had IT ratchet down for some maintenance of their own for a week? Would that work?"

"I thought we came down here to recruit her *away* from all this," Marnes grumbled.

Juliette shot him a look. "And I thought I told you—or your secretary—not to bother. Not that I've got anything against what you do, but I'm needed down here." She raised her arm and checked something dangling from her wrist. It was a timepiece. But she was studying it as if it still worked.

"Look, I'd love to chat more." She looked up at Jahns. "Especially if you can guarantee a holiday from the juice, but I've got a few more adjustments to make and I'm already into my overtime. Knox gets pissed if I push into too many extra shifts."

"We'll get out of your hair," Jahns said. "We haven't had dinner yet, so maybe we can see you after? Once you punch out and get cleaned up?"

Juliette looked down at herself, as if to confirm she even needed cleaning. "Yeah, sure," she said. "They've got you in the bunkhouse?"

Marnes nodded.

"All right. I'll find you later. And don't forget your muffs." She pointed to her ears, looked Marnes in the eye, nodded, then returned to her work, letting them know the conversation, for now, was over.

13

Marnes and Jahns were guided to the mess hall by Marck, a mechanic just getting off second shift. Marnes seemed to take umbrage at needing a tour guide. The deputy possessed that distinctly male quality of pretending to know where he was, even when he didn't. Walking slightly ahead in an attempt to prove this, he would pause at some intersection, point questioningly in one direction, only to have Marck laugh and correct him.

"But it all looks the same," he grumbled as he continued to forge ahead.

Jahns laughed at the manly display and hung back to bend the young mechanic's ear, recognizing that he worked on Juliette's shift. He smelled of the down deep, that odor that wafted in whenever a mechanic came up to repair something in her offices. It was the blend born of their work, a mix of perspiration, grease, and vague chemicals. But Jahns was learning to ignore that. She saw that Marck was a kind and gentle man, a man who took her by the arm when a trolley of rattling parts was hurried past, a man who acknowledged every single person they passed in those dim corridors of jutting pipes and drooping wires. He lived and breathed well above his lot in life, Jahns thought. He radiated confidence. Even in the darkness, his smile threw shadows.

"How well do you know Juliette?" she asked him, once the noisy cart rattled out of earshot.

"Jules? I know her like a sister. We're all family down here."

He said this as though he assumed the rest of the silo operated differently. Ahead of them, Marnes scratched his head at the next intersection before guessing correctly. A pair of mechanics crowded around the corner from the other direction, laughing. They and Marck exchanged a snippet of conversation that sounded to Jahns like a foreign language. She suspected Marck was right, that perhaps things did work differently in the deepest depths of the silo. People down there seemed to wear their thoughts and feelings on the outside, seemed to say exactly what they meant, much as the pipes and wires of the place lay exposed and bare.

"Through here," Marck said, pointing across a wide hall toward the sound of overlapping conversations and the tinking of knives and forks on metal plates.

"So, is there anything you can tell us about Jules?" Jahns asked. She smiled at Marck as he held the door for her. "Anything you think we should know?" The two of them followed Marnes to a handful of empty seats. The kitchen staff bustled among the tables, actually serving the food rather than having the mechanics line up for it. Before they'd even situated themselves on the dented aluminum benches, bowls of soup and glasses of water with lime slices bobbing on top were being set out, and hunks of bread torn from loaves and placed directly on the beaten-up surface of the table.

"Are you asking me to vouch for her?" Marck sat down and thanked the large man who portioned out their food and spoons. Jahns looked around for a napkin and saw most of the men and women using the greasy rags that dangled from their back or breast pockets.

"Just anything we should know," she said.

Marnes studied his bread, sniffed it, then dunked one corner into his soup. A neighboring table erupted with laughter at the conclusion of some story or joke being told.

"I know she can do any job thrown at her. Always could. But I figure you don't need me to talk you into something you've already walked this far to get. I'd imagine your minds are already made up."

He sipped on a spoonful of soup. Jahns picked up her utensil and saw that it was chipped and twisted, the butt of the spoon scratched like it'd been used to gouge at something.

"How long have you known her?" Marnes asked. The deputy chewed on his soggy bread and was doing a heroic job of blending in with his surroundings, of looking like he belonged.

"I was born down here," Marck told them, raising his voice over the din-filled room. "I was shadowing in Electrical when Jules showed up. She was a year younger than me. I gave her two weeks before I figured she'd be kicking and screaming to get out of here. We've had our share of runaways and transfers, kids from the mids thinking their problems wouldn't dare follow them—"

He left the sentence short, his eyes lighting up as a demure woman squeezed in next to Marnes on the other side of the table. This new arrival wiped her hands with her rag, stuffed it into her breast pocket, and leaned over the table to kiss Marck on the cheek.

"Honey, you remember Deputy Marnes." Marck gestured to Marnes, who was wiping his mustache with the palm of his hand. "This is my wife, Shirly." They shook hands. The dark stains on Shirly's knuckles seemed permanent, a tattoo from her work.

"And your mayor. This is Jahns." The two women shook hands as well. Jahns was proud of herself for accepting the firm grip without caring about the grease.

"Pleased," Shirly said. She sat. Her food had somehow materialized during the introductions, the surface of her soup undulating and throwing off steam.

"Has there been a crime, officer?" Shirly smiled at Marnes as she tore off a piece of her bread, letting him know it was a joke.

"They came to harangue Jules into moving up top with them," Marck said, and Jahns caught him lifting an eyebrow at his wife.

"Good luck," she said. "If that girl moves a level, it'll be down from here and into the mines."

Jahns wanted to ask what she meant, but Marck turned and continued where he'd left off.

"So I was working in Electrical when she showed up—"

"You boring them with your shadow days?" Shirly asked.

"I'm tellin' them about when Jules arrived."

His wife smiled.

"I was studying under old Walk at the time. This was back when he was still moving around, getting out and about now and then—"

"Oh yeah, Walker." Marnes jabbed a spoon at Jahns. "Crafty fellow. Never leaves his workshop."

Jahns nodded, trying to follow. Several of the revelers at the neighboring table got up to leave. Shirly and Marck waved good-bye and exchanged words with several of them, before turning their attention back to the table.

"Where was I?" Marck asked. "Oh, so the first time I met Jules was when she arrived at Walk's shop with this pump." Marck took a sip of his water. "One of the first things they have her doing—now, keep in mind this is just a waif of a girl, right? Thirteen years old. Skinny as a pipe. Fresh from the mids or somewhere up there." He waved his hand like it was all the same. "They've got her hauling these massive pumps up to Walk's to have him respool the motors, basically unwrap a mile of wire and lay it back in place." Marck paused and laughed. "Well, to have Walk make *me* do all the work. Anyway, it's like this initiation, you know? You all do that sort of thing to your shadows, right? Just to break 'em down a little?"

Neither Jahns nor Marnes moved. Marck shrugged and continued. "Anyway, these pumps are heavy, okay? They had to weigh more than she did. Maybe double. And she's supposed to wrestle these things onto carts by herself and get them up four flights of stairs —"

"Wait. How?" Jahns asked, trying to imagine a girl that age moving a hunk of metal twice her weight.

"Doesn't matter. Pulleys, ropes, bribery, whatever she likes. That's the point, right? And they've got ten of these things set aside for her to deliver —"

"Ten of them," Jahns repeated.

"Yeah, and probably *two* of them actually needed respooling," Shirly added.

"Oh, if that." Marck laughed. "So Walk and I are taking bets on how long before she cuts and runs back to her old man."

"I gave her a week," Shirly said.

Marck stirred his soup and shook his head. "The thing was, after she pulled it off, none of us had any idea how she'd done it. It was years later that she finally told us."

"We were sitting over at that table." Shirly pointed. "I'd never laughed so hard in my life."

"Told you what?" Jahns asked. She had forgotten her soup. The steam had long stopped swirling from its surface.

"Well, sure enough, I wound the coils on ten pumps that week. The whole time, I'm waiting for her to break. Hoping for it. My fingers were sore. No way she could move all of them." Marck shook his head. "No way. But I kept winding them, she kept hauling them off, and a while later she'd bring another. Got all ten of them done in six days. The little snot went to Knox, who was just a shift manager back then, and asked if she could take a day off."

Shirly laughed and peered into her soup.

"So she got someone to help her," Marnes said. "Somebody probably just felt sorry for her."

Marck wiped his eyes and shook his head. "Aw, hell no. Somebody would've seen, would've said something. Especially when Knox demanded to know. Old man nearly blew a fuse asking her what she'd done. Jules just stands there, calm as a dead battery, shrugging."

"How did she do it?" Jahns asked. Now she was dying to know.

Marck smiled. "She only moved the one pump. Nearly broke her back getting it up here, but only moved the one."

"Yeah, and you rewound that thing ten times," Shirly said.

"Hey, you don't have to tell me."

"Wait." Jahns held up her hand. "But what about the others?"

"Done them herself. I blame Walk, talking his head off while she swept the shop that first night. She was asking questions, badgering me, watching me work on that first pump. When I got done, she pushed the pump down the hall, didn't bother with the stairs, and stowed it in the paint shop right on the trolley. Then she went downstairs, got the next pump, and hauled it around the corner into the tool lock-up. Spent the entire night in there teaching herself how to rewire a motor."

"Ah," Jahns said, seeing where this was going. "And the next morning she brought you the same pump from the day before, from just around the corner."

"Right. Then she went and wound copper four levels below while I was doing the same thing up here."

Marnes erupted with laughter and slapped the table, bowls and bread hopping.

"I averaged two motors a day that week, a brutal pace."

"Technically, it was only one motor," Shirly pointed out, laughing.

"Yeah. And she kept up with me. Had them all back to her caster with a day to spare, a day she asked to take off."

"A day she got off, if I remember right," Shirly added. She shook her head. "A shadow with a day off. The damnedest thing."

"The point is, she wasn't ever supposed to get the task done in the first place."

"Smart girl," Jahns said, smiling.

"Too smart," Marck said.

"So what did she do with her day off?" Marnes asked.

Marck pushed his lime down beneath the surface of his water with his finger and held it there a moment.

"She spent the day with me and Walk, sweeping the shop, asking how things worked, where these wires went to, how to loosen a bolt and dig inside something, that kind of stuff." He took a sip of water. "I guess what I'm sayin' is that if you want to give Jules a job, be very careful."

"Why be careful?" Marnes asked.

Marck gazed up at the confusion of pipes and wires overhead.

"'Cause she'll damn well do it. Even if you don't really expect her to."

14

After their meal, Shirly and Marck gave them directions to the bunk room. Jahns watched as the young married couple exchanged kisses. Marck was coming off his shift while Shirly was going onto hers. The shared meal was breakfast for one and supper for the other. Jahns thanked them both for their time and complimented the food, then she and Marnes left a mess hall nearly as noisy as the generator room had been and followed the winding corridors toward their beds for the night.

Marnes would be staying in the communal bunk room used by junior first-shift mechanics. A small cot had been made up for him that Jahns gauged to be half a foot too short. Down the hall from the bunk room, a small apartment had been reserved for Jahns. The two of them decided to wait there, biding their time in private, rubbing the aches in their legs, talking about how different everything in the down deep was, until there was a knock on their door. Juliette pushed it open and stepped inside.

"They got you both in one room?" Juliette asked, surprised.

Jahns laughed. "No, they've got the deputy in the bunk room. And I would've been happy staying out there with the others."

"Forget it," Juliette said. "They put up recruits and visiting families in here all the time. It's nothing."

Jahns watched as Juliette placed a length of string in her mouth, then gathered her hair, still wet from a shower, and tied it up in a tail. She had changed into another pair of overalls, and Jahns guessed the stains in them were permanent, that the fabric was actually laundered and ready for another shift.

"So how soon could we announce this power holiday?" Juliette asked. She finished her knot and crossed her arms, leaning back against the wall beside the door. "I would think you'd wanna take advantage of the post-cleaning mood, right?"

"How soon can *you* start?" Jahns asked. She realized, suddenly, that part of the reason she wanted this woman as her sheriff was that she felt unattainable. Jahns glanced over at Marnes and wondered how much of his attraction to her, all those many years ago when she was young and with Donald, had been as simply motivated.

"I can start tomorrow," Juliette said. "We could have the backup generator online by morning. I could work another shift tonight to make sure the gaskets and seals—"

"No," Jahns said, raising her hand. "How soon can you start as sheriff?" She dug through her open bag, sorting folders across the bed, looking for the contract.

"I'm—I thought we discussed this. I have no interest in being—"

"They make the best ones," Marnes said. "The ones who have no interest in it." He stood across from Juliette, his thumbs tucked into his overalls, leaning against one of the small apartment's walls.

"I'm sorry, but there's no one down here who can just slip into my boots," Juliette said, shaking her head. "I don't think you two understand all that we do—"

"I don't think you understand what we do up top," Jahns said. "Or why we need you."

Juliette tossed her head and laughed. "Look, I've got machines down here that you can't possibly—"

"And what good are they?" Jahns asked. "What do these machines do?"

"They keep this whole goddamned place running!" Juliette declared. "The oxygen you breathe? We recycle that down here. The toxins you exhale? We pump them back into the earth. You want me to write up a list of everything oil makes? Every piece of plastic, every ounce of rubber, all the solvents and cleaners, and I'm not talking about the power it generates, but everything else!"

"And yet it was all here before you were born," Jahns pointed out.

"Well, it wouldn't have lasted my lifetime, I'll tell you that. Not in the state it was in." She crossed her arms again and leaned back against the wall. "I don't think you get what a mess we'd be in without these machines."

"And I don't think you get how pointless these machines are going to become without all these people."

Juliette looked away. It was the first time Jahns had seen her flinch.

"Why don't you ever visit your father?"

Juliette snapped her head around and looked at the other wall. She wiped some loose hair back from her forehead. "Go look at my work log," she said. "Tell me when I'd fit it in."

Before Jahns could reply, could say that it was family, that there's always time, Juliette turned to face her. "Do you think I don't care about people? Is that it? Because you'd be wrong. I care about every person in this silo. And the men and women down here, the forgotten eight floors of Mechanical, *this* is my family. I visit with them every day. I break bread with them several times a day. We work, live, and die alongside one another." She looked to Marnes. "Isn't that right? You've seen it."

Marnes didn't say anything. Jahns wondered if she was referring specifically to the "dying" part.

"Did you ask him why he never comes to see me? Because he has all the time in the world. He has *nothing* up there."

"Yes, we met with him. Your father seemed like a very busy man. As determined as you."

Juliette looked away.

"And as stubborn." Jahns left the paperwork on the bed and went to stand by the door, just a pace away from Juliette. She could smell the soap in the younger woman's hair. Could see her nostrils flare with her rapid, heavy breathing.

"The days pile up and weigh small decisions down, don't they? That decision not to visit. The first few days slide by easy enough; anger and youth power them along. But then they pile up like unrecycled trash. Isn't that right?"

Juliette waved her hand. "I don't know what you're talking about."

"I'm talking about days becoming weeks becoming months becoming years." She almost said that she'd been through the same exact thing, was still piling them up, but Marnes was in the room, listening. "After a while, you're staying mad just to justify an old mistake. Then it's just a game. Two people staring away, refusing to look back over their shoulders, afraid to be the first one to take that chance—"

"It wasn't like that," Juliette said. "I don't want your job. I'm sure you've got plenty of others who do."

"If it's not you, it's someone I'm not sure I can trust. Not anymore."

"Then give it to the next girl." She smiled.

"It's you or him. And I think he'll be getting more guidance from the thirties than he will from me, or from the Pact."

Juliette seemed to react to this. Her arms loosened across

her chest. She turned and met Jahns's gaze. Marnes was studying all this from across the room.

"The last sheriff, Holston, what happened to him?"

"He went to cleaning," Jahns said.

"He volunteered," Marnes added gruffly.

"I know, but why?" She frowned. "I heard it was his wife."

"There's all kinds of speculation—"

"I remember him talking about her, when you two came down to look into George's death. I thought, at first, that he was flirting with me, but all he could talk about was this wife of his."

"They were in the lottery while we were down here," Marnes reminded her.

"Yeah. That's right." She studied the bed for a while. Paperwork was spread across it.

"I wouldn't know how to do this job. I only know how to fix things."

"It's the same thing," Marnes told her. "You were a big help with our case down here. You see how things work. How they fit together. Little clues that other people miss."

"You're talking about *machines,*" she said.

"People aren't much different," Marnes told her.

"I think you already know this," Jahns said. "I think you have the right attitude, actually. The right disposition. This is only slightly a political office. Distance is good."

Juliette shook her head and looked back to Marnes. "So you nominated me for this, is that it? I wondered how this came up. Seemed like something right out of the ground."

"You'd be good at it," Marnes told her. "I think you'd be damned good at anything you set your mind to. And this is more important work than you think."

"And I'd live up top?"

"Your office is on level one. Near the airlock."

Juliette seemed to mull this over. Jahns was excited that she was even asking questions.

"The pay is more than you're making now, even with the extra shifts."

"You checked?"

Jahns nodded. "I took some liberties before we came down."

"Like talking to my father."

"That's right. He would love to see you, you know. If you came with us."

Juliette looked down at her boots. "Not sure about that."

"There's one other thing," Marnes said, catching Jahns's eye. He glanced at the paperwork on the bed. The crisply folded contract for Peter Billings was on top. "IT," he reminded her.

Jahns caught his drift.

"There's one matter to clear up, before you accept."

"I'm not sure I'm accepting. I'd want to hear more about this power holiday, organize the work shifts down here —"

"According to tradition, IT signs off on all nominated positions —"

Juliette rolled her eyes and blew out her breath. "IT."

"Yes, and we checked in with them on the way down as well, just to smooth things over."

"I'm sure," Juliette said.

"It's about these requisitions," Marnes interjected.

Juliette turned to him.

"We know it probably ain't nothing, but it's gonna come up —"

"Wait, is this about the heat tape?"

"Heat tape?"

"Yeah." Juliette frowned and shook her head. "Those bastards."

Jahns mimed pinching two inches of air. "They had a folder on you this thick. Said you were skimming supplies meant for them."

"No they didn't. Are you kidding?" She pointed toward the door. "We can't get any of the supplies we need because of them. When I needed heat tape – we had a leak in a heat exchanger a few months back – we couldn't get any because Supply tells us the backing material for the tape is all spoken for. Now, we had that order in a while back, and then I find out from one of our porters that the tape is going to IT, that they've got miles of the stuff for the skins of all their test suits."

Juliette took a deep breath.

"So I had some intercepted." She looked to Marnes as she admitted this. "Look, I'm keeping the power on so they can do whatever it is they do up there, and I can't get basic supplies. And even when I do, the quality is complete crap, probably because of unrealistic quotas, rushing the manufacturing chain –"

"If these are items you really needed," Jahns interrupted, "then I understand."

She looked to Marnes, who smiled and dipped his chin as if to say he'd *told* her this was the right woman for the job.

Jahns ignored him. "I'm actually glad to hear your side of this," she told Juliette. "And I wish I made this trip more often, as sore as my legs are. There are things we take for granted up top, mostly because they aren't well understood. I can see now that our offices need to be in better communication, have more of the constant contact I have with IT."

"I've been saying that for just about twenty years," Juliette said. "Down here, we joke that this place was laid out to keep us well out of the way. And that's how it feels, sometimes."

"Well, if you come up top, if you take this job, people will hear you. You could be the first link in that chain of command."

"Where would IT fall?"

"There will be resistance, but that's normal with them. I've handled it before. I'll wire my office for some emergency waivers. We'll make them retroactive, get these acquisitions above-board." Jahns studied the younger woman. "As long as I have your assurance that every one of those diverted supplies were absolutely necessary."

Juliette did not flinch away from the challenge. "They were," she said. "Not that it mattered. The stuff we got from them was crap. Couldn't have fallen apart better if it'd been designed to. I'll tell you what, we finally got our shipment from Supply and have extra tape. I'd love to drop off a peace offering on our way up. Our design is so much better—"

"Our way up?" Jahns asked, making sure she understood what Juliette was saying, what she was agreeing to.

Juliette looked them both over. She nodded. "You'll have to give me a week to sort out the generator. I'm holding you to that power holiday. And just so you understand, I'll always consider myself Mechanical, and I'll be doing this partly because I see what happens when problems are ignored. My big push down here has been preventive maintenance. No more waiting for things to break before we fix them, but to go around and make them hum while they're still working. Too many issues have been ignored, let degrade. And I think, if the silo can be thought of as one big engine, we are like the dirty oil pan down here that needs some people's attention." She reached her hand out to Jahns. "Get me that power holiday, and I'm your man."

Jahns smiled and took her hand, admired the warmth and power in her confident handshake.

"I'll get on it first thing in the morning," she said. "And thank you. Welcome aboard."

Marnes crossed the room to shake Juliette's hand as well. "Nice to have you on, boss."

Juliette smirked as she took his hand. "Well now, let's not get ahead of ourselves. I think I'll have a lot to learn before you go calling me that."

15

IT FELT APPROPRIATE that their climb back to the up top would occur during a power holiday. Jahns could feel her own energy complying with the new decree, draining away with each laborious step. The agony of the descent had been a tease, the discomfort of constant movement disguising itself as the fatigue of exercise. But now her frail muscles were really put to work. Each step was something to be conquered. She would lift a boot to the next tread, place a hand on her knee, and push herself another ten inches up what felt like a million feet of spiral staircase.

The landing to her right displayed the number fifty-eight. Each landing seemed to be in view forever. Not like the trip down, where she could daydream and skip right past several floors. Now they loomed in sight gradually beyond the outer railing and held there, taunting in the dim green glow of the emergency lights, as she struggled upward, one plodding and wavering step at a time.

Marnes walked beside her, his hand on the inner rail, hers on the outer, the walking stick clanging on the lonely treads between them. Occasionally, their arms brushed against one another. It felt as though they'd been away for months, away from their offices, their duties, their cold familiarity. The adventure down to wrangle a new sheriff had played out differently than Jahns had imagined it would. She had dreamed of a return to her youth and had instead found herself haunted by old ghosts. She had hoped to find a renewed vigor and instead felt the years of wear in her knees and back. What was to be a grand tour of her silo was instead trudged in relative anonymity, and now she wondered if its operation and upkeep even needed her.

The world around her was stratified. She saw that ever more clearly. The up top concerned itself with a blurring view, taking for granted the squeezed juice enjoyed with breakfast. The people who lived below and worked the gardens or cleaned animal cages orbited their own world of soil, greenery, and fertilizer. To them, the outside view was peripheral, ignored until there was a cleaning. And then there was the down deep, the machine shops and chemistry labs, the pumping oil and grinding gears, the hands-on world of grease-limned fingernails and the musk of toil. To these people, the outside world and the food that trickled down were mere rumors and bodily sustenance. The point of the silo was for the people to keep the machines running, when Jahns had always, her entire long life, seen it the other way around.

Landing fifty-seven appeared through the fog of darkness. A young girl sat on the steel grate, her feet tucked up against herself, arms wrapped around her knees, a children's book in its protective plastic cover held out into the feeble light spilling from an overhead bulb. Jahns watched the girl, who was unmoved save her eyes as they darted over the colorful pages. The girl never looked up to see who was passing the apartment floor's landing. They left her behind, and she gradually faded in the darkness as Jahns and Marnes struggled ever upward, exhausted from their third day of climbing, no vibrations or ringing footsteps above or below them, the silo quiet and eerily devoid of life, room enough for two old friends, two comrades, to walk side by side on the steps of chipping paint, their arms swinging and every now and then, very occasionally, brushing together.

They stayed that night at the midlevel deputy station, the officer of the mids insisting they take his hospitality and Jahns eager to buttress support for yet another sheriff nominated from outside the profession. After a cold dinner in near darkness and enough idle banter to satisfy their host and his wife, Jahns retired to the main office, where a convertible couch had been made as comfortable as possible, the linens borrowed from a nicer elsewhere and smelling of two-chit soap. Marnes had been set up on a cot in the holding cell, which still smelled of tub gin and a drunk who had gotten too carried away after the cleaning.

It was impossible to notice when the lights went out, they were so dim already. Jahns rested on the cot in the darkness, her muscles throbbing and luxuriating in her body's stillness, her feet cramped and feeling like solid bone, her back tender and in need of stretching. Her mind, however, continued to move. It drifted back to the weary conversations that had passed the time on their most recent day of climbing.

She and Marnes seemed to be spiraling around one another, testing the memory of old attractions, probing the tenderness of ancient scars, looking for some soft spot that remained among brittle and broken bodies, across wrinkled and dried-paper skin, and within hearts callused by law and politics.

Donald's name came up often and tentatively, like a child sneaking into an adult bed, forcing wary lovers to make room in the middle. Jahns grieved anew for her long-lost husband. For the first time in her life, she grieved for the subsequent decades of solitude. What she had always seen as her calling—this living apart and serving the greater good—now felt more like a curse. Her life had been taken from her. Squeezed into pulp.

The juice of her efforts and sacrificed years had dripped down through a silo that, just forty levels below her, hardly knew and barely cared.

The saddest part of this journey had been this understanding she'd come to with Holston's ghost. She could admit it now: a great reason for her hike, perhaps even the reason for wanting Juliette as sheriff, was to fall all the way to the down deep, away from the sad sight of two lovers nestled together in the crook of a hill as the wind etched away all their wasted youth. She had set out to escape Holston, and had instead found him. Now she understood, if not the mystery of why all those sent out to clean actually did so, why a sad few would dare to volunteer for the duty. Better to join a ghost than to be haunted by them. Better no life than an empty one—

The door to the deputy's office squeaked on a hinge long worn beyond the repair of grease. Jahns tried to sit up, to see in the dark, but her muscles were too sore, her eyes too old. She wanted to call out, to let her hosts know that she was okay, in need of nothing, but she listened instead.

Footsteps came to her, nearly invisible in the worn carpet. There were no words, just the creaking of old joints as they approached the bed, the lifting of expensive and fragrant sheets, and an understanding between two living ghosts.

Jahns's breath caught in her chest. Her hand groped for a wrist as it clutched her sheets. She slid over on the small convertible bed to make room and pulled him down beside her.

Marnes wrapped his arms around her back, wiggled beneath her until she was lying on his side, a leg draped over his, her hands on his neck. She felt his mustache brush against her cheek, heard his lips purse and peck the corner of hers.

Jahns held his cheeks and burrowed her face into his shoulder. She cried, like a schoolchild, like a new shadow who felt lost and afraid in the wilderness of a strange and terrifying job. She cried with fear, but that soon drained away. It drained like the soreness in her back as his hands rubbed her there. It drained until numbness found its place, and then, after what felt like a forever of shuddering sobs, *sensation* took over.

Jahns felt alive in her skin. She felt the tingle of flesh touching flesh, of just her forearm against his hard ribs, her hands on his shoulder, his hands on her hips. And then the tears were some joyous release, some mourning of the lost time, some welcomed sadness of a moment long delayed and finally there, arms wrapped around it and holding tight.

She fell asleep like that, exhausted from far more than the climb, nothing more than a few trembling kisses, hands interlocking, a whispered word of tenderness and appreciation, and then the depths of sleep pulling her down, the weariness in her joints and bones succumbing to a slumber she didn't want but sorely needed. She slept with a man in her arms for the first time in decades, and woke to a bed familiarly empty, but a heart strangely full.

In the middle of their fourth and final day of climbing, they approached the midthirties of IT. Jahns had found herself taking more breaks for water and to rub her muscles along the way, not for the exhaustion she feigned but the dread of this stopover and seeing Bernard, the fear of their trip ever coming to an end.

The dark and deep shadows cast by the power holiday followed them up, the traffic sparse as most merchants had closed for the silo-wide brownout. Juliette, who had stayed behind to oversee the repairs, had warned Jahns of the flickering lights from the backup generator. Still, the effect of the shimmering illumination had worn on her nerves during the long climb. The steady pulsing reminded her of a bad lightbulb she'd unhappily endured for the better part of her first term. Two different techs from Electrical had come to inspect the bulb. Both had deemed it too operational to replace. It had taken an appeal to McLain, the head of Supply even back then, to score her a replacement.

Jahns remembered McLain delivering the bulb herself. She hadn't been head of Supply for long and had fairly smuggled the thing up those many flights of stairs. Even then, Jahns had looked up to her, this woman with so much power and responsibility. She remembered McLain asking her why Jahns didn't just do what everyone else did—simply break the bulb the rest of the way.

The fact that this had never occurred to Jahns used to bother her—until she began to take pride in this failing; until she got to know McLain well enough to understand the question was a compliment, the hand-delivery her reward.

When they reached the thirty-fourth, Jahns felt like they were, in a sense, home again: back in the realm of the familiar, at the main landing for IT. She waited by the railing, leaning on it and her walking stick, while Marnes got the door. As it was cracked open, the pale glow of diminished power was swept off the stairwell by the bright lights blooming inside. It hadn't been widely publicized, but the reason for the severe power restrictions on other levels was largely the exemptions IT possessed. Bernard had been quick to point out various clauses in the Pact to support this. Juliette had bitched that servers shouldn't get priority over grow lights but resigned herself to getting the main generator realigned and taking what she could. Jahns told Juliette to view this as her first lesson in political compromise. Juliette said she saw it as a display of weakness.

Inside, Jahns found Bernard waiting for them, a look on his face like he'd swallowed sour fruit juice. A conversation between several IT workers standing off to the side was quickly silenced with their entry, leaving Jahns little doubt that they'd been spotted on the way up and expected.

"Bernard," she said, trying to keep her breathing steady. She didn't want him to know how tired she was. Let him think she was strolling by on her way up from the down deep, like it was no big deal.

"Marie."

It was a deliberate slight. He didn't even look Marnes's way or acknowledge that the deputy was in the room.

"Would you like to sign these here? Or in the conference room?" She dug into her bag for the contract with Juliette's name on it.

"What games are you playing at, Marie?"

Jahns felt her temperature rise. The cluster of workers in silver IT jumpsuits were following the exchange. "Playing at?" she asked.

"You think this *power holiday* of yours is cute? Your way of getting back at me?"

"Getting back—?"

"I've got servers, Marie—"

"Your servers have their full allocation of power," Jahns reminded him, her voice rising.

"But their cooling comes ducted from Mechanical, and if temps get any higher, we'll be ramping down, which we've *never* had to do!"

Marnes stepped between the two of them, his hands raised. "Easy," he said coolly, his gaze on Bernard.

"Call off your little shadow here," Bernard said.

Jahns placed a hand on Marnes's arm.

"The Pact is clear, Bernard. It's my choice. My nomination. You and I have a nice history of signing off on each other's—"

"And I told you this girl from the pits will not do—"

"She's got the job," Marnes said, interrupting. Jahns noticed his hand had fallen to the butt of his gun. She wasn't sure if Bernard had noticed or not, but he fell silent. His eyes, however, did not leave Jahns's.

"I won't sign it."

"Then next time, I won't ask."

Bernard smiled. "You think you'll outlive another sheriff?" He turned toward the workers in the corner and waved one of them over. "Why do I somehow doubt that?"

One of the technicians removed himself from the whispering group and approached. Jahns recognized the young man from the cafeteria, had seen him up top on nights she worked late. Lukas, if she remembered correctly. He shook her hand and smiled an awkward hello.

Bernard twirled his own hand, stirring the air with his impatience. "Sign whatever she needs. I refuse to. Make copies. Take care of the rest." He waved dismissively, turned and looked Marnes and Jahns up and down one final time as if disgusted with their condition, their age, their positions, *something*. "Oh, and have Sims top up their canteens. See that they have food enough to stagger to their homes. Whatever it takes to power their decrepit legs out of here and back to wherever it is they belong."

And with that, Bernard strode off toward the barred gates that led into the heart of IT, back to his brightly lit offices, where servers hummed happily, the temperature rising in the slow-moving air like the heat of angered flesh as capillaries squeezed, the blood in them rising to a boil.

16

THE FLOORS FLEW by faster as they approached home. In the darkest sections of the staircase, between quiet floors of people hunkered down and awaiting a return to normalcy, old hands wrapped around each other and swung between two climbers, brazenly and openly, grasping each other while their other hands slid up the cool steel of the rails.

Jahns let go sporadically only to check that her walking stick was secure against her back or to grab Marnes's canteen from his pack and take a sip. They had taken to drinking each other's water, it being easier to reach across than around one's own back. There was a sweetness to it as well, carrying the sustenance another needed and being able to provide and reciprocate in a perfectly equitable relationship. It was a thing worth dropping hands for. Momentarily, at least.

Jahns finished a sip, screwed on the metal cap with its dangling chain, and replaced it in his outer pouch. She was dying to know if things would be different once they got back. They were only twenty floors away. An impossible distance yesterday now seemed like something that could slip away without her noticing. And as they arrived, would familiar surroundings bring familiar roles? Would last night feel more and more like a dream? Or would old ghosts return to haunt them both?

She wanted to ask these things but talked of trivialities instead. When would Jules, as she insisted they call her, be ready for duty? What case files did he and Holston have open that needed tending to first? What concession would they make to keep IT happy, to calm down Bernard? And how would they handle Peter Billings's disappointment? What impact would this have on hearings he might one day preside over as judge?

Jahns felt butterflies in her stomach as they discussed these things. Or perhaps it was the nerves of all she wanted to say but couldn't. These topics were as numerous as grains of dust in the outside air, and just as likely to dry her mouth and still her tongue. She found herself drinking more and more from his canteen, her own water making noises at her back, her stomach lurching with every landing, each number counting down toward the conclusion of their journey, an adventure that had been a complete success in so many ways.

To start with, they had their sheriff: a fiery girl from the down deep who seemed every bit as confident and inspiring as Marnes had intimated. Jahns saw her kind as the future of the silo. People who thought long-term, who planned, who got things done. There was a precedent of sheriffs running for mayor. She thought Juliette would eventually make a fine choice.

And speaking of running, the trip had fired up her own goals and ambitions. She was excited about the upcoming elections, however unopposed she might be, and had even dreamed up dozens of short speeches during the climb. She saw how things could run better, how she could perform her duties more diligently, and how the silo could have new life breathed into old bones.

But the biggest change was whatever had grown between herself and Marnes. She had even begun to suspect, just in the last hours, that the real reason for his never taking a promotion was because of her. As deputy, there was enough space between them to contain his hope, his impossible dream of holding her. As sheriff, it couldn't happen: too much conflict of interest, too much his immediate superior. This theory of hers contained a powerful sadness and an awe-inspiring sweetness. She squeezed his hand as she thought about this theory, and it filled her with a deep hollowness, a cramp in her gut at all he had silently sacrificed, a massive debt to live up to no matter what happened next.

They approached the landing to the nursery and had no plans for stopping to see Juliette's father, to urge him to receive his daughter on the way up, but Jahns changed her mind as she felt her bladder beg for release.

"I've got to go pretty bad," she told Marnes, embarrassed like a child to admit she couldn't hold it. Her mouth was dry and her stomach churning from so much fluid, and maybe from the fear of getting home. "I wouldn't mind seeing Juliette's father, either," she added.

Marnes's mustache bent up at the corners with the excuse. "Then we should stop," he said.

The waiting room was empty, the signs reminding them to be quiet. Jahns peered through the glass partition and saw a nurse padding through the dark corridor toward her, a frown becoming a slight smile of recognition.

"Mayor," she whispered.

"I'm sorry not to have wired ahead, but I was hoping to see Dr. Nichols. And possibly use your restroom?"

"Of course." She buzzed the door and waved them through. "We've had two deliveries since you last stopped by. Things have been crazy with this generator mess—"

"Power holiday," Marnes said, correcting her, his voice gruff and louder than theirs.

The nurse shot him a look but nodded as if this was duly

noted. She took two robes from the racks and held them out, told them to leave their stuff by her desk.

In the waiting room, she waved toward the benches and said she would find the doctor. "The bathrooms are through there." She pointed at a door, the old sign painted on its surface nearly worn clean away.

"I'll be right back," Jahns told Marnes. She fought the urge to reach out and squeeze his hand, as normal as that dark and hidden habit had lately become.

The bathroom was almost completely devoid of light. Jahns fumbled with an unfamiliar lock on the stall door, cursed under her breath as her stomach churned noisily, then finally threw the stall open and hurried to sit down. Her stomach felt like it was on fire as she relieved herself. The mixture of welcomed release and the burn of having held it too long left her unable to breathe. She went for what felt like forever, remained sitting as her legs shook uncontrollably, and realized she had pushed herself too hard on the climb up. The thought of another twenty levels mortified her, made her insides feel hollow with dread. She finished and moved over to the adjoining toilet to splash herself clean, then dried herself with one of the towels. She flushed both units to cycle the water. It all required fumbling in the darkness, unfamiliar as she was with the spacing and location that were second nature in her apartment and office.

She staggered out of the bathroom on weak legs, wondering if she might need to stay one more night, sleep in a delivery bed, wait until the morning to make the climb to her office. She could barely feel her legs as she pulled open the door and returned to Marnes in the waiting room.

"Better?" he asked. He sat on one of the family benches, a space left conspicuously beside him. Jahns nodded and sat heavily. She was breathing in shallow pants and wondered if he'd find her weak if she admitted she couldn't go any further that day.

"Jahns? You okay?"

Marnes leaned forward. He wasn't looking at her, he was looking toward the ground. "Jahns. What the hell just happened?"

"Lower your voice," she whispered.

He screamed instead.

"Doctor!" he yelled. "Nurse!"

A form moved beyond the dusky glass of the nursery. Jahns laid her head back against the seat cushion, trying to form the words on her lips, to tell him to keep it down.

"Jahns, sweetheart, what did you do?"

He was holding her hand, patting the back of it. He shook her arm. Jahns just wanted to sleep. There was the slapping of footsteps running their way. Lights turned up forbiddingly bright. A nurse yelled something. There was the familiar voice of Juliette's father, a doctor. He would give her a bed. He would understand this exhaustion . . .

There was talk of blood. Someone was examining her legs. Marnes was crying, tears falling into his white mustache, peppered with black. He was shaking her shoulders, looking her in the eye.

"I'm okay," Jahns tried to say.

She licked her lips. So dry. Mouth so damned dry. She asked for water. Marnes fumbled for his canteen, brought it to her lips, splashing water against and into her mouth.

She tried to swallow but couldn't. They were stretching her out on the bench, the doctor touching her ribs, shining a light in her eyes. But things were getting darker anyway.

Marnes clutched the canteen in one hand, smoothed her hair back with the other. He was blubbering. So sad for some reason.

So much more energy than her. She smiled at him and reached for his hand, a miraculous effort. She held his wrist and told him that she loved him. That she had for as long as she could remember. Her mind was tired, loosening its grip on her secrets, mouthing them to him as tears flowed down his face.

She saw his eyes, bright and wrinkled, peering down at her, then turning to the canteen in his hand.

The canteen that he had carried.

The water, she realized, the poison meant for him.

17

THE GENERATOR ROOM was unusually crowded and eerily silent. Mechanics in worn overalls stood three deep behind the railing and watched the first-shift crew work. Juliette was only dimly aware of them; she was more keenly aware of the silence.

She leaned over a device of her own making, a tall platform welded to the metal floor and arrayed with mirrors and tiny slits that bounced light across the room. This light shined on mirrors attached to the generator and its large dynamo, helping her get them in perfect alignment. It was the shaft between the two of them that she cared about, that long steel rod the size of a man's waist where the power of combusting fuel was transformed into the spark of electricity. She was hoping to have the machines on either end of this rod aligned to within a thousandth of an inch. But everything they were doing was without precedent. The procedures had been hurriedly planned in all-night sessions while the backup generator was put online. Now she could only concentrate, could only hope the eighteen-hour shifts had been good for something and trust in plans made back when she'd had some decent rest and could think soundly.

While she guided the final placement, the chamber around her stood deathly quiet. She gave a sign, and Marck and his team tightened several of the massive bolts on the new rubber floor mounts. They were four days into the power holiday. The generator needed to be up and running by morning and at full power that next evening. With so much done to it—the new gaskets and seals, the polishing of cylinder shafts that had required young shadows to crawl down into the heart of the beast—Juliette was worried about it even starting up. The generator had never been fully powered down during her lifetime. Old Knox could remember it shutting itself down in an emergency once, back when he was a mere shadow, but for everyone else the rumble had been as constant and close as their own heartbeats. Juliette felt inordinate pressure for everything to work. She was the one who had come up with the idea to do a refit. She calmed herself with reassurances that it was the right thing to do and that the worst that could happen now was that the holiday would be extended until they sorted out all the kinks. That was much better than a catastrophic failure years from now.

Marck signaled that the bolts were secure, the locknuts tightened down. Juliette jumped off her homemade platform and strolled over to the generator to join him. It was difficult to walk casually with so many eyes on her. She couldn't believe this rowdy crew, this extended and dysfunctional family of hers, could be so perfectly silent. It was like they were all holding their breath, wondering if the crushing schedule of the last few days was going to be for naught.

"You ready?" she asked Marck.

He nodded, wiping his hands on a filthy rag that always seemed to be draped over his shoulder. Juliette checked her watch. The sight of its second hand ticking around in its constant path comforted her. Whenever she had doubts about something working, she looked at her wrist. Not to see the time, but to see a thing she had fixed. A repair so intricate and impossible—one that had taken years of cleaning and setting parts almost too small to see—that it made her current task, whatever it was, feel small by comparison.

"We on schedule?" Marck asked, grinning.

"We're doing fine." She nodded to the control room. Whispers began to stir through the crowd as they realized the restart was imminent. Dozens of them pulled sound protection from their necks and settled the muffs over their ears. Juliette and Marck joined Shirly in the control room.

"How's it going?" Juliette asked the second-shift foreman, a young woman, small and spirited.

"Golden," Shirly said as she continued to make adjustments, zeroing out all the corrections that had built up over the years. They were starting from the ground up, none of the patches and fixes of old to disguise any new symptoms. A fresh start. "We're good to go," she said.

She backed away from the controls and moved to stand near her husband. The gesture was transparent: this was Juliette's project, perhaps the last thing she would ever try to fix in the down deep of Mechanical. She would have the honor, and the full responsibility, of firing the generator up.

Juliette stood over the control board, looking down at knobs and dials that she could locate in utter darkness. It was hard to believe that this phase of her life was over, that some new one was about to begin. The thought of traveling to the up top frightened her more than this project could. The idea of leaving her friends and family, of dealing with politics, did not taste as sweet to her as the sweat and grease on her lips. But at least she had allies up there. If people like Jahns and Marnes were able to get by, to survive, she figured she'd be okay.

With a trembling hand, more from exhaustion than nerves, Juliette engaged the starter motor. There was a loud whine as a small electrical engine tried to get the massive diesel generator moving. It seemed to be taking forever, but Juliette had no idea what normal sounded like. Marck stood by the door, propping it open so they could better hear any shouts to abort. He glanced over at Juliette as she continued to hold the ignition, creases of worry in his brow as the starter whined and groaned in the next room.

Someone outside waved both arms, trying to signal her through the glass.

"Shut it off, shut it off," Marck said. Shirly hurried toward the control panel to help.

Juliette let go of the ignition and reached for the kill switch, but she stopped herself from pressing it. There was a noise outside. A powerful hum. She thought she could feel it through the floor, but not like the vibration of old.

"It's already running!" someone yelled.

"It was already running," Marck said, laughing.

The mechanics outside were cheering. Someone pulled off their ear protection and hurled the muffs up into the air. Juliette realized the starter motor was louder than the rebuilt generator, that she'd been holding the ignition even as it had already started and continued to run.

Shirly and Marck hugged one another. Juliette checked the temps and pressures on all the zeroed gauges and saw little to adjust, but she wouldn't be sure until it warmed up. Her throat constricted with emotion, the release of so much pressure. Work crews were leaping over the railing to crowd around the rebuilt beast. Some who rarely visited the generator room were reaching out to touch it, almost with reverent awe.

Juliette left the control room to watch them, to listen to the sound of a perfectly working machine, of gears in alignment. She stood behind the railing, hands on a steel bar that used to rattle and dance while the generator labored, and watched an unlikely celebration take place in a normally avoided workspace. The hum was magnificent. Power without dread, the culmination of so much hurried labor and planning.

The success gave her a new confidence for what lay ahead, for what lay above. She was in such fine spirits and so fixated on the powerful and improved machines that she didn't notice the young porter hurry into the room, his face ashen, his chest swelling with the deep gulps of a long and frantic run. She barely noticed the way the news traveled from mouth to mouth throughout the room, spreading among the mechanics until fear and sadness registered in their eyes. It wasn't until the celebration died completely, the room falling into a different sort of quiet, one studded with sobs and gasps of disbelief, of grown men wailing, that Juliette knew something was amiss.

Something had happened. A great and powerful thing had fallen out of alignment.

And it had nothing to do with her generator.

PART 3

CASTING OFF

18

THERE WERE NUMBERS on each of the pockets. Juliette could look down at her chest and read them, and so it occurred to her that they must have been printed upside down. They were there for her to read, and for no one else. She numbly stared at them through her helmet visor while the door behind her was sealed. There was another door, a forbidden one, looming in front of her. It stood silently as it waited to be opened.

Juliette felt lost in this void between the two doors, trapped in this airlock full of brightly colored pipes jutting from the walls and ceiling, everything shimmering behind plastic-wrapped shrouds.

The hiss of argon being pumped into the room sounded distant through her helmet. It let her know the end was near. Pressure built against the plastic, crinkling it across the bench and walls, wrapping it tightly around the pipes. She could feel the pressure against her suit, like an invisible hand gently squeezing.

She knew what was to happen next—and part of her wondered how she had gotten here, a girl from Mechanical who had never cared one whit about the outside, who had only ever broken minor laws, and who would've been content for the rest of her life to live in the deepest bowels of the earth, covered in grease and fixing the broken things, little concern for the wider world of the dead that surrounded her . . .

19

Days Earlier

JULIETTE SAT ON THE floor of the holding cell, her back against the tall rows of steel bars, a mean world displayed on the wallscreen before her. For the past three days, while she had attempted to teach herself how to be silo sheriff, she had studied this view of the outside and wondered what the fuss was all about.

All she saw out there were dull slopes of ground, these gray hills rising up toward grayer clouds, dappled sunlight straining to illuminate the land with little success. Across it all were the terrible winds, the frenzied gusts that whipped small clouds of soil into curls and whorls that chased one another across a landscape meant only for them.

For Juliette, there was nothing inspiring about the view, nothing that aroused her curiosity. It was an uninhabitable wasteland devoid of anything useful. There were no resources beyond the tainted steel of crumbling towers visible over the hills, steel it would no doubt cost more to reclaim, transport, smelt, and purify than it would to simply pull new ore from the mines beneath the silo.

The forbidden dreams of the outside world, she saw, were

sad and empty. They were dead dreams. The people of the up top who worshipped this view had it all backward—the future was *below.* That's where the oil that provided their power came from, the minerals that became anything useful, the nitrogen that renewed the soil in the farms. Any who shadowed in the footsteps of chemistry and metallurgy knew this. Those who read children's books, those who tried to piece together the mystery of a forgotten and unknowable past, remained deluded.

The only sense she could make of their obsession was the open space itself, a feature of the landscape that frankly terrified her. Perhaps it was something wrong with *her* that she loved the walls of the silo, loved the dark confines of the down deep. Was everyone else crazy to harbor thoughts of escape? Or was it something about her?

Juliette looked from the dry hills and the fog of soil to the scattered folders around her. It was her predecessor's unfinished work. A shiny star sat balanced on one of her knees, not yet worn. There was a canteen sitting on one of the folders, safe inside a plastic reusable evidence bag. It looked innocent enough lying there, having already done its deadly deed. Several numbers written with black ink on the bag had been crossed out, cases long since solved or abandoned. A new number stood to one side, a case number matching a folder not present, a folder filled with page after page of testimony and notes dealing with the death of a mayor whom everyone had loved—but whom someone had killed.

Juliette had seen some of those notes, but only from a distance. They were written in Deputy Marnes's hand, hands that would not relinquish the folder, hands that clutched it madly. She had taken peeks at the folder from across his desk and had seen the spattered tears that smeared occasional words and caused the paper to pucker. The writing amid those drying tears was a scrawl, not as neat as his notes in the other folders.

What she could see seemed to crawl angrily across the page, words slashed out violently and replaced. It was the same ferocity Deputy Marnes displayed all the time now, the boiling anger that had driven Juliette away from her desk and into the holding cell to work. She had found it impossible to sit across from such a broken soul and be expected to think. The view of the outside world that loomed before her, however sad, cast a far less depressing shadow.

It was in the holding cell that she killed time between the static-filled calls on her radio and the jaunts down to some disturbance. Often, she would simply sit and sort and re-sort her folders according to perceived severity. She was sheriff of all the silo, a job she had not shadowed for but one she was beginning to understand. One of the last things Mayor Jahns had told her had proved truer than she could imagine: people were like machines. They broke down. They rattled. They could burn you or maim you if you weren't careful. Her job was not only to figure out why this happened and who was to blame, but also to listen for the signs of it coming. Being sheriff, like being a mechanic, was as much the fine art of preventive maintenance as it was the cleaning up after a breakdown.

The folders scattered on the floor were sad cases of the latter: complaints between neighbors that got out of hand; reported thefts; the source of a poisonous batch of amateur tub gin; several more cases stemming from the trouble this gin had caused. Each folder awaited more findings, more legwork, more hikes down the twisting stairs to engage in twisted dialogue, sorting lies from truth.

Juliette had read the Law portion of the Pact twice in preparation for the job. Lying in her bed in the down deep, her body exhausted from the work of aligning the primary generator, she had studied the proper way to file case folders, the danger of disturbing evidence, all of it logical and analogous to some part of her old job as mechanic. Approaching the scene of a crime or an active dispute was no different from walking into a pump room where something was broken. Someone or something was always at fault. She knew to listen, to observe, to ask questions of anyone who could have had anything to do with the faulty equipment or the tools they had used, following a chain of events all the way down to the bedrock itself. There were always confounding variables—you couldn't adjust one dial without sending something else off-kilter—but Juliette had a skill, a talent, for knowing what was important and what could be ignored.

She assumed it was this talent that Deputy Marnes had originally seen in her, this patience and skepticism she employed to ask one more stupid question and stumble eventually onto the answer. It was a boost to her confidence that she had helped solve a case before. She hadn't known it then, had been more concerned with simple justice and her private grief, but that case had been an interview and job training all in one.

She picked up that very folder from years gone by, a pale red stamp on its cover reading CLOSED in bold block letters. She peeled the tape holding its edges together and flipped through the notes. Many of them were in Holston's neat hand, a forward-slanting print she recognized from just about everything on and inside her desk, a desk that had once been his. She read his notes about her, refamiliarized herself with a case that had seemed an obvious murder but had actually been a series of unlikely events. Going back through it, something she had avoided until now, gave birth to old pains. And yet—she could also recall how comforting it had been to distract herself with the clues. She could remember the rush of a problem solved, the satisfaction of having answers to offset the hollowness left by her lover's death. The process had been similar to fixing a machine on extra shifts. There was the pain in her body from the effort and exhaustion, offset slightly by the knowledge that a rattle had been wrenched away.

She set the folder aside, not yet ready to relive it all. She picked up another and placed it in her lap, one hand falling to the brass star on her knee.

A shadow danced across the wallscreen, distracting her. Juliette looked up and saw a low wall of dirt spill down the hill. This layer of soot seemed to shiver in the wind as it traveled toward sensors she had been trained to think of as important, sensors that gave her a view of the outside world she had been frightened as a child into believing was worth seeing.

But she wasn't so sure, now that she was old enough to think for herself and near enough to observe it firsthand. This up top's obsession with cleaning barely trickled its way to the down deep, where *true* cleaning kept the silo humming and everyone alive. But even down there, her friends in Mechanical had been told since birth not to speak of the outside. It was an easy enough task when you never saw it, but now, walking by it to work, sitting before this view of a vastness one's brain could not comprehend, she saw how the inevitable questions must have surfaced. She saw why it might be important to squelch certain ideas before a stampede to the exits formed, before questions foamed on people's mad lips and brought an end to them all.

She flipped open Holston's folder. Behind the bio tab was a thick stack of notes about his last days as sheriff. The portion relating to his actual crime was barely half a page long, the rest of the piece of paper blank and wasted. A single paragraph simply explained that he had reported to the up-top holding cell and had expressed an interest in the outside. That was it. A few lines to spell a man's doom. Juliette read the words several times before flipping the page over.

Underneath was a note from Mayor Jahns asking that Holston be remembered for his service to the silo and not as just another cleaner. Juliette read this letter, written in the hand of someone who was also recently deceased. It was strange to think of people she knew that she could never see again. Part of the reason she had avoided her father all these years was because he was, simply put, *still there*. There was never the threat of her not being able to change her mind. But it was different with Holston and Jahns: they were gone forever. And Juliette was so used to rebuilding devices thought beyond repair that she felt if she concentrated enough, or performed the correct series of tasks in the right order, she should be able to bring the deceased back, be able to re-create their wasted forms. But she knew that wasn't the case.

She flipped through Holston's folder and asked herself forbidden questions, some for the very first time. What had seemed trivial when she lived in the down deep, where exhaust leaks could asphyxiate and broken flood pumps could drown everyone she knew, now loomed large before her. What was it all about, this life they lived in underground confines? What was out there, over those hills? Why were they here, and for what purpose? Had her kind built those tall silos crumbling in the distance? What for? And most vexing of all: what had Holston, a reasonable man—or his wife for that matter—been thinking to want to leave?

Two folders to keep her company, both marked CLOSED. Both belonging in the mayor's office, where they should have been sealed up and filed away. But Juliette kept finding herself returning to them rather than the more pressing cases in front of her. One of these folders held the life of a man she had loved, whose death she had helped unravel in the down deep. In the other lived a man she had respected whose job she now held. She didn't know why she obsessed over the two folders, especially since she couldn't stomach seeing Marnes peer forlornly down at his own loss, studying the details of Mayor Jahns's death, going over the depositions, convinced he had a killer but with no evidence to corner the man.

Someone knocked on the bars above Juliette's head. She looked up, expecting to find Deputy Marnes telling her it was time to call it a day, but saw a strange man peering down at her instead.

"Sheriff?" he said.

Juliette set the folders aside and palmed the star off her knee. She stood up and turned around, facing this small man with a protruding gut, glasses perched at the end of his nose, his silver IT overalls snugly tailored and freshly pressed.

"Can I help you?" she asked.

The man stuck his hand between the bars. Juliette moved the star from one palm to the other and reached out to accept it.

"Sorry I'm late getting up here," he said. "There's been a lot going on, what with the ceremonies, that generator nonsense, and all the legal wrangling. I'm Bernard, Bernard Holland."

Juliette felt her blood run cold. The man's hand was so small, it felt like it was missing a finger. Despite this, his grip was solid. She tried to pull back, but he refused to let go.

"As sheriff, I'm sure you already know the Pact inside and out, so you know that I'll be acting mayor, at least until we can arrange a vote."

"I'd heard," Juliette said coolly. She wondered how this man had gotten past Marnes's desk without some sort of violence. Here was their prime suspect in Jahns's death – only he was on the wrong side of the bars.

"Doing some filing, are you?" He relinquished his grip, and Juliette pulled her hand away. He peered down at the paperwork strewn across the floor, his eyes seeming to settle on the canteen in its plastic bag, but Juliette couldn't be sure.

"Just familiarizing myself with our ongoing cases," she said. "There's a little more room in here to . . . well, think."

"Oh, I'm sure a lot of deep thought has taken place in this room." Bernard smiled, and Juliette noticed his front teeth were crooked, one of them overlapping the other. It made him look like the stray mice she used to trap in the pump rooms.

"Yes, well, I've found the space conducive to sorting my thoughts out, so maybe there's something to that. And besides" — she leveled her eyes at him — "I don't expect it to remain empty for long. And once it's occupied, I'll be able to take leave of all this deep thought for a day or two while someone is put to cleaning —"

"I wouldn't count too much on that," Bernard said. He flashed his crooked teeth again. "The word down below is that the poor mayor, rest her soul, plumb wore herself out with that crazy climb of hers. I believe she was hiking down to see *you*, isn't that right?"

Juliette felt a sharp sting in her palm. She loosened her grip on the brass star, the knuckles on both hands white from making fists.

Bernard adjusted his glasses. "But now I hear you're investigating for foul play?"

Juliette continued to level her eyes at him, trying not to be distracted by the reflection of the dull hills visible in his spectacles. "I suppose you should know, as *acting* mayor, that we're treating this very much as a murder," she said.

"Oh my." His eyes widened over a limp smile. "So the rumors are true. Who would do such a thing?" The smile grew, and Juliette realized she was dealing with a man who felt himself invulnerable. It wasn't the first time she'd encountered a dirty and outsized ego such as his. Her time as a shadow in the down deep had been spent surrounded by them.

"I believe we'll find the party responsible was the one with the most to gain," she said dryly. After a pause, she added: "*Mayor.*"

The crooked smile faded. Bernard let go of the bars and

stepped back, his hands tucking into his overalls. "Well, it's nice to finally put a face to the name. I'm aware that you haven't spent much time out of the down deep – and to be honest I've stayed much too insulated in my own office – but things are changing around here. As mayor and sheriff, we will be working together a lot, you and me." He glanced down at the files at her feet. "So I expect you to keep me posted. About everything."

With that, Bernard turned and left, and it required a concerted effort for Juliette to relax her fists. When she finally peeled her fingers away from the star, she found its sharp edges had gouged into her palm, cutting her and drawing blood. A few drops caught the light on the edge of the brass, looking like wet rust. Juliette wiped the star clean on her new overalls, a habit born of her previous life among the sludge and grease. She cursed herself when she saw the dark spot the blood had left on her new clothes. Turning the star over, she peered at the stamped insignia on its face. There were the three triangles of the silo and the word *Sheriff* arched over the top of them. She turned it over again and fingered the clasp that held the sharp spike of the pin. She opened the clasp and let the pin hinge free. The stiff needle had been bent and straightened in several places over the years, giving it a hand-forged look. It wobbled on its hinge – echoing her hesitation to wear the thing.

But as Bernard's footsteps receded, as she heard him say something indecipherable to Deputy Marnes, she felt a new resolve steel her nerves. It was like encountering a rusted bolt that refused to budge. Something about that intolerable stiffness, that reluctance to move, set Juliette's teeth on edge. She had come to believe that there were no fasteners she couldn't unstick, had learned to attack them with grease and with fire, with penetrating oil and with brute strength. With enough planning and persistence, they always gave. Eventually.

She forced the wavy needle through the breast of her overalls and clasped the catch on the back. Looking down at the star was a little surreal. There were a dozen folders at her feet demanding her attention, and Juliette felt, for the first time since arriving at the up top, that this was her job. Her work at Mechanical was behind her. She had left that place in far better condition than she'd found it, had stayed long enough to hear the near-silent hum of a repaired generator, to see a shaft spin in such perfect alignment that one couldn't tell if it was moving at all. And now she had traveled to the up top to find here the rattle and squelch and grind of a different set of gears, a misalignment that was eating away at the true engine of the silo, just as Jahns had forewarned.

Leaving most of the folders where they were, she picked up Holston's, a folder she shouldn't even have been looking at but couldn't be without, and pulled the cell door open. Rather than turn to her office, she first walked the other way toward the yellow steel entrance to the airlock. Peering through the triple-paned glass for the dozenth time in several days, she imagined the man she had replaced standing inside, wearing one of those ridiculously bulky suits, waiting for those far doors to open. What went through a man's thoughts as he waited there alone to be cast off? It couldn't have been mere fear, for Juliette had tasted that well enough. It had to be something beyond that, a wholly unique sensation, the calm beyond the pain, or the numbness past the terror. Imagination, she figured, just wasn't up to the task of understanding unique and foreign sensations. It knew only how to dampen or augment what it already knew. It would be like telling someone what sex felt like, or an orgasm. Impossible. But once you felt it yourself, you could then imagine varying degrees of this new sensation.

It was the same as color. You could describe a new color only in terms of hues previously seen. You could mix the known, but you couldn't create the strange out of nothing. So maybe it was only the cleaners who understood what it felt like to stand there, trembling—or perhaps not afraid one bit—as they waited for their death.

The obsession with *why* played out in whispers through the silo—people wanting to know why they did what they did, why they left a shiny and polished gift to those who had exiled them—but that did not interest Juliette at all. She figured they were seeing new colors, feeling the indescribable, perhaps having a religious experience that occurred only in the face of the reaper. Wasn't it enough to know that it happened without fail? Problem solved. Take it as an axiom. Move on to a real issue, like what it must *feel* like to be the one going through it. *That* was the real shame of the taboos: not that people couldn't pine for the outside world, but that they weren't even allowed to commiserate with the cleaners during the weeks after, to wonder what they had suffered, to properly express their thanks or regrets.

Juliette tapped the yellow door with the corner of Holston's folder, remembering the man in better times, back when he was in love, a lottery winner, telling her about his wife. She nodded to his ghost and stepped away from the imposing metal door with its small panes of thick glass. There was a kinship she felt from working in his post, now wearing his star, even sitting in his cell. She had loved a man once and knew what that felt like. She had loved in secret, not involving the silo in their relationship, ignoring the Pact. And so she also knew what it meant to lose something so precious. She could imagine, if her old lover was out there on that hill—wasting away in plain sight rather than feeding the roots—that she could be driven to cleaning, to wanting to see those new colors for herself.

She opened Holston's file again as she wandered back toward her desk. *His* desk. Here was one man who knew of her secret love. She had told him, once the case was settled in the down deep, that the man who had died, whose case she had helped solve, had been her lover. Maybe it was how he had gone on and on about his wife the days before. Maybe it was his trustworthy smile that made him such a good sheriff, engendering this baffling urge to divulge secrets. Whatever the cause, she had admitted something to a man of the law that could have gotten her in trouble, an affair completely off the books, a wanton disregard for the Pact, and all he had said, this man entrusted with upholding those laws, was: "I'm sorry."

Sorry for her loss. And he had hugged her. Like he knew what she was holding inside, this secret grief that had hardened where her hidden love once lay.

And she had respected him for that.

Now she sat at his desk, in his chair, across from his old deputy, who held his head in his hands and peered down, unmoving, at an open folder dotted with tears. All it took was a glance for Juliette to suspect that some forbidden love lay between him and the contents of that folder as well.

"It's five o'clock," Juliette said as quietly and gently as she could.

Marnes lifted his face out of his hands. His forehead was red from resting it there so long. His eyes were bloodshot, his gray mustache shimmering with fresh tears. He looked so much older than he had a week ago in the down deep, when he had come to recruit her. Swiveling in his old wooden chair, the legs squeaking as if startled by the sudden movement, he glanced at the clock on the wall behind him and surveyed the time imprisoned behind its yellowed and aged plastic dome. He nodded silently at the ticking of the hand, stood up, his back stooping for a moment as he fought to straighten it. He ran his hands down his overalls, reached to the folder, closed it tenderly, and tucked it under his arm.

"Tomorrow," he whispered, nodding to Juliette.

"See you in the morning," she said as he staggered out toward the cafeteria.

Juliette watched him go, feeling sorry for him. She recognized the love behind his loss. It was painful to imagine him back in his small apartment, sitting on a cot wide enough for one, sobbing over that folder until he finally collapsed into his fitful dreams.

Once alone, she placed Holston's folder on her desk and slid her keyboard closer. The keys had been worn bare long ago, but someone in recent years had neatly reprinted the letters in black ink. Now even these handwritten faces were fading and would soon need another coat. Juliette would have to see to that—she couldn't type without looking at her keyboard like all these office workers could.

She slowly pecked out a request to wire down to Mechanical. After another day of getting little done, of being distracted by the mystery of Holston's decision, she had come to a realization: there was no way she could perform this man's job until she first understood why he had turned his back on it, and on the silo itself. It was a nagging rattle keeping her from other problems. So instead of kidding herself, she was going to embrace the challenge. Which meant that she needed to know more than his folder contained.

She wasn't sure how to get the things she needed, how to even access them, but she knew people who might. This was what she missed most about the down deep. They were family there, all with useful skills that overlapped and covered one another. Anything she could do for any of them, she would. And she knew they would do the same, even be an army for her. This was a comfort she sorely missed, a safety net that felt all too far away.

After sending the request, she sat back with Holston's folder. Here was a man, a good man, who had known her deepest secrets. He was the only one who ever had. And soon, God willing, Juliette would uncover his.

20

IT WAS WELL after ten by the time Juliette pushed herself away from her desk. Her eyes had become too sore to stare at her monitor any longer, too tired to read one more case note. She powered down her computer, filed the folders away, killed the overhead lights, and locked the office door from the outside.

As she pocketed her keys, her stomach grumbled, and the fading odor of a rabbit stew reminded her that she'd missed yet another dinner. That made it three nights in a row. Three nights of focusing so hard on a job she barely knew how to perform, a job she had no one to guide her through, that she'd neglected to eat. If her office hadn't abutted a noisy, aroma-filled cafeteria, she might have been able to forgive herself.

She pulled her keys back out and crossed the dimly lit room, weaving around nearly invisible chairs left scattered between the tables. A teenage couple was just leaving, having stolen a few dark moments in the wallscreen's twilight before curfew. Juliette called out for them to descend safely, mostly because it felt like the sheriff thing to do, and they giggled at her as they disappeared into the stairwell. She imagined they were already holding hands and would steal a few kisses before they got to their apartments. Adults knew of these illicit things but let them slide, a gift each generation bestowed on the next. For Juliette, however, it was different. She had made the same choices as an adult, to love without sanction, and so her hypocrisy was more keenly felt.

As she approached the kitchen, she noticed the cafeteria wasn't quite empty. A lone figure sat in the deep shadows by the wallscreen, staring at the inky blackness of nighttime clouds hanging over darkened hills.

It appeared to be the same figure as the night before, the one who had watched the sunlight gradually fade while Juliette worked alone in her office. She adjusted her route to the kitchen in order to pass behind the man. Staring all day at folders full of bad intentions had made her a budding paranoid. She used to admire people who stood out, but now she found herself wary of them.

She moved between the wallscreen and the nearest table, pausing to push chairs back into place, their metal feet scraping on the tile. She kept an eye on the seated man, but he never once turned toward the noise. He just stared up at the clouds, something in his lap, a hand held up by his chin.

Juliette walked right behind him, stepping between the table and his chair, which had been moved strangely close to the wallscreen. She fought the urge to clear her throat or ask him a question. Instead, she passed on by, jangling her master key from the crowded ring that had come with her new job.

Twice, she glanced back over her shoulder before she reached the kitchen door. The man did not move.

She let herself inside the kitchen and hit one of the light switches. After a genial flicker, the overhead bulbs popped on and shattered her night vision. She pulled a gallon of juice from one of the walk-in refrigerators and grabbed a clean glass from the drying rack. Back in the walk-in, she found the stew—covered and already cold—and brought it out as well. She ladled two scoops into a bowl and rattled around in a drawer for a spoon. She only briefly considered heating up the stew as she returned the large pot to its frosted shelf.

With her juice and bowl in hand, she returned to the cafeteria, knocking the lights off with her elbow and pushing the door shut with her foot. She sat down in the shadows at the end of one of the long tables and slurped on her meal, keeping an eye on this strange man who seemed to peer into the darkness as if something could be seen out there.

Her spoon eventually scraped the bottom of her empty bowl, and she finished the last of her juice. Not once through the meal had the man turned away from the wallscreen. She pushed the dishes away from herself, insanely curious. The figure reacted to this, unless it was mere coincidence. He leaned forward and held his outstretched hand out at the screen. Juliette thought she could make out a rod or stick in his grasp—but it was too dark to tell. After a moment, he leaned over his lap, and Juliette heard the squeak of charcoal on expensive-sounding paper. She got up, taking this movement as an opening, and strolled closer to where he was sitting.

"Raiding the larder, are we?" he asked.

His voice startled her.

"W-worked through dinner," she stammered, as if *she* needed to explain herself.

"Must be nice to have the keys."

He still didn't turn away from the screen, and Juliette reminded herself to lock the kitchen door before she left.

"What're you doing?" she asked.

The man reached behind himself and grabbed a nearby chair, slid it around to face the screen. "You wanna see?"

Juliette approached warily, grabbed the backrest, and deliberately slid the chair a few inches further from the man. It was too dark in the room to make out his features, but his voice sounded young. She chastised herself for not committing him to memory the night before when there'd been more light. She would need to become more observant if she was going to be any good at her job.

"What're we looking at, exactly?" she asked. She stole a glance at his lap, where a large piece of white paper glowed faintly in the wan light leaking from the stairwell. It was spread flat across his thighs as if a board or something hard rested beneath it.

"I think those two are going to part. Look there."

The man pointed at the wallscreen and into a mix of blacks so rich and so deep as to appear as one. The contours and shadowy hues Juliette could make out almost seemed to be a trick played by her eyes — as real as ghosts. But she followed his finger, wondering if he were mad or drunk, and tolerated the exhausting silence that followed.

"There," he whispered, excitement on his breath.

Juliette saw a flash. A spot of light. Like someone flicking on a torch far across a dark generator room. And then it was gone.

She bolted out of her chair and stood near to the wallscreen, wondering what was out there.

The man's charcoal squeaked on his paper.

"What the hell was *that?*" Juliette asked.

The man laughed. "A star," he said. "If you wait, you might see it again. We've got thin clouds tonight and high winds. That one there is getting ready to pass."

Juliette turned to find her chair and saw that he was holding his charcoal at arm's length, staring up at the spot where the light had flashed, one eye winked shut.

"How can you see anything out there?" she asked, settling back into her plastic chair.

"The longer you do this, the better you see at night." He leaned over his paper and scribbled some more. "And I've been doing this a long time."

"Doing what, exactly? Just staring at the clouds?"

He laughed. "Mostly, yeah. Unfortunately. But what I'm trying to do is see past them. Watch, we might get another glance."

She peered up in the general area of the last flash. Suddenly, it popped back into view, a pinprick of light like a signal from high over the hill.

"How many did you see?" he asked.

"One," she told him. She was almost breathless from the newness of the sight. She knew what stars were—they were a part of her vocabulary—but she'd never seen one before.

"There was a faint one just to the side of it as well. Let me show you."

There was a soft click, and a red glow spilled over the man's lap. Juliette saw that he had a flashlight hanging around his neck, a film of red plastic wrapped around the end. It made the lens look like it was on fire, but it emanated a gentle glow that didn't barrage her eyes the way the kitchen lights had.

Spread across his lap, she saw a large piece of paper covered with dots. They were arranged haphazardly, a few perfectly straight lines running in a grid around them. Tiny notes were scattered everywhere.

"The problem is that they move," he told her. "If I see that one here tonight"—he tapped one of the dots with his finger; there was a smaller dot beside it—"at the same exact time tomorrow, it'll be a little over here." As he turned to Juliette, she saw that the man was young, probably in his late twenties, and quite handsome in that clean, officelike way. He smiled and added, "It took me a long time to figure that out."

Juliette wanted to tell him that he hadn't been *alive* a long time but remembered what it had felt like as a shadow when people dismissed her the same way.

"What's the point?" she asked, and saw his smile fade.

"What's the point of anything?" He returned his gaze to the

wall and doused the flashlight. Juliette realized she'd asked the wrong question, had upset him. And then she wondered if there was anything illicit in this activity of his, anything that defied the taboos. Was collecting data on the outside any different from the people who sat and stared at the hills? She had just made a mental note to ask Marnes about this when the man turned to her again in the darkness.

"My name's Lukas," he said. Her eyes had adjusted well enough that she could see his hand stretched out toward her.

"Juliette," she replied, grabbing and squeezing his palm.

"The new sheriff."

It wasn't a question, and of course he knew who she was. Everyone up top seemed to.

"What do you do when you're not up here?" she asked. She was pretty sure this wasn't his job. Nobody should get chits for staring up at the clouds.

"I live in the upper mids," Lukas said. "I work on computers during the day. I only come up when the viewing's good." He switched the light back on and turned toward her in a way that suggested the stars weren't the most important thing on his mind anymore. "There's a guy on my level who works up here on dinner shift. When he gets home, he lets me know what the clouds were like during the day. If he gives me the thumbs-up, I come take my chances."

"And so you're making a schematic of them?" Juliette gestured toward the large sheet of paper.

"Trying to. It'll probably take a few lifetimes." He tucked his charcoal behind his ear, pulled a rag from his overalls, and wiped his fingers clean of black residue.

"And then what?" Juliette asked.

"Well, hopefully I'll infect some shadow with my sickness and they'll pick up wherever I leave off."

"So literally, like, several lifetimes."

He laughed, and Juliette realized it was a pleasant one. "At least," he said.

"Well, I'll leave you to it," she said, suddenly feeling guilty for talking to him. She stood and reached out her hand, and he took it warmly. He pressed his other palm to the back of her hand and held it a moment longer than she would have expected.

"Pleasure to meet you, Sheriff."

He smiled up at her. And Juliette didn't understand a word of what she muttered in return.

21

THE NEXT MORNING, Juliette arrived early at her desk having stolen little more than four hours of sleep. Beside her computer, she saw a package waiting for her: a small bundle wrapped in recycled pulp paper and encircled with white electrical ties. She smiled at this last touch and reached into her overalls for her multi-tool. Pulling out the smallest pick from the tool, she stuck it into the clasp of one of the electrical ties and slowly pulled the ratcheting device apart, keeping it intact for future use. She remembered the trouble she'd gotten into as a mechanic's shadow the day she'd been caught cutting a plastic tie from an electrical board. Walker, already an old crank those decades ago, had yelled at her for the waste and then shown her how to tease the little clasp loose to preserve the tie for later use.

Years had passed, and when she was much older, she had found herself passing this lesson on to another shadow named Scottie. He had been a young lad at the time, but she had had a go at him when he had made the same careless mistake she once had. She remembered frightening the poor boy white as a cinder block, and he had remained nervous around her for months after. Maybe because of that outburst, she had paid him more attention as he continued his training, and eventually, the two had grown close. He quickly grew up to become a capable young man, a whiz with electronics, able to program a pump's timing chip in less time than it took her to break one down and put it back together.

She loosened the other tie crossing the package and knew the bundle was from him. Several years ago, Scottie had been recruited by IT and had moved up to the thirties. He had become "too smart for Mechanical," as Knox had put it. Juliette set the two electrical straps aside and pictured the young man preparing this package for her. The request she'd wired down to Mechanical the night before must've bounced back up to him, and he had spent the night dutifully doing this favor for her.

She pried the paper apart carefully. Both it and the plastic ties would need to be returned; they were both too dear for her to keep and light enough to porter on the cheap. As the package came apart, she noticed that Scottie had crimped the edges and had folded these tabs under each other, a trick children learned so they could wrap notes without the expense of glue or tape. She disassembled his meticulous work with care, and the paper finally came loose. Inside, she found a plastic box like the kind used to sort nuts and bolts for small projects down in Mechanical.

She opened the lid and saw that the package wasn't just from Scottie — it must've been hurried up to him along with a copy of her request. Tears came to her eyes as the smell of Mama Jean's oatmeal and cornflour cookies drifted out. She plucked one, held it to her nose, and breathed deeply. Maybe she imagined it, but she swore she noted a hint of oil or grease emanating from the old box — the smells of home.

Juliette folded the wrapping paper carefully and placed the cookies on top. She thought of the people she would have to share them with. Marnes, of course, but also Pam in the cafeteria, who had been so nice in helping her settle into her new apartment. And Alice, Jahns's young secretary, whose eyes had been red with grief for over a week. She pulled the last cookie out and finally spotted the small data drive rattling around in the bottom of the container, a little morsel baked special by Scottie and hidden among the crumbs.

Juliette grabbed it and set the plastic case aside. She blew into the little metal end of the drive, getting any debris out, before slotting it into the front of her computer. She wasn't great with computers, but she could navigate them. You couldn't do anything in Mechanical without submitting a claim, a report, a request, or some other piece of nonsense. And they were handy for logging in to pumps and relays remotely to shut them on or off, see their diagnostics, all of that.

Once the light on the drive winked on, she navigated to it on her screen. Inside, she found a host of folders and files; the little drive must've been stuffed to the brim with them. She wondered if Scottie had gotten any sleep at all the night before.

At the top of a list of primary folders was a file named "Jules." She clicked this one, and up popped a short text file obviously from Scottie, but noticeably unsigned:

> J—
>
> Don't get caught with this, okay? This is everything from Mr. Lawman's computers, work and home, the last five years. A ton of stuff, but wasn't sure what you needed and this was easier to automate.
>
> Keep the ties—I got plenty.
>
> (And I took a cookie. Hope you don't mind.)

Juliette smiled. She felt like reaching out and brushing her fingers across the words, but it wasn't paper and wouldn't be the same. She closed the note and deleted it, then cleared out her trash. Even the first letter of her name up there felt like too much information.

She leaned away from her desk and peered into the cafeteria, which appeared dark and empty. It was not yet five in the morning, and she would have the upper floor to herself for a while. She first took a moment to browse through the directory structure to see what kind of data she was dealing with. Each folder was neatly labeled. It appeared she had an operating history of Holston's two computers, every keystroke, every day, going back a little more than five years, all organized by date and time. Juliette felt overwhelmed by the sheer *amount* of information—it was far more than she could hope to weed through in a lifetime.

But at least she had it. The answers she needed were in there, somewhere, among all those files. And somehow it felt better, *she* felt better, just knowing that the solution to this riddle, to Holston's decision to go to cleaning, could now fit in the palm of her hand.

She was several hours into sifting through the data when the cafeteria crew staggered in to clean up last night's mess and prepare for breakfast. One of the most difficult things to get used to about the up top was the exacting schedule everyone kept. There was no third shift. There was barely a second shift, except for the dinner staff. In the down deep, the machines didn't sleep, and so the workers barely did either. Work crews often stayed on into extra shifts, and Juliette had gotten used to surviving on a handful of hours of rest a night. The trick was to pass out now and then from sheer exhaustion, to just rest against a wall with one's eyes closed for fifteen minutes, long enough to hold the tiredness at bay.

But what had once been necessary for survival was now a luxury. The ability to forgo sleep gave her time in the morning and at night to herself, time to invest in frivolous pursuits on top of the cases she was supposed to be working. It also gave her the opportunity to teach herself how to do the blasted job, since Marnes had become too depressed to help get her up to speed.

Marnes—

She looked at the clock over his desk. It was ten minutes after eight, and the vats of warm oatmeal and corn grits were already filling the cafeteria with the smells of breakfast. Marnes was late. She'd been around him less than a week, but she had yet to see him late to anything, ever. This break in the routine was like a timing belt stretching out of shape, a piston developing a knock. Juliette turned her monitor off and pushed away from her desk. Outside, first-shift breakfast was beginning to file in, food tokens clinking in the large bucket by the old turnstiles. She left her office and passed through the traffic spilling from the stairwell. In the line, a young girl tugged on her mother's overalls and pointed to Juliette as she passed. Juliette heard the mother scolding her child for being rude.

There had been quite a bit of chatter the past few days over her appointment, this woman who had disappeared into Mechanical as a child and who had suddenly reemerged to take over from one of the more popular sheriffs in memory. Juliette cringed from the attention and hurried into the stairwell. She wound her way down the steps as fast as a lightly loaded porter, her feet bouncing off each tread, faster and faster, at what felt like an unsafe pace. Four flights down, after squeezing around a slow couple and between a family heading up for breakfast, she hit the apartment landing just below her own and passed through the double doors.

The hallway beyond was busy with morning sights and sounds: a squealing teapot, the shrill voices of children, the thunder of feet overhead, shadows hurrying to meet their casters before trailing behind them to work. Younger children were lumbering reluctantly off to school; husbands and wives kissed in doorways while toddlers tugged at their overalls and dropped toys and plastic cups.

Juliette took several turns, winding through the hallways and around the central staircase to the other side of the level. The deputy's apartment was on the far side, way in the back. She surmised that Marnes had qualified for several upgrades over the years but had passed on them. The one time she had asked Alice, Mayor Jahns's old secretary, about Marnes, she had shrugged and told Juliette that he had never wanted or expected anything more than second fiddle. Juliette assumed she meant that he never wanted to be sheriff, but she had begun to wonder in how many other areas of his life that philosophy applied.

As she reached his hall, two kids ran by holding hands, late for school. They giggled and squealed around the corner, leaving Juliette alone in the hallway. She wondered what she would say to Marnes to justify coming down, to explain her worry. Maybe now was a good time to ask for the folder that he couldn't seem to be without. She could tell him to take the day off, let her handle the office while he got some rest, or maybe fib a little and say she was already in the area for a case.

She stopped outside his door and lifted her hand to knock. Hopefully he wouldn't see this as her projecting authority. She was just concerned for him. That was all.

She rapped on the steel door and waited for him to call her inside—and maybe he did. His voice over the last few days had eroded into a dull and thin rasp. She knocked again, louder this time.

"Deputy?" she called. "Everything okay in there?"

A woman popped her head out of a door down the hallway. Juliette recognized her from school recess time in the cafeteria, was pretty sure her name was Gloria.

"Hey, Sheriff."

"Hey, Gloria, you haven't seen Deputy Marnes this morning, have you?"

She shook her head, placed a metal rod in her mouth, and started wrapping her long hair into a bun. "I haben't," she mumbled. She shrugged her shoulders and jabbed the rod through her bun, locking her hair into place. "He was on the landing last night, looking as whipped as ever." She frowned. "He not show up for work?"

Juliette turned back to the door and tried the handle. It clicked open with the feel of a well-maintained lock. She pushed the door in. "Deputy? It's Jules. Just checkin' in on ya."

The door swung open into the darkness. The only light spilling in was from the hallway, but it was enough.

Juliette turned to Gloria. "Call Doc Hicks – No, shit . . ." She was still thinking down deep. "Who's the closest doctor up here? Call him!"

She ran into the room, not waiting for a reply. There wasn't much space to hang oneself in the small apartment, but Marnes had figured out how. His belt was cinched around his neck, the buckle lodged into the top of the bathroom door. His feet were on the bed, but at a right angle, not enough to support his weight. His butt drooped below his feet, his face no longer red, the belt biting deep into his neck.

Juliette hugged Marnes's waist and lifted him up. He was heavier than he looked. She kicked his feet off the bed, and they flopped to the floor, making it easier to hold him. There was a curse at the door. Gloria's husband ran in and helped Juliette support the deputy's weight. Both of them fumbled for the belt, trying to dislodge it from the door. Juliette finally tugged the door open, freeing him.

"On the bed," she huffed.

They lifted him to the bed and laid him out flat.

Gloria's husband rested his hands on his knees and took deep breaths. "Gloria ran for Doctor O'Neil."

Juliette nodded and loosened the belt from around Marnes's neck. The flesh was purple beneath it. She felt for a pulse, remembering George looking just like this when she'd found him down in Mechanical, completely still and unresponsive. It took her a moment to be sure that she was looking at the second dead body she had ever seen.

And then she wondered, as she sat back, sweating, waiting for the doctor to arrive, whether this job she had taken would ensure it wasn't the last.

22

AFTER FILLING OUT reports, discovering Marnes had no next of kin, speaking with the coroner at the dirt farm, and answering questions from nosy neighbors, Juliette finally took a long and lonely walk up eight flights of stairs, back to her empty office.

She spent the rest of the day getting little work done, the door to the cafeteria open, the small room much too crowded with ghosts. She tried repeatedly to lose herself in the files from Holston's computers, but Marnes's absence was incredibly sadder than his moping presence had been. She couldn't believe he was gone. It almost felt like an affront, to bring her here and then leave her so suddenly. And she knew this was a horrible and selfish thing to feel and even worse to admit.

As her mind roamed, she glanced occasionally out the door, watching the clouds slide across the distant wallscreen. She debated with herself on whether they appeared light or dense, if tonight would be a good one for viewing stars. It was another guilt-ridden thought, but she felt powerfully alone, a woman who prided herself on needing no one.

She played some more with the maze of files as the light of an unseen sun diminished in the cafeteria, as two shifts of lunch and two shifts of dinner vibrated and then subsided around her, all the while watching the roiling sky and hoping, for no real logical reason, for another chance encounter with the strange star hunter from the night before.

And even sitting there, with the sounds and scents of everyone on the upper forty-eight eating, Juliette forgot to grab a bite for herself. It wasn't until the second-shift staff was leaving, the lights cut down to quarter power, that Pam came in with a bowl of soup and a biscuit. Juliette thanked her and reached into her overalls for a few chits, but Pam refused. The young woman's eyes—red from crying—drifted to Marnes's empty chair, and Juliette realized the cafeteria staff had probably been as close to the deputy as anyone.

Pam left without a word, and Juliette ate with what little appetite she could manage. She eventually thought of one more search she could try on Holston's data, a global spell-check to look for names that might offer clues, and eventually figured out how to run it. Meanwhile, her soup grew cold. While her computer began to churn through the hills of data, she took her bowl and a few folders and left her office to sit at one of the cafeteria tables near the wallscreen.

She was looking for stars on her own when Lukas appeared silently at her side. He didn't say anything, just pulled up a chair, sat down with his board and paper, and peered up at the expansive view of the darkened outside.

Juliette couldn't tell if he was being polite by honoring her silence, or if he was being rude by not saying hello. She finally settled on the former, and eventually the quiet felt normal. Shared. A peace at the end of a horrible day.

Several minutes passed. A dozen. There were no stars and nothing was said. Juliette held a folder in her lap, just to give her fingers something to do. There was a sound from the stairwell, a laughing group moving between the apartment levels below, and then a return to the quiet.

“I’m sorry about your partner,” Lukas finally said. His hands smoothed the paper on the board. He had yet to make a single mark or note.

“I appreciate that,” Juliette said. She wasn’t sure what the appropriate response was, but this seemed the least wrong. “I’ve been looking for stars but haven’t seen any,” she added.

“You won’t. Not tonight.” He waved his hand at the wallscreen. “These are the worst kinds of clouds.”

Juliette studied them, barely able to make them out with the last of the twilight’s distant glow. They looked no different to her than any others.

Lukas turned almost imperceptibly in his seat. “I have a confession, since you’re the law and all.”

Juliette’s hand groped for the star on her chest. She was often in danger of forgetting what she was.

“Yeah?”

“I knew the clouds were gonna be bad tonight. But I came up anyway.”

Juliette trusted the darkness to conceal her smile.

“I’m not sure the Pact has much to say on such duplicity,” she told him.

Lukas laughed. It was strange how familiar it already sounded, and how badly she needed to hear it. Juliette had a sudden urge to grab him, to tuck her chin into his neck, and to cry. She could almost feel her body begin to piece the moves together — even though her skin would not budge. It could never happen. She knew this, even as the sensation vibrated within her. It was just the loneliness, the horror of holding Marnes in her arms, of feeling that lifeless heft of a body that has lost whatever animates it. She was desperate for contact, and this stranger was the only person she knew little enough to want it from.

"What happens now?" he asked, his laughter fading.

Juliette almost blurted out, inanely, *Between us?* but Lukas saved her.

"Do you know when the funeral will be? And where?" he asked.

She nodded in the darkness.

"Tomorrow. There's no family to travel up, no investigation to make." Juliette choked back the tears. "He didn't leave a will, so they left it up to me to make arrangements. I decided to lay him to rest near the mayor."

Lukas looked to the wallscreen. It was dark enough that the bodies of the cleaners couldn't be seen, a welcome relief. "As he should be," he said.

"I think they were lovers in secret," Juliette blurted out. "If not lovers, then just as close."

"There's been talk," he agreed. "What I don't get is why keep it a secret. Nobody would've cared."

Somehow, sitting in the darkness with a complete stranger, these things were more easily aired than in the down deep among friends.

"Maybe *they* would have minded people knowing," she said, thinking out loud. "Jahns was married before. I suspect they chose to respect that."

"Yeah?" Lukas scratched something on his paper. Juliette looked up but was sure there hadn't been a star. "I can't imagine loving in secret like that," he said.

"I can't imagine needing someone's permission, like the Pact or a girl's father, to be in love in the first place," she replied.

"No? How else would it work? Just any two people any time they liked?"

She didn't say.

"How would anyone ever enter the lottery?" he asked, persisting in the line of thought. "I can't imagine it not being out in the open. It's a celebration, don't you think? There's this ritual, a man asks a girl's father for permission —"

"Well, aren't you with anyone?" Juliette asked, cutting him off. "I mean . . . I'm just asking because it sounds like, like you have strong opinions but maybe haven't —"

"Not yet," he said, rescuing her again. "I have a little strength left yet for enduring my mom's guilt. She likes to remind me every year how many lotteries I've missed out on, and what this has done to her overall chances for a bevy of grandchildren. As if I don't know my statistics. But hey, I'm only twenty-five."

"That's all?" Juliette said.

"What about you?"

She nearly told him straightaway. Nearly blurted out her secret with almost no prompting. As if this man, this boy, a stranger to her, could be trusted.

"Never found the right one," she lied.

Lukas laughed his youthful laugh. "No, I mean, how old are you? Or is that impolite?"

She felt a wave of relief. She thought he'd been asking her about being with anyone.

"Thirty-four," she said. "And I'm told it's impolite to ask, but I've never been one for rules."

"Says our sheriff," Lukas said, laughing at his own joke.

Juliette smiled. "I guess I'm still getting used to that."

She turned back to the wallscreen, and they both enjoyed the silence that formed. It was strange, sitting with this man. She felt younger and somehow more secure in his presence. Less lonely, at least. She pegged him as a loner as well, an odd-sized washer that didn't fit any standard bolt. And here he had been, at the extreme other end of the silo, searching for stars, while she'd been spending what spare time she could down in the mines, as far away as possible, hunting for pretty rocks.

"It's not going to be a very productive night for either of us, looks like," she eventually said, ending the silence, rubbing the unopened folder in her lap.

"Oh, I don't know," Lukas told her. "That depends on what you came up here for."

Juliette smiled. And across the wide room, barely audible, the computer on her desk beeped, a search routine having finally pawed through Holston's data before spitting out its results.

23

THE NEXT MORNING, instead of climbing to her office, Juliette descended five flights to the upper dirt farm for Marnes's funeral. There would be no folder for her deputy, no investigation, just the lowering of his old and tired body into the deep soil where it would decompose and feed the roots. It was a strange thought, to stand in that crowd and think of him as a folder or not. Less than a week on the job, and she already saw the manila jackets as places where ghosts resided. Names and case numbers. Lives distilled onto twenty or so sheets of recycled pulp paper, bits of string and darts of random color woven beneath the black ink in which their sad tale had been jotted.

The ceremony was long but didn't feel so. The earth nearby was still mounded where Jahns had been buried. Soon, the two of them would intermingle inside the plants, and these plants would nourish the occupants of the silo.

Juliette accepted a ripe tomato as the priest and his shadow cycled among the thick crowd. The two of them, draped in red fabric, chanted as they went, their voices sonorous and complementing one another. Juliette bit into her fruit, allowing a polite amount of juice to spatter her overalls; chewed; and swallowed. She could tell the tomato was delicious, but only in a mechanical way. It was hard to truly enjoy it.

When it became time for the soil to be shoveled back into the hole, Juliette watched the crowd. Two people dead from the up top in less than a week. There had been two other deaths elsewhere in the silo, making it a very bad week.

Or good, depending on who you were. She noticed childless couples biting vigorously into their fruit, their hands intertwined, silently doing the math. Lotteries followed too closely after deaths for Juliette's tastes. She always thought they should fall on the same dates in the year, just to look as though they were going to happen anyway, whether anyone died or not.

But then, the lowering of the body and the plucking of ripe fruit just above the graves was meant to hammer this home: the cycle of life is here; it is inescapable; it is to be embraced, cherished, appreciated. One departs and leaves behind the gift of sustenance, of life. They make room for the next generation. We are born, we are shadows, we cast shadows of our own, and then we are gone. All anyone can hope for is to be remembered two shadows deep.

Before the hole was completely filled, members of the feast stepped up to the edge of the farm's soil and tossed what remained of their fruit into the hole. Juliette stepped forward and added the rest of her tomato to the colorful hail of rind and pulp. An acolyte leaned on his too-large shovel and watched the last of the fruit fly. Those that missed, he knocked in with scoops of dark, rich soil, leaving a mound that would, in time and with a few waterings, settle.

After the funeral, Juliette began the climb back to her office. She could feel the flights of stairs in her legs, even though she prided herself on being in shape. But walking and climbing were different sorts of exercise. It wasn't turning wrenches or loosening stubborn bolts, and the endurance was of a different kind than merely staying up and alert for an extra shift. She decided it was unnatural, this climbing. Humans weren't meant for it. She doubted they were engineered to travel much beyond a single level of a silo. But then another porter flew down the steps past her, a smile of quick greeting on his fresh face, his feet dancing across steel treads, and she wondered if perhaps it was something that just took practice.

When she finally made it back to the cafeteria, it was lunchtime, and the room was buzzing with noisy chatter and the clinking of metal forks on metal plates. The pile of folded notes outside her office door had grown. There was a plant in a plastic bucket, a pair of shoes, a small sculpture made of colorful wire. Juliette paused over the collection. As Marnes didn't have any family, she supposed it would be up to her to go through it all, to make sure the items went to those who would use them best. She bent down and picked up one of the cards. The writing was in unsure print, scrawled with crayon. She imagined the upper-grade school had spent craft time that day making cards for Deputy Marnes. This saddened Juliette more than any of the ceremonies. She wiped tears out of her eyes and damned the teachers who thought to get the kids involved in the nastiness of it all.

"Leave them out of it," she whispered to herself.

She replaced the card and composed herself. Deputy Marnes would have liked to have seen this, she decided. He was an easy man to figure, one of those who had grown old everywhere but in his heart, that one organ he had never worn out because he'd never dared to use it.

Inside her office, she was surprised to find she had company. A stranger sat at Deputy Marnes's desk. He looked up from the computer and smiled at her. She was about to ask who he was when Bernard—she refused to think of him as even *interim* mayor—stepped out of the holding cell, a folder in hand, smiling at Juliette.

"How were the services?" he asked.

Juliette crossed the office and snatched the folder out of his hand. "Please don't tamper with anything," she said.

"Tamper?" Bernard laughed and adjusted his glasses. "That's a closed case. I was going to take it back to my offices and refile it."

Juliette checked the folder and saw that it was Holston's.

"You do know that you report to me, right? You were supposed to have at least glanced over the Pact before Jahns swore you in."

"I'll hold on to this, thanks." Juliette left him by the open cell and went to her desk. She shoved the folder in the top drawer, checked that the data drive was still jutting out from her computer, and looked up at the guy across from her.

"And you are?"

He stood, and Deputy Marnes's chair let out its customary squeak. Juliette tried to force herself not to think of it as his anymore.

"Peter Billings, ma'am." He held out his hand. Juliette accepted it. "I was just sworn in myself." He pinched the corner of his star and held it away from his overalls for her to see.

"Peter here was actually up for *your* job," Bernard said.

Juliette wondered what he meant by that, or what the point was in even mentioning it. "Did you need something?" she asked Bernard. She waved at her desk, which had piled up the day before as she had spent most of her time managing Marnes's affairs. "Because anything you need doing, I can add it to the bottom of one of these piles, here."

"Anything I give you goes on *top,*" Bernard said. He slapped his hand down on the folder with Jahns's name on it. "And I'm doing you a favor by coming up and having this meeting here rather than have you come down to *my* office."

"What meeting is this?" Juliette asked. She didn't look up at him but busied herself sorting papers. Hopefully he would see how busy she was and leave, and she could start getting Peter up to speed on what little she herself had figured out.

"As you know, there's been quite a bit of . . . *turnover* these past weeks. Unprecedented, really, at least since the uprising. And that's the danger, I'm afraid, if we aren't all on the same page." He pressed his finger onto the folder Juliette was trying to move, pinning it in place. She glanced up at him.

"People want continuity. They want to know tomorrow will be a lot like yesterday. They want reassurances. Now, we've just had a cleaning, and we've suffered some losses, so the mood is naturally a bit raucous." He waved at the folders and piles of pulp paper spilling from Juliette's desk and onto Marnes's. The young man across from her seemed to eye the mound warily, like more of the pile could shift toward him, giving him more of it to work through. "Which is why I am going to announce a forgiveness moratorium. Not only to strengthen the spirits of the entire silo, but to help you two clear the slate so you don't get overwhelmed while you're getting up to speed on your duties."

"Clear the slate?" Juliette asked.

"That's right. All these drunken misdemeanors. What's this one for?" He picked up a folder and studied the name on the label. "Oh, now what's Pickens done this time?"

"He ate a neighbor's rat," Juliette said. "Family pet."

Peter Billings chuckled. Juliette squinted at him, wondering why his name seemed familiar. Then she placed it, recalling a memo he had written in one of the folders. This kid, practically a boy, had been shadowing a silo judge, she remembered. She had a difficult time imagining that, looking at him. He seemed more the IT type.

"I thought owning rats as pets was illegal," Bernard said.

"It is. He's the claimant. It's a countersuit in retaliation" – she sorted through her folders – "for this one right here."

"Let's see," Bernard said. He grabbed the other folder, held the two of them together, and then dropped them both into her recycle bin, all the carefully organized papers and notes spilling out and intermingling in a jumbled pile on top of other scraps of paper to be repulped.

"Forgive and forget," he said, wiping his palms together. "That's going to be my election motto. The people need this. This is about new beginnings, forgetting the past during these tumultuous times, looking to the *future!*" He slapped her on the back, hard, nodded to Peter, and headed for the door.

"Election motto?" she asked before he could get away. And it occurred to her that one of the folders he was suggesting could be forgiven was the one wherein *he* was the prime suspect.

"Oh yes," Bernard called over his shoulder. He grabbed the jamb and looked back at her. "I've decided, after much deliberation, that there is no one better qualified for this job than me. I don't see any problem with continuing my duties in IT while performing the role as mayor. In fact, I already am!" He winked. "Continuity, you know." And then he was gone.

Juliette spent the rest of that afternoon, well past what Peter Billings considered "sensible working hours," getting him up to speed. What she needed most of all was someone to field complaints and to respond to the radio. This was Holston's old job, ranging the top forty-eight and calling on any disturbance. Deputy Marnes had hoped to see Juliette fill that role with her younger, fresher legs. He also had said that a pretty female might "do the public will some good." Juliette had other ideas about his intentions. She suspected Marnes had wanted her away so he could spend time alone with his folder and its ghost. And she well understood that urge. So as she sent Peter Billings home with a list of apartments and merchants to call on the next day, she finally had time to sit down at her computer and see the results from the previous night's search.

The spell-checker had turned up interesting results. Not so much the names she had hoped for, but rather these large blocks of what looked like coded text: gibberish with strange punctuation, indentation, and embedded words she recognized but that seemed out of place. These massive paragraphs were spread throughout Holston's home computer, first showing up just over three years ago. That made it fit the timeline, but what really caught Juliette's eye was how often the data appeared in nested directories, sometimes a dozen or more folders deep. It was as if someone had taken pains to keep them hidden but had wanted multiple copies stashed away, terrified of losing them.

She assumed it was encoded, whatever it was, and important. She tore off bites of a small loaf of bread and dipped these in corn spread while she gathered a full copy of this gibberish to send down to Mechanical. There were a few guys perhaps smart enough to make some sense of the code, starting with Walker. She chewed her food and spent the next hours going back over the trail she had managed to tease out of Holston's final years on the job. It had been difficult to narrow his activities down, to figure out what was important and what was noise, but she had approached it as logically as any other breakdown. Because that's what she was dealing with, she decided. A breakdown. Gradual and interminable. Almost inevitable. Losing his wife had been like a seal or a gasket cracking. Everything that had rattled out of control for Holston could be traced back, almost mechanically, to her death.

One of the first things she'd realized was that his activity on the work computer held no secrets. Holston had obviously become a night rat, just like her, staying up for hours in his apartment. It was yet another commonality she felt between them, further strengthening her obsession with the man. Sticking to his home computer meant she could ignore over half the data. It also became apparent that he had spent most of his time investigating his wife, just as Juliette was now prying into *him*. This was their deepest shared bond, Juliette's and Holston's. Here she was, looking into the last voluntary cleaner as he had looked into his wife, hoping to discover what torturous cause might lead a person to choose the forbidden outside.

And it was here that Juliette began to find clues almost eerie in their connection. Allison, Holston's wife, seemed to be the one who had unlocked the mysteries of the old servers. The very method that had made Holston's data available to Juliette had at some point brought some secret to Allison, and then to Holston. By focusing on deleted e-mails between the couple, and noting the explosion of communication around the time Allison had published a document detailing some undeletion method, Juliette stumbled onto what she felt was a valid trail. She became more certain that Allison had found something on the servers. The trouble was determining what it was—and whether she'd recognize it herself even if she found it.

She toyed with several ideas, even the chance that Allison had been driven to rage by infidelity, but Juliette had enough of a feel for Holston to know that this wasn't the case. And then she noticed each trail of activity seemed to lead back to the paragraphs of gibberish, an answer Juliette kept looking for any excuse to reject because she couldn't make sense of it. Why would Holston, and Allison especially, spend so much time looking at all that nonsense? The activity logs showed her keeping them open for hours at a time, as if the scrambled letters and symbols could be read. To Juliette, it looked like a wholly new language.

So what was it that had sent Holston and his wife to cleaning? The common assumption around the silo was that Allison had gotten the stirs, had gone crazy for the out-of-doors, and that Holston eventually succumbed to his grief. But Juliette had never bought that. She didn't like coincidences. When she tore a machine down to repair it, and a new problem surfaced a few days later, all she usually had to do was go back through the steps from the last repair. The answer was almost always there. She saw this riddle the same way: it was a much simpler diagnosis if both of them were driven out by the *same thing*.

She just couldn't see what it might be. And part of her feared that finding it could drive her crazy as well.

Juliette rubbed her eyes. When she looked at her desk again, Jahns's folder caught her attention. On top of her folder sat the doctor's report for Marnes. She moved the report aside and reached for the note underneath, the one Marnes had written and left on his small bedside table:

It should have been me.

So few words, Juliette thought. But then, who remained in the silo for him to speak to? She studied the handful of words, but there was little to squeeze from them. It was *his* canteen that had been poisoned, not Jahns's. It actually made her death a case of manslaughter, a new term for Juliette. Marnes had explained something else about the law: the worst offense they could hope to pin on anyone was the *attempted* and unsuccessful murder of *him,* rather than the botched accident that had claimed the mayor. Which meant, if they could nail the act on a guilty party, that person could be put to cleaning for what they had *failed* to accomplish with Marnes, while only getting five years' probation and silo service for what had *accidentally* happened to Jahns. Juliette thought it was this crooked sense of fairness as much as anything else that had worn down poor Marnes. There was never any hope for true justice, a life for a life. These strange laws, coupled with the agonizing knowledge that he had carried the poison on his own back, had gravely wounded him. He had to live with being the poison's porter, with the hurtful knowledge that a good deed, a shared walk, had been his love's death.

Juliette held the suicide note and cursed herself for not seeing it coming. It should have been a foreseeable breakdown, a problem solved by a little preventive maintenance. She could have said more, reached out somehow. But she had been too busy trying to stay afloat those first few days to see that the man who had brought her to the up top was slowly unraveling right before her eyes.

The flash of her inbox icon interrupted these disturbing thoughts. She reached for the mouse and cursed herself. The large chunk of data she had sent down to Mechanical some hours earlier must've been rejected. Maybe it was too much to send at once. But then she saw that it was a message from Scottie, her friend in IT who had supplied the data drive.

"Come now," it read.

It was an odd request. Vague and yet dire, especially given the lateness of the hour. Juliette powered down her monitor, grabbed the drive from the computer in case she had more visitors, and briefly considered strapping Marnes's ancient gun around her waist. She stood, went to the key locker, and ran her hand down the soft belt, feeling the indention where the buckle had, for decades, worn into the same spot on the old leather. She thought again of Marnes's terse note and looked at his empty chair. She decided in the end to leave the gun hanging where it was. She nodded to his desk, made sure she had her keys, and hurried out the door.

24

IT WAS THIRTY-THREE levels down to IT. Juliette skipped down the steps so swiftly, she had to keep a hand on the inner railing to keep from flying outward into the occasional upbound traffic. She overtook a porter near six, who was startled by being passed. By the tenth floor, she was beginning to feel dizzy from the round and round. She wondered how Holston and Marnes had ever responded to trouble with any degree of urgency. The other two deputy stations, the one in the mids and the one in the down deep, were nicely situated near the dead center of their forty-eight floors, a far superior arrangement. She passed into the twenties thinking about this: that her office was not ideally positioned to respond to the far edge of her precinct. Instead, it had been located by the airlock and the holding cell, close to the highest form of the silo's capital punishment. She cursed this decision as she considered the long slog back up.

In the high twenties, she practically bowled a man over who wasn't watching where he was going. She wrapped one arm around him and gripped the railing, keeping them both from a nasty tumble. He apologized while she swallowed a curse. And then she saw it was Lukas, his lapboard strapped to his back, nubs of charcoal sticking out of his overalls.

"Oh," he said. "Hello."

He smiled at seeing her, but his lips drooped into a frown when he realized she'd been hurrying in the opposite direction.

"I'm sorry," she said. "I've got to go."

"Of course."

He stood out of the way, and Juliette finally took her hand off his ribs. She nodded, not sure what to say, her thoughts only on Scottie, and then she continued her run down, moving too fast to chance a glance back.

When she finally got to thirty-four, she paused on the landing to catch her breath and let the dizziness fade. Checking her overalls—that her star was in place and the flash drive still in her pocket—she pulled open the main doors to IT and tried to stroll in as if she belonged there.

She sized up the entrance room quickly. To her right, a glass window looked into a conference room. The light was on, even though it was now the middle of the night. A handful of heads were visible through the glass, a meeting taking place. She thought she heard Bernard's voice, loud and nasal, leaching through the door.

Ahead of her stood the low-security gates leading back to IT's labyrinth of apartments, offices, and workshops. Juliette could imagine the floor plan; she'd heard the three levels shared much in common with Mechanical, only without the fun.

"Can I help you?" a young man in silver overalls asked from behind the gates.

She approached.

"Sheriff Nichols," she said. She waved her ID at him, then passed it under the gate's laser scanner. The light turned red and the gate let out an angry buzz. It did not open. "I'm here to see Scottie, one of your techs." She tried the card again, with the same result.

"Do you have an appointment?" the man asked.

Juliette narrowed her eyes at the man.

"I'm the sheriff. Since when do I need appointments?" Again with the card, and again the gate buzzed at her. The young man did not move to help.

"Please do not do that," he said.

"Look, son, I'm in the middle of an investigation here. And you're impeding my progress."

He smiled at her. "I'm sure you're familiar with the unique position we maintain here and that your powers are –"

Juliette put her ID away and reached over the gate to grab the straps of his overalls with both hands. She pulled him almost clear over the gates, her arms bulging with the sinewy muscles that had freed countless bolts.

"Listen here, you blasted runt, I'm coming *through* these gates or I'm coming over them and then through *you.* I'll have you know that I report directly to Bernard Holland, acting mayor, and your goddamned boss. Do I make myself clear?"

The kid's eyes were wide and all pupil. He jerked his chin up and down.

"Then move it," she said, letting go of his overalls with a shove.

He fumbled for his ID – swiped it through the scanner.

Juliette pushed through the spinning arms of the turnstile and past him. Then stopped.

"Uh, which way, exactly?"

The boy was still trying to get his ID back into his chest pocket, his hand trembling. "Th-thataway, ma'am." He pointed to the right. "Second hall, take a left. Last office."

"Good man," she said. She turned and smiled to herself. It seemed that the same tone that got bickering mechanics to snap to back home worked here just as well. And she laughed to herself to think of the argument she had used: your boss is also my boss, so open up. But then, with eyes that wide and that much fear in his veins, she could've read him Mama Jean's bread recipe in the same tone and gotten through the gates.

She took the second hallway, passing by a man and woman in IT silver as they walked the other way. They turned to watch her pass. At the end of the hall, she found offices on both sides and didn't know which one was Scottie's. She peeked first into the one with the open door, but the lights were off. She turned to the other one and knocked.

There was no answer at first, but the light at the bottom of the door dimmed, as if someone had walked across it.

"Who's there?" a familiar voice whispered through the door.

"Open this damn thing," Juliette said. "You know who this is."

The lever dipped, the door clicking open. Juliette pushed her way inside, and Scottie shoved the door closed behind her, engaging the lock.

"Were you seen?" he asked.

She looked at him incredulously. "Was I seen? Of *course* I was seen. How do you think I got in? There're people everywhere."

"But did they see you come in *here?*" he whispered.

"Scottie, what the hell is going on?" Juliette was beginning to suspect she had hurried all this way for nothing. "You sent me a wire, which already seemed desperate enough, and you told me to come now. So here I am."

"Where did you get this stuff?" he asked. Scottie grabbed a spool of printout from his desk and held it in trembling hands.

Juliette stepped beside him. She placed a hand on his arm and looked at the paper. "Just calm down," she said quietly. She tried to read a few lines and immediately recognized the gibberish she had sent to Mechanical earlier that day. "How did you get this?" she asked. "I just wired this to Knox a few hours ago."

Scottie nodded. "And he wired it to me. But he shouldn't have. I can get into a lot of trouble for this."

Juliette laughed. "You're kidding, right?"

She saw that he wasn't.

"Scottie, you're the one who pulled all this stuff for me in the first place." She stepped back and looked hard at him. "Wait, you know what this nonsense is, right? You can read it?"

He bobbed his head. "Jules, I didn't know what I was grabbing for you at the time. It was gigs of crap. I didn't look at it. I just grabbed it and passed it on—"

"Why is this so dangerous?" she asked.

"I can't even talk about it," Scottie said. "I'm not cleaning material, Jules. I'm not." He held out the scroll. "Here. I shouldn't have even printed it, but I wanted to delete the wire. You've got to take it. Get it out of here. I can't be caught with it."

Juliette took the scroll, but just to calm him down. "Scottie, sit down. Please. Look, I know you're scared, but I need you to sit and talk to me about this. It's very important."

He shook his head.

"Scottie, sit the hell down right now." She pointed at the chair, and Scottie numbly obeyed. Juliette sat on the corner of his desk and noted that the cot at the back of the room had been recently slept on, and felt pity for the young man.

"Whatever this is"—she shook the roll of paper—"it's what caused the last two cleanings."

She told him this like it was more than a rapidly forming theory, like it was something she knew. Maybe it was the fear in his eyes that cemented the idea, or the need to act strong and sure to help calm him. "Scottie, I need to know what it is. Look at me."

He did.

"Do you see this star?" She flicked it with her finger, causing a dull ring.

He nodded.

"I'm not your shift foreman anymore, lad. I'm the law, and this is very important. Now, I don't know if you're aware of this, but you can't get into any trouble for answering my questions. In fact, you're obliged to answer them."

He looked up at her with a twinge of hope. He obviously didn't know that she was making this up. Not lying—she would never turn Scottie in for all the silo—but she was pretty sure there was no such thing as immunity, not for anyone.

"What am I holding?" she asked, waving the scroll of printout.

"It's a program," he whispered.

"You mean like a timing circuit? Like a—?"

"No, for a computer. A programming language. It's a—" He looked away. "I don't want to say. Oh, Jules, I just want to go back to Mechanical. I want none of this to have happened."

These words were like a splash of cold water. Scottie was more than frightened—he was terrified. For his *life*. Juliette got off the desk and crouched beside him, placed her hand on the back of his hand, which rested on his anxiously bouncing knee.

"What does the program do?" she asked.

He bit his lip and shook his head.

"It's okay. We're safe here. Tell me what it does."

"It's for a display," he finally said. "But not for like a readout, or an LED, or a dot matrix. There are algorithms in here I recognize. Anyone would . . ."

He paused.

"Sixty-four-bit color," he whispered, staring at her. "Sixty-four bit. Why would anyone need that much *color?*"

"Dumb it down for me," Juliette said. Scottie seemed on the verge of going mad.

"You've seen it, right? The view up top?"

She dipped her head. "You know where I work."

"Well, I've seen it too, back before I started eating every meal in here, working my fingers to the bone." He rubbed his hands up through his shaggy, sandy-brown hair. "This program, Jules – what you've got, it could make something like that wallscreen look *real*."

Juliette digested this, then laughed. "But wait, isn't that what it does? Scottie, there are sensors out there. They just take the images they see, and then the screen has to display the view, right? I mean, you've got me confused, here." She shook the printed scroll of gibberish. "Doesn't this just do what I think it does? Put that image on the display?"

Scottie wrung his hands together. "You wouldn't need anything like this. You're talking about passing an image *through*. I could write a dozen lines of code to do that. No, this, this is about *making* images. It's more complex."

He grabbed Juliette's arm.

"Jules, this thing can make brand-new views. It can show you anything you *like*."

He sucked in his breath, and a slice of time hung in the air between them, a pause where hearts did not beat and eyes did not blink.

Juliette sat back on her haunches, balancing on the toes of her old boots. She finally settled her butt on the floor and leaned back against the metal paneling of his office wall.

"So now you see –" Scottie started to say, but Juliette held up her hand, hushing him. It had never occurred to her that the view could be fabricated. But why not? And what would be the point?

She imagined Holston's wife discovering this. She must've been at least as smart as Scottie – she was the one who came up with the technique he had used to find this in the first place, right? What would she have done with this discovery? Say something out loud and cause a riot? Tell her husband, the sheriff? What?

Juliette could know only what she herself would do in that position, if she were almost convinced. She was by nature too curious a person to doubt what she might do. It would gnaw at her, like the rattling innards of a sealed machine or the secret workings of an unopened device. She would have to grab a screwdriver and a wrench and have a peek . . .

"Jules —"

She waved him off. Details from Holston's folder flooded back. Notes about Allison, how she suddenly went crazy, almost out of nowhere. Her curiosity must have driven her there. Unless — unless Holston didn't know. Unless it was all an act. Unless Allison had been shielding her husband from some horror with a mock veil of insanity.

But would it have taken Holston three years to piece together what she had figured out in a *week?* Or did he already know and it just took three years to summon the courage to go after her? Or did Juliette have an advantage he didn't? She had Scottie. And she was, after all, following the bread crumbs of someone else following more bread crumbs, a much easier and more obvious trail.

She looked up at her young friend, who was peering worriedly down at her.

"You have to get those out of here," he said, glancing at the printouts.

Juliette nodded. She pushed up from the floor and tucked the scroll into the breast of her overalls. It would have to be destroyed; she just wasn't sure how.

"I deleted my copies of everything I got for you," he said. "I'm done looking at them. And you should do the same."

Juliette tapped her chest pocket, felt the hard bulge of the flash drive there.

"And Jules, can you do me a favor?"

"Anything."

"See if there's any way I can transfer back to Mechanical, will you? I don't want to be up here anymore."

She nodded and squeezed his shoulder. "I'll see what I can do," she promised, feeling a knot in her gut for getting the poor kid involved at all.

25

THE NEXT MORNING, exhausted, Juliette arrived late at her desk, her legs and back sore from the climb down to IT and from not getting an ounce of sleep. She had spent the entire night tossing and turning, wondering if she'd discovered a box that was better left unopened, worried she might be raising questions that promised nothing but bad answers. If she went out into the cafeteria and looked in a direction she normally avoided, she would be able to see the last two cleaners lying in the crook of a hill, almost as if in one another's arms. Did those two lovers throw themselves into the rotting wind over the very thing Juliette was now chasing? The fear she'd seen in Scottie's eyes made her wonder if she wasn't being careful enough. She looked across her desk at her new deputy, greener even at this job than she, as he transcribed data from one of the folders.

"Hey, Peter?"

He looked up from his keyboard. "Yeah?"

"You were in Justice before this, right? Shadowing a judge?"

He tilted his head to the side. "No, I was a court assistant. I actually shadowed in the mids' deputy office until a few years ago. I wanted that job, but none came up."

"Did you grow up there? Or the up top?"

"The mids." His hands fell away from his keyboard to his

lap. He smiled. “My dad was a plumber in the hydroponics. He passed away a few years ago. My mom, she works in the nursery.”

“Really? What’s her name?”

“Rebecca. She’s one of the —”

“I know her. She was shadowing when I was a kid. My father —”

“He works in the upper nursery, I know. I didn’t want to say anything —”

“Why not? Hey, if you’re worried about me playing favorites, I’m guilty. You’re my deputy now, and I’ll have your back.”

“No, it’s not that. I just didn’t want you to hold anything against me. I know you and your father don’t —”

Juliette waved him off. “He’s still my father. We just grew apart. Tell your mom I said hi.”

“I will.” Peter smiled and bent over his keyboard.

“Hey. I’ve got a question for you. Something I can’t figure.”

“Sure,” he said, looking up. “Go ahead.”

“Can you think of why it’s cheaper to porter a paper note to someone than it is to just wire them from a computer?”

“Oh, sure.” He nodded. “It’s a quarter chit per character to wire someone. That adds up!”

Juliette laughed. “No, I know what it costs. But paper isn’t cheap, either. And neither is porting. But it seems like sending a wire would be practically free, you know? It’s just information. It weighs nothing.”

He shrugged. “It’s been a quarter chit a character since I’ve been alive. I dunno. Besides, we’ve got a fifty-chit-per-day allowance from here, plus unlimited emergencies. I wouldn’t stress.”

“I’m not stressed, just confused. I mean, I understand why everyone can’t have radios like we carry, because only one person can transmit at a time, so we need the air open for emergencies, but you'd think we could all send and receive as many wires as we wanted."

Peter propped his elbows up and rested his chin on his fists. "Well, think about the cost of the servers, the electricity. That means oil to burn and all the maintenance of the wires and cooling and whatnot. Especially if you have a ton of traffic. Factor that against pressing pulp on a rack, letting it dry, scratching some ink on it, and then having a person who's already heading that way walk it up or down for you. No wonder it's cheaper!"

Juliette nodded, but mostly for his benefit. She wasn't so sure. She hated to voice why, but she couldn't help herself.

"But what if it's for a different reason? What if someone made it expensive on *purpose?*"

"What? To make money?" Peter snapped his fingers. "To keep the porters employed with running notes!"

Juliette shook her head. "No, what if it's to make conversing with each other more difficult? Or at least costly. You know, separate us, make us keep our thoughts to ourselves."

Peter frowned. "Why would anyone want to do that?"

Shrugging, Juliette looked back at her computer screen, her hand creeping to the scroll hidden in her lap. She reminded herself that she no longer lived among people she could implicitly trust. "I don't know," she said. "Forget about it. It's just a silly thought."

She pulled her keyboard toward her and was just glancing up at her screen when Peter saw the emergency icon first.

"Wow. Another alert," he said.

She started to click on the flashing icon, heard Peter blow out his breath.

"What the hell's going on around here?" he asked.

She pulled the message up on her screen and read it quickly, disbelieving what she was seeing. Surely this wasn't the way of the job. Surely people didn't die this often. Had she simply not heard about it before, with her nose always buried in some crankcase or under an oil pan?

The blinking number code above the message was one she recognized without even needing her cheat sheet. It was becoming sadly familiar. Another suicide. They didn't give the victim's name, but there was an office number. And she knew the floor and address. Her legs were still sore from her trip down there.

"No—" she said, gripping the edge of her desk.

"You want me to—?" Peter reached for his radio.

"No, damn it, no." Juliette shook her head. She pushed herself away from her desk, knocking over the recycling bin, which spilled all the pardoned folders across the floor. The scroll from her lap rolled into them.

"I can—" Peter began.

"I got this," she said, waving him away. "Damn it." She shook her head. The office was spinning around her head, the world getting blurry. She staggered for the door, arms wide for balance, when Peter snapped back to his computer screen, dragging his mouse with its little cord behind, clicking something.

"Uh, Juliette—?"

But she was already stumbling out the door, bracing herself for the long and painful descent.

"Juliette!"

She turned to find Peter running behind her, his hand steadying the radio attached to his hip.

"What?" she asked.

"I'm sorry— It's— I don't know how to do this—"

"Spit it out," she said impatiently. All she could think of was little Scottie, hanging by his neck. It was electrical ties in her imagination. That's how her waking nightmare, her morbid thoughts, crafted the scene of his death in her head.

"It's just that I got a private wire and—"

"Keep up if you want, but I've got to get down there." She spun toward the stairwell.

Peter grabbed her arm. Roughly. A forceful grip.

"I'm sorry, ma'am, but I'm supposed to take you into custody—"

She whirled on him and saw how unsure of himself he looked.

"What did you say?"

"I'm just doing my duty, Sheriff, I swear." Peter reached for his metal cuffs. Juliette stared at him, disbelieving, as he snapped one link around her wrist and fumbled for the other.

"Peter, what's going on? I've got a friend I need to see to—"

He shook his head. "The computer says you're a suspect, ma'am. I'm just doing what it tells me to do—"

And with that, the second link clicked around her other wrist and Juliette looked down at her predicament, dumbfounded, the image of her young friend hanging by his neck unable to be shaken loose from her mind.

26

SHE WAS ALLOWED a visitor, but who would Juliette want to see her like this? No one. So she sat with her back against the bars, the bleak view outside brightening with the rising of an unseen sun, the floor around her bare of folders and ghosts. She was alone, stripped of a job she wasn't sure she had ever wanted, a pile of bodies in her wake, her simple and easily understood life having come unraveled.

"I'm sure this will pass," a voice behind her said. Juliette leaned away from the steel rods and looked around to find Bernard standing behind her, his hands wrapped around the bars.

Juliette moved away from him and sat on the cot, turning her back to the gray view.

"You know I didn't do this," she said. "He was my friend."

Bernard frowned. "What do you think you're being held for? The boy committed suicide. He seems to have been distraught from recent tragedies. This is not unheard of when people move to a new section of the silo, away from friends and family, to take a job they're not entirely suited for—"

"Then why am I being held here?" Juliette asked. She realized suddenly that there might be no double cleaning after all. Off to the side, down the hallway, she could see Peter shuffling back and forth as if a physical barrier prevented him from coming any closer.

"Unauthorized entry on the thirty-fourth," Bernard said. "Threatening a member of the silo, tampering with IT affairs, removing IT property from secured quarters—"

"That's ratshit," Juliette said. "I was summoned by one of your workers. I had every right to be there!"

"We will look into that," Bernard said. "Well, Peter here will. I'm afraid he's had to remove your computer for evidence. My people down below are best qualified to see if—"

"*Your* people? Are you trying to be mayor or IT head? Because I looked into it, and the Pact clearly states you can't be both—"

"That will be put to a vote soon enough. The Pact has changed before. It's designed to change when events call for it."

"And so you want me out of the way." Juliette stepped closer to the bars so she could see Peter Billings, and have him see her. "I suppose you were to have this job all along? Is that right?"

Peter slunk out of sight.

"Juliette. Jules." Bernard shook his head and clicked his tongue at her. "I don't want you out of the way. I wouldn't want that for any member of the silo. I want people to be in their *place*. Where they fit in. Scottie wasn't cut out for IT. I see that now. And I don't think you were meant for the up top."

"So, what, I'm banished back to Mechanical? Is that what's going on? Over some ratshit charges?"

"*Banished* is such a horrible word. I'm sure you didn't mean that. And don't you want your old job back? Weren't you happier then? There's so much to learn up here that you've never shadowed for. And the people who thought you best fit for this job, who I'm sure hoped to ease you into it . . ."

He stopped right there, and it was somehow worse that he

left the sentence hanging like that, forcing Jules to complete the image rather than just hear it. She pictured two mounds of freshly turned soil in the gardens, a few mourning rinds tossed on top of them.

"I'm going to let you gather your things, what isn't needed for evidence, and then allow you to see yourself back down. As long as you check in with my deputies on the way and report your progress, we'll drop these charges. Consider it an extension of my little . . . *forgiveness* holiday."

Bernard smiled and straightened his glasses.

Juliette gritted her teeth. It occurred to her that she had never, in her entire life, punched someone in the face.

And it was only her fear of missing, of not doing it correctly and cracking her knuckles on one of the steel bars, that stopped her from putting an end to that streak.

It was just about a week since she had arrived at the up top, and Juliette was leaving with fewer belongings than she'd brought. A blue Mechanical overall had been provided, one much too big for her. Peter didn't even say good-bye—Juliette thought more from shame than anger or blame. He walked her through the cafeteria to the top of the stairs, and as she turned to shake his hand, she found him staring down at his toes, his thumbs caught in his overalls, her sheriff's badge pinned at an angle over his left breast.

Juliette began her long walk down through the length of the silo. It would be less physically taxing than her walk up had been, but more draining in other ways. What exactly had happened to the silo, and why? She couldn't help but feel in the middle of it all, that she should shoulder some of the blame. None of this would have happened had they left her in Mechanical, had they never come to see her in the first place. She would still be bitching about the alignment of the generator, not sleeping at night as she waited for the inevitable failure and a descent into chaos as they learned to survive on backup power for the decades it would take to rebuild the thing. Instead, she had been witness to a different type of failure: a throwing not of switches but of bodies. She felt the worst for poor Scottie, a boy with so much promise, so many talents, gone before his prime.

She had been sheriff for a short time, a star appearing on her breast for but a wink, and yet she felt an incredible urge to investigate Scottie's death. There was something not right about the boy having killed himself. The signs were there, sure. He had been afraid to leave his office—but then, he'd also shadowed under Walker and had maybe picked up the habit of reclusiveness from the old man. Scottie had also been harboring secrets too big for his young mind, had been fearful enough to wire her to come quickly—but she knew him like her own shadow and knew he didn't have it in him. She suddenly wondered if Marnes had ever had it in him as well. If Jahns were here beside her, would the old mayor be screaming for Jules to investigate both their deaths? Telling her that none of this fit?

"I can't," Juliette whispered to the ghost, causing an upbound porter to turn his head as he passed.

She kept further thoughts to herself. As she descended toward her father's nursery, she paused at the landing, contemplating longer and harder the idea of going in to see him than she had on her way up. Pride had prevented her the first time. And now shame set her feet into motion once again as she spiraled down away from him, chastising herself for thinking on the ghosts from her past that had long ago been banished from memory.

At the thirty-fourth, the main entrance to IT, she again considered stopping. There would be clues in Scottie's office, maybe even some they hadn't managed to scrub away. She shook her head. The conspiracies were already forming in her mind. And as hard as it was to leave the scene of the crime behind, she knew she wouldn't be allowed anywhere near his office.

She continued down the staircase and thought, as she considered IT's location in the silo, that this couldn't be an accident either. She had another thirty-two floors to go before she checked in with the first deputy, who was located near the center of the mids. The sheriff's office was thirty-three floors above her head. IT, then, was as far as it could get from any deputy station in the silo.

She shook her head at this paranoid thinking. It wasn't how diagnoses were made. Her father would have told her so.

After meeting with the first deputy around noon, and accepting a piece of bread and fruit, along with a reminder to eat, she made good time down through the mids, wondering as she passed the upper apartments which level Lukas lived on, or if he even knew of her arrest.

The weight of the past week seemed to pull her down the stairwell, gravity sucking at her boots, the pressures of being sheriff dissipating as she left that office far behind. Those pressures were slowly replaced with an eagerness to return to her friends, even in shame, as she got closer and closer to Mechanical.

She stopped to see Hank, the down-deep deputy, on level one-twenty. She had known him for a long time, was becoming surrounded with familiar faces, people who waved hello, their moods somber, as if they knew every detail of her time away. Hank tried to get her to stay and rest awhile, but she only paused long enough to be polite, to refill her canteen, and then to shuffle the remaining twenty floors to the place she truly belonged.

Knox seemed thrilled to have her back. He wrapped her up in a crippling hug, lifting her feet off the ground and roughing up her face with his beard. He smelled of grease and sweat, a mix Juliette had never fully noticed in the down deep because she had never been free from it.

The walk to her old room was punctuated by slaps on her back, well-wishes, questions about the up top, people calling her sheriff in jest, and the sort of rude frivolities she had grown up in and grown used to. Juliette felt more saddened by it all than anything. She had set out to do something and had failed. And yet her friends were just happy to have her back.

Shirly from second shift spotted her coming down the hallway and accompanied Juliette on the rest of the walk to her room. She updated Juliette on the status of the generator and the output from the new oil well, as if Juliette had simply been on vacation for a short while. Juliette thanked her at the door to her room, stepped inside, and kicked her way through all the folded notes slipped under the door. She lifted the strap of her day pack over her head and dropped it, then collapsed onto her bed, too exhausted and upset at herself to even cry.

She awoke in the middle of the night. Her small display terminal showed the time in green blocky numbers: 2:14 a.m.

Juliette sat at the edge of her old bed in overalls that weren't truly hers and took stock of her situation. Her life was not yet over, she decided. It just felt that way. Tomorrow, even if they didn't expect her to, she would be back at work in the pits, keeping the silo humming, doing what she did best. She needed to wake up to this reality, to set other ideas and responsibilities aside. Already, they felt so far away. She doubted she would even go to Scottie's funeral, not unless they sent his body down to be buried where it belonged.

She reached for the keyboard slotted into the wall rack. Everything was covered in a layer of grime, she saw. She had never noticed it before. The keys were filthy from the dirt she had brought back from each shift. The monitor's glass was limned with grease. She fought the urge to wipe the screen and smear the shiny coat of oil around, but she would have to clean her place a little deeper, she decided. She was viewing things with untainted and more critical eyes.

Rather than chase pointless sleep, she keyed the monitor awake to check the work logs for the next day, anything to get her mind off the past week. But before she could open her task manager, she saw that she had over a dozen wires in her inbox. She'd never seen so many. Usually people just slid recycled notes under each other's doors — but then, she had been a long way away when the news of her arrest had hit, and she hadn't been able to get to a computer since.

She logged on to her e-mail account and pulled up the most recent wire. It was from Knox. Just a semicolon and a parenthesis — a half-chit smile.

Juliette couldn't help it; she smiled back. She could still smell Knox on her skin and realized, as far as the big brute was concerned, that all the troubles and problems percolating in whispers down the stairwell about her paled in comparison to her return. To him, the worst thing that had happened in the last week was probably the challenge of replacing her on first shift.

Jules went to the next message, one from the third-shift foreman welcoming her home — probably because of the extra time his crew was putting in to help cover her old shift.

There was more. A day's pay of a note from Shirly, wishing her well on her journey. These were all notes they had hoped she would receive up top, to make the trip down easier, hoping she wouldn't loathe herself or feel humiliated, or even a failure. Juliette felt tears well up at how considerate it all was. She had an image of her desk, Holston's desk, with nothing but unplugged wires snaking across its surface, her computer removed. There was no way she could've gotten these messages when they were meant to be read. She wiped her eyes and tried not to think of the wired notes as money wasted, but rather as extravagant tokens of her friendships in the down deep.

Reading each one, trying to hold it together, made the last message she came to doubly jarring. It was paragraphs long. Juliette assumed it was an official document, maybe a list of her offenses, a formal ruling against her. She had seen such messages only from the mayor's office, usually on holidays, notes that went out to every silo member. But then she saw that it was from Scottie.

Juliette sat up straight and tried to clear her head. She started from the beginning, damning her blurred vision.

> J—
>
> I lied. Couldn't delete this stuff. Found more. That tape I got you? Your joke was truth. And the program—NOT for big screen. Pxl density not right. 32,768 x 8,192! Not sure what's that size. 8″ x 2″? So many pxls if so.
>
> Putting more together. Don't trust porters, so wiring this. Screw cost, wire me back. Need transfr to Mech. Not safe here.
>
> —S

Juliette read it a second time, crying now. Here was the real voice of a ghost warning her of something, all of it too late. And it wasn't the voice of someone who was planning his own death—she was sure of that. She checked the time stamp of the wire; it was sent before she had even arrived back at her office the day before, before Scottie had died.

Before he had been *killed,* she corrected herself. They must have found him snooping, or maybe her visit had alerted them. She wondered what IT could see, if they could break into her wire account, even. They must not have yet, or the message wouldn't have been there, waiting for her.

She leapt suddenly from her bed and grabbed one of the folded notes by the door. Digging a charcoal from her day pack, she sat back down on the bed. She copied the entire wire, every odd spelling, double-checking each number, and then deleted the message. She had chills up and down her arms by the time she finished, as if some unseen person was racing toward her, hoping to break into her computer before she dispensed with the evidence. She wondered if Scottie had been cautious enough to have deleted the note from his sent wires, and assumed, if he'd been thinking clearly, that he would.

She sat back on her bed, holding the copied note, thoughts about the work log for the next day gone. Instead, she studied the sinister mess revolving around her, spiraling through the heart of the silo. Things were bad, from top to bottom. A great set of gears had been thrown out of alignment. She could hear the noise from the past week, this thumping and clanging, this machine lumbering off its mounts and leaving bodies in its wake.

And Juliette was the only one who could hear it. She was the only one who knew. And she didn't know who she could trust to help set things right. But she did know this: it would require a diminishing of power to align things once again. And there would be no way to call what happened next a "holiday."

27

JULIETTE SHOWED UP at Walker's electronics workshop at five, worried she might find him asleep on his cot, but smelling instead the distinctive odor of vaporized solder wafting down the hallway. She knocked on the open door as she entered, and Walker looked up from one of his many green electronics boards, corkscrews of smoke rising from the tip of his soldering iron.

"Jules!" he shouted. He lifted the magnifying lens off his gray head and set it and the soldering iron down on the steel workbench. "I heard you were back. I meant to send a note, but . . ." He waved around at the piles of parts with their work-order tags dangling from strings. "Super busy," he explained.

"Forget it," she said. She gave Walker a hug, smelling the electrical-fire scent on his skin that reminded her so much of him. And of Scottie. "I'm going to feel guilty enough taking some of your time with this," she said.

"Oh?" He stepped back and studied her, his bushy white brows and wrinkled skin furrowed with worry. "You got something for me?" He looked her up and down for something broken, a habit formed from a lifetime of being brought small devices that needed repairing.

"I actually just wanted to pick your brain." She sat down on one of his workbench stools, and Walker did the same.

"Go ahead," he said. He wiped his brow with the back of his sleeve, and Juliette saw how old Walker had become. She remembered him without so much white in his hair, without the wrinkles and splotchy skin. She remembered him with his shadow.

"It has to do with Scottie," she warned him.

Walker turned his head to the side and nodded. He tried to say something, tapped his fist against his chest a few times and cleared his throat. "Damn shame," was all he could manage. He peered down at the floor for a moment.

"It can wait," Juliette told him. "If you need time—"

"I *convinced* him to take that job," Walker said, shaking his head. "I remember when the offer came, being scared he'd turn it down. Because of me, you know? That he'd be too afraid of me bein' upset at him for leaving, that he might just stay forever, so I urged him to take it." He looked up at her, his eyes shining. "I just wanted him to know he was free to choose. I didn't mean to push him away."

"You didn't," Juliette said. "Nobody thinks that, and neither should you."

"I just don't figure he was happy up there. That weren't his home."

"Well, he was too smart for us. Don't forget that. We always said that."

"He loved you," Walker said, and wiped his eyes. "Damn, how that boy looked up to you."

Juliette felt her own tears welling up again. She reached into her pocket and brought out the wire she'd transcribed onto the back of the note. She had to remind herself why she was there, to hold it together.

"Just don't seem like him to take the easy way—" Walker muttered.

"No, it doesn't," she said. "Walker, I need to discuss some things with you that can't leave this room."

He laughed. Mostly, it seemed, to keep from sobbing. "Like I ever leave this room," he said.

"Well, it can't be discussed with anyone else. No one. Okay?"

He bobbed his head.

"I don't think Scottie killed himself."

Walker threw up his hands to cover his face. He bent forward and shook as he started to cry. Juliette got off her stool and went to him, put her arm around his trembling back.

"I knew it," he sobbed into his palms. "I knew it, I knew it." He looked up at her, tears coursing through several days of white stubble. "Who did this? They'll pay, won't they? Tell me who did it, Jules."

"Whoever it was, I don't think they had far to travel," she said.

"IT? Goddamn them."

"Walker, I need your help sorting this out. Scottie sent me a wire not long before he . . . well, before I think he was killed."

"Sent you a wire?"

"Yeah. Look, I met with him earlier that day. He asked me to come down to see him."

"Down to IT?"

She nodded. "I'd found something in the last sheriff's computer—"

"Holston." He dipped his head. "The last cleaner. Yeah, Knox brought me something from you. A program, looked like. I told him Scottie would know better than anyone, so we forwarded it along."

"Well, you were right."

Walker wiped his cheeks and bobbed his head. "He was smarter than any of us."

"I know. He told me this thing, that it was a program, one that made very detailed images. Like the images we see of the outside—"

She waited a beat to see how he would respond. It was taboo even to use the word in most settings. Walker was unmoved. As she had hoped, he was old enough to be beyond childhood fears—and probably lonely and sad enough not to care anyway.

"But this wire he sent, it says something about p-x-l's being too dense." She showed him the copy she'd made. Walker grabbed his magnifiers and slipped the band over his forehead.

"Pixels," he said, sniffing. "He's talking about the little dots that make up an image. Each one is a pixel." He took the note from her and read some more. "He says it's not safe there." Walker rubbed his chin and shook his head. "Damn them."

"Walker, what kind of screen would be eight inches by two inches?" Juliette looked around at all the boards, displays, and coils of loose wire strewn about his workshop. "Do you have anything like that?"

"Eight by two? Maybe a readout, like on the front of a server or something. Be the right size to show a few lines of text, internal temps, clock cycles . . ." He shook his head. "But you'd never make one with this kind of pixel density. Even if it were possible, it wouldn't make sense. Your eye couldn't make out one pixel from its neighbor if it were right at the end of your nose."

He rubbed his stubble and studied the note some more. "What's this nonsense about the tape and the joke? What's that mean?"

Juliette stood beside him and looked over the note. "I've been wondering about that. He must mean the heat tape he scored for me a while back."

"I think I remember something about that."

"Well, do you remember the problems we had with it? The exhaust we wrapped in it almost caught fire. The stuff was complete crap. I think he sent a note asking if the tape had gotten here okay, and I sorta recall writing back that it did, and thanks, but the tape couldn't have self-destructed better if it'd been *engineered* to."

"That was your joke?" Walker swiveled in his stool and rested his elbows on the workbench. He kept peering over the copied charcoal letters like they were the face of Scottie, his little shadow coming back one last time to tell him something important.

"And he says my joke was truth," Juliette said. "I've been up the last three hours thinking about this, dying to talk to someone."

Walker looked back over his shoulder at her, his eyebrows raised.

"I'm not a sheriff, Walk. Never born to be one. Shouldn't have gone. But I know, as sure as everyone, that what I'm about to say should send me to cleaning . . ."

Walker immediately slid off his stool and walked away from her. Juliette damned herself for coming, for opening her mouth, for not just clocking into first shift and saying to hell with it all—

Walker shut the door to his workshop and locked it. He looked at her and lifted a finger, went to his air compressor and pulled out a hose. Then he flipped the unit on so the motor would start to build up pressure, which just leaked out the open nozzle in a steady, noisy hiss. He returned to the bench, the clatter from the noisy compressor engine awful, and sat down. His wide eyes begged her to continue.

"There's a hill up there with a crook in it," she told him, having to raise her voice a little. "I don't know how long it's been since you've seen this hill, but there are two bodies nestled together in it, man and wife. If you look hard, you can see a dozen shapes like this all over the landscape, all the cleaners, all in various states of decay. Most are gone, of course. Rotted to dust over the long years."

Walker shook his head at the image she was forming.

"How many years have they been improving these suits so the cleaners have a chance? Hundreds?"

He nodded.

"And yet nobody gets any further. And never once have they *not* had enough time to clean."

Walker looked up and met her gaze. "Your joke is truth," he said. "The heat tape. It's engineered to fail."

Juliette pursed her lips. "That's what I'm thinking. But not just the tape. Remember those seals from a few years back? The ones from IT that went into the water pumps, that were delivered to us by accident?"

"So we've been making fun of IT for being fools and dullards—"

"But *we're* the fools," Juliette said. And it felt so damned good to say it to another human being. So good for these new ideas of hers to swim in the air. And she knew she was right about the cost of sending wires, that they didn't want people talking. Thinking was fine; they would bury you with your thoughts. But no collaboration, no groups coordinating together, no exchange of ideas.

"You think they have us down here to be near the oil?" she asked Walker. "I don't think so. Not anymore. I think they're keeping anyone with a lick of mechanical sense as far from them as possible. There're two supply chains, two sets of parts being made, all in complete secrecy. And who questions them? Who would risk being put to cleaning?"

"You think they killed Scottie?" he asked.

Juliette nodded. "Walk, I think it's worse than that." She leaned closer, the compressor rattling, the hiss of released air filling the room. "I think they kill *everybody*."

28

Juliette reported to first shift at six, the conversation with Walker playing over and over in her head. There was sustained and embarrassing applause from the handful of techs present as she entered dispatch. Knox just glared at her from the corner, back to his gruff demeanor. He had already welcomed her home and would be damned if he'd do it again.

She said hello to the people she hadn't seen the night before and looked over the job queue. The words on the board made sense, but she had a difficult time processing them. In the back of her mind, she thought about poor Scottie, confused and struggling while someone much larger than him—or several someones—choked him to death. She thought of his little body, probably riddled with evidence but soon to feed the roots of the dirt farms. She thought of a married couple lying together on a hill, never given a chance to make it any further, to see beyond the horizon.

She chose a job from the queue, one that would require little mental exertion on her part, and thought of poor Jahns and Marnes and how tragic their love—if she had been reading Marnes correctly—had been. The temptation to tell the entire room was crippling. She looked around at Megan and Ricks, at Jenkins and Marck, and thought about the small army of tight brotherhood she could form. The silo was rotten to the core, an evil man was acting mayor, a puppet stood where a good sheriff had been, and all the good men and women were gone.

It was comical to imagine: her rallying a band of mechanics to storm the upper levels and right a wrong. And then what? Was *this* the uprising they had learned about as children? Was this how it began? One silly woman with fire in her blood stirring the hearts of a legion of fools?

She kept her mouth shut and made her way to the pump room, riding the flow of morning mechanics, thinking more about what she should be doing above than about what needed repairing below. She descended one of the side stairwells, stopped by the tool room to check out a kit bag, and lugged the heavy satchel to one of the deep pits where pumps ran constantly to keep the silo from filling halfway up with water.

Caryl, a transfer from third shift, was already working near the pit basin patching rotten cement. She waved with her trowel, and Juliette dipped her chin and forced herself to smile.

The offending pump sat idle on one wall, the backup pump beside it struggling mightily and spraying water out of dry and cracked seals. Juliette looked into the basin to gauge the height of the water. A painted 9 was just visible above its murky surface. Juliette did some quick math, knowing the diameter of the basin and that it was almost nine feet full. The good news was they had at least a day before boots were getting wet. Worst case, they would replace the pump with a rebuilt one from spares and deal with Hendricks bitching at them for checking it out instead of fixing what they already had.

As she began stripping the failed pump down, pelted with spray from its smaller, leaking neighbor, Juliette considered her life with this new perspective provided by the morning's revelations. The silo was something she had always taken for granted. The priests said it had always been here, that it was lovingly created by a caring God, that everything they would ever need had been provided for. Juliette had a hard time with this story. A few years ago, she had been on the first team to drill past ten thousand feet and hit new oil reserves. She had a sense of the size and scope of the world below them. And then she had seen with her own eyes the view of the outside with its phantom-like sheets of smoke they called clouds rolling by at miraculous heights. She had even seen a star, which Lukas thought stood an inconceivable distance away. What god would make so much rock below and air above and just a measly silo between?

And then there was the rotting skyline and the images in the children's books, both of which seemed to hold clues. The priests, of course, would say that the skyline was evidence that man wasn't supposed to exceed his bounds. And the books with the faded colored pages? The fanciful imagination of authors, a class done away with for all the trouble they inspired.

But Juliette didn't see fanciful imagination in those books. She had spent a childhood in the nursery, reading each one over and over whenever they weren't checked out, and things in them and in the wondrous plays performed in the bazaar made more sense to her than this crumbling cylinder in which they lived.

She wiggled the last of the water hoses free and began separating the pump from its motor. The steel shavings suggested a chewed-up impeller, which meant pulling the shaft. As she worked on automatic, cruising through a job she'd performed numerous times before, she thought back on the myriad of animals that populated those books, most of which had never been seen by living eyes. The only fanciful part, she figured, was that they all talked and acted human. There were mice and chickens in several of the books that performed these stunts as well, and she knew their breeds were incapable of speech. All those other animals had to exist somewhere, or used to. She felt this to the core, maybe because they didn't seem that fantastical. Each seemed to follow the same plan, just like all the silo's pumps. You could tell one was based on the other. A particular design worked, and whoever had made one had made them all.

The silo made less sense. It hadn't been created by a god—it was probably designed by IT. This was a new theory, but she felt more and more sure of it. They controlled all the important parts. Cleaning was the highest law and the deepest religion, and both of these were intertwined and housed within its secretive walls. And then there was the spacing from Mechanical and the spread of the deputy stations—more clues. Not to mention the clauses in the Pact that practically granted them immunity. And now the discovery of a second supply chain, a series of parts engineered to fail, a reason behind the lack of progress in prolonging survival time on the outside. IT had built this place and IT was keeping them there.

Juliette nearly stripped a bolt, she was so agitated. She turned to look for Caryl, but the younger woman was already gone, her repair patch a darker shade of gray as it waited to dry and blend in with the rest. Looking up, Juliette scanned the ceiling of the pump room where conduits of wire and piping traveled through the walls and mingled overhead. A run of steam pipes stood clustered to the side to keep from melting any of the wires; a ribbon of heat tape hung off one of these pipes in a loose coil. It would have to be replaced soon, she thought. That tape might have been ten or twenty years old. She considered the stolen tape that had caused so much of the mess she was in and how it would've been lucky to survive twenty minutes up there.

And that's when Juliette realized what she had to do. A project to pull the wool back from everyone's eyes, a favor to the next fool who slipped up or dared to hope aloud. And it would be so easy. She wouldn't have to build anything herself—they would do all the work for her. All it would take would be some convincing, and she was mighty good at that.

She smiled, a list of parts forming in her head as the broken impeller was removed from the faulty pump. All she would need to fix this problem was a replacement part or two. It was the perfect solution to getting everything in the silo working properly once more.

Juliette worked two full shifts, wearing her muscles to a numb ache, before returning her tools and showering. She took a stiff brush to her nails over the bathroom sink, determined to keep them up-top clean. She headed toward the mess hall, looking forward to a tall plate of high-energy food rather than the weak rabbit stew from the cafeteria on level one, when she passed through Mechanical's entrance hall and saw Knox talking to Deputy Hank. The way they turned and stared, she knew they were talking about her. Juliette's stomach sank. Her first thought was of her father. And then Peter. Who else could they take away from her that she might care about? They wouldn't know to contact her about Lukas, whatever he was to her.

She made a swift turn and headed in their direction, even as the two of them moved to intercept her. The looks on their faces confirmed her every fear. Something awful had happened. Juliette barely noticed Hank reaching for his cuffs.

"I'm sorry, Jules," he said as they got close.

"What happened?" Juliette asked. "Dad?"

Hank's brow wrinkled in confusion. Knox was shaking his head and chewing on his beard. He studied the deputy like he might eat the man.

"Knox, what's going on?"

"Jules, I'm sorry." He shook his head. He seemed to want to say more but was powerless to do so. Juliette felt Hank reaching for her arm.

"You are under arrest for grave crimes against the silo."

He recited the lines like they were from a sad poem. The steel clicked around her wrist.

"You will be judged and sentenced according to the Pact."

Juliette looked up at Knox. "What is this?" she asked. Was she really being arrested again?

"If you are found guilty, you will be given a chance at honor."

"What do you want me to do?" Knox whispered, his vast muscles twitching beneath his overalls. He wrung his hands together, watching the second metal band clack around her other wrist, her two hands shackled together now. The large head of Mechanical seemed to be contemplating violence – or worse.

"Easy, Knox," Juliette said. She shook her head at him. The thought of more people getting hurt because of her was too much to bear.

"Should humanity banish you from this world . . . ," Hank continued to recite, his voice cracking, his eyes wet with shame.

"Let it go," Juliette told Knox. She looked past him to where more workers were coming off second shift, stopping to see this spectacle of their prodigal daughter being put in cuffs.

"In that banishment, may you find your sins scrubbed, scrubbed away," Hank concluded. He looked up at her, one hand gripping the chain between her wrists, tears streaking down his face.

"I'm sorry," he said.

Juliette nodded to him. She set her teeth and nodded to Knox as well.

"It's all right," she said. She kept bobbing her head. "It's all right, Knox. Let it go."

29

THE CLIMB UP was to take three days. Longer than it should have, but there were protocols. A day trip up to Hank's office, a night in his cell, Deputy Marsh coming down the next morning from the mids to escort her up another fifty levels to his office.

She felt numb during this second day of climbing, the looks from passersby sliding off her like water on grease. It was difficult to concern herself with her own life – she was too busy tallying all the others lost, some of them because of her.

Marsh, like Hank, tried to make small talk, and all Juliette could think to say in return was that they were on the wrong side. That evil ran amok. Instead, she kept her mouth shut.

At the mids deputy station, she was shown to a familiar enough cell, just like the one in Hank's in the down deep. No wallscreen, only a stack of primed cinder blocks. She collapsed onto the bunk before he even had the gate locked and lay there for what felt like hours, waiting for night to come and pass to dawn, for Peter's new deputy to come and march her up the last leg of her journey.

She checked her wrist often, but Hank had confiscated her watch. He probably wouldn't even know how to wind it. The thing would eventually fall into disrepair and return to being a trinket, a useless thing worn upside down for its pretty band.

This saddened her more than it should have. She rubbed her bare wrist, dying to know the time, when Marsh came back and told her she had a visitor.

Juliette sat up on the cot and swung her legs around. Who would come up to the mids from Mechanical?

When Lukas appeared on the other side of the bars, the dam that held back all her emotions nearly broke. She felt her neck constrict, her jaws ache from fighting the sobs, the emptiness in her chest nearly puncture and burst. He grabbed the bars and leaned his head against them, his temples touching the smooth steel, a sad smile on his face.

"Hey," he said.

Juliette barely recognized him. She was used to seeing him in the dark, had been in a hurry when they'd bumped into each other on the stairs. He was a striking man, his eyes older than his face, his light brown hair slicked back with sweat from what she assumed was a hurried walk down.

"You didn't need to come," she said, speaking softly and slowly to keep from crying. What really saddened her was someone seeing her like this, someone she was beginning to realize she cared about. The indignity was too much.

"We're fighting this," he said. "Your friends are collecting signatures. Don't give up."

She shook her head. "It won't work," she told him. "Please don't get your hopes up." She walked to the bars and wrapped her hands a few inches below his. "You don't even know me."

"I know this is ratshit—" He turned away, a tear streaking down his cheek. "Another cleaning?" he croaked. "Why?"

"It's what they want," Juliette said. "There's no stopping them."

Lukas's hands slid down the bars and wrapped around hers. Juliette couldn't free them to wipe her cheeks. She tried to dip her head to use her shoulder.

"I was coming up to see you that day—" Lukas shook his head and took a deep breath. "I was coming to ask you out—"

"Don't," she said. "Lukas. Don't do this."

"I told my mom about you."

"Oh, for God's sake, Lukas—"

"This can't happen," he said. He shook his head. "It can't. You can't go."

When he looked back up, Juliette saw that there was more fear in his eyes than even she felt. She wiggled one hand free and peeled his other one off. She pushed them away. "You need to let this go," she said. "I'm sorry. Just find someone. Don't end up like me. Don't wait—"

"I thought I had found someone," he said plaintively.

Juliette turned to hide her face.

"Go," she whispered.

She stood still, feeling his presence on the other side of those bars, this boy who knew about stars but nothing about her. And she waited, listening to him sob while she cried quietly to herself, until she finally heard his feet shuffle across the floor, his sad gait carrying him away.

That night, she spent another evening on a cold cot, another evening of not being told what she'd been arrested for, an evening to count the hurts she had unwittingly caused. The next day, there was a final climb up through a land of strangers, the whispers of a double cleaning chasing after her, Juliette falling into another stunned trance, one leg moving and then the other.

At the end of her climb, she was moved into a familiar cell, past Peter Billings and her old desk. Her escort collapsed into Deputy Marnes's squeaking chair, complaining of exhaustion.

Juliette could feel the shell that had formed around her during the long three days, that hard enamel of numbness and disbelief. People didn't talk softer; they just sounded that way. They didn't stand further from her; they just seemed more distant.

She sat on the lone cot and listened to Peter Billings charge her with conspiracy. A data drive hung in a limp plastic bag like a pet fish that had gobbled all its water and now lay dead. Dug out of the incinerator, somehow. Its edges were blackened. A scroll was unspooled, only partly pulped. Details of her computer search were listed. She knew most of what they had found was Holston's data, not hers. She wasn't sure what the point would be of telling them this. They already had enough for several cleanings.

A judge stood beside Peter in his black overalls while her sins were listed, as if anyone were really there to decide her fate. Juliette knew the decision had already been made, and who had made it.

Scottie's name was mentioned, but she didn't catch the context. It could have been that the e-mail on his account had been discovered. It could have been that they were going to pin his death on her, just in case. Bones buried with bones, keeping the secrets held between them safe.

She tuned them out and instead watched over her shoulder as a small tornado formed on the flats and spun toward the hills. It eventually dissipated as it crashed into the gentle slope, dissolving like so many cleaners, thrown to the caustic breeze and left to waste away.

Bernard never showed himself. Too afraid or too smug, Jules would never know. She peered down at her hands, at the thin trace of grease deep under her nails, and knew that she was already dead. It didn't matter, somehow. There was a line of bodies behind and before her. She was just the shuffling present, the cog in the machine, spinning and gnashing its metal teeth until that one gear wore down, until the slivers of her self broke loose and did more damage, until she needed to be pulled, cast off, and replaced with another.

Pam brought her oatmeal and fried potatoes from the cafeteria, her favorite. She left it steaming outside the bars. Notes were ported up from Mechanical all day and passed through to her. She was glad none of her friends visited. Their silent voices were more than enough.

Juliette's eyes did the crying, the rest of her too numb to shake or sob. She read the sweet notes while tears dripped on her thighs. Knox's was a simple apology. She imagined he would rather have murdered and done something—even if he were cast out for the attempt—than made the impotent display his note said he would regret all his life. Others sent spiritual messages, promises to see her on the other side, quotes from memorized books. Shirly maybe knew her best and gave her an update on the generator and the new centrifuge for the refinery. She told her all would remain well, and largely because of her. This elicited the faintest of sobs from Juliette. She rubbed the charcoal letters with her fingers, transferring some of her friends' black thoughts to herself.

She was left at last with Walker's note, the only one she couldn't figure out. As the sun set over the harsh landscape, the wind dying down for the night and allowing the dust to settle, she read his words over and over, trying to deduce what he meant.

> Jules—
>
> No fear. Now is for laughing. The truth is a joke and they're good in Supply.
>
> —Walk

• • •

She wasn't sure how she fell asleep, only that she woke up and found notes like peeled chips of paint around her cot, more of them slipped between the bars overnight. Juliette turned her head and peered through the darkness, realizing someone was there. A man stood behind the bars. When she stirred, he pulled away, a wedding band singing with the sound of steel on steel. She rose hurriedly from the cot and rushed to the bars on sleepy legs. She grabbed them with trembling hands and peered through the darkness as the figure melded with the black.

"Dad—?" she called out, reaching through the grate.

But he didn't turn. The tall figure quickened his pace, slipping into the void, a mirage now, as well as a distant childhood memory.

The following sunrise was something to behold. There was a rare break in the low dark clouds that allowed visible rays of golden smoke to slide sideways across the hills. Juliette lay in her cot, watching the dimness fade to light, her cheek resting on her hands, the smell of cold untouched oatmeal drifting from outside the bars. She thought of the men and women in IT working through the past three nights to construct a suit tailored for her, their blasted parts ported up from Supply. The suit would be timed to last her just long enough, to get her through the cleaning but no further.

In all the ordeal of her handcuffed climb, the days and nights of numb acceptance, the thought of the actual cleaning had never occurred to her until now, on the very morning of that duty. She felt, with absolute certainty, that she would not perform the act. She knew they all said this, every cleaner, and that they all experienced some magical, perhaps spiritual, transformation on the threshold of their deaths and performed nonetheless. But she had no one up top to clean for. She wasn't the first cleaner from Mechanical, but she was determined to be the first to refuse.

She said as much as Peter took her from her cell and led her to that yellow door. A tech from IT was waiting inside, making last-minute adjustments to her suit.

Juliette listened to his instructions with a clinical detachment. She saw all the weaknesses in the design. She realized—if she hadn't been so busy working two shifts in Mechanical to keep the floods out, the oil in, the power humming—that she could have made a better suit in her sleep. She studied the washers and seals, identical to the kind employed in pumps, but designed, she knew, to break down. The shiny coat of heat tape, applied in overlapping strips to form the skin of the suit, she knew to be purposefully inferior. She nearly pointed these things out to the tech as he promised her the latest and greatest. He zipped her up, tugged on her gloves, helped with her boots, and explained the numbered pockets.

Juliette repeated the mantra from Walker's note: *No fear. No fear. No fear.*

Now is for laughing. The truth is a joke. And they're in good Supply.

The tech checked her gloves and the Velcro seals over her zippers while Juliette puzzled over Walker's note. Why had he capitalized *Supply?* Or was she even remembering it correctly? Now she wasn't sure. A strip of tape went around one boot, then the other. Juliette laughed at the spectacle of it all. It was all so utterly pointless. They should bury her in the dirt farms, where her body might actually do some good.

The helmet came last, handled with obvious care. The tech had her hold it while he adjusted the metal ring collar around her neck. She looked down at her reflection in the visor, her eyes hollow and so much older than she remembered yet so much younger than she felt. Finally, the helmet went on, the room dimmer through the dark glass. The tech reminded her of the argon blast, of the fires that would follow. She would have to get out quickly or die a far worse death inside.

He left her to consider this. The yellow door behind her clanged shut, its wheel spun on the inside as if by a ghost.

Juliette wondered if she should simply stay and succumb to the flames, not give this spiritual awakening a chance to persuade her. What would they say in Mechanical when that tale spiraled its way through the silo? Some would be proud of her obstinacy, she knew. Some would be horrified at her having gone out that way, in a bone-charring inferno. A few might even think she'd not been brave enough to take the first step out the door, that she'd wasted the chance to see the outside with her own eyes.

Her suit crinkled as the argon was pumped into the room, creating enough pressure to temporarily hold the outside toxins at bay. She found herself shuffling toward the door, almost against her will. When it cracked, the plastic sheeting in the room flattened itself against every pipe, against the low-jutting bench, and she knew the end had come. The doors before her parted, the silo splitting like the skin of a pea, giving her a view of the outside through a haze of condensing steam.

One boot slid through that crack, followed by another. And Juliette moved out into the world, dead set on leaving it on her own terms, seeing it for the first time with her own eyes even through this limited portal, this roughly eight-inch-by-two-inch sheet of glass, she suddenly realized.

30

BERNARD WATCHED THE cleaning from the cafeteria while his techs gathered their supplies in Peter's office. It was his habit to view these things alone—his techs rarely joined him. They lugged their equipment out of the office and headed straight for the stairwell. Bernard was ashamed sometimes of the superstitions, the fears, he fostered even in his own men.

First the dome of her helmet, and then the shiny specter of Juliette Nichols staggered aboveground. She lumbered up the ramp, her movements stiff and unsure. Bernard checked the clock on the wall and reached for his cup of juice. He settled back to see if he could gauge another cleaner's reaction to what they were seeing: a world crisp, bright, and clean, studded with soaring life, grass wavering in a fresh breeze, a glimmering acropolis beckoning from over the hills.

He had watched nearly a dozen cleanings in his day, always enjoying that first pirouette as they took in their surroundings. He had seen men who had left families behind dance before the sensors, waving as if to beckon their loved ones out, trying to pantomime all the false goodness displayed on their visor screens, all to no avail, to no audience. He had seen people reaching madly for flying birds, mistaking them for insects much closer to their faces. One cleaner had even gone back down the ramp and presumably beaten on the door as if to signal something, before finally getting to cleaning. What were any of these various reactions but the proud reminder of a system that worked? That no matter the individual psychology, the sight of all their false hopes eventually drove them to do what they promised they wouldn't.

Perhaps that's why Mayor Jahns could never bear to watch. She had no idea what they were seeing, feeling, responding to. She would come up with her weak stomach the next morning and take in a sunrise, mourn in her own way, the rest of the silo granting her some space. But Bernard cherished this transformation, this delusion he and his predecessors had honed to perfection. He smiled and took a sip of fresh fruit juice and observed this Juliette as she staggered around, coming to her misguided senses. There was the barest coat of grime on the sensor lenses, not even worth a hard scrub, but he knew from double cleanings in the past that she would do it anyway. No one had ever not.

He took another sip and turned to the sheriff's office to see if Peter had summoned the courage to come watch, but the door was closed all but a crack. He had high hopes for that boy. Sheriff today, and maybe one day mayor. Bernard might hold the post for a short while, maybe an election or two, but he knew he belonged in IT, that this was not the job for him. Or rather, that his other duties were far more difficult to replace.

He turned away from Peter's office and back to the view—and nearly dropped his paper cup of juice.

The silvery form of Juliette Nichols was already trudging up the hill. The grime on the sensors was still in place.

Bernard stood abruptly, knocking his chair over backward. He staggered toward the wallscreen, almost as if he could chase after her.

And then he watched, dumbfounded, as she strode up that

dark crease and paused for a moment over the still form of two other cleaners. Bernard checked the clock again. Any moment now. Any moment. She would collapse and fumble for her helmet. She would roll in the dusty soil, kicking up a cloud, sliding down that slope until she came to a dead rest.

But the second hand ticked along, and so did Juliette. She left the two cleaners behind, her limbs still climbing with power, her steady gait guiding her far up to the crest of the hill, where she stood, taking in a view of who knew what, before disappearing, impossibly, out of sight.

Bernard's hand was sticky with juice as he raced down the stairwell. He kept the crushed paper cup in his fist for three levels before catching up to his techs and hurling it at their backs. The ball of trash bounced off and went tumbling into space, destined to settle on some distant landing below. Bernard cursed the confused men and kept running, his feet dangerously close to tripping over themselves. A dozen floors down, he nearly collided with the first hopeful climbers ascending to see the second crisp sunrise in the past weeks.

He was sore and winded when he finally made it down to thirty-four, his spectacles sliding around on the sweaty bridge of his nose. He burst through the double doors and yelled for the gate to be opened. A frightened guard complied, scanning the reader with his own ID right before Bernard slammed through the stubby metal arm. He practically ran down the hallway, taking two turns before he got to the most heavily fortified door in the entire silo.

Swiping his card and punching in his security code, he hurried inside, past the thick wall of solid steel. It was hot in the room full of servers. The identical black cases rose from the tiled floor like monuments to what was possible, to the craft and engineering of human endeavor. Bernard walked among them, the sweat gathering in his eyebrows, light glittering in his vision, his upper lip wet with perspiration. He ran his hands along the faces of the machines, the flashing lights like happy eyes trying to dispel his anger, the electrical hum like whispers to their master, hoping to calm him.

Their soothing efforts were in vain. All Bernard felt was a surge of fear. He went over and over what could have gone wrong. It wasn't as if she would survive; she couldn't possibly survive, but his mandate, second only to preserving the data on these machines, was never to let anyone out of sight. It was the highest order. He understood why and trembled from the repercussions of the morning's failure.

He cursed the heat as he reached the server on the far wall. The vents overhead carried cool air from the down deep and deposited it into the server room. Large fans in the back whisked the heat away and pumped it through more ducts down the silo, keeping the cool and dingy nastiness of the triple-digit levels humanely warm. Bernard glared at the vents, remembering the power holiday, the week of rising temperatures that had threatened his servers, all for some generator, and all because of this woman he had just let out of his sight. The memory stoked the flames under his collar. He cursed the design flaw that left the control of those vents down in Mechanical with those grease monkeys, those uncivilized tinkerers. He thought of the ugly and loud machines down there, the smell of leaking exhaust and burning oil. He had only needed to see it once—to kill a man—but even that was too much. Comparing those noisy engines with the sublime servers was enough to make him never want to leave IT. Here was where silicon chips released their tangy scent as they heated under the strain of crunching data. Here was where one could smell the rubber coating the wires, running in parallel, neatly bundled, labeled and coded, and streaming with gigabits of glorious data every second. Here was where he oversaw the refilling of their data drives with all that had been deleted from the last uprising. Here, a man could think, surrounded by machines quietly doing the same.

Somewhere down those vents, however, was the stench of the unclean. Bernard wiped the sweat from his head and rubbed it on the seat of his overalls. The thought of that woman, first *stealing* from him, then rewarded by Jahns with the highest office of law, and now daring to not clean, to wander off... It raised his temperature dangerously.

He reached the server at the end of the row and squeezed between it and the wall to the back. The key kept around his neck slid into the greased innards of the case locks. As he turned each one, he reminded himself that she couldn't have gotten far. And how much trouble could this really cause? More importantly, what had gone wrong? The timing should always be impeccable. It always had been.

The back of the server came free, revealing the mostly empty innards behind. Bernard slipped the key back into his overalls and set the panel of black steel aside, the metal warm to the touch. There was a cloth case fastened inside the server's belly. Bernard loosened the flap and reached inside, extracting the plastic headset. He pulled it down over his ears, adjusted the mic, and unspooled the cord.

He could keep this under control, he thought to himself. He was head of IT. He was mayor. Peter Billings was his man. People liked stasis, and he could maintain the illusion of it. They were afraid of change, and he could conceal it. With him in both offices, who would oppose him? Who was better qualified? He would explain this. Everything would be okay.

Still, he was mightily, uniquely afraid as he located the correct jack and plugged in the cord. There was an immediate beeping sound in the headphones, the connection automatically taking place.

He could still oversee IT from a distance, make sure this never happened again, be more on top of his reports. Everything was under control. He told himself this as his headphones clicked and the beeping stopped. He knew someone had picked up, even if they refused anything in the way of a greeting. He felt there was annoyance hanging in the silence.

Bernard dispensed with the pleasantries as well. He jumped right into what he needed to say.

"Silo one? This is silo eighteen." He licked the sweat off his lips and adjusted his mic. His palms suddenly felt cold and clammy, and he needed to pee.

"We, uh ... we might have a, uh ... slight problem over here ..."

PART 4

THE UNRAVELING

31

The Tragic Historye of Romeus and Juliette

THE WALK WAS LONG, and longer still for her young mind. Though Juliette took few of the steps with her own small feet, it felt as though she and her parents had traveled for weeks. To impatient youth, all things took forever and any kind of waiting was torture.

She rode on her father's shoulders, clutched his chin, her legs wrapped choking around his neck. Riding so high, she had to stoop her head to avoid the undersides of the steps. Clangs from strangers' boots rang out on the treads above her, and sprinkles of rust dust drifted into her eyes.

Juliette blinked and rubbed her face into her father's hair. As excited as she was, the rise and fall of his shoulders made it impossible to stay awake. When he complained of a sore back, she rode a few levels on her mother's hip, fingers interlocked around her neck, her young head lolling as she drifted off to sleep.

She enjoyed the sounds of the traveling, the footfalls and the rhythmic song of her mother and father chatting about adult things, their voices drifting back and forth as she faded in and out.

The journey became a haze of foggy recollections. She awoke to the squealing of pigs through an open door, was vaguely aware of a garden they toured, woke fully to the smell of something sweet and ate a meal—lunch or dinner, she wasn't sure. She hardly stirred that night as she slid from her father's arms into a dark bed. She awoke the next morning beside a cousin she didn't know in an apartment nearly identical to her own. It was a weekend. She could tell by the older kids playing loudly in the hallway instead of getting ready for school. After a cold breakfast, she returned to the stairs with her parents and the sensation that they'd been traveling all their lives instead of just one day. And then the naps returned with their gentle erasure of time.

After another day they arrived at the hundredth landing of the silo's unfathomable depths. She took the last steps herself, her mom and dad holding a hand each, telling her about the significance. She was now in a place called the "down deep," they told her. The bottom third. They steadied her sleepy legs as she wobbled from the last tread of the ninety-ninth stairway to the landing of the hundredth. Her father pointed above the open and busy doors to a large painted number with an incredible third digit:

100

The two circles captivated Juliette. They were like wide-open eyes peering out at the world for the first time. She told her father that she could already count that high.

"I know you can," he said. "It's because you're so smart."

She followed her mother into the bazaar while clutching one of her father's strong and rough hands with both of her own. There were people everywhere. It was loud, but in a good way. A happy noise filled the air as people lifted their voices to be heard—just like a classroom once the teacher was gone.

Juliette felt afraid of getting lost, and so she clung to her father. They waited while her mom bartered for lunch. It required stopping at what felt like a dozen stalls to get the handful of things she needed. Her dad talked a man into letting her lean through a fence to touch a rabbit. The fur was so soft, it was like it wasn't there. Juliette snapped her hand back in fear when the animal turned its head, but it just chewed something invisible and looked at her like it was bored.

The bazaar seemed to go on forever. It wound around and out of sight, even when all the many-colored adult legs were clear enough for her to see to the end. Off to the sides, narrower passages full of more stalls and tents twisted in a maze of colors and sounds, but Juliette wasn't allowed to go down any of these. She stuck with her parents until they arrived at the first set of square steps she'd ever seen in her young life.

"Easy now," her mother told her, helping her up the steps.

"I can do it," she said stubbornly, but took her mom's hand anyway.

"Two and one child," her father said to someone at the top of the steps. She heard the clatter of chits going into a box that sounded full of them. As her father passed through the gate, she saw the man by the box was dressed in all colors and wearing a funny floppy hat that was much too big for him. She tried to get a better look as her mom guided her through the gates, a hand on her back and whispers in her ear to keep up with her father. The gentleman turned his head, bells jangling on his hat, and made a funny face at her, his tongue poking out to the side.

Juliette laughed but still felt half-afraid of the strange man as they found a spot to sit and eat. Her dad dug a thin bedsheet out of his pack and spread it across one of the wide benches. Juliette's mom made her take her shoes off before she stood on the sheet. She held her father's shoulder and looked down the slope of benches and seats toward the wide-open room below. Her father told her the open room was called a "stage." Everything in the down deep had different names.

"What're they doing?" she asked her father. Several men on the stage, dressed as colorfully as the gatesman, were throwing balls up into the air — an impossible number of them — keeping them all from hitting the ground.

Her father laughed. "They're juggling. They're here to entertain us until the play starts."

Juliette wasn't sure she wanted the play to start. This was it, the thing she wanted to see. The jugglers tossed balls and hoops between each other, and Juliette could feel her own arms windmilling as she watched. She tried counting the hoops, but they wouldn't stay in one place long enough.

"Eat your lunch," her mother reminded her, passing her bites of a fruit sandwich.

Juliette was mesmerized. When the jugglers put the balls and hoops away and started chasing one another, falling down and acting silly, she laughed as loudly as the other kids. She looked constantly to her mom and dad to see if they were watching. She tugged on their sleeves, but they just nodded and continued to talk, eat, and drink. When another family sat close and a boy older than her laughed at the jugglers as well, Juliette felt suddenly like she had company. She began to squeal even louder. The jugglers were the brightest things she had ever seen. She could've watched them forever.

But then the lights were dimmed and the play began, and it was boring by comparison. It started off well with a rousing sword fight, but then it was a lot of strange words and a man and woman looking at each other the way her parents did, talking in some funny language.

Juliette fell asleep. She dreamed of flying through the silo with one hundred colorful balls and hoops soaring all around her, always out of reach, the hoops round like the numbers at the end of the bazaar's level – and then she woke up to whistles and applause.

Her parents were standing and yelling while the people on the stage in the funny costumes took several bows. Juliette yawned and looked over at the boy on the bench beside her. He was sleeping with his mouth open, his head in his mom's lap, his shoulders shaking while she clapped and clapped.

They gathered up the sheet and her father carried her down to the stage, where the sword-fighters and strange talkers were speaking to the audience and shaking hands. Juliette wanted to meet the jugglers. She wanted to learn how to make the hoops float in the air. But her parents waited instead until they could speak to one of the ladies, the one who had her hair braided and twisted into drooping curves.

"Juliette," her father told her, lifting her onto the stage, "I want you to meet . . . Juliette." He gestured to the woman in the fluffy dress with the strange hair.

"Is that your real name?" the lady asked, kneeling down and reaching for Juliette's hand.

Juliette pulled it back like it was another rabbit about to bite her, but nodded.

"You were wonderful," her mom told the lady. They shook hands and introduced themselves.

"Did you like the play?" the lady with the funny hair asked.

Juliette nodded. She could sense that she was supposed to and that this made it okay to lie.

"Her father and I came to this show years ago when we first started dating," her mother said. She rubbed Juliette's hair. "We were going to name our first child either Romeus or Juliette."

"Well, be glad you had a girl, then," the lady said, smiling.

Her parents laughed, and Juliette was beginning to be less afraid of this woman with the same name as her.

"Do you think we could get your autograph?" Her father let

go of her shoulder and rummaged in his pack. "I have a program in here somewhere."

"Why not a script for this young Juliette?" The lady smiled at her. "Are you learning your letters?"

"I can count to a hundred," Juliette said proudly.

The woman paused, then smiled. Juliette watched her as she stood and crossed the stage, her dress flowing in a way that overalls never could. The lady returned from behind a curtain with a tiny book of papers held fast with brass pins. She accepted a charcoal from Juliette's father and wrote her name large and curly across the cover.

The woman pressed the collection of papers into her small hands. "I want you to have this, Juliette of the silo."

Her mother protested. "Oh, we couldn't. That's too much paper—"

"She's only five," her father said.

"I have another," the lady assured them. "We make our own. I want her to have it."

She reached out and touched Juliette's cheek, and this time Juliette didn't pull away. She was too busy flipping through the papers, looking at all the curly notes handwritten along the sides beside the printed words. One word, she noticed, was circled over and over among all the others. She couldn't make out many of them, but this one she could read. It was her name. It was at the beginning of so many sentences:

Juliette.

This was her. She looked up at the lady, understanding at once why her parents had brought her there, why they had walked so far and for so long.

"Thank you," she said, remembering her manners.

And then, after some consideration:

"I'm sorry I fell asleep."

32

A glooming peace this morning with it brings;
The sun, for sorrow, will not show his head.
Go hence, to have more talk of these sad things;
Some shall be pardon'd, and some punished.

IT WAS THE MORNING of the worst cleaning of Lukas's life—and for once he considered going into work, ignoring the paid holiday, to pretend it was a day like any other. He sat at the foot of his bed as he worked up the courage to move, one of his many star charts in his lap. Lightly with his fingers, so as not to smear the marks away, he caressed the charcoal outline of one star in particular.

It wasn't a star like the others. Those were simple dots on a meticulous grid with details of date sighted, location, and intensity. This wasn't that kind of star—not one that lasted nearly so long. It was the five-pointed kind, the outline of a sheriff's badge. He remembered drawing the shape while she was talking to him one night, the steel on her chest glowing faintly as it caught the weak light from the stairwell. He remembered her voice being magical, the way she carried herself mesmerizing, and her arrival into his boring routine had been as unexpected as the parting of clouds.

He also remembered how she had turned away from him in her cell two nights ago, had tried to save his feelings by pushing him away.

Lukas had no more tears. He had spent most of the night shedding them for this woman he hardly knew. And now he wondered what he would do with his day, with his life. The thought of her out there, doing anything for them—cleaning—made him sick. He wondered if that was why he'd had no appetite for two days. Some deep part of his gut must have known he'd never keep anything down, even if he forced himself to eat.

He set the star chart aside and dropped his face into his palms. He rested there, so tired, trying to convince himself to just get up and go to work. If he went to work, at least he'd be distracted. He tried to remember where he'd left off in the server room last week. Was it the number eight tower that had gone down again? Sammi had suggested he swap out the control board, but Lukas had suspected a bad cable. That's what he'd been doing, he remembered now: toning out the Ethernet runs. It's what he should have been doing right then, that very day. Anything but sitting around on a holiday, feeling like he could be physically ill over a woman about whom he'd done little more than tell his mother.

Lukas stood and shrugged on the same pair of overalls he'd worn the day before. He remained there a moment, staring at his bare feet, wondering why he'd gotten up. Where was he going? His mind was completely blank, his body numb. He wondered if he could stand there, unmoving, his stomach twisted in knots, for the rest of his life. Someone would eventually find him, wouldn't they? Dead and stiff, standing upright, a statue of a corpse.

He shook his head and these black thoughts loose and looked for his boots.

He found them; it was an accomplishment. Lukas had done something by getting himself dressed.

He left his room and ambled toward the landing, weaving around kids squealing from another day off school, parents trying to corral them and get their boots and overalls on. The commotion was little more than background noise for Lukas. It was a hum, like the aches in his legs from the long climb down to see her and the even longer climb back up. He stepped out onto the apartment's landing and felt a habitual tug upward toward the cafeteria. All he could think about was all he had thought of for the past week: making it through another day so he could go up top for the chance to see her.

It suddenly occurred to Lukas that he still could. He wasn't one for sunrises — he much preferred the twilight and the stars — but if he wanted to see her, all he had to do was climb to the cafeteria and scan the landscape. There would be a new body there, a new suit with the shine still on it glimmering in whatever weak rays the sun dribbled through those blasted clouds.

He could see the image clearly in his head: her uncomfortable sprawl — legs twisted, arm pinned, helmet turned to the side, gazing back at the silo. Sadder still, he saw himself decades later, a lonely old man sitting in front of that gray wallscreen and drawing not star charts but landscapes. The same landscapes over and over, looking up at a wasting might-have-been, sketching that same still pose while weeping tears that dripped and turned charcoal to mud.

He would be like Marnes, that poor man. And thinking of the deputy, who died with no one to bury him, it reminded Lukas of the last thing Juliette had told him. She had begged him to find someone, to not be like her, to never be alone.

He gripped landing fifty's cool steel railing and leaned over. Looking down, he could watch the stairwell drill its way deep into the earth. The landing for fifty-six was visible below, the several landings between jutting off at unseen angles. It was hard to gauge the distance but he figured it was more than enough. No need to walk down to eighty-two, which most jumpers preferred for its long clear path down to ninety-nine.

Suddenly, he saw himself in flight, tumbling down, arms and legs splayed. He reckoned he would just miss the landing. One of the railings would catch him and saw him near in half. Or maybe if he jumped out a little further, maybe if he aimed his head, he could make it quick.

He straightened, feeling a twinge of fear and a rush of adrenaline from picturing the fall, the end, so vividly. He glanced around and checked the morning traffic to see if anyone was watching him. He had seen other adults peer over railings before. He'd always assumed bad thoughts were going through their heads. Because he knew, growing up in the silo, that only children dropped physical things from the landings. By the time you got older, you knew to keep a grip on all that you could. Eventually, it was something else that slipped away, something else you lost that tumbled down through the heart of the silo, that made you ponder leaping after—

The landing shivered with the beat of a hurrying porter; the sound of bare feet slapping against steel treads came next and spiraled closer. Lukas slid away from the railing and tried to focus on what he was doing that day. Maybe he should just crawl back into bed and sleep, kill some hours with unconsciousness.

As he attempted to summon some sliver of motivation, the speeding porter flew past, and Lukas caught a glimpse of the boy's face twisted in consternation. Even as he sped out of sight—his pace swift and reckless—the image of his worry remained vividly lodged in Lukas's mind.

And Lukas knew. As the rapid patter of the boy's feet wound

deeper into the earth, he knew something had happened that morning, something up top, something newsworthy about the cleaning.

A seed of hope. Some wishful kernel buried deep, where he was loath to acknowledge it lest it poison or choke him, began to sprout. Maybe the cleaning never happened. Was it possible her banishment had been reconsidered? The people of Mechanical had sent up a petition. Hundreds of daring signatures, risking their own necks to save hers. Had the mad gesture from the down deep worn the judges down?

That tiny seed of hope sprang roots. It grew vinelike through Lukas's chest, filling him with an urgency to run up and see for himself. He left the railing, and the dream of leaping after his worries, and pushed his way through the morning crowd. Whispers, he noticed, were already forming in the porter's wake. He wasn't the only one who had noticed.

As he joined the up-bound traffic, he realized the aches in his legs from the days before had vanished. He prepared to pass the slow-moving family in front of him—when he heard the loud squawk of a radio behind him.

Lukas turned to find Deputy Marsh a few treads back fumbling for the radio on his hip, a small cardboard box clutched to his chest, a sheen of sweat on his forehead.

Lukas stopped and held the railing, waiting for the mids deputy to reach him.

"Marsh!"

The deputy finally got the volume down on his radio and glanced up. He nodded to Lukas. The both of them squeezed against the railing as a worker and his shadow passed them, heading upward.

"What's the news?" Lukas asked. He knew the deputy well, and he knew he might spill it for free.

Marsh swiped his forehead and moved the box into the crook of his other arm. "That Bernard is whoopin' my ass this mornin'," he complained. "Done climbed *enough* this week!"

"No, what of the *cleaning*?" Lukas asked. "A porter just hurried by like he'd seen a ghost."

Deputy Marsh glanced up the steps. "I was told to bring her things to thirty-four as quick as grease. Hank nearly killed himself bringing 'em partway up to me." He started up the stairs as if he couldn't afford to stay. "Look, I've gotta keep movin' if I wanna keep my job."

Lukas held his arm, and traffic swelled below them as annoyed climbers squeezed past and against the occasional traveler heading down. "Did the cleaning go through or not?" Lukas demanded.

Marsh sagged against the railing. Quiet chatter popped through his radio.

"No," he whispered, and Lukas felt as though he could fly. He could fly straight up the space between the stairs and the concrete heart of the silo, could soar around the landings, could go fifty levels at a leap—

"She went out, but she didn't clean," Marsh said, his voice low but laced with words sharp enough to pierce Lukas's dreams. "She wandered over them hills—"

"Wait. What?"

Marsh nodded, and sweat dripped from the deputy's nose. "Plumb out of sight," he hissed, like a radio turned down low. "Now I've got to get her things up to Bernar—"

"I'll do it," Lukas said, reaching out his hands. "I'm going to thirty-four anyway."

Marsh shifted the box. The poor deputy seemed liable to collapse at any moment. Lukas begged him, just as he had two days earlier in order to see Juliette in her cell. "Let me take them up for you," he said. "You know Bernard won't mind. He and I are good friends, just like you and I have always been . . ."

Deputy Marsh wiped his lip and nodded ever so slightly, thinking on this.

"Look, I'm going up anyway," Lukas said. He found himself slowly taking the box from an exhausted Marsh, even though the waves of emotion surging through his own body made it difficult to focus. The traffic on the stairs had become background noise. The idea that Juliette might still be in the silo had slipped away, but the news that she hadn't cleaned, that she had made it over the hills — this filled him with something else. It touched the part of him that yearned to map the stars. It meant no one would ever have to watch her waste away.

"You'll be careful with that," Marsh said. His eyes were on the box, now tucked into Lukas's arms.

"I'll guard it with my life," Lukas told him. "Trust me."

Marsh nodded to let him know he did. And Lukas hurried up the stairs, ahead of those rising to celebrate the cleaning, the weight of Juliette's belongings rattling softly in a box tucked tightly against his chest.

33

Thy old groans ring yet in my ancient ears.

Walker the electrician bent over a cluttered workbench and adjusted his magnifier. The great bulbous lens was attached to his head with a hoop that might've been uncomfortable had he not been wearing it for most of his sixty-two years. As he pushed the glass into position, the small black chip on the green electronics board came into crystal focus. He could see each of the silver metal legs bent out from its body like the limbs of a spider, the tiny feet seemingly trapped in silver puddles of frozen steel.

With the tip of his finest soldering iron, Walker prodded a spot of silver while he worked the suction bulb with his foot. The metal around the chip's tiny foot melted and was pulled through a straw, one little leg of sixteen free.

He was about to move to the other—he had stayed up all night pulling fried chips to distract his mind from other things—when he heard the recognizable patter of that new porter skittering down his hall.

Walker dropped the board and hot iron on the workbench and hurried to his door. He held the jamb and leaned out as the kid ran past.

"Porter!" he yelled, and the boy reluctantly stopped. "What news, boy?"

The kid smiled, revealing the whites of youth. "I've got *big* news," he said. "Cost you a chit, though."

Walker grunted with disgust but dug into his coveralls. He waved the kid over. "You're that Samson boy, right?"

The kid bobbed his head, his hair dancing around his youthful face.

"Shadowed under Gloria, didn't you?"

The kid nodded again as his eyes followed the silver chit drawn from Walker's rattling pockets.

"You know, Gloria used to take pity on an old man with no family and no life. Trusted me with news, she did."

"Gloria's dead," the boy said, lifting his palm.

"That she is," Walker said with a sigh. He dropped the chit into the child's outstretched palm, then waved his aged and spotted own for the news. He was dying to know everything and would have gladly paid ten chits. "The details, child. Don't skip a one."

"No cleaning, Mr. Walker!"

Walker's heart missed a beat. The boy turned his shoulder to run on.

"Stay, boy! What do you mean, no cleaning? She's been set free?"

The porter shook his head. His hair was long, wild, and seemingly built for flying up and down the staircase. "Nosir. She *refused!*"

The child's eyes were electric, his grin huge with the possession of such knowledge. No one had ever refused to clean in his lifetime. In Walker's, either. Maybe not ever. Walker felt a surge of pride in his Juliette.

The boy waited a moment. He seemed eager to run off.

"Anything else?" Walker asked.

Samson nodded and glanced at Walker's pockets.

Walker let out a long sigh of disgust for what had become of this generation. He dug into his pocket with one hand and waved impatiently with the other.

"She's *gone,* Mr. Walker!"

He snatched the chit from Walker's palm.

"Gone? As in dead? Speak up, son!"

Samson's teeth flashed as the chit disappeared into his overalls. "Nosir. Gone as in over the hill. No cleaning, Mr. Walker, just strode right over and out of view. Gone to the city, and Mr. Bernard witnessed the whole thing!"

The young porter slapped Walker on the arm, needing, obviously, to strike something with his enthusiasm. He swiped his hair off his face, smiled large, and turned to run along his route, his feet lighter and pockets heavier from the tale.

Walker was left stunned in the doorway. He gripped the jamb with an iron claw lest he tumble out into the world. He stood there swaying, looking down at the pile of dishes he'd slipped outside the night before. He glanced over his shoulder at the disheveled cot that had been calling his name all night. Smoke still rose from the soldering iron. He turned away from the hall, which would soon be pattering and clinking with the sounds of first shift, and unplugged the iron before he started another fire.

He remained there a moment, thinking about Jules, thinking about this news. He wondered if she'd gotten his note in time, if it had lessened the awful fear he'd felt in his gut for her.

Walker returned to the doorway. The down deep was stirring. He felt a powerful tug to go out there, to cross that threshold, to be a part of the unprecedented.

Shirly would probably be by soon with his breakfast and to take away his dishes. He could wait for her, maybe talk a bit. Perhaps this spell of insanity would pass.

But the thought of waiting, of the minutes stacking up like

work orders, of not knowing how far Juliette had gotten or what reaction the others might be having to her not cleaning, pressed him into motion.

Walker lifted his foot and reached out past his doorway, his boot hovering over untrammeled ground.

He took a deep breath, fell forward, and caught himself on it. And suddenly, he felt like an intrepid explorer himself. There he was, fortysomething years later, teetering down a familiar hallway, one hand brushing the steel walls, a corner coming up, around which his eyes could remember nothing.

And Walker became one more old soul pushing into the great unknown, his brain dizzy with what he might find out there.

34

Is there no pity sitting in the clouds
that sees into the bottom of my grief?
O sweet my mother, cast me not away!

THE HEAVY STEEL DOORS of the silo parted, and a great cloud of argon billowed out with an angry hiss. The cloud seemed to materialize from nowhere, the compressed gas blossoming into a whipped froth as it met the warmer, less dense air beyond.

Juliette Nichols stuck one boot through that narrow gap. The doors opened only partway to hold back the deadly toxins, to force the argon through with pent-up pressure, so she had to turn sideways to squeeze past, her bulky suit rubbing against the thick doors. All she could think of was the raging fire that would soon fill the airlock. Its flames seemed to lick at her back, forcing her to flee.

She pulled her other boot through — and she suddenly found herself outside.

Outside.

There was nothing above her helmeted head but clouds, sky, and the unseen stars.

She lumbered forward, emerging through the fog of hissing argon to find herself on an upward-sloping ramp, the corners by the walls caked high with wind-trapped dirt. It was easy to forget that the top floor of the silo was belowground. The view from her old office and the cafeteria created an illusion of standing on the surface of the earth, head up in the wild air, but that was because the sensors were located there.

Juliette looked down at the numbers on her chest and remembered what she was supposed to be doing. She trudged up the ramp, head down, focusing on her boots. She wasn't sure how she even moved, if it was the numbness one succumbed to in the face of execution—or if it was just automated self-preservation, simply a move away from the coming inferno in the airlock, her body delaying the inevitable because it couldn't think or plan beyond the next fistful of seconds.

As Juliette reached the top of the ramp, her head emerged into a lie, a grand and gorgeous untruth. Green grass covered the hills like newly laid carpet. The skies were intoxicatingly blue, the clouds bleached white like fancy linen, the air peppered with soaring things.

She spun in place and took in the spectacular fabrication. It was as if she'd been dropped into a book from her youth, a book where animals talked and children flew and gray was never found.

Even knowing it wasn't real, knowing that she was looking through an eight-by-two-inch fib, the temptation to *believe* was overwhelming. She wanted to. She wanted to forget what she knew of IT's devious program, to forget everything she and Walker had discussed, and to fall instead to the soft grasses that weren't there, to roll around in the life that wasn't, to strip off the ridiculous suit and go screaming happily across the lying landscape.

She looked down at her hands, clenched and unclenched them as much as the thick gloves would allow. This was her coffin. Her thoughts scattered as she fought to remember what was real and what was a false hope laid on top by IT and her visor. The sky was not real. The grass was not real. Her *death* was real. The ugly world she had always known was real. And then, for just a moment, she remembered that she was supposed to be doing something. She was supposed to be cleaning.

She turned and gazed at the sensor tower, seeing it for the first time. It was a sturdy block of steel and concrete with a rusted and pitted ladder running up one side. The bulging sensor pods were stuck like warts on the faces of the tower. Juliette reached for her chest, grabbed one of the scrubbing pads, and tore it loose. The note from Walker continued to stream through her mind: *No fear.*

She took the coarse wool pad and rubbed it against the arm of her suit. The heat tape wrapping did not peel, did not flake away like the stuff she had once stolen from IT, the tape they had engineered to fail. This was the brand of heat tape Juliette was used to working with, Mechanical's design.

They're good in Supply, Walker's note had said. The good had referred to the *people* of Supply. After years of helping Juliette score spares when she needed them most, they had done something extraordinary for her. While she had spent three days climbing stairs and three lonely nights in three different holding cells on her way to banishment, they had replaced IT's materials with those from Mechanical. They had fulfilled their orders for parts in a most devious way, and it must've been at Walker's behest. IT had then – unwittingly and for once – built a suit designed to *last,* not to disintegrate.

Juliette smiled. Her death, however certain, was delayed. She took a long look at the sensors, relaxed her fingers, and dropped the wool pad into the fake grass. Turning for the nearest hill, she tried her best to ignore the false colors and the layers of life projected on top of what was truly there. Rather than give in to the euphoria, she concentrated on the way her boots clomped on the packed earth, noted the feel of the angry wind buffeting against her suit, listened for the faint hiss as grains of sand pelted her helmet from all sides. There was a terrifying world around her, one she could be dimly aware of if she concentrated hard enough, a world she knew but could no longer see.

She started up the steep slope and headed vaguely toward the gleaming metropolis over the horizon. There was little thought of making it there. All she wanted was to die beyond the hills where no one would have to watch her rot away, so that Lukas the star hunter would not be afraid to come up at twilight for fear of seeing her still form.

And suddenly, it felt good to simply be walking, to have some purpose. She would take herself out of sight. It was a more solid goal than that false city, which she knew to be crumbling.

Partway up the hill, she came to a pair of large rocks. Juliette started to dodge around them before she realized where she was, that she had followed the most gentle path up the crook of two colliding slopes, and here lay the most horrible lie of them all.

Holston and Allison. Hidden from her by the magic of the visor. Covered by a mirage of stone.

There were no words. Nothing to see, nothing to say. She glanced down the hill and spotted other sporadic boulders resting in the grass, their position not random at all but where cleaners of old had collapsed.

She turned away, leaving these sad things behind. It was impossible to know how much time she had, how long to hide her body from those who might gloat — and the few who might mourn.

Climbing toward the crest of the hill, her legs still sore from ascending the silo, Juliette witnessed the first rips in IT's deceitful veil. New portions of the sky and the distant city came into view, parts that had been obscured by the hill from down below. There seemed to be a break in the program, a limit to its lies.

While the upper levels of the distant monoliths appeared whole and gleamed in the false sunlight, below these sharp panes of glass and bright steel lay the rotted dinginess of an abandoned world. She could see straight through the bottom levels of many of the buildings, and with their heavy tops projected onto them, they seemed liable to topple at any moment.

To the side, the extra and unfamiliar buildings had no supports at all, no foundations. They hung in the air with dark sky beneath them. This same dark vista of gray clouds and lifeless hills stretched out across the low horizon, a hard line of painted blue where the visor's program met its end.

Juliette puzzled over the incompleteness of IT's deceit. Was it because they themselves had no idea what lay beyond the hills, and so couldn't guess what to modify? Or did they deem it not worth the effort, knowing nobody would ever make it this far? Whatever the reason, the jarring and illogical nature of the view left her dizzy. She concentrated instead on her feet, taking those last dozen steps up the painted green hill until she reached the crest.

At the top, she paused while heavy gusts of wind buffeted against her, causing her to lean into their turbulence. She scanned the horizon and saw that she stood on the divide between two worlds. Down the slope before her, on a landscape her eyes had never before seen, lay a bare world of dust and parched earth, of wind flurries and small tornadoes, of air that could kill. Here was new land, and yet it looked more familiar to her than anything she'd encountered thus far.

She turned and peered back along the path she had just climbed, at the tall grasses blowing in the gentle breeze, at occasional flowers dipping their heads at her, at the bright blue and brilliant white overhead. It was an evil concoction, inviting but false.

Juliette took one last admiring gaze at this illusion. She noted how the round depression in the center of the hills seemed to mark the outline of her silo's flat roof, the rest of her habitable home nestled deep in the belly of the soil. The way the land rose up all around made it look as though a hungry god had spooned out a large bite of the earth. With a heavy heart, she realized that the world she had grown up in was now closed off to her, that her home and her people were safe behind bolted doors, and she must be resigned to her fate. She had been cast off. Her time was short. And so she turned her back on the alluring view and bright colors to face the dusty, the dead, and the real.

As she started down the hill, Juliette pulled cautiously on the air in her suit. She knew Walker had given her the gift of time, time no cleaner before her had ever had, but how much? And for what? She had already reached her goal, had managed to haul herself out of the sensors' sight, so why was she still walking, still staggering down this foreign hill? Was it inertia? The pull of gravity? The sight of the unknown?

She was barely down the slope, heading in the general direction of the crumbling city, when she stopped to survey the unfamiliar landscape before her. The elevation made it possible to choose a path for her final walk, this maiden walk, across the tall dunes of dry earth. And that's when she saw, gazing out toward the rusting city beyond, that the hollow in which her silo resided was no accident. The hills bore a clear pattern as they stretched into the distance. It was one circular bowl after another, the earth rising up between them as if to shield each spooned-out bite from the caustic wind.

Juliette descended into the next bowl, pondering this, watching her footing as she went. She kicked aside the larger rocks and controlled her breathing. She knew from working deep in the flooded basins, swimming beneath the muck that burly men cringed from as she unclogged the drains, that air could be conserved through calmness. She glanced up, wondering if she had enough in the suit to cross this bowl and make it up the next great hill.

And that's when she saw the slender tower rising from the center of the bowl, its exposed metal glinting in the sparse sunlight. The landscape here was untouched by the program in her visor; reality passed through her helmet untarnished. And seeing this, the familiar sensor tower, she wondered if perhaps she'd gotten turned around, if she had surveyed the world one too many times from the crest of the hill, if she was in fact trudging back toward her silo, covering ground already crossed before.

The sight of a dead cleaner wasting away in the dirt seemed to confirm this. It was a bare outline, ribbons of an old suit, the husk of a helmet.

She stopped and touched the dome of the helmet with the toe of her boot, and the shell crumbled and caved in. Whatever flesh and bone had been inside had long ago drifted off on the winds.

Juliette looked down the hill for the sleeping couple, but the crook of those two dunes was nowhere in sight. She suddenly felt bewildered and lost. She wondered if the air had finally worked past the seals and heat tape, if her brain was succumbing to noxious fumes, but no. She was nearer the city, still walking toward that skyline, the tops of which were still rendered whole and gleaming, the sky above them blue and spotted with bright clouds.

It meant this tower below her . . . was not hers. And these dunes, these great mounds of dead earth, were not meant to block out the winds or hold back the air. They were meant to shield curious eyes. To block this sight, this view, of some *other*.

35

One, two, and the third in your bosom.

LUKAS HELD THE SMALL box tightly against his chest as he hiked up to the landing on thirty-eight. Here was a mixed-use level of offices, shops, a plastics factory, and one of the small water treatment plants. He pushed through the doors and hurried down corridors quiet from the day's cleaning until he reached the main pump control room. His IT master key allowed him inside. The room housed a tall and familiar computer cabinet from his Tuesday maintenance schedule. Lukas left the overhead light off to keep the small window in the door darkened to passersby. He slid behind the tall server rack and the wall, scooted to the ground, and fished his flashlight out of his overalls.

In the soft red glow of his night light, Lukas gently peeled the flaps of the box apart, revealing the contents inside.

The guilt was immediate. It punctured the anticipation, the thrill of discovery, of intimacy. It wasn't guilt from defying his boss or lying to Deputy Marsh, nor of delaying the delivery of items he had been told were important. It was the violation of her things. The reminder of her fate. Here were Juliette's remains. Not her body, which was lost and gone, but the remnants of the life she had lived.

He took a heavy breath, considered closing the flaps and forgetting the contents, and then thought of what would become of them anyway. His friends in IT would probably be the ones to paw through them. They would tear open the box and trade items like kids swapping candy. They would desecrate her.

He bent the flaps open further and decided to honor her instead.

He adjusted his light and saw a stack of silo vouchers on top, wrapped in a piece of wire. He pulled these out and flipped through them. They were vacation vouchers. Dozens of them. He lifted them to his nose and puzzled over the tangy scent of grease emanating from the box.

A few expired meal cards lay underneath these vouchers, the corner of an ID badge poking out. Lukas reached for the badge, coded gold from her job as sheriff. He searched for another ID among the various scattered cards, but it appeared it had not yet been replaced with whatever color Mechanical used. There hadn't been that much time between her being fired for one offense and being put to death for another.

He took a moment to study the picture on the badge. It looked recent, just as he remembered her. Her hair was tied back tight, leaving it flat on her head. He could see loose curls sticking out at either side of her neck and remembered the first night he had watched her work, how she had braided her long hair herself while she sat alone in a pool of light, peering at page after page in those folders of hers.

He ran his finger over the picture and laughed when he saw her expression. Her forehead was wrinkled, her eyes narrowed, as if trying to determine what the photographer was attempting or why in the heavens it was taking so long. He covered his mouth to prevent the laugh from becoming a sob.

The vouchers went back into the box, but the ID slid into the breast pocket of his overalls as if by Juliette's own stubborn accord. The next thing that caught his eye was a silver multitool, new looking, a slightly different model from his own. He grabbed this and leaned forward to pull his own tool out of his back pocket. He compared the two, opening a few of the tools on hers and admiring the smooth motion and neat click as each attachment locked into place. Taking a moment to first clean his, wiping his prints off and removing a bit of melted rubber wire casing, he switched the tools. He decided he would rather carry this reminder of her and have his own tool disappear into storage or be pawned off to a stranger who wouldn't appreciate –

Lukas froze at the sound of footsteps and laughter. He held his breath and waited for someone to come in, for the overhead lights to burst on. The server clicked and whirred beside him. The noise in the hallway receded, the laughter fading.

He was pushing his luck, he knew, but there was more in the box to see. He rummaged inside again and found an ornate wooden box, a valuable antique. It was just slightly bigger than his palm, and he took a moment to figure out how to open it. The first thing he saw as the top slid away was a ring, a woman's wedding ring. It could've been solid gold, but it was difficult to tell. The red glow from his flashlight tended to wash out colors, causing everything to appear dull and lifeless.

He checked for an inscription but found none. It was a curious artifact, this ring. He was certain Juliette hadn't been wearing it when he'd known her, and he wondered if it was a relative's, or a thing passed down from before the uprising. He placed it back in the wooden box and reached for the other item inside, a bracelet of some sort. No, not a bracelet. As he pulled it out, he saw that it was a watch, the face so tiny it melded with the design of the jeweled strap. Lukas studied the face, and after a moment he realized his eyes or the red flashlight were playing tricks on him. Or were they? He looked closely to be sure—and saw that one of the impossibly thin hands was ticking away the time. The thing worked.

Before he could contemplate the challenge of concealing such an item or the consequences of being discovered with it, Lukas slid the watch into his chest pocket. He looked at the ring sitting alone in the box, and after a moment's hesitation, palmed this and stashed it away as well. He fished through the cardboard box and gathered some of the loose chits at the bottom and placed these into the antique box before sealing it shut and returning it.

What was he doing? He could feel a trickle of sweat work its way from his scalp and run the length of his jawline. The heat from the rear of the busy computer seemed to intensify. He dipped his head and lifted his shoulder to dab the itchy run of sweat away. There was more in the box, and he couldn't help himself: he had to keep looking.

He found a small notepad and flipped through it. It contained one to-do list after another, all of the items neatly crossed out. He replaced this and reached for a folded piece of paper at the bottom of the box, then realized it was more than a piece. He pulled out a thick collection of papers held together with brass fasteners. Across the top, in handwriting similar to that in the notebook, was printed:

Main Generator Control Room Operation Manual

He flipped it open and found inscrutable diagrams and bulleted notes lining the margins. It looked like something she'd put together herself, either as a reminder from piecing the room's operation together over time, or perhaps as a helpful guide for others. The paper was recycled without being pulped, he saw. She had just written on the back. He flipped the manual over and checked the lines and lines of printed text on the opposite side. There were notes in the margins and a name circled over and over:

Juliette. Juliette. Juliette.

He flipped the manual over and surveyed the rear, only to find it was the original front. *The Tragic Historye of Romeus and Juliette,* it said. It was a play. One Lukas had heard of. In front of him, a fan kicked on in the heart of the server, blowing air over warm chips of silicon and wire. He wiped the sweat from his forehead and tucked the bound play back into the box. He neatly arranged the other items on top and folded the cardboard flaps together. Wiggling back to his feet, Lukas doused his light and shoved it back into his pocket, where it nestled against Juliette's multi-tool. With the box secured under one arm, he patted his chest with his other hand and felt her watch, her ring, and her ID there with its picture of her. All tight against his torso.

Lukas shook his head. He wondered what the hell he was thinking as he stole out of the small and dark room, a tall panel of winking and blinking lights watching him go.

36

Eyes, look your last!
Arms, take your last embrace! And, lips,
O you the doors of breath, seal with a righteous kiss
a dateless bargain to engrossing death!

THE BODIES WERE EVERYWHERE. Covered in dust and dirt, suits worn down by the toxic eaters that lived in the winds. Juliette found herself stumbling over more and more of them. And then, they were constant, a mass of boulders jumbled together. A few were in suits similar to her own, but most wore rags that had been eaten away into streamers. When the wind blew past her boots and across the bodies, strips of clothing waved like kelp in the down deep's fish farms. Unable to pick her way around them all, she found herself stepping over the remains, working her way closer and closer to the sensor tower, the bodies easily in the hundreds, possibly the thousands.

These weren't people from her silo, she realized. However obvious, the sensation was startling. *Other* people. That they were dead did nothing to diminish the soul-shattering reality that people had lived so close and she had never known. Juliette had somehow crossed an uninhabitable void, had gone from one universe to another, was possibly the first ever to have done so, and here was a graveyard of foreign souls, of people just like her having lived and died in a world so similar and so near to her own.

She made her way through dead bodies thick as crumbling rock, the forms becoming indistinguishable from one another. They were piled high in places, and she had to choose her path carefully. As she neared the ramp leading down to this *other* silo, she found herself needing to step on a body or two in order to pass. It looked as though they'd been trying to get away and had scampered over one another, creating their own small hills in a mad attempt to reach the real ones. But then, when she reached the ramp leading down, she saw the crush of bodies at the steel airlock door and realized they had been trying to get *back in.*

Her own imminent death loomed large — a constant awareness, a new sense worn on her skin and felt keenly in every pore. She would soon join these bodies, and somehow she was not afraid. She had passed through that fear on the crest of the hill and was now in new lands, seeing new things, a terrible gift for which she had to be grateful. Curiosity drove her forward, or maybe it was the mentality of this frozen crowd, all in scrambling repose, bodies swimming over each other and reaching toward the doors below.

She swam among them. Waded, where she had to. She stepped through broken and hollow bodies, kicked aside bones and tattered remains, and fought her way to the partly cracked doors. There was a figure there frozen between its iron teeth, one arm in, one out, a scream trapped on a gray and withered face, two eye sockets empty and staring.

Juliette was one of them, one of these others. She was dead, or nearly so. But while they were frozen in motion, she was still pushing ahead. Shown the way. She tugged the body out of the gap, her breathing loud in her helmet, her exhalations misting on the screen before her nose. Half the body pulled free—the other half collapsed inside the door. A mist of powdered flesh drifted down in between.

She wiggled one of her arms inside and tried to push through sideways. Her shoulder slipped through, then her leg, but her helmet caught. She turned her head and tried again, but the helmet still wedged tightly between the doors. There was a moment of panic as she could feel the steel jaws gripping her head, supporting the weight of her helmet, leaving her semi-dangling from its grasp. She swam her arm all the way through, trying to reach around the door for purchase, to pull herself the rest of the way, but her torso was stuck. One leg was in, the other out. There was nothing to push against or pull in order to go the rest of the way. She was trapped, an arm useless on the inside, waving frantically, her rapid breathing using up what remained of her air.

Juliette tried to fit her other arm through. She couldn't turn her waist, but she could bend her elbow and slide her fingers across her belly through the tight space between her stomach and the door. She curled her fingers around the edge of the steel and pulled. There was no leverage in those confines. It was just the strength in her fingers, in her grip. Juliette suddenly didn't want to die, not there. She curled her hand as if to make a fist, her fingers bent around the edge of those steel jaws, her knuckles singing out from the strain. Jerking her head against her helmet, trying to bang her face against the damned screen, twisting and shoving and yanking—she suddenly popped free.

She stumbled forward into the airlock, a boot catching briefly on the gap behind her, arms windmilling for balance as she kicked through a pile of charred bones and sent a cloud of black ash into the air. It was the remains of those who had been caught in the cleansing fire of the airlock. Juliette found herself in a burned room eerily similar to the one she had recently left. Her exhausted and bewildered mind spun with outrageous delusions. Perhaps she was already dead, and these were the ghosts awaiting her. Maybe she had burned alive inside the airlock of her own silo, and these were her mad dreams, her escape from the pain, and now she would haunt this place forever.

She stumbled through the scattered remains toward the inner door and pressed her head against the thick glass porthole. She looked for Peter Billings beyond, sitting at his desk. Or perhaps a glimpse of Holston wandering the hallways, a specter searching for his ghostly wife.

But this was not the same airlock. She tried to calm herself. She wondered if her air was running low, if sucking on her own exhaust was like breathing the fumes of a hot motor, choking off her brain.

The door was sealed. It was real. The thousands were dead, but she wasn't. Not yet.

She tried to spin the large wheel that secured the door, but it was either frozen in place or locked from the inside. Juliette banged on the glass, hoping the silo sheriff would hear her, or maybe a cafeteria worker. It was dark inside, but the thought lingered that someone must be there. People lived *inside* silos. They didn't belong piled up around them.

There was no answer. No light flicked on. She leaned on the large wheel, remembered Marnes's instructions, how all the mechanisms worked, but those lessons felt like so long ago and she hadn't thought them important at the time. But she remembered something: after the argon bath and the fire, didn't the inner door unlock? Automatically? So the airlock could be scrubbed? This seemed like something she remembered Marnes saying. He had joked that it wasn't as if anyone could come back inside once the fire had run its course. Was she remembering this or making it up? Was it the wishful thinking of an oxygen-starved mind?

Either way, the wheel on the door wouldn't budge. Juliette pushed down with all her weight, but it definitely felt locked to her. She stepped back. The bench hanging from the wall where cleaners got suited up before their deaths looked inviting. She was tired from the walk, from the struggle to get inside. And why was she trying to get inside? She spun in place, indecisive. What was she doing?

She needed air. For some reason, she thought the silo might have some. She looked around at all the scattered bones of an uncountable number of bodies. How many dead? They were too jumbled to know. The skulls, she thought. She could count those and know. She shook this nonsense from her head. She was definitely losing her senses.

The wheel on the door is a stuck nut, some receding part of her said. *It's a frozen bolt.*

And hadn't she made a reputation as a young shadow for working them free?

Juliette told herself that this could be done. Grease, heat, leverage. Those were the secrets to a piece of metal that wouldn't budge. She didn't have any of the three, but she looked around anyway. There was no squeezing back through the outer door; she knew she wouldn't make it a second time, not that kind of straining. So she had this room. The bench was secured to the wall along the back edge and hung from two chains. Juliette wiggled the chains but didn't see how they could come free, or what good they would do her anyway.

In the corner, there was a pipe snaking up that led into a series of vents. It must be what delivered the argon, she thought. She wrapped her hands around the pipe, put her feet on the wall, and tugged.

The connection to the vent wiggled; the toxic air had corroded and weakened it. Juliette smiled, set her teeth, and yanked back ferociously.

The pipe came free of the vent and bent at its base. She felt a sudden thrill, like a wild rat standing over a large crumb. She grabbed the free end of the pipe and worked it back and forth, bending and wrenching the fastened end. Metal would snap if you could wiggle it even a little bit, if you did it long enough. She had felt the heat of weakened steel countless times while bending it over and over until it broke.

Sweat beaded on her brow and twinkled in the dim light allowed by her visor screen. It dripped down her nose, fogged the screen, and still she yanked and pushed, back and forth, growing frantic and desperate—

The pipe snapped, taking her by surprise. Just a faint pop bled through her helmet, and then the long piece of hollow metal was free. One end was crushed and twisted, the other whole and round. Juliette turned to the door, a tool now in hand. She slid the pipe through the wheel, leaving as much as she could hanging out the side, just short enough not to brush the wall. With both gloved hands wrapped around the pipe, she hoisted herself and bent at the waist over the pipe, her helmet touching the door. She bounced her weight on the lever, knowing it was a jerking motion that freed a bolt, not a steady force. She wiggled her way toward the end of the pipe, watching it bend a little, worried it might snap in half long before the door budged.

When she got toward the end—maximum leverage—she threw her weight up and down with all her strength, and she cursed as the pipe snapped. There was a loud clang, barely muffled by her suit, and then she collapsed to the floor, landing painfully on her elbow.

The pipe was at an angle beneath her, digging into her ribs. Juliette tried to catch her breath. Her sweat dripped against the visor screen, blurring her view. She got up and saw that the pipe was unbroken. She wondered if it had slipped free, but it was still threaded through the spokes of the large wheel.

Disbelieving, excited, she slid the pipe out the other side. She wrapped her hands around the spokes and leaned into it.

And the wheel.

It budged.

37

For now, these hot days, is the mad blood stirring.

WALKER MADE IT TO the end of the hallway and found himself leaving the comforting confines of a tight corridor to enter the wider entrance hall to Mechanical. The room, he saw, was full of young shadows. They hung out in groups, whispering to themselves. Three boys crouched near one wall, throwing stones for chits. Walker could hear a dozen interwoven voices spilling out of the mess hall across the room. The casters had sent these young ears away while they discussed adult things. He took a deep breath and hurried through that damned open space, focusing on each step, moving one foot ahead of him at a time, each small patch of floor a thing to conquer.

After a short lifetime, he finally crashed into the wall on the other side and hugged the steel panels in relief. Behind him, the shadows laughed, but he was too frightened to care. Sliding across the riveted steel, he grabbed the edge of the mess-hall door and pulled himself inside. The relief was enormous. Even though the mess hall was several times the size of his workshop, it was at least full of crowding furniture and people he knew. With his back to the wall, his shoulder against the open door, he could almost pretend it was smaller. He slumped to the ground and rested, the men and women of Mechanical arguing among themselves, voices rising, agitated, competing.

"She'd be out of air by now, anyway," Ricks was saying.

"You don't know that," Shirly said. She was standing on a chair so she could be at least as tall as the others. She surveyed the room. "We don't know what advances they've made."

"That's because they won't tell us!"

"Maybe it's gotten better out there."

The room quieted with this last. Waiting, perhaps, to see if the voice would dare speak again and break its anonymity. Walker studied the eyes of those facing his way. They were wide with a mixture of fear and excitement. A double cleaning had removed some taboos. Shadows had been sent away. The adults were feeling frisky and free to speak forbidden thoughts.

"What if it *has* gotten better?" someone else asked.

"Since two weeks ago? I'm telling you guys, it's the suits! They figured out the suits!" Marck, an oilman, looked around at the others, anger in his eyes. "I'm sure of it," he said. "They've sorted the suits and now we have a chance!"

"A chance to what?" Knox growled. The grizzled head of Mechanical sat at one of the tables, digging into a breakfast bowl. "A chance to send more of our people out to wander the hills until they run out of air?" He shook his head and took another bite, then jabbed at the lot of them with his spoon. "What we need to be talking about," he said, chewing, "is this sham of an election, this rat-ass mayor, and us kept in the dark down here—!"

"They didn't figure out the suits," Walker hissed, still breathless from his ordeal.

"*We're* the ones who keep this place humming," Knox continued, wiping his beard. "And what do we get? Busted fingers and ratshit pay. And now? Now they come and take our people and send them out for a view we don't care about!" He slammed the table with his mighty fist, sending his bowl hopping.

Walker cleared his throat. He remained crouched on the floor, his back against the wall. No one had seen him enter or heard him the first time. Now, while the room was scared quiet by Knox, he tried again.

"They did *not* figure out the suits," he said, a little louder this time.

Shirly saw him from her perch. Her chin dropped, her mouth hanging open. She pointed, and a dozen other heads turned to follow.

They gaped at him. Walker was still trying to catch his breath and must've looked near death. Courtnee, one of the young plumbers who was always kind to him whenever she stopped by his workshop, left her seat and hurried to his side. She whispered his name in surprise and helped him to his feet, urging him to come to the table and take her chair.

Knox slid his bowl away from himself and slapped the table. "Well, people are just wandering all over the damned place now, aren't they?"

Walker looked up sheepishly to see the old foreman chief smiling through his beard at him. There were two dozen other people staring at him, all at once. Walker half waved, then stared down at the table. It was suddenly too many people.

"All this shouting rouse you, old man? You setting off over the hills, too?"

Shirly jumped down from her chair. "Oh, God, I'm so sorry. I forgot to take him his breakfast." She hurried toward the kitchen to fetch him some food even as Walker tried to wave her off. He wasn't hungry.

"It isn't . . ." His voice cracked. He tried again. "I came because I *heard*," he whispered. "Jules. Out of sight." He made a gesture with his hand, arching it over some imaginary hill running across the table. "But it wasn't them in IT that figured *nothing,*" he said. He made eye contact with Marck and tapped his own chest. "I did it."

A whispered conversation in the corner fell quiet. No one sipped their juice, no one moved. They were still half-stunned to see Walker out of his workshop, much less among the crowd of them. Not one of them had been old enough to remember the last time he'd roamed about. They knew him as the crazy electrical man who lived in a cave and refused to cast shadows anymore.

"What're you *sayin'*?" Knox asked.

Walker took a deep breath. He was about to speak when Shirly returned and placed a bowl of hot oats in front of him, the spoon standing off the rim, the concoction was so thick. Just how he liked it. He pressed his hands against either side of the bowl, feeling the heat in his palms. He was suddenly very tired from lack of sleep.

"Walk?" Shirly asked. "You okay?"

He nodded and waved her away, lifted his head and met Knox's gaze.

"Jules came to me the other day." He bobbed his head, gaining confidence. He tried to ignore how many people were watching him speak, and the way the overhead lights twinkled in his watering eyes. "She had a theory about these suits, about IT." With one hand, he stirred his oats, steeling his resolve to say the unthinkable. But then, how old was he? Why did he care for taboos?

"You remember the heat tape?" He turned to Rachele, who worked first shift and knew Juliette well. She nodded. "Jules sorted that it weren't no accident, the way the tape broke down." He nodded to himself. "She sorted it all, she did."

He took a bite of his food, not hungry but enjoying the burn of the hot spoon on his tongue. The room was silent, waiting. The whispers and quiet play of the shadows outside could just barely be heard.

"I've built up favors and favors with Supply over the years," he explained. "Favors and favors. So I called them all in. Told them we'd be even." He looked at this group of men and women from Mechanical, could hear more standing in the hallway who'd arrived late but could read from the frozen demeanors in the room to stay put. "We've taken stuff out of IT's supply chain before. I know I have. All the best electronics and wire go to them that make the suits—"

"The ratshit bastards," someone muttered, which got more than a few of them bobbing their heads.

"So I told Supply to return the favor. Soon as I heard they took her—" Walker paused and swiped at his eyes. "Soon as I heard, I wired in those favors, said to replace anything them bastards asked for with some of our own. Best of the best. And don't let 'em be the wiser."

"You did *what?*" Knox asked.

Walker dipped his head over and over; it felt good to let out the truth. "They've been making those suits to fail. Not 'cause it ain't bad out there, that's not what I figure. But they don't want your body wandering out of sight, no sir." He stirred his oats. "They want us all right here where they can see us."

"So she's okay?" Shirly asked.

Walker frowned and slowly shook his head.

"I *told* you guys," someone said. "She'd have run out of air by now."

"She was dead *anyway,*" someone else countered, and the argument began to build again. "This just proves they're full of shit!"

Walker had to agree with that.

"Everybody, let's stay calm," Knox roared. But he appeared

the least calm of them all. More workers filed in now that the moment of silence appeared to be over. They gathered around the table, faces full of worry.

"This is it," Walker said to himself, seeing what was happening, what he had started. He watched his friends and coworkers get all riled up, barking at the empty air for answers, their passions stirred. "This is it," he said again, and he could feel it brewing, ready to burst out. "Thisisit, thisisit—"

Courtnee, still hovering over him, tending to him like he was an invalid, held his wrist with those delicate hands of hers.

"What is it?" she asked. She waved down the others so she could hear. She leaned close to Walker. "Walk, tell me, what is it? What is this? What're you trying to say?"

"This is how it starts," he whispered, the room quiet once more. He looked up at all the faces, scanned them, seeing in their fury, in all the exploded taboos, that he was right to worry.

"This is how the uprising begins . . ."

38

Sharp misery had worn him to the bones;
And about his shelves, a beggarly account of empty boxes.

LUKAS ARRIVED AT THIRTY-FOUR breathless and clutching the small box, more exhausted from the laws he had broken than this habitual climb to work. He could still taste the metallic tang of adrenaline in his mouth from hiding behind the servers and rummaging through Juliette's things. He patted his chest, feeling the items there, and also his racing heart.

Once he was better composed, he reached for the doors to IT and nearly cracked a knuckle as they flew outward toward him. Sammi, a tech he knew, burst out in a hurry and stormed past. Lukas called his name, but the older tech was already gone, storming up the stairs and out of sight.

There was more commotion in the entrance hall: voices yelling over one another. Lukas entered warily, wondering what the fuss was about. He held open the door with his elbow and slid into the room, the box tight against his chest.

Most of the yelling, it seemed, was coming from Bernard. The head of IT stood outside the security gates and was barking at one tech after the other. Nearby, Sims, the head of IT security, similarly laid into three men in gray overalls. Lukas remained frozen by the door, intimidated by the angry duo.

When Bernard spotted him there, he snapped his mouth shut and waded through the trembling techs to greet him. Lukas opened his mouth to say something, but his boss was fixated less on him and more on what was in his hands.

"This is it?" Bernard asked, snatching the box from him.

"It—?"

"Everything that greaser owned fits in this little damn box?" Bernard tugged the flaps open. "Is this everything?"

"Uh . . . that's what I was given," Lukas stammered. "Marsh said—"

"Yeah, the deputy wired about his cramps. I swear, the Pact should stipulate an age limit for their kind. Sims!" Bernard turned to his security chief. "Conference room. Now."

Lukas pointed toward the security gate and the server room beyond. "I suppose I should get to—"

"Come with me," Bernard said, wrapping his arm around Lukas's back and squeezing his shoulder. "I want you in on this. There seem to be fewer and fewer ratshit techs I can trust around here."

"Unless y-you want me on the servers. We had that thing with tower thirteen—"

"That can wait. This is more important." Bernard ushered him toward the conference room, the hulking mass of Sims preceding them.

The security guard grabbed the door and held it open, frowning at Lukas as he went by. Lukas shivered as he crossed the threshold. He could feel the sweat running down his chest, could feel guilty heat in his armpits and around his neck. He had a sudden image of being thrown against the table, pinned down, contraband yanked from his pockets and waved in his face—

"Sit," Bernard said. He put the box down on the table, and he and Sims began emptying its contents while Lukas lowered himself into a chair.

"Vacation chits," Sims said, pulling out the stack of paper coupons. Lukas watched the way the man's arms rippled with muscle with even the slightest movement. Sims had been a tech once, until his body kept growing and made him too obviously suited for other, less cerebral, endeavors. He lifted the chits to his nose, took a sniff, and recoiled. "Smells like sweaty greaser," he said.

"Counterfeit?" Bernard asked.

Sims shook his head. Bernard was inspecting the small wooden box. He shook it and rapped it with his knuckles, listening to the rattle of chits inside. He searched the exterior for a hinge or clasp.

Lukas almost blurted out that the top slid, that it was so finely crafted you could barely see the joints and that it took a bit of effort. Bernard muttered something and set the box aside.

"What exactly are we looking for?" Lukas asked. He leaned forward and grabbed the box, pretended to be inspecting it for the first time.

"Anything. A fucking clue," Bernard barked. He glared at Lukas. "How did this greaser make it over the hill? Was it something she did? One of my techs? What?"

Lukas still couldn't figure out the anger. So what if she hadn't cleaned—it would've been a double anyway. Was Bernard furious because he didn't know *why* she'd survived so long? This made sense to Lukas. Whenever he fixed something by accident, it drove him nearly as nuts as having something break. He'd seen Bernard angry before, but this was something different. The man was livid. He was *manic*. It was just how Lukas would feel if he'd had such an unprecedented piece of success with no cause to pin it on.

Sims, meanwhile, found the notebook and began flipping through it. "Hey, boss—"

Bernard snatched it from him and tore through the pages, reading. "Someone'll have to go through all this," he said. He pushed his glasses up his nose. "There might be some sign of collusion in here—"

"Hey, look," Lukas said, holding out the box. "It opens." He showed them the sliding lid.

"Lemme see that." Bernard dropped the notebook to the table and snatched the wooden box away. He wrinkled his nose. "Just chits," he said disgustedly.

He dumped them on the table and was about to toss the box aside, but Sims grabbed it from him. "That's an antique," the large man said. "You think it's a clue, or can I . . . ?"

"Yes, keep it, by all means." Bernard waved his arms out toward the window with its view of the entrance hall. "Because nothing of greater fucking importance is going on around here, is it, shit-for-brains?"

Sims shrugged noncommittally and slid the wooden box into his pocket. Lukas desperately wanted to be somewhere else, anywhere in the silo but there.

"Maybe she just got lucky," Sims offered.

Bernard began dumping the rest of the box onto the table, shaking it to loosen the manual that Lukas knew was tightly wedged in the bottom. He paused in his efforts and squinted at Sims over the rims of his glasses.

"Lucky," Bernard repeated.

Sims tilted his head.

"Get the fuck out of here," Bernard told him.

Sims nodded. "Yeah, you're right."

"No, I mean get out!" Bernard pointed at the door. "Getthefuckout!"

The head of security smiled like this was funny but lumbered for the door. He slid out of the room and gently clicked the door shut behind him.

"I'm surrounded by morons," Bernard said once they were alone.

Lukas tried to imagine this was not meant as an insult directed at him.

"Present company excluded," Bernard added, as if reading his mind.

"Thanks."

"Hey, you at least can fix a goddamn server. What the hell do I pay these other ratshit techs to do?"

He pressed his glasses up the bridge of his nose again, and Lukas tried to remember if the IT head had always cursed this much. He didn't think so. Was it the strain of being interim mayor that was getting to him? Something had changed. It felt strange to even consider Bernard his friend anymore. The man was so much more important now, so much busier. Perhaps he was cracking under the stress that came with the extra responsibility, the pain of being the one to send good people to cleaning—

"You know why I've never taken a shadow?" Bernard asked. He flipped through the manual, saw the play on the reverse side, and turned the bound sheets of paper around. He glanced up at Lukas, who lifted his palms and shrugged.

"It's because I shudder to think of anyone else ever running this place."

Lukas assumed he meant IT, not the silo. Bernard hadn't been mayor very long.

Bernard set the play down and gazed out the window, where muffled voices argued once more.

"But I'll have to, one of these days. I'm at that age where your friends, the people you grew up with, are dropping like flies, but you're still young enough to pretend it won't happen to you."

His eyes fell to Lukas. The young tech felt uncomfortable being alone with Bernard. He'd never felt that before.

"Silos have burned to the ground before because of one man's hubris," Bernard told him. "All it takes is improper planning, thinking you'll be around forever, but because one man disappears" – he snapped his fingers – "and leaves a sucking void behind, that can be enough to bring it all down."

Lukas was dying to ask his boss what the hell he was talking about.

"Today is that day, I think." Bernard walked around the long conference table, leaving behind him the scattered remnants of Juliette's life. Lukas's gaze drifted over the items. The guilt of going through them himself vanished when he saw how they'd been treated by Bernard. He wished instead that he'd stashed away more of them.

"What I need is someone who already has access to the servers," Bernard said. Lukas turned to the side and realized the short, full-bellied head of IT was standing right beside him. He moved his hand up to his chest pocket, making sure it didn't bulge open where Bernard could see.

"Sammi is a good tech. I trust him, but he's nearly as old as I am."

"You aren't that old," Lukas said, trying to be polite, to gather his wits. He wasn't sure what was going on.

"There aren't many I consider friends," Bernard said.

"I appreciate that . . ."

"You're probably the closest thing –"

"I feel the same –"

"I knew your father. He was a good man."

Lukas swallowed and nodded. He looked up at Bernard and realized the man was holding out his hand. Had been for a while. He extended his own to accept, still not sure what was being offered.

"I need a shadow, Lukas." Bernard's hand felt small in Lukas's own. He watched as his arm was pumped up and down. "I want you to be that man."

39

Wisely and slow; they stumble that run fast.

Juliette forced her way through the inner airlock door and scrambled to get it closed. Darkness overwhelmed her as the heavy door squealed on its hinges and settled against its dry seals. She groped for the large locking wheel and leaned on the spokes, spinning it and sealing the door tight.

The air in her suit was growing stale; she could feel the dizziness overtaking her. Turning around, keeping one hand on the wall, she stumbled forward through the darkness. The puff of outside air that she'd allowed inside seemed to claw at her back like a horde of mad insects. Juliette staggered blindly down the hallway, trying to put distance between herself and the dead she'd left behind.

There were no lights on, no glow from the wallscreens with their view of the outside world. She prayed the layout was the same, that she could find her way. She prayed the air in her suit would hold out a moment longer, prayed the air in the silo wouldn't be as foul and toxic as the wind outside. Or – and just as bad – that the air in the silo wouldn't be as devoid of oxygen as what little remained in her suit.

Her hand brushed the bars of a cell just where they should have been, giving her hope that she could navigate the darkness. She wasn't sure what she hoped to find in the pitch black—she had no plan for salvation—she was simply stumbling away from the horrors outside. It hardly registered for her that she had been there, had gone *outside,* and was now in someplace new.

As she fumbled through the office, sucking on the last breaths of air in her helmet, her feet knocked into something and Juliette went sprawling forward. She landed roughly on a soft mound, groped with her hand, and felt an arm. A body. Several bodies. Juliette crawled over them, the spongy flesh feeling more human and solid than the husks and bones outside—and more difficult to move across. She felt someone's chin. The weight of her body caused their neck to turn, and she nearly lost her balance. Her body recoiled at the sensation of what she was doing, the reflex to apologize, to pull her limbs away, but she forced herself forward over a pile of them, through the darkness, until her helmet slammed into the office door.

Without warning, the blow was hard enough that Juliette saw stars and feared blacking out. She reached up and fumbled for the handle. Her eyes might as well have been sealed shut, the utter darkness was so complete. Even the bowels of Mechanical had never seen such deep and perfect shadow.

She found the latch and pushed. The door was unlocked but wouldn't budge. Juliette scrambled to her feet, her boots digging into lifeless bodies, and threw her shoulder against the door. She wanted out.

The door moved. A little. She could feel something slide on the other side and imagined more bodies piled up. She threw herself again and again into the door, grunts of effort and frustrated tiny screams echoing in her helmet. Her hair was loose, sweaty, and matting to her face. She couldn't see. Couldn't breathe. Was growing more faint as she poisoned her own internal atmosphere.

When the door slid open a crack, she tried to force her way through, one shoulder first, squeezing her helmet past, then pulling her other arm and leg after. She fell to the floor, scrambled around, and shoved herself against the door, sealing it tight.

There was a dim light, almost impossible to notice at first. A barricade of tables and chairs was pressed in against her, scattered from her efforts to get through. Their hard edges and spindly legs seemed intent on ensnaring her.

Juliette heard herself wheezing for air and knew her time had run out. She imagined the poison all over her like grease. The toxic air that she'd let in was a cloud of vermin just waiting for her to crawl out of her shell so they could eat away at her.

She considered lying down and letting her air supply run out instead. She would be preserved in this chrysalis of a suit, a well-built suit, a gift from Walker and the people of Supply. Her body would lie forever in this dim silo that shouldn't have existed—but so much better than to rot on a lifeless hill and fly away, piece by piece, on a fickle breeze. It would be a good death. She panted, proud of herself for making it somewhere of her own choosing, for conquering these last few obstacles. Slumping against the door, she very nearly lay down and closed her eyes—but for the nagging of her curiosity.

Juliette held up her hands and studied them in the dim glow from the stairwell. The shiny gloves—wrapped in heat tape and melted to form a bright skin—made her look like a machine of sorts. She ran her hands over the dome of her helmet, realizing she was like a walking toaster. When she had been a mere shadow in Mechanical, she'd had a bad habit of taking things apart, even those that already worked. What had Walker said of her? That she liked nothing more than peering inside of toasters.

Juliette sat up and tried to focus. She was losing sensation, and with it the will to live. She shook her head and pulled herself to her feet, sent a pile of chairs crashing to the floor. She was the toaster, she realized. Her curiosity wanted it open. This time, to see what was *outside.* To take one breath and know.

She swam through the tables and chairs, wanting more and more distance between herself and any bad air she had let in. The bodies she had crawled over in the sheriff's office had felt whole. Naturally dead. Trapped inside and starved or asphyxiated, perhaps. But not rotten. Still, and despite her light-headedness and need to breathe, she wanted to somehow douse herself before cracking the helmet, wanted to dilute the toxins as she would with any other chemical spill back in Mechanical.

She escaped the barrier of tables and chairs and made her way across the open cafeteria floor. The emergency lights in the stairwell leaked a green glow to dimly show the way. She passed through the serving door and into the kitchen, and tried the taps on the large sink. The handles turned, but the spout didn't leak a drop, didn't knock with even a futile try from distant pumps. She went to the dangling hose over the dish station and pulled that lever — and was similarly rewarded. There was no water.

Her next thought was the walk-ins, to maybe freeze the nastiness she could feel crawling all over her suit. She staggered around the cooking stations and pulled the large silver handle on the door, her breath wheezy in her helmet. The light in the back reaches of the kitchen was already so dim she could barely see. She couldn't feel any cold through her suit but wasn't sure if she'd be able to. It was built to shield her, and built well. The overhead light didn't come on, so she assumed the freezer was dead. With the door open, she peered inside, looking for anything fluid, and saw what looked like vats of soup.

She was desperate enough to try anything. Juliette moved inside the walk-in, letting the door swing slowly shut behind her. She seized one of the large plastic containers, a bucket the size of the largest cooking pots, and tore the top off. The door clicked shut, returning her to solid darkness. Juliette knelt beneath the shelf and tipped the massive bucket over. She could feel the liquid soup splatter over her suit, crinkling it and splashing to the floor. Her knees slipped in the stuff. She felt for the next one and did the same, ran her fingers into the puddles and coated herself in it. There was no way of knowing if she was being crazy, if she was making things worse, or if any of it mattered. Her boot slipped, sending her flat onto her back, her helmet cracking against the floor.

Juliette lay there in a puddle of tepid soup, unable to see, her breath raspy and stale. Her time had run out. She was dizzy and could think of nothing else to try, didn't have the breath or energy, anyway. The helmet had to come off.

She fumbled for the latches, could barely feel them through her gloves. Her gloves were too thick. They were going to kill her.

She rolled to her belly and crawled through the soup, her hands and knees slipping. She reached the door, gasping, and fumbled for the handle, found it, threw the door open. There was a rack of knives gleaming behind the counter. She lurched to her feet and grabbed one, held the blade in her thick mitts, and slumped to the floor, exhausted and dizzy.

Turning the blade toward her own neck, Juliette groped for the latch. She slid the point along her collar until it caught in the crack of the button. Steadying herself, her arm shaking, she moved the knife and pressed in, shoving it toward her body against all her most human instincts.

There was a faint click. Juliette gasped and groped along the rim with the blade for the other button until she found it. She repeated the maneuver.

Another click, and her helmet popped off.

Juliette's body took over for her, compelling her to take deep gulps of foul air. The stench was unbearable, but she couldn't stop gasping for more. Rotted food, biological decay, a tepid filth of stenches invaded her mouth, tongue, nose.

She turned to the side and retched, but nothing came out. Her hands were still slippery with soup. Breathing was painful; she imagined a burning sensation on her skin, but it could've been her fevered state. She crawled away from the walk-in, toward the cafeteria, out of the fog of rotting soup, and took another gulp of air.

Air.

She took a lungful, the odor still overpowering, the soup coating her. But beyond the stench, something else was there. Something faint. Something *breathable* that began to force away the dizziness and the panic. It was *oxygen.* Life.

Juliette was still alive.

She laughed madly and stumbled toward the stairwell, drawn to the green glow of light, breathing deeply and too exhausted to appreciate this, the *impossible* life still in her.

40

For you and I are past our dancing days.

KNOX SAW THE UPROAR in Mechanical as just another emergency to overcome. Like the time the basement subwall had sprung a leak, or when the oil rig had hit that pocket of methane and they had to evacuate eight levels until the air handlers made it safe to return. Against the inevitable flow of commotion, what he needed to do was push for order. To assign tasks. He had to break a huge undertaking down to discrete bits and make sure they fell to the right hands. Only this time, he and his people wouldn't be setting out to repair something. There were things the good people of Mechanical meant to *break*.

"Supply is the key," he told his foremen, pointing to the large-scale blueprint hanging on the wall. He traced the stairwell up the thirty flights to Supply's main manufacturing floor. "Our greatest advantage is that IT doesn't know we're coming." He turned to his shift leaders. "Shirly, Marck, and Courtnee, you'll come with me. We'll load up with supplies and take your shadows with us. Walker, you can wire ahead to let 'em know we're coming. Be careful, though. Assume IT has ears. Say we have a load of your repairs to deliver."

He turned to Jenkins, who had shadowed under Knox for six

years before he grew his own beard and moved to third shift. The assumption everywhere was that Knox's job was his in waiting. "Jenks, I want you to take over down here. There are no days off for a while. Keep the place running, but get ready for the worst. I want as much food stockpiled as possible. And water. Make sure the cistern is topped up. Divert from the hydroponics feed if you have to, but be discreet. Think of an excuse, like a leak or something, in case they notice. Meanwhile, have someone make the rounds and check every lock and hinge, just in case the fighting comes to us. And stockpile whatever weapons you can make up. Pipes, hammers, whatever."

Some eyebrows were lifted at this, but Jenkins nodded at the list as if it all made sense and was doable. Knox turned to his foremen. "What? You know where this is heading, right?"

"But what's the larger picture?" Courtnee asked, glancing at the tall blueprint of their buried home. "Storm IT, and then what? Take over running this place?"

"We already run this place," Knox growled. He slapped his hand across the floors of the midthirties. "We just do it in the dark. Like these levels here are dark to us. But now I mean to shine a light in their rat hole and scare them out, see what else they're hiding."

"You understand what they've been doing, right?" Marck turned to Courtnee. "They've been sending people out to die. On purpose. Not because it *had* to happen, but because they wanted it to!"

Courtnee bit her lip and didn't say anything, just stared at the blueprint.

"We need to get going," Knox said. "Walker, get that wire out. Let's load up. And think of something pleasant to chat about while we're on the move. No grumbling about this where some porter can hear and make a chit or two ratting us out."

They nodded. Knox slapped Jenkins on the back and dipped

his chin at the younger man. "I'll send word when we need everyone. Keep the bare bones you think you've gotta have down here and send the rest. Timing is everything, okay?"

"I know what to do," Jenkins said. He wasn't trying to be uppity, just reassuring his elder.

"All right," Knox said. "Then let's get to it."

They made it up ten flights with little complaint, but Knox could begin to feel the burn in his legs from the heavy load. He had a canvas sack stuffed full of welding smocks on his wide shoulders, plus a bundle of helmets. A rope had been strung through their chin straps, and they clattered down his wide back. Marck struggled with his load of pipe stock as they kept trying to slide against one another and slip out of his arms. The shadows brought up the rear, behind the women, with heavy sacks of blasting powder tied together so they hung around their necks. Professional porters with similarly full loads breezed past them in both directions, their glances signaling a mix of curiosity and competitive anger. When one porter – a woman Knox recognized from deliveries to the down deep – stopped and offered to help, he gruffly sent her on her way. She hurried up the steps, looking back over her shoulder before spiraling out of view, and Knox regretted taking his exhaustion out on her.

"Keep it up," he told the others. Even with the small group, they were making a spectacle. And it was growing ever more tiresome to hold their tongues as news of Juliette's amazing disappearance gyred all around them. At almost every landing, a group of people, often younger people, stood around and gossiped about what it all meant. The taboo had moved from thought to whisper. Forbidden notions were birthed on tongues and swam through the air. Knox ignored the pain in his back and lumbered up and up, each step driving them closer to Supply, feeling more and more like they needed to get there in a hurry.

As they left the one-thirties, the grumblings were fully in the air. They were nearing the upper half of the down deep, where people who worked, shopped, and ate in the mids mingled with those who would rather they didn't. Deputy Hank was on the stairwell of one-twenty-eight, trying to mediate between two arguing crowds. Knox squeezed past, hoping the officer wouldn't turn and see his heavily loaded train and ask them what they were doing up this far. As he ascended past the ruckus, Knox glanced back to watch the shadows slink past, hugging the inner rail. Deputy Hank was still asking a woman to please calm down as the landing sank out of sight.

They passed the dirt farm on one-twenty-six, and Knox figured this to be a key asset. The thirties of IT were a long hike up, but if they had to fall back, they would need to hold at Supply. Between their manufacturing, the food on this level, and the machinery of Mechanical, they might be self-sufficient. He could think of a few weak links, but many more for IT. They could always shut off their power or stop treating their water—but he really hoped, as they approached Supply on weary legs, that it wouldn't come to any of that.

They were greeted on the landing of one-ten by frowns. McLain, the elder woman and head of Supply, stood with her arms crossed over her yellow overalls, her stance screaming unwelcome.

"Hello, Jove." Knox fixed her with a wide smile.

"Don't *Jove* me," McLain said. "What's this nonsense you're after?"

Knox glanced up and down the stairwell, shrugged his heavy load higher up his shoulder. "Mind if we step in and talk about it?"

"I don't want any trouble here," she said, her eyes blazing beneath her lowered brow.

"Let's go inside," Knox said. "We haven't stopped once on the way up. Unless you want us collapsing out here."

McLain seemed to consider this. Her arms loosened across her chest. She turned to three of her workers, who formed an imposing wall behind her, and nodded. While they pulled open the gleaming doors of Supply, she turned and grabbed Knox's arm. "Don't get comfortable," she told him.

Inside the front room of Supply, Knox found a small army of men and women in their yellow overalls, waiting. Most of them stood behind the low, long counter where the people of the silo normally waited for whatever parts they needed, whether newly fabricated or recently repaired. The parallel and deep aisles of shelves beyond ran into the gloomy distance, boxes and bins bulging off of them. The room was noticeably quiet. Usually, the mechanical thrumming and clanking sounds of fabrication could be heard worming their way through the space, or one might hear workers chatting unseen back in the stacks while they sorted newly fashioned bolts and nuts into hungry bins.

Now it was just silence and distrustful glares. Knox stood with his people, their sacks and loads slumping exhaustedly to the floor, sweat on their brows, while the men and women of Supply watched, unmoving.

He had expected a more amicable welcome. Mechanical and Supply had a long history together. They jointly ran the small mine beneath the lowest levels of Mechanical that supplemented the silo's stockpile of ores.

But now, as McLain followed her boys back inside, she graced Knox with a look of scorn he hadn't seen since his mother passed away.

"What in the hell is the meaning of this?" she hissed at Knox.

He was taken aback by the language, especially in front of his people. He thought of himself and McLain as equals, but now he was being snapped at as if by one of Supply's dogs. Made to feel small and worthless.

McLain's gaze ranged down the exhausted line of mechanics and their shadows before turning back to him.

"Before we discuss how we're cleaning up this problem, I want to hear how you're handling your employees, whoever was responsible." Her eyes bored through him. "I *am* correct in assuming you had nothing to do with this, right? That you've come to apologize and shower me with bribes?"

Shirly started to say something, but Knox waved her off. There were a lot of people in the room just waiting for this to go undiplomatically.

"Yes, I do apologize," Knox said, grinding his teeth together and bowing his head. "And no, I just learned of this earlier today. After I found out about the cleaning, in fact."

"So it was all your electrician," McLain said, her thin arms crossed tightly over her chest. "One man."

"That's right. But—"

"I've meted out punishment to those involved here, let me tell you. And I suppose you'll have to do more than banish that old fart to his room."

There was laughter behind the counter. Knox put a hand on Shirly's shoulder to keep her in place. He looked past McLain to the men and women arranged behind her.

"They came and took one of our workers," he said. His chest may have been heavy, but his voice still boomed. "You know how it happens. When they want a body for cleaning, they *take* it." He thumped his chest. "And I *let* them. I stood there because I trust this system. I *fear* it, just as any of you."

“Well—” McLain began, but Knox cut her short, continuing in that voice that routinely gave calm commands over the racket of machines run amok.

“One of my people was taken, and it was the oldest of us, the wisest of us, who intervened on her behalf. It was the weakest and most scared who braved his neck. And whoever of you he turned to for help, and who gave it, I owe you my life.” Knox blinked away the blur and continued. “You gave her more than a chance to walk over that hill, to die in peace and out of sight. You gave *me* the courage to open my eyes. To see this veil of lies we live behind—”

“That’s quite enough,” McLain barked. “Someone could be sent to cleaning for even *listening* to such nonsense, to such *drivel.*”

“It’s not nonsense,” Marck cried down the line. “Juliette is dead because of—”

“She’s dead because she broke these very laws!” McLain snapped, her voice high and shrill. “And now you march up here to break even more? On *my* level?”

“We aim to break heads!” Shirly said.

“Leave it!” Knox told them both. He saw the anger in McLain’s eyes, but he also saw something else: the sporadic nods and raised brows among the rank and file behind her.

A porter entered the room with empty sacks in each hand and looked around at the tense silence. One of the large Supply workers by the door ushered him back onto the landing with apologies, telling him to return later. Knox composed his words carefully during the interruption.

“No person has ever been sent to cleaning for *listening,* however great the taboo.” He allowed that to sink in. He glared at McLain as she moved to interrupt, but she seemed to decide against it. “So let me be sent to cleaning by any of you for what I’m about to say. I will welcome it if these facts do not move you to instead push forward with me and my men. For this is what Walker and a few of you brave souls have shown us this morning. We have cause for more hope than they dare give us. There's more at our disposal to broaden our horizons than they'll allow. We have been raised on a pack of lies, made to fear by the sight of our kinsmen rotting on the hills, but now one of us has crossed over that! They have seen new horizons! We have been given seals and washers and told that they should suffice, but what are they?"

He stared down the men and women behind the counter. McLain's arms seemed to loosen across her chest.

"Designed to fail, that's what! Fake. And who knows what other lies there are. What if we'd taken any cleaner back and done our best by them? Cleaned and disinfected them? Tried whatever we could? Would they survive? We can no longer trust IT to tell us they wouldn't!"

Knox saw chins rise and fall. He knew his own people were ready to storm the room if need be; they were as amped up and driven mad by all this as he was.

"We are not here to cause trouble," he said, "we are here to bring *order!* The uprising has already happened." He turned to McLain. "Don't you see? We've been *living* the uprising. Our parents were the children of it, and now we feed our own children to the same machine. This will *not* be the start of something new, but the end of something old. And if Supply is with us, we stand a chance. If not, then may our bodies haunt your view of the *outside,* which I now see as far less rotten than this blasted silo!"

Knox bellowed this last in open defiance of all taboo. He threw it out and savored the taste of it, the admission that anything beyond those curved walls might be better than what was inside them. The whisper that had killed so many became a throaty roar shouted from his broad chest.

And it felt good.

McLain cringed. She took a step away, something like fear in her eyes. She turned her back on Knox and made to return to her people, and he knew he had failed. There had been a chance, however slim, in this silent and still crowd to inspire action, but the moment had slipped him by or he had scared it off.

And then McLain did something. Knox could see the tendons in her slender neck bulge. She lifted her chin to her people, her white hair in its tight knot high on her head, and she said, quietly, “What say you, Supply?”

It was a question, not a command. Knox would later wonder if it had been asked in sadness; he would wonder if she had taken poor stock of her people, who had listened patiently during his madness. He would also wonder if she was just curious, or if she was challenging them to cast him and his mechanics out.

But now he wondered, tears streaming down his face, thoughts of Juliette swelling inside his heart, if he could even hear his handful of compatriots shouting, so drowned out were they by the angry war cries of the good men and women of Supply.

41

And too soon marr'd are those so early made.
The earth hath swallow'd all my hopes but she.

LUKAS FOLLOWED BERNARD THROUGH the halls of IT, nervous techs scattering before them like night bugs startled by the light. Bernard didn't seem to notice the techs ducking into offices and peering through windows. Lukas hurried to keep up, his eyes darting side to side, feeling conspicuous with all these hidden others watching.

"Aren't I a little old to be shadowing for another job?" he asked. He was pretty sure he hadn't accepted the offer, not verbally anyway, but Bernard spoke as if the deal was done.

"Nonsense," he said. "And this won't be shadowing in the traditional sense." He waved his hand in the air. "You'll continue your duties as before. I just need someone who can step in, who knows what to do in case something happens to me. My will—"

He stopped at the heavy door to the server room and turned to face Lukas. "If it came to it, in an emergency, my will would explain everything to the next head, but—" He gazed over Lukas's shoulder and down the hall. "Sims is my executor, which we'll have to change. I just don't see that ever going smoothly."

Bernard rubbed his chin and lost himself in his thoughts. Lukas waited a moment, then stepped beside him and entered his code on the panel by the door, fished his ID out of his pocket —made sure it was *his* ID and not Juliette's—and swiped it through the reader. The door clicked open, snapping Bernard out of his thoughts.

"Yes, well, this will be much better. Not that I expect to go anywhere, mind you." He adjusted his glasses and stepped through the heavy steel doorway. Lukas followed, pushing the monstrous enclosure shut behind them and waiting for the locks to engage.

"But if something did happen to you, I would oversee the cleanings?" Lukas couldn't imagine. He suspected there was more to learn about those suits than the servers. Sammi would be better at this, would actually *want* this job. Also—would he have to abandon his star charts?

"That's a small part of the job, but yes." Bernard guided Lukas through the servers, past number thirteen with its blank face and still fans, all the way to the back of the room.

"These are the keys to the true heart of the silo," Bernard said, fishing a jangling set out of his overalls. They were strung on a cord of leather that hung around his neck. Lukas had never noticed them before.

"There are other features to this cabinet that you'll learn about in time. For now, you simply need to know how to get downstairs." He inserted the key into several locks on the back of the server, locks designed to look like recessed screws. What server was this? Twenty-eight? Lukas glanced around the room and tried to count its position, and realized he'd never been assigned to maintain this tower.

There was a gentle clang as the back came off. Bernard set it aside, and Lukas saw why he'd never worked on the machine. It was practically empty, just a shell, like it had been scrapped for parts over the long years.

"It's crucial that you lock this after coming back up."

Lukas watched Bernard grab a handle in the bottom of the empty chassis. Bernard pulled it toward him, and there was a soft grinding noise nearby. "When the grate's back in place, you simply press this down to secure it."

Lukas was about to ask *What grate?* when Bernard stepped aside and dug his fingers into the metal slats of the floor. With a grunt, he pulled the heavy surface of the flooring up and began sliding it over. Lukas jumped around to the other side and bent down to help.

"Wouldn't the stairs . . . ?" he started to ask.

"They don't access this part of thirty-five." Bernard waved at a ladder leading down through the floor. "You go first."

Lukas's head spun from the day's sudden turn. As he bent to grab the ladder he felt the contents of his breast pocket shift and shot a hand up to hold the watch, ring, and ID steady. What had he been thinking? What was he thinking now? He lowered himself down the long ladder, feeling like someone had initiated an automated routine in his brain, a rote program that had taken over his actions. From the bottom of the ladder, he watched as Bernard lowered himself down the first rungs before sliding the grate into place, sealing them both inside the dark dungeon beneath the already-fortressed server room.

"You are about to receive a great gift," Bernard said in the darkness. "Just as I was once granted the same."

He flicked on a light, and Lukas saw that his boss was grinning maniacally, the anger from before gone. Here was a new man before him, a confident and eager man.

"All the silo and everyone in it hinges on what I'm about to show you," Bernard said. He beckoned Lukas down the brightly lit but narrow corridor toward a wider room beyond. The servers felt very far above. Lukas felt closed off from every other soul in the silo; he was curious, but also afraid. He wasn't sure he wanted such responsibility and cursed himself for going along with this.

And yet, his feet moved. They carried him down that hidden passageway and into a room full of the strange and curious, a place that made the charting of stars seem insignificant, a den where the sense of the world's scale, of *size,* took on wholly new proportions.

42

I'll bury thee in a triumphant grave; A grave?
O no! a lantern, slaughter'd youth, For here lies Juliet,
and her beauty makes this vault a feasting presence full of light.

JULIETTE LEFT HER SOUP-SLATHERED helmet on the floor and moved toward the pale-green glow of light. It seemed brighter than before. She wondered how much of the darkness had been because of her helmet. As her senses returned, she remembered that it wasn't a piece of glass she'd been looking through, but some infernal screen that took the world as she saw it and overlaid it with half a lie. Maybe it had dimmed her view in the process.

She noticed the stench from her drenched suit followed her, the smell of rotten vegetables and mold—or possibly the toxic fumes from the outside world. Her throat burned a little as she crossed the cafeteria toward the stairwell. Her skin began to itch, and she couldn't tell if it was from fear, her imagination, or truly something in the air. She didn't dare risk finding out, so she held her breath and hurried as fast as her weary legs would take her, around the corner to where she knew the stairs would be.

This world is the same as my world, she thought to herself, stumbling down the first flight of stairs in the wan glow of emergency-light strips. *God built more than one.*

Her heavy boots, still dripping with soup, felt unsteady on the metal treads. At the landing on two, she paused and took in a few big gulps of air, less painful gulps, and considered how best to remove the infernal and bulky outfit that made every movement awkward, that reeked of the fetid smell of rot and outside air. She looked down at her arms. The thing had required help to put on. There were double zippers in the back, layers of Velcro, miles of heat tape. She looked at the knife in her hand, suddenly grateful that she hadn't dropped it after using it to remove her helmet.

Gripping the knife with one clumsy glove, she carefully inserted the tip through the other sleeve, right above the top of her wrist. She forced the point through, pushing the blade over the top of her arm so it wouldn't jab her even if it pierced all the way. The fabric was difficult to cut, but a tear finally formed as she worked the handle in small circles. She slid the knife into this tiny rip, the dull side of the blade facing her skin, and slid it down her arm and toward her knuckles. When the tip of the blade ripped through the fabric between her fingers, she was able to free her hand from the long gash she'd made, the sleeve flopping from her elbow.

Juliette sat down on the grating, moved the knife to her newly freed hand, and worked on the other side. She freed it as well while soup dripped from her shoulders and down her arms. She next started a tear at her chest, having better control of the knife now without the thick gloves on. She ripped the metal foil exterior away, peeling herself like an orange. The solid collar for her helmet had to stay—it was attached to her charcoal fabric undersuit as well as the reinforced zippers up her back—but piece by piece she removed the shiny outer coat, which was slathered with a nastiness she attributed partly to the soup and partly to her trek over the hills.

Next came her boots, which were cut free around the ankles until she was able to work them off, sawing a slit down the outside edge and popping one foot free, then the other.

Before she cleaned up the hanging tatters of fabric any further, or worried about the material still attached to the zipper at her back, she got up from the landing and hurried down the steps, putting more distance between herself and the air above, which seemed to scratch at her throat. She was another two flights down, swimming through the green glow of the stairwell, before she appreciated the fact that she was alive.

She was alive.

For however much longer, this was a brutal, beautiful, and brand-new fact for Juliette. She had spent three days climbing long stairs similar to these as she came to grips with her fate. Another day and night had been spent in a cell made for the future corpses who dotted the landscape. And then — *this.* An impossible trek through the wilderness of the forbidden, breaking into the impenetrable and the unknown. Surviving.

Whatever happened next, for this moment, Juliette flew down foreign steps in bare feet, the steel cool against her tingling skin, the air burning her throat less and less with each gulp of new air, the raw stench and memory of death receding further and further above her. Soon, it was just the patter of her joyous descent ringing out and drifting down a lonely and empty darkness like a muffled bell that rang not for the dead, but for the living.

She stopped on six and rested while she worked on what remained of her protective suit. With care, she sliced her black undersuit by her shoulders and collarbone, working the tear all the way around and clawing at her back as it ripped free, strips of heat tape still attached. Once the helmet collar was detached from the fabric—just the zipper hanging like a second spine along her back—she could finally remove it from her neck. She pulled it off and dropped it to the ground, then stripped off the rest of the black carbon fabric, peeling away the arms and legs and leaving all the material in a rough pile outside the double doors to level six.

Six should be an apartment level, she thought. She considered going inside and yelling out for help or looking for clothes and supplies in the many rooms, but her greater impulse was to descend. The up top felt poisoned and too close. It didn't matter if it was all in her imagination or from her miserable experiences living in the up top of her own silo—her body felt a revulsion for the place. Safe was the down deep. It had always felt this way.

One hopeful image did linger from the upper kitchen: the rows and rows of canned and jarred food for the lean harvests. Juliette figured there would be more in the lower mess halls as well. And the air in the silo seemed decent as she regained her breath; the sting in her lungs and on her tongue had faded. Either the vast silo held a lot of air that was now being consumed by no one, or there was still a source. All these thoughts gave her hope, these tallies of resources. So she left her spoiled and tattered clothing behind, and armed with only a large chef's knife, she stole down the curved stairs naked, her body becoming more and more alive with every step taken, her mind becoming more determined to keep the rest of her that way.

On thirteen, she stopped and checked inside the doors. There was always the chance that this silo was laid out completely differently, floor to floor, so it made little sense to plan ahead if she didn't know what to expect. There were only a handful of areas in the up top that she was intimately familiar with, and every bit of overlap so far had seemed a perfect copy. Thirteen she would definitely know. There were certain things, learned so young and remembered so deep that they felt like little stones in the center of her mind. These would be the parts of her that rotted last, the bits left over once the rest skittered off on the wind or was drunk deep by the roots. In her mind, as she pushed the door open a crack, she wasn't in a different silo, an abandoned husk of a silo, but in her past, pushing open a door on her youth.

It was dark inside, none of the security or emergency lights on. There was a different smell. The air was stagnant and had a tinge of decay.

Juliette shouted down the hallway: "Hello?"

She listened to her voice echo back from the empty walls. The voice that returned sounded distant, weaker, higher than her own. She imagined herself at age nine, running through these very halls, crying out to her older self across the years. She tried to picture her mother chasing behind that girl, attempting to scoop her up and force her to be still, but the ghosts evaporated in the darkness. The last of the echoes faded, leaving her alone and naked in the doorway.

As her eyes adjusted, she could just barely make out a reception desk at the end of the hall. Light reflected off glass windows just where they should have been. It was the exact same layout as her father's nursery in the mids, the place where she had been not just born but raised. It was hard to believe that this was someplace *different*. That *other* people had lived here, other children had been born, had played and had been raised just over a hill and down a dip, had given chase or challenged each other to Hop or whatever games they had invented, all of them unaware of the others. Maybe it was from standing in the doorway of a nursery, but she couldn't help but think of all the lives this place had contained. People growing up, falling in love, burying their dead.

All those people *outside*. People she had desecrated with her boots, scattering their bones and ashes as she kicked her way into the very place they had fled. Juliette wondered how long ago it had happened, how long since the silo had been abandoned. What *had* happened here? The stairwell was still lit, which meant the battery room still held juice. She needed paper to do the math, to figure how recently or how long ago all this life had turned to death. There were practical reasons for wanting to know, beyond the mere itch of curiosity.

With one last look inside, one final shudder of regret for not stopping to see her father the last few times she'd passed his nursery, Juliette shut the door on the darkness and the ghosts and considered her predicament. She could very well be perfectly alone in a dying silo. The thrill of being alive at all was quickly draining away, replaced with the reality of her solitude and the tenuousness of her survival. Her stomach grumbled its agreement. She could somehow still smell the fetid soup on her, could taste the stomach acid from her retching. She needed water. She needed clothes. These primal urges were pushed to the forefront, drowning out the severity of her situation, the daunting tasks before her, leaving the regrets of the past behind.

If the layout was the same, the first hydroponic farm would be four floors below and the larger of the two upper dirt farms would lie just below that. Juliette shivered from an updraft of cold air. The stairwell was creating its own thermal cycle, and it would only be colder the further down she went. But she went anyway—lower was better. At the next level, she tried the door. It was too dark to see past the first interior hallway, but it seemed like offices or workrooms. She tried to remember what would be on the fourteenth in her own silo but didn't know. Was it incredible not to know? The up top of her own home had somehow been strange to her. That made this silo something completely alien.

She held the door to fourteen open and stuck the blade of her knife between the slits of metal that formed every landing's grating. The handle was left sticking up to form a stop. She allowed the door to close on its sprung hinges until it rested on the handle, holding it open. This let in enough light for her to steal inside and grope around the first handful of rooms.

There were no overalls hanging on the backs of the doors, but one room was set up for conferences. The water in the pitchers had long evaporated, but the purple tablecloth looked warm enough. Warmer than being naked. Juliette moved the assortment of cups, plates, and pitchers and grabbed the cloth. She wrapped it around her shoulders, but it was going to slip off when she moved, so she tried knotting the corners in front of her. Giving up on this, she ran back to the landing, out into the welcomed light, and removed the fabric completely. Grabbing the knife — the door squealing eerily shut behind her — she pushed the blade through the center of the tablecloth and cut a long gash. Her head went through this, the cloth falling past her feet in front of and behind her. A few minutes with the blade and she'd cut away the excess, forming a belt out of one long strip and tying another shock of fabric over her head to keep it warm.

It felt good to be making something, to be engineering her way through one particular problem. She had a tool, a weapon if need be, and clothes. The impossible list of tasks had been whittled down a few shavings. She descended further, her feet cold on the stairs, dreaming of boots, thirsty for water, very much aware of all that remained for her to do.

On fifteen, she was reminded of another necessity as her weary legs nearly gave way. Her knees buckled, she grabbed the railing, and she realized, as the adrenaline left her veins, that she was deathly tired. She paused on the landing, hands on her knees, and took a few deep breaths. How long had she been going? How much further could she push herself? She checked her reflection in the blade of the knife, saw how horrible she looked, and decided she needed rest before she went any further. Rest now, while it was still warm enough not to shiver to pieces.

It was tempting to explore that level for a bed, but she decided against it—there would be little comfort in the pitch black behind those doors. So she curled up on the steel grating of landing fifteen, tucked her arms under her head, and adjusted the tablecloth so every patch of bare skin was covered. And before she could go over the long list forming in her head, exhaustion took over. She drifted off to sleep with only a moment's panic that she shouldn't be so tired, that this might be the sort of nap one never woke up from, that she was destined to join the residents of this strange place, curled up and unmoving, frozen and lifeless, rotting and wasting away . . .

43

But old folks – many feign as they were dead;
Unwieldy, slow, heavy and pale as lead.

"Do you understand what you're proposing we do?"

Knox looked up at McLain, met her wrinkled and wizened eyes with as much confidence as he could muster. The tiny woman who controlled all the silo's spares and fabrication cut an oddly imposing figure. She didn't have Knox's barrel chest or thick beard, had wrists barely bigger than two of his fingers, but she possessed a wizened gray gaze and the weight of hard years that made him feel but a shadow in her presence.

"It's not an uprising," he said, the forbidden words moving easily with the grease of habit and time. "We're setting things to right."

McLain sniffed. "I'm sure that's what my great-grandparents said." She pushed back loose strands of silver hair and peered down at the blueprint spread out between them. It was as if she knew this was wrong but had resigned herself to helping rather than hindering it. Maybe it was her age, Knox thought, peering at her pink scalp through hair so thin and white as to be like filaments of glass. Perhaps, with enough time in these walls, one could become resigned to things never getting better, or even changing all that much. Or maybe a person eventually lost hope that there was anything worth preserving at all.

He looked down at the blueprint and smoothed the sharp creases in the fine paper. He was suddenly aware of his hands, how thick and grease limned his fingers appeared. He wondered if McLain saw him as a brute, storming up here with delusions of justice. She was old enough to consider him young, he realized. Young and hot tempered, while he thought of himself as being old and wise.

One of the dozens of dogs that lived among Supply's stacks grunted discontentedly under the table as if all this war planning were spoiling its nap.

"I think it's safe to assume IT knows something is coming," McLain said, running her small hands across the many floors between them and thirty-four.

"Why? You don't think we were discreet coming up?"

She smiled up at him. "I'm sure you were, but it's safe to assume this because it would be dangerous to assume otherwise."

He nodded and chewed on the part of his beard below his lower lip.

"How long will the rest of your mechanics take to get here?" McLain asked.

"They'll leave around ten, when the stairwell is dimmed, and be here by two, three at the latest. They'll be loaded down."

"And you think a dozen of your men is sufficient to keep things running down below?"

"As long as nothing major breaks, yeah." He scratched the back of his neck. "Where d'ya think the porters will fall? Or the people from the mids?"

She shrugged. "The mids see themselves as toppers mostly. I know, I spent my childhood up there. They go for the view and eat at the café as much as they can, justifying the climb.

The toppers are another question. I think we have more hope among them."

Knox wasn't sure he heard her correctly. "Say again?"

She looked up at him, and Knox felt the dog nuzzling against his boots, looking for company or warmth.

"Think about it," McLain said. "Why are you so riled up? Because you lost a good friend? That happens all the time. No, it's because you were *lied* to. And the toppers will feel this ever more keenly, trust me. They live in sight of those who've been lied to. It's the mids, the people who aspire upward without knowing and who look down on us without compassion, that will be the most reluctant."

"So you think we have allies up top?"

"That we can't get to, yeah. And they would take some convincing. A fine speech like you poisoned my people with."

She gifted him with a rare grin, and Knox felt himself beaming in return. And right then he knew, instantly, why her people were devoted to her. It was similar to the pull he had on others, but for different reasons. People feared him and wanted to feel safe. But they respected McLain and wanted to feel loved.

"The problem we're gonna have is that the mids are what separate us from IT." She drew her hand across the blueprint. "So we need to get through there quick but without starting a fight."

"I thought we'd just storm up before dawn," Knox grumbled. He leaned back and peered under the table at the dog, who was half sitting on one of his boots and looking up at him with its foolish tongue hanging out, tail wagging. All Knox saw in the animal was a machine that ate food and left shit behind. A furry ball of meat he wasn't allowed to eat. He nudged the filthy thing off his boot. "Scram," he said.

"Jackson, get over here." McLain snapped her fingers.

"I don't know why you keep those things around, much less breed more of 'em."

"You wouldn't," McLain snapped back. "They're good for the soul, for those of us who have them."

He checked to see if she was serious and found her smiling a little more easily now.

"Well, after we set this place right, I'm gonna push for a lottery for them, too. Get their numbers under control." He returned her sarcastic smile. Jackson whined until McLain reached down to pet him.

"If we were all as loyal as this to each other, there'd never need to *be* an uprising," she said, peering up at him.

He dipped his head, unable to agree. There had been a few dogs in Mechanical over the years, enough for him to know that some people felt this way, even if he didn't. He always shook his head at those who spent hard-earned chits on food that would fatten an animal that would never repay the favor. When Jackson crossed under the table and rubbed against his knee, whining to be petted, Knox left his hands spread out on the blueprint, defiant.

"What we need for the trip up is a diversion," McLain said. "Something to thin the numbers in the mids. It'd be nice if we could get more of them to go up top, because we're going to make a racket moving this many people up the stairs."

"We? Wait, you don't think you're coming—"

"If my people are, then of course I am." She inclined her head. "I've been climbing ladders in the stockroom for over fifty years. You think a few flights of stairs will give me grief?"

Knox wasn't sure *anything* could give her grief. Jackson's tail thumped the leg of the table as the mutt stood there, looking up at him with that dumb grin his breed habitually wore.

"What about welding doors shut on the way up?" Knox asked. "Keep them in until this is all over."

"And do what afterward? Just apologize? What if this takes weeks?"

"Weeks?"

"You don't think it'll be that easy, do you? Just march up and take the reins?"

"I'm under no delusions about what comes next." He pointed at her office door, which led out to the workshops full of clacking machinery. "Our people are building the implements of war, and I aim to use them if it comes to that. I will gladly take a peaceful transfer, would be satisfied pushing Bernard and a few others out to clean, but I have never shied away from getting dirty, either."

McLain nodded. "Just so we're both clear—"

"Clear as glass," he said.

He clapped his hands, an idea forming. Jackson ducked away from the sudden noise.

"I've got it," he told her. "A diversion." He pointed to the lower floors of Mechanical on the blueprint. "What if we have Jenkins cascade a power outage? We could start a few levels above this, or even better, with the farms and the mess halls. Blame it on the recent generator work—"

"And you think the mids'll clear out?" She narrowed her eyes.

"If they want a warm meal. Or they'll hunker down in the dark."

"I think they'll be in the stairwell gossiping, wondering what all the fuss is about. Even more in our way."

"Then we'll tell them we're going up to fix the problem!" Knox felt himself getting frustrated. The damn dog was sitting on his boot again.

"*Up* to fix a problem?" McLain laughed. "When's the last time *that* made any sense?"

Knox pulled on his beard. He wasn't sure what was so complicated. There were a lot of them. They worked with tools all day. They were going to beat in tech heads, little men like Bernard who sat on their butts and clacked on keyboards like secretaries. They just needed to go up there and *do* it.

"You got any better ideas?" he asked.

"We need to keep in mind the *after,*" McLain said. "After you've bludgeoned some people to death and the blood is dripping through the grates, what then? Do you want people living in fear of that happening again? Or of whatever you put them through to get there?"

"I only want to hurt those that lied," he said. "That's all any of us want. We've *all* lived in fear. Fear of the outside. Fear of cleaning. Afraid to even talk about a better world. And none of it was true. The system was rigged, and in a way to make us hang our heads and *take* it—"

Jackson barked up at him and began to whine, his tail swishing the floor like a dropped air hose with a stuck nozzle that had gone out of control.

"I think when we're done," he said, "and we start talking about using our know-how to explore a world we've only ever looked out at, I think that's gonna inspire some people. Hell, it gives me hope. Don't you feel anything?"

He reached down and rubbed Jackson's head, which stopped the animal from making so much noise. McLain looked at him for a while. She finally bobbed her head in agreement.

"We'll go with the power outage," she said with finality. "Tonight, before any who went to see the cleaning return disappointed. I'll lead up a squad with candles and flashlights, make it look like a goodwill mission headed by Supply. You'll follow a few hours later with the rest. We'll see how far the repair story gets us before we run into trouble. Hopefully, a good number will be staying in the up top, or back in their beds in the mids, too exhausted from climbing for a meal to care about the commotion."

“There’ll be less traffic those early hours,” Knox agreed, “so maybe we won’t run into too much trouble.”

“The goal will be to hit IT and contain it. Bernard is still playing mayor, so he probably won’t be there. But either he’ll come to us or we’ll push up after him once the thirties are secure. I don’t think he’ll put up much of a fight, not once his floors are ours.”

“Agreed,” Knox said, and it felt good to have a plan. To have an ally. “And hey, thanks for this.”

McLain smiled. “You give a good speech for a greaser,” she said. “And besides”—she nodded toward the dog—“Jackson likes you, and he’s hardly ever wrong. Not about men.”

Knox looked down and realized he was still scratching the mutt. He pulled his hand away and watched the animal pant, staring up at him. In the next room, someone laughed at a joke, the voices of his mechanics mixing with those of the members of Supply, all gently muffled by the wall and door. This laughter was joined by the sounds of steel rods bending into shape, flat pieces hammered sharp, machines for making rivets turned instead into making bullets. And Knox knew what McLain meant about loyalty. He saw it in that dumb dog’s eyes, that it would do anything for him if only he would ask. And this weight bearing down on his chest, of the many who felt that way for him and for McLain—Knox decided that *this* was the heaviest burden of them all.

44

Death's pale flag is not advanced there.

THE DIRT FARM BELOW filled the stairwell with the rich smell of fresh rot. Juliette was still waking up as she descended another level and began noticing the scent. She had no idea how long she'd slept—it had felt like days but could've been hours. She had woken with her face pressed to the grating, a pattern of red lines marking her cheek, and had gotten under way immediately. Her stomach was gnawing at her, the odor from the farm hurrying her along. By twenty-eight, the pungency hung in the air so thick it felt like she was swimming *through* the scents. It was the smell of death, she decided. Of funerals. Of loamy soil turned over, releasing all those tangy molecules into the air.

She stopped on thirty—the hydroponic farms—and tried the doors. It was dark inside. There was a sound down the hallway, the whir of a fan or a motor. It was a strange encounter, this small noise. For over a day, she had heard nothing but the sounds she made herself. The green glow of the emergency lights was no company; it was like the heat of a dying body, of batteries draining with the leak of photons. But this was something *moving,* some sound beyond her own breathing and footfalls, and it lurked deep in the dark corridors of the hydroponic farms.

Once again, she left her only tool and defense behind as a doorstop to allow in a trickle of light. She stole inside, the smell of vegetation not as strong as in the stairwell, and padded down the hallway with one hand on the wall. The offices and reception area were dark and lifeless, the air dry. There was no blinking light on the turnstile, and she had no card or chit to feed it. She placed her hands on the supports and vaulted over, this small act of defiance somehow powerful, as though she had come to accept the lawlessness of this dead place, the complete lack of civilization, of rules.

The light spilling from the stairwell barely reached the first of the growing rooms. She waited while her eyes adjusted, thankful for this ability honed by the down deep of Mechanical and the dark interiors of broken machines. What she saw, barely, when she was finally able, did not inspire her. The hydroponic gardens had rotted away. Thick stalks, like ropes, hung here and there from a network of suspended pipes. It gave her an idea of how long ago these farms had succumbed, if not the silo. It hadn't been hundreds of years, and it hadn't been days. Even a window that wide felt like a treasure of information, the first clue toward an answer to this mysterious place.

She rapped one of the pipes with her knuckles and heard the solid thud of fullness.

No plants, but water! Her mouth seemed to dry out with just the prospect. Juliette leaned over the railing and into the growing room. She pressed her mouth to one of the holes in the top of a pipe where the stalk of a plant should have been growing. She created a tight seal and sucked. The fluid that met her tongue was brackish and foul—but wet. And the taste was not of anything chemical or toxic, but stale organics. Dirt. It was only slightly more distasteful than the grease and oil she had practically been drenched in for two decades.

So she drank until she was full. And she realized, now that she had water, that if there were more crumbs to find, more clues, she might just live long enough to gather them.

Before she left, Juliette snapped a section of pipe off the end of a run, keeping the cap intact on one side. It was only a little over an inch in diameter and no more than two feet long, but it would work as a flask. She gently bent the broken pipe that remained down, allowing water to flow from the remaining loop. While she topped up her pipe, she splashed some water on her hands and arms, still fearful of contamination from the outside.

Once her pipe was full, Juliette stole back toward the lit doorway at the end of the hall. There were three hydroponic farms, all with closed loops that wound through long and twisting corridors. She tried to do a rough calculation in her head, but all she could come up with was enough to drink for a very long time. The aftertaste was awful, and she wouldn't be surprised if her stomach cramped from the contents, but if she could get a fire going, find enough fabric or leftover paper to burn, even that could be helped with a good boil.

Back in the stairwell, she returned to the rich odors she had left behind. She retrieved her knife and hurried down another thick slice of the silo, almost two times around the stairwell to the next landing, and checked the door.

The smell was definitely coming from the dirt farms. And Juliette could hear that whirring motor again, louder now. She stopped the door, propped her flask against the railing, and checked inside.

The smell of vegetation was overpowering. Ahead, in the dim green glow, she could see bushy arms reaching over the railings and into the pathway. She vaulted the security gate and explored the edge, one hand on the wall while her eyes adjusted again. There was definitely a pump running somewhere. She could also hear water dripping, either from a leak or a functioning tap. Juliette felt chills from the leaves brushing her arms. The smell of rot was distinguishable now: it was the odor of fruit and vegetables decaying in the soil and withering on the vine. She heard the buzz of flies, the sounds of life.

She reached into a thick stand of green and felt around until her hand hit something smooth. Juliette gave it a tug and held a plump tomato up to the light. Her timeline estimate suddenly shrank. How long could the dirt farms sustain themselves? Did tomatoes require seeding, or did they come back every year like the weeds? She couldn't remember. She took a bite, the tomato not yet fully ripe, and heard a noise behind her. Another pump clicking on?

She turned just in time to see the door to the stairwell slamming closed, plunging the dirt farm into absolute darkness.

Juliette froze. She waited for the sound of her knife rattling down through the staircase. She tried to imagine that it could've slipped and fallen on its own. With the light extinguished, her ears seemed to hijack the unused portion of her brain. Her breathing, even her pulse, seemed audible, the whirring of the pump louder now. Tomato in hand, she crouched down and moved toward the other wall, arms stretched out to feel her way. She slid toward the exit, staying low to avoid the plants, trying to calm herself. There were no ghosts here, nothing to be spooked about. She repeated this to herself as she slowly crept forward.

And then an arm was on her, reaching over her shoulder. Juliette cried out and dropped the tomato. The arm pinned her, holding her in a crouch as she tried to stand. She slapped at this intruder, tried to pull away from it, the tablecloth bonnet yanked from her head—until finally she felt the hard steel of the turnstile, one of the waist bars jutting out in the hallway, and felt the fool.

"You 'bout gave me a heart attack," she told the machine. She reached for its sides and lifted herself over. She would come back for more food once she had light. Leaving the turnstile and heading for the exit, one hand on the wall and another groping ahead of herself, Juliette wondered if she would start talking to objects now. Start going crazy. As the darkness absorbed her, she realized her mind-set was changing by the minute. Resigned to her death the day before, now she was frightened of mere insanity.

It was an improvement.

Her hand finally bumped into the door, and Juliette pushed it open. She cursed the loss of the knife; it was certainly missing from the grating. She wondered how far it might have fallen, if she'd ever find it again, or maybe a replacement. She turned to grab her flask—

And saw that it was missing as well.

Juliette felt her vision narrow, her heart quicken. She wondered if the closing of the door could have toppled her flask. She wondered how the knife had slipped through a gap in the grating narrower than its handle. And as the pounding in her temples receded, she heard something else.

Footsteps.

Ringing out on the stairwell below her.

Running.

45

These violent delights have violent ends.

THE COUNTERTOP IN SUPPLY rattled with the implements of war. Guns, freshly milled and wholly forbidden, were lined up like so many sticks of steel. Knox picked one up — could feel the heat in a barrel recently bored and rifled — and hinged the stock to expose the firing chamber. He reached into one of the buckets of shiny bullets, the casings chopped from thin tubes of pipe and packed with blasting powder, and slotted one into the brand-new gun. The operation of the machine seemed simple enough: point and pull the lever.

"Careful where you aim that," one of the men of Supply said, leaning out of the way.

Knox raised the barrel toward the ceiling and tried to picture what one of these could do. He'd only ever seen a gun once, a smaller one on the hip of that old deputy, a gun he'd always figured was more for show. He stuffed a fistful of deadly rounds in his pocket, thinking how each one could end an individual life and understanding why such things were forbidden. Killing a man should be harder than waving a length of pipe in their direction. It should take long enough for one's conscience to get in the way.

One of the Supply workers emerged from the stacks with a tub in his hands. The bend of his back and sag of his shoulders told Knox the thing was heavy. "Just two dozen of these so far," the man said, hoisting the bin to the counter.

Knox reached inside and pulled out one of the heavy cylinders. His mechanics and even some of the men and women in yellow eyed the bin nervously.

"Slam that end on something hard," the man behind the counter said, just as calmly as if he were doling out an electrical relay to a customer and giving some last-minute installation advice, "like a wall, the floor, the butt of your gun – anything like that. And then get rid of it."

"Are they safe to carry?" Shirly asked as Knox stuffed one into his hip pocket.

"Oh yeah, it takes some force."

Several people reached in the tub and clattered around for one. Knox caught McLain's eyes as she took one for herself and slotted it into a pocket on her chest. The look on her face was one of cool defiance. She must have seen how disappointed he was in her coming, and he could tell at a glance that there would be no reasoning with her.

"All right," she said, turning her gray-blue eyes toward the men and women gathered around the counter. "Listen up. We've got to get back open for business, so if you're carrying a gun, grab some ammo. There are strips of canvas over there. Wrap these things up as best you can to keep them out of sight. My group is leaving in five minutes, got that? Those of you in the second wave can wait in the back, out of sight."

Knox nodded. He glanced over at Marck and Shirly, both of whom would join him in the second wave; the slower climbers would go first and act casual. The stouter legs would follow and make a strong push, hopefully converging on thirty-four at the same time. Each group would be conspicuous enough –

combined, they might as well sing their intentions while they marched.

"You okay, boss?" Shirly rested her rifle on her shoulder and frowned at him. He rubbed his beard and wondered how much of his stress and fear was shining through.

"Fine," he grumbled. "Yeah."

Marck grabbed a bomb, stashed it away, and rested a hand on his wife's shoulder. Knox felt a pang of doubt. He wished the women didn't have to get involved — at least the wives. He continued to hope that the violence they were preparing for wouldn't be necessary, but it was getting harder and harder to pretend as eager hands took up arms. They were, all of them, now capable of taking lives, and he reckoned they were angry enough to do so.

McLain stepped through the opening in the counter and sized him up. "This is it, then." She reached out a hand.

Knox accepted it. He admired the strength in the woman. "We'll see you on thirty-five and go up the last level together," he said. "Don't have all the fun without us."

She smiled. "We won't."

"And good climbing." He looked to the men and women gathering up behind her. "All of you. Good luck and see you soon."

There were stern nods and clenched jaws. The small army in yellow began to file for the door, but Knox held McLain back.

"Hey," he said. "No trouble until we catch up, okay?"

She slapped his shoulder and smiled.

"And when this does go down," Knox said, "I expect you at the very back, behind the —"

McLain stepped closer, a hand gripping Knox's sleeve. Her wrinkled face had suddenly hardened.

"And tell me, where will you be, Knox of Mechanical, when the bombs fly? When these men and women who look up to us are facing their gravest test, where will you be?"

Knox was taken aback by the sudden attack, this quiet hiss that landed with all the force of a shout.

"You know where I'll—" he started to answer.

"Damn straight," McLain said, releasing his arm. "And you'd better well know that I'll see you there."

46

I dreamt my lady came and found me dead

JULIETTE STOOD PERFECTLY STILL and listened to the sound of footsteps retreating down the stairwell. She could feel the vibrations in the railing. Goose bumps rushed up her legs and down her arms. She wanted to call out, to yell for the person to stop, but the sudden surge of adrenaline made her chest feel cold and empty. It was like a chill wind had forced itself deep into her lungs, crowding out her voice. People were alive and in the silo with her. And they were running away.

She pushed away from the railing and dashed across the landing, hit the curved steps at a dead run and took them as fast as her legs could take her. A flight down, as the adrenaline subsided, she found the lungs to yell "Stop!" but the sound of her bare feet on the metal stairs seemed to drown out her voice. She could no longer hear the person running, dared not stop and listen for fear they would get too far ahead, but as she passed the doorway on thirty-two, she worried that they might slip inside some level and get away. And if there were only a handful of them hiding in the vast silo, she might never find them. Not if they didn't want to be found.

Somehow, this was more terrifying than anything else: that

she might live the rest of her days foraging and surviving in a dilapidated silo, talking to inanimate objects, while a group of people did the same and stayed out of sight. It so stressed her that it took a while to consider the opposite: that this might instead be a group who *would* seek her out, and not have the best intentions.

They wouldn't have the best intentions, but they would have her knife.

She stopped on thirty-two to listen, hands clamped to the railing. Holding her breath to keep quiet was almost impossible—her lungs were crying out for deep gulps of air. But she remained still, the pulse in her palms beating against the cool railing, the distinct sound of footsteps still below her and louder now. She was catching up! She took off again, emboldened, taking the steps three at a time, her body sideways as she danced down the stairs as she had in youth, one hand on the curving railing, the other held out in front of her for balance, the balls of her feet just barely touching a tread before she was flying down to the next, concentrating lest she slip. A spill could be deadly at such speeds. Images of casts on arms and legs and stories of the unfortunate elderly with broken hips came to mind. Still, she pushed her limits, positively flying. Thirty-three went by in a blaze. Half a spiral later, over her footfalls, she heard a door slam. She stopped and looked up. She leaned over the railing and peered down. The footfalls were gone, leaving just the sound of her panting for air.

Juliette hurried down another rotation of the steps and checked the door on thirty-four. It wouldn't open. It wasn't locked, though. The handle clicked down and the door moved, but it caught on something. Juliette tugged as hard as she could—but to no avail. She yanked again and heard something crack. With a foot braced on the other door, she tried a third time, yanking sharply, snapping her head back, pulling her arms toward her chest and kicking with her foot—

Something snapped. The door flew open, and she lost her grip on the handle. There was an explosion of light from inside, a bright burst of illumination spilling out the door before it slammed shut again.

Juliette scrambled across the landing and grabbed the handle again. She pulled the door open and struggled to her feet. One broken half of a broomstick lay inside the hallway; the other half hung from the handle of the neighboring door. Both stood out in the blinding light all around her. The overhead lamps inside the room were fully lit, the bright rectangles in the ceiling marching down the hall and out of sight. Juliette listened for footsteps but heard little more than the buzzing of the bulbs. The turnstile ahead of her winked its red eye over and over, like it knew secrets but wouldn't tell.

She got up and approached the machine, looked to the right where a glass wall peeked into a conference room, the lights full on in there as well. She hopped over the stile, the motion a habit already, and called out another hello. Her voice echoed back, but it sounded different in the lit air, if that were possible. There was life in here, electricity, other ears to hear her voice, which made the echoes somehow fainter.

She passed offices, peeking in each one to look for signs of life. The place was a mess. Drawers dumped on the floor, metal filing cabinets tipped over, precious paper everywhere. One of the desks faced her, and Juliette could see that the computer was on, the screen full of green text. It felt as though she'd entered a dream world. In two days—assuming she'd slept that long—her brain had gradually acclimated to the pale-green glow of the emergency lights, had grown used to a life in the wilderness, a life without power. She still had the taste of brackish water on her tongue, and now she strolled through a disheveled but otherwise normal workplace. She imagined the next shift (did offices like these have shifts?) returning, laughing, from the stairwell, shuffling papers and righting furniture and getting back to work.

The thought of work had her wondering what they did here. She had never seen such a layout. She almost forgot her flight down the stairs as she poked about, as curious about the rooms and power as the footsteps that had brought her there. Around a bend she came to a wide metal door that, unlike the others, wouldn't open. Juliette heaved on it and felt it barely budge. She pressed her shoulder against the metal door and pushed it, a few inches at a time, until she could squeeze through. She had to step over a tall metal filing cabinet that had been yanked down in front of the heavy door in an attempt to hold it closed.

The room was massive, at least as big as the generator room and far larger than the cafeteria. It was full of tall pieces of furniture bigger than filing cabinets but with no drawers. Instead, their fronts were covered with blinking lights, red, green, and amber.

Juliette shuffled through paper that had spilled from the filing cabinet. And she realized, as she did so, that she couldn't be alone in the room. Someone had pulled the cabinet across the door, and they had to have done this from *inside.*

"Hello?"

She passed through the rows of tall machines, for that's what she figured they were. They hummed with electricity, and now and then seemed to whir or clack like their innards were busy. She wondered if this was some sort of exotic power plant — providing the lighting perhaps? Or did these have stacks of batteries inside? Seeing all the cords and cables at thc backs of the units had her leaning toward batteries. No wonder the lights were blaring. This was like twenty of Mechanical's battery rooms combined.

"Is anyone here?" she called out. "I mean you no harm."

She worked her way through the room, listening for any movement, until she came across one of the machines with its door hinged open. Peering inside, she saw not batteries but boards like the kind Walker was forever soldering. In fact, the guts of this machine looked eerily similar to the inside of the dispatch room's computer—

Juliette stepped back, realizing what these were. "The servers," she whispered. She was in this silo's IT. Level thirty-four. Of course.

There was a scraping sound near the far wall, the sound of metal sliding on metal. Juliette ran in that direction, darting between the tall units, wondering who the hell this was running from her and where they planned to hide.

She rounded the last row of servers to see a portion of the floor moving, a section of metal grate sliding to cover a hole. Juliette dived for the floor, her tablecloth garb wrapping around her legs, her hands seizing the edge of the cover before it could close. Right in front of her, she saw the knuckles and fingers of a man's hands gripping the edge of the grate. There was a startled scream, a grunt of effort. Juliette tried to yank back on the grate but had no leverage. One of the hands disappeared. A knife took its place, snicking against the grate, hunting for her fingers.

Juliette swung her feet beneath her and sat up for leverage. She yanked on the grate and felt the knife bite into her finger as she did so.

She screamed. The man below her screamed. He emerged and held the knife between them, his hand shaking, the blade catching and reflecting the overhead lights. Juliette tossed the metal hatch away and clutched her hand, which was dripping blood.

"Easy!" she said, scooting out of reach.

The man ducked his head down, then poked it back up. He looked past Juliette as if others were coming up behind her. She fought the urge to check—but decided to trust the silence just in case he was trying to fool her.

"Who are you?" she asked. She wrapped part of her garment around her hand to bandage it. She noticed the man, his beard thick and unkempt, was wearing gray overalls. They could've been made in her silo, with just slight differences. He stared at her, his dark hair wild and hanging shaggy over his face. He grunted, coughed into his hand, seemed prepared to duck down under the floor and disappear.

"Stay," Juliette said. "I mean you no harm."

The man looked at her wounded hand and at the knife. Juliette glanced down to see a thin trace of blood snaking toward her elbow. The wound ached, but she'd had worse in her time as a mechanic.

"S-s-sorry," the man muttered. He licked his mouth and swallowed. The knife was trembling uncontrollably.

"My name's Jules," she said, realizing this man was much more frightened of her than the other way around. "What's yours?"

He glanced at the knife blade held sideways between them, almost as if checking a mirror. He shook his head.

"No name," he whispered, his voice a dry rasp. "No need."

"Are you alone?" she asked.

He shrugged. "Solo," he said. "Years." He looked up at her. "Where did"—he licked his lips again, cleared his throat; his eyes watered and glinted in the light—"you come from? What level?"

"You've been by yourself for *years?*" Juliette said in wonder. She couldn't imagine. "I didn't come from any level," she told him. "I came from another silo." She enunciated this last softly and slowly, worried what this news might do to such a seemingly fragile man.

But Solo nodded as if this made sense. It was not the reaction Juliette had expected.

"The outside . . ." Solo looked again at the knife. He reached out of the hole and set it on the grating, slid it away from both of them. "Is it safe?"

Juliette shook her head. "No," she said. "I had a suit. It wasn't a far walk. But still, I shouldn't be alive."

Solo bobbed his head. He looked up at her, wet tracks running from the corners of his eyes and disappearing into his beard. "None of us should," he said. "Not a one."

47

Give leave awhile,
we must talk in secret.

"WHAT IS THIS PLACE?" Lukas asked Bernard. The two of them stood before a large chart hanging on the wall like a tapestry. The diagrams were precise, the lettering ornate. It showed a grid of circles evenly spaced with lines between them and intricacies inside each. Several of the circles were crossed out with thick red marks of ink. It was just the sort of majestic diagramming he hoped to achieve one day with his star charts.

"This is our Legacy," Bernard said simply.

Lukas had often heard him speak similarly of the mainframes upstairs.

"Are these supposed to be the servers?" he asked, daring to rub his hands across a piece of paper the size of a small bedsheet. "They're laid out like the servers."

Bernard stepped beside him and rubbed his chin. "Hmm. Interesting. So they are. I never noticed that before."

"What are they?" Lukas looked closer and saw each was numbered. There was also a jumble of squares and rectangles in one corner with parallel lines spaced between them, keeping the blocky shapes separate and apart. These figures contained no detail within them, but the word *Atlanta* was written in large letters beneath.

"We'll get to that. Come, let me show you something."

At the end of the room was a door. Bernard led him through this, turning on more lights as he went.

"Who else comes down here?" Lukas asked, following along.

Bernard glanced back over his shoulder. "No one."

Lukas didn't like that answer. He glanced back over his own shoulder, feeling like he was descending into something people didn't return from.

"I know this must seem sudden," Bernard said. He waited for Lukas to join him, threw his small arm around Lukas's shoulder. "But things changed this morning. The world is changing. And she rarely does it pleasantly."

"Is this about . . . the cleaning?" He'd nearly said *Juliette*. The picture of her felt hot against his breastbone.

Bernard's face grew stern. "There was no cleaning," he said abruptly. "And now all hell will break loose, and people will die. And the silos, you see, were designed from the ground down to prevent this."

"Designed," Lukas repeated. His heart beat once, twice. His brain whirred through its circuits and finally computed that Bernard had said something that had made no sense.

"I'm sorry," he said. "Did you say *silos?*"

"You'll want to familiarize yourself with this." Bernard gestured toward a small desk which had a fragile-looking wooden chair tucked up against it. There was a book on the desk unlike any Lukas had ever seen, or even heard of. It was nearly as thick as it was wide. Bernard patted the cover, then inspected his palm for dust. "I'll give you the spare key, which you are never to remove from your neck. Come down when you can and read. Our history is in here, as well as every action you are to take in any emergency."

Lukas approached the book, a lifetime's worth of paper, and hinged open the cover. The contents were machine printed, the ink pitch-black. He flipped through a dozen pages of listed contents until he found the first page of the main text. Oddly, he recognized the opening lines immediately.

"It's the Pact," he said, looking up at Bernard. "I already know quite a bit of—"

"This is the Pact," Bernard told him, pinching the first half inch of the thick book. "The rest is the Order."

He stepped back.

Lukas hesitated, digesting this, then reached forward and flopped the tome open near its middle.

- In the Event of an Earthquake:
- For casement cracking and outside leak, see airlock breach (p. 2180)
- For collapse of one or more levels, see support columns under sabotage (p. 751)
- For fire outbreak, see . . .

"Sabotage?" Lukas flipped a few pages and read something about air handling and asphyxiation. "Who came up with all this stuff?"

"People who experienced many bad things."

"Like . . . ?" He wasn't sure if he was allowed to say this, but it felt like taboos were allowed to be broken down there. "Like the people before the uprising?"

"The people before *those* people," Bernard said. "The one people."

Lukas closed the book. He shook his head, wondering if this was all a gag, some kind of initiation. The priests usually made more sense than this. The children's books, too.

"I'm not *really* supposed to learn all this, am I?"

Bernard laughed. His countenance had fully transformed from earlier. "You just need to know what's in there so you can access it when you need to."

"What does it say about this morning?" He turned to Bernard, and it dawned on him suddenly that no one knew of his fascination, his enchantment, with Juliette. The tears had evaporated from his cheeks; the guilt of possessing her forbidden things had overpowered his shame for falling so hard for someone he hardly knew. And now this secret had wandered out of sight. It could be betrayed only by the flush he felt on his cheeks as Bernard studied him and pondered his question.

"Page seventy-two," Bernard said, the humor draining from his face and replaced with the frustration from earlier.

Lukas turned back to the book. This was a test. A shadowing rite. It had been a long time since he'd performed under a caster's glare. He began flipping through the pages and saw at once that the section he was looking for came right after the Pact, was at the very beginning of the Order.

He found the page. At the very top, in bold print, it said:

- In the Event of a Failed Cleaning:

And below this rested terrible words strung into awful meaning. Lukas read the instructions several times, just to make sure. He glanced over at Bernard, who nodded sadly, before Lukas turned back to the print.

- In the Event of a Failed Cleaning:
- Prepare for War.

48

Poor living corpse, closed in a dead man's tomb!

JULIETTE FOLLOWED SOLO THROUGH the hole in the server-room floor. There was a long ladder there and a passageway that led to thirty-five, a part of thirty-five she suspected was not accessible from the stairwell. Solo confirmed this as they ducked through the narrow passageway and followed a twisting and brightly lit corridor. A blockage seemed to have come unstuck from the man's throat, releasing a lone-stricken torrent. He talked about the servers above them, saying things that made little sense to Juliette, until the passageway opened into a cluttered room.

"My home," Solo said, spreading his hands. There was a mattress on the floor in one corner, a tangled mess of sheets and pillows trailing from it. A makeshift kitchen had been arranged across two shelving units: jugs of water, canned food, empty jars and boxes. The place was a wreck and smelled foul, but Juliette figured Solo couldn't see or smell any of that. There was a wall of shelves on the other side of the room stocked with metal canisters the size of large ratchet sets, some of them partially open.

"You live here alone?" Juliette asked. "Is there no one else?" She couldn't help but hear the thin hope in her voice.

Solo shook his head.

"What about further down?" Juliette inspected her wound. The bleeding had almost stopped.

"I don't think so," he said. "Sometimes I do. I'll find a tomato missing, but I figure it's the rats." He stared at the corner of the room. "Can't catch them all," he said. "More and more of them—"

"Sometimes you think there's more of you, though? More survivors?" She wished he would focus.

"Yeah." He rubbed his beard, looked around the room like there was something he should have been doing for her, something you offered guests. "I find things moved sometimes. Find things left out. The grow lights left on. Then I remember *I* did them."

He laughed to himself. It was the first natural thing she'd seen him do, and Jules figured he'd been doing a lot of it over the years. You laughed either to keep yourself sane or because you'd given up on staying that way. Either way, you laughed.

"Thought the knife in the door was something I did. Then I found the pipe. Wondered if it was left behind by a really, really big rat."

Juliette smiled. "I'm no rat," she said. She adjusted her tablecloth, patted her head, and wondered what had happened to her other scrap of cloth.

Solo seemed to consider this.

"So how many years has it been?" she asked.

"Thirty-four," he said, no pause.

"Thirty-four *years?* Since you've been *alone?*"

He nodded, and the floor seemed to fall away from her. Her head spun with the concept of that much time with no other person around.

"How *old* are you?" she asked. He didn't seem all that much older than her.

"Fifty," he said. "Next month, I'm pretty sure." He smiled. "This is fun, talking." He pointed around the room. "I talk to things sometimes, and whistle." He looked straight at her. "I'm a good whistler."

Juliette realized she probably had only just been *born* when whatever happened here took place. "How exactly have you *survived* all these years?" she asked.

"I dunno. Didn't set out to survive for years. Tried to last hours. They stack up. I eat. I sleep. And I . . ." He looked away, went to one of the shelves and sorted through some cans, many of them empty. He found one with the lid hinged open, no label, and held it out toward her. "Bean?" he asked.

Her impulse was to decline, but the eager look on his poor face made it impossible. "Sure," she said, and she realized how hungry she was. She could still taste the brackish water from earlier, the tang of stomach acid, the unripe tomato. He stepped closer, and she dug into the wet juice in the can and came out with a raw green bean. She popped it into her mouth and chewed.

"And I poop," he said bashfully while she was swallowing. "Not pretty." He shook his head and fished for a bean. "I'm by myself, so I just go in apartment bathrooms until I can't stand the smell."

"In *apartments?*" Juliette asked.

Solo looked for a place to set down the beans. He finally did, on the floor, among a small pile of other garbage and bachelor debris.

"Nothing flushes. No water. I'm by myself." He looked embarrassed.

"Since you were sixteen," Juliette said, having done the math. "What happened here thirty-four years ago?"

He lifted his arms. "What always happens. People go crazy.

It only needs to happen once." He smiled. "We get no credit for being sane, do we? I get no credit. Even from me. From myself. I hold it together and hold it together and I make it another day, another year, and there's no reward. Nothing great about me being normal. About not being crazy." He frowned. "Then you have one bad day, and you worry for yourself, you know? It only takes one."

He suddenly sat down on the floor, crossed his legs, and twisted the fabric of his overalls where they bunched up at his knees. "Our silo had one bad day. Was all it took." He looked up at Juliette. "No credit for all the years before that. Nope. You wanna sit?"

He gestured at the floor. Again, she couldn't say no. She sat down, away from the reeking bed, and rested her back against the wall. There was so much to digest.

"How did you survive?" she asked. "That bad day, I mean. And since."

She immediately regretted asking. It wasn't important to know. But she felt some need, maybe to glimpse what awaited her, maybe because she feared that surviving in this place could be worse than dying on the outside.

"Staying scared," he said. "My dad's caster was the head of IT. Of this place." He nodded. "My dad was a big shadow. Knew about these rooms, one of maybe two or three who did. In just the first few minutes of fighting, he showed me this place, gave me his keys. He made a diversion, and suddenly I became the only one who knew about this place." He looked down at his lap a moment, then back up. Juliette realized why he seemed so much younger. It wasn't just the fear, the shyness, that made him seem that way—it was in his eyes. He was locked in the perpetual terror of his teenage ordeal. His body was simply growing old around the frozen husk of a frightened little boy.

He licked his lips. "None of them made it, did they? The ones who got out?" Solo searched her face for answers. She could feel the dire hope leaking out of his pores.

"No," she said sadly, remembering what it felt like to wade through them, to crawl over them. It felt like weeks ago rather than days.

"So you saw them out there? Dead?"

She nodded.

He dipped his chin. "The view didn't stay on for long. I only snuck up once in the early days. There was still a lot of fighting going on. As time went by, I snuck out more often and further. I found a lot of the mess they made. But I haven't found a body in" — he thought carefully — "maybe twenty years?"

"So there were others in here for a while?"

He pointed toward the ceiling. "Sometimes they would come in here. With the servers. And fight. They fought everywhere. Got worse as it went along, you know? Fight over food, fight over women, fight over fighting." He twisted at the waist and pointed back through another door. "These rooms are like a silo in a silo. Made to last ten years. But it lasts longer if you're solo." He smiled.

"What do you mean? A silo in a silo?"

He nodded. "Of course," he said. "Sorry. I'm used to talking with someone who knows everything I know." He winked at her, and Juliette realized he meant himself. "You don't know what a silo is."

"Of course I do," she said. "I was born and raised in a place just like this. Only, I guess you could say that we're still having good days and not giving ourselves credit for them."

Solo smiled. "Then what's a silo?" he asked, that teenage defiance bubbling to the surface.

"It's . . ." Juliette searched for the words. "It's our home. A building like those over the hill, but underground. The silo is the part of the world you can live in. The *inside,*" she said, realizing it was harder to define than she thought.

Solo laughed.

"That's what the word means to *you.* But we use words all the time without really understanding them." He pointed toward the shelf with all the metal canisters. "All the real knowing is in those. Everything that ever happened." He shot her a look. "You've heard the term 'raging bull'? Or someone being 'bullheaded'?"

She nodded. "Of course."

"But what's a bull?" he asked.

"Someone who's careless. Or mean, like a bully."

Solo laughed. "So much we don't know," he said. He studied his fingernails. "A silo isn't the world. It's nothing. The term, this word, comes from a long time ago, back when crops grew in the outside further than you could see" — he waved his hand over the floor like it was some vast terrain — "back when there were more people than you could count, back when everyone had lots of kids." He glanced up at her. His hands came together and kneaded one another, almost as if embarrassed to bring up the making of kids around a woman.

"They grew so much food," he continued, "that even for all these people they couldn't eat it all, not at once. So they stored it away in case times got bad. They took more seeds of grain than you could count and they would pour them into these great silos that stood aboveground —"

"Aboveground," Juliette said. "Silos." She felt as though he must be making this up, some delusion he'd concocted over the lonely decades.

"I can show you pictures," he said petulantly, as if upset by her doubt. He got up and hurried to the shelf with the metal canisters. He read the small white labels on the bottom, running his fingers across them.

"Ah!" He grabbed one—it looked heavy—and brought it to her. The clasp on the side released the lid, revealing a thick object inside.

"Let me," he said, even though she hadn't moved a muscle to help. He tilted the box and let the heavy object fall onto his palm, where it balanced expertly. It was the size of a children's book, but ten or twenty times as thick. Still, it was a book. She could see the edges of miraculously fine-cut paper.

"I'll find it," he said. He flipped pages in large chunks, each flap a fortune in pressed paper clapping solidly against more fortunes. Then he whittled his search down more finely, a pinch at a time, before moving to a single page at a time.

"Here." He pointed.

Juliette moved closer and looked. It was like a drawing, but so exact as to almost seem real. It was like looking at the view of the outside from the cafeteria, or the picture of someone's face on an ID, but in color. She wondered if this book had batteries in it.

"It's so real," she whispered, rubbing it with her fingers.

"It *is* real," he said. "It's a picture. A photograph."

Juliette marveled at the colors, the green field and blue sky reminding her of the lies she had seen in her visor's false images. She wondered if this was false as well. It looked nothing like the rough and smeared photos she'd ever seen.

"These buildings"—he pointed to what looked like large white cans sitting on the ground—"these are silos. They hold seed for the bad times. For until the times get good again."

He looked up at her. They were just a few feet apart, Juliette and him. She could see the wrinkles around his eyes, could see how much the beard concealed his age.

"I'm not sure what you're trying to say," she told him.

He pointed at her. Pointed at his own chest. "We are the

seeds," he said. "This is a silo. They put us here for the bad times."

"Who? Who put us here? And what bad times?"

He shrugged. "But it won't work." He shook his head, then sat back on the floor and peered at the pictures in the massive book. "You can't leave seeds this long," he said. "Not in the dark like this. Nope."

He glanced up from the book and bit his lip, water welling up in his eyes. "Seeds don't go crazy," he told her. "They don't. They have bad days and lots of good ones, but it doesn't matter. You leave them and leave them, however many you bury, and they do what seeds do when they're left alone too long . . ."

He stopped. Closed the book and held it to his chest. Juliette watched as he rocked back and forth, ever so slightly.

"What do seeds do when they're left too long?" she asked him.

He frowned.

"We rot," he said. "All of us. We go bad down here, and we rot so deep that we won't grow anymore." He blinked and looked up at her. "We'll never grow again."

49

If you had the strength of twenty men,
it would dispatch you straight.

THE WAITING BEYOND THE stacks of Supply was the worst. Those who could napped. Most engaged in nervous banter. Knox kept checking the time on the wall, picturing all the pieces moving throughout the silo. Now that his people were armed, all he could hope for was a smooth and bloodless transfer of power. He hoped they could get their answers, find out what had been going on in IT—those secretive bastards—and maybe vindicate Jules. But he knew bad things could happen.

He saw it on Marck's face, the way he kept looking at Shirly. The worry there was evident in the man's frown, the tilt of his eyebrows, the wrinkles above the bridge of his nose. Knox's shift leader wasn't hiding the concern for his wife as well as he probably thought he was.

Knox pulled out his multi-tool and checked the blade. He flashed his teeth in the reflection to see if anything from his last meal was stuck there. As he was putting it away, one of Supply's shadows emerged from behind the stacks to let them know they had visitors.

"What color visitors?" Shirly asked as the group gathered their guns and lurched to their feet.

The young girl pointed at Knox. "Blue. Same as you."

Knox rubbed the girl's head as he slipped between the shelving units. This was a good sign. The rest of his people from Mechanical were running ahead of schedule. He made his way to the counter while Marck gathered the others, waking a few, the extra rifles clattering as they were gathered up.

As Knox rounded the counter, he saw Pieter enter through the front door, the two Supply workers guarding the landing having allowed him past.

Pieter smiled as he and Knox clasped hands. Members of Pieter's refinery crew filed in behind, their customary black overalls replaced with the more discreet blue.

"How goes it?" Knox asked.

"The stairs sing with traffic," Pieter said. His chest swelled as he took in and held a deep breath, then blew it out. Knox imagined the pace they'd maintained to shave off so much time.

"Everyone's under way?" He and Pieter slid to the side while their two groups merged, members of Supply introducing themselves or embracing those they already knew.

"They are." He nodded. "I'd give the last of them another half hour. Though I fear the whispers on porters' lips travel even faster than we do." He looked toward the ceiling. "I'd wager they echo above our heads even now."

"Suspicions?" Knox asked.

"Oh, aye. We had a run-in by the lower market. People wanted to know the fuss. Georgie gave them lip, and I thought it'd come to blows."

"God, and not in the mids yet."

"Aye. Can't help but think a smaller incursion would've had a greater chance of success."

Knox frowned, but he understood Pieter's thinking so. The man was used to doing a great deal with only a handful of strong backs. But it was too late for them to argue over plans already in action. "Well, the blackouts have likely begun," Knox said. "There's nothing to it but for us to chase them up."

Pieter nodded gravely. He looked around the room at the men and women arming themselves and repacking their gear for another quick climb. "And I suppose we mean to bludgeon our way up."

"Our plan is to be heard," Knox said. "Which means making some noise."

Pieter patted his boss on the arm. "Well then, we are already winning."

He left to pick out a gun and top up his canteen. Knox joined Marck and Shirly by the door. Those without guns had armed themselves with fearsome shanks of flattened iron, the edges bright silver from the shrill work of the grinder. It was amazing to Knox that they all knew, instinctively, how to build implements of pain. It was something even shadows knew how to do at a young age, knowledge somehow dredged up from the brutal depths of their imagination, this ability to deal harm to one another.

"Are the others running behind?" Marck asked Knox.

"Not too bad," Knox said. "More that these guys made good time. The rest'll catch up. You guys ready?"

Shirly nodded. "Let's get moving," she said.

"All right, then. Onward and upward, as they say." Knox scanned the room and watched his mechanics meld with members of Supply. More than a few faces were turned his way, waiting for some sign, maybe another speech. But Knox didn't have another one in him. All he had was the fear that he was leading good people to their slaughter, that the taboos were falling in some runaway cascade, and it was all happening much too quickly. Once guns were made, who would unmake them? Barrels rested on shoulders and bristled like pincushions above the crowd. There were things, like spoken ideas, that were almost impossible to take back. And he reckoned his people were about to make many more of them.

"On me," he growled, and the chatter began to die down. Packs rustled into place, pockets jangling with danger. "On me," he said again to the quieting room, and his soldiers began to form up in columns. Knox turned to the door, thinking this was certainly all *on him*. He made sure his rifle was covered, tucked it under his arm, and squeezed Shirly's shoulder as she pulled the door open for him.

Outside, two workers from Supply stood by the railing. They had been turning the sparse traffic away with a made-up power outage. With the doors open, bright light and the noise of Supply's machinery leaked out into the stairwell, and Knox saw what Pieter meant by whispers traveling swifter than feet. He adjusted his pack of supplies — the tools, candles, and flashlights that made it seem as if he were marching to aid rather than war. Beneath this beguiling layer were secreted more bullets and an extra bomb, bandages and pain salve for just in case. His rifle was wrapped in a strip of cloth and remained tucked under his arm. Knowing what it was, he found the concealment ridiculous. Looking at the others marching with him, some in welding smocks, some holding construction helmets, he saw their intentions were all too obvious.

They left the landing and the light spilling from Supply behind and began their climb. Several of his people from Mechanical had changed into yellow overalls, the better to blend in the mids. They moved noisily up the dimmed nighttime glow of the stairwell, the shiver of traffic from below giving Knox hope that the rest of his people would be catching up soon. He felt sorry for their weary legs but reminded himself that they were traveling light.

He tried his damnedest to picture the coming morning as positively as he could. Perhaps the clash would conclude before any more of his people arrived. Maybe they would end up being nothing more than a wave of supporters coming to join in the celebrations. Knox and McLain would have already entered the forbidden levels of IT, would have yanked the cover off the inscrutable machinery inside, exposing those evil whirring cogs once and for all.

They made good progress while Knox dreamed of a smooth overthrow. They passed one landing where a group of women were hanging laundry over the metal railing to dry. The women spotted Knox and his people in their blue overalls and complained of the power outages. Several of his workers stopped to hand out supplies and to spread lies. It wasn't until after they had left and had wound their way up to the next level that Knox saw the cloth had come unwrapped from Marck's barrel. He pointed this out and it was fixed before the next landing.

The climb turned into a silent, grueling ordeal. Knox let others take the lead while he slid back and checked on the status of his people. Even those in Supply he considered his responsibility. Their lives were hanging in the balance of decisions he'd made. It was just as Walker had said, that crazy fool. This was it. An uprising, just like the fables of their youth. And Knox suddenly felt a dire kinship with those old ghosts, those ancestors of myth and lore. Men and women had done this before—maybe for different reasons, with a less noble anger caught in their throats, but somewhen, on some level, there had been a march like this. Similar boots on the same treads. Maybe some of the same boots, just with new soles. All with the jangle of mean machines in hands not afraid to use them.

It startled Knox, this sudden link to a mysterious past. And it wasn't that terribly long ago, was it? Less than two hundred years? He imagined, if someone lived as long as Jahns had, or McLain for that matter, that three long lives could span that distance. Three handshakes to go from that uprising to this one. And what of the years between? That long peace sandwiched between two wars?

Knox lifted his boots from one step to another, thinking over these things. Had he become the bad people he'd learned about in youth? Or had he been lied to? It hurt his head to consider, but here he was, leading a revolution. And yet it felt so right. So *necessary.* What if that former clash had felt the same? Had felt the same in the breasts of the men and women who'd waged it?

50

Methinks I see thee, now thou art so low,
As one dead in the bottom of a tomb.

"It would take ten lifetimes to read all these."

Juliette looked up from the pile of scattered tins and stacks of thick books. There was more to marvel at in their text-heavy pages than in any of the children's books of her youth.

Solo turned from the stove, where he was heating soup and boiling water. He waved a dripping metal spoon at the scattered mess she'd made. "I don't think they were meant to be read," he told her. "At least, not like I've been reading them, front to back." He touched his tongue to the spoon, then stuck it back in the pot and stirred. "Everything's out of order. It's more like a backup to the backup."

"I don't know what that means," Juliette admitted. She looked down at her lap, where pictures of animals called "butterflies" filled the pages. Their wings were comically bright. She wondered if they were the size of her hands or the size of people. She had yet to find any sense of scale for the beasts.

"The servers," Solo said. "What did you think I meant? The backup."

He sounded flustered. Juliette watched him busy about the

stove, his movements jerky and manic, and realized *she* was the one cloistered away and ignorant, not him. He had all these books, decades of reading history, the company of ancestors she could only imagine. What did she have as her experience? A life in a dark hole with thousands of fellow ignorant savages?

She tried to remember this as she watched him dig a finger in his ear and then inspect his fingernail.

"The backup of what exactly?" she finally asked, almost afraid of the cryptic answer to come.

Solo found two bowls. He began wiping one out with the fabric in the belly of his overalls. "The backup of *everything,*" he said. "All that we know. All that ever was." He set the bowls down and adjusted a knob on the stove. "Follow me," he said, waving his arm. "I'll show you."

Juliette closed the book and slotted it into its tin. She rose and followed Solo out of the room and into the next one.

"Don't mind the mess," he said, gesturing at a small hill of trash and debris piled up against one wall. It looked like a thousand empty cans of food, and smelled like ten thousand. Juliette wrinkled her nose and fought the reflex to gag. Solo seemed unaffected. He stood beside a small wooden desk and flipped through diagrams hanging from the wall on enormous sheets of paper.

"Where's the one I want?" he wondered aloud.

"What are these?" Juliette asked, entranced. She saw one that looked like a schematic of the silo, but unlike any they'd had in Mechanical.

Solo turned. He had several sheets flopped over one shoulder, his body practically disappearing between the layers of them. "Maps," he said. "I want to show you how much is out there. You'll shit yourself."

He shook his head and muttered something to himself. "Sorry, didn't mean to say that."

Juliette told him it was fine. She held the back of her hand to her nose, the stench of rotting food intolerable.

"Here it is. Hold this end." Solo held out the corner of a half-dozen sheets of paper. He took the other side and they lifted them away from the wall. Juliette felt like pointing out the grommets at the bottom of the maps and how there were probably sticks or hooks around here somewhere for propping them up, but held her tongue. Opening her mouth just made the smell of the rotting cans worse.

"This is us," Solo said. He pointed to a spot on the paper. Dark, squiggly lines were everywhere. It didn't look like a map or schematic of anything Juliette had ever seen. It looked like children had drawn it. Hardly a straight line existed anywhere.

"What's this supposed to show?" she asked.

"Borders. Land!" Solo ran his hands over one uninterrupted shape that took up nearly a third of the drawing. "This is all water," he told her.

"Where?" Juliette's arm was getting tired of holding up her end of the sheet. The smell and the riddles were getting to her. She felt a long way from home. The thrill of survival was in danger of being replaced with the depression of a long and miserable existence looming for years and years before her.

"Out there! Covering the land." Solo pointed vaguely at the walls. He narrowed his eyes at Juliette's confusion. "The silo, *this silo,* would be as big around as a single hair on your head." He patted the map. "Right here. All of them. Maybe all of us left. No bigger than my thumb." He placed a finger in a knot of lines. Juliette thought he seemed so sincere. She leaned closer to see better, but he pushed her back.

"Let those go," he said. He slapped at her hand holding the corners of paper and smoothed the maps against the wall. "This is us." He indicated one of the circles on the top sheet. Juliette eyeballed the columns and rows, figured there were four dozen or so of them. "Silo seventeen." He slid his hand up. "Number twelve. This is eight. And silo one up here."

"No."

Juliette shook her head and reached for the desk, her legs weak.

"Yes. Silo one. You're probably from sixteen or eighteen. Do you remember how far you walked?"

She grabbed the small chair and pulled it out. Sat down heavily.

"How many hills did you cross?"

Juliette didn't answer. She was thinking about the *other* map and comparing the scales. What if Solo was right? What if there were fifty or so silos and all of them could be covered by a thumb? What if Lukas had been right about how far away the stars were? She needed something to crawl inside, something to cover her. She needed some sleep.

"I once heard from silo one," Solo said. "A long time ago. Not sure how well any of these others are doing—"

"Wait." Juliette sat up straight. "What do you mean, you *heard* from them?"

Solo didn't turn from the map. He ran his hands from one circle to another, a childlike expression on his face. "They called. Checking in." He looked away from the map and her, toward the far corner of the room. "We didn't talk for long. I didn't know all the procedures. They weren't happy."

"Okay, but how did you do this? Can we call someone now? Was it a radio? Did it have a little antenna, a small black pointy thing—" Juliette stood and crossed to him, grabbed his shoulder, and turned him around. How much did this man know that could help her but that she couldn't get out of him? "Solo, how did you talk to them?"

"Through the wire," he said. He cupped his hands and covered his ears with them. "You just talk in it."

"You need to show me," she said.

Solo shrugged. He flipped up a few of the maps again, found the one he wanted, and pressed the others against the wall. It was the schematic of the silo she had seen earlier, a side-on view of it divided into thirds, each third side by side with the others. She helped him hold the other sheets out of the way.

"Here are the wires. They run every which way." He traced thick branches of lines that ran from the exterior walls and off the edges of the paper. They were labeled with minuscule print. Juliette leaned closer to read; she recognized many of the engineering marks.

"These are for power," she said, pointing at the lines with the jagged symbols above them.

"Yup." Solo nodded. "We don't get our own power anymore. Borrow it from others, I think. All automatic."

"You get it from others?" Juliette felt her frustration rise. How many crucial things did this man know that he considered trifling? "Anything else you want to add?" she asked him. "Do you have a flying suit that can whisk me back to my silo? Or are there secret passages beneath all the floors so we can just stroll there as easy as we like?"

Solo laughed and looked at her like she was crazy. "No," he said. "Then it would be *one* seed, not many. One bad day would ruin us all. Besides, the diggers are dead. They buried them." He pointed at a nook, a rectangular room jutting off from the edge of Mechanical. Juliette peered closer. She recognized every floor of the down deep at a glance, but this room wasn't supposed to exist.

"What do you mean, *the diggers?*"

"The machines that removed the dirt. You know, that made this place." He ran his hand down the length of the silo. "Too heavy to move, I guess, so they poured the walls right over them."

"Do they work?" Juliette asked. An idea formed. She thought

of the mines, of how she'd helped excavate rock by hand. She thought of the sort of machine that could dig out an entire silo, wondered if it could be used to dig *between* them.

Solo clicked his tongue. "No way. Nothing down there does. All toast. Besides—" He chopped his hand partway up the down deep. "There's flooding up to—" He turned to Juliette. "Wait. Are you wanting *out?* To *go* somewhere?" He shook his head in disbelief.

"I want to go *home,*" Juliette said.

His eyes widened. "Why would you go *back?* They sent you away, didn't they? You'll stay here. We don't want to leave." He scratched his beard and shook his head side to side.

"Someone has to know about all of this," Juliette told him. "All these other people out there. All that space beyond. The people in my silo need to know."

"People in your silo already *do,*" he said.

He studied her quizzically, and it dawned on Juliette that he was right. She pictured where they currently stood in this silo. They were in the heart of IT, deep inside the fortress room of the mythical servers, below the servers in a hidden passage, hidden probably even from the people who had access to the innermost kernels of the silo's mysteries.

Someone in her own silo *did* know. He had helped keep these secrets for generations. Had decided, alone and without input from anyone, what they should and should not know. It was the same man who had sent Juliette to her death, a man who had killed who knew how many more . . .

"Tell me about these wires," Juliette said. "How did you talk to the other silo? Give me every detail."

"Why?" Solo asked, seemingly shrinking before her. His eyes were wet with fear.

"Because," she said. "I have someone I very much wish to call."

51

This day's black fate on more days doth depend:
This but begins the woe others must end.

THE WAITING WAS INTERMINABLE. It was the long silence of itchy scalps and trickling sweat, the discomfort of weight on elbows, of backs bent, of bellies flat against an unforgiving conference table. Lukas peered down the length of his fearsome rifle and through the conference room's shattered glass window. Little fragment jewels remained in the side of the jamb like transparent teeth. Lukas could still hear, ringing in his ears, the incredible bang from Sims's gun that had taken out the glass. He could still smell the acrid scent of gunpowder in the air, the looks of worry on the faces of the other techs. The destruction had seemed so unnecessary. All this preparation, the toting of massive black guns out of storage, the interruption of his talk with Bernard, news of people coming from the down deep, it all made little sense.

He checked the *slide* on the side of the rifle and tried to remember the five minutes of instruction he'd been given hours earlier. There was a *round* in the *chamber.* The *gun* was *cocked.* More *bullets* waited patiently in the *clip.*

And the boys in security gave *him* a hard time for his tech jargon. Lukas's vocabulary had exploded with new terms. He thought about the rooms beneath the servers, the pages and pages of the Order, the rows of books he'd only gotten a glimpse of. His mind sagged under the weight of it all.

He spent another minute practicing his *sighting,* looking down the *barrel* and lining up the small cross in the tiny circle. He aimed at the cluster of conference chairs that had been rolled into an obstructing jumble by the door. For all he knew, they would be waiting like this for days and nothing would ever happen. It had been a while since any porter had brought an update on what was going on below.

For practice, he gently slid his finger into the guard and against the *trigger.* He tried to get comfortable with the idea of pulling that lever, of fighting the upward kick Sims had told them to expect.

Bobbie Milner—a shadow no more than sixteen—made a joke beside him, and Sims told them both to shut the fuck up. Lukas didn't protest at being included in the admonishment. He glanced over at the security gate, where a bristle of black barrels poked through the stanchions and over the metal duty desk. Peter Billings, the new silo sheriff, was over there fiddling with his small gun. Bernard stood behind the sheriff, doling out instructions to his men. Bobbie Milner shifted his weight beside Lukas and grunted, trying to get more comfortable.

Waiting. More waiting. They were all waiting.

Of course, had Lukas known what was coming, he wouldn't have minded.

He would've begged to wait there forever.

Knox led his group through the sixties with just a few stops for water, a pause to secure their packs and tighten their laces. They passed several curious porters with overnight deliveries who prodded for details about where they were heading, about the blackouts. Each porter left unhappy. And hopefully, empty-headed.

Pieter had been right: the stairwell was singing. It vibrated with the march of too many feet. Those who lived above were generally moving upward, away from the blackouts and toward the promise of power, of warm food and hot showers. Meanwhile, Knox and his people mobilized behind them to squelch a different *kind* of power.

At fifty-six, they had their first spot of trouble. A group of farmers stood outside the hydroponic farm lowering a cluster of power cables over the railing, presumably toward the small group they had seen the last landing down. When the farmers spotted the blue overalls of Mechanical, one of them called out, "Hey, we keep you fed, why can't you keep the juice on?"

"Talk to IT," Marck replied from the front of the queue. "They're the ones blowing fuses. We're doing what we can."

"Well, do it faster," the farmer said. "I thought we just had a rat-damned power holiday to prevent this nonsense."

"We'll have it by lunchtime," Shirly told them.

Knox and the others caught up with the head of the group, creating a jam by the landing.

"The faster we get up there the faster you'll get your juice," Knox explained. He tried to hold his concealed gun casually, like it was any other tool.

"Well, how about giving us a hand with this tap then? They've had power on fifty-seven for most of the morning. We'd like enough to get our pumps cranking." He indicated the trunk of wires coiling over the railing.

Knox considered this. What the man was asking for was technically illegal. Challenging him about it would mean delays, but telling him to go ahead might look suspicious. He could sense McLain's group several levels up, waiting on them. Pace and timing were everything.

"I can spare two of my men to help out. Just as a favor. As long as it doesn't get back to me that Mechanical had shit to do with this."

"Like I care," the farmer said. "I just want water moving."

"Shirly, you and Courtnee give them a hand. Catch up when you can."

Shirly's mouth dropped open. She begged with her eyes for him to reconsider.

"Get going," he told her.

Marck came to her side. He lifted his wife's pack and handed her his multi-tool. She begrudgingly accepted it, glowered at Knox a moment longer, then turned to go, not saying a word to him or her husband.

The farmer let go of the cables and took a step toward Knox. "Hey, I thought you said you'd lend me two of—"

Knox leveled a glare harsh enough to make the man pause. "Do you want the best I got?" he asked. "Because you've got it."

The farmer lifted his palms and backed away. Courtnee and Shirly could already be heard stomping their way below to coordinate with the men on the lower landing.

"Let's go," Knox said, hitching up his pack.

The men and women of Mechanical and Supply lurched forward once more. They left behind the group of farmers on landing fifty-six, who watched the long column wind its way upward.

Whispers rose as the power cables were lowered. Powerful forces were merging over these people's heads, bad intentions coming together and heading for something truly awful.

And anyone with eyes and ears could tell: some kind of reckoning was coming.

There was no warning for Lukas, no countdown. Hours of quiet anticipation, of insufferable nothingness, simply erupted into violence. Even though he had been told to expect the worst, Lukas felt like the waiting so long for something to happen just made it a fiercer surprise when it finally did.

The double doors of landing thirty-four blew open. Solid steel peeled back like curls of paper. The sharp ring made Lukas jump, his hand slip off the stock of his rifle. Gunfire erupted beside him, Bobbie Milner shooting at nothing and screaming in fear. Maybe excitement. Sims was yelling impossibly over the roar. When it died down, something flew through the smoke, a canister, bouncing toward the security gate.

There was a terrible pause — and then another explosion like a blow to the ears. Lukas nearly dropped his gun. The smoke by the security gate couldn't quite fog the carnage. Pieces of people Lukas had known came to a sick rest in the entrance hall of IT. The people responsible began to surge through before he could take stock, before he could become fearful of another explosion occurring right in front of him.

The rifle beside him barked again, and this time Sims didn't yell. This time, several other barrels joined in. The people trying to push through the chairs tumbled into them instead, their bodies shaking as if pulled by invisible strings, arcs of red like hurled paint flying from their bodies.

More came. A large man with a throaty roar. Everything moved so slowly. Lukas could see the man's mouth part, a yell in the center of a burly beard, a chest as wide as two men. He held a rifle at his waist. He fired at the ruined security station. Lukas watched Peter Billings spin to the floor, clutching his shoulder. Bits of glass shivered from the window frame in front of Lukas as barrel after barrel erupted across the conference table, the shattered window seeming insignificant now. A prudent move.

The hail of bullets hit the man unseen. The conference room was an ambush, a side-on attack. The large man shook as some of the wild fire got lucky. His beard sagged open as his mouth parted. His rifle was cracked in half, a shiny bullet between his fingers. He tried to reload.

The guns of IT loosed their own bullets too fast to count. Levers were held, and springs and gunpowder did the rest. The giant man fumbled with his rifle but never got it reloaded. He tumbled into the chairs, sending them crashing across the floor. Another figure appeared through the door, a tiny woman. Lukas watched her down the length of his barrel, saw her turn and look right at him, the smoke from the explosion drifting toward her, white hair flowing about her shoulders as if the smoke were a part of her.

He could see her eyes. He had yet to shoot his gun, had watched, jaw slack, as the fighting took place.

The woman bent her arm back and made to throw something his way.

Lukas pulled the trigger. His rifle flashed and lurched. In the time it took, the long and terrible time it took for the bullet to cross the room, he realized it was just an old woman. Holding something.

A bomb.

Her torso spun and her chest blossomed red. The object fell. There was another awful wait, more attackers appearing, screaming in anger, until an explosion blew the chairs and the people among them apart.

Lukas wept while a second surge made a futile attempt. He wept until his clip was empty, wept as he fumbled for the release, shoved a spare into the butt, the salt bitter on his lips as he drew back that bolt and let loose with another menacing hail of metal—so much stouter and quicker than the flesh it met.

52

I have seen the day
that I have worn a visor
and could tell a whispering tale.

BERNARD CAME TO AT the sound of shouting, his eyes burning from the smoke, his ears ringing with a long-ago blast.

Peter Billings was shaking his shoulders, yelling at him, a look of fright in his wide eyes and on his soot-stained brow. Blood stained his overalls in a wide rust-colored pool.

"Hrm?"

"Sir! Can you hear me?"

Bernard pushed Peter's hands away and tried to sit up. He groped about his body, looking for anything bleeding or broken. His head throbbed. His hand came away from his nose wet with blood.

"What happened?" he groaned.

Peter crouched by his side. Bernard saw Lukas standing at a distance behind the sheriff, rifle on his shoulder, peering toward the stairwell. There was shouting in the distance, and then the patter of gunfire.

"We've got three men dead," Peter said. "A few wounded.

Sims led a half dozen into the stairwell. They got it a lot worse than us. A *lot* worse."

Bernard nodded. He checked his ears, was surprised they weren't bleeding as well. He dotted his sleeve with blood from his nose and patted Peter on the arm. He nodded over his shoulder. "Get Lukas," he said.

Peter frowned but nodded. He spoke with Lukas, and the young man knelt by Bernard.

"Are you okay?" Lukas asked.

Bernard nodded. "Stupid," he said. "Didn't know they'd have guns. Should've guessed about the bombs."

"Take it easy."

He shook his head. "Shouldn't have had you here. Dumb. Could have been us both—"

"Well, it was *neither* of us, sir. We've got 'em running down the stairwell. I think it's over."

Bernard patted his arm. "Get me to the server," he said. "We'll need to report this."

Lukas nodded. He knew which server Bernard meant. He helped Bernard to his feet, an arm around his back, Peter Billings frowning as the two of them staggered down the smoky hallway together.

"Not good," Bernard told Lukas, once they were away from the others.

"But we won, right?"

"Not yet. The damage won't be contained here. Not today. You'll have to stay below awhile." Bernard grimaced and tried to walk alone. "Can't risk something happening to us both."

Lukas seemed unhappy about this. He entered his code into the great door, pulled out his ID, wiped someone else's blood off it and his hand, then swiped it through the reader.

"I understand," he finally said.

Bernard knew he'd picked the right man. He left Lukas to close the heavy door while he made his way to the rearmost server. He staggered once and fell against number eight, catching himself and resting a moment until the wooziness went away. Lukas caught up and was pulling his copy of the master key out of his overalls before Bernard got to the back of the room.

Bernard rested against the wall while Lukas opened the server. He was still too shaken up to notice the flashing code on the server's front panel. His ears were too full of a false ringing to notice the real one.

"What's that mean?" Lukas asked. "That noise?"

Bernard looked at him quizzically.

"Fire alarm?" Lukas pointed up at the ceiling. Bernard finally heard it as well. He stumbled toward the back of the server as Lukas opened the last lock, pushed the young man out of the way.

What were the chances? Did they already know? Bernard's life had become unhinged in two short days. He reached inside the cloth pouch, grabbed the headset, and pulled it over his tender ears. He pushed the jack into the slot labeled "1" and was surprised to hear a beep. The line was *ringing.* He was making a call.

He pulled the jack out hurriedly, canceling the call, and saw that the light above "1" wasn't blinking; the light above "17" was.

Bernard felt the room spin. A dead silo was calling him. A survivor? After all these years? With access to the servers? His hand trembled as he guided the jack into the slot. Lukas was asking something behind him, but Bernard couldn't hear anything through the headphones.

"Hello?" he croaked. "Hello? Is anyone there?"

"Hello," a voice said.

Bernard adjusted his headphones. He waved for Lukas to

shut the fuck up. His ears were still ringing, his nose bleeding into his mouth.

"Who is this?" he asked. "Can you hear me?"

"I hear you," the voice said. "Is this who I think it is?"

"Who the fuck is this?" Bernard sputtered. "How do you have access to—?"

"You sent me out," the voice said. "You sent me to die."

Bernard slumped down, his legs numb. The cord on the headphones uncoiled and nearly pulled the cups from his head. He clutched the headphones and fought to place this voice. Lukas was holding him by the armpits, keeping him from collapsing onto his back.

"Are you there?" the voice asked. "Do you know who this is?"

"No," he said. But he knew. It was impossible, but he knew.

"You sent me to die, you fuck."

"You knew the rules!" Bernard cried, yelling at a ghost. "You *knew!*"

"Shut up and listen, Bernard. Just shut the fuck up and listen to me very carefully."

Bernard waited. He could taste the copper of his own blood in his mouth.

"I'm coming for you. I'm coming home, and I'm coming to *clean.*"

The world is not thy friend nor the world's law.
Villain and he be many miles asunder.
And all these woes shall serve
for sweet discourses in our time to come.
He that is strucken blind cannot forget
the precious treasure of his eyesight lost.
One fire burns out another's burning,
one pain is lessen'd by another's anguish.

—The Tragic Historye of Romeus and Juliet

PART 5

THE STRANDED

53

Silo 18

MARCK STUMBLED DOWN THE great stairway, his hand sliding against the cool railing, a rifle tucked under his arm, his boots slipping in blood. He could barely hear the screams all around him: the wails from the wounded as they were half dragged down the steps, the horrified cries from the curious crowds on every landing who witnessed their passage, or the shouts of promised violence from the men chasing him and the rest of his mechanics from level to level.

The ringing in his ears drowned out most of the noise. It was the blast, the god-awful blast. Not the one that had peeled open the doors of IT – he had been ready for that one, had hunkered down with the rest. And it wasn't the second bomb, the one Knox had lobbed deep into the heart of their enemy's den. It was the *last* one, the one he didn't see coming, the one that spilled from the hands of that small white-haired woman from Supply.

McLain's bomb. It had gone off right in front of him, had taken his hearing as it took her *life*.

And Knox, that stout and unmovable head of Mechanical – his boss, his good friend – gone.

Marck hurried down the steps, wounded and afraid. He was a long way from the safety of the down deep—and he desperately wanted to find his wife. He concentrated on this rather than the past, tried not to think of the explosion that had taken his friends, had wrecked their plans, had engulfed any chance at justice.

Muffled shots rang out from above, followed by the piercing zing of bullets striking steel—only steel, thank God. Marck stayed away from the outer railing, away from the aim of the shooters who hounded them from the landings above with their smoothly firing rifles. The good people of Mechanical and Supply had been running and fighting for over a dozen levels; Marck silently begged the men above to stop, to give them a chance to rest, but the boots and the bullets kept coming.

Half a level later, he caught up to three members of Supply, the one in the middle wounded and being carried, his arms draped over shoulders, blood dotting the backs of their yellow overalls. He yelled at them to keep moving, couldn't hear his own voice, could just feel it in his chest. Some of the blood he was slipping in was his own.

With his injured arm tight against his chest, his rifle cradled in the crook of his elbow, Marck kept his other hand on the railing to keep from tumbling headfirst down the steep stairwell. There were no allies behind him, none still alive. After the last shootout, he had sent the others ahead, had barely gotten away himself. And yet they kept coming, tireless. Marck would pause now and then, fumble with the unreliable ammunition, chamber a shot, and fire wildly up the stairwell. Just to *do* something. To slow them down.

He stopped to take a breath, leaned out over the railing, and swung his rifle toward the sky. The next round was a dud. The bullets buzzing back at him *weren't*.

Huddling against the stairwell's central post, he took the

time to reload. His rifle wasn't like theirs. One shot at a time and difficult to aim. They had modern things he'd never heard of, shots coming as fast as a frightened pulse. He moved toward the railing and checked the landing below, could see curious faces through a cracked doorway, fingers curled around the edge of the steel jamb. This was it. Landing fifty-six. The last place he'd seen his wife.

"Shirly!"

Calling her name, he staggered down a quarter turn until he was level with the landing. He kept close to the interior, out of sight from his pursuers, and searched the shadowed faces.

"My wife!" he yelled across the landing, a hand cupped to his cheeks, forgetting that the incredible ringing was only in *his* ears, not theirs. "Where is she?"

A mouth moved in the dark crowd. The voice was a dull and distant drone.

Someone else pointed down. The faces cringed; the cracked door twitched shut as another ricochet screamed out; the stairway shook with all the frightened boots below and the chasing ones above. Marck eyed the illicit power cables draped over the railing and remembered the farmers attempting to steal electricity from the level below. He hurried down the stairs, following the thick cords, desperate to find Shirly.

One level down, positive that his wife would be inside, Marck braved the open space of the landing and rushed across. He threw himself against the doors. Shots rang out. Marck grabbed the handle and tugged, shouting her name to ears as deaf as his own. The door budged, was being held fast with the sinewy restraint of unseen arms. He slapped the glass window, leaving a pink palm print, and yelled for them to open up, to let him in. Eager bullets rattled by his feet—one of them left a scar down the face of the door. Crouching and covering his head, he scurried back to the stairwell.

Marck forced himself to move downward. If Shirly was behind those doors she might be better off. She could strip herself of incriminating gear, blend in until things settled down. If she was below — he needed to hurry after her. Either way, *down* was the only direction.

At the next landing, he caught up with the same three members of Supply he'd passed earlier. The wounded man was sitting on the decking, eyes wide. The other two were tending to him, blood on their sides from supporting his weight. One of the Supply workers was a woman Marck vaguely recognized from the march up. There was a cold fire in her eyes as Marck paused to see if they needed help.

"I can carry him," he shouted, kneeling by the wounded man.

The woman said something. Marck shook his head and pointed to his ears.

She repeated herself, lips moving in exaggeration, but Marck wasn't able to piece it together. She gave up and shoved at his arm, pushing him away. The wounded man clutched his stomach, a red stain ballooning out from his abdomen all the way to his crotch. His hands clasped something protruding there, a small wheel spinning on the end of a steel post. The leg of a chair.

The woman pulled a bomb from her satchel, one of those pipes that promised so much violence. It was solemnly passed to the wounded man, who accepted it, his knuckles white, his hands trembling.

The two members of Supply pulled Marck away — away from the man with the large piece of office furniture sprouting from his oozing stomach. The shouts sounded distant, but he knew they were nearby. They were practically in his ear. He found himself yanked backward, transfixed by the vacant stare on the face of this doomed and wounded man. His eyes locked onto Marck's. The man held the bomb away from himself, fingers curled around that terrible cylinder of steel, a grim clench of teeth jutting along his jawline.

Marck glanced up the stairwell where the boots were finally gaining on them, coming into view, black and bloodless, this tireless and superior enemy. They came down the dripping trail Marck and the others had left behind, coming for them with their ammo that never failed.

He stumbled down the stairwell backward, half dragged by the others, one hand on the railing, eyes drifting to the swinging door opening behind the man they'd left behind.

A young face appeared there, a curious boy, rushing out to see. A tangle of adult hands scrambled to pull him back.

Marck was hauled down the curving stairs, too far down to see what happened next. But his ears, as deadened as they were, caught the popping and zinging of gunfire, and then a blast, a roaring explosion that shook the great stairwell, that knocked him and the others down, slamming him against the railing. His rifle clattered toward the edge—Marck lunged for it. He grabbed it before it could escape and go tumbling into space.

Shaking his head, stunned, he pushed himself up to his hands and knees and managed to rise slowly to his feet. Senseless, he staggered forward down the shuddering steps, the treads beneath his feet ringing and vibrating as the silo around them all continued its spiral into dark madness.

54

Silo 18

THE FIRST MOMENT OF true rest came hours later at Supply, on the upper edge of the down deep. There was talk of holding there, of setting up some kind of barrier, but it wasn't clear how the entire stairway could be blocked to include the open space between the railing and the concrete cylinder beyond. This was the gap where the singing bullets lived, a place where jumpers were known to meet their ends, and where their enemy could surely find some way to scamper down.

Marck's hearing had improved during the last leg of his run. Enough to grow weary of the rhythmic clomp of his own boots, the sound of his pained grunts, the noise of his exhausted pants for air. He heard someone say that the last explosion had wrecked the stairway, had impeded the chase. But for how long? What was the damage? No one knew.

Tensions ran high on the landing; the news of McLain's death had unsettled the people of Supply. The wounded in yellow overalls were taken inside, but it was suggested—and not gently—that Mechanical's injured would be better off receiving treatment further below. Where they belonged.

Marck waded through these arguments, the voices still somewhat muffled and distant. He asked everyone about Shirly, several in yellow shrugging as if they didn't know her. One guy said she'd already gone down with some of the other wounded. He said it a second time, louder, before Marck was sure he'd heard him.

It was good news, and he'd figured as much. He was about to leave when his wife emerged without warning from the anxious crowd, startling him.

Her eyes widened as she recognized him. And then her gaze fell to his wounded arm.

"Oh, God!"

She threw her arms around him, pressed her face against his neck. Marck hugged her with one arm, his rifle between them, the barrel cold against his quivering cheek.

"Are you okay?" he asked.

She latched on to his neck, her forehead finding his shoulder, and said something he couldn't hear but could feel against his skin. She made room to inspect his arm.

"I can't hear," he told her.

"I'm fine," she said, louder. She shook her head, her eyes wide and wet. "I wasn't there. I wasn't there for any of it. Is it true about Knox? What happened? How bad was it?"

She focused on his wound, and her hands felt good on his arm—strong and confident. The crowd was thinning as members of Mechanical retreated further down the stairwell. Several in Supply yellow treated Marck to cold stares, eyeing his wound as if worried it would soon be *their* problem.

"Knox is dead," he told her. "McLain, too. A few others. I was right there when the blast went off."

He looked down at his arm, which she had exposed by tearing away his ripped and stained undershirt.

"Were you shot?" she asked.

He shook his head. "I don't know. It happened so *fast*." He looked over his shoulder. "Where's everyone going? Why aren't we holing up here?"

Shirly set her teeth and jerked her head at the door, which was two deep with yellow overalls. "Don't think we're wanted," she said, her voice raised so he could hear. "I've got to clean this wound. I think some of the bomb is in you."

"I'm fine," he insisted. "I've just been looking for you. I've been worried sick."

He saw that his wife was crying, unbroken tear tracks standing out amid the beads of sweat.

"I thought you were gone," she said. He had to read her lips to make it out. "I thought they had . . . that you were . . ."

She bit her lip and stared at him with uncharacteristic fear. Marck had never seen his wife fazed, not by a sprung casement leak, not by a cave-in deep in the mine that trapped several of their close friends, not even when Juliette was sent to cleaning. But heaps of dread were locked up in her expression now. And that scared him in a way the bombs and bullets couldn't.

"Let's hurry after the others," he said, taking her hand. He could feel the exposed nerves on the landing, the gazes begging them to be off.

When shouts rang down from above once more and the members of Supply retreated to the safety of their doorway, Marck knew this brief moment of respite was over. But it was okay. He'd found his wife. She was unharmed. There was little anyone could do to him now.

When they reached one-thirty-nine together, Marck knew they'd made it. His legs had somehow held out. The blood loss hadn't stopped him. With his wife helping him along, they passed the last landing before Mechanical, and all he could think about was holding the line against those bastards who were taking shots at them from above. Inside Mechanical, they would have power, safety in numbers, the advantage of home turf. More importantly, they would be able to bandage wounds and get some rest. That's what he sorely needed: rest.

He nearly tripped and fell down the last few steps, his legs not used to an end to the descent, a flat piece of ground rather than one more tread to sink to. As his knees buckled, and Shirly caught him, he finally noticed the jam of people at the security station leading into Mechanical.

The crew that had stayed behind while the rest marched up to fight had been busy. Steel plates had been welded solid across the wide security entrance. The diamond-studded sheeting stood from floor to ceiling, wall to wall. Sparks hissed along one edge as someone worked to complete the job from the inside. The sudden flurry of refugees and wounded amassed in a crowd desperate to get in. Mechanics shoved and jostled against the barrier. They screamed and beat on the steel plates, mad with fear.

"What the hell?" Marck cried. He followed Shirly as she pressed into the back of the crowd. At the front, someone was crawling on the floor, wiggling on their belly through the tightest of gaps, a rectangle left open below the security turnstile wide enough to slide through, easy enough to defend.

"Easy! Wait your turn," someone ahead of them shouted.

Yellow overalls were mixed in with the others. Some were mechanics who had donned disguises—some seemed to be from Supply, helping the wounded, mixed up in the wrong crowd or not trusting their own level for safety.

As Marck attempted to usher Shirly toward the front, a shot rang out, the thwack and clatter of a hot ball of lead striking nearby. He changed direction and pulled her back toward the stairs. The crush around the impossibly small entrance grew frantic. There was a lot of yelling back and forth through the hole, people on this side shouting that they were being shot at, those on the other side yelling, "One at a time!"

Several were on their bellies, scrambling for the tiny hole. One got his arms inside and was pulled through, sliding across the steel grating and disappearing into the dark space. Two others tried to be next, jostling for position. They were all exposed to the open stairwell above. Another shot rang out, and someone fell, clutching a shoulder and screaming, "I'm hit!" The throng dispersed. Several ran back to the stairs, where the overhang of the treads protected them from the gunfire. The rest were in chaos, all trying to fit through a space expressly designed to allow no more than one at a time.

Shirly screamed and squeezed Marck's arm as another person was shot nearby. A mechanic fell to the ground and doubled over in pain. Shirly yelled at her husband, asking him what they should do.

Marck dropped his rucksack, kissed her cheek, and ran with his rifle back up the stairs. He tried to take them two at a time, but his legs were too sore. Another shot rang out, the ricochet of a miss. His body felt incredibly heavy, slow like in a bad dream. He approached the landing of one-thirty-nine with his gun level, but the shooters were further up, peppering the crowd from higher above.

He checked that he had a fresh round in the home-built gun, cocked it, and edged out onto the landing. Several men in the gray of Security were leaning out over the railing above, barrels trained down toward the ground floor of Mechanical. One of the men tapped his neighbor and pointed toward Marck. Marck watched all this down the length of his own barrel.

He fired a shot, and a black rifle tumbled toward him from above, the arms of its wielder slumping over the railing before sagging down and disappearing.

Gunfire erupted, but he was already diving back toward the stairs. The shouting grew furious both above and below him. Marck went to the other side of the stairs, away from where he'd last been seen, and peered down. The crowd was thinning by the security barrier. More and more people were being pulled through. He could see Shirly looking up, shielding her eyes against the stairway lights above.

Boots rang out behind him. Marck reloaded, turned, and aimed at the highest step he could see along the upward spiral. He waited for whatever was heading down toward him.

When the first boot appeared, he steadied himself, allowed more of the man to sink before his barrel, and then he pulled the trigger.

Another black rifle clattered against the steps and bounced through the railing; another man sagged to his knees.

Marck turned and ran. He lost his grip on his own gun, felt it bang against his shins as it skittered away from him, and he didn't stop to retrieve it. He slid down the steps, lost his footing, landed on his ass, and bounced back up. He tried taking the steps two at a time, was running as if in a dream, not fast enough, legs like rusted steel—

There was a bang, a muffled roar behind him, and somehow, someone had caught up, had punched him in the back, had hit him.

Marck sprawled forward and bounced down the steps, his chin striking the steel treads. Blood poured into his mouth. He tried to crawl, got his feet beneath him, and stumbled forward.

Another roar, another punch to the back, the feeling that he'd been bitten and kicked at the same time.

This is what it feels like to be shot, he thought numbly. He spilled down the last few steps, lost sensation in his legs, crashed to the grating.

The bottom floor was nearly empty. One person stood beside the tiny hole. Another was half in and half out, boots kicking.

Marck saw that it was Shirly, on her belly, looking back at him. They were both lying on the floor. So comfortable on the floor. The steel was cool against his cheek. There were no more steps to run down, no bullets to load, nothing to shoot.

Shirly was screaming, not as happy as he was to be lying there.

One of her arms extended back out of that small black rectangle, reached for him past the rough cuts in the steel plates. Her body slid forward, pulled by some force beyond, pushed by this nice person in yellow still standing by the strange wall of steel where the entrance to his home used to be.

"Go," Marck told her, wishing she wouldn't scream. Blood flecked the floor before him, marking his words. "I love you —"

And as if by command, her feet slid into the darkness, her screams swallowed by that rectangular, shadowy maw.

And the person in yellow turned. The nice man's eyes grew wide, his mouth fell open, and then his body jerked from the violence of gunfire.

It was the last thing Marck saw, this man's deathly dance.

And he only distantly felt, but for a tremble of time, the end of him that came next.

55

Three Weeks Later
Silo 18

WALKER REMAINED IN HIS cot and listened to the sounds of distant violence. Shouts echoed down his hallway, emanating from the entrance to Mechanical. The familiar patter of gunfire came next, the *pop pop pop* of the good guys followed by the *rat-a-tat-tat* of the bad.

There was an incredible bang, the roar of blasting powder against steel, and the back-and-forth crackle ended for a moment. More shouting. Boots clomping down his hallway, past his door. The boots were the constant beat to the music of this new world. He could hear this music from his cot, even with the blankets drawn over his head, even with his pillow on top, even as he begged, out loud, over and over, for it to please stop.

The boots in the hallway carried with them more shouting. Walker curled up into a tight ball, knees against his chest, wondering what time it was, dreading that it was morning, time to get up.

A brief respite of silence formed, that quiet of tending to the wounded, their groans too faint to penetrate his sealed door.

Walker tried to fall asleep before the music was turned

back up. But, as always, the quiet was worse. During the quiet, he grew anxious as he waited for the next patter of gunfire to erupt. His impatience for sleep often frightened that very sleep away. And he would grow terrified that the resistance was finally over, that the bad guys had won and were coming for him—

Someone banged on his door—a small and angry fist unmistakable to his expert ears. Four harsh knocks, and then she was gone.

Shirly. She would have left his breakfast rations in the usual place and taken away last night's picked-over and mostly uneaten dinner. Walker grunted and rolled his old bones over to the other side. Boots clomped. Always rushing, always anxious, forever warring. And his once-quiet hallway, so far from the machines and pumps that really needed tending to, was now a busy thoroughfare. It was the entrance hall that mattered now, the funnel into which all the hate was poured. Screw the silo, the people above and the machines below, just fight over this worthless patch of ground, pile the bodies on either side until one gives, do it because it was yesterday's cause, and because nobody wants to remember back any further than yesterday.

But Walker did. He remembered—

The door to his workshop burst open. Through a gap in his filthy cocoon, Walker could see Jenkins, a boy in his twenties but with a beard that made him appear older, a boy who had inherited this mess the moment Knox died. The lad stormed through the maze of workbenches and scattered parts, aiming straight for Walker's cot.

"I'm *up,*" Walker groaned, hoping Jenkins would go away.

"No you're not." Jenkins reached the cot and prodded Walker in the ribs with the barrel of his gun. "C'mon, old man, up!"

Walker tensed away from him. He wiggled an arm loose to wave the boy away.

Jenkins peered down gravely, a frown buried in his beard, his young eyes wrinkled with worry. “We need that radio fixed, Walk. We’re getting battered out there. And if I can’t listen in, I don’t think I can defend this place.”

Walker tried to push himself upright. Jenkins grabbed the strap of his overalls and gave him some rough assistance.

“I was up all night on it,” Walker told him. He rubbed his face. His breath was awful.

“Is it fixed? We need that radio, Walk. You do know Hank risked his life to get that thing to us, right?”

“Well, he should’ve risked a bit more and sent a *manual,*” Walker complained. He pressed his hands to his knees, and with much complaint from his joints, he stood and staggered toward the workbench, his blankets spilling to the floor in a heap. His legs were still half-asleep, his hands tingling with the weak sensation of not being able to form a proper fist.

“I got the battery sorted,” he told Jenkins. “Turns out that wasn’t the problem.” Walker glanced toward his open door and saw Harper, a refinery worker turned soldier, standing in the hallway. Harper had become Jenks’s number two when Pieter was killed. Now he was peering down at Walker’s breakfast, practically salivating into it.

“Help yourself,” Walker called out. He waved dismissively at the steaming bowl.

Harper glanced up, eyes wide, but that was as long as he hesitated. He leaned his rifle against the wall and sat down in the workshop doorway, shoveling food into his mouth.

Jenkins grunted disapprovingly but didn’t say anything.

“So, see here?” Walker showed him the arrangement on the workbench where various pieces of the small radio unit had been separated and were now wired together so everything was accessible. “I’ve got constant power.” He patted the transformer he had built to bypass the battery. “And the speakers work.” He keyed the transmit button, and there was a pop and hiss of static from his bench speakers. “But nothing comes through. They aren’t *saying* anything.” He turned to Jenkins. “I’ve had it on all night, and I’m not a deep sleeper.”

Jenkins studied him.

“I would’ve heard,” he insisted. “They aren’t talking.”

Jenkins rubbed his face, made a fist. He kept his eyes closed, his forehead resting in one palm, a weariness in his voice. “You think maybe something *broke* when you tore it apart?”

“Disassembled,” Walker said with a sigh. “I didn’t *tear it apart.*”

Jenkins gazed up at the ceiling and relaxed his fist. “So you think they aren’t using them anymore, is that it? Do you reckon they know we have one? I swear, I think this damn priest they sent is a spy. Shit’s been fallin’ apart since we let him in here to give last rites.”

“I don’t *know* what they’re doing,” Walker admitted. “I think they’re still using the radios; they’ve just excluded this one somehow. Look, I made another antenna, a stronger one.”

He showed him the wires snaking up from the workbench and spiraling around the steel-beam rafters overhead.

Jenkins followed his finger, then snapped his head toward the door. There was more shouting down the hallway. Harper stopped eating for a moment and listened. But only for a moment. He dug his spoon back into the cornmush.

“I just need to know when I’ll be able to listen in again.” Jenkins tapped the workbench with his finger, then picked his rifle up. “We’ve been shooting blind for almost a week now. I need results, not lessons on all this”—he waved a hand at Walker’s work—“all this *wizardry.*”

Walker plopped down on his favorite stool and peered at the myriad circuits that had once been jammed into the radio’s cramped innards. “It’s not wizardry,” he said. “It’s electrics.”

He pointed at two of the boards, connected by wires he had lengthened and resoldered so he could analyze all the bits more closely. "I know what most of these do, but you've gotta remember that nothing about these devices is known, not outside of IT, anyway. I'm havin' to theorize while I tinker."

Jenkins rubbed the bridge of his nose. "Just let me know when you've got something. All your other work orders can wait. This is the only thing that matters. Got that?"

Walker nodded. Jenkins turned and barked at Harper to get the hell off the floor.

They left Walker on his stool, their boots picking up the beat of the music again.

Alone, he stared down at the machine strung out across his workbench, its little green lights on its mysterious boards lit up and taunting him. His hand drifted to his magnifiers as if by its own accord, as if by decades of habit, when all Walker really wanted was to crawl back into his cot, to wrap his cocoon around himself, to disappear.

He needed help, he thought. He looked around at all that required doing and, as ever, his thoughts turned to Scottie, his little shadow, gone to work in IT where they hadn't been able to protect him. There had been a slice of time, sliding away from him now and fading into the slippery past, when Walker had been a happy man. When his life should've ended to keep him from enduring any of the suffering beyond. But he had made it through that brief bliss and now could hardly recall it. He couldn't imagine what it felt like to rise with anticipation in the morning, to fall asleep with contentment at the end of the day.

It was only fear and dread anymore. And also regret.

He had started all this, all the noise and violence. Walker was convinced of that. Every life lost was on his wrinkled hands. Every tear shed was due to his actions. Nobody said it, but he could feel them thinking it. One little message to Supply, one favor for Juliette, just a chance at dignity, an opportunity to test her wild and horrible theory, to bury herself out of sight—and now look at the cascade of events, the eruption of anger, the senseless violence.

It wasn't worth it, he decided. This was how the math always added up: not worth it. Nothing seemed worth it anymore.

He bent over his workbench and set his old hands to tinkering. This was what he did, what he had always done. There was no escaping it now, no stopping those fingers with their papery skin, those palms with their deep lines that seemed to never end, not when they should. He followed those lines down to his bony wrists, where weak little veins ran like buried wire with blue insulation.

One snip, and off he would go to see Scottie, to see Juliette.

It was tempting.

Especially since, Walker figured, wherever they were, whether the priests were onto something or simply ratshit mad, both of his old friends were in far better places than him . . .

56

Silo 17

A TINY STRAND OF COPPER wire stood at a right angle to the rest. It was like a silo landing shooting off the great stairway, a bit of flat amid the twisted spiral. As Juliette wrapped the pads of her fingers around the wire and worked the splice into place, this jutting barb sank into her finger, stinging her like some angry insect.

Juliette cursed and shook her hand. She very nearly dropped the other end of the wire, which would've sent it tumbling several levels down.

She wiped the welling spot of blood onto her gray overalls, then finished the splice and secured the wires to the railing to keep the strain off. She still didn't see how they had come loose, but everything in this cursed and dilapidated silo seemed to be coming apart. Her senses were the least of it.

She leaned far out over the railing and placed her hand on the hodgepodge of pipes and tubing fastened to the concrete wall of the stairwell. She tried to discern, with hands chilled by the cool air of the deep, any vibration from water gurgling through the pipe.

"Anything?" she called down to Solo. There seemed to be the

slightest tremor in the plastic tubing, but it could've been her pulse.

"I think so!"

Solo's thin voice echoed from far below.

Juliette frowned and peered down the dimly lit shaft, down that gap between steel step and thick concrete. She would have to go see for herself.

Leaving her small tool bag on the steps—no danger of anyone coming along to trip over it—she took the treads two at a time and spiraled her way deeper into the silo. The electrical wiring and the long snake of pipes spun into view with each rotation, drips of purple adhesive marking every laborious joint she'd cut and fastened by hand.

Other wiring ran alongside hers, electrical cables snaking from IT far above to power the grow lights of the lower farms. Juliette wondered who had rigged this stuff up. It hadn't been Solo; this wiring had been strung during the early days of silo seventeen's downfall. Solo had simply become the lucky beneficiary of someone else's hard and desperate work. Grow lights now obeyed their timers, the greenery obeyed the urge to blossom, and beyond the stale stench of oil and gas, of floods and unmoving air, the ripe tinge of plants growing out of control could be nosed from several landings away.

Juliette stopped at the landing of one-thirty-six, the last dry landing before the flood. Solo had tried to warn her, had tried to tell her even as she lusted over the image of the massive diggers on the wall-sized schematic. Hell, she should've known about the flood without being told. Groundwater was forever seeping into her own silo, a hazard of living below the water table. Without power to the pumps, the water would naturally make its way in and rise.

Out on the landing, she leaned on the steel railing and caught her breath. A dozen steps below, Solo stood on the single dry tread their efforts had exposed. Nearly three weeks of wiring and plumbing, of scrapping a good section of the lower hydroponics farm, of finding a pump and routing the overflow to the water treatment facility tanks, and they had uncovered a single step.

Solo turned and smiled up at her. "It's working, right?" He scratched his head, his wild hair jutting at all angles, his beard flecked with a gray that his youthful jubilance denied. The hopeful question hung in the air, a cloud visible from the cold of the down deep.

"It's not working *enough,*" Juliette told him, annoyed with the progress. She peered over the railing, past the jutting toes of borrowed boots to the colorful slick of water below. The mirrored surface of oil and gas stood perfectly still. Beneath this coat of slime, the emergency lights of the stairwell glowed eerily green, lending the depths a haunting look that matched the rest of the empty silo.

In that silence, Juliette heard a faint gurgle in the pipe beside her. She even thought she could hear the distant buzz of the submerged pump a dozen or so feet below the oil and gas. She tried to *will* the water up that tube, up twenty levels and hundreds of joints to the vast and empty treatment tanks above.

Solo coughed into his fist. "What if we install another—?"

Juliette raised her hand to quiet him. She was doing the math.

The volume of the eight levels of Mechanical was difficult to calculate, so many corridors and rooms that may or may not have been flooded, but she could guess the height of the cylindrical shaft from Solo's feet to the security station. The lone pump had moved the level of the flood a little less than a foot in two weeks. Eighty or ninety feet to go. With another pump, say a year to get to the entrance of Mechanical. Depending on how watertight the intervening levels were, it could be much more. Mechanical itself could take three or four times as long to clear.

"What about another pump?" Solo insisted.

Juliette felt nauseous. Even with three more of the small pumps from the hydroponic farms, and with three more runs of pipe and wiring to go with them, she was looking at a year, possibly two, before the silo was perfectly dry. She wasn't sure if she had a year. Just a few weeks of being in that abandoned place, alone with a half-sane man, and she was already starting to hear whispers, to forget where she was leaving things, finding lights on she swore she'd turned off. Either she was going crazy, or Solo found humor in making her feel that way. Two years of this life, of her home so close but so impossibly far away . . .

She leaned over the railing, feeling like she really might be sick. As she gazed down at the water and through her reflection cast in that film of oil, she suddenly considered risks even crazier than two years of near-solitude.

"Two years," she told Solo. It felt like voicing a death sentence. "Two years. That's how long this'll take if we add three more pumps. Six months at least on the stairwell, but the rest will go slower."

"Two years!" Solo sang. "Two years, two years!" He tapped his boot twice against the water on the step below, sending her reflection into sickening waves of distortion. He spun in place, peering up at her. "That's no time!"

Juliette fought to control her frustration. Two years would feel like forever. And what would they find down there, anyway? What condition would the main generator be in? Or the diggers? A machine submerged under fresh water might be preserved as long as air didn't get to it, but as soon as any of it was exposed by the pumps, the corrosion would begin. It was the nastiness of oxygen working on wet metal that spelled doom for anything useful down there. Machines and tools would need to be dried immediately and then oiled. And with only two of them –

Juliette watched, horrified, as Solo bent down, waved away the film of grease at his feet, and scooped up two palms of the brackish filth below. He slurped noisily and happily.

– Okay, with only *one* of them working diligently at salvaging the machines, it wouldn't be enough.

Maybe she'd be able to salvage the backup generator. It would require less work and still provide plenty of power.

"What to do for two years?" Solo asked, wiping his beard with the back of his hand and looking up at her.

Juliette shook her head. "We're not waiting two years," she told him. The last three *weeks* in silo seventeen had been too much. This, she didn't say.

"Okay," he said, shrugging. He clomped up the stairwell in his too-big boots. His gray overalls were also baggy, as if he were still a young boy trying to wear clothing tailored for his father. He joined Juliette on the landing, smiled at her through his glistening beard. "You look like you have more projects," he said happily.

She nodded silently. Anything the two of them worked on, whether it was fixing the sloppy wiring of the long-ago dead, or improving the farms, or repairing a light fixture's ballast, Solo referred to as a "project." And he professed to *love* projects. She decided it was something from his youth, some sort of survival mechanism he'd concocted over the years that allowed him to tackle whatever needed doing with a smile instead of horror or loneliness.

"Oh, we've got quite a project ahead of us," Juliette told him, already dreading the job. She started making a mental list of all the tools and spares they'd need to scrounge on their way back up.

Solo laughed and clapped his hands. “Good,” he said. “Back to the workshop!” He twirled his finger over his head, pointing up at the long climb ahead of them.

“Not yet,” she said. “First, some lunch at the farms. Then we need to stop by Supply for some more things. And *then* I need some time alone in the server room.” Juliette turned away from the railing and that deep shaft of silver-green water below. “Before we get started in the workshop,” she said, “I’d like to make a call—”

“A call!” Solo pouted. “Not a call. You spend all your time on that stupid thing.”

Juliette ignored him and hit the stairs. She began the long slog up to IT, her fifth in three weeks. And she knew Solo was right: she *was* spending too much time making calls, too much time with those headphones pulled down over her ears, listening to them beep. She knew it was crazy, that she was going slowly mad in that place, but sitting at the back of that empty server with her microphone close to her lips and the world made quiet by the cups over her ears—just having that wire linking her from a dead world to one that harbored life—it was the closest she could get in silo seventeen to making herself feel sane.

57

Silo 18

... was the year the Civil War consumed the thirty-four states. More American lives were lost in this conflict than in all the subsequent ones combined, for any death was a death among kin. For four years, the land was ravaged, smoke clearing over battlefields of ruin to reveal brother heaped upon brother. More than half a million lives were lost. Some estimates range to almost twice that. Disease, hunger, and heartbreak ruled the life of man ...

The pages of the book flashed crimson just as Lukas was getting to the descriptions of the battlefields. He stopped reading and glanced up at the overhead lights. Their steady white had been replaced with a throbbing red, which meant someone was in the server room above him. He retrieved the loose silver thread curled up on the knee of his overalls and laid it carefully into the spine of the book. Closing the old tome, he returned it to its tin case with care, then slid it into the gap on the bookshelf, completing the vast wall of silvery spines. Padding silently across the room, he bent down in front of the computer and shook the mouse to wake the screen.

A window popped up with live views of the servers, only distorted from such wide angles. It was another secret in a room overflowing with them, this ability to see distant places. Lukas searched through the cameras, wondering if it was Sammi or another tech coming to make a repair. His grumbling stomach, meanwhile, hoped it was someone bringing him lunch.

In camera four, he finally spotted his visitor: a short figure in gray overalls sporting a mustache and glasses. He was slightly stooped, a tray in his hands dancing with silverware, a sloshing glass of water, and a covered plate, all of it partly supported by his protruding belly. Bernard glanced up at the camera as he walked by, his eyes piercing Lukas from a level away, a tight smile curling below his mustache.

Lukas left the computer and hurried down the hallway to get the hatch for him, his bare feet slapping softly on the cool steel grating. He scrambled up the ladder with practiced ease and slid the worn red locking handle to the side. Just as he lifted the grate, Bernard's shadow threw the ladderway into darkness. The tray came to a clattering rest as Lukas shifted the section of flooring out of the way.

"I'm spoiling you today," Bernard said. He sniffed and uncovered the plate. A fog of trapped steam billowed out of the metal hood, two stacks of pork ribs revealing themselves underneath.

"Wow." Lukas felt his stomach rumble at the sight of the meat. He lifted himself out of the hatch and sat on the floor, his feet dangling down by the ladder. He pulled the tray into his lap and picked up the silverware. "I thought we had the silo on strict rations, at least until the resistance is over."

He cut a piece of tender meat free and popped it in his mouth. "Not that I'm complaining, mind you." He chewed and savored the rush of proteins, reminded himself to be thankful for the animal's sacrifice.

"The rations haven't been lifted," Bernard said. "We had a pocket of resistance flare up in the bazaar, and this poor pig found himself in the crossfire. I wasn't about to let him go to waste. Most of the meat, of course, went to the wives and husbands of those we've lost."

"Mmm?" Lukas swallowed. "How many?"

"Five, plus the three from that first attack."

Lukas shook his head.

"It's not bad, considering." Bernard brushed his mustache with his hand and watched Lukas eat. Lukas gestured with his fork while he chewed, offering him some, but Bernard waved him away. The older man leaned back on the empty server that housed the uplink and the locking handle for the ladderway. Lukas tried not to react.

"So how long will I need to stay in here?" He tried to sound calm, like any answer would do. "It's been three weeks, right?" He cut off another bite, ignoring the vegetables. "You think a few more days?"

Bernard rubbed his cheeks and ran his fingers up through his thinning hair. "I hope so, but I don't know. I've left it up to Sims, who's convinced the threat isn't over. Mechanical have themselves barricaded pretty good down there. They've threatened to cut the power, but I don't think they will. I think they finally understand that they don't control the juice up here on our levels. They probably tried to cut it before they stormed in and then were surprised to see us all lit up."

"You don't think they'll cut the power to the farms, do you?" He was thinking of the rations, his fear of the silo being starved.

Bernard frowned. "Eventually. Maybe. If they get desperate enough. But that'll just erode whatever support those greasers have up here. Don't worry, they'll get hungry enough and give in. It's all going by the book."

Lukas nodded and took a sip of water. The pork was the best he thought he'd ever had.

"Speaking of the book," Bernard asked, "are you catching up with your studies?"

"Yeah," Lukas lied. He nodded. In truth, he had hardly touched the book of Order. The more interesting details were found elsewhere.

"Good. When this annoyance is over, we'll schedule you some extra shifts in the server room. You can spend that time shadowing. Once we reschedule the election—and I don't think anyone else will run, especially not after all this—I'll be up top a lot more. IT will be *yours* to run."

Lukas set down the glass and picked up the cloth napkin. He wiped his mouth and thought about this. "Well, I hope you're not talking weeks from now. I feel like I've got years of—"

A buzzing noise cut him off. Lukas froze, the napkin falling out of his hand and flopping to the tray.

Bernard startled away from the server as if it had physically shocked him or its black metallic skin had grown suddenly warm.

"Goddamn it!" he said, banging the server with his fist. He fumbled inside his overalls for his master key.

Lukas forced himself to take a bite of food, to act normal. Bernard had grown more and more agitated by the constant ringing of the server. It made him irrational. It was like living with his father again, back before the tub gin finally bored him a hole beneath the potatoes.

"I fucking swear," Bernard grumbled, working the series of locks in sequence. He glanced over at Lukas, who slowly chewed a piece of meat, unable suddenly even to taste it.

"I've got a project for you," he said, wiggling the last lock free, which Lukas knew could stick a bit. "I want you to add a panel on the back here, just a simple LED array. Figure out some code so we can see who's calling us. I wanna know if it's important or if we can safely ignore it."

He yanked the back panel off the server and set it noisily against the front of server forty, behind him. Lukas took another sip of water while Bernard peered into the machine's dark and cavernous interior, studying the blinking lights above the little communication jacks. The black guts of the server tower and its frantic buzzing drowned out Bernard's whispered curses.

He pulled his head out, which was bright red with anger, and turned to Lukas, who set his cup on his tray. "In fact, what I want right here is *two* lights." Bernard pointed to the side of the tower. "A red light if it's silo seventeen calling. Green if it's *anyone else.* You got that?"

Lukas nodded. He looked down at his tray and started cutting a potato in half, thinking suddenly of his father again. Bernard turned and grabbed the server's rear panel.

"I can pop that back on." Lukas mumbled this around a hot mouthful of potato; he breathed out steam to keep his tongue from burning, swallowed, and chased it with water.

Bernard left the panel where it was. He turned and glared angrily into the pit of the machine, which continued to buzz and buzz, the overhead lights winking in alarm. "Good idea," he said. "Maybe you can knock this project out first thing."

Finally, the server quit its frantic calls, and the room fell silent save for the clinking of Lukas's fork on his plate. This was like the moments of rye-stench quiet from his youth. Soon—just like his father passing out on the kitchen floor or in the bathroom—Bernard would leave.

As if on cue, his caster and boss stood, the head of IT again throwing Lukas into darkness as he blocked the overhead lights.

"Enjoy your dinner," he said. "I'll have Peter come by later for the dishes."

Lukas jabbed a row of beans with his fork. "Seriously? I thought this was lunch." He popped them into his mouth.

"It's after eight," Bernard said. He adjusted his overalls. "Oh, and I spoke with your mother today."

Lukas set his fork down. "Yeah?"

"I reminded her that you were doing important work for the silo, but she really wants to see you. I've talked with Sims about allowing her in here —"

"Into the server room?"

"Just inside. So she can see that you're okay. I'd set it up elsewhere, but Sims thinks it's a bad idea. He's not so sure how strong the allegiance is among the techs. He's still trying to ferret out any source of leaks —"

Lukas scoffed. "Sims is paranoid. None of our techs are gonna side with those greasers. They're not going to betray the silo, much less you." He picked up a bone and gnawed at the remaining meat.

"Still, he has me convinced to keep you as safe as possible. I'll let you know if I can set something up so you can see her." Bernard leaned forward and squeezed Lukas's shoulder. "Thanks for being patient. I'm glad to have someone under me who understands how important this job is."

"Oh, I understand completely," Lukas said. "Anything for the silo."

"Good." Another squeeze of his hand, and Bernard stood. "Keep reading the Order. Especially the sections on insurrections and uprisings. I want you to learn from this one just in case, God forbid, it ever happens on *your* watch."

"I will," Lukas said. He set down the clean bone and wiped his fingers on the napkin. Bernard turned to go.

"Oh —" Bernard stopped and turned back to him. "I know you don't need me to remind you, but under no circumstances are you to answer this server." He jabbed his finger at the front of the machine. "I haven't cleared you with the other IT heads yet, so your position could be in . . . well, *grave* danger if you were to speak with *any* of them before the induction."

"Are you kidding?" Lukas shook his head. "Like I want to talk with anyone who makes *you* nervous. No frickin' thanks."

Bernard smiled and wiped at his forehead. "You're a good man, Lukas. I'm glad I've got you."

"And I'm glad to serve," Lukas said. He reached for another rib and smiled up at his caster while Bernard beamed down at him. Finally, the older man turned to go, his boots ringing across the steel grates and fading toward that massive door that held Lukas prisoner among the machines and all their secrets.

Lukas ate and listened as Bernard's new code was keyed into the lock, a cadence of familiar but unknown beeps — a code Lukas no longer possessed.

For your own good, Bernard had told him. He chewed a piece of fat as the heavy door clanged shut, the red lights below his feet and down the ladderway blinking off.

Lukas dropped the bone onto his plate. He pushed the potatoes aside, fighting the urge to gag at the sight of them, thinking of where his father's bones lay. Setting the tray on the grating, he pulled his feet out of the ladderway and moved to the back of the open and quiet server.

The headphones slid easily out of their pouch. He pulled them down over his ears, his palms brushing the three-week growth of beard on his face. Grabbing the cord, he slotted it into the jack labeled "17."

There was a series of beeps as the call was placed. He imagined the buzzing on the other side, the flashing lights.

Lukas waited, unable to breathe.

"Hello?"

The voice sang in his earphones. Lukas smiled.

"Hey," he said.

He sat down, leaned back against server forty, and got more comfortable.

"How's everything going over there?"

58

Silo 18

WALKER WAVED HIS ARMS over his head as he attempted to explain his new theory for how the radio probably worked. "So the sound, these transmissions, they're like ripples in the air, you see?" He chased the invisible voices with his fingers. Above him, the third large antenna he'd built in two days hung suspended from the rafters. "These ripples run up and down the wire, up and down"—he gesticulated to show the length of antenna—"which is why longer is better. It snags more of them out of the air."

But if these ripples are everywhere, then why aren't we catching any?

Walker bobbed his head and wagged his finger in appreciation. It was a good question. A damn good question. "We'll catch them this time," he said. "We're getting close." He adjusted the new amplifier he'd built, one much more powerful than the tiny thing in Hank's old hip radio. "Listen," he said.

A crackling hiss filled the room, like someone twisting fistfuls of plastic sheeting.

I don't hear it.

"That's because you aren't being quiet. *Listen.*"

There. It was faint, but a crunch of transmitted noise emerged from the hiss.

I heard it!

Walker nodded with pride. Less for the thing he was building and more for his bright understudy. He glanced at the door, made sure it was still closed. He only spoke with Scottie when it was closed.

"What I don't get is why I can't make it clearer." He scratched his chin. "Unless it's because we're too deep in the earth."

We've always been this deep, Scottie pointed out. *That sheriff we met years ago, he was always talking on his radio just fine.*

Walker scratched the stubble on his cheek. His little shadow, as usual, had a good point.

"Well, there *is* this one little circuit board I can't figure out. I think it's supposed to clean up the signal. Everything seems to pass through it." Walker spun around on his stool to face the workbench, which had become dominated by all the green boards and colorful tangles of wires needed for this most singular project. He lowered his magnifier and peered at the board in question. He imagined Scottie leaning in for a closer inspection.

What's this sticker? Scottie pointed to the tiny dot of a white sticker with the number "18" printed on it. Walker was the one who had taught Scottie that it's always okay to admit when you don't know something. If you couldn't do this, you would never truly know *anything.*

"I'm not sure," he admitted. "But you see how this little board is slotted into the radio with ribbon cables?"

Scottie nodded.

"It's like it was meant to be swapped out. Like maybe it burns up easy. I'm thinking this is the part that's holding us up, like a blown fuse."

Can we bypass it?

"Bypass it?" Walker wasn't sure what he meant.

Go around it. In case it's burned out. Short it.

"We might blow something else. I mean, it wouldn't be *in* here if it weren't truly needed." Walker thought for a minute. He wanted to add that the same could be said of Scottie, of the boy's calming voice. But then, he never was good at telling his shadow how he felt. Only what he knew.

Well, that's what I would try—

There was a knock at the door followed by the squeal of hinges left purposefully loud. Scottie melted into the shadows beneath the workbench, his voice trailing off in the hiss of static from the speakers.

"Walk, what the hell's going on here?"

He swiveled around on his stool, the lovely voice and harsh words soldered together as only Shirly could. She came into his workshop with a covered tray, a thin-lipped frown of disappointment on her face.

Walker lowered the volume on the static. "I'm trying to fix the—"

"No, what's this nonsense I hear about you not eating?" She set the tray in front of him and pulled off the cover, releasing the steam from a plate of corn. "Did you eat your breakfast this morning, or did you give it to someone else?"

"That's too much," he said, looking down at three or four rations of food.

"Not when you've been giving yours away it isn't." She slapped a fork into his hand. "Eat. You're about to fall out of your overalls."

Walker stared at the corn. He stirred the food with his fork, but his stomach was cramped beyond hunger. He felt like he'd gone without for so long, he'd never be hungry again. The cramp would just tighten and tighten into a little fist and then he'd be just fine forever—

"Eat, damn it."

He blew on a bite of the stuff, had no desire to consume it, but put some in his mouth to make Shirly happy.

"And I don't want to hear that any of my men are hanging around your door sweet-talking you, okay? You are *not* to give them your rations. Got that? Take another bite."

Walker swallowed. He had to admit, the burn of the food felt good going down. He gathered up another small bite. "I'll be sick if I eat all this," he said.

"And I'll murder you if you don't."

He glanced over at her, expecting to see her smiling. But Shirly didn't smile anymore. Nobody did.

"What the hell is that *noise?*" She turned and surveyed the workshop, hunting for the source of it.

Walker set down his fork and adjusted the volume. The knob was soldered onto a series of resistors; the knob itself was called a potentiometer. He had a sudden impulse to explain all of this, anything to keep from eating. He could explain how he had figured out the amplifier, how the potentiometer was really just an adjustable resistor, how each little twist of the dial could hone the volume to whatever he—

Walker stopped. He picked up his fork and stirred his corn. He could hear Scottie whispering from the shadows.

"That's better," Shirly said, referring to the reduced hiss. "That's a worse sound than the old generator used to make. Hell, if you *can* turn that down, why ever have it up so loud?"

Walker took a bite. While he chewed, he set down his fork and grabbed his soldering iron from its stand. He rummaged in a small parts bin for another scrap potentiometer.

"Hold these," he told Shirly around his food. He showed her the wires hanging off the potentiometer and lined them up with the sharp silver prods from his multimeter.

"If it means you'll keep eating." She pinched the wires and the prods together between her fingers and thumbs.

Walker scooped up another bite, forgetting to blow on it. The corn burned his tongue. He swallowed without chewing, the fire melting its way through his chest. Shirly told him to slow down, to take it easy. He ignored her and twisted the knob of the potentiometer. The needle on his multimeter danced, letting him know the part was good.

"Why don't you take a break from this stuff and eat while I'm here to watch?" Shirly slid a stool away from the workbench and plopped down on it.

"Because it's too hot," he said, waving his hand at his mouth. He grabbed a spool of solder and touched it to the tip of the hot soldering iron, coating it with bright silver. "I need you to hold the black wire to this." He lightly touched the iron to the tiny leg of a resistor on the board labeled "18." Shirly leaned over the bench and squinted at the one he was indicating.

"And then you'll finish your dinner?"

"Swear."

She narrowed her eyes at him as if to say that she took this promise seriously, then did as he had shown her.

Her hands weren't as steady as Scottie's, but he lowered his magnifier and made quick work of the connection. He showed her where the red wire went and tacked that one on as well. Even if none of this worked, he could always remove it and tinker with something else.

"Now, don't let it get cold," Shirly told him. "I know you won't eat it if it cools, and I'm not going back to the mess hall to warm it up for you."

Walker stared at the little board with the numbered sticker on it. He grudgingly picked up the fork and scooped a sizable bite.

"How're things out there?" he asked, blowing on the corn.

"Things are shit," Shirly said. "Jenkins and Harper are arguing over whether or not they should kill the power to the entire silo. But then some of the guys who were there, you know, when Knox and . . ."

She looked away, left the sentence unfinished.

Walker nodded and chewed his food.

"Some of them say the power in IT was up to the max that morning, even though we had it shut down from here."

"Maybe it was rerouted," Walker said. "Or battery backups. They have those, you know." He took another bite but was dying to spin the potentiometer. He was pretty sure the static had changed when he'd made the second connection.

"I keep telling them it'll do us more harm than good to screw with the silo like that. It'll just turn the rest of them against us."

"Yeah. Hey, can you adjust this? You know, while I eat?"

He turned the volume up on the static, needing two hands to work the potentiometer as it dangled from its bright wires. Shirly seemed to shrink from the noise crackling out of his home-built speakers. She reached for the volume knob as if to turn it down.

"No, I want you to spin the one we just installed."

"What the hell, Walk? Just eat your damn food already."

He took another bite. And for all her cussing and protests, Shirly began adjusting the knob.

"Slowly," he said, his mouth full of food.

And sure enough, the static from the speakers modulated. It was as if the crunching plastic had begun to move and bounce around the room.

"What am I even doing?"

"Helping an old man—"

"—yeah, I might need you up here on this one—"

Walker dropped his fork and held out his hand for her to stop. She had gone past it though, into the static once more. Shirly seemed to intuit this. She bit her lip and wiggled the knob the other way until the voices returned.

“Sounds good. It’s quiet down here anyway. You need me to bring my kit?”

“You did it,” Shirly whispered to Walker, as if these people could hear her if she spoke too loudly. “You fixed —”

Walker held up his hand. The chatter continued.

“Negative. You can leave the kit. Deputy Roberts is already here with hers. She’s sweeping for clues as I speak —”

“What I’m doing is working while he does nothing!” a faint voice called out in the background.

Walker turned to Shirly while laughter rolled through the radio, more than one person enjoying the joke. It had been a long time since he’d heard anyone laugh. But *he* wasn’t laughing. Walker felt his brow furrow in confusion.

“What’s wrong?” Shirly asked. “We did it! We fixed it!” She got off her stool and turned as if to run and tell Jenkins.

“Wait!” Walker wiped his beard with his palm and jabbed his fork toward the strewn collection of radio parts. Shirly stood a pace away, looking back at him, smiling.

“Deputy *Roberts?*” Walker asked. “Who in all the levels is *that?*”

59

Silo 17

JULIETTE FLICKED THE LIGHTS on in the Suit Lab as she hauled in her latest load from Supply. Unlike Solo, she didn't take the constant source of power for granted. Not knowing where it came from made her nervous that it wouldn't last. So while he had the habit, the compulsion even, of turning every light on to full and leaving it there, she tried to conserve the mysterious energy as much as possible.

She dropped her recent scavenges on her cot, thinking of Walker as she did so. Is this how he ended up living among his work? Was it the obsession, the drive, the need to keep hammering away at a series of never-ending problems until he couldn't sleep more than a few paces from them?

The more she understood the old man, the farther away from him she felt, the lonelier. She sat down and rubbed her legs, her thighs and calves tight from the most recent hike up. She may've been gaining her porter legs these last weeks, but they were still sore all the time, the ache in them a constant new sensation. Squeezing the muscles transformed that ache into pain, which she somehow preferred. The sharp and definable sensations were better than the dull and nameless kind. She liked feelings she could understand.

Juliette kicked her boots off—strange to think of these scavenged things as *hers*—and stood up. That was enough rest. It was as much rest as she could allow herself to have. She carried her canvas sacks to one of the fancy workbenches, everything in the Suit Lab nicer than what she'd had in Mechanical. Even the parts engineered to fail were constructed with a level of chemical and engineering sophistication she could only begin to appreciate now that she understood their evil intent. She had amassed piles of washers and seals, the good from Supply and the leftover bad from the lab, to see how the system worked. They sat along the back of her main workbench, a reminder of the diabolical murderousness with which she'd been sent away.

She dumped the parts from Supply and thought about how strange it was to have access to, to *live* in this forbidden heart of some *other* silo. It was stranger still to appreciate these workbenches, these immaculate tools, all arranged for the purpose of sending people like her to their death.

Looking around at the walls, at the dozen or so cleaning suits hanging from racks in various states of repair, it was like living and working in a room full of ghostly apparitions. If one of those suits jumped down and started moving about on its own, it wouldn't have surprised her. The arms and legs on each one were puffy, as if full, the mirrored visors easily concealing curious faces. It was like having company, these hanging forms. They watched her impassively while she sorted her finds into two piles: one of items she needed for her next big project, the other of useful tidbits she had snagged with no specific idea of what she might use them for.

A valuable rechargeable battery went in this second group, some blood still on it that she hadn't been able to wipe off. Images flashed through her mind of some of the scenes she'd found while scrounging for materials, like the two men who had committed suicide in the head office of Supply, their hands interlocked, opposite wrists slit, a rust-colored stain all around them. This was one of the worst scenes, a memory she couldn't shake. There was more evidence of violence scattered about the silo. The entire place was haunted and marred. She completely understood why Solo limited his rounds to the gardens. She also empathized with his habit of blocking off the server room every night with the filing cabinet, even though he had been alone for years. Juliette didn't blame him. She slid the dead bolts on the Suit Lab every night before she went to sleep. She didn't really believe in ghosts, but that conviction was being sorely tested by the constant feeling of being watched by — if not actual people — the silo itself.

She began her work on the air compressor and, as always, it felt good to be doing something with her hands. *Fixing* something. Staying distracted. The first few nights, after surviving the horrible ordeal of being sent to clean, of fighting her way inside this carcass of a silo, she had searched long and hard for someplace that she could actually sleep. It was never going to be below the server room, not with the stench of Solo's debris piles pervading the place. She tried the apartment for IT's head, but thoughts of Bernard made it impossible even to sit still. The couches in the various offices weren't long enough. The pad she'd tried to put together on the warm server-room floor was nice, but the clicking and whirring of all those tall cabinets nearly drove her insane.

The Suit Lab, strangely enough, with the specters and ghouls hanging about, was the only spot where she'd won a decent night of sleep. It was probably the tools everywhere, the welders and wrenches, the walls of drawers full of every socket and driver imaginable. If she was going to fix anything, even herself, it would be there in that room. The only other place she'd felt at home in silo seventeen was in the two jail cells she sometimes slept in on trips up and down. There, and sitting behind that empty server, talking to Lukas.

She thought about him as she crossed the room to grab the right-size tap from one of the expansive metal tool chests. She pocketed this and pulled down one of the complete cleaning suits, admiring the heft of the outfit, remembering how bulky it had felt when she'd worn one just like it. She lifted it onto a workbench and pulled off the helmet's locking collar, took this to the drill press and carefully bored a starter hole. With the collar in a vise, she began working the tap into the hole, creating new threads for the air hose. She was wrestling with this and thinking about her last conversation with Lukas when the smell of fresh bread entered the lab, followed by Solo.

"Hello!" he called from the doorway. Juliette looked up and jerked her chin for him to enter. Turning the tap required effort, the metal handle digging into her palms, sweat forming on her brow.

"I baked more bread."

"Smells great," she grunted.

Ever since she'd taught Solo how to bake flatbread, she couldn't get him to stop. The large tins of flour that had been holding up his canned-goods shelves were being removed one at a time while he experimented with recipes. She reminded herself to teach him more things to cook, to put this industriousness of his to good use by having him mix it up a little.

"And I sliced cucumbers," he said, proud as if it were a feast beyond compare. In so many ways, Solo was stuck with the mind of a teenager — culinary habits included.

"I'll have some in a bit," she told him. With effort, she finally got the tap all the way through the pilot hole, creating a threaded connection as neat as if it had come from Supply. The tap backed out easily, just like a fitted bolt would.

Solo placed the plate of bread and vegetables on the workbench and grabbed a stool. "Whatcha working on? Another pump?" He peered at the large wheeled air compressor with the hoses trailing off it.

"No. That was going to take too long. I'm working on a way to breathe underwater."

Solo laughed. He started munching on a piece of bread until he realized she wasn't joking.

"You're serious."

"I am. The pumps we *really* need are in the sump basins at the very bottom of the silo. I just need to get some of this electricity from IT *down* to them. We'll have the place dry in weeks or months instead of years."

"Breathe underwater," he said. He looked at her like *she* was the one losing her mind.

"It's no different from how I got here from my silo." She wrapped the male end of the air hose coupler with silicone tape, then began threading it into the collar. "These suits are airtight, which makes them watertight. All I need is a constant supply of air to breathe, and I can work down there as long as I like. Long enough to get the pumps going, anyway."

"You think they'll still work?"

"They should." She grabbed a wrench and tightened the coupler as hard as she dared. "They're designed to be submerged, and they're simple. They just need power, which we've got plenty of up here."

"What will *I* do?" Solo wiped his hands, sprinkling bread crumbs on her workbench. He reached for another piece of bread.

"You'll be watching the compressor. I'll show you how to

crank it, how to top it up with fuel. I'm going to install one of the portable deputy radios in the helmet here so we can talk back and forth. There'll be a whole mess of hose and electrical wire to play out." She smiled up at him. "Don't worry, I'll keep you busy."

"I'm not worried," Solo said. He puffed out his chest and crunched on a cucumber, his eyes drifting to the compressor.

And Juliette saw — just like a teenager with little practice but great need — that Solo had not yet mastered the art of lying convincingly.

60

Silo 18

. . . boys from the other side of the camp. These results were closely observed by the experimenters, who were posing as camp counselors. When the violence got out of hand, the experiment was halted before it could run its full course. What began at Robber Cave as two sets of boys, all with nearly identical backgrounds and values, had turned into what became known in the field of psychology as an in-grouping and out-grouping scenario. Small perceived differences, the way one wore a hat, the inflections in speech, turned into unforgivable transgressions. When stones started flying, and the raids on each other's camps turned bloody, there was no recourse for the experimenters but to put an end to—

Lukas couldn't read any more. He closed the book and leaned back against the tall shelves. He smelled something foul, brought the spine of the old book to his nose and sniffed. It was *him,* he finally decided. When was the last time he'd showered? His routine was all out of whack. There were no screaming kids to wake him in the morning, no evenings hunting for stars, no dimmed stairwell to guide him back to his bed so he could repeat it all the following day. Instead, it was fitful periods of tossing and turning in the hidden bunk room of level thirty-five. A dozen bunks, but him all alone. It was flashing red lights to signal that he had company, conversations with Bernard and Peter Billings when they brought him food, long talks with Juliette whenever she called and he was free to answer. Between it all, the books. Books of history out of order, of billions of people, of even more stars. Stories of violence, of the madness of crowds, of the staggering timeline of life, of orbited suns that would one day burn out, of weapons that could end it all, of diseases that nearly had.

How long could he go on like this? Reading and sleeping and eating? The weeks already felt like months. There was no keeping track of the days, no way to remember how long he'd worn this pair of overalls, if it was time to change out of them and into the pair in the dryer. Sometimes he felt like he changed and washed his clothes three times a day. It could easily have been twice a week. It smelled like longer.

He leaned his head back against the tins of books and closed his eyes. The things he was reading couldn't all be true. It made no sense, a world so crowded and strange. When he considered the scale of it all, the idea of this life burrowed beneath the earth, sending people to clean, getting worked up over who stole what from whom – he sometimes felt a sort of mental vertigo, this frightening terror of standing over some abyss, seeing a dark truth far below, but unable to make it out before his senses returned and reality snatched him back from the edge.

He wasn't sure how long he'd been sitting like that, dreaming of a different time and place, before he realized the throbbing red lights had returned.

Lukas slid the book back in its tin and struggled to his feet. The computer screen showed Peter Billings at the server-room door, as deep as he was allowed into the room. A tray with Lukas's dinner sat on top of the work-log filing cabinet inside the door.

He turned away from the computer, hurried down the corridor, and scrambled up the ladder. After removing the grate, he carefully dropped it back into place and picked a circuitous path through the tall humming servers.

"Ah, here's our little protégé." Peter smiled, but his eyes narrowed at the sight of Lukas.

Lukas dipped his chin. "Sheriff," he said. He always had this sense that Peter was silently mocking him, looking down on him, even though they were about the same age. Whenever Peter showed up with Bernard, especially the day Bernard had explained the need to keep Lukas safe, there had seemed some sort of competitive tension between the two more junior men —a tension Lukas was aware of, even if he didn't share it. In private, Bernard had committed Lukas to secrecy and told him that he was grooming Peter for the eventual job of mayor, that he and Lukas would one day work hand in hand. Lukas tried to remember this as he slid the tray off the cabinet. Peter watched him, his brow lowered in thought.

Lukas turned to go.

"Why don't you sit and eat here?" Peter asked, not budging from where he leaned against the thick server-room door.

Lukas froze.

"I see you sitting here with Bernard while you eat, but you're always in a hurry to scurry off when I come by." Peter leaned out and peered into the stacks of servers. "What is it you do in here all day, anyway?"

Lukas felt trapped. In truth, he wasn't even all that hungry, had thought about saving it for later, but eating his food to completion was usually the fastest way out of these conversations. He shrugged and sat down on the floor, leaned against the work-log cabinet, and stretched his legs out in front of him. Uncovering the tray revealed a bowl of unidentifiable soup, two slices of tomato, and a piece of corn bread.

"I work on the servers mostly, just like before." He started with a bite of the bread, something bland. "Only difference is I don't have to walk home at the end of the day." He smiled at Peter while he chewed the dry bread.

"That's right, you live down in the mids, don't you?" Peter crossed his arms and seemed to get even more comfortable against the thick door. Lukas leaned to the side and gazed past him and down the hallway. Voices could be heard around the corner. He had a sudden impulse to get up and run, just for the sake of running.

"Barely," he answered. "My apartment's practically in the up top."

"All the mids are," Peter laughed, "to those who live there."

Lukas worked on the corn bread to keep his mouth occupied. He eyed the soup warily while he chewed.

"Did Bernard tell you about the big assault we've got planned? I was thinking of going down to take part."

Lukas shook his head. He dipped his spoon into the soup.

"You know that wall Mechanical built, how those idiots boxed themselves in? Well, Sims and his boys are gonna blast it to smithereens. They've had all the time in the world to work on it from our side, so this little rebellion nonsense should be over in a few days, max."

While he slurped the hot soup, all Lukas could think about were the men and women of Mechanical trapped behind that wall of steel, and how he knew precisely what they were going through.

"Does that mean I'll be out of here soon?" He pressed the edge of his spoon into an under-ripe tomato rather than use the knife and fork. "There can't be any threat out there for me, can there? Nobody even knows who I am."

"That's up to Bernard. He's been acting strange lately. A lot of stress, I suppose." Peter slid down the door and rested on his heels. It was nice for Lukas not to have to crane his neck to look up at him. "He did say something about bringing your mother up for a visit. I took that to mean you might be in here at least a week longer."

"Great." Lukas pushed his food around some more. When the distant server started buzzing, his body practically jerked as if tugged by some string. The overhead lights winked faintly, meaningful to those in the know.

"What's that?" Peter peered into the server room, rising on his toes a little.

"That means I need to get back to work." Lukas handed him the tray. "Thanks for bringing this." He turned to go.

"Hey, the mayor said to make sure you ate everything—"

Lukas waved over his shoulder. He disappeared around the first tall server and began to jog toward the back of the room, wiping his mouth with his hand, knowing Peter couldn't follow.

"Lukas—!"

But he was gone. He hurried toward the far wall, digging his keys out of his collar as he went.

While he worked on the locks, he saw the overhead lights stop their flashing. Peter had closed the door. He removed the back panel and dug the headphones out of their pouch, plugged them in.

"Hello?" He adjusted his microphone, made sure it wasn't too close.

"Hey." Her voice filled him up in a way mere food couldn't. "Did I make you run?"

Lukas took a deep breath. He was getting out of shape living in such confinement, not walking to and from work every day. "No," he lied. "But maybe you should go easy with the calling. At least during the day. You-know-who is in here all the time. Yesterday, when you let it ring so long, we were sitting *right beside* the server while it buzzed and buzzed. It really pissed him off."

"You think I care if he gets angry?" Juliette laughed. "And I *want* him to answer. I'd love to talk to him some more. Besides, what would you suggest? I want to talk to you, I need to talk to *someone*. And you're always right there. It's not like you can call me and expect me to be here waiting. Hell, I'm all over the damn place over here. You know how many times I've been from the thirties to Supply in the last week? Guess."

"I don't want to guess." Lukas rubbed his eyelids.

"Probably a half dozen times. And you know, if he's in there all the time, you could just do me a favor and kill him for me. Save me all this trouble—"

"*Kill* him?" Lukas waved his arm. "What, just *bludgeon* him to death?"

"Do you really want some pointers? Because I've dreamed up a number of—"

"No, I don't want pointers. And I don't want to *kill* anybody! I never *did*—"

Lukas dug his index finger into his temple and rubbed in tiny forceful circles. These headaches were forever popping up. They had been ever since—

"Forget it," Juliette said, the disgust in her voice zipping through the wires at the speed of light.

"Look—" Lukas readjusted his mic. He hated these conversations. He preferred it when they just talked about nothing. "I'm sorry, it's just that … things are crazy over here. I don't know who's doing what. I'm in this box with all this information, I've got this radio that just blares out people fighting all the time, and yet I seem to know ratshit compared to everyone else."

"But you know you can trust me, right? That I'm one of the good guys? I didn't do anything wrong to be sent away, Lukas. I need you to know that."

He listened as Juliette took in a deep breath and let it out with a sigh. He imagined her sitting over there, alone in that silo with a crazy man, the mic pressed close to her lips, her chest heaving with exasperation, her mind full of all these expectations of him.

"Lukas, you do know that I'm on the right side here, don't you? And that you're working for an insane man?"

"Everything's crazy," he said. "Everyone is. I do know this: we were sitting here in IT, hoping nothing bad would happen, and the worst things we could think of came to *us*."

Juliette released another deep breath, and Lukas thought about what he had told her of the uprising, the things he had omitted.

"I know what you say my people did, but do you understand why they came? Do you? Something needed to be done, Luke. It *still* needs doing."

Lukas shrugged, forgetting she couldn't see him. As often as they chatted, he still wasn't used to conversing with someone like this.

"You're in a position to help," she told him.

"I didn't *ask* to be here." He felt himself growing frustrated. Why did their conversations have to drift off to bad places? Why couldn't they go back to talking about the best meals they'd ever had, their favorite books as kids, the likes and annoyances they had in common?

"None of us asked to be where we are," she reminded him coolly.

This gave Lukas pause, thinking of where she was, what she'd been through to get there.

"What we control," Juliette said, "is our actions once fate puts us there."

"I probably need to get off." Lukas took a shallow breath. He didn't want to think of actions and fate. He didn't want to have this conversation. "Pete'll be bringing me my dinner soon," he lied.

There was silence. He could hear her breathing. It was almost like listening to someone think.

"Okay," she said. "I understand. I need to go test this suit anyway. And hey, I might be gone awhile if this thing works. So if you don't hear from me for a day or so . . ."

"Just be careful," Lukas said.

"I will. And remember what I said, Luke. What we do going forward defines who we are. You aren't one of them. You don't belong there. Please don't forget this."

Lukas mumbled his agreement, and Juliette said good-bye, her voice still in his ears as he reached in and unplugged the jack.

Rather than slot the headphones into their pouch, he slumped back against the server behind him, wringing the ear pads in his hands, thinking about what he had done, about who he was.

He felt like curling up into a ball and crying, just closing his eyes and making the world go away. But he knew if he closed them, if he allowed himself to sink into darkness, all he would see there was *her*. That small woman with the white hair, her body jumping from the impacts of the bullets, *Lukas's* bullets. He would feel his finger on the trigger, his cheeks wet with salt, the stench of spent powder, the table ringing with the clink of empty brass, and the jubilant and victorious cries of the men and women he had aligned himself with.

61

Silo 18

"— SAID THURSDAY THAT I'D get it to you in two days."

"Well, damn it, it's been two days, Carl. You do realize the cleaning's tomorrow morning, right?"

"And you realize that today is still today, don't you?"

"Don't be a smart-ass. Get me that file and get it up here, pronto. I swear, if this shit falls through because you were —"

"I'll bring it. C'mon, man. I'm busting your balls. Relax."

"Relax. Screw you, I'll relax tomorrow. I'm getting off the line. Now don't dick around."

"I'm coming right now . . ."

Shirly held the sides of her head, her fingers tangled in her hair, elbows digging into Walker's workbench. "What in the depths is going on?" she asked him. "Walk, what is this? Who *are* these people?"

Walker peered through his magnifiers. He dipped the single bristle plucked from the cleaning brush into the white paint on the wet lid of primer. With utmost care, his other hand steadying his wrist, he dragged the bristle across the outside of the potentiometer directly opposite the fixed mark he'd painted on the knob itself. Satisfied, he counted the ticks he'd made so far, each one marking the position of another strong signal.

"Eleven," he said. He turned to Shirly, who had been saying something, he wasn't sure what. "And I don't think we've found ours yet."

"*Ours?* Walk, this is freaking me out. Where are these voices *coming* from?"

He shrugged. "The city? Over the hills? How should I know?" He started spinning the knob slowly, listening for more chatter. "Eleven besides us. What if there's more? There has to be more, right? What're the chances we've found them all already?"

"That last one was talking about a cleaning. Do you think they meant . . . ? Like . . . ?"

Walker nodded, sending his magnifiers out of whack. He re-adjusted them, then went back to tuning the dial.

"So they're in silos. Like us."

He pointed to the tiny green board she'd helped him wire the potentiometer to. "It must be what this circuit does, modulates the wave frequency, maybe." Shirly was freaking out over the voices; he was more fascinated by these other mysteries. There was a crackle of static; he paused in turning the knob, scrubbed back and forth across it, but found nothing. He moved on.

"You mean the little board with the number *eighteen* on it?"

Walker looked at her dumbly. His fingers stopped their searching. He nodded.

"So there's at least *that* many," she said, putting it together quicker than he had. "I've got to find Jenkins. We've got to tell him about this." Shirly left her stool and headed for the door. Walker bobbed his head. The implications made him dizzy, the bench and walls seeming to slide sideways. The idea of *people* beyond these walls—

A violent roar rattled his teeth and shook the thought loose.

His feet slipped out from underneath him as the ground trembled, decades of dust raining down from the tangle of pipes and wires crisscrossing overhead.

Walker rolled to his side, coughing, breathing the musky mildew drifting in the air. His ears were ringing from the blast. He patted his head, groped for his magnifiers, when he saw the frame lying on the steel decking before him, the lenses broken into gravel-sized shards.

"Oh, no. I need . . ." He tried to get his hands underneath him, felt a twinge in his hip, a powerful ache where bone had smacked steel. He couldn't think. He waved his hand, begging Scottie to come out of the shadows and help him.

A heavy boot crunched on what remained of his magnifiers. Strong, young hands gripped his overalls, pulling him to his feet. There was shouting everywhere. The pop and rattle of gunfire.

"Walk! You okay?"

Jenkins held him by his overalls. Walker was pretty sure he would collapse if the boy let go.

"My magni—"

"Sir! We've gotta go! They're inside!"

Walker turned toward the door, saw Harper helping Shirly to her feet. Her eyes were wide, stunned, a film of gray dust on her shoulders and in her dark hair. She was looking toward Walker, appearing as dazed as he felt.

"Get your things," Jenkins said. "We're falling back." He scanned the room, his eyes drifting to the workbench.

"I fixed it," Walker said, coughing into his fist. "It works."

"A little too late, I think."

Jenkins let go of his overalls, and Walker had to catch himself on his stool not to go tumbling back to the ground. The gunfire outside drew nearer. Boots thundered by, more shouting, another loud blast that could be felt through the floor. Jenkins and Harper were at the doorway shouting orders and waving their arms at the people running past. Shirly joined Walker at his workbench. Her eyes were on the radio.

"We need this," she said, breathing hard.

Walker looked down at the glittering jewels on the floor. Two months' wages for those magnifiers –

"Walk! What do I grab? Help me."

He turned to find Shirly gathering up the radio parts, the wires between the boards folded up, tangled. There was a single loud pop from one of the good guns right outside his door, causing him to cower, his mind to wander.

"Walk!"

"The antenna," he whispered, pointing to where the dust was still drifting from the rafters. Shirly nodded and jumped up on his workbench. Walker looked around the room, a room he had promised himself he would never leave again, a promise he really had meant to keep this time. What to grab? Stupid mementos. Junk. Dirty clothes. A pile of schematics. He grabbed his parts bin and dumped it on the floor. The radio components were swept in, the transformer unplugged from its outlet and added. Shirly was yanking down the antenna, the wires and metal rods bundled against her chest. He snatched his soldering iron, a few tools; Harper yelled that it was now or never.

Shirly grabbed Walker by the arm and pulled him along, toward the door.

And Walker realized it wasn't going to be *never.*

62

Silo 17

THE PANIC SHE FELT from donning the suit was unexpected.

Juliette had anticipated some degree of fear from slipping into the water, but it was the simple act of putting on the cleaning suit that filled her with a hollow dread, that gave her a cold and empty ache in the pit of her stomach. She fought to control her breathing while Solo zipped up the back and pressed the layers of Velcro into place.

"Where's my knife?" she asked him, patting the pockets on the front and searching among her tools.

"It's over here," he said. He bent down and fished it out of her gear bag, out from under a towel and change of clothes. He passed her the knife handle-first, and Juliette slotted it into the thick pocket she'd added on the suit's belly. It was easier to breathe just having it within reach. This tool from the upper café was like a security blanket of sorts. She found herself checking for it the way she used to check her wrist for that old watch.

"Let's wait with the helmet," she told Solo as he lifted the clear dome from the landing. "Grab that rope first." She pointed with her puffy mitts. The thick material and the two layers of undersuit were making her warm. She hoped that boded well for not freezing to death in the deep water.

Solo lifted the coils of spliced rope, a large adjustable wrench the length of his forearm knotted at the end.

"Which side?" he asked.

She pointed to where the gracefully curving steps plunged into the green-lit water. "Lower it over steady. And hold it out so it doesn't get caught on the steps below."

He nodded. Juliette checked her tools while he dropped the wrench into the water, the weight of the hunk of metal tugging the rope straight down to the very bottom of the great stairwell. In one pocket, she had a range of drivers. Each one was tied to the pocket with a few feet of string. She had a spanner in another pocket, cutters behind pocket number four. Looking down at herself, more memories flooded back from her walk outside. She could hear the sound of fine grit pelting her helmet, could sense her air supply running thin, could feel the clomp of her heavy boots on the packed earth . . .

She gripped the railing ahead of her and tried to think of something else. Anything else. Wire for power and hose for air. Concentrate. She would need a lot of both. She took a deep breath and checked the tall coils of tubing and electrical wire laid out on the deck. She had flaked them in figure eights so they would be impossible to tangle. Good. The compressor was ready; all Solo had to do was make sure everything fed down to her, didn't get caught up—

"It's on the bottom," Solo said. She watched him knot the line to the stairway railing. He was in good spirits today. Lucid and energetic. This would be a good time to get it over with. Shifting the flood to the treatment plant would've been an inelegant, temporary solution. It was time to get those big pumps down below churning through that water properly, pumping it through the concrete walls and back into the earth beyond.

Juliette shuffled to the edge of the landing and looked down at the silvery surface of the foul water. Was this plan of hers crazy? Shouldn't she be afraid? Or was it the years of waiting and doing this safely that was more terrifying to her? The prospect of going mad, inch by inch, seemed the greater risk. This would be just like going outside, she reminded herself, which she had already done and had survived. Except ... this was safer. She was taking an unlimited supply of air, and there was nothing toxic down there, nothing to eat away at her.

She gazed at her reflection in the still water, the bulky suit making her look enormous. If Lukas were standing there with her, if he could see what she was about to do, would he try to talk her out of it? She thought he might. How well did they really know each other? They had had what, two, three encounters in person?

But then there were the dozens of talks since. Could she know him from just his voice? From stories about his childhood? From his intoxicating laughter when everything else in her day made her want to cry? Was this why wires and e-mails were expensive, to prevent this kind of life, this kind of relationship? How could she be standing there, thinking of a man she hardly knew rather than the insanity of the task before her?

Maybe Lukas had become her lifeline, some slender thread of hope connecting her to home. Or was he more like a tiny spot of light seen occasionally through the murk, a beacon guiding her return?

"Helmet?" Solo stood beside her, watching her, the clear plastic dome in his hands, a single flashlight strapped to its top.

Juliette reached for it. She made sure the flashlight was securely fastened and tried to clear her head of pointless ruminations.

"Hook up my air first," she said. "And turn on the radio."

He nodded. She held the dome while he clicked the air hose

into the adapter she'd threaded through the collar. There was a hiss and spit of residual air from the line as it locked into place. His hand brushed the back of her neck as he reached in to flick on the radio. Juliette dipped her chin, squeezing the handmade switch sewn into her undersuit. "Hello, hello," she said. There was a strange squeal from the unit on Solo's hip as her voice blared out of it.

"Little loud," he said, adjusting his volume.

She lifted the dome into place. It had been stripped of its screen and all the plastic linings. Once she'd scraped the paint off the exterior, she was left with an almost completely transparent half sphere of tough plastic. It felt good to know, clicking it into the collar, that whatever she saw out of it was really there.

"You good?"

Solo's voice was deadened by the airtight connection between the helmet and the suit. She lifted her glove and gave him a thumbs-up. She pointed to the compressor.

He nodded, knelt down by the unit, and scratched his beard. She watched him flick the portable unit's main power, push the priming bulb five times, then yank the starting cord. The little unit spat out a breath of smoke and whirred to life. Even with its rubber tires, it danced and rattled the landing, sending vibrations up through her boots. Juliette could hear the awful acoustics through her helmet, could imagine the violent racket echoing up through the abandoned silo.

Solo held the choke an extra second, just like she'd shown him, and then pushed it all the way in. While the machine pattered and chugged, he looked up at her, smiling through his beard, looking like one of the dogs in Supply staring up at its faithful owner.

She pointed to the red can of extra fuel and gave him another thumbs-up. He returned the gesture. Juliette shuffled toward the steps, her gloved hand on the railing for balance. Solo squeezed past and went to the railing and the knotted rope. He held out a hand to steady her while she lumbered down the slippery treads in the suit's clunky boots.

Her hope was that it would be easier to move once she was in the water, but she had no way of knowing, just an intuitive feel for the physics of it all, the way she could gauge a machine's intent simply by poring over it. She took the last dry steps, and then her boots broke the oily surface of the water and found the step below. She waded down two more, anticipating the frigid cold that would seep through, but it never came. The suit and her undergarments kept her toasty. Almost too warm, in fact—she could see a humid mist forming on the inside of her helmet. She dipped her chin into the radio switch and told Solo to open her valve to let the air in.

He fumbled at her collar and twisted the lever to allow the flow of air. It hissed by her ear, quite noisily, and she could feel the suit puff out around her. The overflow valve she'd screwed into the other side of the collar squealed as it opened and let out the excess pressure, preventing her suit—and her head, she suspected—from bursting.

"Weights," she said, clicking the radio.

He ran back to the landing and returned with the round exercise weights. Kneeling on the last dry step, he strapped these below her knees with heavy Velcro, then looked up to see what was next.

Juliette struggled to lift one foot, then the other, making sure that the weights were secure.

"Wire," she said, getting the hang of working the radio.

This was the most important part: the power from IT would run the lifeless pumps below. Twenty-four volts of juice. She had installed a switch on the landing so Solo could test it while she was down there. She didn't want to travel with the wires live.

Solo unspooled a dozen feet of the two-connector wire and tied a loop around her wrist. His knots were good, both with the rope and the wire. Her confidence in the endeavor was growing by the minute, her discomfort in the suit lessening.

Solo smiled down through her clear plastic dome from two steps above, yellow teeth flashing in his scraggly beard. Juliette returned the smile. She stood still while he fumbled with the flashlight strapped to her helmet, clicking it on. The battery was freshly charged and would last a full day, much longer than she possibly needed.

"Okay," she said. "Help me over."

Releasing the radio contact with her chin, she turned and leaned against the railing, worked her belly up onto it, then eased her head over. It was an incredible sensation, throwing herself over that rail. It felt suicidal. This was the great stairwell; this was her silo; she was four levels up from Mechanical; all that space below her, that long plummet only madmen dived into, and she was going just as willingly.

Solo helped with her weighted feet. He splashed down onto the first wet step to assist her. Juliette threw her leg over the railing as he lifted. Suddenly, she was straddling that narrow bar of slippery steel, wondering if the water would truly hold her, if it would catch and slow her fall. And there was a moment of raw panic, the taste of metal in her mouth, the sinking of her stomach, and the dire need to urinate, all while Solo heaved her other foot over the railing, her gloved hands clawing madly for the rope he'd tied, her boots splashing noisily and violently into the silvery skin of the flooded waters.

"Shit!"

She blew her breath out into the helmet, gasping from the

shock of splashing in so quickly, her hands and knees wrapping around the twisting rope, her body moving inside the puffy suit like a layer of too-large skin had become detached.

"You okay?" Solo shouted, his hands cupped around his beard.

She nodded, her helmet unmoving. She could feel the tug of the weights on her shins, trying to drag her down. There were a dozen things she wanted to say to Solo, reminders and tips, words of luck, but her mind was racing too fast to think of using the radio. Instead, she loosened her grip with her gloves and knees, felt the rope slide against her body with a distant squeak, and she began her long plummet down.

63

Silo 18

LUKAS SAT AT THE little desk constructed from an embarrassment of wood and stared down at a book stuffed with a fortune in crisp paper. The chair beneath him was probably worth more than he'd make in a lifetime, and he was *sitting* on it. If he moved, the joints of the dainty thing twisted and squeaked, like it could come apart at any moment.

He kept his boots firmly planted on either side, his weight on his toes, just in case.

Lukas flipped a page, pretending to read. It wasn't that he didn't want to be reading, he just didn't want to be reading *this.* Entire shelves of more interesting works seemed to mock him from within their tin boxes. They sang out to be perused, for him to put away the Order with its rigid writing, bulleted lists, and internal labyrinth of page references that led in more circles than the great stairwell itself.

Each entry in the Order pointed to another page, every page another entry. Lukas flipped through a few and wondered if Bernard was keeping tabs on him. The head of IT sat on the other side of the small study, just one room of many in the well-stocked hideaway beneath the servers. While Lukas pretended to shadow for his new job, Bernard alternated between fiddling with the small computer on the other desk and going over to the radio mounted on the wall to give instructions to the security forces in the down deep.

Lukas pinched a thick chunk of the Order and flopped it to the side. He skipped past all the recipes for averting silo disasters and checked out some of the more academic reference material toward the back. This stuff was even *more* frightening: chapters on group persuasion, on mind control, on the effects of fear during upbringing; graphs and tables dealing with population growth . . .

He couldn't take it. He adjusted his chair and watched Bernard for a while as the head of IT and acting mayor scrolled through screen after screen of text, his head notching back and forth as he scanned the words there.

After a moment, Lukas dared to break the silence. "Hey, Bernard?"

"Hm?"

"Hey, why isn't there anything in here about how all this came to be?"

Bernard's office chair squealed as he swiveled it around to face Lukas. "I'm sorry, what?"

"The people who made all this, the people who wrote these books. Why isn't there anything in the Order about them? Like how they built all this stuff in the first place."

"Why would there be?" Bernard half turned back to his computer.

"So we would *know*. I dunno, like all the stuff in the other books—"

"I don't want you reading those other books. Not yet." Bernard pointed to the wooden desk. "Learn the Order first. If you can't keep the silo together, the Legacy books are pulp. They're as good as processed wood if no one's around to read them."

"Nobody *can* read them but the two of us if they stay locked up down here—"

"No one *alive*. Not today. But one day, there'll be plenty of people who'll read them. But only if you study." Bernard nodded toward the thick and dreadful book before turning back to his keyboard and reaching for his mouse.

Lukas sat there awhile, staring at Bernard's back, the knotted cord of his master keys sticking out of the top of his undershirt.

"I figure they must've known it was coming," Lukas said, unable to stop himself from perseverating about it. He had always wondered about these things, had suppressed them, had found his thrills in piecing together the distant stars that were so far away as to be immune to the hillside taboos. And now he lived in this vacuum, this hollow of the silo no one knew about where forbidden topics were allowed and he had access to a man who seemed to know the precious truth.

"You aren't studying," Bernard said. His head remained bent over his keyboard, but he seemed to know that Lukas was watching him.

"But they had to've seen it coming, right?" Lukas lifted his chair and turned it around a little more. "I mean, to have built all these silos before it got so bad out there . . ."

Bernard turned his head to the side, his jaw clenching and unclenching. His hand fell away from the mouse and came up to smooth his mustache. "These are the things you want to know? How it happened?"

"Yes." Lukas nodded. He leaned forward, elbows on his knees. "I want to know."

"Do you think it matters? What happened out there?" Bernard turned and looked up at the schematics on the wall, then at Lukas. "Why would it matter?"

"Because it *happened*. And it only happened one way, and it kills me not to know. I mean, they saw it coming, right? It would take years to build all—"

"Decades," Bernard said.

"And then move all this stuff in, all the people—"

"That took much less time."

"So you know?"

Bernard nodded. "The information is stored here, but not in any of the books. And you're wrong. It *doesn't* matter. That's the past, and the past is not the same thing as our Legacy. You'll need to learn the difference."

Lukas thought about the difference. For some reason, a conversation with Juliette sprang to mind, something she was forever telling him—

"I think I know," he said.

"Oh?" Bernard pushed his glasses up his nose and stared at him. "Tell me what you *think* you know."

"All our hope, the accomplishments of those before us, what the world *can* be like, that's our Legacy."

Bernard's lips broke into a smile. He waved his hand for Lukas to continue.

"And the bad things that can't be stopped, the mistakes that got us here, that's the past."

"And what does this difference mean? What do *you* think it means?"

"It means we can't change what's already happened, but we can have an impact on what happens next."

Bernard clapped his small hands together. "Very good."

"And this"—Lukas turned and rested one hand on the thick book, then continued, unbidden—"the Order. *This* is a road map for how to get through all the bad that's piled up between our past and the future's hope. *This* is the stuff we can prevent, that we can fix."

Bernard raised his eyebrows at Lukas's last statement, as if it were a new way of looking at an old truth. Finally, he smiled, his mustache curling up, his glasses rising on the wrinkled bridge of his nose.

"I think you're almost ready," he said. "Soon." Bernard turned back to his computer, his hand falling to his mouse. "Very soon."

64

Silo 17

THE DESCENT TO MECHANICAL was oddly tranquil, almost mesmerizing. Juliette slid through the green flood, pushing herself away from the curved railing each time the staircase spiraled around beneath her feet. The only sounds anywhere were the hiss of air entering her helmet and the excess gurgling out the other side. A never-ending stream of bubbles rolled up her visor like beads of solder, drifting up in defiance of gravity.

Juliette watched these silver spheres chase one another and play like children through the metal stairs. They broke up where they touched the railing, leaving just minuscule dots of gas stuck to the surface, rolling and colliding. Others marched in wavy lines inside the stairway. They gathered in crowds beneath the hollow steps, bubbles becoming pockets of air that wobbled and caught the light radiating from the top of her helmet.

It was easy to forget where she was, what she was doing. The familiar had become distorted and strange. Everything seemed magnified by the plastic dome of her visor, and it was easy to imagine that she wasn't sinking at all, but that the great stairway was rising, pushing up through the deep earth and heading toward the clouds. Even the sensation of the rope sliding through her gloved hands and across her padded belly felt more like something tugged inexorably from above rather than a line she was descending.

It wasn't until she arched her back and looked straight up that Juliette remembered how much water was stacking up above her. The green glow of the emergency lights faded to an eerie black in the space of a landing or two. The light from her flashlight barely dented it. Juliette inhaled sharply and reminded herself that she had all the air in the silo. She tried to ignore the sensation of so much liquid piled up on her shoulders, of being buried alive. If she had to, if she panicked, she could just cut the weights free. One flick with the chef's knife and she would bob right back to the surface. She told herself this as she continued to sink. Letting go of the rope with one hand, she patted for the knife, making sure it was still there.

"SLOWER!" her radio barked.

Juliette grabbed the rope with both hands and squeezed until she came to a stop. She reminded herself that Solo was up there, watching the air hose and electrical wires as they spooled off their neat coils. She imagined him tangled up in the lines, hopping around on one foot. Bubbles raced out of her overflow valve and jiggled through the lime-green water back toward the surface. She leaned her head back and watched them swirl around the taut rope, wondering what was taking him so long. In the undersides of the helical steps, the air pockets danced mercury silver, wavering in the turbulence of her passing—

"OKAY." The radio speaker behind her neck crackled. "GOOD HERE."

Juliette cringed from the volume of Solo's voice and wished she'd checked that before closing up her helmet. There was no fixing it now.

With ears ringing and the silence and majesty of the tranquil descent broken, she slid down another level, keeping her pace steady and slow as she studied the slack in the wire and the air hose for any sign of their pulling taut. As she passed close to the landing of one-thirty-nine, she saw that one of the doors was missing; the other door had been wrenched violently from its hinges. The entire level must have been flooded, which meant more water for the pumps to move. Just before the landing rose out of sight, she saw dark forms down the corridor, shadows floating in the water. The flashlight on her helmet barely illuminated a pale and bloated face before she drifted past, leaving the long-dead to rise out of sight.

It hadn't occurred to Juliette that she might come across more bodies. Not the drowned of course — the flood would've risen too slowly to take anyone by surprise — but any violence that occurred in the down deep would now be preserved in its icy depths. The chill of the water around her seemed to finally penetrate the layers of her suit. Or perhaps it was just her imagination.

Her boots thumped to the lowermost floor of the stairwell while she was still looking up, keeping an eye on the slack in the lines. Her knees were jarred by the startling end to her descent. It had taken her far less time than a dry hike would have.

With a grip on the rope for balance, Juliette let go with her other hand and waved it through the thick atmosphere of green groundwater. She dipped her chin against the radio switch. "I'm down," she transmitted to Solo.

She took a few lumbering and tentative steps, waving her arms and half swimming toward the entrance to Mechanical. The light from the stairwell barely penetrated past the security gates. Beyond, the oily depths of a home both foreign and familiar awaited her.

"I HEAR YOU," Solo answered after some delay.

Juliette felt her muscles tense up as his voice rattled around inside her helmet. Not being able to adjust the volume was going to drive her mad.

After a dozen halting steps, she eventually got the hang of the awkward wading motion and learned to drag her weighted boots across the steel decking. With the suit inflated and her arms and legs brushing around on the inside, it was like guiding a bubble by throwing oneself against its skin. She paused once to look back at her air hose, making sure it wasn't getting caught on the stairs, and she gave the rope she had descended one last glance. Even from this distance it appeared as an impossibly slender thread, a thread hanging in that submerged straw of a stairwell. It wavered slightly in the wake she was causing, almost as if saying good-bye.

Juliette tried not to read anything into it; she turned back to the entrance to Mechanical. *You don't have to do this,* she reminded herself. She could hook up two, maybe three more small pumps plus a few additional runs of hydroponic piping. The work might take a few months, the water level would recede for years, but eventually these levels would be dry and she could investigate those buried diggers Solo had told her about. It could be done with minimal risk—other than to her sanity.

And if her only reason for getting back home was vengeance, if that was her only motivation, she might have chosen to wait, to take that safe route. She could feel the temptation even then to yank the weights off her boots and float up through the stairwell, to fly past the levels like she used to dream she could, arms out, buoyant and free . . .

But Lukas had kept her apprised of the horrible mess her friends were in, the mess her leaving had caused. There was a radio mounted to his wall below the servers that leaked violence day and night. Solo's underground apartment was equipped with an identical radio, but it could communicate only with silo seventeen's portables. Juliette had given up fiddling with it.

A part of her was glad she couldn't hear. She didn't want to have to listen to the fighting—she just wanted to get home and make it stop. This had become a desperate compulsion: returning to her silo. It was maddening to think that she was only a short walk away, but those doors were only ever opened to kill people. And what good would her return do, anyway? Would her surviving a cleaning and revealing the truth be enough to expose Bernard and all of IT?

As it happened, she had other, less sane plans. It was a fantasy, maybe, but it gave her hope. She dreamed of fixing up one of the diggers that had built this place, a machine buried and hidden at the long end of its vertical toil, and driving it through the earth itself to eighteen's down deep. She dreamed of breaking that blockade, of leading her people back to these dry corridors and getting this dead place *working* again. She dreamed of operating a silo without all the lies and deceptions.

Juliette waded through the heavy water toward the security gate, dreaming these childish dreams, discovering that they somehow steeled her resolve. She approached the security turnstile and saw that the lifeless and unguarded gate would pose the first true obstacle of her descent. Getting over it wouldn't be easy. Turning her back to the machine, she placed her hands on either side and pushed, squirming and kicking her heavy heels against the low wall, until she was just barely sitting on the control box.

Her legs were too heavy to lift . . . at least high enough to swing over, anyway. The weights had ended up being more than she'd needed to counter the suit's buoyancy. She wiggled backward until her butt was more secure and tried to turn sideways. With a thick glove under her knee, she strained and leaned back until her boot was on the edge of the wall. She rested a moment, breathing hard and filling her helmet with muffled laughter. It felt ridiculous, all this effort to do something so outrageously simple, so benign. With one boot already up, the other was easier to lift. She felt the muscles in her abdomen and thighs, muscles sore from weeks of a porter's hustle, finally help her lift her own damn foot up.

She shook her head in relief, sweat trickling down the back of her neck, already dreading repeating the maneuver on the return trip. Dropping to the other side was easy: the weights did all the work. She took a moment to make sure the wires knotted around her wrist and the air hose attached to her collar weren't getting tangled and then started down the main corridor, the flashlight on top of her helmet her only illumination.

"YOU OKAY?" Solo asked, his voice startling her again.

"I'm fine," she said. She held her chin down against her chest, leaving the contact open. "I'll check in if I need you. The volume is a little high down here. Scares the hell out of me."

She released the contact and turned to see how her lifeline was doing. All along the ceiling, her overflow bubbles danced in the glow of her flashlight like tiny jewels—

"OKAY. GOTCHA."

With her boots hardly leaving the floor, pushing forward on them one at a time, she slowly made her way across the main intersection and past the mess hall. To her left, if she made her way down the hallway and took two turns, she could reach Walker's workshop. Had it always been a workshop? She had no idea. In this place, it might be a storeroom. Or an apartment.

Her small apartment would be in the opposite direction. She turned to peer down that hallway, her cone of light brushing away the darkness to reveal a body pressed up against the ceiling, tangled in the runs of pipe and conduit. She looked away. It was easy to imagine that being George or Scottie or someone else she had cared about and lost. It was easy to imagine it being herself.

She shuffled toward the access stairs, her body wavering in

the thick but crystal-clear water, the weight of her boots and the buoyancy of her torso keeping her upright even though she felt on the verge of toppling. She paused at the top of the square steps leading down.

"I'm about to descend," she said, chin down. "Make sure you keep everything feeding. And please don't respond unless there's a problem. My ears are still ringing from the last time."

Juliette lifted her chin from the contact switch and took the first few steps, waiting for Solo to blare something in her ear, but it never came. She kept a firm grip on the wire and hose, dragging it around the sharp corners of the square stairwell as she descended into the darkness. The black water all around was disturbed only by her rising bubbles and the feeble cone of her sweeping, flashlit gaze.

Six floors down, the hose and wire became difficult to pull, too much friction from the steps. She stopped and gathered more and more of it around herself, letting the slack coil drift in the weightlessness of the water. Several of her careful splices in both the wire and tubing slid through her gloves. She paused and checked the taped and glued joints of the latter to see how they were holding up. Minuscule bubbles were trailing out of one joint, leaving a perforated and wavy line of tiny dots in the dark water. It was hardly anything.

Once she had enough slack at the bottom of the stairs to reach the sump basin, she turned and marched purposefully toward her work. The hardest part was over. The air was flowing in, cool and fresh and hissing by her ear. The excess streamed out through the other valve, the bubbles shooting up in a curtain whenever she turned her head. She had enough wire and hose to reach her goal, and all of her tools were intact. It felt like she could finally relax now that she knew she wouldn't be going any deeper. All she had to do was hook up the power lines, two easy connections, and make her way out.

Being so close, she dared to think of getting free, of rescuing this silo's Mechanical spaces, resuscitating one of its generators and then one of its hidden and buried diggers. They were making progress. She was on her way to rescuing her friends. It all seemed perfectly attainable, practically in her grasp, after weeks of frustrating setbacks.

Juliette found the sump room just where it was supposed to be. She slid her boots to the edge of the pit in the center. As she leaned forward, her flashlight shone down on the numbers signifying how deep the waters had risen. They seemed comical under so many hundreds of feet of water. Comical and sad. This silo had failed its people.

But then Juliette corrected herself: these *people* had failed their *silo*.

"Solo, I'm at the pump. Gonna hook up the power."

She peered down at the bottom of the pit to make sure the pump's pickup was clear of debris. The water down there was amazingly clear. All the oil and grime she'd worked hip-deep in at the bottom of her own basin had been made diffuse, spread out into who knew how many gallons of groundwater seepage. The result was crystal-clear stuff she could probably have drunk.

She shivered, suddenly aware that the chill of the deep water was making its way through her layers and wicking away her body heat. Halfway there, she told herself. She moved toward the massive pump mounted on the wall. Pipes as thick as her waist bent to the ground and snaked over the edge of the pit. The outflow ran up the wall in a similarly sized pipe and joined the jumble of mechanical runs above. As she stood by the large pump and worked the knotted wires off her wrist, she remembered the last job she'd ever performed as a mechanic. She had pulled the shaft on an identical pump and had discovered a worn and broken impeller. As she selected a Phillips driver from her pocket and began loosening the positive power terminal, she took the time to pray that *this* pump had not been in a similar condition when the power had blown. She didn't want to have to come down and service it again. Not until she could do it while keeping her boots dry.

The positive power line came free more easily than she had hoped. Juliette twisted the new one into place. The sound of her own breathing rattled in the confines of her helmet and provided her only company. As she was tightening the terminal around the new wire, she realized she could hear her breathing because the air was no longer hissing by her cheek.

Juliette froze. She tapped the plastic dome by her ear and saw that the overflow bubbles were still leaking out, but slower now. The pressure was still inside her suit; there just wasn't any more air being forced inside.

She dipped her chin against the switch, could feel the sweat form around her collar and drip down the side of her jaw. Her feet were somehow freezing, while from the neck up she was beginning to sweat.

"Solo? This is Juliette. Can you hear me? What's going on up there?"

She waited, turned to aim her flashlight down the air hose, and looked for any sign of a kink. She still had air, the air in her suit. Why wasn't he responding?

"Hello? Solo? Please say something."

The flashlight on her helmet needed to be adjusted, but she could feel the ticking of some silent clock in her head. How much air would she have starting *right then?* It had probably taken her an hour to get down there. Solo would fix the compressor before her air ran out. She had plenty of time. Maybe he was pouring in more fuel. Plenty of time, she told herself as the driver slipped off the negative terminal. The damn thing was stuck.

This, she didn't have time for, not for anything to be corroded. The positive wire was already spliced and locked tight. She tried to adjust the flashlight strapped to her helmet; it was aimed too high: good for walking, horrible for working. She was able to twist it a little and aim it at the large pump.

The ground wire could be connected to any part of the main housing, right? She tried to remember. The entire case was the ground, wasn't it? Or was it? Why couldn't she remember? Why was it suddenly difficult to think?

She straightened the end of the black wire and tried to give the loose copper strands a twist with her heavily padded fingers. She jabbed this bundle of raw copper into a cowling vent on the back, a piece of conducting metal that appeared connected to the rest of the pump. She twisted the wire around a small bolt, knotted the slack so it would hold, and tried to convince herself that this would work, that it would be enough to run the damn thing. Walker would know. Where the hell was he when she needed him?

The radio by her neck squawked — a burst and pop of static — what sounded like part of her name in a faraway distance — a dead hiss — and then nothing.

Juliette wavered in the dark, cold water. Her ears were ringing from the outburst. She dipped her chin to tell Solo to hold the radio away from his mouth, when she noticed through the glass window of her helmet's visor that there were no more bubbles spilling from the overflow valve and rising in that gentle curtain across her vision. The pressure in her suit was gone.

A different sort of pressure quickly took its place.

65

Silo 18

WALKER FOUND HIMSELF SHOVED down the square stairs, past a crew of mechanics working to weld another set of steel plates across the narrow passage. He had most of the home-built radio in the spare-parts tub, which he desperately clutched with two hands. He watched the electrical components rattle together as he jostled through the crowd of mechanics fleeing from the attack above. In front of him, Shirly carried the rest of the radio gear against her chest, the antenna wires trailing behind her. Walker skipped and danced on his old legs so he wouldn't get tangled up.

"Go! Go! Go!" someone yelled. Everyone was pushing and shoving. The rattle of gunfire seemed to grow louder behind him, while a golden shower of fizzling sparks rained through the air and peppered Walker's face. He squinted and stormed through the glowing hail as a team of miners in striped overalls fought their way up from the next landing with another large sheet of steel.

"This way!" Shirly yelled, tugging him along. At the next level, she pulled him aside. His poor legs struggled to keep up. A duffel bag was dropped; a young man with a gun spun and hurried back for it.

"The generator room," Shirly told him, pointing.

There was already a stream of people moving through the double doors. Jenkins was there, managing the traffic. Some of those with rifles took up position near an oil pump, the counterweighted head sitting perfectly still like it had already succumbed to the looming battle.

"What is that?" Jenkins asked as they approached the door. He jerked his chin at the bundle of wires in Shirly's arms. "Is that . . . ?"

"The radio, sir." She nodded.

"Fat lot of good it does us now." Jenkins waved two other people inside. Shirly and Walker pressed themselves out of the way.

"Sir—"

"Get him inside," Jenkins barked, referring to Walker. "I don't need him getting in the way."

"But, sir, I think you're gonna want to hear—"

"C'mon, go!" Jenkins yelled to the stragglers bringing up the rear. He twirled his arm at the elbow for them to hurry. Only the mechanics who had traded their wrenches for guns remained. They formed up like they were used to this game, arms propped on railings, long steel barrels trained in the same direction.

"In or out," Jenkins told Shirly, starting to close the door.

"Go," she told Walker, letting out a deep breath. "Let's get inside."

Walker numbly obeyed, thinking all the while of the parts and tools he should have grabbed, things a few levels overhead now that were lost to him, maybe for good.

"Hey, get those people out of the control room!"

Shirly ran across the generator room as soon as they were inside, wires trailing behind her, bits of rigid aluminum antenna bouncing across the floor. "Out!"

A mixed group of mechanics and a few people wearing the yellow of Supply sheepishly filed out of the small control room. They joined the others around a railing cordoning off the mighty machine that dominated the cavernous facility and gave the generator room its name. At least the noise was tolerable. Shirly imagined all these people being stuck down there in the days when the roar of the rattling shaft and loose engine mounts could deafen a person.

"All of you, out of my control room." She waved the last few out. Shirly knew why Jenkins had sealed off this floor. The only power they had left was the literal kind. She waved the last man out of the small room studded with sensitive knobs, dials, and readouts and immediately checked the fuel levels.

Both tanks were topped up, so at least they had planned *that* properly. They would have a few weeks of power, if nothing else. She looked over all the other knobs and dials, the jumble of cords still held tightly against her chest.

"Where should I . . . ?"

Walker held his box out. The only flat surfaces in the room were covered with switches and the sorts of things one didn't want to bump. He seemed to understand that.

"On the floor, I guess." She set her load down and moved to shut the door. The people she'd hurried outside gazed longingly through the window at the few tall stools in the climate-controlled space. Shirly ignored them.

"Do we have everything? Is it all here?"

Walker pulled pieces of the radio out of the box, tsking at the twisted wires and jumbled components. "Do we have power?" he asked, holding up the plug of a transformer.

Shirly laughed. "Walk, you do know where you are now, right? Of course we have power." She took the cord and plugged it into one of the feeds on the main panel. "Do we have everything? Can we get it up and running again? Walk, we need to let Jenkins hear what we heard."

"I know." He bobbed his head and sorted the gear, twisting some loose wires together as he went. "We need to string that out." He jerked his head at the tangled antenna in her arms.

Shirly looked up. There were no rafters.

"Hang it from the railing out there," he told her. "Straight line, make sure that end reaches back in here."

She moved toward the door, trailing the loops out behind her.

"Oh, and don't let the metal bits touch the railing!" Walker called after her.

Shirly recruited a few mechanics from her work shift to help out. Once they saw what needed doing, they took over, coordinating as a team to undo the knots while she went back to Walker.

"It'll just be a minute," she told him, shutting the door behind her, the wire fitting easily between it and the padded jamb.

"I think we're good," he said. He looked up at her, his eyes sagging, his hair a mess, sweat glistening in his white beard. "Shit," he said. He slapped his forehead. "We don't have speakers."

Shirly felt her heart drop to hear Walker swear, thinking they'd forgotten something crucial. "Wait here," she told him, running back out and to the earmuff station. She picked one of the sets with a dangling cord, the kind used to talk between the control room and anyone working on the primary or secondary generators. She jogged past the curious and frightened-looking crowd to the control room. It occurred to her that she should be more afraid, like they were, that a real war was grinding closer to them. But all she could think about were the voices that war had interrupted. Her curiosity was much stronger than her fear. It was how she'd always been.

"How about these?"

She shut the door behind herself and showed him the headphones.

"Perfect," he said, his eyes wide with surprise. Before she could complain, he snipped the jack off with his multi-tool and began stripping wires. "Good thing it's quiet in here," he said, laughing.

Shirly laughed as well, and it made her wonder what the hell was going on. What were they going to do, sit in there and fiddle with wires while the deputies and the security people from IT came and dragged them away?

Walker got the ear cones wired in, and a faint hiss of static leaked out of them. Shirly hurried over to join him; she sat down and held his wrist to steady his hand. The headphones trembled in them.

"You might have to . . ." He showed her the knob with the white marks he'd painted on.

Shirly nodded and realized they'd forgotten to grab the paint. She held the dial and studied the various ticks. "Which one?" she asked.

"No." He stopped her as she began dialing back toward one of the voices they'd found. "The other way. I need to see how many—" He coughed into his fist. "We need to see how many there are."

She nodded and turned the knob gradually toward the black unpainted portion. The two of them held their breath, the hum of the main generator barely audible through the thick door and double-paned glass.

Shirly studied Walker while she spun the dial. She wondered what would become of him when they were rounded up. Would they all be put to cleaning? Or could he and a few of the others claim to be bystanders? It made her sad, thinking about the consequences of their anger, their thirst for revenge. Her husband was gone, ripped from her, and for what? People were dying, and for what? She thought how things could've gone so differently, how they'd had all these dreams, unrealistic perhaps, of a real change in power, an easy fix to impossible and intractable problems. Back then she'd been unfairly treated, but at least she'd been safe. There had been injustice, but she'd been in love. Did that make it okay? Which sacrifice made more sense?

"A little faster," Walker said, growing impatient with the silence. They'd heard a few hits of crackling static but no one talking. Shirly very slightly increased the rate she spun the knob.

"You think the antenna—?" she started to ask.

Walker raised his hand. The little speakers in his lap had popped. He jerked his thumb to the side, telling her to go back. Shirly did. She tried to remember how far she had gone since the sound, using a lot of the same skills she'd learned in that very room to adjust the previously noisy generator—

"—Solo? This is Juliette. Can you hear me? What's going on up there?"

Shirly dropped the knob. She watched it swing on its soldered wire and crash to the floor.

Her hands felt numb. Her fingertips tingled. She turned, gaped at Walker's lap where the ghostly voice had risen, and found him looking dumbly down at his own hands.

Neither of them moved. The voice, the name, they were unmistakable.

Tears of confused joy winked past Walker's beard and fell into his lap.

66

Silo 17

JULIETTE GRABBED THE LIMP air hose with both hands and squeezed. Her reward was a few weak bubbles rolling up her visor — the pressure inside the tube was gone.

She whispered a curse, tilted her chin against the radio, and called Solo's name. Something had happened to the compressor. He must have been working on it, maybe topping up the fuel. She had told him not to turn it off for that. He wouldn't know what to do, wouldn't be able to restart it. She hadn't thought this through clearly at all; she was an impossible distance from breathable air, from any hope of survival.

She took a tentative breath. She had what was trapped in the suit and the air that remained in the hose. How much of the air in the hose could she suck with just the power of her lungs? She didn't think it would be much.

She took one last look at the large sump pump, her hasty wiring job, the loose trail of wires streaming through the water that she'd hoped to have time to secure against vibration and accidental tugs. None of it likely mattered anymore, not for her. She kicked away from the pump and waved her arms through the water, wading through the viscous fluid that seemed to impede her while giving her nothing to push or pull against.

The weights were holding her back. Juliette bent to release them and found she couldn't. The buoyancy of her arms, the stiffness of the suit . . . she groped for the Velcro straps but watched her fingers through the magnified view of helmet and water as they waved inches from the blasted things.

She took a deep breath, sweat dripping from her nose and splattering the inside of her dome. She tried again and came close, her fingertips nearly brushing the black straps, both hands outstretched, grunting and throwing her shoulders into the simple act of reaching her damned shins . . .

But she couldn't. She gave up and shuffled a few more steps down the hallway, following the wire and hose, both visible in the faint cone of white light emanating from above her head. She tried not to bump against the wire, thinking of what one accidental pull might do, how tenuous the connection was that she'd made to the pump's ground. Even as she struggled for a deep breath, her mind was ever playing the mechanic. She cursed herself for not taking longer to prepare.

Her knife! She remembered her knife and stopped dragging her feet. It slid out of its homemade sheath sewn across her belly and gleamed in the glow from her flashlight.

Juliette bent down and used the extra reach of the blade; she slid the point of the knife between her suit and one of the straps. The water was dark and thick all around her. With the limited amount of light from her helmet, and being at the bottom of Mechanical under all that heap of flood, she felt more remote and alone, more afraid, than she had in all her life.

She gripped the knife, terrified of what dropping it could mean, and bobbed up and down, using her stomach muscles. It was like doing sit-ups while standing. She attacked the strap with a labored sawing motion, cursed in her helmet from the effort, the strain, the pain in her abdomen from lurching forward, from throwing her head down ... when finally the exercise weight popped free. Her calf felt suddenly naked and light as the round hunk of iron clanged mutely to the plate-steel flooring.

Juliette tilted to the side, held down by one leg, the other trying to rise up. She worked the knife carefully beneath the second strap, fearful of cutting her suit and seeing a stream of precious bubbles leak out. With desperate force, she shoved and pulled the blade against the black webbing just like before. Nylon threads popped in her magnified vision; sweat spattered her helmet; the knife burst through the fabric; the weight was free.

Juliette screamed as her boots flew up behind her, rising above her head. She twisted her torso and waved her arms as much as she could, but her helmet slammed into the runs of pipes at the top of the hallway.

There was a bang—and the water all around her went black. She fumbled for her flashlight, to turn it back on, but it wasn't there. Something bumped her arm in the darkness. She fumbled for the object with one hand, knife in the other, felt it spill through her gloved fingers, and then it was gone. While she struggled to put the knife away, her only source of light tumbled invisible to the ground below.

Juliette heard nothing but her rapid breathing. She was going to die like this, pinned to the ceiling, another bloated body in these corridors. It was as if she were destined to perish in one of those suits, one way or another. She kicked against the pipes and tried to wiggle free. Which way had she been going? Where was she facing? The pitch black was absolute. She couldn't even see her own arms in front of her. It was worse than being blind, to *know* her eyes were working but somehow taking nothing in.

It heightened her panic, even as the air in her suit seemed to grow more and more stale.

The air.

She reached for her collar and found the hose, could just barely feel it through her gloves. Juliette began to gather it in, hand over hand, like pulling a mining bucket up a deep shaft.

It felt like miles of it went through her hands. The slack gathered around her like knotted noodles, bumping and sliding against her. Juliette's breathing began to sound more and more desperate. She was panicking. How much of her shallow breaths were coming from the adrenaline, the fear? How much because she was using up all her precious air? She had a sudden terror that the hose she was pulling had been cut, that it had been sawn through on the stairwell, that the free end would at any moment slip through her fingers, that her next frantic reach for more of the lifeline would result in a fistful of inky water and nothing else . . .

But then she grabbed a length of hose with tension, with *life*. A stiff line that held no air but led the way out.

Juliette cried out in her helmet and reached forward to grab another handhold. She pulled herself, her helmet bumping against a pipe and bouncing her away from the ceiling. She kept reaching, lunging one hand forward in the black to where the line should be, finding it, grasping, yanking, hauling herself through the midnight soup of the drowned and the dead, wondering how far she'd get before she joined them and breathed her very last.

67

Silo 18

LUKAS SAT WITH HIS mother on the thick jamb of the open server-room door. He looked down at her hands, both of them wrapped around one of his. She let go with one of them and picked a piece of lint off his shoulder, then cast the offending knot of string away from her precious son.

"And you say there'll be a promotion in this?" she asked, smoothing the shoulder of his undershirt.

Lukas nodded. "A pretty big one, yeah." He looked past her to where Bernard and Sheriff Billings were standing in the hallway, talking in low voices. Bernard had his hands tucked inside the stretched belly of his overalls. Billings looked down and inspected his gun.

"Well, that's great, sweetheart. It makes it easier to bear you being away."

"It won't be for much longer, I don't think."

"Will you be able to vote? I can't believe my boy is doing such important things!"

Lukas turned to her. "Vote? I thought the election was put off."

She shook her head. Her face seemed more wrinkled than it

had a month ago, her hair whiter. Lukas wondered if that was possible in so brief a time.

"It's back on," she said. "This nasty business with those rebels is supposed to be just about over."

Lukas glanced toward Bernard and the sheriff. "I'm sure they'll figure out a way to let me vote," he told his mother.

"Well, that's nice. I like to think I raised you proper." She cleared her throat into her fist, then returned it to the back of his hand. "And they're feeding you? With the rationing, I mean."

"More than I can eat."

Her eyes widened. "So I suppose there'll be some sort of a raise . . . ?"

He shrugged. "I'm not sure. I'd think so. And look, you'll be taken care of—"

"Me?" She pressed her hand to her chest, her voice high. "Don't you worry about me."

"You know I do. Hey, look, Ma—I think our time's up." He nodded down the hallway. Bernard and Peter were heading toward them. "Looks like I've got to get back to work."

"Oh. Well, of course." She smoothed the front of her red overalls and allowed Lukas to help her to her feet. She puckered her lips, and he presented his cheek.

"My little boy," she said, kissing him noisily and squeezing his arm. She stepped back and gazed up at him with pride. "You take good care of yourself."

"I will, Ma."

"Make sure you get plenty of exercise."

"Ma, I will."

Bernard stopped by their side, smiling at the exchange. Lukas's mother turned and looked the silo's acting mayor up and down. She reached out and patted Bernard on his chest. "Thank you," she said, her voice cracking.

"It's been great to meet you, Mrs. Kyle." Bernard took her

hand and gestured toward Peter. "The sheriff here will see you out."

"Of course." She turned one last time and waved at Lukas. He felt a little embarrassed but waved back.

"Sweet lady," Bernard said, watching them go. "She reminds me of my own mother." He turned to Lukas. "You ready?"

Lukas felt like voicing his reluctance, his hesitation. He felt like saying, *I suppose,* but he straightened his back instead, rubbed his damp palms together, and dipped his chin. "Absolutely," he managed to say, feigning a confidence he didn't feel.

"Great. Let's go make this official." He squeezed Lukas's shoulder before heading into the server room. Lukas walked around the edge of the thick door and leaned into it, slowly sealing himself in as the fat hinges groaned shut. The electric locks engaged automatically, thumping into the jamb. The security panel beeped, its happy green light flicking over to the menacing red eye of a sentry.

Lukas took a deep breath and picked his way through the servers. He tried not to go the same way as Bernard, tried never to go the same way twice. He chose a longer route just to break the monotony, to have one less routine in that prison.

Bernard had the back of the server open by the time he arrived. He held the familiar headphones out to Lukas.

Lukas accepted them and put them on backward, the microphone snaking around the rear of his neck.

"Like this?"

Bernard laughed at him and twirled his finger. "Other way around," he said, lifting his voice so Lukas could hear through the muffs.

Lukas fumbled with the headphones, tangling his arm in the cord. Bernard waited patiently.

"Are you ready?" Bernard asked, once they were in place. He held the loose jack in one hand. Lukas nodded. He watched Bernard turn and aim the plug at the banks of receptacles. He pictured Bernard's hand swinging down and to the right, slamming the plug home into number seventeen, then turning and confronting Lukas about his favorite pastime, his secret crush . . .

But his boss's small hand never wavered; it clicked into place, Lukas knowing exactly how that felt, how the receptacle hugged the plug tightly, seemed to welcome it in, the pads of one's fingers getting a jolt from the flicking of that spring-loaded plastic retainer—

The light above the jack started blinking. A familiar buzzing throbbed in Lukas's ears. He waited for her voice, for Juliette to answer.

A click.

"Name."

A thrill of fear ran up Lukas's back, bumps erupting across his arms. The voice, deep and hollow, impatient and aloof, came and went like a glimpse of a star. Lukas licked his lips.

"Lukas Kyle," he said, trying not to stammer.

There was a pause. He imagined someone, somewhere, writing this down or flipping through files or doing something awful with the information. The temperature behind the server soared. Bernard was smiling at him, oblivious to the silence on his end.

"You shadowed in IT."

It felt like a statement, but Lukas nodded and answered. "Yessir."

He wiped his palm across his forehead and then the seat of his overalls. He desperately wanted to sit down, to lean back against server number forty, to relax. But Bernard was smiling at him, his mustache lifting, his eyes wide behind his glasses.

"What is your primary duty to the silo?"

Bernard had prepped him on likely questions.

"To maintain the Order."

Silence. No feedback, no sense if he was right or wrong.

"What do you protect above all?"

The voice was flat and yet powerfully serious. Dire and somehow calm. Lukas felt his mouth go dry.

"Life and Legacy," he recited. But it felt wrong, this rote façade of knowledge. He wanted to go into detail, to let this voice, like a strong and sober father, understand that he *knew* why this was important. He wasn't dumb. He had more to say than memorized facts –

"What does it take to protect these things we hold so dear?"

He paused.

"It takes sacrifice," Lukas whispered. He thought of Juliette – and the calm demeanor he was projecting for Bernard nearly crumbled. There were some things he wasn't sure about, things he *didn't* understand. This was one of them. It felt like a lie, his answer. He wasn't sure the sacrifice was worth it, the danger so great that they had to let people, *good* people, go to their –

"How much time have you had in the Suit Lab?"

The voice had changed, relaxed somewhat. Lukas wondered if the ceremony was over. Was that *it?* Had he passed? He blew out his held breath, hoping the microphone didn't pick it up, and tried to relax.

"Not much, sir. Bernar – Uh, my boss, he's wanting me to schedule time in the labs after, you know . . ."

He looked to Bernard, who was pinching one side of his glasses and watching him.

"Yes. I do know. How is that problem in your lower levels going?"

"Um, well, I'm only kept apprised of the overall progress, and it sounds good." He cleared his throat and thought of all the sounds of gunfire and violence he'd heard through the radio in the room below. "That is, it sounds like progress is being made, that it won't be much longer."

A long pause. Lukas forced himself to breathe deeply, to smile at Bernard.

"Would you have done anything differently, Lukas? From the beginning?"

Lukas felt his body sway, his knees go a little numb. He was back on that conference table, black steel pressed against his cheek, a line from his eye extending through a small cross, through a tiny hole, pointing like a laser at a small woman with white hair and a bomb in her hand. Bullets were flying down that line. His bullets.

"Nosir," he finally said. "It was all by the Order, sir. Everything's under control."

He waited. Somewhere, he felt, his measure was being taken.

"You are next in line for the control and operation of silo eighteen," the voice intoned.

"Thank you, sir."

Lukas reached for the headphones, was preparing to take them off and hand them to Bernard in case he needed to say something, to hear that it was official.

"Do you know the worst part of my job?" the hollow voice asked.

Lukas dropped his hands.

"What's that, sir?"

"Standing here, looking at a silo on this map, and drawing a red cross through it. Can you imagine what that feels like?"

Lukas shook his head. "I can't, sir."

"It feels like a parent losing thousands of children, all at once."

A pause.

"You will have to be cruel to your children so as not to lose them."

Lukas thought of his father.

"Yessir."

"Welcome to Operation Fifty of the World Order, Lukas Kyle.

Now, if you have a question or two, I have the time to answer, but briefly."

Lukas wanted to say that he had no questions; he wanted to get off the line; he wanted to call and speak with Juliette, to feel a puff of sanity breathed into this crazy and suffocating room. But he remembered what Bernard had taught him about admitting ignorance, how this was the key to knowledge.

"Just one, sir. And I've been told it isn't important, and I understand why that's true, but I believe it will make my job here easier if I know."

He paused for a response, but the voice seemed to be waiting for him to get to the question.

Lukas cleared his throat. "Is there . . . ?" He pinched the mic and moved it closer to his lips, glanced at Bernard. "How did this all begin?"

He wasn't sure – it could have been a fan on the server whirring to life – but he thought he heard the man with the deep voice sigh.

"How badly do you wish to know?"

Lukas feared answering this question honestly. "It isn't crucial," he said, "but I would appreciate a sense of what we're accomplishing, what we survived. It feels like it gives me – gives us a purpose, you know?"

"The reason *is* the purpose," the man said cryptically. "Before I tell you, I'd like to hear what you think."

Lukas swallowed. "What I think?"

"Everyone has ideas. Are you suggesting you don't?"

A hint of humor could be heard in that hollow voice.

"I think it was something we saw coming," Lukas said. He watched Bernard, who frowned and looked away.

"That's one possibility."

Bernard removed his glasses and began wiping them on the sleeve of his undershirt, his eyes at his feet.

"Consider this . . ." The deep voice paused. "What if I told you that there were only fifty silos in all the world, and that here we are in this infinitely small corner of it."

Lukas thought about this. It felt like another test.

"I would say that we were the only ones . . ." He almost said that they were the only ones with the resources, but he'd seen enough in the Legacy to know this wasn't true. Many parts of the world had buildings rising above their hills. Many more could have been prepared. "I'd say we were the only ones who *knew*," Lukas suggested.

"Very good. And why might that be?"

He hated this. He didn't want to puzzle it out, he just wanted to be told.

And then, like a cable splicing together, like electricity zipping through connections for the very first time, the truth hit him.

"It's because . . ." He tried to make sense of this answer in his head, tried to imagine that such an idea could possibly verge on truth. "It's not because we knew," Lukas said, sucking in a gasp of air. "It's because we *did it*."

"Yes," the voice said. "And now you know."

He said something else, just barely audible, like it was being said to someone else. "Our time is up, Lukas Kyle. Congratulations on your assignment."

The headphones were sticky against his head, his face clammy with sweat.

"Thank you," he managed to say.

"Oh, and Lukas?"

"Yessir?"

"Going forward, I suggest you concentrate on what's beneath your feet. No more of this business with the stars, okay, son? We know where most of them are."

68

Silo 18

"HELLO? SOLO? PLEASE SAY something."

There was no mistaking that voice, even through the small speakers in the dismantled headset. It echoed bodiless in the control room, the same control room that had housed that very voice for so many years. The location was what nailed it for Shirly; she stared at the tiny speakers spliced into the magical radio, knowing it couldn't be anyone else.

Neither she nor Walker dared breathe. They waited what felt like forever before she finally broke the silence.

"That was Juliette," she whispered. "How can we . . . ? Is her voice *trapped* down here? In the air? How long ago would that have been?"

Shirly didn't understand how any of the science worked; it was all beyond her pay grade. Walker continued to stare at the headset, unmoving, not saying a word, tears shining in his beard.

"Are these . . . these *ripples* we're grabbing with the antenna, are they just bouncing around down here?"

She wondered if the same was true of *all* the voices they'd heard. Maybe they were simply picking up conversations from the *past*. Was that possible? Like some kind of electrical echo? Somehow, this seemed far less shocking than the alternative.

Walker turned to her, a strange expression on his face. His mouth hung partway open, but there was a curl at the edges of his lips, a curl that began to rise.

"It doesn't work like that," he said. The curl transformed into a smile. "This is *now*. This is *happening*." He grabbed Shirly's arm. "You heard it too, didn't you? I'm not crazy. That really was her, wasn't it? She's alive. She made it."

"No . . ." Shirly shook her head. "Walk, what're you saying? That Juliette's *alive?* Made it where?"

"You heard." He pointed at the radio. "Before. The conversations. The cleaning. There's more of them *out there*. More of *us*. She's *with* them, Shirly. This is *happeningrightnow*."

"Alive."

Shirly stared at the radio, processing this. Her friend was still *somewhere*. Still breathing. It had been so solid in her head, this vision of Juliette's body just over the hills, lying in silent repose, the wind flecking away at her. And now she was picturing her moving, breathing, talking into a radio somewhere.

"Can we talk to her?" she asked.

She knew it was a dumb question. But Walker seemed to startle, his old limbs jumping.

"Oh, God. God, yes." He set the mishmash of components down on the floor, his hands trembling, but with what Shirly now read as excitement. The fear in *both* of them was gone, drained from the room, the rest of the world beyond that small space fading to meaninglessness.

Walker dug into the parts bin. He dumped some tools out and pawed into the bottom of the container.

"No," he said. He turned and scanned the parts on the ground. "No, no, no."

"What is it?" Shirly slid away from the string of components so he could better see. “What’re we missing? There’s a microphone right there.” She pointed to the partially disassembled headphones.

“The transmitter. It’s a little board. I think it’s on my workbench.”

“I swiped everything into the bin.” Her voice was high and tense. She moved toward the plastic bucket.

“My *other* workbench. It wasn’t needed. All Jenks wanted was to *listen in.*” He waved at the radio. “I did what he wanted. How could I have known I’d need to transmit—?”

“You couldn’t,” Shirly said. She rested her hand on his arm. She could tell he was heading toward a bad place. She had seen him go there often enough, knew he had shortcuts he could take to get there in no time. “Is there anything in here we can use? Think, Walk. Concentrate.”

He shook his head, wagged his finger at the headphones. “This mic is dumb. It just passes the sound through. Little membranes vibrating . . .” He turned and looked at her. “Wait—there *is* something.”

“Down here? Where?”

“The mining storehouse would have them. Transmitters.” He pretended to hold a box and twist a switch. “For the blasting caps. I repaired one just a month ago. It would work.”

Shirly rose to her feet. “I’ll go get it,” she said. “You stay here.”

“But the stairwell—”

“I’ll be safe. I’m going *down,* not up.”

He bobbed his head.

“Don’t change anything with that.” She pointed to the radio. “No looking for more voices. Just hers. Leave it there.”

“Of course.”

Shirly bent down and squeezed his shoulder. “I’ll be right back.”

Outside, she found dozens of faces turning her way, frightened and questioning looks in their wide eyes, their slack mouths. She felt like shouting over the hum of the generator that Juliette was alive, that they weren't alone, that other people lived and breathed in the forbidden outside. She wanted to, but she didn't have the time. She hurried to the rail and found Courtnee.

"Hey—"

"Everything okay in there?" Courtnee asked.

"Yeah, fine. Do me a favor, will you? Keep an eye on Walker for me."

Courtnee nodded. "Where are you . . . ?"

But Shirly was already gone, running to the main door. She squeezed through a group huddled in the entranceway. Jenkins was outside with Harper. They stopped talking as she hurried past.

"Hey!" Jenkins seized her arm. "Where the hell're *you* going?"

"Mine storeroom." She twisted her arm out of his grasp. "I won't be long—"

"You won't be *going*. We're about to blow that stairwell. These idiots are falling right into our hands."

"You're *what?*"

"The stairwell," Harper repeated. "It's rigged to blow. Once they get down there and start working their way through . . ." He put his hands together in a ball, then expanded the sphere in a mock explosion.

"You don't understand." She faced Jenkins. "It's for the radio."

He frowned. "Walk had his chance."

"We're picking up a *lot* of chatter," she told him. "He needs this one piece. I'll be right back, swear."

Jenkins looked at Harper. "How long before we do this?"

"Five minutes, sir." His chin moved back and forth, almost imperceptibly.

"You've got four," he said to Shirly. "But make sure —"

She didn't hear the rest. Her boots were already pounding the steel, carrying her toward the stairwell. She flew past the oil rig with its sad and lowered head, past the row of confused and twitching men, their guns all pointing the way.

She hit the top of the steps and slid around the corner. Someone half a flight up yelled in alarm. Shirly caught a glimpse of two miners with sticks of TNT before she skipped down the flight of stairs.

At the next level, she turned and headed for the mine shaft. The hallways were silent, just her panting and the clop, clop, clop of her boots.

Juliette. Alive.

A person sent to *cleaning*, alive.

She turned down the next hallway and ran past the apartments for the deep workers, the miners and the oilmen, men who now bore guns instead of boring holes in the earth, who wielded weapons rather than tools.

And this new knowledge, this impossible bit of news, this secret, it made the fighting seem surreal. Petty. How could anyone fight if there were places to go beyond these walls? If her friend was still out there? Shouldn't they be going as well?

She made it to the storeroom. Probably been two minutes. Her heart was racing. Surely Jenkins wouldn't do anything to that stairway until she got back. She moved down the shelves, peering in the bins and drawers. She knew what the thing looked like. There should have been several of them floating about. Where were they?

She checked the lockers, threw the dingy overalls hanging

inside them to the ground, tossed work helmets out of the way. She didn't see anything. How much time did she have?

She tried the small foreman's office next, throwing the door open and storming to the desk. Nothing in the drawers. Nothing on the shelves mounted on the wall. One of the big drawers on the bottom was stuck. Locked.

Shirly stepped back and kicked the front of the metal drawer with her boot. She slammed the steel toe into it once, twice. The lip curled down, away from the drawer above. She reached in, yanked the flimsy lock off its lip, and the warped drawer opened with a groan.

Explosives. Sticks of dynamite. There were a few small relays that she knew went into the sticks to ignite them. Beneath these, she found three of the transmitters Walker was looking for.

Shirly grabbed two of them, a few relays, and put them all in her pocket. She took two sticks of the dynamite too—just because they were there and might be useful—and ran out of the office, through the storeroom, back toward the stairs.

She had used up too much time. Her chest felt cool and empty, raspy, as she labored to breathe. She ran as fast as she could, concentrating on throwing her boots forward, lunging for more floor, gobbling it up.

Turning at the end of the hall, she again thought about how ridiculous this fighting was. It was hard to remember why it had begun. Knox was gone, so was McLain. Would their people be fighting if these great leaders were still around? Would they have done something different long ago? Something more sane?

She cursed the folly of it all as she reached the stairs. Surely it had been five minutes. She waited for a blast to ring out above her, to deafen her with its concussive ferocity. Leaping up two treads at a time, she made the turn at the top and saw that the miners were gone. Anxious eyes peered at her over homemade barrels.

"Go!" someone yelled, waving their arms to the side, hurrying her along.

Shirly focused on Jenkins, who crouched down with his own rifle, Harper by his side. She nearly tripped over the wires leading away from the stairwell as she ran toward the two men.

"Now!" Jenkins yelled.

Someone threw a switch.

The ground lurched and buckled beneath Shirly's feet, sending her sprawling. She landed hard on the steel floor, her chin grazing the diamond plating, the dynamite nearly flying from her hands.

Her ears were still ringing as she got to her knees. Men were moving behind the railing, guns popping into the bank of smoke leaking from a new maw of twisted and jagged steel. The screams of the distant wounded could be heard on the other side.

While men fought, Shirly patted her pockets, fished inside for the transmitters.

Once again, the noise of war seemed to fade, to become insignificant, as she hurried through the door to the generator room, back to Walker, her lip bleeding, her mind on more important things.

69

Silo 17

JULIETTE PULLED HERSELF THROUGH the cold, dark waters, bumping blindly against the ceiling, a wall, no way to tell which. She gathered the limp air hose with blind and desperate lunges, no idea how fast she was going—until she crashed into the stairs. Her nose crunched against the inside of her helmet, and the darkness was momentarily shouldered aside by a flash of light. She floated, dazed, the air hose drifting from her hands.

Juliette groped for the precious line as her senses gradually returned. She hit something with her glove, grabbed it, and was about to pull herself along when she realized it was the smaller power line. She let go and swept her arms in the blind murk, her boots bumping against something. It was impossible to know top from bottom. She began to feel turned around, dizzy, disoriented.

A rigid surface pressed against her; she decided she must be floating *up,* away from the hose.

She kicked off what she assumed was the ceiling and swam in the direction that she hoped was down. Her arms tangled in something—she felt it across her padded chest—she found it with her hands, expecting the power cord, but was rewarded with the spongy nothingness of the empty air tube. It no longer offered her air, but it did lead the way out.

Pulling in one direction gathered slack, so she tried the other way. The hose went taut. She pulled herself into the stairs again, bounced away with a grunt, and kept gathering line. The hose led up and around the corner—and she found herself pulling, reaching out an arm to fend off the blind assaults from walls, ceiling, steps—bumping and floating up six flights, a battle for every inch, a struggle that seemed to take forever.

By the time she reached the top, she was out of breath and panting. And then she realized she wasn't out of breath, she was out of *air.* She had burned through whatever remained in the suit. Hundreds of feet of exhausted hose lay invisible behind her, sucked dry.

She tried the radio again as she pulled herself through the corridor, her suit rising slowly toward the ceiling, not nearly as buoyant as before.

"Solo! Can you hear me?"

The thought of how much water still lay above her, all those levels of it pressing down, hundreds of feet of solid flood—it was suffocating. What did she have left in the suit? Minutes? How long would it take to swim or float to the top of the stairwell? Much, much longer. There were probably oxygen bottles down one of those pitch-black hallways, but how would she find them? This wasn't her home. She didn't have time to look. All she had was a mad drive to reach the stairwell, to race to the surface.

She pulled and kicked her way around the last corner and into the main hallway, her muscles screaming from being used in new ways, from fighting the stiff and bulky suit, the viscous atmosphere, when she realized the inky water had lightened to something nearer charcoal instead of pitch black. There was a *green tint* to her blindness.

Juliette scissored her legs and gathered in the tubing, bumping along the ceiling, sensing the security station and stairwell ahead. She had traveled corridors like these thousands of times, twice in utter darkness when main breakers had failed. She remembered staggering through hallways just like this, telling coworkers it would be okay, just to stay still, she'd handle it.

Now she tried to do the same for herself, to lie and say it would all be okay, to just keep moving, don't panic.

The dizziness began to set in as she reached the security gate. The water ahead glowed lime green and looked so inviting, an end to the blind scrambling, no more of her helmet bumping into what she couldn't see.

Her arm briefly tangled with the power cord; she shook it free and hauled herself toward that tall column of water ahead, that flooded straw, that sunken stairway.

Before she got there, she had her first spasm, like a hiccup, a violent and automatic gasp for air. She lost her grip on the line and felt her chest nearly burst from the effort of breathing. The temptation to shed her helmet and take a deep inhalation of water overpowered her. Something in her mind insisted she could breathe the stuff. Just give her a chance, it said. One lungful of the water. Anything other than the toxins she had exhaled into her suit, a suit designed to keep such things *out*.

Her throat spasmed again, and she started coughing in her helmet as she pulled her way into the stairwell. The rope was there, held down by the wrench. She swam for it, knowing it was too late. As she yanked down, she felt the slack coming—the loose end of the rope spiraled in sinking knots toward her.

She drifted slowly toward the surface, very little of the built-up pressure inside her suit, no quick ride to the top. Another throat spasm, and the helmet had to come off. She was getting dizzy, would soon pass out.

Juliette fumbled for the clasps on her metal collar. The sense of déjà vu was overpowering. Only this time, she wasn't thinking clearly. She remembered the soup, the fetid smell, crawling out of the dark walk-in. She remembered the knife.

Patting her chest, she felt the handle sticking out from its sheath. Some of the other tools had wiggled out of their pockets; they dangled from lines meant to keep them from getting lost, lines that now just made them a nuisance, turned them into more weights holding her down.

She rose gently up the stairwell, her body shivering from the cold and convulsing from the absence of breathable air. Forgetting all reason, all sense of where she was, she became singularly aware of the noxious fog hanging all around her head, trapped by that dome, killing her. She aimed the blade into the first latch in her collar and pressed hard.

There was a click and a fine spray of cold water against her neck. A feeble bubble lurched out of her suit and tumbled up her visor. Groping for the other latch, she shoved the knife into it, and the helmet popped off, water flooding over her face, filling her suit, shocking her with the numbing cold and dragging her, sinking, back down to where she'd come from.

The freezing cold jolted Juliette to her senses. She blinked against the sting of the green water and saw the knife in her hands, the dome of her helmet spinning through the murk like a bubble heading in the wrong direction. She was slowly sinking after it, no air in her lungs, hundreds of feet of water pressing down on her.

She jabbed the knife into the wrong pocket on her chest, saw the drivers and spanners hanging by their cords from her struggle through the blackness, and kicked toward the hose that still led through four levels of water to the surface.

Bubbles of air leaked out of her collar and across her neck, up through her hair. Juliette seized the hose and stopped her plummet, pulled upward, her throat screaming for an intake of air, of water, of anything. The urge to swallow was overpowering. She started to pull herself up, when she saw, on the undersides of the steps, a shimmering flash of hope.

Trapped bubbles. Maybe from her descent. They moved like liquid solder in the hollow undersides of the spiral staircase.

Juliette made a noise in her throat, a raw cry of desperation, of effort. She pawed through the water, fighting the sinking of the suit, and grasped the railing of the submerged stairway. Pulling herself up and kicking off of the railing, she made it to the nearest shimmer of bubbles, grabbed the edge of the stairs, and pushed her mouth right up to the metal underside of the step.

She inhaled a desperate gasp of air and sucked in a lot of water in the process. She ducked her head below the step and coughed into the water, which brought the burn of fluids invading her nose. She nearly sucked in a lungful of water, felt her heart racing and ready to burst out of her chest, stuck her face back up against the wet rusty underside of the step and, her lips pursed and trembling, managed to take in a gentle sip of air.

The tiny flashes of light in her vision subsided. She lowered her head and blew out, away from the step, watching the bubbles of her exhalation rise, and then pressed her face close for another taste.

Air.

She blinked away underwater tears of effort, of frustration, of relief. Peering up the twisted maze of metal steps, many of them moving like flexible mirrors where the trapped air was stirred by her mad gyrations, she saw a pathway like no other. She kicked off and took a few steps at a time, pulling herself hand over hand in the gaps between, drinking tiny bubbles of air out of the inches-deep hollow beneath each tread, praising the tight welds where the diamond-plate steps had been joined many hundreds of years ago. The steps had been boxed in for strength, to handle the traffic of a million impacts of boots, and now they held the gaseous overflow from her descent. Her lips brushed each one, tasting metal and rust, kissing her salvation.

The green emergency lights all around her remained steady, so Juliette never noticed the landings drifting past. She just concentrated on taking five steps with each breath, six steps, a long stretch with hardly any air, another mouthful of water where the bubble was too thin to breathe, a lifetime of rising against the tug of her flooded suit and dangling tools, no thought for stopping and cutting things free, just kick and pull, hand over hand, up the undersides of the steps, a deep and steady pull of air, suck this shallow step dry, don't exhale into the steps above, easy now. Five more steps. It was a game, like Hop, five squares in a leap, don't cheat, mind the chalk, she was good at this, getting better.

And then a foul burn on her lips, the taste of water growing toxic, her head coming up into the underside of a step and breaking through a film of gas stench and slimy oil.

Juliette blew out her last breath and coughed, wiping at her face, her head still trapped below the next step. She wheezed and laughed and pushed herself away, banging her head on the sharp steel edge of the stairs. She was free. She briefly bobbed below the surface as she swam around the railing, her eyes burning from the oil and gas floating on top. Splashing loudly, crying for Solo, she made it over the railing. With her padded and shivering knees, she finally found the steps.

She'd survived. Clinging to the dry treads above her, neck bent, gasping and wheezing, her legs numb, she tried to cry out that she'd made it, but it escaped as a whimper. She was cold. She was freezing. Her arms shivered as she pulled herself up the quiet steps, no rattle from the compressor, no arms reaching to assist her.

"Solo . . . ?"

She crawled the half-dozen treads to the landing and rolled onto her back. Some of her tools were caught on steps below, tugging at her where they were tied to her pockets. Water drained out of her suit and splashed down her neck, pooled by her head, ran into her ears. She turned her head—she needed to get the freezing suit off—and found Solo.

He was lying on his side, eyes shut, blood running down his face, some of it already caked dry.

"Solo?"

Her hand was a shivering blur as she reached out and shook him. What had he done to himself?

"Hey. Wakethefuckup."

Her teeth were chattering. She grabbed his shoulder and gave him a violent shake. "Solo! I need help!"

One of his eyes parted a little. He blinked a few times, then bent double and coughed, blood flecking the landing by his face.

"Help," she said. She fumbled for the zipper at her back, not realizing it was Solo who needed *her.*

Solo coughed into his hand, then rolled over and settled once again on his back. The blood on his head was still flowing from somewhere, fresh tracks trickling across what had dried some time before.

"Solo?"

He groaned. Juliette pulled herself closer, could barely feel her body. He whispered something, his voice a rasp on the edge of silence.

"Hey—" She brought her face close to his, could feel her lips swollen and numb, could still taste the gasoline.

"Not my name . . ."

He coughed a mist of red. One arm lifted from the landing a few inches as if to cover his mouth, but it never had a chance of getting there.

"Not my name," he said again. His head lolled side to side, and Juliette finally realized that he was badly injured. Her mind began to clear enough to see what state he was in.

"Hold still," she groaned. "Solo, I need you to be still."

She tried to push herself up, to will herself the strength to move. Solo blinked and looked at her, his eyes glassy, blood tinting the gray in his beard crimson.

"Not Solo," he said, his voice straining. "My name's Jimmy—"

More coughing, his eyes rolling up into the back of his head.

"—and I don't think—"

His eyelids sagged shut and then squinted in pain.

"—don't think I was—"

"Stay with me," Juliette said, hot tears cutting down her frozen face.

"—don't think I ever *was* alone," he whispered, the lines on his face relaxing, his head sagging to the cold steel landing.

70

Silo 18

THE POT ON THE stove bubbled noisily, steam rising off the surface, tiny drops of water leaping to their freedom over the edge. Lukas shook a pinch of tea leaves out of the resealable tin and into the tiny strainer. His hands were shaking as he lowered the little basket into his mug. As he lifted the pot, some water spilled directly on the burner; the drops made spitting sounds and gave off a burned odor. He watched Bernard out of the corner of his eye as he tilted the boiling water through the leaves.

"I just don't understand," he said, holding the mug with both hands, allowing the heat to penetrate his palms. "How could anybody—? How could you *do* something like this on *purpose?*" He shook his head and peered into his mug, where a few intrepid shreds of leaf had already gotten free and swam outside the basket. He looked up at Bernard. "And you knew about this? How—? How could you *know* about this?"

Bernard frowned. He rubbed his mustache with one hand, the other resting in the belly of his overalls. "I wish I *didn't* know it," he told Lukas. "And now you see why some facts, some pieces of knowledge, have to be snuffed out as soon as they form. Curiosity would blow across such embers and burn this silo to the ground." He looked down at his boots. "I pieced it together much as you did, just knowing what we have to know to do this job. This is why I chose you, Lukas. You and a few others have some idea what's stored on these servers. You're already prepped for learning more. Can you imagine if you told any of this to someone who wears red or green to work every day?"

Lukas shook his head.

"It's happened before, you know. Silo ten went down like that. I sat back there" — he pointed toward the small study with the books, the computer, the hissing radio — "and I listened to it happen. I listened to a colleague's shadow broadcast his insanity to anyone who would listen."

Lukas studied his steeping tea. A handful of leaves swam about on hot currents of darkening water; the rest remained in the grip of the imprisoning basket. "That's why the radio controls are locked up," he said.

"And it's why *you* are locked up."

Lukas nodded. He'd already suspected as much.

"How long were you kept in here?" He glanced up at Bernard, and an image flashed in his mind, one of Sheriff Billings inspecting his gun while his mother had visited him. Had they been listening in? Would he have been shot, his mother too, if he'd said anything?

"I spent just over two months down here until my caster knew I was ready, that I had accepted and understood everything I'd learned." He crossed his arms over his belly. "I really wish you hadn't asked the question, hadn't put it together so soon. It's much better to find out when you're older."

Lukas pursed his lips and nodded. It was strange to talk like this with someone his senior, someone who knew so much more, was so much wiser. He imagined this was the sort of conversation a man had with his father—only not about the planned and carried-out destruction of the entire world.

Lukas bent his head and breathed in the smell of the steeping leaves. The mint was like a direct line through the trembling stress, a strike to the calm pleasure center in the deep regions of his brain. He inhaled and held his breath, finally let it out. Bernard crossed to the small stove in the corner of the storeroom and started making his own mug.

"How did they do it?" Lukas asked. "To kill so many. Do you know how they did it?"

Bernard shrugged. He tapped the tin with one finger, shaking out a precise amount of tea into another basket. "They might still be doing it for all I know. Nobody talks about how long it's supposed to go on. There's fear that small pockets of survivors might be holed up elsewhere around the globe. Operation Fifty is completely pointless if anyone else survives. The population has to be homogenous—"

"The man I spoke to, he said we were *it*. Just the fifty silos—"

"Forty-seven," Bernard said. "And we *are* it, as far as we know. It's difficult to imagine anyone else being so well prepared. But there's always a chance. It's only been a few hundred years."

"A few *hundred?*" Lukas leaned back against the counter. He lifted his tea, but the mint was losing its power to reach him. "So hundreds of years ago, we decided—"

"*They.*" Bernard filled his mug with the still-steaming water. "They decided. Don't include yourself. Certainly don't include me."

"Okay, *they* decided to destroy the world. Wipe everything out. Why?"

Bernard set his mug down on the stove to let it steep. He pulled off his glasses, wiped the steam off them, then pointed them toward the study, toward the wall with the massive shelves of books. "Because of the worst parts of our Legacy, that's why. At least, that's what I *think* they would say if they were still alive." He lowered his voice and muttered, "Which they aren't, thank God."

Lukas shuddered. He still didn't believe anyone would make that decision, no matter what the conditions were like. He thought of the billions of people who supposedly lived beneath the stars all those hundreds of years ago. Nobody could kill so many. How could anyone take that much life for granted?

"And now we *work* for them," Lukas spat. He crossed to the sink and pulled the basket out of his mug, set it on the stainless steel to drain. He took a cautious sip, slurping lest it burn him. "You tell me not to include us, but we're a part of this now."

"No." Bernard walked away from the stove and stood in front of the small map of the world hanging above the dinette. "We weren't any part of what those crazy fucks did. If I had those guys, the men who did this, if I had them in a room with me, I'd kill every last goddamned one of them." Bernard smacked the map with his palm. "I'd kill them with my bare hands."

Lukas didn't say anything. He didn't move.

"They didn't give us a *chance*. That's not what this is." He gestured at the room around him. "These are prisons. Cages, not homes. Not meant to protect us, but meant to force us, by pain of death, to bring about *their* vision."

"Their vision for *what?*"

"For a world where we're too much the same, where we're too tightly invested in each other to waste our time fighting, to waste our resources guarding those *same* limited resources." He lifted his mug and took a noisy sip. "That's my theory, at least. From decades of reading. The people who did this, they were in charge of a powerful country that was beginning to crumble. They could see the end, *their* end, and it scared them suicidal. As the time began to run out—over decades, keep in mind—they figured they had *one* chance to preserve themselves, to preserve what they saw as their way of life. And so, before they lost the only opportunity they might ever have, they put a plan into motion."

"Without anybody knowing? How?"

Bernard took another sip. He smacked his lips and wiped his mustache. "Who knows? Maybe nobody could believe it anyway. Maybe the reward for secrecy was inclusion. They built other things in factories bigger than you can imagine that nobody knew about. They built bombs in factories like these that I suspect played a part in all this. All without anyone knowing. And there are stories in the Legacy about men from a long time ago in a land with great kings, like mayors but with many more people to rule. When these men died, elaborate chambers were built below the earth and filled with treasure. It required the work of hundreds of men. Do you know how they kept the locations of these chambers a secret?"

Lukas lifted his shoulders. "They paid the workers a ton of chits?"

Bernard laughed. He pinched a stray tea leaf off his tongue. "They didn't have chits. And no, they made perfectly sure these men would keep quiet. They killed them."

"Their own men?" Lukas glanced toward the room with the books, wondering which tin this story was in.

"It is not beyond us to kill to keep secrets." Bernard's face hardened as he said this. "It'll be a part of your job one day, when you take over."

Lukas felt a sharp pain in his gut as the truth of this hit. He caught the first glimmer of what he'd truly signed on for. It made shooting people with rifles seem an honest affair.

"We are not the people who made this world, Lukas, but it's up to us to survive it. You need to understand that."

"We can't control where we are right now," he mumbled, "just what we do going forward."

"Wise words." Bernard took another sip of tea.

"Yeah. I'm just beginning to appreciate them."

Bernard set his cup in the sink and tucked a hand in the round belly of his overalls. He stared at Lukas a moment, then looked again to the small map of the world.

"Evil men did this, but they're gone. Forget them. Just know this: they locked up their brood as a fucked-up form of their own survival. They put us in this game, a game where breaking the rules means we all die, every single one of us. But *living* by those rules, obeying them, means we all suffer."

He adjusted his glasses and walked over to Lukas, patted him on the shoulder as he went past. "I'm proud of you, son. You're absorbing this much better than I ever did. Now get some rest. Make some room in your head and heart. Tomorrow, more studies." He headed toward the study, the corridor, the distant ladder.

Lukas nodded and remained silent. He waited until Bernard was gone, the muted clang of distant metal telling him that the grate was back in place, before walking through to the study to gaze up at the big schematic, the one with the silos crossed out. He peered at the roof of silo one, wondering just who in hell was in charge of all this and whether they too could rationalize their actions as having been foisted upon them, imagine themselves as not really being culpable but just going along with something they'd inherited, a crooked game with ratshit rules and almost everyone kept ignorant and locked up.

Who the fuck were these people? Could he see himself being *one* of them?

How did Bernard not see that *he* was one of them?

71

Silo 18

THE DOOR TO THE generator room slammed shut behind her, dulling the patter of gunfire to a distant hammering. Shirly ran toward the control room on sore legs, ignoring her friends and coworkers asking her what was going on outside. They cowered along the walls and behind the railing from the loud blast and the sporadic gunfire. Just before she reached the control room, she noticed some workers from second shift on top of the main generator toying with the rumbling machine's massive exhaust system.

"I got it," Shirly wheezed, slamming the control-room door shut behind her. Courtnee and Walker looked up from the floor. The wide eyes and slack jaw on Courtnee's face told Shirly she'd missed something.

"What?" she asked. She handed the two transmitters to Walker. "Did you hear? Walk, does she know?"

"How is this possible?" Courtnee asked. "How did she survive? And what happened to your face?"

Shirly touched her lip, her sore chin. Her fingers came away wet with blood. She used the sleeve of her undershirt to dab at her mouth.

"If this works," Walker grumbled, fiddling with one of the transmitters, "we can ask Jules herself."

Shirly turned and peered through the control room's observation window. She lowered her sleeve away from her face. "What's Karl and them doing with the exhaust feed?" she asked.

"They've got some plan to reroute it," Courtnee said. She got up from the floor while Walker started soldering something, the smell reminding her of his workshop. He grumbled about his eyesight while Courtnee joined her by the glass.

"Reroute it where?"

"IT. That's what Heline said, anyway. The cooling feed for their server room runs through the ceiling here before shooting up the Mechanical shaft. Someone spotted the proximity on a schematic, thought of a way to fight back from here."

"So, we choke them out with our fumes?" Shirly felt uneasy about the plan. She wondered what Knox would say if he were still alive, still in charge. Surely all the men and women riding desks up there weren't the problem. "Walk, how long before we can talk? Before we can try and contact her?"

"Almost there. Blasted magnifiers . . ."

Courtnee rested her hand on Shirly's arm. "Are you okay? How're you holding up?"

"Me?" Shirly laughed and shook her head. She checked the bloodstains on her sleeve, felt the sweat trickling down her chest. "I'm walking around in shock. I have no idea what the hell's going on anymore. My ears are still ringing from whatever they did to the stairwell. I think I've screwed up my ankle. And I'm starving. Oh, and did I mention my friend isn't as dead as I thought she was?"

She took a deep breath.

Courtnee continued to stare at her worryingly. Shirly knew none of this was what her friend was asking her about.

"And yeah, I miss Marck," she said quietly.

Courtnee put her arm around her friend and pulled her close. "I'm sorry," she said. "I didn't mean to –"

Shirly waved her off. The two of them stood quietly and watched through the window as a small crew from second shift worked on the generator, trying to reroute the outpouring of noxious fumes from the apartment-sized machine to the floors of the thirties high above.

"You know what, though? There are times when I'm *glad* he's not here. Times when I know I won't be around much longer either, not once they get to us, and I'm glad he's not here to stress about it, to worry about what they'll do to us. To me. And I'm glad I haven't had to watch him do all this fighting, living on rations, this sort of craziness." She dipped her chin at the crew outside. She knew Marck would have been either up there leading that terrible work or outside with a gun pressed to his cheek.

"Hello. Testing. Hello, hello."

The two women turned around to see Walker clicking the red detonate switch, the microphone from the headset held beneath his chin, furrows of concentration across his brow.

"Juliette?" he asked. "Can you hear me? Hello?"

Shirly moved to Walker's side, squatted down, rested a hand on his shoulder. The three of them stared at the headphones, waiting for a reply.

"Hello?"

A quiet voice leaked out of the tiny speakers. Shirly clapped a hand to her chest, her breath stolen from the miracle of a reply. It was a fraction of a second later, after this surge of desperate hope, that she realized this wasn't Juliette. The voice was different.

"That's not her," Courtnee whispered, dejected. Walker waved his hand to silence her. The red switch clicked noisily as he prepared to transmit.

"Hello. My name is Walker. We received a transmission from a friend. Is there anyone else there?"

"Ask them where they are," Courtnee hissed.

"Where exactly are you?" Walker added, before releasing the switch.

The tiny speakers popped.

"We are nowhere. You'll never find us. Stay away."

There was a pause, a hiss of static.

"And your friend is dead. We killed him."

72

Silo 17

THE WATER INSIDE THE suit was freezing, the air cold, the combination lethal. Juliette's teeth chattered noisily while she worked the knife. She slid the blade into the soggy skin of the suit, the feeling of having already been here, having done all this before, unmistakable.

The gloves came off first, the suit destroyed, water pouring out of every cut. Juliette rubbed her hands together, could barely feel them. She hacked away at the material over her chest, her eyes falling to Solo, who had gone deathly still. His large wrench was missing, she saw. Their supply bag was gone as well. The compressor was on its side, the hose kinked beneath it, fuel leaking from the loose filling cap.

Juliette was freezing. She could hardly breathe. Once the chest of the suit was cut open, she wiggled her knees and feet through the hole, spun the material around in front of herself, then tried to pry the Velcro apart.

Her fingers were too senseless even to do this. She ran the knife down the joint instead, sawing the Velcro apart until she could find the zipper.

Finally, squeezing her fingers until they were white, she

pulled the small tab free of the collar and threw the suit away from herself. The thing weighed double with all the water in it. She was left in two layers of black undersuit, still soaking wet and shivering, a knife in her trembling hand, the body of a good man lying beside her, a man who had survived everything this nasty world could throw at him except for her arrival.

Juliette moved to Solo's side and reached for his neck. Her hands were icy; she couldn't feel a pulse, wasn't sure if she would be *able* to. She could barely feel his neck with her frozen fingers.

She struggled to her feet, nearly collapsed, hugged the landing's railing. She teetered toward the compressor, knowing she needed to warm up. She felt the powerful urge to go to sleep but knew she'd never wake up if she did.

The fuel can was still full. She tried to work the cap, but her hands were useless. They were numb and vibrating from the cold. Her breath fogged in front of her, a chilly reminder of the heat she was losing, what little heat she had left.

She grabbed the knife. Holding it in both hands, she pressed the tip into the cap. The flat handle was easier to grasp than the plastic cap; she spun the knife and cracked the lid on the jug of fuel. Once the cap was loose, she pulled the blade out and did the rest with her palms, the knife resting in her lap.

She tilted the can over the compressor, soaking the large rubber wheels, the carriage, the entire motor. She would never want to use it again anyway, never rely on it or anything else for her air. She put the can down, still half-full, and slid it away from the compressor with her foot. Fuel dripped through the metal grating and made musical impacts in the water below, drips that echoed off the concrete walls of the stairwell and added to the flood's toxic and colorful slick.

Wielding the knife with the blade down, the dull side away

from her, she smacked it against the metal fins of the heat exchanger. She yanked her arm back with each strike, expecting the whoosh of an immediate flame. But there was no spark. She hit it harder, hating to abuse her precious tool, her only defense. Solo's stillness nearby was a reminder that she might need it if she were able to survive the deadly cold—

The knife struck with a snick, and there was a pop, heat traveling up her arm, a wash of it against her face.

Juliette dropped the knife and waved her hand, but it wasn't on fire. The compressor *was*. Part of the grating, too.

As it began to die down, she grabbed the can and sloshed some more fuel out of it, large balls of orange flame rewarding her, leaping up in the air with a whoosh. The wheels crackled as they burned. Juliette collapsed close to the fire, felt the heat from the dancing flame as it burned all across the metal machine. She began to strip, her eyes returning now and then to Solo, promising herself that she wouldn't leave his body there, that she would come back for him.

Feeling returned to her extremities—at first gradually, but then with a tingling pain. Naked, she curled into a ball next to the small and feeble fire and rubbed her hands together, breathing her warm and visible breath into her palms. Twice she had to feed the hungry and stingy fire. Only the wheels burned reliably, but they kept her from needing another spark. The glorious heat traveled somewhat through the landing's grated decking, warming her bare skin where it touched the metal.

Her teeth chattered violently. Juliette eyed the stairs, this new fear coursing through her that boots could rumble down at any moment, that she was trapped between these other survivors and the freezing water. She retrieved her knife, held it in front of her with both hands, tried to will herself not to shiver so violently.

Glimpses of her face in the blade caused her to worry more. She looked as pale as a ghost. Lips purple, eyes ringed dark and seeming hollow. She nearly laughed at the sight of her lips vibrating, the clacking blur of her teeth. She scooted closer to the fire. The orange light danced on the blade, the unburned fuel dripping and forming silvery splashes of color below.

As the last of the gas burned and the flames dwindled, Juliette decided to move. She was still shaking, but it was cold in the depths of the shaft so far from the electricity of IT. She patted the black underlinings she'd stripped off. One of them had been left balled up and was still soaked. The other she had at least dropped flat; if she'd been thinking clearly she would've hung it up. It was damp, but better to wear it and heat it up herself than allow the cold air to wick her body temperature away. She worked her legs in, struggled to get her arms through the sleeves, zipped up the front.

On bare, numb, and unsteady feet, she returned to Solo. She could feel his neck this time. He felt warm. She couldn't remember how long a body stayed that way. And then she felt a weak and slow thrumming in his neck. A beat.

"Solo!" She shook his shoulders. "Hey . . ." What name had he whispered? She remembered: "Jimmy!"

His head lolled from side to side while she shook his shoulder. She checked his scalp beneath all that crazy hair, saw lots of blood. Most of it was dry. She looked around again for her bag —they had brought food, water, and dry clothes for when she got back up—but the satchel was gone. She grabbed her other undersuit instead. She wasn't sure about the quality of the water in the fabric, but it had to be better than nothing. Wrenching the material in a tight ball, she dripped what she could against his lips. She squeezed more on his head, brushed his hair back to inspect the wound, probed the nasty cut with her fingers. As soon as the water hit the open gash, it was like pushing a button. Solo lurched to the side, away from her hand and the drip from the undersuit. His teeth flashed yellow in his beard as he screamed in pain, his hands rising from the landing and hovering there, arms tensed, still senseless.

"Solo. Hey, it's okay."

She held him as he came to, his eyes rolling around, lids blinking.

"It's okay," she said. "You're gonna be okay."

She used the balled-up undersuit to dab at his wound. Solo grunted and held her wrist but didn't pull away.

"Stings," he said. He blinked and looked around. "Where am I?"

"The down deep," she reminded him, happy to hear him talking. She felt like crying with relief. "I think you were attacked . . ."

He tried to sit up, hissing between his teeth, a powerful grip pinching her wrist.

"Easy," she said, trying to hold him down. "You've got a nasty cut on your head. A lot of swelling."

His body relaxed.

"Where are they?" he asked.

"I don't know," Juliette said. "What do you remember? How many were there?"

He closed his eyes. She continued to dab at his wound.

"Just one. I think." He opened his eyes wide as if shocked by the memory of the attack. "He was *my* age."

"We need to get up top," she told him. "We need to get where it's warm, get you cleaned up, get me dry. Do you think you can move?"

"I'm not crazy," Solo said.

"I know you're not."

“The things that moved, the lights, it wasn’t me. I’m not crazy.”

“No,” Juliette agreed. She remembered all the times she had thought the same thing of herself, always in the down deep of this place, usually while rummaging around Supply. “You aren’t crazy,” she said, comforting him. “You aren’t crazy at all.”

73

Silo 18

LUKAS COULDN'T FORCE HIMSELF to study, not what he was supposed to be studying. The Order sat flopped open on the wooden desk, the little lamp on its thousand-jointed neck bent over and warming it in a pool of light. He stood before the wall schematics instead, staring at the arrangement of silos, which were spaced out like the servers in the room above him, and listened to the radio crackle with the sounds of distant warring.

The final push was being made. Sims's team had lost a few men in an awful explosion, something about a stairwell—but not the great stairwell—and now they were in a fight they hoped would be the last. The little speakers by the radio crackled with static as the men coordinated themselves, as Bernard shouted orders from his office one level up, always with the crackle of gunfire erupting behind the voices.

Lukas knew he shouldn't listen, and yet he couldn't stop. Juliette would call him any time now and ask him for an update. She would want to know what had happened, how the end had come, and the only thing worse than telling her would be admitting he didn't know, that he couldn't bear to listen.

He reached out and touched the round roof of silo seventeen.

It was as though he were a god surveying the structures from up high. He pictured his hand piercing the dark clouds above Juliette and spanning a roof built for thousands. He rubbed his fingers over the red X drawn across the silo, those two slashes that admitted to such a great loss. The marks felt waxy beneath his fingers, like they'd been drawn with crayon or something similar. He tried to imagine getting the news one day that an entire people were gone, wiped out. He would have to dig in Bernard's desk – *his* desk – and find the red stick, cross out another chance at their Legacy, another pod of buried hope.

Lukas looked up at the overhead lights, steady and constant, unblinking. Why hadn't she called?

His fingernail caught on one of the red marks and flaked a piece of it away. The wax stuck under his fingernail, the paper beneath still stained blood red. There was no taking it back, no cleaning it off, no making it whole again –

Gunfire erupted from the radio. Lukas went to the shelf where the little unit was mounted and listened to orders being barked, men being killed. His forehead went clammy with sweat. He knew how that felt, to pull that trigger, to end a life. He was conscious of an emptiness in his chest and a weakness in his knees. Lukas steadied himself with the shelf, palms slick, and looked at the transmitter hanging there inside its locked cage. How he longed to call those men and tell them not to do it, to stop all the insanity, the violence, the pointless killing. There could be a red X on them all. *This* was what they should fear, not each other.

He touched the metal cage that kept the radio controls locked away from him, feeling the truth of this and the silliness of broadcasting it to everyone else. It was naïve. It wouldn't change anything. The short-term rage to be sated at the end of a barrel was too easy to act on. Staving off extinction required something else, something with more vision, something impossibly patient.

His hand drifted across the metal grating. He peered inside at one of the dials, the arrow pointing to the number "18." There were fifty numbers in a dizzying circle, one for each silo. Lukas gave the cage a futile tug, wishing he could listen to something else. What was going on in all those other distant lands? Harmless things, probably. Jokes and chatter. Gossip. He could imagine the thrill of breaking in on one of those conversations and introducing himself to people who weren't in the know. "I am Lukas from silo eighteen," he might say. And they would want to know why silos had numbers. And Lukas would tell them to be good to each other, that there were only so many of them left, and that all the books and all the stars in the universe were pointless with no one to read them, no one to peer through the parting clouds for them.

He left the radio alone, left it to its war, and walked past the desk and its eager pool of light spilling across that dreary book. He checked the tins for something that might hold his attention. He felt restless, pacing like a pig in its pen. He knew he should go for another jog among the servers, but that would mean showering, and somehow showering had begun to feel like an insufferable chore.

Crouching down at the far end of the shelves, he sorted through the loose, untinned stacks of paper there. Here was where the handwritten notes and the additions to the Legacy had amassed over the years. Notes to future silo leaders, instructions, manuals, mementos. He pulled out the generator control-room manual, the one Juliette had written. He had watched Bernard shelve the papers weeks ago, saying it might come in handy if the problems in the down deep went from bad to worse.

And the radio was blasting the worse.

Lukas went to his desk and bent the neck of the lamp so he could read the handwriting inside. There were days that he dreaded her calling, dreaded getting caught or Bernard answering or her asking him to do things he couldn't, things he would never do again. And now, with the lights steady overhead and nothing buzzing, all he wanted was a call. His chest ached for it. Some part of him knew that what she was doing was dangerous, that something bad could've happened. She was living beneath a red X, after all, a mark that meant death for anyone below it.

The pages of the manual were full of notes she'd made with sharp lead. He rubbed one of them, feeling the grooves with his fingers. The actual content was inscrutable. Settings for dials in every conceivable order, valve positions, electrical diagrams. Riffling through the pages, he saw the manual as a project not unlike his star charts, created by a mind not unlike his own. This awareness made the distance between them worse. Why couldn't they go back? Back to before the cleaning, before the string of burials. She would get off work every night and come sit with him while he gazed into the darkness, thinking and watching, chatting and waiting.

He turned the manual around and read some of the printed words from the play, which were nearly as indecipherable. In the margins sat notes from a different hand. Lukas assumed Juliette's mother, or maybe one of the actors. There were diagrams on some pages, little arrows showing movement. An actor's notes, he decided. Directions on a stage. The play must've been a souvenir to Juliette, this woman he had feelings for whose name was in the title.

He scanned the lines, looking for something poetic to capture his dark mood. As the text flowed by, his eyes caught a brief flash of familiar scrawl, not the actor's. He flipped back, looking for it a page at a time until he found it.

It was Juliette's hand, no mistaking. He moved the play into the light so he could read the faded marks:

> George:
>
> There you lay, so serene. The wrinkles in your brow and by your eyes, nowhere seen. A touch when others look away, look for a clue, but only I know what happened to you. Wait for me. Wait for me. Wait there, my dear. Let these gentle pleas find your ear, and bury them there, so this stolen kiss can grow on the quiet love that no other shall know.

Lukas felt a cold rod pierce his chest. He felt his longing replaced by a flash of temper. Who was this George? A childhood fling? Juliette was never in a sanctioned relationship; he had checked the official records the day after they'd met. Access to the servers afforded certain guilty powers. A crush, perhaps? Some man in Mechanical who was already in love with another girl? To Lukas, this would have been even worse. A man she longed for in a way she never would feel for him. Was that why she'd taken a job so far from home? To get away from the sight of this George she couldn't have, these feelings she'd hidden in the margins of a play about forbidden love?

He turned and plopped down in front of Bernard's computer. Shaking the mouse, he logged in to the upstairs servers remotely, his cheeks feeling flush with this sick feeling, this new feeling, knowing it was called jealousy but unfamiliar with the heady rush that came with it. He navigated to the personnel files and searched the down deep for "George." There were four hits. He copied the ID number of each and put them in a text file, then fed them to the ID department. While the pictures of each popped up, he skimmed their records, feeling a little guilty for the abuse of power, a little worried about this discovery, and a lot less agonizingly bored having found something to do.

Only one of the Georges worked in Mechanical. Older guy. As the radio crackled behind him, Lukas wondered what would become of this man if he was still down there. There was a chance that he was no longer alive, that the records were a few weeks out of date, the blockade a barrier to the truth.

A couple of the hits were too young. One wasn't even a year old yet. The other was shadowing a porter. It left one man, thirty-two years old. He worked in the bazaar, occupation listed as "other," married with two kids. Lukas studied the blurry image of him from the ID office. Mustache. Receding hair. A sideways smirk. His eyes were too far apart, Lukas decided, his brows too dark and much too bushy.

Lukas held up the manual and read the poem again.

The man was dead, he decided. *Bury these pleas.*

He did another search, this time a global one that included the closed records. Hundreds of hits throughout the silo popped up, names from all the way back to the uprising. This did not dissuade Lukas. He knew Juliette was thirty-four, and so he gave her an eighteen-year window, figured if she were younger than sixteen when she'd had this crush, he wouldn't stress, he would let go of the envious and shameful burn inside him.

From the list of Georges, there were only three deaths in the down deep for the eighteen-year period. One was in his fifties, the other in his sixties. Both died of natural causes. Lukas thought to cross-reference them with Juliette, see if there had been any work relations, if they shared a family tree perhaps.

And then he saw the third file. *This* was his George. *Her* George. Lukas knew it. Doing the math, Lukas saw he would be thirty-eight if he were still alive. He had died just over three years earlier, had worked in Mechanical, had *never married.*

He ran the ID search, and the picture confirmed his fears. He was a handsome man, a square jaw, a wide nose, dark eyes. He was smiling at the camera, calm, relaxed. It was hard to hate the man. Difficult, especially, since he was dead.

Lukas checked the cause and saw that it was investigated and then listed as an industrial accident. *Investigated.* He remembered hearing something about Jules when the up top got its new sheriff. Her qualifications had been a source of debate and tension, a wind of whispers. Especially around IT. But there had been chatter that she'd helped out on a case a long time ago, that this was why she'd been chosen.

This was the case. Was she in love with him before he died? Or did she fall for the memory of the man after? He decided it had to be the former. Lukas searched the desk for a charcoal, found one, and jotted down the man's ID and case number. Here was something to occupy his time, some way of getting to know her better. It would distract him, at least, until she finally got around to calling him back. He relaxed, pulled the keyboard into his lap, and started digging.

74

Silo 17

JULIETTE SHIVERED FROM THE cold as she helped Solo to his feet. He wobbled and steadied himself, both hands on the railing.

"Do you think you can walk?" she asked. She kept an eye on the empty stairs spiraling down toward them, wary of whoever else was out there, whoever had attacked him and nearly gotten her killed.

"I think so," he said. He dabbed at his forehead with his palm, studied the smear of blood he came away with. "Don't know how far."

She guided him toward the stairs, the smell of melted rubber and gasoline stinging her nose. The black undersuit was still damp against her skin, her breath billowed out before her, and whenever she stopped talking, her teeth chattered uncontrollably. She bent to retrieve her knife while Solo clutched the curved outer railing. Looking up, she considered the task before them. A straight run to IT seemed impossible. Her lungs were exhausted from the swim, her muscles cramped from the shivering and cold. And Solo looked even worse. His mouth was slack, his eyes drifting to and fro. He seemed barely cognizant of where he was.

"Can you make it to the deputy station?" she asked. Juliette had spent nights there on supply runs. The holding cell made for an oddly comfortable place to sleep. The keys were still in the box – maybe they could rest easy if they locked themselves inside and kept the key with them.

"That's how many levels?" Solo asked.

He didn't know the down deep of his own silo as well as Jules. He rarely risked venturing so far.

"A dozen or so. Can you make it?"

He lifted his boot to the first step, leaned into it. "I can try."

They set off with only a knife between them, which Juliette was lucky to have at all. How it had survived her dark pull through Mechanical was a mystery. She held it tightly, the handle cold, her hand colder. The simple cooking utensil had become her security totem, had replaced her watch as a necessary thing she must always have with her. As they made their way up the stairs, its handle clinked against the inner railing each time she reached over to steady herself. She kept her other arm around Solo, who struggled up each step with grunts and groans.

"How many of them do you think there are?" she asked, watching his footing and then glancing nervously up the stairway.

Solo grunted. "Shouldn't be any." He wobbled a little, but Juliette steadied him. "All dead. Everyone."

They stopped to rest at the next landing. "*You* made it," she pointed out. "All these years, and you survived."

He frowned, wiped his beard with the back of his hand. He was breathing hard. "But I'm Solo," he said. He shook his head sadly. "They were all gone. All of them."

Juliette peered up the shaft, up the gap between the stairs and the concrete. The dim green straw of the stairwell rose into a tight darkness. She pinned her teeth together to keep them from chattering while she listened for a sound, for any sign of life. Solo staggered ahead for the next flight of stairs. Juliette hurried beside him.

"How well did you see him? What do you remember?"

"I remember — I remember thinking he was just like me."

Juliette thought she heard him sob, but maybe it was the exertion from tackling more of the steps. She looked back at the door they were passing, the interior dark, no power being leached from IT. Were they passing Solo's assailant? Were they leaving some living ghost behind?

She powerfully hoped so. They had so much further to go, even to the deputy station, much less to anyplace she might call home.

They trudged in silence for a level and a half, Juliette shivering and Solo grunting and wincing. She rubbed her arms now and then, could feel the sweat from the climb and from helping to steady him. It was nearly enough to warm her but for the damp undersuit, and she was so hungry by the time they cleared three levels that she thought her body was simply going to give out. It needed fuel, something to burn and keep itself warm.

"One more level and I'm going to need to stop," she told Solo. He grumbled his agreement. It felt good to have the reward of a rest as their goal — the steps were an easier climb when they were countable, finite. At the landing of one-thirty-two, Solo used the railing to lower himself to the ground, hand over hand like the bars of a ladder. When his butt hit the decking, he laid out supine and folded his hands over his face.

Juliette hoped it was nothing more than a concussion. She'd seen her fair share of them working around men who were too tough to wear helmets — but not so tough when a tool or a steel beam caught them on the head. There was nothing for Solo but to rest.

The problem with resting was that it made her colder. Juliette stomped her feet to keep the blood circulating. The slight sweat from the hike was working against her. She could feel a draft cycling through the stairwell, cold air from below passing over the chilled waters like a natural air-conditioning unit. Her shoulders shook, the knife vibrating in her hand until her reflection became a silvery blur. Moving was difficult; staying in one place would kill her. And she still didn't know where this attacker was, could only hope he was below them.

"We should get going," she told Solo. She looked to the doors beyond him, the windows dark. What would she do if someone burst out at that very moment and attacked them? What kind of fight could she hope to put up?

Solo lifted his arm and waved it at her. "Go," he said. "I'll stay."

"No, you're coming with me." She rubbed her hands together, blew on them, summoned the strength to continue. She went to Solo and tried to grab his hand, but he withdrew it.

"More rest," he said. "I'll catch up."

"I'll be damned if I'm —" Her teeth clacked uncontrollably. She shivered and turned the involuntary spasm into an excuse to shake her arms, waggling them and forcing the blood to her extremities. "Damned if I'm leaving you alone," she finished.

"So thirsty," he told her.

Despite having seen quite enough water for a lifetime, Juliette was thirsty as well. She glanced up. "One more level and we're at the lower farms. C'mon. That'll be far enough for today. Food and water, find me something dry. C'mon, Solo, up. I don't care if it takes us a week to get home, we aren't giving up right here."

She grabbed his wrist. This time he didn't pull away.

The next flight took forever to climb. Solo stopped several times to lean on the railing and gaze senselessly at the next step. There was fresh blood trickling down his neck. Juliette stomped her frozen feet some more and cursed to herself. This was all stupid. She'd been so damned stupid.

A few steps from the next landing, she left Solo behind and went to check the doors to the farms. The jury-rigged power cables descending from IT and snaking their way inside were a legacy from decades ago, a time when the survivors, like Solo, were cobbling together what they could to stave off their demise. Juliette peeked inside and saw that the grow lights were off.

"Solo? I'm gonna go hit the timers. You rest here."

He didn't answer. Juliette held the door open and tried to slot her knife into the metal grating by her feet, leaving the handle to prop it open. Her arm shook so violently, it took her considerable effort just to aim it into a gap. Her undersuit, she noticed, smelled like burning rubber, like the smoke from the fire.

"Here," Solo said. He held the door open and slumped down against it, pinning it to the railing.

Juliette clutched the knife against her chest. "Thanks."

He nodded and waved his hand. His eyes drooped shut. "Water," he said, licking his lips.

She patted his shoulder. "I'll be right back."

The farm's entrance hall gobbled up the emergency lights from the stairway, the dim green quickly fading to pitch black. A circulating pump whirred in the distance, the same noise that had greeted her in the upper farms so many weeks ago. But now she knew what the sound was, knew there would be water available. Water and food, perhaps a change of clothes. She just needed to get the lights on so she could see. She cursed herself for not bringing a spare flashlight, for the loss of her pack and their gear.

The darkness accepted her as she climbed over the security gate. She knew her way. These farms had been nourishing her and Solo for weeks while they worked on the pathetic hydroponics pump and all that plumbing. Juliette thought of the new pump she'd wired; the mechanic in her was curious about the connection, wondered whether the thing would work, if she should've thrown the switch on the landing before they left. It was a crazy thought, but even if she didn't live to see it, some part of her wanted that silo dry, that flood removed. Her ordeal in its depths already seemed oddly distant, like something she had seen in a dream but hadn't really gone through, and yet she wanted it to have *mattered* for something. She wanted Solo's wounds to have mattered for something.

Her undersuit swished noisily while she walked, her legs rubbing together, her damp feet squeaking as she lifted them from the floor. She kept one hand on the wall, her knife comforting her in the other. Already, she could feel the residual warmth in the air from the last burn of the grow lights. She was thankful to be out of that frigid stairwell. In fact, she felt *better.* Her eyes began to adjust to the darkness. She would get some food, some water, find them a safe place to sleep. Tomorrow, they would aim for the mids deputy station. They could arm themselves, gather their strength. Solo would be stronger by then. She would need him to be.

At the end of the hall, Juliette groped for the doorway to the control room. Her hand habitually went to the switch inside, but it was already up. It hadn't worked in over three decades.

She fumbled blindly through the room, arms out in front of her, expecting to hit the wall long before she did. The tip of the knife scraped one of the control boxes. Juliette reached up to find the wire hanging from the ceiling, tacked up by someone long ago. She traced the wire to the timer it had been rigged to, felt for the programmable knob and slowly turned it until it clicked.

A series of loud pops from the relays outside rattled down the growing halls. A dim glow appeared. It would take a few minutes for them to warm all the way up.

Juliette left the control room and headed down one of the overgrown walkways railed off between the long plots of dirt. The nearest plots were picked clean. She pushed through the greenery, plants from either side of the hall shaking hands in the middle, and made her way to the circulation pump.

Water for Solo, warmth for herself. She repeated this mantra, begging the lights to heat up faster. The air around her remained dim and hazy, like the view of an outside morning beneath the heavy clouds.

She made her way through the pea plants, long neglected. Popping a few pods off their vines, she gave her stomach something to do besides ache. The pump whirred louder as it worked to push water through the drip pipes. Juliette chewed a pea, swallowed, slipped through the railing, and made her way to the small clearing around the pump.

The soil beneath the pump was dark and packed flat from weeks of her and Solo drinking there and refilling their containers. A few cups were scattered on the ground. Juliette knelt beside the pump and chose a tall glass. The lights above her were slowly brightening. She already imagined she could feel their warmth.

With a bit of effort, she managed to loosen the drain plug at the bottom of the pump a few turns. The water was under pressure and jetted out in a fine spray. She held the cup tightly against the pump to minimize the spillage. The cup gurgled as it was filled.

She drank out of one cup while filling another, some loose dirt crunching between her teeth.

Once both were full, she screwed them into the wet dirt so they wouldn't tip over and then twisted the plug until the spray stopped. Juliette tucked the knife under her arm and grabbed the two cups. She went to the railing, passed everything through, then threw her leg over the lowermost bar and scrambled out.

Now she needed warmth. She left the cups where they were and grabbed the knife. There were offices around the corner, a dining room. She remembered her first outfit in silo seventeen: a tablecloth with a slit in the middle. She laughed to herself as she turned the corner, feeling like she was regressing, like her weeks of working to make things better were taking her back to where she'd started.

The long hallway between the two grow stations was dark. A handful of wires hung from the pipes overhead, drooping between the spots where they'd been hastily attached. They marched in these upside-down leaps toward the hum and glow of the growing plots in the distance.

Juliette checked the offices and found nothing for warmth. No overalls, no curtains. She moved toward the dining hall, was turning to enter, when she thought she heard something beyond the next plot of plants. A click. A crackle. More relays for the lights? Stuck, perhaps?

She peered down the hall and into the grow station beyond. The lights were brighter there, warming up. Maybe they had come on sooner. She crept down the hallway toward them, drawn like a shivering fly to a flame, her arms bursting with goose bumps at the thought of drying out, of getting truly warm.

At the edge of the station, she heard something else. A squeal, maybe metal on metal, possibly another circulation pump trying to kick over. She and Solo hadn't checked the other pumps on this level. There was more than two people could eat or drink in the first patches.

Juliette froze and turned around to look behind herself.

Where would she set up camp if she were trying to survive in this place? In IT, for the power? Or here, for the food and water? She imagined another man like Solo squeezing through the cracks in the violence, lying low and surviving the long years. Maybe he'd heard the air compressor earlier, had come down to investigate, got scared, hit Solo over the head, and ran. Maybe he grabbed their gear bag just because it was there, or maybe it had been knocked under the railing by accident and had sunk to the pits of Mechanical.

She held the knife out in front of herself and slid down the hallway between the burgeoning plants. The wall of green before her parted with a rustle as she pushed through. Things were more overgrown here. Unwelcoming. Not picked over. This filled her with a mix of emotions. She was probably wrong, was probably hearing things again, just as she had for weeks, but part of her *wanted* to be right. She wanted to find this man who was like Solo. She wanted to make contact. Better that than living in fear of someone lurking in every shadow, behind every corner.

But what if there was more than one of them? Could a group of people have survived this long? How many could there be and go undetected? The silo was a massive place, but she and Solo had spent *weeks* in the down deep, had been in and out of these farms several times. Two people, an oldish couple, no more. Solo had said the man was his age. He would have to be.

These calculations and more ran through her mind, convincing her that she had nothing to be afraid of. She was shivering, but her adrenaline was pumping. She was armed. The leaves of wild and unkempt plants brushed against her face; Juliette pushed through this dense outer barrier and knew she'd found something on the other side.

The farms here were different. Groomed. Tamed. Recently guided by the hand of man. Juliette felt a wash of fear and relief, those two opposites twisting together like staircase and rail. She didn't want to be alone, didn't want this silo to be so desolate and empty, but she didn't want to be attacked. The first part of her felt an urge to call out, to tell whoever was in there that she meant no harm. The second part tightened its grip on the knife, clenched chattering teeth together, and begged her to turn and run.

At the end of the groomed grow station, the hallway took a dark turn. She peered around the corner into more unexplored territory. A long patch of darkness stretched toward the other side of the silo, a distant glow of light emanating from what was probably yet another crop station sucking juice from IT.

Someone was here. She knew it. She could feel the same eyes she'd felt for weeks, could sense the whispers on her skin, but this time she wasn't imagining it; she didn't have to fight the awareness or think she was going crazy. With her knife at the ready and the welcomed thought that she was between this someone and the defenseless Solo, she moved slowly but bravely into the dark hall, passing open offices and tasting rooms to either side, one hand on the wall to guide and steady herself—

Juliette stopped. Something wasn't right. Had she heard something? A person crying? She backed up to the previous door, could barely see it in front of herself, and realized it was closed. The only one she could see along the hall that was closed.

She stepped away from the door and knelt down. There had been a noise inside. She was sure of it. Almost like a faint wail. Looking up, she saw in the wan light that some of the overhead wires diverted perpendicularly from the rest and snaked through the wall above the door.

Juliette moved closer. She crouched down and put her ear to the door. Nothing. She reached up and tried the knob, felt that it was locked. How could it be locked, unless—?

The door flew open—her hand still on the knob—yanking her into the darkened room. There was a flash of light, and then a man over her, swinging something at her head.

Juliette fell onto her ass. A silver blur moved past her face, the crunch of a heavy wrench slamming into her shoulder, knocking her flat.

There was a high-pitched scream from the back of the room, drowning out Juliette's cry of pain. She swung the knife out in front of her, felt it hit the man's leg. The wrench clattered to the ground, more screams, people shouting. Juliette kicked away from the door and stood, clutching her shoulder. She was ready for the man to pounce, but her attacker was backing away, limping on one foot, a boy no more than fourteen, maybe fifteen.

"Stay where you are!" Juliette aimed the knife at him. The boy's eyes were wide with fear. A group of kids huddled against the back wall on a scattering of mattresses and blankets. They clung to one another, their wide eyes aimed at Juliette.

The confusion was overwhelming. She was seized by the sensation of wrongness. Where were the others? The adults? She could feel people with bad intentions sliding down the dark hallway behind her, ready to pounce. Here were their kids, locked away for safety. Soon, the mother rats would be back to punish her for disturbing their nest.

"Where are the others?" she asked, her hand trembling from the cold, the confusion, the fear. She scanned the room and saw that the boy standing, the one who had attacked her, was the oldest. A girl in her teens sat frozen on the tangle of blankets, two young boys and a young girl clinging to her.

The eldest boy glanced down at his leg. A stain of blood was spreading across his green overalls.

"How many are there?" She took a step closer. These kids were obviously more afraid of her than she was of them.

"Leave us alone!" the older girl screamed. She clutched something to her chest. The young girl beside her pressed her face into the older girl's lap, trying to disappear. The two young boys glared like cornered dogs but didn't move.

"How did you get here?" she asked them. She aimed the knife at the tall boy but started to feel silly for wielding it. He looked at her in confusion, not comprehending the question, and Juliette knew. Of course. How would there be decades of fighting in this silo without that second human passion?

"You were born down here, weren't you?"

Nobody answered. The boy's face screwed up in confusion, as if the question were mad. She peeked back over her shoulder.

"Where are your parents? When will they be back? How long?"

"Never!" the girl screeched, her head straining forward from the effort. "They're dead!"

Her mouth remained open, her chin trembling. The tendons stood out on her young neck.

The older boy turned and glared at the girl, seemed to want her to remain quiet. Juliette was still trying to comprehend that these were mere kids. She knew they couldn't be alone. Someone had attacked Solo.

As if to answer, her eyes were drawn to the wrench on the decking. It was Solo's wrench. The rust stains were distinctive. How was that possible? Solo had said . . .

And Juliette remembered what he'd said. She realized these kids, this young man, were the same age that he still saw himself as. The same age he'd been when he'd been left alone. Had the last survivors of the down deep perished in recent years, but not before leaving something behind?

"What's your name?" Juliette asked the boy. She lowered her knife and showed him her other palm. "My name's Juliette," she said. She wanted to add that she came from another silo, a saner world, but didn't want to confuse them or freak them out.

"Rickson," the boy snarled. He puffed out his chest. "My father was Rick the plumber."

"Rick the plumber." Juliette nodded. She saw along one wall, at the end of a tall dune of supplies and scavenges, the gear bag they'd stolen. Her change of clothes spilled out the gaping mouth of the bag. Her towel would be in there. She slid toward the bag, an eye on the kids huddled together on the makeshift bed, the group nest, wary of the older boy.

"Well, Rickson, I want you to gather your things." Kneeling by her bag, she dug inside and searched for the towel. She found it, pulled it out, and rubbed it over her damp hair, an indescribable luxury. There was no way she was leaving them here, these kids. She turned to face the other children, the towel draped across the back of her neck, their eyes all locked on hers.

"Go ahead," she said. "Get your things together. You're not going to live like this—"

"Just leave us," the older girl said. The two boys had moved off the bed, though, and were going through piles of things. They looked to the girl, then to Juliette, unsure.

"Go back to where you're from," Rickson said. The two eldest children seemed to be gaining strength from each other. "Take your noisy machines and go."

That's what this was about. Juliette remembered the sight of the compressor on its side, more heavily attacked maybe than Solo had been. She nodded to the two smaller boys, had their ages pegged for ten or eleven. "Go on," she told them. "You're gonna help me and my friend get home. We have good food there. Real electricity. Hot water. Get your things—"

The youngest girl cried out at this, a horrible peal, the same cry Juliette had heard from the dark hallway. Rickson paced back and forth, eyeing her and the wrench on the floor. Juliette slid away from him and toward the bed to comfort the young girl, when she realized it wasn't her squealing.

Something moved in the older girl's arms.

Juliette froze at the edge of the bed.

"No," she whispered.

Rickson took a step toward her.

"Stay!" She aimed the point of the knife at him. He glanced down at the wound on his leg, thought better of it. The two boys froze in the act of stuffing their bags. Nothing in the room moved save the baby squealing and fidgeting in the girl's arms.

"Is that a child?"

The girl turned her shoulders. It was a motherly gesture, but the girl couldn't have been more than fifteen. Juliette didn't know that was possible. She wondered if that was why the implants went in so early. Her hand slid toward her hip almost as if to touch the place, to rub the bump beneath her skin.

"Just go," the teenager whimpered. "We've been fine without you."

Juliette put down the knife. It felt strange to relinquish it but more wrong to have it in her hand as she approached the bed. "I can help you," she said. She turned and made sure the boy heard her. "I used to work in a place that cared for newborns. Let me . . ." She reached out her hands. The girl turned further toward the wall, shielding the child from her.

"Okay." Juliette held up her hands, showed her palms. "But you're not going to live like this anymore." She nodded to the young boys, turned to Rickson, who hadn't moved. "None of you are. This isn't how anyone should have to live their days, not even their last ones."

She nodded to herself, her mind made up. "Rickson? Get your things together. Only the necessities. We'll come back for anything else." She dipped her chin at the younger boys, saw how their overalls had been chopped at the knees, their legs covered in grime from the farms. They took it as permission to return to packing. These two seemed eager to have someone else in charge, maybe anybody other than their brother, if that's who he was.

"Tell me your name." Juliette sat down on the bed with the two girls while the others rummaged through their things. She fought to remain calm, not to succumb to the nausea of kids having kids.

The baby let out a hungry cry.

"I'm here to help you," Juliette told the girl. "Can I see? Is it a girl or a boy?"

The young mother relaxed her arms. A blanket was folded away, revealing the squinting eyes and pursed red lips of a baby no more than a few months old. A tiny arm waved at its mother.

"Girl," she said softly.

The younger girl clinging to her side peeked around the mother's ribs at Juliette.

"Have you given her a name?"

She shook her head. "Not yet."

Rickson said something behind her to the two boys, trying to get them not to fight over something.

"My name's Elise," the younger girl said, her head emerging from behind the other girl's side. Elise pointed at her mouth. "I have a loose tooth."

Juliette laughed. "I can help you with that if you like." She took a chance and reached out to squeeze the young girl's arm. Flashes of her childhood in her father's nursery flooded back, the memories of worried parents, of precious children, of all the hopes and dreams created and dashed around that lottery. Juliette's thoughts swerved to her brother, the one who was not meant to be, and she felt the tears well up in her eyes. What had these kids been through? Solo at least had normal experiences from before. He knew what it meant to live in a world where one could be safe. What had these five kids, six, grown up in? Seen? She felt such intense pity for them. Pity that verged on the sick, wrong, sad desire for none of them to have ever been born . . .

Which was just as soon washed over with a wave of guilt for even considering it.

"We're going to get you out of here," she told the two girls. "Gather your things."

One of the young boys came over and dropped her bag nearby. He was putting things back into it, apologizing to her, when Juliette heard another strange squeak.

What now?

She dabbed her mouth on the towel, watching as the girls reluctantly did an adult's bidding, finding their things and eyeing one another to make sure this was okay. Juliette heard a rustling in her gear bag. She used the handle to separate the zippered mouth, wary of what could be living in the rat's nest these kids had created, when she heard a tiny voice.

Calling her name.

She dropped the towel and clawed through the bag, past tools and bottles of water, under her spare overalls and loose socks, until she found the radio. She wondered how Solo could possibly be calling her. The other set had been ruined in her suit—

"—please say something," the radio hissed. "Juliette, are you there? It's Walker. Please, for God's sake, answer me—"

75

Silo 18

"WHAT HAPPENED? WHY AREN'T they responding?" Courtnee looked from Walker to Shirly, as if either of them could know.

"Is it broken?" Shirly picked up the small dial with the painted marks and tried to tell if it had accidentally moved. "Walk, did we break it?"

"No, it's still on," he said. He held the headphones up by his cheek, his eyes drifting over the various components.

"Guys, I don't know how much longer we have." Courtnee was watching the scene in the generator room through the observation window. Shirly stood up and peered out over the control panel toward the main entrance. Jenkins and some of his men were inside, rifles pinned against their shoulders, yelling at the others. The soundproofing made it impossible to hear what was going on.

"Hello?"

A voice crackled from Walker's hands. The words seemed to tumble through his fingers.

"Who's there?" he called, flicking the switch. "Who is this?"

Shirly rushed to Walker's side. She wrapped her hands around his arm, disbelieving. "Juliette!" she screamed.

Walker held up his hand, tried to quiet her and Courtnee both. His hands were trembling as he fumbled with the detonator and finally clicked the red switch.

"Jules?" His old voice cracked. Shirly squeezed his arm. "Is that you?"

There was a pause, and then a cry from the speakers, a sob. "Walk? Walk, is that you? What's going on? Where are you? I thought . . ."

"Where is she?" Shirly whispered.

Courtnee watched them both, her cheeks in her palms, mouth open.

Walker hit the switch. "Jules, where are you?"

A deep sigh hissed through the tiny speakers. Her voice was tiny and far away. "Walk, I'm in *another silo*. There's more of them. You wouldn't believe . . ."

Her voice drifted off to static. Shirly leaned against Walker while Courtnee paced in front of them, looking from the radio to the window.

"We know about the others," Walker said, holding the mic below his beard. "We can hear them, Jules. *All* of them."

He let go of the switch. Juliette's voice returned.

"How are you — Mechanical? I heard about the fighting. Are you in the middle of that?" Before she signed off, Juliette said something to someone else, her voice barely audible.

Walker raised his eyebrows at the mention of the fighting.

"How would she have heard?" Shirly asked.

"I wish she were here," Courtnee said. "Jules would know what to do."

"Tell her about the exhaust. About the plan." Shirly waved for the microphone. "Here, let me."

Walker nodded. He handed Shirly the headset and the detonator.

Shirly worked the switch. It was stiffer than she'd thought it'd be. "Jules? Can you hear me? It's Shirly."

"Shirly . . ." Juliette's voice wavered. "Hey, you. You hanging in there?"

The emotion in her friend's voice brought tears to Shirly's eyes. "Yeah—" She bobbed her head and swallowed. "Hey, listen, some of the others are routing the exhaust feed to IT's cooling vents. But remember that time we lost back pressure? I'm worried the motor might . . ."

"No," Juliette said. "You have to stop them. Shirly, can you hear me? You have to stop them. It won't do anything. The cooling is for the *servers*. The only people up there who—" She cleared her throat. "Listen to me. Make them stop—"

Shirly fumbled with the red switch. Walker reached over as if to help, but she finally got the device under control. "Wait," she transmitted. "How do you know where the vents lead?"

"I just do. This place is laid out the same. Goddamn it, let me talk to them. You can't let them—"

Shirly hit the switch again. There was a blast of sound from the generator room as Courtnee threw open the door and ran outside. "Courtnee's going," she said. "She's going right now. Jules— How did you—? Who are you with? Can they help us? It's not looking good over here."

The tiny speakers crackled again. Shirly could hear Juliette take a deep breath, could hear other voices in the background, heard her give commands or orders to some other person. Shirly thought her friend sounded exhausted. Weary. Sad.

"There's nothing I can do," Juliette said. "There's no one here. One man. Some kids. Everyone's gone. The people who lived here, they couldn't even help themselves." The line went silent, and then she clicked through again. "You have to stop the fighting," she said. "Whatever it takes. Please— Don't let it be because of me. Please stop—"

The door opened again, Courtnee returning. Shirly heard shouts in the generator room. Gunfire.

"What is that?" Juliette asked. "Where are you guys?"

"In the control room." Shirly looked up at Courtnee, whose eyes were wide with fear. "Jules, I don't think we have much time. I—" There was so much she wanted to say. She wanted to tell her about Marck. She needed more time. "They're coming for us," was all she could think to relate. "I'm glad you're okay."

The radio crackled. "Oh God, make them stop. No more fighting! Shirly, listen to me!"

"It doesn't matter," Shirly said, holding the button and wiping her cheeks. "They won't stop." The gunfire was getting closer, the pops audible through the thick door. Her people were dying while she cowered in the control room, talking to a ghost. Her people were dying.

"You take care of yourself," Shirly said.

"Wait!"

Shirly handed the headset to Walker. She joined Courtnee by the window and watched the crush of people cower on the other side of the generator, the flash and shudder of barrels leaning against the railing, someone in the blue of Mechanical lying still on the ground. More faded pops. More distant and muted rattles.

"Jules!" Walker fumbled with the radio. He shouted her name, was still trying to talk to her.

"Let me talk to them!" Juliette yelled, her voice impossibly far away. "Walk, why can I hear you and not them? I need to talk to the deputies, to Peter and Hank. Walk, how did you call me? I need to talk to them!"

Walker blubbered about soldering irons, about his magnifiers. The old man was crying, cradling his boards and wires and electrics as if they were a broken child, whispering to them and rocking back and forth, salt water dripping dangerously onto this thing he'd built.

He babbled to Juliette while more men in blue fell, arms draped over railings, inadequate rifles dropping noiselessly to the ground. The men they had lived in terror of for a month were inside. It was over. Shirly groped for Courtnee, their arms entangling, while they watched, helpless. Behind them, the sobs and mad ravings of old Walk mixed with the jitter of deadened gunfire, a popping noise like the grumble of a machine losing its balance, sliding out of control . . .

76

Silo 18

LUKAS TEETERED ON THE upturned trash can, the toes of his boots denting the soft plastic, feeling as if it could go flying out from under him or collapse under his weight at any moment. He steadied himself by holding the top of server twelve, the thick layer of dust up there telling him it had been years since anyone had been in to clean with a ladder and a rag. He pressed his nose up to the air-conditioning vent and took another whiff.

The nearby door beeped, the locks clanking as they withdrew into the jamb. With a soft squeal, the massive hinges budged and the heavy door swung inward.

Lukas nearly lost his grip on the dusty server top as Bernard pushed his way inside. The head of IT looked up at him quizzically.

"You'll never fit," Bernard said. He laughed as he turned to push the door shut. The locking pins clunked, the panel beeped, and a red light resumed its watch over the room.

Lukas pushed away from the dusty server and leapt from the trash can, the plastic bucket flipping over and scooting across the floor. He wiped his hands together, brushed them on the seat of his pants, and forced a laugh.

"I thought I smelled something," he explained. "Does it look smoky in here to you?"

Bernard squinted at the air. "It always seems hazy in here to me. And I don't smell anything. Just hot servers." He reached into his breast pocket and brought out a few folded pieces of paper. "Here. Letters from your mother. I told her to porter them to me and I'd pass them along."

Lukas smiled, embarrassed, and accepted them. "I still think you should ask about . . ." He glanced up at the air-conditioning vent and realized there was no one in Mechanical to ask. The last that he'd heard from the radio below was that Sims and the others were mopping up. Dozens were dead. Three to four times that many were in custody. Apartment wings were being prepped in the mids to hold them all. It sounded like there would be enough people to clean for years.

"I'll have one of the replacement mechanics look into it," Bernard promised. "Which reminds me, I'd like to go over some of that with you. There's going to be a massive shift from green to blue as we push farmers into Mechanical. I was wondering what you'd think of Sammi heading up the entire division down there."

Lukas nodded as he skimmed one of the letters from his mother. "Sammi as head of Mechanical? I think he's overqualified but perfect. I've learned a lot from him." He glanced up as Bernard opened the filing cabinet by the door and flipped through work orders. "He's a great teacher, but would it be permanent?"

"Nothing's permanent." Bernard found what he was looking for and tucked it into his breast pocket. "You need anything else?" He pressed his glasses up his nose. Lukas thought he looked older from the past month. Older and worn down. "Dinner'll be sent over in a few hours . . ."

Lukas did have something he wanted. He wanted to say that

he was ready, that he had sufficiently absorbed the horror of his future job, had learned what he needed without going insane. And now could he please go home?

But that wasn't the way out of there. Lukas had sorted this out for himself.

"Well," he said, "I wouldn't mind some more reading material . . ."

The things he had discovered in server eighteen burned in his brain. He feared Bernard would be able to read them there. Lukas thought he knew, but he needed to ask for that folder in order to be sure.

Bernard smiled. "Don't you have enough to read?"

Lukas fanned the letters from his mother. "These? They'll keep me busy for the walk to the *ladder*—"

"I meant what you have below. The Order. Your studies." Bernard tilted his head.

Lukas let out a sigh. "Yeah, I do, but I can't be expected to read that twelve hours a day. I'm talking about something less dense." He shook his head. "Hey, forget it. If you can't—"

"What do you need?" Bernard said. "I'm just giving you a hard time." He leaned against the filing cabinet and interlocked his fingers across his belly. He peered at Lukas through the bottom of his glasses.

"Well, this might sound weird, but it's this case. An *old* case. The server says it's filed away in your office with all the closed investigations—"

"An *investigation?*" Bernard's voice rose quizzically.

Lukas nodded. "Yeah. A friend-of-a-friend thing. I'm just curious how it was resolved. There aren't any digital copies on the serv—"

"This isn't about Holston, is it?"

"*Who?* Oh, the old sheriff? No, no. Why?"

Bernard waved his hand to dismiss the thought.

"The file is under Wilkins," Lukas said, watching Bernard closely. "George Wilkins."

Bernard's face hardened. His mustache dropped down over his lips like a lowered curtain.

Lukas cleared his throat. What he'd seen on Bernard's face was nearly enough. He started to say, "George died a few years ago down in Mech—"

"I know how he died." Bernard dipped his chin. "Why would you want to see that file?"

"Just curious. I have a friend who—"

"What's this friend's name?" Bernard's small hands slid off his belly and he tucked them into his overalls. He moved away from the filing cabinet and took a step closer.

"What?"

"This friend, was he involved with George in any way? How close a friend was he?"

"No. Not that I know of." Lukas wanted simply to ask, to ask why he'd done it. "Look, if it's a big deal, don't worry about—"

"It's a very big deal," Bernard said. "George Wilkins was a dangerous man. A man of *ideas*. The kind we catch in whispers, the kind who poisons the people around him—"

"What? What do you mean?"

"Section thirteen of the Order. Study it. All insurrections would start *right there* if we let them, start with men like him."

Bernard's chin had lowered to his chest, his eyes peering over the rims of his glasses, the truth coming freely without all the deceit Lukas had planned.

Lukas never needed that folder; he had found the travel logs that coincided with George's death, the dozens of wires asking Holston to wrap things up. There was no shame in Bernard. George Wilkins hadn't died; he'd been murdered. And Bernard was willing to tell him why.

"What did he do?" Lukas asked quietly.

"I'll tell you what he did. He was a mechanic, a greaser. We started hearing chatter from the porters about these plans circulating, ideas for expanding the mine, doing a lateral dig. As you know, lateral digs are forbidden—"

"Yeah, obviously." Lukas had a mental image of miners from silo eighteen pushing through and meeting miners from silo nineteen. It would be awkward, to say the least.

"A long chat with the old head of Mechanical put an end to that nonsense, and then George Wilkins came up with the idea of expanding *downward.* He and some others drew up schematics for a level one-fifty. And then a level one-sixty."

"*Sixteen* more levels?"

"To begin with. That was the talk, anyway. Just whispers and sketches. But some of these whispers landed in a porter's ear, and then *ours* perked up."

"So you killed him?"

"Someone did, yes. It doesn't matter who." Bernard adjusted his glasses with one hand. The other stayed in the belly of his overalls. "You'll have to do these things one day, son. You know that, don't you?"

"Yeah, but—"

"No buts." Bernard shook his head slowly. "Some men are like a virus. Unless you want to see a plague break out, you inoculate the silo against them. You remove them."

Lukas remained silent.

"We've removed fourteen threats this year, Lukas. Do you have any idea what the average life expectancy would be if we weren't proactive about these things?"

"But the cleanings—"

"Useful for dealing with the people who want *out.* Who dream of a better world. This uprising we're having right now is full of people like that, but it's just one sort of sickness we deal with. The cleaning is one sort of cure. I'm not sure if someone with a different illness would even clean if we sent them out there. They have to want to *see* what we show them for it to work."

This reminded Lukas of what he'd learned of the helmets, the visors. He had assumed this was the only kind of sickness there was. He was beginning to wish he'd read more of the Order and less of the Legacy.

"You've heard this latest outbreak on the radio. All of this could have been prevented if we'd caught the sickness earlier. Tell me that wouldn't have been better."

Lukas looked down at his boots. The trash can lay nearby, on its side. It looked sad like that. No longer useful for holding things.

"Ideas are contagious, Lukas. This is basic Order material. You know this stuff."

He nodded. He thought of Juliette, wondered why she hadn't called in what felt like forever. She was one of these viruses Bernard was talking about, her words creeping in his mind and infecting him with outlandish dreams. He felt his entire body flush with heat as he realized he'd caught some of it too. He wanted to touch his breast pocket, feel the lumps of her personal effects there, the watch, the ring, the ID. He had taken them to remember her in death, but they had become even more precious knowing that she was still alive.

"This uprising hasn't been nearly as bad as the last one," Bernard told him. "And even after *that* one, things were eventually smoothed over, the damage welded back together, the people made to forget. The same thing will happen here. Are we clear?"

"Yessir."

"Excellent. Now, was that all you wished to know from this folder?"

Lukas nodded.

"Good. It sounds like you need to be reading something else, anyway." His mustache twitched with half a smile. Bernard turned to go.

"It was you, wasn't it?"

Bernard stopped but didn't turn to face him.

"Who killed George Wilkins. It was you, right?"

"Does it matter?"

"Yeah. It matters to— To me— It means—"

"Or to your *friend?*" Bernard turned to face him. Lukas felt the temperature in the room go up yet another notch. "Are you having second thoughts, son? About this job? Was I wrong about you? Because I've been wrong before."

Lukas swallowed. "I just want to know if it's something I'd ever have to . . . I mean, since I'm shadowing for . . ."

Bernard took a few steps toward him. Lukas felt himself back up half a step in response.

"I didn't think I was wrong about you. But I was, wasn't I?" Bernard shook his head. He looked disgusted. "Goddamn it," he spat.

"Nosir. You weren't. I think I've just been in here too long." Lukas brushed his hair off his forehead. His scalp was itchy. He needed to use the bathroom. "Maybe I just need some air, you know? Go home for a while? Sleep in my bed. What's it been, a month? How long do I need—?"

"You want out of here?"

Lukas nodded.

Bernard peered down at his boots and seemed to consider this awhile. When he looked up, there was sadness in his eyes, in the droop of his mustache, across the wet film of his eyes.

"Is that what you want? To get out of here?"

He adjusted his hands inside his overalls.

"Yessir." Lukas nodded.

"Say it."

"I want out of here." Lukas glanced at the heavy steel door behind Bernard. "Please. I want you to let me out."

"Out."

Lukas bobbed his head, exasperated, sweat tickling his cheek as it followed the line of his jaw. He was suddenly very afraid of this man, this man who all of a sudden reminded him even more of his father.

"Please," Lukas said. "It's just . . . I'm starting to feel cooped up. Please let me out."

Bernard nodded. His cheeks twitched. He looked as if he were about to cry. Lukas had never seen this expression on the man's face.

"Sheriff Billings, are you there?"

His small hand emerged from his overalls and raised the radio to his sad, quivering mustache.

Peter's voice crackled back. "I'm here, sir."

Bernard clicked the transmitter. "You heard the man," he said, tears welling up in his eyes. "Lukas Kyle, IT engineer first class, says he wants *out* . . ."

77

Silo 17

"HELLO? WALK? SHIRLY?"

Juliette shouted into the radio, the orphans and Solo watching her from several steps below. She had hurried the kids through the farms, made hasty introductions, checking the radio all the while. Several levels had gone by, the others trudging up behind her, and still no word from them, nothing since she'd been cut off, the sound of gunfire sprinkled among Walker's words. She kept thinking if she just got higher, if she tried one more time . . . She checked the light by the power knob and made sure the battery wasn't dead, turned the volume up until she could hear the static, knew that the thing was working.

She clicked the button. The static fell silent, the radio waiting for her to speak. "Please say something, guys. This is Juliette. Can you hear me? Say anything."

She looked to Solo, who was being supported by the very man who had dazed him. "We need to go higher, I think. C'mon. Double-time."

There were groans; these poor refugees of silo seventeen acted like she was the one who'd lost her mind. But they stomped up the stairs after her, their pace dictated by Solo, who had seemed to rally with some fruit and water but had slowed as the levels wore on.

"Where are these friends of yours we talked to?" Rickson asked. "Can they come help?" He grunted as Solo lurched to one side. "He's heavy."

"They aren't coming to help us," Juliette said. "There's no getting from there to here." *Or vice versa,* she told herself.

Her stomach lurched with worry. She needed to get to IT and call Lukas, find out what was going on. She needed to tell him how horribly awry her plans had gone, how she was failing at every turn. There was no going back, she realized. No saving her friends. No saving this silo. She glanced back over her shoulder. Her life was now going to be one of a mother to these orphaned children, kids who had survived merely because the people who had been left, who had been committing the violence on each other, didn't have the stomach to kill them. Or the *heart,* she thought.

And now it would fall to her. And to Solo, but to a lesser degree. He would probably be just one more child for her to attend to.

They made their gradual way up another flight, Solo seeming to regain his senses a little, progress being made. But still a long way to go.

They stopped in the mids for bathroom breaks, filling more empty toilets that wouldn't flush. Juliette helped the young ones. They didn't like going like this, preferred to do it in the dirt. She told them that was right, that they only did this when they were on the move. She didn't tell them about the years Solo had spent destroying entire levels of apartments. She didn't tell them about the clouds of flies she'd seen.

The last of their food was consumed, but they had plenty of water. Juliette wanted to get to the hydroponics on fifty-six before they stopped for the night. There was enough food and water there for the rest of the trip. She tried the radio repeatedly, aware that she was running down the battery. There was no reply. She didn't understand how she'd heard them to begin with; all the silos must have used something different, some way of not hearing each other. It had to be Walker, something he'd engineered. When she got back to IT, would she be able to figure it out? Would she be able to contact him or Shirly? She wasn't sure, and Lukas had no way of talking to Mechanical from where he was, no way of patching her through. She'd asked a dozen times.

Lukas . . .

And Juliette *remembered.*

The radio in Solo's hovel. What had Lukas said one night? They were talking late and he'd said he wished they could chat from down below where it was more comfortable. Wasn't that where he was getting his updates about the uprising? It was over the radio. Just like the one in Solo's place, beneath the servers, locked behind that steel cage for which he'd never found the key.

Juliette turned and faced the group; they stopped climbing and gripped the rails, stared up at her. Helena, the young mother who didn't even know her own age, tried to comfort her baby as it began to squeal. The nameless infant preferred the sway of the climb.

"I need to go up," she told them. She looked to Solo. "How're you feeling?"

"Me? I'm fine."

He didn't look fine.

"Can you get them up?" She nodded to Rickson. "Are you okay?"

The boy dipped his chin. His resistance had seemed to crumble during the climb, especially during the bathroom break. The younger children, meanwhile, had been nothing but excited to see new parts of the silo, to feel that they could raise their voices without terrible things happening to them. They were coming to grips with there being only two adults left, and neither seemed all that bad.

"There's food on fifty-six," she said.

"Numbers —" Rickson shook his head. "I don't —"

Of course. Why would he need to count numbers he'd never live to see, and in more ways than one?

"Solo will show you where," she told him. "We've stayed there before. Good food. Canned stuff as well. Solo?" She waited until he looked up at her, the glazed expression partly melting away. "I have to get back to your place. I have people I need to call, okay? My friends. I need to find out if they're okay."

He nodded.

"You guys will be fine?" She hated to leave them but needed to. "I'll try to make it back down to you tomorrow. Take your time getting all the way up, okay? No need to rush home."

Home. Was she already resigned to that?

There were nods in the group. One of the young boys pulled a water bottle out of the other's bag and unscrewed the cap. Juliette turned and began taking the stairs two at a time, her legs begging her not to.

Juliette was in the forties when it occurred to her that she might not make it. The sweat she'd worked up was chilling her skin; her legs were beyond the ache, beyond the pain: they were numb with fatigue. She found her arms doing a lot of the work as she lunged ahead, gripped the railing with clammy hands, and hauled herself up another two steps.

Her breathing was ragged; it had been for half a dozen levels. She wondered if she'd done damage to her lungs from the underwater ordeal. Was that even possible? Her father would know. She thought of spending the rest of her life without a doctor, of teeth as yellow as Solo's, of caring for a growing child and the challenge of seeing that more weren't made, not until the children were older.

At the next landing, she again touched her hip where her birth control rode under her skin. Such things made more sense in light of silo seventeen. So *much* about her previous life made sense. Things that had once seemed twisted now had a sort of pattern, a logic about them. The expense of sending a wire, the spacing of the levels, the single and cramped stairway, the bright colors for particular jobs, dividing the silo into sections, breeding mistrust . . . it was all designed. She'd seen hints of this before but never knew why. Now this empty silo told her, the presence of these kids told her. It turned out that some crooked things looked even worse when straightened. Some tangled knots only made sense once unraveled.

Her mind wandered while she climbed, wandered in order to avoid the aches in her muscles, to escape the day's ordeals. When she finally hit the thirties it gave her, if not an end to the suffering, a renewed focus. She stopped trying the portable radio as often. The static never changed, and she had a different idea for contacting Walker, something she should have pieced together sooner, a way to bypass the servers and communicate with other silos. It was there all along, staring her and Solo in the face. There was a small sliver of doubt that she might be wrong, but why else lock up a radio that was already locked up two other ways? It only made sense if that device was supremely dangerous. Which is what she hoped it would be.

She stomped up to thirty-five dead on her feet. Her body had never been pushed this hard, not even while plumbing the small pump, not during her trek through the outside. Will alone helped her lift each foot, plant it, straighten her leg, pull with her arm, lunge forward for another grab. One step at a time now. Her toe banged on the next step: she could barely lift her boot high enough. The green emergency lights gave her no sense of the passing of time, no idea if night had come, when morning would be. She desperately missed her watch. All she had these days was her knife. She laughed at the switch, at having gone from counting the seconds in her life to fending for each and every one of them.

Thirty-four. It was tempting to collapse to the steel grating, to sleep, to curl up like her first night in that place, just thankful to be alive. Instead, she pulled the door open, amazed at the effort this required, and stepped back into civilization. Light. Power. Heat.

She staggered down the hallway with her vision so constricted it was as if she could only see through a straw at her center, everything else out of focus and spinning.

Her shoulder brushed the wall. Walking required effort. All she wanted was to call Lukas, to hear his voice. She imagined falling asleep behind that server, warm air blowing over her from its fans, the headphones tight against her ears. He could murmur to her about the faraway stars while she slept for days and days . . .

But Lukas would wait. Lukas was locked up and safe. She had all the time in the world to call him.

She turned instead into the Suit Lab, shuffled toward the tool wall, didn't dare look at her cot. A glance at her cot, and she'd wake up the next day. Whatever day that was.

Grabbing the bolt cutters, she was about to leave but went back for the small sledge as well. The tools were heavy, but they felt good in her hands, one tool in each, pulling down on her arms, stretching her muscles and grounding her, keeping her stable.

At the end of the hall, she pressed her shoulder against the heavy door to the server room. She leaned until it squeaked open. Just a crack. Just wide enough for her. Juliette hurried as much as her numb muscles would allow toward the ladder. Shuffling. Fast as she could go.

The grate was in place; she tugged it out of the way and dropped the tools down. Big noise. She didn't care—they couldn't break. Down she went, hands slick, chin catching a rung, floor coming up faster than she'd anticipated.

Juliette sank to the floor, sprawled out, shin banging the sledge. It took a force of will, an act of God, to get up. But she did.

Down the hall and past the small desk. There was a steel cage there, a radio, a big one. She remembered her days as sheriff. They had a radio just like it in her office; she'd used it to call Marnes when he was on patrol, to call Hank and Deputy Marsh. But this one was different.

She set the sledge down and pinched the jaws of the cutter on one of the hinges. Squeezing was too hard. Her arms shook. They trembled.

Juliette adjusted herself, put one of the cutters' handles against her neck, cradled it with her collarbone and shoulder. She grabbed the other handle with both hands and pulled toward herself, hugging the cutters. Squeezing. She felt them move.

There was a loud crack, the twang of splitting steel. She moved to the other hinge and did it again. Her collarbone hurt where the handle dug in, felt like it might be the thing to crack, not the hinge.

Another violent burst of metal.

Juliette grabbed the steel cage and pulled. The hinges came away from the mounting plate. She tore hungrily at the box, trying to get to the prize inside, thinking of Walker and all her family, all her friends, the sound of people screaming in the background. She had to get them to stop fighting. Get everyone to stop fighting.

Once she had enough space between the bent steel and the wall, she wrapped her fingers in this gap and tugged, bending the protective cage on its welds, tilting the cage away from the wall, revealing the entire radio unit beneath. Who needed keys? Screw the keys. She wrenched the cage flat, then bent her weight on it, making a new hinge of its front, warping it out of the way.

The dial on the front seemed familiar. She turned it to power the unit on and found that it clicked instead of spinning. Juliette knelt down, panting and exhausted, sweat running down her neck. There was another switch for power; she turned this one instead, static rising in the speakers, a buzz filling the room.

The other knob. This was what she wanted, what she expected to find. She thought it might be patch cables like the back of the server, or dip switches like a pump control, but it was tiny numbers arranged around the edge of a knob. Juliette smiled, exhausted, and turned the pointer to "18." Home. She grabbed the mic and squeezed the button.

"Walker? Are you there?"

Juliette slumped down to the ground and rested her back against the desk. With her eyes shut, mic by her face, she could imagine going to sleep like that. She saw what Lukas meant. This was comfortable.

She squeezed again. "Walk? Shirly? Please answer me."

The radio crackled to life.

Juliette opened her eyes. She stared up at the unit, her hands trembling.

A voice: "Is this who I think it is?"

The voice was too high to be Walker. She knew this voice. Where did she know it from? She was tired and confused. She squeezed the button on the mic.

"This is Juliette. Who is this?"

Was it Hank? She thought it might be Hank. He had a radio. Maybe she had the wrong silo completely. Maybe she'd screwed up.

"I need radio silence," the voice demanded. "All of them off. Now."

Was this directed at her? Juliette's mind spun in circles. A handful of voices chimed in, one after the other. There were pops of static. Was she supposed to say something? She was confused.

"You shouldn't be transmitting on this frequency," the voice said. "You should be put to cleaning for such things."

Juliette's hand fell to her lap. She slumped against the wooden desk, dejected. She recognized the voice.

Bernard.

For weeks, she had been hoping to speak to this man, had been silently begging for him to answer. But not now. Now she had nothing to say. She wanted to talk to her friends, to make things okay.

She squeezed the radio.

"No more fighting," she said. All the will was drained from her. All desire for vengeance. She just wanted the world to quiet itself, for people to live and grow old and feed the roots one day—

"Speaking of cleanings," the voice squeaked. "Tomorrow will be the first of many more to come. Your friends are lined up and ready to go. And I believe you know the lucky one who's going first."

There was a click, followed by the hiss and crinkle of static. Juliette didn't move. She felt dead. Numb. The will was drained from her body.

"Imagine my surprise," the voice said. "Imagine when I found out a decent man, a man I trusted, had been poisoned by you."

She clicked the microphone with her fist but didn't raise it to her mouth. She simply raised her voice instead.

"You'll burn in hell," she told him.

"Undoubtedly," Bernard said. "Until then, I'm holding some things in my hand that I think belong to you. An ID with your picture on it, a pretty little bracelet, and this wedding ring that doesn't look official at all. I wonder about that . . ."

Juliette groaned. She couldn't feel any part of her body. She could barely hear her thoughts. She managed to squeeze the mic, but it required every ounce of effort that she had left.

"What are you going on about, you twisted fuck?"

She spat the last, her head drifting to the side, her body craving sleep.

"I'm talking about Lukas, who betrayed me. We found some of your things on him just now. Exactly how long has he been talking to you? Well before the servers, right? Well, guess what? I'm sending him your way. And I finally figured out what you did last time, what those idiots in Supply helped you do, and I want you to be assured, be very assured, that your friend won't have the same help. I'm going to build his suit personally. Me. I'll stay up all night if I have to. So when he goes out in the morning, I can be sure that he gets nowhere *near* those blasted hills."

78

Silo 18

A GROUP OF KIDS THUNDERED down the staircase as Lukas was escorted to his death. One of them squealed in delighted horror as if being chased. They spiraled closer, coming into view, and Lukas and Peter had to squeeze to one side to let them pass.

Peter played the sheriff role and yelled at the kids to slow down, to be careful. They giggled and continued their mad descent. School was out for the day; no more listening to adults.

While Lukas was pressed against the outer railing, he took a moment to consider the temptation. Freedom was just a jump away. A death of his own choosing, one he had considered in the past when moods turned dark.

Peter pulled him along, hand on his elbow, before Lukas could act. He was left admiring that graceful bar of steel, watching the way it curved and curved, always spinning the same amount, never ending. He pictured it corkscrewing through the earth, could sense its vibrations like some cosmic string, like a single strand of DNA at the silo's core with all of life clinging to it.

Thoughts like these swirled as they gained another level on

his death. He watched the welds go by, some of them neater than others. A few were puckered up like scars; several had been polished so smoothly he almost missed them. Each was a signature by its creator: a work of pride here, a rushed job at the end of a long day there, a shadow learning for the first time, a seasoned pro with decades of practice making it look all too easy.

He brushed his shackled hands over the rough paint, the bumps and wrinkles, the missing chips that revealed centuries of layers, of colors that changed with the times or with the supply of dyes or cost of paint. The layers reminded him of the wooden desk he'd stared down at for almost a month. Each little groove marked the passage of time, just as each name scratched into its surface marked a man's mad desire to have *more* of it, to not let that time whisk his poor soul away.

For a long while they marched in silence, a porter passing with a bulky load, a young couple looking guilty. Exiting the server vault had not been the stroll to freedom Lukas had longed for the past weeks. It had been an ambush, a march of shame, faces in doorways, faces on landings, faces on the stairway. Blank, unblinking faces. Faces of friends wondering if he was their enemy.

And maybe he was.

They would say he had broken down and uttered the fateful taboo, but Lukas now knew why people were put out. He was the virus. If he sneezed the wrong words, it would kill everyone he knew. This was the path Juliette had walked, and for the same absence of reason. He believed her, always had, always knew she'd done nothing wrong, but now he *really* understood. She was like him in so many ways. Except he would not survive; he knew that. Bernard had told him so.

They were ten levels up from IT when Peter's radio buzzed

with chatter. He took his hand off Lukas's elbow to turn up the volume, see if it was for him.

"This is Juliette. Who is this?"

That voice.

Lukas's heart leapt up a little before plummeting a very long way. He fixed his gaze on the railing and listened.

Bernard responded, asked for silence. Peter reached for his radio, turned it down but not off. The voices climbed with them, back and forth. Each step and each word ground down on Lukas, chipped away at him. He studied the railing and again considered *true* freedom.

A grab and a short leap up; a long flight.

He could feel himself going through the motions, bending his knees, throwing his feet over.

The voices in the radio argued. They said forbidden things. They were sloppy with secrets, thinking other ears couldn't hear.

Lukas watched his death play out over and over. His fate awaited him over that rail. The visual was so powerful, it wrecked his climbing pace, it affected his legs.

He slowed, Peter slowing with him. Each of them began to falter, to waver in the conviction of their climb as they listened to Juliette and Bernard argue. The strength in Lukas drained away, and he decided not to jump.

Both men were having second thoughts.

79

Silo 17

JULIETTE WOKE UP ON a floor, someone shaking her. A man with a beard. It was Solo, and she was passed out in his room, by his desk.

"We made it," he said, flashing his yellow teeth. He looked better than she remembered him looking. More alive. She felt as though she were dead.

Dead.

"What time is it?" she asked. "What day?"

She tried to sit up. Every muscle felt torn in half, disconnected, floating beneath her skin.

Solo went to the computer and turned on the monitor. "The others are picking out rooms and then going to the upper farms." He turned to look at her. Juliette rubbed her temples. "There are *others,*" he said solemnly, like this was still news.

Juliette nodded. There was only one other that she could think of right then. Dreams came back to her, dreams of Lukas, of all her friends in holding cells, a room of suits being prepped for each of them, no care for whether they cleaned or not. It would be a mass slaughter, a symbol to those who remained.

She thought of all the bodies outside of *this* silo, silo seventeen. It was easy to imagine what came next.

"Friday," Solo said, looking at the computer. "Or Thursday night, depending on how you like it. Two in the morning." He scratched his beard. "Felt like we slept longer than that."

"What day was it yesterday?" She shook her head. That didn't make sense. "What day did I dive down? With the compressor?" Her brain wasn't working.

Solo looked at her like he was having similar thoughts. "The dive was Thursday. Today is tomorrow." He rubbed his head. "Let's start over . . ."

"No time." Juliette groaned and tried to stand up. Solo rushed to her and put his hands under her arms, helped lift her. "Suit Lab," she said. He nodded. She could tell he was exhausted, maybe half as much as she was, but he was still willing to do anything for her. It made her sad, someone being this loyal to her.

She led him down the narrow passage, and the climb up the ladder brought back a legion of aches. Juliette crawled out to the server-room floor; Solo followed up the ladder and helped her to her feet. They made their way to the Suit Lab together.

"I need all the heat tape we've got," she told him, prepping him while he escorted her. She staggered through the servers, bumped into one of them. "It needs to be the kind on the yellow spool, the stuff from Supply. Not the red kind."

He nodded. "The good kind. Like we used on the compressor."

"Right."

They left the server room and shuffled down the hallway. Juliette could hear the kids shouting excitedly around the bend, the patter of their feet. It was a strange sound, like the echoes of ghosts. But something normal. Something normal had returned to silo seventeen.

In the Suit Lab, she got Solo busy with the tape. He stretched out long strips on one of the workbenches, overlapping the edges, using the torch to cauterize and seal the joints.

"At least an inch of overlap," she told him when it looked like he was being shy with the stuff. He nodded. Juliette glanced at her cot and considered collapsing into it. But there was no time. She grabbed the smallest suit in the room, one with a collar she knew might be a tight fit. She remembered the difficult squeeze to get into silo seventeen and didn't want to repeat it.

"I'm not gonna have time to make another switch for the suit, so I won't have a radio." She went through the cleaning outfit, piece by piece, pulling out the parts engineered to fail and hunting through her hauls from Supply for a better version of each. Some she'd have to seal over with the good tape. The suit wouldn't look as neat and tidy as the one Walker had helped arrange, but it would be a world away from what Lukas was getting. She grabbed all the parts she'd spent weeks puzzling over, marveling at the engineering it took to make something weaker than it appeared. She tested a gasket from a pile she wasn't sure about by pinching her fingernails together. The gasket parted easily. She dug for another.

"How long?" Solo asked, noisily stretching another piece of tape out. "You'll be gone a day? A week?"

Juliette looked up from her workbench to the one Solo was working over. She didn't want to tell him she might not make it. This was a dark thought she would keep to herself. "We'll figure out a way to come for you," she said. "First, I have to try to save someone." It felt like a lie. She wanted to tell him she might be gone for good.

"With this?" Solo rustled the blanket of heat tape.

She nodded. "The doors to my home never open," she told him. "Not unless they are sending someone to clean."

Solo nodded. "It was the same here, back when this place was crazy."

Juliette looked up at him, puzzled, and saw that he was smiling. Solo had told a joke. She laughed, even though she didn't feel like it, and then found that it helped.

"We've got six or seven hours until those doors open," she told him. "And when they do, I want to be there."

"And then what?" Solo shut down the torch and inspected his work. He looked up at her.

"Then I want to see how they explain my being alive. I think—" She changed out a seal and flipped the suit around to get to the other sleeve. "I think my friends are fighting on one side of this fence, and the people who sent me here are fighting on the other. Everyone else is watching, the vast majority of my people. They are too scared to take sides, which basically means they've checked out."

She paused while she used one of the small extractors to remove the seal that linked the wrist to the glove. Once she had it out, she reached for a good one.

"You think this will change that? Saving your friend?"

Juliette looked up and studied Solo, who was almost done with the tape.

"Saving my friend is all about saving my friend," she said. "What I think will happen, when all those people on that fence see that a cleaner has come home, I think it'll make them come down on the right side of things, and with that much support, the guns and the fighting are meaningless."

Solo nodded. He began to fold up the blanket without even being asked. This bit of initiative, of knowing what needed to happen next, filled Juliette with hope. Maybe he needed these kids, needed someone to take care of. He seemed to have aged a dozen years already.

"I'll come back for you and the others," she told him.

He dipped his head, kept his eyes on her awhile, his brain seeming to whir. He came to her workbench and set the neatly folded blanket down, patted it twice. A quick smile flashed in his beard, and then he had to turn away, had to scratch his cheek as if he had an itch there.

He was still a teenager like that, Juliette saw. Still ashamed to cry.

Nearly four of Lukas's final hours were burned hiking the heavy gear up to level three. The kids had helped, but she made them stop one level down, worried about the air up top. Solo assisted her in suiting up for the second time in as many days. He studied her somberly.

"You're sure about this?"

She nodded and accepted the blanket of heat tape. Rickson could be heard a level below, commanding one of the boys to settle down.

"Try not to worry," she told him. "What happens, happens. But I have to try."

Solo frowned and scratched his chin. He nodded. "You're used to being around your people," he said. "Probably happier there anyway."

Juliette reached out and squeezed his arm with one of her thick gloves. "It's not that I would be miserable here, it's that I would be miserable knowing I let him go out without trying something."

"And I was just starting to get used to having you here." He turned his head to the side, bent over, and grabbed her helmet from the decking.

Juliette checked her gloves, made sure everything was

wrapped tightly, and looked up. The climb to the top would be brutal with the suit on. She dreaded it. And then navigating the remains of all those people in the sheriff's office and getting through the airlock doors. She accepted the helmet, scared of what she was about to do despite her convictions.

"Thanks for everything," she said. She felt like she was doing more than saying good-bye. She knew there was a very good chance that she was doing willingly what Bernard had attempted so many weeks ago. Her cleaning had been delayed, but now she was going back to it.

Solo nodded and stepped around her to check her back. He patted the Velcro, tugged on her collar. "You're good," he said, his voice cracking.

"You take care of yourself, Solo." She reached out and patted his shoulder. She had decided to carry the helmet one more flight up before putting it on, just to conserve her air.

"Jimmy," he said. "I think I'm going back to being called Jimmy now."

He smiled at Juliette. Shook his head sadly, but smiled.

"I'm not going to be alone anymore," he told her.

80

JULIETTE MADE HER way through the airlock doors and up the ramp, ignoring the dead around her, just focusing on each step, and the hardest part was over. The rest was open space and the scattered remains she wished she could pretend were boulders. Finding her way was easy. She simply turned her back on that crumbling metropolis in the distance, the one she had set off for so very long ago, and began to walk away from it.

As she picked her way across the landscape, the sight of the occasional dead seemed sadder now than during that previous hike, more tragic for having shared their home for a while. Juliette was careful not to disturb them, passed them with the solemnity they deserved, wishing she could do more than feel sorry for them.

Eventually, they thinned, and she and the landscape were left alone. Trudging up that windswept hill, the sound of fine soil peppering her helmet became oddly familiar and strangely comforting. *This* was the world in which she lived, in which they all lived. Through the clear dome of her helmet, she saw it all as clearly as it could be seen. The speeding clouds hung angry and gray; sheets of dust whipped sideways and low to the ground; jagged rocks looked like they'd been sheared from some larger piece, perhaps by the machines that had crafted these hills.

When she reached the crest, she paused to take in the vista around her. The wind was fierce up there, her body exposed. She planted her boots wide so she wouldn't topple over and peered down into the inverted dome before her, at the flattened roof of her home. There was a mix of excitement and dread. The low sun had only barely cleared the distant hills, and the sensor tower below was still in shadow, still in nighttime. She would make it. But before she started down the hill, she found herself gazing, amazed, at the scattering of depressions marching toward the horizon. They were just like the silo schematic, evenly spaced depressions, fifty of them.

And it occurred to her, suddenly and with a violent force, that countless others were going about their days nearby. People *alive.* More silos than just hers and Solo's. Silos unaware, packed with people waking up for work, going to school, maybe even to cleaning.

She turned in place and took it all in, wondering if maybe there was someone else out on that landscape at the exact same time as her wearing a similar suit, a completely different set of fears racing through their mind. If she could have called out to them, she would have. If she could have waved to all the hidden sensors, she would have.

The world took on a different scope, a new scale, from this height. Her life had been cast away weeks ago, likely should have ended — if not on the slope of that hill in front of her home, then surely in the flooded deeps of silo seventeen. But it hadn't ended like that. It would probably end here, instead, this morning with Lukas. They might burn in that airlock together if her hunch was wrong. Or they could lie in the crook of that hill and waste away as a couple, a couple whose kinship had been formed by desperate talks lingering into the night, an intense bond between two stranded souls that was never spoken or admitted to.

Juliette had promised herself never to love in secret again, never to love at all. And somehow this time was worse: she had kept it a secret even from him. Even from *herself.*

Maybe it was the proximity of death talking, the reaper buffeting her clear helmet with sand and toxins. What did any of it matter, seeing how wide and full the world was? Her silo would probably go on. Other silos surely would.

A mighty gust of wind struck her, nearly ripping the folded blanket out of her hands. Juliette steadied herself, gathered her wits, and began the much easier descent toward her home. She ducked down below the crest with its sobering views and saddening heights, out of the harsh and caustic winds. She followed that crook where two hills met, winding her way toward the sad sight of a couple buried in plain view, who marked her fateful, desperate, and weary way home.

She arrived at the ramp early. There was no one on the landscape, the sun still hidden behind the hills. As she hurried down the slope, she wondered what anyone would think if they saw her on the sensors, stumbling toward the silo.

At the bottom of the ramp, she stood close to the heavy steel doors and waited. She checked the heat-tape blanket, ran through the procedure in her mind. Every scenario had been thought of during her climb, in her mad dreams, or during the walk through the wild outside. This would work, she told herself. The mechanics were sound. The only reason no one survived a cleaning was because they never had help; they couldn't bring tools or resources. But she had.

Time seemed to pass not at all. It was like her delicate and precious watch when she forgot to wind it. The trapped soil along the edge of the ramp shifted about impatiently with her, and Juliette wondered if maybe the cleaning had been called off, if she would die alone. That would be better, she told herself. She took a deep breath, wishing she had brought more air, enough for a return trip, just in case. But she had been too worried about the cleaning actually happening to consider that it might not.

After a long wait, her nerves swelling and heart racing, she heard a noise inside, a metallic scraping of gears.

Juliette tensed, her arms rippling with chills, her throat constricting. This was it. She shifted in place, listening to the great grind of those heavy doors as they prepared to disgorge poor Lukas. She unfolded part of the heat blanket and waited. It would all go so quickly. She knew. But she would be in control. No one could come in and stop her.

With a terrible screech, the doors to silo eighteen parted, and a hiss of argon blasted out at her. Juliette leaned into it. The fog consumed her. She pushed blindly forward, groping ahead of herself, the blanket flapping noisily against her chest. She expected to run into him, to find herself wrestling a startled and frightened man, had prepared herself to hold him down, get him wrapped up tightly in the blanket—

But there was no one in the doorway, no body struggling to get out, to get away from the coming purge of flames.

Juliette practically fell into the airlock; her body expected resistance like a boot at the top of a darkened stairway and found empty space instead.

As the argon cleared and the door began to grind shut, she had a brief hope, a tiny fantasy, that there was no cleaning. That the doors had simply been opened for her, welcoming her back. Maybe someone had seen her on the hillside and had taken a chance, had forgiven her, and all would be okay . . .

But as soon as she could see through the billowing gas, she

saw that this was not the case. A man in a cleaning suit was kneeling in the center of the airlock, hands on his thighs, facing the inner door.

Lukas.

Juliette raced to him as a halo of light bloomed in the room, the fire nozzles spitting on and reflecting off the shimmering plastic. The door thunked shut behind her, locking them both inside.

Juliette shook the blanket loose and shuffled around so he could see her, so he would know he wasn't alone.

The suit couldn't hide the shock. Lukas startled, his arms leaping up in alarm, even as the flames began to lance out.

She nodded, knowing he could see her through her clear dome, even if she couldn't see him. With a sweeping twirl she had practiced in her mind a thousand times, she spread the blanket over his head and knelt down swiftly, covering herself as well.

It was dark under the heat tape. The temperature outside was rising. She tried to shout to Lukas that it was going to be okay, but her voice sounded muffled even inside her own helmet. Tucking the edges of the blanket down beneath her knees and feet, she wiggled until it was tightly pinned. She reached forward and tried to tuck the material under him as well, making sure his back was fully protected.

Lukas seemed to know what she was doing. His gloved hands fell to her arms and rested there. She could feel how still he was, how calm. She couldn't believe he was going to wait, had chosen to burn rather than clean. She couldn't remember anyone ever making that choice. This worried her as they huddled together in the darkness, everything growing warm.

The flames licked against the heat tape, striking the blanket with enough force to be felt, like a buffeting wind. The temperature shot up, sweat leaping out on her lip and forehead, even with all the superior lining of her suit. The blanket wouldn't be enough. It wouldn't keep Lukas alive in his suit. The fear in her heart was only for him, even as her skin began to heat up.

Her panic seemed to leach into him, or maybe he was feeling the burns even worse. His hands trembled against her. And then she literally felt him go mad, felt him change his mind, begin to burn, *something*.

Lukas pushed her away from himself. Bright light entered their protective dome as he began to crawl out from under it, kicking away.

Juliette screamed for him to stop. She scrambled after him, clutching his arm, his leg, his boot, but he kicked out at her, beat her with his fists, frantically tried to get away.

The blanket fell off her head, and the light nearly blinded her. She felt the intense heat, could hear her dome pop and make noises, saw the clear bubble dip in above her and warp. She couldn't see Lukas, couldn't feel him, just saw blinding light and felt searing heat, scorching her wherever her suit crinkled against her body. She screamed in pain and yanked the blanket back over her head, covering the clear plastic.

And the flames raged on.

She couldn't feel him. Couldn't see him. There would be no way to find him. A thousand burns erupted across her body like so many knives gouging her flesh. Juliette sat alone under that thin film of protection, burning up, enduring the raging flames, and wept hot tears. Her body convulsed with sobs and anger, cursing the fire, the pain, the silo, the entire world.

Until eventually—she had no more tears and the fuel ran its course. The boiling temperature dropped to a mere scalding, and Juliette could safely shrug off the steaming blanket. Her skin felt as if it were on fire. It burned wherever it touched the interior of her suit. She looked for Lukas and found she didn't have to look far.

He was lying against the door, his suit charred and flaking in the few places it remained intact. His helmet was still in place, saving her the horror of seeing his young face, but it had melted and warped far worse than hers. She crawled closer, aware that the door behind her was opening, that they were coming for her, that it was all over. She had failed.

Juliette whimpered when she saw the places his body had been exposed, the suit and charcoal liners burned away. There was his arm, charred black. His stomach, oddly distended. His tiny hands, so small and thin and burned to a—

No.

She didn't understand. She wept anew. She threw her gloved and steaming hands against her bubbled dome and cried out in shock, in a mix of anger and blessed relief.

This was not Lukas dead before her.

This was a man who deserved none of her tears.

81

Silo 18

AWARENESS, LIKE SPORADIC JOLTS of pain from her burns, came and went.

Juliette remembered a billowing fog, boots stomping all around her, lying on her side in the oven of an airlock. She watched the way the world warped out of shape as her helmet, a viscous thing, continued to sag toward her, melting. A bright silver star hovered in her vision, waving as it settled beyond her dome. Peter Billings peered through her helmet at her, shook her scalded shoulders, cried out to the people marching around, telling them to help.

They lifted her up and out of that steaming place, sweat dripping from faces, a melted suit cut from her body.

Juliette floated through her old office like a ghost. Flat on her back, the squeal of a fussy wheel below her, past the rows and rows of steel bars, an empty bench in an empty cell.

They carried her in circles.

Down.

She woke to the beeping of her heart, these machines checking in on her, a man dressed like her father.

He was the first to notice that she was awake. His eyebrows lifted, a smile, a nod to someone over her shoulder.

And Lukas was there, his face — so familiar, so strange — was in her blurry vision. She felt his hand in hers. She knew that hand had been there awhile, that he had been there awhile. He was crying and laughing, brushing her cheek. Jules wanted to know what was so funny. What was so sad. He just shook his head as she drifted back to sleep.

It wasn't just that the burns were bad; it was that they were everywhere.

The days of recovery were spent sliding in and out of pain-killer fogs.

Every time she saw Lukas, she apologized. Everyone was making a fuss. Peter came. There were piles of notes from down deep, but nobody was allowed up. Nobody else could see her but the man dressed like her father and women who reminded her of her mother.

Her head cleared quickly once they let it.

Juliette came out of what felt like a deep dream, weeks of haze, nightmares of drowning and burning, of being outside, of dozens of silos just like hers. The drugs had kept the pain at bay — but had dulled her consciousness, too. She didn't mind the stings and aches if it meant winning back her mind. It was an easy trade.

"Hey."

She flopped her head to the side — and Lukas was there. Was he ever not? A blanket fell from his chest as he leaned forward, held her hand. He smiled.

"You're looking better."

Juliette licked her lips. Her mouth was dry.

"Where am I?"

"The infirmary on thirty-three. Just take it easy. Do you want me to get you anything?"

She shook her head. It felt amazing to be able to move, to respond to words. She tried to squeeze his hand.

"I'm sore," she said weakly.

Lukas laughed. He looked relieved to hear this. "I bet."

She blinked and looked at him. "There's an infirmary on thirty-three?" His words were on a delay.

He nodded gravely. "I'm sorry, but it's the best in the silo. And we could keep you safe. But forget that. Rest. I'll go grab the nurse."

He stood, a thick book spilling from his lap and tumbling into the chair, burying itself in the blanket and pillows.

"Do you think you can eat?"

She nodded, turned her head back to face the ceiling and the bright lights, everything coming back to her, memories popping up like the tingle of pain on her skin.

She read folded notes for days and cried. Lukas sat by her side, collecting the ones that spilled to the floor like paper planes tossed from landings. He apologized over and over, blubbering like he was the one who'd done it. Juliette read all of them a dozen times, trying to keep straight who was gone and who was still signing their name. She couldn't believe the terrible news about Knox. Some things seemed immutable, like the great stairway. She wept for him and for Marck, wanted desperately to see Shirly, was told that she couldn't.

Ghosts visited her when the lights were out. Juliette would wake up, eyes crusted over, pillow wet, Lukas rubbing her forehead and telling her it would be okay.

Peter came often. Juliette thanked him over and over. It was all Peter, all Peter. He had made the choice. Lukas told her of the stairway, his march to cleaning, hearing her voice on Peter's radio, the implications of her being alive.

Peter had taken the risk, had listened. That had led to him and Lukas talking. Lukas had said forbidden things, was in no danger of being sent anyplace worse, said something that confused her about being a bad virus, a catching cold. The radio barked with reports from Mechanical of people surrendering. Bernard sentenced them to death anyway.

And Peter had a decision to make. Was he the final law, or did he owe something to those who put him in place? Did he do what was right or what was expected of him? It was so easy to do the latter, but Peter Billings was a good man.

Lukas told him so on that stairwell. He told him that this was where they'd been put by fate, but what they did going forward defined them. That was who they were.

He told Peter that Bernard had killed a man. That he had proof. Lukas had done nothing to deserve this.

Peter pointed out that every ounce of IT security was a hundred levels away. There was only one gun up top. Only one law.

His.

82

Weeks Later
Silo 18

THE THREE OF THEM sat around the conference table, Juliette adjusting the gauze bandage on her hand to cover the raised lace of scar tissue peeking out. The overalls they'd given her were loose to minimize the pain, but the undershirt itched everywhere it touched. She sat in one of the plush chairs and rolled back and forth with the push of her toes, impatient, ready to get out of there. But Lukas and Peter had things to discuss. They had escorted her this close to the exit, this close to the great stairwell, only to sit her down in that room. To get some *privacy,* they had said. The looks on their faces made her nervous.

Nobody said anything for a while. Peter used the excuse of sending a tech for some water, but when the pitcher came and the glasses were filled, nobody reached for a drink. Lukas and Peter exchanged nervous glances. Juliette grew tired of waiting.

"What is it?" she asked. "Can I go? I feel like you've been delaying this for days." She glanced at her watch, wiggled her arm so it would fall from the bandage on her wrist and she could see the tiny face. She stared across the table at Lukas and had to laugh at the worry on his face. "Are you trying to keep me here forever? Because I told everyone in the deep that I'd be seeing them tonight."

Lukas turned to Peter.

"C'mon, guys. Spit it out. What's troubling you? The doc said I was fine for the trip down and I told you I'd check in with Marsh and Hank if I had any problems. I'm gonna be late enough as it is if I don't get a move on."

"Okay," Lukas said, letting out a sigh. It was as though he'd given up on Peter being the one. "It's been a few weeks—"

"And you two've made it feel like months." She twisted the dial on the side of her watch, an ancient tic returning like it had never left.

"It's just that"—Lukas coughed into his fist, clearing his throat—"we couldn't give you *all* the notes that were sent to you." He frowned at her, looked guilty.

Juliette's heart dropped. She sagged forward, waiting for it. More names would be coming to move from one sad list to another—

Lukas held up his palms. "Nothing like that," he said quickly, recognizing the worry on her face. "God, sorry, nothing like that—"

"*Good* news," Peter said. "Congratulatory notes."

Lukas shot him a look that told Juliette she might think otherwise.

"Well . . . it is *news*." He looked across the table at her. His hands were folded in front of him, resting on the marred wood, just like hers. It felt as though they might both move them several inches until they met, until fingers interlocked. It would be so natural after weeks of practice. But that was something worried friends did in hospitals, right? Juliette pondered this while Lukas and Peter went on about elections.

"Wait. What?" She blinked and looked up from his hands, the last part coming back to her.

"It was the *timing*," Lukas explained.

"You were all anyone was talking about," Peter said.

"Go back," she said. "*What* did you say?"

Lukas took a deep breath. "Bernard was running unopposed. When we sent him out to cleaning, the election was called off. But then news got around about your miraculous return, and people showed up to vote anyway—"

"A *lot* of people," Peter added.

Lukas nodded. "It was quite a turnout. More than half the silo."

"Yeah, but ... *mayor?*" She laughed and looked around the scratched conference table, bare except for the untouched glasses of water. "Isn't there something I need to sign? Some official way to turn this nonsense down?"

The two men exchanged glances.

"That's sorta the thing," Peter said.

Lukas shook his head. "I *told* you—"

"We were hoping you'd accept."

"Me? *Mayor?*" Juliette crossed her arms and sat back, painfully, against the chair. She laughed. "You've gotta be kidding. I wouldn't know the first thing about—"

"You wouldn't have to," Peter said, leaning forward. "You have an office, you shake some hands, sign some things, make people feel better—"

Lukas tapped him on the arm and shook his head. Juliette felt a flush of heat across her skin, which just made her scars and wounds itch more.

"Here's the thing," Lukas said as Peter sat back in his chair. "We *need* you. There's a power vacuum at the top. Peter's been in his post longer than anyone, and you know how long that's been."

She was listening.

"Remember our conversations all those nights? Remember you telling me what that other silo was like? Do you understand how close to that we got?"

She chewed her lip, reached for one of the glasses, and took a long drink of water. Peering over the lip of the glass, she waited for him to continue.

"We have a chance, Jules. To hold this place together. To put it *back* to—"

She set the glass down and lifted her palm for him to stop.

"If we were to do this," she told them coolly, looking from one of their expectant faces to the other. "*If* we do it, we do it my way."

Peter frowned.

"No more lying," she said. "We give truth a chance."

Lukas laughed nervously. Peter shook his head.

"Now, listen to me," she said. "This isn't crazy. It's not the first time I've thought this through. Hell, I've had weeks of nothing *but* thinking."

"The truth?" Peter asked.

She nodded. "I know what you two are thinking. You think we need lies, fear—"

Peter nodded.

"But what could we invent that's scarier than what's *really out there?*" She pointed toward the roof and waited for that to sink in. "When these places were built, the idea was that we were all in this together. Together but separate, ignorant of one another, so we didn't infect the others if one of us got sick. But I don't *want* to play for that team. I don't agree with their cause. I refuse."

Lukas tilted his head. "Yeah, but—"

"So it's us against them. And not the people in the silos, not the people working day-to-day who don't know, but those at the top who *do.* Silo eighteen will be different. Full of knowledge, of *purpose.* Think about it. Instead of manipulating people, why not *empower* them? Let them know what we're up against. And have *that* drive our collective will."

Lukas raised his eyebrows. Peter ran his hands up through his hair.

"You guys should think about it." She pushed herself away from the table. "Take your time. I'm going to go see my family and friends. But either I'm in, or I'll be working against you. I'll be spreading the truth one way or the other."

She smiled at Lukas. It was a dare, but he would know she wasn't joking.

Peter stood and showed her his palms. "Can we at least agree not to do anything rash until we meet again?"

Juliette crossed her arms. She dipped her chin.

"Good," Peter said, letting out his breath and dropping his arms.

She turned to Lukas. He was studying her, his lips pursed, and she could tell he knew. There was only one way this was going forward, and it scared the hell out of him.

Peter turned and opened the door. He looked back at Lukas.

"Can you give us a second?" Lukas asked, standing up and walking toward the door.

Peter nodded. He turned and shook Juliette's hand as she thanked him for the millionth time. He checked his star, which hung askew on his chest, and then left the conference room.

Lukas crossed out of sight of the window, grabbed Juliette's hand, and pulled her toward the door.

"Are you kidding me?" she asked. "Did you really think I would just accept that job and—?"

Lukas pressed his palm against the door and forced it shut. Juliette faced him, confused, then felt his arms slide gently around her waist, mindful of her wounds.

"You were right," he whispered. He leaned close, put his head by her shoulder. "I'm stalling. I don't want you to go."

His breath was warm against her neck. Juliette relaxed. She forgot what she was about to say. She wrapped an arm around his back, held his neck with her other hand. "It's okay," she said, relieved to hear him say it, to finally admit it. And she could feel him trembling, could hear his broken and stuttered exhalations.

"It's okay," she whispered again, pressing her cheek against his, trying to comfort him. "I'm not going anywhere for good—"

Lukas pulled away to look at her. She felt him searching her face, tears welling up in his eyes. His body had started shaking. She could feel it in his arms, his back.

And then she realized, as he pulled her close and pressed his lips against hers, that it wasn't fear or panic she was sensing in him. It was *nerves.*

She whimpered into their kiss, the rush to her head better than the doctor's drugs. It washed away any pain caused by his hands clutching her back. She couldn't remember the last time she'd felt lips move against her own. She kissed him back, and it was over too soon. He stepped away and held her hands, glanced nervously at the window.

"It's a . . . uh . . ."

"That was nice," she told him, squeezing his hands.

"We should probably . . ." He jerked his chin toward the door.

Juliette smiled. "Yeah. Probably so."

He walked her through the entrance hall of IT and to the landing. A tech was waiting with her shoulder bag. Juliette saw that Lukas had padded the strap with rags, worried about her wounds.

"And you're sure you don't need an escort?"

"I'll be fine," she said, tucking her hair behind her ears. She shrugged the bag higher up her neck. "I'll see you in a week or so."

"You can radio me," he told her.

Juliette laughed. "I know."

She grabbed his hand and gave it a squeeze, then turned to the great stairwell. Someone in the passing crowd nodded at her. She was sure she didn't know him but nodded back. Other chins were turning to follow her. She walked past them and grabbed that great curved bar of steel that wound its way through the heart of things, that held those pouting and worn treads together as life after life was ground away on them. And Juliette lifted her boot to that first step on a journey far too long in coming—

"Hey!"

Lukas called after her. He ran across the landing, his brows lowered in confusion. "I thought you were heading *down,* going to see your friends."

Juliette smiled at him. A porter passed by, loaded down with his burdens. Juliette thought of how many of her own had recently slipped away.

"Family first," she told Lukas. She glanced up that great shaft in the center of the humming silo and lifted her boot to the next tread. "I've got to go see my father first."

Q&A WITH AUTHOR HUGH HOWEY

Q: Is this really the end?!
A: To quote every one of my favorite kung-fu movies: Every end is a new beginning. There are many more stories to tell. Not just the rest of silo 18's story, but the future of silo 17, which is about to change. And then there are all the other silos crowding in around them. You won't believe what's going on in silo 40!

Q: Why no elevator?
A: The same reason communication is expensive. Those in power fear our ability to come together and share ideas, thoughts, and dreams.

Also: The Union of Amalgamated Porters.

Q: Why do so many people die in your books?
A: To make room for all the new ones!

Q: Can I tell you how awesome I think these books are?
A: Why, yes, you can! Even better if you tell others or write a review. I read every single review on Amazon, even though some of them upset my tummy. If you want to help other readers discover the stories you love, take a few minutes and craft a review.

Do it for all the books you enjoy. As writers, our souls subsist on your feedback. It means a lot to us!

Q: When will this book become a movie?!
A: What if we do an epic TV show instead . . . ?

Q: What's next?
A: I'm working on a sequel to *Sand* right now. If you haven't read that one, it's about a family of sand divers who live in that narrow and inhospitable strip of earth between the Sand Mountains and the constant warring in No Man's Land. It is a truly dreadful place. Silo 17 would be their Shangri-la. Anyone who's ever tried to leave Sand Land has either perished or has never been heard from again.

That is, until a young girl comes back from that elsewhere with stories from the other side . . .

Q: How can I keep up with your writing?
A: That's an awfully convenient question! Thanks for asking.
You can follow me on Twitter: @hughhowey
You can visit my website regularly: hughhowey.com
And you can e-mail me: hughhowey@gmail.com

Q: Tell the truth: Did you come up with all these questions yourself?
A: Yes.

EPILOGUE

Silo 17

"THIRTY-TWO!"

Elise danced up the steps of the down deep, her breath trailing in long curls of steam behind her, the clumsy feet of youth making a racket with their heavy boots on the wet steel.

"Thirty-two steps, Mr. Solo!"

She made it back up to the landing, tripped over the last step, and caught herself on her hands and knees. Elise stayed there a minute, head down, probably deciding if she would cry or be okay.

Solo waited for her to cry.

Instead, she looked up at him, a wide smile telling him she was fine. There was a gap in that smile where a loose tooth had come out and not yet been replaced.

"It's going *down*," she said. She wiped her hands on her new overalls and ran over to him. "The water's going down!"

Solo grunted as she threw herself into his hip and hugged his waist. He draped an arm across her back while she squeezed him.

"Everything's gonna be great!"

Solo held the railing with one hand and looked down past the rust-colored stain of old blood beneath his feet, looked past that memory and into the receding waters far below. He reached for the radio on his hip. Juliette would be the most excited to know.

"I think you're right," he told little Elise, pulling his radio free. "I think everything's gonna be just fine . . ."

A HISTORY OF THE DARKEST YARNS

IS THE WORLD a good place or not? Is it safe or is it dangerous? Beyond the horizon, are there more wonders or more terrors?

These questions haunt us, whether we're aware of them or not. They determine whether we love to travel to foreign lands, or if we feel better staying home. They influence how we feel about immigration, how we feel about other countries, other states, even other neighborhoods. Some of us dread the future, while for others it can't get here soon enough. Some people long for the days of the past, while others see nothing but progress.

Many of us vacillate between the two extremes, hope and dread flowing and ebbing like the tide. Some days we want to venture forth, other days we want to stay in bed with the covers over our heads. We have at times felt everything in between.

I'll never forget the first time I sailed to Cuba, back when I was twenty-five. I was captaining a steel trawler for an Australian client who was sailing to Hong Kong. A dozen miles off the north coast of Cuba, we started picking up radar contacts of Cuban ships. The VHF squawked with Spanish chatter. We were approaching Havana with little knowledge of what would greet us there.

My whole life up to that point had been one of anti-Cuban propaganda. Like the most effective propaganda, the first germs were based on slivers of truth. There was indeed a history of conflict between our two countries. Here was the site of perhaps our nearest brush with nuclear war, and communists were the enemy in all my favorite childhood action films. These people wanted me dead. I fully expected warning shots to be fired across our bow. I expected hostility. This journey was surely a mistake.

Cuba is a complex place, an island of paradoxes, but one thing it most certainly was not was dangerous. Nor was it a place where Americans were unwelcome or loathed. We were greeted with open arms everywhere we went. My months spent in Cuba over the years have been an absolute delight. My childhood perception of Cuba could have kept me from visiting. Fortunately, I made the decision to go see for myself.

This idea of needing to see with my own eyes was a foundational idea for *Wool* and the books to follow. The wallscreens are our televisions, our web browsers, our search engines, our newspapers, the local news, our cellphones. We are bombarded constantly by talking heads telling us what the world is like. They say it's mostly car wrecks, traffic jams, murders, war, hurricanes, and things that might kill your children, which we'll tell you about at eleven.

The temptation might be to blame the media, but we're the same people who slow down traffic even when the accident is on the other side of the median. We have to look. We are captivated by the awful. We want to know if it's something we should be concerned about. It makes perfect sense: we are descendants of a million generations of humans, apes, shrews, and lizards who were better safe than sorry. In nature, optimists taste great.

The modern challenge has been to overcome our base instincts and look at the world with rational eyes. Or, even more challenging, dare to look with hope.

As I write this, I'm sitting in Portugal while the United States enacts travel restrictions and quarantines. Spain, our neighbor on all sides, is shutting down. Italy is closed for business. The world is dealing with a pandemic that has already claimed more lives than the morning of September 11. Fear, needless to say, is rampant.

One would be crazy to have hope in these times, and yet some of us do. Some of us see countries rallying together to battle this disease. There are nurses and doctors everywhere being superheroes. There are Italians singing from their balconies to keep each other company and to keep each other entertained. Zion Williamson, a nineteen-year-old NBA rookie, is pledging to cover the lost wages of those who work in his arena as professional sports shut down. And all these closings are signs that we have the courage to win this fight. The actions being taken are ones of hope. Already in China, Singapore, and South Korea, we can see signs that this hope is not without reason.

For me, *Wool* has never been a story about the end of humanity. It's been a story about humanity prevailing against all odds. And the heroes of this story are those who go against the grain of pessimism, fear, doubt, and despair. The heroes are Allison, who will not trust a single screen to tell her what's out there. And Juliette, who believes that anything broken can be repaired.

The first self-published edition of *Wool* was dedicated: *For Those Who Dare to Hope.* To this day, I commonly sign these books with my name and a simple *Dare to hope!* as a reminder of what the story is really about. I'm not always as brave as I'd like to be. I falter and fail and give in to the screens in my life. And yet, sailing across vast oceans and into ports unknown taught me something vital: there is nothing out there as dark as our doubts, nor as dangerous as our inaction. Go out. See for yourselves. And if what you find there is broken, know that together we can fix it.

. . .

Despite all the reasons we should have hope, it seems we are instead obsessed with stories about the end times. Post-apocalyptic tales and disaster flicks dominate our popular culture.

At the time I wrote *Wool,* Hollywood was inundating us with stories about floods, monster waves, and tornadoes full of sharks. We got earthquakes and asteroids destroying the Earth, snakes hijacking planes, aliens raining hell down upon us, and zombies doing zombie things. The Empire State Building has been particularly accosted over the years, going down to UFO strikes and meteors and volcanoes and Superman. It was a terrible time to be planet Earth or a very tall building.

In this climate, *Wool* became kind of a big deal. The book went to auction at publishing houses and got snapped up by Ridley Scott for a film adaptation. I landed a literary agent (Kristin Nelson, the best in the business), and we started doing deals around the world. I was asked to do interviews and give talks all over the place, and foreign publishers were flying me to far-flung locales to sign books and do yet more interviews and signings.

Everywhere I went on book tour, I kept getting the same questions from fans and media alike: Why are we obsessed with these stories? What is up with this fad? And when will it end?

I didn't have a good answer. But as it kept coming up over and over, time and time again, I realized I needed to have something decent to say. So I mulled it over. I wondered why I wanted to tell a story about the end of times. What did that say about me? Or the fact that I love reading stories like this and watching movies where the Empire State Building fares poorly. I'm a happy, optimistic guy. What gives? What was so unique about the world we were living in that this trend emerged and came to dominate popular culture?

This last question about the uniqueness of our place and

time helped unlock the answer. I've learned over the years to reject any question that gives preeminence to a particular place or time. This bias of our centrality almost always leads us astray. It took forever to accept that the Earth is not the center of the universe, or that our solar system is one of many, or that those fuzzy spots among the stars are entire other galaxies, or that our universe might be part of a multi-verse, or that it's all a simulation with some really crappy coders.

We have an even stronger bias toward the time we live in. Part of this is egocentrism, but it's mostly that we know far more about present events than we do a past that we barely study. The pace of innovation, for instance, feels like it's moving at its swiftest pace ever, but there is a good argument to be made that the world was changing more rapidly a century ago than it is today. Cries of record partisanship and nastiness in politics ignore the fact that politicians once shot each other in the streets and had fist fights in Congress.

Every generation thinks it lives in unique times. This bias is almost always wrong.

And yet the explosion in popularity of post-apocalyptic fiction was difficult to deny and required some sort of explanation. It really was everywhere, from *The Hunger Games* and *The Maze Runner* to *World War Z* and *Armageddon*. How could I argue that no time in history was all that unique or special under the onslaught of so many stories in which our world ends?

I was thinking about this during the West Coast swing of my big *Wool* book tour. Flying over the Rockies, I looked out the window at the rough terrain and thought about the unbelievable challenges that American settlers faced. That was when I realized that westerns had once been a cultural obsession similar to post-apocalyptic fiction. In the first half of the twentieth century, pulp westerns were being published at a frenzied clip, and western films were far more numerous than the dystopian and apocalyptic fare of the twenty-first century. From 1930 to 1954, nearly three thousand western films were made!

Suddenly, both of these cultural obsessions made perfect sense. Westerns are also stories about survival along the edges of civilization. They are stories about barely getting by in new lands where laws are tenuous, strangers are dangerous, and harsh conditions bring out the best in our heroes and the worst in everyone else.

It occurred to me in that airplane that there might be something bigger here, something old and universal that provides an insight into the human condition. Did the pattern go back further than westerns?

As someone who used to live on a sailboat in my twenties, I'd long been fond of lost-at-sea stories. There were a lot in my local library to choose from, even among the classics. Because when humans began to travel across the ocean, we became obsessed with tales of piracy, sunken treasure, shipwrecks, uncharted and deserted islands, and all that can go wrong at sea. The ocean was the great frontier at the time. It was a place where civilization ended and the wilds began.

What about before that? Of course! It was the spooky tales of being lost in the woods, the "Hansel and Gretel" stories, tales of witches and demons, the underworld, the wrath of gods. It was Dante's *Inferno, Gulliver's Travels, The Odyssey, Sir Gawain and the Green Knight.*

Throughout human history, we have told stories as much for warning as for entertainment. Don't stray too far from safety because bad things might happen. An expression of our internal fears and external exhortations, the disaster story became a fixture. There is reason to suspect that the origin of storytelling lies here. Our lives have always felt tenuous. We depend on each other and on our technology. But we also rely on our cleverness and guile. Disaster stories are horrors wherein we are separated from the former, but also fantasies where we are rescued by the latter. We wonder if we were left alone in the wilderness with nothing more than our courage and our imaginations, would we survive? It's almost like we would really enjoy a TV show about being naked and afraid in the middle of nowhere, or a reality show where strangers are dropped on a deserted island and forced to knock each other off one by one.

If we've always been obsessed with wilderness and survival stories, why have we moved on to world-ending tales and post-apocalyptic fiction?

I believe it's because we no longer have a wilderness on Earth to explore and fear. It's all been mapped and photographed from orbit. The exceptions to this prove the rule: *Lost* with its island that is magically uncharted. *The Martian,* where if we can't have a wilderness on this planet we can always head next door. These days, when we want to tell a wilderness story, we have to look beyond horizons of distance and think about horizons of time. We need to imagine a future where we might be exploring other worlds, or a future where our world returns to the wilderness that we fear.

Seen in this light, the popularity of apocalyptic fiction makes perfect sense. We are simply removing the social bonds and the tools that we rely upon and asking how we would fare with our wits alone. It's a wonderful problem to explore, and one that has served us as a species for thousands and thousands of years. It keeps us sharp, alert, and mentally trained. Our oldest and fondest stories are of just this sort.

The Odyssey tells a story of the wilderness, the sea, wrathful gods, all our physical and emotional worlds ending, and how our hero can somehow survive and prevail in the end. It's a story as old as time. The reason this story resonates with us today, even though it was written millennia ago and was told in a different language by people from a different culture, is because no era and no people are all that unique. Which is a marvelous thing.

It's a lesson I learned in my own Odyssean travels as I sailed around the world. I met people on hundreds of islands, and I found far more in common than unique among us. We are not special . . . which *is* special. We have the same fears, the same hopes, the same love of overcoming odds, the same addiction to our fellow man and our tools, such that the loss of them fills us with the greatest of dreads. That's what makes us human. That's our story. And it's a story as old as time.

So it's not surprising that I wrote a story about humanity on the precipice. These stories have always been popular. What is very surprising is that it ever became the novel you currently hold in your hands. The simple truth is this book should not exist. In fact, when I see a copy, I marvel at how it got there.

This disbelief does not come from the twenty years I tried in vain to write my first novel, giving up after a few chapters every single time. Nor does it come from the fact that I was in my thirties, working in a bookshop in North Carolina, writing in my spare time, self-publishing my science fiction, when I came up with the story.

No, the reason this book should not exist is that I never even considered it a novel.

Which is strange, because everything is potentially a novel for me. Every news story, every wacky idea, every morning dream. I have more book ideas than I know what to do with. At any one time, at least a dozen fully formed novels are tossing around in my head like a pack of caffeinated Jack Russell terriers.

But this was not one of those ideas. When I sat down to write

Wool, I was already in the end stages of writing my next novel, which would've been my sixth published work. *Wool* was just an idea for a short story. It was a bit of therapy following the death of my beloved dog, Jolie. I wanted to write something dark; I wanted to wallow in my misery; I wanted to craft a story where the ending was obviously going to be a good and happy one, but in the twist of all twists during a twist-happy time in our culture, the twist in this twisted tale was that there was no twist after all.

Things are bad. Good people die. The end.

I'll never forget the feeling I had when the first line came to me. It just felt right. It captured my mood. I dashed it off to myself in an e-mail on my lunch break at work: *The children were playing while Holston climbed to his death.* Naivete and gaiety as a suicide shuffles by. The beginning of life and the end of life. Possibility and the collapse of wave functions. Kids skipping rope while a man ponders graver uses.

I've always been a positive guy. Even in the wake of that death (which only non–dog owners will dismiss as simply being the loss of a pet), I was keeping my chin up and knew that life would go on and continue to be amazing. But the absence of my best friend was palpable. I felt her missing every time I came home. There was a pocket of air just her size at my feet while I wrote. The fact that I would never get her back tormented me. That was the origin of this story. It was also its conclusion.

Or so I thought.

A lesson on the origins of storytelling would follow, a lesson that I was slow to realize and appreciate. I used to think of storytellers as authors absconded away in remote cabins, pecking out stories in solitude, which they then delivered to readers bound and on a platter. The truth is that storytelling has almost always been an oral tradition. There is supposed to be a live audience, and the energy of that audience influences the storytelling and even the story itself.

Heresy! many authors cry. *The art must stand alone! No one may influence the endeavor!*

Which makes me wonder what kind of awful art those people create. Art is influence, and it works both ways. The audience gasps, and the storyteller knows they struck the right note. They laugh, and the storyteller knows their wit landed a blow. They snooze, and the storyteller recalibrates. It is the joy of theater and live music that the audience plays a role in the energy received, absorbed, augmented, transmitted, transmogrified. Any live performer will tell you this. Any live audience will agree.

Wool was originally the first seven chapters of the book you hold in your hand. Technically it was a novelette, too long to be a short story and too short to be a novella. It was nothing, really. Some self-therapy. Until I discovered I was not alone.

I tossed the story online and priced it at 99 cents, the lowest option available at the time. I would have gladly made it free if I could have. Once I published it, I forgot about it. I went back to my novel. I did zero promotion. The cover art was something I threw together in five minutes, though I would not blame anyone for assuming it was more like three.

Within weeks, I noticed something strange was happening. My online sales dashboard, which usually ticked up one or five sales a day of my various novels (enough to buy a coffee and keep the stories coming), had suddenly gone up a dozen. The next day, a dozen more. Then by the dozens each day.

A thousand copies of the original *Wool* sold in a single month, a number that was absolutely astonishing to me (and to anyone who knows anything about how books are meant to be sold). The next month, 3,000 copies flew off virtual shelves. I was making roughly 35 cents for every copy sold, so this was real money to a guy who made $300 a week before taxes shelving other people's books (yeah, seriously).

I didn't understand what was happening. As far as I could tell, no one I knew was talking about the story. It wasn't my friends and family. I certainly wasn't telling anyone about it. And then I noticed the reviews. Oh my god the reviews.

They were almost all five stars, and they all had the same complaint: *Where was the rest? Where could they find more?*

There was no more. Spoiler alert: Holston is dead! Allison is dead! There is no more story to tell. My dog died and I was broken inside and I needed to put myself back together one sentence at a time. Little did I know that my therapy was really a group session. Something about this world I had created and these emotions I was venting had resonated with a random reader, who had told someone else, who had written a review, who had accosted one more person to read this damn thing, it's only 99 cents, you can finish it on your lunch break, and so on.

Yes, the story has twists that keep most readers second-guessing themselves. Yes, in a world of twist endings the idea of playing it straight caught most people off-guard. (I spoil the story in the first sentence, let's remember!) Yes, there is nothing more to tell. But readers asked me to tell it to them anyway.

It was October of 2011. I had a novel outlined for the upcoming NaNoWriMo, an annual tradition that involves writing a fifty-thousand-word novel in a single month. I'd participated in the last few of these, writing novels like *Molly Fyde and the Land of Light, Half Way Home,* and *The Hurricane.* That year, I was going to write the fourth and final Molly Fyde novel. But as sales clicked past 1,000 on October 31, I decided to heed the reviewers clamoring for more. I dashed together a hasty outline. I started with the few named characters who were still alive (Marnes and Jahns), but I had in mind a new character, one who lived deep down inside me, who had always been there, who could fix even the most broken of things, and who would rise up with hope and audacity and make things right in my world and hers.

Juliette was born that month. Out of the ashes of my grief, formed by an interaction with my audience, art and story bouncing back and forth from the speaker and the hearer, this novel took shape. Over the month of November, I wrote parts two, three, and four of this book. In December, I began work on part five. By January, every bit of this story was published online and rocketing up the bestseller charts. I only ever combined the stories into a single novel because a few readers complained about having to click five times to get all the parts.

The simple truth is that I never would have written the rest of the story without you, the reader. I never would have known we were going through similar things, feeling the same stuff, longing for similar stories. The following year, I started to better understand the word-of-mouth that allowed me to become a full-time writer when I went on book tours and met my audience in person. I heard how people fell in love with this serialized tale and told all their friends and family to read it. I met people who bought dozens of copies and sent them to everyone they could think of. I met the people who wrote the reviews imploring others to discover this world, Juliette's world. I realized that the success of these books came as much from the reader's reaction to it as from what skill I exerted there.

My life has been forever changed, not just because I've been able to do more of what I love and tell more and wilder stories since, but because of my appreciation for the storytelling and story-loving animal in all of us. We crave human connection. We long for stories that drag us through agony but give us a glimmer of hope. We want to read disaster stories that teach us how to survive. Above all, we are hooked on the relationships we form with our favorite fictional characters, and the relationships we form with the authors who create them and our fellow readers who adore them as much as we do.

This story lives and breathes in its current form because you haven't stopped. Because of you, the book continues to find new readers year after year. Because of you, perhaps there will be more. A TV series, maybe. Another trilogy of life beyond the silos for any who dare to hope. Or more short stories about life in other silos. It's impossible for me to say. It's all up to you.

For those who left a review or told a friend, thank you. For those who are about to leave a review or tell a friend, I look forward to seeing where our journey takes us next. It might be a journey through a broken world, but there's a Juliette in each of us, ready to make things right.

Hugh Howey
Quarantined in Silo 06
Portugal, Earth
02020 AD